# HAPPY ENDINGS

Sadie Grey, widow of the recently assassinated US President, has to cope with her bereavement in the full glare of the media spotlight. Despite her grief she is determined to make a life of her own, a life that offers more than memories and photo-opportunities. Throwing herself energetically into a programme fund raising for medical research, Sadie meets a brilliant and charismatic doctor who intrigues and excites her, and against her better judgement she begins to hope for more. Allison Sterling is the best reporter on the nation's most powerful newspaper. Her relationship with Des Shaw has always been a volatile one, complicated by his clandestine relationship with the former First Lady. *Happy Endings* explores the lives of Sadie and Allison as they cope with the pain of life and the challenges of love with two handsome and fascinating men. It is the story of two extraordinary women who have had it all and want more.

# HAPPY ENDINGS

## Sally Quinn

**EAGLE LARGE PRINT**

HAMPTON, NEW HAMPSHIRE

Library of Congress Cataloging-in-Publication Data

Quinn, Sally.
  Happy endings / by Sally Quinn.
    p.  cm.—(Eagle large print)
  ISBN 0–7927–1378–8 (Hardcover: lg. print)
  ISBN 0–7927–1377–X (Softcover: lg. print)
  1. Large type books.  I. Title.  II. Series.
[PS3567.U349H37  1992]                                     92–20788
813′.54—dc20                                                      CIP

Published in Large Print by arrangement with Simon & Schuster.

'To those I love' by Isla Paschal Richardson, originally published in *My Heart Waketh: Poems* (Boston: Bruce Humphries, Inc., 1947). Used by kind permission of Isla Paschal Richardson Poe.

*Printed in Great Britain*

To my mother and father,
and to Ben and to Quinn,
the four people I love most
I.T.W.W.W.

# HAPPY ENDINGS

# CHAPTER ONE

'I'm scared, I'm always scared. There are just too many nuts out there.'

Sadie Grey was sitting in her private study in the family quarters of the White House talking to her press secretary, Jenny Stern.

'I think you should try not to overreact, Sadie. My God, the President couldn't be more secure. You've practically got a battalion traveling with him now every time he sets foot out of the White House. It's almost a joke.'

'Don't patronize me, Jen. I know how many threats there are against Rosey, not to mention me and even Willie, for lord's sake.'

She had jumped up from the chair and walked to the window overlooking Lafayette Park, her back to Jenny. She didn't want her to see the tears.

Even in the sweltering June heat the protesters with their placards were standing around on the sidewalk facing the White House, a constant reminder of her vulnerability.

Jenny was taken aback. Sadie had never spoken to her in that tone and Jenny couldn't remember her being so overwrought since before the election. At the time, Sadie was having an affair with Desmond Shaw, and she had every reason to be overwrought.

'I'm sorry,' said Jenny. 'I didn't realize you were so upset.'

'Look at them out there,' said Sadie. 'And any of those lunatics could have a gun or a bazooka. They could fire right in here and kill me this very instant.

1

You call that protection? Every time I send Willie out to his play group with Monica I'm terrified I'll never see him again, that some maniac will blow up his car or kidnap him. I just can't bear it.'

Jenny stood up and went over to Sadie, taking her by the arms.

'Sadie, what's wrong? I've never seen you like this. What on earth brought this on?'

Jenny guided her over to the sofa. Sadie slumped down.

'I've been having these awful dreams every night that something terrible is going to happen.'

'What?'

'I don't know exactly and I'm afraid to even talk about it.'

'Have you told Rosey?'

'He knows I've been having nightmares. I wake up screaming in the middle of the night and he has to shake me and calm me down. I just say I had a bad dream and he accepts that and goes back to sleep. But they are so vivid and they go on night after night. I can't help believing in them.'

'Tell me about it.'

Sadie leaned back against the cushion.

'We're standing somewhere, in a field or garden, surrounded by flowers, soft pastel summer flowers. We're laughing and happy. There is a green gauzy curtain or something and I sense that there is some menace behind it, but I don't know where it is. Then suddenly all of the pastel flowers turn red, blood red. Everything is covered with blood and I am being tossed away, discarded. I don't know where Rosey is. I never see him again. I'm screaming because I don't know where I am and I can't find Rosey or Willie or anybody. I've never

2

had anything affect me like this, and I can't talk to anybody about it because they'll think I'm crazy. The ones who don't already.'

She managed a weak laugh.

'Look, do you want to talk to the head of the Secret Service? Maybe that would make you feel better.'

'That would scare me to death. Just the fact that we have to have so many people around us all the time is bad enough. It means they know what targets we are. The details would only make me feel worse. I can't see what other precautions we can take unless we never leave this place. We're already prisoners enough as it is.'

The phone on Sadie's desk rang. Jenny picked it up.

'It's Lorraine Hadley. Shall I tell her you'll call back?'

Sadie made a face. There was nothing worse than a former hostess in a city where parties weren't that important anymore. Lorraine was a dinosaur and didn't even know it. Yet she was so desperate to be a part of things that Sadie felt sorry for her.

'No, I'll talk to her. If I don't take it now she'll only keep calling back.'

'Darling,' said Lorraine. 'In case you've forgotten, your birthday is coming up.'

'It's really a nothing birthday,' said Sadie. 'Forty-four. I have absolutely no feeling about it at all.'

'So we'll just do a small party, then?'

'Lorraine, you're sweet to think of it, but I really don't want a birthday party.'

'Don't be ridiculous. We've got to get you out of that House before you forget how to behave in

3

polite company. We must remind the natives that there really is a First Lady. How about six or eight of us, just family? It really will do you good.'

She was right. It would be good to get out of the White House. She had been practically a recluse for the past two years, since Willie was born. She knew Rosey would enjoy it. He kept trying to persuade her to go out to dinner, but it was such a production that it never seemed worth it.

'Oh, why not,' said Sadie. 'But absolutely no more than six or eight.'

'Wonderful!' said Lorraine. 'I know you won't be sorry. Now, if only this dreadful humidity will clear up, we'll eat in the garden.'

*      *      *

'Really, Sadie, this is insane!'

Lorraine had been on the phone with Sadie's staff for days trying to arrange the birthday party, and her exasperation was beginning to show.

'I've had everyone in my household identified and checked by the Secret Service. They all feel like criminals. Police have been swarming over the place for days. The telephone people have strung up wires outside my house. There is a command post set up in my living room and a hospital upstairs in my library. I had a huge fight with one of those faceless agents—really, they are so incredibly rude, all of them ...' She paused at the silence on the other end of the line. '... About whether we could have cocktails outside or not. He wouldn't even hear of eating outside. I made such a stink about drinks that he finally gave in, but he wasn't happy about it. And then, this is too ridiculous, he told me

4

I couldn't greet you and Rosey at the door. I have to wait until you're inside. For God's sake, Sadie, this is Georgetown after all. It's not the ghetto.'

All this talk about security made Sadie even more anxious.

'I don't like it any more than you do, Lorraine, but we have no choice. It goes with the territory. It's frightening to think that there are people who would go to such lengths to harm us. But if it's too much for you, we can always just forget it. I won't mind. I promise.'

'Oh no, darling. Not at all. My God, I don't want you to think . . .'

That got her. The evening was going to put Lorraine back on the map for at least a year. Besides, she loved all the security. It made her feel important.

'It's just that bringing your own water? And your own drinks? And having to have the wine uncorked by a Secret Service agent? I mean, honestly . . .!'

'Lorraine.'

'All right, all right, I'll shut up. But I do think it would be nice if someone would tell me exactly how many support staff are coming so I could arrange to have them fed.'

'That won't be necessary,' said Sadie. 'They eat beforehand, and if they don't somebody will send out for fast food.'

'Don't be silly,' said Lorraine. 'Ezio's a wonderful chef. I'd be happy to provide for them.'

'I don't think you will when you hear how many there are. I've just asked.'

'How many?'

'Forty-five.'

★　　　★　　　★

It was shortly before five the evening of the birthday party when Lorraine called Sadie. She had just returned from the hairdresser to find several large dogs sniffing out the place. One of the waitresses had been held outside because the house had already been sealed, and Archie, Lorraine's husband, was having a fit because two marksmen with long-range rifles were sitting in his bedroom facing the window.

The Secret Service had put up a hideous gauze curtain in the garden to shield the President from the next-door neighbor's upstairs window. So humiliating for the neighbors. They were from such a good old Washington cave-dweller family. The agents had also wanted to put curtains up in front of the holly trees, but then her guests wouldn't have been able to see her beautiful English border—they gave in on that one. They had moved the garden furniture in close to the house so the President would be shielded by the L-shaped wing and protected by the high fence behind the holly trees. They had even designated specific chairs for the Greys.

The President's valet was in the kitchen checking out the food and Ezio was fuming. It seemed that his salad included tomatoes and the President hadn't eaten any of the garden tomatoes that had been served him at Camp David the previous weekend. Perhaps he had developed an allergy? Lorraine had managed to convince Ezio that red peppers would be even better and a little more unusual. The President's water was brought in in a large gallon container as was Sadie's favorite summer drink, sangria.

6

Why hadn't somebody just told her that Sadie like sangria? She certainly could have managed to provide that. But when Rosey's valet began uncorking the wine she decided to go upstairs and take a hot bath. She understood that presidents in this day and age needed to be protected but it was really getting ridiculous.

Sadie had requested that Abigail and Malcolm Sohier be invited. They were one of the most attractive couples in Washington and favorites of the Greys. Malcolm was the Democratic senator from Massachusetts, bright, charming, and witty. Abby was well read and fun. They were a rarity in Washington, a political couple who had not been corrupted by power and who continued to care about issues. Malcolm might well be the Democratic candidate for President when Rosey left the White House. Sadie had hoped last time that Rosey would choose him for his running mate, but he had refused to get rid of the dreadful Freddy Osgood, claiming it would be political suicide in the West and Midwest. He was probably right, but it was still too bad.

Lorraine had wanted to include a prominent columnist and his wife, but Sadie had put her foot down. She liked journalists and found them exciting and irreverent, but she had learned a lesson from Des. You could never really trust them. Nothing was ever off the record, especially if you were the President.

At any rate, having accepted the idea of a birthday party, Sadie was looking forward to a cosy evening with just the six of them.

★    ★    ★

Sadie was used to the motorcycles, the police cars, and the sirens accompanying them wherever they went. She knew it was exciting to others, seeing the presidential motorcade. As they pulled up to Lorraine's house and stopped, a long black limousine with flags kept going. It was the decoy. Behind them was the ambulance, which stopped and parked directly across the street. There were several cars both in front and in back of their limousine. What appeared to be an army, most in dark glasses, earphones, and three-piece suits, headed up the stone stairs to the elegant federal pink-brick house. Standing in the doorway of the central hall, Lorraine moved aside as people with briefcases pushed past her. Rosey and Sadie got out of the limousine and headed up the stairs. Lorraine stepped out on the front landing to greet them as they neared the door. Before she could put out her hand, a burly agent grabbed her and sent her reeling back into the house, nearly knocking her down.

'Not out here,' he hissed.

Lorraine steadied herself and managed to smile as she extended her hand to Rosey and Sadie, who acted oblivious to what had just happened. Miraculously, most of the support team had disappeared. One group had gone to the upstairs study to set up a medical center. The other group went to a small breakfast room off the kitchen to set up a command and communications center, including an entire separate phone system.

Lorraine took her cue from the Greys.

'Darlings,' she said, as though nothing had happened, 'I'm thrilled that you could come. Let's go out on the terrace and have a drink.'

She led them down the hall, past the elegant drawing room, and out the back French doors to where the Sohiers were waiting. The seven or eight Secret Service agents had more or less vanished into the garden, taking up unobtrusive positions among the trees.

She was greeted by a chorus of 'Happy Birthdays.'

'I'd almost forgotten it was my birthday, actually,' drawled Sadie in her soft Savannah accent. 'And I wasn't the only one.' She glanced pointedly at her husband.

'Well, Sugar, as the man said, "it ain't over till it's over." We still have a few more hours left.'

'Mr President, don't tell me you still haven't given your wife a present,' exclaimed Malcolm in mock horror.

'You're going to eat your heart out, Sohier,' laughed Rosey.

The Greys kissed the Sohiers warmly. Archie, a renowned bore, was greeted with less enthusiasm.

'Sadie,' said Archie, recognizing the coolness, 'you look positively ravishing.'

Sara Adabelle Grey did look great. Her auburn hair was longer than it had been since she had come to the White House four years earlier. It was parted to the side and brushed smoothly so that it fell slightly over her eye. She looked more like thirty-four than forty-four. Her skin was pale, which set off her turquoise eyes, and she wore a strapless linen dress of the same color. William Rosewell Grey III, graying noticeably at the temples now, was tall and distinguished-looking in a tan linen suit. They were a gorgeous couple, and the

9

way they looked at each other, it seemed to the observer that after twenty-some years of marriage they were still in love.

Lorraine insisted that her guests be seated. There were six white wrought-iron chairs set out, and she perched on a corner of one, not wanting to wrinkle her silk caftan, and nervously smoothed back a hair on her chignon.

She turned to the waiter who was hovering behind her with champagne glasses filled with peach-colored liquid.

'We have bellinis here, or Sadie, if you prefer, the White House sent over sangria.' She wanted to make her point.

Sadie didn't bite.

'Oh, bellinis sound heavenly,' she said. 'I'll have one.' Rosey reached for one as well.

After the guests had been served, they turned to admire the garden.

It did look spectacular. Typically English, it had a perennial border along the back and sides, directly in front of a bank of hollies that screened the row of houses behind the wall.

A large crepe myrtle graced the center of the yard, a pretty cherry tree stood to the left, and a small fountain lent a cooling sound to the summer air. The grass was deep and green, which contrasted beautifully with the pastel flowers. The only thing that marred the scene was the silk tent-like curtain erected to the left of the patio, which was billowing in the breeze. Sadie and Rosey seemed not to notice it.

'How's Willie?' asked Abby.

'Fabulous!' said Rosey before Sadie could reply. His face brightened. 'What a great little kid! I never would have believed what joy there is having a late baby like this. He is the light of my life. He came down to my office today and all hell broke loose. He had the entire cabinet on their toes right before the meeting with his toy airplanes and his tanks. There's no question he's going to be a general when he grows up. I'm thinking of sending him to the Citadel in the finest Southern military tradition.'

'He's completely bananas about Willie and vice versa,' said Sadie in mock despair. 'Willie is in Rosey's lap every chance he gets. I feel rather left out.'

'The fact is that I'm besotted. You appreciate your kids so much more when you're older. When you're young you're so involved with your career and travel that you don't really have the time to concentrate on them. Being in the White House is like working at home. I'm always there. I can run up and see him anytime I want or he can come down and visit me. I always play tennis in the evenings and then throw the ball around with Willie afterwards. It's great.'

'We could get to be real bores about Willie.' Sadie laughed. 'How about your kids?' she asked the Sohiers. 'Are you going on vacation with them this summer?'

'I think we'll just take them to the North Shore as usual,' said Abigail. 'Massachusetts is so great in the summer. And after Washington it's such a relief. When are you going to Easthampton?'

'I was supposed to go up at the beginning of July with Willie and have Rosey come up on weekends and join us in August. But he's gotten so grouchy about the two of us being away that I've decided to wait and go up with him. Besides, it's just too

11

complicated to go separately.'

Washington conversation never strays too far away from politics, and Malcolm Sohier was already getting a little restless with the casual chitchat. He changed the conversation as soon as he thought it was acceptable.

'Mr President,' he said, 'what's happening with the murder investigation of those DEA agents?'

Rosey leaned forward and frowned.

'You know things are getting serious when they start murdering our Drug Enforcement people,' he said. 'But the normal recourse, which would be to go through diplomatic channels, isn't an option. These guys are killing their own judges, journalists, politicians, police, and ordinary citizens who dare to protest, mowing them down in cold blood. The drug dealers have more or less taken over their governments. Even the armies are intimidated. There's just nobody for us to complain to. They're either scared or dead. Those who are running the countries are mostly on the payrolls of the dealers. If you can't lick 'em, join 'em. I've asked Freddy and his friend Roy Fox to head up a task force to look into the situation. I have to say, right now, it is definitely one of my number-one priorities.'

'But Mr President,' said Abigail, 'what's to stop these drug dealers from doing the same thing in this country? Drugs are rampant. I work with ghetto kids in drug programs. Malcolm and I have done fund raising in Los Angeles and we're told everybody out there uses them. We're talking about intelligent, educated, wealthy people who should know better. If you can't get the message across to them—'

'Oh, please, Abby, everyone,' interjected

12

Lorraine. 'This is such a depressing subject. Can't we just have fun tonight instead of being so serious? After all, it is Sadie's birthday.'

'I'll drink to that,' said Malcolm, raising his glass.

'To Sadie. Happy Birthday. And what a wonderful evening.'

'To Sadie,' they all chorused, then laughed, as they raised their bellinis to her.

Rosey, who had been engrossed in the talk about the drug problem, seemed to relax when the subject was changed.

'Lorraine,' he said, 'I must compliment you on your garden. It is really spectacular. Do you have an English gardener?'

'As a matter of fact, I do.'

'Let's just take a walk around the border,' he said and stood up.

Lorraine noticed that all the agents in the garden suddenly stiffened.

'Foxglove,' he was saying as he took her arm and began to walk toward the back border. 'It's always been my favorite. Do you know that they are terribly poisonous? In medieval times they used to make a potion of them and put it in the king's mead to kill him.'

'For God's sake, Rosey, don't say things like that. It gives me the willies.'

Rosey laughed. 'What's the matter with you, Lorraine?'

'I don't know. It's all these men around with their dark glasses and their earphones and those bulges under their arms. I don't remember there being so many. Doesn't it ever bother you?'

'Oh, you get used to it. It's part of being

President. To tell you the truth, I never even give it a thought. Sadie worries about it . . . these lilies are amazing. I've never smelled such strong perfume.'

He leaned toward one of the tall white spires.

Sadie had been sipping her peaches and champagne. She just happened to glance up as the bullet struck Rosey in the front of his chest splattering the white lilies, the pink phlox, and the yellow and white daisies with his bright red blood.

At first he stood up straight. Since his back was partly toward her, Sadie didn't quite believe he had been hit. But the second shot knocked him backward, seeming to tear his whole torso apart, and sent him flat against the ground.

Sadie watched as everything shifted into slow motion. Within seconds he was surrounded by Secret Service agents, who covered his body and the area around him with their bodies. More shots rang out as the high-ground men in Archie's bedroom began shooting back. She could hear the shouting as the call for medical assistance went out. The doctor came rushing through the door with a hypodermic. As she tried to run to Rosey, several agents threw themselves around her and pulled her roughly into the house, shielding her body with theirs. She saw the medics rush in with their stretcher and out to the garden. She could hear a command to 'neutralize' the attack. She didn't know what that meant. As she struggled to get out of their strong grip she tried to scream or shout Rosey's name but nothing came out of her mouth but whimpers.

'Are there more than one? Where did it come from? Will they try again? Evacuate with as much cover as possible to the ambulance,' she heard

14

people saying as others carried her out the front door and down the steps. The medics were just behind her with the stretcher, and when they passed her she looked over and saw Rosey lying there, his body soaked with blood and a small trickle coming out of his mouth. His eyes were open and he gave her a stunned, questioning look. For the first time she was able to make a sound, and when she did she heard her voice whisper, 'Rosey, Rosey, what have they done to you?'

It occurred to her only after she had said it that it was the first time she realized he wasn't dead. They reached the bottom of the steps and she saw the ambulance door open and a medic jump in as they slid the stretcher into the back. The agents had slightly loosened their grip on her and she leapt to the back of the ambulance scrambling in and grabbing Rosey's legs. Now she had her full voice back and she could hear herself screaming his name.

'Rosey, oh my God, are you all right?'

'Get her the fuck out of there,' shouted a voice behind her. 'There isn't room. We need an agent.' She felt somebody pulling her out by her legs as her skirt rode up almost to her waist.

'Leave me alone, goddammit,' she shrieked.

'The ambulance isn't armored,' the voice said.

'It's my husband in there. I have a right. I'm going with him.'

'No, ma'am,' said one of Rosey's grim-faced agents. 'It's the President of the United States in there.'

With that, he pushed her out of the way, jumped in the back of the ambulance, and slammed the door in her face. Another two agents jumped on the

15

running board of the ambulance and the siren started up as it pulled away from the house.

'Roseyyyyyyyyy,' she cried out, piercing the atmosphere with her pain. Two agents picked her up and carried her to the presidential limousine, threw her in, and jumped in on top of her.

'Rosey, my husband, where are they taking him?' she demanded.

'George Washington University Hospital, Mrs Grey.'

The noise from the sirens was deafening. She couldn't see the ambulance or its police escort because the follow-up van with the agents was in between them and the limousine. The only thing she could see, and what she would remember later, were the two flags on either side of the front of the limousine. The American flag and the presidential flag. The next day would be the Fourth of July.

\*      \*      \*

The President's ambulance pulled up under the canopy of George Washington University Hospital just as Sadie's limousine was rounding Washington Circle behind it. She saw a group of men surround her husband's stretcher as they carried him to the emergency room entrance.

When she entered, the corridor to the emergency room was already filled with Secret Service agents. She turned to her left, accompanied by her own two agents, and started running through the emergency room to the back where one area to the left was filled with people and partially curtained off. She heard someone shout for 'an I.V. for the President.' Then she heard a frighteningly calm voice say

16

something about the wound being to the abdomen and asking for a chest tube.

There were so many men with their backs to her that she couldn't see over them. She couldn't see anything and she tried to claw her way past the front row of them. Her own agents grabbed her again and turned her away, leading her back down the hallway.

'For God's sake,' she shouted, 'let me see my husband. Is he still alive? Please, I beg you, don't keep me away from him.'

'He's alive, Mrs Grey,' said the agent who had her arm. 'But there's no space in the resuscitation area. They're preparing the President for surgery. They want you to wait in here.'

They ushered her into a tiny holding room, no larger than a broom closet, at the entrance to the emergency room. There was a telephone, a small table, two metal chairs, and a tray of half-eaten food—meat-loaf, soup, kale, and half a can of soda. The room smelled of stale food, and the dark blue wall on one side seemed to come down on her as she stood there. For a moment she thought she might throw up or faint, and she closed her eyes, only to be steadied by four strong hands. Then she heard someone say that the President was being taken to the operating room. She saw a horde of people from the resuscitation room coming around the corner in front of her, heading down the hall.

She jumped out the door just as they wheeled her husband by. Rosey caught her eye as she stood staring at him in shock. He had lost all of his color. His skin was white and his lips were blue. He had a ghostly appearance, partially wrapped as he was in a sheet. His shirt had been ripped off his chest. There

17

seemed to be tubes coming from everywhere. She had never seen so much blood in her life. It was not only on Rosey but also on the white-coated doctors who were escorting him.

She had grabbed onto the side of the gurney so she could walk holding his hand as they wheeled him rapidly to the O.R.

'My wife,' Rosey whispered to one of the doctors standing above him as they approached the operating room. 'I want to speak to my wife. It's very important.'

'We have to move quickly, Mr President. You're losing a lot of blood.'

'Please.'

The doctor hesitated a moment, then nodded.

Rosey held up his hand to gesture to the agents for privacy, and they backed away a few steps. She leaned down toward his face.

He reached up and grabbed the back of her head so that her lips were almost touching his. He stared deeply into her eyes.

'You're going to be just fine, darlin', I know you will,' she said, gasping, as her tears fell onto his lips.

'My precious Sadiebelle... I love you. And I forgave you ... a long time ago.'

'Oh God, Rosey, don't talk like that. Not now. Please, you don't need—'

'Hush, angel. I have to tell you...'

He was squeezing her other hand so hard that it hurt.

'I know Willie is not my son.'

The sound that came from her mouth was a guttural moan. Before she could shake her head, Rosey continued.

'It's all right. I've known all along . . . I love him like my own. It doesn't matter . . . All that matters was having you back. I know it's not easy . . . you tried . . . sorry I couldn't make you more happy.'

'Oh, Rosey, I do love you. More than you will ever know. Oh Jesus, God in heaven, I'm so sorry, so sorry. I can't bear this.'

She began to sob uncontrollably.

'Mr President, we really have to get you in there, sir. We can't wait any longer,' said the doctor, the urgency unmistakable in his voice.

'You have to,' Rosey almost shouted, summoning up his last bit of energy.

'Promise me, Sadiebelle.'

Before she could answer he continued.

'Never tell him the truth. Raise him as my son. Make him proud of me.'

'I will, I promise, Oh Rosey, I—'

'I'm sorry, Mr President, we're going in,' said the doctor as forcefully as he could. He pushed the gurney forward, leaving Sadie, her hand torn from his, standing helplessly in the middle of the hall, tears streaming down her face, her turquoise dress covered in blood.

\*     \*     \*

Someone, she couldn't remember who, had taken her arm and led her to an elevator. There were a lot of agents and people in white in the elevator. They showed her into a corner office, all glass, overlooking Washington Circle. It was twilight now, a little after nine, and the cars had their lights turned on. She had driven around this circle so many times. The Kennedy Center was only a few

19

blocks away. All she had ever noticed were the beautiful little apple trees, especially in the spring when they were in bloom. Now all those people in those cars were speeding home to people they loved and here she was, in a hospital, waiting to see if her husband would die.

There seemed to be a lot of noise around her, a lot of people asking her if she wanted anything, a lot of phones ringing, a lot of motion. She was numb, oblivious to it all except from some sort of vague, faraway place. It occurred to her that she was cold, freezing, in fact, in her strapless dress in this air-conditioned room. Some words to that effect came out of her mouth and immediately a man's gray jacket was over her shoulders. She mentioned something about hot tea and a mug was placed in her hand a few minutes later.

She alternated between staring hypnotically out at the swirling traffic and concentrating on the red, white, and gray love seat she was sitting on. She noticed that the chair in front of her was an off-white velvet desperately in need of cleaning.

There were bookcases with medical books and plaques and family pictures ... family pictures. She suddenly thought of her two older children, Outland and Annie Laurie. They were both away for the summer. Someone would have to notify them about their father.

She broke out of her reverie for a moment, looking up at one of the agents in the room.

'My children...' she began.

'They're on their way, ma'am.'

Shortly, her husband's chief of staff walked in, looking exceptionally solemn, and rushed over to give her a hug. He was accompanied by several

20

aides and the attorney general.

'Jesus, Sadie,' he said. 'I can't believe this thing. What the hell happened? . . . Never mind, you're hardly in shape to answer that. I've just been downstairs. They're still in surgery. One of the doctors is coming up pretty soon to give you a report.'

'Is he, is he . . .'

'He's alive.'

Period. That was all he said. Not doing well, or going to make it, or hanging in there. Just . . . alive.

'The Vice President was in Tennessee. He's flying in.'

She couldn't have cared less where Freddy Osgood was.

'George Manolas is in the next room trying to handle the press situation. Things are already going crazy. And if . . .' he froze before he said it. She stared at him, disbelieving.

'I'm going down to see where the hell that doctor is. I'll be right back.' He gave her a squeeze, not looking her in the eye, and disappeared.

She stood up and began pacing. The clock on the wall said it was after 10:00 p.m. Had she really been waiting an hour? She walked over to a wall and read one of the plaques:

'Most people fear change more than disaster,' one of them read.

It seemed ironic. Here she had opted against change in her life in order to avoid disaster, and now she had both.

The door was ajar and she could see into the open office area beyond and into a conference room adjacent to the one she was in. Already WHCA, the White House Communications Agency, had set up

21

the command post there, and the place was swarming.

She walked out of the executive office and stood outside the conference room door staring in.

The first thing she heard was her husband's press secretary telling someone on the telephone that 'it doesn't look good; in fact, it looks terrible.'

A moment later someone noticed her. Then Manolas felt the silence and turned. His face turned ashen at the sight of her.

'Mrs Grey,' he said, mumbling an apology. 'I didn't realize you were there.'

'It's all right,' she said quietly and walked back to the executive office.

It was only a few minutes later that the doctor came up. His green surgical garb was splattered with blood and his hair was disheveled.

He simply stood in front of her. She begged him with her eyes.

'The uh, the uh President . . .' he cleared his throat. 'We went into his chest, and when we opened him up we discovered that the entrance of the bullet was high. This is a very dangerous area to repair. We put him on cardiopulmonary bypass. We clipped the aorta and exposed it above the renal arteries. Not only the aorta but the superior mesenteric artery had been hit. A good part of the aorta was destroyed by the bullet. We keep finding new sites of bleeding and we continue to clamp them, but his pressure keeps dropping. The anesthesiologist is trying to keep up with the blood loss. You see, as you clamp the aorta you deprive the lower body of blood, including the abdomen and kidneys. The body becomes acidotic and the shock can become irreversible . . . The heart slows down ... the pressure drops ... '

'What are you telling me?'

'It, uh, it looks grim.'

She stood there for a moment taking it all in. Then, before she even thought about what she was doing, she dashed for the door. She pushed the doctor aside as she had been pushed aside so many times that evening, and ran out of the office, through the open executive suite, out into the corridor. In front of her was a sign identifying Stairway No. 1. She opened the door and began running down the stairs as fast as she could in her high heels, grasping at the red railings to steady herself. When she came out at the bottom she was confused for a moment, then she saw a lot of men to the right and turned toward them.

She went down another corridor until she saw a room full of people in green surgical outfits, patients with oxygen masks, tubes, and I.V.s. There was another sign: 'No admittance or throughway.' She burst through it, going as fast as she could, leaving a number of bewildered people behind her.

As she raced out of the Post-Anesthesia Care Unit she saw the double swinging doors to the O.R. and the phalanx of Secret Service agents blocking them. They were waiting for her, as was the doctor who had spoken to her earlier.

'Please,' she said to the doctor. 'Please.'

'We just can't let anyone into the O.R., Mrs Grey. You'll have to understand.' His face could not hide his anguish. 'There's a small room right here you can wait in.'

He took her arm and led her into a tiny windowless office with three chairs and a small

23

desk. It was airless and she became claustrophobic.

'I'm having trouble breathing,' she said, sinking into the chair and putting her head in her hands.

The doctor called for a nurse and instructed her to bring the First Lady some smelling salts and a glass of ice water.

Just then there was a commotion coming from the O.R. A blood-spattered nurse appeared at the door, a look of sheer desperation on her face.

'Dr Sokolow, we need you in here,' she said.

The doctor started as though he'd been shot himself and dashed out of the little room.

It was about fifteen minutes later when the double doors opened from the operating room. People came pouring out, all of them grim-faced. Sadie leapt out of her chair and went to stand by the door of her little room waiting for the gurney to come rolling out, carrying Rosey to the recovery room. There was no gurney.

Several doctors began walking toward her, all of them now in what appeared to be red clothes. Their masks were pulled down around their necks and their faces were contorted with emotion.

Sadie started shaking her head slowly in horror as she backed into the room, waiting for what she now knew would be the news.

The one called Sokolow spoke first.

'We tried. We tried. We really tried. We did everything we could. We made every effort. But there was just too much damage. He went into shock, we couldn't get the pressure . . .'

One of the other doctors put his arm on Sokolow's shoulder to steady him.

'We're very sorry, Mrs Grey. The President is dead.'

24

She didn't say a word for several moments. Then finally she spoke.

'May I see him now?'

'Of course.'

He led her into the operating room where the now motionless body of her husband lay.

Several nurses and doctors and a few Secret Service agents dressed in green hospital garb were still in the room. They were all in tears.

As she approached Rosey, who was covered with a sheet, except for his head, she motioned for the others to stay away.

They discreetly turned their backs on her.

She stood for a long moment memorizing his features. The wavy light brown hair with the perfectly graying temples. The high forehead with a few more lines than when he became President. The fair eyebrows, slightly arched. The pale lashes. The beautiful aquiline nose—his best feature. His cheekbones, high and etched. His mouth, nicely shaped, though his lips could have been fuller. He had a strong chin. Altogether it was an extraordinarily handsome face, a patrician face, a kind face.

'Oh, Rosey,' she whispered. 'I did love you. I was just stupid and silly and immature. I never stopped loving you. And in my heart Willie is your child. You are his father. You always will be. To him and to me. Nothing can ever change that. I was never worthy of you. But why do you have to leave me now when I'm just learning from you what real love is? You've taught me everything that's noble and fine in my life. I don't want to lose you now. I can't lose you now.'

She leaned over and softly kissed his lips,

25

brushing them gently with her own. For just a moment she felt his energy surround her and nearly lift her off the ground. The force was so strong that she gasped for breath and then looked up as the charged atmosphere moved from around her arms and neck to her head and then above her.

'Rosey, it's you. It's you. You are there. Don't leave me now. Please come back.'

She could feel the desperate tears begin to come now as she felt him slipping out of her grasp. She raised an arm to catch him as his energy seeped away.

'Rosey, I love you. I love you. I always will,' she whispered.

But he had gone, leaving his beautiful, empty body on the bed.

'Goodbye, my darling,' she said finally and turned away.

Dr Sid Sokolow, who had gotten control of himself, came up to her. He held a package in his hand, which he gave to her.

'One of the nurses found this in the President's pocket,' he said. 'It's for you.'

It was a gaily wrapped present, with pink and blue paper and blue ribbon. The paper was badly cut and the Scotch tape was put on wrong. He had tried to curl the ribbons with scissors and taken all the body out of it. She had always teased him about how hopeless he was at wrapping presents. There was a tiny envelope that said 'Happy Birthday.' It had her name on it.

She tore off the paper and found a small box.

She held her breath as she opened it.

Inside was an exquisite antique ring of turquoise and marquise diamonds in a gold setting. She recognized it right away. It had belonged to his paternal grandmother, who had been raised in India. It was the only thing that had belonged to Rosey's mother, Miz G., that she actually coveted.

But the ring was even more significant than that. She had asked Rosey recently if they couldn't renew their wedding vows privately. He had told her he wasn't ready to forgive her yet.

She slipped the ring on her finger slowly before she opened the note.

Inside, in his bold handwriting in black ink, it said:

'I take thee Sadie to be my wife for better or for worse, for richer or for poorer, in sickness and in health, 'til death do us part.'

# CHAPTER TWO

Allison had had too much to drink. Julian had ordered endless bottles of vintage red wine, a huge extravagance, and she had obliged him by practically drinking two all by herself. Not that she didn't have a good excuse. A person's fortieth birthday was not an everyday occurrence. And though she hadn't really worried too much about her age, the idea of being forty and childless suddenly depressed her. Forty, unmarried, and childless. She had to stop thinking negatively. The positive aspects of her life, that's what she should concentrate on.

She was the London correspondent for the *Washington Daily*. She had a bright future at the paper. She was the goddaughter of former president

Roger Kimball and one of the most powerful women in American journalism. She was blond, thought to be quite beautiful, intelligent, talented, witty ... and forty, unmarried, and childless. This was ridiculous. She was supposed to be having a good time.

It was not like Julian to throw her a birthday party. He usually didn't show his emotions. He preferred to be known as cool and elusive. And most of the time he was.

'I'm a cold, cruel sadistic Brit, so what do you want?' he would say, with those taunting pale blue eyes.

Generally, Allison didn't find British men very attractive, or at least sexually attractive. Most of them seemed devoid of a basic animal magnetism or whatever it was that made American men so appealing. Maybe they were too studied, too effete, too anemic.

Julian was different.

He was tall with a lithe, sensuous body, blond hair, and perfect features. He looked every bit the aristocrat he was, but he had a roguish quality that belied his upper-class manners. Julian was a renegade, a bad boy, always doing the unexpected, shocking the establishment, outraging his titled father. He was the delight of the journalistic left except when he occasionally turned on them for their sanctimonious moralizing. Julian belonged to nobody. He was his own person. His father had been ambassador to Saudi Arabia. He had lived in the desert, spoke fluent Arabic, and had written several books on terrorism in the Middle East. Everyone called him Julian of Arabia.

Julian had chosen the Groucho Club for her

28

birthday party, a rather funky private club in Soho named for the famous Groucho Marx line about not wanting to join any club that would have him as a member. There was a comfortable lounge bar on the first floor with deep overstuffed sofas and chairs and a decidedly undecorated look. Upstairs were private rooms for parties and a small restaurant. The club catered to the publishing crowd, journalists, and television types of some reputation and little money. It was the scene of most of London's book parties and literary magazine launchings. Allison had wanted to keep the party small, so they had stuck to twelve. As it happened, her two closest American friends were out of the country on assignment, so there were only Brits at the party.

Julian was looking down the table at her now. She caught his glance though she was feigning a deep conversation with her dinner partner. Julian had seated himself next to a rather icily beautiful British fashion magazine writer who was clearly infatuated with him. Not that Julian had any interest in Clarissa. It was just his way of getting Allison's attention. Because Julian was in love with Allison and Allison was not in love with him. They had never discussed it. It was simply understood. One day she would go back to America and that would be the end.

Julian was standing now. He had rapped on his glass to signal a toast. Everyone was only too happy for another opportunity to drink a little more of the amazing claret. 'I would like everyone to drink to our smashing expatriate . . . and to hope that this is not the last birthday she will spend on our fair isle.'

It was the closest he would ever come to asking

29

her to stay.

Allison smiled. He was brilliant and clever, facile and sexy. And titled and rich. Why couldn't she be in love with him? He had such pride, too. That appealed to her. She hated men who made passes. She liked to be the one to select her partners. Julian would rather be left in the desert to die of thirst than to ever suggest she marry him. Even when they had first met it was she who had invited him to her house for dinner, not once but several times, before he asked her out. It was she who seduced him.

Clarissa was reaching a hand up to draw him down to the table again. She had not liked the long smoldering look he was giving Allison. He gracefully shrugged her away and began walking down toward Allison's end of the table, wineglass in hand. He sat down, leaning his arm on the back of her chair and taking a handful of her hair. She could see that he was a little drunk, but his eyes were as clear as most people's were when sober.

'Why don't we get the hell out of here,' he whispered in her ear.

'Your lips are purple from the claret,' she said. Their faces were so close they were almost touching.

'Bugger off.'

'I bet you don't talk to Lady Clarissa that way.'

'I don't have to.'

'Do you want to go to bed with her?'

'Compared to what?'

'What a dumb question. You'd fuck a camel.'

'They don't call me Julian of Arabia for nothing.'

He smiled wickedly and bit her lower lip. She didn't even bother to see if anyone was watching.

30

She didn't care either. They were all so smashed that it hardly mattered.

'I suppose she made a pass at you.'

'Not at all. She merely invited me to visit her in Barbados next month. Her parents have a house there. Very grand. Quite the toffs, you know.'

'I don't give a damn if she is Lady Clarissa, she's nothing but a clapped-out slagette.'

Allison was quite pleased with herself over this shot. It annoyed her that Clarissa wouldn't even be at the party except that Julian's best friend had brought her. She pulled back a little to show the proper indignation.

Julian threw back his head and laughed.

'Good girl,' he said. It always sounded like 'gel'. 'It's been a tough go but you're finally learning to speak our native tongue.'

'Your tongue is purple, too,' she said.

'Well,' he whispered very softly, moving his head closer to her and lowering his eyes to her mouth. 'I can arrange for you not to have to see it.'

He took her head in his hands pulling her to him as he covered her mouth with his. She could feel herself giving in, letting her body relax into his arms, only vaguely aware that there were people around them laughing and talking.

Then suddenly there was a shout, and someone came running into their private dining room.

'The President has been shot!'

Allison rose out of her chair as though she had been submerged and was coming up for air. She had had so much to drink and was so engrossed in Julian that it took her a moment to focus on what had been said.

'What? What did he say?' she asked nobody in

31

particular.

'The President of the United States has been shot.'

'Rosey? Oh no. Oh God. Oh no.'

Allison looked wildly around the room as if for confirmation that what she had heard was false.

She looked at Julian, comprehending at last. He was grim and suddenly very sober. He stared at Allison's ashen face.

'Bloody hell,' he said softly.

★     ★     ★

She couldn't imagine how Julian, as drunk as he was, had managed to navigate his car from the West End to her office on Upper Brook Street. Within minutes she was on the phone with the desk in Washington. The *Daily* was in an uproar and she could hardly make sense of what Muchnick, the foreign editor, was saying. The President had been shot on deadline, just as the paper was being put to bed, and had been rushed to George Washington University Hospital. Nobody knew anything more except that he was in surgery.

'Get reaction' was all Muchnick would say.

'But what happened?' she demanded. 'You know: who, what, where, when and why?'

'I don't have time for this now, Sterling,' he said testily and hung up.

'God, I hate that asshole,' she shouted. She was standing at her desk, the phone cradled under her arm, pacing back and forth. Julian came into her office just as she finished her conversation, two cups of black coffee in his hands.

'Drink,' he ordered. 'It's just possible that you

are the asshole at this moment, and a slightly drunken one at that.'

'How drunk am I?'

'Too drunk to call the Prime Minister's office and too drunk to call the American ambassador. Why don't you call Reggie?'

Reggie was the palace spokesman, a jovial party boy himself and good friend to most of the foreign press.

'I'm not that drunk . . . Do you think Muchnick could tell I was drunk?'

'I don't think it occurred to him.'

'Well, why the hell shouldn't I be drunk? It's my fortieth birthday and it's two o'clock in the morning. How was I supposed to know the President would be shot? . . . Christ, the President's been shot. Rosey's been shot!'

The realization stunned her only momentarily as it had when she first heard the news. But her head was compartmentalized. Emotions and news were in separate compartments. This was news. It would not register until much later that Rosey was a friend. Somebody she cared about, somebody with whom she had shared a great deal of pain.

She grabbed her Rolodex and began thumbing through it for numbers as she turned on the BBC radio. The clackety-clack of wire machines in the hall churned out the mounting details of the shooting. Julian ripped off the streams of white paper and carried them into Allison's office. Her shoes were off, her hair was tied back, and she had put on a sweater. She seemed oblivious to anything but The Story.

The black coffee, or maybe it was the story itself, sobered her up fast. She placed a call to the Prime

33

Minister's national security guy, a frequent lunch partner and sometime source whose home phone number she happened to have. Jeremy gave her some colorful reaction that she wouldn't have gotten from the Prime Minister's press secretary. Then she placed a call to the PM. She wanted to get the Brits out of the way and file before she called the American ambassador.

It was about four in the morning when she finally called E. Cotesworth Tennant III. He was one of Rosey Grey's closest friends and had been chairman of his reelection campaign in Virginia. They were both from Richmond, both First Families of Virginia, roommates at the Episcopal High School, clubmates in Saint Anthony Hall at the University of Virginia, classmates at Virginia Law School.

Allison had never really known Cotes when she was in Washington. He had stayed in Richmond because his wife was dying of cancer. Even though Rosey had been President for two years before he actually ran for office, it wasn't until after the election that he had named Cotes to the Court of St. James's.

They had become friendly when, two years earlier, they both arrived in London. She knew the conversation with Cotes would be difficult. She didn't know how difficult.

He picked up the phone on the first ring.

'Cotes, it's Allison.'

'Do you know anything?'

'Only what's come over the wire. He's in surgery at G.W.'

'Jesus Christ, Allison. I can't believe it. I was only just talking to him yesterday on the phone. He was all excited about Sadie's birthday present.'

Allison stiffened at the mention of Sadie's name even now. But Cotes wouldn't have known why.

'Goddamn Secret Service, where the hell were they anyway ...' he stopped in midsentence, his voice cracking.

She could hear another phone ringing in the background.

'Hang on,' he said. He didn't put her on hold. There was a long silence after he answered.

'You're sure?' he said finally. 'Yes, no, no, nothing. I'll get back to you.'

'Allison?'

'Yes?' She held her breath.

He took a deep breath of his own.

'He's, um ... he's uh ... Allison?'

'Yes.'

'He's dead, Allison. He's dead. The President's dead. Rosey's dead.'

'Yes.' Her mind was whirling. She couldn't just hang up on him. He was so distraught. But she had to get on the story. Get more reaction. Get to Downing Street.

'I'll let you go then,' she said. 'I know you must have a lot to do. When will you ...? I'll call you later this morning. And Cotes ... I'm terribly sorry.'

Her first file had had only a few bland quotes that she knew the desk wouldn't use. Now she had to call everybody again and file a real react story for the late edition. By the time she had finished it was almost six in the morning and Julian had fallen asleep on the sofa in her office. She wasn't the least bit drunk anymore. Her adrenaline had taken over and she was on a deadline high. She had so much energy she felt as if she would jump out of her skin.

The fact of Rosey's death still hadn't sunk in. The emotion compartment was still closed.

She had an overwhelming rush of sexual desire. She desperately needed the release. It was probably the combination of Rosey's death and working on a tight deadline. She had read about people often wanting to make love after a death. It was supposedly a confirmation of their own aliveness. It was not an unfamiliar feeling either after finishing an emotionally charged story. Des used to say he felt a post-coital slump after finishing a big story, then an enormous surge of sexual energy.

Des. She didn't want to think about him now. She missed him terribly. Was he still in love with Sadie? She knew they hadn't seen each other for three years. But now Sadie was free. Well, she had finished with Desmond Shaw. If Sadie wanted him now, she could have him. If she really believed that, why did she feel sick to her stomach?

She looked over at Julian, sleeping quite soundly on the sofa. He was beautiful and he loved her. He loved her because he couldn't have her. She knew that much.

She walked over to the sofa and knelt down beside him, kissing him softly on the lips, the neck, the ears.

He pretended to be asleep at first, but as her kisses became more insistent, he reached out to her silently, pulling her on top of him, then rolling her easily off the sofa onto the carpet. She raised her arms behind her head and he grabbed her wrists with his hands, pressing them against the floor. She was slipping away into a state of distracted desire as Julian made love to her as if he were expecting her to evaporate any moment.

Neither of them spoke afterward. They lay in each other's arms on the floor, their clothes disheveled, listening to the noise from the wire machine with its urgent clacking, its insistent little bells.

'So,' he said after a long while. 'What will all of this mean?'

He was trying to sound casual.

Allison pretended not to understand.

'It means that we now have a very liberal President from Tennessee. Freddy Osgood. It means that our country will go through another tormenting and soul-searching period about where we went wrong. It means that in about an hour . . . what time is it anyway?'

'Half six.'

'It means that any minute now my phone will start ringing with requests for me to go on British television to talk about the moral decay of America, the inadequacy of our gun control laws, and the wild west mentality of our countrymen.'

'What will this mean for you?'

He couldn't bring himself to say 'us.'

'It means I'll have to go back to the States for the funeral. Muchnick will insist that I stay here to cover British reaction, but the Prime Minister will go, so nothing will be happening here. Besides, Rosey was a friend. Uncle Rog will be there. This will be tough on him. He adored Rosey. I think he was almost relieved when he had a stroke and had to step down from the presidency. I think he really believed Rosey was a better President than he was. He was right. I want to be there with Uncle Rog and Aunt Molly. God, I can't believe I'm talking about Rosey's funeral.'

37

She was talking rapidly.

'Well, then, I shall miss you, my sweet,' he said rather flippantly.

'I'm sure Lady Clarissa will be overjoyed to hear that I'm out of the country.'

'She won't hear it from my lips.'

'I think I'll seal them myself right now, just to make sure,' she said and climbed on top of him, straddling him and this time pinning his arms back behind his head as she playfully began to munch at his mouth, taking little bites and then pulling away.

'Ah, a lovely little farewell fuck,' he said, grabbing her and pulling her down to him, pressing her mouth against his.

The phone rang. It rang again.

'Shit,' said Julian.

'Right on the button,' she said, as she pulled away from him and ran to get it.

'The *Daily*,' she answered. 'Oh, hi, Nigel. Yes, it's horrible. I know, right. What time? Yeah, I don't. I'll have to talk to my desk to see what they want. Moral decay, gun control laws, the usual. I got it. Right. I'll get back to you. Yes, I'm sorry, too.'

She turned to Julian.

'BBC,' she said. 'I'd better check in with the desk again.'

She started to place the call when the phone rang again. It was Cotes.

'Allison? Are you going back?' He sounded very businesslike.

'Yes, though I haven't informed the desk yet.'

'Will you go with me?'

'Oh Cotes, I have to think about this. When are you leaving?'

38

'Late this afternoon or early evening. I talked to Sadie. She just got back from the hospital a few minutes ago. She's still in shock. She wants me to be an honorary pallbearer. She wants me back as soon as I can get there. I've got to go over to Downing Street and advise the PM on their plans to attend the, uh'—he cleared his throat—'the, uh, funeral. I'll be going on an Air Force plane.'

'I don't know, Cotes. How will I pay for it?'

'You don't have to pay for it. You'll be my guest.'

'You know better than that. I'm not even sure the paper will let me even if we can figure out a way to pay for it.'

'Allison, find a way, please. I don't want to go by myself. I don't want that plane ride alone.'

'Okay, Cotes. I'll call you back.'

Her conversation with Muchnick was worse than she had feared. At first he refused to let her come back at all, claiming he couldn't leave England uncovered and he couldn't spare any of his correspondents in Europe to cover for her.

'Look, Muchnick,' she told him finally. 'This is not negotiable.'

She had to go over his head to the managing editor, Walt Fineman, to get them to allow her to go back with Cotes. They would figure out the problem of payment later. She convinced Walt that it would be to their advantage to have access to the ambassador for six hours alone. He would be in touch with the White House from the plane and that would be invaluable to the paper later. She felt a little sleazy even arguing the case that way. What she wanted to say was that her friend was hurting. But journalists weren't supposed to talk that way.

39

The story always came first. So she sold it as a story and he bought it.

She wondered when she would start feeling sad. She hoped not until after the funeral. She had too much work to do.

Julian drove her to the embassy, a block from her office on Upper Brook Street. They hadn't had time to talk all day because she was so busy.

She cold tell he was trying to be nonchalant about her departure, yet both of them sensed that this trip was going to be a turning point.

He stopped the car and turned off the ignition. He didn't look at her right away. She instinctively clutched at her bag, wrapping both her arms around it on her lap. They sat in silence for a moment.

'I think the script calls for an embrace,' he said.

She tried to smile, then reached up and wrapped her arm around his neck, burying her head in his chest. The only sound was the rustle of her raincoat and the rain pelting the roof of the car.

'Don't stay away too long, luv, or I shall soon be beating them away with clubs.'

'If only that weren't true.'

'Actually, I think I'll go down to Sussex and bury myself in my work.'

'Great idea. You'll be safer there.'

'I don't know; Clarissa is rather persistent.'

She blinked back the tears. Fatigue and the events of the day had brought her emotions to the edge.

'Goodbye, Julian.'

He took her chin gently in his hand, leaned over, and kissed her softly on the lips.

'I love you,' he said under his breath.

40

She did not respond.

It was only later on the plane that she realized he had never told her that before.

*       *       *

Cotes was waiting for her in one of the seats at the back of the little Air Force Gulfstream 3. She took the seat facing him. She was relieved to see they were alone.

Cotes, with his choirboy face and mop of sandy hair, actually looked his age at the moment. There were dark circles under his bloodshot eyes.

He wore a crewneck sweater. She had slipped into a knit pullover and socks. He was sipping a bourbon on the rocks. She ordered a beer, a proper antidote to her hangover.

As the plane took off, the steward brought Cotes another drink and a cheese tray, then disappeared into the galley to the rear.

Cotes seemed calm as they compared notes about what had happened to Rosey.

By now they knew that the gunman had been a Vietnam veteran and a former communications expert at the White House who had gotten deeply involved in drugs and been fired as a result. He had tapped into the White House communications system to learn the President's habits and schedule, had rented an apartment in the building behind Lorraine Hadley's house in Georgetown, and had waited for an opportunity to kill Rosewell Grey. He had been diagnosed recently as psychotic. He had left a note saying he was acting on his own, that he wanted to punish the President personally for destroying his life.

41

He had been gunned down by the Secret Service minutes after they discovered him on the other side of the wall from Lorraine's backyard. There appeared to be no conspiracy.

Cotes consumed an entire bottle of wine at dinner. Against her better judgment she had submitted to his pressure and had drunk over a half bottle herself.

It was only after the steward had retired that Cotes, sufficiently plastered and working on a brandy, let down his guard.

'Jesus,' he said at last. 'Jesus, I loved that som'bitch.'

Cotes's accent by now was so Southern it was almost unintelligible.

'He was closer to me than my goddamn brother. He was so private. He never let on about his problems; he never bragged on his triumphs. But he talked to me. And he was the one I talked to. We were each other's only confidants.'

Tears rolled down Cotes's face and Allison, who had tried to keep herself together all day, found his grief catching. He put his head down on the table between them and began to sob. She hadn't heard a man cry like that since her father, Sam, wept when her mother died. It was her first memory. She was two. Sam had been dead for over ten years, murdered by a burglar. Now, exhausted and confronting Rosey's death for the first time all day, the anguish of Sam's death overwhelmed her.

She was crying softly when Cotes raised his head and began to howl like some wounded animal.

Then he began to sing, quietly at first, almost whispering, until finally he was belting out 'Amazing Grace' in a beautiful baritone.

Allison listened, tears streaming down her face. Once she had allowed herself to start she couldn't stop.

When he finished, they were both so drained that there were no tears left. She closed her eyes, hoping that Cotes would let her sleep. She was drifting away when he called her name.

'I just want you to know that I know everything,' he said abruptly.

'What do you mean?' She was still half asleep and confused.

'I know about Sadie and Desmond Shaw.'

'Sadie and Des?'

She was awake now. She knew very well what he meant. She waited to let him tell her. And old reporter's trick. He might not know everything. Or he might know more than she did.

'Rosey told me. It damn near killed him.'

Allison just stared at him. Why did it still hurt as though it had happened yesterday and not two years ago?

'Sonny, I know that Sadie and Des had an affair. I know you found out about it and broke up with him. That's why you requested a foreign assignment. Sadie told Rosey everything when she ended it with Des before the convention. I could have strangled her for it. I still don't see how she could have done it. Christ. The risk. The humiliation for Rosey if it had gotten out. The First Lady fucking the bureau chief of the *Weekly*. Bitch. That's what I called her to Rosey's face. Bitch. It was the only time he's ever been really mad at me. Gentleman to the end, he blamed himself. But she was. She was a goddamn bitch.'

Allison closed her eyes again.

43

'Cotes,' she said, 'I really don't want to talk about it. Please.'

'You're still in love with that bastard, aren't you?'

'I hate his guts.'

'It's worse than I thought.'

She didn't respond.

'What about Julian?'

'I care deeply about Julian.'

'That's the kiss of death. Well, I can't say I'm pained to hear it. He's managed to knock off every great piece of ass in London. In fact, you're the only woman who's given him any trouble at all. The elusive Miss Allison Sterling.'

'If I fell in love with him he'd lose interest in me in a minute.'

Despite herself, Cotes had drawn her into the conversation.

'So what are you saving yourself for? You're not getting any younger.'

Cotes's tone had suddenly changed and she stiffened slightly.

'What's that supposed to mean?'

'Well, I mean you're forty years old. You're a very beautiful woman. I can't imagine any man not wanting you. Time's running out if you want to have babies.'

'That's *my* problem, Cotes.'

She was just tired enough and had had enough to drink that she didn't feel like being diplomatic.

'Well, I might be able to help you out.'

'Cotes, what the hell are you talking about?'

'I'd like to throw my hat in the ring, Sonny, I'm just drunk enough and just pitiful enough tonight to have the courage to ask you.'

'Oh God,' she said and buried her face in her hands.

'I probably didn't say it right. I mean, I know this isn't the best timing, it's just that I've admired you for so long, but I thought you were in love with Julian so I didn't, then tonight when you ... I just wondered ... oh, shut up, Tennant. You're making an ass out of yourself. Forget I said anything. It's just the booze talking. I don't know. Sometimes I get so goddamned lonely. God, I get lonely. And now ... now Rosey's dead. My buddy, my best friend is dead.'

He put his head down on the table. Allison reached over and put her hand on the top of his head, stroking it gently.

He was asleep in seconds. She leaned her head back and immediately fell asleep as well.

The steward didn't wake them until the plane was landing. They avoided each other's glance as they took turns going to the bathroom to freshen up. Cotes disappeared up to the cockpit to chat with the pilots until they were on the ground.

The White House had sent a car to meet Cotes. Allison accepted a ride, insisting that she sit in front while a staffer briefed Cotes. They dropped him at the White House first.

'Goodbye, Allison. I'll probably see you tomorrow,' he said, matter-of-factly, as he got out. 'Thank you for coming with me.'

Once she had checked into her room at the Jefferson Hotel, a block from the *Daily*, she called the desk. It was after ten.

Unfortunately Muchnick was still there.

'So, did you get a story?'

'There was no story, but ...'

'Great. That nonstory probably will cost us a cool five thousand bucks. Well, how was the food?'

'I'm going to bed. It's been a long day. I'll see you in the morning.'

'Yeah, well, don't be late. We've got a funeral to cover.'

'So I'm told.'

## CHAPTER THREE

Willie woke her up, bounding into her room and jumping up onto the bed. She could feel his warm breath on her cheek, his pudgy fingers around her neck. It was his usual morning ritual. Released by his nanny to attack them he would come wake them up, sometimes earlier than they had hoped. Still half asleep, she wound her arms around his body.

'Ummmm,' she said, burrowing her face into the sweet folds of his neck. 'I'm gon' get me some sugar.' She began to kiss him until he giggled with delight. She squeezed him even tighter and began to rock back and forth with him from side to side.

'Where's my daddy?' he asked suddenly.

She felt a shock as she realized she had forgotten. She had been sound asleep when he came in.

Rosey was dead. There was no daddy. Their world was shattered. She let go of Willie, helpless in front of this two-year-old child. A numbness began to creep up her body. She hadn't read the books that tell you what to say.

'Mommy, where's my daddy?'

He gestured to the empty side of the bed. Queen-size. Rosey hated king-size.

'I like to hold on to you,' he had said. 'You get lost in a kingsize bed.'

She looked over at the fresh pillow, undented; the sheets neat and tucked in. Willie was right. He wasn't there. She touched his pillow just to make sure it wasn't an illusion. Acceptance hadn't really taken hold yet.

Willie was watching her as she moved her hand along the pillow, as though she saw something he could not. As though it were some sort of magic trick where his daddy would come leaping out from behind the pillow.

'Wheeeeeeeeeeeere's Daddy?' squealed Willie with pleasure and pounced on the pillow, picking it up and looking underneath. But nobody said, 'There he is!' and popped out.

Willie, undaunted, tried again. 'Wheeeeeeeeeeeere's Daddy?' Sadie buried her face in her hands.

Willie quieted down. He put his hand on her arm and said softly, 'Mommy?'

'Mommy's very sad, Willie.'

Willie put his arms around her.

She really believed that he understood, because he didn't let her go for the longest time.

Then he asked again. 'Where's my daddy?'

'Daddy's gone to heaven.'

'What's heaven?'

'It's a beautiful place where everybody's very happy. And Daddy can sit in a big chair and watch over us. He can protect us in heaven and make sure everything is okay. He's watching us right now, and he wants us to be happy too.' She could barely speak.

'Do they have candy there?'

47

'Yes, lots of candy and everything.'

'I want to go there, too.'

'So do I, my precious. So do I.'

*      *      *

There were so many things to think about. So many things to do, to plan. She had never really thought that Rosey might die despite the premonition. They'd never even discussed it. He'd left everything to her to be divided among the three children. He'd told her that once. That was the extent of their talks about death. He never said where he wanted to be buried. What kind of funeral. It never occurred to either one of them that he would die so soon. That was probably unrealistic, his being President. What did they think all those Secret Service had been for? They were there because there were people who wanted to kill the President. But there was something invincible about Rosey, some inherent belief he had about himself that he imparted to others. Maybe it was his upper-class background, his WASP mentality. They wouldn't dare.

Rosey hadn't been dead 24 hours.

Now, here she was sitting in her little office on the second floor of the White House besieged with questions, requests, demands, other people's needs, and almost worse, sympathy. The sympathy was what was so debilitating. She could function all right until she saw someone looking at her with sympathy. Then she would respond appropriately by becoming pitiful.

She hated the way Jenny was looking at her. Her eyebrows would knit together in a solemn way

48

every time she glanced at Sadie, every time she said, 'How are you?'

'Damn it, Jenny, stop looking at me that way. I'm okay until you look at me like that. You're not helping me any. And for God's sake stop asking me how I am. You know how I am.'

Jenny looked stricken.

'I'm sad, Jen. I'm very, very sad.' The tears began to come. She couldn't stop them any more than she could stop breathing. They were streaking down her cheeks.

'My husband is dead. My husband, whom I loved and whom I betrayed. My husband, who was the father of my children'—she stopped in midsentence and sucked in her breath—Rosey was the father of two of her children. She buried her face in her hands. 'Oh my God, my God,' she said. 'What kind of pain I must have caused him. I can't bear it, Jenny. I just can't bear it.'

She was talking to herself now, oblivious of Jenny's presence.

'Oh Rosey, please don't be dead. Please don't leave now. You have to forgive me. I wanted to make it up to you. How can I ever make you understand? I can't live with this kind of grief. I can't do it.'

Jenny got up and put her arms around Sadie, holding her, rocking her, the two of them swaying in unison to the sounds of their sobs.

'What am I going to do? How can I go through with this?' she asked softly. 'I can't control myself. The whole world is going to be staring at me. And I can't stop crying. I've got to be controlled and I can't. I'll shame my husband and my country and myself . . . Can't we say I've had a stroke? The shock of it has been too much. They can do it without me. That would be better than having the President's widow hysterical and flinging her body on the coffin. Nobody would want that, would they?'

Jenny said nothing. It was better just to let her talk.

'Jenny, I'm not kidding. I'm about to become one of the great national embarrassments in the history of this country. You know how I am anyway. I cry at the drop of a hat. I cry at insurance company commercials. I've always marveled at those women who can go to their husbands' funerals and remain stoic throughout the whole ceremony. Stiff upper lip. Head held high. And afterward everybody says, "Oh, wasn't she wonderful, wasn't she incredible. So brave. So courageous. So dignified." Well, not me. Forget it. I'm simply not capable of it. I'm already a basket case. You know what they'll say about me? "Could you believe her? What an incredibly bad scene. Really, it was inexcusable. You'd think she'd be able to control herself for a few hours, in front of the whole world. She has a position to uphold. She's not representing herself, she's representing the country. Class tells. It's lucky the President isn't alive to see this humiliating display of emotion. Grotesque is the only word for it."'

Jenny still said nothing. She could see that Sadie was working herself up into a frenzy and she felt helpless to do anything about it. Sadie had created such a devastating scenario that even Jenny was becoming apprehensive. She had seen Sadie when she was obsessed before, and she worried that she might not be able to calm her down.

50

'I can't do it, Jenny. You better tell them now so they can plan for my not being there. We'll have to think of some really legitimate excuse.'

'Sadie,' said Jenny gently. 'You know you're going to have to go to the funeral...'

'Jenny, don't you understand? It's not that I don't want to. I want nothing more than to be there, to honor my husband before the world. But I'm not capable of it. I would only dishonor him. I can't do that to him ... Not again.'

'Sadie, why don't I go get Cotes? He's out there with Manolas and Harry Saks. They're desperate to see you. They've got to start going over the plans. It's Sunday evening already. The funeral is Wednesday; tomorrow you've got all the memorial services in the East Room. You haven't even decided yet whether Rosey should be buried in Arlington or Richmond. Your parents want to talk to you; Rosey's parents want to talk to you. Your children need you. Outland and Annie Laurie are wandering around like lost souls. Annie Laurie is a basket case. The baby is the only one who's fine. Willie thinks it's like somebody's birthday party.'

Sadie started to smile, then felt herself losing control again.

'Everything makes me cry now, Jenny. You see.'

'I'll go get Cotes.'

'Jenny?'

'You've got to convince them that I can't do it. I'm dead serious. There's just no way I'm going to be able to hold it together. If I have to I'll drug myself so I really am incapacitated. I'm just too sad, Jenny. I'm just too sad.'

She leaped up from her chair when she saw him and flung her arms around his neck as if he might

51

disappear.

'Cotes, thank God you're here.'

'Oh Sadie, I'm so sorry,' he said, embracing her. They stood there in the middle of the room, holding on to each other.

'Lordy, lordy, I'm not doing too well either, now am I? I'm supposed to be here to console you and look at me.' He tried to smile as he wiped his eyes with the back of his hand.

She took his arm and sat him down on the sofa next to her, putting her head on his shoulder. He took her hand and stroked it. The two of them sat there for a long time in silence.

'Miss Sadiebelle. What can I do? How can I help?'

'Get me out of this, Cotes. I can't go through it. I know I won't be able to control myself. It will be too humiliating.'

'Just let me tell you one thing, darlin'. You can do it and you will. You're a strong woman, Sadie. Hell, you're a lot stronger than I am and I went through it with Mary Louise. Granted, I didn't have to do it in front of millions of people, but honestly, Sadie, it doesn't make it any easier to grieve in private. The pain is still there ... and the guilt.'

She winced when he said that. She turned to him and looked him in the face for the first time.

'He told you?'

'Jesus, Sadie. He had to talk to somebody. Just because he was President of the United States didn't mean he wasn't suffering. And he was scared. Scared somebody might find out. He had to worry about damage control. We got awful close in those last months before Mary Louise died. I told

52

him everything. I really bared my soul. He did, too.'

'How can you not hate me then?'

'I did. I did for a long time. I still get angry. I couldn't bloody well believe it. Not only the personal pain you caused him but the political jeopardy. But godammit, Sadie. Who am I to criticize anybody? I did the same thing. Then I had to contend with the guilt. If I had it, you've got it in spades. But if he forgave you, I can, too.'

Cotes stood and looked down at her. His face was flushed with conviction.

Sadie smiled in spite of herself. He looked like the Southern Episcopal High School graduate he was.

'Oh Cotes, thank you for that. I couldn't stand it if you hated me now. I need you. If I'm going to go through with this I am going to need you.'

'You're going to go through with this, Sadie. You have no choice and you know it.'

Her lack of response was an acknowledgement.

'There are a lot of people who are going to need you now, Sadiebelle. Your children. Especially Annie Laurie. She's been queen of the hill at Sweetbriar and in Richmond. She was her daddy's little darlin'. She had a real special relationship with Rosey. I know you and Annie Laurie have always had your problems. But she is devastated by this; she's going to need her mama. Outland's being very brave. He feels he's the man of the family now and he's going to have to take care of you. That puts a lot of pressure on him. He told me this afternoon he was thinking of not going back to Stanford and staying here so you wouldn't be lonely. There's going to be a lot of attention focused on those two

53

kids. And they are still kids. We forget that once they're grown and out of the house, off to school. But no two teenagers will ever have the responsibility to carry themselves with dignity the way your two will in the next few days. You are going to have to set an example for them. Nobody else can do it.'

He paused. She was taking it all in. Still saying nothing.

'I don't mean to be harsh on you, Sadie. I'm just trying to be realistic. You are the President's wife.'

She looked up at him quickly.

'Widow.'

She glanced down at her hands. She had begun twisting the ring Rosey had meant for her on her birthday. She kept staring at it, twisting it back and forth until the skin underneath was raw.

'Sadie, say something. I'm just shooting off my mouth and you're just sitting there. What are you thinking?'

'You're not going to approve. Jenny's not going to approve,' she said quietly.

'Well, what is it for Christ's sake? I told you I'll do anything to help you. And you're going to have to do whatever it takes to get you through this. What do you want?'

She hesitated for a moment, still pulling at the ring. Then she looked up at Cotes, standing in front of the sofa. Her eyes were clear and direct and when she spoke, her voice was determined.

'I want to see Des.'

★          ★          ★

She hadn't slept all night. The doctor had given her

a tranquilizer but instead of putting her to sleep it had hyped her up. She always had had a weird reaction to drugs. They seemed to have the opposite effect. Valium made her nervous, jumpy. When she did begin to doze, dreams invaded her sleep. For some odd reason she dreamt of Allison Sterling. She hadn't thought of her for a long time. There was no reason to. She knew Allison had gone to London. She saw her byline often enough in the *Daily*. Jenny had told her Allison and Des were finished.

She had managed to put the whole thing with Des out of her head for the past few years. She had tried to be a good wife to Rosey. She had succeeded. She loved Rosey. She had never stopped loving him, which was one reason the whole thing had been so complicated. Even now she wasn't sure if she had ever really been in love with Des. She had been tremendously attracted to him. He had been an obsession. It was as if it had been beyond her control. But she never really trusted him. Or trusted his love. The specter of Allison had always been there, even though he had denied it.

There had never been any doubt with Rosey. He adored her. She was his life. After she had stopped seeing Des, Rosey's love for her had been so comforting that her own feelings for him had deepened more than she had ever expected.

She had learned a powerful lesson about marriage. You could never have everything in one person. She had known she would never be totally sexually satisfied with Rosey. But she had gotten so much more of value from him that it was an acceptable trade-off. In the end, she had to admit that even though sex was important to her it was not as important as security. Something her relationship with Des was lacking in spades. If she could get along better with Annie Laurie, if they could be friends, she would try to tell her about marriage. Nobody ever tells young brides what to expect. Nobody ever tells you how much pain and compromise and anger and disappointment there is in even the happiest marriage. When she became attracted to Des she didn't know what it meant. She didn't know how you were expected to know whether your own marriage was finished or not. What were the signs that a marriage was over, that it was time to pack it in? How could you tell whether you were just going through a rough patch, as all marriages do?

Now that it was too late, she realized that she had misread the signs. She had mistaken her infatuation with Des for real love when in fact it was just that, infatuation. Granted she had been under a lot of stress. Roger Kimball, the President, had suffered a stroke and had to step down. Rosey was thrust into the presidency after only three years in Washington.

Becoming a prisoner in a fishbowl had been too much for her. She had lost control. Des had helped her find herself and her identity. He had encouraged her to write again, get her own office, be her own person. He had saved her. It was almost like having an affair with your shrink. But when it had come to a choice of leaving Rosey, she had backed down. The idea of leaving Rosey was too terrifying. When she was honest with herself she knew why. Des wanted her to stand on her own. She had never been on her own in her life. She had always had a man to take care of her. She always would. She couldn't survive without one. Rosey

56

had taken care of her, protected her, provided for her. It was primitive, perhaps, but there it was. Her affair with Des had been instructive in one sense. It had shown her her needs. Des didn't, wouldn't, couldn't fulfill them. Rosey had.

Now here she was without him. The realization as she tossed and turned in her empty bed in the White House suddenly overwhelmed her.

Goddamn Rosey for dying. For getting killed. It was his fault. The Secret Service never wanted him to go outside at Lorraine's house in the first place. She knew because she had overheard a conversation at the hospital. They had warned Lorraine and told him not to go out in the garden. He did it anyway. He obviously didn't care about her or Willie or the other children either. To deliberately risk his life that way. It was so irresponsible. Every President knows you have to be careful. You're just a sitting duck. Why did he do it? Just to look at some stupid garden. Probably just to show off to Lorraine that he knew a lot about flowers. Suddenly she was consumed with rage at her husband. Her fingernails were digging into her palms and her jaw was so tight she felt as if her teeth would break. Goddamn him. She hated him at this moment more than she had ever hated anyone in her life. Because of him she would have to be put through this horrible public spectacle. Alone. But maybe not. The hell with Rosey.

There was one person who could give her the emotional strength to get through it all. And not just the funeral either. The next few days, weeks, months, maybe even years. Willie's father: Des. He didn't know he was Willie's father. She would have to tell him. He would be more reliable now. He

57

would have to be because of Willie. He wouldn't expect her to be so independent now. She was the President's widow. Just because Rosey was dead didn't mean she was a different person. She was still the same woman with the same needs. She needed a man and Des was the only candidate. She wasn't even thinking about sex now. She was thinking about her emotional and psychological state. When she asked to see Des she hadn't thought of resuming a relationship with him. She had needed to cleanse herself of her guilt. To make her confession. He was Catholic. He would understand. He was the only person who could rid her of that horrible pain. He could not only help her with her guilt, he could get her through this.

Toward dawn Sadie fell asleep, exhausted. She was also relieved. Just the idea of having Des to call on, if nothing else, gave her a sense of security. As it was, she felt as though she were drowning. Des might be a life raft with a hole in it, but it was better than nothing.

*      *      *

The first service in the East Room for family and close friends was at 11:00 a.m. The rest of the day was given over to other ceremonies for members of Congress and diplomats, then the press corps. She wished Des were coming, but she didn't dare ask him. Nobody would understand, and Cotes wouldn't have let her anyway. She would have to rely on Cotes for the ceremony.

She looked at her face in the mirror and was horrified at what she saw. She was pale and drawn, her face drained of all color. She thought she looked at least fifty years old. Tiny lines were beginning to show around her eyes. The only good thing was that she hadn't eaten anything in the last two days so she looked a bit thinner. Rosey liked them tall and slim. She always accused him of liking those overbred, horsey, Foxcroft, Virginia, hunt-country women with long legs and no sense of humor. He was delighted when he thought she might, after all, be a little jealous.

But Rosey was dead. Why was she thinking about what Rosey liked? He had died and left her alone. It didn't matter what Rosey had liked. Damn him. She was by herself. Now she could do as she pleased.

She wondered whether she should add a little color to her cheeks, then decided not to. Let them see her pain.

There was a knock on the door and Cotes came in, looking quite upset and flustered.

'Christ, Sadie,' he said. 'We forgot to invite the President to any of the memorial services in the East Room today.'

The President. He said the word and she flinched. Rosey was dead. He wasn't the President anymore. She wasn't the First Lady anymore either. The White House wasn't her home. She had no home.

'Don't you think we ought to invite the Osgoods to the family service? Roger Kimball is coming. I think it would be a nice gesture.'

'I'm not having those people at the family service,' she said. There was a finality to her voice that left Cotes speechless.

'They're not friends of ours. Rosey only picked him to balance the ticket because he was a liberal

59

Democrat. I can't stand her. I can't stand the way she talks, that ridiculous platinum beehive, the ankle bracelet, all those country-western songs she sings every time anybody blinks at her, the low-cut tight dresses. She looks like a hooker for God's sake ... and he's vulgar and uncouth.'

She didn't know why she had exploded about the Osgoods. She didn't hate Blanche at all. She thought she was tacky but she sort of felt sorry for her. It was Freddy she wasn't crazy about.

Her anger at Rosey was pouring out of her and everyone was suffering because of it, even her children.

'I'm sorry, Cotes. It's just that, I don't know. It's too soon. It's too hard. Can't they go to the congressional service later? I need just one private family moment for myself before it all goes public. They're not my family. They're not close friends. They're political. It isn't fitting. I'll do it all according to protocol after this morning. But I need this morning, please.'

'I'll tell the President myself.'

He started to walk out of the room, then turned to her.

'Sadiebelle,' he said.

'Yes?'

'I hate to tell you this, but you have a run in your stocking.'

She glanced down at her black stocking and saw the dreaded white line running up the side of her leg. Her face began to crumple. Without warning she felt herself going to pieces. She started to cry, burying her face in her hands.

'Oh my God, Des, what am I going to do? I don't have another pair. I never wear black stockings. I

60

don't own any. I have three more days of this and no black stockings. I can't bear it.'

She was sobbing so hard that Cotes could hardly understand her. He walked over and put his arms around her, rocking her back and forth until she quieted.

'It's all right. It's okay. I'll send somebody to get you a dozen pairs right now. Don't worry. We'll take care of it. It'll be just fine.'

Finally she pulled away.

'I'm sorry again,' she said. 'I really am a basket case, aren't I?'

He looked down at her and smiled sympathetically.

'Sadie,' he said, almost apologetically.

'Yes?'

'My name is Cotes.'

## CHAPTER FOUR

What struck Allison when she walked in was how silent the newsroom was. It was 5:00 p.m., closing in on deadline, a time when the entire paper is normally in a frenzy. Yet there was an eerie hush, broken only by the occasional sound of a ringing telephone.

She found herself almost tiptoeing across the room to the managing editor's office. She knew protocol demanded that she see the executive editor, Alan Warburg, first, but Walt Fineman was her friend. She walked with such determination that the colleagues she passed barely had time to nod to her. She would see them later. She needed

Walt right now.

When he saw her he leaped up from his desk and ran toward her taking her in his arms and crushing her till she could barely breathe. She could hear him stifle a sob.

'I'm sorry,' he said finally, letting her go. He wiped his eyes, then put his arm around her and led her to the sofa. She found herself losing control and bit down on her lip to stop it. Not in the newsroom.

'It's okay, Sonny. Everybody's doing it,' he said.

'What's happened, Walt? Jesus, what happened?'

'We don't know any more than we did last night. Some nut case. A Vietnam vet who used to be with White House communications. Got fired for his drug problem and wanted to punish the President. Tapped into the private phone line, monitored their activities. Rented an apartment behind Lorraine's house and wasted him on Sadie's birthday.'

'It can't be that simple.'

'We think it is. But the conspiracy theorists are still crawling out of the fucking woodwork. The usual liberal media stuff. Don't want to look too closely because the assassin was antiwar, anti-Vietnam.'

She hesitated before she asked the next question. Trying to be as casual as she could.

'How's Sadie taking it?'

Walt looked at her carefully, then looked down. She wondered if he knew.

'Hard. She's pretty broken up, actually. I've talked to Jenny a couple of times. Funny, I never really thought the Greys had that great a relationship.'

'Wonder what Jenny's going to do now?' She wanted to change the subject.

'I'm afraid she's going to ask for her old job back on the national staff.'

'What will you do?'

'You can't go home again, Sonny. Not after you've been the First Lady's press secretary. You're tainted.'

'They do it all the time at the *New York World*.' She was half-hearted about her old best friend.

'Yeah, and look what happens. The revolving-door policy just doesn't work very well. Their allegiances are confused. She ought to go into PR.'

Allison shivered. That was the kiss of death for a true journalist.

They were silent for a moment. It only made the silence of the newsroom more noticeable.

'I can't believe how quiet it is,' she said.

'It's been like this. And everybody's being so nice. Even Muchnick sent out for coffee and sandwiches.'

'Sterling, you're back!' Alan Warburg said as he walked into Walt's office.

Allison, guilty, jumped up from the sofa.

'Alan, I was just coming in to see you.'

'Sure, sure. I get no respect around here.'

Normally brittle and tense, the executive editor seemed gentler than Allison had ever seen him. She put out her hand to shake his, but as he grabbed it he embraced her with his free arm. The hug brought tears to her eyes, as it did to his.

'It's a bitch, huh?' he said.

'Oh Alan, it's just so horrible.'

'Well,' he said stiffening, 'we've got to get on with the show. What are you up to, Sonny? Muchnick tells me you flew over with Tennant.

He's one of the pallbearers. Did you get anything?'

'Background. Nothing for a story. He's pretty broken up, too. Muchnick will probably take my head off.'

'Not today. He's a pussy cat. What about your godfather? Surely he'll be here. All the former Presidents are coming. We don't have a confirm on him though. It'll be hard for him in that wheelchair.'

'Jesus, I forgot to call him. I'll do that right now. Aunt Molly just had heart surgery so she won't be coming.'

'Well, you obviously need to keep an eye on the Brits. But I think you'd be more valuable to us at the White House right now. You know all the players. Are you and Cotes Tennant pretty tight?'

'I think he'll keep me informed.' There was something about Alan's question that seemed a little too personal. Maybe it was her imagination. She hadn't had much sleep lately and wasn't going to get much in the next few days either.

'Good. Well, you'd better get over there. We're almost on deadline.'

'I need to make a quick pass through the newsroom to check in and get a fill. Then I'll call Uncle Rog. Then I'll go over to the White House.'

She was talking to Walt as Alan walked out of the office.

'Sonny,' said Walt.

'Yes?'

'Des will be there.'

\* \* \*

The White House press room had changed since

64

she'd been away. Gone were the filthy suede sofas and chairs that had been at least comfortable and where the regulars had hung out. They had been replaced with blue folding theater chairs with the names of the major papers and networks marked on them. They were lined up to face the dais.

The place was packed. It was hot and humid and smelled of too many damp bodies. The unusually dry July Washington weather that had allowed Lorraine to have cocktails outside had reverted to the familiar swamplike mugginess that was summer in the nation's capital. There were so many people coming in and out of the press room that somebody had just propped the door open so the overworked air-conditioning was hardly cooling the room at all. People were sprawled in the theater chairs, cameramen were dozing on the raised platform at the end of the room where their equipment was set up, ready for the occasional announcements, bulletins, and briefings. In contrast to the *Daily*'s newsroom the noise was deafening. Reporters shouting at press aides, cameramen and technicians shouting at each other, people yelling at editors on the telephones, everyone's tempers frayed trying to get the story and get it out. In the back, where some of the major papers had their cubicles and the networks had their mini-booths, the place was also in chaos. It was 6.00 p.m., deadline for the news broadcasts, too. The door to the tiny ladies' room was locked. One of the TV reporters had holed up inside to do her hair and makeup in time for the broadcast. Several women were pounding on it in outrage, telling her to get out. In the small room beyond, where the food machines were squeezed in between extra camera equipment, there were empty

65

coffee cups, candy wrappers, and plastic bags strewn around on the few tables and on the floor. If one didn't know the President had been assassinated the day before, there was certainly no evidence of it here.

Even though she had had dinner on the plane. Allison was suddenly hungry, and she also realized that she was beginning to have a hangover. There was hardly anything left to eat in the food machines. A bruised apple and a bag of pork rinds. She put her money in the machine and stood for a moment, unable to make a decision. She knew she should have the apple but she really wanted...

'Oh, go ahead. Have the pork rinds.'

There it was. That sensation in her gut just hearing his voice. She had hoped it might be gone. She didn't want to look at him, afraid of what she would see, would feel.

She pressed the knob for the apple and it fell into the bin in front of her.

She picked it up, polished it against her skirt, held it up as if to take a bite, and turned to look at him triumphantly.

'That's my girl.' It was his dazzling grin that got her.

'Bastard.'

'And they're off...'

Before she could respond they both noticed people rushing from their cubicles in the back up to the front room where George Manolas, the President's press secretary, had appeared at the lectern for an announcement.

They both stopped what they were doing, ran into the front room, took places standing against the wall since the *Daily* and the *Weekly* seats were

66

taken by the correspondents who regularly covered the White House. They all took out their notebooks and waited.

Manolas stood quietly in front of the crowd as people found places. His eyes were red and swollen, his face grim, but he seemed relatively composed.

Looking at Manolas forced reality on everyone and the room became still, almost as if people had stopped breathing.

'As you know,' he said, clearing his throat, 'the assassin was killed and we have no new information on him since we last spoke. The plans for the funeral are progressing. The President's body...' his voice broke slightly. Several of the journalists wiped tears away as they tried to take notes. '... has been autopsied and has just been brought into the East Room to lie in state. I don't need to tell you that today's Fourth of July activities across the nation were cancelled. The First Lady and the family are gathering in the family quarters where they will be dining alone tonight. We'll be passing out schedules as plans are firmed up. But briefly, tomorrow, Monday, there will be services in the East Room for the family and close friends, then for members of Congress and the administration, then for members of the diplomatic corps. Tuesday the body will lie in state at the Capitol, and Wednesday is the funeral. Right now it has not been decided whether the President will be buried in his family plot in Richmond or at Arlington Cemetery. Any questions?'

The room erupted in shouts, everyone was on deadline now. Some were running for phones without even waiting for details.

'What's the magazine doing?' Allison asked Des.

'We're holding the issue until tomorrow. We have to go a day late. Those little fuckers on duty last night didn't bother to show up for the pool with the President. There was no press there when he got shot, only a photographer. They really got caught with their pants down this time.'

'Are you serious?' She paused. 'I don't know why I sound so surprised. The magazines skip the pool all the time on weekends. They were bound to get caught sometime. But the President gets shot and there's no pool, my God. What about the networks?'

'Nobody.'

She looked at Des in amazement. Amazement at her ability to compartmentalize. One minute she was weeping over the assassination of her friend, the President of the United States, the next her heart was pounding at seeing Des again, after almost two years, the next she was a hard-core professional oblivious to anything but THE STORY. Maybe that was what had been wrong with their relationship in the first place. Maybe that was why he had left her.

He was taking notes and she studied him almost clinically for several moments. Damn him, he looked better than he ever had. There was more gray, but it only served to soften his wavy black hair. Maybe a few more laugh lines around the eyes, but nothing diminished those long lashes and that insolent twinkle. He had a sexy mouth. Sensuous. And a strong jaw, good teeth. Her eyes moved down to his wrinkled navy linen blazer, loosened tie with . . . without a spot! That was an improvement. And could that bold striped shirt be an old British one she had given him? Somewhat frayed around

68

the white collar but his one concession to decent dressing. His hands were her favorite thing about him. They were short and square and tanned. Very masculine. She didn't have to see his body to remember it. Broad shoulders, a hairless muscular chest, and the greatest ass on any man she had ever seen.

He looked up from his notebook and caught her eye.

She blushed. She could have killed herself. Giving him the edge.

'Remembering what a great ass I have, Sterling?'

'Actually, I was remembering what a pain in the ass you were, Shaw.'

'Ah, how I've missed you, Sonny.'

They looked at each other directly for the first time. She couldn't tell whether he was joking or not. He knew it, too. She just smiled an enigmatic smile.

'Des, I've got all I need and I'm walking back to the bureau, coming?'

A tall, dark-haired, attractive young woman in her early thirties walked up to Des and spoke to him, completely ignoring Allison. Her tone was overly familiar, Allison thought. It was obvious that she had something going with him or thought she did.

'Julie Fensterer, Allison Sterling,' he said, stepping back a little, as though he expected the two of them to tear into each other.

Julie Fensterer stopped dead and turned to look at Allison. What Allison saw in her eyes was fear. Julie quickly checked Allison out and what she saw did not alleviate her apprehension.

'I've read you for years,' she said. 'You're the

69

reason I decided to go to journalism school.'

Allison suddenly felt old, but she refused to respond to Julie's subtle dig. Des looked relieved.

'Why don't you go on ahead, Julie,' he said. 'It's going to be tight tonight. I'll be along shortly.'

Julie flushed. She glanced at Allison, then back at Des, then reluctantly she said, 'Fine,' stuffed her tape recorder in her bag and started out the door.

'What are your plans?' he asked Allison.

'I've got to talk to Manolas briefly, then I'm going across the street to Blair House to see Uncle Rog. Apparently he's just arrived. I've promised Cotes Tennant I'd have a drink with him at the Hay Adams later.'

'You're not filing?'

'I've already called in some stuff on the Brits for foreign. The Opinion section wants me to do a piece. I told them I'd think about it. I just don't feel like writing anything, though. I've been away too long. And I feel so conflicted about Rosey in so many ways.'

'Tell me about it.'

His jaw hardened and his eyes welled up. She was afraid he was going to cry right there in the midst of all the pandemonium. She could feel herself start to break down. There were so many emotions to deal with between them. It was too much.

'I gotta get out of here,' he said. 'I'm losing it.'

He turned and walked quickly out the door and up the walkway toward the gate. It was twilight, and though it was still uncomfortably hot and muggy it had cooled down in the time she had been in the press room. The TV crews were still standing in front of the White House doing their standups. Allison followed Des almost to the gate before they were alone again.

'Des?'

'I'd like to see you, Sonny.'

He wasn't kidding this time.

'What's your schedule?'

'Call me when you've finished with Tennant. I'll be at the bureau all night. Maybe we can get together for a drink then?'

It wasn't a command. Still, she hesitated. Even after all this time, just having a drink with him would be putting in for more pain than she needed. She could see that already.

'I don't know, I . . .'

'Please.'

'Okay.'

He squeezed her arm. His eyes were still filled with tears as he turned and walked away.

\*        \*        \*

The bar at the Hay Adams Hotel, across Lafayette Square from the White House, was packed. Even so you could have heard a pin drop. People sat in corner banquettes, on sofas and chairs in small clusters whispering to each other as they might have done in a funeral home. There was no one to disturb, but it didn't seem to matter. The bar was a fitting room to mourn. In faux olde English, with dark wood paneling, antlers, tapestries, and heavy paisleys, it lacked only suits of armor for the final touch. A pianist normally serenaded the guests, but there was none this Sunday summer Fourth of July.

Allison was seated in a corner by the fireplace. Cotes hadn't arrived yet so she ordered a light beer.

Her visit with Uncle Rog at Blair House, where

71

all the former Presidents were staying, had depressed her. As if she wasn't depressed enough already. He was still in terrible shape nearly four years after the stroke that had forced him to turn the presidency over to Rosey. His left arm and leg were still partially paralyzed and he spoke with a slight slur. She had had a quick bite with him but he had tired so easily, she decided to leave him so he could get a good night's sleep. Rosey's death had hit him very hard. He had broken down more than once while they talked, finally pushing his tray aside, unable to eat. He had been asked by Sadie to join the family for the first service in the East Room and he had insisted that Allison come along for moral support.

He had an attendant who had traveled with him from Colorado, but she could see he needed more than that. Allison had reluctantly agreed to be there though she wasn't at all sure how Sadie would feel about it.

This was the first time she had ever worried about Sadie's feelings, though she realized Sadie must have suffered a great deal in the last few years. Only now could Allison really sympathize with the enormity of the guilt and grief that Sadie must be experiencing. She didn't want to make it any more difficult for her. The next few days, trying to deal with all that in front of the whole world, would be more than anyone should have to go through. She had no desire to add to it. Yet she couldn't let Uncle Rog go through it alone either. She was genuinely worried that he might not be able to handle it. Tomorrow would be a difficult day for everyone.

Cotes found her at once and collapsed next to her

72

on the banquette. He put an arm around her and buried his head on her shoulder. At first she though he was making a pass at her and she tried with some embarrassment to pull away. Several people looked at them disapprovingly and she was about to say something when she realized that he was weeping.

'I'm sorry, Sonny. I know I'm a basket case. I can't help it. I've just come from Sadie. My God, it's so goddamned sad. So sad.'

Allison's emotions were already on edge and Cotes's sorrow didn't help any. She could feel the tears sliding down her cheeks, and she noticed that once people saw that Cotes was crying they began to take out their handkerchiefs, too. Several people noisily broke down. Everyone was raw. It was exhausting, this kind of emotion. And there were days more of it to come.

Allison wanted to ask about Sadie but she didn't dare. She wanted to know and she didn't. But Cotes was ready to talk. He had already confided to her on the plane. Now it didn't even seem to be indiscreet.

'She wanted to talk about what happened with Des. That's all she wanted to talk about,' said Cotes. Allison caught her breath.

'It was as if she needed the expiation. She talked about how much she had hurt Rosey and how hard she had tried to make it up to him. She was so damned pitiful, Sonny. I've just hardly ever seen anybody in so much pain. She asked me over and over if I thought Rosey believed that she was sorry for what she had done, if he knew at the end that she really loved him.'

'Did she?' She couldn't help herself.

He thought about it for a minute. 'Lord only knows,' he said finally. 'I think she did love him. I

73

think she truly cared for the guy. But if I had to put money on it I'd say she's still in love with Des. Which is what is tearing her up inside.'

Allison felt engulfed in fear. For the past few years she had put Des out of her mind, as if he had never existed. But she knew Des was the reason she hadn't been able to fall in love with Julian—or anyone else for that matter. She hadn't even sorted out her feelings for him in the last few hours except to know that she was extremely agitated.

She didn't want to see him later, but she seemed not to be in control of her own will. She had to see him. Things had been so unresolved when she left for London. When she had found out about him and Sadie that was it. There was no official breaking up or parting of the ways. They never even said goodbye. But they had loved each other too long and too deeply. She knew why she had agreed to see him now. If nothing else, she needed to tell him goodbye.

Seeing him this evening had confused her. Knowing now, as she had suspected all along, that Sadie still loved him, confused her even more. Part of her wanted to forget him and go back to London. But she was also a competitor; she didn't want to lose.

'She wants to see him, Sonny.'

She thought she was going faint. How could she possibly go up against the beautiful bereaved widow of the President, especially when Des had loved her?

'Cotes, I suddenly feel very tired and a little bit sick. I think it was all that booze on the plane. I've got to get some sleep or I'm not going to make it. Do you mind? I can walk back to the Jefferson.'

74

'Miss Sterling?'

A waiter was standing in front of her with a telephone. Without thinking she took it.

'Sonny?'

'Yes.'

'I can get away for a while now. I'm really starving. I'll pick you up in front of the Hay Adams in about twenty minutes if that's all right.'

He was being so uncharacteristically polite.

'That's fine.'

'Great. See you then.'

'Goodbye.'

Why had she agreed to see him? She was exhausted. Not in control. She was a mess. This was a terrible mistake.

'The office?'

'Yes. I'm afraid I'm going to have to go back before I go to the hotel.'

'I'll walk you over.'

'Don't be silly. Aren't you staying here?'

'Yes, but...'

'I'll take a cab if that will make you feel better, but I'm not going to let you walk me over there. You're just as exhausted as I am. Just go to bed.'

'Okay, but let me put you in a cab.'

'Cotes, I appreciate your chivalry, but I'm a grown woman. I have traveled all over the world by myself and I can get my own taxi for God's sake.'

'Okay. Then you can walk me to my room.'

She burst out laughing in spite of herself.

'You jerk. Let's get out of here.'

He paid the bill. She didn't fight him. They walked to the elevator.

'Are you going to write anything, Sonny?'

'I don't know yet. They want me to. I just don't

know. It may be too complicated. Too hard.'

'Do me a favor?'

'What?'

Whatever you write, no crap, no maudlin crap. Okay?'

'I promise. Goodnight, Cotes. See you at the White House.'

★        ★        ★

She had time to go to the ladies' room and do something about her face. She was shocked at what she saw. The lights were too harsh and every tiny line was emphasized. They all seemed to point downward, giving her normally slim face a heavy, dour look. What was left of her mascara was slightly smudged under her eyes from too many tears and she had chewed off most of her lipstick. She wet a tissue and wiped her eyes, then powdered over her face. In the light it looked as if she was wearing a Kabuki mask. She gargled, squirted some breath spray, put on fresh lipstick, and teased her hair with a brush. Counteract the downward trend of her face with an uplift. Create an optical illusion. Who could tell? Julie 'I went to journalism school because of you' Fensterer could tell. That's who.

She glanced at her watch, grabbed her purse, and ran up the stairs to the lobby, trying to straighten out her black cotton knit skirt as she went.

Des was just pulling into the driveway when she came out the door.

He was smiling. Why was it her instinct to wipe that smile off his face? It wasn't just now. It had always been that way. There had always been an inherent anger in her about him, through their

76

entire relationship. He would approach her with a happy-go-lucky attitude and she would be, deep down inside, mad. Just mad. There was something about him that just pissed her off. Maybe the fact that he was always so optimistic about their relationship. That he never expected to work at it. That he didn't give it the time and energy she did. Maybe . . . None of it made sense. Seeing him smile now, tentative though this smile was, reminded her again of her anger. It wasn't just Sadie either. It had been long before Sadie. God knows she had spent enough hours with Rachel trying to figure it out. Yet all that shrinking hadn't helped. Could it be that women were just always genetically angry at men? That was too pat. Yet Des had been right on some level when he periodically accused her of wanting to make him pay. Pay for what? For his very existence? She just didn't know. So how could she explain it to him? Or stop being mad? She couldn't. Poor son of a bitch, she thought as the doorman opened the car door for her. Or am I the one to feel sorry for?

He didn't greet her when she got in. He didn't have to. It was as if they had never been apart. Except that they didn't kiss. Normally there would have been a perfunctory kiss on the lips—at least it would start out perfunctory. But what were they to do now? Shake hands? Better nothing.

'Where are we going?'

'I thought we'd go to Paolo's in Georgetown. There's not much choice on a Sunday night, on the Fourth of July on the night after the President of the United States has been assassinated. It's noisy. It won't be so depressing.'

'Let me tell you about the Hay Adams.'

'I can imagine.' There was a silence as he drove down Pennsylvania toward Georgetown. Not uncomfortable.

'So how's Cotesworth Tennant?'

It was his way of asking her if they'd had an affair in London. If she were in love with him. The way he said his name had an edge. As in how's-that-little-candy-ass-preppy.

He was wrong about Cotes. Cotes was a good ole boy, not a candy ass. But it wouldn't do to argue the point. It pleased her anyway, that slight intimation of jealousy.

'Devastated. Rosey got him through the death of his wife.' She didn't say that Cotes had gotten Rosey through Sadie's affair with Des. But there it was looming up in the car between them like some giant mushroom. Cold and clammy and grotesque.

They didn't say anything else to each other. The air seemed to have become thinner in the car. They both breathed in deeply and heaved sighs simultaneously. It almost made her laugh. She rolled down the window, even though the car was air-conditioned, to get some oxygen. The hot wind against her face was even more stifling.

Des parked the car on N Street and they walked in silence around the corner to the restaurant.

He had been right. It was packed and noisy. There were several bar-height round tables with stools in the front, a bar to the right, and booths to the left. In the back, beyond the pizza ovens, was the real restaurant, informal but just as crowded and noisy as the front.

They were lucky to get a corner table where at least they could hear themselves. The place was mostly filled with yuppies and college students. The

78

atmosphere was shrill, almost hysterical. People were laughing too loudly and occasionally someone would burst into tears and the rest of the group would move to console him or her. It was a contrast to the funeral hush at the Hay Adams.

They ordered light beers. Des patted his middle. She looked, half hoping, for a paunch but saw none. She was so thirsty, her mouth so dry, she could hardly speak.

'This,' said Des, 'is the restaurant where the President's staff and the pool photographers were having dinner when he was shot. The pool reporters would have been eating here too—if they'd been on duty like they were supposed to be.'

'What's going to happen to them?'

'Well, it's not just the *Weekly*. It's the other magazines as well. Not to mention the papers. But they're not usually around on weekends. It was our job and we blew it.'

'What were you doing at the White House earlier? I thought you didn't do the hands-on reporting anymore. I completely forgot to ask you.'

'Trying to get as many details out of Manolas as I could. We're in a jam having to go tomorrow before the funeral. The funeral will have been over for a half a week by the time next Monday's edition comes out. We've got a lot to nail down early.'

'So who's Julie Fensterer?'

He grinned.

'You don't miss anything, do you?'

'Are you in love with her?'

He stopped smiling and looked directly into her eyes.

'No, Sonny. I'm not in love with her.'

'Are you still in love with Sadie?'

79

She couldn't believe that she'd asked that. She only got scared after she'd said the words.

He didn't take his eyes off her for the longest time. He searched her face as though he were trying to learn something. He started to speak several times and then stopped. He clasped his hands together on the table and looked down at them.

'I don't know how to answer that question, Sonny.'

Dear God, at least he hadn't said yes.

'Why?'

'You hurt me a lot you know.'

How could he say that? To her. She was the one who had been destroyed when she discovered he was sleeping with Sadie Grey. Discovered by accident on a presidential trip to Israel. And after they had been in bed together all night. Jesus.

'Now I'm at a loss for words,' she said.

She had to control herself. She wanted to find out what happened. If she was ever to be at peace with herself—or with him, for that matter—she had to clear this up. She had to resolve this. It was eating at her and had been for the past three years. She needed to get on with her life.

'You left me. You walked away from me,' he said. 'Just kissed me off. In Jerusalem. Without a word of explanation. I thought we had gotten back together again. I loved you, Sonny. God, did I love you. I wanted you back. That night in the King David I was happy for the first time since we broke up. I thought I loved Sadie but I realized then that it was you, baby, and nobody else. Then you just kicked sand in my face.'

'Des! You were fucking the First Lady!'

She was almost yelling at him now. Lucky the

80

place was so noisy. Nobody was paying attention to them.

'And I didn't know about it. How was I supposed to feel when I found out? After you had just spent the night in my bed telling me you loved me. I felt like the biggest asshole in the entire world. I couldn't believe it. And I believed that you loved me. That was what was so pathetic.'

He was stunned.

'You found out the next morning? How?'

'Never mind how. I just did.'

'That explains a lot.'

'I didn't think you needed an explanation. I figured when I walked off you'd know why. Anyway, I was too angry and hurt and humiliated to explain anything.'

'I thought you knew all along I was seeing Sadie. I just assumed Jenny would have told you. You were best friends. I knew you couldn't have believed I was in love with Jen all that time. You know me too well. You would have had to know I was getting laid somewhere. You're too smart not to have figured out Jenny was the beard for Sadie and me.'

'How could I have known and not mentioned it? It's me, Des. Allison. You know me too well for that. I'd have had to have been lobotomized not to bring it up. Are you kidding?'

Des looked beaten, defeated.

'Oh Sonny.'

'I guess we didn't know each other that well after all, Des.'

★     ★     ★

Des had to go back to the office. He dropped her off at the Jefferson. This time he squeezed her hand as she got out of the car. She thought about the rest of their dinner as she got ready for bed. They had dropped the discussion of their relationship from exhaustion if nothing else. It was as if they were both on such emotional overload from the assassination and from seeing each other again that they couldn't handle any more. They had ended the evening with polite conversation about London and journalistic gossip. It was not unpleasant, just distant. It amazed her how they could have gone from such intense passion to such noncommittal chitchat. She felt so drained then and at this moment she could barely dial the operator for a wake-up call. She didn't even remember putting her head on the pillow, she fell asleep so quickly.

Her dreams were murky and confused, punctuated, she thought, with loud knocking. There was a coffin and the knocking was coming from inside it. She rushed to open the coffin before they lowered it into the ground. Rosey Grey stepped out of it. 'Thank God,' he said. 'I really wasn't dead at all.' Sadie threw her arms around him. He embraced her and they walked off together. Des looked at Allison, then put his arms around her. 'Thank God he's not dead,' he said. 'Because I really do love you.' She embraced him and they walked off together.

But the knocking persisted. Finally she realized somebody was at the door. She sat up in bed, then looked at the alarm. It was 7:00 a.m. Noon London time.

'Who is it?' she called out. A muffled voice responded, 'Room service.' She hadn't remembered

82

ordering breakfast the night before, but she was so tired she might well have. She jumped out of bed and tossed a robe over her satin nightshirt, opened the door, and stuck out her head to see who it was.

Des was standing at the door, totally disheveled, unshaven, circles under his eyes, with a bag in his hand.

'I believe you ordered croissants and tea, madame.'

Even a simple French word like madame he could fracture.

Before she was able to respond he had brushed past her and placed the bag on the table. He took off his jacket and began setting up the meal.

'It's hot as bastard out there already,' he said, opening the plastic top to her tea.

'Sugar and cream, I'm afraid. No honey or skim milk.'

He remembered.

She had shut the door and was watching him with stunned amusement.

'I've got marmalade and black raspberry.' He glanced at her over his shoulder. 'Go ahead and get back in bed. I'm serving you breakfast in style this morning, milady.'

'Not before I brush my teeth.'

She disappeared into the bathroom for a moment, then got back in bed, propped up the pillows, and pulled the covers over her.

'*Et voilà*,' he finished with a flourish as he presented her with her croissants and tea. She couldn't help laughing.

'Hey, Des,' she said. 'You know what?'

'What?'

'You're an asshole.'

83

'I can't believe such vulgar language would come from the mouth of such a delicate angel,' he said, taking off his shoes and plunking down on the other side of the bed, his coffee in hand.

'I just want you to know that I've noticed that you're on the bed with me.'

'Damn, you don't miss a trick,' he said shaking his head in amazement.

She took a sip of her tea and looked him directly in the eye. She was feeling slightly less groggy since she had splashed cold water on her face and run a brush through her hair.

He looked back at her and they both smiled.

'I'm suddenly starving,' she said. She took a huge bite out of her croissant.

'Me, too.' He did the same.

He was still smiling as he reached over and wiped the flakes off her mouth with his thumb.

She reached over and gently brushed his lips as well.

He caught her hand and held it there.

She looked at him again. This time they were both serious.

'What do you want, Shaw?'

'I want you.'

She could feel his words reverberate through her body.

'Take off your bathrobe.'

Almost as if in a trance she slowly removed her robe, pulling it out from under her so she was still under the covers.

They hadn't taken their eyes off each other.

He reached his arm around her neck behind the pillow, then leaned over and softly brushed her lips with his.

Before she could respond, he had pulled away, moved his arm back and was leaning against his own pillow again.

'Take off your nightshirt.'

She swallowed hard. This was a mistake. She reached down and slowly unbuttoned each button until the last one was undone. She carefully opened it and let it slide off her shoulders. Only her breasts were bare, the rest of her was still covered.

Des reached over and pulled back the covers so that her whole body was exposed.

'Oh God,' he breathed.

Her heart was beating so loudly that she could hear it and she was unable to swallow at all.

He leaned over and began to trace her body with his finger. First the eyes, then the nose, the mouth, the throat ... taking in each part of her with his eyes as he went.

He wet his finger with his tongue and traced her again, so gently that it was hard to believe such a strong hand was on her.

When he had finished he looked at her again and she began to shiver. This time he traced her with his tongue, starting with her eyes, then her mouth ... downward, until she began to moan.

'What do you want, Sterling?' he whispered.

'I want you.'

*     *     *

The air-conditioning in the East Room had been turned up full blast and Allison was glad she was wearing her London clothes. She had been sweltering only a few minutes ago in the oppressive heat. Now everyone sat on their little gold caterers'

85

chairs shivering in their black linen dresses and dark summer suits.

It was overcast outside and you could cut the humidity with a knife. Inside, the White House was even more depressing. The President's casket had been set up in the center of the East Room with a small altar in front of it. The altar and the bier were hung with black crepe and there were swags of black crepe over the doorways and windows. Large standing candelabra were on the corners of the altar and at the entrances into the room, lending an Elizabethan quality to the already lugubrious atmosphere.

She had met Uncle Roger at Blair House, and his attendant had driven them across the street to the White House and helped him in.

She was horrified to find that they had been seated almost directly behind where Sadie and her family were to sit. Allison felt like running and hiding.

Someone was playing hymns on the piano. It was such a small tinkly sound in that vast room overwhelmed with the raised bier that it seemed somewhat ludicrous. Yet it broke the weight of the silence mercifully, a curious hint of life in a deadened atmosphere. No one had spoken a word since Allison and Uncle Rog had taken their seats. No one even looked up as others filed in and took their seats. People sat as if in a trance.

An Episcopalian minister entered the room and took his place at the makeshift altar. Everyone sat up at attention. The minister was an old family friend of the Greys from Richmond. He had married Rosey and Sadie and christened their children. Allison was surprised not to see Cotes. He

86

must be with Sadie.

Then a slight murmur arose as everyone looked toward the door.

Sadie was standing alone, with Willie, his hand clasped in hers. Her normally flushed skin was absolutely white, contrasting sharply with her auburn hair and black silk dress.

She looked so beautiful and so sad that Allison found herself fighting back tears.

What flashed through Allison's mind was the first time she had ever seen Sadie Grey. She was the wife of the newly elected Vice President just up from Richmond for her first real Washington party. She had arrived late at Lorraine Hadley's for dinner. When she and Rosey had walked in the door everyone had gasped at the gorgeous couple.

This was six years and a lot of pain later. Sadie had seemed, that night, so young and radiant and so full of expectation. They really had had it all, those two. Now look what it had come to.

Willie was tugging at his mother's hand and she looked down at her son. He had his mother's coloring, dark curly hair, with a hint of auburn. His features were heavier, stronger than those of his patrician father. His lips were fuller and his nose as aquiline as Rosey's had been. He was his mother's child.

He was pointing toward his father's coffin.

'Mommy, Mommy,' he cried out. 'Daddy's in the box. Open the box, Mommy. I want to see Daddy.'

Everyone in the room heard and their eyes went immediately to Sadie's face, which seemed to shatter at the sound of her son's voice.

Before anyone could stop him, Willie had broken

away from his mother and raced toward the coffin. He pulled himself up on the platform and was beginning to climb up on the coffin when Outland, his older brother, rushed forward and grabbed him, kicking and screaming, up into his arms.

'I want to see my daddy,' he cried. 'I want my daddy.'

Cotes appeared from behind Sadie, grasped her arm just in time, Allison thought, and led her to her seat in the front row. Sadie's daughter, Annie Laurie, her face red and streaming with tears, followed and sat beside her brother. Outland had taken a seat next to his mother with Willie on his lap.

Allison had not seen Outland in years. He had been at Stanford, having rejected his father's alma mater, the University of Virginia. He was a strikingly handsome young man, dark and brooding, with long black lashes and a thin mouth. He had his father's lithe body and aristocratic bearing. Annie Laurie, a sophomore at Sweetbriar, was a clone of Rosey. The same narrow face, long thin nose, light brown hair, slightly haughty look.

Outland turned to look at the rows behind him and spotted Uncle Roger in his wheelchair on the end. He smiled and nodded briefly. Allison prayed Sadie would not turn around. She didn't want Sadie to see her and she didn't want to have to acknowledge Sadie herself.

What if Sadie still loved Des? What if she wanted him back? She hadn't even dared mention Sadie's name to Des again after they'd made love. It seemed inappropriate, almost sacrilegious. She couldn't believe Des would have made love to her this time if he had any intention of going back to

88

Sadie. He knew Sadie was free now. He knew he could probably have her back. To sleep with Allison under those circumstances, if that had been his intention, would have been too cruel. Des was not a cruel person. She really believed him this time when he said he loved her.

God, how could she be thinking like this in front of Rosey's coffin? He hadn't even been dead two days. He was lying only a few feet from her and she was wondering whether Sadie was going to take Des away.

It had to be the last thing on Sadie's mind. Allison glanced in her direction. Sadie's head was bowed in grief as the eulogy began.

## CHAPTER FIVE

'Des is here.'

Jenny stood in the doorway of Sadie's office in the family quarters. She was trying to hide the disapproving look on her face.

Sadie was standing by the window looking out at all the mourners in Lafayette Square. There were so many of them. Mostly dressed in black, standing in the summer heat, sweltering in the humidity, weeping or simply staring at the White House with its flag at half mast.

'She wore the same black silk dress she had had on at the memorial service that morning. It had been even more painful than she had expected and she had lost control as she had expected. When Willie climbed up on Rosey's coffin it was just too much. She was still somewhat in shock, but her

89

worst fears about her own lack of composure had been confirmed. She really didn't know how she was going to get through the next few days. Des was her only hope. Maybe he could give her strength.

She wondered whether or not she should mention Allison. She had seen Allison the moment she walked into the East Room that morning. She couldn't believe that Allison had been invited, much less that she had come, even if it was to comfort Roger Kimball. She had to admit Allison had looked miserable and had done everything she could to disappear. They had avoided looking at each other. Still, Allison's presence had made her guilt and grief more acute. If she mentioned it it would only upset Des and distract him. She would leave it alone. It was done now and she needed him too much to make him feel conflicted. She had not attended any other service. There were too many plans to be made and she had to be involved in all of them. Visiting dignitaries and heads of state, what to do with them? The rotunda, Tuesday morning, the funeral services at the National Cathedral, the burial later in Arlington, not Richmond. Transportation, flowers, invitations, music, seating, not to mention clothes for herself and her children, her hair, a veil ... it was endless. At least it kept her occupied. Then there were the notes and letters and newspapers that reminded her of her loss. Most of the televisions in the White House were on, so there was an echo through the rooms of various channels and TV anchormen reporting the latest events and rerunning newsreels of important people arriving. Thank God at least there were no pictures of the assassination or of their ambulance ride to the hospital.

The appointment with Des had been for 4:00 p.m., immediately after the service for journalists. Jenny had told her that the crowd for that one was bigger than at any of the others. She had also told her that Des seemed stunned that Sadie would want to see him.

'How can I say no, Jen?' he had asked.

'You can't,' she replied.

Jenny had told him nothing except that Sadie wanted to see him, and she had disappeared as soon as she announced him.

Des stood in the doorway. Sadie's back was to him.

'You wanted to see me.' It was a statement as much as a question.

She turned and faced him.

'Yes.'

She looked lovelier than he had remembered. Grief became her. She wore very little makeup. What little there was had been cried off during the day. Even though she had freshened up for Des, she hadn't dared put on mascara. Her hair was brushed back from her face with little regard for style. She looked simple and natural and beautiful.

He said nothing.

She noticed his eyes were red and puffy. He had been crying. She had never seen him cry. But then everybody had been crying. Men she never believed were capable of any emotion had totally lost control.

She had cried in front of him enough times. Oddly, now she felt emptied of all emotion.

He looked wonderful. Tanned, strong. That square jaw, that cocky stance, those eyes that could always tell what she was thinking. Only now he had absolutely no idea.

'I thought you might want an interview.'

'How are you, Sadie?'

'I don't know.'

'I'd like to hug you.'

'I thought it might help.'

He took a step forward.

'To do an interview, I mean.'

'I don't think it's right.'

'It would be a big scoop.'

'I can live without it.'

'I needed to see you.'

He took another step forward. She still did not move.

'I'm here.'

'I can't do this alone.'

'What can I do?'

'Stay here.'

'How can I?'

'Please?'

'I . . .'

'Des?'

She ran into his arms before he could get to her and held him tightly.

Now the emotions returned and she broke down. It was all too much for her. She felt so conflicted, so confused, so hopeless. She didn't know what she felt anymore. It was so good to be back in his arms again after these past two years and so comforting to have a man to hold on to after these past two days. Yet she was overcome with guilt, remorse, anger, self-pity, grief, loss, pain. Was there any emotion she wasn't feeling now except happiness?

'Oh God, Des. I'm so sorry. So sorry to do this to

you.'

Her arms were wrapped around his waist, his around her back. They held on to each other though she had felt him begin to pull away slightly before she apologized.

'It's all right, Sadiebelle,' he said. 'It's all right.' It surprised her that he had used her nickname, that it had come back so quickly and automatically. It seemed to have a soothing effect on her.

He loosened his grip on her and led her to the sofa where they sat down together. He continued to hold her hand, fighting back his own tears as she wept.

'I want to give you an interview,' she said, when she had quieted down.

'Don't be ridiculous, Sadie. I couldn't take advantage of you like that. You're distraught. You don't know what you're saying. You don't need this.'

She managed a smile.

'Where's the old Des? He would have leapt at it.'

'The old Des died a little over two years ago.'

'So now both men in my life are dead.'

Oh Sadie ... what can I do? How can I help you?'

'Where's your notebook?'

'I don't ...'

She looked at him, imploringly.

He reached into his pocket and pulled out a notebook and pen, opened it, and looked up at her.

It was the first time their eyes had met since he walked in. He swallowed hard, remembering why he had loved her. She had always been so vulnerable, unlike Allison, who could be so aloof, so self-sufficient.

Sadie brought out his most primitive instincts for protecting a woman. She had always seemed to need him and never more than now.

'I want you to write that what people will see in the next few days is a spectacle, a ceremony filled with pictures. The pictures are of a family, a young widow, her two teenaged children and her toddler, grieving over the loss of their father and husband, who also happened to be the President of the United States. He was young and vital, rich, well born, and handsome. He was also intelligent, honest, courageous, and decent. He had more integrity than any man I have ever known. He cared deeply about his family and his country. He believed in them. When he was betrayed, he could be the most forgiving of all men. He was everything he appeared to be and more.'

She was speaking in a quiet voice, tears sliding softly down her cheeks. Des was writing steadily, not looking up at her.

'But people shouldn't color this picture perfect. Because it's much sadder even than it looks. Because this model wife, the First Lady of the United States, betrayed her husband. She had an affair while he was President...'

'Sadie, stop it.' Des dropped his pen and took hold of her arm, shaking it.

'No, let me finish. Hear me out, please. I need to talk about it... She risked humiliating him before the world, destroying his presidency, her family, and deeply hurting the country. She risked everything for her own pleasure. She even considered leaving him.'

'Why didn't she?' His curiosity and the depth of her emotion had gotten the better of him.

'Because she was afraid. She was afraid that her lover didn't really love her for herself. That he was enamored by the fact that she was the First Lady. That he expected too much of her. That he wanted her to be independent, to take care of herself, and she wasn't capable of that. That she had no talent, except perhaps writing silly novels, and he believed she was better than she was. That he had no money and neither did she. That her husband threatened to give up the presidency if she left him. That her two children would have been devastated by it. That it would have hurt the country. And that she was pregnant.'

She said that sentence almost under her breath and waited. But he didn't pick up on it.

'Did she love him?'

She caught her breath and looked him in the eye.

'She loved him with all her heart. More than he loved her.'

'Then why didn't she tell him that when she broke it off so abruptly?'

'Because she was afraid he wouldn't let her go if she told him the truth.'

'She was right.'

★　　　★　　　★

She had insisted on the side entrance to the National Cathedral. That way she would walk right in front of the pulpit and go immediately to the front-row pew. She wouldn't have to walk all that distance down the main aisle past all those people.

Outland, Annie Laurie, and Willie were in the presidential limousine with her. Her parents and Rosey's parents were in the car behind them.

95

Thank God for Willie. She hadn't counted on his presence being such a distraction. He was her incentive for maintaining control, much more so that the thought of the millions of people watching her.

Willie had climbed all over her during the ride from the White House to the cathedral, and she was desperate to keep him from wrinkling her long-sleeved black silk suit. He had almost pulled off one of the braid buttons and had managed to snag her black stockings with his fingernails.

She had started out with her black veil drawn over her face but William had complained loudly, 'Mommy, I can't see you,' and pulled at the veil until he pushed it back over her tiny black pillbox. Finally he had climbed into her lap, put his arms around her neck, and given her a wet kiss right on the mouth that smeared her lipstick. Outland tried to get him to leave her alone but Willie seemed to sense that she was sad and instinctively wanted to help her out. Annie Laurie was a mess, sobbing most of the way to the cathedral. Sadie was trying very hard not to be irritated with her, but Annie Laurie seemed to be wallowing in her grief. Oddly, rather than make Sadie more emotional, Annie Laurie's wailing served to strengthen her.

Sadie's mother had given her several white lace handkerchiefs. 'Every lady should have them,' said her mother, not intending a reproach. They were already in damp little balls, not from tears but from her perspiring hands. Ceremonies of any kind always made her sweat, made her heart race, made her adrenaline pump, made her cry. Sometimes it was embarrassing. A retirement ceremony for someone she hardly knew would have her in a state.

96

Yet this was the most intense physical reaction she had ever experienced. Despite the debilitating heat she had been having such chills that she had been sitting outside on the Truman balcony wrapped in a blanket rather than stay inside in the air-conditioning. Even now her teeth were clenched to keep from chattering. Still, she perspired. Her hands were like melting ice cubes.

If only she could get through the next few hours, through the church ceremony and the burial at Arlington, then she could collapse.

As the door to the limousine opened at the side entrance, Toby Waselewski, her Secret Service agent, leaped out of the car and was standing there, ready to assist her, waiting to take Willie under his wing when he began to squirm. The bishop was standing on the steps in his imposing purple robes to embrace her and lead her up the stairs. She pulled her veil over her face and got out of the car.

There was such a swirl and swarm of people it made her momentarily dizzy and she worried she might faint. Willie was tugging at her hand and Outland—strong, gorgeous, lovely Outland—was supporting her with his arm firmly under her elbow.

It wasn't until she was well inside the cathedral that she looked up and saw the rose window, the circular stained-glass morality play she had studied when she first began coming to the cathedral with Rosey.

The top of the window, twelve o'clock, represented heaven, she had been told. The bottom, six o'clock, was hell. She had been so ashamed that day, thinking how primitive religion was. She had been unfaithful to her husband. She had committed adultery and the Lord punished her by taking her husband away.

This was six o'clock in spades. She wasn't all that sure how much she believed in the Lord—up until now, that is.

Hers was a just and fitting punishment, after all. Could there also be a redemption?

She walked over the green-and-brown marble floor, stepping lightly over the cross and into her brown leather seat on the right side of the front row, flanked by her children.

She sank to her knees to pray.

Dear God. I'm so sorry. Please forgive me. Please help me. Don't punish me anymore. I can't bear it. You've made your point. I don't mean that to be flip. I want to be a good person. I genuinely do. I've been selfish. I don't want to hurt anybody anymore. I just want to make people happy. I'm so afraid, God. I'm afraid you're mad because I don't know whether I really believe in you. But I try. I'm afraid you're so mad you'll ... I can't bring myself to think this because maybe you haven't thought of it yet... I'm so scared you'll take Willie away from me. She stifled a sob. It was only a matter of seconds before she would lose control. She had to finish this prayer. It was too important. Just because he's Des's son and not Rosey's. But you really can't do that. You just can't. I know people say that the Lord doesn't give you any burden you can't shoulder. I think I can shoulder this one. Barely. But Willie, losing Willie, I couldn't take that. I'll be a really good mother. I'll go to church and I'll teach him about you. This sounds so stupid trying to make a deal, to bargain with you, but I don't know what else to do. I feel desperate. I can't

98

take back any of the terrible things I've done. You've shown me about punishment. Help me now to redeem myself. Amen.

She sat back up on her seat and put her arm around Willie, her precious Willie. That mop of black curly hair, those long black eyelashes and dark eyebrows, that half-curled lower lip and those mischievous eyes, the fruit of her sins. Kill him and her sins would be eradicated? No. No. She had paid enough already. She put her arm around him and held him as tightly as she could, staring at the cross in front of her.

God is good. God is good. She chanted under her breath. Ward off evil. God is good.

A surge of organ music broke her reverie. The people behind her were standing up and she realized that the coffin was about to be carried down the aisle. The coffin. Not Rosey. What an impersonal word. She turned slightly to her left. Enough so she would be facing the aisle but not so much that anyone could see her face through the veil. They had decided to allow TV cameras in the church but only in the back. None were allowed in the front or facing her or the congregation. There had been a major controversy about it, and she had finally acquiesced. Rosey was the President. People should be allowed to mourn like the others in the church.

It was Cotes's face that caused her to begin to break down. Cotes, listing under the weight of the coffin, his face bright red with strain and grief, the perspiration pouring off his brow, was trying so hard. But when he saw her standing there, in black, clutching Willie's hand, his whole demeanor crumpled and he started to cry.

99

She could hear G. and Miz G., Rosey's parents, crying softly behind her. Cotes was like a second son to them. For the first time in her marriage she felt sorry for them. Their grief was as real as her own.

The coffin was set in front of the altar, between the pulpit and the lectern. Behind the rood screen sat members of the clergy from all faiths, and the choir. The cathedral was packed. There were over a thousand people and yet there was utter silence except for muffled sobs and coughs.

Try not to concentrate on Rosey. Try not to think of him in the coffin. Look at the stained-glass windows, they each tell a story. Look at the state flags . . .

'Mommy, it's Daddy in the box. I want to see my daddy,' said Willie and started straining at her hand. This time she didn't have the strength to deal with him. As she felt his hand slip from hers, she saw Outland pick him up and hand him to Toby. He was standing unnoticed behind a huge column just to the right of the altar. Toby motioned as if to say he would take him out the side door but she shook her head. She wanted Willie there. She was scared to let him get too far away from her.

Her glance went back to the coffin. Suddenly she felt overwhelmed with grief. Rosey, tall and handsome and elegant and loving, was lying in that coffin. Her husband. Her heart seared with pain against her chest. She wanted to run up to it and throw her body on the coffin and scream and wail and cry and keen. Somehow that would be more fitting than this horrible Anglo-Saxon control she was forced to exhibit. For the first time, she understood suttee, the Hindu custom of wives

100

flinging themselves on their husbands' funeral pyres. Her life was over. Rosey was her life and now he was dead. She wanted to die, too.

She didn't die. She stood there tall and erect, in control except for the silent tears. No shrieks of anguish. Very Widow of the President. The country would be proud.

Most of the ceremony was a blur. People kept kneeling and standing, reaching for the Book of Common Prayer, then the Hymnal. She concentrated on the green-and-rust needlepoint kneelers with their yellow crosses, their leaves and pinecones. How many hours and bleeding fingers did they represent?

They were singing now.

Oh God, our help in ages past, our hope for years to come. Our shelter from the stormy blast and our eternal home...'

The bishop, tall and imposing, was standing in the pulpit.

'I am the resurrection and the life saith the Lord; he that believeth in me, though he were dead, yet shall he live; and whosoever liveth and believeth in me shall never die.'

'I believe. I believe,' she chanted under her breath. Take no chances.

'Let us pray.'

She bowed her head.

'O God, whose mercies cannot be numbered, accept our prayers on behalf of thy servant William Rosewell Grey and grant him an entrance into the land of light and joy...'

He already lived in the land of light and joy. He loved his life, his job, his wife, his children ... his children, my child whom he loved as his. Except for the pain I caused him. She could hear a soft giggle from Willie on the other side of the column and Toby's gentle, 'Shh.'

'The Lord is my shepherd, I shall not want. He maketh me to lie down in green pastures, he leadeth me beside the still waters, he restoreth my soul. He leadeth me in the paths of righteousness for his name's sake...'

'I have never really heard these words before,' she said to herself. 'Let them be true.'

'... Surely goodness and mercy shall follow me all the days of my life and I will dwell in the house of the Lord forever. Amen.'

I promise.

Cotes was approaching the lectern. Had she known he was going to speak? Of course. Why had she allowed it? She wasn't going to make it through this. She could tell. She reached for Outland's hand.

She could see Cotes shaking as he took out the piece of paper he was to read from. She took a deep breath and tried not to look at the coffin. Where to look? Not at Cotes, certainly. Try to concentrate on something else. It will be over soon. Nothing worked, not the stained glass or the flags or the benches or the marble-patterned floor.

All she could think about was Rosey, lying dead in that box. And his beautiful birthday present.

'I would like to dedicate this poem to Mrs Grey, whom the President loved with all his heart,' said Cotes, then nodded to Sadie.

She caught her breath. She hadn't expected this.

'If I should ever leave you whom I love,' Cotes's voice wavered as he began to read.

*To go along the Silent Way, grieve not,*
*Nor speak of me with tears, but Laugh and talk*
*Of me as if I were beside you, for*
*Who knows but that I shall be oftentime?*
*I'd come, I'd come, could I but find a way!*

She let go of Outland's hand to wipe her eyes under her veil. She had abandoned all efforts at control now. Cotes continued.

*But would not tears and grief be barriers?*
*And when you hear a song I used to sing*
*Or see a bird I love—Let not the thought*
*Of me be sad, for I am loving you*
*Just as I always have ... You were so good*
*To me ...*

Cotes paused to compose himself.
Outland had to put his arm around his mother.

*So many things I wanted still*
*To do ... So many, many things to say to*
     *you ...*
*Remember that I did not fear ... It was*
*Just leaving you I could not bear to face ...*

She was crying now.

*We cannot see beyond ... But this I know;*
*I loved you so—'twas heaven here with you.*

Oh God, I can't stand it, she said to herself. I can't stand it.

She didn't have much sense of the rest of the ceremony. It was mercifully brief. A prayer, then

103

'The Battle Hymn of the Republic.'

Then the bishop was coming to escort her out to the right.

Toby was standing at the door with Willie in his arms.

Willie strained to get away from Toby and into her arms, and she took him and held him. Then, with Willie in her arms, she emerged into the sodden daylight of Washington summer, to the waiting cameras and her limousine.

She started to put Willie down but he gently touched her veil and lifted it up to see her tear-stained face.

'Mommy sad?' he asked softly.

'Yes, Willie,' she answered. 'Mommy very, very sad.'

# CHAPTER SIX

'So, this is the hot spot,' said Allison.

i Ricchi was packed, as usual, and the bustle of waiters and customers in front made it seem even more crowded.

She and Walt Fineman were seated at one of the tables in the center, which afforded them a good view of everyone who came and went.

i Ricchi was very pretty, light, and airy, with lots of glass in front, walls painted to look like old Italian stucco, trompe l'oeil vines done in muted pastels. There was a large pizza oven at the back of the front room that emitted a warm glow despite the air-conditioning.

'It's a good day for power lunches,' said Walt. 'It

almost never happens anymore, since everybody cut out expense-account lunches. Half the town is here. You can feel the energy in this room, the jockeying for position. I've never seen anything like it. It's wild.'

'It's desperate, it's frantic is what you mean,' she said. 'Not like an ordinary transition. This is happening so fast. Nobody is prepared for it. Now everything is up for grabs. All of Rosey's people are history and Freddy Osgood's rubes own the town. It would be funny if it weren't so awful. Look at them. Trying to maintain some sense of decorum in the wake of an assassination, all the while glad-handing and sucking up as if there were no tomorrow. God, I love Washington, I'd forgotten how much I love it.'

'Great. Because you're coming back.'

'Excuse me.' Allison nearly choked on her Virgin Mary.

'I said, you're coming back.'

'Wrong, Walt. Warburg promised me four years in London. I've only been there a little over two. Am I doing a lousy job? Is that it? Besides, if you think I'm coming back to sit on the foreign desk and deal with that little shit Muchnick, forget it. I'll go work for the *New York World* first.'

Walt was smiling. 'You're coming back to be assistant managing editor for national affairs. The third most powerful job on the paper—in case you need to be reminded. You will be the first woman to ever hold that job—as if I need to tell you.'

'As you pointed out, Walt, I'm coming back.'

'God, you're an easy lay.'

'I couldn't help overhearing that,' said a tall, white-haired man approaching the table. 'And I'm
105

shocked, totally shocked that you would say such a thing about this virtuous woman here.'

It was Howard Heinrich, lawyer, lobbyist, socialite, ladies' man, pol, and super source. One of the most powerful and well-connected men in Washington, Heinrich was professionally outrageous.

'However, just in case it might be true, how about dinner tonight, lovely lady?'

'Oh, Howard, promise me you won't tell anybody what you just overheard,' said Allison in mock distress.

'Who would I tell?'

Howard had sat down, nodding to his lunch date who was leaving. He motioned to the waiter and asked for another cup of coffee, never asking either Allison or Walt if they minded.

'I couldn't help noticing that you were having lunch with Freddy Osgood's new chief of staff,' said Allison innocently. 'An old and dear friend, I presume?'

'Precisely,' said Howard.

'I suppose he'll have to do for a lunch partner while Sadie's in mourning'.

'Poor woman,' said Howard, lowering his eyelids for a moment.

'How are you going to handle this one, Howard? I know Sadie's not all that fond of the Osgoods. You won't want to seem disloyal, especially now.'

'I know, it's a problem,' he said, not quite catching the sarcasm in Allison's voice. 'I discussed it with her on the phone this morning. She's in pretty bad shape. But then it's only been two weeks. Anyway, I told her that Washington is a tough town. Power is all that matters. She's going to have to get used to all these disloyal sons of bitches who worked for her husband. Now they've got their noses halfway up the Osgoods' redneck asses. The Osgoods are not unaware of what's going on either. I had a long talk with them about it last night over dinner at the White House in the family dining room. They can't believe how many close friends they suddenly have.'

'Are you ready to order?' The waiter appeared just as Heinrich was delivering his one-two punch. 'Well, I won't keep you,' he said, jumping up from his seat. 'As a matter of fact, I see someone over there I wanted to say hello to.'

Before they had a chance to even guess, Heinrich managed to get it in. 'Shirley Walker. An old girl of mine.' He lowered his voice. 'I hear she's about to be made head of the Environmental Protection Agency. Big job. Rosey never gave much of a damn about the environment, but Freddy Osgood's extremely high on it. Anyway, good to see you.'

Heinrich was about to break his neck to get over to Shirley Walker's table. And not a moment too soon because Allison and Walt had barely been able to contain themselves.

'Jesus, what a piece of work,' said Walt. 'That was beautiful. One of the best I've ever seen.'

'I'm in awe,' agreed Allison. 'The guy has no peers. The most skillful power fucker I've ever seen in my entire experience. He takes my breath away. It's like watching one of the old masters at work. He is a true artist. I only appreciate him more after being away for two years. We don't have anything comparable in London. But then the stakes aren't as high. To be El Supremo you have to operate in the power capital of the world.'

107

'What I don't understand,' said Walt, 'is what's in it for him? What does he want? He's already loaded. He's one of the most powerful lawyer/lobbyists in the country. He doesn't want a job. He does much better freelancing. He's had and still has the ear of every President since I can remember. So what does he want?'

'Walt, Walt, Walt, it's the game. The pursuit, the big score. What do all those guys on Wall Street want with another billion? What do the leveraged-buyout artists want? They can't begin to spend it all. They want it because it's there. Another conquest. It's like playing championship chess. When there's a change in administrations . . . for them it's the Olympics. Howard trains for four years.'

She looked over at Shirley Walker's table and watched her turn girlish as Howard moved in for the kill.

'I mean this boy is in shape. Do you realize how much work goes into his vocation? Not only does he have to know who's in with the President, their best friends, relatives, and staffs, at least three levels down, but also the enemies. That's just for starters. He's got to know everything about the Vice President, the secretary of state, all the top cabinet officers, senators, congressmen, Embassy Row, the top lawyers and lobbyists . . . and don't forget the press. He's got to keep tabs on all the governors of both parties. One of them is always sure to run. He's got to stay in favor with whatever hostesses are left who haven't gone broke or died of old age. Plus, he's got to be very careful, being a bachelor, about who he takes out. He can only take out people who don't matter in case he upsets them. He can't take out his "old flame" Shirley, for instance, because if he takes her to bed and there are hard feelings afterward he could get in trouble. He can't take out anybody too cute or sexy or too famous or successful or too smart or opinionated. But they can't be stupid, ugly, or without some social graces either. They have to be totally inoffensive, boring, neutral. What you might call a Swiss lay.'

Walt was laughing when the waiter brought their risotto.

'Quite a change from the old lunch hangouts,' she said.

'Yeah,' he said. 'It gets a little trendy sometimes.'

'I still pine for good ole Chez Camille with its grungy decor and those fabulous moules marinières,' said Allison.

'God, Sonny. It'll be good to have you back. I really have missed you.'

He began to put his hand over hers. His eyes looked a little misty. He could feel her pull back a bit. Not physically. He pulled back, too, taking her cue.

'It's the historical perspective I miss,' he said, and smiled.

'Historical perspective! You can go fuck yourself. I'm not that old.'

They were both relieved when the emotional moment had passed.

'So tell me more about Howard Heinrich. How does the guy do it? It must be exhausting.'

'It is exhausting. It's exhausting training for the decathlon, too. I was once ruminating with Heinrich over lunch. It was while Uncle Roger was having such a rough time in the White House. Before his stroke. I said I couldn't understand why

109

anybody would want to be President. And Howard said to me, "I can't understand anybody not wanting to be President. At least I can't understand why anybody would want to live in this town and not be President. It's the only game in town. If you can't be President then the name of the game is to be as close as possible to whoever the son of a bitch is.'''

'Who's doing the interview over there?' Walt was craning to see what was going on as bright lights went on. There was a sudden commotion at one of the center tables in the middle of the restaurant.

The waiter who was clearing the table answered Walt's question. 'It's Jules Lowen and a camera crew from "Good Night." They're doing a piece on business as usual in Washington after the assassination.'

The waiter looked embarrassed as he left to get their coffee.

'I don't believe it,' said Allison. 'That's disgusting. But then Benton Halloran was never known for his taste. Is he still a lush?'

'Yep. But you'd never know it on the air. I'm told he can be three sheets to the wind and still put on a flawless performance. Anyway, that's not Halloran. That's his new correspondent, Jules Lowen.'

'How can they do this?'

'Sonny, you've been in Colorado with Roger Kimball for nearly a week. This town has made its transition. The king is dead, long live the king. Besides, you're a journalist. It's a good story. Less than two weeks after the President has been assassinated let the game begin. With your old pal Heinrich carrying the torch. This scene is part of

110

the story. Don't tell me you've lost your touch?'

'No, I, it's just that I . . .' she felt on the verge of tears.

'Sorry, Sonny. I guess I'm just too cynical. Oh, oh. Look. Heinrich is about to make his move on the correspondent. He's circling around the table making sure they see him as he passes. Now they've caught him. Now he's resisting. Ladies and gentlemen, this is touch and go. Will they be able to persuade him? Ah ha. Got him. He's down in the seat, next to the correspondent. This is risky, ladies and gentlemen. A real high-risk move. A gamble. He could come across looking crass and insensitive. But no. I think he's pulled it off. He's looking mournful. Wait. Oh God, he's beautieeeful. He's pulled out his handkerchief. He's wiping his eyes. He's blowing his nose. He's sighing heavily. He's motioning to the rest of the room. He's patting the correspondent on the hand, now the arm. He's standing up. He's walking slowly, sadly, head slightly bowed out of the restaurant as the camera follows—bravo.'

'Take me out, Coach,' whispered Allison.

'Jules is a pretty nice guy. He probably hated this assignment. Here he comes . . . Hey, Julie. I see you've just interviewed the quarterback. What did he have to offer?'

Lowen sat down with relief.

'Christ, the guy is something. He was crying actual tears. He was saying that the city was so grief-stricken that people just wanted to be together, to mourn together. That's why the restaurant was so full. It was like a giant wake. Nobody wanted to be alone. But it was too much for him, he said. He was going home before his

111

meal arrived. He couldn't swallow. But it helped to be with friends when you were in such pain.'

'He's only just finished his third meal,' said Allison.

'Do you enjoy your work, Jules?' asked Walt.

'Oh, give me a break. This is not my idea. Although it's not a bad story, given the results. Anyway, I've got to run. Nice to see you back in town, Allison.'

'That's television for you,' said Allison, after he had left.

'Speaking of which, Des has become quite the TV star, you know. He's doing "Dateline: Washington" regularly on Sundays and he's really good at it.'

Allison was surprised. Des hadn't mentioned it. But then, they were hardly having a career talk the only time she had seen him.

'So I gather,' she said.

'What's with Mr Wonderful?'

'You can't help it, can you?'

'Sorry.'

'I'm having dinner with him tonight.'

'Is he the reason why you accepted the new job so quickly?'

'Sure, Walt. I'm just an airhead bimbo who makes all her career decisions based on the men in her life.'

'Sonny, I don't know why I react this way to Des. I apologize. It's just that he hurt you once very badly and I don't want to see you get hurt again.'

'I can't be angry with you, Walt. I know you care about me. But you've got to trust me. I haven't been in London for two years for nothing. I'm older and wiser. In other words, I have historical

112

perspective.'

He was signing the check. He looked up at her, his eyebrows furrowed.

'Well, in that case,' he said, 'I hope Des is history.'

\*     \*     \*

Nora's restaurant was as crowded at dinnertime as i Ricchi had been at lunch. The public Washington 'wake' was clearly in full force.

Allison had agreed to meet Des there at 9:30 because it was Thursday night and the magazine would be closing.

She had had a chance to go back to her hotel and shower and change and she felt a lot fresher and more relaxed.

The afternoon had been exhausting and, though she wouldn't admit it to anybody, scary. She had accepted Walt's offer to be assistant managing editor for national affairs without really thinking about it. It was one of those offers you couldn't refuse. Then, later, thinking about it, it made her crazy. How could she possibly have accepted this job? She had never been an editor except for filling in occasionally on the national desk when people were away on vacation. People would resent her, she'd been away for two years, and she was a woman, which would make it tougher. There were a lot of negatives.

But they had all insisted. Walt, Alan, even Calhoun, who was leaving. Nobody would resent her. They all respected and admired her as a reporter. She was the best. And the toughest. Being away for two years gave her a fresh view of things,

113

she'd ask the right questions. In the end, what it all boiled down to, and what none of them would come right out and admit, was that she was a woman. They needed a woman. They had to have a woman. They were desperate for a woman in one of the top management jobs. They didn't have anybody remotely close in the other sections. She was to be the sacrificial lamb. If she screwed up she would blow it for all the other women at the paper. Not to mention journalism, not to mention the fate of all women in the entire world. Not that she was being melodramatic or anything.

She hadn't decided whether to tell Des tonight. What if he thought she was coming back just because of the other night? She didn't want to put any pressure on him. On the other hand, she'd had it with London. There was really no story there. She'd done all the great eating trips in Europe, she'd O.D.'d on English country weekends, and she was never going to be an Anglophile. Then there was Julian. She had to break it off with Julian. She just needed help. Maybe it was convenient to have a profession that allowed you to move every time you ran into man trouble.

The truth was, it was time. Washington was the news center of the world, she was a journalist, and this was where the story was. She wanted to be here. If Des misunderstood, that was just too bad.

She was thinking all this as she walked into Nora's, fully expecting him not to be there. In all the time they had lived together and met at restaurants, he had never managed to get there ahead of her.

She was greeted effusively by the owner, an old friend.

'Des is here. He's waiting for you at your table in the back corner. Welcome home.'

'Being here really makes me feel like I am home,' she said.

He led her through the small room filled with print tablecloths, soft candles, and quilted walls to 'their' table in the back, small and round and intimate.

Des was sitting to the side, having saved the back corner seat for her so that she would be facing the room, her favorite place.

He looked quite spiffy for Des, especially for Des having come directly from a hard day at the office. His hair was combed, his shirt was buttoned at the top, and his tie seemed devoid of spots. He had shaved and the minty smell of his breath when he leaned down to kiss her hello indicated that he had brushed his teeth. A bottle of champagne stood in a cooler next to the table.

'Okay, what's wrong?'

She hadn't meant to sound accusatory. When Des was on his best behavior it meant bad news.

'What have I done now?' His look was one of surprise and a little hurt.

'Nothing. That's the problem. It's all too perfect.'

'Jeez. A guy wants to take his gal for dinner, a little champagne, a little hearts and flowers, and all he gets is shit.'

'I'll have a glass of champagne.' She nodded to the waiter.

She turned to Des and they both smiled uneasily. When the waiter had filled her glass she held it up to his and he clinked his glass to hers. They looked at each other and smiled again. Then they both

115

looked down at the table.

'It's warm in here,' said Allison. 'I think I'll take off my jacket.'

She slid her white linen jacket off and let it drop on the back of her chair as Des leaned over with one hand to help her. She was wearing a white camisole top. She rubbed her arms nervously, gazing around the restaurant for something to talk about.

'Good idea,' he said. He took off his jacket, crumpled it up in a little ball, and stuck it on the empty seat next to him.

'I feel like I've been living out my whole life in restaurants lately,' she said, with a slight laugh.

'Yeah, I know what you mean.'

'Being single,' they both said in unison. They looked up at each other in surprise and laughed.

'Which reminds me,' he said and began fumbling in his pocket.

'I have some news,' she said, running her hand through her hair.

'Save it.'

'What?'

'It can wait.'

She was puzzled and relieved at the same time. She was really dreading telling him she was going to move back. The way this dinner was going it was clear he wasn't going to be too thrilled.

'I think I'll have another glass of champagne,' she said, reaching for the bottle.

'No, here, let me help.'

'Des, you're being so goddamned polite. I can't stand it.'

What she didn't say was that it reminded her of a night years ago. He had broken up with her after she scooped him so badly on a cabinet nomination

116

story. She had humiliated him in front of the whole town. Afterward, he had taken her to dinner. He had been so polite and gentlemanly all the way through that it had given her the creeps. He had even opened the car door for her. She had known all along that something was terribly wrong, even before he dropped her off at her door and said goodbye, not goodnight, and drove away. This, when they had been living together. He'd never even told her he was mad. Just goodbye. Just like that.

'Well, don't get used to it. It'll never happen again.'

He had pulled something out of his pocket.

'Shall we order?'

This whole scene was making her edgy. It was not going at all the way she had planned. She picked up the menu and began to scan it. She couldn't concentrate. She put the menu down and reached for a sip of her champagne.

Something sharp and metallic hit her lip and she jerked her head back in surprise.

'My God!'

'What's the matter?'

'I don't know. There's something in my glass.'

She put down her glass and peered into it. Before she could reach in Des had put his finger in her champagne and pulled out something gold. Without saying anything he took her left hand and slipped it on her finger.

It was a moment before she realized what was happening.

Then she looked down at her hand. A gold ring was on her finger, two hands holding a crown over a heart. It was so worn and old-looking that it was

117

hard to discern the design. Just the outlines were clear.

'A claddagh ring. My great-grandmother's claddagh ring. It was her wedding ring when she was married as a girl in Ireland.'

He cleared his throat.

Allison stared at him, then stared down at the ring, then looked back at him. She didn't know whether to laugh or not. She didn't know how to behave. Was this a joke? What was he saying to her? What was she supposed to say to him? She was afraid to respond.

'Des, I'm not sure I understand.'

'Sonny?'

Suddenly he looked so vulnerable and sweet and scared. He cleared his voice again.

'I love you and I want to marry you.'

She couldn't answer. She could only feel her jaw drop slightly as she stared at him in disbelief. This was the last thing in the world she had expected from him tonight. She said the only thing that came into her mind.

'Now you'll think that the only reason I'm taking the job as national editor is so that I can come back to marry you.'

'I take it that means yes.'

He was grinning with relief.

'No one's ever said those words to me before.'

She was talking out loud, musing to herself more than speaking to Des.

'I've never said those words before.'

'Not even to Chessy?'

'Never. She proposed to me, steamrollered me into marriage before I knew what had happened. I was too smitten at the tender age of twenty-one to

118

know what a bad idea it was.'

They sat quietly for a moment. She took another sip of champagne.

'What about Nick? I thought Nick asked you to marry him.'

'Nick asked me to go with him to Vietnam when we graduated from Columbia Journalism School. He had a great job offer. So did I. In New York. He didn't ask me to marry him. He asked me to give up my job and follow him around the world. I presume he meant to marry me, but he never asked. Not like that.'

There was another silence. They had never been this awkward with each other.

The waiter took their order. Allison couldn't remember, after he left, what she had asked for. She didn't care. She couldn't have been less hungry.

'So what's the job?' Des was backing away from the proposal.

'Assistant managing editor for national affairs. Replacing Calhoun. He wants to go off and write books. I guess I'll start out as national editor. Basically, Plumley and I will exchange jobs. Then after I've completed my apprenticeship, approximately six months, I'll move into Calhoun's job.'

'That's a pretty big job.'

'For a woman.'

'I didn't mean that. You're the most capable person I know. I just mean you've been out of the country for two years, you've never been an editor and you're a woman. Meaning a lot of those guys are not going to want to take it from somebody in a skirt.'

119

Her impulse was to get defensive, tough it out. But Des was not challenging her. He was clearly being sympathetic, and she really needed to talk to somebody. She'd spent the whole afternoon pretending to be cool. Besides, she was on her third glass of champagne. And somewhere in the dark recess of her mind was the recognition that she had just been proposed to for the first time in her life at age forty.

'Des, I'm scared. I don't know whether I can handle it or not. I mean, I know I'm smarter than Plumley and I'm just as smart as Calhoun, but there's something different about them. They exude a certain attitude. Like they're owed. Like it's their due to be editors, to be in charge, to lead people. I don't feel that way. I feel as if I don't want to be responsible for anybody but myself. I also feel it's my duty. They need a woman. They don't have one. If I don't do it who will? I'm surely the most capable woman in the office right now. It would be a disaster for them to go outside, bring a woman in as AME national from some other paper. But if I fail . . . even if I don't like it and want out . . . I've told them I'll do it but I still haven't really decided.'

'You'll do it,' he said firmly.

She felt relieved at his decisiveness.

'You'll do it because it's a good excuse to come back to Washington to be near me.'

She was briefly surprised and then he burst out laughing.

'You bastard.'

They had been picking at their food, neither one as enthusiastic about their meal as they had been about the champagne. Des had ordered another bottle and the waiter had just opened it and placed

120

it in a bucket.

'Let's get out of here,' he said and grabbed her by the arm. He took the bottle of champagne and pulled her, as she reached for her purse and jacket, out of the restaurant into the steamy night.

'Where are we going?' she giggled.

'We're going for a walk.'

'Are you crazy? From what I've been reading about Washington we're liable to get blown away by drug addicts with Uzis.'

'Okay, we'll go for a ride.'

'Taking me for another ride are you? Why should I trust you, Desmond Shaw?'

She was half in the bag but pretending to be sober. He could always tell when she'd had too much to drink. She pronounced his name Dezzzzmond. Heavy on the zzzz's.

'Shut up,' he said, and took her by the back of the head. He held her to him, kissing her fiercely on the mouth. Then he gripped her with the arm that held the champagne while his other slid down to grab her behind.

'Actually, I think we'll go back to my house.'

'And what are we going to do there?'

'Talk.'

He had taken her by the waist and was leading her down the block and around the corner to his house on 21st Street, stopping every few steps to kiss her.

'How can we talk when you keep kissing me?'

'You're the one who's looking for challenges.' He reached in his pocket for the key and let them both in. They dropped their jackets and her bag on the floor, putting the bottle he had been carrying on the hall table. He pressed her against the door jamb and

121

continued to kiss her, this time holding her from behind with both hands.

She was the one who unzipped his zipper. But not before he had magically removed her underpants and had her skirt above her waist. He had backed up to the table and was leaning against it to allow her to wrap her legs around his waist and support her. His mouth was feverishly searching her mouth, her neck, as he moved frantically inside her. She was gasping for breath and begging him not to stop—'Oh God, Dezzz . . .'—when suddenly there was a loud crash.

The champagne bottle had fallen over and was pouring bubbles and foam all over the table and down the floor.

'Shit,' said Des. Allison jerked away in surprise from the noise, leaving him exposed in all his glory.

Before he had a chance to do anything she had pulled off her camisole and skirt and crouched on the floor next to the table. She let the champagne run into her mouth, down her chin, across her breasts and dribble toward her belly button.

Des knelt beside Allison on the floor and began licking the champagne off her face with his tongue, then moved downwards.

'Hurry, Des,' she moaned, 'before it loses its fizz.'

'More challenges,' he mumbled.

He moved his body on top of her and soon they were in perfect, if slightly drunken, rhythm.

It was Allison who began to cry first after they had come together, deep, heaving sobs.

Then Des was crying, too, guttural noises ringing up out of his chest. The two of them lay on the hard wooden floor of the foyer crying until they were exhausted, holding on to each other as though they expected somebody to come and wrench them apart.

'Oh God, Des. Rosey's dead. The President is dead. I can't bear it. I just can't stand it. Somebody shot him and it's as if nobody cares. This whole horrible city doesn't give a damn about it. All they care about is getting in with the new administration. It's so grotesque. There's no time even for mourning.

She was still crying, but softly now, tears flowing from her eyes.

He pulled himself off of her and sat up, burying his face in his hands. 'I'm sorry,' he said, 'I've just lost it. I can't seem to get control of myself.'

Allison sat up next to him and rested her head on his shoulder.

It was catching, this crying. As soon as her tears would subside, he would cry and she would start up again. The two of them sat there for a long while in the dark, naked and wet in their grief.

'It's Sadie, isn't it, Des? You're crying for Sadie.'

She had never dared to bring it up before, but now she had to know the truth.

'I'm crying for us all, Sonny. I'm crying for Sadie. I loved her once and she's hurting. I want to help her and I can't because she wants too much from me. I'm crying for Rosey, poor fucker. He was a decent President and he didn't deserve to die. I'm crying for those kids. Willie, who will never know his dad. I'm crying for the country. What kind of a place is this where people murder each other and murder their Presidents? I'm crying for me. For all the guilt I feel for Rosey and the pain I caused him. I'm crying for you. For causing you so

123

much pain, too.'

His voice cracked again and he buried his face in his hands once more and she circled him with her arms to stop the shaking.

'Do you still love her?'

She couldn't go on another minute without asking.

Des was silent for a long time.

'I care about her. Maybe I love her. But it's more protective. She's not the woman for me. It would never have worked. She's too dependent, too needy. She's a sensational dame, though.'

Allison felt sick. This wasn't exactly what she wanted or needed to hear. Des was thinking out loud more than speaking directly to her, and she knew he was being totally honest. He was searching his feelings to come up with the right words.

'Do I love her? God, how many times I've asked myself that question. I love many things about her. Am I in love with her? I was very sexually attracted. How much of it was the idea that she was the President's wife? That she was forbidden fruit? How much was the challenge, the excitement, the danger? She believes that's all it was. She may be right. I don't think so. I don't want to think so. It doesn't say much for me if it's true. I don't think I behaved very well. I'm not going to get any prizes for moral superiority. I did wrong. No question. But sometimes love, sex, passion, whatever you want to call it, makes you crazy. I don't remember having a brain during that period. I don't recall having a rational moment. I recall thinking I was nuts, out of control, certifiable. I recall thinking my cock had replaced my brain and I was a prisoner of its whims. I was obsessed. I was possessed. I don't think, but I'm not sure, that I should really be held accountable, because I had no control over the demons that forced me to act the way I did. So the answer is I don't know.'

She waited. She'd never heard him talk so openly about himself. Des was not, to say the least, introspective. She felt ill. She had not understood the depth of his feelings for Sadie. It was her fault for bringing it up. She should have known better. Yet she listened in horrified fascination the way she might have watched the amputation of one of her own limbs.

'What I do know is ...'

It was dark outside, but the light from the streetlamp shone through the living-room windows and they could see each other in shadow. She traced his profile against the white of the walls in her mind because up until now he had been speaking to no one, not looking in her direction.

She felt suddenly overwhelmed with her love for him, her need for him. She could feel the fear in her throat, fear that he might not want her after all, when they had come so close. She was still wearing his claddagh ring. She wrapped her arms around his neck and squeezed him as hard as she could, grasping one hand with the other to protect the ring from being pulled off should he change his mind.

'I know I love you. I'm in love with you. I'm crazy about you. I want you. I need you. I have never doubted that feeling for one moment since I first met you. Even when I was seeing Sadie I always loved you and missed you. You are my life and I want you with me for the rest of it. I want you to marry me and I want you to say that you will. You haven't answered me yet, you know.'

Now he was looking down at her. He took her chin in his hand and kissed her lips, then brushed her eyelids with his mouth, then her nose, then her lips again. He pulled back from her and looked directly into her eyes.

'I love you, Sonny, and I want to marry you. Will you marry me?'

She could sense all the fear and tension being siphoned out of her body, replaced with sureness and calm.

She closed her eyes and whispered.

'Yes, Des. I will marry you.'

He pulled her to him, back down on the dark wood floor and they made love softly, gently, until they were both spent.

## CHAPTER SEVEN

'Dear Des, It's been two months. I need you. Love, Sadie.'

She had written the note in desperation and sent it off before she could change her mind. Now she was sorry but it was too late. He would have to answer her. He had no choice. What would he say? It almost didn't matter. The fact was that she needed to talk to him. She had to.

Her phone rang. It was the White House operator. Des was on the line. She hadn't given him the number.

'Des?'

'Hi, how are you?'

'Can you come see me?'

'Sure.'

126

'Tonight?'

'Uh, I don't see why not.'

'You'll have dinner?'

She was too anxious.

'Yes.'

That wasn't enough.

'I'd be happy to.'

'Good.'

She wondered if he could hear the relief in her voice.

'Well, I guess I'll see you tonight then.'

'Right.'

'Goodbye.'

'Bye.'

\*    \*    \*

It was hot, but a dry heat, not the killing humidity of Washington summers. Early September brought with it a hint of fall, which usually disappointed by the end of the month when the dampness returned. There was a slight breeze this particular evening and the crickets seemed especially loud as Des drove from Dupont Circle over to Sadie's house in Georgetown.

He was perspiring quite profusely despite the breeze, despite the fact that the top was down on his Thunderbird, and the fact that he had just showered and changed. He found a parking space near the corner of Dumbarton and Wisconsin right next to a little flower stand. On impulse he stopped and bought a small bouquet of anemones, which he carried up the stairs to the large federal brick house like a teenage boy going courting.

The housekeeper let him in the front door and

127

led him down the hallway past the living room, out to a small private stone terrace dominated by a huge shady oak tree.

Sadie was standing by a wrought-iron chair as he walked outside. She took a step forward to greet him, then stopped.

He walked over to her. They looked at each other for a moment, before Des, who had his navy blazer slung over his shoulder, dropped it on the chair and took both of her hands.

'Sara Adabelle,' he said.

'I like it when you call me that.'

He searched her face, looking for evidence of pain. It was there. Tiny lines had appeared around the corners of her eyes as though she had been squinting in the sun. He noticed for the first time a few gray hairs mingled in with the McDougald auburn. It was more an indication, he suspected, of less than religious attendance at her hairdresser's than any real sign of aging.

She was still in mourning, but her black silk dress was casual and slinky and wrapped around the waist to reveal her lovely figure.

They stared at each other for a moment, then she stepped back and beckoned to a chair.

'Please.'

He sat down and automatically loosened his tie, then crossed and uncrossed his legs, shifted in his seat.

'Irish, neat?'

'Actually, I think I'll have a beer. It's so hot.'

She seemed disappointed that he had rejected her attempt at intimacy.

'I'll get it.'

'Here, let me help.' He jumped up.

128

'No, no. It's right here in the bar. Besides, it feels kind of good to be able to do things for myself now. Not always have somebody at your beck and call every second. I always found that a little claustrophobic.'

She disappeared into the house and came back a few minutes later with a beer and a kir for herself. She took a chair opposite him and the two of them sat there for a moment in silence listening to the breeze rustle the leaves.

'I thought you might have called,' she said.

'I ... I didn't want to bother you. I know you must be swamped.'

'Actually I was, in a way. But so much of it has been obligation rather than solace. I've needed a friend. Jenny's been great, but she was close to Rosey and it's been hard for her. She's pretty broken up. I can't lean on the kids. It's tough enough on them already. And Lorraine, well, forget Lorraine. She's completely useless. All I hear is that it's her fault, she never should have insisted on having cocktails in the garden. She overruled the Secret Service, she can't possibly go on living in that house now. There are bloodstains all over the terrace that she can't get out ... God, it makes me crazy just to hear her voice. She acts as if she's the only person who is suffering over this. I've heard that she's collapsed several times at parties and has had to be taken home. It's really ridiculous.'

'I've never heard you use that tone about Lorraine.'

'Well, I've had it. This has ruined what was left of our friendship. Though she did help me find this wonderful house. In the same way her house reminds her of Rosey's death, she reminds me. I

129

can't stand to be around her. That leaves you.'

'How can I help you?'

'You can be here for me. You can listen to me cry. You can hold me when I'm feeling sad. You can talk to me and tell me funny stories. You can give me reasons for wanting to go on living.'

'I don't know what to say.'

'Say you're going to marry Allison. That would be the truth. Then we can stop being so awkward with each other.'

'I'm going to marry Allison.'

'When?'

'How the hell should I know?'

He was clearly irritated.

'Sorry. It's just that she's in England and can't leave until her replacement's wife has a baby. It's all very complicated.'

'It's right for you, Des. She's right for you. I wasn't enough. You need a strong, independent woman. I'm not like that. I can see your annoyance with her now. But you know, there's a touch of pride in your voice. You kind of like it that she's not just hopping on a plane the minute you snap your fingers, don't you?'

'I think I like it in theory more than in practice.'

They sat in silence once again.

'Would you like another drink?'

'Not just yet, thanks.'

'She'll probably want to have babies.'

'Oh, no, not Allison. She's not the type. Too career-orientated.'

'Don't count on it.'

'Besides, I don't want to get into that again. I've done it. The midnight feedings, changing diapers, nannies, pediatricians, getting into the right

130

schools. It's a nightmare. I'm too old for it. Christ, by the time the kid was twenty I'd be in my seventies. No way.'

'You've discussed it then?'

'No. What's to discuss?'

'I don't know. It just seems to me that if you're about to marry someone the topic of children might happen to come up.'

'Mommy! Mommy!'

They both looked up as a dark curly-haired child with a filthy face tumbled out onto the terrace. He was followed closely behind by a round-faced, buxom, heavy-set young woman, looking exasperated.

'Mommy, I don't want a bath,' Willie whined as he crawled up into Sadie's lap.

'Willie, I let you play in the dirt an extra hour because you promised you'd take a bath,' said Monica. 'It's almost your bedtime. Now come here.'

She went over to Sadie and grabbed the kicking bundle from her arms.

'Look, you're getting Mummy all dirty.'

Sadie's face lit up for the first time since Des had come in.

'Willie,' she said, laughing. 'I want you to mind Monica. It's almost your bedtime anyway. You should have had a bath long ago. If you go take one now you can have a popsicle before you go to bed.'

'Posicle?'

His eyes widened at this unexpected windfall. Before Monica could turn around, Willie was headed into the house, desperate that she might change her mind.

'Sadie,' said Monica reprovingly. 'That's bribery.

131

Besides, he hardly touched his dinner and it's not good for his teeth.'

'You're absolutely right, Monica, and that's why you're the world's most fabulous nanny and I'm not. If his teeth rot out because of tonight, so be it. Monica, this is Desmond Shaw, an old friend of mine. Des, this is Monica Meehan. Monica's from Ireland. She came when Willie was born. She's promised to stay until he's twenty-one, at which point she will need a nanny.'

Monica laughed and ran after Willie.

'God, what would I do without her? I can't imagine. Willie is a terror. And does he have a mind of his own. Stubborn as a mule.'

'Who does he take after? Rosey was such a conciliatory person. A real diplomat, a total consensus guy. That's what made him so effective. Willie's genes must come from your side of the family. He's so sturdy. He looks like a little mick street kid. Like a lot of the kids in my neighbourhood when I was growing up. But I guess the Scots were like that, too. Must be McDougald blood.'

He didn't notice how she was looking at him.

'I think it's time for dinner,' she said.

They drank too much. Red wine, good red wine. Sadie had had the cook grill the veal chops outside and they had pasta and a salad.

After a few glasses of wine they both relaxed. Sadie found herself telling Des about her children, Rosey's parents, her parents, what demands the family was putting on her. It felt so easy to talk to him. He knew all the players, or at least knew all about them from hearing so much during the two years they were together.

132

The cook brought their sherbet and fresh fruit and Sadie gave her the rest of the evening off. She and Des would clear. Monica stuck her head in to say Willie was down and Sadie let her off, too.

Soon the house was quiet. It had grown dark outside. The French doors to the family dining room off the terrace were open and the candles flickered in the air as they talked.

'This evening has been good for me, Des,' she said. 'I feel alive for the first time in two months. I've felt somewhat detached, as though I've been observing an experience somebody else has lived through. This is the first time I've been able to talk about Rosey without crying. I didn't get you over here under false pretenses, you know. I really did need you.'

'I know that. It's just that I feel so conflicted about you, Sadiebelle. I don't know what I can give you.'

'How can you say that after tonight? You can give me hope. I can't count on my children for that. They have their own lives to lead. Even now they're in Richmond. Annie Laurie and Outland have to go back to college. I can't ask them to stay and take care of me.'

'You've got Willie.'

'Yes, my sweet little fatherless Willie.'

Her eyes welled up.

'He's going to need someone, some man around, Des. Outland won't be here. I was thinking...'

She saw that he was uncomfortable. She laughed self-consciously and wiped the tears away with her napkin.

'I guess that's the wine talking.'

'Sadie. You're right. But you've got to be

133

realistic. I'm about to get married. Chances are you'll get married again yourself. I can't give Willie what he needs. I'm not his father.'

Sadie didn't say a word. She looked carefully at Des, sat back in her chair, reached over to her wineglass, picked it up, and took a long sip. She continued to look at him. He found himself reaching nervously for his glass, then staring into it after he had taken a gulp. Something made him start to perspire again. He took another gulp.

'I'm not his father,' he said, quietly, but without conviction.

Sadie felt a chill go through her. Her teeth were clenched so tight that she could almost feel them start to grind. She clasped her arms around her body and began rubbing them as though she were cold. How could she have dared? She had sworn to herself she would never tell him. But now, here she was; it was almost midnight, she was drunk. Des was drunk, and she had a desperate need to have him know.

Still, she wasn't going to tell him. She couldn't bring herself to tell him. He would just have to figure it out. How could he not know? How could he look at Willie, call him a little mick street kid, and not know? Because he didn't want to know, that's how. Well, the hell with him. He was going to know. Why should she have to keep this hellish secret all to herself for the rest of her life? She had to share it. Somehow she couldn't put Rosey to rest until that was off her conscience.

'Am I?'

It was more a statement than a question.

She didn't answer.

'Am I?'

Still she said nothing.

'Jesus Mary Mother of God.'

His voice was a whisper.

'Holy Mother.'

Now his eyes filled with tears. He looked at Sadie, who was crying softly.

'I am.'

The two of them sat there looking at each other. Then Des slowly got up and went to her, taking her in his arms and holding her as tightly as he possibly could for a very long time.

He was the first to break the silence.

'Did Rosey know?'

She nodded. Now she began to sob and he held her tightly again.

'He told me he knew as he was dying.'

'Oh Jesus, oh no. Oh my Sadie, my Sadiebelle. I'm so sorry. So sorry for everything.'

He pulled away from her and took her hand.

'Let's go upstairs,' he said, without asking. 'I want to see him. I need to see him. My Willie. My son.'

*     *     *

Des tiptoed into Willie's room and saw the toddler sprawled across the bed on his tummy, his head at the foot of the bed, his pudgy arms hanging through the child guard. He knelt down on the floor and put his face next to Willie's. He stared at him for the longest time, then sat up. With a strong, tan finger he gently traced Willie's profile from his forehead down along his little turned-up nose, over his pink lips, down his firm chin, then stroked his fat cheeks. Willie sighed but didn't wake up. Des took one of Willie's hands in his and placed his other hand on top of Willie's head, stroking the black curls back and forth. Finally he leaned down and put his body on top of the child while he knelt, embracing as much of him as he could, and then just held him.

Sadie leaned against the doorjamb, her arms crossed as she watched. She felt as though her heart would break looking at the two of them, how much they looked alike. How could anyone not have guessed the moment Willie was born? The idea that Rosey wouldn't have known seemed so absurd to her now. The idea that Des never even thought of it was appalling.

'Des,' she said quietly.

'I know.'

He got up, walked to the door, then turned and looked once again at Willie, before he walked out.

'Come,' she said, and led him across the hall into her bedroom. He sank to the canopied bed and put his head in his hands.

She sat next to him and put her hand on his back, stroking him gently. The house was eerily quiet except for the night noises from the open windows.

'Tell me what to do, Sadie. I've never had a son before. I've never had a son by a woman who was married to a President of the United States. What do I do? What do we do?'

She could feel her heart respond. She knew she was treading on dangerous ground. But she was drunk and lightheaded and emotional and she loved him, saw his pain, his confusion. She had to say what she needed to say, what she wanted, what she had always wanted.

'We could marry and tell him the truth, tell

everyone the truth.'

Someone else must have said it. She couldn't have been the one to utter those words, they were so preposterous. How could she take them back? She almost reached out in the air and tried to retrieve them, then had this image of how ridiculous she would look and nearly giggled. How could such intense emotion turn so suddenly from pain to humor? She felt ashamed.

Des sat up straight and looked at her, his expression one of total shock.

'I didn't mean that. I'm sorry. It's crazy,' she sputtered before he could say anything. 'It doesn't make any sense. I don't know why I even said it. It's just that I love him so much. I want him to have a father, his father. And because I loved you so much . . .'

'Sadie.'

'I do, Des. I love you. I've never stopped loving you. In my fantasy Rosey disappeared and you and Willie and I lived happily ever after. I know I shouldn't be telling you this, but I don't care because I'm too drunk to control myself. I'll never have the courage to say it again and I'll have to pretend that I don't love you from now on. So I figured I might as well tell you now so you would always know, no matter what, that I have loved you and I will forever.'

She paused for breath, and then whispered.

'Willie is our love child. Our child of love.'

Des couldn't take his eyes off her, off her brimming eyes, her beautiful, sweet, vulnerable face. He was drunk, too, and the soft, Southern lilt to her voice, the subtle smell of her perfume made him feel somehow transported by her need.

137

He reached over and put his arm around her and kissed her first on the mouth, then on her face, her eyes.

'Oh Des,' she murmured.

She leaned back on the silk blanket cover and pulled Des with her, holding him tightly as he kissed her.

He pulled away and looked down at her.

He caressed her hair, searching her face, then sat up abruptly.

'I can't do this, Sadie. I care too much about you. And I've just been hit by a bomb. I need some time to absorb this. I don't know what's right, but I do know what's wrong and that would be to tell the truth about Willie. That child is the President's son. We'll have to think of another way. A way where the fewest people get hurt. And I'm afraid that those fewest people are you and me.'

★     ★     ★

It was the first of October and she still hadn't heard from him. He had said he needed time and that he would call her in a few weeks. He had said that he loved . . . no, he didn't say he loved her. He said he cared about her. A very different thing.

She wanted to die. She couldn't believe she had told him she loved him and wanted him to marry her. Each time she thought about it she shuddered with humiliation and despair. If only she hadn't lost control he probably would have called her the next day. She could have lured him back. Maybe she shouldn't have told him about Willie. But that was impossible. It had been nearly impossible not to tell him even before Rosey died. He had to know. Now he was going to marry Allison. She had tried not to show how much she cared when he told her. Somewhere down deep she had always hoped she and Des would be together, unrealistic as it seemed. Maybe he was trying to decide between her and Allison. He could always marry her and they could still pretend that Willie was Rosey's son. That way he could be a father to him and not hurt Willie, the kids, their families, the country ... not cause a scandal. Sometimes it was so hard to have one's life be determined by national considerations. It sounded so heavy, just saying it. It was even more ponderous living it. But that wasn't even the point. She had never known she was capable of hurting so much.

She was sitting at her desk in the upstairs sitting room, a sunny yellow room at the front of the house facing south. She was wearing black sweats and black sneakers and she was trying to answer her mail, which was taking up a whole room in the house. She hated it. It was tedious and depressing, and when Joyce, her secretary, wasn't around it was even worse because she had nobody to complain to. She hadn't really thought about getting back to her writing. She was too drained to write anything but a letter, and even that took all she had. It was impossible to go out without being mobbed and stared at. All she had was the telephone. And here she sat, waiting for it to ring. It rang.

'Darling, you're there.'

'Where the hell else would I be, Lorraine?'

Just hearing Lorraine's voice now irritated her.

'Oh sweetheart. Is it a bad day?'

'Oh no. I'm having a great day, Lorraine. How about you?'

139

Mistake.

'It comes and goes. Yesterday I just couldn't stop crying. But today I've gotten my chin up a bit.'

'Good for you.'

Lorraine would have made a great presidential widow. In fact, she would make a great widow period. In fact, she probably couldn't wait for the day old Archie would keel over and she could collect all his millions.

'Nothing like a good bit of gossip to cheer one up,' said Lorraine.

'Absolutely.'

'Well, it seems that our beloved First Lady ... one Blanche Osgood ... oh, that woman is so common. I don't see how Rosey could have chosen Freddy Osgood as his running mate. It's really too much ... anyway ...'

At that moment Willie came tumbling into Sadie's study, his sturdy little legs and arms flying all at the same time, and landed in her lap. He grabbed the telephone and pulled the receiver away from her, as she started to laugh.

'Hey, tubby, where've you been all morning?'

'Me not tubby. Me Willie.'

'Oops, excuse me,' she said, covering her mouth in mock horror to his delight. 'I thought you were tubby.' And she grabbed his leg and began to munch on his thigh. Then she heard Lorraine barking at the end of the dangling phone.

'I can see this is not a good time to talk,' said Lorraine in her most irritated voice.

'Let me call you back,' said Sadie, gagging, as Willie wrapped the phone cord around her neck. Gratefully, she hung up.

'You know what I'm going to do? I'm going to

eat you up,' she said. She began to make gobble noises, pretending to eat his limbs until she had him convulsed with giggles.

'Oh Monica, this is delicious,' she said and the nanny appeared behind Willie. 'Come and have some. He tastes better than candy.' And she continued to gobble until the three of them were rolling on the floor, infected with Willie's hilarity.

'Oh my chile, you do my poor ole heart good,' said Sadie, sitting up to catch her breath. But only for a moment, until Willie jumped on her and knocked her down again.

'God,' she said, 'Willie, you're getting so strong. You know Mommy hates to roughhouse. What do mommies like to do?'

'Cuddle,' squealed Willie with delight, throwing his arms around her and climbing into her lap. He buried his head in her shoulder, then looked up and grinned.

'Daddy like roughhouse.'

Sadie saw Monica's face fall and she suddenly felt the wind go out of her.

'Okay, fats, we're off to play group,' said Monica quickly, sweeping Willie off the floor into her arms.

'Give Mommy a big kiss.'

She held Willie over to Sadie while he planted a wet kiss on her cheek and whisked him out of the room before Sadie could protest.

It was interesting how, now that the initial grieving phase was over, all conversations that even touched on Rosey or the assassination were cut off in midsentence or changed. Even her closest friends did it. It was not that she really needed to talk about Rosey. But people seemed so uncomfortable with it that it made her reluctant to force the

141

conversation. If only Des would call her. He didn't seem to mind talking about it. Yet she may have ruined the one relationship that could have helped her the most.

The phone rang. It was Lorraine again.

'I've been on the phone and I thought you might have tried to call back,' she said.

'No, actually I was playing with Willie.'

She could tell Lorraine was annoyed.

'Well, there was one little morsel I thought you should know about.' She paused for effect.

'Desmond Shaw is going to marry Allison Sterling.'

There was a note of triumph in her voice, almost as if she knew about Sadie and Des. Of course she didn't.

'I know,' Sadie said, trying to sound casual. Trying not to sound as though she hadn't just fallen down a dark well. So he was really going to marry Allison. They were announcing it. Her evening with Des hadn't changed anything. He hadn't even bothered to tell her. How could he hurt her like this? It was hard to imagine.

'What do you mean, you know? How could you know and not tell me. This is incredible news.'

'I guess maybe I just have other things on my mind. Listen, Lorraine, I've got to see to Willie. I'll call you later, okay?'

She had just put the phone down when it rang again.

'Sadie? It's Jen.' She hesitated.

'I'm afraid I have something to tell you.'

'About Des and Allison?'

'Yes.'

'Lorraine beat you to it. I knew they were

142

thinking of it. Des came over for dinner a few weeks ago. He told me.'

'Des came for dinner? Oh Sadie, was that a good idea?'

'As it turns out, no.'

'Well, I thought I ought to tell you before somebody else did. I should have known Lorraine would get there first. I heard it last night from some reporters at the *Daily*. How the hell did Lorraine hear it?'

'Probably from some of her pals in London. Isn't Allison still over there?'

'I guess you're right.'

'How do you feel about it?'

'How do I feel about it? Oh great, Jen. Just ecstatic. I'm so happy for them both.'

'I'm sorry. I'm just trying to be sympathetic. I'm not doing a very good job.'

'No, I'm the one who's sorry. I didn't mean to ... it's just that ... oh God, Jen, I don't know how much more I can take.'

Her voice cracked.

'Sometimes I think if it weren't for Willie I'd—'

'Do you want me to come over?'

'You don't have to.'

'I'm coming over.'

Sadie put the receiver down and stared out the window. It was a gorgeous fall day. The leaves were beginning to turn and the maple in front of the house, the one she had always admired even before she moved, was about to come ablaze with scarlet. It reminded her of the day, years ago, when Rosey was still Vice President, that she had first had lunch with Des.

She had refused him at first, then had thought of

a zany way to meet him without being seen. She had gotten her gardener to smuggle her out of the Vice President's mansion in a garbage can in the back of his van.

It had been such a daring thing to do. She could hardly believe now that she had ever been that silly and carefree. Des had met them on the George Washington Parkway and had taken her to the Auberge Chez François, a romantic country inn in Virginia. The restaurant was normally closed on Mondays, but the proprietor had opened it especially for them because Des was an old friend.

They had fallen in love that day, drinking wine, basking in the autumn sunlight that streamed into the empty restaurant, watching the colored leaves swirl past the window.

On the way back to Washington, Des had abruptly pulled off the winding road to a deserted spot overlooking the falls, and they had made passionate love in the car.

It wasn't until much later, after Rosey was in the White House, that she and Des had resumed their affair. She would always remember that lunch as the most magical day of her life.

Des. God she had loved him. Enough to have told Rosey she was leaving him for Des. Then she had gotten pregnant and sent Des away with no explanation. She had hurt him badly. Why shouldn't he do the same?

A knock at the door broke her reverie. It was her housekeeper, Asuncion, with a letter that had been hand delivered. It was really the only way, these days, that anything got through to her.

It wasn't until she saw the *Weekly* logo that she lost her breath. She stared at the envelope in her

144

hand as though inside there might be either a horrible poisonous snake or a beautiful piece of jewelry. Which would it be? Dare she open it?

She got up and paced the floor several times. She put the envelope down, went into her dressing room and combed her hair, put on lipstick. No matter whether it was acceptance or rejection, she had to look her best. She went downstairs to the kitchen to get a mug of tea. Soothing tea. Inspired, she added a touch of brandy to it. It was cool enough outside to justify. She went back upstairs to her study and stared once more at the menacing envelope. This was ridiculous. This was like being back at Smith and not opening your grades. This was like being a struggling young career girl in New York and not opening your bills. She grabbed the letter with resolve. Viper or jewel, so be it. She ripped it open.

'My dearest Sadiebelle,' it began.

She took a deep breath, walked over to the sofa by the fireplace, sank into the pillows and took a large swig of tea.

I know it's been three weeks and I know what you must have been going through. It hasn't been much fun for me either.

This thing has hit me like a bombshell. I feel devastated.

Yes, I had planned to marry Allison. We hadn't set a date but we had talked about sometime around Christmas.

Sadie couldn't help her excitement over his tenses. I had planned, not I plan.

But that [he continued] was before I knew about Willie.

Willie changes everything.

It would be a heartless and difficult thing for me to do now, to marry Allison. Dearest Sadie, I don't see how I can offer myself to you either. I don't believe you would want a husband who was in love with someone else.

He had said it. Finally. He didn't love her. She felt momentarily nauseated. She swallowed hard and kept reading.

I've been wrestling night and day with the fact that Allison probably wouldn't want me either if she knew I was the father of your child, of the President's child. I've already caused her so much pain. Somehow I don't see how I can avoid causing her more.

Christ, I've ruined so many lives, even potentially the life of my son, our child. I wish to God I knew how to resolve this situation without hurting anyone, but for the life of me I don't see how. It's an unbelievable quandary for me.

I can't do my duty toward Willie without causing him and you to be heaped with scorn and without losing Allison. I can't help but ask myself who am I to have assumed this vital role in three different lives almost casually. I've come to realize, in the last few weeks, after considerable soul searching, that that's one of the things I do in life. I do things too casually without thinking of the consequences.

But there it is. A rather fatal flaw in my character.

I don't know what to do, Sadie. I don't see how I can turn my back on the child I know I would love, on you whom I have loved, and on the woman I do love. I just can't see my way out. I can't run away. I don't know what to do.

Des

\*      \*      \*

'I know what they think, Sadie. I just look stupid. They think I'm common as pig's tracks. Well, I'm gonna tell you somethin', honey. They can just take their ole Washington establishment and shove it up where the sun don't shine, 'cause I don't give a plug nickel about any of 'em. And I'll tell you somethin' else. They're all gonna kiss my ass for the next two years anyhow, so it doesn't matter. My husband is the President of the United States of America. Ha!'

Blanche Osgood lit up a cigarette, took a long slow drag, blew out the smoke in perfectly symmetrical rings, and picked a piece of tobacco off her tongue. She crossed her legs and settled back smugly into the folds of the sofa in the family sitting room of the White House.

Sadie took a sip of her Coke and smiled in spite of herself.

'What're you smilin' about, Sadie?'

'I'm smiling because you make me laugh, Blanche. I'm smiling because you're right. And I'm smiling in spite of myself because that's exactly the same attitude I had when I first came to Washington as the Vice President's wife. I was going to be myself, do my own thing, the hell with all of them. I actually did try to live that way. But you know what, my friend. It didn't work. They

147

always get you in the end.'

'They didn't get you.'

'Oh, yes they did.'

'How?'

'Slowly. Subtly. There's an undercurrent of derision for anything that you do that is not part of their habits, their mores. You're the outsider and you have to go through a series of initiation rites to be one of them, to be part of their culture. It's almost like a religion. I did it though. I'm one of them now. I learned their language and their rituals. Mostly I learned their taboos. I did that early on. If I hadn't, I would have been destroyed. It is a deadly game, Blanche. For all your bravado you can be devastated by them. You're only one person, and even if you have the power, if your husband has the power, you can't win against them. You can't 'lick them, so you have no choice but to join them. Some people don't join them. And they leave without a trace. Without a footprint. It's as if they've never even been here. The establishment—and that includes the journalists as well—always prevails.'

'Sweet Jesus, Sadie. You make it sound so serious. We're talkin' about a bunch of horses' asses here, not the court of Louis the Fourteenth. Lordy, listen to this gal talk. You'd think I was educated or somethin'.'

Sadie smiled again.

'Blanche, give me a cigarette, will you?'

'I thought you didn't smoke.'

'I started again after ... I just started again.'

Sadie shivered though the heat was turned up full blast against the November chill. Blanche liked it warm. Why did she suddenly feel cold? She pulled her shawl tightly around her shoulders and tucked her feet up underneath her on the chair, glad she had decided to wear pants.

She looked around the large sitting area, what was the end of the great hall, really, and out the Palladian window toward the West Wing. How many times had she sat there and wished she could get out of her prison as First Lady, get out of her marriage with Rosey and marry Des? She had gotten her wish. She was free of everything she thought she hated about the White House and all she could think of was how much she envied Blanche.

Poor tacky Blanche. Poor platinum-blond Blanche. Poor white trash Blanche. She was First Lady and Sadie was not.

Sadie had hesitated at first when Blanche invited her over for lunch. It hadn't been the first invitation to the White House. The Osgoods had made an effort but she had put them off, saying that it was too painful, which was the truth. This time, when Blanche asked her for lunch, the obligatory once-a-week invitation, she had decided to go. She had never had much use for Blanche when Rosey was President. In fact, she had been actively critical of her to close friends. She had tried to persuade Rosey not to pull Osgood out of the Senate and appoint him Vice President when Roger Kimball had his stroke. Freddy had only been in Washington a few years and Blanche had never really even made the move. Her budding career as a country music singer and songwriter in Nashville had kept her back in their home state most of the time. She had gotten some initial publicity when Freddy was first elected to the Senate from

149

Tennessee, but she had no real profile in Washington and was rarely seen. When Osgood became Vice President, she kept pretty much the same schedule, coming to Washington only for command performances. Every time she did come she said something outrageous that got her in trouble. Rosey had even had to speak to Freddy about it several times. Sadie felt a certain sympathy for Blanche, having had similar problems herself when she first came to Washington.

By the time Freddy became Vice President, however, Sadie had taken on the protective coloration of an insider and she was totally uninterested in helping Blanche out. She had her own problems. Not the least was her affair with Des. If it didn't actually take up most of her time, it certainly took up most of her emotional energy.

Now Sadie was alone, lonely, and, if the truth be known, bored. She needed something to keep her occupied, keep her mind off her pain and her boredom. Blanche looked to be a worthy project. From the moment she had set foot in the White House in July it had been a disaster. She had had to leave her beloved Nashville and move to Washington, which was bad enough. But moving into the goldfish bowl that was the White House was more than she had bargained for. She had become the laughingstock of Washington with her hair, her clothes, her music, her friends, and her big mouth.

Her all-too-frequent, from Sadie's point of view, comments in the press reflected an outward sanguinity and toughness. Yet Sadie gathered from the persistent luncheon invitations that Blanche was in trouble and needed help.

150

Freddy was visibly anguished over his bride's inability to adjust, and Blanche, who had only married him a short time before he was elected to the Senate, was thrown into the most horrible position of having to be something she had never put in for. As Sadie well knew, the White House was not the ideal place to work on one's marriage. Whatever problems they had were going to have to be dealt with in public unless Blanche could find a confidante and mentor to guide her through the treacherous shoals of Washington's political and social life. Sadie appeared to have been appointed.

In fact, though Blanche didn't know it, it had been Freddy's call that had finally prompted Sadie to come to the White House. There had been an urgency to Freddy's voice that surprised her.

'I know it's hard, Sadie,' he had said, 'and it's probably the last thing on earth you have a mind to do. But honey, Blanche needs help real bad. She's just goddamn miserable up here locked in this gilded cage. My little songbird needs her freedom. Frankly, if she doesn't get it, I'm afraid there's going to be all hell to pay somewhere along the line. Unless she learns some Washington manners... I don't need to tell you, Sadie, that everybody's makin' fun of her. She's trying to put on a brave face but it's eatin' her up inside. It isn't makin' my life any easier either, I'll tell you that. Sadie, I'm askin' you to see Blanche, talk to her, have lunch with her, be her friend. She doesn't have a single friend in this goddamn town. She's not goin' to change all that much, but at least she can learn what's acceptable and what's not. Blanche is not a stupid woman. I wouldn't've married somebody stupid. They ain' no flies on her head. But she can't know what she doesn't know. You've got to tell her. Will you do that for me, Sadie? I'll be eternally grateful. And please, for Christ's sweet sake, do not tell her I called you. I'm in enough hot water already.'

A servant had appeared and announced lunch, which Sadie and Blanche were to eat in the family dining room. Blanche deferred to Sadie, letting her lead the way as though Sadie were still First Lady and Blanche the humble guest.

The waiter served a cheese soufflé and Sadie's face lit up.

'Oh, my favorite thing for lunch.'

'Well, I just tell them, when we entertain, to do it the way you liked to do it, serve what you liked to serve. It seems to make them happy and then I don't have to get mad at the raised eyebrows, which is what happens when I try to suggest something.'

Blanche had lost some of her veneer of confidence in the short time that Sadie had been there. Sadie found herself warming to this blowsy, improbable-looking woman who seemed so forlorn and out of place.

'They all think you were perfect, you know.'

There was pain mixed with envy and admiration in her voice as she looked up shyly at Sadie, then took a mouthful of the perfect soufflé. Sadie's perfect soufflé.

'Oh Blanche, if only you could know how unperfect I felt most of the time. Nobody in this job ever feels as if they know what they're doing. Nobody can ever please everybody. There's always somebody who thinks you're a disaster.'

'Nobody ever thought that about you. You're beautiful and smart and well educated and you've got taste and class. Lady, you got class comin' out your ears. I'm just a tacky ole country singer. What do I know?'

'Blanche, you've got a career. You're a well-known singer. You've made your own records. You have your own life and your own identity. That's more than I ever had. I envy you that.'

'Not anymore I don't. I don't have nuthin'. It surprises me that that's what you think of me. I can't imagine somebody like you envying me.'

'Now look. You've got to get out of this frame of mind. You just can't allow yourself to sink into this black hole or you'll never get out of it.'

Blanche's eyes welled up as the salad was served. The perfect green salad with Sadie's vinaigrette.

After lunch they both reached simultaneously for a cigarette and nearly knocked over a glass. Blanche held out the pack for Sadie, then took one herself. Sadie picked up the white matches embossed in gold with The President's House, lit Blanche's cigarette, then her own. She put the matches down and began to finger them, turning them around and around in her hands.

It had been at this table more than three years earlier that she had lit up a cigarette in front of Rosey. She knew he hated her smoking and she had done it to provoke a fight. She had wanted to provoke a fight that Sunday morning, because she had decided to tell her husband she was leaving him for Des. She had been trying to get up her courage when she looked at the matches with The President's House stamped on them and she had suddenly become enraged. She could remember even now her anger at the idea that it was indeed The President's House. Not her house, not the

153

First Lady's House, not even the First Family's House. Just the President. Where did that leave her? Out of there with Des, that's where. It had been those silly matches that had propelled her, finally, to tell her husband about her love affair, to inform him that she was leaving him and His House for a home of her own with the man she loved.

That was such a long time ago. Yet she could still remember the fear she felt when Rosey said nothing. The loneliness she felt when he left the room and stayed away for the rest of the day. The sorrow she felt when he came to her that night and cried. The pity she felt when he begged her to stay. And the despair she had felt later when she learned she was pregnant and didn't know who the father was.

She had had no choice then but to stay. It would have been a scandal if she had left. And Rosey had threatened not to run again if she left him for Des. So she had had to tell Des she would not go with him. She had taken the coward's way out, refusing to answer his phone calls, refusing to see him. She had let him know at the convention. He had written her a two-word note, 'Regrets Only,' and sent it up to her on the platform through a Secret Service agent just as Rosey accepted the nomination. She had responded to him turning toward him in the *Weekly* box below and shaking her head no. She had never seen him again. She had watched him on the Sunday morning news show when she could, when Rosey wasn't around. When she could steal a moment or two.

Then she had had his baby. Beautiful, curly black-haired, blue-eyed little mick, Willie. Her angel. Their love child.

154

Rosey was ecstatic. He always acted as though this was the child of their love. Until the day he died.

A pack of matches brought it all back.

*     *     *

By four that afternoon both Sadie and Blanche were drunk.

They had moved into the bedroom and Blanche's dressing room to go through her closet. Sadie had agreed to advise Blanche on entertaining, clothes, and other important matters including finding a 'project'.

Blanche was in a very good mood by this time. She had put on some CD's of her friends singing country music hits and was singing along with them. She had a deep, soulful, quite powerful voice, almost a gospel voice, that resonated through the family quarters as she sang.

Sadie had sat down on the sofa for a rest and to pour herself another glass of white wine. She hadn't counted on missing the White House or Rosey as much as she had that afternoon. She had stayed away because she knew it might be hard and because she had had no real interest in Blanche. This was really anguish. Everywhere she looked were reminders of their four years in the White House, the good times and the bad. The worst part was that it was still her house. Everything was exactly as she had left it. Not an ashtray out of place. The beautiful, soft chintz in the bedroom, the flowered prints, the throws and pillows. All her little touches. The bed where she and Rosey had spent their first terrified night, the night after Roger

155

Kimball had his stroke and Rosey was sworn in as President. The bed where she had made such infrequent love to her husband and where she had lain awake at night longing for Desmond Shaw. The bed where Rosey had cried the night she told him about Des. The same bed where she lay weeping the night Rosey died. The bed Willie pounced on the next morning looking for his daddy.

How ungrateful she had been for all she had. A wonderful husband who adored her, fabulous children. She was the First Lady, with an opportunity to really make a difference and to change things. And what had she done with it? Nothing but mope and whine and feel sorry for herself. What an awful person she had been. Shallow and frivolous and self-involved. Now that it was too late she saw it. How sad that she had had so much and not taken advantage of it. She could see Blanche falling into the same self-pitying trap that beset so many First Ladies. Blanche needed to be taken out of herself. To see how much she could do, what opportunities were available to her. To see how this could be a joyous and fulfilling time of her life. If Sadie had done nothing truly worthwhile as First Lady, she might have a second chance if she could help Blanche.

Blanche flopped down on the chaise longue, let her backless mules drop off, and sighed.

'I know what you think of my wardrobe, Sadie. It's written all over that polite face of yours. You think it's a dog's lunch, don't you?'

'Well, Blanche, I didn't say that.'

'You don't have to, honey. It just ain't gonna do, is it?'

156

'Here's the problem. Your wardrobe is perfect for a country music singer from Nashville. Some of it is not really appropriate for the White House. But before we go any further with this, we have to take a broader view of this whole situation.'

She found she was slurring her words and trying to sound sober by using pompous-sounding phrases.

'Exactly my sentiments,' said Blanche, rising to the occasion.

'Now, we don't want you to become a different person, to hide your light under a bushel, so to speak. We want you to be yourself, right?'

'To thine own self be true,' nodded Blanche, pouring herself just a teeny bit more wine.

'So what we want is to let Blanche be Blanche in the context of the White House. In other words, you've got to clean up your act.'

'How'm I gonna do that?' Blanche looked perturbed.

'First of all, you've got to keep your mouth shut until we figure out how you're going to do it. Then you'll reemerge as the new, improved First Lady. The sad thing is that your image has nothing to do with who you really are. You came at this with a chip on your shoulder about Washington, the White House, and if I'm not totally mistaken—tell me if I'm out of line—your husband.'

Blanche was silent for a moment and she seemed to sober up.

'No, you're wrong.'

Sadie waited but Blanche said nothing more. The problem was deeper than she had thought.

'So what we've got to do,' she said quickly, 'is to have you portrayed as a kind, sweet, warmhearted, funny, slightly, and I mean slightly, irreverent, bright career woman who has moved to Washington and is delighted in discovering her new environment. A sort of country Alice in Wonderland.'

'A hooker with a heart of gold is what you're saying.'

Sadie didn't respond.

'You've got to knock off this business of being a prisoner in the White House. You know and I know how difficult it is, but you're not going to get any sympathy from anybody out there. You are the Queen and queens have no right to complain. They like to know you're human and have human problems like everyone else, but they only want to know about epic problems. They say they want details but when they get them they only use them against you. So when they ask you about how you're going to continue with your singing career as First Lady, you have to say that it will be a challenge for you.'

'Freedom's just another word for nuthin' left to lose,' warbled Blanche as she got up from her chaise and struck a pose at the window, looking out on the mall towards the Washington Monument.

'Here's what we'll do. Plan A,' said Sadie, warming to her subject. 'We'll invite a selected group of tame reporters to an on-the-record tea. That way the news organizations can't object if we select whomever we want. It's not an interview, it's a social occasion that we are going to allow to be on the record. You and I will rehearse beforehand, maybe I'll get Jenny Stern to advise, though we'll have to let your own press secretary at least think she's involved. We'll talk about her later.'

158

'What about my clothes?'

'I don't know, Blanche. You've got such a good figure, a little busty maybe, damn you. Simple plain suits and dark dresses in solid colors would work really well for you. Save the buttons and bows and frills for Nashville. I'll help you shop. That's easy. There are two other things that need to be addressed right away. One is your project, the other is the Washington establishment.'

'How can I have a project if I'm supposed to be a career woman?'

'All you have to do to have a project as First Lady is just say you have one. Then you get your staff to do it, and you do as much or as little as you want. The main thing is to get something that will fly, something that will enhance your image as a ministering angel.'

'Ha, that'll be the day.'

'I had historic preservation and Planned Parenthood as the Vice President's wife. I had to low-key both of those when I got to the White House. Preservation is too elitist and Planned Parenthood too controversial. Children. That was the key. It's the most worthwhile thing you can do and nobody can be against children. I chose Children's Hospital and sick children and it was terrific. I never got any bad press on it at all.'

'Well, if you did it how can I do it? I've already got the same damn soufflé and salad dressing. I haven't so much as moved a vase since you left. It's still your house in my mind. You're still First Lady in spirit. I'm just an interloper. It's all a charade. Any minute Rosey will walk in the door and I can get out of here, go back to Nashville and sing my heart out. I think my attitude shows. I think people

159

think I'm so pathetic that I couldn't think up my own project, that all I can do is copy you. I'm just a poor woman's Sadie Grey.'

'We need to get a different approach. Babies with AIDS, for instance. Children with AIDS. Or even AIDS period. You can do a lot to lower the fear quotient of the public about it.'

'That's all I need.'

'Blanche, AIDS is a danger for everybody. You can call for education about the disease. There are ways you can do it that would be helpful and courageous, like holding AIDS babies, things like that.'

'It's already started to affect the music industry.'

'Okay. You can get some of your famous music friends to do concerts to raise money for hospices or homes for children with AIDS.'

'What if I get it by holding one of those babies? I don't know, Sadie. I'm not so sure this is such a red-hot idea.'

'You can't get AIDS that way. You should go out to NIH and see what they're doing. There's that doctor out there who's always being quoted about AIDS, what's his name? Michael Lanzer. You ought to talk to him. It can't hurt. Freddy has just set up a commission to deal with the AIDS problem. It's a good issue.'

'Okay, okay. Jesus Lord, you're persistent. I'll do it. Now talk to me about Washington. The establishment, you call it.'

'It's very hard to be a part of it, very hard to understand. Some people can live in this city a lifetime and never get it. Lorraine Hadley took me under her wing when I first got here and she saved me a lot of time and a lot of grief. It's ironic now that she has allowed herself to be left behind. You really have to be an anthropologist in a way. People in this city think of themselves as so open-minded, so ready to accept anything new because almost everybody here came from someplace else. Nobody is actually from Washington. In fact, it's really a very close-minded culture. They're very set in their ways and they don't even know it. They're rigid the way converts are to a new religion. The establishment is composed of people who have been in former administrations and stayed on. It's comprised of lawyers and lobbyists, which are the same thing, journalists, some longtime members of the Congress and the Senate, and some longtime diplomats. In the old days there used to be a number of extremely rich women, widows or wives of establishment men who acted as hostesses or catalysts. They held salons where members of the establishment could get together and socialize, compare notes, exchange political gossip, commiserate, collude.'

'This sounds pretty serious, Sadie. I think I'll have some black coffee and sober up.'

Blanche stood up and wobbled across the floor to ring for the butler. 'Maybe I should get a pad and pencil and take notes.'

'I didn't mean to sound so pedantic, but it's the first time I've ever really analyzed it. It's kind of interesting.'

'What ever happened to all those hostesses? I know your friend Lorraine is one of them, but she doesn't impress me as somebody I need to make up to.'

'There are almost none left. Most of them have died off or gone broke, and the younger ones have all gone out and gotten jobs. Nobody in her right mind today would call herself a hostess. It's not serious, it's too frivolous. Even if a woman had the money, the house, the staff, and the time, she still wouldn't consider it in today's Washington. The few who are still left are looked upon as anachronisms. They don't draw the power crowd. People just don't play that game anymore. The city is too big and too diverse. It's not a small Southern town anymore. Lorraine is finished. She's had it, to answer your question. She doesn't even realize it yet. It's sad really.'

'Well, how'm I going to survive if the savviest hostess in Washington doesn't even know when her number's up?'

'You're treading water every day of your life in this town, kiddo, even if you're in power. The sharks are always circling. Just remember that. They never go away. Right now they've got a whiff of your blood.'

'Did I just order coffee? I think I'll switch to bourbon on the rocks.'

Just then there was a knock at the door and the butler appeared with a tray of coffee, and tea for Sadie.

Blanche thanked him, waited till he was out of the room, then went into the family sitting area. She grabbed a bottle of bourbon and poured some into her coffee. Sadie declined. She was wound up now, involved in her little sociology lesson.

'You should write a book about Washington, Sadie. You really know your stuff.'

'Oh, I don't know. I might.'

She would never admit to Blanche or anyone else that she was writing a novel when Rosey was killed.

Only Jenny and Des knew about it. Des had encouraged her and had actually helped edit it while they were still seeing each other.

'So what do I do? Let's skip the lecture and get me on a lifeboat quick.'

'Only if we can drown this metaphor,' said Sadie with a chuckle.

'Huh?'

'Never mind. You want tips. I'll give you some. Number one: You have to know everything that's going on in Washington. You have to look at the news. You have to know who everybody is. Number two: You can't be ostentatious about anything. Money, clothes, looks, sex—anything. Three: If you're a woman you have to do something. You can't just be a wife anymore. It doesn't work. That's why we need to work on a project. Four: You have to walk a very fine line between being a character, being controversial, and being an outrage. Controversial is fine as long as everybody agrees with you. That's a neat trick to pull off. You can be controversial in word but not in deed. A controversial style will get you noticed. You'll be labelled a character of sorts. People will want to be around you, invite you, even lionize you. However, be politically controversial, deviate in the least from the norm of Republican or Democrat and you're dead. The thing about you, Blanche, is that you're only a step away from being an adorable character, revered and held in affection.'

'Why should I give a damn about any of them?' said Blanche, suddenly becoming belligerent.

'For one very good reason,' said Sadie, 'you love your husband.'

Blanche just stared at her in silence. Then took a

163

large swig of her 'coffee.'

★    ★    ★

They were still talking in the bedroom when Freddy came up the elevator to the family quarters at seven o'clock.

'Hey honey,' he called out. 'I'm home. We've got company.'

'Baby Jesus,' said Blanche. 'It's Freddy and here we are loaded and it's . . .' she looked at the clock. 'Oh my God, it's seven o'clock. Now try to act sober, Sadie. He'll kill me if he thinks I'm drunk. I've been having a few cocktails before he gets home lately and he doesn't like it. Be out in one minute!' she yelled back.

Sadie and Blanche quickly straightened themselves up and walked to the sitting room.

'Well, glory be, girls,' said Freddy, looking at both of them and bursting out laughing. 'I do believe you've been hittin' the moonshine.'

They were trying hard to look proper but neither of them was having much luck. Blanche held her liquor better than Sadie, who had been trying to sober up for hours while Blanche was drinking her bourbon-laced coffee.

'How dare you suggest such a thing of the First Lady of the Land and the former First Lady?' said Blanche in a phony British accent, her nose in the air.

'Kiss my naked ass, woman,' said Freddy. 'Can you believe this, Foxy? We got two gorgeous women here totally soused.'

He went over to Blanche and gave her a robust kiss, then turned to Sadie who was still standing

164

there trying to look proper and sober.

'Sadie, glad to see you,' he said, a bit self-consciously. 'Blanche didn't tell me you were coming over for *lunch*. He emphasized 'lunch' then glanced pointedly at his watch. 'I can't tell you how happy I am that you finally did,' he added.

Sadie realized that Freddy was taking liberties with them, with her in particular, that he never would have done had she been sober. She tried to pull herself up to full height.

'We've had a wonderful afternoon, haven't we, Blanche?' she said.

'So I can see,' said Freddy.

He noticed that Sadie was glancing uncomfortably toward his guest.

'Oh, excuse me, where are my manners? I don't think you've met the new attorney general, Roy Fox. Roy and I grew up together in Tennessee. Everybody calls him Foxy. You probably know that already. Roy's a bachelor, too.'

The minute he had gotten the words out of his mouth he realized how gauche it was to even suggest such a thing, and turned quite red-faced.

Sadie looked at both of them thinking what a contrast they were to Rosey. Rosey who had been so elegant, who had such class and style.

Roy Fox's appointment had been extremely controversial and Freddy had had to call in a lot of chits to get him confirmed. Though Sadie had never met him, she had certainly read about him during the confirmation hearings. Foxy had had a rather checkered past and there was a definite overtone of sleaze about him. He had never been involved in any illegal dealings but had played fast and loose with women and booze all his life. The storm of

165

criticism left both him and Freddy undaunted, and he managed to squeal through the hearings and the votes. They were given high marks for their masterful manipulation of Congress. The trial by fire and subsequent victory had given Freddy a leg up as he took over the difficult job of following an assassinated President.

Foxy and Freddy were interchangeable in terms of style, and Sadie could see that now as she watched the two of them together.

Freddy Osgood was a perfectly good match for Blanche from a taste standpoint, though he had been taken in hand by the image makers after he'd become Vice President. During the last campaign he had ended up looking like an investment banker even if he still talked like a truck driver.

He also had a proprietary way with women. He looked upon them as though they had all been made for his personal enjoyment. His audacious behavior had earned him a reputation as a successful ladies' man as the bachelor governor of Tennessee before he married Blanche and ran for the Senate. He had even been rumored to have had an affair with a famous hooker.

Sadie had never heard any rumors about Freddy screwing around after he had married Blanche, but given the way he looked at other women, including her, the bereaved widow of his predecessor, she could only guess that he probably had. Blanche's reticence when Sadie had referred to their marriage made her even more suspicious.

'Freddy, name your poison, buddy,' said Foxy, walking over to the bar in the family sitting area.

'Whatever these two gals are having will suit me just fine.'

166

Foxy poured himself some bourbon, neat, and bolted it down in one gulp. He poured Freddy another, handed it to him and settled down on the sofa as though he were the President and not Freddy. He seemed totally at home in the White House, totally comfortable with Freddy, not at all subservient or even overly respectful.

It occurred to her that he might actually be a little nervous around her, though, an unusual feeling for him to have around women. Where Freddy was appraising her as a woman and no doubt wondering what she would be like in bed, or more specifically what it would be like to make love to a grieving widow, Foxy seemed much more deferential.

'So, ladies, what'll it be?' Freddy asked with a comical expression. 'Milk? Black coffee?'

'I'll have you know I've been drinking black coffee all afternoon,' said Blanche.

'Mind if I taste it?'

'Freddy Osgood...'

'Now, kids,' said Foxy good-naturedly, 'let's not start so early. What will Mrs Grey think?'

Whatever they were about to 'start,' they stopped.

Freddy walked over to the armchair next to where Sadie had seated herself.

'Sadie, I'm mighty glad you decided to come by today.' He winked. 'I know Blanche appreciates it. I guess you're one of the few people who really knows how hard it is for a First Lady and how lonely you can get sometimes.'

This was all for Blanche's benefit and it seemed to work. She noticed Blanche's skeptical face soften.

167

'What did y'all talk about? Did you change the world?'

'Well, one thing we talked about was having a series of small, intimate dinner parties upstairs here in the private quarters,' said Sadie. She had brought this up with Blanche shortly before the two men appeared and Blanche had seemed receptive, though a bit uncomfortable.

'It's rarely done. In fact, Rosey and I never actually did it. We'd have friends to dinner in the family dining room and we'd have state dinners, but we never really entertained in the White House the way most people in political life would do at home. You might think of having twenty-four people at a time, two round tables of twelve or three tables of eight, something like that.' She paused and waited for his reaction.

'Who'll we invite?'

'The point would be to invite journalists, people in Congress, lawyers, mixed in with some in your own administration. It would give people a chance to get to know you on a more personal level, to see you and Blanche at your best. It benefits those in your administration who need to do a little business on the Hill, cozy up to the press a little, meet and greet. It's the kind of thing that used to be done by Washington hostesses who don't exist anymore. The hostesses used to have kind of a marketplace where things got done, contracts were made. It was really invaluable to a lot of people. I don't see why the President and his wife couldn't fill the social vacuum. Plus the fact that just getting invited to the White House is a big thrill for anybody. Nobody would turn you down. It couldn't hurt. There's really no downside if your guest lists are good.'

168

'Hell of an idea,' piped up Foxy, who had been assessing Sadie while she talked. 'Not only is she beautiful but smart, too,'

All three of them looked at Foxy, who suddenly seemed embarrassed at his heavy-handed compliment. He even appeared to be blushing, something he probably hadn't done since he was fourteen.

'I think we were talking about parties,' reminded Sadie, but with a smile on her face.

'I told Sadie I thought it was a good idea,' said Blanche, 'but it's just somethin' I've never done before. A state dinner they can put on without me. There's a whole office that does that. If Freddy were a bachelor they'd still have state dinners. But this would be so personal. I am here to tell you that I have never had a seated dinner in my life except for the dinner before our wedding. I like to have killed myself by the time that wedding was over. I just don't want to end up being a laughingstock.'

'You've got to make it personal. You can even bring up some singing stars and other entertainers who helped during the campaign. People like to be with interesting successful people in the power center of the world. Period. If you make that possible and if you can be yourself, it's a piece of cake.'

'She's right, honey. I think it's a great idea. We'll do it.'

'You know what, though, Sadie?' said Blanche. 'I still think a lot of those people are horses' asses. There are a lot of big mouths and big egos in this city, a lot of hypocrites and phonies and climbers. You're nothing but a title or a job to them. I'll do it. I'll have these parties. But that doesn't mean I have

169

to like it, or them for that matter.'

'That was quite a speech, gal,' said Foxy. 'You're turning into a true patriot. Next thing I know I'll be coming in here for a little bourbon and finding you sewing a flag.'

'Shut up, Foxy,' said Blanche, 'and get your sorry ass into the dining room. We're getting ready to eat. Sadie, you might as well stay. Too bad you didn't bring a nightgown and toothbrush, you could spend the night.'

Sadie laughed, though a cloud of gloom spread over her at the idea of ever staying another night in the White House again. Too many sad memories.

Freddy and Foxy joined in the invitation and she finally agreed to stay for dinner. She called Monica to ask her to put Willie to bed without her. This was the first night she hadn't been home to tell him goodnight since Rosey died. She didn't want to think about that. She was actually enjoying herself. Though she was sitting in the room where she had known more pain than she had ever known in her life, she still was having the best time she had had since she left. These people amused her, and she wasn't thinking about Des either.

'What are we having for dinner, doll?' asked Freddy.

'Barbecued spareribs, butter beans, spoon bread, and peach pie.'

'Blanche's perfect spareribs, Blanche's perfect butter beans, spoon bread, and Blanche's perfect peach pie,' said Sadie in a mocking sing-song voice.

'My, my, how things are changing around the White House.'

# CHAPTER EIGHT

'So who makes the coffee around here?'

Several male heads turned to look at Allison. She was standing next to the national desk. Nobody said a word.

'Did I say something wrong?'

Still nothing.

'Hey, guys, give me a break. I'm new around here. Let me try again. Who gets coffee around here?'

Dead silence.

'Okay, I'm going down to the cafeteria for coffee. Can I get anybody anything?'

'I'll have mine light with no sugar and a glazed doughnut.'

'Make that two lights with no sugar and a bagel.'

'I like it black and a danish.'

They were all talking at once as they reached into their pockets for change.

'You can all go fuck yourselves,' she said with a sweet smile, and headed toward the cafeteria.

\*     \*     \*

It was 11:00 a.m. on her second day back at the *Daily* from London. She had just had two meetings: a breakfast meeting at the Sheraton Carlton with Walt Fineman, the managing director, and then a second with Fineman that included Alan Warburg, the executive editor. She was scared to death but she didn't dare show it.

She had arranged to see Walt first. He was one of

171

her closest friends and she knew he would make her feel more secure. She was wrong.

'Brainard quit Friday.' Walt had just finished ordering bacon and eggs. He said it casually, as though it were a part of the order.

'What? Brainard can't quit. He's my deputy. He's the only one who knows what's going on. How can he quit? You promised me Brainard. Why did he quit? Don't tell me. He quit over me. I knew this was a mistake. I should have stayed in London. I should have married Julian and had babies. Who needs this career-girl bullshit. I quit. Now you don't have a national editor or a deputy national editor. I like the sound of those words. I quit.'

Walt was smiling by the time Allison finished.

'You're more nervous than I thought you'd be, Sonny.'

'God, Walt. I've never been an editor in my life except for that brief stint on the desk a couple of summers ago. Now I'm supposed to waltz in as the first woman national editor having just learned that my deputy has quit because of me. I don't have a clue what I'm doing. My all-male staff is demoralized and hostile. I'm jet-lagged. And it's Des's birthday today. He's taking me out tonight and I know he's going to want to set a date for the wedding. All I can say is it's a good thing I don't have premenstrual syndrome.'

'And to think they call you the iron butterfly.'

'You're not taking me seriously.'

'On the contrary. I take you so seriously I recommended you for the job.'

'Let's get this clear, Fineman. Did you or did you not recommend me because I was a woman? Wasn't that my major qualification?'

172

'I cannot tell a lie.'

'How much of a bubblehead would I have had to have been to have been passed over? Just out of curiosity.'

'Let's put it this way. You wear a skirt?'

'You noticed.'

That's it. That's all it took. You were the lucky winner.'

'This is outright reverse discrimination. No wonder Brainard quit.'

'Yeah, well, tell it to the EEOC.'

'It really makes me sick.'

'Let's look at the bright side. You're not a total airhead and you're a great-looking piece of ass.'

'You better watch it, buster, or I'll slap you with a sexual harassment suit so fast it will make your head swim.'

'God, Sonny, I've missed you.'

She grinned, then leaned over impulsively and gave him a kiss on the cheek.

'I've missed you, too, Walt. I wouldn't have taken this job if it weren't for you. But what are we going to do about Brainard? I really am scared without him. As pompous as he was, he did know his stuff. And he'd been on the campaign with all the guys. That's such a tight little clique out there you can't get near them unless you've been one of the recent boys on the bus. Brainard is a political genius. Where's he going by the way? I hope not to the *New York World*.'

'He's taking a leave to write a book. Big six-figure advance. Then he'll come back for the next election as a reporter. I think he's using you as an excuse, frankly. I don't think he gives a shit about being an editor. He just liked the title political editor.

Malkin's actually a better editor and easier to get along with. You're lucky.'

'So what else do I need to be warned about before we go see Warburg?'

'Two items on the agenda: Lauren Hope. Pregnant. Wants six months' maternity leave and then to work part-time after that.'

'Oh, no. She covers the Hill. She can't cover the Hill part-time.'

'She's already having problems with morning sickness. We've missed a couple of stories. Plumley was in a real bind about it before he went to London. He felt that a man has a rougher time trying to deal with women in that situation. You're going to have to handle it.'

'Great. One of three women on the staff and the way my luck is going the other two will probably get pregnant immediately. What's the other problem? You might as well lay it on me.'

'We hired a new reporter. Pulitzer Prize winner from Savannah, Georgia. You might remember the stories. Corruption on the docks in Savannah and the drug connections. Really first-rate reporting and writing. The guy's got balls. Risked his life several times. He's covering Justice. He'd never been to Washington before we hired him. He reports to you. He's got this theory that the drug connection is all over the place. Possibly on the Hill and in Justice.'

'What's his name?'

'Tyson. Sprague Tyson. Mid-thirties. Attractive. Married. One child. You may like him. But I warn you. The story is tricky. And this guy takes no prisoners. It'll be a challenge to control him.'

'Well, that's some good news, anyway.'

Walt signaled for the check.

'What's with you and Des? When's the big day?'

Walt had never liked Des. And he had always liked her too much.

'I don't know, Walt. He was really anxious to set a date at first. Now he seems reluctant. He's pissed that I stayed in London so long. Frankly, I'd like to get settled in this job before we get married. Des is talking about Christmas. But I just can't think about that right now. I've got to get in there and kick ass and take names.'

'Atta girl.'

'Atta person, atta person.' She laughed. 'By the way, who makes the coffee around the newsroom?'

'Boy, have you got a lot to learn.'

★　　　★　　　★

'Vision,' said Warburg. 'That's what I want from you: vision. Where have we been, where are we, where are we going?'

'What about the daily story?' asked Allison. 'I mean, I don't want to sound prosaic, but...'

'Ah, the daily story,' he said, waving his hand. 'The daily story will take care of itself.'

'I'll remind you of that when we lose out on the Pulitzer for spot coverage.'

They were sitting in Warburg's glass office looking out over the newsroom, and Allison was remembering what it was about Warburg that drove her crazy. She had never known anyone who was so brilliant and so stupid at the same time.

Warburg was short and pudgy with dark wavy hair and a heavy five o'clock shadow even after he had just shaved. He had piercing black eyes and zero sense of humor. He didn't talk so much as he elocuted. He did not suffer fools, except for his kind of fools, and he had no time for small talk, gossip, or fun. There were those who thought he was mean, even cruel. Allison believed he was unaware of his impact on people, most of whom were scared of him. She wasn't scared of him, but she did find it difficult to communicate with him. If his advice to her was going to be 'vision,' she would have to look elsewhere for a mentor. Warburg was the brains of the operation. Walt Fineman was the soul. Maybe 'vision' was his way of saying she had to be the heart.

'The hell with the Pulitzer,' said Warburg. 'They're worthless and everybody knows it. We don't need the Pulitzer. Half the reporters who win Pulitzers couldn't get hired here and half the stories that win them wouldn't be fit to run in this newspaper.'

'I hope you don't talk that way when you go to judge them,' said Walt. 'You'd guarantee us getting aced out. Come to think of it . . .'

'Well, I'm certainly not going to play politics and kiss ass just to win a few meaningless prizes, that's for certain.'

'Have you apprised the staff of your attitude?'

'Don't be ridiculous. It gives them incentive.'

'If you think the whole thing is so stupid, why don't you resign from the board?'

'Actually, I'm thinking about it. They don't have a woman now. They need a woman. I've got the perfect person in mind. A real politician, an infighter, somebody mean enough to face down all those idiots. A killer.'

'Just who is this lovely person?' asked Allison.

176

'Ah, and lovely, too. I forgot about that. She's sitting right in front of me.'

'Moi? Alan, you flatter me. But now you're being ridiculous. I haven't even started work yet. I don't even know what I'm doing. Besides, I think I would get too angry, sitting on that board.'

'That's precisely what you're supposed to do. I get bored and contemptuous and it's hurting the paper. Besides, you've already been at the job two days. You've got them hopping over there on the national desk. That's what we need. Just a word of warning, Allison.'

'What's that, Alan?'

'Don't let those boys bully you into making coffee every morning.'

★       ★       ★

'Lunch,' said Malkin, wolfing down another roll. 'Lunch is the key.'

'What do you mean, lunch?' asked Allison, picking at her salmon.

'You've got fifty egos sitting out there on the national staff. Every one of them feels neglected, even the biggest stars. But particularly those who are doing yeoman's work, covering the agencies, unsexy beats they think nobody gives a shit about. They're right, but the fact remains, somebody's got to do it. It's our job to keep them relatively happy doing it. They all have gripes and insecurities. They need hand-holding and baby-sitting. They need lunch. Get my drift?'

They were eating at the McPherson Grill, a popular lunchtime spot a block away from the White House, all mauve and gray bleached wood
177

and ferns.

'I've gained five pounds just today. I thought when I took this job I was making the easy choice between my career and my private life. Now I see it's more serious. I'm choosing between my career and my figure. I'm not sure this isn't too large a price to pay.'

'No problem. Just join a fitness center. They're terrific at lunchtime and on weekends. Every great single piece of ass, male and female, I hasten to add, shows up to check out the action. Thirty minutes on the stairway to hell, as we lovingly call it, and you're into maintenance.'

'What is going on with all you yuppies in this city? I haven't been gone that long, but all anybody talks about is running and cholesterol and fitness. It's so uncivilized. That's one of the things I loved about the English. They just don't bloody well bother.'

'Get real, Sonny. This is the nineties. It's also called middle age.'

'Gee, I'm glad I came back. Every hour of my day so far has been chockablock with good news and upbeat conversation. Moving right along, since you asked me to get real: Why did Brainard really quit? Was he using me as an excuse to leave and write his book, or was it more personal?'

'I think it was a combination of things,' said Malkin. 'He did want to write a book. And he did want national editor. But I think the guy's just vintage male chauvinist pig. He didn't want to work for a woman. He didn't dare say so but it was pretty clear to me.'

'How do you feel about it?'

'If you're good, fine. If you're not, I'm outta

178

here.'

'That's fair. Are you going to help me or are you going to stand around and watch me fall on my face?'

'I hadn't really decided that—until now.'

'So put me out of my misery.'

'I like your way of being straightforward. I'll do everything I can to make it work for you. For us. For the paper. I only ask one thing in return.'

'And what is that, Malkin?'

'Lunch.'

★       ★       ★

Malkin did the 2:30 story conference. Allison sat on the banquette against the side wall as he pitched the stories to Fineman. Warburg sat at the other end of the conference table and quietly raised an eyebrow now and then but never said a word. Warburg was not a nuts-and-bolts guy. He would only interject when there was a need for 'vision.'

Allison had been to a lot of story conferences but she'd never pitched a story. Malkin was good. He had a solid understanding not only of the stories but of the reporters covering them and the implications.

He was also subtle. To the outside observer, story conferences looked very casual, fast-paced, matter-of-fact. It was like anything else that required a lot of work and expertise. It looked easy the way juggling or tap dancing looked easy. In fact, story conferences required some of the same skills.

She pretended to take notes, working from the mimeographed schedule of potential stories that was distributed as everyone came in. She wasn't studying content. She was studying style. Men's style. Not that she wanted to be like them. She had never played dress-for-success-anything-they-can-do-I-can-do-better. She just wanted to know how they operated. She didn't want to be one of the boys but neither did she want to be 'the girl.' She knew what they thought and said about aggressive, outspoken women, even the men who paid lip service to feminism. As she established herself she couldn't allow herself to break their rules. At least not at first. If they didn't take her seriously she would never be effective. She'd have to be circumspect, watch and listen. Then, when she had her own confidence and the confidence of her staff, she could tell them all to shove it.

Today's stories were routine. A plane crash investigation, yet another British espionage story, which happily Allison knew more about than anybody else though it was on foreign's budget. There was a stock market scandal and an investigative story on the oil and gas industry and the environment that was ready to run.

Fineman had his feet on the conference table. After everyone had had his turn, he went down the list.

'We've got three extra columns on oil and gas, stay in touch with the people who are dummying foreign front and national front. We'll look at scandal, possible front, more than a key. If we get a front-page lead on stocks, then we can key to the plane crash.'

With that everyone was up. Allison got outside the door, then remembered something she wanted to ask Malkin. As she walked back in several of the men were standing around Fineman laughing.

'So then the guy says, "Well, if that's pussy I'll eat it . . ."'

More laughter.

Then someone saw Allison. They all stopped abruptly. A couple of them coughed with embarrassment and they quickly left the room without looking at her.

Finally just she and Walt were left.

Walt didn't say anything at first, then he simply shrugged.

'I don't want to be one of the local jocks and sit around laughing at dirty jokes, Walt. I don't want to be one of the boys.'

'So what do you want to be, Sonny?'

'I want to be neuter.'

'That'll be the day.'

'You watch. I am going to be so sexless in this job that after a while nobody will think of me as a woman.'

'A hundred bucks says someone will come on to you before six months is up.'

'You got it,' she said, slapping his hand.

'On second thought, make it a night with you at the Inn at Little Washington.'

'Are you coming on to me?'

'Yeah. You just lost your bet.'

\*     \*     \*

It was the cutback at 3:00 p.m. Allison and 'the boys' stood around the national desk discussing length of stories. Once again she watched Malkin to see how he conducted his business. Soon to be hers.

'Spill. Gulf of Mexico. Twenty-five inches long. Everybody happy with that? Who's unhappy? Did you address Jack's concerns?'

'Not all of it,' was the reply.

'Well, I'm not going to change the lead.'

'What about the tanker? Can we keep it to sixteen?'

'I still don't see why they can't be one story.'

Allison found her mind wandering as she listened to the men discuss stories. She was still jet-lagged and her concentration wasn't the greatest. And, she felt a bit shell-shocked. There was so much to learn and the terrain was perilous. Not only that, she had a long evening with Des coming up. She would have killed to be able to go home, have a glass of wine, a hot bath, and collapse into bed. But Des had planned a birthday dinner and probably a long talk. She didn't know whether she could get through it. All she knew was that she wanted to have an unstressful time. But Des's voice had sounded so full of meaning.

She was musing to herself when she looked up and saw, standing halfway across the newsroom, one of the best-looking men she had ever seen in her life. He was talking on the telephone and taking notes, his notebook balanced on the top of his computer, his phone cupped under his chin. She thought she knew everyone in the newsroom, but she had certainly never seen him before. His sandy hair was flopping over one eye, his tie was loosened around his neck, his khaki suit jacket wrinkled.

He finished his conversation, hung up the phone, and took off his jacket, tossing it in a heap on his already hopelessly messy desk. His shirtsleeves were already rolled up but he jerked his tie even looser and began riffling through the pile of papers. Finally he looked up, seeming to search the newsroom for somebody. As he did he met her eyes and they stared at each other for a moment before he looked down again and continued to go through his papers.

'Malkin,' she said, without taking her eyes off the stranger. 'Who's that guy over there, the one in shirtsleeves standing up? I've never seen him before.'

'Oh, that's Tyson. From Savannah. Hot shit. Fearless little fucker. He's after the drug boys. The way he's going about it he's likely to get his brains blown out before he's through. He's a pain in the ass, too. He's got his own agenda, and if it coincides with ours fine, if not that's tough.'

'He doesn't look little to me.'

'I mean age. He's only in his thirties.'

'I guess I should introduce myself to him.'

'Hey, Sonny, just stand warned. The guy is not a piece of cake. He's very difficult and if he weren't a major talent he'd have been outta here so fast it would make your head swim.'

'I hear you.'

As she walked toward his desk she instinctively ran her fingers through her hair and smoothed her skirt. He watched her approach but there was neither a hint of a smile nor any sign of recognition on his face. Or appreciation for that matter. Allison was not used to having men look at her and not appreciate her.

She stuck out her hand.

'Hi, I'm Allison Sterling. I've just started as national editor. I think you're the only person on the staff I've not met. You came when I was in London.'

'Tyson,' he said, taking her hand and giving it a

cursory shake. 'Sprague Tyson.'

His glance was cool and appraising. Not of her as a woman but of her as a boss.

'Look forward to working with you,' she said, trying to sound warm, though his gaze gave her a chill. 'You have quite a reputation.'

'I'll try to live up to it.'

There was only a trace of a Southern accent, and strangely it hardened rather than softened him. He had not taken his eyes off hers, and she finally glanced away to avoid his penetrating stare.

'Well, at any rate,' she began. She couldn't believe she sounded nervous. 'I'd like to take you to lunch sometime in the next few weeks. I'm trying to get around and talk to everybody on the staff—'

'I don't do lunch.'

There was almost a contemptuous tone.

'It's a waste of time. I'm usually out on the streets then anyway.'

That last sentence. An afterthought. Had he realized how rude he sounded?

'Fine. Then at your earliest convenience I'd appreciate it if you'd come to my office so we can discuss your project.'

She saw him wince and she realized he was about to speak up. She hurriedly finished what she was about to say.

'I realize that you are reporting to Warburg but he and Fineman have asked me to work directly with you on a day-to-day basis. Why don't you check your schedule and let me know tomorrow when you would like to sit down and talk? Or do you not sit down either?'

Before he could answer she had turned and walked away. She was stunned to find herself

184

shaking slightly. She wondered if he realized how angry she was. She didn't want him to see that he had gotten to her, but she also didn't like the fact that he had managed to upset her so. She never got angry like that. And here was someone she was going to have to work with very closely.

She was sitting at her desk when Malkin walked in with a grin on his face.

'Not a scratch on you,' he said reassuringly.

'What a prick,' she said. 'I can't believe him. Who does that little son of a bitch think he is?'

'He's not that little.'

'Age, Malkin. I'm talking about his age.'

\* \* \*

'Sonny?'

'Oh, hi, Des.'

'What's the matter. You sound depressed.'

'Oh, nothing. Nothing that a case of sleeping pills wouldn't cure.'

'That bad, huh?'

'I don't know, Des. Maybe I'm just not cut out to be an editor. Particularly an editor of men. Men on the national staff. Arrogant, cocky men who think they know everything and think because you're a woman you're basically a piece of ass or an airhead or at least not worthy of respect. It's been a very tough day. Happy birthday, by the way. I'm afraid I'm not going to be a million laughs tonight. Poor Des. I came all the way back from London early so I could be here for your birthday and now I'm an exhausted mess.'

'We'll fix that. I thought you might be a little strung out after today, not to mention jet-lagged. So

185

I've planned a little dinner at home tonight. That way we can talk.'

There was something in his tone that made her uneasy, but she decided it was just her imagination.

'Oh, Des, you angel, I love you, I adore you. I'm mad about you.'

'How does caviar, baked potato, and champagne sound?'

'Perfect, and if I can have a hot bath and dinner in bed, I'm yours.'

'I've even got my own birthday cake for dessert.'

He wasn't going along with her suggestive teasing, very unlike Des.

'Well, I've got a can of chocolate icing I plan to smear all over your body and lick off for dessert.'

'What time do you think you'll be out of there?'

'In time to light your candle and blow it out.'

She felt he was struggling not to respond to her silliness. Though after her last remark he did begin to chuckle, almost, it seemed, in spite of himself.

'You should have more terrible days like this,' he said.

'Is that your birthday wish?'

'We'll discuss that later.'

\*　　　\*　　　\*

'May I see you for a second, Allison?'

Lauren Hope, the congressional correspondent, stuck her head into Allison's little glass cubicle just as she was hanging up with Des. She glanced quickly at her watch. It was a little after five-thirty. She was desperate for a cup of tea, a habit she had picked up in London. The evening story conference was at six-thirty, so she had an hour.

186

'I was just going down to the cafeteria for a cup of tea. Why don't you join me?' she said.

'Great, just let me get my purse.'

Allison tried not to stare at Lauren's belly as they went down in the elevator. She still showed no visible signs of pregnancy. Allison was curious as to what it felt like in a way she had never been before. It surprised her. She didn't want to bring it up. She was embarrassed, even though she knew that that was what Lauren wanted to talk about. She didn't even know why she thought it was embarrassing. Perhaps because she had always looked at pregnancy as an affliction of some kind. She had always felt somewhat contemptuous of women who were pregnant, as though they had allowed themselves to become inferior, lesser beings.

Lauren chatted amiably as she poured herself some coffee.

'Decaf,' she was saying. 'It's driving me crazy. I can't function without caffeine. But no caffeine while I'm pregnant. No anything. No booze, no cigarettes, no medicine. They're really so strict now about what you can have and do. It's terrible.'

They were sitting at a table near the window and Lauren was smiling as she looked out the window and watched the turning October leaves swirl around in the breeze.

'Just think, it will be spring when I'm due. New buds on the trees. What a perfect time to have a baby.'

Allison felt awkward. She couldn't think of a thing to say but Lauren didn't seem to notice.

'If only I can just get through the next couple of months. This morning sickness is really getting me down. It's as bad as they say it is. Worse.'

187

Here was this redhead, freckle-faced woman just jabbering away about her stupid pregnancy as though it were something to be proud of. In fact, she was not doing her job and should be apologizing, should be asking for a second chance. Allison was appalled. At what point was she going to tell Allison she knew she was letting the paper down and ask for a less demanding assignment? This attitude was not acceptable.

'So when do you plan to take your leave?' Allison was trying to sound nonjudgmental.

'Well, the *Daily* only allows six weeks paid maternity leave and I plan to take at least three months off after the baby comes. So I guess I'll just keep on working until the big day. Or as near as possible, depending on how I feel.'

'Well, we'll have to work out some accommodation for that time. You'll need some backup in your job. I was thinking about giving Estrella some of your assignments now. He can fill in for you on the days you don't feel well and during the time you're away. Which I suspect will be longer than three months.'

Lauren's face went white.

'Estrella? He wants my job in the worst way. He's sick of covering the agencies. He's been trying to weasel his way up on the Hill for the last year and now that I'm pregnant he sees his big chance.'

She was now very angry.

'Really?'

Allison was genuinely surprised, both at what Lauren had to say and at the depth of her anger.

'Yes, really. I'd just as soon keep that little shit away from my beat if you don't mind, Allison.'

'I didn't know you felt so strongly about him,
188

Lauren,' she said carefully. 'I'm sorry. But he is a good reporter and he is hungry and available and he does know the Hill. I don't see that we have any choice. I'm sure you agree that the paper needs to be covered in Congress. If you continue to have morning sickness we can't let ourselves get beat by not sending anyone. This way Estrella will be conversant enough with the beat that he'll be able to take over for a few months while you're gone.'

'I'm sorry, too, Allison. But I can't hack Estrella. The guy is a snake. We'll have to find another solution.'

'I'll be happy to consider any suggestions, Lauren. What did you have in mind?'

She couldn't help but be aware that they were calling each other by name with each sentence and the tone was getting testier and testier.

'I had in mind that I would do my own job. Occasionally somebody who might be free on the national staff would fill in if I couldn't make it. I did not envision having someone actually assigned to take over my job on a semi-permanent basis, Allison.'

Lauren's eyes were beginning to get misty and Allison could see she was going to have to calm her down. But the more Lauren talked the madder Allison got. She seemed oblivious to the needs of the desk or the paper. It was all about what was good for her.

'Look, Lauren. I know this is a difficult and emotional time for you. I understand that and I respect that.'

She didn't do either but she felt she had to say it.

'But your job is to cover the story and my job is to make sure the story gets covered. If you can't do

189

your job, then it's my job to make sure somebody can. It makes more sense to have someone who's on top of things cover your beat on a regular basis when you're not around than to assign some hit-and-run artist. We'll get creamed if we do that and if we get creamed who is going to have to answer for it? What am I going to say? Lauren didn't want Estrella to do it because she was scared he would run away with her job? Think about it.'

Lauren was fighting back the tears now. She reached into her handbag, pulled out a Kleenex and tried to wipe her eyes without anyone else in the cafeteria seeing her.

Finally she turned to Allison.

'I can't believe I'm having this conversation with you, of all people. Everyone else, the men, have been wonderful, so understanding and supportive. The few stories I've missed, they just picked up the wires. It was no big deal. Now you come in here, the first woman national editor, well-known feminist, and chew my ass off. What's going on with you, Allison?'

'I'll tell you what's going on, Lauren. What's going on is that I am the first woman national editor and that means I have to do a better job than any national editor before me. Because if I don't they'll say that women can't hack it. You don't have any idea what's going on behind our backs. These guys are just sitting there waiting for us to fail. They like to think they're such liberal feminists but in their very guts they'd like to see us all barefoot and pregnant. You are conforming to their vision of what a woman should be and do. You have now attained nonperson status. If you don't do your job now they can forgive you because you're just a

190

woman anyway and a pregnant woman at that. They'd rather lose a story than lose their perception of what women should be. Well, Lauren, I'm sorry, but I'm not buying into that. You do your best work or you're history. I don't mean to be cold-hearted. I'm just realistic. If I let it happen once it hurts all of us. You included. My attitude about pregnancy is the same as if somebody took a leave to write a book. This is not an illness. This is elective. If you took a leave to write a book I'd put Estrella on your beat and you wouldn't dare say a word about it. Having a baby doesn't make you special. I like you, Lauren, and I think you're a great reporter. There's nobody covering the Hill who does a better job. But if you're not cutting it, you, more than anyone, should have pride enough and guts enough to say that you're not. You should step aside and let someone else do it until you can cut it again. Any other attitude is unprofessional and you are a professional.'

Lauren didn't say anything for a while. She just sat there twisting her tissue and trying not to cry.

'Jesus, Allison. You're tough. You're really tough.'

'Am I right, Lauren?'

'I can't say you're not.'

'So tell me what you think I should do?'

'So get Estrella, the little fucker. I'll beat his ass when I come back.'

'Atta girl!'

'Atta person, Allison. Atta person.'

★      ★      ★

'So, how was your day?'

191

'Walt Fineman. You haven't had your eyes off me for one minute. I've seen you in that glass office of yours peering out over your newspaper. You don't fool me for a second. You're like a mother on her child's first day in kindergarten.'

'You noticed.'

'You're my security blanket, Walt. I had to make sure you were out there for me if things fell apart.'

'Did they?'

'Let's just say it was not the easiest day I ever had in my life.'

'Are you discouraged?'

'Yes, but I'm not quitting, if that's what you're asking.'

'You already quit this morning at breakfast, remember.'

'Yeah, well, I take it back.'

'Why? What changed your mind?'

'It's too much of a challenge. It's going to be a lot tougher than I imagined, but I like my chances.'

'What do you see as the biggest challenges?'

'Making the women be honest with themselves, face up to the truth. Not just Lauren either. All of them. They have a sense of entitlement that they don't deserve any more than anybody else on the staff. The boys. Making them respect me and see me as a person not as a woman. And Tyson. I'm looking forward to having his balls for breakfast.'

'Sonny, I have never made the mistake of underestimating you before. But I think you've met your match this time. The guy is one of the toughest people I've ever met, a real cool customer. I wouldn't count on it.'

'With syrup on them.'

192

Allison was lying in the bath, bubbles up to her neck, her head resting on a rubber pillow on the back of the tub. Her left hand held a flute of champagne. The sounds of Gershwin wafted through the room from the hall. All the lights were out in the bathroom and several candles flickered in the darkness. Des was perched on the toilet seat, leaning up against the wall, his feet on the edge of the tub. His tie was loosened, his shirt unbuttoned at the neck, his sleeves rolled up. He needed a haircut. His hair was curling around the back of his ears and though it looked sexy it still looked unkempt. Though no more so than most journalists.

He was singing along off key and grinning at Allison.

'Embrace me, my sweet embraceable you. Embrace me you irreplaceable you.'

He had relaxed considerably since she had gotten home. The strain of their being apart had taken its toll. At first he had refused to join her in the bathroom, but a few glasses of champagne and he was on his way.

'Scorpio,' she mused aloud. 'The most sensual sign in the zodiac. Cancer-Scorpio, a magnetic, harmonious combination.'

'I thought you thought astrology was a bunch of crap.'

'Well, I did actually. Maybe I still do. But I knew a lot of Arabs in London. One of them had this great astrologer he sent me to and I got hooked. I'm not really sure I believe it at all, but it's egotistically satisfying and it's a lot more fun than religion.

193

Besides, some of the things the guy told me were uncanny.'

'Like what?' he asked, taking another sip. It was clear he couldn't care less about astrology, but he was amused.

'Like that I was going to marry a tall, dark, handsome man.'

She noticed, or thought she noticed, his smile disappear for a moment, but then he laughed and she figured she had imagined it.

'He talked a lot about the importance of compatible signs. How you can never go wrong with a Cancer-Scorpio combination. He says you and I are karmically linked.'

'What the hell is that?'

'That we have been together in many past lives. Our karmas are linked so that we find one another in each life.'

'That's the worst thing I've ever heard of. I thought you were supposed to work through your karma. Now you tell me I'm stuck with you for eternity.'

'Fuck you. It could be a lot worse. Do you realize how many men would kill to be stuck with me for eternity? You happen to be extremely lucky.'

'Do I get to get laid in other lives outside the relationship or is this it?'

'I don't like your attitude, Desmond Shaw. If you keep this up you may not get laid in this one. I need more champagne.'

'I get no kicks from champagne,' he sang as he leaned over and poured her another glass.

'You actually have a pretty good voice,' she said. 'Aging choirboy.'

'Considerably better than yours.'

'You're really pressing your luck,' she said, holding her leg up out of the bubble bath and rubbing it with soap.

Des leaned over and kissed her big toe.

'Mere alcohol doesn't thrill me at all...'

She put her foot on his chin and gently pushed him away.

'But I get a kick out of you.'

'Towel please.'

'Madame,' he said holding up a large terry-cloth bath sheet. He was not as steady on his feet as he might have been.

She stepped out of the tub, the water dripping from her body onto the bath mat. She looked directly at him with a challenging smile as he appraised her, then she turned her back to him so that he could wrap her up.

He lifted her in his arms and carried her into the bedroom, where he laid her on the bed up against the pillows. A fire was going in the fireplace, taking the slight chill of the November air out of the room. There were more candles, candles everywhere, the music was still playing, and on the chest at the foot of the bed was a tray of toast with lemon wedges, a tin of translucent gray caviar, two large baked potatoes, sour cream, and a tossed salad.

'I thought this was your birthday, my darling Shaw. What's in it for you?'

He reached over and touched her damp hair, then leaned down slowly and kissed the back of her neck, her earlobes, her shoulders. He stopped abruptly and pulled back, cupping her face in his hand, then got up quickly and walked over to the fireplace. He stared into the fireplace for a moment, then took the poker and began to attack the logs

195

ferociously.

'Des? What's wrong?'

'Nothing. Everything. Nothing.'

'Are you all right?'

'Yes ... no.'

She was sitting up now, holding the damp towel around her.

'Des, what in God's name is the matter? You look like you've just seen a horrible accident.'

'Sonny, I ...' He had his arms out in front of him, then turned back to the fireplace.

'Shit,' he said with such forceful exasperation that it propelled her off the bed and over to where he was standing.

'Des?'

She touched his arm tentatively and he turned to look at her.

'Sonny. I just want you to know how much I love you. And how much I need you and want you.'

'Oh Des,' she said with a relieved laugh. 'Is that terrible? Are you so afraid of being pussy-whipped by me that you can't stand to love me? You really are such an idiot. Honest to Christ. I thought there was something really wrong. Now kiss me and let's eat. I'm famished.'

She held up her mouth toward his and allowed him to kiss her lightly. She turned and let her towel fall to the floor in a mock seductive way. She put on her negligee, leaving the front slightly open, and sat on the edge of the bed, leaning back, her legs crossed.

'So am I,' he said, with obvious relief. He sat in the armchair next to the bed while she piled caviar on a baked potato and handed it to him. He poured her a glass of champagne, then one for himself. She

196

fixed her own potato, then leaned back against the pillows and took a long bite, savoring it with her eyes closed, moaning as she ate.

'Oh God, that's good,' she said when she had swallowed it. 'Oh that is so good. If I had a choice between good caviar and great sex I....'

'Let me guess.'

'Great sex. No contest.'

'What if it's a choice between great caviar and good sex.'

'Ooooo, that's a tough one.'

'Let me guess.'

'Good sex. No contest.'

'What if...'

'Shut up you gorgeous brute and come here.'

'Sonny, we haven't finished eating. Have you lost control?

'Well, you've done such a brilliant job of keeping my mind off my hideous first day at work, I think you should keep it up. Over here, big guy.' She patted the bed and smiled at him.

'You have no shame, woman.'

Something was off. He seemed nervous to her, the usual confidence, cockiness were missing, but she just couldn't place what the problem was.

Normally he would have been all over her by now, but he hadn't made a single real advance. She was so tired she would have been content just to go to sleep, though she felt it was expected that they should make love. She didn't see any way around it. Particularly since he seemed reluctant. He was clearly waiting for her to make the overture.

Now that she thought of it, he had been acting reticent on the telephone for the past several weeks. Or was it longer? There was something in his voice.

He was holding something back. But what? Was he having an affair? Was he in love with someone else? No. She didn't think so. Not that fast. Besides, if he were, he would have told her. He'd been waiting for her for a long time. They'd been through too much for him to let a little flirtation get in his way. It was not another woman. She was sure of that. So what was the problem?

Des got on the bed with her and for a long time they lay together kissing each other quietly. He caressed her hair and looked at her with so much love that she nearly wept.

She began to undress him, slowly, taking off his tie, then unbuttoning his shirt, caressing his chest. She unbuckled his belt, undid his pants, unzipped his fly. He watched her as she reached inside and pulled him out. When he didn't harden right away she took him in her mouth and gently caressed him with her tongue.

She smiled at the results, looking up at him smugly.

'Ha,' she crowed. 'Look what I've done. How can anyone ever say women don't have all the power.'

'Pretty pleased with yourself, aren't you?' he chuckled. He pulled her up to him and kissed her, then quickly finished undressing himself. He turned her over and let his weight descend on her as she let out a sigh.

'Oh Des,' she whispered. 'I've missed you so. Make love to me now, please.'

'Baby, oh Sonny, I love you,' he said. 'I love you.'

She moved under him to receive him and as she did she felt him grow soft. She moved her pelvis against him several times to stimulate him but nothing happened. He was completely limp. She paused and they were still for a long time.

'I'm sorry, Sonny,' he said after a while, his voice cracking with emotion. 'God, I'm sorry.'

She caressed his back, his hair, his body, hugging and holding him as hard as she could.

'It's okay, Des. It's okay. I understand. Don't feel sorry. It's all right.'

'It's not you, baby. Do you understand. It has nothing to do with you.'

'Is there somebody else?' She held her breath. She couldn't bear to hear the word *yes*.

'Not another woman.'

She was so tense now that she began to giggle out of sheer nervousness.

'You mean there's another man?'

'Jesus, you're an asshole.'

Des pushed himself up off of her and laughed. They could both feel the tension dissipate.

They were sitting up now, grinning nervously at each other.

'Well, what then?'

'I don't know, Sonny.'

He looked at her and she could see the pain.

'I don't know how to explain it to you. Maybe it's my old Catholic training coming back to haunt me. I'm wrestling with some demons and I need to work it out. I know I'm already divorced. But the idea of remarrying seems like a major step. I've done a lot of thinking about it and I think that's what I want. But I've got to have some more time. I don't want to be a two-time loser. I've got to square things with my maker. I'm not too happy with some of the things I've done in my life, with the way I've hurt some people. I want to make sure I never do it again. I love you too much to give you less than you deserve, and that's what you'd be getting if you married me right now.'

Allison listened quietly as she leaned against the pillows. She had pulled the sheet up over her breasts.

'Oh Des, did you think I wouldn't understand? I do. We've been away from each other for so long. We've caused each other too much anguish. I've been desperate about the fact that we would leap into marriage so quickly after I got back. It's only six or seven weeks until Christmas and I've got a new job. Boy, do I ever have a new job. It just wouldn't be fair to either one of us to race into marriage without spending more time together. The pressure was making me crazy. It was just unrealistic.'

She threw herself back on the bed, her arms and legs spread out around her.

'God, I feel so relieved. I feel like a new person. Thank you for being honest. I was too afraid to say anything for fear of losing you again, maybe this time forever.'

He was still sitting on the edge of the bed and she put her arms around his back, kissing his neck and his cheek from behind.

'Why don't we go to sleep now? I'm exhausted.'

'Same,' he said, more than convincingly.

They lay down on the bed holding hands.

Allison closed her eyes and yawned.

'Goodnight, Des. I love you.'

'Goodnight, Sonny. I love you, too.'

She sensed he was still awake even though she was dozing off. She could feel his eyes on her. She could hear his deep sighs.

After a long while she turned over and one eye fluttered open to find Des looking longingly at her. 'Do you think,' she mumbled softly, 'that in another life, you might be able to get it up again?'

## CHAPTER NINE

Des's package for Willie had arrived a few days before Christmas, his birthday.

She opened up the box with some trepidation. She didn't know what she was expecting. A silver cup inscribed 'To William from your loving father, Desmond Shaw'?

When she saw what was inside it made her smile. It was a tiny baseball mitt. The note said, 'Sadie. Tell Willie this is from his special friend. D.'

It reminded her of why she loved Des so. There was so much unspoken love and hurt in his simplicity. There was something masculine, shy, and brave about it.

She missed him. She missed Rosey, too. Not just for herself but for Willie. He needed a father, a man. Now the man who would have been his father was dead and the man who was his father couldn't be.

The weather had become bleak around Thanksgiving. That had to have been the most depressing period in all her life. They said that six months after a loss was when it really hit you. They weren't whistling 'Dixie.'

She had no choice but to have Thanksgiving at her house on Dumbarton Street. Rosey's parents had wanted them all to come to Richmond, but the Greys condescended to them and her parents felt uncomfortable there. Her parents had wanted to do it in Savannah but that would have been just as uncomfortable for everyone.

In the end it didn't matter. The whole thing was a disaster. The minute G., Rosey's father, stood to say Grace: 'Bless, oh Lord, this food to our use and us to thy service,' Miz G., Rosey's mother, had started to cry. Then, of course, Sadie's father had insisted on saying Grace: 'Lord make us truly thankful for these blessings we are about to receive for Christ's sake. Amen.' Her mother burst into tears. When Outland, sitting in his father's place at the head of the table, began carving the turkey, Annie Laurie started to sniffle. What had caused Sadie to lose control was poor sweet Outland, mutilating this monstrous bird.

When she began to cry, Outland let the tears stream down his cheeks, standing at the table carving knife and fork in hand.

Only Willie remained unmoved. 'Mommy, everybody always crying,' he said.

'You're right, darling. Everybody's always crying around here. Especially Mommy, and it's got to stop. Mommy has done nothing but cry for nearly six months and she can't stand it anymore.'

She went around to the other end of the table where Outland stood, trying to regain control of his emotions, and put her arm around him, holding Willie's hand. Then she went over to Annie Laurie and rather formally kissed her. Finally, she returned to her place at the table, raised a glass and said, with as much composure as she could muster, 'To absent friends.'

She took a sip and everyone followed suit. 'Now, everyone. Let's try to enjoy our Thanksgiving dinner, please.'

That had more or less saved the day. But it had still been tense and gloomy and she was relieved when she was able to put Willie down at seven and plead a headache for herself.

When she crawled into bed after soaking in a hot tub for nearly an hour, she vowed she would not spend Christmas at home.

★ ★ ★

La Samanna. It looked the way it sounded. Azure blue and white, golden, pinks and corals. Tropical, remote, pristine, lyrical.

They had taken the last villa on the crescent beach. It was at the end of a winding path hidden by lush foliage, vines, and bougainvillea. Far up on a rock ledge was the main villa with the Moroccan bar, tiled pool, and dining terrace overlooking the ocean.

She was right on the beach with a bedroom, living room, kitchen, and terrace. It was landscaped with palm trees and flowers for privacy. Willie and Monica had a room adjoining her living room. Outland and Annie Laurie had separate entrances upstairs. The Secret Service agents had the ground-floor room on the other side of Willie's.

She had discouraged her parents and the Greys from coming. She knew they wouldn't enjoy it and it would have made her more depressed. Jenny had volunteered, too, but she had been persuaded that Sadie wanted to be alone with the kids, though the two older ones had each brought a friend from

203

school.

She had made a deal with the kids. They had to eat with her on the dining terrace, at least dinner. Otherwise they were on their own. She didn't want to be alone with just Monica and Willie. The rest of the time she would be content to play with them on the beach or read. She had brought a huge pile of novels. She hadn't had a binge like that in years.

When she walked into her villa, the view from the open French doors took her breath away. Far in the distance a small purplish speck stuck out on the horizon, the tiny island of Saba. Kicking off her shoes, she stepped down off the tiled terrace and let the sand slide between her toes. She walked out to the water and stood gazing at the horizon. The sun was beginning its descent, there was a slight breeze and the air was warm and dry. Just the sound of the waves on the shore was soothing. She felt the tension begin to dissolve for the first time since Rosey died. It wasn't much, but it was enough to fill her with a small feeling of hope.

She had the urge to be in the water, to symbolically wash away her sorrows. She rushed back to her room, pulled out her bathing suit, and raced down to the ocean, running into it as though she were finishing a marathon and bursting through the ribbon.

She had considered ordering dinner in her room the first night even though the hotel discouraged it. Then she decided, what the hell, she needed to celebrate in some way. Outland's and Annie Laurie's friends would lend a note of gaiety to the evening. She would even invite Monica and let Willie come, too. It would be fun. She would take the bottle of champagne that the manager had sent to the room and they would have a toast. But to what?

Suddenly she felt guilty. How could she feel like celebrating, like making a toast, when her husband was dead? What kind of person was she?

She was a live person, she concluded. Not a dead one. She had decided not to throw herself on the funeral pyre after all. Her life would go on. If she were to live, then she damn well ought to do it. Not sit around and feel sorry for herself.

In truth, she had already tried. She had tried in September calling Des, trying to rekindle that romance. She hadn't heard from him after their exchange of letters. She had written him back after she had received that wrenching letter in October. He had responded with the short note that said he was trying to sort things out and that Allison was returning in November. The plan was for her to move in with him. He didn't know what to do about Allison and their wedding plans. He was agonizing about her, about Willie. He would write again, he had said. He cared deeply for her, for his son. Time only made his dilemma more painful. He signed it 'Love, Des.'

She hadn't written back. What was she supposed to say? Oh great, take your time. Don't worry about us. There was no question that Des's reaction to her and to Willie had slowed her down. She didn't feel guilty about trying to renew her relationship with Des. She told herself she had done it for Willie. In some way, too, Rosey had given Des his blessing by acknowledging that Willie was Des's child on his deathbed.

Rosey. Her feelings about him were so confused. She had tried so hard after she got pregnant with

Willie and broke off with Des. She did love Rosey. She was content with him. What was so hard to accept, even now, was that she had never really been in love with him. There was never the passion she had felt with Des.

Her emotions now were so erratic—one minute she missed Rosey terribly and didn't want to go on living, the next she longed for the kind of romantic relationship she never had with him. The ambivalence was not new—no wonder Des was wary of her.

At first she had been angry and hurt by Des. But the more she thought about it, the more she realized that he had every right to feel the same way. She had left him. She had his baby and never told him. He tried to make a life for himself, her husband was shot, and then she wanted him to give up everything for her. That wasn't fair. But if she couldn't blame Des, who could she blame? How could she deal with her pain without somebody to lay it off on? Maybe the answer was to deal with it. Get on with it. Rosey would have wanted it that way, as they say. But *would* Rosey have wanted it that way? Probably. He was a bigger person than she. He wouldn't want her to be unhappy. The fact was that the sooner she pulled herself together the better it would be for Willie.

She had done nothing but cry for six months. It was time to stop.

★　　　★　　　★

They had a round table on the terrace overlooking the ocean. The manager had taken the table in front of theirs as protection against the unlikely gawker

206

or autograph seeker. The Secret Service agents were at the next table.

La Samanna prided itself on being safe for celebrities and guarded their privacy as if they were heads of state. There were several other well-known people there this Christmas—a Hollywood producer, a rock singer and his entourage, a tennis star. They all avoided each other as if they were invisible, as the protocol required.

When they walked out onto the terrace she felt everyone trying hard to keep from looking. Most had succumbed and were peeking around their menus. She didn't mind, really. She looked great and she wanted people to see that she wasn't the pathetic widow. She knew she had to walk a fine line about her bereavement. She couldn't appear too happy. It was too soon. People wanted and expected her to be brave and courageous in the face of tragedy. The black dress she had chosen was subdued but sexy. It was a way to say she was still mourning but ready to go on living.

The waiter opened the champagne. Sadie lifted her glass to her family.

'Here's to a great Christmas vacation, everyone,' she said, taking a sip.

They did the same.

Outland eyed her strangely.

'What's the matter, darling?' she asked.

'You look . . . different, Mom, that's all,' he said. 'No. You're acting different.'

'How?'

'You seem, sort of . . . well, I don't know . . . sort of happy.'

She smiled.

'Well, I feel sort of happy tonight. We're still sad

207

about your father, of course. I'll always be sad. But I look around this table and I see that I have so much to be thankful for.'

The two young guests were silent, awed by the intimacy.

'I feel happy that we have each other and that we're alive. I'm going to try very hard not be sad for you all. You don't need a mother who drags you down and makes you feel guilty for having a good time. I'm determined we will have a great vacation. Okay?'

'All right!' said Outland, raising his glass. 'Here's to Mom. The greatest—'

'Don't say anything nice about me,' she interrupted, 'or I'll cry and that will destroy the whole thing.'

They all laughed,

'Here's to all the girls we're going to love in St Martin,' said Outland, lifting his glass to his roommate.

'I can't believe I've raised a male chauvinist pig for a son,' said Sadie.

'Oh, please,' said Annie Laurie. 'This is a two-way street, you know,' and lifted her own glass. 'Here's to all the men we're going to love in St Martin,' she added. She and her friend toasted each other and giggled.

'I'll drink to that one', said Sadie playfully.

They were starting on their second bottle of wine and chattering happily away. Willie had fallen asleep in Monica's arms. Sadie was more relaxed than she had been in months. She wasn't paying attention to anyone around them. Then she saw one of her Secret Service agents get up and block the path of a man heading over to their table. At first she assumed it was an autograph seeker or a well wisher. She started to turn back to the table when she recognized him. It was one of the doctors who had operated on Rosey at George Washington Hospital.

She felt sick to her stomach. This man had come out of the operating room to tell her her husband was dead. Dr Sokolow, with the sympathetic face, the worried eyes, was heading her way to destroy her happy mood, her first night of vacation. What she really wanted was to have the agent pick him up and fling him off the side of the terrace over the rock cliff and down into the water,

'Dr Sokolow,' she said, smiling to alert the agent that it was all right. 'How wonderful to see you.'

He looked relieved and grateful that she had called off her agent.

'Mrs Grey, how are you?'

That look. They all had it when they spoke to her. That sad look. The Bereaved. We mustn't expect too much of the bereaved. There was something so demeaning about it, belittling, as though she were demented. They all meant well. They had her best interests at heart, but it was as if Sadie Grey had totally disappeared and they were talking to some cutout replica. Nobody saw her as a real person anymore. They all treated her with deference when Rosey was Vice President. When he became President it only got worse. Now it was in the realm of the ridiculous. It was as if she had become some sort of spiritual goddess, a sacred totem in which they placed their concerns and fears. She had always found it burdensome, but never so much as after Rosey was killed. Mostly it upset her. Tonight, oddly, it only tickled her. She

209

had to resist the urge to laugh.

'I couldn't be better, Dr Sokolow. I'm here for the Christmas vacation with my children and their friends. We're having a wonderful time.' She saw the look of surprise and quickly turned to introduce him to the children before he saw her smile.

'Won't you sit down?' she offered without enthusiasm.

'No, no thanks,' he said. 'I didn't mean to intrude. I'm having dinner with my wife and another couple we're vacationing with. I just wanted to come over and say hello.'

'Well, then, it's nice to see you.' Her tone was polite, if slightly dismissive.

'Perhaps you'd like to join us for a drink one evening? We're here until after New Year's.'

'Thank you. That might be nice,' she said.

'Actually, our son is at Harvard and the Lanzers' son and daughter are both at Harvard. They're here with us,' he said, looking at the kids. 'Or rather, they flew down here with us. We haven't seen much of them since we got here. Perhaps you kids might like to hook up with them. They seem to have discovered all of the island's hot spots. Mrs Grey, we'd love to have you join our party any time.'

'That's terribly nice of you,' said Sadie. She wondered how many more times she was going to say 'nice.'

'I'll let you finish your meal,' he said, smiling as he walked away.

Sadie tried to turn discreetly to see who he was with. She couldn't manage it without seeming too obvious. All she could see were two dark-haired women laughing hysterically, their attention directed to the other man at the table. She couldn't see his face, but he had sandy-colored hair and was gesturing animatedly, clearly entertaining them. She turned back to her children forlornly.

'Don't worry, Mom,' said Outland. 'We won't abandon you.'

★     ★     ★

The next day, Christmas Eve, Sadie spent buried in her novel, although she did take a long walk on the beach with Annie Laurie. She had always had a rather strained relationship with her daughter, particularly since Annie Laurie entered adolescence. She was her father's daughter. She looked like him, talked like him, thought like him. Rosey had worshiped her. Outland, on the other hand, was *her* child. He took after the McDougalds. He looked like her. His hair was black, not auburn, but he had her turquoise eyes and dark eyelashes. With Rosey gone she felt closer to Annie Laurie than she ever had. She could feel, too, that her daughter wanted to be closer. Sadie was her only parent now.

They never discussed Rosey. They talked about clothes and hair-dos and college. But she was beginning to feel an intimacy that had never been there and it made her happy.

They had another pleasant dinner on Christmas Eve before the kids all went out on the town. They had finally met the Sokolow and Lanzer children on the beach. Sadie went to her room to devour another novel.

On Christmas Day, except for 'Merry Christmas' in the morning, there was no mention of the holiday. Presents had been exchanged in

211

Washington and strict pacts had been made prohibiting more.

It was Willie's birthday, though, and that made it special for everyone. As if to erase Christmas, they made a big deal over him with lots of presents and balloons and streamers. The ice cream and cakes would be for later that afternoon to string out the celebration.

Before lunch she gave Willie Des's mitt. He immediately put it on his hand. Outland picked up a ball and threw it to Willie. Willie caught it and yelled with delight, then seemed to lose interest in his other gifts.

When they went up for lunch, Willie insisted on wearing his mitt and held on to it all the way up to the terrace. Sadie wished that she had never given it to him. She had wanted to put everything out of her mind, and seeing Willie with the mitt reminded her of Des.

It was another cloudless day. The water was calm and clear, the waves gentle. There was a big buffet lunch with cold lobsters and salads. They sat at the same table and the kids went to get her a plate so she wouldn't have to stand in line.

She saw Dr Sokolow's party at the buffet. The sandy-haired man was quite attractive. She had the feeling that she had met him before.

Outland carried Sadie's plate, followed by three young people, the Lanzer and Sokolow children. He introduced them to Sadie and they returned to their parents' table.

'We were thinking about going with them tonight to the other side of the island for dinner, but we didn't want to leave you alone,' said Outland. 'Dr Sokolow says they would love you to join them for dinner. Would that be okay? I mean, we don't have to. It's no big deal.'

Sadie's heart sank. She wasn't ready for this. She really didn't want to have dinner with strangers, but she couldn't ask the kids to stay with her. She knew it wasn't all that much fun for them. And she really didn't want to eat alone in the villa. That would be too depressing. After being alone most of the day she needed a break.

'Yes, of course, it would be fine,' she replied.

'Great,' said the kids, and Outland went over to the Sokolows' table to break the news. Dr Sokolow immediately offered to escort Sadie up to the bar for a drink before dinner.

'That won't be necessary,' she said. 'I'll just meet you at the table. Around eight-thirty?'

She was nervous. She didn't know these people. She really wasn't in the mood to make conversation. The only thing she had in common with the doctor was Rosey's death. She had been lulled into contentment and security by her little cocoon of family plus the sun and sand and water. Now she would have to gear up, be on stage, although the idea of adult conversation was not unappealing.

★    ★    ★

She did not want to look like a widow. She wanted to look pretty and sexy, but she had to be careful about that, too.

Turquoise. That would be appropriate. A good Caribbean color. An ankle-length jersey skirt and pullover. She hated to have to plot every move, every costume, as though she were about to perform, but that was her life now.

She was ready shortly before eight-thirty. She must have gone back to the bathroom ten times to check her mascara, her lipstick, take another hit of breath spray, brush her hair. It was stage fright.

Dr Sokolow, 'Sid, please,' sat her between himself and the sandy-haired man. He introduced Sadie to his wife, Judy, and then to Michael Lanzer. Lanzer's wife wasn't there.

Michael Lanzer stood up to shake her hand and looked at her directly, something most men never did. He was even better-looking up close. He had remarkable blue eyes, a square jaw, and high cheekbones lending him almost oriental or Indian features which belied his coloring.

Unlike most men who looked at her, his gaze was inquisitive, challenging.

'Isn't your wife joining us?' Sadie asked as he held her chair.

'She's not feeling well. Some kind of Caribbean bug.'

'Oh dear, I hope it's nothing serious,' she said, searching for something to say. 'At least you have a doctor here in case she really does get sick. I gather the medical care on this island is generally not the best.'

'Dr Lanzer is one of the great doctors in the country,' said Dr Sokolow. 'He's head of the National Cancer Institute at the NIH. Perhaps you've read about him. Dr Lanzer developed the drug that slows down the effects of the AIDS virus.'

'Oh, Dr Lanzer, of course. I've read about you. I was talking about you the other day . . .'

'I hope it won't be the last time,' he said with a mischievous smile.

She looked at him startled.

214

Was there something flirtatious in his tone of voice or did she imagine it? It was not possible. Nobody flirted with her. Certainly not now.

The wine steward had brought a bottle of red wine and Sid Sokolow turned to her.

'Will you do the honors?'

'Certainly.' She nodded. She hated this ritual of tasting the wine. It made everyone uncomfortable and insecure except for true wine connoisseurs or snobs. She was always afraid, though she knew wines, that she would fail to detect a deficient wine and someone else would have to send it back.

She held the glass to her nose and sniffed, then swirled it around. It smelled odd and when she tasted it there was no doubt that it had gone bad.

'Uhhhhh,' she said, making a face unintentionally. 'I'm afraid it's no good.'

'Certainly, Madame,' said the sommelier and whisked the bottle away.

'It was to the uh, I mean, I was talking about you to . . .'

'You don't need to explain,' Lanzer said. He was still smiling.

She was blushing. God. She hadn't blushed in so long she wasn't sure that was what she was doing.

'Well, I, it . . .'

'Is this your first time at La Samanna, Mrs Grey?' said Judy Sokolow, changing the subject. Sadie detected a reproving look to Lanzer.

'Sadie, please.'

'Sadie. Have you been here before?'

'Yes, but not for a long time. Not since my husband was governor. We tried to get here a couple of times after we came to Washington but we just never seemed to make it. And it's such a big

215

deal to travel as President. It's almost not worth it.'

There was a sympathetic silence and she realized everyone was thinking of the safety factor involved in a presidential trip.

'Before that,' she hurriedly continued, 'we tried a whole series of Caribbean resorts. None of them was what we were looking for until we found this place. They all seemed to be filled with people who speak in Long Island Lockjaw.'

Lanzer laughed appreciatively, more than a little surprised.

She found herself flustered again.

The wine steward brought another bottle, which, when she tasted it, mercifully was fine.

'We found La Samanna through the Lanzers,' said Judy Sokolow. 'Dr Lanzer's wife is French. They've been coming to the island for years.

'Never here though,' said Lanzer. 'I've never been able to afford it. Giselle's parents are giving us this trip.'

'You seem to fit right in,' said Sadie. 'Nobody would ever guess that you were just a poor doctor.'

She said it with a perfectly straight face. Judy and Sid Sokolow burst out laughing. After a moment so did Lanzer.

'Oh, all right,' he said slowly with an amused grin. 'So that's the way it's going to be.'

\* \* \*

Sadie wasn't tired when she returned to her villa. She had actually had the first meal in six months without talking about Rosey, or death, or anything depressing. Judy Sokolow had made sure the conversation stayed light. Sid was protective and

216

sympathetic. He knew. He had been there. But it was Michael Lanzer with his slightly flirtatious razzing that had made the evening. He had bordered on the irreverent the whole time. It had made Judy a nervous wreck.

She couldn't stop thinking about Michael Lanzer. She had never met anyone quite like him.

Who was this man and why was she reacting to him this way? She needed a cigarette. She got one off her bedside table, lit up, and tried to decide what to do with all her energy. It was only eleven. The kids wouldn't be home for hours. She would try not to worry about them.

What she really felt like doing was dancing. She would have killed to go out to some discotheque and dance her head off all night long. That, of course, was impossible. Lanzer had walked her back to her villa after dinner. As they had passed the Moroccan bar on the way down the path she had heard the sounds of disco music and had seen people dancing as they did every night after dinner. It made her itch to break out of her prison.

She paced around puffing on cigarettes. She felt as though she were going to jump out of her skin. She hadn't had sex for over six months. She hadn't really missed it all that much either. The sex anyway. Not with Rosey. What she did miss was being loved.

This evening, though, she really wanted, she really needed a man. And there wasn't one available.

She decided to take a walk on the beach. At least that would make her tired. Then maybe she'd be able to sleep. It was a lot better than reading. She kicked off her sandals, put out her cigarette, and

217

opened the sliding doors. The moon was almost
full. It lit up the beach so that she could see
practically to the end. She didn't want her agents to
follow her so she crept out around the bushes. Then
she began to run.

It wasn't until she had nearly reached the point
that she noticed him sitting near the rocks, his arms
on his knees. He was wearing an open-necked shirt
and his white pants were rolled up. Frightened, she
hesitated, not knowing what to do. Before she could
decide, he turned toward her. The moon was so
bright that she could distinguish his features right
away.

'Hi,' he said.

'Hi.'

Why did she feel so nervous?

'How did you know I'd be here?' he asked.

'I didn't. I just decided to take a walk and . . .'
She was flustered. Only then did she realize that he
was putting her on.

He patted the ground next to him. She sat down.

'You're really terrible, you know,' she said. She
was partially amused, partially irritated, partially
impressed.

'I was just pulling your chain.'

'Are you always this fresh, Dr Lanzer?'

'Mike.'

'You're not a Mike. I'm sorry. You're a Michael.
Are you always this fresh, Michael?'

'Only with really beautiful women.'

'Why is that?'

'To hide my insecurity. I like to make them think
I'm not impressed. They have so many men falling
all over them. They don't need me. Besides,' he
grinned, 'it works.'

218

'Are you always this arrogant, Michael?'

'Only with shiksas.'

'What's a shiksa?'

'God,' he said, 'I've got a real live one.'

'What is it?'

'A female goy. The blond, blue-eyed—only in your case, auburn-haired—Christian. The one who went out with the captain of the football team and never looked at the kid in the thick glasses with the slide rule who got all the grades.'

'Are you always this honest?'

'No,' he said. His face was serious for the first time.

'I didn't know you were Jewish.'

'Most people don't. I don't talk about it.'

'So why are you talking to me about it now?'

'I don't know. Maybe it's being away on an island. On a deserted beach at night. After a few drinks with a beautiful woman. Or maybe it's just being lonely.'

She leaned back on her elbows.

'How's your wife feeling?' she asked after a slight pause.

He looked over at her and saw that she had brought up his wife deliberately.

'Not great. I probably should get back and check on her.' He looked at his watch. 'I've been out here more than an hour.'

'Oh, no, is it that late? I'm going to have to try and sneak back without the agents finding out that I've flown the coop.'

She stood up quickly and brushed the sand from her skirt. He jumped up, too, rubbing the sand from his hands.

'Are they always around?'

219

She felt as though his question was not just idle. 'Always.'

'That must be intrusive.'

They had begun walking back to the villas. She was walking on the edge of the water, letting it wash up over her feet. It felt cool and refreshing.

'Terribly.'

'How can you have any life?'

'It was easier in the White House.'

Her words were loaded. Why did she have the sudden, crazy impulse to tell him about Des?

'Oh?'

She resisted. 'And since Rosey died I haven't really had any life. My life belongs to the country, for the time being anyway. I know that sounds grandiose and preposterous, but then so is my life.'

They walked in silence the rest of the way back, a totally comfortable silence. When they reached the edge of her villa, where she would have to make a run for it, they stopped, facing each other.

'I enjoyed our talk,' she said. 'Despite the fact that you are utterly impossible, Michael Lanzer.'

She looked up at him directly and he met her gaze. She had the desperate urge to fling herself into his arms. Did he want to do the same? They stood there smiling at each other in the moonlight.

'So did I, Sadie Grey.'

'I do hope we can be friends.'

'We will be.'

'See you tomorrow,' she said quickly and turned to run up to her villa, afraid that if she didn't she might well have done or said something she would be sorry for.

★　　★　　★

220

The next day she took her walk early in the morning so as not to run into him. Then she stayed away from the beach most of the day, sitting on her private patio. When she wanted to swim she ran down to the edge of the water, unwrapped the towel around her waist, and quickly went in, not lingering when she came out of the water.

It wasn't so much to avoid seeing Michael as it was to avoid having him see her. In a bathing suit.

She and the kids had a late lunch. The kids had been off snorkeling all morning. As they walked out onto the dining terrace, she noticed the Sokolows and Michael getting up from their table. As soon as he spotted her he walked over. She was surprised at her nervous reaction.

'Would you care to join us for dinner tonight?' he asked.

Judy Sokolow was directly behind him.

'Oh, please do,' said Judy. 'Giselle is still sick. It would be so much more fun.'

'Well, I, uh, the kids...'

'Oh, do, Mom. We were sort of thinking of going out, if that's okay with you.'

'I guess I have no choice.' She laughed, trying not to show her excitement. 'I'd be delighted.'

'Good. We'll see you at eight-thirty. Perhaps you'd care to join us in the bar at seven-thirty?'

'I don't see why not.'

'I'll come to get you,' said Michael.

'Oh, that won't be necessary,' she said quickly. She was afraid of looking too obvious. 'The agents will walk me up.'

'See you then,' said Judy.

The dinner that night was long with good wine

221

and lots of relaxed conversation. At one point Sadie got a cigarette from her purse and put it in her mouth. Michael reached over and took it away as she was about to light it.

Sadie was shocked. So were the Sokolows. Nobody said a word until Michael spoke up.

'I don't want you to smoke. When we get back to Washington I'd like you to come out to the NIH for a tour of the cancer ward. I don't want to watch you kill yourself.'

'Yes, sir,' she said, giving him a little salute. She feigned annoyance but was secretly pleased that he seemed to care about her.

Later, on the path, as he was escorting her back to her villa, she turned to him.

'I must say. That was pretty cheeky of you, taking my cigarette away from me and lecturing me in front of the Sokolows.'

'You call me cheeky,' he said with a grin. 'After you sent back the wine the other night. I've never seen anybody actually do that before in my life. I bet it was fine, too.'

'What are you talking about? It was terrible. It had gone bad. It was undrinkable.'

'I would rather have drunk it and been sick all night than send it back,' he said.

'That's perfectly ridiculous.'

They stopped on the path, out of breath, and giddy with their own mutual audacity. They looked at each other in amazement and burst out laughing.

'So,' she said, smiling. 'We're even.'

She wondered if he was resisting putting his arm around her. She distanced her body from him so that they didn't accidentally touch. She hoped he realized it was a gesture of affection. Why was she so afraid to touch him? If she hadn't cared she wouldn't have had to move away. They didn't speak the rest of the way down the path.

It wasn't until they reached her villa that he said, rather matter-of-factly, 'See you on the beach in an hour.'

Before she had a chance to protest he turned and left, disappearing up the path behind the bougainvillea and palm trees.

She didn't quite know how to react. She wanted nothing more than to join him. Yet she was annoyed that he would take for granted that she would come. And she was intrigued. She was also fearful of getting caught. She knew how angry her agents would be if they knew she was sneaking out. It was stupid and dangerous. She was a great kidnap target. Toby Waselewski, her favorite agent, had been with her ever since Rosey was Vice President. He knew she was mischief. He knew about her affair with Des. She could trust him. Unfortunately Toby was on day duty.

They had arranged with the St Martin police force to guard her at night. It was a matter of courtesy and protocol to allow the local government to perform some service. Sadie knew that local police were never as vigilant.

What the hell. Nothing was going to happen. He was married. She was who she was. They were just going to talk. It was perfectly innocent. She would go. But why did she feel so guilty? she wondered, as she squirted cologne on the backs of her wrists and the nape of her neck.

He was waiting for her at the same place as the night before.

'You're late.'

'You said an hour.'

She was already on the defensive.

'It's been an hour and eleven minutes.'

'I'm terribly sorry.' She was amused. 'But I did have to escape from half of the St Martin police force.'

'I had to get out without my wife seeing me, and believe me that takes a lot more ingenuity.'

'How so?'

'The level of surveillance in my family is very intense.'

'You are awful.'

'So you keep telling me. It's not good for my ego.'

'I don't think your ego needs any encouragement at all, if you want the truth, Dr Lanzer.'

'You're wrong about that,' he said, turning serious.

She couldn't think of anything to say so they sat in silence for a while, listening to the waves lap up against the sand.

'Tell me about Giselle,' she said finally.

'She's French. You know that already. She's what the French call gamine. She's brilliant. She's a wonderful and very Jewish mother.'

She wanted to ask what that meant but didn't.

'How long have you been married?'

'Twenty years.'

'How old are you anyway?'

'Forty-one. I got married the year I graduated from college.'

'That makes me feel like an old hag.'

'That's how I would have described you.'

'What made you fall in love with her?'

'I don't know. I thought I was in love. Maybe she

224

reminded me of my mother. Maybe I thought I was going to escape my destiny by studying in France for a year before medical school; by marrying a Frenchwoman. She was attractive, exotic, different, interesting, smart—really smart. She was everything I had ever wanted. Maybe I thought she was the closest thing I was going to get to a shiksa with big tits.'

Sadie burst out laughing.

'What! Is that the ultimate fantasy?'

'Of course.'

'So why didn't you just marry one and be done with it?'

'Because that would have meant going over the wall and I was unsure of what I'd find. I was afraid that I might be alone with a bunch of vacuous, shallow, paper-thin WASPs.'

'How flattering.'

He paused for a moment, then looked at her questioningly.

'It's not unusual, is it? We just turned out differently for each other than we had expected. It's no more her fault than mine. I thought I was getting one thing and I got something else. It was my fantasy that I put off on her. But this is mishegoss.'

'What's mishegoss?'

'Insanity,' he said. 'It means sitting on a beach spilling my guts to you.'

'You sound like a man who is contemplating an affair.'

She couldn't believe she had said this.

'Are you kidding?' He laughed. 'I would never survive the guilt.'

Sadie was giggling so hard she was breathless.

225

'You are so funny,' she said, gasping.

He stopped for a moment and stared at her intensely.

'You are so beautiful.'

She met his eyes and the two of them sat there for a long time, looking at each other. She had never wanted to kiss anyone as much as she wanted to kiss him that minute. She couldn't imagine him not wanting to kiss her. Yet he didn't make a move and neither did she.

Finally she found the strength to look down.

'I'm enjoying your company too much,' he said quietly.

She stood up. So did he.

Again they walked in silence until they neared her villa.

'We're going to St Bart's tomorrow,' she said. 'Some friends have lent me their yacht. We'll be gone for a few days.'

'When will you be back?' he asked, his tone much too casual.

'Monday.'

'Tuesday is New Year's Eve. Will you be here for that?'

Again his voice was studiedly casual.

'Yes.'

He smiled.

'See you,' she said.

This time it was he who turned away first.

\*　　　\*　　　\*

She remembered nothing of the trip to St Bart's. She was in a dream world the entire time. All she could think about was Michael. She woke up

226

thinking about him. She lay in her bed on the yacht for hours fantasizing about him. She dreamed about what it would be like to make love to him. Who would make the first move? She knew he wanted her. Or at least she thought he did.

He was so different, so hard to read. If he didn't want to make love to her, then what was going on between them? She had never felt so drawn to anyone; her feelings for him were so complicated, she didn't quite understand them.

For one thing, she was drawn to him intellectually. He was smart, sensitive, so perceptive about her, about who she was. He seemed to sense her need. That was it. She needed Michael. She wanted him, too, but it was need that was drawing her to him. That thought frightened her. She had never thought of herself as a needy person. Yet if anyone was or should be, it was she.

Michael was striking the most intense chord in her. He was playing to her almost instinctively and she was responding in kind. Whether it was real or not didn't matter. It was there, he was there, and she needed him and wanted him.

★   ★   ★

The three days away from La Samanna seemed like months. They returned after lunch on Monday. By then she was so frantic to see him that she took a walk up the beach hoping to bump into him, but he was nowhere in sight.

By six-thirty she had resigned herself to eating with the kids when the phone in her room rang.

'Hello.'

'May I speak to Mrs Grey.'

She recognized his voice, low, melodious, sexy, almost hypnotic.

'It's me,' she said.

'Hi me.'

There was a pause and they both sighed.

'Could you ... I mean, would you consider joining us for dinner?'

'Your wife, is she...?'

'She's better. She'll be at dinner.'

She paused.

'What time do you...?'

'See you at seven-thirty.'

★　　★　　★

Sadie had the Secret Service agents walk her up to the Moroccan bar a little after seven-thirty. The Sokolows were sitting together on the banquette. Michael and Giselle were seated in chairs around a wicker table.

The men stood as she approached. Even in the dim light she could see everyone in the bar peering at her.

Her own curiosity was focused on Giselle.

She looked her over as carefully as Giselle was inspecting her.

Giselle was petite and very gamine, as Michael had said. Very French-looking. She had a pixie haircut that flattered her small face. She wore a stylish bronze-colored mini-skirt that showed off her slim, shapely legs, and a wrapped jersey top that covered what Sadie could tell with a sinking heart were beautiful full breasts.

Seeing Giselle and Michael together for the first time, Sadie felt physically sick. When she saw the

228

way Giselle looked at her she knew in that instant that she felt the same way, too.

Michael started to introduce them. His voice did not have the usual confident ring.

'Mrs Lanzer,' Sadie said before Michael could speak, 'I'm so happy to meet you. I'm sorry you've not been feeling well.'

She had spoken too quickly. Did it sound forced? Part of the reason, she realized, was that she felt horribly guilty.

'Madame,' said Giselle, 'I am so happy to meet you also. I am only sorry that I haven't been able to join you before. This flu is a really terrible one. The only thing good I can say is that I am getting a lot of rest. And I have been able to read a little.'

She spoke in a husky French accent but her English was perfect. She had a natural charm and seemed friendly.

The cocktail hour was pleasant if a bit awkward as everyone concentrated on keeping the conversation going. Sadie and Michael and the Sokolows had formed a bond over the past few days and Giselle seemed the outsider.

Sadie was aware that Giselle felt it, too. As they walked into the dining room to dinner Giselle linked her arm in Michael's. Then she grabbed the seat next to him so that he was seated between her and Judy Sokolow.

'What do you think, Sadie?'

Judy was asking her a question. She had no idea about what. Fortunately, if she seemed a little removed she could be excused. She was a recently widowed First Lady. Nobody would possibly imagine that she was thinking about Michael's mouth on his wife's breast, his hand between her

229

legs. This was ridiculous.

'I'm sorry, Judy,' she said. 'What do I think about what?'

'About Blanche Osgood. Do you think she'll choose some sort of project? She's going to have to do something. She's not getting very good press.'

'Well, actually, I was just talking to her about that the other day. In fact, the other night when I said I'd been talking about you'—she turned to Michael—'that's what I meant.'

They had been avoiding each other. Now, when he smiled at her she almost lost track of what she was saying.

'Well—' she cleared her throat—'I was suggesting to Blanche that perhaps AIDS or even children with AIDS would be an important project for her. She's in the entertainment business. She's had friends who've died of AIDS. She's desperate to go back to her singing but she feels funny about giving country music concerts. I thought if she did it for a cause like AIDS it would be okay. I was actually planning to discuss it with you. I was hoping you might give her some guidance.'

'That is a wonderful idea,' said Judy. 'Don't you think so. Michael?'

'I, uh, I don't know,' he said. 'I'll have to give it some thought.' He seemed uncomfortable.

'Would you be working on the project, too?' asked Giselle.

Her question was directed at Sadie. The look on her face gave her away, even if the offhand tone of her voice did not.

'Well, I, I don't know,' said Sadie. 'I suppose she might ask me to be involved. It was just an idea.'

'Bon alors...' said Giselle looking directly at

230

Michael.

She stood up, suddenly looking drained.

'I'm so sorry,' she said. 'But I am still feeling a bit under the weather.'

She reached across the table to where Sadie was sitting and extended her hand.

'Mrs Grey, I hope you will forgive me if I leave a little early.'

Michael stood and pushed his chair back.

They said goodnight and left.

There hadn't been a glance or a nod from Michael.

*　　　*　　　*

She had no idea whether or not he would try to get away and meet her. Still she felt compelled to go even if he didn't show up.

She waited almost an hour. Dejected, she was about to leave when she saw him in the moonlight coming toward her.

When he reached her he was out of breath.

'I've taken a walk every night, sometimes staying away for two or three hours, just so I wouldn't arouse suspicions when you came back,' he said dropping to the sand next to her. 'If she knew I had been meeting you on the beach she would go completely berserk.'

'Why? Nothing's happened.'

'Tell it to the judge.'

'Nothing has. We're just friends.'

'All I can say, Sadie Grey, is that this is the damnedest friendship I've ever had.'

The way he looked at her made her get up and walk closer to the water, into the waves, holding up

231

her long full jersey skirt. She stood, letting the waves wash over her, cooling off. Then she walked back to where he was sitting and lowered herself next to him.

'I thought Giselle was terrific,' she said. 'She's extremely attractive and bright. Very charming.'

'She thought you were very nice.'

That was it. But there was a warning note in his voice.

She changed the subject.

'Tell me what you do?' she said. 'Talk to me about your work. You've hardly mentioned it. I know you discovered AZT and you're head of the National Cancer Institute. But what do you actually do? What is your day like?'

'It's changed a lot. I'm hardly a scientist anymore. Every day I feel I'm getting farther and farther away from the lab and from the clinic. I've really become a politician now and a p.r. man. The first fifteen years at NIH I lived under a rock. I got up, went to work, worked eighteen hours, came home, and went to bed. I spent most of my time in a laboratory with rats.'

'Maybe that's why you're so socially retarded.'

'Now it begins,' he said, with expectant pleasure.

'You seem to like it.'

'I'm just more comfortable with the notion that someone who looks like you and talks like you would want to give someone like me a lot of lip.'

'What on earth are you talking about?'

'I'm talking about what my dear sister Naomi calls shiksa madness.'

'Okay, I'll bite. What's that?'

'How much time do you have?'

'I have all night. You're the one with a curfew.'

232

He looked at his watch and groaned.

'I'm going to have to get back.' He paused. 'Thank God, I need protection from myself.'

'C'mon. Tell me. What is it really?'

'What do you want to know except that I've obviously got a terminal case of it.'

'No, I'm serious. What is it about? Explain it to me.'

'When I was in high school, we were all seated alphabetically. Jennings, Jenkins, Jones, and Klein were in front of me. They were all girls. Three gentiles and one of us. I would get so excited by my fantasies that I used to hold a book over my lap in case I might embarrass myself in class. It was interesting that my fantasies were always about Jennings, Jenkins, or Jones. Never about Klein. That's shiksa madness!'

'Have you ever been in love with a shiksa?'

'I'm not sure. I don't think so. No.'

'How much about that is a fantasy?'

'I'm not sure.'

'You would be sure if you'd ever been to bed with one.'

She was fishing.

'Sadie.' He said this very slowly, very carefully. 'I've never been to bed with another woman besides Giselle in my life.'

She was so stunned that she didn't know what to say. She was aware that her mouth was open.

'You look as if I've just told you I've tested positive for the AIDS virus.'

'I couldn't be more surprised if you had,' she said. 'Michael, I'm not sure I believe you. How is this possible?'

'Because that's what you do if you're a nice boy.

233

You grow up, you go to religious school, you go to college, you meet a nice girl, and you get married—forever. My father told me that if I had to go to bed with a girl before I was married, I should only do it with a shiksa, not one of our kind. Of course I never took him up on his advice. I was too young and too scared at the time. You see, shiksas were the forbidden fruit. Obtaining one was a perverted form of accomplishment. Now I realize that the advice was a terrible degradation of both Jewish and gentile women.'

'And what's in it for the shiksa?' she said. 'Being a trophy? Assuming she succumbs.'

'In order for her to want to buy into the trophy thing she has to need something that she's not getting where she is. She has to want intimacy and involvement that she is not getting in her present life. She has to want to share the pain. Some people believe that with WASPs there's no intimacy, no involvement, no pain allowed. Their culture doesn't permit it. They have to deny and suppress. The man she is looking for has the passion, the sensitivity, the intimacy, the trust, the capability of sharing pain. She's got to know that somebody else can share her pain. She needs to know she's needed. She's never had a man tell her what's in his heart.'

'So what if I get a man who'll tell me what's in his heart. What indication do I have that he's interested in what's in mine? He hasn't talked about me, asked about me, shown any curiosity about me since he met me. It all seems very one-sided.'

'Did it occur to you that he's afraid of seeming to be too interested? That he knows you can have any man you want? That you've always had any man you wanted.'

234

'What makes you say that?'

'I know you. I know who you are.'

'Don't be so sure.'

'You've probably had affairs. You're having this little flirtation for your own amusement. It's just a dalliance.'

It was the first time she had any idea how sensitive he was. So much of what he said was couched in humor that it was hard to tell how serious he was about anything.

'Oh Michael,' she said, angry and hurt at the same time, 'please don't talk like that.'

'Am I wrong?'

'About what?'

'About anything I just said.'

She felt bewildered and a little afraid. She didn't know what she thought or felt about anything.

'Are you asking if I've ever had an affair?'

'Yes.'

'Yes.'

She was provoked into telling him and it stunned her as much as it did him.

'His name is Desmond Shaw. It was three years ago. While Rosey was President. I've been in love with him ever since. At least until now.'

'Sadie, I . . .'

'Don't say anything more, Michael. I think we should say goodnight.'

She had the frantic urge to be alone, to think things out.

He jumped up and reached down to help her. When he did they found themselves face to face. He still had her hand in his. It was the first time they had touched each other. Greetings were too threatening. They had never even shaken hands except the very first time they were introduced.

They pulled their hands away from each other as if they had felt an electric shock and turned to walk down the beach.

What was she doing? Her husband had only been dead for six months. She had loved him and she mourned him now. How could she have forgotten that love? How could she feel this way about Michael when she was still in love with Des? Could she have gotten over Des so quickly when he had been the grand passion, the great love of her life? It didn't make sense. Was it just that she was terribly wounded and he was sympathetic? She didn't trust herself anymore. Newly widowed women often took lovers to affirm their existence. It was normal for people in her situation to feel vulnerable and confused. But nothing had prepared her for this . . . this mishegoss, as Michael would say.

When they got back to her villa he turned to her.

'Tomorrow night is New Year's Eve,' he said. 'I hope you'll join us. There's going to be a party on the terrace.'

'Oh Michael, I'd love to, but I'm afraid I'd feel so conspicuous. Like a fifth wheel.'

He burst out laughing.

'What's so funny?'

'The idea of you as a fifth wheel.'

'What matters is how I would feel.'

'If it will put your mind at ease, Giselle is still feeling really lousy. I don't think she'll be up for it even by tomorrow night. Besides, she hates holidays. She always refuses to go out on New Year's Eve. So you don't have to worry about being a fifth wheel.'

'I'll think about it.'

236

Sadie loved New Year's Eve. It was festive and sexy. New Year's Eve always held out some promise to her of good things to come, of romance.

They were to meet for dinner at nine-thirty. Giselle had conveniently had a relapse and would not be joining them. Just as Michael had predicted. She was giddy with anticipation. She worried a little that she might be thought callous to be enjoying New Year's Eve so soon after Rosey's death. She had to be careful tonight not to look as if she were having too good a time. She probably shouldn't dance. She decided to wear black again, off the shoulder, ankle length. Sexy but covered up. It was appropriate for the holiday, it didn't look too mournful, and it sent the right message. The kids were going to be at dinner at their own table, then they planned to go into town.

What did she think was going to happen tonight? Her fantasy was that he would come back to her villa and they would make love. That was impossible. He was married. Monica and Willie were in the bedroom on the other side of the living room. The agents were all around them.

The Secret Service! Oh God, she had forgotten about them. She wouldn't stay at the party until midnight. But if she left with him her agents would follow. She'd better talk to Toby. Make sure he was on duty. He'd already been through her affair with Des and had proved his discretion. He let her have her privacy and made sure that she was protected at the same time. And he never gave any indication that he disapproved of her activities. Now she

237

wasn't even married, so she wouldn't be doing anything wrong, but Michael was. Very married. She didn't know why that should make a difference but she sensed that it did to him. She sensed that no matter how attracted to her he was, even how much in love with her he might be, that it would be very hard for him to have an affair, much less leave his wife. What was she thinking of? She really was obsessing on this man. It was making her crazy.

She also felt guilty about her kids, though they seemed to be having a wonderful time. She was there for them in body if not in spirit. A few times on the yacht trip to St Bart's they had remarked about how remote she seemed.

She decided to spend the day with Willie, or rather Willie and his baseball mitt—the two were now surgically joined. It was spooky the way he had attached himself to that mitt, as though it were an extension of himself. It was almost as if he knew who had given it to him and why.

Just as interesting was her own reaction to watching Willie play with the mitt. She realized that it no longer caused her pain. In less than a week she had gone from feeling intense sorrow to lightheaded hopefulness. She could only attribute that fact to her newfound attraction to Michael. It shocked her to realize that she could have changed so much in such a short time. Now, instead of trying to forget Des, it was Michael she wanted to put out of her mind.

Spending the day with Willie would help take her mind off Michael and assuage her guilt about her child. A trip to town for lunch and ice cream would be fun and a nice treat for Monica. Maybe a little drive around the island. Then when they came back

there would be only a few hours until he came for
her.

*    *    *

'You look beautiful.'
She knew he meant it. It embarrassed and
pleased her at the same time. She never knew quite
how to respond when he complimented her. It
wasn't that she was unused to compliments. It was
just that Michael was so different from other men.
She couldn't count on her old wiles to work with
him. He saw through her too easily. She knew he
enjoyed her flirtatiousness with him but she also
knew with certainty that one false move could turn
him off just as easily as she could turn him on. In
normal circumstances he would have been a
challenge. She would have gone after him for the
pleasure of the chase, for the sport, because he was
so unpredictable and so elusive. In this case, the
chance of losing him was too upsetting. In fact it
was unthinkable.
He looked wonderful. He was tanned, which
made his high cheekbones look even more exotic.
He was wearing a blue shirt with the sleeves rolled
up and it showed off the muscles of his wiry body
and made his eyes look even bluer. She wondered if
he had thought of that or whether it was just
coincidental. Still, she could not bring herself to
compliment him.
'How's Giselle?'
'I gave her sleeping pills.' He grinned.
'You didn't! Isn't that malpractice or something?'
'She asked for them.'
'What kind of a dose?'

239

'She ought to wake up in time for the Fourth of July.'

She choked with laughter.

'Don't say it. I know I'm terrible.'

'I didn't say a word.'

'I like to make you laugh.'

'You're pretty successful at it.'

He turned serious on her, the way he did so often. One minute the jester, the next so solemn.

'I'd like to make you cry, too.'

She pulled back in shock.

'Why would you want to do that?'

'Just to know that I was capable of arousing such emotions in you.'

'Why would you want to hurt me?'

'I don't. I just want to know that I could.'

'I never know whether to take you seriously or not. I think you're putting me on but I'm not sure.'

'Good. I like it that way.'

'I'm going to have to think about that.'

They walked up the path, deliberately not touching each other, although their arms were swinging so closely together that their hands nearly met by accident several times.

The Sokolows were waiting for them at the table. They had been drinking champagne in the bar earlier and seemed well on their way toward having a good time. Was it her imagination or were they particularly pleased about her being there with Michael? She felt they were almost encouraging a romance, though she and Michael had both been very careful not to pay too much attention to each other in front of Sid and Judy.

Michael ordered a bottle of Sadie's favorite champagne. Did he know it was her favorite? They all proceeded to get quite high.

Sadie brought up her idea of getting Blanche Osgood interested in an AIDS project, perhaps giving country music concerts as benefits.

'When I suggested that she get in touch with you to see if you had any ideas for her,' said Sadie, 'she seemed to like the idea. So did Freddy. He's even more desperate than she is for her to have a project. It's awfully hard being cooped up in the White House when you've had your own career. I know only too well what it's like and I didn't even have a career.'

'Oh great,' said Michael. 'Just what I need. To be the mentor for a country music-singing First Lady who's desperate for a project and who's being advised by a former First Lady who's a sadist and wants to punish me. I think I'll go back to my rats. There is nothing in it for an innocent country doctor but pain and anguish.'

They were all quite loose by now and Sadie began to tease Michael about Blanche. She predicted that Blanche would certainly fall in love with him, which would make it easier to deal with her.

Judy and Sid joined in making him the butt of their jokes as well. He seemed to revel in the attention, especially since the teasing, led by Sadie, had a rather intimate quality to it. After dinner they went into the Moroccan bar where dancing had already begun. Michael and Sadie settled into a dark corner while Sid asked Judy to dance to the schmaltzy music.

'I love this song,' said Sadie spontaneously. 'You're probably such a music snob you can't stand it.'

'On any other occasion I would have said you

241

were right. But not tonight. Tonight I wouldn't want to hear anything else.'

'I wish I could dance. It's driving me insane that I can't. I just don't think it's appropriate, though, do you?'

'Just as well. I'm a terrible dancer. You're probably great.'

'I am. And I don't believe you're terrible either.'

'It's a WASP sport, dancing. I was always waiting tables at the country club and watching all the debutantes two-stepping with their horribly bland, boring boyfriends. I never understood it, frankly. Why would you bother to dance? Why put your arms around a woman and hold her close unless you're going to make love to her?'

'Maybe it's better than nothing.'

He looked at her a long time. She had no place and nothing to hide when he looked at her like that. And she didn't want to.

'Would you like to dance?'

'I'd love to . . . but not here.' Her voice was almost a whisper.

He looked at his watch.

'It's almost midnight.'

'We've got to get out of here anyway. I don't want to be here when the clock strikes twelve.'

'Let's go.'

When Sid and Judy returned to the table, they embraced Sadie, saying their farewells, as they were leaving the next morning.

Sadie and Michael slipped out of the bar and down the stone stairway to the beach rather than take the more traveled path to the villas. Her agents, led by Toby, kept a discreet distance.

They had reached the bottom of the steps to the

beach, which was hidden by bougainvillea and a small cluster of palm trees. Sadie kicked off her sandals. They could hear the words from a popular musical drifting down from the terrace.

'Say you love me ... one love, one lifetime ... that's all I ask of you.'

'May I?' He held out his arms.

She went to him, put one arm gently around his neck, her hand in his. She moved closer so that their bodies were barely touching. She put her head in the crook of his neck, her cheek softly grazing his. He began to move slightly, swaying to the music, though they were both standing in place.

'I take back what I said about dancing.'

She could feel his breath on her shoulder and she began to tremble.

'Ten, nine, eight, seven, six...' on the terrace they were counting down to midnight, 'five, four, three, two, one ... Happy New Year!'

'Auld Lang Syne' began to play. Michael stopped moving. He pulled back from her just slightly so that he could look down into her face. Then he slowly brought his mouth toward hers. They kissed so softly that for a moment she wasn't even sure they were actually kissing.

He pulled back again and looked at her with sadness. He reached out, touching the hair at her temple, stroking the side of her cheek with the backs of his fingers.

'Who are you? she whispered. 'Where have you been?'

'You break my heart, Sadie Grey,' he said finally.

They held hands as they made their way back through the palm trees. There were several people on the beach. It was too risky for them to walk down to the end tonight. Besides, they had Toby trailing them.

When they got to her villa, they turned to each other as they had each night before.

'I'll... I guess I should'—he cleared his throat—'I should say goodnight here. Or goodbye. We're taking the early flight in the morning.'

'I don't want you to go.'

He looked at her for a moment as though he were torn, then reached out and grabbed one of her hands. He squeezed it, then let it go as quickly as he had taken it.

'I have to,' he said.

Before she could reply, he was gone.

*　　*　　*

The next morning as she was having breakfast there was a knock on the door. It was one of her agents with a small package. She took it out to her terrace and carefully opened it. Inside was a beautiful conical seashell. It was ridged on the exterior in pink gradually turning to seafoam as it swirled to the mother-of-pearl pointed top. It was rubbed silky smooth from the sand and the sea.

There was a note inside.

Dear Sadie,

I found this shell on the beach this morning. It reminded me of you. Also, it's an unusual shell in that if you hold it up to your ear you can hear the sound of a man's heart beating. You are a kind and thoughtful friend and you have given me a perfect and unforgettable week.

M.D.L.

When she got back to Washington she wrote two letters.

Dear M.D.L.,

I'm returning the shell to you. You found it. It's your talisman. I held it to my ear but I couldn't hear the sound of a man's heart beating. Perhaps because the sound of my own was so loud.

Love, S.G.

Dear Des,

The mitt was wonderful, a huge success. It is removed from his pudgy little hand only for baths and meals and then amidst great protest. Thank you for remembering.

Dearest Des, I want to release you from what I know must be almost unendurable torment and guilt about me. I know you will always feel it about Willie as will I. There is nothing either of us can do about that.

I now know that you are right about one thing. Willie must always believe he is Rosey's son. It would be too devastating for him, for you and me, for our families, for everyone, to reveal the truth.

That is not to say that you won't always have a certain obligation to him. You will. As his 'special friend.'

The point of this note is to tell you that you needn't feel that obligation to me anymore.

I have met someone else. I'm not sure yet what it is that he and I feel for each other, but it is enough to make me realize that I have the strength to let you go.

You will always own a piece of my heart. I love you.

Sadie.

# CHAPTER TEN

It was a gray and drizzling January day. Allison was tempted to have lunch downstairs in the cafeteria and skip her exercise class. The luncheon in the boardroom for the President of Argentina had been canceled and she had a rare free hour in the middle of the day.

She was so depressed all she wanted to do was curl up somewhere with a fashion magazine and eat brownies. Instead, she was going to have another unpleasant session with Sprague Tyson over the drug story. God forbid it should be over lunch. She was still annoyed about that. He was as good professionally as advertised and also, as advertised, a prick. Tyson was working on an important and dangerous story about the Medellin cartel infiltrating the Justice Department. Half the time she thought she might kill him if the Colombians didn't. But nobody on the staff could touch him as an investigative reporter, and she figured he was probably a pretty good bet to win the Pulitzer. She would just have to put up with his arrogance and hostility.

That was not, however, why she was so depressed. She was depressed because of Des.

Since she had come back Des had been remote and distracted, just generally not himself.

He had barely made love to her. Maybe four or five times in two months since they'd been together. He refused to discuss their relationship or marriage, not that she had pressed him. She felt it was important for her to get a handle on her new job before she went off and got married, but it would have been nice if he had mentioned it, since that was one of the reasons she had come back in the first place. She wanted the editorship, certainly, but she was in love with Des. She had no doubt about that. She had always been in love with him. For her sins, she always would be. But she wanted to be capable of having a life without him. Des had insisted that they keep their respective houses. Even though they spent most nights together, he would often disappear over to his house in the evening and on weekends—to be alone, he said.

She had gone through several stages of emotions. At first she was so absorbed by her job that she didn't really have time to concentrate fully on the fact that Des was on another planet. The fact was she was relieved that he didn't pressure her to be with him every minute. She was spending twelve to fourteen hours a day at work and still feeling overwhelmed. When she came home at night she was so exhausted all she wanted was a couple of glasses of wine, a good meal, and a hot bath. Usually they went around the corner to Nora's if they were at his house or the Bistro Français if they were at her house in Georgetown. They rarely cooked. Des was better at it than she was but he wasn't interested in shopping or cleaning up. Besides, it was easier to go out. Their conversations were mostly about the news—news-related subjects, people in the news, or people who reported the news. They managed to avoid anything remotely intimate.

As Christmas neared, however, Des withdrew even more. She knew him well enough, though they had been apart for those few years, to sense that it didn't have anything to do with her. She began to probe about his work. She knew he was a bit discontented with the bureau chief job, that he missed writing; he felt bored and unchallenged. He admitted all of this, discussed it matter-of-factly without much emotion. Clearly, this was not what was causing his mood.

Even though Allison had hoped they wouldn't get married at Christmas as they had originally discussed, she was annoyed that the holiday was approaching without so much as a word about their plans. It wasn't that she was desperate to get married. She just wanted him to want to get married. What she really wanted was for him to get down on his knees and beg her. He had asked her once, at that dinner at Nora's, formally. Now they were in some limbo and she was not liking it one bit.

She was more or less determined to say something to him if he didn't bring it up by Christmas Day. How could he not? How could he let Christmas come and go without mentioning it? It was inconceivable. But he did.

Christmas was a nightmare. She had never liked Christmas anyway. Christmases had always been glum after her mother was killed in an automobile accident while on assignment in France when Allison was two. Her father would get terribly depressed around Christmastime. His mother, Nana, had lived with them, and it was only because of her that the holidays were bearable. Then her father, Sam, had been murdered by an intruder in their house in Georgetown. Since then, even though she celebrated Christmas, it made her sad.

Now all three were dead. The only family she had left were Uncle Rog and Aunt Molly, and Des. Uncle Rog and Aunt Molly were celebrating Christmas in Colorado, and though they had invited her out there neither one was in good enough health to really handle a visitor. Des was almost family. At least that was the idea. His daughter, Fiona, now in her early twenties, would be spending Christmas with her mother, Chessy, in her house in Barbados. Happily. Allison didn't much like Fiona anyway. She was too much like her mother, a spoiled little rich brat. It was all Chessy's money, so Des had no real control over Fiona. He saw her only occasionally and then there was no real warmth between them. Fiona had been a major disappointment in Des's life. That was another reason she was puzzled by his attitude. They had never discussed children but Allison thought Des wanted more. At least he wanted a son. Now was his chance to marry and have another child. Assuming that, at forty, she could still get pregnant. They didn't have much time left. She hadn't quite come to terms yet with how she felt about children, but her attitude had begun to change until Des started to disappear on her. She was afraid that if he didn't bring it up soon she would start to withdraw. She knew herself. Then he would never be able to reach her until it was too late.

*　　*　　*

On Christmas morning Allison had pretended to be asleep when Des got up and went downstairs for breakfast. She kept putting off getting up herself. She didn't want to face what she knew was going to be a disappointment when they finally did get around to opening presents.

Des had told her long ago how much he had always hated Christmas. It reminded him of his childhood, when his parents anguished over not being able to give their children nice presents. He knew how sad Christmas was for her. However, they each dealt with their sadness in different ways. Des's way was to ignore it, Allison's was to go overboard. The only thing she had liked about being in England was that the British really went in for it in a big way and she hadn't had to cope with Des's Scrooge act.

It was 11:00 a.m. She couldn't put off any longer what they both had been dreading.

She put on her robe and slippers, brushed her teeth, combed her hair, and trudged down to the tiny library on the second floor. They had put the tree there, in a small, raised altarlike cubicle surrounded by windows. She heard the fire crackling and peered in. Des was reading the paper and sipping coffee. He was already dressed in jeans and a turtleneck.

'Hi,' she said, trying to sound cheery.

'Hi. Merry Christmas.'

'Merry Christmas to you, too.'

She hadn't meant to sound sarcastic.

'Are you going to get some breakfast?'

'Yeah. I thought I'd get a muffin and some tea.'

'Oh, good. Well, bring it up here.'

'I will.'

He sounded as miserable as she did.

When she was settled on the sofa in front of the fire, facing Des's favorite chair and footstool, they looked at each other and smiled nervously. She was damned if she was going to be the one to suggest they open their presents. They could rot for all she cared. She had gotten him some great stuff, all things he would like, too, but if he hadn't got her something comparable he would be embarrassed and their whole day would be ruined.

She picked up the paper and began to read. He didn't say anything for a few minutes, then cleared his throat.

'You want to, uh, open the presents?'

'Sure.'

She looked down at her claddagh ring, the one he had given her at Nora's the night he asked her to marry him. It had been less than four months yet it seemed so long ago, that night when they had been so in love. There had been years when she had hoped to find a ring under the tree. Now she had his ring, but it didn't seem to be doing her much good. At least he hadn't asked for it back, although she couldn't be all that certain he wouldn't.

It occurred to her that he had never bought her jewelry. He knew her favorite store in Washington was the Tiny Jewel Box. She had bought the few pieces that she owned there. She had always bought her own jewelry. She was not the kind of woman men bought jewelry for. She used to take pride in

251

that. Now suddenly it upset her. She found herself wanting to be spoiled for once, to be loved and cherished as the vows said. Here was the man who had asked her to marry him, sitting across from her in almost total silence, having never mentioned 'holy matrimony' since September.

Des handed her a present that he had picked out from under the tree. The poor little tree, with only a few lights and bulbs and even fewer presents under its branches. It was certainly not a family Christmas tree, not a tree for children. It was a perfunctory tree. Perfect for a perfunctory holiday and a perfunctory relationship.

Before she opened it he told her what it was.

'It's a new laptop,' he said. 'I know yours is broken.'

That was true. Her traveling computer was on its last legs. But then she was no longer a foreign correspondent. She had her own PC at home, which was hooked up to the office. She had absolutely no use for a new one, which of course was why she hadn't bothered to get another one.

She looked up at him. Their eyes met briefly. In that instant she saw pain and remorse and guilt. And worry. He was obviously unsure of his present. But he had also, obviously, tried to give her the least personal present he could think of.

She glanced quickly away. She didn't want him to see how disappointed she was.

'Oh Des, it's great,' she said, knowing how halfhearted she sounded. 'You've been paying attention.'

A compliment. Maybe he wouldn't guess.

'Yeah, well, I thought you might need a new one.'

He sat back down on the sofa. She went over to the tree, picked up her present and brought it to him.

He unwrapped it slowly, with trepidation. As well he might have.

Inside was a beautiful box, handcrafted of smooth walnut. It was about a foot in length and a little under that in width. When he opened it he found a small gold plaque inside engraved with his name, Desmond Fitzmaurice Shaw. It was filled with small packages, each one wrapped. As he opened them one by one his eyes watered.

Allison had gone to his parents, and his brother, a priest. She had gone through his drawers and taken the family treasures that he owned. His grandfather's gold watch, which was chainless and had a cracked face, she had repaired, polished, and fitted with a new chain. An old pair of cufflinks with the backs off she had had mended. Pictures of his grandparents on both sides, she had had framed in a three-sided dark leather frame with his parents in the center. A tiny music box that played the William Tell Overture, which he had listened to every night as a child, she had had repainted and refitted so that when he opened it the tinkling sound filled the silence.

She stood as he opened them, fascinated by his reaction, not prepared for the depth of his emotions.

Finally, he got up and grabbed her in his arms. He squeezed her until she thought the breath would leave her, burying his head in her shoulder.

'Oh Sonny, Sonny, I'm so sorry for what I've put you through.'

'Why, Des? Why have you done this to me? I

don't understand.'

'I know. It's something . . . I can't . . .'

'Is it me? Have I done something?'

'Christ no! It has nothing to do with you. I only wish it were that simple.'

'Is it somebody else? If it is, just tell me, but don't make me—'

'No, Lord no, it's not somebody else the way you might think . . .'

'Well, what then, Des? Goddammit! Don't put me through this anymore. I can't stand it.'

'Sonny, it's something I'm going to have to work out for myself. Just know this. I love you more than I've ever loved any woman in my life and I always will. I want to marry you. But it just may take some time. That's all I can tell you.'

'Des.' She said his name quietly, evenly. 'I gave up my job in London, which I adored, a wonderful life, many good friends, and a man I cared about to come back and marry you. I am in love with you. That love has sustained me through a lot of pain. But I'm really not sure how much more I can take. You should know this. I just may not have that time.'

With that, she turned and went upstairs to get dressed for the O'Grady Christmas goose dinner.

★      ★      ★

The O'Gradys had invited them for Christmas. Colin O'Grady, the bureau chief of the *Boston Gazette*, was Des's oldest friend. They had grown up together on Boston's south side in a rundown Irish Catholic neighborhood. O'Grady was a man's man, one of the last of the old-time journalists

254

around Washington. He was hard-working, hard-drinking, a great storyteller, and a colorful character. His wife, Patricia, used to be what Allison considered, though she had always liked her, a Washington wife. She had been one of the few women in their crowd who stayed home to raise her children. But all that had changed. Pat O'Grady had gotten a job after her two kids started school. Now she was the environmental person on the staff of Malcolm Sohier, the Massachusetts senator who was a good friend of all of theirs. Pat had never looked or been better. She was full of confidence, loved her work, and was managing her life better than most. O'Grady, Allison suspected, was probably not all that unhappy to relax and bend a little. It was hard not to, since everyone adored Sohier.

★     ★     ★

It all seemed a blur to her, that dinner. O'Grady was already hitting the eggnog by the time they got there—he had the reddest nose of any Irishman she'd ever seen. He persuaded Des, which took no effort, to have a 'wee taste', and the two of them were off. There was a funny lopsided Christmas tree decorated with homemade ornaments, lots of popcorn strings, and flashing colored lights. Toys were strewn all over the floor and a great big fluffy dog named Muffin tussled with the children who ran excitedly from room to room playing hide-and-seek.

The O'Gradys had put together a group of strays, all journalists. It was normally the kind of crowd Allison would have loved. Instead, she was

255

overcome with depression at seeing this happy, loving family and this ragtag assortment of merry people.

She was only beginning to allow herself to admit that this was what she wanted—a husband, children, a family. She wasn't going to go as far as to want a dog. But who knew?

When Des had proposed to her she had started thinking about children for the first time in her life. It was scary how quickly her mind, her body, had responded. She had repressed any maternal desire for so long that she actually believed she didn't want children. Now an overwhelming baby hunger engulfed her. She had never felt such a strong emotion in her life, not even sexual. She walked down the street and everyone was pregnant. Every belly was swollen, every woman pushed a carriage with a bouncing, rosy-cheeked baby. Sometimes she felt such an emptiness in her womb that she doubled over, cradling herself as though she were a baby. Still, if someone asked her, Des for instance, if she wanted a child, she wasn't sure she was ready to say yes. Emotionally and physically she wanted, needed, craved a baby. Only psychologically was she unable to make the commitment.

She had just begun to acknowledge her longing, even to herself, when Des pulled back on her. Then it was too late. Once unleashed, the baby hunger, the insatiable need, was too strong to stave off, and she was left feeling vulnerable and exposed.

She looked around the room from where she was standing, alone, near the Christmas tree. Des was leaning against the mantel in his tweed jacket and turtleneck. She studied him for a while. He looked suddenly older. Funny, she hadn't noticed it

256

before. His hair was shot through with gray and there were deep furrows in his brow. He was beginning to get that craggy look that worked so well on men and so disastrously on women. Too much sun only became him. When he was young, he told her, they called him Boston Blackie because he tanned so dark in the summer. She noticed, too, that his eyebrows were bushier, a little unruly. It made him look intellectual. That would make him laugh. He did have the single sexiest mouth of any man alive, a very full lower lip that sort of curled downward in a humorous, mocking way. And those dancing black eyes. He was gesturing and laughing with O'Grady and a couple of men. She was certain they were talking sports. He really was a man's man, which made him even more attractive. His energy, his enthusiasm for what he was doing were boundless. When all that was focused on her was positively irresistible.

God, she wanted him. She wanted him to be her husband. She wanted him to be the father of her children.

She glanced at some of the other women there, the ones who were mothers, the ones whose kids were causing such jolly chaos. They had lines in their faces and pot bellies and spreading hips and thighs. Their clothes were rather dowdy and practical, their hair cut in short, easy-to-keep bobs, their faces unmade up except for a touch of lipstick. These women were the ones she used to scorn. Now she felt only envy.

Pat was calling everyone to the table. Allison came out of her reverie to be told she was seated between two Brits.

'To make you feel less homesick,' said Pat.

257

The dining room was jammed. There was one large table for sixteen, then a smaller table on the glassed-in porch for the children. There were candles and holly and toys on the table and two huge geese ready for carving.

Pat, now the working wife, had hired a waiter, so different from her earlier entertaining ventures when she had lurked, the martyr, in the kitchen, rarely emerging to join her guests.

As they sat down O'Grady asked them all to bow their heads. Allison was somewhat taken aback. Grace was not something most journalists did.

'Bless us, Oh Lord, and these thy gifts...' he said.

Allison raised her head and looked around the table. She noted with surprise that Des had his head bowed and his eyes tightly shut. He was praying. It shocked her. The idea that somebody she loved actually believed in God and prayed was unsettling. They never talked about religion. Once or twice he had told her about his growing up Catholic in Boston and how he had gotten sick of the Church and the priests, finally telling a priest in confession to 'Fuck off, Padre.'

It had never been an issue with them. She had told him she was an atheist, he had accepted it, and that had been the end of it. Now, here he was, praying. It was so weird. And frightening. Whatever it was that was bothering him had driven him to this.

'... which we are about to receive from thy bounty through Christ our Lord. Amen.'

Des's was the loudest amen.

He caught her looking at him and the look in his eyes was one of betrayal. What she didn't know was

258

whether he felt he was betraying her because of religion or because of something or somebody else.

The meal was lively and fun, with everyone shouting and arguing about politics and the new administration.

Blanche Osgood, or Blanche Baker as she liked to be called professionally, was the subject of nearly every Washington party. Practically everyone at the table had written something about her and nobody had the same opinion, which always made for great Washington conversations.

Allison, seated between Brits, began thinking about Julian. She wondered where he was this Christmas and whether he was happy. She wished at that very moment that she was with him and not Des. At least there wouldn't be this terrible strain. She had always felt good and somewhat contented with Julian. It occurred to her that she might well have made a mistake, giving up her job in London, giving up Julian.

The two British journalists had written exactly the opposite kinds of pieces about Blanche, and immediately they began to berate each other in such a subtle yet lethal manner that there was a hush.

Augustine Wormley, on Allison's right, had written a vicious piece describing the First Lady as a blowsy no-talent tart. Simon Lancaster, on her other side, rather liked Blanche. He insisted she was a true American primitive, an original who dared to be her own person in the face of ferocious criticism from the Washington establishment. Which, he added, included several people at this very party.

Within minutes the entire table had erupted into a mud-wrestling match, with everyone screaming and shouting and interrupting, disagreeing, insulting one another, and generally behaving in a manner unsuitable for polite conversation.

Allison was uncharacteristically quiet. She had her thoughts about Blanche, but she'd been away for so long she hadn't really had a chance to focus on her.

Des, on the other hand, was adamantly agreeing with Lancaster that this was some broad and that given a chance she would take Washington by storm.

'The only reason,' Des contended, 'that women don't like her is that she has such huge knockers.' Des looked so pleased with himself for having made such an outrageous statement that it became funny and the women could only laugh and guffaw and beat the table in mock indignation.

'And the men who don't like her are threatened and insecure about their own sexuality,' piped up Pat O'Grady.

'Bloody good point,' chimed in Lancaster.

'This woman is without redeeming qualities,' said Wormley, 'and you all know it and you are all being perverse. It's reverse snobbism of the worst kind. This is a disaster for Washington. She's an embarrassment to the country.'

'Allison, your silence has not gone unnoticed,' said O'Grady. 'I can't believe you're not going to weigh in here.'

Everyone looked at her.

'I feel as if I'm on a talk show,' she said, laughing. 'Why doesn't everyone start yelling at me instead of staring solemnly?'

'Maybe because we all respect what you have to say,' said O'Grady, with the slightest tinge of sarcasm.

'If it weren't Christmas, O'Grady . . .' she said with a vicious smile.

'I know, I know you'd tell me to—'

'Enough, you two,' said Pat. 'Let's hear what Allison has to say.'

'I haven't quite decided what I think about Blanche Baker. However, just knowing that Augustine thinks she is a worthless tart makes me want to love her.'

Everyone chuckled at that and Augustine swelled up with pride at having once again been the center of controversy.

'But if I may be serious for a moment.'

'Oh boo, Allison,' said Wormley, 'this is supposed to be festive. If you go serious on us we'll have to start being pompous.'

'We can't have that, now can we?' Allison feigned horror. 'God, I've missed Washington. Do you know what you sound like, Wormley? You sound like Lorraine Hadley and all those Georgetown hostesses. They can't stand it that somebody like Blanche would come into town and not pay attention to them. Unlike Sadie Grey, who won them over by turning to them for advice and counsel.'

She hadn't meant to invoke Sadie's name. It had come out before she realized what she was saying. She saw Des wince. She hadn't mentioned Sadie once to Des since she had come back. Who needed it? It was over and done with now. But now, the pain on his face almost made her lose her train of thought.

Was it over and done with? It hadn't even occurred to her for a second that Des might still be

261

seeing her or that she might be the issue. But his expression made her wonder.

She didn't want Des to think she was being bitchy about Sadie. It would backfire. She hadn't really meant it that way, anyway. 'It seems like another century,' she said quickly. 'Things have changed so much in Washington since the Greys arrived six years ago. Those hostesses were on the way out then and they just don't matter anymore. The Washington salon is dead. But those ladies still can gossip. In fact, that's all they do since they don't have parties that anybody goes to anymore. What better person to gossip about than Blanche Baker? She's, as they would say, N.Q.O.C.'

'Translation please,' shouted O'Grady. 'I bet that's some WASP expression that's not flattering to the Harps.'

'"Not quite our class," or "not quite our crowd,"' said Allison. 'But just to fool you they sometimes will say N.O.C.D.'

'Okay, I give up.'

'"Not our class, dear," or "not our crowd, dear."'

'For five bucks what's N.I.N.A.?' challenged O'Grady.

'No Irish need apply,' said Des.

'Forget it, Shaw, you don't collect any five dollars from me. Harps aren't allowed to play.'

'Still stings, does it, me boy?' laughed Des.

Allison was glad to see O'Grady had eased him back into the land of the living.

'We were talking about Blanche,' said Lancaster.

'I think this could be a seminal moment for First Ladies,' said Allison. 'For one thing, she's the first First Lady to ever have a career. If she manages to

262

keep it and work it into her job description without disrupting the presidency it would be fabulous. But from what I understand, the men in the West Wing are adamant that she give up her music while Freddy is in office. I think that would be a disaster.'

'We're not talking about her career, darling Allison,' said Wormley. 'We are talking about her mouth. She hasn't said one thing in the nearly six months that Freddy's been in office that doesn't make her sound like a stupid bimbo. Whoever is advising her to take on the Washington establishment surely must have some sadistic plans to destroy her husband. As we have seen in several past administrations, it does not work. We now know that you can't lick 'em. You simply must join 'em, as you Americans say.'

'I think you're right, Augustine. She did start out with a chip on her shoulder. But there hasn't been any of that in the last six weeks or so. Before that there was a bombshell coming out of the White House nearly every week. Somebody must have gotten to her. My feeling is, with a good press person, she could do very well. She seems to be well motivated and I think her instincts are essentially decent. I wouldn't write her off. She does, however, have a long way to go. The backless mules and peroxide-blond wig are not going to take her very far.'

'Thus spake Allison.' Wormley sat back smugly and took a long gulp of red wine. 'I think I'll use that quote in my next piece on Washington.'

'Oh, fuck off, Wormley,' said Allison under her breath, mindful of the children at the next table. 'Christmas is off the record.'

'That's my gal,' said Des, smiling from his end of

the table. 'I was afraid with all this levity, it wasn't really you inhabiting that gorgeous body.'

'You can go fuck yourself, too, Shaw.'

'Now, now, my children. This language is not befitting the birth of our little Lord Jesus,' said O'Grady. 'Besides, it's time for Christmas carols. So if you will all join me at the piano we'll have a little champagne and song.'

Allison walked over to the mantel where Des had been standing earlier. He sauntered over and put another log on the fire. The others had gathered around O'Grady, who was playing 'O Holy Night'.

It was beginning to get dark.

'Look, it's snowing,' said Des. Allison turned to see tiny white flakes swirling past the window making a beautiful pattern against the sunset and the silhouettes of pine trees. It was such a perfect day or should have been, with good friends, and rosy-cheeked children, and so much to look forward to. She really wanted to put her arms around Des but something about him put her off.

'Be right back,' he said, touching her lightly on the shoulder as he went upstairs.

She remembered the last time she had been in that bathroom. She and Des had tried to make love in the midst of one of O'Grady's parties. Des was still married to Chessy, who was downstairs in the living room. Now he wasn't married. Yet she had a rival she didn't know or even know about. It was so much worse, not knowing whatever or whoever this thing or person was that was coming between them. She could fight another woman. This ghost she could not.

Nobody had noticed Des leave. She could easily follow him. Why not?

She slipped out of the living room and crept up the stairs. The door to the bathroom was shut. She knocked gently. He opened it. He was just zipping up his fly.

She said nothing, just looked down at his crotch and began nervously chewing her lip.

'Looking for a re-creation of the scene we last played here?'

She couldn't tell whether or not he was amused.

'Maybe just for what we felt for each other then.'

'It hasn't changed for me.'

'Prove it.'

'Oh, Sonny. It's just so much more complicated now.'

'How much more complicated can you get than to have been married to Chessy?'

'Trust me, it's possible.'

'I'm not sure I can trust you anymore, Des. Not when you're hiding something from me.'

'Jesus, Sonny,' he said. 'This thing is killing me.' He turned away from her and pounded his fist against the bathroom wall.

'It can't hurt you more than it's hurting me. I just ache so, Des.'

She was pleading.

'I want you so badly. I want you to marry me. I want to have a baby. I have to have a baby. Listen to what I'm saying. I can't bear this anymore. I'm not even angry. Don't you see? I'm not mad. I just need you. And you're not here. You've got to help me.'

Des let himself down on the toilet seat lid and pulled her over to him, resting his head against her stomach. She thought he was struggling for the words. Instead he said nothing. He just squeezed

265

her as tightly as he could.

Just as he did, she slipped on the wet floor and stepped on a rubber duck, which squealed loudly.

As she had that night, many years before, Allison was suddenly trying not to giggle. There was something almost hilarious about this scene, the two of them in anguish in somebody else's bathroom, Des perched on the toilet seat, she standing on the wet bath mat with rubber ducks dispersed under her feet.

'We've got to stop meeting like this,' she said and cracked up.

'You witch.' Des had leaped up when he heard the squeal and grabbed for her.

She slipped away from his grasp and turned toward the door.

He grabbed her arm and twisted it, pulling her back to him until she was pressing up against his chest.

He started to kiss her but she jerked her head away and fell back from him. Her mirth had turned to anger she hadn't known she felt, or at least had pretended not to feel. She reached down and picked up the duck and flung it at him, hitting him in the face. He looked stunned at first, then angry. She was afraid, all of a sudden, that he might hit her. His black eyes had changed color the way they did when he got really furious. She always thought he looked like some comic-strip character whose eyes turned into kaleidoscopes when he was upset. She didn't care. She wanted to hurt him the way he had hurt her.

He came toward her and she flung open the door and raced down the stairs. He followed her, grabbing for her hair, her skirt, anything that would stop her. She kept going, until she reached the landing, tripping slightly, then catching her balance and running out the front door. The guests had migrated toward the kitchen and the sun porch in back so nobody saw them leave, though that was the last thing on her mind. She was scared. She didn't know what he would do.

The ground was covered with snow by now and they were caught in a near blizzard of whiteness as they ran across the lawn to the bushes. She saw one of the children's soccer balls and threw it at his feet, tripping him and causing him to fall in the snow.

'Shit,' he said and picked himself up, now lightly dusted all over. It was dark, and he had obviously lost sight of her, but she was breathing heavily in the silence.

'Sonny, goddammit, where are you?'

'Don't you goddammit me, goddamn you. Just get away from me, do you hear? Just leave me the fuck alone.'

He came at her then, lunging through the dark. She picked up a handful of snow and pushed it into his face, temporarily blinding him.

He swung out at her hand to knock it away and hit her in the face. The crack of his hand against her jaw stunned her. He was close enough now that even in the darkness she could see him. He was even more shocked than she was.

The rage welled up inside her. She had never known what it was like to want to hit somebody, even kill somebody. All she knew was that she had to strike out at him, had to hurt him.

She raised her arm and brought it down as hard as she could, striking the side of his head. The thud gave her enormous pleasure and she did it again, even harder. She was breathing heavily, letting out low guttural noises. She felt a thrill, a sensation of such satisfaction that she began pummeling him until she had worked herself up into a frenzy. Des had been caught by surprise when she hit him. He lost his balance and fell to his knees, giving her an even better vantage.

It seemed as if she had been going at him for hours when she realized that he was not hitting back, not trying to protect himself. It was almost as if he wanted to be beaten.

'Goddamn you, Desmond Shaw. Get up and fight like a man!' she screamed at him. She hit him again.

'You bastard, get up off your knees, you shit. I hate your very guts.'

No movement.

'Okay, then I'll get you up.' She reached down and put her hands under his arms, attempting to pull him up off his knees, but he wouldn't let her. She tugged again but he was just too heavy for her.

'All right then, you want to be punished,' she yelled, even more angry than before. 'I'll punish you.'

She pushed his body as hard as she could until he fell over in the snow and then she began to kick him in the side.

Tears were rolling down her cheeks as she continued her assault.

'I know what you're doing, you asshole. This is some sick Catholic penance game you're playing here. You're so wracked with guilt that you think you have to pay for it so you're letting me do it for you. Forgive me, Father, for I have sinned.' She began mocking him, chanting the penance in a singsong voice. 'Forgive me, Father, for I have sinned! Just let Allison beat the crap out of me and then I'll feel better. I will have paid for my sins. In fact, I can just keep on sinning. That's the good ole Catholic way. Jesus, what hypocrisy! You know what, Desmond Shaw. You are sick.'

She was shrieking, choking on the snow as it swirled into her mouth. She kicked him again, trying to provoke some response.

'You are desperately, hopelessly, irrevocably sick.'

Then, suddenly, she realized what was making her so angry. It wasn't just that Des had been so withdrawn recently. It was everything. All the humiliation of having to hide their affair when they first met because he was married to Chessy. The anger at him for caring more about his work than he did about her, more about his work than hers. The unbearable pain of breaking up, of his leaving her. The years of loneliness and self-imposed isolation after they split; and finally the agony of finding out that he was having an affair with Sadie Grey, the First Lady, her greatest rival.

Looking at him in the snow, she thought she had never hated anyone so much in her entire life.

'You have caused me more pain than anybody has ever caused me in my life, and I'm not going to buy into it anymore. I loathe your very guts, do you hear me. I despise you and I never want to see you again. Merry Christmas, you prick.'

She turned and ran into the house, leaving Des like an amputated statue kneeling in the snow. She grabbed the keys to the car from his coat pocket, got her jacket, and dashed out of the house. She started his car and drove to her house. She left the keys inside under the car seat and made a mental note to call his service and leave a message to that effect.

By the time she got inside she realized her clothes were soaked and she was chilled through. She fixed a cup of hot tea with honey, lemon, and rum and took it upstairs. She drew a steaming hot bath, put on some old blues tapes, got into the tub, and went into as close to a Zen state as she could manage.

She didn't even consider the consequences of her actions earlier. All she cared about was getting into bed. She put on a flannel night-gown, slid under the down comforter, and slowly dozed off to sleep. She was only distantly aware of the phone ringing and her answering machine recording several insistent voices.

★　　　★　　　★

Julian. One of the calls had been from Julian, whom she had not spoken to since she left England, whom she adored but was not in love with. Julian who wanted to marry her.

She would return his call first.

She would call Pat O'Grady later.

She would call Des . . . maybe never. He hadn't even identified himself. He didn't need to. His message was simple.

'We need to talk.'

Fuck Des. She was all talked out. It was Julian she wanted to talk to. Julian who loved her.

When she called him it was late afternoon his time. He was having a Boxing Day party at his father's estate in Cornwall and the noise level in the background was high. He had already had a few toddies himself.

'I just bloody well missed you and wondered how you were getting on. I hadn't heard news of your marriage and thought perhaps something had got buggered up.'

'Oh Julian, I miss you. I've had a terrible fight with Des. Literally. I'd get on a plane this instant but I can't leave work. I've got the duty this week. I'm the junior person and everyone else has taken off.'

'Darling, say no more. Julian of Arabia is on the next Concorde to Dulles.'

'Oh Julian, don't tease me.'

'My sweet, I'm jolly well not kidding. I've been dying for an excuse to get out of here. There's a ghastly New Year's Eve party scheduled where several of my lady friends are threatening to converge on me and tear me to bits. So you see it's a matter of life or death. I'll see you tomorrow. Leave a key under the mat. Ciao.'

She should have stopped him. It wasn't fair. Just because she was hurting was no reason she should use someone else. But she was in a weakened condition. She needed Julian now. After all, he had called her. He had always had a sixth sense about her. It must have come from spending so much time in the desert with all those Arabs.

\* \* \*

New Year's Eve was cozy and undemanding with Julian trying to be brave and understanding. They had cooked at home because she hadn't wanted to be seen with him. Everyone believed she was engaged to Des. She didn't want the hassle of trying

271

to explain, especially since she didn't have a clue what to explain. Des had called and left several messages on her machine, but she had not returned his calls. So that was where they were at the moment. She didn't feel like seeing him and certainly not making love to him. She didn't want to make love to Julian either, for that matter. She had managed to keep him at arm's length with body language. She knew he loved her and it made her sad. She had realized immediately that 'Julian of Arabia' didn't seem quite as romantic in Georgetown as he had in Chelsea or Cornwall. He must have realized it, too. He left the next day, pleading a meeting with his editor in London. She was relieved as well as disappointed. Relieved because she wouldn't feel cheated at having given him up for Des, disappointed because she had nobody to turn to if things really didn't work out with Des, which was the way things were looking.

*     *     *

Dwelling on her Christmas Day fight with Des wasn't getting her anywhere. She went outside her glass cubicle and peered through Walt Fineman's window to see if it was still raining. The January drizzle had stopped but it was still dreary. Still, she had no excuse to skip the exercise class since it wasn't wet anymore. She needed it, that was for sure. She'd been drowning her sorrows in calories since their fight. She needed the energy for her battle with Sprague later in the afternoon.

She walked back to her office and sat down at her desk, looking at the mounds of paperwork that had piled up in front of her. It seemed to her to have

272

little to do with daily journalism and a lot to do with boring administrative duties. Other people's expense accounts. Doing her own was torture enough. This was not her strong point.

She should skip exercise and go down to the cafeteria, get a salad, bring it up and eat at her desk.. The idea depressed her even more. She leaned back in her desk chair and stared at the newsroom through the glass. She was paralyzed with indecision and inertia.

The phone rang. Everybody was out to lunch so she answered it herself.

'Sonny?'

It was Des. For some reason she hadn't counted on that.

'Yes?'

'I've got to see you.'

'Des, I . . .'

'Please.'

'I just can't do it anymore.'

'That's not what I'm asking for.'

'I'm not just talking about the last few months. I'm talking about ever since we met.'

'I understand that.'

'I've got a hole in my gut. Every time I see you or talk to you or make love to you or live with you or promise to marry you or break up with you or fight with you it gets bigger.'

'I know, Sonny. I've got the same problem. That's why we need to talk.'

She didn't say anything, she didn't know what to say.

'Sonny?'

'I just feel so tired.'

'Please.'

273

'When?'

'Now. Lunch.'

'You bastard. I was just about to eat bean sprouts at my desk while I did expense accounts.'

'Baby, you shouldn't be worrying your pretty head with things like that.'

'You're right. Talk me out of it.'

'The Willard Hotel dining room. In half an hour.'

'You're so convincing.'

'See you there.'

'Bye.'

God, she was a wreck. Her hair was a mess. She had on an old gray knit suit and a white turtleneck. Drab. She had a serious case of premenstrual syndrome. Her skin was blotchy. She had worn hardly any makeup. She looked like the weather. Even twenty minutes in the ladies' room wasn't going to do it. But then so what. He was probably going to tell her he wanted out for good. It would make it easier for them both if she looked like a dog.

She caught a taxi to Pennsylvania Avenue. She didn't want to mess up the salvage job she had done on herself by walking. Why was she doing this? she wondered, as the cab rounded Lafayette Square. She could still turn back, she thought as they passed the White House. But she didn't stop the driver. She deserved all the pain she was going to get for being so stupid. Curiosity. That's what. Always a reporter. She couldn't stand not knowing.

She walked through the doors of the elegant old restored hotel and walked down Peacock Alley to the dining room. It wasn't a place where she normally ate. It was so grand and Victorian and formal. The few times she had eaten there had been with sources.

Des was waiting for her. He stood up when she approached the table. Not his usual style. A bad sign. She remembered the night he had broken up with her years ago after she had humiliated him on a story. He had picked her up for dinner and had been so polite. Opening doors, pulling back her chair.

'Hi.' She sounded too bouncy.

'Hi.' He sounded ominous.

They both sat down.

She was so self-conscious. She looked gratefully at the glass in front of her as a distraction.

'Water,' she said and took a huge gulp.

'Martini,' he said with a grin, taking a gulp out of his own glass.

'That bad, huh?'

'Depends on how you look at it.'

'Spare me the suspense, Shaw. What's the headline?'

'Let's get married.'

'We've already run that story.'

'Not with a double byline.'

'Gag me with chopsticks, as the copy aides say.'

'You started it.'

'Are you referring to the metaphor or the relationship?'

'I don't know what the hell we're talking about.'

'Boy, this sure is romantic.'

'Oh, shut up, you asshole.'

'Why Desmond Shaw, you do say the—'

Des had jumped up from his chair and was pulling her from hers.

'Get your purse.'

She stooped down to get her bag, still trying to wrest her arm away from him. She didn't know whether to be angry or amused. He was practically dragging her out of the dining room and down the hall.

'Where are we going, if you don't mind my asking?'

'You'll see.'

They reached the elevator, which opened just as he was pressing the button, and he pulled her inside.

'What the hell?'

'Just let me run the show, for once, okay?'

She stood silently against the wall of the elevator on the opposite side.

When the elevator door opened on the twelfth floor she got out and waited. He took her hand and led her down the hall. They stopped at a door, he reached in his pocket, pulled out a key, and opened it.

They were in a pretty blue suite overlooking Pennsylvania Avenue with a step up to a study and a bedroom. On the table was a bucket with a bottle of champagne in it.

She was determined not to say a word until he explained.

'This is the honeymoon suite.'

He announced it with such boyish satisfaction that she laughed.

His face fell.

'So?'

'It's ours.'

'But we're not on our honeymoon.'

'It's a preview of coming attractions. Maybe you'd understand the trailer better. Isn't that what the Brits call it?'

'So you heard Julian was here and you're jealous.'

'Of course I'm jealous. I don't want you fucking anybody else, goddamn you.'

He really was jealous. She debated telling him that she hadn't been to bed with Julian, then decided against it. Let him suffer.

There was still a lot of anger and tension between them. 'I love you. Don't you understand that?'

He was shouting.

'Then why have you been putting me through hell for the last three months?'

She was shouting, too. She certainly had not meant to.

'Sonny, I . . .' he looked defeated. 'I can't tell you. But you have to trust me. I didn't want to hurt you. It was killing me. But something had to be resolved. And it has been. All I want now is to make it up to you. Let me try. Marry me, please.'

'Oh Des. I just don't see how it can work. I'm a reporter. I can't stand not knowing something. It would make me crazy. You're telling me that for the last three months you have made me absolutely miserable, treated me like shit, hidden something from me that nearly ruined my life, and now I should just forget it? Marry you? Get on with our lives? You've got to be kidding. I'd spend the rest of our lives trying to get it out of you. And if I didn't I'd end up hating your guts. Is that what you want?'

'Yes, if that's the only way I can have you.'

'For God's sake, Des. Tell me what it was.'

'I think I've changed my mind. I don't think I could stand your interrogations for the next thirty or forty years. You're right. Forget the whole thing.

Forget I ever asked you to marry me. It would be a disaster. I've seen you at work. You're too formidable. I'm no match. You'd destroy me.'

It took her a moment to realize that he was putting her on.

'You fucker. This is serious.' He looked at her a long time, trying to make up his mind.

'As usual, you are a brilliant reporter,' he said. 'I knew I couldn't hide it completely from you. But yes, if it will make you feel better, it did have something to do with my family. I was sworn to secrecy. I have to protect that secret or it could destroy this person's life. You have to trust me with the rest, Sonny.'

'Don't tell me. Let me guess.' Now she was putting him on. 'I think I know what it is. I'm going to tell you and I don't expect you to respond. I just want to watch your face. Your Jesuit priest brother confides in you that he's just tested positive for the AIDS virus. The last time you were in Boston you shared a razor and cut yourself. But wait, we've made love since then so it couldn't be that...'

Des broke into a huge grin.

'Or maybe ... your mother confessed that you are not your father's natural son, and that your real father has died of a degenerative disease that is hereditary...'

Des walked over and put his arms around her, pulled her to him, and kissed her while she was still talking.

'Just tell me if I'm warm,' she said, when she came up for air.

'You're warm,' he said, kissing her again. 'You're very warm.'

278

'Des, I can't do this. I have to get back to the office. I have a meeting with Sprague Tyson.'

'Fuck Sprague Tyson.'

This time when he kissed her his hands were caressing her body, moving to undress her. 'On the other hand, I have an even better idea.'

\*　　　\*　　　\*

'I thought maybe we could go down to the cafeteria and get some tea . . . or do you not do tea either?'

She was standing in front of Sprague Tyson's desk in the middle of the newsroom. It was a little after four. She had just gotten back from the Willard. Her face was flushed and her hair, despite desperate attempts at combing, still looked disheveled. She hoped she seemed composed.

He looked up from his notes. He studied her for a moment. His eyes flickered a bit in . . . appreciation? He certainly wasn't going to give her the satisfaction of reacting,

'Actually, I'd rather we went somewhere more private. There's a lot of confidential stuff I need to discuss with you. Why don't you go down and get your tea and then maybe we could go to the conference room. It's empty. I checked.'

'Fine. I'll be back shortly.'

She was certainly not going to ask him if she could bring him something.

When she came back he was already in the conference room.

She sat at the table, deliberately leaving one chair between them.

He had spread out his papers.

'So,' she started out. She felt a little out of her

279

element. She was an experienced reporter, but investigative reporting was a different kind of talent. She wasn't completely confident dealing with this particular subject.

'What have you got?'

'It's complicated.'

Was he questioning her ability to deal with it?

'Try me.'

He looked at her hard.

'The problem is, I don't know exactly what I do have. It's little bits and pieces of the puzzle but nothing really tracks so far.'

'Well, why don't we start at the beginning. How did you get onto the story? What was the first thing that you learned?'

Walt had taught her a trick early on. 'You can't let the fuckers intimidate you,' he had told her, 'which they will always try to do. They know more and if it isn't in your area of expertise you can feel very insecure. The fact is that it's your ass on the line, not theirs. Eventually you're going to have to explain it to the people above you and if you can't you're in deep shit. So ask the stupidest questions you can think of, as if you're the reporter and you're going to have to go back and write the story and you're going to have to understand it.'

'I think,' said Tyson, 'that would be a waste of time. Why don't I just give you the overall picture?'

'Actually, Sprague, why don't you start at the beginning? Tell me what was the first thing you learned that made you think you had a story.'

'You have to establish that you're the boss,' Walt had told her. 'They are reporting to you. It's your right to know everything they know and they have to tell you.'

280

'There's a drug problem in this country,' he said.

This was going to be difficult. He was belittling her.

'Very good. Now go to the head of the class.'

'I don't think this is going to work, Allison,' he said. The muscles in his jaw were twitching.

'It has to work, Sprague. I'm your editor. It goes to me first. You went to the Citadel, I'm told. You understand the chain of command. Perhaps you have a problem with my being a woman?'

'No. I have a problem with your not knowing anything about the drug scene.'

'And do you have a problem with Alan Warburg not knowing anything about it? Because he is the executive editor and he'll have to make the final decision about whether this story will run.'

'Presumably it will have been edited carefully before it gets to him.'

'Ah yes. And by whom? Walt Fineman, the managing editor and well-known drug expert?'

'So what's your point, ma'am?'

'Insubordination will not be tolerated. You work with me or you work with nobody.'

'Yes, ma'am.'

This was not the end of it. She didn't have the feeling she had won. But at least he didn't get up and storm out.

'Now, do you want to tell me what you know?'

'I've been nosing around the Drug Enforcement Agency.' He was very businesslike. She noticed he didn't say DEA. Was he patronizing her?

'Who was your contact?'

He paused.

'An agent I met on a story in New Orleans while I was at the Savannah paper. When I got up here I
281

called him. We've had lunch a couple of times. He's put me on to something big. But I don't know yet. He tells me the head of the DEA, Mike Garcia, is worried about what's going on over at Justice. Apparently our illustrious attorney general, Roy Fox, has become friendly with some Colombian dame named Antonia Alvarez. She's with the embassy working in the military liaison office. Her father's one of the big landowners and tight with Alberto Mendez, the Foreign Minister. Foxy met her at some embassy party and has taken her out a couple of times. DEA have had their eye on Mendez for a while in connection with some drug barges that came in through New Orleans that were connected to one of his family's companies. Anyway, Garcia apparently talked to the A.G. and he says he wants to keep it in Justice and has steered the DEA away from the story. Plus, he's making noises about trying to consolidate the DEA into the FBI, which is driving Garcia crazy.'

'It sounds like you've got several stories here. And maybe some that ought to go in the paper sooner rather than later. The FBI merger with DEA, for instance.'

'Well, I hadn't thought of it ... I mean, I don't want to blow my sources...'

She had him. He hadn't seen two stories. Clearly the FBI merger plan with DEA was a great daily story and one that might not hold. It hadn't occurred to him. She was in command—certainly for the first time ever with Tyson. Though she hadn't really worked closely with him before. He had been out on his own since August developing sources. He was just now coming up with something.

'As soon as we finish here we'll go see Fineman about the merger story. And we'd better talk to Estrella. He's covering the FBI and he might know something. Have you discussed this with him?'

'No, but this is my—'

'We can't have him pick up the paper and read an FBI story. Maybe he's working on the same lead.'

'Whoa. Wait just a minute. I've been working on this one for three months—'

'Tyson.' She was getting more self-assured by the second. 'We're all in the same army.'

'Knock off the military metaphor, will ya.'

She burst out laughing, in spite of herself, and detected a flicker of appreciative amusement.

'Okay, back to the story. You've got one source so far. Your DEA friend from New Orleans. How good is he and where's your second source?'

'My source is the guy who won me the Pulitzer Prize in Savannah. My second source is Garcia. I was getting to that. I had lunch with him last week and I've been following up on some stuff he told me. The guy is ballistic about the possible merger. It's not going to happen, at least I don't think so, but morale in the DEA is in the toilet for a lot of reasons and one of them is this merger thing. His guys are getting paid shit, they're getting their brains blown out all over Central America, they have no authority compared to the other agencies, and they have no political power where it counts. Also, Garcia does not trust Foxy. He's worried about the A.G.'s relationship with Antonia Alvarez. He says she's a real piece of work. Checkered past. The best private schools, university education, a lot of dough. She's very much the ruling class but a real hell-raiser and has a perverse set of values. He's

283

also got several of his guys onto Mendez. Frankly, I think Mendez is in up to his neck in the Medellin cartel but I can't prove it. I've got to go back to New Orleans and then I'll have to go down and spend some time in Colombia. Garcia will keep talking to me. He's so fed up he's about to take a walk. I'm dead and so is he if anybody finds out that he's talking to me. That includes Estrella. Do you understand what I'm telling you?'

'I do. So here's what we're going to do. The merger thing is a story. You can get on that and do it yourself unless you think it will blow your sources for you. If you don't want to do that we can let Estrella have it without revealing your sources. Let him use his own, check it out himself. We'll go to Fineman on that right now. On the Antonia Alvarez-Foxy story, that may not hold either. Get on that and see what you come up with. The Mendez thing is big. Particularly if there is any possibility of a cover-up on the part of the A.G. I'd spend some more time at Justice. Hang around, develop some sources, see what you come up with. And see if they've gotten any wind of it up on the Hill. Lauren's got to get cut in on the fact that you're over there. The Hill is her beat and she'll get her nose out of joint if you don't.'

'You don't get it. Sterling. I can't just tell them—'

'You don't get it, Tyson. These people cover these departments. That's their job. If you go in there and big-foot them, they're going to get pissed. You don't have to tell them what you're after, but you've got to let them know you're around. Don't be so sure they can't help you. It's so easy. All you have to do is flatter them, ask their advice, they'll

284

be happy to help. If you stumble on a story they can use they'll love you. Trust me.'

'What about Colombia?'

'Check out the Antonia-Foxy thing first. If that'll hold then go to Colombia.'

'Okay.'

She could tell he was impressed. She felt as though she had cleared a major hurdle in her job. Tyson was a challenge for any editor, new or old, male or female.

'Now let's go see Fineman.'

She picked up her notebook and pencil while he gathered his papers from the table.

As they started toward the door of the conference room she turned to him.

'Oh, and Tyson.'

He looked up and his eyes met hers.

'Yes, ma'am?'

'Don't get yourself killed.'

'Is that an order?'

'That's an order.'

&#42;   &#42;   &#42;

'Jesus, I'd rather be a lion tamer. I had no idea it would be like this. You've got to keep them up on their little perches and keep that whip cracking all the time or they'll maul you.'

They were having dinner at Le Steak in Georgetown. It was the night after their 'lunch' at the Willard. Allison had told him then that she needed to think about marriage. She had thought about it. She had called him that day to suggest dinner. She loved Le Steak on a snowy night, dim lighting, candles on the table, the Côte du Rhône,

285

steamy French bread and sweet butter, tangy salad dressing, juicy steak with fabulous sauce, and incredible french fries. Five thousand calories and the loss of a night's sleep on a full stomach was worth the pleasure.

Des was in a great mood, pleased with himself. He obviously thought she was going to say yes. He looked gorgeous.

She felt quite shy. She wanted to keep the conversation on an impersonal level at first. There was so much to talk about it was easier to talk about nothing.

She had already told him about Sprague. Now she was bubbling over with enthusiasm about his change, though slight, in attitude toward her.

Des was less impressed than she thought he should be.

'I say send the fucker back to Savannah and let him rot there. You don't need to put up with that kind of shit from anybody.'

'I know, Des. But he could win the Pulitzer on this one.'

'So what? What's the Pulitzer worth these days, anyway? It's a total farce and everyone knows it. It's politics. It has nothing to do with merit. Look what happens when these prizewinners from small papers are hired away by the big ones after they've won. Most of the time they can't hack it. They're in over their heads. But they can't just keep giving prizes to the same top papers every year. So these guys get screwed year after year in favor of people who can't hold a candle to them. I don't see why the big papers don't just get out of the prize game altogether.'

'We've been over this before. It means a lot to the

286

reporters. We can't do that to them. You sound like Alan and Walt. It ruins their spring every year.'

'I still say that Tyson is overrated, and I can't stand the idea of that little shit giving you a hard time.'

'Well, then, why don't you go beat him up? That will show him. My great big macho man.'

'Maybe I'll just do that. How about another glass of wine, baby? It will relax you.'

'Are you trying to get me drunk, Desmond Shaw?'

'Just trying to loosen you up for the kill.'

'I'm loose.'

'So how about next week?'

'That doesn't give us much time.'

'Time for what?'

'Planning.'

'What do we need to plan? We get the license, we get the blood tests, we get the judge, we do it.'

'Des, for Christ's sake, we're getting married, not registering to vote. There's a little more to it than that. We have to send out invitations, plan the party, get a caterer, get a dress, get wedding rings—'

'Wait, wait, wait—'

'There's a lot to do.'

'Sonny.'

'What?'

'I can't go through all that again.'

'All what?'

'I can't go through a wedding. I've done that. It would be humiliating. I just want to do it. We can celebrate later with our friends. But I just don't want it to be a big fucking deal.'

'Excuse me, Des. But I haven't done it before

and it's my wedding, too, and it is a big fucking deal.'

'Oh God, I was afraid this would happen.'

'You mean you were afraid that the bride might want a wedding? What an outrageous thing to want. What kind of a person would want to ruin a perfectly decent marriage with an actual wedding?'

'I'm not saying that.'

'Well, what exactly are you saying?'

'I'm not good at this, Sonny. I'm not trying to be a hard ass. I'm not trying to deprive you of something that's important to you, though I honestly didn't think you would want a wedding. But I feel I owe you an explanation.'

He poured each of them another glass of red wine. Then he took her hand and looked at her.

'I love you, Sonny. Just know that.'

She could feel herself wavering.

'I'm Catholic.'

'A lapsed Catholic.'

'I've never bought this lapsed business. There's no such thing. You can't let it go. I'm not practicing in that I don't go to Mass every Sunday, but I need a slow steady drizzle of Catholicism in my life to feed my soul.'

She fell back in the chair. 'I have to tell you, I'm stunned.'

'I don't talk about it. Mostly I don't even think about it. It's just there.'

'What does that have to do with having a wedding?'

'In the eyes of the Church I'm already married.'

She started to speak but he interrupted her.

'I'm legally divorced. But part of me believes it doesn't count. I have seriously contemplated having

288

my marriage to Chessy annulled or something.'

'How could you even think of such a thing? How do you explain Fiona? Does she not exist or do you propose to make her a bastard overnight?'

'Of course I'm not going to do it. I'm trying to give you some understanding of the depths of my feeling. A second marriage is hard for me. I'm going against everything I've been brought up to believe. I'm going to do it because intellectually I know it's the right thing to do. But it ain't easy.'

'Intellectually? You're going to marry me because intellectually you know it's the right thing to do? Screw that, Des. What about emotionally? How do you think this makes me feel? It's as if I'm dragging you into some horrible bondage. Well, I don't want that.'

'God, Sonny. You want to know how I feel and then when I tell you you get all bent out of shape. I'm trying to explain to you why I don't want some big public wedding.'

'Des, I'm not exactly asking for the National Cathedral and twelve bridesmaids. But I want our friends to be part of it. I'm happy and proud to be your wife. Either you feel that way about me or there's not going to be a wedding. I can't marry somebody who's ashamed to be marrying me.'

'Christ, you drive a tough bargain.'

'I'm not angry. I'm just telling you how I feel.'

'Why don't we tell the man how we want our steaks and get another bottle of wine. I think this is a two-bottle night.'

He dispatched the waiter, and turned to her, this time with amusement, but she sensed there was respect in his glance.

'All right, Miss Sterling. What sort of wedding

would you like?'

'I'd sort of pictured myself in a white silk suit. I'd like to get married someplace pretty like the living room of the F Street Club in front of the fireplace with about fifty or so friends, champagne, a small supper, and some nice music if we want to dance. And a cake at the end. With a bride and groom on top.'

He had been listening approvingly until the cake. Then he winced.

'That's going too far.'

'Give me a break, Shaw. It's a wedding.'

'Okay. Okay. A bride and groom on the cake. So who marries us?'

'How about Judge Frankel?'

'Okay, I'll agree to all of that. It is a compromise. And I have one request, I'd like my brother, Martin, to say a prayer at the ceremony.'

Her face fell. She sighed.

'A priest saying a prayer at my wedding? God. What kind of prayer? I mean, I would feel so hypocritical being an atheist and having to listen—'

'It's my wedding, too. You don't have to believe a word he says. This one is for me. I'll ask him to write it himself.'

'Okay, Martin will say a prayer.'

Their dinner was served and they both dug in without saying a word to each other.

'Compromise is so exhausting,' Allison said finally, with a mock sigh, and they both laughed with relief.

'You know, you're more trouble than any dame I could ever have hooked up with. Why do I do this to myself?'

'Because everybody else bores your ass, that's

290

why.'

'Is that it?'

'Des, while we're hammering out issues, can we get a few other things out of the way?'

'Do we have to?'

'This will only take a minute. Babies?'

'How many?'

'One.'

'Okay, next?'

'Does it have to be Catholic?'

'I wish you could see the expression on your face,' he said, chuckling. 'No, I believe the mother determines a child's religion. I was never good at that. God knows what Fiona is.'

'Two wedding rings?'

'I've never worn a wedding ring in my life. It is the ultimate sign of the pussy-whipped male. I can't believe that you really want me to wear one. Do you?'

She thought about this for a moment, then smiled.

'Actually, you're right. I don't want you to. It shows that I have the ultimate confidence.'

'So that's it, I hope. Mary and Joseph, I feel as if I've conducted the Arab-Israeli summit. Yet all I've done is negotiate with the future Mrs Desmond Shaw.'

'Uh, Des?'

'Yes.'

'There's one more thing...'

Dear Sadie,

By now you've probably heard that Allison and I will be married today.

I thank you for releasing me.

291

I hope your guy knows how lucky he is. I hope he makes you happy.

Give my 'special friend' a hug for me.

And one for yourself with more feeling than you know.

Always,<br>
Des

## CHAPTER ELEVEN

'Blanche, it's Sadie.'

'Well, hey here, lady. Did you bring me back a gorgeous island native? Like the ones with the machetes and the sharks' teeth hanging down on their bare bronze chests?'

'Actually I was saving him for myself,' Sadie laughed.

'Languishing on a tropical beach while I had to spend Christmas at Camp David with all of my horrible stepchildren. It was like being with the Beverly Hillbillies—and I should know.'

Blanche tickled Sadie, but it was clear why she had a problem with the press.

'So, did you have a great time?'

'Actually, I did, believe it or not,' said Sadie. 'I surprised even myself. There was a doctor there who was in the emergency room the night Rosey was shot.'

'Oh, that sounds like fun.'

'No. I mean, yes. He and his wife have kids the same ages as mine. They were with another couple. Michael Lanzer and his wife. He's the head of the National Cancer Institute at NIH. I told you we ought to get ahold of him for the AIDS project.'

'Oh yeah, the one who discovered that drug, what's it called—AZT?'

'I talked to him about the idea of AIDS being a project for you and he was interested. He has lots of ideas about things you could do. I really think this could be a great thing for you, especially with somebody like him. He's extremely articulate and very funny. You'd love him and he would love you.'

'Is he cute?'

'He's married.'

'So, he's that cute, huh? Nobody ever says "he's married" unless the guy's real cute.'

'Blanche.'

She found herself becoming flustered. She couldn't let Blanche detect how she felt about Michael. Maybe she had already.

'I thought you might want to set up a meeting with him.' She was intent on being serious. 'It's been six months. You've got to get some project going.'

'I know. I know. You're right. Freddy's been on my case, too. Okay, how do we do this?'

'Why don't I call him and tell him you're interested. Then I'll call your secretary and she can set something up with the three of us.'

'Oh, you're going to chaperone? Or am I the chaperone?'

'Blanche!'

'Don't be so touchy. I'm just teasing... A cute doctor? That doesn't sound bad at all. What if he has AIDS? Did you think of that?'

Sadie laughed in spite of herself.

'You're hopeless. Goodbye, Blanche.'

'May I speak to Dr Lanzer, please, this is Mrs Grey calling.'

Why did she feel so guilty? The secretary didn't even know she was the former First Lady. The secretary heard 'This is Mrs Grey calling' not 'This is Mrs Grey calling. You know the former First Lady and I'm crazy about Dr Lanzer and I intend to make mad passionate love to him and take him away from his adoring wife and destroy his family.'

'Oh yes, Mrs Grey. Dr Lanzer said you might be calling. Just a moment and I'll let him know you're on the line.'

What! Dr Lanzer had told his secretary that she might be calling. What arrogance! What had made him so certain she might be calling? She had a good mind to hang up. At least that would force him to call her. But it was too late for that.

'Dr Lanzer will be right with you if you don't mind holding for just a moment.'

'No, that's okay, that's fine, thank you.'

It seemed like five minutes before he came on the line. With no apology.

'Hey, how are ya?'

'Exhausted.'

'Why?'

He cared.

'From the anticipation of waiting for you to come on the line.'

'Happy New Year to you, too.'

'Oh, yes. I knew there was something I'd forgotten to say to you.'

Bring him back to the beach. Make him remember. He wasn't going to get away with this clipped, professional, businesslike tone with her.

'More than that, I hope.'

Good. She had him back now.

'Did you get my note?'

'I did.'

'Good.'

There was a silence. She didn't know how to keep him there. She couldn't think of anything else to say.

'I talked to Blanche Osgood this morning.'

'About?'

'Excuse me, you are the Dr Lanzer who was at La Samanna in St Martin last week, aren't you?'

'Oh, we're going to play hardball today, are we?'

'Well, I did talk to you at length about Blanche needing a project and how we had thought AIDS might be the perfect answer for her.'

'I think I repressed it.'

'Oh Michael.'

'Why do I have a horrible feeling about this? That I'm being sacrificed to the First Lady for the good of the country. Why don't you just take me up to the roof of the temple of the Sun God and put a dagger through my heart? It will be quicker and less painful that way.'

She began to giggle.

'Here you go.'

'So. You talked to Blanche Osgood. And what did she say?'

Sadie could barely stop laughing.

'She wanted to know if you were cute.'

'Cute! Cute? She wanted to know if I was cute? People are dying all over the country from this plague and she wants to know if I'm cute? Is this your revenge for La Samanna? The First Lady's a

295

disaster. Something has to be done about her. Sacrifice a Jew for the cause. No problem.'

Sadie was laughing uncontrollably now.

'You really turn yourself on, don't you?' she said.

'Not as much as you do.'

He hadn't meant to say that, she could tell. She didn't respond. She just let it sink it. Torture him.

'So,' he said, clearing his throat. 'How do we proceed?'

'Since I'm the unofficial sponsor of this project I thought you might like to invite me out to the NIH so that you could tell me something about what the institute does. We could talk about some of the possible ways Blanche could get involved. I think it would be better if you and I were united—'

'This sounds dangerous.'

She ignored him.

'Anyway, I've got my calendar in front of me if you wanted to give me a date. I thought it would be nice if you gave me lunch.'

'I haven't had lunch with anybody in twenty years . . . where do you want to eat?'

'How about in your office? Can't we get them to bring a sandwich up or something? That way we won't have to go out and be stared at.'

'That's fine.'

'How's Monday?'

'Monday? Let's see. I, uh, I guess Monday is fine.'

'You don't sound excited.'

'Sorry. I have a very busy schedule. I have to be out of town two days next week and—'

'I'm flattered that you're able to work me in.'

'My reluctance only reflects a healthy sense of self-preservation.'

'Good. Then we have a mutual goal. I'll see you at ten on Monday. Bye now.'

★ ★ ★

This was not at all how she had imagined their first conversation. He was like a different person on the phone. Nothing like the romantic he had been at La Samanna. There was no warmth in this Dr Lanzer at all. Humor, yes. Reminiscent of the arrogance he had first displayed when she met him. But this humor was meant to intentionally erect a wall between them. The famous wall he had talked of on the beach. She thought the wall had come down. Or that he had scaled it. Now she found herself standing on the other side of it from him.

She had found this magical person on the island. She had allowed herself to be vulnerable. She had trusted him to treat her gently. Now he was pushing her away. She had thought her attraction to him sexual at first, but over the week her feelings had grown so intense that she didn't want only to make love to him. That was certainly something new. She had no idea who or what she was dealing with. She didn't understand him or herself. On the beach one evening he told her about a saying of the Hasidic Jews. 'While pursuing happiness we are in flight from contentment.' It sounded like something he was trying to convince himself of. Perhaps she represented happiness to him. Did Giselle represent contentment? He was drawn to happiness but the consequences were too frightening.

It was so complicated. Any other man would have tried to make love to her. She knew goddamn well he wanted her. So why didn't he try? Perhaps

297

she should just leave him alone. But she couldn't. She had Blanche and the AIDS thing to deal with. It was an excuse to see him again; it was a project for her. Finishing the novel she had started to write before Willie was born wasn't possible now. She couldn't concentrate. She needed to be around people.

She needed to be around him. She couldn't rid herself of the longing that overwhelmed her every time she thought of him, pictured him in her mind, remembered his voice, his touch, his kiss.

*       *       *

Her agents accompanied her up to the top floor of the Claude Pepper Building, through the wide glass double doors into the director's office of the National Cancer Institute.

Lanzer's secretaries were standing by the door waiting for her arrival. One of them took her coat, the other ushered her into the conference room.

'Dr Lanzer is on the phone but he will be with you in just a moment,' she said.

'Fine,' said Sadie. 'Thank you.'

The secretary closed the door, leaving Sadie alone.

She quickly took out a mirror and examined her face. She was pleased with the way she looked. She still had a blush of color from the tropical sun. Not too much makeup. This was a business meeting. Her simple black suit and white silk blouse with pearls would more than match his mood of the other day.

Her palms were perspiring and her teeth were actually chattering. She sat down at the conference table, but she couldn't sit still so she stood up and paced around the room.

The secretary had left two steaming cups of black coffee in black National Cancer Institute mugs on the table. At the head of the table were two pads—one yellow, one white—with several sharpened pencils.

On the wall on the cabinet was a sign that read: 'What part of "no" don't you understand?'

Was this a personal note to her?

No, I will not have an affair with you. No, I will not fall in love with you. No, I will not leave my wife for you. No, I will never marry you. What part of no don't you understand, you stupid shiksa?

This was ridiculous. She was working herself up over nothing. She walked over to the blackboard at the other end of the room. On it were diagrams notated with 'halogenated congeners of ddn: a new class of lipophillic prodrug'—completely undecipherable. So that's who he was. No wonder she didn't understand him. She would certainly never understand what he did.

It was fifteen minutes after ten. She had been there at ten sharp.

She walked over to the window. Directly across the street was Bethesda Naval Hospital and beyond was the Mormon temple, the silvery spires in contrast to the clear blue winter sky. Beyond that were rolling wooded hills all covered with powdery white snow. She shivered. Her body temperature still hadn't adjusted to the freezing temperatures since she had returned from St Martin.

She looked up at the clock on the wall. It was twenty-five minutes past ten. Now she was beginning to get angry. She couldn't help thinking

299

that he was deliberately keeping her waiting. Just to show her he was not impressed with who she was.

She walked over to the table and picked up a mug of coffee, putting in a little powdered cream and sugar. She'd wait five more minutes. She walked back over to the window and stared out at the spires of the Mormon temple again. It reminded her vaguely of the National Cathedral from that distance. It had only been six months since Rosey's funeral.

'I'm really sorry. I didn't mean to keep you waiting.'

'You're coffee's getting cold.' she said.

She could see he didn't know how to greet her. He paused, then walked over to her and put out his hand.

She looked at him, then withdrew beneath his gaze. She looked down at her hand gripping the black mug and transferred it to her other hand.

'My hands are cold,' she said self-consciously.

'I won't respond to that.'

He looked very appealing. He was wearing a blue buttoned-down shirt and tie with no jacket. His sleeves were rolled up and the hair on his arms was still slightly bleached from the sun. His eyes looked even bluer against his tan.

'You look great,' he said.

She was furious with herself for being so nervous.

She turned to walk over to the table, clearing her throat.

She sat down in her chair, leaned back, and crossed her legs. Maybe that would throw him off balance. Then they'd be even.

'Have you come up with any ideas we might think about for our project?' she asked.

300

'What do you mean "we," paleface?' he asked, laughing.

'Oh, no, you're not going to start that again, are you?'

'Actually, I have,' he said. 'Of course, it all depends on where you want to go with it.'

He sat in the chair at the head of the conference table and he immediately got down to business.

'What I would suggest,' he said, 'is to use this opportunity to convey a message, to convey certain information, to simplify, to acquire enthusiasm. Get the First Lady to be an informed advocate for the institute. Adopt a mission. Reward excellence, commitment, achievements. The enemy here is ignorance. It is essential to convey how important this is. Make people aware that AIDS is occurring in children. Get her to take a tour of the AIDS unit at Children's Hospital. Make people understand that we need to anticipate problems, identify problems.'

She looked at his hands.

'Now the issue is runaway children using sex to get money at risk of AIDS,' he was saying. His hands were arranging pencils in a neat row.

'The recent emergence of crack shows women exchanging sexual favors for drugs, which exposes them to AIDS. The First Lady can speak out. Make it unfashionable for people to harbor discrimination about AIDS. Human nature can't be changed. What can be changed is the guidance our leaders give us.'

He glanced up at her, met her eyes, and immediately looked away. He caressed his coffee cup. He was so earnest she had no choice but to pretend to listen.

301

'Everyone in Washington is so media hip that they deny or denigrate symbols of power or authority. They don't abide by them, they don't tap into where they are important. But symbols are important outside the beltway. You want the First Lady to feel affirmed by it, to lend support in discussions?'

It was a rhetorical question. She knew it was a question only because she heard the inflection at the end of his sentence..

She nodded. Now his hands were caressing his tie. Everything but her.

'I think you ought to get the President to set up a special committee on AIDS, something a little bit different from what's been done. This would be a committee of volunteers whose job would be to inform the public about all aspects of AIDS. Get him to appoint the First Lady as its chairperson. You be vice chair. Have meetings once a month. Get her to go around the country and give country music concerts to raise money for AIDS research and draw attention to the problem. It's important to get people to contribute in a way that suits them. Don't encourage her to try to be an expert on AIDS. She's not—neither are you for that matter. That's not to say that you two shouldn't both be as informed as possible yourselves.'

'Everything you say sounds brilliant. I'm sure the President and Blanche will think so too.'

She smiled at him.

For a moment it seemed he had lost track of what he was saying.

'My job has three parts really. Running the institute, seeing patients, and running the lab. That's the creative part. I have an intense feeling

302

that our success or failure determines the pattern of death and suffering for people we don't even know. Those are the consequences of not doing our job right. That's reality. If we don't do a good job people will die or suffer and won't know why.'

She had never heard a man talk that way about what he did. She couldn't imagine a politician, or a journalist for that matter, speaking with such passion. It wasn't that they didn't believe in what they did, or that what they did wasn't honorable, but that there was a different kind of commitment here. It was uncynical, a quality that was a hopeless impediment in the world of politics or journalism.

She understood for the first time what people meant when they said the brain was the true erogenous zone.

'I don't have time to visit the clinic today but I'd like to take you over there sometime. I'm good with my patients. I care about them.'

She didn't say anything.

'I'm a very good doctor, you know. I may not be very good at other things, but I am a good doctor.'

He said this with a mixture of shyness and pride.

Why was he telling her this? Trying to convince her? As if she needed convincing. She was so concerned about impressing him that it never occurred to her that he might actually want to impress her.

'I'm sure you're good at lots of things.'

She hadn't intended the double entendre, but they both flushed slightly.

He stood up.

'I've asked a few of our people to join us for lunch,' he said, looking out the window with his back to her. 'I thought it might be good for you to

303

get different perspectives on what we do here.'

He was putting up more barriers between them. Another wall?

Several men had appeared at the door of the conference room and Michael walked over to greet them, then introduced them to Sadie.

The meeting was virtually over for her. She knew perfectly well that she would have to make the first move if she were to see him the next time. And the next. And the next.

*　　*　　*

'Des and Allison are getting married.'

'I know. He sent me a note.'

'Are you all right?'

'I don't know. I think so. Yes. Sure. I'm fine.'

'Why?'

'What kind of question is that, Jenny?'

It was Sunday. Monica was off. Sadie and Jenny had walked Willie up to Montrose Park in his stroller. She had had to get out of the house. It was almost worse being the widow of an assassinated President than being the First Lady. Before she had been a celebrity, now she was some sort of sanctified object. People looked grim when they saw her.

Georgetown was a small community and most people respected her privacy. She could put on pants, boots, a knit cap, a parka with a hood, and dark glasses and people wouldn't necessarily recognize her as long as she stayed off the main streets. The park was empty. The day was overcast and cold and there was still a lot of snow on the ground. Willie was irresistible with those fat rosy

304

cheeks poking out of his hood, romping in the snow, then running over for reassuring hugs before going back at it again.

They had found a bench at the back of the park where they could see if anyone was approaching and keep an eye on Willie at the same time. The Secret Service agents, happy to get out, were throwing snowballs at Willie. Sadie had brought a thermos with some hot chocolate and they were sipping it when Jenny brought up the wedding.

'You amaze me, that's all,' said Jenny. 'One minute you are desperate over Des. The next minute he's getting married and you are totally sanguine about it. This is not the first time you have done this about-face with him. What's with you, anyway? I thought you were madly in love with him.'

'I was.'

'So. What's changed all that?'

She debated whether to tell her about Michael. What was there to tell? There must be something or she would be crushed about Des. Actually, she was dying to confide in someone. If she could confide in Jenny while she was having an affair as First Lady, she could certainly trust her now. Not that trust was the problem. In some ways, she just liked the idea of keeping Michael to herself. But she wasn't going to. She knew it.

'I've met somebody else.'

'Oh?'

'Speaking of which, he's Jewish.'

'Oh really?'

'He's five years younger.'

'Great.'

'He's a doctor.'

305

'A Jewish doctor, the worst kind.'

'He's married.'

'On the oy vey scale of one to ten, this is a ten.'

'I knew you'd approve.'

'What are you going to do about it?'

'Marry him.'

Sadie smiled when she said it. She had meant it as a joke. But once the words were out it didn't sound so funny.

Jenny stared at her, then smiled and shrugged. 'Mazel tov.'

★    ★    ★

This was going to be her first social outing in Washington since Rosey was shot. She found herself thinking and even saying 'since Rosey was shot' rather than 'since Rosey was killed' or 'since Rosey died.' Rosey had been shot and she didn't want to forget it or to let anyone else forget it either. 'Shot' was abrupt, violent, literal, shocking. When she said it people winced. She knew they would rather she used something more euphemistic. But euphemisms didn't convey what she wanted to say. She remembered a sign at Dachau, the German concentration camp which she had visited on a trip to Europe. *'Denket Daran.'* 'Think about it.' Remember it. The President of the United States, your President, my husband, my children's father was shot. Assassinated. Think about it.

Blanche had taken her up on the idea of having some small dinner parties upstairs in the family quarters. Make the first one a Valentine's Day party, Sadie had suggested. Something very un-Washington, fun, and friendly. Sadie had given

306

her a basic guest list of about forty people to cull
from. She thought three or four round tables of
eight would be about right. And a good mix. She
had suggested that they take this opportunity to
announce the President's Committee on AIDS. She
had also convinced Blanche that she ought to
surprise everyone by singing a few songs for them.
Invite the top male country singer and do a few
duets. Then explain that she was going to start
having concerts to raise money and awareness of
AIDS. Sadie even jotted down a few ideas for
Blanche to use for her remarks. She had persuaded
Blanche to invite the Lanzers.

Sadie had already introduced Michael to Blanche
and the President. Freddy seemed satisfied that
Blanche and Sadie were happy and arranged for
Michael to meet with Freddy's chief of staff.
Blanche thought Michael 'real smart' and 'kind of
cute' but pronounced him 'not my type.'

Sadie had planned on controlling the guest list,
but it had gotten away from her. The Sohiers were
her suggestion, as were the Warburgs. She had also
suggested Worth Elgin, the editor of the Opinion
section of the *Daily*, and his social-climbing wife,
Clare. She had insisted on Lorraine Hadley even
though she was on the wane. Gossip was still a large
part of Washington and Lorraine a key purveyor.

Senator and Mrs Corwin would be crucial. He
had banked his whole career on Defense but after
*glasnost*, he had been quick to see that Defense
issues were going to take a backseat. He had
quickly adopted health care as his new issue. The
new head of Health and Human Services was a
woman, a doctor, and quite well thought of.

The anchor of 'Good Night,' Benton Halloran,

was somebody who got around town, although he was known to have an alcohol problem.

The whole point of the evening was to make Blanche look good.

Unbeknownst to Sadie, however, Blanche had invited Foxy, who did not have the greatest press in Washington and who, as a bachelor attorney general, was clearly on his way to becoming an embarrassment to the administration. Foxy was bringing his new girlfriend, the second secretary at the Colombian embassy, Antonia Alvarez. Sadie had read about her in the Feature section of the *Daily*. Antonia was making quite a splash. She was the daughter of a very wealthy landowner in Colombia who had spent some time in Cuba in a period of revolutionary fervor before returning home to join the Foreign Ministry. Antonia was young, beautiful, sexy, and outspoken, which had gotten her a lot of publicity.

Blanche had also invited Des and Allison. She would have no way of knowing about Sadie and Des. Nobody knew. Des was the *Weekly* bureau chief and a regular on the weekend Sunday morning talk show. Allison was the *Daily*'s national editor. They could influence a lot of people. If they decided Blanche was on the level, it would be a big help.

Sadie tried to explain to Blanche that inviting Allison and Des to a small intimate party with Foxy and the Alvarez woman was inviting trouble. She was, in effect, serving up Foxy on a platter. They were not coming to the White House for a cozy evening. They were coming to get a story. They were good journalists, which meant they were killers. Nobody was safe around them, particularly not a man like Foxy who was not housebroken. And

308

certainly not White Housebroken.

Blanche was adamant. Freddy had insisted he couldn't have a party where there would be country singers from Nashville, people who were friends of Foxy's, and not have his old buddy. And Freddy was certain he could handle them. When Blanche told her Des and Allison were coming, Sadie had nearly dropped out of the party.

It was Jenny who had talked her into going. Jenny had persuaded her that she was going to be running into them from now on and she might as well have the first time be in a controlled environment. Besides, Jenny had reminded her, Michael Lanzer would be there. Michael Lanzer, the man she would one day marry.

★          ★          ★

'You can't turn down an invitation to the White House, Michael. You know that. It just isn't done unless you're making some grand gesture of political protest.'

'But I don't want to go to this dinner party.'

'Why not?'

'Because I hate parties.'

'You don't hate parties. You love parties. You're extremely gregarious.'

'Oh, I see. I love parties. Sorry. I must have gotten confused.'

'C'mon, Michael, don't be silly. This is serious.'

Sadie was completely exasperated. Michael had gotten his invitation from the White House and had called her to complain. At least he had called her. It was, in fact, the first time. What she had to remember was that he was a married man. Still, she was used to getting what she wanted. It was frustrating and challenging at the same time.

'You're right, it's serious. I'm serious. I don't want to go.'

'Look, you've gone to lots of parties. I've seen your picture in the feature section of the *Daily* several times at these cancer and AIDS benefits.'

'Right. And it's surrealistic. I feel like I'm external graft, some foreign transplant with all those Hollywood types. I've done that in one era and I don't want to do it anymore. I didn't feel genuine. There's a certain artificial camaraderie, conviviality at these things.'

'Michael, we're talking about a few hours out of your life for a cause you care desperately about.'

'A few hours. You just put your finger on it. I've got to prioritize. I can't spend fifteen or sixteen hours a day here and then go out at night. Time is the most important thing I've got.'

'There's always the chance you might meet somebody interesting, learn something. Have you ever thought of that?'

She was getting more frustrated by the minute, even though he was obviously enjoying their little sparring match.

'Look, I just don't feel comfortable in that role. So I meet some countess or some industrialist. So what? There's nothing in that for me. If there were a group of scientists or clinicians or family support groups, then there's some role for me.'

'Okay, Michael. What's the real reason? Is it Giselle?'

'Giselle has nothing to do with it,' he said curtly.

'Well, then, what is it?'

'You want to know what the real reason is. I'll

tell you what the real reason is: I hate, loathe, and despise wearing a tuxedo.'

'Ha! I knew it. I knew it was something incredibly dumb.'

'Dumb? You know what's dumb? Having to buy one. What that meant to me was a demarcating line, a dividing point in my life, a symbol of change. I'd never owned a tuxedo. I'd always rented one for the rare wedding or bar mitzvah. Then after this AZT thing and this job I had to start going to these black tie parties. It gets pretty expensive to rent them and if you go to more than three a year you're better off buying one. Then there are all the accessories. You have to understand, a tuxedo is not my uniform. A tie is as far as I want to go. With the exception of weddings and a few scientific awards ceremonies I rarely do anything I respect in a tuxedo. It's kind of an indignity.'

'I bet you look smashing in a dinner jacket.'

'Don't try that on me, Mrs Grey.'

'Let me try this one on you, then.'

'It better be good.'

'I need you. I'm asking you to go as a favor to me.'

He could tell she wasn't teasing anymore.

'Why?'

'Des and Allison will be there. They just got married.'

'So I read.'

'Please.'

'Okay, you got me.'

'God, you're easy, Dr Lanzer,' she said and hung up before he could respond.

★    ★    ★

311

Blanche had asked her advice about the seating, as with everything else. Sadie was a master at seating. Seating was everything. It was an art. Any diplomat would tell you that thoughtless seating has been responsible for starting wars. Lorraine would never forget, she told Sadie, the night the French ambassador stormed out of her house before dinner because he felt he had been insulted by his seat.

'Below the salt' was the most dreaded phrase in Washington, Sadie had learned. That was why she had taken to round tables. It solved so many problems, not only protocol, but from the standpoint of enjoyment. At a small round table nobody could have a terrible time. If one's dinner partner was a disaster one could always get a group discussion going.

Of course, Sadie didn't really take much of what Lorraine had to say these days to heed. Not only was Lorraine a dying breed, the Washington Party was going the way of the Washington Hostess, as well.

The problem was that Washington was in effect in its third-term presidency. Roger was a Democrat, then Rosey, now Freddy. Though the latter two had brought some of their own people in with them, they had inherited the office. So they had kept most of the same people on. Not only that, but they had drawn from Democrats who had been in office twenty and twenty-five years earlier, long before the Republican administration that preceded Roger had come into power. What this meant to Washington was that everybody knew everybody else.

Washington parties were working events. People

312

went to parties to meet people, make contacts, exchange information, more or less like a Middle Eastern bazaar. Parties were neutral territory where people from opposite political camps could lay down their arms and break bread together without hostility or animosity. They were the arena where those from the Hill, from the administration, from the press corps, diplomatic corps, military, and the vast numbers of lobbyists could meet and trade.

Parties were an extension of the workday. Only the clothes changed. Black tie was becoming rarer and rarer, so even the uniform remained the same.

If people were going to continue to work after they left the office they needed a pretty good reason since work ended around eight. The reason for parties had always been to meet people. But Washington was no longer a transient stopover. Now everyone knew everyone else. Their children had grown up together. There was no point in entertaining anymore. With no forum, the would-be hostesses had all gone out and gotten jobs.

This was relaxing for the social and political climbers, and for those who put in twelve-hour days. For journalists and writers, however, it was nothing short of deadly. No forum, no gossip, no news.

This was one reason Blanche was in such trouble. If there had been a lot going on, the press would have been distracted by substantive issues and events. But with the town so dull, anybody was fair game, especially the First Lady.

\*   \*   \*

313

Blanche was annoyed with Foxy for inviting Antonia Alvarez because she had wanted him as an extra man for Sadie, but Sadie had persuaded her that that was a terrible idea. The 'Good Night' anchor's wife was away so there was an extra man. Still, it would be the first time she had attended a party since Rosey had been shot, and the idea of walking into a room, particularly at the White House, particularly alone, was terrifying.

What made it even more difficult was that Michael would be there with his wife and Des would be there with his wife.

Even though she knew it was going to be hard, Sadie hadn't quite anticipated the trepidation she felt as she got out of her car and was escorted into the diplomatic entrance as a guest at a White House party for the first time in six years.

She did know she had to look perfect. Maybe it was frivolous, but if she looked great she wouldn't feel like such a pitiful person. She had read about widows who felt a loss of self-esteem when their husbands died. It had never occurred to her she would be one of them. She had too much going for her. Yet now she was feeling it. It didn't make things easier that she was the widow of a President.

She knew that even though the fitted turquoise cut-velvet dress became her, even though her hair seemed to have more body than it ever had, framing her face provocatively, even though she still had a little honey-coloured glow from the sun at La Samanna—it was worth a couple of wrinkles later—and her hands and feet had been manicured and she had spent what seemed like hours on her makeup, and was wearing sexy new underwear to give herself more confidence and she had had a

314

massage to relax her ... even so, she was a mess.

She had planned to arrive late. That would irritate Blanche, since Blanche had billed it as Sadie's coming-out party. However, she hadn't actually put it on the invitations. She had a choice between standing with Freddy and Blanche as the guests arrived or making an entrance after everyone was there. She chose the latter. That way nobody would feel sorry for her. She could stand anything but that.

★     ★     ★

Everyone was there when she got off the elevator on the second floor of the White House. She only saw two faces. She saw Michael and she saw Des. She wanted to get back on the elevator and disappear. This was going to be too hard. Then she saw the President. Freddy. Not Rosey—the idea of Freddy as President was still grotesque. She and Rosey had argued over it many times before he chose him. Politics had won out. Rosey had been right. But then Rosey had thought of himself as invincible. Rosey hadn't counted on getting shot.

Sadie looked around the room and saw that all eyes were on her. Curiosity was what she saw first. Faces that had prepared to be sympathetic turned to admiration.

'Well, don't you look scrumptious, Miss Sara Adabelle,' said Freddy Osgood.

He took both her hands in his and held them up to his mouth to kiss them.

Blanche, who was only just recovering from the sight of Sadie, walked over to her right behind Freddy.

315

'Oh Freddy, don't be such a cornball. Who do you think you are, some kinda French count?'

'How 'bout President of the U-nited States?' he asked.

'Well, excuuuuuuuse me,' she said, raising one eyebrow.

'Come on, you two,' said Sadie smiling. 'Everybody's looking at us.'

'That's right, Freddy. They'll think we're Maw and Paw Kettle.'

Sadie pretended to miss the edge in their voices.

The President turned to take her into the crowd.

'I'm sure you know everybody, Sadie, but let me just take you around the room.'

Sadie glanced over at Blanche. She could see her eyes were moist as she forced a smile.

Blanche was a disaster. Her platinum hair was piled on top of her head with several rhinestone clips. Her dress was a white form-fitting number covered with rhinestones and beads. It had a rectangular-shaped cutout right above her ample breasts. She didn't look as if she belonged in Washington, much less in the White House.

'What's wrong?' Sadie whispered.

'What's wrong is that you look like the First Lady and I look like fifty dollars for all night upstairs—that's what's wrong.'

Before Sadie could say a word Freddy was guiding her into the group.

He introduced her to the country music singers Blanche had invited from Nashville, then to the Corwins, the Warburgs, and the Elgins whom she knew, of course. At last she was in front of Des and Allison. She thought she felt perspiration on her forehead. She wondered if Allison would notice.

316

Des looked straight at her. There was conflict in his eyes, and guilt. And love?

They leaned slightly toward each other, neither sure whether they should kiss or shake hands. He took her hand and leaned further forward, giving her the option. She took his hand and offered a cheek, which he brushed lightly and pulled away quickly.

'How are you?' he asked, aware that the whole room and Allison were watching.

'Congratulations,' said Sadie. Her own voice sounded odd to her. 'And I should say best wishes to the bride.'

She turned to Allison.

Allison looked gorgeous.

She had on a satin floor-length dress that was pale blue-gray, the color of her eyes. The only jewelry she wore was a pair of blue-gray pearl earrings. She was elegant and simple and understated. Suddenly Sadie felt like fifty dollars for all night upstairs.

'Thank you,' said Allison.

They stared at each other awkwardly, Allison searching Sadie's face for clues. Sadie knew Allison was wondering whether she was going to leave Des alone, or whether she would have a go at him again if things got rough.

'How's Willie?' asked Allison abruptly.

'Jenny was telling us she'd spent the day with you and Willie recently,' said Des quickly. 'She talks about him all the time. You'd think she was the real mother.'

Des froze as he said this. So did Sadie. But Allison laughed innocently and Sadie relaxed.

'Y'all monopolizin' Sadie,' said Freddy. 'Let me finish taking you around.'

317

Benton Halloran, the 'Good Night' anchor, was talking to Foxy and leering at Antonia Alvarez. He was already half in the bag, Sadie was disturbed to note. She had been so preoccupied with Des that she hadn't focused on the fact that Freddy was leading her to the head of HHS, Rose Horowitz, who was talking earnestly to Michael and Giselle. She could tell Michael was trying desperately to pay attention to her as he followed Sadie's progress through the room.

Sadie felt like an Olympic sprinter who had just cleared a major hurdle, only to have to repeat her feat.

'I guess I don't have to introduce the good doctor, do I?' said Freddy.

Sadie realized he'd forgotten Michael's name.

Giselle stiffened.

Sadie was ready, once more, to turn and flee. She decided to address Giselle first.

'Giselle, I'm so happy to see you,' she exclaimed. 'I'm only sorry we're not at La Samanna. I hope you recovered from your illness.'

'Yes, thank you,' said Giselle.

She turned to Michael casually.

'Michael,' she said.

They shook hands formally.

'Let's go see how Blanche is doing,' Freddy proposed, and Sadie moved away gratefully.

Blanche was hyperventilating.

'Sadie, what do you think, how does everything look? Do you think we should go in for dinner?'

'Blanche, relax. It's perfect. You look wonderful and everything looks heavenly. Everyone's going to have a great time. It's already a success. You can just tell.'

318

'Thanks to you. You did it all.'

That was, in fact, the truth.

Sadie had chosen the French tablecloths with hearts on them, overseen the flower arrangements, talked to the chef about the menu, helped with the heart-shaped decorations, and suggested to Blanche that she and her music guests from Nashville entertain everyone after dinner.

'You don't think people will think it's tacky?' Blanche had asked.

'Blanche, it will be different. It will be un-Washington. It will be totally you. That's the point.'

But now Sadie was observing the fruits of her labors with satisfaction. She knew that giving Blanche the credit was smart. It didn't hurt for people to know she had an influence over the First Lady and, therefore, the President. Not that she cared for social reasons. It just made it easier for her to get things done. What she wanted to get done now was to help Michael make AIDS an important project for Blanche.

The cocktails were held at one end of the great hall, which also doubled as a living room for the family.

Sadie had suggested putting tables in the oval room, which was normally used as the formal reception room in the family quarters to make the dinner cozy. Candles were the only lighting.

Sadie, of course, had done the seating. She had put herself at Freddy's table on his right so she could act more or less as hostess. He had wanted her there too for moral support more than anything else. On his other side she had put Abigail Sohier, who could make anyone feel comfortable. On her other side was the now-tipsy Benton Halloran. She had never met him, but Des had told her, when he was doing the Sunday morning talk show, what a lush the guy was. She was curious about him. He was so appealing on the air. She had placed Michael at her table but not next to her. He was seated between the head of Health and Human Services and Antonia Alvarez. That should keep him awake.

Des and Allison were at other tables. She had put Des next to Blanche. Let's see how he fared with this First Lady. But Des would like Blanche, she knew. He liked sexy 'dames' and she would amuse him. Allison she had put next to Lorraine's boring husband, Archie, in an uncharitable moment, but had compensated by putting Foxy on her other side. Sadie thought Foxy was bad news. Allison would have a field day with Foxy.

The noise level was very high during dinner. A sure sign of success. Sadie could see that Blanche had relaxed and was having a good time with Des as well as with Alan Warburg on her other side. She had put her between two journalists. Blanche wanted good press. This was her chance.

Sadie had begun at her table by talking first to Halloran. Halfway through the main course she turned the table. Just as she turned to Freddy she heard Antonia Alvarez ask Michael, in a pronounced Spanish accent, 'Why aren't you afraid to get AIDS yourself, Dr Lanzer?'

Sadie looked at Michael only to see him glance quickly at her.

The table quietened as everyone looked at Lanzer.

'There is,' said Michael carefully, 'an unspoken camaraderie among people working in a lab where

320

there is a live AIDS virus. People have acquired AIDS in the lab.'

'And how do you know you don't have it now?'

'People are screened once or twice a year.'

'How often do you get tested?'

'Twice a year.'

'That must mean that you are more at risk than the others. Have you had an accident?'

'Actually, yes.'

Michael looked at Sadie. He was in fact, talking to her. Not to anyone else at the table.

'What happened?'

'I was stuck by a contaminated needle.'

'How long ago?'

'Two years ago.'

Everyone at the table was on the edge of their chairs.

'Are the tests conclusive?' persisted Antonia.

Sadie held her breath.

'No.'

She looked at him in desperation.

'Forgive me for being so inquisitive, Dr Lanzer,' said Antonia, 'but it's a subject that fascinates everyone.'

'Not at all,' said Michael. He was speaking in a calm voice. 'I'm happy to answer any questions. It's too important for people to be kept in the dark.'

'What kind of testing is available, Dr Lanzer?' asked Freddy.

'There's the ELISA test, which can be false positive,' said Lanzer. 'If that's positive, you do the Western test, which, by the way, is named after a Dr Southern. If that's positive it's likely the person is infected but you can still do the PCR test. That can also be false positive and that can send people

321

into a panic. There's a fourth test that also determines the CD-four to CD-eight ratio. If that's low you get alarmed.'

'Do most people who are told they've tested positive get all of those tests?' Freddy asked.

'No. But now it's really important to do early screening because the good news is that early treatments are working. DDX, not AZT, is a dramatic new weapon against AIDS.'

'Why don't more people know about it?' asked Freddy.

'That's a good question, sir,' said Michael. 'And that's what we're hoping will happen now that the First Lady has taken an interest in this issue. Communication is essential.'

'What would be the most effective way to do it?'

'I would suggest a national AIDS screening test, sir. And nothing could be more effective than if you were the first person screened.'

'Oh, Mr President, what a good idea,' said Abigail Sohier.

'And so dramatic. You should definitely do that,' said Antonia, just the slightest bit mischievously.

'That's a very interesting idea, Dr Lanzer, and I shall certainly consider it,' said Freddy.

'Dr Lanzer, what part of the population is most at risk?' asked Abigail.

'Nobody can say anything with certainty about anything. However, if you're a drug addict you've got a real problem. Or if you are the wife or lover of a drug addict.'

Sadie noticed Antonia's smile fade.

'Gay men are at risk and you're at risk if you're the lover of a bisexual. In the Bronx, one in eighty children are born of mothers who are infected.

Runaway children are going to be the next big risk.'

'What about the normal average American boy?' asked Freddy.

'Probably fairly safe,' said Michael, 'although everyone should take precautions, even those least at risk.'

'How can you get AIDS other than through drugs or transfusions or intercourse?' asked Abigail.

'For instance,' said Sadie, 'you can't get AIDS by kissing. Am I right, Dr Lanzer?'

'It has never been documented.'

'But would you recommend kissing someone who was at risk for AIDS?'

'I can't see where a superficial kiss would do any harm.'

'How does your wife deal with your being at risk?' asked Antonia.

'You'd have to ask her.'

He looked at Sadie now and it was her turn to lower her eyes.

'Dr Lanzer, tell us,' Halloran interrupted. 'Why is it that AIDS in this country is predominantly homosexual and in Africa it is more or less heterosexual?'

'If I knew the answer to that,' he said with enormous relief, 'I would spend the rest of my life basking in glory.'

★   ★   ★

'Freddy, I think it's time for the entertainment,' whispered Sadie to Freddy.

Freddy leaped to his feet. He thanked everyone for being there, made a few remarks about Valentine's Day and how he was hoping this dinner would be the beginning of a love affair between the White House and the Washington establishment, and then turned it over to his wife. Blanche spoke about her two male friends, both well-known country music singers who had done duets with her in the past, and took the opportunity to announce that she was about to do a number of concerts with them and others to benefit AIDS.

'But tonight,' she said, 'we're going to do strictly love songs for lovers. And I'd just like to remind everybody, as I'm sure Dr Michael Lanzer would tell you, that abstention is the most effective form of safe sex.'

She laughed and everyone else in the room tittered and glanced at one another, not knowing quite what to make of their new First Lady.

There wasn't a person in the room who wasn't impressed. Blanche was a marvelous singer, had great presence, and she and 'the boys,' as she called them, had done several moving songs together. It was unlike any White House dinner ever given and people felt quite excited to have been included. Despite Blanche's outrageous appearance and her questionable remarks about safe sex, Sadie felt the evening had been a relative success.

After the singing, Sadie stood up, indicating to the rest of the guests that they could do so as well.

Butlers came around with trays of liqueurs, orange juice, and water, and everyone seemed eager to stay on rather than disappear the way people normally do at a Washington dinner party the minute dinner is over.

Sadie noticed that Foxy was bringing Allison over to meet Antonia, who was in deep conversation with Michael and hadn't yet stood up. Allison had that killer look in her eye, and Sadie chuckled to herself with satisfaction.

Sadie moved to Dr Horowitz and began a conversation with her, half-turned so she could overhear what the others were saying.

'Antonia,' said Foxy, placing a proprietary hand on her shoulder. 'I want you to meet someone.'

Antonia looked slightly annoyed as she turned to greet Allison.

'This little gal is the only person I've met who could be a match for you, Antonia.'

Antonia put out her hand, dismissing Foxy's clumsy introduction.

'I am Antonia Alvarez of the Colombian embassy,' she said.

'Allison Sterling.'

'Ah yes. You recently got married? Congratulations.'

'Thank you.' Allison was looking Antonia over carefully. 'You're a friend of the Foreign Minister, Mendez?'

'Boy, you two girls sure have done some intelligence work on each other. Who needs a CIA or a secret police? Didn't I tell ya?'

Foxy, too, was drunk.

Michael stood now and introduced himself to Allison.

'Dr Lanzer,' said Allison. 'I'm national editor at the *Daily*. One of our new reporters has been assigned to the medical beat. She's going to be calling on you shortly. You've been so helpful to everyone it's really refreshing. You're one of the few people who has a reputation for actually answering the phone.'

Michael beamed as Sadie watched.

'Would you ever consider having lunch with me?' I'd love to come out and see NIH and talk to you, learn something about the place. I never covered it as a reporter and I'm trying, as an editor, to get out and see what it is the reporters are doing. I sometimes feel very isolated in my job.'

'I'd love to show you around.'

Sadie wondered if Dr Horowitz knew that she hadn't heard a word being said to her. All she could think about was that she had lost Des to Allison. She couldn't bear to lose Michael, too, even if he wasn't hers to lose.

'Well, you just broke my heart,' said Foxy. 'I thought when you asked me for lunch it was because you thought I was irresistible. And now, right before my very eyes, you go and jilt me with this . . . this doctor.'

Allison was obviously having a hard time being civil to Foxy, but she was a journalist and she made a joke out of it.

'Well, just to show you I'm not discriminating, I'll ask Antonia to lunch, too. Would that make you feel better?'

'Oh, you go both ways, do you?'

Michael stiffened. He seemed stunned that a cabinet officer could act this way at the White House.

'Foxy, please!' Even Antonia was provoked. It was clear she had no use for Foxy except for political reasons. She had been careful to humor him up to this point.

'Certainly for lunch,' laughed Allison. Sadie was impressed at how well she was handling the situation.

'I'll call you next week, Antonia. I think you may

be in dire need of advice on how to protect yourself in Washington.'

Antonia burst out laughing.

'And I'm not talking about the drug wars either,' continued Allison innocently.

Antonia's laugh subsided rather too quickly.

'What's going on over here?' asked Blanche as she walked over to the group.

'I'm afraid Foxy's been misbehaving terribly,' said Sadie with an indulgent smile.

'Not Foxy,' said Blanche, 'that ole devil, I can't believe it.'

'I just don't think he's housebroken yet,' said Sadie, shooting Foxy a warning look. 'Perhaps you should consider sending him to training school.'

Everyone laughed, leaving Foxy no choice but to join in.

'Well, darlin', we got plenty of newspapers in the family sitting room,' said Blanche. 'Maybe that's where we ought to keep you the next time we have a party.'

'Whooooeeeeeee,' said Foxy. 'These Washington gals are too much for me. I'm going back to Nashville.'

He turned to Blanche.

'Where are the boys? I think I'm going over to talk to them.'

'Y'all givin' poor Foxy a bad time over there?' asked the President, walking over to the group.

'Not as bad as he deserves, from what I can see,' said Blanche.

'Well, don't underestimate him,' said Freddy. 'He ain't called Foxy for nothing.'

'We'll see,' said Allison with a mischievous smile.

Freddy didn't smile back.

'I think it's time to leave,' said Sadie, and then under her breath to Freddy, 'before the fox gets treed by the hounds.'

★    ★    ★

'Lunch?'

'Yes. Lunch. You don't have to make it sound like an indecent offer, Michael. I'm inviting you to lunch with me. Just lunch.'

'I already told you I don't do lunch.'

'God, you're a pain,' said Sadie.

He burst out laughing, clearly enjoying their now established repartee.

'What do you think I'm running out here, a health spa? I'm working fourteen or fifteen hours a day trying to save people's lives and I'm supposed to drop everything and come into town to spend three hours with you for lunch, probably lose a couple of patients while I'm at it? No problem.'

'This is a working meeting. I have an agenda.'

'I'll bet.'

'How about next Wednesday at noon? My house.'

'You really think I'm just going to—'

'See you then, bye,' she said in a lilting voice as she hung up.

★    ★    ★

She was even more nervous this time.

This would be the first time she would be seeing him alone since La Samanna. She missed their long talks on the beach.

Since they had been back she had felt estranged.

328

Being with him only in public hadn't helped; but she needed to see how he fit into her world. They both had to know what they were dealing with.

In her bereaved state she didn't trust her judgment. And no matter how hard she tried to talk herself out of him, it didn't work.

The phone would ring and his voice would bring her to her knees. She would see him, and his eyes would burn a hole right through her.

To make it even more difficult, he had been wonderful at the White House, witty, intelligent, and charming. She was so proud of him. She had to keep reminding herself that he wasn't hers.

Now he was coming to lunch at her house. She had an uneasy feeling that she could lose him this time if she didn't do it right. What was right with him, though? She just didn't know. He defied all the rules.

He stood there with a smile in the raw March mist. He looked so young and boyish that she longed to take his head in her hands and kiss him on the forehead.

'Aren't you going to ask me in? Or is there a separate entrance for Jews?'

'Oh, for God's sake, Michael,' she said, laughing. 'You really are awful.'

He walked into the entrance hall of the house with its old wood-plank floor and soft oriental rugs, antique chests and grandfather clocks, porcelain lamps and crystal chandeliers.

'Is this a house or an apartment building? I've never been in anybody's house that was this big except the White House.'

She knew he was trying to bait her and she ignored his remark, leading him into the sunny

329

yellow library filled with books. She motioned him to an armchair next to the fire and then walked to the bar.

'I'm having a Virgin Mary, how about you?'

He didn't answer right away and she was pleasantly aware that he was distracted by her well-fitting white wool pants and cashmere sweater.

'Uh, fine,' he said.

She handed him the drink, then sat in the chair opposite him, curling her feet up under her.

'I'm happy to see you,' she said. 'I've missed you.'

He smiled but said nothing, looking down at his drink.

She took a chance.

'Haven't you missed me?' She was partly playful, partly serious.

'Yes, actually.'

He looked directly at her this time and there was no mistaking how he felt.

'Oh Michael, I—'

'Excuse me, Mrs Grey,' Monica interrupted, sticking her head in the room. 'Willie and I are off to play group. Would you like a hug?'

'Of course.'

Even though Michael had been at La Samanna, he had never met Willie, and she wanted him to know her youngest child. She wanted him to know anything that would establish more intimacy.

Willie came toddling in on sturdy legs, a bundle of energy and movement. He had Des's swagger already.

'Hey, Willie,' said Michael, picking him up, and holding him in the air like an airplane. 'Where did you get all that curly black hair?'

330

Willie giggled and Michael looked over at Sadie. Her face was drained. He took one more look at Willie, then quickly put him down.

She gave Willie an extra-strong hug and handed him to Monica.

'Y'all have a good time. I'll see you back here around four?'

'Righto,' said Monica.

'You must be hungry,' Sadie said to Michael. 'I'll see about lunch.'

When she returned she led him back to the informal dining room off the kitchen, a cozy wood-paneled room with a large fireplace and an old English table and chairs. Two places were set, with two bowls of steaming hot soup. On the sideboard was a salad, sandwiches, fruit, and brownies.

'Everything's fine, Asuncion,' said Sadie to the invisible housekeeper in the kitchen. 'I won't be needing you until around five. Would you mind answering the phone while we have our meeting?'

They sat down in silence, took their napkins rather formally into their laps, and picked up their spoons.

Michael took a sip of his soup.

'What's this?' he asked her.

'Crab bisque. Don't you like it?'

'It's trayf.'

'What?'

'Food that's not kosher.'

'Oh, dear, Michael, I'm sorry. I had no intention of offending you.'

She was genuinely upset. She got up and started to remove his soup dish.

He put his hand on her wrist and held it.

'Sit down.'

331

'But if you can't eat it . . .'

He burst out laughing.

'I'll eat it. I'll eat it.'

They finished their soup. She couldn't wait to clear the offending soup bowls. He got up this time to help.

She grabbed his wrist and held it.

'Sit down.'

They looked at each other and smiled.

'You're so domestic,' he said.

When she came back she tossed the salad and placed the sandwiches in front of him.

He took a bite.

'What is this?'

'It's a Croque Monsieur, a French grilled ham and chee . . . oh God.' She started to giggle. 'Pork.'

'Not just pork. This is the ultimate trayf. Meat and dairy together.'

'Well,' she said defensively, 'I have lots of Jewish friends who eat ham and bacon . . . Oh the hell with it.'

'Relax. Can't you see I'm just teasing you?'

'Yes, but . . .'

'There's no reason for you to know this stuff,' he said. 'Besides, the thinking is, if we can maintain self-control in our diets, then it will help us to control ourselves when we face other temptations.'

'I guess you'll have to be content with salad and fruit,' she said mischievously.

'Who said I had any self-control?' He grinned, taking a large bite of his sandwich.

'I talked to Blanche about the President being tested for HIV.'

'And?'

'And she thinks it's brilliant.'

332

'So?'

'Freddy is reluctant.'

'I have to admit he didn't seem all that pleased when I suggested it the other evening.'

'You know, Freddy has a rather checkered past. There were lots of women between the time he got divorced and married Blanche. I mean lots. And some of them were not exactly the kind you'd want to take home to Mother. Party girls, I think is the description. Freddy and Foxy were what you might call tail hounds in the old days. So I think he's just scared.'

'Will he do it anyway?'

'I don't see how he can avoid it. You suggested it in front of a table full of people. If he doesn't do it, it will be headlines all over the country, thanks to Des or Allison. Blanche is already furious at him for not agreeing immediately. She's now threatening to cut him off if he doesn't get tested. She says if he doesn't he must think he might have it, and if he does, she's going to be hog-tied if she'll sleep with him and risk her life.'

Michael laughed.

'Poor guy. I didn't really mean for this to happen.'

'What would you do?'

He didn't see where she was headed.

'If I were Freddy? I'd have the test.'

'And if it's positive?'

'I'd do the test again.'

'Would you do it again if you tested negative?'

'No.'

'Why not? You said yourself the tests are inconclusive. Surely if they test false positive they could test false negative.'

'Yes.'

'Do you do more in-depth tests on yourself twice a year or just the superficial test?'

'Just the superficial test.'

'Don't you want to know?'

'No.'

'I thought you said there were all these great new drugs.'

'I'd rather not prolong death.'

'Aren't you scared?'

'No. We all have to die sometime.'

'Isn't Giselle scared?'

'She doesn't think about it. If I've got AIDS then she's got AIDS.'

It was the first time he had indicated they still slept together. The confirmation was more painful than she would have expected.

'Blanche would cut Freddy off so fast it would make your head swim. Giselle wouldn't refuse you?'

'Never.'

'Why not? What if she doesn't feel like it. What if there's no passion?'

'Sex is a currency. You can spend it. Give it as a down payment. Sex is fealty. If your man is having sex with you it confirms that you are his woman, his wife. You have control.'

'That doesn't sound too thrilling. What's in it for him?'

'It is a sign of his obedience, his devotion, his fealty.'

'How depressing.'

'Not really. You can use sex to get intimacy, for loneliness. It's easy to be lonely when you're married. Sex is only one kind of dialogue. For most women sex is more dialogue than orgasm...'

He looked at her and smiled gently.

'You should know all this better than most.'

'I didn't expect you to resist that one. I expect our scenarios are not all that different.'

'You have dinner. Then you do the dishes...'

'While the husband reads the paper...' she said.

'Well, sometimes,' he said. 'Then you do homework with the kids...'

'Who are arguing about God knows what, somebody borrowed something of someone's...'

'Then you go upstairs to get ready for bed. He brushes his teeth...'

'She takes a bath,' said Sadie.

'He showers.'

'Where are we? Oh yes. She puts on a nightgown.'

'He gets into his pajamas.'

'They get in bed.'

'He gets something out of his briefcase.'

'She picks up a fashion magazine.'

'The sign of wanting to have sex is prolonged reading.'

'If you don't fall asleep,' she said.

'If you haven't fallen asleep and if you do want to have sex you turn out your light. If your partner wants to have sex, too, then she turns out her light.'

They were both immensely pleased with their neat little pas de deux.

'Oh God, this is so exciting,' she said. 'But wait.'

'What?'

'Birth control. She has to get up and do something about birth control.'

'Damn, just when it's getting exciting,' he said.

'Okay, she's back in bed. They're kissing.'

'In the dark.'

335

'What about oral sex?' She couldn't believe she was asking him that.

'No experimentation.'

'None?'

He was describing her sex life with Rosey completely. Here was one area where there were no cultural differences.

'Only shiksas give blow jobs,' he said with a chuckle. 'That's what the whole reformation was about. Although I'm told Jewish women do, too, now. It's really the end of the culture.'

★   ★   ★

Sadie and Michael had only spoken once since lunch at her house. Naturally it was she who called him. She had called to tell him that Blanche had persuaded Freddy to have the first AIDS blood test to launch their program.

Michael seemed pleased when she called. He was also slightly distant and noncommittal, as if their intimate conversation had never happened.

This was the way it was with him. Each time they met or talked on the phone, she had to reestablish the relationship. Then, just as they were getting warmed up, he would have to go. This time was no different. She had no sooner told him about Freddy when he had to run off to a meeting.

It was incredibly frustrating. Every goddamned thing was a test with him. He was so judgmental. It was trial by fire just to have lunch, have a telephone call, accept an invitation. Would she be able to measure up? Would she bridge the gap? Would she clear the hurdle? And then when she succeeded, when she knew absolutely that she had met his

336

approval, he would put forth another set of tasks, obstacles, evaluations, appraisals. He made her feel so unworthy. Guilty until proven innocent. And proven and proven and proven. It was exhausting. Especially when all she wanted to do was to love him.

## CHAPTER TWELVE

'Great buns. World-class buns.' Allison smacked Des's behind appreciatively.

'You think so?'

He was lying on his stomach, his head resting on his arms.

It was Sunday afternoon in February. They had been to a brunch, had a few bloodys and had come home to her house on Olive Street, where they were now more-or-less living, to finish the papers and take a nap. The nap had turned into something more interesting.

'Not only do I think so, every woman I know thinks so. It's a big topic of conversation, your ass.'

'Really?' He lifted his head and looked around to see if she was kidding. He grinned skeptically.

'Really.'

'Well,' he chortled, quite pleased with himself now that he was convinced she was sincere, 'can't drive a spike with a tackhammer.'

'Speaking of spikes . . .'

'The girls talk about that, too?'

He had put his head back down on his arms. She was sitting next to him cross-legged, nude, tousled, stroking his back with her left hand as she talked.

337

'What would they know about yours, my darling husband?'

'I mean anybody's.'

'I don't care about anybody's. Let's talk about yours. Or rather ours. Why don't you turn over so I can get a better grip.'

With that she tried reaching under him, but he pushed her away, then grabbed her wrists.

'Oh, you great big strong brute, you.'

He had turned over by now and he pulled her down on top of him and kissed her, still holding her wrists away from him.

She pulled back and kissed her way down from his stomach, finally taking his erection in her hands.

'Desi, my best friend,' she said, giggling. 'Even in the bleakest of times, when Des and I were apart, I always knew you cared about me.'

'Don't belittle my cock,' he said from above her head.

'That would be impossible under the circumstances. But we're awfully proprietary, aren't we? I thought once we were married I could take liberties.'

'You're on thin ice, sweetheart.'

She leaned over and kissed the tip of him gently.

'Don't go away Desi, dear, you gorgeous thing. I'll be right back as soon as I soothe Papa's ruffled feelings.'

She kissed her way back up to his mouth.

'Now where were we?' she asked, between kisses.

'We were talking about my awesome equipment.'

'Oh, yes,' she said, sitting up, suddenly distracted. 'I referred to you as my husband. My husband, "I'd like you to meet my husband,

338

Desmond Shaw." "I happen to be the wife of Desmond Shaw." You have no idea how that feels for me. You've been married before, I never have. You've had a wife. You've been a husband. You want to hear something really silly? I've been sitting in my office writing "Mrs Desmond Shaw" on yellow pads over and over again. Even "Allison Shaw." I'll never be called Allison Shaw, but I wrote it. Just like I did in fifth grade when I was in love with Jamie Laurents. "Mrs Jamie Laurents. Allison Laurents." "Sonny Shaw." Actually that sounds quite good. A great fifties housewife name. Oh, God. Can you believe it? Me? The iron woman? What has become of me? You can see how our society has conditioned us into believing that the worst thing that could happen would be to end up an old maid. Even though that word has gone out of style the concept is still alive. It's really sick. Why does it matter? Why should I care? Yet I did. I do. I think it's all bullshit and yet I do. Do you realize how many times I've been asked in the last few years why I never married. Never married for Christ's sake! I wasn't even forty. It was as if I were dead. And now that I'm married I feel like a totally different person. A legitimate person in the eyes of society. It's disgusting, but it's true. I hate to say it. I had no idea it would feel so different. It's kind of like what it might feel like if you were white all your life and suddenly one day you were black. You had always known there was racism out there but you never knew how awful it was until you were black. I called the car dealer to get my car serviced and announced myself very officiously as "Mrs Shaw." Those bastards were so courteous and so polite as opposed to their usual hostile behavior.

You'd think I'd told them I was the queen of fucking England. And you know what? That's what I felt like. I like being Mrs Desmond Shaw. It's really pathetic. If you ever tell a living soul I said that I will call you a liar. I like saying "my husband." I like being a wife. In fact, there are a couple of other nouns I wouldn't mind the sound of either.'

'I'll bite.'

'Mother. Daughter. Son.'

'How about Mother. Son.'

'You pig! After what I've just said. How can you even think like that? What's wrong with a daughter?'

'Nothing,' he said carefully. 'It's just that I don't seem to be a very good father to girls.'

'How do you know that your alleged lack of talent as a father is limited to girls? You've never had a son.'

He didn't say anything for a moment and she was surprised by the odd expression on his face. She couldn't decide if she had hurt his feelings, but she knew she had said something wrong.

'Every man would like to have a son,' he said quietly.

'You do know, don't you, that it's the male who determines the sex of the child?'

'I'm aware of that.'

'Well, I'd like to have a girl. A beautiful little girl who I can play with on weekends. If I have a boy he'll end up watching sports with you and I'll still be lonely . . . But really, I don't care. All I want is a normal, healthy baby.'

'Me, too. Why don't we make one. Now.'

'Allison, it's Jenny.'

There was a pause.

'I haven't forgotten your name. It's just been a while, that's all. I'm surprised to hear from you.'

'I know,' Jenny said nervously. 'Too long really. I've missed you.'

Allison didn't quite know what to say. She said nothing.

'Well, you must wonder why I'm calling.'

'Actually, I do.'

She knew she sounded cold, but that was all right. She felt cold. She could tell Jenny was nervous. That was all right, too. She deserved to be nervous. Jenny had been her best friend since they had started out at the *Daily* years ago. They had been reporters together. They had spent holidays together. Jenny had been through Des with her. Jenny had been like family to her since she had no mother or father. Then Jenny went to work at the White House as Sadie Grey's press secretary and virtually dropped Allison. Soon afterwards she began dating Des. Allison was confident that Des could never be in love with Jenny. She also knew that Jenny had always been secretly in love with him. She thought it an act of betrayal to go out with him knowing how devastated Allison was after the breakup. It was later, when she learned that Des had been having an affair with Sadie and that Jenny was acting as the beard, that she realized the extent of that betrayal. She had vowed never to have anything to do with Jenny again. Jenny had to feel guilty. She sounded guilty. Allison was not about to put her out of her misery.

341

'I thought we might ... I mean ... I'd like to take you to lunch.'

'Why?'

'Well, uh, I just thought, um, it seemed like we hadn't seen each other in a long time and I thought it might be nice to get together.'

Another silence.

'Would you have lunch with me? I'd like to pick your brain about something.'

'Fine. You name the date and time.'

'How about next week? Thursday? Mo and Joe's at noon. I know you have to get back at two-thirty for story conference.'

'Fine. See you then.'

'Bye.'

Allison had already hung up.

★　　　★　　　★

Allison arrived a few minutes late. Jenny was waiting in the dimly lit underground restaurant at a corner banquette. Allison glanced absentmindedly at the autograph pictures and book jacket covers of various writers and journalists about town that adorned the walls of the foyer. She walked down the stairs past the bar, lined with the all-male regulars, to her table.

'Look at this place,' she said to Jenny without apologizing for being late. 'It hasn't changed a bit. They are still ninety-five percent men in here. We're the only table of women lunching alone without male companions. So much for the advancement of women on the power-lunch circuit.'

'I don't think it's that,' said Jenny. 'It's just that the food is so terrible that women won't eat here.

342

It's jock food. They're not big on spa cuisine. In fact, I'm not sure why I suggested we come here.'

She seemed anxious. Allison did nothing to put her at ease.

'So,' said Jenny, after they had both ordered sparkling water, 'how do you like being king of the hill, or should I say queen of the hill? I have to admit I never expected them to name a woman national editor. You deserve a lot of credit for overcoming the prejudices of some of those male chauvinist pigs in that newsroom. Most of them are really uncomfortable with women, particularly with women in roles of authority.'

'They still are. Especially the women.'

'You're kidding!'

'They think I'm tougher than the men are.'

'Are you?'

'Yes. But I'm not tougher on them than I am on the men. I treat them equally. They don't like that. The men are so afraid of women. They don't understand feminism. They're terrified that if they tell a woman that she looks great she'll sue them for sexual harassment. They don't know how to act. They're afraid that if they ask a pregnant woman to do something they'll be perceived as insensitive. So what they do is worse. They're patronizing and paternalistic and lenient. They just opt out because it's easier. I know that most of the women have gone to Walt and complained about me. Of course the men see that as whining. I had an argument last week with a woman editor from the Living section about a story they were doing that overlapped a story one of my reporters—female, by the way—was doing. Alan Warburg asked Walt if we had resolved the issue and Walt said, "No, it's still

343

at the level of women screaming at each other." I went totally ballistic. If it had been two men it would have been a serious dispute. The point is, I treat everybody the same. The women on my staff are used to maumauing the male editors. Unfortunately for them, it doesn't work with me.'

'You sound very tough. It must be hard to make friends.'

'I have to be tough, Jenny. About everything. Besides, I haven't had much luck with friendship.'

Just then the waiter appeared with his notebook. They both ordered salads without looking at the menu.

Jenny looked down, took a sip of her drink, and swizzled the lime around.

'How's Des?'

'Cut to the chase, Jenny. Why are we here?'

Jenny looked taken aback. It took her a moment to get her bearings.

'We're here because I wanted to apologize. I wanted to tell you I'm sorry.'

Allison said nothing.

'I'm sorry for abandoning you as a friend, particularly when you were in such pain. I didn't mean to do it. I just got caught up in a situation and I didn't know how to get out of it. By the time I had gotten involved it was too late.'

'Why did you take that stupid job in the first place, Jenny? Being the First Lady's press secretary is not honest work for a serious journalist, and besides, you knew I wasn't crazy about Sadie Grey. You were supposed to be my best friend.' There was a pleading note to her voice that she had not anticipated. The hurt was still raw.

'I took it because Walt Fineman, your close and

344

dear friend, told me I should look for work, that I had no future at the *Daily*.'

'You're kidding.' Allison was clearly surprised.

'I wish I were. I was desperate. I got this offer from Sadie about the same time and it seemed like an exciting challenge and a way out. If only I had had any idea what kind of challenge.'

'You're talking about Des's affair with Sadie?'

Jenny looked startled. The waiter appeared with their lunch. They both stopped talking until he walked away.

'Of course I know about it. I guessed long before Des told me. Sadie had sent him a message in Jerusalem several years ago and I saw it, unbeknownst to him. That's when we almost got back together and then broke up for good. That's what propelled me to go to London. I had to get out of town. I had lost my best friend, then the man I loved. It was too much.'

'Oh Sonny, I'm just so sorry. Sadie had started the affair with Des after you broke up the first time. I didn't know about it until she asked for my help with the logistics. She told me if I didn't help her she'd just have to fend for herself. She was obsessed with Des. Without me they would have been caught and I couldn't let that happen. I couldn't. It would have been awful for the President and the country. Especially after Roger Kimball had to step down. Everybody was already shaky.'

'Why couldn't you still be my friend?'

'Number one because you're too good a reporter and you know me too well. You would have figured it out eventually. Especially since I had to start going out with Des in case his being around the White House or the E.O.B. caused suspicion.

345

Number two, not necessarily in order of importance, I felt I was betraying you and I hated myself for it. I missed you terribly and I had nobody to talk to. I've never been so miserable in my life. You were the one person I couldn't go to. That's why I wanted to see you today. I've wanted for so long to apologize and explain. But I felt I had to wait until you and Des were married. I didn't know whether or not you knew so I had to sort of feel you out about it. I didn't want to betray Des if he hadn't told you.'

Sonny began to soften. She knew Jenny was telling the truth, and for the first time she felt sorry for her. She could understand what a horrible position she'd been in and she couldn't be sure she would have acted any differently herself.

'It was a very difficult time for me, very stressful, Sonny. I resented Sadie and Des a lot for putting me in that position and I told them so. But they really did love each other.'

She saw Allison's face tighten.

'Or at least she really loved him. I'm not so sure he wasn't just infatuated with the idea of fucking the First Lady.'

Allison relaxed, taking comfort in Jenny's last comment, though she wasn't sure she believed her. She wanted to. She hadn't realized how much she had missed her until now. She wanted to be her friend again. She didn't see why it wasn't possible.

'All of that kind of upstaged the job itself,' Jenny was saying. 'It was okay, but the truth is I always felt a little like I was selling out. I figured afterward I could write another White House book, then maybe do lots of lectures and get some sort of lucrative consulting job.'

346

'And?'

'It's not what I really want to do.'

'What do you really want to do.'

'I think I'd like to try editing.'

So that was it. Jenny wanted a job. All this time she thought Jenny wanted to be her friend and now it turned out she just wanted a job. It made her feel so used. And betrayed again. How could she have been so wrong about Jenny twice? Well, it wouldn't happen again. She was not that dumb.

'I don't think you'd really like editing,' Allison said tightly. 'I'm having a very hard time adjusting, especially from being a foreign correspondent. I worked more hours as a reporter but they were my hours. This is like being a prisoner, like having a ball and chain around your ankle sitting at that desk. Your time is never your own. Everybody has claims on it. If you're not within the line of sight, if you go to the ladies' room, they put out an A.P.B. The worst part is the temptation to rewrite. You know you're a better writer than the person you're editing but you have to try not to. That's really the most painful part.'

'Oh, I don't know. I think I would like it.'

The silence this time was especially awkward.

'You don't ... I mean, you don't think there might be something on the desk at the *Daily* for me, do you? It doesn't have to be national, although that's what I know best. It could be the Living section or the federal page or even metro, I don't know. Health? Could there be something there? It's just that I really miss the paper and—'

'Forget it, Jenny. It isn't going to work. I would have said no even if you hadn't told me about your conversation with Walt. Unfortunately, I think he's right. There really is no future for you at the *Daily*, especially after having been in the White House. You've priced yourself out of a job at the *Daily*. Besides, you really can't go home again.'

'You really are tough, aren't you, Sonny.'

'As I said earlier, I have to be.'

For the rest of the lunch they made tense small talk. Jenny got the bill as quickly as she could. Neither one of them could wait to get up from the table.

Walking up the stairs to the exit, Allison stopped by the bowl of chocolate mints to grab a few.

A hand went in on top of hers, practically pushing her aside, and she looked up to see who the rude person was.

It was Sprague Tyson. Beside him was a rather disreputable-looking guy who could easily have been a Mafia type or a gunrunner.

She just stared at Sprague.

'Sorry,' he said unconvincingly.

She stared at his luncheon companion.

'Allison Sterling, Manny Peligroso.'

'Enchanted,' said Allison with mock politeness, reaching out to take Manny's beefy paw.

'Same,' said Manny.

Manny turned to leave.

'I thought you didn't do lunch,' said Allison out of the corner of her mouth against her better judgment.

'Not with lady editors anyway.'

Only the slightest turn on the corner of his mouth belied his seriousness.

'Prick,' hissed Allison under her breath after he had walked away.

'Who is he?' asked Jenny. 'He's gorgeous.'

348

'I don't know,' said Allison. 'I just don't know.'

\*       \*       \*

Coffee. The coffee thing was serious. If anybody had told her that her biggest problem as national editor would be coffee etiquette she would have died laughing. Now here she was lying awake at night trying to figure out how to deal with it. And she was a tea drinker.

The problem was this: She had inherited from her predecessor a coffeepot that was in her office. There was a constant stream of people in and out of her office, at all times of day or evening, watching press conferences, speeches, announcements, resignations, plane crashes, and whatever news happened to be occurring. All of these people functioned on caffeine. When she first arrived she would fill up the pot with water for her tea. Then she found that while she was having meetings or on deadline someone would get up and disappear down to the cafeteria for coffee. It was disruptive and time consuming—cream, sugar or black; who's got the money—the key person for the discussion was inevitably the one who had gone for coffee. In self-defense, Allison had started bringing in instant coffee, but that meant that everybody was making coffee in her office and the pot had to be refilled several times during the day. She found herself trooping to the ladies' room to fill the pot. She was getting bored and outraged that not a single one of 'the boys' would ever take the pot to be filled. Or bring in their own instant. Or cream. Or sugar.

One day she rebelled. She didn't fill the pot with water. She went down to the cafeteria to get her tea.

For three days the empty pot sat there, a rebuke to her entire male staff. She might as well have put a sign on it saying, 'Go get your own fucking water.' For three days nobody did anything.

On the fourth morning she arrived to find the water in the pot. As she went over nonchalantly to pour water for her tea she noticed Malkin hovering near the door. She said nothing. They soon ran out of water and the pot stayed empty for the rest of the day.

The next morning the same thing happened. There was Malkin hovering. But still the pot stayed empty.

The following Monday when the pot was full and Malkin appeared he couldn't resist.

'Did you notice the pot was filled for the last few days?' he asked.

'Yes, I did,' said Allison.

'I filled it.' He beamed with pride.

'Did you?'

'Yes, I did.'

'That's terrific, Malkin. Congratulations. That's really nice of you. Above and beyond and all that. Good job. Great work.'

'Thanks. Thanks a lot,' he said. Pleased with her praise, he turned and headed back toward the desk, a special spring to his step.

It was that night she lay awake until dawn.

The next day she unplugged the coffeepot and put it away. When 'the boys' came in for her morning meeting at eleven with their empty mugs and saw it had disappeared they quickly shoved their mugs behind them and never said a word. From then on they would get their coffee before the meetings. Nobody ever mentioned coffee around her again.

★ ★ ★

It was a slow day in late March when the story broke. Allison was in her office. She had just called the morning meeting. Suddenly the newsroom was chaos. Malkin rushed in with the wires. One of the local TV stations in Washington had been bombed. It had been a small mail bomb and nobody was hurt. Within minutes there were reports of similar bombings in New York and Los Angeles. Then minutes later the wires had more. TV stations in Miami, San Antonio, and New Orleans had been hit. Phone calls from people who claimed they represented the Colombian drug cartel took the credit. One of the four top drug kingpins in Colombia had been arrested and was about to be extradited. The callers said the American people could expect more bombings if they carried out the extradition.

Allison stood at her desk and looked through the glass partition around the room. She was looking for heads. Bobbing heads. Any heads she could find. She did a 360-degree turn and yelled at Malkin.

'Get Tyson, get Conlon, get Lefkowitz. I want Tyson in Miami immediately. That's the biggest hit. He's got a lot of contacts down there. See who else you can find. Get somebody on plane reservations. We need rental cars, we need hotels, pull the clips on the drug kingpins. We need money, we need computers...'

She was dispatching people as quickly as she could as she walked through the newsroom. She

351

was making her way over to Walt Fineman, who was headed her way with a list in his hands, reeling off instructions to two editors who were trailing him.

We've got to cover five cities here,' he said. 'We only have correspondents in one. Who've we got?'

Malkin raced over to them.

'We've got problems,' he said. 'Tyson refuses to go to Miami. He says he's working here on the big picture, which is more important.'

Allison was stunned.

'You're kidding. Did you tell him I assigned him to go?'

'Yep,' said Malkin with an unhappy expression on his face. It was clear he did not want to get in the middle of this battle.

'I don't believe this. Who does he think he is? Tell him to get his ass in gear. He's going to Miami. We've already sent Robeson from Atlanta to Louisiana. Who else have we got?'

'Jacobs overheard Tyson say he wasn't going. She's volunteered,' said Malkin.

'Great!' said Allison.

'Jacobs is almost eight months pregnant, Allison. They won't let her on a plane,' said Malkin. 'Besides, she shouldn't travel anyway.'

'Shouldn't that be her decision?'

'I don't think so,' said Fineman. 'She's insisting. She feels she has to prove to you that she's not a candy ass. The women think you're tough, Allison. I think it's our responsibility to refuse her.'

'Okay. Tell her to forget it,' she said finally. 'I don't need one of my reporters going into labor in the middle of a terrorist bombing out in the field. Did you get Corey in Denver? We need him in

352

Texas right away.'

'He says he can't go. His son's birthday is tomorrow and he's taking him and all his friends on a camping trip. They're all there ready to go and he's rented a camper...'

'Shit, Malkin. What is this? Are we running a day-care center or a newsroom? I don't get it. Walt, we need to talk.'

By this time everyone was aware that Allison was upset, and a silence had descended over the newsroom as they stopped what they were doing to gaze at Allison and Walt and Malkin. Many of the reporters had begun to gather around the national desk as the wires kept coming over with more stories of the bombings, and there was the usual atmosphere of collective excitement over a breaking story.

Allison headed toward Walt's office with Walt and Malkin close behind. Alan Warburg had seen the commotion with Allison and had come out of his office to see what was going on.

'What's the problem?' Alan was always curt and to the point.

'We need to talk,' said Allison as she made her way into Walt's office with the three of them now following. As Walt came in he closed the door behind them. Allison, without sitting down, turned to the three and began to speak, a scene that became a pantomime to the rest of the newsroom, all of whom were riveted by the spectacle behind the glass wall.

'I'm having a hard time dealing with the attitudes on the national staff,' Allison said. 'On foreign we never got into trouble by expending too many resources. You can never not do enough, or so I was trained to think. You get a breaking story, you get people on planes, and then you worry about whether or not you have too many. I'd rather have three people too many than not enough or none. But on national everybody always has a problem. On foreign you're not allowed to have a problem. On foreign everybody is general assignment. On national everybody has a beat. You're only responsible for what you're responsible for. I don't want to be put in the position of having to ask, no, beg my reporters to cover a goddamn story. It's their job. They shouldn't have the right of refusal. I could order them to go, but then I'd pay for it in spades. We've got a newspaper to put out. How am I supposed to cover this story with a bunch of prima donnas for reporters?'

'Amen, sister,' said Walt.

'You're absolutely right, Allison,' said Alan.

There was dead silence. Then they all burst out laughing. Allison, too, in spite of herself.

'So what am I supposed to do, forget the story? Just accept the fact that national can't handle the "crash and burn" stuff? No way. I'm the editor of this section and we have a job to do and if we can't chase fires with the people we have we're just going to have to get some new firemen.'

'Look, you've got to realize a couple of things here,' said Alan. 'These people are older than the metro reporters. They get set in their ways, they get attached to their beats. They're not as hungry as they used to be. Plus the fact that they can't cut corners on their commitments at home like they once could.'

'So what you do,' said Walt, 'is go over to metro and find some young tiger and send him on the story.'

'What about the bureau people?' asked Alan. 'They're used to this.'

'The bureau people. That's a laugh. I'm having just as much trouble with them.'

'Then do something meshugge. Send someone from Boston to Texas.'

'I'll tell you what I'm going to do first. I'm going to get Tyson off his ass and to Miami. He khadnows these players better than anybody. He keeps saying he has to stay here for the big picture.'

'Allison,' said Warburg carefully, 'the cost of winning this fight is losing. You understand that don't you? It would be unheard of for a reporter to turn down an assignment flat out if he is forced unless he has a very, very good excuse. It's grounds for dismissal. You have the right to force him. But you have to ask yourself what the price is. He may quit. If the price of victory is too much, it's defeat.'

'Alan, I understand what you're saying. I'm listening. But we have a little male-female problem here I suspect. It's a new problem for this newsroom. If I don't get over this hurdle now, it will be left for the next woman editor in this paper to do it. I venture to say that Sprague Tyson would not have refused this assignment from a male editor, and he's not going to refuse it from me. You've got to let me handle this my own way. If I lose this one I'll lose face with the whole staff, and then I won't have any credibility at all and I might as well go back to being a reporter. Tyson's going to Miami.'

'Good luck and may God be with you,' laughed Walt, as Allison marched out of his office and headed toward Sprague Tyson's desk.

355

He was on the phone, as usual, head buried to avoid being overheard by the person next to him. He didn't see Allison coming.

'Tyson,' she said as she reached his desk.

He looked up, frowned, shook his head, and leaned down into the phone again.

'Excuse me, Tyson, I need to talk to you, right away.'

She moved her body closer to his head so that he was staring down directly at her feet, one of which was tapping. Her arms were crossed, more to contain her anger than anything else.

Tyson mumbled something into the phone and hung up. When he looked up at her his face was stone cold. Rather than sit there and look up at her he chose to stand. He was over six feet tall and his slim body was all muscle. Standing, he looked down on her. She felt suddenly extremely nervous. She was also aware that the entire newsroom had stopped all activity and everybody was staring at the two of them with dread and fascination.

'What seems to be the problem, Tyson?' She hoped her voice held more conviction than it sounded to her.

'I don't have a problem.'

'Oh, great, then you'll be going to Miami?'

'Actually, I won't. As I explained to your little lapdog, Malkin, I'm already working on the story, and I think I can make a better contribution to the paper here than there.'

Allison was outraged but she realized that she could not make a scene in this atmosphere, which had now taken on the silence of a religious service.

'Actually, I think that it is my job to make that decision, don't you?'

356

That sounded weak. She shouldn't have ended with a question mark. What if he didn't back down? He would quit. The paper would lose the best investigative reporter in the country. He would be snatched up by the competition and win ten Pulitzers. She would lose her job and go down in infamy as the first and last woman editor of the *Daily*. People would say women just coudn't be managers because they couldn't handle men. She would ruin it for all women forever in journalism. So what the hell, she might as well kill herself. If she didn't die right here of humiliation in front of everyone. Nothing like a little overdramatizing in moments of tension and stress. What would a male editor do now? Deck the son of a bitch, probably. No. That was just the way she liked to think men reacted. They never did what they were supposed to do. A man would never have gotten himself into this spot in the first place. Warburg had made that perfectly clear. But then she wasn't a man. She was exploring new territory. She had to win and she had to do it on her terms.

'It might have been, if that decision had been well considered. But it wasn't. You never discussed it with me at all. You just sent Malkin over here to order me to Miami.'

'By the same token you never considered what went into my decision,' she said. She was so angry that her voice was starting to shake, and her mouth was dry. She could tell that he knew she was about to lose it.

'You had no idea what my problems were,' she said. 'You just refused.'

He looked surprised. He had unnerved her when he made the point that she hadn't considered what

357

he was working on. He had been taken aback with the same complaint. It was a standoff. But she was the boss and she had to win.

They stood and stared at each other for a long moment, squaring off.

Finally she lowered her voice to a whisper.

'Tyson,' she said. 'You went to military school, as we discussed earlier. The way I understand it, the first rule you learn in the military is to follow orders. "Ours is not to reason why, ours but to do or die." This is not the military. But we have a breaking story that is our equivalent of battle. I have my orders from my superiors to cover that story. They didn't tell me how. They just want the story and they want it first and they want it better. You can do the job better than anyone else. You're the best. I have no doubt that you can be valuable to us on the phone. But it is my judgment, and I reserve the right to be wrong, that you will be more effective if you're there. Therefore, I respectfully request that you do as I ask. If we don't get that story it's my ass. And if it's my ass it's your ass. Do you read me, Tyson?'

She had seen that hint of a smile on his lips only once before, in the conference room. There was something about his eyes, the way he was looking at her, something behind that stony glare. She couldn't tell whether it was mocking or appreciative. She didn't want to test it. She was barely able to stand up, much less analyze his expression.

'Yes, sir,' he whispered. Then in a loud voice that surprised her and everyone around them, all of whom were pretending not to notice, he said, 'Well, what the hell are we waiting for? I need airplane reservations. If we don't get on it now the networks will have booked every plane to Miami. I need clips, I need money. I'll need a computer ... I'll need a car when I get there. I'm going home to pack and I want everything ready when I get back.'

'Yes, sir,' she whispered.

She went quickly to Malkin who was grinning.

She shook her head in warning as she headed into her office with Malkin behind her. She didn't want either of them to be perceived as gloating.

There was a crowd around the national desk watching television and reading wires. Whenever any big story broke everyone wanted a piece of the action, even if it meant just hanging around and knowing what was going on. Some of the younger reporters were making themselves highly visible in hopes of being sent off on the story when their elders couldn't make it. They were all watching Allison.

'Don't gloat,' she said to Malkin under her breath. 'I don't want anyone to think I'm enjoying this. And for God's sake, make sure everything is ready for him when he gets back.'

'We've got him booked to Miami. I made sure of that while you were still, uh, negotiating with him. He's got a car and a hotel room. We've got a problem with the machine. I've sent someone over to Systems to get him a computer and the fucking door is locked.'

'Well, find somebody with a key. This is not acceptable. What about money?'

'Doris doesn't have enough in petty cash.'

'Shit. I don't believe this. All we need are computers and money and we can't get either. This is supposed to be one of the great metropolitan newspapers of the free world and nothing works around here. I'll go to the bank next door and get some money out of my own account. But Malkin, please make sure we've got clips.'

When she came back with her last five hundred dollars in cash Malkin was waiting for her, looking glum.

'There's not a computer working. They're all broken,' he said.

'Try to get Tyson at home before he leaves and see if he has one he can take. And talk to some of the others about using theirs. I can send somebody back to my house for mine. If worse comes to worse we can go downstairs to the computer store and buy one. I might as well be running a pawn shop.'

Walt and Alan both stuck their heads into her office.

'Nice work on the Tyson thing,' said Walt with a lascivious grin. 'What did you have to promise to get him to—'

'Don't even finish that thought, much less that sentence, Walt,' she said, smiling.

'Okay, so how'd you do it?' Alan asked, 'I'm impressed.'

'Some people just have leadership ability and some haven't,' she said.

They both laughed as they walked back toward the national desk.

'I think, Malkin, we've already spent far too much time on Sprague Tyson,' she said. 'We've got a huge story breaking and too many other cities and too many other reporters to deal with to worry about him. Why don't you round up the boys and let's figure out strategy.'

Just as Malkin left, the phone rang. It was Des.

'What a story,' he said.

His juices were flowing. She could tell. He just wanted to share the excitement with her. They couldn't really share information even though he worked for the *Weekly* and didn't have a next-day deadline. They had long ago decided that was unwise.

Allison decided to tell him about her contretemps with Sprague. She knew Des was predisposed not to like him just from what little she had told him. She was also curious to know how he would react to what she had done. He listened carefully while she recounted the details of her standoff. When she was finished he said nothing.

'Well,' she said rather proudly. 'How do you think I handled it?'

'I think,' said Des carefully. 'That when you cut off a guy's nuts in public you have either created a eunuch, in which case he will no longer be the kind of reporter he is now, or you have created a monster bent on revenge. Or he will mull it over for a long time and say to himself, "That is some kinda dame." In any case, you have not heard the last of him.'

★　　　★　　　★

'Allison? Allison!'

Allison was vaguely aware of somebody saying her name but she couldn't bring herself out of her stupor.

'Allison? Are you all right?'

'Huh? Uh, what, huh?'

She was aware she wasn't making any sense. She was trying to come out of her groggy state but she

361

still couldn't orient herself. She didn't know where she was or who was talking to her. All she knew was that the lights were too bright.

'I'm so sorry,' she said, still trying to get her bearings. She pulled herself up in her blue chair. Blue chair? Where was she? She wasn't in her office. She blinked her eyes. At the head of the conference table she saw Walt leaning forward with a worried expression on his face. Several people were crowded around her.

'What happened?' she asked.

'You just blacked out,' said Walt.

She looked around and saw the rest of the national staff sitting around a large table staring at her. It must be the weekly national staff meeting.

'Do you feel okay? Do you want me to take you down to the nurse?' Walt was asking.

She could make out Lauren Hope's face across the table and next to her Sprague Tyson. God, how humiliating. She felt as if she had been drugged. What was happening to her? This was the second time she had just passed out like this. She was beginning to be frightened.

'I'm fine, just fine, thank you, I just, if I could have some water ... I'll be fine.'

She didn't sound very convincing, but somebody got her a drink with ice. She managed to get herself together enough to go to the ladies' room, with Lauren nervously accompanying her, and splash cold water on her face.

When she came back Tyson was talking. He was discussing the fight between the DEA, the Justice Department, the FBI, and the CIA over the drug strategy and the President's cleanup operation in the District of Colombia.

362

'This is small potatoes for the cartels,' Tyson was saying. 'The Colombians...'

He looked up as she walked back in and lost his train of thought.

'The uh, the, uh...'

'The Colombians,' said Walt. Sprague's reaction to Allison did not go unnoticed by Walt.

'Oh, right. Sorry. The Colombians are just laughing at the whole group, at how inept they are.'

'How could they have been so stupid as to have this press conference?' Walt asked.

'Foxy persuaded the President that it was a great idea. He told him they were on a roll, getting all this great coverage. Foxy obviously likes the publicity. A lot of thought had not gone into this.'

'What about Foxy?' asked Walt. 'What's his role here and what kind of clout does he really have with the President?'

'Tight. Very tight. Nobody closer. And Foxy's down on the head of DEA. Not that he's high on the FBI or CIA heads either. He'd rather oversee all of those agencies himself as far as I can tell. But he really wants a bit out of Garcia's ass. And if I know Foxy he's going to get it.'

Allison was having a hard time following the conversation, even after the drink and the splash of cold water. She should be involved in the discussion. This was her story. The staff would be looking to her to see if she was on top of it. Yet she was so preoccupied with her blackout and she felt so groggy that she didn't dare open her mouth. Besides, she wasn't sure what to say anyway. She really didn't want Tyson to know she was out of it either. She decided to say nothing.

'New business,' Walt was saying. 'Honoraria. Do

we have a policy?'

This was a subject that was intensely interesting to all of the staff—whether or not they could accept speaking fees and from whom.

'Everybody needs to read the Style book,' Walt said. 'You know you can't accept money from the government or anything you cover. Then we'll look at it on a case-by-case basis to see if there's a conflict. In any event, your assistant managing editor should approve it in advance. And if your editor has a problem he or she should come to me.'

Allison felt strongly about this issue. She had assigned one of her reporters to do a story not only on Hill people taking speaking fees but on journalists as well. It had had a mixed reaction at the *Daily*. Many reporters refused to cooperate and tell how much they got and from whom.

'Does it trouble you, Allison,' asked one of the reporters, 'that if an increasing amount of income comes from outside the *Daily* then the question arises as to who the real master is?'

Allison tried to answer but she found herself slurring her words. Walt jumped in.

'Some people are in demand and it's a very heady experience,' he said quickly.

'Did everyone at the paper who was asked to, cooperate, and are we going to continue that practice?' asked another.

'No, they didn't,' Allison mustered a response. 'It's Alan's idea that we continue to look into it occasionally.'

She leaned back in her chair. Walt looked relieved.

'Well, I think from looking at the situation closely,' said Lauren Hope, 'that people who don't take honoraria, inside or outside the paper, are rich and people who do are not rich.'

Everyone laughed appreciatively.

'It's always open to discussion, outside writing and speaking,' concluded Walt. 'I'll be meeting with each staff to discuss this further and I'm sure there will be a lot of reaction.'

Walt stood up, signaling the end of the meeting.

He grabbed Allison and took her arm.

'I'm okay,' she said.

'Well, we're going to talk about this. Come down to my office right now.'

They took the elevator down to the fifth floor in silence. Unfortunately Tyson was on the elevator. He never looked at Allison, though several other reporters were glancing suspiciously at her out of the corners of their eyes. When they got out of the elevator Tyson put his hand lightly on Allison's shoulder as he walked away. It was obviously a gesture of support. It stunned her. She couldn't get it out of her mind.

'Okay, what's going on?' asked Walt, once they were in his office.

'I don't know.'

'What do you mean, "you don't know"?'

She didn't say anything.

'How long has this been going on?'

She looked down at her watch. She didn't want him to see her eyes tear up.

'I don't know what's happening to me, Walt,' she finally managed to choke out. 'I'm really scared.' She was on the verge of breaking down but she couldn't because of the glass office. Everyone was watching. Damn these stupid glass offices. There was no privacy in a newsroom.

'Have you seen a doctor?'

'No.'

'Have you mentioned anything to Des?'

She shook her head again.

He picked up the phone and dialed a number while she was sitting there.

'This is Walt Fineman. Please tell Dr Goldberg that I'm sending over Allison Sterling right away to be examined. It's urgent. Extremely urgent.'

Goldberg was everybody's doctor. They also shared the same therapist, the same agent, the same dentist, and the same personal trainer at the health club. It was part of the pack journalism syndrome.

Before she could protest he was standing up and pulling her out of her chair. 'If you don't go I'll physically take you there.'

'Walt, I've got too much to do. I'm supposed to have lunch with Jennifer Conlon about her maternity leave. Do you know she wants to work only part-time when she comes back from having the baby? I can't believe how self-indulgent these people are. Honest to Christ. How are you supposed to run a newspaper like this? This is Marie Roger's first week back and she's going home several times a day to nurse. And have you seen her tits? They're leaking like a faucet. She's got these horrible little wet spots on her silk blouses. It's really disgusting.' She shuddered.

Walt laughed.

'I must say this conversation certainly brought you back from the dead.'

She looked up at him and a shadow crossed her face.

'I'm sorry, Sonny. I didn't mean to joke like that. You're really scared, aren't you?'

366

She managed a weak smile.

'I'm too mean to die,' she said to Walt. 'Besides, I'm not finished yet with Tyson.'

★     ★     ★

Riding over to 19th Street in the taxi she broke out in a cold sweat. It was the first of May and unseasonably warm for this time of year. She took her suit jacket off and leaned her head against the back of the seat.

All she could think about were her parents. They both died young. Maybe that was her fate, too. She was probably going to die of a brain tumor. There. She actually allowed herself to think the worst. What else could it be? Please, please don't let it be cancer, she said out loud. Who was she whispering to? Not the cabdriver, who said, 'I beg your pardon?' Not herself. Not God. There wasn't any God. She knew that for sure. Despite Des's feeble attempts to ease his way back into the Church since they'd gotten together again ... it was odd. He'd been so contemptuous of it before. Now he was constantly making oblique references to it. She didn't think he even meant to. He was even talking more to his priest brother. She was terrified he'd be sucked back into his religion. It wasn't just one thing. It was sort of creeping up on him like the invasion of the body snatchers. You fall in love with one person, marry him, and the next minute he becomes somebody else, someone you don't even know. Praying and going to mass. It was like marrying a normal person and then having them start jogging. The next minute they're running marathons and talking about cross-training. This was ridiculous. What was she thinking about? Here she was afraid she was dying of a brain tumor and then thinking about being married to a jogger.

The taxi pulled up to Dr Goldberg's building. Her heart was pounding when he ushered her into his office.

'I think I should tell you right away that I'm afraid I have a brain tumor,' she blurted out. 'I know I always come in here even if I have a hangnail and tell you I think it's cancer but this time'—she found her eyes going blurry again—'this time I really think it is. I've been sort of passing out for the past week or so. I can feel my eyelids get heavy and then I'm gone. Maybe, I don't know, maybe, I was hoping it could be some kind of seizure disorder. But I'm really afraid, David. I just don't think I can deal with this.'

Goldberg was her friend as well as her doctor. He was funny, smart, and attractive and he understood completely what babies tough-minded journalists were. He chuckled reassuringly, examined her carefully, then sent her to the nurse for a blood test, with instructions to go home and get some rest.

At first she protested, but when she finally got home she had barely gotten out of her clothes before she went under again.

It was Des who woke her when he got home. It was already dark.

'Sonny, Sonny, wake up, are you okay?'

She could hear his voice in the distance, urgent and frightened.

'Oh Des ... I, Des,' she could feel herself drifting away again.

'Sonny, what's the matter? I just called the office to see when you were coming home and they said you went home sick at noon. What the hell's going on? I'm going to call Goldberg.'

'No, no, Des, I saw him...'

She couldn't keep her eyes open and she flopped back against the pillow. She just wanted to be left alone.

'Well, what did he say? Sonny! Wake up for Christ's sake.'

'I can't wake up, Des. Please, just let me sleep.'

'We're going to the emergency room, right now if you don't wake up. I'll carry you if I have to.'

'Please, Des. I'm okay, I think. I'll wake up. I promise,' she mumbled. 'Just give me a few minutes, please.'

Des picked her up, placed her arms around his neck, and carried her into the bathroom. He pulled off her wrapper, turned on the shower and held her under it, all the while ignoring her vehement protests. It did, however, wake her up. When she got out of the shower she was cursing Des at the top of her lungs.

'You motherfucker!' she yelled, grabbing a towel. 'You had absolutely no right to do that. I was just fine, a little sleepy, that's all,' she said, furiously drying herself off.

Des smiled for the first time since he'd come in.

'You had me worried there for a while. Let's go downstairs. I could use a wee taste of Irish after this.'

'I think I'll have some camomile tea,' she said. 'Something soothing.'

She slipped on her robe and slippers and they went down to the study, which had a tiny kitchen-wet bar tucked into a closet. She made her tea while Des fixed a drink.

They sat on the love seat, the French doors open to the tiny patio below. There was a soft spring breeze. They were silent for a long time, the only sound the clink of ice in Des's glass. Allison moved closer to him and he put his arms around her. She snuggled up against him and rested her head on his shoulder. He rubbed his hands up and down her arm, stroking her like a kitten.

It was his gentleness that made her cry and soon the tears were rolling down her cheeks.

'Sonny, what is it? What's the matter?'

'Oh Des. It isn't fair. It just isn't fair. After all that we've been through. I can't bear it. I'm so scared.'

'Scared of what?'

'I don't want to die.'

*    *    *

The next morning she felt better. Actually, she felt pretty good. She got up, got dressed, and went to work.

She felt fine but she couldn't keep her eyes off her watch. She was waiting for David Goldberg to call Des. Even though he hadn't been able to find anything wrong with her in the exam, he had ordered up a battery of tests and she knew that was where the bad news would be. She had given Goldberg strict instructions to call Des with the results of the test. She didn't want to hear bad news over the phone.

At about eleven the phone rang. It was Des.

'How about lunch?' he said.

'David Goldberg called you and told you I have a brain tumor and you're taking me to lunch to tell me. That spineless bastard. Why can't he do his own dirty work?'

'Wrong,' Des laughed. 'I was just worried about you and I knew you were worried. I wanted to cheer you up, take your mind off things.'

'Are you sure?' She still wasn't convinced.

'Positive. Where would you like to eat?'

'Let's go to Bice's. I might as well make my last meal a good one.'

\*    \*    \*

Bice's was a popular new restaurant off Pennsylvania Avenue. It was all bleached woods and green plaids, banquettes and glass. Des had staked it out early on as his new favorite restaurant and had even been awarded his own table by the maître d'hotel. It was on the side of the front room next to the window with a view of the whole room and the entrance stairs.

Allison was a little nervous that they were in full view of everyone, given what she expected the news to be.

'God, I need a drink,' said Allison, once they were seated across from each other. 'I think I'll have a glass of white wine. I know I'll be sorry at four when I get a tiny hangover, but I don't care.'

When the waiter came over Des ordered a martini for himself and a glass of Perrier for her.

Allison was so shocked she couldn't respond and the waiter took their order and scurried away.

'Excuse me,' she said in a very controlled voice. 'But I think there's been some mistake here.'

'Oh, what's that?'

'I was under the impression that I had ordered a

371

glass of white wine.'

'You can't have that!'

'And why not?'

'Because you're pregnant.'

'I am not! ... I mean ... how do you know? I mean ... I am?'

Des smiled. Des beamed. Des lifted his arm and flexed his muscles.

'I am?' she asked weakly. 'You mean I don't have a brain tumor? I'm not dying?'

Des got up and moved over to her side of the table, put his arm around her and kissed her on the forehead, then gently on the lips. It was a very un-Des-like gesture. He was usually so uncomfortable about what he called P.D.A., or public display of affection.

'Oh Des, it's true, isn't it?' She could feel her throat constrict with relief and happiness.

'I love you, Sonny. I'm so pleased and proud that you're going to have my baby.'

It was such a sweet speech it almost made her cry. He looked like the little Catholic altar boy he once was, a Des she had never known and rarely seen any evidence of.

'I love you, too.' She didn't know what more to say and she was afraid if she did she would start to cry. She couldn't possibly have a scene here in Bice's. Already several people they knew were looking at them.

The waiter was the only one who dared approach them with their drinks. Des took his glass after the waiter had left and lifted it to her.

'Here's to Junior,' he said.

'I'm so happy to know that I'm going to live, not to mention that I'm going to have a baby, that I'm not even going to get annoyed with you for assuming it will be a boy.'

'If this is what pregnancy does to you, I'm all for it. The mellowing of Sonny Sterling.'

'I'm mellow because neither of us has any control over whether it's a boy or a girl. Anyway, we'll soon find out. They have a new test now that's much faster than amniocentesis. It's called something like chorionic villus sampling. You take it three to six weeks into your pregnancy and you get the results within a week or so. That way, if there's a problem...'

She was talking so quickly and so excitedly that it took her a moment to notice that Des's face had stiffened.

'What do you mean, amniocentesis? You're not going to consider that, are you?' There was an urgent tone to his voice.

'Well, no, I just told you, there's an earlier test. I'll have to discuss it with my gynecologist but...'

'Sonny.'

'What?'

'We can't do this. You can't do this.'

'Do what? What are you talking about, Des?'

'I'm talking about amniocentesis or whatever the hell the other test is. Those tests. We can't do those tests. Any of them.'

'Why not?' She was genuinely puzzled.

'Well, suppose they showed that something was wrong with the child?'

'Then, unfortunately, I'd have to have an abortion.'

'No.'

'No what?'

'I can't let that happen. I can't allow you to abort

373

our child. My child.'

'First of all, I would be aborting a fetus, not a child. Second, you can't not allow me to do anything. And third, what the hell is the matter with you? You've always been pro-choice. Or at least you haven't been anti-abortion. What's this about?'

'We weren't talking about my baby.'

'Des, let me get this straight. I am forty years old. You are over fifty. We are older parents. The risk of having a defective fetus is much greater for us. You are saying that you will take a chance on having a seriously damaged child rather than abort a fetus early on.'

He didn't answer for a minute or so but she could see that he was struggling and that it was very painful for him.

'I guess that's what I'm saying.'

'Well, Des, I'm the mother. And I couldn't hack it. I know myself too well. Frankly, I know you too well. You'd leave it to me to deal with. You are not the most liberated soul I've ever met. I am not prepared to be a single parent to a severely retarded or handicapped child. That's all there is to it.'

'And I can't stand by and let you destroy our baby.'

They stared at each other, stone-faced and determined.

'It's not negotiable, Des. It's simply not negotiable.'

\*        \*        \*

She felt so illicit, reading a baby book in the office. She hid it under her desk and brought it up under the newspaper to take a peek whenever she had a free moment.

No sooner would 'the boys' leave after her morning meeting than she found her heart racing. She would look around furtively, carefully spread the paper out and hold it completely open. Then she would reach down and slide whichever book she was obsessed with at the moment into her lap. Like a man taking clandestine glances at a girlie magazine, she would thumb through until she found her favorite mother/baby profile.

She was particularly interested in the descriptions of the working mothers and how they coped with their new babies, how they divided their time and still managed to be relatively guilt-free. It was becoming clear that they didn't. In fact, now that she was watching the working mothers in the office more closely, she was beginning to see all kinds of things she hadn't been aware of before. She felt as if she had been living in a dark closet and suddenly somebody had turned on the lights. The women in the office had a sort of underground system of sympathy and support. And well they might have. The stress, the compensation, juggling of schedules, covering up, all to care for their children and present a facade of professionalism in the face of the most daunting obstacles was a revelation to her. And it was so obvious for anyone who took the time, who knew to look for it, right out there.

She hadn't told anyone yet she was pregnant. She wanted to wait until after the test. The bloody test. She had seen her doctor. He had presented the options: amnio or chorionic villus sampling. Amnio you took after four months, and didn't get the results until you were into your fifth month. If you had to 'terminate the pregnancy' it would be really awful. The baby would have started kicking. She knew somebody it had happened to. Her friend never even tried to get pregnant again. Besides, she had to consider Des. She had been appalled at his position on prenatal testing, stunned that he was so deeply emotionally opposed to it. He had always been pro-choice, at least nominally, yet not when it involved his own child. This was the second time now that religion had intruded into their relationship and it was profoundly upsetting to her. First, it was having his brother, the priest, be part of his marriage, or rather their marriage ceremony. Now this. He couldn't stop her from having either test. He couldn't stop her from aborting a defective fetus. But the depth of his feeling had shaken her. It had convinced her that their marriage could not survive the abortion of his five-month-old-plus baby. Which is the way he would see it. There was a slightly greater risk of having a miscarriage with the chorionic villus sampling, especially for a woman of forty-one, and she would be forty-one in July. She could, however, take the test at ten weeks and have the results in one week. She wouldn't even be three months pregnant. She wouldn't tell Des she was having the test. If the results were bad she could have a simple D and C and tell him she'd miscarried. He'd never know the difference. He might suspect, but he'd never know for sure. The question then would be, could she live with the lie?

This was such a macabre line of thinking. She would find herself wandering off. Then she would pull herself back to the baby book and a chapter on how the mother could bond with the child and not feel her role usurped by the baby-sitter.

Actually, she found herself wandering off constantly, about everything. She couldn't concentrate on any one subject for more than a few minutes at a time.

The whole idea of being pregnant had come as such a shock to her even though they had discussed it before they were married. She had gone so long without having a baby or even wanting one that the idea of a child was more a fantasy or an illusion; she never really expected it to be a reality. It was only when she and Des first talked about getting married this time that she had developed this terrible physical longing, this baby hunger. Even then it seemed she was destined to be denied this final gift. She was so used to personal losses that she had accepted the fact she would never be a mother. Now she was going to be and she was having a difficult time coming to terms with it.

Part of that had to do with her job. Her new job. She hadn't even been back from London a year. She was a workaholic, obsessed with her office, her career; so much so that it was even difficult making time for Des, her husband. Now that she was pregnant, she was strangely, unexpectedly of two minds about it.

Her time of adjustment had been endless, it seemed to her, like going from freedom to prison. The subject matter—from foreign to national—had been completely different. Even though she had been on the national staff before, there had been three years of politics to learn. Washington had changed drastically in those three years. In just that short time it had gone from being a company town to a corporate metropolis. It wasn't just about politics and government anymore. The White

House no longer wielded the influence on the city that it used to, either politically or socially. The Congress was never in town, always on the road, politicking and raising money. Congressmen and senators were isolated and disillusioned. The diplomatic corps was irrelevant. The lawyer/lobbyists were in such proliferation and had been so exposed as fixers that they no longer had the kind of influence or stature that once commanded huge amounts of money. The glamour of the press had worn thin. They had become as institutional as the other 'estates.' They were now too cautious and establishment to have the cachet they had in the seventies or even early and mid-eighties. The new breed of journalists were more like yuppie accountants, more concerned with their mortgages than with throwing bombs.

It had taken her the entire past year just to absorb all of this, the kind of thing that she would have automatically understood if she had stayed as a reporter covering the White House.

This was all on top of just plain information that she had had to learn, not to mention learning how to be a boss. As much as Des teased her about finally finding her metier, it was difficult for her to order people around. She did it and she gradually learned how to make it look easy, but much of the time her stomach was in knots trying to take in as much as she could and convince people that she knew what she was talking about. It was only in the past few months that she had become comfortable with her role as editor, as a supervisor. She had always been used to being her own agent, doing things for herself. Now she was responsible for other people. For that reason she was conflicted about the baby, about the timing. Just as she had gotten her feet on the ground, she was going to be distracted for months, then away for at least three months, then distracted forever after. If the other women on her staff were any indication of how she would be pulled back and forth, she was going to be in for some tough times.

There was another side to it that pleased her, though. She had finally allowed herself to admit that she needed a child to make her feel fulfilled. She wanted someone of her own, some family of her own. Somebody with her own blood. It was visceral. Her grandparents were all dead. Her parents were dead. She had no brothers or sisters. Uncle Rog and Aunt Molly were all she had and they weren't going to be around much longer. She needed kin. Des was her husband but he didn't count. He wasn't a blood relation. He could leave her anytime. That wasn't the same. This was a very primitive, tribal feeling she had. She had always felt so lost. So alone. Early on with no mother, no siblings. Even more so after Nana died. Sam never remarried so it was just the two of them. When Sam was murdered she didn't think she could bear it. Now she had a chance to feel whole again. To feel found. Her baby would give her that.

She was also tired. She hadn't thought about it before. When she calculated the amount of leave she had taken over the years in London it probably didn't add up to more than a few weeks. There was always something and her vacation time had been expendable. Her career always came first, even over her private life. It used to annoy Julian no end. Now she couldn't think of a greater luxury than to be able to take three months off and do nothing.

Not that having a baby was nothing. She would have a baby nurse full time, around the clock. Doing nothing to her meant doing anything but newspapering. This would be enforced time off with something more important to do than putting out a paper. With no guilt. She had worked so hard over the years, canceled so many plans, so much of her private life, that she felt no guilt at all. She knew it would be a big pain in the ass for Walt and Alan, but she also knew that they were enlightened enough to think it was a good thing. In the end, it all balanced out. She felt really happy about her circumstances. In fact, she was happier than she had been for as long as she could remember.

'That's yesterday's paper.'

She started as though she'd been shot, then quickly pushed the paper on top of the baby book, covering it up so that he couldn't see what she was reading.

'What?' She looked up to see Sprague smiling knowingly at her.

'Yesterday's paper,' he said and gestured toward the journal lying on her desk. 'What've you got under it, *Playboy*?'

What was it about him that rattled her so? He made her angry and frustrated in a way that nobody else did or could. He had this combination of Southern gentlemanly manners and confrontational arrogance that drove her crazy. He managed to be hostile and courtly at the same time. She prided herself on never being outdone by anyone, especially by a man, giving as good as she got, being quick with a comeback. With Sprague, she always felt tongue-tied and it infuriated her. She could never decide whether she was angrier at him or

380

herself.

'*Playgirl*,' she said, pleased that she could think of anything to say, yet she felt the blood surge to her face.

He didn't say anything. He just smiled.

She blushed even redder. Damn him!

He reached over and pulled the glass door to her office closed.

'May I?' he asked after the fact.

Without waiting for an answer he sat down.

'May I?' he asked again, as an afterthought.

Now it was her turn to say nothing. She waited to see what was on his mind.

'I need to go to Colombia.'

'This doesn't sound too safe.'

'I've got a lead on Mendez. I think Antonia Alvarez and he are working together and there is some evidence that they have sucked Foxy in. They may be blackmailing him. There is a limo that pulls up every week in the early morning in front of the Jefferson Hotel. The doorman is Colombian and he says the limo driver is from the Colombian embassy. The driver always delivers a package to Foxy's suite. He delivers it in person. He will never leave it at the desk or let anyone else take it up to him.'

'What do you think is in it?'

'I think it's drugs. Cocaine.'

'Holy shit!' she said.

'Holy shit!' was an expression in the newsroom reserved for only the most incredible stories. It was sparingly used.

'Tyson, you're talking about the attorney general. You're telling me that the attorney general of the United States has been turned on to drugs by the

381

deputy chief of mission of the Colombian embassy while he's fucking her? That she's delivering drugs to him at his residential hotel on a regular basis? That she is blackmailing him into God knows what—we'll get to that later? And that she is in cahoots with the Foreign Minister of Colombia?'

'That's what I'm telling you.'

'That, my friend, is a great story. Go for it, baby. It will bring glory to us all. You have my blessing for your trip to Colombia.'

'That's a switch. You're usually so reluctant to let me do anything.'

'Ah, but now I can see my own name in lights.'

Why was she talking to him in such a flip manner? She never talked to any other reporter this way.

'However,' she added, 'we are forgetting one small thing.'

'What's that?'

'I think we need to run this one by Fineman and Warburg. They're upstairs in a meeting right now, but the minute they get back we're going in to see them.'

'But you have no objection?'

'Absolutely none.'

'What about my safety? Aren't you concerned about my safety anymore?'

'You have to be fatalistic about this. We all have to die sometime. It might as well be for the Pulitzer Prize.'

'You're tough, boss,' he said, picking up her flip tone, as he walked out of her office. 'You're very, very tough.'

He paused, then stopped and looked back at her.

'Or are you?'

382

Slightly chagrined, she watched him make his way through the newsroom, his walk so confident and assured that he might have owned the place. If only he had known that the minute he left she had picked up the baby book and flipped through the section on breast feeding.

She sat there for a moment intent on breast preference, delay in the mother's milk, is the baby getting enough, and the manual expression of breast milk, when suddenly she broke out in a cold sweat.

One of her reporters had just walked in and dropped a bomb in her lap, what might be the hottest story of the decade, the greatest scandal in Washington since she could remember, and she was reading about breast feeding. This was pathetic. This was terrifying. Ten minutes pregnant and her brain was turning to pablum. Is this why so many normally bright, talented, ambitious women turned into cows overnight simply because they were going to have a baby? It was like being married with three children and then discovering in middle age that you were a repressed homosexual. She had to get a grip on herself before it was too late. She took the baby book and shoved it into her briefcase under the desk, determined to take it home and never bring it to work again. Never mind that it would be like a chain smoker having a pack of cigarettes in her briefcase for the rest of the afternoon.

She jumped up and walked out of her office. Maybe she should go down to the cafeteria and get some tea, talk to one of the boys about the budget, go back to the Living section and raise hell about a profile they were doing that encroached on national's territory. She was having strange crampy feelings in her abdomen, her stomach was making

383

weird gurgling noises and there was a sense of something quickening in her body. Was that the way it would be until the baby was born? But then there would be the baby. Then it would be forever. Is this what she really wanted? What if she didn't want to come back to work? Or worse, what if she came back and was distracted and uninterested or preoccupied? How would Des feel about this change in her? The bastard. He'd probably love it. Just keep 'em barefoot and pregnant. She had to stop this. She was driving herself crazy. Maybe the problem was that nobody knew. Once she'd had the test, once it was out, then she could talk about it and she wouldn't have to obsess. Des had persuaded her not to tell anyone for three months. That was the danger period for older women for miscarriages. She hadn't known how hard it would be. Especially since she was going to have the test without telling him. This was when she really missed having a friend like Jenny. She had almost called her several times after she found out she was pregnant, but she had been so hurt at their lunch that she resisted. Oh well. By the time three months were up she would know anyway. Until then she had to get herself together or she would not be able to do her job.

She looked across the city room to see Walt and Alan coming in from their meeting upstairs. She signaled to Sprague, who was standing at his desk, the phone cradled under his chin, to meet her in Alan's office.

They were standing there when Alan and Walt reached the door. Seeing the urgent looks on their faces, Alan told his secretary to hold his calls and ushered them in.

384

Allison presented the situation as Sprague had explained it to her.

'Holy shit!' said Alan.

Sprague then went into details, explaining why he needed to get to Colombia quickly and who he needed to see.

'They're blowing up journalists right and left down there, not to mention Supreme Court justices and presidential candidates,' said Alan. 'Are you sure it's safe?'

'This story is too big not to pursue. If there's danger involved, Sprague is prepared to face it,' said Allison without a moment's hesitation.

'You're tough, Sterling,' said Walt with an appreciative laugh.

Sprague couldn't help but smile.

Alan looked at both Sprague and Allison, then nodded his assent.

'Okay,' he said, 'but I don't want any dead reporters on my hands. No heroics, Tyson. It's not worth any fucking prize to get your ass blown away.'

'Sir, that's exactly the opposite of what your national editor just told me.'

'The problem with my national editor, Tyson, is that she doesn't realize that she's not a man.'

★　　　★　　　★

'The baby's fine. It's a girl.'

Her gynecologist had called her just before story conference.

She was eleven weeks pregnant. She was having a baby girl. It was real. It wasn't just fantasy.

It was also July 3, her forty-first birthday.

385

She was totally unprepared for the phone call even though she had jumped every time the phone rang. She was equally unprepared for the flood of tears that came so quickly. There she sat in the middle of the city room in her little glass box, holding the phone and weeping. She couldn't control it so she didn't even bother to hide the fact that she was crying.

One of 'the boys' had seen her and had rushed into Walt's office. Walt was standing at her desk within seconds. She had obviously never given him her doctor's report after her blacking-out spells, so he expected the worst.

'Sonny, what is it? Are you okay? Let's get out of here. I'll take you next door and we can get a drink and talk.'

'It's all right, Walt. It's ... I can't talk about it yet. I'll tell you tomorrow. I'm going to the ladies' room and fix my face in a minute. Don't worry. I promise, everything is fine.'

She said it with such conviction that she could tell he believed her, but he only reluctantly left her office when she insisted.

She couldn't tell him until she told Des.

She didn't want to tell Des right away. She needed to sit with it for a while. She needed to be alone with it. She felt an urgent need to get out of the office, away from everybody. As soon as she had pulled herself together she managed to walk through the newsroom and into the ladies' room without having everyone staring at her. She freshened up and then just walked out of the office. She grabbed a taxi and went down to the Potomac River, to Thompson's boathouse. She had the taxi let her off in the parking lot and she walked across the little bridge that covered the end of the Rock Creek before it poured into the larger river.

It was a beautiful sunny day and there was a soft breeze that rustled the leaves and created ripples on the surface of the water. She walked down the bank and found a grassy spot under a large pin oak.

She had nothing specific she wanted to think about. She just wanted to be alone. She sat there, her mind blank, staring at the water. She felt as though she had been transported into some sort of impressionist painting. The sky was so vivid and the leaves of the oak tree hung down in front of her so delicate and graceful. They seemed to frame the view of Roosevelt Island across the river, all green and full and lush at this time of year. She always thought of it as Fantasy Island, a place where one could go and hide out from the rest of the world, peering out from the privacy of the undergrowth at the Washington monuments and watching the rat race without actually having to be a part of it. She had always wanted to canoe over to it and get out and walk around. But there was never enough time. The sun flickered on top of the water, casting bright shards of light into her eyes even though she was sitting in the shade, but she resisted getting out her dark glasses. She didn't want anything to mitigate the colors of her reverie. She was totally alone by the river. It wasn't lunchtime yet and there were no picnickers spreading their blankets and enjoying the view. Could it be that this was undiscovered, this place? She had never been here before to sit and meditate.

A plane lifted up from National Airport and soared above her. She could see from behind the bushes the people beginning to take their seats on the terrace of the Sequoia restaurant on the waterfront to her right. The cars whizzed past the Kennedy Center to her left, out of hearing distance so that they seemed a hasty blur. Where was everyone going in such a hurry?

The sightseeing boat, the *Dandy*, went by in front of her, with gay little flags strung around it. You could have dinner on board and cruise up and down the river. They had never done that. Always too busy with more high-powered things.

One lone man in a scull rowed up the river on the side closest to the island. A few speedboats passed by. He was whistling and he seemed happy, content to do just that. The wake of the speedboats left the waves lapping up against the shore.

She felt totally calm, totally serene. She always felt spiritually renewed by being near water. Rivers, lakes, oceans, beaches. Especially beaches. Des had God. She had water.

She wished she could feel this way forever. All the baby books talked about how important it was to stay calm during your pregnancy, that anxiety was not good for the baby. She wondered whether she would be able to do that. There was much she felt anxious about in her everyday life. Except at this moment she had never felt more peaceful. Was this what it was going to be like? Being pregnant, having a baby? Maybe that's why so many women had babies all the time. If it was like this it was better than any drug, any high she'd ever had.

A girl. She had wanted a girl. To replace the mother she had never had? A little child-mother. She had an image of her daughter—beautiful, blond, blue-eyed—taking care of her in her old age. But that wasn't fair. She'd had to grow up so fast herself as a child that she never got to be one. Sam wanted her mother back and she had felt obligated to transform herself into a wife for Sam instead of being his daughter. Now she was going to try to do the same thing to her own child? They both wanted her mother back but she would have to guard against letting that happen.

She would call her Katherine. She needed to honor her mother at any rate. To assuage her guilt at being angry at her. Angry because her mother had left her to go abroad for a story. Angry at her for caring more about a story than her daughter. A story she had died for. And left her alone. Nana had instilled that in her enough times, this hostility for her mother. Nana hadn't believed women should work in the first place, much less be foreign correspondents, much less go abroad on assignment with a two-year-old child at home.

Suddenly she was infused with sadness. Sadness for the loss, for missing someone she had never really known and yet knew intimately. She leaned over and began to rock herself. She heard herself whisper 'Mommy, Mommy,' words she didn't remember ever having said until now. Soon she would be somebody's mommy. Then she would hear the word and it would make her happy instead of making her ache with emptiness. At least now she didn't feel empty. She felt full. How Sam would have been thrilled at the news. How he would have looked forward to having a grandchild, a beautiful granddaughter named Katherine.

What would she call her? Her mother was called Kay but that would be too painful a reminder. Katherine sounded too formal and too grand for a baby. Kitty was too old-fashioned. Kate, no, it was a great name but too popular now. Kay Kay maybe. That sounded better with Shaw as a last name anyway. She wasn't going to go the hyphenated last name route.

Oh, she would have such fun dressing her in beautiful clothes with pink lace and frills and smocking and little flowers. She had been haunting baby and maternity stores in the last few weeks.

What would she look like pregnant? She wondered if Des would still find her sexually attractive though he seemed even more turned on by her than before. She couldn't wait for her breasts to get big. Lungs. Knockers, melons, jugs. All her life she had longed to have them. Now she would. She would nurse her baby, too. She hadn't thought she would before she got pregnant. There had been something sort of bovine and disgusting about the idea of it. Now that she was actually pregnant she couldn't wait.

She wanted to bask in her joy before she told Des. He would be upset that she had had the test without telling him. He would always suspect she might have had a secret abortion. He would be thrilled that the child was healthy. He would be disappointed that he was to have another daughter. Thank God she had had the early test, so that she knew her child was normal and healthy. That would dilute some of Des's anger.

More than that, it would give her a chance, knowing the sex, to bond with her daughter.

It was such a good omen, even though she wasn't the least bit superstitious, to find out about it on her birthday. She was sure it was good luck, that good things were going to happen to all of them.

A buoy was bobbing in the water as another

speedboat went by and the wake pushed the waves up again on the banks. A helicopter, probably the President's, whirred overhead, toward the White House.

She felt completely at peace with herself.

She rubbed her stomach in a round, soothing circular motion.

'Happy Birthday, Sonny,' she said. 'Happy Birthday to you, too, Kay Kay. You're the best present any mommy could ever have.'

\*    \*    \*

Forty-one was sort of a nothing birthday. She had told Des she really didn't care about having a party. She had her baby now and that was enough. Besides, it was the first anniversary of Rosey's being shot and neither one of them really felt like celebrating. They would stay at home alone together and have caviar and ... soda water. Des would have his usual Irish. She would tell him about Kay Kay. Then what?

She had called Walt to tell him she was taking the rest of the day off. She reassured him that everything was fine and arranged to meet him for breakfast the next morning. After she left the river she spent the day looking at baby clothes at the Foxhall Shopping Mall in Wesley Heights. She stood and stared longingly at a blue silk dress in the window of the maternity shop next to the baby store. She decided to wait until she told Des. Then she went home, fixed a peanut butter and jelly sandwich—peanut butter and jelly? She hadn't eaten one of those since she was twelve—a glass of skim milk, and went up to her bedroom where she put on a wrapper and curled up in bed with her baby books. Bliss!

Des came home about seven. She had the caviar, the toast, and the lemon wedges all prepared. There was chilled vodka in case he wanted that. She had bought fresh flowers, which were arranged in the little study on the second floor. It was cool, and dry for July, so she left the French doors open and put on a Mozart piano concerto. She sighed deeply. She couldn't remember ever having been so happy. Seeing him standing shyly in front of her with a box wrapped in pretty papers and ribbons, all she wanted to do was fling herself in his arms and hug him—which she did.

'Oh Des, I'm so happy. I love you so much.' She could barely get it out, she was choking with emotion.

'Hey, what is this? I thought women weren't supposed to be happy about their birthdays.'

She had planned to tell him after dinner, after she'd softened him up.

'Des we're having a girl and she's fine. She's healthy and normal.'

She had blurted it out.

'Please don't be angry with me for having the test. Please don't be disappointed that it's a girl. I'm so happy and I love you so much I'll be devastated if anything spoils it now.'

She had blurted that out too.

She could see Des trying to take it all in, the expressions on his face fast-forwarding a series of emotions as he absorbed the news in segments. In the end, he smiled and she could see that what he had settled on was relief. He reached out and pulled her close to him.

'Oh, thank God, Sonny. Thank God for both of us.'

He was holding her tightly and her face was buried in his shoulder. He rocked her back and forth.

'Yes, I'm angry with you for having the test and not telling me. It makes me crazy to know what you might have done if the news were not good. Yes, a part of me would like to have a son. I can't deny that. But you must know that I'm overwhelmed with happiness and relief that everything is fine and now I'm glad you did it so that we don't have to worry anymore. Nothing can ruin this for us. We're blessed.'

They stood and held on to each other for several moments until he remembered her birthday present.

'Great timing,' he said, pleased with himself.

She ripped off the wrapping to find the blue silk dress she had seen in the window of the maternity shop that day.

She looked up at Des stunned. 'How did you know. I just...'

'I told the woman you were tall and blond and beautiful and just pregnant and she said she'd seen someone fitting that description staring at the dress earlier in the day. So I bought it.'

'I'll tie a pillow on my stomach and try it on later, but first, let's eat.' She beamed with pride. 'I'm suddenly starving.'

Later that evening, out on their tiny terrace, Allison, against her better judgment, brought up the subject of the test. It was after Des had had several drinks and practically a whole bottle of wine, and after a splendid meal that she all too rarely fixed. She knew it was risky, but it had been weighing on her mind. She had been so undone at the time that she had called O'Grady for lunch. She had needed him to explain to her why Des was as upset as he was. Particularly since he had always claimed to be a lapsed Catholic and had always been pro-choice. His explanation had depressed her.

'I've said it before and I'll say it again. There's no such thing as lapsed,' he had said. 'You, my dear atheist, are married to a Catholic. You had better get used to it.'

She brought it up with Des now, but gingerly. She didn't want to make him angry. She really didn't want to spoil this perfect birthday evening. They had had such a wonderful time at dinner planning their daughter's future, talking about what she would be like.

'She is going to be one little piece of work,' said Des, 'if she's anything like her mother. I can barely handle one of you. I'm not sure I can take on two.'

'She'll be a total Daddy's girl. She'll wrap you around her little finger. You'll be hopelessly in love with her and I'll be completely left out.'

'Ah, already competitive, are we now?'

'I'm not, I mean, I don't want to be, I just want to love her and to love you and for all of us to love each other.'

'If you love her half as much as I love you then she'll be the most loved little girl in the whole world.'

He took her hand and held it, looking at her in the candlelight with such adoration that she was overwhelmed.

'Oh Des, aren't you glad now that I've had the test. That we know. That we don't have to worry

394

anymore.'

He took his hand away and looked down.

'I've told you I'm relieved.'

'Des, I know I shouldn't bring this up and I really don't want to destroy our mood. I don't want you to be angry with me and I don't want an argument, I just feel that there's such a large part of you that I don't know, that I don't understand. The whole Catholicism thing. You've always said that you were a lapsed Catholic and left it at that. I've never seen any signs of religious belief or actions. You've always been pro-choice. I've talked to O'Grady and he says there's no such thing as a lapsed Catholic. I'm beginning to believe him. It just seems to me that sometime last fall you changed. Something happened to you and you've been different. That whole period right before we were married, when you seemed so depressed and distracted and I didn't understand it. I thought you might be in love with someone else. Then you snapped out of it and asked me to marry you, but we had to have your brother present at the ceremony. Now your reaction to the baby's test. I feel that we need to talk about this. You're my husband and about to be the father of my child. I don't know who you are. I love you and I like you better than I used to, but I don't know you. Help me out here.'

'O'Grady's right. I guess you're never really lapsed. I just thought I was. It's not like I'm completely back in the fold. But I've been doing a lot of thinking this past year. You say you don't know me. Well, that makes two of us, baby. I've never been particularly introspective. The whole process makes me uncomfortable. Especially

395

knowing your beliefs, or lack of.'

'But what about the test? Have you totally changed your mind about abortion?' She was trying to sound calm and unjudgmental.

'I didn't know I had until you mentioned the test. The idea of it just blew me away. Not the knowing. The having to make a decision if there was a problem. I couldn't face that. Then I had to figure out why.'

'So why?'

'It's God's will. You have to accept what He gives you. That spares you the moral decision. You don't want to be tempted to do the wrong thing. You don't want to put yourself in the wrong position. Especially since I'm not sure I'd be good enough to be the father of a seriously defective child. I'm not sure I could cope. Not having to make a decision makes it easier somehow. If the amnio or whatever the test is doesn't turn out right and you have an abortion, you're asking me to jeopardize my soul.'

'Do you really believe that?'

She wasn't challenging him. She was just being matter-of-fact. She understood that he found the whole subject challenging on a much higher level. It wasn't a personal conversation anymore.

'I may have rejected the art form of the Catholic church, but the intensity of it survives. It just does. I've had many late night talks about this with O'Grady and, privately, we always end up agreeing that it may not make any sense. Yet we say to each other, "Yeah, but who's going to take the chance?"'

She didn't know what to say so she didn't say anything. Very unusual for Allison. This was so unlike Des, this sort of reflection. He had never

396

talked about anything like this to her in all the time she'd known him. Part of her was thrilled with his new openness, his new depth. It was so exciting to learn that somebody you thought you knew so well was more complicated than you could have guessed. Part of her was a little embarrassed. She found the mere discussion of anything religious embarrassing. Partly she felt angry. She had bought into one thing and she was getting another. She had believed Des was not religious and she had married him, gotten pregnant by him. Now she was being told that her husband, this man she was to spend the rest of her life with and raise a child with, was not only religious but a Catholic. How would that affect Kay Kay? Would he try to indoctrinate her? She couldn't allow that. Yet she could see how strongly he was affected by it. Could he control it? This was something she had not bargained for. She was going to have to think about this one. It was clear to her, though, that the most important thing for both of them now was to be honest.

Des broke the silence.

'If you had found out that there was something wrong with the baby ... would you have had an abortion without telling me?'

She had no choice but to lie.

'I don't know.'

$$\star \qquad \star \qquad \star$$

Walt had been more relieved than she was. He got up from his desk and came around and hugged her, right in his glass office in front of the entire newsroom.

'I really thought you were dying of a brain

tumor,' he confessed.

'Des doesn't want me to tell anyone yet,' she said. 'He says it makes for a very long pregnancy. But I don't care. Now that I know everything is fine I want to tell everybody.'

'Well, now's your chance. Let's do it at my so-called Wednesday morning meeting. It's just about that time.'

This particular meeting was routine and boring. There was an announcement of a brown bag lunch. Each week, a different person from the *Daily* was chosen to speak at lunchtime to anyone in or out of the paper who was interested in that person's topic. There was a change in the TV section layout . . . an announcement of a personnel change in the top management of the company, and the birth announcement from two foreign correspondents married to each other. Everyone in the meeting was shuffling through papers, staring at the ceiling, glancing at their watches and doodling.

'Oh, I almost forgot,' said Walt. 'Allison is going to have a baby girl.'

Somehow adding 'baby girl' made it seem almost like a fait accompli. Even Allison was startled.

Pencils dropped and so did jaws.

Everyone stared at her as though Walt had announced she was going to give birth to a baby elephant. She burst out laughing.

The men looked down at the table and shuffled their papers. They seemed to be almost embarrassed. The Living editor, who was a woman, smiled encouragingly.

'What's the matter, guys?' Allison could feel her own face redden unexpectedly. 'Walt didn't exactly announce that I've got a brain tumor.'

398

One by one they got up self-consciously, as the meeting was over, and came over to her, shook her hand, congratulated her, and then left quickly. Walt smiled at her as he rushed out explaining that he had an early lunch and would talk to her later. Only she and the Living editor, with whom he had never gotten along, were left.

'That's very exciting,' she said, smiling warmly and putting her hand on Allison's shoulder. 'When are you due?'

'Christmas Day, actually.'

The two women chatted about Lamaze classes, breast feeding, biodegradable diapers, nannies, things Allison would never have dreamed of discussing before.

'There's a mother's lunch once a month where we all get together and talk about coping,' said the editor. 'I hope you'll join us this month. It might be helpful.'

Some sort of door had been opened and she had been invited into a secret society.

For the rest of the day there was a steady stream of women coming by her office, stopping her in the aisle, introducing themselves to her in the ladies' room—many of them she had never even met before—offering playpens, clothes, names of baby sitters, advice.

The men were interesting, too. Out of earshot of other men, they confided in her about their wives, their children, their home life. She began to realize that this made her a human being in their eyes, a woman, instead of the hard-nosed ambitious automaton. In fact, it seemed all she had to do was tell people she was pregnant and she was immediately turned into the bloody Virgin Mary.

It was time. She felt fulfilled in a way she hadn't ever imagined possible, and Kay Kay wasn't even born yet. Professionally she had done everything she had wanted to do, been everywhere she had wanted to go, visited more countries, flown on more airplanes, attended more parties. This was like embarking on a new adventure, a new assignment. It would be good for her marriage, good for her and Des. It had been too easy for them to spend all their time working. Without Kay Kay she could see how they could look at each other in another five years and say, 'Now what?'

And what a perfect due date. What a fabulous present. For once in her life she really would have a Merry Christmas.

★      ★      ★

'I'm having lunch with Sadie.'

'You've got to be joking.'

'I'm not,' said Des.

'Have you already asked her?'

'Yes.'

'So there's nothing I can say about it?'

'It's an interview.'

'Give me a break.'

'It's a one-year-after-the-assassination story.'

'You called and asked her for an interview? Des. You couldn't have been that insensitive.'

'She called to congratulate us about the baby. She offered.'

'Just like that. Hi, Des. It's your old girlfriend, Sadie, you remember the widow of our assassinated President. Well, in case you've forgotten it's one year ago and I thought you might want to tell the

400

world how I'm feeling about the whole thing. It would be a big scoop for you, an exclusive. Whaddya say, big guy?'

'Sonny.'

'Don't Sonny me, Des. I'm not stupid.'

'She's in love with someone else.'

'What? Did she tell you that? This is terrific. What a ploy. I'm safe. I'm in love with somebody else. So it's okay to have lunch. Allison won't mind. Just who is she in love with anyway? The doctor who took care of Rosey in the emergency room? That would make a great story. Is she going to tell all at lunch? On the record? How many millions of dollars would you like to bet that this interview never sees print?'

'This is not like you.'

'This is exactly like me. Where are you going to take her anyway, i Ricchi so everybody in town will see you together?'

'If I wanted to be with Sadie, I wouldn't have married you.'

'It's just that I . . .'

'You're pregnant and you don't want me running off with another woman, is that it?'

'That's it.'

'Sonny, I love you. I love our baby already. I've never been happier and we have only more happiness ahead of us. I have no interest in Sadie Grey and I never will for the rest of my life. Is that what you wanted to hear?'

'Those are the magic words.'

'Good. We're over that hump.'

'Still,' mused Allison. 'She's very attractive, very tragic, she's a single parent. And she needs a father for her child. I can't believe she's not interested in

401

you. You would be the perfect father for Willie.'

'What makes you say that?'

'Oh, I don't know. Just intuition.'

*　　*　　*

Allison was furious with Des.

He had been on 'Meet the Media' that weekend and had blasted the administration, the President, and Foxy over the way they were handling the Colombian drug situation.

Watching it in their bedroom on TV, Allison had practically had an anxiety attack. It was October and she was seven months pregnant; she did not need the aggravation of having Des go out on such a limb. She had just been reading one of her baby books, which emphasized the notion that expectant women should be as calm and serene as possible during their pregnancy so that the fetus would not experience any stress in the womb.

This particular Sunday morning he had really outdone himself, which of course the host and the producers loved since they made news that way and it made the show more interesting.

Des had barely walked in the door when the phone started ringing. It was the editor of the *Weekly* calling from New York, a social-climbing horse's ass of major proportions who saw his invitations to the White House going right down the drain. Des held the phone at elbow length so Allison could hear what he was saying.

'I think you should give up that show,' Allison began in a murderously controlled voice, after he hung up.

'Why? Just because that asshole thinks his social

402

life is in jeopardy?'

'I'm just beginning to think that journalists should be read and not seen or heard.'

'Since when? I've noticed you've appeared on plenty of these goddamn opinion shows. More than I have, in fact, since they're always desperate for women who can put two words together and don't have two heads.'

'We obviously can't have a conversation without you getting competitive.'

'Competitive? What the hell do you think you are?'

'I'm trying to make a point here if you would just listen. I'm saying that I think journalists are getting too self-congratulatory, too involved with what they think and not with what they're reporting. I think television has done this to many of us and I don't think it's healthy. It's all about airtime and exposure and money and big book contracts and not a whole hell of a lot about "seeking the truth," if I may be so corny. It's just all very self-serving and I don't like it.'

'Since when did you get religion?'

'You may have noticed I haven't done it for a while. It just made me uneasy. Too often I felt tempted to say something, not just because I believed it but because I wanted attention, I wanted to be controversial, I wanted to be talked about, a star. I didn't like what it was doing to me and I don't like what it's doing to you. I don't think you feel as strongly about the President's drug programs and Colombia and Foxy as you said you did. I think you wanted to stir things up. I don't blame your editor for being furious. I would be, too. You don't need it and the magazine doesn't need it and I don't

403

need it and Kay Kay doesn't need it.'

'Oh for Christ's sweet sake,' he said. 'You can all go fuck yourselves. I have a good mind to just quit the magazine and do television full time. I'm sick of it, sick of him, and I could become sick of you if you don't get off my back.'

With that he walked out of the bedroom and slammed the door. They didn't speak for the rest of the day and that night he slept in the guest room. Kay Kay kicked and rolled around in Allison's stomach all night as though it were she who had had the fight with Des. Allison spent the whole time talking to her in a soothing voice, playing classical music and rubbing her stomach. Finally at dawn Kay Kay quieted down and they both went to sleep.

Des's discontent with his work hadn't been lost on her. She had never heard him express it so strongly before and she wanted to get over their fight so they could talk about it.

She brought it up again the next evening when they came home from work. They were sitting in the little study. She waited until he had lit a fire and fixed himself an Irish on the rocks. She was curled up in her usual spot on the sofa. Only now she needed a pillow to place against her stomach to lean on, it was so big. She found it interesting about herself that she not only didn't mind having a large belly but she rather liked it. So many women seemed to feel ugly and ungainly when they were pregnant. She only felt prettier, sexier, more radiant the more she grew. The only downside was the fatigue. She had barely made it through the day, she was so tired, but she didn't dare let anyone know it. Not only that, but she was so preoccupied with Kay Kay and now Des and his problems, that she was finding it difficult to concentrate on her work. It was getting harder and harder and she was feeling guilty. The fact was that she really didn't want to be at work anymore. She wanted to be home knitting booties. Home with her husband and her baby. A year ago the whole idea of it would have made her gag. Now it seemed the most natural thing in the world.

Des was ready to talk. He clearly didn't want to prolong their fight any more than she did, and she could see that he was probably feeling ashamed of his behavior the day before. It didn't take much for him to open up once he saw that she really wanted to be sympathetic.

'This job burns people out, Sonny,' he said.

He was standing leaning over the mantel. It gave him a better view of her girth, he liked to tell her.

'I have to deal with overbearing editors in New York who think they know more about Washington than I do. New York always thinks Washington's in bed with their sources, that we whore for various sources, that we don't have enough access, that we will practically commit fellatio for access. Frankly, and this may surprise you considering what you said about me last night, but I don't give a shit about access journalism. I think it's dangerous and essentially unhealthy. I can't stand the fights anymore. I'm sick of them. Everybody thinks Washington gets too much space. They're right even though it's heresy to admit it. I can't stand the interbureau hassles. Who owns the national security staff, the White House reporters or the State reporters? I'm bored with the screaming matches on the squawk box with New York. Last Friday we had everybody in the room giving the bird to the

405

box. You don't know who's in the meeting in New York, you don't know who you're insulting.'

He was pacing the floor, rubbing his hands through his hair.

He had kept all this from her the past year. Why was he bringing it up now when she didn't have the strength or the ability to deal with it? Why was he doing this to her? Was this his way of getting attention? That's what fathers-to-be were supposed to do. Yet she surmised that if she didn't give him the attention and sympathy he needed from her she wouldn't get it from him. She couldn't risk that—not now, anyway. She would just listen.

'I hate having to go to New York to schmooze and hang out,' he was saying, 'just to keep them from thinking this is a hostile outpost. Even one day away from here can be a mistake. The animals get loose from their cage. It drives me crazy that the New York writers have their own opinions and go off half-cocked, completely ignoring our reporters and their files. The story this week on drugs was so fucking screwed up that they had to rewrite the whole thing. The writers were exhausted and all they wanted to do was go home. Tempers were short, conversations were edgy. At one point I could hear the phone clattering as the writer in New York threw it against the wall. Then he said, "Excuse me, I've got to calm down." Just another happy Saturday close at the *Weekly*. It's enough to make you go find a quart of vodka and get totally shit-faced.'

'It would seem you're not a very happy camper,' she said, with some affection and a little fear.

'I'm not, Sonny, I'm bored out of my gourd. I've done everything I want to do at this magazine. I'm proud of what I've done, but it's time for me to leave.'

Allison felt her stomach turn. This was not the time for Des to decide to quit his job. She needed a sense of security, not upheaval, in her life.

'But what will you do, Des?'

'I don't know. More television, maybe. Maybe write a novel. I'll do something.'

'But what will we do? You and I and Kay Kay?'

'We'll be fine. We'll be just fine.'

## CHAPTER THIRTEEN

'Wonder of wonders. Miracle of miracles.' Michael had invited her to a Passover seder. Not that she had any idea what a seder was. Except that it was sort of like Easter Sunday lunch. In Savannah they always had a big ham at Easter. At least now she knew enough to know they wouldn't have ham.

After she had accepted she realized what he was trying to do. He was trying to pile another row of bricks on the cultural wall between them. Get her at the seder, out of her element the way she got him at the White House. Show her what different worlds we live in, how impossible the gap is. Make her understand why it could never work, even an affair. That was clearly his thinking.

She didn't want to make any mistakes this time. Giselle would be watching her. She didn't know whether Giselle suspected there had been anything between them at La Samanna. She didn't imagine Giselle was too thrilled at the idea of inviting her to the seder. There had been a definite coolness

407

between them at the White House dinner. Certainly not because of her. She had tried. She had been very friendly toward Giselle. But this was not a stupid woman. This was also a Frenchwoman. Sadie couldn't help but notice that the invitation for the seder had come from Michael. She had hoped Giselle might invite her as well, but she hadn't, and the lack of a call from the hostess made her ill at ease before she even set foot in the door.

Jenny. She would have to discuss this with Jenny. She wanted to be prepared.

'A seder, huh? I've been to a seder. Let's see now. Lots of wine, everybody gets drunk, they tell stories, sing songs, eat a lot of food, it's great. You'll have a good time.'

'Jenny Stern. You are not being at all helpful. I have to know what they do so I don't make a stupid mistake. His wife doesn't like me. She will love it if I screw up.'

'His wife hates you? That bitch. Just because you're trying to steal her husband away from her. What nerve!'

'Whose side are you on, anyway?'

'Yours, dearie. That's why I'm being so skeptical.'

'What do you mean?'

'Sadie, I love you. I care about you. You have just been through a major trauma. Your husband, who just happened to be President of the United States, father of your children, was assassinated before your very eyes. You went through a public funeral with the kind of scrutiny no human being should be required to experience. It's only been nine months, Sadie. You are still in mourning. I daresay you've got your share of guilt, too, which

408

makes it even harder. You meet this nice doctor who falls for you. He's unthreatening, he's married, he's noble, compassionate, sympathetic, and Jewish. Perfect. Irresistible. Only it's totally unreal. You're not in control of your emotions yet. You don't know what the hell you're doing. You can't possibly be in love with anybody right now. You're too raw. This relationship is inappropriate at best and ridiculous at worst. You complain that he never calls, that you have to be the aggressor. Well, thank God the guy has got some sense, even if you don't. If he's as smart as you say he is, and I'm sure you're right, then he knows, in spite of his feelings for you, that it just isn't right and isn't to be trusted. I feel sorry for him. It must be difficult for him to control his emotions in the face of a determined Sadie Grey. I've seen you go after what you want before, and I sure as hell would not want to be in your way. I only hope this Michael Lanzer is strong. Otherwise he is going to get destroyed. Because one day you are going to wake up and say, "What the hell am I doing with him?" I just pray that when you do he's not lying in the bed next to you.'

'It's not true that I always get what I want. I didn't get Des.'

She was upset and her voice rose when she answered Jenny defensively.

'Bullshit, Sadie. You didn't want Des. You turned him down once. You could probably have persuaded him not to marry Allison, if you'd wanted to. Des is no dummy. He knew you had reservations. So did he. He might have tried to overcome his but he certainly couldn't have overcome yours. You didn't want him.'

'Well, I want Michael.' She surprised herself by not arguing back.

'I don't think you really do. I think you are bereaved and lonely. Maybe even a little horny. Michael might be the perfect transitional person right now. He's kind and gentle and totally safe. But I think you're fooling yourself if you think he's your man for the long haul.'

'I think you're saying this only because he's Jewish.'

'You could be right.' Jenny's face softened and she smiled. 'I find most Jewish men insufferable. They're a bunch of spoiled little princes. I should know. I have two of them for brothers.'

'But you adore your brothers.'

'That's because they are brilliant, funny, noble, sympathetic, kind, and gentle.'

'Jenny,' said Sadie with an exasperated laugh. 'Why don't you want me to marry him?'

'Marriage? We're talking marriage? Has he told his wife yet? Or is he waiting to break it to her at the seder?'

'Jen?'

'Because it just wouldn't be right.'

'So tell me about the seder.'

★      ★      ★

Jenny was a reform Jew. Very Reform. She hadn't been to a seder in a while and didn't remember much about it. She did explain that it was the Feast of Freedom and it celebrated the flight of the Israelites from Egyptian slavery. Jenny found a Haggadah for her, a book of the Passover service that Sadie had practically memorized by the time

410

the Friday night in April rolled around.

Judy Sokolow had called to tell her that they were going to the seder. Their children and her sister and her husband would also be going, as well as a distant cousin of Michael's who was a resident at G.W. Hospital and Michael's parents. The Lanzers' kids would also be there. Michael had said nothing to her about bringing her own children and she was just as glad. She thought they might have felt awkward, especially Annie Laurie, and she didn't want to have to worry about that, too. She was worried enough about herself. She was also somewhat leery about meeting Michael's parents—especially his mother. That had upped the anxiety level. She didn't tell Judy that Giselle had not formally invited her. She almost mentioned it to Michael. Was it possible that Giselle didn't know she was coming? But Judy and Giselle would have talked, that's how Judy must have known. Still, she did think it was odd of her not to call. She was, after all, the widow of the President. Giselle must be very annoyed.

Judy assured her that a dressy white wool suit would be appropriate and reassured her that she would do just fine. Each person has a Haggadah and everyone takes turns reading from it. The leader, Michael, would make sure that she could follow. Judy and Sid would watch out for her, she would be fine. Thank God for Judy. She was so warm and sympathetic and made Sadie feel comfortable.

By the time she got in the car that April Friday evening at sundown she felt positively relaxed. She also felt smug. She had brought a box of homemade cookies, Asuncion's specialty, with no yeast. She had been doing her homework. Jews ate matzoh

411

only, unleavened bread with no yeast, on Passover.

★  ★  ★

Michael opened the door. He was wearing a yarmulke. For a moment she was shocked. He looked different.

He could see what she was thinking, how nervous and ill at ease, how out of place she felt. He had his laser eyes focused right on her. He smiled and took her arm, bringing her into the room. His other hand rested lightly on her back. There was something oddly proprietary about the way he did it. In a way, it was a mixed signal, like putting up a few more bricks on the wall and then taking them down before the mortar was dry. It was the first time he had touched her since La Samanna, except for shaking hands.

Giselle came forward to greet her. Everyone else was already there. She had deliberately come late, as was her habit, so as not to have to stand around and make small talk. Aside from being easier on her, it was less strain on the others as well, not having to be saddled with the icon for cocktails.

She scanned the room to see what kind of taste Giselle had, how Michael lived. This way, when she was thinking of him later, she would be able to imagine where he was. It made him seem closer. The room was tasteful in an extremely modern and rather cold way. The house had lots of glass overlooking a terrace and yard. In front of the fireplace were two white square wool and chrome sofas, a glass coffee table, and two black leather-and-chrome chairs. A modern, geometric-patterned rug covered the floor. Over the mantel was a purple glass vase with one long-stemmed white flower. Only the fire in the fireplace gave warmth to the room. Giselle was looking extremely chic in a simple red silk dress that complemented her dark hair. Her eyes were wary and unhappy.

'Madame,' she said. 'What a pleasure it is to have you here.'

Ah, Giselle was torn. It was a feather in her cap to have Sadie at her seder. She wanted to play the gracious hostess for the benefit of her guests. On the other hand, she was scared. Her husband obviously cared about this woman, perhaps too much. Suddenly, Sadie felt sorry for Giselle. She wanted to reassure her. Yet, despite Michael's yarmulke, her painful memories, and her growing conviction that Jenny had been right, she knew that it would be a lie. Watching him making everyone at home, glancing around into the dining room to see the exotic table setting and the candles, the only thing she felt was need.

'I brought you these,' she said to Giselle shyly, holding out the colorful flowered canister.

'Thank you,' said Giselle, a little taken aback as she reached for it.

'They're homemade cookies,' said Sadie, beaming, as she handed them to Giselle.

A brief look passed over Giselle's face, and she accidentally let go of the canister. It fell to the floor, burst open, and scattered cookies and crumbs everywhere.

Giselle stood in silence for a second, staring at the floor, then cast a look at Michael.

'Chametz,' someone mumbled, and then they were all down on the floor gathering up the crumbs.

It was obvious something wasn't quite right.

413

'I, they're kosh ... I mean they're specifically, they don't have any yeast in them,' Sadie said to Michael.

'It's all right,' he whispered.

Giselle almost ordered Michael to go into the kitchen and get the vacuum cleaner.

Judy Sokolow came over to her, seeing her confusion. She took Sadie aside with a gentle smile.

'Michael's mother is Orthodox,' she said quietly. 'It's forbidden to have anything with flour in the house. It's called chametz. Giselle doesn't keep kosher. She has spent three days scouring the house for crumbs because Michael's mother was coming. She's absolutely exhausted, and she's had it up to here with Mrs Lanzer. Maybe this will bring them together. Meanwhile, try to relax. This will only give everybody something to talk about. You've made the seder!'

Michael had returned with the vacuum and within minutes things were cleaned up, and everyone was crowding around Sadie wanting to talk to her. It wasn't every day that a former First Lady came for Passover. Sid and their children and Michael's kids came over and began to giggle with Sadie about her little faux pas.

Michael walked over to their group.

'Well, Madame,' he said, imitating his wife's accent, 'I know you like to make grand entrances, but don't you think this is somewhat excessive?'

Everyone laughed and Sadie felt the tension drain out of her.

'Let's go meet some people,' he said, smiling at her. He took her around the room, introducing her to the guests, many of whom seemed starstruck and were terribly reassuring about the dreaded chametz.

414

Sadie sometimes forgot how people viewed her. She could be forgiven almost anything. At least by everyone but Giselle.

Michael finally got to his mother and father after she had met everyone else in the room.

His mother was short, plump, and in her seventies. His father was slim and wiry and with a full head of white hair and a large expectant grin on his face. Michael seemed amused.

'Mother,' he said formally, 'I would like to introduce you to Sadie Grey. Sadie, this is my mother, Esther Lanzer. And this is my father, Abe. Sadie Grey.'

'So Michael,' said his mother. 'We're not good enough to be introduced first. We have to wait until last.'

At least she didn't mention the incident.

'Mother, I'm just saving the best till last,' he said, smiling indulgently at her, not in the least perturbed.

'Mrs Grey,' said his father. 'You are even more beautiful than your pictures.'

'In that case, Mr Lanzer,' she said with relief, 'I insist that you call me Sadie.'

'And I am Abe.' He beamed and took both of her hands in his.

'Well, what have we got here? A little romance already?' said his mother.

Michael burst out laughing.

'Maybe two?' she said with a look at Michael.

'We had better get started with the seder,' he said quickly. 'It's going to be a very long evening.

\*　　\*　　\*

415

Michael was at the head of the table, with a beautiful black velvet pillow embroidered in gold with symbols and Hebrew letters, which he leaned against. His mother was on his right and Judy's mother on his left. Sadie, seated in the center of the table, was between Sid Sokolow and Michael's father, who were both trying very hard to make her feel comfortable. Giselle was opposite Michael at the other end. It occurred to Sadie that Michael had placed her as far away from his wife and his mother as was possible and she couldn't have been more grateful.

She looked at the table, set with a beautiful lace cloth, special gold and white plates, and glasses at each place, filled.

She was still trying to find a way to recoup from the cookies. She wanted to compliment Giselle on the table, but that was such an inane thing to do. The china, the cloth, the glasses were attractive but not anything to exclaim about specifically. It was the candlesticks that caught her eye. They were obviously very old, crudely crafted, slightly bent, scratched, and made up of some sort of chrome. They were out of place with the finery.

Sadie reached out to touch them, turning to Giselle's end of the table.

'What charming candlesticks,' she said, as she fondled one of them with her fingers. 'They must be very old.'

'Shiksa!' Michael's mother muttered from her end of the table. Sadie recoiled as though she had touched the flame, jerking her hand away quickly.

She looked up at Giselle anxiously only to find her staring at Michael. Then she looked imploringly at Michael. What had she done now?

416

'You're not supposed to touch the Sabbath candles,' whispered Sid. 'It's the Sabbath as well as Passover. But don't worry. It's all right. Nobody cares except Esther and if it weren't you it would be somebody else.'

She didn't see how she would make it through the rest of the evening. And if she did, how she would ever recover. Whatever chance she had thought she had with Michael was lost tonight. She could see it in his eyes, not to mention Giselle's sudden high spirits.

The only thing to do was to concentrate on the seder. She looked around the table, trying to take her mind off what had happened. There were strange coverings on the flat bread or matzoh. There was a large platter with a shankbone, an egg, horseradish, a pasty-looking mixture, some parsley, a bowl of water, and a mixture of finely chopped apples, walnuts, and wine made to resemble the mortar that the Jewish slaves had used to build pyramids for the Egyptians. There was a large silver chalice in the center of the table.

In each place was a small booklet. She recognized the Haggadah. It was not unlike the one Jenny had given her. She was relieved to see that people were picking up their booklets and reading them as they began the seder service. At least she would be able to follow the proceedings.

Then Michael stood and raised his cup of wine.

He began by saying a prayer. With dread she realized that the strange language he was speaking was Hebrew and that the Haggadah was in half Hebrew, half English. So she wouldn't be able to follow it completely. What had she been thinking about when she agreed to come? Here was this man she thought she loved reciting Hebrew from memory—and everyone else was following in their books—in this exotic setting. She felt as if she had come upon some remote tribe in the wilderness and was peering at them through the palm fronds as they performed their bizarre rituals.

She did not have any sense of being at the home of some cute guy she just happened to have a crush on.

When she finally consulted the Haggadah she saw what he was saying. 'Behold this cup of wine! Let it be a symbol of our joy tonight as we celebrate the festival of Pesach.

'On this night, long years ago, our forefathers hearkened to the call of freedom. Tonight that call rings out again, sounding its glorious challenge, commanding us to champion the cause of all the oppressed and the downtrodden, summoning all the peoples throughout the world to arise and be free.

'We are taught,' continued Michael, 'in every generation all are obliged to regard themselves as if they had personally gone forth from the land of Egypt.'

Everyone washed their hands, Michael divided the matzoh and he began, in Hebrew, the story of Israel's redemption from Egypt.

Thank God she had read, and practically memorized, the Haggadah Jenny had lent her. At least, even though he was reciting in Hebrew, the English was alongside. She was beside herself with gratitude when the others began to read passages in English

At one point a small child, around seven years old, the son of Michael's cousin, stood up to ask the four questions . . . in English.

'Why is this night of Pesach so different from all other nights of the year?' he began with a quavering voice and a trembling lip.

Sadie thought she had never identified so totally with anyone in her entire life as she had with this frightened little boy.

Why was this night different from all other nights? Because she had made a total ass out of herself on this night, that's why. Because she was placing herself in a situation that was completely unviable, because she had obviously lost another man she cared about. Each person began reciting various portions of the story, the legend of how Moses led the Jews out of slavery in Egypt and into freedom. When the story was finished Michael then gave a short speech about the meaning of freedom to the Jews. It was heartfelt and moving.

'The slavery the Israelites suffered in Egypt, and the freedom they won, inspired many of the more beautiful of the teachings in the Torah. Let us now read some of them together.'

They read several verses, then Michael said, and she repeated in English after him, 'The stranger that sojourneth with you shall be unto you as the native among you, and thou shalt love him as thyself; for ye were strangers in the land of Egypt: I am the Lord.'

She looked up at him and saw that he was looking at her.

Everyone else was looking down at their text and when he spoke next he spoke directly to her. She listened to the words in English as the others read them.

'And a stranger thou shalt not oppress, for ye know the heart of a stranger, seeing ye were strangers in the land of Egypt.'

She smiled at him and he smiled back.

'How many wonderful deeds did God perform for us!' Michael was saying.

'Had he brought us out of Egypt and not split the sea for us—'

And everybody, including Sadie, said in a loud chorus, 'Dayenu!' which the Haggadah explained meant, 'For that alone we should have been grateful!'

'Had he split the sea for us and not brought us through dry-shod—'

'Dayenu!'

'Had he brought us through dry-shod, and not sustained us in the wilderness for forty years—'

'Dayenu!'

'Had he sustained us in the wilderness for forty years, and not fed us with manna—'

'Dayenu!'

'Had he fed us with manna, and not given us the Sabbath—'

'Dayenu!'

'Had he given us the Sabbath, and not brought us to Mount Sinai—'

'Dayenu!'

'Had he brought us to Mount Sinai and not given us the Torah—'

'Dayenu!'

'Had he given us the Torah, and not brought us into the land of Israel—'

'Dayenu!'

'How much more, then, are we to be grateful to God for the wonderful deeds he performed for us! For he brought us out of Egypt, and split the Red Sea for us, and brought us through dry-shod, and sustained us in the wilderness for forty years, and fed us with manna, and gave us the Sabbath, and brought us to Mount Sinai, and gave us the Torah, and brought us into the land of Israel!'

The chorus of voices rose in a joyous crescendo with everyone almost laughing as they sang out Dayenu; when Michael finished they burst into actual song, singing, 'Day, Day, enu; Day, Day, enu!' as loudly and as boisterously as they could.

Sadie was surprised by how quickly the service went from somber to gay, but she saw that Michael was laughing and smiling and she relaxed even more. Maybe this was going to be all right after all. If they ever got any food.

Mercifully the service was only a little longer and then they stopped for the meal.

The happy mood carried over to dinner, which was delicious. Both Abe and Sid turned to Sadie and almost surrounded her with warmth and attention. They obviously had sensed how uncomfortable she had been at the beginning of the seder.

'Let me tell you about those forbidden candlesticks,' Abe said to her with a mischievous grin, glancing surreptitiously toward his wife, who was probably giving Michael a piece of her mind.

'They were brought over to America by my father from Russia. The only thing they were able to take with them. He had no money of his own and he was able to afford only a cheap metal-like chrome for his Shabbes candlesticks. He was a wonderful craftsman. After my father died my mother took very good care of them, telling me always that they were more precious than real silver because they were made with love and used with

421

love. She said they had kept the flame of hope burning on every Shabbes, even in the darkest times. They are very important to this family.'

'I understand and I'm sorry I touched them,' said Sadie. 'It's just that I had no idea...'

'Dahlink,' said Abe, putting his hand on hers. 'Don't say another word. You did a wonderful thing. You admired them. You recognized their beauty despite what they are made out of. You did the right thing.'

'Tell me about your mother. She sounds like a wonderful woman,' said Sadie. 'She must have led a very hard life.'

'My mother, oy.' He laughed and looked heavenward. 'My mother. You want to know about my mother, I'll tell you about my mother.'

Abe turned out to be a comedian. Sadie could see where Michael got his sense of humor. Before long she was laughing so hard she was nearly in tears about Abe's mother. Then Sid got into the act.

'My mother always favored my younger brother, who was a complete loser,' said Sid. 'I was getting straight A's in school and keeping a part-time job to help out with expenses. I played the violin in the school orchestra, I was editor of the school paper, head of the science club. I got a full scholarship to college and paid my way through medical school. And all I ever got was, "Lou did this" and "Lou said this" and "Lou said that." One day I was so angry that I just screamed at my mother. "Mother, I'm the one who's successful. I'm the one who's supporting you and Lou, too, and you've never once said, "Well done" in my life. Can't you ever just say one nice thing to me?"'

'See what you've done?' said Abe. 'You've got a

422

couple of Jews talking about their mothers.' He started to say, 'Now Michael...' and she leaned forward intently, but Michael had begun to speak in Hebrew again.

'What now?' she whispered to Sid. 'Is this the last part of the service?'

'Yes. We're not supposed to eat any more. But there is plenty of drinking to be done.'

'Why this egg and why these flowers?' Michael was asking in Hebrew as Sadie followed the English text.

'The egg is the form of life and rebirth. These flowers rise up against winter as our forebears rose up against Pharaoh. They remind us to sing the Song of Songs, of liberation through love.'

She looked up at him and saw that he had stolen another glance at her and that he was speaking to her again.

'Come with me, my love, come away,' he said, reciting from memory from the Haggadah.

'For the long wet months are past,
The rains have fed the earth
And left it bright with blossoms.

'Birds wing in the low sky,
Dove and songbirds singing
In the open air above,

'Earth nourishing tree and vine,
Green fig and tender grape,
Green and tender fragrance.

'Come with me, my love, come away.'

She felt sad.

Next came the cup of Elijah.

The cup was filled with wine. Michael rose and went to open the door so that the Prophet Elijah, who comes to set the Jewish people free, could symbolically enter.

He sent the little boy who had asked the first question to close the door, then quickly emptied the cup so the child would think Elijah had drunk it.

Then everyone sang joyously as the child rushed to the door to see where Elijah had gone.

The last part of the seder was mostly singing and responses, and although Sadie enjoyed it she didn't know the tunes, and the words were all in Hebrew. The final song was called 'L'Shanah Ha'Ba'Ah Be'Yurushalayim'. The mood in the room became sober again as it had been in the beginning, and everyone sang together. At the end, they all raised their hands and their voices and shouted, 'Next year in Jerusalem.'

It was that line that did her in. There would be no next year for her and Michael. Even if there were, it certainly wouldn't be in Jerusalem. He was Jewish. She was not. It was that simple. And that complicated. He had finished building the wall between them so high that she couldn't see him over the top anymore. The mortar that built this wall was made of finely chopped apples, walnuts, and wine.

★        ★        ★

It had been over a month—six weeks to be exact. They hadn't spoken since the seder. She had written an effusive thank-you note to him and

424

Giselle at home. She had gotten no reply.

She was going crazy.

So many times she had started to call him; even held on as the line rang and the secretary answered. In the end she always hung up. What was she going to say? 'All right. So you're Jewish. I'm not. So big fucking deal.'

No. She was not going to say that. She wasn't going to say it because it was a very big deal. At least for him. For her the fact that Michael was Jewish was completely irrelevant except for the fact that it wasn't to him. That's what made it a big fucking deal. That and the absolute certainty that she could never go through another religious ceremony with him again. Not with his mother and his wife present, anyway. That wasn't the issue at the moment, however, since he hadn't exactly asked her to participate in a meeting, much less a religious ceremony.

Meetings she had been to. She had never quite understood the meaning of the phrase 'bury yourself in your work' until the last six weeks. She had been a whirlwind of activity, throwing herself into Blanche's AIDS project with a vengeance. She had organized Blanche's every moment. She had set up Blanche's tour of the AIDS program at Children's Hospital, which had gotten an enormous amount of good publicity. She had arranged for her to visit every AIDS hospice in the city, every shelter for abandoned babies with AIDS. She had persuaded Blanche to fly to San Fransisco to talk to the people in the arts and entertainment worlds, and to tape an AIDS message to be aired during prime time on all of the networks. She had convinced Blanche to start rehearsals for her first

425

Live AIDS concert with her music friends.

Sadie had practically taken up residence in the East Wing of the White House, and Blanche's staff more or less answered to Sadie. Blanche was only too happy to have Sadie run her life. She was also thrilled with the turnaround in publicity and the new image Sadie had managed to create for her in little over two months.

Two meetings of the President's Committee on AIDS had been planned. Blanche had had to postpone one, and Michael was out ot town for the other and sent a substitute. Sadie was crushed. This was the only legitimate way she had to see him. She had gotten into this thing, and gotten Blanche into it, because of Michael. Then, after the seder, she had thrown herself into it to distract herself and to prove to him that she was a good person, a worthwhile human being. Finally, however, she had found herself genuinely involved and deeply committed. She was also surprised to find how important it had become to her in such a short time.

Blanche had eventually persuaded Freddy to actually take the first AIDS test for the national testing program. There had been a huge amount of publicity as the President had driven out to NIH for the test. The photo opportunity had been impressive, with the President smiling with a needle in his arm. Never mind that his smile seemed a bit frozen in the photographs. Michael Lanzer was in all the pictures. She cut them all out. She put them in a folder. She looked at them every day. His pictures made her smile. He had a surprised look in all of them. 'What am I doing in this picture?' his expression seemed to say. It was an expression she had never seen on him before. He was either terribly serious with her, talking about medicine and science, or funny, making jokes, loving. Rarely loving, but she had seen that side of him. Surprise was not anything she expected of him. He'd seen it all. Even talking about sex, an area in which he was hardly experienced, he had a worldly aura. Part of that obviously came from being a doctor, of dealing with life and death on an everyday basis, of dealing with human bodies. But another part of it, she decided, was being Jewish, for him, anyway. It was the sense that he had seen or experienced another kind of human suffering that left no room for surprise.

She liked the idea of the camera capturing something about him that even he didn't seem to be aware of. Stealing something of him that nobody knew about. It intrigued her that the photograph seemed to have abducted a piece of his soul. She wanted it. She cut it out. Now she had it.

And why not? It was only fair. After all, he had a piece of hers.

★          ★          ★

'Sadie. It's Blanche.'

The voice on the other end of the line sounded shaky and scared.

'Blanche, what is it?'

'Oh Sadie, I, I'm so scared.' Blanche burst into tears.

'Tell me what's the matter.'

'It's Freddy and that goddamn test,' she said finally. 'I knew I shouldn't have pushed it. I should have listened to him. He didn't want to do it.'

Sadie's voice was very quiet.

427

'What are you saying, Blanche?'

'We haven't gotten the results yet. At least I don't think so. When they took the test they told us it would be a couple of days. We didn't hear anything for a week. I asked Freddy every night and he kept getting more and more upset and yelled at me to get off his back. Then yesterday Michael Lanzer came to the White House to see him.'

Sadie held her breath.

'What did he say?'

'I don't know. Freddy wouldn't tell me. But he was white as a sheet when he came back to the family quarters last night. He wouldn't talk to me at all. He just got bowl-huggin' drunk and went to bed. He had already left for his office when I woke up this morning.'

'How do you know Michael saw him? Did he tell you? Was it on the schedule? There wasn't anything on the news last night or in the papers this morning about it?'

'I found out from his press secretary. He came up to see me yesterday evening. He wanted me to persuade Freddy to get NIH to give out the results of his test. The press was beginning to ask. He also said it won't be long before they find out that Michael was here. And if they don't release the results it'll look like it was positive.'

'Blanche, do you want me to come over there?'

'No. I just don't know what to do. I'm so scared. What if he has . . . I mean, what if . . . it's just so awful I can't even think about it.'

'Do you want me to call Michael?'

'Oh, would you, Sadie? I'm just too scared. Would you please?'

She knew she shouldn't. It wasn't ethical. But it

428

would give her an excuse to talk to him.

'Yes. I'll call him.'

'Just do me a favor.'

'What's that?'

'If it's bad news, I don't want to know.'

★　　★　　★

His secretary, for once, put him on right away.

'Hey.' He sounded too casual.

'Hi,' she said.

'How are you?' He sounded as if he really wanted to know.

'Fine.' Oh, no! She was going to lose it. Her voice was wavering. 'Not fine, actually.'

'What's wrong?' He was alarmed.

'I miss you.' Oh God! How could she have said that?

He didn't answer.

'I'm sorry,' she said.

'What have you been up to?' He acted as if he hadn't heard her.

She pulled herself together and related her activities of the past two months.

'Good for you. I'm proud of you. You're really doing it.'

'You patronizing bastard.' Make him pay.

'I've seen your picture everywhere peering over the President's shoulder and smiling for the cameras,' she said. 'How does it feel to be famous?'

'I wasn't trying to get in the pictures, I was trying to avoid the pictures.'

Ha! She had got him.

'That's not how it looked to me. It looked like you were desperate to get the glory, like you had

429

surgically joined yourself to the President in order to get the maximum publicity.'

'Did it look like that? Because I . . .' He was upset.

'It's all right, Michael. I'm sure it's good for AIDS. So I wouldn't worry about it. If it gives you a little ego boost at the same time, well then, no harm done.'

'You really are bad, you know that?' He was laughing.

'Why sugar,' she said in her deepest drawl, 'you do say the sweetest things.'

'I have missed you, Sadie Grey.'

'Really?' She couldn't help the sarcastic tone.

'Yes.' He was serious. 'God help me.'

'I gather you went to see the President yesterday.'

'Where did you hear that?' he said carefully after a slight hesitation.

'Blanche called me this morning. She's hysterical, Michael. She said that they were told the results would be in in a couple of days. It's been almost a week and the press is beginning to agitate. Then you make this secret unannounced visit to the White House. The President comes back to the family quarters in a foul mood, gets, if you'll pardon the expression, "bowl-huggin' drunk," and won't talk to her.'

'You know I can't talk to you about this.'

His voice was distant.

'Michael. I'm not asking you to tell me about the President. I'm asking you to do something. This is not just an everyday AIDS test. This is a national public relations campaign and we're talking about the President of the United States. Not to mention his wife, the person he sleeps with. At least get him to announce the results. He can't just stonewall this.'

'Sadie, he's my patient. I can't discuss this.'

Just his saying that gave her chills. He had inadvertently told her by calling the President a patient. Or did he know what he was doing?

'He's got to make some kind of announcement.'

'This is not my problem. I'm a doctor and a scientist, not a flack.'

'Dammit, Michael. You can't do this. It was your idea. You got the President into this mess. You suggested it at dinner in front of everyone, making it impossible for him not to do it. You must have considered the consequences of an unfortunate outcome. You can't get away with this. "What do you mean we, paleface?" routine.'

'Is this our first fight?'

'Stop patronizing me.'

'Look, Sadie. First of all, you're jumping to conclusions. You don't know anything. Second, assuming I did meet with the President, you have no idea what I said to him. Third, assuming I met with the President and that I briefed him on the results of the test, you can also assume that I would have discussed various options with him about how best to proceed. Beyond that, I have no role. Okay?'

'Okay.' She was calmer now. 'Then what can we do?'

'What happens now is completely up to the President.'

*     *     *

431

'Sadie, it's Jen.'

'Hi. What's up?'

'Well, nothing. I'm just relieved to see that the President does not have AIDS. That was a weird thing, they did, though, waiting for over a week to announce the results of the test. I was beginning to wonder there for a while. I bet ole Manolas must have been sweating bullets. This is not your press secretary's favorite scenario. Frankly, I was surprised that Freddy agreed to take that test. A little risky considering his rather checkered past. I must say, the announcement was a little tacky though. Kissing Blanche on the lips in front of the entire White House press corps. I'm surprised they didn't have intercourse. It would have made a great photo.'

'Oh Jenny, you're terrible.'

'By the way, how's the good doctor?'

'Who?'

'Oh, please.'

'Oh, Michael. You mean Michael Lanzer?'

'That's the one.'

'I wouldn't know. I haven't seen him in a couple of months. Not since the disastrous seder.'

'Trouble in paradise?'

'There's certainly no trouble. There's nothing.'

'So you haven't converted yet.'

'C'mon, Jen.'

'Sorry. I really am sorry.'

'Let's change the subject. Tell me some gossip. There is absolutely nothing happening in this town. It's boring, boring, boring. Totally dead.'

'I do have one thing.'

'Oh great. I knew I could count on you. I used to be able to rely on Lorraine for gossip but she's totally dried out. It's all over for her. She's finished. Tell me, what do you know?'

'Allison is pregnant.'

★     ★     ★

She felt about the first anniversary of Rosey's death the same way she had felt about Christmas. She just did not want to be in Washington.

Everyone had offered. Invitations from people she didn't even know had been pouring in. Come stay with us, get away from everything, don't let yourself be alone.

She had insisted that Annie Laurie and Outland go to Europe with friends. Spare them. She really didn't want to be with her parents and certainly not with Rosey's. What she wanted was to be somewhere she couldn't be found, haunted, trailed, photographed, on display. She figured that if she had managed to carry on an affair for two years in the White House as First Lady without getting caught, then she could certainly find some place to go on the anniversary of Rosey's death without being found out. It was a challenge. One that she felt up to.

The invitation came unexpectedly from Rosey's dear friend Cotes Tennant, the former ambassador to England, who had a hunting preserve in Georgia, near the Florida border. He had thousands of acres with a small comfortable house in the midst of mossy glades and groves of live oaks. Near the swamps were a string of outer islands, miles of white sand dunes inhabited by wild horses. The house was staffed year-round by the offspring of family retainers who cooked and cleaned and were

433

ready to care for guests who came down to shoot dove at a moment's notice. There was an airstrip on the property, and Cotes offered his own Lear jet for the trip. He couldn't be there but she was welcome to take anyone she wanted.

It was perfect. She would take Willie and Monica and Jenny and go down for a long weekend. She would read, take canoe trips, jeep and pony rides, Willie would be in heaven and she would be in privacy. She accepted.

The date of Rosey's death was July 3, her birthday.

The papers and magazines were already in a feeding frenzy about it. She would tell nobody about Georgia. She would drive out of her house several days before the anniversary, hiding on the floor of the car. She would send Willie and Monica out in another car and have Jenny meet them at some private isolated airport in southern Maryland. From there they would fly directly to Georgia and Beau Rivage. Afterward, she would drive up to Savannah and spend a few days with her parents. She was extremely pleased with her plan.

She was certainly not expecting Michael's call.

'How are you?' His voice sounded formal.

'Fine.' She tried to sound nonchalant.

'I'm calling because it's two weeks away from your birthday and the first anniversary of your husband's death.'

'Oh? I guess I must have forgotten.'

'I'd forgotten, too.'

'What?' She was confused.

'How much I miss you when I don't talk to you.'

'Do you just refrain from calling me for months at a time so you can get to say things like that?'

434

She was hurt that he never called, that he hadn't talked to her since she'd called about Freddy. She just wasn't in the mood for playful sparring.

'I'm calling you now, Sadie.'

'I'm supposed to keel over with excitement?'

She hadn't meant to sound so defensive but she was depressed and she wanted him to know how she felt. She didn't feel like playing it cool. Her life was not a game and if that's what he wanted he could look somewhere else. She was a human being with feelings and pain and he didn't seem to be aware of that, or if he was he didn't give a damn.

He ignored her remark.

'We have a custom. It's called Yahrzeit. It means a year's time. The year after someone has died. The bereaved spend that day with people they love. And who love them.'

'That's exactly what I plan to do, thank you. I'm spending that day with Willie and Monica and Jenny. We're going away someplace where nobody will find us.'

'I'd like to spend that day with you, too.'

'You'd what?'

'I want to be with you. I'll go wherever it is you're going. I'll meet you there. It's important to me, Sadie.'

'Why?'

'Because I . . . I care about you.'

She was so overwhelmed that she couldn't reply. It seemed that he was trying to tell her that he loved her. Why was she enraged at him?

'Jesus Christ, Michael! We haven't spoken in almost two months. And it was almost two months before that. And then it was I who called you. What the hell do you think you're doing now? You call up

435

two weeks before my birthday and the anniversary of Rosey's death and insinuate yourself into my life as though you had some claim on me. It's so arrogant I can't even believe it. What do you think I'm doing with my life here anyway? Do you think I'm just sitting here day after day waiting for you to call? Then when you do I'll just leap with joy and rearrange all of my plans for you? Is this your way of showing me how much you care about me? Well, forget it. Is this what you call a friendship? Because if it is it's the damndest friendship I've ever seen. Friends are people who care about each other, who are always there for you when you need them. You don't fit that description. I offered you my friendship and I've given it wholeheartedly. I've been supportive of you and your work. You may have noticed that this has not exactly been the easiest year of my life. In fact, there aren't too many people who've been through what I've been through. I can use all the help I can get. I must have been demented to think that you were going to be my friend. You must have thought so, too. You'll just have to forgive me my delusions. I've not been myself lately. But I'll get over it. I promise you. Now I have a suggestion for you. The weekend of my birthday and the Yahrzeit, or whatever you call it, is also the Fourth of July weekend. It just happens to be one of the few holidays that Jews and gentiles celebrate alike. I happen to know something about this one. I suggest that you and your family go watch fireworks and eat hotdogs together. Hebrew National makes very good kosher hot dogs, I'm told. And while you're at it why don't you take one of those firecrackers and shove it.'

When she had finished speaking she slumped

436

with exhaustion. She had been standing up, holding the phone in her hand, pacing back and forth in her upstairs study as though she were on drugs. Now she had no energy at all.

'You're really hurt, aren't you?'

He seemed surprised.

'Oh Michael. What do you think, for God's sake?'

'I'm sorry, Sadie. I am so sorry. I apologize. I had no idea. I couldn't imagine that someone like you could be hurt by someone like me. I never thought that you would care about something like that. I didn't know. I didn't understand.'

'I guess there's just a lot about each other we don't understand, isn't there?'

*     *     *

So Michael was coming to Beau Rivage. He had sent flowers the day after their conversation. He had been truly bewildered by her outburst. She had called to thank him and he had asked again to be with her on Yahrzeit.

She couldn't resist. She had told him yes. The plan was that he would fly to Jacksonville the morning of her birthday, drive an hour to Beau Rivage, spend the day, and then drive back to Jacksonville. He would spend the night there and take the early flight out the next morning. She would drive to Savannah to visit her parents for a few days. What he didn't know was that she was going to persuade him to stay overnight at Beau Rivage and drive back with her to Savannah. He would put up a fight. But he was feeling so guilty about hurting her that she felt sure she could

437

convince him to go to the moon with her.

She wanted him to meet her parents. She had met his. She wanted him to know more about her. She hadn't decided yet when she was going to tell him about Savannah.

When she told Jenny that Michael was coming, Jenny just rolled her eyes. Sadie knew that Jenny was dying to meet him so she got no opposition there.

Now that Michael was coming she was ecstatic. He must know how much she needed him. He had pulled her out of a depression and sent her soaring with one phone call. He was the only person capable of doing that. He seemed to have some sort of magic hold over her. She reveled in it and resented it all at once.

\* \* \*

Beau Rivage. She hadn't been there since before Rosey was President. Cotes had more or less given them the key when Rosey sent him off to London to be ambassador. For lots of reasons they had never had a chance to use it. It was almost a second home to her. When she and Rosey were first courting in Richmond they would all go down to Beau Rivage for weekends. Pretty drunken weekends, too. Her first years there were mostly remembered in a haze of alcohol. Not that she could hold booze at all. Her idea of drinking in those days was disgusting things like Grasshoppers, silly crème de menthe frappés, anything that would hide the taste and make her look sophisticated—usually make her throw up, too.

They had left Washington several days before her

birthday, before the reporters started gathering outside her house. She had worried that it might be too unbearably hot and humid in Georgia, but the air was, though Southern summer sultry, actually quite dry for that time of year.

Driving up the three-mile dirt road, through the slash pines, past the kennels and stables, by the old slave quarters, and on to the house she felt a sense of freedom she hadn't had since Rosey became Vice President. The simple graveyard was still there, the inviting circle of boxwood and bricks. What she loved about it was its informality, its simplicity. This was not some white-columned, antebellum mansion. Beau Rivage was designed to be a shooting preserve for the Tennants, never a permanent residence.

It was situated high up on a bluff overlooking the St Mary's River, a river that was pitch black, and often called the Black River by the locals. The river wound out of the Okeefenokee Swamp and eventually ended up in the ocean. But at Clarks Bluff, where the house was perched, it was still deep in swampland.

The house itself was small, an unassuming one-story building of old weathered cypress. Pale pink shutters were a welcoming touch. It was diminished in size even more by the surrounding giant live oak trees, which hung with pale gray Spanish moss, the color of the facade. It was almost indistinguishable from its surroundings, like a desert creature that blends into the landscape. Overgrown camellia bushes, holly trees, and mistletoe clumped around the outside gave one the sense that the house had been there forever. The tiny palmetto trees gave the illusion of being in the tropics.

Inside was a large comfortable room dominated by a huge fireplace made with river stones and an enormous picture window overlooking the live oaks and the river below. Overstuffed furniture was slip-covered in faded bird chintz. Worn oriental rugs covered the floors, and Audubon and Currier and Ives prints hung on the walls.

Every room was inviting. Every room had a place to flop down. There was nothing you could not put your feet on. It was heavenly for a man. It was attractive and cozy for a woman. It felt like home. It was also, if she saw it through Michael's eyes, what one might call throw-away goyish chic.

The staff had been there forever, certainly as long as she could remember. Pearl, the cook, fixed the best oyster stew she had ever tasted, black-eyed peas, shrimp, quail with stewed tomatoes, and grits with lots of gravy. They were warm and hospitable and she and Jenny were soon settled in their rooms and into their shorts and T-shirts.

Sadie had brought a pile of novels, as she had done when she went to La Samanna, but she found she was having trouble concentrating, anticipating Michael's arrival.

She was up by six, glancing at the clock every fifteen minutes or so. He was taking the 9:00 a.m. flight, the earliest flight out of Washington to Jacksonville, so he wouldn't be getting there until lunchtime. She spent the morning playing with Willie in the little plastic baby pool they had brought, squirting him with a hose. He really was the most delectable child. She couldn't stop hugging and kissing him. By the time Michael was expected to arrive she was drenched and had to go change her clothes. From one pair of rolled-up khakis and a blue work shirt to another.

She was nervous about seeing him. Nervous about seeing him in another beach environment, nervous about spending time alone with him, nervous about having Willie get to know him, nervous about Jenny. She wanted Jenny's approval, her blessing. If Jenny liked Michael, felt he was right for her, then somehow the Jewish thing wouldn't seem like such an obstacle. Not to mention the married thing. She felt like a young girl about to introduce her would-be fiancé to her father for the first time.

Finally she heard his car in the drive.

She took a deep breath, ran a brush through her hair, checked her lipstick, and walked outside to greet him.

★　　★　　★

The ancient little wooden ChrisCraft puttered slowly through the swampy river. It passed under streams of hanging moss, palm trees, vines, and through marsh grass so high you couldn't see anything beyond. There wasn't a noise to be heard except the hum of the engine, the buzz of an occasional bumblebee, the crickets chirping, and an occasional whoosh, which sounded ominously like an alligator sliding into the water from the muddy banks.

Sadie and Michael sat together on the front seat of the boat eating fried chicken and bread-and-butter sandwiches while Jed, the burly caretaker of Beau Rivage, sat in the back, steering. It was after three and the sun was still hot, but they had avoided the scorching midday heat. Happily the air was still unseasonably dry and the sky was clear. It was a perfect Georgia summer day, and Sadie felt a million miles away from everywhere.

And once again, she had outsmarted her beleaguered Secret Service agents, sneaking down to the boat soon after Michael arrived without anyone seeing them.

Jed was taking them to Cumberland Island. It was about two hours down the river past the sleepy town of St Mary's, where the river widened and opened up to the savannahs and the sea. It was just a short ride across to Cumberland Island. One of the magical Sea Islands, it had miles of white rolling deserted dunes, forests of mossy live oaks, and enchanting wild ponies.

Jed knew a secret dock with a small boathouse where he kept an old beat-up pickup truck. He would stay there and fish and drink beer and gossip with his pals while Sadie and Michael went exploring.

They had been completely silent in the boat. Sadie hadn't wanted to talk at all. She was content just to be near him. It all seemed so silent and mysterious, like heading into the tunnel of love.

When they got to the island Jed lifted a small cooler from the boat, took out a couple of beers for himself and put it into the back of the pickup. He gave Michael the keys, pointed them in the right direction, and they were off.

Michael gunned the motor and began speeding down the beach as though they were in a movie car chase scene, bouncing up and down the dunes. Sadie held on to the handle for dear life, both of them laughing and giggling, exhilarated at their sense of freedom.

They drove for miles, occasionally looking across the seat at each other in happy disbelief at their good fortune. They were completely alone, alone really for the first time. The notion was intoxicating.

As he drove, Sadie had a chance to study him. She never really got a chance to look at him except for quick looks when they were in meetings. He was tan, which made him look handsome, made his eyes bluer and deeper. His eyes always seemed so laserlike that it gave him a steely look, especially when he wasn't smiling. From the side his mouth looked gentle and his face kind. She had an irresistible urge to stroke his cheek.

They came to a small grove of scrub oak trees right off the dunes, on a small promontory overlooking the ocean. The sun was low by now, and the air a bit cooler, as the breezes were coming from the water. They left the pickup on the dunes and took their picnic bag to the grove. In front of them lay the dunes, and as they approached the promontory they could hear the rumbling of horses' hoofs. Then, seemingly out of nowhere, came a small herd of wild ponies, pale whites and grays running and prancing in the sand. Just as quickly they disappeared in a cloud. Michael and Sadie were both left breathless by this magical apparition. The grove served as the entranceway into the forest behind them. It was quite dense, with scruffy trees and bushes, then it became almost enchanted, as the scrubs were replaced by live oaks, replete with Spanish moss and wild berry trees.

Michael was the first to spot a path, and without saying anything he entered it, beckoning her to

443

follow.

Soon they were deep into the woods, brushing moss away from them in front as they followed the narrow path. The only sounds they heard were the whippoorwills and the scratching of armadillos against the trees.

After about ten minutes they came to a small clearing. They both stood a bit awkwardly for a moment, then Michael, with a sudden sense of purpose, cleared away some brush, smoothed the sand, and made a small cushion of moss. He sat down and patted the sand next to him.

When they were seated she looked at him and he met her eyes for the first time that day. She blushed and looked down, making small patterns in the sand.

He pulled something out of his pocket and held it in front of her so that she could see it with her eyes lowered. It was a small box, carefully wrapped and tied with a ribbon.

'Happy birthday,' he said.

She looked up at him in surprise. He was smiling as if anticipating her surprise.

'What did I do to deserve this?' she asked. She hadn't intended that tone.

'Put up with me as a friend.'

'Since when did we become humble?'

'Open it.'

She opened the package carefully. Inside was a plain fluted glass containing a flat candle.

She looked up, puzzled. 'What?'

'It's a Yahrzeit candle. You burn it on the first anniversary of the death.'

He took out a package of matches.

'Light it.'

'Am I allowed to touch it?'

'I'm sorry about that,' he said. 'I apologize. you were made uncomfortable in my home and that's unforgivable. Especially at Passover.'

She didn't say anything. She just took the small candle, set it in the sand, and lit it as he had told her. Then she looked at him quizzically. She didn't know what she was supposed to do, though she sensed that the moment was solemn.

He began to chant in Hebrew, his voice a lilting, singsong sound as he prayed.

She felt somewhat embarrassed. She didn't understand what he was saying. She didn't know where to look. Then the prayer began to take hold of her and she found the haunting sound hypnotic and especially moving. She felt as though she were in a trance, not just because of Michael's voice, but because of the eerie setting and the hush of the forest. She was overcome with images of Rosey—when they first met, their wedding, when the children were born, his election as governor of Virginia, then as Vice President. She remembered the day that Roger had been stricken and Rosey had been sworn in as President. She could see Rosey's face when she told him she was leaving him for Des, remembered that he had wept and begged her to stay. She saw his joy when she told him she was pregnant and how delighted and happy he was at the birth of Willie. She remembered the birthday party a year ago, Rosey smiling and happy, so secretive and smug about his present for her one minute, and then the shock on his face and the blood everywhere. And finally, Rosey telling her he loved her and that he knew Willie was not his son. She felt such a rush of anguish she didn't think she could bear it.

From a distance she heard her voice keening and she felt the tears.

Michael put his arms around her and held her until she stopped crying.

'Do you want to talk?' he asked her after a while.

'Yes,' she said. 'I want to tell you about Willie.'

        ★        ★        ★

She talked for almost an hour. It was odd, her doing the talking. Usually it was the other way around. She needed to tell someone she trusted. She talked about Rosey and her feelings for him. She told him about Des and Willie and the breakup with Des both times, including just before she went to La Samanna.

When she finished her story, Michael, without a word, built a little mound around the candle so it couldn't set fire to the brush.

Then he stood up and took her hand.

'Let's go,' he said, and pulled her toward the path to the beach.

She turned to look at the Yahrzeit candle flickering softly.

'Goodbye, Rosey,' she whispered.

        ★        ★        ★

It was almost six, but she had told Jed that they would be back by dark, so they had a while. They were still holding hands when they emerged from the forest onto the bluff overlooking the dunes. Oddly, after all her fantasizing about making love, she only wanted to be close to him now. To have

446

him hold her or touch her. She was feeling devoid of sexuality. It was such a relief for a change, considering that for six months she had been practically obsessed with the idea of going to bed with him.

She was ravenous and so was he. They opened their picnic baskets and took out sandwiches and deviled eggs and finished off the fried chicken. They hardly talked at all while they were eating. They had bouts of silence, followed by bouts of talking, followed by more silence. All they could hear now was the sound of the waves splashing up on the beach. For as far as they could see the beach was deserted. They were completely alone.

'Well,' she said, when she had finished eating. 'I must say, it did feel good to be the one talking for a change.'

'Just as I was beginning to go soft on you,' he laughed, 'you turn on me.

'I know how difficult it must have been for you, poor baby. Doing all that listening. But now it's your turn. Talk to me. Tell me about yourself. Why are Jewish men so funny?'

'We're more able to laugh at ourselves because we've felt exclusion and pain. That's why there are so many Jewish comedians. To survive you've got to find humor in life. You have to be able to laugh at your predicament.'

'You keep talking about pain. I don't really understand what you mean. Look how successful you are. Being Jewish hasn't hurt you at all. Actually I'd say you were in hog heaven.'

'You know what they say?' he flashed her a wicked smile.

'I give up. What do they say?'

447

'When you're in love, the whole world looks Jewish.'

⋆ ⋆ ⋆

By the time they got back everyone had gone to bed. It was after nine. They were both exhausted. Earlier in the day, especially after their conversation, it had seemed that there might have been another romantic encounter like at La Samanna. But the day had been too emotional for that. The longer and the better she knew him, the more reluctant she was to chance ruining what they had with physical intimacy. It was certainly an unusual situation. Like some sort of long Victorian engagement. She had the conviction that if she went to bed with him now he would never see her again. There were barriers of trust that had to be overcome. Their talk had convinced her even more.

They said goodnight in the living room. There had really been no need to convince him to stay overnight because it was too late and he was too tired to drive back to Jacksonville. She had even convinced him to drive with her to Savannah the next morning, meet her parents, and take a plane from there.

'I'll send Willie in to wake you in the morning,' she said. 'Just in case you have a hard time getting up.'

'Oh great,' he said, laughing. 'Just what I was going to suggest.'

'Unless you'd rather have me.'

'I'd rather have you.'

They were standing in that strange zone of double entendre that always left them so

448

unbalanced.

They were standing rather close together in the dimly lit room, both wrinkled, sweaty, sandy, hot, and slightly sunburned from their outing. He had never looked more attractive to her.

He reached out, almost in spite of himself, and brushed her tangled hair out of her eyes.

'It was a nice day, wasn't it,' she said.

'Yeah,' he said, his voice catching. 'The whole world looked Jewish.'

\* \* \*

The day after Sadie's birthday and the first anniversary of Rosey's death was the Fourth of July. Sadie's parents had gone to their beach cottage at Tybee, known more formally as Savannah Beach, some twenty miles out of town on the ocean.

Instead of driving to Savannah, their little group—Sadie, Michael, Willie, Monica, Jenny, and the agents—went directly to Tybee, where Sadie's parents were planning a picnic for Willie before the fireworks.

The cottage was a small informal white wooden house with a screened-in porch overlooking the ocean. At the end of the narrow street leading up to the beach, it was virtually indistinguishable from most of the other houses around it, all of them surrounded by swaying palms and picket fences, all of them raised on stilts to protect them from flooding. Tybee was not exactly Newport, but it was the only good beach near Savannah and therefore the fashionable beach, despite the size of the cottages and their close proximity to each other.

Sadie adored Tybee. She had spent her summers there since she was a child, there and in Statesboro, and it held only the sweetest memories. Tybee was boardwalks and jukeboxes, the smells of hamburgers and french fries, suntan oil and 'co-colas,' bare feet and sunburns, sandy sheets and fireflies, sunsets and the soothing sound of the ocean. Tybee was palm trees and laziness and Southern accents and very, very Protestant.

Tybee was everything that was strange and foreign to Michael Lanzer, and she could feel his uneasiness as they walked into her parents' cottage.

Her mother couldn't have been more cordial. Too cordial. She nearly talked him to death, offered him boiled peanuts and Cokes every other minute. Her father was remote; his politeness was forced, to say the least. It was obvious that neither one of them could wait until he was gone. Michael clearly felt the same way. He kept glancing at his watch, finally standing up after about an hour and announcing that he had a plane to catch. Sadie knew his plane wasn't until much later but she didn't protest.

She walked him out to the porch and shrugged a helpless apology.

'Well, at least you didn't touch the candlesticks,' she said

His face, which had been so open and receptive yesterday, last night, this morning, had closed on her. A little veil had come down over his eyes. The wall had gone up. The gates were closed. Their whole relationship was like a game of Simon Says. Simon Says take two baby steps forward. Simon Says take one giant step backward.

'More importantly,' he said, 'I didn't touch you.'

She put out her hand, almost as a challenge.

He took it and she looked directly at him as she squeezed tightly.

'I promise I won't tell,' she whispered.

⋆     ⋆     ⋆

Monica and Jenny had taken Willie to the beach along with a picnic lunch.

Sadie was ravenous, so her mother got out the fried chicken and pimento cheese sandwiches and sweetened ice tea and the three of them sat down in silence and began to eat. The silence became more and more uncomfortable. Finally she couldn't stand it any longer.

'So, how d'y'all like Michael?'

They both looked at each other.

'Mama? Daddy?'

'He certainly seem like a fine doctor. I'm sure he's brilliant, finding that drug, what is it? AZT that can help AIDS? Although I'm not so sure I would want to work with that virus. You just never know what can happen. Why I read in the paper just the other day about a nurse in some hospital who got stuck with a needle. I mean one little stick and...'

Her father hadn't said a word. He was gnawing on a drumstick.

'Mama, didn't you think he was attractive?'

'He's certainly not ugly, for heaven's sake. I mean he's not my type, but I can understand that ... but I don't see what difference it makes...'

'I'm in love with him.'

There was dead silence.

'Well, don't you have anything to say at all?' Her

451

voice was shrill. She was more upset than she had thought she would be. She didn't know what she had expected. Maybe that they would be happy for her after the tragedy she had experienced, knowing that she had somebody. Or at least sort of had somebody. She hadn't told them anything about him, just that he was going to Beau Rivage and she was bringing him by to meet them. But they had to have figured something out. Now they just looked at her in shock.

'Sadie, darlin',' her mother said finally. 'The man is married.'

'Daddy?'

He finished chewing his chicken bone and set it down on the plate. He carefully wiped his mouth with his napkin, then deliberately wiped each finger. When he had finished he put his napkin on the table and looked at her.

'That's not the only problem,' he said, almost impatiently, to her mother.

'What is it then?' asked Sadie.

'He's Jewish,' said her father.

*　　　*　　　*

Des was the last person she expected to hear from when she picked up the telephone.

It was the last week in July and she was packing to go up to Easthampton for August. Normally she would have spent a large part of June and July there, certainly weekends, and this year she and Willie had been up for a few weekends already. But there was something depressing about being at a resort when you were alone or in mourning. It just didn't work. The whole point was to relax and have

452

a good time. That's just not what she felt. Besides, she had two things to keep her in Washington despite the heat and the humidity. One was her AIDS project, which had become practically a full-time job now.

Freddy Osgood had agreed to let her keep her old office in the old Executive Office Building that Rosey had designated for her when she was First Lady. He had also provided a secretary for her. She was now an official member of the President's Commission on AIDS. Not only that, but Freddy was being almost pathologically solicitous of Michael. Whatever the National Cancer Institute wanted, they got. And he had put a number one presidential priority on AIDS research.

Blanche was going along full blast with her Live AIDS concerts, which had been Sadie's idea and had given her a wonderful project. It had taken her out of Washington, put her on the front pages with positive press, and effectively gotten her out of Sadie's way. Sadie was now representing the First Lady and the commission was more or less under her control. It was interesting and distracting. It also put her in constant contact or communication with Michael. At least on the phone.

Michael was the other reason she wanted to be in town. Not that anything was happening there. Their relationship had resumed its abstract state after his visit to Georgia.

He wasn't ready to leave his marriage. She hadn't finished mourning Rosey. She hadn't dealt with her guilt about Des and Willie. She wasn't sure she was completely over Des. The obsession she had had for Michael wasn't normal, it wasn't healthy, it wasn't realistic. She needed to heal herself before she

453

thought about loving someone else.

'Congratulations,' she said when she picked up the phone and heard Des's voice. 'I hear Allison is pregnant.'

She was surprised that her heart had started beating faster.

'Yes. We're having a baby girl. We just found out.'

What he didn't say was that Willie was having a baby sister. What he didn't say was that he wasn't disappointed at not having a boy because he already had a son. Des had once expressed his disappointment to her about never having a son. He really didn't like his daughter, Fiona, now in her twenties. She was Chessy's daughter all the way, he had said, a spoiled little rich girl ashamed of her father's poor Boston Irish upbringing, ashamed of his family. 'Every man wants a son,' he had once said to Sadie. When they had actually talked about her leaving Rosey he had fantasized about their having a son. With two nearly grown children, the idea of a baby in her forties appalled Sadie, but she never let on to Des. It was ironic that she had accidentally gotten pregnant and then had to raise the child as Rosey's.

'That's wonderful, Des.' She really meant it. She had known Allison was pregnant. Why was she so thrilled it was a girl? Because it kept Willie special to him. For whatever that was worth. He never saw Willie. He sent him presents every once in a while from 'his special friend' but that was awkward, too. She didn't quite know how to explain them to him. Uncle Des? That's what she told him.

'When's the baby due?'

'Around Christmas. Actually Christmas Day, I

454

think. Willie's birthday, in fact. That will be interesting for more reasons than one. Sonny is militantly antireligion.'

He sounded a bit regretful. That was not a compliment about Allison, she felt. She didn't quite know what to say.

'Do you have a name for her yet?' That was neutral.

'We think we'll call her Katherine Kimball Sterling Shaw after Sonny's mother; she died in an automobile accident in France when Sonny was two.'

'Oh, yes. She was quite a famous journalist, wasn't she?'

'Very. One of the first women war correspondents in World War Two. Sonny worships her. Always wanted to be like her.'

'Well, she certainly succeeded.'

They were both being so restrained, so polite.

He cleared his throat.

'Well, I called because I wanted to see Willie ... and you. I thought you might like to ask me over for lunch.'

'Oh. Well, that would be great. I mean, I'd love for you to see Willie. You won't recognize him. He's a real little bruiser.'

'Yeah?' He laughed. His voice was hoarse with pride. 'Has he, uh, does he have anyone to roughhouse with? Boys need to roughhouse.'

'Only Outland, but he's never here. Monica tries, and she's very bouncy and loving. But Willie's more interested in her enormous bosoms than in roughhousing. I don't think it's quite the same.'

'That's my boy.'

'You pig. You haven't changed a bit.'

'You've missed me, I can tell.'

She laughed, then said spontaneously, 'Des, why don't you take me out to lunch? I've just been cooped up here for so long I feel like a hothouse flower. Except for a brief trip to Georgia and my AIDS meetings I stay home. I've got a serious case of cabin fever. We're leaving for Long Island at the end of the week and it will be same thing there. I'd love to go to a real restaurant like a real person, for a change.'

'I don't know. It's just that I'd really like to see Willie.'

'Come by here first and spend some time with him. That's all you'd see of him anyway even if we ate here.'

'It's kinda public.'

'We're just talking about eating lunch.'

He didn't say anything.

'You haven't told Allison you're going to see me.'

'Right.'

Okay. I'll give you an interview. I'll tell you what it's like a year later. Everybody in America is dying for this interview. It's yours. You can take your bloody notebook and put it on the table so everyone can see. Even Allison couldn't object to that. It's all in the line of duty.'

'Sadie, I hate to appear to use you like that ... you've got a deal.'

'That was a hard sell.'

'Where do you want to eat?'

'Let's go to the new Galileo's. Obviously, I've never been there but it sounds great.'

'Good. We can sit in the back. It's fairly private there. We can talk. I'll come by the house about eleven-thirty to see Willie and we can go from

456

there.'

'I promise you you won't be sorry.'

'That remains to be seen.'

The last time he had interviewed her she was the First Lady, they were in the third-floor solarium, and halfway through they had fallen on each other and made passionate love. It had been the beginning of their dangerous love affair.

That would not happen this time. She was certain. But Des still cared about her. She was certain of that, too.

*　　*　　*

Des and Willie made her cry, they were so wonderful together. Des roughhoused with him, rolling around on the floor, wrestling, punching. Willie climbed all over him, rode him, laughing and giggling. They were both bright red.

Des had come loaded down with sports equipment for Willie. Tiny bats and soccerballs and racquets.

'I didn't bring books,' he said, rather apologetically. 'I figured you'd probably handle that department. I wanted to do for him what a father should do. Get him what he's not getting.'

'He loves it,' she said reassuringly. 'Can't you tell? He adores you, too.'

Des looked as though she had given him the greatest present in the world.

'Mommy, can I go home with Uncle Des?' asked Willie, clinging to Des's neck.

Des and Sadie looked at each other, stricken.

'Oh Willie, angel, I don't know...'

'Sure, I'll take you home with me sometime,

457

dumpling.'

Des looked as if he was going to expire. He pulled Willie to him and hugged him tightly. It was only then that Sadie began to realize the extent of Des's pain over Willie. The idea that she might be in Des's situation was unthinkable. That she would not have access to her own child, and be able to claim her own child. Love her child and never have him know that she was his mother? It was too awful to contemplate. Yet that was what Des had to deal with every day of his life. Des, who was so bad at revealing his feelings, even to himself, looked suddenly vulnerable. She felt she could see through him. The X-ray showed him bleeding inside. It was hard enough on her. But it was her fault. She was the one who had caused this pain for two people she loved dearly, first Rosey, then Des. How could he ever forgive her?

'We better get going or we'll be late for lunch,' Sadie said. She had to get out or she would fall apart.

'Right,' said Des, reluctantly prying Willie off him.

Sadie called Monica, who appeared smiling and grabbed Willie into her arms.

'Bye buddy,' said Des, mussing his hair, still unable to take his hands off him.

'I love you, Uncle Des,' said Willie.

'Yeah,' said Des and turned away quickly.

★       ★       ★

Galileo's was packed when Des and Sadie came in and the place came to a halt as they were shown to their table in the back. As soon as they had passed

458

through the front room the entire restaurant began to buzz with excitement. This was the first time Sadie Grey had gone out to a restaurant for lunch since her husband had been assassinated.

The new Galileo's was not as cozy as the little hole in the wall they had all been accustomed to. The old one had become so popular it had outgrown its space on P Street and they had been forced to move to a larger location farther down on 21st Street. Now, unfortunately, it looked like just another uptown Italian restaurant with tiles, white tablecloths, and tapestries. Still, the food was good and the atmosphere welcoming. Des had requested one of the tables in the back cloistered in a small cozy niche.

She was happy to be there but also very glad Des had suggested they sit in the back corner where the tables next to them were filled with her own Secret Service agents. In spite of the fact that she didn't dare go out for that reason, it was a shock. She hadn't been prepared for the sensation she was causing. Washington had become so boring, nothing was going on; so to have Sadie appear at a restaurant was a very big deal. It would be talked about for weeks.

They ordered their drinks, she a sparkling water, Des, on his best behavior, a beer.

'What? No martini?' she teased.

'I have to keep my wits about me.'

'Don't tell me you've given them up?'

'I wish I had. I'm afraid I may be one of the last people in town to still have a martini at lunch.'

'And just a wee taste of Irish at night?'

'You remember.'

'I have forgotten nothing about you, Des.'

They both looked a little uncomfortable.

'I hadn't forgotten your curly black hair either,' she went back to teasing. 'I was surprised to see how much gray there is now. You're going to look very romantic with all white hair. Very Irish. Very poetic.'

'It won't be long now.'

'So,' she said, changing the subject, 'where's your notebook?'

'We're not doing an interview.'

'Why not?' She was really surprised.

'It's nobody's goddamned business what you've been doing or what you're feeling. Fuck 'em.'

'How will you explain this lunch to your office ... to Allison?'

'I don't care about the office. I told Allison that I had called you to tell you about the baby and to suggest that I drop by and see you and that you wanted to go out to lunch.'

'And that was fine with her? I don't believe it.'

'I told her you were in love with somebody.'

'You didn't! It will be all over town. Des, how could you?'

'I had to see Willie ... and you. I didn't want to lie to her. I want to be able to continue seeing Willie. This was the only way. Sonny won't tell. You'll just have to trust me on that one.'

'I guess I don't have any choice, do I?'

'You are, aren't you? I mean, in love with somebody?'

'In love? I don't ... I think so ... I mean I ... yes. Yes, I am. I am in love with somebody.'

'Good. Great. That's terrific. I'm happy for you.'

'Do you want to know who it is?'

'Not necessarily. I mean, I don't really care. I

460

don't need to know. You don't have to tell me. Yeah, sure. Who?'

'This is not for Allison. Okay? You can tell her you don't know.'

'Of course.'

'He's a doctor. He's younger than I am. He's Jewish. He's married.'

Des gave a low whistle.

'His name is Michael Lanzer. He's head of the National Cancer Institute. He's helping Blanche and me with the AIDS project. You met him at the White House in February.'

'No kidding? That guy? You're in love with that guy?'

'Surprised?'

'No, it's just that ... you really go for the ethnics, don't you? First a Mick, now a Jew. What next?'

'There isn't going to be a next. This is it.'

'How long has this been going on?'

'Nothing's going on.'

'I don't get it.'

'Neither do I, actually. I've never had a relationship quite like this one before.'

'Pardon me for asking, but does he know he's the lucky guy?'

'I've never told him.'

'Has he told you he loves you?'

'Never.' She laughed at the look on his face. 'I must say, Des, it's unlike you to be this inquisitive about somebody's personal life. I can't believe it's you.'

'What does he know?'

Des was irritated, she could tell. She wasn't quite sure why.

461

'He knows about you. He knows about Willie.'

'Shit, Sadie? You've got to be kidding.'

'Now it's your turn to be upset. He won't tell. You'll have to trust me on this one.'

He smiled in spite of himself.

'So what has this momzer got to offer for himself?'

'Momzer?'

'Jewish for bastard.'

'Des, what is it you're upset about?'

She was pleased that he was so agitated.

'It's just that you're a pretty fabulous dame. Not to mention a national treasure. I hate to see you waste yourself on some married . . . guy who you're not even sure loves you. Besides,' he said as an afterthought, obviously to be more persuasive, 'I have to consider Willie. Any man you end up with is going to be the stepfather to my son. I have a stake in this relationship.'

He liked that idea. She could see he was going to pursue it.

'I want to know that Willie is going to end up with somebody who loves him, who is going to help him grow into a man.'

'Des, you can't run my life or Willie's life from the sidelines as the mood suits you. I have to live the way I feel is best for me and Willie. You have your own life now with Allison and little Katherine on the way. I wish things could have been different, but God didn't plan it that way for us. I loved you once, with all my heart. Letting you go was the hardest thing I've ever had to do. But I had to. Now I see a chance for happiness for me and my child. And if it's meant to be, I'm going to grab it. And I hope you'll understand and give me your

462

blessing.'

He paused a long time.

'I will. But it doesn't mean I have to like it.'

'Des?'

'Yeah?'

'Does this whole conversation sound like it's right out of a soap opera?'

'Yes, but then, as it turns out, so are our lives.'

*     *     *

She had talked to him a few times from Easthampton in August. It was always she who called him. He seemed happy to hear from her and often they would have quite long talks if she called at the end of the day. He was usually much more accessible on the phone than he was in person, except for La Samanna and Cumberland Island. Beaches. That was it. He was vulnerable on beaches. She had tried to get him to come up to Long Island but he wouldn't. Besides, except in the winter, it was too public. She had found that out the hard way when she was First Lady and she had been spotted with Des in early spring on a cold, wintry beach. That was in another life, though. She had been obsessed with Des. Now there was Michael to think about. She had missed him terribly while she was away. It wasn't that she was used to seeing him—she wasn't. It was just that in Washington she knew he was there and that she could see him if she needed him, if she had to.

Now she was back. She had closed the Easthampton house the week after Labor Day. She had returned to Washington in time to enroll Willie in nursery school. She had gone back to her office uninspired and depressed at the prospect of her life, of her future.

\*     \*     \*

Except for those few phone calls, Michael had been out of her life for months. After their time in Georgia they both seemed to have sensed that the differences between them were too great.

The only problem was that even though she had tried to put him out of her mind, she began to miss him terribly. For one thing, having dismissed him psychologically, she had nobody to think about. That left a terrible emptiness in her life. But more than that, oddly enough, as the weeks passed, she began to miss the Jewishness of him. What had seemed to her overwhelming now seemed fascinating.

She had begun to associate him with holidays, almost as if he were family. In her mind he was, or had been, ever since she had made up her mind to marry him. Now Christmas was coming, and New Year's, and Chanukah. She was actually beginning to think that way now. She knew he was not going to La Samanna again, so she had decided not to go either. She knew she would be absolutely miserable there without him even though she had decided not to see him anymore.

It was all too complicated. She was in a sort of weird emotional limbo. The holiday season was upon her and she was not handling it at all well. She needed to talk to someone. She needed to talk to Jenny.

\*     \*     \*

They were in her office at the E.O.B.

It reminded her of the days when she was First Lady and they would sit for hours and talk about Des. It was in her office there that she and Des used to meet, where they had their affair, always with Jenny, then her very unhappy press secretary, sitting in the outside office guarding the door.

Then she used her office for Des and for writing her novel, with which Des was ostensibly helping her. He had come to see her under the guise of being her editor. The novel was on the shelf at the moment. She hadn't felt like writing in a long time, not since she had gotten pregnant with Willie. One day she would get back to it...

Now her office was for AIDS and Michael, talking to Michael, that is, because she had never met him there. Now she was sitting in front of the fire, sipping her tea, her feet curled up under her on the sofa, talking to Jenny about her new love. Or rather her new ex-love.

'Tell me what to do, Jen. I'm really in love with him, at least I think I am, although I don't trust it. I don't trust shiksa madness either. I don't know whether he's really infatuated with me or just my shiksaness. I don't know anything anymore. All I know is that I'm a mess. But Jenny, he's so feeling and caring and understanding. He's the most sensitive man I've ever met.'

Jenny rolled her eyes.

'Sadie, let me tell you about the famously sensitive Jew, who doesn't exist because they are all narcissists.'

'But he's not. Not when he's with me! Don't you find him attractive?'

465

'I can see where he would be very attractive to a lot of women. It's just that I don't buy into that thing, at least not anymore. That doesn't mean that you shouldn't. I really believe that Jewish men should be with gentile women. The bad part about a Jew marrying a Jew is that he will turn her into his mother. The thing is that he won't be tempted to make a shiksa his mother. It is much harder for a Jewish man to work his pathology on a shiksa wife. Jewish men behave better with shiksas, that's the truth.'

'So what's the downside?'

'The downside, need I remind you, is that he's married, Sadie.'

'Suppose he weren't?'

'The downside is that when Jewish men and gentile women have children and she wants to send them to Sunday school and have little creches under the Christmas tree and dress them up for Easter, he goes berserk. And there's another downside.'

'What's that?'

'For him, once the sexual desire for his gorgeous shiksa ebbs he'll look at her and think, "For this I've given up my culture?"'

'What if she converts?'

Jenny rolled here eyes again.

'Please don't tell me you're thinking about that.'

'No, but what if she did?'

'Then he wouldn't be in love with her.'

'Why not?'

'Because she would be neither Jewish nor a shiksa, which is even worse.'

★      ★      ★

466

It was Christmastime and on television everyone was wishing everyone a happy Chanukah. The newspapers and magazines all had Chanukah stories. The stores, even the few she went to and always early in the morning before the crowds came, all had Chanukah signs, greeting cards, wrapping paper, food, toys, candles, six-pointed stars. Where everything at Christmas used to be red and green, now it was blue and white.

Had it always been that way? Had she just never noticed before? Had her consciousness been that changed?

Now she saw the endless array of Christmas ads, carols, toys, foods, presents, the inundation of Santa Clauses, reindeer, elves, baby Jesuses, mangers, wise men, Christmas trees, tinsel, fake snow, and twinkling lights as being anti-Semitic at worst, bad for the Jews at best.

It was no use. Her brain had been irrevocably washed. She might as well give in. It had been months since they had spoken. She called him.

He was pleasant and polite. He wouldn't allow himself to seem surprised or happy to hear from her. Only a nervous laugh gave him away. She, on the other hand, was in such a state that her mouth was dry and she felt as if she were talking with a wad of cotton between her teeth.

She invited him to have a holiday lunch with her. She deliberately said holiday. She invited him to the house because she knew how he hated being stared at when he was out with her, and because she wanted to be alone with him.

They set a date a week before Christmas, in the middle of Chanukah. He was to come at noon. Their goodbyes were slightly awkward.

467

She was so excited she barely slept the night before. She lay awake trying to decide what to wear. Red or green was out. So was blue. Finally she chose white. Neutral. She always seemed to end up in white. This time a simple white skirt and sweater.

She was drying her hair when the phone rang around 10:00 a.m. It was Maureen, Michael's secretary. She sounded worried.

'You haven't heard from Michael?' she asked.

'No,' said Sadie. 'Is anything wrong?'

'He usually comes in by seven at least,' she said. 'But he hasn't been in all morning. He has an important meeting here in his office. Everyone's here and he still hasn't shown up. I've tried bleeping him but there's no answer. Giselle is in France for the holidays with her parents. I know you're supposed to have lunch with him at noon. Please have him call if he gets there. If he doesn't, please call me right away. Something may have happened.'

Sadie was surprised at her reaction. She tried his home number, letting it ring. Her stomach was in knots. Her imagination went wild. She imagined him having been mugged and shot, lying bleeding in his house, unable to reach the phone. She imagined him having been in an automobile accident on the way to work, lying bleeding on the road or in an ambulance somewhere. She imagined him having had a heart attack, lying gasping for his last breath, unable to call for help. She was unable to sit down. She paced back and forth, her heart beating at an alarming rate, as she glanced at the clock every five minutes. She found herself praying over and over in desperation that nothing had

468

happened to him.

By the time noon came she was beside herself. When he did not ring the bell exactly on the dot of twelve she called Maureen.

'I'm going to his house,' she said. 'I've got my Secret Service agents with me in case there's a problem. I'll call you from there.'

It had started to snow and it was coming down quite heavily on Wisconsin Avenue as they headed out to his house in Bethesda. Cars were beginning to skid on the slippery street; yet despite the weather it only took them twenty minutes to get there. Sadie begged them to go as fast as they could without attracting attention.

The front door was locked. She rang the doorbell. They walked around to the back and found a bedroom window above the porch slightly open, shades down. One of the agents climbed up on the shoulders of another and pulled himself up to the porch. Once up there he peered through the crack, then called down.

'There's a guy in the bed. He's not moving. He looks like he's asleep but the phone is ringing and it's not waking him up.'

'Climb in and see if he . . . if he's all right,' said Sadie, her voice quavering.

The agent climbed in through the window. Sadie stood there shivering in the freezing cold, waiting for an eternity until he came back to the window.

'He's alive,' he said. 'But he's very sick. He's pretty hot, too. He must have a high temperature. He seems kind of delirious. Maybe we should call an ambulance.'

'Come down and open the front door,' she said.

Michael was lying on the bed, in an icy-cold

room, covered to his waist in only a sheet, his body flushed and hot to the touch. His breathing was shallow and he was shaking slightly.

'Michael! Michael!' she shouted.

He opened his eyes, which were glazed.

'Sadie,' he whispered. 'What are you doing here, you dumb shiksa?'

'Oh God, I don't believe this,' she said, laughing with relief. 'You are hopeless.'

He couldn't be that sick if he was able to tease her.

She turned to the agents.

'I think we should do what I do with Willie when he gets a fever. Put him in a lukewarm tub and keep squeezing water over his head while I call the White House physician.'

Michael, it turned out, had a severe virus that had peaked that morning. By the time Dr Medver had left, having come over in a White House sedan, Michael was propped up in bed with a robe on, in a warm room, sipping some canned broth Sadie had found in the kitchen. He was weak and feverish and stayed awake for short periods.

Sadie had called Maureen to tell her what had happened and assured her that she had everything under control. She had called her housekeeper, Asuncion, and gotten her to bring over some food and tidy up the house a bit. It looked as if a bachelor had been living there alone for a while. Sadie was curious to look around. She wanted to see if she could discover some things about Giselle and their marriage but she didn't dare just yet. She wondered what was going on between them. She dreaded the phone ringing for fear it might be Giselle. Michael was really too sick to answer the phone. Yet if Giselle called Maureen and found out what had happened, she might just come right home. Sadie didn't want that. She wanted to take care of him herself. She suspected they might be having some sort of fight. It was odd that she would have left him alone during the holidays. Apparently the kids were in France as well. She would find out all of that soon enough.

She stayed with him until about seven that night. She left Asuncion there while she went home to have dinner with Willie, put him to bed, shower and wash her hair, and pack an overnight bag. Then she went back to Michael's house. He lived in a quiet little cul-de-sac completely protected by evergreen trees and shrubs. He also had a private driveway that went to the side entrance, so she could come and go without having to worry about being spotted.

Her agents weren't too thrilled with the idea. She let them stay downstairs in the living room while she pulled the mattress and comforter off his daughter's bed, dragged them into his room, and slept on the floor next to his bed. He was too weak even to go to the bathroom by himself so she got her agents to come up and help him when he needed to. She bathed his head constantly with lukewarm washcloths, made him sip broth and some freshly squeezed orange juice, and even eat some toast. He didn't want to eat much. He seemed grateful for her attention. Mostly he just seemed really sick.

By morning, when he finally woke up, he had turned the corner and was actually somewhat alert. She had gotten up early, put on some black sweats, and had brought him some hot tea and toast and a

471

boiled egg. He was able to get to the bathroom himself, took a shower and shaved while she changed his sheets and made his bed. He barely made it back to bed, though.

'You are looking at one sick Jew,' he said, smiling weakly, after he had finished his breakfast.

'You're not as sick as you were,' she said.

'You look great, you look beautiful. I like you with no makeup on, your hair straight, dressed like that.'

'Oh this,' she blushed. 'I look like an old hag. I just thought it would be more comfortable.'

'Old hag. You took the words right out of my mouth. That's what I meant to say.' He paused. 'I'd also like to say thank you. You didn't have to come out here, you know.'

'I don't like being stood up for lunch.'

'It was the only way I could think of to get you to spend the night.'

He was clearly in a weakened condition. He would never have said anything like that normally. It was the closest thing he had ever come to making a pass or even hinting that he wanted to go to bed with her.

She chose to smile at him and say nothing. She was afraid anything she might say would scare him off.

'Speaking of lunch,' she said, 'what would you like? I'll get you anything you want.'

'You're so domestic. It's wonderful. It's a whole side of you I didn't know existed. But forget lunch. I just had breakfast. I can't even think about eating. I'm not hungry.'

'Well, you've got to get your strength back and you're going to eat lunch so you might as well have

472

what you want.'

'Fine. I want chicken soup with knaydlach.'

'Okay, I give up. What are knaydlach?'

'They're matza balls.'

'I've often wondered why they never use any other part of the matza.'

Michael looked at her stunned, then started to howl with laughter. He laughed until there were tears in his eyes. Finally, when he had quit, he looked at her skeptically.

'You are kidding, aren't you?'

'About what?' But she couldn't help grinning.

'I really had you for a minute.'

'Sadie Grey, I love you. You're wonderful.'

He slipped it in so she wouldn't notice. He hadn't dared look at her when he said it for fear she would see that he meant it.

'Where would I find this delicacy?'

'There are hundreds of delicatessens around here. Of course, if it's too much trouble I just won't eat.'

It was her turn to laugh at the martyred tone and the pitiful expression on his face. Despite his teasing, though, one thing she understood for sure: he was testing her. And she was goddamned well going to find the best chicken soup and matza balls he had ever had in his entire life.

She found the soup at a deli nearby and had Asuncion pick it up and bring it over. She served it to him in bed, on a nice tray with a clean cloth napkin that she found while inspecting Giselle's household. She had discovered, to her chagrin, that the house was immaculate. Giselle was obviously a brilliant homemaker.

Michael made a big ceremony of tasting the chicken soup, which even she had to admit was delicious. The matza balls passed his inspection as well. He didn't say much, but she could tell he was pleased and touched that she would go to so much trouble for him. He was still quite weak, and just eating and talking to her had tired him out. She took the tray away, took one of his pillows, turned out the light, and pulled the covers over him. He turned over to go to sleep. She stood at his back for a moment, then reached over and stroked his head. He pulled his hand out from under the covers and put it over hers and held it for a moment.

'I'll be back,' she whispered. Before she had left the room he was sound asleep.

She wanted to spend some time with Willie if she was coming back to spend the night. The question was, did she really have to spend the night? Was he that sick? She rationalized that he was still weak even though his fever had broken. He might need something in the night or he might have a relapse. Certainly he would need breakfast in the morning. If she didn't stay she wouldn't be able to get there until late. In any case, she convinced herself that he needed her. She had Asuncion fix a big pot of minestrone and some Italian bread to take back with her.

When she got back after putting Willie down at seven, he was awake, lying in the dark room listening to classical music on his radio.

'I was afraid you weren't coming,' he said.

'Of course I was coming. I told you I would. Why didn't you call me?'

She sat down on the edge of the bed and automatically felt his forehead.

'I never call you, remember?'

'That's right, you bastard, so suffer.'

474

'I must not have a fever or you wouldn't be calling me a bastard.' He chuckled.

'You don't. You haven't all day. Are you feeling any better?'

'Will you be staying tonight?' She had the feeling that he was afraid to admit he was feeling better for fear she might not stay.

'Yes.'

'I am feeling a little better . . . but I'm still pretty weak,' he added hastily.

It was so dark he couldn't see her smiling.

She turned on the lights and made him get out of bed and take a shower while she dragged the mattress back into his daughter's room. She didn't want to give him a chance to protest. She made his bed, then went downstairs and fixed them both a tray and brought it back. They ate in silence with just the sound of the radio playing softly in the background.

'Jenny says I shouldn't convert.'

'To what?'

'To Judaism.'

He laughed, nearly knocking over his soup bowl.

'I presume,' he said, 'that you are joking.'

'I just wanted to see how you would react.' She was smiling mischievously.

'To even consider it would be to not understand the very basis of my existence.'

'What would be so terrible about it?'

'It would combine the worst of both. It would be the most disastrous combination.'

'Namely?'

'A Jewish woman with a shiksa brain.'

'Thanks a lot.'

'Actually, I'm reluctant to admit this, but you

have a yiddishe kopf.'

'What's that?'

'A Jewish head. A Jewish brain.'

'What does that make me?'

'The best combination.'

'I'm flattered.'

'You should be.'

'Do you ever have fantasies about Jewish women?'

'Never.'

'Why not?'

'I'm not evolved enough.'

★　★　★

He never mentioned that the mattress had been moved.

She asked him when she brought him a fresh glass of ice water if she could get him anything else before he went to sleep. She was standing by the edge of the bed. He reached up and took her hand in his.

'Thank you,' he said.

His eyes were so compelling that she had to pull away. What she really wanted to do was to sit down on the bed and put her arms around him. To kiss him. To make love to him. But she didn't. All he needed to do was to pull ever so gently on her hand and she would have come to him. But he didn't. She could tell he wanted to. But he didn't. Somehow it was important to her that when it happened, if it happened, he had to make the first move.

She didn't sleep well that night. All she could think about was making love to him.

Sometimes it seemed impossible, the idea of it. So forbidden and scary, not only for her, but she knew for him as well. Other times the idea of not making love to him was impossible.

Sometimes sex seemed so immediate, so natural to her, just another bodily function. She felt she knew him so well that it would only be an extension of what they already had. Everybody did it. All the time. There was really nothing mysterious about it. Other times the notion of making love to Michael was the ultimate in mystery, in intimacy, of belonging. It was something so deep that she couldn't imagine sharing it with anybody, so frightening that she couldn't dwell on it. She wondered if he had such conflicting thoughts about her.

Des always said that everybody fucked. Everybody cheated on their spouses. If you ever suspected people were fucking they were surely fucking. Everybody in the royal family fucked. Everybody in Hollywood fucked. Everybody in New York and Washington fucked. The difference was that in Washington they didn't think about it or enjoy it. In fact, she was a perfect example. She did it when she was married to Rosey. It wasn't just an ordinary affair either. She was, after all, the First Lady and she was fucking. That's why Des found it so astonishing and even unbelievable that she and Michael weren't.

Somehow, with Michael, she wasn't about to reduce it to that. Anything that happened with him would have to be more spiritual than just sex. That sounded corny but it was true. It couldn't be just an affair.

She wondered what he would be like in bed.

477

Certainly not a seasoned lover. How could he be? But would he be shy and awkward, or assured?

She had fantasized so much about making love to him, but her fantasies were always based on perfect love and perfect sex and never on what the reality might be. It never even occurred to her that she could be disappointed. She was too much in love.

Sometimes she was amazed at her own interest in him, the level of her desire and obsession with him. Five years ago, even two years ago, she would never have been ready for him, never even entertained the notion of him, certainly never would have been attracted to him. He had said that to her many times. In high school they would have hated each other, he said. She would have thought him a nerd, a creep, with his nose buried in his books, his slide rule and short white socks, probably playing the clarinet in the school band. He would have thought her a stuck-up shiksa bitch.

He was right, too. He had her number. She had always gone for the preppy jocks. Des wasn't preppy but he was a jock and more macho than any man she had ever gone out with. Michael would never qualify for macho. Somehow, now, that all seemed so irrelevant.

   &#9733;  &#9733;  &#9733;

He was like a new person the next morning, energetic and playful. She had been thumbing through the magazines on his bedside table and found one called *A Pictorial Guide to Sexually Transmitted Diseases*.

'God, that's attractive,' she said.

'I don't have AIDS,' he said. He knew what she

478

had been thinking.

'How do you know?'

'I got tested.'

'When?'

'Recently.'

'I thought you said you didn't want to know.'

'I changed my mind.'

★　　★　　★

She brought him breakfast before she left to see Willie. He gave her several Christmas presents he had gotten for Willie, all obviously wrapped by him in red-and-green Santa Claus paper. He explained to her what they were. They were actually Chanukah presents. One was a draydl, a little top that spun around and miraculously ended up rewarding the spinner with gold-wrapped chocolate coins, of which there were many. The draydl, he explained, was a phony game made up by Jews in the Middle Ages to fool their persecutors into thinking they were playing rather than meeting to study the Torah, which was forbidden. The other gift was a tiny menorah, or candelabrum with nine little candles to light, one on each night of Chanukah. She was touched that he would think of Willie, even more that he would want to include Willie. For that was what he was offering. Up until then Willie had been totally separate from what they had together.

'I can't really pretend to be sick enough to need waiting on anymore,' he said.

'You're still not well enough to go out, particularly in this freezing weather. Thank God it's Friday. At least you can spend the weekend at

479

home. I'll come back after I've put Willie down for his nap and bring you a surprise.'

He looked as young and excited as Willie did when she told him the same thing. She had to smile at the expression on his face, though it made her feel torn between them this week. Willie had been the major focus of her attention since the minute he was born, and only this week had she actually had to choose between him and somebody else for her time. Willie was out of sorts, especially at not having her there in the mornings to get up with him. She would have to make it up to him, but she was a tiny bit resentful that she was being pulled in two directions.

When she came back that afternoon Michael had just gotten out of the shower and was wearing boxer shorts and a La Samanna T-shirt.

He also had on his robe, which she had found in the closet and which he claimed he didn't know he had.

It was snowing heavily outside and she still had flakes glistening in her hair and on her face. She had put on bright turquoise blue sweats, which she said reminded her of the Caribbean and La Samanna and the fact that the first anniversary of their meeting was coming up in another week. She had stopped at the deli and brought him a corned-beef sandwich and some kosher pickles. She pulled a chair up to the side of his bed while they ate. Michael ate every bite. After lunch she handed him two presents that she had carefully wrapped in white paper with blue ribbon.

'Happy Chanukah,' she said.

He opened one present to find a box of Christmas cookies with little red and green sprinkles on them.

That one was from Willie, she explained, who was thrilled with his presents. It was also from her because she wanted to try again with the cookies to make up for the horrible scene at Passover.

The other present was a tape of the song that was played New Year's Eve in La Samanna when they were dancing together on the beach.

'Now we have a first anniversary and a song,' she said laughing.

'You really are a romantic, aren't you?'

'You once said I was the deepest person you knew and the shallowest,' she said. 'My romantic tendencies represent both of those sides.'

He put the tape into the tape recorder on his bedside table and they listened to it together. When the lyrics, 'Say You Love Me,' were sung, she reached over to turn off the tape, but he put his hand on hers and stopped her.

'Why won't you look at me?'

She reddened and shrugged. It was making her uncomfortable and embarrassed. It was too close to the bone, words that she wanted to be said and hadn't been.

She waited until the song was finished, then turned the tape off.

'I have another surprise for you,' she said, pulling a small bottle of oil with an almond in it out of her bag.

'This looks kinky,' he said with a grin. 'I have a feeling I'm going to like this.'

'You are, trust me,' she said. 'If you aren't well now, you will be when I'm finished with you. Take off your bathrobe and your T-shirt and turn over.'

'This is kinky,' he said with an expectant grin, as he quickly undressed.

481

He had a lot of hair on his chest. She hadn't expected that. She had an almost uncontrollable urge to bury her head in his chest and wrap herself around him. Instead, she got up and pulled down the shades and turned off the lights. Sitting on the side of the bed, she pulled the covers down to his buttocks, pushing his shorts down as far as she could with decency.

She poured a tiny bit of oil on her hands, rubbed them together and began massaging his back with an almost professional smoothness that came from being massaged many times over the years. She did this for about ten minutes until he began to moan and she realized that she herself was about to explode from sexual tension and desire.

Finally he turned over and grabbed her wrists.

'I can't stand this anymore, Sadie Grey,' he said. His face was almost grim. 'Why are you doing this? Why are you here? Why are you taking care of me?'

She couldn't stand it anymore either.

'Because I love you.'

It had been so simple to say.

He pulled her to him and began to kiss her softly on the mouth, then more passionately. She thought she would faint. The energy had been drained out of her and she nearly went limp. All the fantasies she had had about this moment drifted away as she allowed herself to be touched and held and loved by this man. She realized that she needed desperately to be pleasured by him, to be filled up by him and his love, emotionally, intellectually, and especially physically. She needed to let it happen, to let him take charge, to have him make love to her the way he talked to her. She needed to take it all in. Later, the next time, she could participate, but this time she wanted to be taken by him, to belong to him completely, and the only way that could happen was to let him do it. Unlike other men she had made love to, where she was an active participant, this time she wanted him to please her. She felt he needed that, and that the greatest gift she could give him, and therefore them, was to let him do it. Later there would be time for her involvement. Now she wanted only to give herself completely to Michael.

He didn't disappoint her. How did he know to kiss her and lick her softly on her neck and shoulders until she wanted to scream? Most men weren't that subtle. The pressure of his fingers on the rest of her body was perfect, gentle and eager at the same time. He knew exactly what to do with his tongue and his hands, and as he moved slowly down her body with his mouth until he rested between her legs she could hear herself as if she were in another room letting out little whimpers and gasps of pleasure. He was literally playing her body like a musical instrument. She had never known what that meant before. Now, when he entered her, she was so ready for him she came in a series of orgasms, like rushes of heat and electricity passing through her over and over again. She felt literally paralyzed with pleasure. She couldn't make a sound, and only when he cried out and she felt him shudder did she remember to breathe again.

They lay together quietly, entwined in each other's arms for a long time. She was the one who spoke first.

'Had you only kissed me and not made love to me, Dayenu!'

He reached over and brought her to him, enclosing her in his arms.

'Oh Sadie,' he whispered.

'Say you love me,' she said.

'I love you.'

It was then that she felt the rush of emotion and it surprised her when the tears started in her eyes. She flung herself against his chest and buried her face in it, only realizing after several minutes that the tears were not all hers.

★     ★     ★

They were both emotionally exhausted but she needed to talk.

'My love for you has been making me crazy ever since I met you,' she said. 'I've been totally obsessed by you to the point of doing really stupid things like writing Sadie Lanzer and Mrs Michael Lanzer on a piece of paper over and over. I've even called your house and hung up when Giselle answered. This is not normal healthy behavior and I don't know whether to trust it or not. Am I just a bereft widow who is not functioning? Is it because you're exotic to me, because I've never known any Jews before? Is it because you are a scientist, from a different world? Is it because you were effectively a virgin, although not inexperienced, I must say? All I know is that I love you and I can't live without you. It seems so inappropriate, you and me. We're so different. We have nothing in common. We don't like to do the same things. Yet I feel more comfortable with you than I ever have with anyone in my life. It seems so totally right. I love the way you talk. Your words turn me on. My mind is my erogenous zone. Or was until just now.' She started rubbing her foot.

'You know, I used to get a cramp in my left foot just talking to you on the phone. Then I got one when we were making love. Maybe that's my erogenous zone. You've saved my life, you know. Now you'll be forever indebted to me, as the Chinese say. I was lost and now I'm found. You're stuck with me, Lanzer. I'm not making any sense, am I?'

'Just keep talking,' he said, stroking her hair. 'You need to talk. I'm listening.'

'I loved Rosey. I was in love with Des. But I love you and I'm in love with you, too. I've learned so much from you. I've thought, many times, that I wouldn't have been ready for you even a year and a half ago. You're like somebody from another planet. Now everything you says sounds wise and funny and brilliant. Somehow what you're doing about AIDS, what you've done, seems so much more important than what people in my world are doing. You're saving people's lives. You've caused me to totally reevaluate everything I believe in, everything I stand for. I feel so shallow and boring and frivolous around you, and yet you don't make me feel that way. I see only understanding and sympathy and empathy in your eyes.'

'And love. You should see love.'

'I do.'

'Then make love to me,' he said. 'It's your turn.'

'You noticed.'

'I did. Thank you.'

'There's nothing you don't get, is there?'

'Shut up, will you, and come over here.'

She took him in her mouth this time. Though she had done this before, she had never had the sensation she had with Michael. For him it was the

485

first time, and watching him experience ecstasy heightened her own pleasure almost more than she could bear.

When they had finished making love, they fell away from each other, lying back separately on the bed, exhausted, breathing heavily, covered with perspiration.

After a while, Sadie spoke dreamily.

'I had this incredible sense when I had you in my mouth of doing something totally animalistic and primitive that people have been doing for thousands of years. It gave me such a sense of subjugation and power. I am completely yours, cavemanlike, your woman, down on my knees, bent to your will and your pleasure. And yet...'

'And yet?'

'At the same time I have total power over you.'

'How so?'

'I could bite it off.'

'That's comforting. You're really playing into my pathology here, aren't you?'

She smiled and kissed him on the cheek. Presently she began to hum.

'Why are you humming "It Had to Be You"?'

'It's one of my favorite songs.'

'Sing the lyrics.'

'It had to be you, you wonderful Jew, it had to be you.'

He smiled, took her head in his hands and kissed her forehead.

'I could go over the wall for you,' he said.

★   ★   ★

Giselle came back at the end of the weekend.

His letter arrived the day before Christmas, their first anniversary.

Dear Sadie,

I love you more than I have ever loved anyone in my life. But I cannot see you again. This piece from Proverbs explains it better than I could. You will never know how sorry I am.

For the lips of a strange woman drop honey,
And her mouth is smoother than oil;
But her latter end is bitter as wormwood,
Sharp as a two-edged sword.
Her feet go down to death:
Her steps take hold on Sheol;
So that she findeth not the level path of life;
Her ways are unstable and she knoweth it not.
Michael

## CHAPTER FOURTEEN

She hadn't been to the Colombian embassy since she was in her early twenties, since she had gone with her father one night. Sam had known the ambassador in his old days as a spook. She had forgotten how beautiful it was with its red-brick facade, long large windows, and paneled walls inside. It was right off Dupont Circle, a location not as desirable as upper Massachusetts Avenue and Kalorama, where many of the other major embassies were.

Allison hadn't wanted to go. It was mid-December, a week before her due date, and by this time she was so heavy and bloated she felt like a slob. She hadn't slept through the night in months. It was all she could do to get to the office, get through a day, and get home. She was, however, determined to go from story conference to the labor room lest anybody accuse her of letting down on the job. It was the most miserable time she could imagine. She longed to just take off and lie in bed reading and daydreaming and talking to Kay Kay. Her unborn child had become her best friend; she wondered how she had ever lived without her. It appalled her that she didn't give a damn about what was going on in the office, and it took everything in her to feign attention. Sprague was getting particularly upset with her for not getting more involved with the drug story, but he was too much of a Southern gentleman to complain about her to Walt or Alan while she was in her delicate state. She knew that he wouldn't do it for political reasons either. It would be unpopular for a male to complain about a female being pregnant even if she wasn't doing her job—unfair but true. The feminists had mau-maued their male colleagues into submission.

Des had talked her into going because the *Weekly* was working on a drug story. She was sure that Des had no idea that Sprague was also working on a lead that the Foreign Minister was involved in the drug business. Somehow Sprague had managed to get an invitation to the dinner. His wife would be there. She had never met Jane and was terribly curious about her, about what kind of woman Sprague would be married to. They had stayed pretty remote from the usual fare of book parties that brought most journalists together in Washington. So tonight was unusual. She had to admit that

Sprague was a dedicated reporter. As antisocial as he seemed to be, he would actually turn up at an embassy dinner for a story.

This was one of the first big embassy parties in a long time. The embassies were essentially dead. They just didn't matter anymore since shuttle diplomacy, television, direct dial, and the fax had replaced the need for ambassadors.

The only reason anyone cared about this particular embassy party was that everyone knew that the President of Colombia was a puppet and that the Foreign Minister really ran the country. So the party was more like a party for the President of Colombia. Then, too, Antonia Alvarez had hit like a storm, the only new glamorous face in Washington. She was sought after as a diversion, if nothing else. Antonia and Foxy had become the glitzy couple. Also, the word was out that Sadie Grey was going to be there. It would be her first official party since the White House dinner the previous February. Sadie was now an icon and everybody wanted to be where she went. Unlike most embassy parties, nobody had turned down this invitation. It was definitely the party to be invited to.

Allison wore the only cocktail maternity dress she could still get into, a blue-gray silk with long sleeves and a round neck with pearls. She was sick of the dress by now, and sick of being huge, but she knew that no matter how dowdy she looked there would be other women there who looked worse. Washington was not exactly the fashion capital of the world.

Allison hadn't seen quite so much press at a party in Washington in years. She had made sure that the

*Daily*'s Living section covered it, but she was surprised to see that even the networks had sent camera crews. Nothing like drugs and celebrities to bring them out. She and Des were late getting there and most everyone had arrived. The receiving line was starting to break up. It was a ratfuck of the first order. Reporters had surrounded Foxy and Antonia looking for good quotes early in the evening so they could make their deadlines. Another group surrounded Sadie Grey and Foreign Minister Mendez, who had obviously broken away from the receiving line to be near her. Mendez had grafted himself to Sadie and was not about to allow her to be more than an inch or so away from him. Mendez was an attractive man in his mid-sixties, tall, tanned, suave, beautifully dressed, and even more beautifully mannered. He was rich, he was internationally known for his reputation with women, gambling, racing, and business. He also had a vast art collection and impeccable taste. It amused Allison to see how he was using Sadie and pouring on the charm. She knew, or at least was fairly sure, he was one of the biggest drug dealers in the world.

Sadie, to her credit, seemed uncomfortable with his attention and his attempt to attach himself to her.

Des grabbed Allison by the hand and squeezed it reassuringly.

'We have to go say hello to Sadie,' he said.

Before she had a chance to reply they were standing in front of her. Sadie looked more beautiful than ever and Allison couldn't help but feel slightly sick to her stomach. Would she ever be able to look at this woman and not have that clutch of fear in her gut?

Before, whenever she had seen Sadie and Des together, there had always seemed to be something unspoken between them, some secret look, something that made her think he might still be in love with her. This evening Sadie greeted Des warmly, but there was a detached friendliness about their handshake that made Allison think that Sadie really was in love with somebody else. She greeted Allison warmly and asked immediately about the baby, about her pregnancy.

'I hear it's a girl and you're going to name her Katherine. I just love that,' she said in her charming Southern accent.

As she talked, Allison had an odd feeling that Sadie was more interested in her pregnancy for reasons she didn't understand.

'You look just superb,' she said. 'So much better than I did. I think it gets worse every time. I was as big as a house with Willie.'

Des took Allison's hand quickly and made an excuse to move on, leaving Allison totally perplexed about the exchange they had just had.

Allison felt rather detached from the scene, anyway. Des went off to work the room leaving her on her own for a while.

One of the many things she had learned since she'd been pregnant was the way pregnant woman were treated. The bigger you got the more invisible you got. Men in Washington, and particularly men in power, discounted a woman the minute she started to show. It was as if they expected your brain to shrink as your stomach swelled. Here she was, a woman in an extremely powerful position, who was considered very attractive and one of the best-known women in the city, and not a single man in any official position had even attempted to strike up a conversation. They would look at her face, smile in initial recognition, their eyes would instinctively travel downward, and immediately glaze over.

More interesting than the men's response to her pregnancy was her response to them. Normally, she herself would have been all over everybody in power as well, trying to pick up as much information as she could. She could see the secretary of state surrounded by several ambassadors, senators, and columnists. Any other time she would have been in the center of that conversation. Now she didn't really care. Her current major concern was fending off the wives who were desperate to find somebody to talk to them. They were the American equivalent to the Indian 'untouchables' in the cruel caste system that was Washington politics and power.

Lorraine Hadley was talking to the wife of one of the ambassadors. Worth and Clare Elgin were working overtime to amuse Foxy and Antonia. Several television superstars had staked out their territory in the middle of the room in competition with the secretary of state and a number of cabinet officers and senators. They were now as sought after and seen to be as powerful as the people they covered, at least by themselves. It had made things a bit disconcerting for those in the administration and Congress who were used to being the center of attention. No one quite knew what the protocol was now that journalists commanded equal billing and top seating. Before, it was the journalists who were the supplicants, always going after the officials for tidbits or even recognition. Now it seemed almost the other way around, with government officials seeking the recognition of the media. At best, it was a mutual courtship comprised of scores of separate little duchies all over town.

The jockeying for position hadn't changed and never would. That was just human nature. Nor had the raw manipulation of and seeking of power. It was just that for her, especially now in her detached frame of mind, as she looked around the room, it all seemed so ridiculous, so absurd, so pointless. It just didn't matter.

So somebody gets a hot story or a scoop today. So somebody loses an election tomorrow. So somebody else gets appointed to a powerful job. So what? In the end, what would it matter? She always deplored those earnest news or administration types who had covered the White House or worked for the government for years and then wrote their memoirs. It was all about 'and then I met' and 'the President said to me' and 'I asked the king' and after a while they were all the same. One self-touting account bled into another until they were indistinguishable. No lessons learned, no values improved, no morals to the story. Everyone in Washington suddenly seemed so self-involved and aggrandized. She had once believed that people came here for noble reasons. That journalists really cared about seeking the truth and politicians really wanted to make the world a better place. That thought made her laugh now. Cynicism had replaced idealism. Had she really become so jaded? Or was she just being realistic and the rest of them jaded? This was a dangerous way for the national editor of the *Daily* to think. Particularly the first

493

woman national editor of the *Daily*.

She noticed Sprague standing in a group of men near the secretary of state. Next to him was a rather pretty dark-haired woman who was hanging back, peripheral at best to the conversation. It had to be his wife. She walked over to where they were standing and introduced herself.

Jane was taller than Allison by several inches. She wore almost no makeup and a very simple navy silk dress with a collar and an antique pearl pin. Savannah Junior League all the way. She was probably his age, late thirties. Her hair showed signs of gray, and there were quite a few lines around her eyes and mouth, which she made no attempt to hide. She must have been quite stunning when she was young. May queen material; most popular debutante. She had the look of a woman who was brought up in a small, privileged community and took it for granted. Not smug, but satisfied. She was not dumb—Sprague had told Allison she was a teacher—but her eyes didn't sparkle with humor.

Allison looked for a bond between them but when Sprague looked at his wife he did not look at her the way Allison would want her husband to look at her. He was proper, polite, gentlemanly.

'Allison, I'd like you to meet my wife, Jane. Jane, this is Allison Sterling.'

'Yes, Sprague told me about you.'

No smile. Nothing. What was that supposed to mean? My husband had told me all about what a terrible bitch you are? She certainly couldn't be jealous of Allison. Sprague had never so much as looked sideways at her. Besides, Allison was weighting in at around one hundred fifty pounds

494

these days.

'I'm sure it's all been incredibly flattering, whatever he's told you,' said Allison with a slight smile.

She turned to look at Sprague. He was inscrutable.

Dinner was announced and she went off to find Des. Everyone filed into the beautiful paneled dining room. It was lit with massive silver candelabras and set with one huge long dining-room table that held all sixty-some people. The Foreign Minister sat at the center of the table with Sadie on his right, the ambassador across the table from him with the wife of the secretary of state on his right. Allison was somewhere about halfway down, on the other side of the table from the Foreign Minister. Des was at one end. She had drawn as her dinner partner on one side, the chairman of the Senate Foreign Relations Committee, a rotund blustery man with zero sense of humor. On the other side was a high-level Colombian diplomat who was extremely good-looking and sexy.

The senator looked at her belly and his face fell. 'When's the baby due?' he asked, his voice heavy with dread, fearing he might get the answer and more.

'Tonight, actually,' said Allison. 'In fact, I've just started having labor pains.'

The poor man blanched.

Just as she said it, though, she felt an odd twinge in her stomach. Could that be a labor pain? How would she know? It didn't hurt. Probably just gas.

She started a conversation with the Colombian, smiling to herself at how out of the question that choice would have been a year ago. Then she would have honed in on the senator and grilled him all through dinner. She had already sized up the Colombian as not terribly plugged in and probably completely unaware of what Mendez was up to. Also she had noticed Sprague introducing himself to him earlier, chat for a few minutes, and then start looking around. Sprague had spent a lot of time with the Foreign Minister or at least in the group that surrounded him. If this guy had been a source Sprague would not have approached him. So she figured he was probably just an innocent bystander.

Then the pain really came and jolted her like an electric shock. It must be the start of labor. She had just been to the doctor the day before and she wasn't even dilated. So she didn't need to worry. They didn't even want to hear from you until the pains were at least five minutes apart.

She needed a distraction.

'What is it like,' she asked the Colombian, 'to be a member of a government that is always under siege, where your life is threatened and your colleagues are being murdered? Are you always afraid?'

When in doubt interview them. Ask them the tough question.

He looked at her for a moment as his smile faded, then glanced at her stomach, as they all did.

'You really want to know?' he said. His accent was thick and heavy, his voice grim. 'I will tell you. It is terrible. I live in constant fear, not only for myself but for my wife and children. I shouldn't say this to you because you are going to have a baby. Very soon you will understand what real fear and real pain is like.'

Why did she feel a chill throughout her whole body as though someone had just cast an evil spell over her? She glanced around to see if a window had been opened. She turned away from the Colombian, more out of superstition than anything else.

'Have you picked out names for the baby?' the senator asked.

She knew he was trying, but she also knew he didn't give a damn and was really being patronizing.

'We haven't decided yet, Senator. I'd much rather talk about how you feel about the fight going on between the attorney general and the head of the DEA over the Colombian drug-trafficking situation. Are you going to get involved in it?'

Another pain. This time she grabbed her stomach and leaned forward.

The senator mopped his brow and she noticed his hand was trembling. He was really nervous about her being in labor. Or was it her question? She suppressed a giggle when the pressure subsided. Should she get Des? She decided not to. It would be a long while before they needed to go to the hospital. She might as well stay here and be distracted. She felt surprisingly calm and serene, not at all afraid or even terribly excited.

'Well, Allison,' he said. 'Of course, as the chairman of the Foreign Relations Committee, I insist on being involved in what is going on over at the White House. And as I told the President the other day...'

It was everything she could do not to burst out laughing. Couldn't they hear themselves?

There was a tinkling of glass and Allison looked

up to see the ambassador stand to begin the toasts and to introduce his Foreign Minister.

'Mr Secretary, Mr Minister. Ambassadors, Senators, Congressmen, Mr Justice, and all of our other distinguished guests...' he began.

Somehow the phrase 'distinguished guests' tickled Allison as she looked around the room and saw so many smug faces nod appreciatively. She started to smile and lowered her head so she wouldn't be noticed.

'... the strong friendship and important cooperation of our two countries...' the ambassador continued.

It was so patently untrue that Allison had to stifle a giggle. She continued to keep her head down.

'... to welcome the man who will be the savior of our country, who by his honesty, his integrity, and his loyalty will lead us out of the quagmire of crime and drug dealing...'

Normally, Allison would have been disgusted by the cynicism and hypocrisy inherent in these diplomatic toasts. But tonight she found it more comical than anything else. She accidentally caught Sprague's glance. He rolled his eyes and bit his lip over the last sentence. That did her in. She gasped with laughter, then desperate to control herself she bit down on her finger until she practically drew blood.

'... And his lovely wife, the beauteous Señora Mendez...'

All eyes focused on the heavy-set, dark-haired woman with the mustache. Allison lost it completely, sputtering with laughter, her shoulders shaking as she buried her head even closer to the table. Without looking up she could feel the senator on her right and the young Colombian on her left start to laugh too. She thought about holding her breath, biting through her finger, getting up and leaving the dining room, anything that would stop her from humiliating herself, but nothing worked. The ambassador droned on.

She felt another electrifying pain and she gasped, grabbing her stomach as if the baby was about to burst out of it. Even the pain didn't help her regain control. Once the pain subsided, the absurdity of the idea that she was in labor at this insane embassy party had her convulsed with laughter even more, and now she wasn't even trying to hide it. Tears of mirth were rolling down her cheeks and the Colombian was on the verge of losing it as well.

Mercifully the toasts ended with only the speakers oblivious to her outbreak of hysteria. She didn't know how she was ever going to recoup from this appalling performance. But at the moment, she didn't really care.

Des had got up and rushed over, a frantic expression on his face.

'Sonny, are you all right?'

She nodded, unable to speak from exhaustion. She was still trying to catch her breath.

'Thank God. I thought you had gone into labor.'

'I have.'

'Holy Mary, Mother of God, let's get out of here.'

'Relax, Des. I'm fine. The pains are almost twenty minutes apart. The doctor said I shouldn't even call until the contractions come between five and seven minutes apart. I'm nowhere near going to the hospital.'

'Are you sure?'

'Positive. But it doesn't mean I don't want to get out of here. I'll explain later what the problem was at dinner.'

As the valet was getting their car, Sprague and his wife were standing on the curb, having just discovered that their car wouldn't start. Allison overheard the exchange and walked over to offer them a ride.

'Even though I could shoot you for making that face at the dinner table,' she said. 'I was okay until you started mugging.'

'Okay? Are you kidding? You took a dive five seconds after the guy was on his feet. I know because I was watching you the whole time.'

He hadn't meant to say that. Jane shot him a look. Allison smiled slightly and raised her eyebrow.

'Were you now?' she said.

He stuttered. It was the first time he had lost his cool in front of her.

'I thought, I, uh, thought you might be in labor.'

'Actually, I am.'

Another pain caught her and she grimaced and leaned over.

'I've offered them a ride. Their car won't start,' Allison said after she had recovered.

'Don't be crazy, Allison,' said Sprague. 'We live in Bethesda.'

Des nearly exploded. 'Are you out of your mind? You're in labor, remember? Your hospital is George Washington, which is five minutes from here and five minutes from our house.'

'Des, calm down. I'm perfectly fine. The pains are too far apart and I wasn't even dilated yesterday. I'd like us to take them home. I'd rather

500

do that than go home and stare at the wall.'

'She's right,' said Jane, 'it's really too early to go to the hospital. This will take her mind off of it.'

The two men looked at each other uncertainly.

'Please, I promise I'll be fine,' insisted Allison.

Finally they both shrugged helplessly and helped Allison into the car.

Sprague immediately brought up Allison's hysteria at the dinner table. She explained what happened and they all began to laugh, except Jane, who didn't say a word as they drove up Massachusetts Avenue. Allison started to pump Sprague about what he had picked up at the party. They were just coming around Ward Circle near American University when she suddenly had a sick feeling. A wave of chills rushed over her, she began shaking uncontrollably, and a gush of fluid poured out between her legs. It was as if somebody had stuck a huge vacuum cleaner inside her and was sucking her gut out.

'Des,' she whispered as she clutched the car door. 'Des,' she said, this time almost shrieking. 'She's coming, Des, Kay Kay's coming. I can feel her, oh God, oh God.'

'Holy Mary, Sonny. Oh Jesus.'

'Des,' she looked at him and her eyes were filled with terror. 'Hurry. Please, please hurry. I'm scared.'

There was a horrible pressure in her groin and she cried out despite herself.

'Lean back and put your feet up,' Jane said.

Sprague reached over from the backseat and put his hands on her shoulder.

'Take it easy, Sonny,' he said. 'Just relax. Try to relax. It will be okay. Just keep breathing.'

501

'I can't, I can't,' Allison was saying. 'She's coming, oh my God, Des, please, somebody.'

'Get her to Sibley,' Jane said. 'Quickly, Des.'

Des was so frantic he drove around the circle one more time, unable to focus. He was about to circle once more when Allison cried out again.

'Sibley, get her to Sibley, Des. It's off to the right. Hurry!' yelled Sprague. He seemed as upset as Des was.

'I don't think I'm going to make it!'

She could feel the baby's head between her legs. It felt like it was on a greased chute, just propelling out of her body. Her clothes were completed soaked and she spread her legs and slumped down in the seat to get in a better position. Des stepped on the gas and headed down Nebraska past the university toward Sibley Hospital, going about ninety miles an hour.

'Hold on, Sonny, hold on. We're almost there. We're almost there, baby.'

Sprague was gripping her shoulder as if that would help keep the baby in.

'Ah, ah, ah,' Allison was panting and crying at the same time as the most horrendous searing pain she had ever felt shot through her abdomen and down to her thighs.

'She's coming out. Oh no, oh please, oh Jesus, oh God,' Allison was pleading as she felt the baby trying to slither out of her body.

She was trying to grapple with the folds of her long gray skirt, now soaked in blood, when Des pulled up to the emergency room entrance, screeching the car to a halt and rushing in to get help while Sprague jumped out of the car and opened Allison's door.

502

Des came running out with two men and a stretcher and they ran around to Allison's side of the car and reached inside for her.

'The cord!' one of them yelled. 'It may be around the neck.'

Allison could feel herself start to faint.

'Oh,' she whispered, as she was about to go under. 'Oh Kay Kay, no. I love you. I love you. I love you.'

*       *       *

When she came to several minutes later she was in the emergency room. It was total chaos. There must have been ten doctors and nurses staring down at her. The lower part of her body was numb and there was a sheet over her legs. They were shouting words that floated through her brain, which was almost as numb as her body '. . . breech, partial abruption of the placenta . . . bleeding . . . emergency C section . . . asphyxia . . . big baby . . . dystocia . . . hung up by its neck . . . cesarean . . . heart rate going down . . . put her on a monitor . . . it's less than one hundred . . . blue . . . limp.'

She looked around frantically for Des but couldn't see him.

'Des,' she called out. 'Where's Des?'

Nobody seemed to hear her.

She saw them take a silent bundle away from the table and over to another table where several white coats hovered, their arms moving rapidly as they bent over to examine it.

'Apgar zero at one minute,' she heard. 'One at five minutes . . . three at ten minutes . . . there's no meconium below the cord.'

503

'What's happening? For God's sake will somebody tell me what's happening? Where's my baby? Somebody tell me something. I want my baby.'

One of the doctors with a mask on leaned down to her.

'There's a problem,' he said. 'The cord was around its neck. We're working on it now.'

'It.' He had called Kay Kay 'It.' Not 'she.' Not 'her' but 'It.' 'Its.'

'She' would have a brain, a soul. 'It' would not.

'Why is she so quiet?'

The white coat looked at her. He put his hand on her shoulder.

'Doctor, it's seizing!' There was a note of urgency in the nurse's voice.

He walked quickly over to the table and left her with the blinding light overhead searing her eyes and the deafening silence of her newborn daughter grating in her ears.

More voices, 'severe . . . call Children's Hospital . . . ambulance.'

'Des, somebody, please, help me. Please. I can't bear it. Des, my baby. Kay, Kay, what are they doing to you? I want my baby.'

Somebody had put an I.V. in her arm and she began to rapidly drift away.

'I want my baby,' she could hear herself say from afar. 'I want my baby.'

★    ★    ★

Des was standing by the window, his back to her, staring out. He was hunched over, the posture of a defeated man.

She watched him for a while, not saying anything to let him know she was awake. She looked around the bare hospital room. It was so stark and unappealing. Yet for some reason it made her feel calm and almost peaceful, like a blank canvas. She didn't want to talk to Des right then. She knew that he would paint on the canvas and it would be black. Now, just for a moment, she could lie there and be the mother of a baby girl and Des could be the father and she could pretend that Kay Kay was in the nursery and any minute they would bring her to the room and she could hold her and kiss her and love her. Kay Kay would look up at her with her beautiful blue eyes and they would finally meet face to face, two best friends who had been like pen pals for nine months. She would coo and gurgle and wrap her tiny pink finger around Allison's and she would smile even though new babies aren't supposed to smile. Allison would take her finger and put it in Kay Kay's mouth and let her suck it and she would fall in love like she had never been in love or even imagined was possible. Des would come and sit on the edge of the bed and put his arm around her and look proudly down at them and call them his two precious girls and she would be happier than she had ever been in her whole life. She would finally have a family.

She lay there in her reverie until Des finally turned and looked at her, his face ravaged. He seemed a hundred years old, lines and wrinkles emerging that she had never noticed before. She smiled at him, still dreaming of Kay Kay, knowing that in a second or two he would pick up his paintbrush and splatter the canvas with anguish.

He walked over to the bed and handed her a

Polaroid. She looked down and there in the picture was the most beautiful baby she had ever seen. Her hair wasn't blond but dark, and there was one large curl on top of her head. Her eyes were closed but her lips were little rosebuds and her cheeks were round and plump and her tiny hands were perfect, five fingers on each one. She was wrapped in a blanket and she looked like an angel and Allison's heart leaped as she looked at Des silently pleading, hopeful.

'She's so beautiful, isn't she?'

'Yes. She is.'

Now her heart was about to pound its way out of her chest. He hadn't said 'was.' He said 'is.'

'Where is she?' she asked, the accent on 'is.'

'At Children's Hospital.'

'I want to go see her.' She threw back the covers and started to get up when she felt a surge of pain in her abdomen that made her gasp.

'Not today. Tomorrow. They said you can go in an ambulance and a wheelchair tomorrow ... if she's ...'

Now she could feel her throat close up.

'If she's what?'

'Sonny. She lost a lot of oxygen. There are problems.'

The phone rang. Allison picked it up.

'Is this Mrs. Shaw?'

'Mrs. Shaw?'

At first she didn't know who they were talking about and she paused. 'Uh ... this is Allison Sterling, uh, yes, uh, Mrs. Shaw.'

'Katherine's mother?'

'Katherine?'

'I'm Tamsin Cooper. I'm a social worker at

506

Children's Hospital. I believe your daughter, Katherine, was admitted last night.'

Katherine's mother—that was she. Your daughter—that was Kay Kay. There was a person, a child, her child. She was a mother. This was the first time anyone had called her a mother, had said the word daughter to her. She felt elated. Kay Kay was alive. She was real.

'Yes, of course.' She recovered her voice. 'It's just that we call her Kay Kay. I'm sorry. I was a little confused. It's all so new and...'

'I understand.'

Her voice sounded sympathetic. Too sympathetic.

'How ... how is she?'

Now the pause was on the other end of the phone.

'She's in the N.I.C.U.—that's the neonatal intensive care unit. I know you'll want to come and see her as soon as you're able. But for now I just wanted to give you a call and let you know that I'm here and that there is a chaplain available at the hospital if you should care to see one.'

'A chaplain?' She caught her breath again. She could feel the dread now permeating her body. She seemed unable to do anything but repeat everything the woman said with a question mark on the end.

'Sister Madeleine is Catholic but she works with people of all faiths.'

She couldn't speak.

'Mrs. Shaw?'

She managed a whispered 'Yes, thank you for calling' before she hung up.

Des was looking at her, his face creased with worry.

507

'Des. I have to go see her. Now.'

'Sonny, I just told you what the doctor . . . '

'Fuck the doctor, Des,' she said in a murderously low, even voice. 'If you love me, if you've ever cared about me, you will get me over there. Even if you have to carry me out of here. I'm not kidding. If you don't I will never speak to you again and I have never been more serious about anything in my life. If my child dies without me I will damn you to hell for eternity.'

Des looked at her for only a moment before he said, 'I'll go get the car and pull it around to the front. Then I'll come back up here and put your coat on and wheel you down. You'll have to carry your I.V. bag yourself. I'll be right back.'

*　　　*　　　*

It was odd how she instinctively knew exactly where Kay Kay was before Des could even wheel her to the right isolette. He had purloined a wheelchair and an I.V. holder in the emergency room and they had arrived unannounced at the N.I.C.U. Within minutes the chairman of neonatology had been summoned, Allison and Des had been robed and scrubbed down and they were heading toward a row of babies in the dimly lit, silent, peach-colored room.

Her first reaction was horror when she saw her daughter's tiny naked body splayed out with what seemed like hundreds of needles and tubes and wires coming out of every part of her. Allison could almost feel the punctures in her own skin, wanted to feel them instead of having her child have to endure them.

508

Every fiber of her being overwhelmed her with the need to touch and hold her baby. Her breasts began to throb and she reached out to the isolette and put her face up against it, almost pawing in her desperation to get at Kay Kay. She could hear herself make what was almost a panting noise. Kay Kay's eyes were closed, sleeping, Allison told herself. She looked so calm and peaceful and healthy. She was such a big baby, plump and pink and gorgeous. It was impossible to imagine there was anything wrong with her even with all the monitors and alarms and flashing lights and beeps and needles and tubes.

'Would you like to touch her?'

The doctor had opened a small hole in the isolette where her hand was and Allison stuck her fingers in. When she gently touched the soft smooth skin of her newborn baby she thought she had never felt such joy and such pain in one moment. She began to stroke Kay Kay with her finger and croon under her breath to her, 'Mommy's here. Mommy loves you. Mommy's right here, Kay Kay. Mommy will never leave you. Mommy's here. Mommy loves you.'

She felt Des put his arm on her shoulder, heard him choke back a sob. She kept on speaking to Kay Kay in a quiet calm voice. Somehow she was unable to cry. She couldn't and wouldn't let Kay Kay know that she was sad or depressed. If her baby was going to survive she would have to use all her strength, her optimism, her power to make it happen. Crying would be for later. She couldn't think that way now. Now all she could think about was that Kay Kay was going to live. She was going to be fine. Anything else was unthinkable,

509

unbearable, unacceptable.

★     ★     ★

She spent the night at Sibley Hospital. They had given her a sedative, and the combination of that and emotional exhaustion helped her to sleep straight through.

She felt stronger the next day and not in as much physical pain as she had been. She went back to Children's the next morning after they had removed her I.V. Des stayed a while but she insisted he go to the office and leave her there alone. She needed to be by herself with Kay Kay.

She sat in her wheelchair dressed in one of her corduroy maternity dresses, the only thing that felt comfortable over her incision. It was slightly chilly in the room and she pulled her sweater closer around her. She had worried that Kay Kay might be too cold with nothing on, but the nurses assured her that she was warm enough. She just sat there and stared at her, all of her senses taking in everything about her daughter that she could. Memorizing. The smells of alcohol, the tubes taped to her mouth, taped to her feet, such perfect little feet. The way her breath was coming in short little takes, up and down, up and down. Allison tried doing it for her . . . just in case. The machines were all functioning. She didn't know what they all meant. There were lights blinking and a blue box over her with bags hanging from it. Somewhere she heard the faint sound of light rock Christmas carols coming from a radio at the nurses' station. How weird. She had no sense of Christmas at all. Yet now that she thought of it there were Christmas

510

decorations around the unit. Subtle, subdued, but still there. Christmas was what, a week away? A few days? There had been Christmas without Mama, then Christmas without Nana, then Christmas without Sam. Would this be Christmas without Kay Kay? A nurse had put on a yellow robe to administer to a baby nearby. A doctor appeared and turned on a bright light over another isolette. Down a row there were several people conferring over a baby. What looked to be a social worker and a nun. The mother was crying. There was a crack baby in one of the isolettes wearing minuscule dark glasses to protect its eyes from the light. Several deflated balloons floated from one of the isolettes. A tiny pair of blue boxing gloves from another. Des had commented on those the day before and he had had a hard time controlling himself when he'd seen them. There was the tinny sound of a baby crying in the background but most of the babies were too sick to cry.

Allison looked up at the clock. It was 2:30 in the afternoon. She would have had no way of knowing. She didn't want to know the time. Each hour that passed would be ticking away Kay Kay's life. But she couldn't think that way. The clock made time seem unrealistic, just a bunch of irrelevant numbers. In this spaceship of a room, humming away, they could easily be hurtling through the universe. It was so quiet and calm and restful.

All there was was Allison and the baby and the slight whoosh of the air pressure and the silence. She felt safe and secure there, and she had the sense that this would never end, that she would never leave, simply stay there forever in this giant isolette, just her and Kay Kay, and everything would be all

511

right as long as they were together.

*　　*　　*

She hadn't wanted to hear it, hadn't wanted to deal with it. The longer she put off the talk with the doctors the longer she could have Kay Kay. She was making Des crazy, making him talk to the doctors, literally putting her hands over her ears when he tried to talk to her. It was so unlike her, denying the truth. It was against everything she had ever been. But this time the truth was too hard and she didn't want to face it until she had to.

She had seen Kay Kay have a seizure, seen how they all rushed to her, wheeling Allison out of the way as they worked over her. She could read their body language, see the worry on their faces, and worse, see the sympathy in their eyes. If there was one thing she couldn't stand it was to have people feel sorry for her. Anything but pity. It was repulsive, to be avoided at all cost.

The social worker had been hovering around.

'How's Mom?' she had asked in a tone Allison felt was extremely patronizing.

'Get her out of here,' she had told Des fiercely. 'I don't need her help and I don't need her sympathy. I just want to be left alone with my baby.'

She had managed to shake Tamsin Cooper. But now the neonatologist insisted on talking to them. Together. It could not be avoided any longer. Either the meeting would be there, out in front of everyone, next to Kay Kay. Or privately in the parents' consulting room. She didn't want Kay Kay to hear any bad news. She chose the private room.

Des came to get her. He had brought Kay Kay a

512

present. A tiny pair of pink ballet slippers, which he hung on the edge of her isolette. He cried. This time openly. He didn't even try to hide it. Not Allison. She would not cry. They were not going to make her cry. She gave Kay Kay's tiny hand a squeeze before she left. She hadn't yet had a response from her of any kind. Kay Kay had never opened her eyes, never cried, never grasped her finger. But she breathed. There was that. She hadn't stopped breathing.

Allison was walking now. She walked into the small conference room and sat down. There were several books on the desk. She glanced at them and quickly looked away. *The Saddest Time, Our Baby Died. Why?, Children Die, Too, Dear Parents. Letters to Bereaved Parents, You Are Not Alone.*

Wrong. Nobody could know what it felt like. Nobody could understand the excruciating pain that she was feeling now. No matter how many times the doctors and nurses and social workers and nuns had seen it, they had never been through it so they didn't know. And Des was the father. He couldn't know either. Only a mother could feel this anguish. She was a mother. She was a mom. Only she could know.

Dr Farmer, the chairman of neonatology, came into the room with them and sat down at the desk. She was very crisp and clear. She was slim and young-looking with a shiny brown page boy and long slim fingers with short immaculate nails. She was sympathetic in the way that doctors are, withholding in order to protect themselves from too much emotional involvement, from the relentless parade of pain that passed by them every day.

Allison sat next to Des on the chair, but she was

so numb that she was hardly aware of his presence. She was trying very hard to concentrate on what the doctor was saying, but all she heard were words. Some of them made sense, some did not. Mostly they seemed disconnected.

'The baby has seizures that are hard to control ... She has an abnormal EEG. She has gasping respiration. There is every indication that she has sustained severe brain damage. But even when there is severe damage to the brain ...' she had glossed over the phrase 'brain damage' so quickly that it took a moment to sink in. 'Severe brain damage.' What was she talking about? Not Kay Kay. It couldn't be possible. She knew Kay Kay was in trouble but not this.

'... there is room for a decision. What is in the baby's best interest and the parents' best interest. If we wait too long the cerebrum could be much more sturdy and the baby will breathe and suck but the EEG will be flat. The baby will be brain dead, there will be cessation of all functions, including mid-brain, but the baby will not be dead. Time is limited, therefore, to make the decision, and this is the hardest decision you will ever make in your life.'

Allison couldn't speak for a moment. She was trying to assimilate what this woman had been saying to her. She leaned forward and squinted at her as if that would help her understand. It didn't work.

'What are you telling us?' she asked.

Dr Farmer looked at Allison and realized that she was not taking it all in.

'Kay Kay is a very beautiful baby,' she said. 'I know how hard this is for you.'

514

For a brief moment Allison saw behind her eyes, felt that she knew what Allison was feeling. Then shut it off.

'We know she cannot do well in the long run. If you take her off the ventilator she will be a "no code," which means that if she decided to die we would not resuscitate.'

'How long,' Des began, then cleared his throat. He reached for her hand. It was freezing cold and limp. He grasped it and held it tightly but she did not respond. 'How long will, uh, would it take?'

'Sometimes a few hours, sometimes a few days.'

'What if we didn't? I mean, what if we let her live? Is there any chance that she might . . . that she might, uh, recover?' asked Allison.

Dr Farmer looked very sad. She shook her head.

'The best case is that you have a baby who can breathe. You will not have a thinking, feeling baby who can walk and talk and coo. You will have difficulty with seizure control, probably with infection. You could take it home, but it would be extremely hard to find care, especially the twenty-four-hour kind of care that it would need. And eventually there would come a time when you'll say you've given it a good try and you've seen the outcome.'

'It.' There was that horrible word again. Kay Kay was she now. If they let her die she would get to stay a she. But if she lived she would revert back to an it. And Allison wouldn't be a mother anymore. She would be a caretaker. But this was not a decision she could possibly make. How could she decide to kill her child? How bad could it be anyway, if she had this beautiful baby to hold for the rest of her life? She hadn't been allowed to hold

515

her yet.

'I want to hold her,' she said. She knew she wasn't focussing but she didn't want to focus. She wanted to hold her baby.

'What will it be like?' asked Des.

What the fuck was he asking that for, as if it were a foregone conclusion? She hadn't decided at all that Kay Kay should die.

'The oxygen levels go down very quickly once you withdraw support,' the doctor said softly. 'There is some terminal gasping but it's unlikely there is any real suffering. We give the baby fentanyl just in case ... after death the heart will often beat for an hour or so ... '

Allison put her hands over her ears.

'I don't want to hear this,' she said, choking on her words. She jumped up.

'I want to hold her. I want to hold her now. I'm not ready to make this decision.'

Dr Farmer stood up. She put her hand on Allison's arm.

'You don't have to decide right now. I'll convene the ethics committee and you two will have a chance to talk it over together. We can meet later with the social worker, the chaplain, anyone you like. But the most important thing now is that you should hold Kay Kay. Let's do that first.'

They took her into the family room and wheeled in the isolette. Pale pinks and blues, with a bed and a comfortable rocking chair. It looked like somebody's bedroom, not a hospital room at all, a place where you could pretend everything was normal.

Allison sat in the rocking chair. They took Kay Kay out of her isolette, still hooked up to all the

516

tubes, and placed her in Allison's arms.

It was as if all the love she had ever felt in the whole world, in her entire life, all the emotions she had repressed, all the feelings she had ever had, began to flow out of her body and into her baby's body and back again in a circular motion. She could actually sense this forceful gush of love, almost like exchanging bodily fluids, like she was transfusing her blood into Kay Kay and back, so strong was the sensation. She had never known anything like it before.

She looked down at this tiny bundle and saw herself, saw Des, saw her mother and her father, and she was overpowered with happiness and anguish. She felt her body clutch Kay Kay to her and she knew that she could never let her die, even if this was all she would ever be able to have of her. She could not give this up. Her skin was rough and red now, slightly dehydrated. She smelled of alcohol and medicines. But she was still the most beautiful baby Allison had ever seen.

She put her finger in Kay Kay's mouth and felt her begin to suck. Suddenly she had an enormous tingling sensation and surge of pain in her breasts as milk began to flow out of them. She had forgotten about her breasts. She had planned to breastfeed. Now that would be impossible. They were feeding Kay Kay through tubes. She would have to pump her breast milk in case Kay Kay recovered ... or pack them with ice in case Kay Kay ... didn't recover.

The doctors had left them alone with their baby. She really didn't want to be alone with Des. She had not been able to look him in the eye since this had happened. Part of it was because she felt inexplicably ashamed. Ashamed that they had had this imperfect child? This child who would never be normal? Ashamed that they, these two successful, take-charge people, were rendered so helpless in the face of such a calamity? Partly she couldn't look him in the eye because she was angry. It was odd how Allison felt now about Des, how angry she was at him for no reason that she could determine. Maybe she was angry because he wasn't doing anything to stop it. He was so rational, so calm, so reasonable. Unplug the baby and let her die? Okay, sure, no problem. Only they didn't call it that here. They called it 'withdrawal of support,' a fancy euphemism for killing the mother. Because that's what would really happen.

Maybe she was angry at him because she was angry and there was nobody else to blame it on. She didn't believe in God so she couldn't blame it on Him/Her. If only she could. It might make the whole thing so much easier. She could pray. Get down on her knees and pray to this humane, loving, caring, all-powerful being who had decided in His/Her wisdom to make her suffer like this. 'Thank you, God, for lending me your baby even for so short a time.' That's probably what a really religious person would say. It was such bullshit, such utter outrageous bullshit.

'I would like to have her baptized.'

She heard Des's voice somewhere in the background saying those words. It was almost as if he had read her mind and was playing some cruel trick on her. She couldn't believe she was hearing it. How could he possibly even suggest such a thing, knowing how she felt? It would be a violation of everything she believed in, it would make a mockery of her pain.

She didn't answer. She wanted to make him say it again. If she felt shame, she wanted him to feel it, too.

'There's a nun here, Sister Madeleine. She's a chaplain to all faiths,' he added quickly. 'I've spoken to her about it. She says it's important to do it sooner rather than later. I've called my brother. He can get here from Massachusetts . . . '

She sat there holding Kay Kay, her breath coming in short little gasps exactly the way her baby's were. She couldn't have spoken even if she had wanted to.

'I thought maybe tomorrow morning.'

There was a pleading tone to his voice.

'I remember you saying that you had a christening dress that belonged to Sam somewhere in a trunk. We could get that out and—'

'Stop it. Stop it right this minute, Des. You can forget a baptism. I will not allow my child to be a part of some pagan rite, some celebration of this monstrous God you worship. Besides, there's no need. There's no need. She's not going to die. She's not. I won't let her. You have to have the consent of both parents. I won't let them or you persuade me to kill her. Ever. Under any circumstances.'

There was silence. Des didn't speak.

'Don't you see?' she said very quietly. 'It just hurts so much.'

Even though she wasn't looking directly at him as she spoke, she could see through the corner of her eye that his cheeks were streaked with tears. She still couldn't cry.

★　　　★　　　★

He had gone to the office for a few hours to catch up on things and, she suspected, to get away from her and the intensity of everything. She had taken a taxi home after he left, to get some clothes. It was late afternoon. She wouldn't leave the hospital overnight now that she had been discharged from Sibley. She was still in a great deal of physical pain, but she didn't want to be away from Kay Kay in case . . . in case they needed her. Children's had a wonderful parents' waiting room, a special bathroom with showers and lockers and a sleeping room with recliners for parents with kids in the I.C.U. or the N.I.C.U. When she wasn't with Kay Kay she was sleeping or resting in the darkened room on a recliner.

The doctors had come to do some procedures on Kay Kay, so she had stopped off at the cafeteria to get something to eat. There would be nothing at home. She wasn't hungry but she knew she had to force herself or she wouldn't be strong enough to stay. She had eaten something, was it mashed potatoes? Apple sauce? She had already forgotten, but it was something comforting, baby food.

In the cab on the way home the driver had gone past St Matthew's, the Catholic church at the corner of Connecticut Avenue. There was a big sign on the front that said, 'Come Home for Christmas.' Passersby were scurrying to and fro with packages under their arms, their bodies braced against the freezing December wind.

As they drove by, Allison looked and up and saw Des. He was coming out of the large doors, looking disheveled and exhausted, his tie askew, his hair rumpled, circles under his eyes, his trench coat open, oblivious to the cold. He looked so sad that it broke her heart. She realized for the first time that she was not the only one suffering. In some way, if she was feeling helpless and alone and ashamed, then he must be feeling it, too. Even worse because he was a man and the man is supposed to protect his wife and his child. It was so primitive on one level. Yet it was that primitive side of Des that she had fallen in love with in the first place; that side of him that she called masculine when she was feeling good about him and macho when she wasn't.

She realized she didn't know this person she was married to. This man she would have sworn was not religious until their first confrontation over their wedding. Now he wanted to have his daughter baptized, now he was going into a Catholic church to pray. Who was he, except a person in a great deal of pain? Would it really be so terrible to let him have this silly little ceremony for Kay Kay if that would help him? She only wished there were something that she had that would help her. How could she deny him this? It would be too cruel, like denying someone in physical pain an anesthetic even though it was ineffective for her. She would let him have the baptism. It wouldn't hurt Kay Kay, and that was all she really cared about.

$$\star \quad \star \quad \star$$

Kay Kay couldn't wear Sam's christening dress because of all the tubes, so they had to lay it on top of her little body. Des had brought a camera.

The had the ceremony in the family room. The three of them stood up. Somehow it seemed right. More formal. Dr Farmer was there and Tamsin

Cooper and all of the nurses and doctors who were taking care of Kay Kay. Everyone had gotten so involved with her, with Allison, with Des.

Des's brother had come. Sister Madeleine officiated, though he assisted as he had at their wedding. He brought the Shaw family Bible with him. When he and Des hugged each other, for some strange reason, it nearly brought Allison—Allison of the stoic face—to tears. Men's grief always seemed so much more touching to her, perhaps because one saw it so rarely.

Sister Madeleine was tiny and round, like a miniature female Santa Claus, with wide twinkling eyes, rosy cheeks, a curled-up lip, and a nose like a cherry. She had such a sympathetic manner, so unproselytizing or unctuous, that she won Allison over despite her dismay at the mere fact that anyone could be a nun.

Allison had a red, green, and black plaid full shirtwaist dress that hid her still expanded figure and leaking breasts. It was pretty and dressy and Christmasy and cheerful. This was to be a happy occasion. She held Kay Kay tightly.

Sister Madeleine began solemnly.

'Kay Kay was conceived through love, carried in love, nurtured in love, and born into love,' she said. 'Allison and Des have shared with each other and now they share with this beautiful baby.'

Des reached over and put his arm around her, encompassing Kay Kay as though he were trying to shelter both of them from any more pain or sorrow.

Sister Madeleine touched Kay Kay's forehead.

'It is with great joy that we welcome you, but it is also with sadness that you are here in the hospital. It is also a time of sadness for your mother and dad who love you so much and know that they will have to let you go.'

Allison froze. She looked up panic-stricken at Des. He squeezed her arm. She didn't say anything. She didn't want to spoil this for Kay Kay.

Sister Madeleine made a sign of the cross over the baby.

'Des, Allison, I invite you to do the same so that Kay Kay may have eternal life as she goes to the Lord.'

Des made a sign of the cross. Allison did not.

'Allison, would you like, in your own way to bless your baby? All of us bless our children in special ways. We may kiss, touch, stroke, or lay our hands on them.'

As turned off as she was by the sign of the cross, she was grateful to Sister Madeleine for including her. She did all four, surrounding her child with as much physical love as she possibly could.

'Mom,' Sister Madeleine continued, 'I know that your consent for this baptism was a real struggle and that you are doing it to help Dad. That's what love is all about. It shows character and integrity and respect for him. It's almost harder than if you were both two consenting Christians.'

'Katherine Kimball Sterling Shaw, I baptize you . . .

'Father in heaven, I ask you to be with Allison and Des as they continue their journey with Kay Kay, a journey that is filled with pain and tears and wondering why because "it just hurts so much." We stand here in silence before you and in silence we cry out. Our Father, who art in heaven, hallowed be thy name . . .'

Des began to repeat the Lord's Prayer, as did the

523

others. Allison didn't but she found the repetition familiar and comforting, like a nursery rhyme or a Christmas carol.

'Their journey is walked in love and courage. Be with them Lord. Fill them with peace and your healing presence. Amen.'

## CONFIDENTIAL PATIENT CARE CONFERENCE ON BABY S. DEC. 24

... At the case review, the neurologist presented her findings, which consisted of the following: (1) a large cystic, circumscribed lesion in the right frontal lobe of the brain which is believed due to an infarct rather than primary hemorrhage; (2) jitteriness; (3) paresis of the left upper arm; and (4) a 'dysmature' EEG. She felt that it was extremely likely that Baby S. will be severely mentally retarded and will probably need custodial care. Because of poor prognosis for cognitive function and the possibility that the child cannot be weaned from the ventilator, it was felt that parental discretion should carry more weight than it might if the child were less severely affected.

Attendees at the meeting agreed that it was reasonable to try to reach an agreement with the parents as to when extubation might be tried and, if the child failed without the ventilator, whether she should be reintubated. Furthermore, there should also be agreement with the parents as to whether sedation (which might hasten her death) should be given if she shows evidence of discomfort while off the ventilator.

Although the parents expressed satisfaction that they were now more informed, my

524

impression was that the mother did not accept everything that was told to her. Discussion centered on Baby S.'s unstable condition, questions about her degree of suffering, and future expectations. It was apparent during the discussion that there was some difference in the views of the parents in terms of steps to be taken for Baby S. They were encouraged to reevaluate the situation and to meet with the doctors at the end of the day.

Merle Johnson, M.D.
Office of Ethics

Christmas Day. Her first Christmas as a mother. Her last day as a mother. Kay Kay was to die today. It had been decided.

The doctors had decided for her, really. Des had decided for her. She had not decided. She would not take responsibility for killing her child.

'They' had decided that Kay Kay was to have her support 'withdrawn' at 10:00 a.m. Christmas morning. She had sat with her all night, alone, and she had asked to be alone with Kay Kay in the family room for about an hour after they had 'withdrawn' the support. No doctors or nurses, no social workers or nuns, no Des. She hadn't thought about friends. She hadn't seen or talked to any of her friends since the night Kay Kay was born. She hadn't wanted to. Sprague apparently had been at the hospital every day, but she had refused to see him. She couldn't bear the idea of people feeling sympathy for her. Any sign of sympathy only made it harder for her to control her emotions. Des relayed messages, brought notes, told about flowers being sent to the house. She tried to put it out of

525

her mind. As long as she stayed in this silent humming cocoon nothing was real and none of this was happening and she was safe and Kay Kay was safe.

Des had gone home to shower and change, then had come back and had gone into the parents' waiting room and slept most of the night on the recliner.

She couldn't possibly sleep or leave Kay Kay alone. She kept her vigil. This was her last night and she had so much to tell her child. She told her about her father Des and how proud of her he was. She talked to Kay Kay about her grandmother Katherine, about how much she had loved her even for the short time she knew her. She told her about Sam and about Nana. She talked about Uncle Rog and Aunt Molly, Jenny, about her old boyfriend Nick and about Julian. She wanted her to know everything before she died. She told her fairy tales and sang her nursery rhymes. She and Kay Kay had their own song. She sang it softly to her over and over.

'You are my Kay Kay, my only Kay Kay, you make me happy when skies are gray. You'll never know dear, how much I love you. Please don't take my Kay Kay away.'

It was the happiest night of her life, being able to sit there in the rocker with her baby and croon to her, and she pushed everything else out of her mind. Until the morning. Until they came. Until it was time.

There were so many of them. They all wore white coats except for Tamsin Cooper and Sister Madeleine and Des. They hovered around. They all had worried and sympathetic expressions on their faces. They kept patting her. Des kept putting his arm around her, trying to get her to meet his eyes. She couldn't look at him. From some other zone she recognized that he must be in pain, but she couldn't focus on it, deal with it.

They took Kay Kay out of her isolette. They had removed the tubes. They handed her to Allison with Des sort of holding on, too. Both of them stood there for a while, just looking at Kay Kay.

'She has to be one of the most beautiful babies I ever saw,' Tamsin said. Everyone murmured in agreement.

'When you're ready,' said the doctor.

Allison tried to speak but no words came out of her mouth.

'You can remove the tube,' said Des in a choked voice.

The doctor gently removed the tube from Kay Kay's mouth.

They had told them it would take hours for her to die. There was a tiny gasping sound from her mouth. Des nodded to everyone and slowly they left the room. The two of them sat on the end of the bed together staring down at this precious, plump little body, this beautiful round face, the rosy cheeks, the perfect little nose, the little rosebud mouth.

'She is so beautiful, isn't she, Des?'

'She is.' He was so broken up he could barely get a word out.

'She has your toes, look at her toes. And I think she has your nose, too.'

'Her mouth is yours,' he said. 'She's beautiful and delicate like you. She would have been so spectacular when she grew up ...' he couldn't

527

finish.

'I'm going to give her a bath and get her dressed,' said Allison, almost matter of fact.

They had set up a bathinette, and Allison gently held her baby and put her in the warm soapy water and bathed her. Her skin felt so good and Allison found herself massaging Kay Kay, touching every part of her body. She picked her up after she had bathed her and wrapped her in one of the new towels in her layette, a white terry-cloth towel with a little hood and pink binding. She diapered her carefully, putting on Vaseline, then baby powder, and she rubbed her body with soothing lotion. Then she dressed her in a soft white velour dress with tiny red and green sprigs of holly embroidered in the smocking on the front and white leggings. All the while she was humming softly to the tune of 'You Are My Sunshine.' When she had finished she turned to Des.

'Now I need some time alone with her if that's okay with you.'

Des hugged her and left the room. He looked relieved. It was obviously too much for him.

When she was by herself with Kay Kay she sat down in the rocker. She wrapped her in a soft blanket and sat staring at her, rocking back and forth for a while, just looking at her baby. Then she unbuttoned the front of her shirtwaist dress and unhooked her bra. Her breasts were engorged and aching as though they would burst. She felt a tingling sensation, then pressure, then a surge of milk flowing as the white liquid began to dribble from her breasts. She put Kay Kay's mouth to her left breast and fixed her lips to her nipple. Kay Kay's body had begun to turn a bit colder and her breathing was coming in little gasps but as her lips touched her mother's nipple she began to suck, making tiny little sucking motions with her mouth, little suckling noises. It didn't hurt at all the way she had expected, and the relief was tremendous. It was the most exhilarating, sensual, overwhelming sensation she had ever had, including an orgasm. Kay Kay would suck for a moment, then stop and take little labored breaths, then suck again. Allison turned her around when she stopped the next time and put her on her other breast and felt the milk surge forward again.

Tears welled up in her eyes as her milk was welling up in her breasts, but still she didn't cry, though she didn't know whether or not she would be able to bear the pain she was feeling at this moment. When Kay Kay seemed to have finished sucking Allison wiped her mouth, then hooked up her bra and buttoned up her dress.

She couldn't get enough of her daughter and she knew that she would have to call Des back in shortly. The breathing was becoming more labored. Each breath was so excruciating to her that she began to breathe in little gasps like Kay Kay. She was overcome with a desire to devour Kay Kay, somehow taking her all in, getting her back inside her womb, making her part of her body again so they couldn't take her away. She reached down and took her hand, held it up to her mouth and began to lick her fingers. She licked her hand, then her arm. Then she held her face up to her and licked her cheeks and her neck and the downy fuzz at the top of her head. She pulled up her dress and licked her tummy, then pulled down her leggings and licked her legs and her toes. She dressed her again, licked

529

her face one more time, held her as closely as she could, got up, and went to the door to get Des.

Kay Kay died an hour later. Allison handed her over to the doctor. She handed her life, her heart and soul over to the doctor.

Somebody handed her some Polaroids of Kay Kay in her Christmas dress, a lock of her hair, her hospital I.D. bracelet, the crib card, her blood pressure cuff. Des and the doctor discussed cremation arrangements. Sister Madeleine said the last rites. That seemed to satisfy Des's need for a funeral. She didn't really care. She didn't really know what was happening. She was aware that they were saying goodbye and thanking people. People were coming up to her and hugging her. She remembered walking out of the hospital with Des and driving home. It was beginning to get dark. It was snowing. He asked her if she wanted something to eat. She had forgotten about food. The house was filled with food people had brought over. There were hams and turkeys with dressing and all the trimmings. Somebody had put up a small Christmas tree.

She felt exhausted. She was only vaguely aware of Des's presence. He kept trying to hug her, to put his arm around her, to comfort her, but she kept pushing him away. She didn't want to look at him. She was suddenly too tired to even think why. She decided to go upstairs and take a hot shower. Slowly she got undressed and into the shower. She stood under the water for a very long time letting it pour over her, washing her large swollen breasts, her misshapen belly.

Then it started, a horrible wrenching pain deep in her gut that welled up inside her chest and up and up until she let out a long low cry of anguish and then the tears came with the wails and then the sobs and she cried out Kay Kay's name and she hugged her body and she begged whatever unknown power had made this happen to not let this be true and she cried so hard that she doubled over and finally ended up on her knees in the shower with the hot water pummeling down on her head and then she was slumped on the floor of the shower, crying so hard that she was too weak to move. She didn't know how long she was in there until Des found her and cut off the water and pulled her out and wrapped her in a huge towel, but she couldn't stop crying and shrieking with pain and she wrenched herself away from him and fell to the floor of the bathroom where she lay heaving with sobs. Des, distraught, got down on the floor with her and tried to comfort her but she kept pushing him away.

She lay there and cried for what seemed like hours. Des never moved, but she could hear him crying, too. After a long time she was silent. Finally he got up and gave her a sedative and a glass of water. Exhausted, she took it. He lifted her up and led her to the bed where he helped her into a flannel nightgown and covered her with a duvet. He tried to take her hand. She pulled it away.

'Why won't you let me help you, Sonny?' he pleaded. 'I love you. I want to help you. I need you. We need each other.' He lay down on top of the duvet and put his body next to hers, trying to hold her, trying to get close.

'Because it is your God who took my baby away from me. You don't need me. You have Him. You can go pray to Him. I have nobody now.'

'Jesus, Sonny don't do this to me, please. I loved Kay Kay. I love you. I know how you're hurting but so am I. Please, let's try to help each other. We won't get through this otherwise. Please, baby?' His voice cracked again.

She felt strangely detached from him, from everything. The sedative was beginning to take effect and she was getting drowsy. He put his head on top of her stomach. She didn't push it away.

'Goodnight, Des,' she said as she drifted off to sleep. 'Merry Christmas.'

## CHAPTER FIFTEEN

It was leap year, the last day of February, the day the girls are supposed to ask the boys.

She had just returned from La Samanna. She hadn't wanted to go at Christmas. In fact, she hadn't wanted to go at all this year. It would only remind her of Michael—but the kids had talked her into it. Outland and Annie Laurie. So they had gone, George Washington's birthday week. She had been both glad and sad. It was wonderful to be with her children again like that alone, just enjoying them. It was the first time, really, that they had been like a family since the year before. They always seemed to be off somewhere.

Willie loved it, too. He adored Outland and followed him around like a puppy dog, imitating everything he did. Annie Laurie was at her best with Willie. Her chip-on-the-shoulder attitude softened around her little brother. Monica was very much a part of the family now, and at night, after

532

dinner and after Willie was in bed, the two older ones would go down to the little town of Marigot and take Monica along, leaving Sadie to baby-sit.

The nights had been the hardest. Just watching the moon shimmering on the water, listening to the waves against the sand, smelling the tropical flowers, feeling the soft night air reminded her of Michael. Memories were everywhere. She felt pulled, drawn toward the end of the beach where they had met at night, yet with nobody to watch Willie she couldn't go. Somehow she kept thinking that Michael would guess she was at La Samanna, that he would fly down and be sitting there on the rocks waiting for her if only she could get away to meet him. But she knew that that would never happen. It was the kind of corny romantic scenario you would find in a novel, not in real life.

Still, just being there made her feel closer to him. Closer than she had in Washington these past two months when she wasn't able to see him or talk to him.

These past two months had been agony. She had felt such euphoria after they had made love, after he told her he loved her. She had felt complete in a way that she never had before. She had felt hope that the two of them might actually be able to have a life together. When she got his letter she had been devastated. She couldn't understand it. She couldn't understand him. How could he not want to see her when he even admitted that he had never loved anyone as much as he loved her? She knew that. She believed it with all her heart. What kind of person, then, would not want to see her? He wasn't in love with Giselle anymore. She probably wasn't in love with him. Their children were out of the house. There was no reason for them to stay together. He knew, he had to know, how much she loved him. Divorce was commonplace. What was wrong with him?

She fluctuated between total despair and a kind of resolute optimism. The despair was not only about losing Michael. At least for now. It was about losing Rosey, losing Des. Was she destined to lose every man she loved? It would seem so. When she was in these moods only the thought of Willie kept her going. Then she would pull herself together and determine to keep on.

She would be angry at herself for empowering Michael to cause her such pain, for allowing him to destroy her peace of mind. If he wanted to be an asshole that was his problem. She was not going to buy into it. He loved her. That she knew. Given that fact, she had confidence that she could—would—ultimately, get him back. Let him torment himself a little while longer over this greatly exaggerated cultural gap. Then, when he was missing her terribly, she would swoop down on him and destroy his resolve. She had done it before, she would do it again.

That was her mood when she returned from La Samanna.

★   ★   ★

She would be seeing him on that very day, leap-year day. The National Commission on AIDS was having a conference at the Pan American Health Organization Building. Freddy Osgood had appointed her a commissioner, one of two seats he had at his disposal. It was something she had really wanted, partly because she thought it was one of the most important issues, partly because she needed something to do, and partly because it gave her opportunities to be directly involved with Michael.

Michael's sense of mission had infused her with a sense of responsibility and caring which she had only given lip service to as First Lady. She found now, being with him, that she was emotionally involved with the issue. This had never happened to her before, this sense of social commitment, and she liked the way it made her feel. Particularly since she was in a position to make something happen. More than anything she had ever done except raising her children it made her feel worthwhile. As First Lady she had been so concerned with finding a project to make Rosey look good that the personal involvement never was there. They had made her give up Planned Parenthood, which she really cared about, because they said it was politically dangerous. Then, her affair with Des and the subsequent birth of Willie consumed her. There had been no time for others.

The truth was that she needed Blanche. Working with Blanche, advising her, helping her be First Lady gave her something to do, distracted her from her thoughts. She couldn't exactly go out and get a job. In fact it was hard for her even to go out. Without Blanche she would go crazy with boredom and depression.

She had thrown herself into the AIDS movement with a vengeance, learning as much as she could, studying, meeting people, reading, going to meetings, lectures, conferences, symposiums. She had gotten Blanche heavily involved and it had improved her public image considerably. Her country music concerts had been huge hits and had raised a lot of money for AIDS research. Blanche had been very popular as a singer and once she had gotten back into it and stopped trying to be something she wasn't, people began to respond to her and respect her.

Sadie had asked Freddy to appoint her to the AIDS commission and she had spent so much time down at their offices on K Street that they had given her one of the storage rooms and let her set up her own office there.

She made speeches, met with CEOs of large companies to solicit funds, lobbied Congress, anything that would help. She had been extremely effective and in less than a year had become widely respected in the field. Since Michael had written her at Christmas saying he didn't want to see her again she had worked even harder.

It was she who had called the conference for the end of February. She wanted to discuss vaccines and drugs that were in use against the AIDS virus. It had been brought to her attention by a source at the FDA that several drug companies had been misrepresenting the side effects of some of their products. She had arranged for the most distinguished group of doctors and scientists in the world to be there, flying them in from Paris, Geneva, Africa, San Francisco, New York. She also arranged for Michael to give a presentation.

The program was designed to make Michael look good. And she would make sure he knew she had planned it that way. Blanche would be there. The presence of the First Lady and former First Lady and dozens of world-famous doctors and scientists would guarantee great coverage. Flushed with

536

success, all thanks to her, he wouldn't be able to resist seeing her again, if only for lunch. That's when she would clinch it. He would understand once and for all that she really loved him and cared about him and he wouldn't run away again. That was the plan.

*　　*　　*

It was a beautiful bright winter day, blustery and freezing cold.

Sadie woke at dawn, having rehearsed all night how she would behave when she saw Michael. Casually, she decided. Assuming she wasn't fainting or throwing up from nerves. She felt pretty confident about her role. She planned to ask Michael a couple of 'spontaneous' questions after his presentation that were designed to allow him to show off. She had decided to dress down. A simple pale blue-green Irish tweed suit. In fact, there was nothing she hadn't planned, down to having her hair trimmed a week earlier and her nails done the day before. She made sure her underwear didn't have any rips or tears in case she got in an accident and he had to take her clothes off to examine her bleeding body.

The director of the commission came to her house that morning to go over the agenda and they drove together to the Pan American Health Organization Building around the corner from the State Department. She was thankful that she didn't have to walk in alone with only her Secret Service agents. She always felt so on display.

Michael wasn't there yet. She could relax, meet a few of the commissioners, get her bearings, and be prepared to greet the First Lady, who was coming with her White House entourage.

The place was crawling with reporters, photographers, and television cameras. When Blanche and her crew arrived and made their way to Sadie there was quite a commotion. She had been right about press interest.

The meeting began promptly at nine to a packed house. Michael had still not arrived when it started and she found herself glancing nervously toward the back of the room, unable to concentrate on the first panelists. Michael's presentation was not until after the eleven o'clock coffee break, so there was no need to panic. When he finally did walk in she happened to be staring at the door. Their eyes met for just an instant until, embarrassed and blushing, she quickly looked away and pretended to be engrossed in what the speaker was saying. She was too distracted to ask any questions during the first two sessions. The other commissioners all wanted their place in the sun, the huge press turnout was irresistible, and it was no problem.

By the coffee break Sadie was practically hyperventilating. She and Blanche were ushered off to the head of the PAHO's private bathroom to freshen up and then escorted down the winding marble stairs to where the coffee was being served in the glass-enclosed foyer.

She got a cup of coffee and casually made her way through the crowd, stopping to chat briefly with a few of the panelists from that morning. Finally she came to where Michael was standing with Frank Biondi, the head of the National Institute of Allergy and Infectious Diseases. Biondi was short, fat, and bald and considered himself quite a ladykiller for reasons that were not altogether clear to Sadie. He also happened to be a good doctor.

Michael had his back to her but she knew he could feel her presence behind him. She was so close to him she saw him stiffen. She felt an urge to kiss him on the back of the neck. Pulling herself up to her full height and wiping her perspiring palms on a tissue in her pocket she came around to face Michael and Dr Biondi.

'Dr Biondi,' she said in her most First Lady voice, completely ignoring Michael. 'You were absolutely marvelous this morning. What a brilliant presentation. But then we all know you are brilliant, which is why you were chosen to lead off the session.'

Dr Biondi puffed up like a peacock.

God, men were so easy.

'May I return the compliment by saying that you've put together a brilliant conference. And I happen to know it was you who put it together. We are all so lucky to have you on our team, someone with your clout, not to mention brains and beauty.'

He was playing right into her little act.

She bestowed a radiant smile on Dr Biondi and then, almost as an afterthought, turned to Michael.

'Michael,' she said flashing him another equally impersonal smile. 'We're so pleased you could be here today, too. Everyone is looking forward to hearing you.'

She forced herself to meet his eyes. The pain she saw surprised her. She had expected him to be amused at her little performance despite himself. Yet there was no twinkle, no humor in the black despair she saw.

He didn't respond and she couldn't immediately

force her eyes away from his. The three stood there in awkward silence.

'Well,' said Biondi a little too jovially, turning to Michael. 'I guess congratulations are in order. Doris tells me that Giselle is expecting. They don't call you "The Lance" for nothing, eh, Lanzer?' He chortled at his own wit.

She could hear the sound of her own breath. She knew she looked shocked, but she couldn't help it. There was nothing that could have prepared her for this. His expression changed to anguished apology.

'Oh yeah,' he said. 'We, uh, I mean, I didn't realize Giselle had told people.'

'Oh, sorry,' said Biondi. At last he was uncomfortable. 'I didn't realize it was supposed to be a secret.' He glanced uncertainly at Sadie and then back to Michael. 'I guess I shouldn't have shot my mouth off like that.'

'No, no, it's all right,' muttered Michael. 'It's just that it's, well, it's awfully early. Just under two months and . . .'

He stopped. The timing was not lost on Sadie. Christmas week. He had made love to Giselle the week she got back from France. The week he had told Sadie he loved her, the week she had given herself to him, the week she had dared to hope they might have a future together.

Giselle was pregnant. He was going to be a father again. She knew how seriously he took family. He would never leave her. Never leave his newborn child. It was over.

She had to say something. She couldn't just stand there staring at him. Biondi would notice.

'Oh Michael, how wonderful for you,' she said finally, amazed at how calm her voice sounded. 'I'm sorry if I seem a bit surprised.'

'Doctors do have extracurricular activities, too, Mrs Grey,' said Biondi with a lascivious expression.

'In any case...' she dismissed him, 'I'm very happy for you. Please give Giselle my congratulations.'

She barely made it away from them and over to Blanche next to the coffee table. She was horrified. She had to regain control but she was on the edge of losing it completely.

'Come over to the window with me,' she whispered to Blanche.

They walked over to the glass wall facing the State Department. Outside the wind was blowing the lifeless dead branches of the trees. What was left of the muddied brown leaves on the ground were swirling through the air. It seemed desolate, just the way she felt. 'Désolée,' the French would say; Giselle would say. 'Je suis désolée.' 'I am desolate.'

'Are you okay?'

'I'm just, something just reminded me of Rosey,' she lied. 'It still happens sometimes. It catches me off guard. I'll be fine. Really. Just stay here with me a minute.'

She got out a tissue and surreptitiously wiped under her eyes so as not to smear her mascara as she watched the gray metaphor for her life out the window. Melodramatic, but that's how she saw it.

They were signaling that the conference was to resume. She took a deep breath and walked back through the crowd, up the stairs, and to her seat, smiling and nodding at people as she went. The show must go on.

Michael had already taken his seat at the table in the center of the horseshoe. Something about his confident, cocky air suddenly infuriated her and all the sorrow she had just felt turned within seconds to a white rage.

How dare he do this to her? He had taken her when she was most vulnerable and toyed with her, played his stupid mind games with her, lured her into his culture and then rejected her in the cruelest manner. It was inexcusable. Hatred for him welled up in her for his having used her, taken advantage of her, humiliated her. All she could think of now was that she wanted to do the same to him. Now. Right this minute.

Michael's talk was on sources and budgets for new vaccines that were already on the market and those that were being developed. It was comprehensive and well delivered, if not particularly sexy or controversial. She had had a pretty good idea from his staff what he would be talking about.

She had not told them certain information she had been given from one of her FDA sources. There had been lethal side effects because of the toxicity in a new AIDS vaccine being tested in what was called the Alpha Omega project. People had died. She had not intended bringing it up at the conference because it had not been checked out, and she didn't have any idea whether Michael knew about it or not. She had planned to discuss it with him afterward.

She had just changed her mind.

When Michael finished, she waited as he fielded a number of respectful questions, then she raised her hand.

He looked surprised, then apprehensive. After a moment he nodded.

542

'Mrs Grey?'

'Are you aware of the Alpha Omega project?'

'Yes.'

'Is that going according to plan?'

'To the best of my knowledge.'

'Have you shared with the committee everything you know about it?'

'To the best of my ability.'

'Isn't it true,' she asked, taking the harsher tone of cross-examination, 'that there have been twenty deaths associated with this experimental drug?'

He looked as though she had slapped him. He turned red. 'I would say the number is closer to five.' His voice was tight.

'So you did know about it?'

'We have heard there were problems. There has been no concrete evidence that the deaths are directly related to the drug.'

'Why didn't you bring it up?'

'We are still trying to check it out. We felt it would be irresponsible and alarmist at this time to make that information public.'

His teeth were clenched now. Only his eyes reflected the hurt. The atmosphere in the room was tense. The only sounds between the questions and answers were nervous coughing, the rattling of papers, and the clicking of the photographers' flashbulbs.

'Wouldn't you say, then, that this problem has been a big setback to the program?'

'No, not really. We are moving along as planned. Unexpected delays or problems do not change the fundamental mission.'

'Thank you, Dr Lanzer.'

There was another long silence as Michael stood

up, gathered his papers, and strode away. Only she saw him turn as he got to the door. She thought he mouthed something to her but she wasn't sure. He seemed to be asking, 'Why?'

★　　　★　　　★

'Sadie Grey, you're just as skinny as an ole rail, you bitch. How do you do it? Oh God, just look at these damn thighs. I'll never get rid of this. The good Lord is making me pay a mighty high price for my glorious tits.'

Sadie laughed in spite of herself. Blanche was going through her usual exercise lament. It was a running commentary about her behind and her thighs. Sadie was used to it by now. Several months ago the two of them had taken up exercising together in the third-floor solarium of the White House with a personal trainer, a bossy woman in her early forties named Ricky who had obviously been a WAC drill sergeant before she got into the fitness biz. The aerobics class usually lasted between thirty and forty-five minutes, depending on how long they could take Ricky. Then they would dismiss her and do spot exercises while they gossiped.

Sadie looked forward to this little break whenever she could, which was usually a couple of times a week, depending on everyone's schedules. She loved getting the workout and she loved being up in the solarium.

Being in the solarium allowed her to daydream about her life before, with Rosey, with Des, with Michael—as painful as it was remembering them, it was better than the stark loneliness she felt now. It reminded her of Des and the first time they had made love in the White House. He had been doing a cover story on her for the *Weekly* and came to interview her. She had set up the interview in the solarium so they could have privacy. Somewhere down deep she must have suspected that something like that might happen. It had happened only once before, when Rosey had been Vice President and she and Des had had lunch. They had made love surprisingly, unexpectedly, completely carried away by passion in the front seat of his car at Great Falls overlooking the water. She had refused to see him again after that, so frightened was she of her own lack of control and the potential consequences of such an act. The interview in the solarium had been the first time they were together alone since they had made love in his car.

She could still remember feeling overwhelmed by him that day in the heat of summer, sipping lemonade and watching the back of his hand, wishing he would caress her body with it. She had been utterly reduced to helplessness, unable to resist even if she had wanted to. All those years being married to Rosey and having an unsatisfactory sex life, she had devalued in her own mind the importance of his love for her. With Des the sex had been spectacular. His love for her turned out to be secondary. Since Rosey had died she had had neither and though often she thought she would crawl the walls if she had to stay celibate, she found she could relieve the tension and satisfy herself if she had to. It was the lack of love that had gnawed at her soul. Michael had given her that love. Then he had taken it away. He had totally crushed her spirit.

Michael had been different. With Des it was sheer reckless abandon and obsessive behavior. With Michael it had been deep and true and measured and totally thoughtful.

Michael. She didn't want to think of him. Why did his face, his name, his voice pop into her head with such maddening regularity. She had even thought of going to a hypnotist to help her forget him, put him out of her mind. She couldn't bear thinking about him. It hurt too much. And the idea that Giselle was pregnant . . . a nightmare she could never have anticipated.

'Sadie. You're in such a dream world. What are you thinking about? I know you haven't heard a word I've said. What's the matter with you? You're losing weight, you've got your head in the clouds. I think I recognize the symptoms. Are you in love, girl?'

Blanche was scrutinizing her. She couldn't get away with much around Blanche, at least in the female department. That was her field. Blanche knew about boys and girls, the birds and the bees, and that was all she really wanted to talk about. Girl talk.

Sadie blushed.

'Sure, Blanche. With one of my Secret Service agents. They're the only men I ever really get to see.'

She thought she had recouped nicely. Blanche was thrown off the track.

'Well, we're just gonna have to fix that. We've got to find you a boyfriend. You're too young to go without sex this long. It's been a year and a half. It's not good for your complexion.'

Suddenly her expression changed from one of

546

animation to sadness and she stroked her cheeks absentmindedly.

'Come to think of it, my complexion doesn't look so good these days either.'

Sadie was glad to take the attention off of her own sex life, or lack thereof. Nobody knew, obviously, about Michael except for her agents. And they didn't really know. It was just too private. For one thing, it wasn't about sex as much as it was about love, and that surprised her.

'Well, we know in your case it can't be from lack of sex, Blanche.'

Blanche was solemn for a moment, trying to decide whether or not to confide in Sadie.

'Don't be too sure,' she said. Then, without warning, her face cracked and she began to sob.

'Blanche? Blanche, what is it? What's the matter?'

'Oh Sadie, I'm so scared. I'm just so terrified.'

'What is it? Tell me. Has there been a threat on Freddy's life?'

'No, no,' said Blanche.

'Well, what then?'

'It's Freddy. He hasn't made love to me, hasn't touched me since last summer. He's even had a bed put in his study and he sleeps there. He won't look at me and he'll barely talk to me. I don't know what the matter is, Sadie. And I'm afraid to think about it.'

Sadie had felt a foreboding ever since Michael had been to the White House. She had never been able to get him to talk about it.

'When was it that he stopped, Blanche? Do you remember exactly?'

'Yes.'

She looked directly at Sadie for the first time.
'When?'

'When Michael came to see him.'

'Oh, Blanche.'

Blanche buried her head on Sadie's shoulder and the two of them sat there on the floor of the solarium in their leotards while Blanche cried.

'What about you, Blanche? Have you been tested?'

'Yes. I'm fine—so far.'

'Has Freddy said anything to you about this?'

'No. I've begged him to tell me what's the matter, but he just says he's got some problems he has to work through and it doesn't have anything to do with me. I've even asked him if he was having an affair with anybody else just to see if I could prod the truth out of him, but he's just stonewalling me.'

'Have you talked to Michael about it?'

'I can't. I'm too scared about what he'll tell me. As long as I don't have to hear it I can pretend it isn't happening.'

There was something about Blanche's story that didn't ring true, but Sadie decided to let it go. Blanche was too upset. That was genuine.

'You've got to, Blanche. This is not just your problem. You've got to be able to plan. Michael is in a horrible position if what we suspect is true. He has to honor Freddy's privacy if that's what Freddy wants. But Freddy has a greater responsibility here. You have to talk to Michael.'

'Well, I had just about worked myself up to it when I heard about Giselle.'

'You mean that she's pregnant?'

'You mean you haven't heard?'

'Heard what?'

'Giselle lost the baby.'

'Oh God!' Her heart was beating so fast she knew Blanche must hear it. 'Poor Michael.' Did she sound convincing?

'That's not the worst of it.'

'Oh?'

'Giselle has left him and gone back to France. I hear it's for good.'

*　　*　　*

This time she was not going to lose him. This time she was going to do it right.

She had to make him understand that not only did she love him but she could bridge any gap between them.

Jenny had been a help, but she was Jewish the way all the Jews she knew were. Not very. As far as Jenny was concerned, Michael could have come from another planet. She needed someone to explain him to her. She needed a rabbi.

Rabbi Benjamin from the Washington Hebrew Congregation would be happy to see her. Jenny had called and made the appointment. The former First Lady, she explained, had a family matter she needed to discuss.

It was mid-March, St Patrick's Day. Ironic. Going to see a rabbi about your Jewish love on St Patrick's Day. Des's favorite holiday. Why did everything always remind her of somebody? She felt like a computer. Press a button and out came a preprogrammed memory designed to cause pain.

It was freezing cold, and sleeting, the way it always was on St Patrick's Day. Weather designed for big pots of corned beef and cabbage, Irish stew, thick soda bread and steaming mugs of Irish coffee. But she had to get the Irish Catholic thing out of her head. She was on her way to see a rabbi. She had to think lox and bagels, kosher pickles and cheese blintzes.

It was a Reform synagogue so she didn't have to worry about wearing the wrong thing or spilling chametz all over the floor or touching the candlesticks. She only had to worry about how to explain to the rabbi why she was there.

Once she met him she realized she needn't have worried.

Daniel Benjamin was great. Short and dark-haired with an engaging smile, he was adorable, funny, smart, and sensitive. She would have no trouble confiding in him. Within five minutes she felt as if he were her best friend.

His office was a small room in the back of the temple with a large glass window looking out on the icy bleak day. They sat in two comfortable chairs in a corner, close enough to have an intimate conversation.

She didn't quite know how to begin, because she didn't really know why she was there, what she wanted from him.

He immediately put her at ease.

'You seem a little nervous,' he said reassuringly. 'You shouldn't be. You're not going to do anything wrong or say anything to offend me. I promise you. You have some family situation you want to discuss,' he said. 'So who doesn't. You've come to the right place. Tell me anything. Ask me anything. I've heard it all. Nothing will surprise me.'

She laughed and relaxed even more.

'That's almost a challenge, Rabbi Benjamin. Now

I feel as though I'll have to come up with something that will shock you.'

'Daniel. Call me Daniel, please. If you're going to tell me something that incredible we should at least be on a first-name basis.'

'Well, then, I guess I should drop the ruse that I wanted to talk about a family problem.'

'Good idea for starters. It will save time.'

He leaned back in his seat and studied her, making a frank appraisal of her.

'I'm in love with a Jewish man. He's recently unmarried.'

Well it wasn't a total lie.

'He's from an Orthodox background but I don't really know what kind of a Jew he is. He's not really religious; he's a physician, a scientist. But culturally he's very Jewish. We've had a brief affair. He's in love with me, too. But he's told me he doesn't want to see me again. He feels the differences between us are too great. I don't feel that way and I want to make him understand that we can bridge those differences.'

'What do you want from him?'

'I want ... well, I want ...' she cleared her throat and recrossed her legs, smoothing out the folds of her blue jersey skirt, tugging absentmindedly at her suede boots. He waited.

'I think I want ...' she giggled. 'This must sound stupid to you, but nobody's ever really asked me that. I mean, I guess I would have to say that I think I want to marry him. But marriage is so complicated and difficult. I was sure before that I wanted to marry him, at least I was at first. But now I don't know. I know I want to be with him. I know I'm in love with him. It's just that he's made such a

551

thing about our differences that he's beginning to convince me of it. In the beginning, when I first met him over a year ago, I just sort of laughed it off. But now, every time I make any progress with him, he manages to throw up another barrier. A lot of it is just mind games, but I don't have the stamina for it that he does. Besides, he has all the advantages. He knows how many more barriers there are out there and I don't. If I thought he was running out of them I'd feel more confident that we could be together and be happy. But I'm not so sure. That's why I'm here. I need advice. I want to know how to convince him I'm right about us before he convinces me that I'm wrong. I want to know how to show him that what he calls a "dumb shiksa" can be part of his world and have both of us comfortable. I want to know how to get him. In other words, I want you to be my Miss Lonelyhearts.'

'First of all, we have to deal with the issue of being involved with a divorced man.'

She didn't say anything. Let him assume for her purposes. It wouldn't hurt.

'It must be difficult for you.'

'Well, I guess it is. But it's more difficult for him.'

'Which means in his mind he's not a good Jew. He just talks about it. Just as there's a difference between talking about sex and doing it.'

'What does that have to do with me?'

'Everything. You say he calls you a "dumb shiksa." That's a pejorative term. It's an insult. It's a slap in the face. It's as if someone called me a "Jewboy."'

'But I thought it was funny.'

552

'It isn't funny. It's like saying somebody has a goyisheh kop, a gentile mind, or calling somebody a shaygets, the male equivalent of a shiksa. A good Jew has to respect a non-Jew. If he's not a good Jew then he won't respect himself and he won't be able to respect you. If you want to know what I think, I think you're setting yourself up. I think you're going to get your head kicked in. A Jew like this one has been taught all his life that you play around with a shiksa but you don't marry one.'

'What if you did?'

'You're dealing with stereotypes here, the forbidden fruit syndrome. What would happen once you have this forbidden fruit? The typical Jewish male from the gentile woman's point of view has an irreverent sense of humor, is a good provider, is a good family man, he takes care of his woman, he is loyal, a good father, he hustles. His fantasy is to leave his wife who is a stereotypical Jewish wife, a JAP or Jewish American Princess, which to me is an infuriating and equally denigrating term. She is demanding, whiny, pushy, controlling, and domineering. There is pressure from her family, the kids are a headache, the house is noisy, and their lives lack dignity. He falls in love with and walks off into the sunset with the perfect shiksa. She is a blue-eyed blonde. She is cool, refined, comes from old money. She went to an Ivy League college but more importantly her father went to an Ivy League college. Her father is not a businessman. They belong to a country club, they have relatives in New England.'

Sadie laughed. 'You sound as if you've given this some thought.'

'I'm not exactly making this up. It's hardly

original.'

'So then what happens? They live happily ever after?'

'On the contrary. Once he has her there would be a fall-off. The relationship would change. There is no more spice. The attraction, possessing the forbidden, is the basis of the whole thing. Once you have it, it's gone. Then it will crash.'

Sadie took this in for a moment, then got up from her chair and walked to the window. She felt so helpless and so frustrated. It really was going to be impossible.

It looked like a blizzard out there with the snow swirling around so frantically. She suddenly had an intense longing to be at a ski lodge in someplace like Stowe, Vermont, with a gorgeous, tall, blue-eyed, sandy-haired, aquiline-nosed, blueblooded WASP sitting by the fire after a good rousing day on the slopes, eating fondu and drinking mulled wine. His name would be E. Winthrop Aldrich III and he would be called 'E Three' by his family and close friends. His humor would be collegiate, clubby, he would never talk about his feelings, he would be bright but not brilliant. His father would be an investment banker and belong to the best country club. His mother would do needlepoint kneelers for the Episcopal church. His sister, Muffy, would be a post-debutante. He would be a banker like his father or a lawyer. He would be a terrific athlete, great squash player, would have a muscular body, bare chest, and a great ass. He would believe in God but only go to church for weddings, funerals, christenings, and Christmas Eve. They would never fight or argue, would be contented and compatible. If they did have problems they would keep a stiff

554

upper lip. Bliss.

Now all she had to do was extricate herself from this rabbi, get out of this synagogue, go home, fix a dry martini, and figure out where to find this Mr Right. It only occurred to her much later that she had already been married to him.

'Have you ever thought of conversion?' the rabbi was saying.

'Conversion?' She was stunned. Was he going to try to convert her right here? She had to get out before it was too late. This was taking a nasty turn. She could feel her whole body tense up.

'It's always a possibility.'

'But what good would that do?' There was an edge to her voice. 'I'm not Jewish. Even if I studied and learned and passed tests or whatever you're supposed to do I still wouldn't be Jewish. I'd still be me. And besides, I can't be circumcised.' She hadn't meant to say it. It just popped out.

The rabbi started to laugh. She had relieved the tension, which he obviously was beginning to feel, too.

'A convert is as good a Jew as a born Jew,' he said. 'You would be given a Hebrew name, but you already have one. Sara is your name, isn't it? It means princess, royalty. Very fitting.'

She was relaxing again. He had seen her anxiety and had immediately rushed to put her at ease once more. Typical sensitive Jewish male.

'I bring up conversion only to leave the option open. But I would encourage you to look at it. If you converted you would be able to experience Judaism as a Jew together with him. You could have an enriched family life and there would be more for you to share.'

'I should tell you, Daniel, that I once brought up conversion with him, not about me but as a hypothetical, and he said it was the worst possible idea, that a shiksa who converted to Judaism combined the worst qualities of the two.'

'Some converts are more zealous. And some Jewish guys don't want to get involved with this. They get shown up by their wives.'

'I don't think that's what he was talking about. I think he was talking about the combination of the dumb shiksa with the controlling wife.'

'Possibly. But I think if you love a Jew you ought to study Judaism in any case. That way at least you'll have a better understanding of what you're getting into. You can love a Jew and not love Judaism. The point of study is to see whether you can love Judaism. And to get you to think about your relationship to your own religion.'

'I know I believe in God, but I wouldn't say I was very religious.'

'What's your connection to Jesus? Do you pray to Jesus? Do you believe in the resurrection? Is your husband in heaven? Even if you didn't convert you could come out of this study as a better Christian.'

'All I really want to do is make Michael feel closer to me. If studying Judaism would help I would do it. I don't want to convert. Especially in my situation, given who I am, and with three Christian children, it would look ridiculous. I don't want to be a "better" Christian, whatever that means. I frankly don't understand conversion. How can you give up who you are and what you believe in just because you love something else? Imagine Michael converting to the Episcopal faith.'

At that she cracked up. Daniel was laughing, too.

'It's hard,' he had agreed. 'The first Christmas, particularly. There's inevitably a big blowup. She may have to have a tree. All he can see when he looks at the tree is a big cross. Then there are some Christian converts who refuse to have a tree and their husbands want them to. It's complicated. It's hard for some of them to feel the Friday night service, to feel part of Jewish history, to feel that little tug when they hear about Israel. I've said no to two conversions because I felt they were doing it for the wrong reasons, because they were in love with Jews but didn't really feel they wanted to be Jewish. You don't just pop conversion on somebody as a present.'

'Suppose we wanted to get married with my feeling the way I do about conversion and not being particularly interested in his religion. How would you feel about it?'

'I can't marry you unless you convert. Because part of the ceremony says you're married to him according to the laws of Moses and Israel. If you're not a Jew, what's the point of saying it?'

'I see. So you won't marry us. I can accept that. But I think we're being a little premature anyway, talking about marriage. What I really want to do is get him to make love to...'

She couldn't believe she had said that. She had even shocked herself. She gasped at her own nerve and put her hand over her mouth.

'Oh, I'm sorry, I didn't mean to say that. I can't imagine what got over me. It's just that you've made me feel so relaxed that I...'

She hoped he would take it the right way. And he did. He interrupted her, laughing, shook his head, and threw up his hands

557

'Okay, you win. I've never been asked before by a woman to help her bed somebody. I thought I'd heard it all.'

'You did challenge me, remember,' she said.

'All right. I'll help. How about the Sabbath meal? I think that's just your ticket. You can make a Sabbath meal for him. A Jewish guy could not help but be touched by that.'

'How do I do that?'

'I'll tell you.'

He was very patient, walking her through the meal, what to prepare, how to light the candles, where to buy the challah, the special bread, how to say the prayer.

He gave her several books to study so she could memorize the blessing, then he took her down the hall to the Judaica shop in the temple to show her the candlesticks, challah covers, and Kiddush cups that were for sale in case she wanted to buy them.

Back in his office he went through it again and told her to call him for advice and to talk it over before she actually did it.

'There's one last thing I should tell you,' he said. 'It's about sex on the Sabbath. We call it oneg or the joy of the Sabbath. Onah is the principle of sexual pleasure. It is considered by Orthodox Jews to be a mitzvah or divine commandment to make love that night.'

The rabbi smiled.

They looked at each other for a moment. He was so understanding and unjudgmental. Yet simply by not making judgments he had caused her to think about so many things she hadn't thought about before. For one thing, he had caused her to wonder whether she was doing the right thing, not only for herself but for Michael.

She gave a deep weary sigh.

'What do you think about all of this?' she asked him. 'You haven't told me what you really think.'

'I think you're dealing with a guy who doesn't want to be the court Jew,' he said. 'You've been the queen. You've lived at the White House. Now you're a national icon. You still spend time with the rich and famous and powerful. He's always been on the outside. Now he's had a taste of what it's like on the inside. He's finally made it. But he's got mixed feelings. He owes something to his ex-wife. Especially if they had a terrible marriage, terrible sex; he's feeling guilty. He takes sex so seriously. He's had this fantasy for a long time, to have sex with someone else. But he's had it hammered into him since he was a child that it's wrong and that gets him emotionally. Also, he's used to pushing aside his own comforts. He's a scientist, remember. That stoicism got him through medical school. He's used to reaching for a higher goal, and that's an emotional thing with him, too. He can hold her off as long as he has to; using work, religious or cultural differences, his former marriage, whatever, as an excuse. But in the end, none of it has any relevance to what he's really feeling.'

'And what is that, Rabbi?'

'If he really loves you he will want to take you at your word. This Jewish issue is nothing more than a smokescreen. What he's really doing is asking you, "Do you love me?"'

★          ★          ★

Books. Her office at home was piled with books.

559

Jewish books. Books on Yiddish, on running a Jewish household, on Jewish prayers and customs, books on conversion. The Old Testament. And she still had the Haggadah from the seder at Michael's house last year. She had compiled quite a Jewish library. She was collecting Jewish artifacts. She had bought a challah cover and plate and a beautiful Kiddush cup at the Judaica store when she went back to see Daniel Benjamin. He had gone over the Sabbath ceremony in detail with her and she felt she was ready, having memorized the prayer that the woman is supposed to say when lighting the candles.

Now all she had to do was get up the courage to do it.

Her plan was this: she would find out from Michael's secretary Maureen, with whom she had become pals, when he was going home on Friday. He usually went home early on Fridays when he had the weekend duty, and she wanted to be there before sundown to light the candles. Even though Michael wasn't Orthodox himself, she wanted to make sure she got every aspect of the ritual absolutely correct. She didn't want him to catch her out on anything and then feel that she would never be able to learn. She had to be perfect.

Maureen seemed to be on Sadie's side. She must have seen how Michael was suffering and suspected that part of the reason was because he wasn't seeing Sadie anymore. She had no real way of knowing that except that the telephone calls had stopped, both ways, since Christmas. So she was more than happy, that last Friday in April, to tell Sadie that he had left early.

It was a very warm night, but then in Washington the weather was always so erratic there was no telling. Spring was definitely in the air.

She had sent Asuncion to the store for the fresh challah that Friday, and Daniel Benjamin had produced some drinkable kosher wine for her. He had been coaching her and she had run through the ritual with him so many times she was confident she wouldn't make a mistake. This was more nerve-racking than her first holy communion. The menu was all planned. She had had Asuncion cook it, so all she had to do when she got to his house was heat it up. She didn't want to be distracted from the ritual by also having to actually cook. There would be the challah, of course, two loaves. Then roasted chicken and potatoes, tsimmes—a delicious-sounding concoction of carrots, sweet potatoes, and sliced apples—and kugel or noodle pudding for dessert.

What to wear was always a problem with Michael. She was in the mood for pink or blue, but she didn't want to look like an Easter egg either. She settled on a pale pink silk shirtwaist dress.

It was around five. She had better leave if she wanted to be there before sundown. Part of her really wanted to do this, the other part dreaded every second of it. She had this sinking feeling that no matter what she did, she was doomed. And she hadn't seen him or spoken to him since that awful day when she humiliated him in front of everyone at the commission meeting. Her father had always told her the worst thing you could ever do to a man was to humiliate him. It was possible that he would

561

never forgive her; and she would never even have a chance to prove to him that she could be part of his life. On the other hand, what did she have to lose by trying? She had already lost him. She had nothing to lose and everything to gain.

Asuncion had loaded up the car. The Secret Service were in the backup car. It was time. She would go.

His car was parked in front. He was home. She took the bags of still-warm food and the flowers. Juggling them with her purse, she walked up to the front door. The sun was lowering in the west but it was still visible. She was okay on time. Shabbat comes automatically with the setting of the sun. After that, candles cannot be lit.

When she got to the door she heard piano music, Mozart. He must have the radio on. She was afraid if she rang the bell and he answered he might slam the door in her face. She tried the door. It was not locked. Typical. She pushed it open gingerly. Michael was sitting at the piano. She had had no idea that he played. She put her bags down on the hall floor and closed the door behind her. He was so absorbed in his music that he didn't hear her come in. She took off her jacket and threw it on a chair. She walked slowly to the door of the living room and stood there quietly listening. He was a good pianist. After a while he stopped. In the still he felt her presence and without starting turned around. He looked as though he had seen an apparition. She could see him, even across the room, blink his eyes several times trying to determine if she were real.

'It's Friday night,' she said in a halting voice. 'I've come to prepare you a Sabbath meal.'

He didn't speak. He just kept staring at her.

562

'It's right here. In these bags,' she turned and pointed to the bags in the hall. 'I've brought everything. You don't have to do a thing. I know how to do it. I've got the challah, and...'

'Sadie.' He interrupted her.

'It's all cooked, it just needs to be warmed up. But we better hurry because we only have about half an hour until sundown and we won't be able to light the candles if we don't—'

'Sadie.'

'I know ... this is intrusive...'

'Sadie!'

She stopped talking. He got up and walked toward her. When he got right up to her she couldn't tell at first whether he was going to hit her or embrace her. But then she had the overwhelming feeling that he wanted to put his arms around her. She had never wanted so badly to be held by anyone as she did at that moment.

Instead he just stood there looking at her.

'I'm glad to see you,' he said finally.

'Oh, Michael, I...'

'Here, let me help you with these bags. We don't have much time until sundown.'

He took the food into the kitchen and helped her unpack it. She put the food in the oven to warm up, then set the table. She had brought a white cloth and silver. She arranged the flowers, then carefully placed the two symbolic loaves of challah on the special plate.

She brought out her best silver candlesticks that she had inherited from her grandmother McDougald in Statesboro, Georgia, and put two candles in them for the two forms of the commandment 'remember' and 'observe.' Then she

563

brought out the beautiful, ornate hand-crafted sterling silver Kiddush cup that she had bought at the Judaica shop at the synagogue.

When the food was ready she brought it to the table and put it in serving bowls and plates so that she wouldn't have to be jumping up and down.

'Oh God. Matches. I've forgotten the matches.'

'I've got matches.'

He handed them to her and she set them next to her place at the table, then excused herself. In the bathroom she took a small white lace scarf out of her bag and placed it on top of her head. She had tried it out at home in front of the mirror to make sure she would look pretty, not ridiculous.

When she returned, she beckoned him to take his place at the table, as she stood before him. She looked at her watch. It was twenty minutes before sunset. She had gotten the times from the rabbi. Shabbat begins eighteen minutes before sunset and after that the candles cannot be lit.

She took the matches from the table and lit one, then lit the candles, laying the match down on her place. After sunset one cannot extinguish the match. Then with her hands, she encircled the candlelight three times, as though to welcome the Sabbath in. Next she covered her eyes and recited the blessing.

'Baruch ata Adonai Elohainu melech ha'olam asher kidshanu b'mitzvotav v'tzivanu l'hadlik ner shel Shabbat.' (Blessed are You, O Lord our God, ruler of the universe, Who has sanctified us with His commandments and commanded us to kindle the lights of the Sabbath.)

Michael smiled, though he was clearly touched and quite solemn for her sake. Now it was time for

564

him to pour the wine and recite the Kiddush. This was the moment, if he chose to, for the husband to recite from Proverbs 31 in praise of his wife. It never occurred to her that Michael might do this for her. She was completely surprised when he began:

'A woman of valor—seek her out,
for she is to be valued above rubies.
Her husband trusts her,
and they cannot fail to prosper.
All the days of her life
she is good to him.
She opens her hands to those in need
and offers her help to the poor.
Adorned with strength and dignity,
she looks to the future with cheerful trust.
Her speech is wise,
and the law of kindness is on her lips.
Her children rise up to call her blessed,
her husband likewise praises her:
"Many women have done well,
but you surpass them all."
Charm is deceptive and beauty short-lived,
but a woman loyal to God has truly earned
     praise.
Give her honor for her work;
her life proclaims her praise.'

'You didn't have to do that.'
'I wanted to.'
He had been looking directly into her eyes and now it was she who looked away. She had put the Kiddush cup in the center of the table for the two of them to share, an extremely romantic notion, she thought.

565

'Now you're supposed to—'

'Pour the wine? I know.'

She had been worried that he might not observe the ritual the same way Daniel had taught her and she would be stuck, not knowing what to do. He opened the wine and poured it to the very top of the cup, then recited in Hebrew. She knew what it meant—'Then God blessed the seventh day'—but it was exotic and mysterious the way he said it, almost singing or chanting. By now the sun had set and it was growing dim. The candles were the only light in the house and the glow reflected on both their faces as they sat at the Sabbath table.

Michael reached over and took the gold-embroidered velvet challah cover from the bread, recited the blessing, then with both hands he tore off a large chunk, then tore that in half, and gave her half of his.

He took the Kiddush cup and brought it to his lips, taking a sip from it, then handed it to her. He never took his eyes off hers the entire time. She was mesmerized by his gaze as she took her own sip of the wine.

'Thank you for this,' he said, as she put the cup down.

'I'm just glad you're not still angry at me for embarrassing you at the commission.'

'I was. I'm not now.'

'So was I.'

'I know. I'm sorry.'

'I'm sorry, too.'

The intensity of the moment was too much for him.

'I'm starving,' he said. He reached over and began to carve the chicken, serving her plate first,

566

then his. He helped himself to the vegetables and potatoes, passing them to her. After his first bite he moaned.

'If you tell me you cooked every morsel of this I'll really be impressed.'

'Well, let's just say I oversaw the cooking. Asuncion...'

'Where is she? Hiding in the kitchen?'

'Oh go to hell.'

'On Shabbas? You don't mean that. Besides, Jews don't have hell. You'll have to think of some other curse.'

'What happens to bad Jews then if they don't have hell?'

'They have confusing, upsetting, conflicted, anxiety-ridden relationships with gorgeous shiksas.'

She was surprised that he had brought up the subject so easily. It made her more nervous than she would have expected. She didn't want to pursue it. Not yet, anyway.

'Rabbi Benjamin says the word *shiksa* is a terrible insult.'

'It is, but only if you're Jewish. To shiksas it's not. Who's Rabbi Benjamin?'

'My coach.'

'Ah,' he said and smiled, then took a long sip of wine.

'I went to talk to him about converting.'

She said it with a perfectly straight face.

He practically spat out his wine.

'Excuse me?'

'I don't even need a new name. I already have a Hebrew name. Sara.'

'Let's run that one by again, if you don't mind.'

'Don't you think it would be a good idea? You

567

can see what a quick study I am. Baruch ata
Adonai...'

'Okay, okay, I get the picture. But Sadie...'
'Sara, please.'

'Sara. You're not Jewish. You will never be
Jewish. It's impossible.'

'Elohainu melech ha'olam...'

'You're like a Japanese who's learned a few words
of English. It's charming but it won't work.'

'... asher kidshanu ...'

'I don't care what the rabbi says. You can't
become Jewish just because you want to be.'

She picked up the noodle pudding, and offered it
to him.

'Keegel?'

'It's pronounced kugel. You see what I mean?'
They looked at each other and laughed.

'The rabbi pronounced it "keegel". But taste it
and you won't care how it's pronounced.'

He put some in his mouth, savored it, and
groaned with pleasure.

'Umm.'

'Do you like it? I actually made that all by
myself.'

'It reminds me of you. Soft and sweet and a
complete noodle.'

'I'm going to take that as a compliment. Gosh, if
I'm lucky maybe you'll even call me keegel.'

'Kugel.'

'Yes, bubeleh?'

'You're hopeless, Sadie.'

'Sara.'

He burst out laughing, partly out of frustration,
partly out of delight.

'There's an old saying that if a woman can't make
568

a decent kugel—divorce her.'

'Is there a saying that if a woman can make a decent keegel, uh, kugel—marry her?'

He reddened. 'I, uh, never heard that one.'

'Why don't you believe in conversion?' she asked, suddenly serious.

'I think the whole idea is stupid. Besides, part of what makes you attractive is that you are different.'

'That's what the rabbi said.'

'What else did the rabbi say?' He was laughing. She raised her eyebrows and smiled seductively.

'He just explained the meaning of various mitzvahs ... are you allowed to wash dishes on Shabbat?' she asked, getting up to clear the table and change the subject. He jumped up to help her clear.

'Not in my house.'

'I'll clear,' she protested. 'Why don't you play the piano for me?'

'You're not allowed to play the piano.'

'What are you allowed to do?'

She looked directly at him and he nearly dropped the plates. Without answering he went into the kitchen and brought back another bottle of wine, since the first one had been drained. They sat down and he opened it, poured it into the cup and handed it to her.

'L'chayim.'

She took a sip and handed him the cup. He took a sip himself. They were both silent.

'There's a wonderful story my grandfather used to tell at Shabbat dinners,' he said. 'His family came from Russia. When he was growing up in a Russian village there were pogroms. The cossacks would ride into town, rape the women, kill the men, loot and destroy everything. The Jews would move to avoid it, but the same thing kept happening. My grandfather was in love with a beautiful young girl named Tuva whose family was a close friend of his family. They were betrothed. But once when the cossacks came, they had to get out of town in a hurry and somehow their group got separated. My grandfather's family went southwest and never saw Tuva's family again. He was heartbroken, knowing that he had lost the love of his life. His family eventually ended up in Prague. Now, there is an ancient and very famous Jewish cemetery in Prague. The graves are so close together in this cemetery that the gravestones are actually touching each other. The cemetery was a small piece of land given to the Jews, and when they ran out of space they just kept having to bury their dead stacked one on top of the other. It's very beautiful, very eerie. It's in a parklike space with huge trees that look as if they're sitting shiva for the dead, all bent and gnarled and hunched over. In one corner of the cemetery is the grave of a very famous rabbi, Rabbi Löw. They have a custom where if you want to say a blessing over someone's grave or a prayer or make a wish, you write it on a small piece of paper and put it on top of their grave with a stone. Many of the graves in the Jewish cemetery have those pieces of paper with stones but none has as many as Rabbi Löw's grave, which is the Jewish equivalent of the wishing well. My grandfather went to the grave and wished that he would find Tuva. He wrote it on a piece of paper and placed it on top of the rabbi's grave with a stone. When he was old enough, he emigrated to the United States and ended up in Connecticut in a small Jewish community. And who should be there? Tuva and her family. They had found their way to America via Poland and the Baltic Sea. That beautiful young Russian girl who was lost in Central Russia was my grandmother.'

'Oh Michael, what a fabulous story! Why haven't you ever told me that story before?'

'I don't know. I don't actually think I've ever told anyone that story. I don't like talking about my background or my family. For some reason I don't mind talking to you about it. But you're different from any other woman I've ever known. I feel I can talk to you. I can tell you things and you'll listen. You won't make judgments.'

She was terribly flattered and touched. It was his way of thanking her for the evening. She didn't know what to say so she didn't acknowledge it.

'But that's like a fairy tale. And it has such a happy ending.'

'I don't believe in happy endings.'

'I do.'

They each took a sip of wine. Neither looked at the other. Neither one had mentioned Giselle or the baby. She felt she ought to say something, anything just to acknowledge that she knew. After all, that was why she was there.

'I'm sorry about the miscarriage.'

He winced and when he looked up she could see the sorrow.

'I'm sorry about Giselle, too.'

He didn't respond to her.

'I don't mean to be intrusive,' she said, 'but are you ... are you okay?'

'I'm fine.'

'It's really hard for you, isn't it? Is there anything

571

I can do?'

She thought she saw his eyes glistening in the candlelight.

'Does Giselle know ... I mean, did she find out about...'

'No.'

She noticed for the first time that he was still wearing his wedding ring.

'Michael.' She reached over the table and touched his hand.

He got up and walked over to where the glass doors faced out to the yard.

This wasn't going at all the way she had anticipated. She had expected him to feel somewhat sad. That would have been only normal. But she also knew that he loved her, so she had assumed that part of him would be happy to be free.

Something compelled her to get up and follow him. She walked over to where he was standing and stood slightly behind him, not touching but so close that she could feel his electricity.

'You asked me what else the rabbi told me. The rabbi told me about Oneg Shabbat, about the Friday night being mitzvah night...'

Michael turned and took her in his arms.

'Oh Sadie' was all he said under his breath.

They stood holding on to each other for the longest time, her head buried in his shoulder.

She pulled back and looked up at him.

He looked at her with such longing that it surprised her. He began to stroke her hair.

'My God, the pain I've caused you. The pain I've caused so many people I love.'

He kissed her on the forehead.

'We can't do a mitzvah, Sadie. That can only be

done with "a joyous heart." I'm just not there yet. Please understand.'

She couldn't hide her disappointment.

She went into the kitchen and gathered her things. He didn't try to stop her, he only stood and watched.

When she had finally put everything away she went to the hall and got her coat.

It was only then that Michael came over to her and helped her on with it. Then he reached down and pulled her into his arms one last time, still saying nothing.

When he released her she turned and opened the door. Then, as she was about to leave, she looked back at him and smiled.

'Her ways are unstable,' she said, 'and she knoweth it not.'

⋆      ⋆      ⋆

It was the jawline that had really begun to bother her. The eyelids had always drooped a little. She had thought it made her look kind of sexy. Although lately, if she hadn't enough sleep, they drooped so low over her eyes that it made it difficult to see. They felt heavy. Still, she could live with that. What she couldn't live with was the sagging chin and neck. It had taken on grotesque proportions and was becoming an obsession with her.

The photographs she had seen of herself lately had been shocking. She looked like an old hag. Suddenly her hair looked too long, her makeup wrong, all the lines in her face pulling downward. It was a disaster. And she wasn't even forty-six yet.

573

How had this happened?

Lorraine had told her to expect this. Lorraine was an expert on facial skin. She had said that all widows go through a period after their husbands die when they decide they are dying too and suddenly begin to look and feel old. This was why, Lorraine said, nobody should have a facelift for at least a year after one's husband had died. It wasn't a good idea because one wasn't in one's right mind. The best plastic surgeons, Lorraine said, wouldn't even consider a widow until after the first year.

It was true that right after Rosey died she had felt that she was looking old and that no man would ever look at her again. Then Des rejected her for Allison and she knew it had to be because she was aging so badly and was no longer attractive.

When Michael came along and loved her she felt beautiful, but then he rejected her, too. Even now, when she sensed that he still cared about her, he wasn't exactly banging down the door to see her. He hadn't called since their Sabbath meal. She hadn't called him either. She was too embarrassed. She had really blown it, misjudged the moment and him. The fact that he hadn't called her was proof that she had made a mistake. No matter how sad he might be feeling, if he really loved her he would have called. If only to say that he appreciated the dinner but couldn't see her now. It was obvious that the reason he wasn't calling was because she looked like an old crone. If she looked younger, fresher, more relaxed, rested, he wouldn't be able to resist. Besides. It was almost two years since Rosey died. She wasn't the grieving widow anymore, at least not in the traditional sense. Emotionally, she had passed several milestones. Her birthday was July 3.

574

She could not face another birthday, another anniversary of Rosey's death, looking the way she looked. Even Lorraine had been asking lately if she was feeling all right, implying that she looked exhausted. The bitch. That was socialese for 'run, don't walk, to your nearest plastic surgeon.' She had made up her mind. She would definitely have a facelift.

In mid-May there was a meeting of the National Commission on AIDS at the NIH. She had planned it as an excuse to see Michael. It was obviously the only way she would get to see him. He was going to speak to the commission members and give a tour. If she had her facelift now, she would be ready to go out and see people by then. It would give her a full mouth. She knew she could get an appointment right away. Lorraine had hinted all along that Dr Granta, her plastic surgeon, owed her. She had dropped so much money on him for every possible procedure (to no avail, she was afraid) and recommended him to so many friends that he would drop everything for her. Sadie had never mentioned to Lorraine that she planned to do it, but she would certainly use Lorraine's name as a reference. And then there was the fact, not to be overlooked, that she was the former First Lady. There would be no problem about timing. He would fit her in. Confidentiality was her only concern now.

*　　*　　*

She was a nervous wreck. There was something so demeaning and undignified about the idea. She couldn't explain why. She highlighted her auburn hair as the few gray strands appeared. She wore

575

makeup. She did everything she could think of to make herself more attractive. Why not plastic surgery? Nevertheless she didn't like the way it made her feel. Which was dishonest. She wasn't going to tell anyone. People would guess, though. She wondered if Michael would guess. She wondered what he would think about her doing it if he knew. She knew what he would think. He would be appalled. He would tell her it was horrible and grotesque and disgusting. He would say he loved her the way she was. He would say she was beautiful now and part of her beauty was her life lived on her face. He would say that she had character and depth in her face and that if she had plastic surgery it would just iron out all the grace and dignity and loveliness that was her. He would tell her that she didn't want to look like a stretched, plastic mask of a doll's face. He would say that her face reflected her soul and that to touch it would be destroy her spirit. He would say all of that because he loved her. Fuck Michael. Where was he when she needed him anyway? Certainly not here in New York on Park Avenue in the backseat of her car waiting to get out and be escorted into the doctor's office after hours in dark glasses with a scarf wrapped around her head. She felt as if she was about to see a back alley abortionist.

She took a deep breath and sailed in as casually as she possibly could, given the fact that her legs were barely holding her up. Dr Granta's personal assistant met her at the door, as arranged. The large attractive waiting room with several sofas and coffee tables was completely empty. The assistant led the way down a hall and into a small room with an examining table, medical instruments, and several mirrors. Before she had a chance to sit down or even look around, the door burst open and Dr Granta appeared, smiling. He was tall and distinguished-looking, graying at the temples, with a warm smile and slightly mischievous eyes.

'Hi,' he said, completely forgoing any kind of protocol, which immediately put her at ease.

'Hi,' she said back. Her teeth were chattering so she couldn't say any more. This was silly.

He grabbed her by the shoulders and propelled her over to a mirror. Standing behind her he reached around and pinched the skin over her eyelids, then took his hand away. To her amazement, the skin remained in a hideous fold hanging over her eye.

She gasped.

'See that,' he said, 'that's what gives your eyes that tired look.'

'Tired!' She was horrified. 'Actually,' she said, trying to muster up as much self-confidence as she could, 'I prefer to think of them as bedroom eyes.'

'Whatever,' he said with a knowing look and shrugged. 'Why don't you join me in my office?'

They walked across the hall into another room, this one pine-paneled, lined with bookcases, filled with antiques, a comfortable sofa, and two chairs facing the desk. It looked like a very expensive library in a Park Avenue apartment.

She took a seat across the desk from him. He leaned back in his chair and looked at her.

'I'm not even forty-six yet,' she said defensively.

This was his cue to gasp. 'No!' he was supposed to say. 'You can't mean it. My God, I've never seen anyone look as young as you do for your age. It's not possible. You don't look a day over

577

twenty-nine, thirty at most.'

Instead he said, 'Chronological age doesn't matter. What matters is the way you look.' Given his tone he might as well have added, 'You hag!'

Well, of course he wouldn't have been shocked at her age. She was probably one of the most famous women in the world. He would know how old she was. Why hadn't she considered that right away? But he might have at least told her she looked great or something. Good even.

'What I had in mind—' she started to say, in her most calm voice.

'I would do the eyes and clean up the jawline and the neck, get rid of some of that fat around the jowls ...' he interrupted.

'Fat? Around the j-jowls?' She grabbed her chin and neck, feeling frantically for the offending fat.

'You don't need the forehead, you don't need the cheeks or under the eyes, not now at least.'

'Not now?' Her voice quavered with gratitude.

'But you're on the fence.'

'On the fence?'

Now she was reduced to repeating everything he said, just to make sure she understood each atrocity.

'You have maybe two good years before it's too late.'

'Too late? For what?'

'Now you have a certain elasticity in your skin. The longer you wait, the less elasticity. In another two years the operation will be riskier, more extensive, and the change will be more noticeable. If you do it now you can wait another seven to ten years before you have to do it again. The eyes will last ten years. And the jowls will require a touch-up

578

in about seven years. In and out. Same day.'

'If I do it now will I stay in the hospital?'

'Oh, yes. We would keep you overnight. Two if you like. There's always the possibility of a hematoma, or blood clot, usually in the cheek near the ear. We would have to come in and open that up and suction out the excess blood...'

Sadie could see his face begin to blur and his voice sounded very distant in her ears. She knew he was talking to her, and she was conscious enough to grab onto the arms of the chair and brace herself for a fall in case she actually fainted dead away, which is what she thought she was going to do.

She could vaguely hear words in the background ... best anesthesiologist ... ice packs ... sleep propped up ... no smoking ... no drinking ... no aspirin...

'Do you have any questions?'

Her only question was whether she would be able to actually get up and walk out of the office on her own or would she humiliate herself in front of him by blacking out and crashing to the floor.

He said a few more things about his assistant, who would be giving her a fact sheet, and to call if there were any more questions and to go home and think about it before making an appointment and of course he would be able to squeeze her in at her convenience. There were always cancellations.

The assistant had put an envelope in her hand and was showing her to the door and the Secret Service agent was there and she grasped his arm and held on until they reached the car and she was inside. It was only then that she allowed herself to pass out.

It wasn't until she had gotten back to Washington that she opened up the envelope. She was in bed, ready to go to sleep in case she began to feel faint.

It was a list of instructions for 'a facial and eyelid plasty.' There were twenty-eight items on the list, several of which she vaguely remembered he had mentioned to her.

Written in capital letters were the words YOU MUST STOP SMOKING. You could dye or tint your hair ten days before or three weeks after surgery. You could wash your hair one week after surgery but you couldn't set it for three weeks. You could not brush your hair for two weeks. It was six weeks until you could use normal makeup. No indoor exercise for one month. No alcohol for two weeks after. No sexual relations for three weeks after surgery. Well, that wouldn't be a problem. No false eyelashes for four weeks. She supposed she could live with that, too. No driving for two weeks. She had a car and driver. You had to be careful when removing clothing overhead so as not to tear earlobes sutures. She started to feel woozy.

At this point she still hadn't decided whether she was going to do it or not. What she knew absolutely in her heart and in her gut was that she didn't want to do it. She really didn't want to do it. But the words *on the fence* and *two more years before it's too late* kept echoing in her head. Not to mention "tired" and "fat in the jowls." She had spent hours when she got back examining her face in the mirror from all angles. One minute she thought she looked gorgeous and young, then the light would catch an angle the wrong way and all she saw was sagging skin. One minute she knew she had no choice but to do it, the next she had convinced herself it wasn't necessary. She couldn't ask anyone. She was looking for some sign, some reason not to do it short of calling up Michael and asking him what he thought. Then she saw it. Like a bolt from heaven, an answer to her prayers, at the bottom of the page. In large type, just like the no-smoking exhortation: PLEASE AVOID USING THE TELEPHONE FOR TWO WEEKS AFTER SURGERY AS IT IS A SOURCE OF INFECTION.

There was a God.

She would simply have to wear tinted glasses and hold up her chin very high from now on when she was out in public.

\*　　　\*　　　\*

He seemed haggard, and he had lost weight. His white doctor's coat hung on his shoulders. Just as well, given the way she thought she looked, jowls and all. Though she had to admit he was still gorgeous and incredibly sexy. Almost more so being thinner—it emphasized his eyes.

When they talked on the phone it was his voice that overwhelmed her, his hypnotic voice, and often she had difficulty picturing him. In person it was his eyes, his penetrating eyes. He could look at her and know everything she was thinking and feeling. It was annoying, frustrating, and an enormous relief at the same time.

She always forgot, until she saw him again, what effect those eyes had on her. When they were apart, she missed him but he faded in her memory. Then she would see him and fall in love with him all over

581

again. He knew it too. Sometimes when she didn't want to tell him the truth about something, didn't want to let him in, he would force her to look at him and stun her with his ability to make her come clean. There were no defenses against those eyes.

She had arranged for the members and staff of the National Commission on AIDS plus representatives from the National Hemophilia Foundation, the American Foundation for AIDS Research, the Institute of Medicine, Project Inform, ACT UP, and the American Association of Physicians for Human Rights to meet at the NIH.

The meeting had been called for 5:00 p.m. Most of the daytime business would be over with so there were fewer people around. Michael was to greet them, give them a briefing and a tour of the Clinical Center's labs and patient facilities. There were about thirty of them in all and they gathered in the auditorium first to hear him speak. He was not on the stage—the group was too small—but stood in the midst of them to give an update on AIDS research and experimental trials. She sat in the front row, having greeted him when she arrived.

They were exceptionally polite when they met. Too polite, really, but there with so many others around they had to be.

'Hello, Michael,' she had said with a lilt in her voice.

'Hi, there,' he had responded, a little too brightly.

The entire time he spoke he never looked in her direction. During the question-and-answer session afterward he would look over her head to call on someone as though she weren't there.

After this talk he led the group on a tour through

the corridors, into research rooms, never addressing a single word to her or even glancing at her. Yet she could feel his eyes on her when he wasn't speaking, even when she couldn't see him.

Michael's talk had been a great success. He was a dynamic speaker and everyone was impressed. The tour was rather pedestrian. The Clinical Center didn't look any different from a regular hospital. She could understand why he had resisted giving the tour when the staff had asked him to.

Even though it was after hours the place still seemed to be bustling and they had to squeeze their way past an AIDS support group meeting in one of the larger waiting areas. Michael was racing along the corridors, obviously bored and trying to get it over with as quickly as possible. At one point he took the group into his own private lab. The outer room looked like any research lab, strewn with old coffee cups and diet drink cans, sweaters rolled up and stuck in bookcases, cartoons Scotch taped to the refrigerator, books piled high, a radio playing classical music, posters of the Swiss Alps pasted on the door. He opened the door to the adjoining room and peered in to see an attractive young Asian woman working with test tubes. He closed the door and turned to the people surrounding him.

'I'd be happy to show any of you through this room, but I feel I should warn you that there are live AIDS viruses in here.'

Why was it she detected a slight note of a challenge in his voice? Was it her imagination or did he direct the last sentence to her? Did he want her to go in there or was he warning her not to? Was he trying to scare her? I could get AIDS so stay away. She couldn't figure it out. She looked up at him and saw he was looking at her. She was tempted to accept his challenge and go in. But she really didn't want to. She had Willie to think about, if there was any risk at all. Besides, what did she care what he thought. Why should she let him get to her like that?

'I think I'll pass, Dr Lanzer,' she said with a smile. 'I have a small child to worry about.'

Several of the medical types asked to see the lab and several others decided to wait outside with her. A few minutes later he emerged with the rest of the group.

'Why did you warn us about the live AIDS virus?' Sadie asked, in front of the group. 'Was there really any danger to us? How likely would it be for anyone to get AIDS by going in there?'

He seemed surprised by her question.

'Just by walking around?' he asked. 'Probably zero.' She sensed he was reluctant to admit it. 'But if anyone messed around with anything, touched anything, knocked anything over, well, then it's possible.'

'How much at risk are you or any of your researchers, then? You deal with this stuff every day, don't you?'

'Actually I don't really do it anymore. I have too much administrative business to attend to. It wouldn't be fair to the researchers if I just stuck my two cents' worth in now and then. As far as risk is concerned, we have never had anyone become zero-converted in our lab. We test everyone every three to six months. There is very, very little chance of becoming infected by working with it the way we do. Although when we first started out no one knew that and there were actually people who refused to

584

work on it. Now, though, I think people can consider themselves pretty safe.'

This was the first time he had actually said that he didn't work with the AIDS virus anymore. He more or less had to admit it in front of this group. They were too savvy. But if that were so, why would he try to warn her away? Was it just another barrier to keep them apart? Sometimes with Michael she felt as if their relationship was an Olympic decathlon competition. If she wasn't jumping hurdles, she was throwing javelins or sprinting. She never seemed to get to the end, she never seemed to be able to win. It was so exhausting. She had actually begun to wonder whether it was worth it.

It was toward the end of the tour that one of her Secret Service agents approached her.

'Mrs Grey,' he said. 'We've just had a call from the White House. Mrs Osgood needs to talk to you. She says it's urgent. You can take the call in here. It's secure.' He pointed the way to an office near where they were standing.

She slipped away quietly. Michael had noticed her leaving the back of the group and he couldn't help following her with his eyes as she disappeared into the next room.

She rang through to Blanche's private number.

'Oh Sadie, thank the Lord! Are you with Michael Lanzer?'

'Well, sort of. He's giving us a tour. I told you about it on the phone this morning. What's the matter, Blanche? You sound frantic.'

'It's Freddy. Sadie, something's awful wrong with him. I'm scared to tell anyone. He refuses to see the White House doctor. He finally agreed to let

585

me call Michael. Do you think you could get him to come over here? I want you to come too.'

Sadie found this request unnerving for many reasons. She was horrified at the idea that Freddy might have tested positive. She was torn about going to the White House with Michael. It would be awkward. They were virtually not speaking to each other, except in public. He hadn't tried to communicate with her since their Sabbath dinner. What would they say to each other?

She didn't want to go back and join the group. If she went directly to Michael it would be too obvious. She asked one of her agents to get him and have him join her in the small office when there was a break.

Several minutes later he came in with a worried expression and closed the door.

'What is it, Sadie?'

'I've just had a call from Blanche. The President is sick and he won't see anyone but you. She wants us both to come to the White House now. The President is in the family quarters.'

His face tensed.

'I'll get my coat. I'll meet you in your car in front of the clinic in five minutes.'

Sadie slipped out the back corridor without saying anything to anyone and, accompanied by her agents, she went down the elevator to her car and waited for Michael.

They rode to the White House in silence. There were so many things she wanted to talk to him about, tell him, ask him. She had missed him so terribly. She wondered what he had been doing these last six weeks or so. She had talked to Judy Sokolow occasionally, and she had said that Michael had gone into seclusion, that he didn't want to see anybody, do anything. As far as Judy knew he hadn't spoken to Giselle. There was no thought that she might come back from France. It was so frustrating to be sitting so near him and not be able to touch him or talk to him about anything real. Yet anything she wanted to say was personal and with the agents sitting in the front seat it wasn't possible. It was like being in a crowded elevator. They couldn't discuss Freddy for that reason either. She was not supposed to know anything about him, anyway. Certainly Michael would never have discussed it with her.

He was leaning up against the door of the opposite side of the car as if to avoid even the barest physical contact with her. She found herself staring at his hand, which was on the seat between them, another barrier. The line of demarcation. Do not come any closer. She now knew what those hands, those strong gentle hands, felt like on her body, touching her, holding her. It was all she could do not to reach out and put her hand over his. Instead, she put her hand next to his, so close she could feel the warmth of his skin.

He looked down at her hand, then up at her. He hadn't expected her to be looking at him. When their eyes met he couldn't look away. Neither could she. Those eyes. God!

'Hi,' she said and smiled.

It was such an intimate moment. He was stunned. His eyes became kaleidoscopes, changing emotions like colors and shapes. Grief, anger, hurt, pain, fear, confusion, suspicion, conflict, longing, need, relief, happiness.

'Hi.'

She moved her hand slightly until it covered his. She held her breath. Slowly he turned his hand around until their palms were touching and squeezed her hand, never changing his distant posture on the other side of the car.

They were just turning into the south gate of the White House.

The Secret Service agent turned to speak to her and they pulled their hands away quickly as if they had each touched a hot frying pan.

The usher was waiting at the diplomatic entrance for them and took them immediately upstairs to the family quarters. Blanche was waiting, perched on the sofa in the sitting area nervously thumbing through a fashion magazine. She leaped up when she saw them and ran over to embrace Sadie. She looked a mess. Her platinum hair, usually done up and sprayed to perfection, was loose and tangled, hanging below her shoulders. Her lipstick was worn off and her mascara was smudged under her eyes from crying. Her face was so pale that it made her look like a frightened doll. She was wearing stretch leggings and a cotton pullover. Sadie had to suppress a smile. Blanche did not exactly present the image one normally had of a First Lady.

'Where is he?' Michael, standing next to them, was grim and all business.

'He's in his study. He's been coughing a lot and he's real short of breath. He has a fever. He didn't let me take his temperature but he's burnin' up. And he's sweating like a pig.'

'I'll need to see him,' said Michael, and Blanche led him over to the door that went into the President's private upstairs office. She started to go in with him but Sadie heard Freddy bark out

'Leave me alone with him' and then dissolved into fits of coughing.

Blanche turned back to Sadie, took her by the arm, and led her to the sofa where she collapsed in tears.

'I think he's positive, Sadie.'

Sadie looked shocked.

'How do you know? Did Michael tell him?'

'No, he won't talk about it. All he does is drink himself to sleep at night. But he hasn't touched me since Michael came to see him after the test and he used to be all over me. He's always been real horny but now he just doesn't seem interested at all. Which is just as well since I'd be scared to death. The White House doctors are bound to find out pretty soon. I don't see how we can keep this quiet. What are we going to do, Sadie? What am I going to do?' She started crying again. 'Oh God, what a mess. Just when things were starting to go great.'

Sadie tried to comfort Blanche while her mind raced. Blanche was very convincing. Freddy must have tested positive or else he wouldn't be acting and looking the way he did. This could be a disaster, and one that the country surely did not need. First one President, Roger Kimball, having a stroke and having to resign. Then Rosey assassinated. Now Freddy testing positive for HIV. It was too much. Somehow this thing had to be contained. But how? It was more than she really wanted to deal with now. She would have to discuss it with Michael. If he would discuss it with her.

Michael came out of Freddy's room after about half an hour. Sadie and Blanche were still on the sofa, Blanche puffing nervously on a cigarette.

He walked over and pulled up a chair next to
589

Blanche.

'I think the President has pneumonia,' he said. 'I've told him I'm going to have to examine him, do some X-rays, take a sputum test, and give him intravenous antibiotics. He's going to have to come back with me to the NIH.'

'Is that all you're going to tell me, Michael? said Blanche, her voice shaking.

'That's all I can tell you now. I'm sorry.'

'Goddammit, Michael. I'm his wife. And he hasn't had sex with me since you came to see him after his test, not since his test.' She was extremely upset. 'He won't even talk to me. And you can't talk to me?'

Sadie had never felt so sorry for anybody as she did for Blanche. As much as she herself had been through, at least she had managed to keep her dignity and Rosey had died a hero. This was the ultimate degradation, and so undeserved for Blanche. She also felt sorry for Michael. He was clearly under severe constraints given the doctor-patient relationship and his duty to maintain privacy. But on a human and a political level he was going to come up against it pretty soon. He couldn't just keep this to himself. Michael had some serious decisions to make. Soon it wouldn't be up to just Freddy and him.

He watched Blanche for a moment, then went to her, put his arms around her, and held her while she cried. He was very gentle with her, very tender, and Sadie was reminded once more why she loved him. Beneath the flip, stoic, aloof facade was a person who understood and responded to human suffering.

'Michael, I'm so scared. What are we going to

do?'

'I know how you must feel. I've asked the President to talk to you. I don't think he understands how agonizing it has been for you to be shut out like this. Carrying this burden by yourself. He needs you now, too. As soon as he gets better the three of us will sit down together and figure this thing out, okay? Now I want you to help him get ready. He'll need an unmarked car. Can you arrange this with the Secret Service? If he doesn't want to be recognized you might think of some kind of disguise. A hat or something. Many of our celebrity patients do it. It's not unusual. I'll call my staff and get them set up to receive him. It will be after seven by the time we get there. We can go in through the underground garage and up to an examining room with not much chance of being seen. It shouldn't take more than a few hours.'

'I'm coming with you,' Blanche announced.

'I wouldn't advise it even with a disguise,' he said. 'It will greatly reduce your chances of being able to keep this private. We'll use an assumed name. But if you're with us . . . I just don't see how . . . the clinic is about the least secure place I can think of.'

'Just give me a minute. Sadie, I want you to come with me. I don't want to be alone.'

'There's no way you can keep this under wraps with the three of you walking in there together. The three most famous people in the world. We might as well get the presidential limousine and alert the press corps downstairs and get up a pool.'

'Trust me, Doctor,' she said. 'You go on and make your phone calls, we'll be ready when you get back.'

Blanche grabbed Sadie and dragged her into the bedroom while Michael went to the phone.

When they finally emerged, Michael didn't recognize either one of them. Sadie was wearing one of Blanche's wigs and Blanche wore a mousy brown wig and horned-rim glasses. Freddy came out of his room a few minutes later in a cowboy hat and dark glasses and a long wool scarf covering most of his face.

'I've called the Secret Service,' said Blanche without a smile. 'You and Freddy will go together in his car. Sadie and I will follow in hers. Let's go.'

      ★      ★      ★

Freddy's car led the way with Sadie following. When they reached the Clinical Center at the NIH they pulled into the underground garage. There were two men waiting at the garage elevator with a wheelchair. As they all got out of their cars Michael explained that Freddy would be better disguised if he were in a wheelchair covered with a blanket, holding his head down so that nobody could see his face. Michael also asked that Sadie and Blanche stay back for several minutes and let Freddy and Michael go first. With all the Secret Service it would be too obvious for them to go at the same time.

Freddy was wheeled onto the elevator, which had to be unlocked by the waiting guard since it stopped operating at 7:00 p.m. They watched the two men and the entourage disappear. Shortly after that the other man who had been waiting for them as they arrived escorted Blanche and Sadie up to the floor where they were to examine Freddy. As they

592

walked down the long empty corridors Sadie was amazed at how eerily silent they were compared to how crowded and bustling they had been earlier in the afternoon. She was relieved that, except for one nurse who seemed oblivious to them, they didn't see another living soul. Michael took the President into one small, windowless examining room while the two women waited in an adjoining examining room. Freddy refused to go down to X-ray so Michael had an X-ray machine brought up to him, though he explained that this would not be the optimum care. After the X-ray he gave Freddy an injection of antibiotics, then returned to Blanche and Sadie. He offered to talk to Blanche privately but she wouldn't hear of it and insisted that Sadie stay with them.

'She's my only real friend now and the only one who understands what I'm going through. I'll need her help and advice. Whatever you can say to me you can say to her.'

'Freddy has asked me to tell you the truth,' said Michael, as he took Blanche's hands in his. Sadie swallowed hard. There was no question now what the news was.

'The results of his first test were positive. He had refused to have a second one, although we've just given him another one now.'

'What does that mean?' Blanche's face cracked into tiny lines of anguish, and the tears started coming again.

'It means that he might go for years with no symptoms and never develop AIDS or he could develop AIDS within a year or so. We have no way of knowing. Once we've gotten the results of these tests we'll probably start him on AZT. We'll do an experimental combination of AZT and DDC, which is a cousin of AZT. That will help avoid the emergence of the resistant strain. The two drugs act synergistically, which means they work together. We'll also get him started on aerosolized pentamidine, which he will inhale biweekly.'

'But the campaign. We're right in the middle of the campaign. The convention is only two months away and the election is in November. What are we going to do? Freddy is sure to win the election.'

'I'm a doctor, not a politician,' Michael said. 'I can't advice you on that. I'm sorry.'

'Oh my God,' said Blanche, burying her face in her hands. 'This is just too much for me, Sadie. I can't do this. I just want to go home and forget the whole thing. I never wanted to be here in the first place. I hate being First Lady. I've always felt like an outsider. I know they all make fun of me behind my back. Just wait till they hear about this. I always wished he wouldn't run this time. Now I know he shouldn't. But he'll never drop out of the campaign. I've seen what power does to people in this town. Once they get a taste of it they can't let it go.'

She was beginning to babble.

'Lord,' she said, wiping away her tears and trying to smile. 'Just listen to me carryin' on, and makin' no sense.'

'I'm going to check on the President,' said Michael, 'and then I'm going to send you both home. You need some rest.'

He got up and walked out of the room.

'Sadie,' Blanche said. 'You've got to help me. You've got to tell me what to do. I can't do this without you. I can't do this alone.'

594

*          *          *

It was almost nine when Michael escorted Freddy
down to his car, with Blanche and Sadie following.
Blanche got in the car with Freddy and Sadie
hugged and kissed her. When their car pulled away
Michael walked Sadie to her car.

'Michael, would you, uh, would you like to come
home with me and have supper?' she asked
tentatively. 'I don't want to go home alone. I just
feel like having somebody to talk to.'

What she didn't say was that she really wanted to
be with him, but then, she didn't have to. He knew
it.

'I . . . actually I'm supposed to be having dinner
with the Sokolows. I called them a while ago and
told them an emergency had come up but they said
they'd hold dinner. Maybe they could scrape
enough together for one more. Knowing Judy,
she'll have enough to feed an army. If you could
drive me over to my office, I'll get my coat and call
her from there.'

He jumped into her car and she couldn't help
letting out an enormous sigh of gratitude and relief.
He wanted to be with her, too. She could tell.

A few minutes later he was back with a smile.
Judy not only had enough food, she was thrilled,
they were to come immediately.

Sadie loved the Sokolows but never more than
this night. They were warm and hospitable and
made her feel completely at home. She realized that
she had never been to their house before. It was a
smallish house near American University with a
central hallway and a living room, a dining room,

595

and a kitchen-family room downstairs. It had a round table and French doors that opened onto a deck, letting in the warm spring night air. The table was set there.

They all had a little too much wine, sitting around the candlelit table. The evening was cozy and relaxed and the four of them fell into the same camaraderie they had established at La Samanna. They even let Sadie help clear the dishes and serve the dessert. Nobody ever let her do that and she loved it. She was sick of being treated like a First Lady instead of a friend. This was just perfect. It was also a nice distraction from the sadness of the evening.

After dinner Sid announced that since Judy had done all the cooking he was going to clean up.

'Oh, I'll help,' said Sadie.

'Great,' said Judy. 'That will give me a chance to talk some more with Michael. C'mon,' she said to him, picking up her wineglass and a bottle. 'Let's go out on the deck. It's so nice out tonight.' And the two of them disappeared outside.

Sadie and Sid stayed in the kitchen, where Sid began rinsing the dishes while Sadie scraped and put things away in the ice box. They had taken their wineglasses into the kitchen with them and another bottle of wine. Sadie knew she had had too much to drink but she didn't care. She was enjoying herself for the first time in ages.

When they finished, Sid made no move to join Judy and Michael outside. He poured them each another glass of wine.

As he was refilling hers he looked up at her.

'You're in love with him, aren't you?'

She considered pretending she didn't know what

he was talking about.

'Yes.'

'That's what I thought . . . you know what you're getting into?'

'You mean what I've already gotten into? As my friend Jenny Stern would say, on the oy vey scale of one to ten this is a ten.'

'This is a very complicated guy, Sadie.'

'That was part of the attraction.'

'Was?'

'Is.'

'Of course he's in love with you. I can't blame him for that. But he may not be able to deal with it.'

'Why not, Sid? That's what I don't understand. He is in love with me. He's told me so. I'm not married and now he's separated.'

She paused, not knowing whether to ask the next question. What the hell. They'd had enough wine.

'Why did they separate anyway?'

'They were too young when they married. They just grew apart. It happens.'

That was it. That was pretty much what Michael had told her on the beach at La Samanna. Sid clearly didn't want to discuss it any further.

'Why did she get pregnant?' she couldn't help asking. She had to know.

Sid looked at her, clearly trying to decide whether to say any more.

'I suspect it was just a foolish last attempt on her part to hold onto a dying marriage. But it backfired. Her pregnancy only served to crystallize all the free-floating hostility in their relationship. It blew the whole thing apart.'

'Do you think she'll come back to him?'

597

'I doubt it. But who can tell about those things? I don't think he wants her back. He's in love with you.'

'So what's the problem?' she asked. 'I just don't get it. I've even been to a rabbi for advice. You've got to help me. You're his best friend. You know him better than anyone. I just can't figure him out.'

'Sadie, what's to figure? The guy is scared to death.'

'Of what? I love him.'

'That's not enough. Look. He's fallen in love with you. He's very sexually attracted to you. You are the former First Lady. You're gorgeous, you're very rich, you transcend famous. And you're a gentile. That would be enough to put off almost any man alive. He's just a nice Jewish boy who grew up on the fringes of society. He's afraid he wouldn't be able to live up to your expectations. You live on a different planet. He's worried about getting his kids through college, paying his mortgage, supporting himself in his old age. You live in a rarefied atmosphere where money and society are concerned. You're used to seeing captains of industry, heads of state, movie stars. The whole world is at your feet. There is nowhere you are not accepted, welcomed. And all this you take for granted.'

'But Sid, none of that means anything to me. You must believe me.'

'I'm not sure you know that. You've never lived without it. Do you remember that Italian movie about the beautiful rich woman on the private yacht trip. A member of the crew falls in love with her but she never notices him. She even lets him see her in a state of partial undress because he is invisible to her. Then they are shipwrecked and end up together on a desert island. They fall in love. She wants to stay with him forever on the island, but he is driven to find out if their love will survive once they are back in the real world. Finally they flag a passing ship and are rescued. The final scene is of him sitting on the deck alone watching as she is borne away on a private helicopter, never looking back. This is Michael's nightmare.'

'But this is absurd. I don't know what more I can do to convince him.'

'To allow himself to love you he would be taking an astonishing risk. You know who you are. He can't come to terms with the notion that you wouldn't replace him with a flick of your finger with the slightest change of mood or circumstance. All this is a very complicated way of saying that he doesn't really believe that you could love him, do love him. Before he can do anything about his feelings for you he has got to know that you love him in a way that won't cost him anything. That won't cause him the ultimate pain.'

'How do I do that?'

'You're a woman, Sadie. You'd have a lot better shot at figuring that out than I would. All I can say is that it won't be easy.'

★     ★     ★

Michael had agreed to come in with her for a cup of coffee after they left the Sokolows.

It was clearly a mistake. They were both drunk. Sadie was feeling a little woozy. They decided to go out to the garden for a few minutes until her head cleared. There was still a slight chill in the air even

599

though it was June, and Michael gave her his jacket. Her teeth were chattering, less because of the chill than because she was so nervous. They walked around the yard, chatting about the Sokolows, looking up at the stars. There was a full moon. They stopped by the high stone wall at the back of the garden.

'I'm at the height of my powers tonight,' she told him.

'So what else is new?'

'No, I mean astrologically. I'm a Cancer. Cancerians are ruled by the moon.'

'So that's what they mean when they talk about loony. They're talking about people like you.'

'Oh you,' she said, and gave him a playful shove with her elbow. He stepped back to avoid her jab and she lost her balance. He reached out to catch her and she fell into his arms, pushing him back against the wall.

Before she knew what was happening his mouth was on hers, his hands were grasping at her body. She put her arms around his neck, as much to steady herself as from passion, and clung to him submissively. He was kissing her mouth, her neck, her shoulders. One hand was inside her silk blouse caressing her breast, the other hand reached inside the elastic waist of her jersey skirt, and had found its mark between her legs, then inside her.

She grabbed at his crotch and began to unzip his zipper. There was a frenzied, desperate quality to their passion. They were almost biting at each other rather than kissing; gasping, clawing, grunting, moaning.

'Michael, I can't, we can't do this,' she heard herself saying. Why was she saying this? She

600

wanted nothing more than to make love to him. But there was too much left unspoken.

'It's too late. We're doing it, Sadie Grey.'

He didn't stop kissing her and she felt weak with lust. She was close to coming and her knees were about to give way. Yet she didn't feel right about it. In her drunken state she didn't understand at first but then, as they were sinking to the grass, she realized what the problem was. The only time they had made love before he had been sick, weak, feverish. This time he was drunk. Both times he was not of sound mind. It was as if he needed an excuse, he needed to be out of it in order to have anything to do with her sexually. She didn't want it that way. She wanted him to be sane, rational, sober, and then decide to make love to her.

She was lying on the grass and he was lying to one side, frantically pulling down her skirt and unbuttoning her blouse.

'No, Michael. No. I'm not going to do it this way. It isn't right. Not this way,' she was gasping now.

The moonlight was shining on one exposed breast, her nipple hardened with desire. His pants were down, too, and he was exposed as well, equally hard.

'Oh God, Sadie. You're so beautiful. I want you so,' he whispered and began licking her nipple, using a slow caressing motion with his hands around her abdomen, then between her legs.

She was so close now, so close, she could have let him keep on, she wanted him to keep on but something in her made her stop him.

'Stop, stop, stop,' she cried out, then sat up abruptly and pushed him away, grabbing her blouse

601

around her, pulling up her skirt. She managed to get herself up off the ground and run into the house, leaning up against the door to the family dining room when she finally got in, panting and gasping for breath.

A few minutes later he appeared in the doorway, disheveled and breathless.

They both stood staring at each other, in different doorways, breathing heavily, not speaking.

When their breathing had subsided Sadie spoke first.

'Would you like some coffee?'

'Tea.'

'Twining's English Breakfast or decaf?'

'What is this, a commercial break?'

She burst out laughing. He had managed to relieve the tension, as usual.

She turned and went into the kitchen to put the water on to boil.

He came in and sat down at the end of the table, leaning back on his chair.

She sat next to him, tucking her feet up on the chair, pulling her knees close to her with her arms. She still needed to protect herself from him. They were both a little more sober than before but not a lot. They had obviously both decided not to mention what had just happened.

The water was boiling so she got up, fixed two mugs with tea and milk and honey, and handed one to him.

'You're so domestic,' he said.

She decided to just come right out and say it.

'Is there nothing I can do, Michael? I love you. You've said you love me. How can I make you trust me?'

She had turned serious so quickly it took him aback. He hadn't expected this.

He looked away from her.

'Do you understand how disturbing this is to me?' he asked finally. 'It's making me nuts. I'm in a state of complete chaos. You're everything I've always wanted. You're like heroin to me. The forbidden fruit, you're warm and luscious...'

He got up from the table and walked around the room, running his hand through his hair.

'You're too different. I just don't think it could work.'

'But what about love? If you're in love, nothing else matters.'

'I could never be so much in love that being Jewish wouldn't matter.'

★　　　★　　　★

It was late evening in early July, the day before her birthday, the second anniversary of Rosey's death. Michael had written her, inviting her to have lunch with him that day. He had also apologized in his note for his behavior the evening they had had dinner with the Sokolows. She had called him to accept his invitation, though reluctantly. The conversation was short and awkward. She really didn't want to see him. In fact, she dreaded the lunch. She didn't know what to say to him. She hated the way their last conversation had ended and she didn't see any way he would be able to make it better. She felt they had reached some sort of impasse but she didn't quite know how to deal with it. She still loved him. He still loved her. It, whatever it was, wasn't over, but then it had never really started in the first place. She found herself getting tired just thinking about it. What she really wanted was a break from Michael, from it. She couldn't wait until she left for Long Island that weekend. It couldn't come a moment too soon.

She was upstairs in her dressing room packing some of her things. She had just had an early supper with Willie and Monica in the family dining room and Monica had taken Willie outside in the garden to catch fireflies. The window was open to the patio and she could hear him laughing with delight as he barreled about grabbing at the little lightning bugs. She walked to the window and stood looking out in the twilight at her son and she felt overwhelmed with love and sadness. He really had been her major solace since Rosey died. Without Willie she didn't think she would have made it. If only Rosey could be here to see him grow, even knowing he wasn't his son. If only Des could be here to enjoy these moments. Poor Des. What tragedy he had known. Unable to acknowledge his only son, his newborn daughter dead on Christmas Day, Willie's birthday. His wife grieving so. And poor Willie, with no father. If only there were some way to allow Des more time with Willie without arousing suspicion, without having Allison know. Allison must never know. She had been through too much pain as it was. But maybe seeing more of Willie would help Des. And Willie certainly needed a man around. She was determined, after their summer vacation, to work it out.

She turned to go back to her packing. All of a sudden she heard a bloodcurdling cry, then a shriek, and finally Monica shouting at the top of her lungs.

'Willie! Oh, no. Willie! Oh my God. Sadie, come quick! Oh, no. Oh, please God. Willie!'

Sadie felt her heart drop to her feet. She ran to the window but the light had grown too dim and the shouts were coming from the other side of the house.

She ran down the stairs as fast as she could, nearly tumbling down them. She raced out the door to the patio and around to the side until she reached the stone stairwell to the basement. There at the bottom of the stairwell was Willie.

His arms and legs were twitching in uncontrollable spasms. His eyes had rolled back in his head. Monica was kneeling beside him, screaming his name, but there was no response. Sadie practically leaped down the stairs to her child, afraid to touch him for fear of breaking something. There was no blood. His body had gone totally limp. His face and lips had turned blue. He appeared to have stopped breathing.

'Willie! Willie!' screamed Sadie, grabbing his face in her hands. He was unarousable.

'Oh my God, I think he's dead. Willie! Oh, please. Monica, go get Toby, get an ambulance!'

The Secret Service agents had heard the noise and had run down behind Sadie, before Monica could move.

'We can get him to Georgetown faster than it would take an ambulance to come,' said one of the agents.

He bent down to pick up Willie and she could see that Willie was breathing, but just barely. He was blue and unconscious.

The agent carefully cradled Willie in his arms and rushed him up the stairs and around the corner to the driveway. Sadie ran alongside him, holding Willie's limp hand in hers with Monica right behind her. When they reached the car Sadie and one of the agents got in the back holding Willie. As Monica was about to get in with them Sadie looked up at her.

'Monica,' she said. 'Go call Desmond Shaw. Tell him what's happened. Ask him to meet us at the hospital.'

Monica started to protest.

'Monica,' Sadie said firmly. 'Call him. Please.'

*    *    *

The car must have gone a hundred miles an hour but it seemed to take centuries to get to the emergency room. Sadie was screaming Willie's name at him, and screaming at the agent to hurry up. He had alerted the police and an escort had shown up almost immediately. Sirens were going, the agent was sitting on the horn, they were going through red lights and stop signs, people were scurrying for the sidewalk as they sped by.

Willie, his head on his mother's lap, was like a lifeless doll. Even in the dark, with only the street lamps to illuminate them, she could see the deathly pallor of his face. His mouth was open, slack jawed, and a little drool came out of one corner. She couldn't tell whether he was breathing or not. There was the slightest motion in his chest but not enough to reassure her. He could be dead.

Please, God. You promised. We had a deal. If I believed in you you wouldn't take Willie away. You can't take Willie away. I won't let you.

She pressed her face against his and began rocking back and forth, a primitive sound of pain coming out of her mouth, one she didn't recognize as ever having made. It was halfway between a grunt and a whimper and she repeated it over and over again as she rocked Willie's body, almost like a mantra.

As they pulled up to the emergency room there were several doctors at the door waiting for them with a stretcher and they rushed Willie inside. Sadie was right beside him as they pulled him into a cubicle and began to examine him.

'Tell me he's not dead. Please tell me he isn't dead.' She heard herself say it and then she had the same eerie out-of-body experience she'd had with Rosey, as she had stood over his body asking the same question. She could see in their eyes that they had suddenly focused on the fact that exactly two years ago the president had been assassinated, and now his widow was standing here begging them to tell her her child was not dead.

'Oxygen,' someone was saying as they fitted a mask over Willie's curly head.

'Ringer's lactate,' someone else said and they were sticking an I.V. into Willie's arm.

It had all happened so fast that they really hadn't had time to respond, but she said it again, almost yelling this time.

'Is he alive? Somebody tell me, please, is my child alive?'

There were kind voices and reassuring words. Yes, he was alive. But they needed to hear what had happened.

She explained that he had fallen down a steep

607

stone staircase and had hit his head at the bottom. He became unconscious and limp. She heard someone mention a neurosurgeon and she just stood there helplessly at the end of Willie's bed while they worked on him, unable to hold him or kiss him. She should have made him go to bed after supper instead of chasing fireflies. She was in a rage at Monica for allowing him to fall down those stairs. She wanted him to be laughing on her lap and giving her a big wet kiss on the lips as he was wont to do. And she wanted Des. She needed Des. She couldn't go through this alone.

At least one prayer was answered. Des walked in the door at that moment.

'Sadie,' he started toward her. 'I came as ... what the...'

'Oh Des,' she cried out, running to him and grabbing him. 'Thank God you're here. Willie fell down the stairs and hurt his head and I thought he was dead but now he's breathing and...'

Des held her by the arm but kept walking until he was right at the bed.

'How is he?' he asked, his face etched with fear.

'I'm sorry, sir,' said one of the doctors, who, in the confusion, hadn't seen Sadie greet Des, 'but we can only allow parents here with the child.'

Sadie and Des both froze.

It was Sadie who recovered first.

'This is my son's godfather,' she said firmly. 'As I'm sure you're aware, his father is dead.'

The poor doctor turned bright red and stammered an apology to Des.

'Has he seen a pediatric neurosurgeon?' asked Des.

'I'm sorry,' said another doctor who had

608

introduced himself to Sadie as being in charge of the emergency room that night. 'We don't have a full-time pediatric neurosurgeon on the staff. I suggest he be transferred to Children's Hospital.'

'How fast can we get him there?'

'You've got the police here. They can call for a helicopter. They can have it on the field in minutes. We'll call Children's and alert them.'

'Let's go then.'

As soon as Des began to take charge she almost collapsed.

They both managed to fit in the helicopter and within minutes they were setting down on the roof of the Children's Hospital helipad. She had been so intent on watching Willie, making sure he was still breathing, that she didn't even notice the landing. They were met by a team with a stretcher, taken immediately down on the elevator to the trauma room where the head of the trauma unit and a neurosurgeon were waiting. All of them acknowledged Des with surprise. They had all gotten to know him and Allison when Kay Kay had been there. Nobody asked any questions but Des felt he had to say something.

'I'm the child's godfather,' he mumbled. Everyone nodded. Nobody wanted to intrude.

A physical examination, laboratory tests, and an emergency CAT scan were done on Willie, after which the emergency physician, the radiologist, and the neurosurgeon huddled for a few minutes. Sadie and Des stood by Willie, who was once again fitted with an oxygen mask and an I.V. This time they were both stricken with fear.

Finally the doctors stopped talking and came over to them.

'We've taken a very close look at these films and so far it looks pretty good. The CAT scan shows nothing at all to worry about. It looks perfectly normal. However, we'd like to put him in the intensive care unit for the next twelve hours and observe him.'

Sadie didn't even hear the rest. All she heard was 'normal.' Willie was alive. He was breathing.

They accompanied Willie on his stretcher up to the I.C.U. When the wide double doors swung open she suddenly heard a gasp and a sob and turned to look at Des. His face was shattered with pain and he had covered his eyes with his fists.

'I don't think I can do this again, Sadie. It's too soon. God, I'm sorry. Give me a minute to get myself together.'

She looked at Des and stopped. How could she have forgotten? She had been so selfish, thinking only of Willie and not about what Des had been through. It was only six months since his child had died in this hospital, on this floor. And now here he was back again with another child, one he couldn't even claim, who might be dying.

She put her arms around him and hugged him. He draped his arms around her and they held on to each other for several moments.

'Ah, Holy Mother,' he said, sucking his breath and then heaving it out. 'I think I'll be okay. Let's go in with Willie.'

He had been placed on another bed and assigned a nurse. A doctor explained that his I.V. would be changed to 5 percent dextrose and quarter normal saline and that they were allowed to sit with him. The hospital had made available one of the private parents' rooms, rooms in which Des had already

610

spent too much time.

They decided to wait with Willie. Sadie sat on a chair on one side of the bed holding one hand while Des sat on a chair on the other side of the bed holding the other. Neither one of them talked, but when they did look at each other it was with the understanding of shared suffering. Sadie found herself kissing Willie's hand. Des rubbed his forehead. She was struck again, as always, by how much they looked alike; the shape of the eyebrows, the nose, the square jaw, the full lower lip, not to mention the black curly hair. How could anyone not guess immediately that Des was the father? Probably because it was so out of the question. Willie was the President's son. It wouldn't occur to anyone to think otherwise.

She was devouring his handsome little face when suddenly he moaned and began to move around; he blinked his eyes and opened them for a second.

'Willie, angel. Are you awake?' she was breathless. 'Mommy's here. Mommy's here and I love you.'

'Mommy?' came this tiny, weak voice. 'Mommy?'

'Yes, angel. I'm right here. Mommy's here.'

He started to whimper and then fell back asleep.

The nurse had seen Willie and came over to check on him.

'He's starting to wake up now,' she said and smiled. 'He'll be in and out for the rest of the night. Do you want to go to the parents' waiting room and try to get some sleep? I think he'll be fine. I can get someone to call you if he wakes up again.'

'I think I'll stay here,' said Sadie. 'I don't want him to wake up and be frightened about where he

611

is. But Des, why don't you go and lie down. I'll be okay.'

Des looked relieved but he came around to the other side of the bed and put his hand over hers, the one that was holding Willie's. For just a moment the three hands were entwined.

\*　　　\*　　　\*

The next morning the doctors and nurses couldn't wait to get Willie out of the I.C.U. He was sitting up, wide awake, wiggling, trying to get off the bed, chatting up a storm, so full of energy it was exhausting to look at him. Everyone in the I.C.U. was all smiles at his plucky little grin, at the look of love and relief on his mother's face.

Des couldn't keep his hands off Willie and insisted on carrying him up to Four Blue, where he had been assigned for the rest of the day as a precautionary measure.

Monica, devastated and racked with guilt, had arrived with a few cosmetics for Sadie, tea and coffee for both of them, and a change of clothes for Willie. She was planning to spend the day. There was really no need for Des to say.

He went over to the bed where Willie was playing with a toy Monica had brought him. He picked him up, giving him a huge hug, holding on so tightly Sadie thought he would never let go.

'I'm glad you're okay, ole buddy,' Des said. 'You had your ole man pretty scared there for a while.'

Sadie glanced quickly at Monica but she had not picked up on what Des had said.

'Don't go, Uncle Des.'

'I have to, pal,' said Des, trying to tear himself

612

away.

'Will you come back and roughhouse with me?'
He pronounced it 'wufhouse.'

'Yes, I will. I'll come back and wufhouse with
you. That's a promise.'

Dear Des,

You were wonderful the other night with
Willie and me. I could never have gotten through
that ordeal without you. I know how awful it
must have been for you for so many reasons.
What happened made me realize how important
you are to Willie and to me. There must be a way
that you can play a larger part in his life without
compromising your own situation. You are his
father. He needs you. So do I.

Love,
Sadie

Dear Michael,

I'm sure Monica explained why I had to cancel
lunch. I had such a terrible scare with Willie I
don't think I'll ever get over it.

I've been thinking a lot about you recently.
And about you and me. It's very painful for me
to admit it, but I think you may be right. I don't
think it could work. Even if I could ever manage
to convince you that I love you, I think you
would always be suspicious and that lack of trust
would ultimately cause you to hurt me.

We've talked so much about you in this
relationship. Your pain, your fears, your
conflicts, your needs. I feel as if I've been almost
peripheral. But the fact is this latest episode with

613

Willie reminded me that I've had a great deal of pain in my life, too. I have fears and needs and conflicts, the same as you. But you seem to be so busy concentrating on yourself that there's no room for me. You said, when we first met at La Samanna, that you wanted someone with whom to "share the pain." But you don't want to share mine. You don't want me to share yours. You want it all to yourself. You don't want to share love either. You have never learned to give love or to take love. Until you do, I'm afraid you'll never really be able to make it work with anyone.

It's a shame. Because I really have loved you.

We seem to have been relying rather heavily on Proverbs in our communications. This time around, I think First Corinthians expresses best what I want to say to you.

> Love is patient and kind,
> Love is not jealous or boastful,
> It is not arrogant or rude.
> Love does not insist on its own way,
> It is not irritable or resentful,
> It does not rejoice at wrong,
> But rejoices in the right.
> Love bears all things,
> Believes all things,
> Hopes all things,
> Endures all things.

We don't have that. I'm sorry.

Love,
Sadie

# CHAPTER SIXTEEN

She was having trouble sleeping. She had finally agreed to pills, though she hated being medicated. It was admitting weakness but she was exhausted. She simply couldn't do her work, and without her work she couldn't survive. It was the only thing that kept her going.

Even with the sleeping pills she had terrible dreams. Des would have to wake her because she was screaming almost every night. She would sit up in bed, her body trembling, trying to remember where she was. It was when she remembered that the pain struck, compressing her like a vise, squeezing the life out of her.

Three a.m. That's when it happened. She never got back to sleep after that. If she hadn't gone to bed early enough she would be wiped out for the rest of the day. Fatigue made her depressed. Depression made her drink. The booze and the pills kept her from sleeping all night. Then she could barely function the next day. Around and around and around.

But no matter whether she was rested or tired, drunk or sober, she could never, not for one second of one minute of one hour of one day, forget Kay Kay. Her dead child's image was engraved on the inside of her brain, a scrim she had to look through in order to see the world.

\* \* \*

On this particular Thursday evening in February

she had had too much to drink. She knew it was a mistake. She didn't care. Usually Des would try to keep a lid on her drinking, which she only did after work. Des, who was well known for enjoying his 'wee taste' of Irish whiskey, was hardly drinking at all. Allison, who only drank wine, and then rarely more than a glass or two, was beginning to consume nearly a whole bottle every night. Thursday was the late night at the *Weekly*'s bureau. Des wouldn't be around to put ice and soda in her glass. The ugliest word in any language had become spritzer. She had knocked off a bottle and more or less passed out around eleven o'clock before Des came home. She had begun dreaming right away.

She was on an ocean liner. It wasn't a very beautiful ship. The floors were covered with sewage and garbage. Mold, spores, and fungus grew on everything. She didn't want to touch anything. She tried to find her way out of the mire but everywhere she walked green slime came oozing through her toes. It was horrible and disgusting.

Everyone she loved was on the ocean liner. Her mother, her father, her grandmother, Uncle Rog and Aunt Molly, Des and Kay Kay.

There was also a famous movie star on board. He wanted Allison to sleep with him. He was tantalized by the fact that she wore only sweat pants and no top, leaving her breasts fully exposed. She wanted to have sex with him, too, not because she had any emotional feeling for him. It was pure lust.

Finally he pushed her up against a wall and took her. After it was over he yawned and walked away. She felt dirty.

The ocean liner capsized and it was complete turmoil and she couldn't find anyone. She managed to get out and get on a lifeboat. She thought Des had followed her and was safe. But when she turned around she realized that her whole family, everyone she loved, had gone down with the ship.

Back on land there was a huge parade, with thousands of people lining the streets and in the stands. They were there to welcome back the survivors. Des was supposed to be leading the parade but he had died in the shipwreck. With no one to lead it, the parade was canceled. The crowd became very angry at Allison. They blamed her for the fact that everyone had died. Someone booed loudly at her and then everyone picked up on it. They booed and hissed and screamed, chanting her name in an ominous way. Then somebody threw a rotten tomato at her and hit her in the face. Then more rotten food. Then pails of slop and garbage and sewage. This time she didn't just have it oozing through her toes. This time her entire body, every single pore, was covered with green slime, as the crowd kept up their chant, 'Allison!'

'Allison! Allison! Allison!' Des was leaning over her, shaking her awake.

Her nightshirt was completely soaked, her hair damp and matted. Her teeth were chattering. She was breathing rapidly, as if she had been running very fast.

'Sonny. Wake up. You're having nightmares again.'

She sat up, still half asleep.

'I'm sorry. I'm sorry. I'm so sorry,' she muttered.

'Sonny,' said Des. 'It's all right. It's okay. It's just a dream. It'll be okay.'

He tried to hold her to him but she pulled away,

trembling.

'Oh Des,' she said finally, when her breathing had slowed and her body had quieted down. 'I don't think I can stand this anymore. Nothing works. I drink or don't, I take sleeping pills or don't. I still keep having these horrible nightmares. They're always the same theme. I'm a vile terrible, disgusting person. They stick with me all day, like the green slime in my dreams sticking to my body. I can't get them out of my head. I dread the night so. I don't know what to do.'

'Poor Sonny,' he said. 'Poor Sonny.'

He coaxed her to lie back down and he stroked her head gently.

'It won't help, Des. The only thing that will help is if I have a lobotomy, if they remove half of my brain and destroy my memory. That would help.' She sounded completely defeated.

They lay together for a while. It was very windy outside and the branches of their dogwood tree were hitting up against the back side of the house. The combination of the wind and the brushing noise made it sound as though someone were being beaten and moaning in pain.

'Have you thought of . . . of calling Rachel?'

'I've thought of it. I can't see what good it would be. My baby's dead. A shrink won't bring her back. I would be crazy if I weren't upset.'

'I know that.' He was careful not to sound critical, patronizing. 'I'm talking about the dreams. She might be able to help you figure them out. She might have some exercises to help you get rid of them. That's all I meant. She's really smart and she's helped you before.'

'I don't know. Maybe. Maybe I'll think about it.

I'm just too tired. So very tired.'

\*   \*   \*

She had been to Rachel Solomon before. When she and Des split up the first time, several years ago. It had been a major crisis and she had finally come to the conclusion that she didn't want to buy into the pain anymore. It was a very mature, evolved discovery. Rachel had helped her understand that on some level she had been pushing Des away. She had already lost the three people she loved most in the world. As painful as it was, it was familiar. She was used to it. She didn't know anything else. To lose Des fit into that same old familiar, comfortable pattern regardless of how much anguish it caused.

She adored Rachel. Rachel was wise and caring. She had learned a lot from her. If she had stayed in Washington she probably would have continued to see her. But then she went to London and was traveling so much she never seemed to have the time to get back into therapy. Besides, it hurt too much. She was much better off, she decided, if she could repress the pain. When she came back, she and Des got together right away and it looked as if they were going to have a happy ending. But it seemed that, for her, happy endings didn't exist.

She had thought of seeing Rachel again in the two months since Kay Kay had died. It was the first time she had actively considered it since she had left for London. But as she said to Des, Rachel wouldn't bring back her baby. She had managed to throw herself into her work right after the New Year. Everyone tried to persuade her to take some time off, go somewhere, not rush it. Not rush it?

Where the hell was she supposed to go? What was she supposed to do? Would lying on a beach in Bali eradicate the awful sorrow that was in her soul?

It was only at the office, where she now spent at least twelve to fourteen hours a day, that she wasn't in absolute hell. Even exhausted, even enveloped in sadness, it was the only thing that remotely served as an antidote to her pain. The newsroom was open, busy, noisy, and, late in the afternoon, frenzied. There was no possibility of being contemplative, of thinking about herself, of dwelling on Kay Kay's death.

For this reason she had not called Rachel. She would only have to deal with it if she did. She didn't want to deal with it. She had not cried once since that night in the shower. She had tried to steel herself against thinking about it. She had tried to shove it way back in the recesses of her brain. She did not want to grieve. She did not want to mourn. It was over and done with. It was time to move on. She had to move on to survive. If only she weren't having these horrible dreams.

She also didn't want to be around Des. The only time they saw each other lately was late in the evening or early in the morning. In the evening she was drunk. In the morning she had a hangover. This was just as well because Des was dealing with his grief differently and it was making her extremely angry.

Des had fallen back on his religion. He was getting up early every morning to go to Mass, which he had never done in his life. He had a Bible on his bedside table that he read at night. Sundays he would often go to Mass twice. Several days a week he would meet with a priest he had befriended at

Holy Trinity Church in Georgetown. He talked regularly to his brother on the phone.

If Allison had felt excluded before, she was feeling totally alone now. Not only did she not believe in God, but if there was a God it was Des's God who had taken Kay Kay away. How he could get down on his knees and pray to this evil was beyond her. How he could worship a God capable of, responsible for, this monstrous act was appalling to her. How he could love and look to this hateful God for guidance simply enraged her.

As if this weren't bad enough, while she was fighting fiercely to contain her grief and her emotions, Des was also a basket case. She had never seen him cry before Kay Kay died. Now he cried all the time. He cried during commercials while they were watching the news at bedtime. He cried reading the newspaper in the morning. Every time he mentioned Kay Kay he would cry. He would try to hold on to her in bed at night and he would cry. So far he hadn't tried to make love to her. She didn't think she could bear that. She was devoid of any sexual feeling. The idea of it made her sick. In fact, she didn't really want to be touched by anyone. Des seemed to have just the opposite reaction. He got a great deal of solace out of touching her, embracing her. All she wanted to do was push him away. She felt violated when he tried to put his arms around her. It was as if he were intruding on her privacy, invading the invisible shield she had surrounded herself with in order to protect herself from more pain. Sometimes she felt like screaming at him, 'Just leave me alone. Stay away. Don't inflict your grief on me.' She also didn't want to ever love anyone again. It hurt too

621

much to lose them. As trite as that sounded she understood at the very core of her being that if she were to survive, this was the only way.

She was filled with rage. Everything Des did made her angry. Everything he said sent her into a frenzy of fury. That was one of the reasons she didn't want to be around him. On some level she knew she was blaming him irrationally for Kay Kay's death, as if he really had anything to do with it. It was his God who was responsible and she didn't even believe in him, so she took it out on Des. She just couldn't help it even though she knew it really didn't make sense.

*    *    *

Rachel Solomon was not surprised when she called. She had heard about the baby's death and had written Allison. Allison thanked her politely for the note and made an appointment to see her.

'I'm having these terrible nightmares,' she told her, very matter-of-factly. 'They're keeping me awake and then I'm almost too exhausted to do my work. I really need to find some sort of exercise to get rid of them and I thought you might be able to help.'

Her voice was completely without emotion. It was just this little problem of nightmares, actually. Nothing serious. Maybe a few shrink-type tricks to cure it and everything would be just fine. No problem.

'Let's talk about it,' said Rachel, equally matter-of-factly. Allison did pick up a slightly sympathetic tone in Rachel's voice, which made her uneasy. She did not want sympathy. That was exactly what she couldn't handle.

'I'll probably only need one session,' she said. 'I'm sure that's all it will take to deal with this problem. You know me.' She laughed. 'I'm the original can-do girl. Let's get in there and get this thing solved. Let's not spend five years on the couch.'

'Right,' said Rachel.

Why did Allison get the impression that Rachel was just humoring her? It really did annoy her a little. Maybe it was just her imagination. Maybe she was just paranoid. In any case, they had made the appointment. She would go to see Rachel once. What she didn't tell Rachel was that once was all she would see her.

*     *     *

'Well,' said Allison, very chipper, very in control. 'I guess I'd better start out with the dreams.'

Rachel was sitting across from Allison in her tiny little cubbyhole of an office, all cozy and secure and womb-like. She had forgotten how reassuring that room and Rachel's presence were. Yet now she only felt dread. Dread that she would have to talk about what had happened. Rachel was good at getting her to open up about things she didn't want to deal with. This time she would outwit her. She had braced herself against any of Rachel's overtures. They would talk about the dreams. Period. She was in charge.

Rachel's eyebrows were turning downward, a sign of concern. She didn't say anything. She just looked at Allison. Allison felt as if Rachel had X-ray vision. She didn't want anyone to look inside her

623

just now, so she avoided Rachel's gaze.

She told Rachel the dream about the ship and the slime, everyone blaming her. Rachel was writing it all down on a yellow pad.

'So. What do you make of it? What does it all mean, Coach?'

Rachel looked at her again with that damned compassionate look.

'How are you, Sonny? You've just been through an enormous tragedy. What you've been through is very, very hard.'

Allison suddenly felt very lightheaded and slightly nauseated. She couldn't decide whether she was going to faint or throw up. She could feel the blood drain from her face, her breath quickened. Her hands grasped the arms of the chair. She closed her eyes and leaned her head against the back of the chair. She had to get a grip. Rachel was trying to do it to her again. To bring it up. She wasn't going to let her. Very clever, the way she had done it, too.

It seemed like hours before she managed to speak. Strangely, she hadn't felt like crying. She felt dead inside. Nevertheless, Rachel had stirred something. It didn't feel good either.

With her eyes still shut, she spoke very softly in a dull voice.

'I can't do this, Rachel. I don't want to do this. I don't have the strength for it. It's a matter of survival. If you want to help me, then help me with my dream. Tell me what it means. If you do anything more I promise you I will get up and leave. Tell me what the dream means and maybe if I understand it it will stop.'

She hadn't opened her eyes. She just sat there very quietly, waiting.

'It's not unusual for parents of deformed, disabled, or handicapped children to have a death wish for their children,' Rachel said softly. 'They wish their children were not that way. They wish they would die. When you realized Kay Kay was brain-damaged you wanted her to die. It's one thing to wish it to happen. It's quite another to make it happen. In your case you were forced to make it happen. You decided for her to die. Now you can't help but feel you are a terrible person for not wanting a vegetable for a daughter. You feel you are a terrible person for making her die. You feel you are a terrible person because the people you have loved the most have died. You feel maybe you have been responsible for their deaths. You feel you must be punished because of it.'

There was another long silence. Allison still did not move, still kept her eyes closed.

'Right,' she said after a while. 'That makes sense. Even though rationally I know that I am not responsible for everyone's death, sub-consciously I have taken the blame. Even though Des and I made the decision along with all the doctors and the board of ethics and even though we clearly had no choice, I am taking the blame for Kay Kay's death, too. I know I'm not to blame but I can't help feeling like a terrible person.'

Her voice had a stilted, even, zombielike quality as she recited her little catechism.

She opened her eyes and sat up in her seat.

'Thank you,' she said to Rachel. 'That helps. That's exactly what I needed. Now we'll just have to see.'

She got up and put on her coat, grabbed her bag, and walked to the door. Rachel hadn't moved.

625

Allison turned to look at her. Rachel's eyebrows were down around her chin.

'I'll call if this doesn't work,' said Allison, 'and insist on my money back.'

★    ★    ★

It was a Monday and a very slow news day. Nothing was happening. It meant she had time to think. That was not acceptable. Total distraction was her only means of survival. She had had her morning meeting with the national staff and she was looking for a lunch date. She walked out of her office and surveyed the newsroom. She needed to find the right person. Too often lately she'd ended up at lunch, ostensibly to talk about work, and the person she was having lunch with would bring up Kay Kay. They would inevitably get teary and maudlin and she would have to cheer them up. She could do it but it wiped her out emotionally, and she found that it exhausted her physically as well. She hadn't figured it out at first. She would have one of these lunches and then collapse by the time she got to story conference at 2:30. She had recently fallen asleep at a story conference. It was especially puzzling because she hadn't been having the shipwreck dream since the session with Rachel. It was only after the third or fourth time it happened that she made the connection. Nobody ever mentioned Kay Kay in the office. It seemed that didn't follow protocol. But just have a bloody cup of tea in the cafeteria with someone and it was the first thing they brought up. Once she got the picture she began getting Walt to speak to her lunch dates beforehand to warn them off. Even so, there were still people who couldn't help alluding to it. Especially the women. They were the criers, too.

She spotted Sprague talking to the foreign editor. She hadn't really talked to him since the night Kay Kay was born. He and Jane had sent food and flowers to the house and they had both written notes. Sprague's note surprised her. It was long and very personal, steeped in emotion and a sense of the tragic that Southerners seemed given to. There was also something chivalrous about it. It was as though he felt it his personal duty to protect her from anymore pain, honor bound to throw an emotional cloak over the mud puddle for her to step on. She had never seen that side of him. What she got, what everyone at the *Daily* got, was the stoic, steely, distant warrior. Sprague, she often thought, was the journalistic equivalent of a samurai. Honor bound, single-minded, focused, deceptively gentlemanly ... and a killer.

Perfect for lunch. He wouldn't cry, for one thing. And he was sure to distract her, for another. She had yet to have a conversation with him since he had come to the *Daily* where they hadn't fought or argued or where she hadn't gotten mad at him. He wouldn't fail her now.

More important, Sprague had just come back from Colombia, this time a trip she had vetoed. She had thought it too dangerous and she had not been wrong. An American freelancer doing a television documentary had been kidnapped in Bogotá a few weeks earlier and had not been heard from. She would have to debrief Sprague and dissuade him from another trip.

She had never had lunch with Sprague. He didn't do lunch. This time he would. She'd like to see him try to refuse her now. The bastard.

She waited until he had returned to his desk, then walked over to him. He was reading some sort of document. She didn't say anything. She just stood next to him until he looked up at her.

'Lunch?' she asked.

'What time?'

'Twelve-thirty.'

'Meet you at the elevator.'

She went immediately to Walt in triumph. it was the first moment of pleasure she had had in two months.

'Guess who I'm having lunch with?'

'Sprague.'

'How did you . . . ?'

'I saw you talking to him. Besides, you wouldn't have bothered to tell me about anyone else.'

'I needed someone to fight with today and you looked too nice.'

'Shall I give him the usual prelunch briefing?'

'Are you kidding? Of course not. Why do you think I picked him?'

'Sorry. Of course you're right. Do you have an agenda?'

'Drugs. I haven't really had a chance to talk to him about where he is in all of that since . . . since . . . Anyway, I'm sure he'll have some outrageous request that I'm going to have to veto and the fur will fly. At least that's what I'm hoping. I'm really in the mood today for a little combat. I can't take it out on Des anymore. So Sprague will do just fine.'

'Is everything okay with you and Des?'

Walt's flippant tone had altered.

'Oh, sure. Everything's fine. It's just that we tend to take everything out on each other. You

628

know. I guess it's inevitable.'

'Anything you want to talk about?'

She hesitated. 'I don't think so really. But thanks, Walt. I know if I need somebody to talk to I can come to you. That's a big help . . .'

She looked at her watch. 'Oh Christ, it's almost twelve-thirty. I've got to go. I think we'll go to The Palm. If I'm not back for story conference, call the rescue squad.'

\*　　\*　　\*

The Palm. It was a man's restaurant. Actually, it was a guy's restaurant. If she had to go head to head with Sprague she had to be one of the guys. No fancy French restaurants with fresh flowers and sycophantic waiters. She wanted rude waiters so she could be rude back. Demonstrate her toughness. She wanted to eat a man-sized steak or veal chop, something that needed cutting with a real knife, not some sissy knife. Sprague had gone to the Citadel. He was a military man. He had managed to intimidate all of the male editors at the *Daily*. He would do the same to her if she let him. But she was not going to. She wanted Sprague to see her as his equal. What hadn't occurred to her was that Sprague, who was not only an 'officer' but a 'gentleman,' would not be seeing her as an editor he had to take on, but as a woman whose baby had just died.

Allison was puzzled. Sprague wasn't acting as he usually did, confrontational. He practically held her chair out for her. Solicitous.

They had been seated right near the entrance at a round table in the center of the room so they could be seen. They were a hot-ticket item that day, she realized. They both ordered sparkling water.

'To what do I owe this honor?' he asked after the waiter had disappeared.

'We haven't had a chance to talk about your project for a while,' she said. 'I thought I ought to catch up. You'll be thrilled to know that I'm back on your case.'

'Great.'

She couldn't read him. Was he being sarcastic? She didn't think so.

The waiter approached them.

'Okay folks. What'll it be?'

It seemed so intrusive today when usually it was amusing and fun. She realized she had made a mistake with the choice of restaurants. The Palm was great for its ample food, cheeky waiters, and rough, noisy barroom atmosphere. Usually she enjoyed the paintings of local celebrities—hers and Des's included—on the walls, and the glad-handing of the insider lawyers, journalists, and politicians. It just wasn't what she needed now. She needed someplace quiet. She needed a womb-like atmosphere. She sensed that Sprague felt the same way.

'It'll be another table,' she said to the waiter. 'Like one of those booths in the very back, preferably with nobody on either side of us. I don't think it will be a problem. It looks like a slow day.'

He seemed unhappy about her request but acquiesced when he saw she was serious. Sprague didn't say a word but she could tell he was pleased. Once they were seated he suggested they order immediately so they could dispense with the waiter.

'I'll have whatever you're having,' she said. 'I

don't really care what I eat.'

She hadn't meant to sound hopeless but it was there, oozing out of her. She hadn't meant to arouse his sympathy, to allude in any way to what had happened. Nevertheless, he had picked up on it and cast a questioning glance at her.

'Thank you for your note,' she said. 'It was . . . beautiful.'

What was she doing? This was exactly what she had been trying to avoid.

'You sound surprised.'

'I was, a little, to tell you the truth. I just hadn't seen that side of you before. You don't talk all that much. At least to me.'

'"The deepest feeling always shows itself in silence; not in silence, but restraint"—that's a line from one of my favorite poems.'

They both seemed slightly embarrassed. She cleared her throat.

The waiter appeared to take their orders: veal piccata, home fries, fried onions, and creamed spinach. She nearly gagged at the idea of eating all that food.

'So,' she said, trying to sound as brisk and full of enthusiasm as she could, 'where are we in the saga of Foxy and Antonia Alvarez? Not to mention Mendez, the distinguished Foreign Minister of Colombia, my new favorite person.'

'I'd say it's more like the saga of Sprague and Jane.'

'What?'

'I've had to send Jane and Melissa back to Savannah.'

'Oh, Sprague, I'm sorry. I had no idea you two were having problems.'

631

'We aren't.'

'Then why . . . ?'

'I've had a threat on my life. I've gotten a message that unless I lay off this story my life and that of my family will not be worth that of a "mule." That's the way the cocaine cowboys describe the little guys who do the small deals for the big guys. A "mule's" life expectancy is jack shit in case you're interested. They're always getting blown up by car bombs.'

She suddenly thought she was having a panic attack . . . the same symptoms she'd had at Rachel's, the dizziness, the cold sweats, the nausea. Once again, she leaned her head back, this time against the wooden booth. Someone else was going to die. Someone else she cared about.

Sprague? She cared about Sprague? She certainly found him attractive and interesting, there was no question about that. But would she be terribly upset if anything happened to him? Her throat constricted. Yes. She would. The realization of the fact shocked her. Could it be that she just couldn't bear the idea of anyone else dying? It could, but it wasn't. It was Sprague. She cared about Sprague. It was that simple.

She waited a second to steady herself, then took a sip of water. Just then the waiter appeared with their food. She didn't think she would be able to swallow even a bite.

'What kind of a threat?' she asked, after the waiter had left. She thought she sounded pretty cool. She didn't want him to know how upset she was.

'Telephone. Over a period of several nights. Three a.m. to be exact. The phone would ring. Jane

632

answered. It was always a man with a German accent. He would tell me what I had been doing. For instance, I was up at Justice two weeks ago and met with Foxy's righthand guy for about an hour. He told me about that. He told me practically everyone I had talked to on this last trip to Colombia. He even knew about my meetings with Garcia. I've been meeting him for lunch at this Mex joint called Jaimalitos on the Georgetown waterfront. Garcia is my Deep Throat at the DEA. He would shit if he knew we were being followed.'

'Have you noticed anyone following you?'

'No, but it doesn't matter. When I knew they were serious was when they gave me Melissa's schedule, including her gymnastics.'

'Oh my God.'

'The point is that they know what I'm doing and how close I'm getting. I've almost got it nailed that Foxy is on drugs and being blackmailed by Antonia and the Foreign Minister, their chief money launderer. They don't like it.'

'What makes you think they're serious about the threat?'

'They've done it before. They own one of the small islands down in the Bahamas called Jenkins's Cove. Some guy who owned a house on the island got suspicious and started making trouble for them, calling the Nassau police and contracting the Nassau papers. They threatened him and he didn't back off so they blew up him and his wife and two kids. Oil fire on their boat. Nothing left but one tiny orange life jacket. "Tragic accident" is how it was reported.'

'How do you know?'

'They told me and I checked it out. It's true.'

She closed her eyes.

'Have you told anyone else?'

'You're the first. I wanted to get Jane and Melissa out of here and get them to a safe place. They're in hiding.'

'But why? You're obviously not going to stay on this story, are you?'

'You're fuckin' A.'

'Sprague. They'll kill you. And they could track down Jane and Melissa, too.'

'I'm not going to let a bunch of cowboys intimidate me. They've got to be stopped. Somebody has to do it. If I don't now, when I'm in a position to, it's just going to get harder and harder.'

'I don't care. I will not have one of my reporters risk his life over a stupid story. It's not worth it.'

'Is this the same editor who couldn't wait to send me off to Colombia?'

'You're fuckin' A.'

'Ally! Does this mean you care?'

She was stunned. It was so un-Sprague-like. For one thing, he had never called her Ally before. In fact, nobody had ever called her that. Sonny had always been her nickname. She couldn't tell from his tone whether he was mocking her or not. Only his eyes had a glint of humor. What did he mean? What was he asking for? It couldn't be what she thought. Not given the circumstances.

'I care about all of my reporters. It's my job.' She hoped he didn't notice how nervous she was.

Was there a flicker of disappointment in those eyes this time?

'Ah. The consummate editor.'

'Speaking of which, we've got to get back to the

634

office and discuss this immediately with Alan and Walt. I can't eat, anyway. This conversation has not done much for my appetite.'

She noticed he had cleaned his plate.

'Funny, I'm just the opposite,' he said with a grin. 'Danger always improves my appetites.'

She couldn't be sure whether he had added the 's' or whether she had just imagined it.

★　　　★　　　★

They got back from lunch just as the gong sounded for story conference. She didn't have a chance to discuss anything with Alan and Walt beforehand except to tell them she had to see them.

As soon as the meeting was over she signaled Sprague and Walt and they all went into Alan's office.

Sprague looked ashen as he walked in and she noticed that he was carrying a small package.

'Sprague's life has been threatened,' she blurted out before anyone could speak. She realized that she was visibly upset even though she was making a special effort to stay cool. She had to be professional about this.

Alan and Walt looked at her, then at Sprague. He did not refute her.

'How do we know the threat is real?' asked Alan.

Sprague threw the package on Alan's desk.

'This just came in the mail.'

Alan opened the package. Inside was a small coffin fashioned out of balsa wood, the kind used to make model airplanes.

'What else?'

Allison was always amazed at how calm,

635

measured, and rational Alan was under pressure. Sprague told Alan and Walt what he had told her at lunch.

'Well, I think that's evidence enough that the threat is real,' he said. 'Sprague, you've been dealing with these jokers for several years. I'll trust your instincts. Still, before we make any decision about how to proceed, I'll like to have you and Allison sit down with Garcia at the DEA and tell him what's going on. Get his response.'

'He's not going to be too thrilled about meeting with an editor. He's already getting squeamish about me. If Foxy got wind that he was leaking to me he'd be in deep shit. And I don't just mean out of a job.'

'Well, try him. If Allison determines that this stuff is real I probably ought to speak to him myself. We've got to take this seriously. These guys don't fuck around.'

Just then Alan's secretary stuck her head in the door.

'Sorry to disturb you, Mr Warburg,' she said, 'but the head phone operator is on the line. She wants to speak to you.'

Alan nodded, picked up the phone, and grunted an acknowledgement. When he hung up he looked grim.

'One of the operators has just received a bomb threat. They say they'll blow up the *Daily*.'

'How seriously do we take that, Tyson?' asked Walt.

'We can't dismiss it, though it's unlikely. If I had to guess I would say it's more of a nuisance threat. The threat against me, however, I take very seriously.'

'What are we going to do?' asked Allison.

'We'll handle the two cases separately,' said Alan. 'We'll beef up the security around here; make sure the guards take extra precautions but nothing more. As far as you're concerned,' he turned to Sprague, 'do you want off the story?'

'No way.'

'You're sure?'

'Absolutely.'

'I can't order you off a life-threatening story, Tyson. But I'm not interested in heroics. If you insist on pursuing this we'll have to get you round-the-clock armed security guards; extra life insurance. You may want to stay in an apartment or hotel. I'm not sure you should drive your own car. You've got to let us be more aware of your movements. And I want to be convinced in my own mind that Jane and Melissa are safe.'

'I feel pretty sure they are,' said Sprague.

'Okay. I'm going to call Sam the Superlawyer and see what advice he's got. He may have some ideas about the FBI we could use. Walt, would you check with foreign and some of the other beat reporters to see if they've got any thoughts? There may be some contacts out there with information we could pursue, people we could get to persuade them that this is a rotten idea.'

As they walked out Allison asked to see Sprague alone.

She was aware as they walked back to her office, that the whole newsroom was watching them. Reporters had an uncanny sense of something important going on. She was in and out of Alan's office, sometimes with Walt, every day. Yet somehow they knew that this was big. She could see

637

them begin to cluster. Even if she and Walt and
Alan and Sprague never said a word about it, like
magic, the story would be out within a day,
absorbed like osmosis into their pores.

She shut the door, sat down, and turned to
Sprague.

'Okay. Now what?'

'I want to go to the Bahamas.'

'Sounds terrific but is this really the time to take
a vacation?'

He laughed. 'On assignment.'

'I can tell I'm not going to like this.'

'I want to go check out Jenkins's Cove.'

'I knew it. Sprague, that's insane. You'd have no
protection down there at all. You'd be a sitting
duck, what could you possibly learn? They'd never
let you on the island and even if they did you'd
never get off alive. You've been reading too many
spy novels. I never thought I'd say this but why
don't you go back to Colombia?'

'This is radical.' He laughed. She got the distinct
impression that he was enjoying this, that he was
teasing her with it.

'I don't think it would be useful right now to go
back to Colombia. I'm not really making any new
contacts the way I did in the beginning. When I
first went down there I could talk to anyone, go
anywhere. I had a grand ole time. Now they're
beginning to notice me. I'm too visible and my
sources are going underground. Most of them are
journalists anyway. They've all got horror stories
they don't dare print because they're afraid of being
killed or kidnapped. They feed them to me, I run
them, then they boost my stories by quoting the
*Daily*. But even they have gotten more confidential.

638

Medellin is too dangerous. I'm just not going to have much success working in Colombia right now. That's why I want to try Jenkins's Cove. At least if I sail there and observe from the water for a few days I can get some idea of the scale of the operation.'

'Can you at least wait until we've met with Garcia?'

'I can. In fact, I'll go set that up right now.' He stood up to leave, then turned to her. 'By the way, how do you feel about Mexican food?'

'It's too spicy.'

'Your problem is you have no adventure in your soul.'

'I used to.'

It had started as a teasing remark and she had meant to keep up the light tone. Her response startled her as much as it did him and reminded her that she had actually been distracted enough to forget about Kay Kay for a short time. But when she said it she could see a look of sympathy cross his face. She wondered if the pain she felt showed on hers.

'Oh, Allison, I'm sorry.'

'Me, too.'

He stood looking at her for a moment, then left and walked back toward his desk.

Walt stuck his head in her office.

'Got a sec?' He came in before she answered and shut the door.

'We're going to have to have a little conference about Sprague. This is a nasty business. It is also a major story that could topple the government. It's bigger than Sprague now. Alan doesn't show it but he's worried as hell. So am I. Sprague is a cowboy himself. He could be in a lot of trouble.'

'I know. I was thinking the same thing. But now it's not just Sprague. It's the whole paper. Why don't we get him and a couple of the other investigative reporters who are working on Justice, the White House, and DEA and their editors and meet at my house one day? I think we've got to brainstorm this. We've also got to work as a team. Up until now everyone has been acting as a free agent. I don't like it. I don't feel we have a handle on it. I need to get an idea of what's going on and who's doing what and who knows what before the whole thing gets out of control.'

'Great idea. Do you want to set it up?'

'Yes. And Walt?'

'Yeah?'

'Let's line up those security guards for Sprague. I don't want to lose anyone . . . else.'

\*　　　\*　　　\*

Des had suggested they go out to dinner. That was going to be a million laughs. Des had given up booze for Lent. It had been almost a month now since he'd had a drink. It wasn't working out too well for them since Allison was smashed by her second glass of wine every night.

During the day she was an emotional robot. As the evening approached she would begin to unravel. By the end of the second story conference at 7:30 she was close to losing it. She never did. By some miracle she had managed to cauterize her feelings. She had always heard about this out-of-body experience, this numbness, but had never believed it. Now she understood how people managed to sustain tragedies. Their minds put up shields to protect them from the pain. Rachel called it denial, telling her once she had no capacity for it. She had asked for tricks to learn it. Now she didn't need tricks. It just happened.

Somewhere in the back of her brain there was a part of her that wanted to mourn, wanted to remember Kay Kay. When she drank she had more of a connection to those parts of herself. The booze didn't unleash any emotions, but it allowed her to relax a little and helped her to sleep. She wasn't having those terrible dreams anymore. Now the dreams were of her and Kay Kay floating on clouds. Kay Kay was round and plump and pink and she held her in her arms. It was silent and tranquil and serene and they were both happy. She loved going to sleep. She loved to drink so she could go to sleep and have her dreams. She still hadn't cried since the day Kay Kay died.

She got home before Des did and poured herself a large glass of white wine. It was after eight, too late for the news. She was not in the mood to be intellectually challenged. The tension at the *Daily* over Sprague and the threats was getting to her. He was still trying to convince Garcia to meet with her and he was still insisting on going to Jenkins's Cove. Meanwhile he had gotten round-the-clock security guards and was very much on the story. Everyone in the building knew about the bomb threats and it had the whole newsroom, including her, on edge. They believed the threats were nuisance threats but no one could be sure.

Des had heard about it and asked her what was going on. She had told him as much as she could. It was hard not to be able to talk to him about it, but he was from another news organization and she couldn't really trust him not to divulge anything. She had been spending more time with Sprague because they could confide in each other. She could tell he was lonely without Jane and Melissa. He had started calling her at night when Des was there to talk about the story. Often it was something that could have waited until the next day. Des was getting pissed. He hated it when she got up and went into another room to talk. Their professional competitiveness had always been a problem. She scooped him years ago, then humiliated him by letting him get the story wrong. They had broken up over it and Allison suspected he had never really forgiven her. Now when there was a story the *Daily* was working on and she couldn't talk about it, it only opened the old wound.

The evening phone calls, in fact her whole relationship with Sprague, made it difficult for her. She felt responsible for him, she worried about him, but more than that she needed him.

She couldn't talk to Des about Kay Kay. Des couldn't stand Allison's way of dealing with it—drinking, overworking, her refusal to mourn. Allison couldn't bear Des's self-indulgent wallowing in pain. With Sprague she didn't actually talk about it but his letter had made it possible for her to allude to her feelings. It was an odd about-face from their adversarial relationship. They had become each other's protector.

★        ★        ★

She had just settled in to this stupid TV show when the front door opened downstairs and she heard

Des come in. He was talking to someone. She heard a woman's voice respond and they both laughed. He hadn't mentioned bringing anyone home with him. She felt particularly annoyed that he would presume to inflict someone on her without discussing it first. She was feeling antisocial. She just wanted to get something to eat quickly and go to bed with her dreams.

When they got to the top of the stairs he called her name.

'Sonny! Sonny, I've got someone here to see you.'

She didn't get up. She waited until they walked into the study. Des came in first, an excited but wary smile on his face. Behind him, looking even more apprehensive, was Jenny.

She hadn't seen Jenny since the baby. Jenny had written her a long letter asking to be friends again, but she hadn't answered it. She hadn't answered any notes. To answer them was to deal with it. She was still ambivalent about Jenny. She knew Jenny was free-lancing and still looking for a job. She felt guilty about that but she still felt Jenny had betrayed her. She knew Jenny hadn't really had a choice, yet she had never forgiven her for breaking off their friendship. She wasn't angry anymore. She just didn't trust her. So she was surprised at her own reaction now. She was glad to see her. Jenny was her best friend, her only real friend. It had been very lonely without her.

'Jen, how 'bout a drink?' Des asked before either of them spoke.

'Oh, great. That would be great. A glass of white wine?'

'Easy. It's already opened.'

643

Was that a reproach? My, how the tables had turned. Or was she just a little sensitive?

He poured Jenny a glass of wine and handed it to her. Then poured himself a diet soda.

'I, for my sins, am off the sauce for Lent.'

'What a revolting custom.' Jenny laughed. 'Lent always reminds me I'm glad to be Jewish.'

'I couldn't agree more,' said Allison. There was just the tiniest edge in her voice.

'I'm going upstairs to get a sweater,' he said quickly. 'I'll be right down.'

'God, I hope I didn't offend him,' Jenny said, after Des had left the room.

'No. I did.'

They looked at each other.

'I've missed you, Sonny. You're still my best friend, you know.'

Allison took a sip of her wine. She didn't know quite how to respond.

'What about Sadie?'

She might as well bring it up. Taboo subject that it was.

'She's one of my closest friends, probably the closest after you. But you and I have known each other much longer.'

'This last year and a half hasn't exactly been the happiest time for your two friends, has it?'

'Sadie was extremely upset about . . . about Kay Kay's death.'

'I got her note.'

'You would like her.'

'It's not to be.'

Her voice was firm but her tone was resigned rather than bitter.

'How are you, Sonny? I worry about you. You're

644

driving yourself.'

'I'm fine.'

She got up to pour herself another glass of wine and found that she was weaving slightly. Only a few more hours and she would be asleep in her bed.

'Thank God for my work,' she said, stretching out on the sofa. 'It's been my salvation. It's Des I worry about. He's more and more unhappy at the *Weekly*. I'm afraid he's going to take a hike any day now. He's bored and unfulfilled and he thinks the whole team in New York is a bunch of social-climbing assholes. Without his work to fall back on he's suddenly gotten religion in a big way. It's really scary, Jen. He's turning into somebody I don't know. This Catholic thing is like a cult, like the Moonies. He goes to Mass every morning. I feel like I can't communicate with him anymore. And we can't talk about Kay Kay. It's too painful for both of us. He gets teary and I get angry and the whole thing is a disaster.'

She had been rattling on.

'I don't believe it. What am I doing laying all of this on you? You walk in the door and get mugged. I'm sorry. It's just that I don't really have anyone else I can talk to about Des.'

'That's what I'm here for, Sonny. I love you and I love Des and you know I will be loyal.'

She had forgotten how good it felt to have a woman friend she could confide in, someone she could trust.

'What am I going to do about Des, Jen, before the body snatchers come and take him away?'

'You know he's just as worried about you, don't you? He says the only thing that's gotten him through is his religion. The fact that you don't

645

believe the things he believe worries him because you have nowhere to turn for solace. Have you seen Rachel?'

'Once. It helped a little. I was having some bad dreams and after talking to her about them, figuring them out, they went away. But I don't need a shrink. I know what the problem is. I would be crazy if I weren't sad. I'll be fine. Really. It will just take some time. The question is, will I be able to stand being married to a religious nut? The answer is, I'm not so sure.'

'He really loves you. This is always a hard time for people, for couples who lose a child. I do volunteer work in the oncology section at Children's Hospital now. A surprising percentage of the parents whose children die split up. The just can't take the stress on the marriage and it affects each person in a different way. One partner will resent the way the other one handles his or her grief. They have nobody to take out their anger on except each other. It's a double tragedy. Don't let it happen to you and Des. You're both strong people and you love each other. You need each other to get through this. Don't try to be superwoman, Sonny. It won't work anymore. You've gone beyond that now. Let yourself grieve. You'll work through the pain a lot faster if you do. It will help your friends, too, you know. It's awfully hard on everyone to watch you suffer so.'

'That was quite a speech. Have you been saving it up?'

'Yes, actually. It's taken me a while to get my courage up.'

They could hear Des coming down the stairs.

'We'll talk more later,' said Jenny.

'Promise?' said Allison.

Jenny looked as if Allison had slapped her in the face and Allison realized that she had sounded sarcastic. She hadn't intended to.

She looked up at Jenny and gave her a reassuring smile just as Des walked into the room.

'Uh oh,' he said. 'What are you two girls cooking up? I'm not so sure I'm in favor of this renewed friendship anymore. It could be dangerous for me.'

'It will be if you keep calling us girls,' said Allison.

'God you're tough, both of you. I'm outnumbered and I haven't even had a drink. What chance do I have?'

'Not much if you don't take us out to eat,' said Jenny. 'I'm starved.'

\*       \*       \*

Allison was practically blotto when they got home. She staggered around the bathroom struggling to get undressed, get her nightgown on, and get her makeup off. Finally she gave up, stripped down, and collapsed into the bed, the merciful bed, and completely gave herself up to it.

Des climbed in and snuggled up behind her reaching his arm around her waist. This had always been their usual sleeping position until Kay Kay had died. After that she didn't want to be near him, near to anyone, and she had been making excuses every night about why she needed space on her side of the bed. She had even put pillows between them to prevent him from touching her. She could tell it upset him and hurt him but she couldn't help it. She simply couldn't bear the idea of being close to

647

him. Part of it was her anger and her need to take it out on someone. Des was convenient because he was there and he believed in God. But there was a much more compelling reason. She had decided she couldn't allow herself to be close to anyone, ever again. The pain of losing them was too great. She had loved Des and she had let herself become dependent on him, physically, psychologically, emotionally. She had allowed herself to have faith in their love. It had not been easy for her. She had had to learn to trust. Trust that the person she loved wouldn't die, wouldn't desert her. She had had to overcome her fear. Letting herself love completely was like the old acting class exercise where you have to fall backward and trust the person behind you to catch you. She had done that, first with Des, then by getting pregnant. That was the greatest act of faith of all. To have a child was surely too open yourself up to the possibility of more pain than anyone could imagine. Yet she had done it willingly, believing that fate couldn't possibly deal her another blow, that if there was a God he had already punished her enough. She had been wrong. She had suffered the worst anguish a person could suffer. She had lost her child. Now she had to discover a way to survive. And she had. She would never love again. That meant, of course, that she had to start distancing herself from Des. This was painful because she needed him now more than ever. It was exactly that need that sent her into a state of terror. It was even more painful watching Des suffer. First over the loss of Kay Kay, now over losing her. It broke her heart watching him, night after night, trying to hold her, comfort her, and comfort himself. Night after night she rejected him. She knew he thought she was just having a difficult time, and eventually things would get better. He didn't realize and she couldn't tell him that things would only get worse. She was strong, but not strong enough to do it all at once. That's why it was gradual. She needed time to wean herself away from his love, his touch, her need.

It surprised her, then, that it felt so good having his arms around her like that. It must be because she was so drunk. She hadn't made love to him, hadn't even been naked in bed with him, since Kay Kay died. Three months now. It had been a cold winter, a good excuse to wear long nightgowns, a good way to keep a barrier between them. She knew he had wanted to make love to her but had not made a move. For the first two months she had not been completely free of pain. In the last few weeks he had tried to press up against her and she could feel him getting hard. Sometimes he disappeared into the bathroom and stayed for a while and she knew he was taking care of his need. She tried to pretend she didn't notice. She didn't want to notice because then she would have to do something about it.

Now she felt him very hard against the back of her thighs. His hand had begun to move, first up to her breasts, cupping them, caressing them, then down her stomach, between her legs, stroking her, then back up to her breasts. He continued this circular motion, rotating his hand back and forth, up and down. It was so soothing, so comforting, so wonderful to be held like this again, to be enveloped like that. In her drunkenness she wondered how she could have wanted to reject him. She was overwhelmed with a sudden need to be loved. She seemed to have been temporarily stripped of her protective armor. Her eyes were closed and the room was pitch black and she lay there in a half-drunken, half-dream-like state letting herself be stroked. If she could only just die like that, right now. If only they could both just die like that together, lying there, loving each other, then she would never have to worry about pain again.

He began to kiss her. He kissed her shoulders and her neck, then pulled her over so that she was lying on her back and kissed her mouth.

She raised her arms up over her head and spread her legs slightly. She didn't have the energy to actively participate. All she wanted to do was submit, succumb, to lie there and receive his love. It was an odd feeling for her. She wasn't exactly sexually aroused. It was more like she was spiritually aroused. When he eased his body on top of hers and reached up to take her hands in his, she thought she must be having a religious experience. She felt warm and soft and adored and completely cherished for the first time in her life.

He had his mouth on hers and he was moaning.

'Des, oh Des,' she whispered.

'My God, how I've missed you,' he said, his voice almost a sob. 'Baby, baby, baby. I love you so. So much, I love you so much,' he kept saying over and over as he covered her body completely with his. She felt him hard between her legs and she opened herself to him, wanting nothing more than to be engulfed by him, absorbed.

Then he entered her and shock waves coursed through her whole body.

'No! No!' she shrieked.

She pulled her face away from his and tried to

push his shoulders away from her.

'Please, no! I can't do this! I can't do this!'

She pulled herself up so that he slid out of her and she slithered her body out from under him.

She was overcome with terror. Not only was she allowing herself to be close to him, to love him again, but she was risking getting pregnant again, risking the most ultimate of pains. It was out of the question. She couldn't, wouldn't let it happen.

In the darkness she could make out the shadows of Des's face, stunned and anguished.

'Sonny, what . . . ?'

But she wouldn't let him speak.

'No, Des. I'm sorry. I'm so sorry. You must understand. I can't do this. It hurts too much. I can't bear it.'

She was gasping for air, the fear having robbed her of her breath.

'Sonny, my baby, my precious, I'm the one who's sorry. I didn't mean to hurt you. Oh God, I should have realized. The scars haven't had a chance to heal yet. Oh Sonny, forgive me. I would rather die than cause you any pain.'

It was her turn to be stunned. He thought he had physically hurt her. He had totally misunderstood.

When she spoke she spoke very quietly, very carefully.

'No, Des. That isn't it. The scars have healed. It's my heart that hasn't. I can't love you anymore. I can't let you love me. I can't love anyone. That's what hurts too much.'

She had moved to the edge of the bed and she sat with her arms hugging her knees. She was cold and she had begun to shiver. She could see the outline of Des's body crouched on the other side of the bed. She watched his posture, saw the signs of defeat.

'Jesus, Mary, Mother of God,' he said finally, under his breath. 'She's had enough. Can't you grant her some peace. For Christ's sake.'

She realized that he was praying. For her.

'Don't you dare pray for me!' She practically screamed, the rage welling up in her. 'Don't you dare pray to your fucking God. He took my child away from me. He took everyone away from me. Now He's taking you away from me, too. You're turning into some kind of weirdo. The next thing you'll be walking around in robes, chanting and waving incense. Well, He must be having a great laugh right now up there in heaven. He's got you by the balls and it's pathetic. You're completely brainwashed. I don't even know you anymore. But I do know this. I hate Him. And I'm beginning to hate you.'

The rage had given her strength, had propelled her out of her grief. It felt good and comfortable. She had come so close to losing it when she let Des love her. Now she felt better, more in control. It was such a relief. She wasn't at all sure, though, that she would be able to sustain it if she stayed there in the same bed, in the same room with him. She had to get out.

She grabbed a pillow and started to walk out, but then she remembered her bathrobe, which was lying at the foot of the bed. When she turned to pick it up she saw Des in the gloom, sitting on the edge of the bed, his shoulders hunched over, his head buried in his hands.

★   ★   ★

It was Holy Week. Easter had never been her favorite holiday. To her it was never the resurrection. It was about death. She had never bought the resurrection thing. Even as a child. She stopped believing in the resurrection before she stopped believing in the Easter Bunny.

The only thing she really liked was getting a new dress every year. Nana always took her to pick it out. She remembered her favorite dress when she was about seven. It was a beautiful pale peach cotton with smocking on the front, little puffed sleeves, and a sash in the back. She got peach-colored socks to match and black patent leather Mary Janes. Nana bought her a gorgeous pale beige gabardine flared coat with a brown taffeta bow and she had a straw hat with a peach grosgrain band. Nana said that the color combination was very smart. It was important, Nana said, not to look like an Easter egg.

The big problem with Easter was that it was always such a disappointment. The Easter Bunny came and brought you a basket with a bunch of dumb candies in it and a few little toys. Then you had to go out and hunt for all the eggs, which always seemed incredibly stupid to Allison because you had already dyed them, so who cared. Besides, what did anyone want with a bunch of hard-boiled eggs? The eggs were beautiful, that was true. Only she wasn't very artistic and never got the dye on right and she hated the little stickers with Easter lilies and Christ on the cross. Then there was Sunday school, which was really boring and made no sense to her at all. What was really maddening was that Sam didn't ever go to church, so Nana would take her and drop her off. No matter how much she complained Sam still made her go. This was her first real experience with hypocrisy, which she never ceased to throw up to Sam long after she grew up. She had to swallow very hard when she sang 'Jesus loves me this I know, for the Bible tells me so.' She didn't know.

As if Sunday school weren't bad enough, there was the inevitable Easter egg hunt. In the inevitable cold, damp drizzle. Since she couldn't stand to be cold, didn't really care, couldn't bear the aggressive competitiveness and never tried that hard, she often came away with no eggs at all. None. She had figured out quite early on that there were always two prizes given. One for the person who found the most eggs and a consolation prize for the one who found the least. Every Easter Allison got the consolation prize. For doing nothing.

This was her view of Easter and to this day she still hadn't quite figured out how it all tied in with Christ getting crucified and rolling away the stone. Behind all the pink and blue and eggs and chicks and bunnies was all this pain and blood and gore. Friday the thirteenth with Gidget. It hadn't been hard for her, much to Sam's chagrin, to make the leap from Episcopalian to atheist.

'Can't you just call yourself an agnostic?' he would say with exasperation.

'It's all a matter of semantics, Sam,' she told him when she was thirteen. 'We're all agnostics because nobody can know for sure if there a God. My belief that there is no God is just as legitimate as for those who believe there is a God. If they don't call themselves agnostics, if they claim a belief, then why shouldn't I claim a disbelief? It's really just being a little more specific. A theist is someone who believe in a deity. A deity is something you worship. I don't worship any thing or any person. Therefore I am a-theistic. Furthermore, I haven't devoted my life to antireligion the way some people devote their lives to religion. You aren't contemptuous; in fact, you are respectful of priests, and nuns, and clerics. Yet they have chosen to give their lives to something they can't possibly know for sure even exists. That's what I call absurd.'

It drove Sam bananas. He couldn't argue with her. She really had him with her newly discovered techniques of debate. It made her feel even more grownup than the smart color combination of her peach and beige and brown Easter outfit.

★      ★      ★

Father Herlihy had been extremely receptive on the telephone. It was Holy Week, he reminded her. Easter was the coming Sunday and he was terribly busy, but he would certainly be happy to make some time to see her. He didn't seem surprised that she had called.

She was the one who was surprised. She hadn't ever intended to call him, although it did seem to be appropriate timing. She and Des had been working long hours, barely speaking the rare times they saw each other. She certainly didn't need religious counseling. She did need to talk to someone about Des. Someone who would understand what he was doing. Even though she knew she could talk to Rachel and Jenny, they were Jewish and wouldn't understand the Catholic thing any more than she did. Why not just go to the source?

Walking over to his office near Georgetown University on this beautiful spring day full of buds and blossoms and hope, she tried to collect her thoughts. She felt very scattered and unsure of her approach. She was angry, she was confused, she was sad. More than any of those things she felt empty, lost, and defeated. She didn't know what she wanted of this man. Did she just want to attack him for being Catholic, for believing in this horrible God? Did she want to confront him, assert herself as an atheist, challenge him? Did she want to find a way to understand Des in hopes of keeping their marriage together or did she want a way out of the marriage by trying to justify her rage? Maybe she was jealous of Des for being able to find something that could comfort him, something she clearly did not have. Was she just curious? Did she only want to know what it was Des talked with him about or was it more? Did she hope to discover what gave Des the solace he got from his visits with the priest? Was there possibly something there for her, too? Something that might salve the pain?

\*     \*     \*

The first thing she noticed were his eyes. They were deep and dark and penetrating. Though his name was Irish he looked more Latin, with his pale skin, slim body, slicked-back black hair, and aquiline nose. Without the black shirt and white collar he might have passed for a Spanish bullfighter.

It didn't matter what he looked like. His eyes virtually obliterated everything else about him. It was all she saw when she walked into his small, sunny, book-lined office. He rose to welcome her and she became locked into his gaze. The only word she could think of to describe the look, the expression, the emotion in his eyes was understanding. He didn't know her but he understood. He was accepting. He was without judgment. She sat down and began to feel her anger dissipate. Usually she got scared when that happened. Her anger was her armor. This time, however, she felt relieved. Relieved and immediately comfortable. It was ironic. She was used to feeling relief when the rage welled up.

They sat down. He waited for her to speak.

'You didn't sound particularly surprised when I called.'

He didn't respond. He just smiled. Smart. It would have been wrong for him to have demurred. Arrogant to have agreed.

'I wanted to see you,' she began again, 'because of Des. Because of Des and me, I guess would be more honest. I don't know what you talk about but I can't imagine you don't know about our baby.'

He nodded.

'Since Kay Kay ... the baby died, we've both seemed to deal with it in very different ways and it's driving us apart.'

She might as well get to the point.

'Des has turned to the Church, or returned to the Church, I should say. He's gotten more and more religious in the past few months and I find it terrifying. When we first got together he told me he was a lapsed Catholic. He never went to church, never prayed, actually made fun of religion. It was just never an issue with us. Now I'm told there's no such thing as a lapsed Catholic. Now he's practically surgically joined to his rosary. For me,

657

it's like having him behave irrationally and discovering he has a brain tumor. I'm sure he's told you that I don't understand how an intelligent person can believe in God. Especially a God who would be capable of such evil.'

He nodded again, unfazed.

'I feel that Des is changing. That he will end up being someone I don't know, someone I can't communicate with. I'm afraid I'll end up losing him, that we'll end up losing each other.'

He had been listening carefully. Now he responded for the first time. His face was full of sympathy.

'I understand how much pain you're in and I want to tell you how sorry I am about your daughter's death. I would like to try to help you if I can.'

'I don't need any help, really. I just want to understand what's happening to my husband.'

He looked at her for a moment, clearly trying to determine how to proceed.

'Many people who come to me, including Catholics, come because they have crises and they lose their faith,' he said finally. 'In order to be able to help them talk about it, I take the strongest case against God. There would be no way for me to get anywhere with them unless I dealt with their intellectual problem. Ultimately, life doesn't make sense. The moral challenge of life is how to live with integrity in a world that doesn't make sense. As Dostoevsky says, the death of one innocent child is enough to destroy a belief in God.'

Now it was her turn to nod. She liked this man. He didn't get defensive or hostile with her. He understood what her problem was. He wanted to

658

help her.

'I know it sounds like a contradiction,' she said, 'like some sort of hidden fault line, that I could be an atheist and at the same time be mad at a God who does these terrible things. I can't really reconcile this. I need to be angry. I'm angry at God, your God, Des's God, until I remember that I don't believe in God. Then I have no one to be angry with but Des. Or myself. I was mad at myself but I couldn't sleep so I've transferred the anger to Des.'

She had tried to make a little joke but it wasn't funny and neither of them laughed.

'What faith provides,' he said, picking up on her question, 'is not answers but meanings to all the questions we have to deal with. As a child, Des may have been exposed to people whose lives took on a pattern of meaning; they were able to deal with their questions because of that meaning. The power of this tragedy has stripped the resources. It has driven him back to look for the meaning of the questions. St John's Gospel says "to believe is to see." It is a way to see through this tragedy and make sense. Faced with the most devastating event of his whole life he searches for meaning in a way he hasn't done in a long time. My guess is he's finding something.'

'Something new?'

'Not at all. This harking back got him in the door. Once he's in the door, he finds what he knows.'

'But Des has always called himself a lapsed Catholic. He has insisted since the first time I knew him that he wasn't religious at all, that he detested the Church and everything it stood for, that he would never, under any circumstances, go back. He has always said that the Church is corrupt and has nothing to offer him. I remember him once telling me a story about having an automobile accident. They pulled him out of the car, broken bones, half dead. The medics were so sure he was going to die that they asked him what religion he was. He told them "none."'

'To be lapsed is not to be disconnected. You never leave. Your baptism is the fundamental act of life. Nothing is so fundamental to your existence as having been baptized. You are joined to the body of Christ. You can reject it. But to the Church you are still a member. Coming home is another way to put coming back to your faith.'

'You've told me what lapsed is not. What is it?'

'A lapsed Catholic is one who is not fulfilling the obligations of faith, not practicing the faith ... praying daily, going to Mass every week, using the Eucharist every week.'

'Remind me what that means.'

'Receiving communion. However, you ought not to receive the Eucharist if you are in serious sin.'

'Is Des?'

She had been having a hard time with this. Now she was incredulous.

'In his situation, because of being divorced and remarried outside the Church, technically, he should not receive the Eucharist.'

'But what if it helps him with his pain? Isn't that what the Church is for? To give solace? If he were married in the Church would that do it? Or remarried? Would I, I mean the spouse, have to convert to Catholicism?'

'No she wouldn't have to be Catholic, but...'

Allison leaned back in her chair. She found

660

herself becoming truly angry. Not at this intelligent, kind priest, but at what she considered the absolute cruelty of what he was telling her in such good faith.

'You're angry. I can see that I've made you mad.'

He understood before she had even shown a trace of her emotions. He was very smart.

'I'm sorry. Yes, you have. You sit there in your little black shirt basically pronouncing life and death sentences on people with impunity. And if I may be perfectly honest, it sounds like total nonsense to me. And worse, it's unforgiving.'

'Are you sure you want to talk about this?' he said. 'I don't feel I'm helping you.'

He had that sympathetic look on his face again. She didn't want sympathy. She couldn't deal with sympathy. She wouldn't let him comfort her. She wanted an intellectual discussion. Or at least she wanted to believe she did. What she really wanted was to vent her anger at someone.

'All I wanted to know is if you think you have the answers to some of my questions.'

'I don't have ready-made answers. I'm not that smart. Things aren't that simple.'

'But you must have an answer for why a supposedly all-powerful good God would cause suffering. Otherwise you wouldn't have devoted your life to him.'

In her mind, God was always spelled with a little 'g,' him with a little 'h.'

He nodded again.

'I believe there is a good God who holds the universe in his hands. What makes it hard is if you believe that God is all powerful and all knowing, all good, and wills the best for his creatures. What do you do about suffering? Essentially, the way one approaches this, is that God has created a universe that has intrinsic human limits. Into this world that is without sin, there is in fact sin. A world without the possibility of sin is a world without freedom. The essence of sin is to choose against God. If God creates a world in which there is no sin He creates a world with no higher form of life than animals and things.'

This made absolutely no sense at all to Allison.

'Well, if God is all powerful, why couldn't he create a world where there was no sin and there was also freedom?'

'Catholics believe God can't be a contradiction. God is the source of all truth. God in a sense obeys the laws of rational truth, a world in which there was no sin but there was freedom is a contradiction.'

'Why?'

'Because the meaning of freedom, when one engages God, is the ability, in spite of God's love for us, to say "no" to God. There is the possibility to reject God. The essence of sin is when a person wants something they cannot have and have God, too.'

'Like chocolate cake?'

She was now insistent on throwing a little levity into this discussion.

'Like chocolate cake.' He smiled. 'There has to be the possibility of saying no to God. If that possibility doesn't exist, then there is no way to sin.'

She was appalled.

'So what's wrong with that? Is this what people mean when they talk about Catholic fear? That they fear they will say no to God and not have him in the end? Is this what hell is? What is hell, anyway? Do you believe in it?'

'Yes, I believe in hell.'

'With the devil and flames and everything?'

He smiled. 'The picture of hell has been distorted. The essence of hell is to know that God is the ultimate good and that I will never be with Him. Heaven is to know that the God whom I have known I now choose finally and totally to rest with Him forever.'

'I think that's something you have to be brought up with,' she said. For a moment neither of them spoke.

Then, with no warning, Kay Kay's face appeared in her brain, as though it were a wide screen, completely wiping out everything else that was in her mind. Up until this point they had been having a perfectly rational conversation, arguing points, answering questions. Ironically, she had forgotten about Kay Kay while they had been talking, forgotten the reason she was there. Now she felt a searing pain and she remembered the rage that had propelled her into this priest's office in the first place. His god had killed her child and now he was robbing her of her husband as well. Yet she couldn't fight against him, with a small 'h,' because he had not chosen to reveal himself to her. It was like fighting marshmallows. In her mind, he didn't even exist except to cause her pain, except to mock her through the faith of others, particularly through Des. This god they all believed in had the face of the Devil to her. She could more easily believe in the Devil At least He, let's give the Devil his due with a capital 'H,' didn't pretend to be something

663

other than what He was. He was no hypocrite. He claimed His Evil. God hid behind the face of good. God was the real Devil, holding out this pathetic hope of eternal salvation to these poor assholes who believed in him, putting them through their paces, forcing them down on their knees to pay him homage, to praise him. Love thy god and watch me kill the person you cherish most and if you praise me afterward I'll kill somebody else you love and make you grovel for my blessings so that I can cause you even more grief. Believe in me and watch me fuck you over. Amen. Ah. But if you refuse to believe in me, if you just don't buy it; wait. I've got something better in store for you. I'll make you pay even worse because I won't even hold out the promise of eternal salvation. You'll just be damned to hell. Neat little trick. I have the power to make you believe in me but I'm not going to do it and I'm going to punish you for not believing in me. Your choice, pal. Don't believe in me and watch me fuck you over.

Her voice was shaking when she finally spoke. She tried to control her anger but she could feel it spilling out all over this good Catholic's desk like Christ's blood. Lick it up, receive the sacrament, don't hate, desecrate. She was losing it. If she didn't get a grip she might start foaming at the mouth.

'Well, either there is a god or there isn't,' she said. 'And if he's all powerful then he can choose to whom he wants to reveal himself. He has revealed himself to all of those born-again Christians, these evangelical preachers who steal their flocks' money and screw their secretaries. Why has he chosen not to reveal himself to me? Am I not good enough? I

664

think I live a good, moral life compared to many "Christians" I can think of. Are all of my decent atheists and agnostic friends not good enough, but thousands, millions of truly evil people who hide behind the cross more worthy? More evil has been done in the name of religion than in the name of anything else. Maybe that is the proof that God is really the Devil with a mask on.'

Father Herlihy sighed. Those dark eyes bored into her. She couldn't be sure what she saw in them. Certainly sorrow, and frustration.

'We are faced with a leap of faith here,' he said quietly. 'Faith is ultimately not the result of a rational conclusion.'

'Bingo!' She practically leaped from her chair, elated. 'Now that makes sense to me. I've been sitting here straining to understand what you've been saying for two hours. It's like listening to someone trying to explain physics or trigonometry and you've finally given me something I can grasp on to. You've just said the magic words.'

He shrugged, almost apologetically.

'One never does it as well as one should. You keep trying to understand and to respond. A priest is supposed to be able to live it and explain it, to help other people live it and share it.'

She returned to her seat and leaned back in the chair, oddly exhausted. She felt as though she had just gone twelve rounds in a boxing ring. She hadn't won but she certainly hadn't lost. There was no knockout.

'I guess this is all pretty redundant and boring to you,' she said. 'You probably have to go through this all the time, answering these questions.'

'Look,' he said, leaning forward intently, 'I don't

mean to sit here and say that I have all the answers and you have none.'

'I don't see it that way at all,' she said, a note of triumph in her voice. 'I see it that you have all the faith and I have none.'

*　　*　　*

She was still shaking as she walked out of his office and back down O Street. What she needed to do was to go to the health club and work out on the 'stairmonster' for about three days to get rid of the anxiety she felt. If only she could exhaust herself physically with exercise her jaw would stop aching from clenching her teeth and her stomach would untie itself.

She turned right on 36th Street toward N and was almost at the corner when she looked up and saw a woman walk out of Holy Trinity Church. It surprised her, from a security standpoint, that the church would be open on a weekday. Then she remembered that Catholics have Mass every day. This was the church where Des went every morning before work. She had never been inside. Her curiosity overcame her. She walked up the stairs and pulled open the door.

The church was large and open inside with the sun pouring through the beautiful stained-glass windows. It had already been decorated for Easter with tiny blooming cherry trees, tulips, and azaleas. There were two aisles on either side of the main altar, each leading to the small nave. On the left there was a miniature chapel with its own crucifix and altar. Sitting in the front row facing that chapel, his head bowed in prayer or concentration was a man in a camel corduroy jacket, with curly black hair. She knew instantly that it was Des.

She slid quietly into the very back row on the right-hand aisle, pulled a scarf out of her pocket, and put it on. If he happened to get up quickly to leave she could always kneel and bow her head.

Two women came in and walked down Des's side of the aisle to the front. They genuflected, then crossed themselves and sat down. One of them walked up to the small chapel and knelt for a while, then returned to her seat. Finally they left. Des never moved.

Now it was just the two of them. It was very quiet. From somewhere near the tiny chapel came the sound of running water, like a fountain. She couldn't see it but the noise was quite loud and blotted out any street sounds she might have heard.

She sat there perfectly still for a long time, listening to the tinkling of the water, watching the sun sparkle through the stained-glass windows, smelling the flowers. She could feel the tension begin to drain out of her body. She closed her eyes so that only the sound of the water dominated her senses and waited while the anger dissipated. She was almost afraid to breathe, the silence was so soothing that she began to be overcome with a sense of calm and total peace.

At first she had this odd sensation that maybe god was going to reveal himself to her.

Okay, okay. You want me to reveal myself I'll do it. I can't stand any more of this bitching. Here I am. I'm not Santa Claus, I'm not the Easter Bunny, I'm really God. With a capital G. White robes, long beard, and everything. Now do you believe in me? It doesn't get any better than this.

She waited.

Nothing happened.

Still, she felt more peaceful. She was more relieved than anything else. If god had actually revealed himself to her she would have felt unbelievably stupid. Ironically, she was even more convinced now that there was no god.

She let her mind go completely blank. She didn't have to hear anyone talk, she didn't have to talk to anyone, she didn't have to think. She could just sit there and listen to the water. Des had god. She had water.

She saw Des out of the corner of her eye. He sat up on the bench, then genuflected and crossed himself. Before she could move he had started up the aisle. She quickly pulled the scarf around her face, bowing her head, and knelt down. She waited until he had left the church, until the large doors had closed and she was all alone.

She didn't get up and leave right away. She sat there for a few moments more, not wanting to give up the serenity.

She had learned something from coming here. Even though god had not revealed himself to her. She had found some measure of peace, of spiritual solace, a salve for her wounded soul. If that's what Des got out of his religion, then how could she be angry with him for it? How could she possibly deny it to him? It didn't mean that his belief and her disbelief wouldn't cause some separation or lack of communication. What it did mean was that they were both hanging on by their fingernails, and if this is what worked for him, so be it.

★　　★　　★

She got home before Des that night. She didn't feel like having a drink. It was the first time since Kay Kay died that she hadn't had a glass of wine immediately when she got home from work. She fixed a glass of sparkling water and lime and went upstairs to get out of her office clothes and put on sweats and sneakers. While she was changing she noticed the Bible on Des's bedside table. She remembered Father Herlihy quoting the Gospel of St John. She had never read the Bible, except in English class at college, never read St John. She picked it up and found chapter three.

'There was a man of the Pharisees named Nicodemus, a ruler of the Jews,' it began. In the text, the famous sayings of Jesus were printed in red ink. Her eyes scanned the words very quickly, looking to see what it was that was so important, so meaningful that Father Herlihy would choose to quote St John above all other passages. She immediately came across one of the most famous quotations from the Bible, one even she recognized.

15  That whosoever believeth in him should not perish but have eternal life.
16  For God so loved the world, that he gave his only begotten Son, that whosoever believeth in him should not perish, but have everlasting life.
17  For God sent not his Son into the world to condemn the world; but that the world through him might be saved.
18  He that believeth on him is not condemned: but he that believeth not is condemned already, because he hath not

669

believed in the name of the only begotten Son of God.

She was stunned. How could this be? It was so judgmental, so unforgiving, so hateful, so ... un-Christian. This was the Bible. The Good Book. This was the book that taught love and forgiveness. The cruelty of those passages seemed to be the antithesis of everything the Bible, religion, Christianity were supposed to stand for. How could any decent person read those words and not be outraged? It was exclusive, bigoted, arrogant. How could Father Herlihy have recommended this to her? God gave us freedom so we could choose to believe in him but then tells us that if we don't we are condemned? What kind of a god would do that?

Here she had just decided that she would accept Des's religion because it gave him strength and solace and now she was finding out that his religion would not only not accept her lack of belief but would actually punish her for it. She was appalled.

She skipped down further, perhaps expecting to find something that would mitigate the unrelenting horror of those last lines. She got to the end of chapter three, to the last passage in black ink.

36    He that believeth on the Son hath everlasting life: and he that believeth not the Son shall not see life; but the wrath of God abideth on him.

The wrath of God had nothing on hers.

She threw the Bible as hard as she could across the room. It hit the full-length mirror on the back of the door and shattered it, scattering the

670

glistening shards throughout the room.

She stood up, walked around the bed and through the door, out the hall, not stopping to pick up the Bible or the shards. She could hear the sound of crunching glass under her sneakers as she walked.

She went down the stairs and into the study, heading straight for the bar. She found Des's bottle of Irish whiskey and poured a large glass, neat. No water. She sat down on the sofa and began to drink. By the time Des got home that night she was completely blotto.

*　　*　　*

It was freezing cold, gloomy, and pouring rain. It reminded her of London and made her a bit nostalgic. Her life then had been so simple compared to her life now. The bedroom scene with Des the week before had left her even more determined to put everything but working out of her mind. She had become a genius at compartmentalizing.

Sprague had offered to pick her up at her house on Olive Street to drive the few blocks down to the Georgetown waterfront.

He honked the horn and she ran out, startled to see a big burly man sitting in the backseat. She jumped in the front seat and shot Sprague a quizzical look.

'This is Ralph,' he said. 'Ralph is my bodyguard. Ralph is a killer. Ralph is one mean son of a bitch. Right, Ralph?'

'You got it, boss.'

'So don't mess with me, woman.'

671

She turned to get a good look at Ralph. He had a crewcut, a nose that had been broken many times, a shiny suit, and several diamond rings.

'Ralph?'

'Yes, ma'am?'

'I'm the boss. I'm also a killer.'

Ralph seemed somewhat startled and a little skeptical of the admission by this slim, blond woman.

'If anything happens to him, Ralph, you'll have to answer to me.'

'Yes, ma'am.'

Ralph's eyes were on sticks.

'And Ralph?'

'Yes, ma'am?'

'If anything does happen to him, it's your ass.'

It was all Sprague could do not to run off the road.

They parked in the underground garage, took the elevator up to the terrace level, and walked past the fountain to Jaimalitos. The Mexican restaurant was almost completely empty except for a few people sitting in the front by the large glass window overlooking the river.

Sprague told Ralph to position himself at a corner table next to the entrance to the back of the restaurant. Then he led the way around the adobe wall to the dimly lit room behind it and took the farthest booth, tucked away between more fake adobe walls and piled high with brightly coloured Mexican pillows. She slid in first and Sprague slid in beside her, much to her surprise.

'I want both of us to be on the same side,' he said. 'When he comes, you'll see why.'

She had never been close to him before and it was

672

slightly awkward sitting next to him like that, wedged into the banquette. She had to lean back against the pillows to talk to him. There was something almost suggestive about the two of them being there alone.

They waited for almost half an hour eating tortilla chips and sipping sparkling water. They talked about nothing in particular.

Finally Garcia came in, hurriedly, casting furtive glances around to see if anyone was watching. He looked like a grade-B actor in a low-budget movie. It was all Allison could do not to laugh. He slid into the other side of the booth as though he had done it many times before, and pounced on the tortilla chips. Even though she had seen him in photographs and on television, she was surprised at how sinister he looked in person: swarthy, paunchy, darting eyes. He was, after all, the head of the DEA, the good guy. She had to take Sprague's word for it that he was smart, crafty, and a good source. Garcia hardly said a word. After ordering a margarita, a huge plate of nachos, and an equally large portion of fajitas, he ate and listened as Sprague outlined the death threats and what he and the paper had done about them.

Garcia wiped his mouth.

'Don't fuck with them, man,' he said to Sprague in a heavy Hispanic accent, completely ignoring Allison. 'They're bad. They don't joke around. There is a saying in the drug trade: "A marijuana deal is done with a handshake, and a coke deal is done with a gun." If they think you're getting close to the big enchilada you're dead meat.'

'Then you think this threat is serious?' Allison asked.

673

He looked around again as though he were being followed.

'I think,' he said, looking at her for the first time, 'that if this guy doesn't get off the story, you better start looking for a new investigative reporter.'

'What do you mean by—?'

Allison had barely gotten the words out when Garcia slid out of his side of the banquette and disappeared as fast as he had come.

Frightened as she was by what Garcia had said, she started to laugh.

'He's got to be kidding. You've got to be kidding. What was that? And who is the big enchilada?'

'The big enchilada is Foxy, and that was the guy who spends a lot of time identifying the mutilated bodies of his agents who have not taken death threats seriously.'

She pondered that for a moment.

'I think I need a margarita,' she said.

'Good idea.'

As cool as he was, she could see that Sprague too was unnerved.

They both took long sips, Allison licking the salt off the side of her glass.

'Sprague,' she said, not looking up, 'I don't want you to get killed.'

He didn't say anything.

She looked up from her glass.

'Please be careful. Please don't do anything dumb. I've said it before. It's just not worth it for a story.'

He could see the pleading in her eyes. He was not smiling. There was no mischief in his eyes, no 'I didn't know you cared' teasing.

'It's an important story, Ally.'

There was the Ally again. She liked it. It was proprietary on his part, presumptuous. But she liked it.

'I don't care. I ... I just don't care, that's all.'

'We're talking about bringing down the government, getting rid of a bunch of sleazeballs and corrupt bastards who are hell-bent on screwing up the country. We're talking about saving thousands of innocent people's lives. We're talking about crime. The people who are running the country, the attorney general for Christ's sake, the top law enforcement officer in the nation, is sponsoring this bad business. I'm on to them. I'm this close. I think if I can get these two guys on Jenkins's Cove connected to the Foreign Minister I can get them to lead me to Antonia and Foxy. It's the DEA report on them that Foxy's trying to squelch. They're blackmailing him through Antonia. If I can get them I can blow this thing. I've got to go down there.'

'I don't care.'

She knew that what she was saying, the way she was saying it, was unprofessional. She couldn't help it. She felt overwhelmed by the idea that something might happen to Sprague. Somehow, Sprague had filled a part of that yawning, empty crater inside her. Des couldn't do it for her. Des had nothing to give her. He had his own emptiness to deal with. Besides, she loved Des. She was trying to get away from love. Sprague was a distraction. If she thought about Sprague she didn't have to think about herself or Des or Kay Kay, so she found she was thinking about him all the time. She was almost obsessive about it. But it was a therapeutic

675

obsession.

'Spoken like a true editor.'

Maybe it was the margarita, which she had practically consumed in one gulp, but the whole conversation had her on the verge of tears. She hadn't cried for four months, but the thought of Sprague dead, killed, panicked her.

'I can't deal with this,' she said, blinking and looking away.

He hadn't quite realized how upset she was.

'Look,' he said gently. 'I'll be careful. I won't do anything stupid. I promise. I have a wife and a child, remember?'

The mention of Jane jarred her. Her expression showed it.

'My child needs me. I won't take any chances.'

She smiled. He returned the smile.

The waiter reappeared with the bill. Sprague ordered two more margaritas.

'You'll have to carry me out of here,' she said.

'I can think of worse assignments.'

'Like going to Jenkins's Cove with Ralph?'

'To name one.'

'I don't know,' she said. 'Marooned out on that sailboat or on a desert island Ralph might start to look pretty good.'

'There are others I'd rather be stranded with.'

They were both surprised that he had said it and they both laughed self-consciously.

Sprague looked down at his watch.

'Oh Lord, we've got to get out of here,' he said. 'I've got a five o'clock plane to Miami.'

'You're leaving today?' she said a little quickly.

'I have to. I've got to go back to the hotel and get my suitcase and leave the car.'

'I knew you'd moved to a hotel. Which one?'

'Right around the corner from you. At the Georgetown Dutch Inn on Thomas Jefferson Street.'

'I remember that place. I once had a love tryst there with a famous movie star in my wild single girl days. It seems like another life.'

The jaw muscles started to work the way they did when he got angry. She realized he wasn't at all happy to hear that she had had another life. Could he be jealous? That pleased her. She had told him that story to make him jealous. She knew what she was doing. And she had gotten the desired response.

'I knew there must be a reason why I chose to stay there,' he said. Cool, very cool.

He stood up abruptly, threw some cash on the table, and signaled to the ever alert Ralph that they were leaving.

It was still pouring when they got outside so she accepted a ride home from him. They rode in silence up to Olive Street. When they got to her house, she opened the door, then turned to Ralph in the backseat. She had intended to say something smart and funny but as she started to speak she realized she was about to choke up.

'Don't let anything happen to him, Ralph. Please.'

Before either one of them could answer she had jumped out of the car into the downpour.

\* \* \*

'Sterling,' she said, picking up the phone.

It was after eight-thirty, after deadline, and the

newsroom was pretty quiet. She was sitting back in her chair with her feet up on her desk going over expense accounts.

'Ally?'

She bolted up in her chair.

'Sprague? Thank God! You're all right?'

She was so relieved to hear his voice that she forgot how furious she was at him for not calling for almost a week.

'Where the fuck have you been?' she said. 'I've . . . we've been worried sick about you. You promised you'd call the minute you got off that boat.'

'Yeah, well, I cruised around a little longer than I had planned to.'

'What happened? Did you learn anything?'

'I'll tell you all about it when I get back.'

He obviously didn't want to talk on the phone.

'Where are you now . . . can you say?'

'I just stopped off for a day or so on the way back to see my father.'

She knew his father was dead. So he must have decided to go visit Jane and Melissa.

'When will you be back?'

'I'm getting in tomorrow night.'

'Okay, I'll set up that meeting at my house for Wednesday morning. Alan and Walt are anxious for us to brainstorm this thing. It's getting out of control. Too many cooks. Everybody wants a piece. Nobody knows what anybody else is doing. We're falling all over each other. It's a mess.'

'Fine with me. What time?'

'Nine-thirty sharp. I need you there at the beginning to lend a note of cohesiveness to the enterprise.'

'I'll be there.'

She hadn't been joking. The whole project was so confusing that even she, who had been involved from the beginning, was losing track. Everyone knew that Sprague was working on something big. A lot of them resented him for his cool, standoffish style, his privileged background, his Pulitzer. But they had to admit he was good. The best. He was like a vacuum cleaner. Wherever he went he just turned it on and sucked up every bit of information available. Allison had never seen anything like it. he was dazzling as an investigative reporter. He knew where to go, who to go to, and how to make people talk. He was dogged, persistent, he never gave up. Where most reporters would try a couple of times, he'd go back forty or fifty times until the person was worn into submission. He worked day and night. Other reporters watching him saw visions of Pulitzers dancing in their heads. Whatever he was working on, they wanted to work on. He had been at this story long enough that several of the reporters who sat next to him and covered some of the beats he'd been sniffing around were beginning to pick up bits of the story here and there. They would come to Allison with their findings. They were getting close to the DEA stuff, the Foxy stuff, the Antonia Alvarez stuff. Sprague's trips to Colombia had intrigued everyone. They all knew he had won his Pulitzer for a series on drugs for the Savannah paper. They also knew he had had his life threatened, and that he was off again on another dangerous assignment. Plus, there had been lots of grim-faced meetings in Alan's glass office with the door shut. All of this was enough to have any self-respecting reporter hyperventilating to be a part of the action, to agitate until they found out what was going on. Allison had decided to coopt the ones who were causing the most trouble with this meeting at her house. They would share the information and proceed as a team. They were disgruntled that Sprague had had a series of drug stories on page one already and had not cooperated with any of them on what they were doing. If she could get them all working on this together they might really have a crack at the Pulitzer, maybe this one for the paper. Once they got a whiff of the possibilities, like the fact that they could bring the whole government down, she was certain she could bring them in line.

★　　★　　★

The meeting was at her house so as not to arouse any more suspicion than necessary in the newsroom. Walt Fineman would be there; Malkin, her deputy; Sprague; Estrella, the bombthrower who covered the agencies; Lauren Hope, back from maternity leave, covering Congress; Rod Taylor, the diplomatic correspondent; and Robin, the woman researcher on the national staff. She had asked Robin to stop off at the American Café and pick up some croissants and muffins and she had made a big pot of coffee and had a large pitcher of fresh orange juice.

Des had an early breakfast meeting so he was out by seven-thirty. She took a shower and washed her hair, then thumbed through her wardrobe looking for just the right thing to wear. She usually didn't pay that much attention to her work clothes. But today she wanted to look good. She picked out a white gabardine skirt and a pale pink cashmere sweater set with white trim, springy but warm enough for the chilly April weather. As she put on her makeup she realized that she was dressing for Sprague. That embarrassed her. She didn't want to think about him. For one thing, it was pointless. For another, it was wrong.

She knew that he had always elicited strong emotions in her, usually anger and exasperation. But he had been talking to her differently lately, looking at her differently. He seemed less challenging to her now, gentler, more sensitive, more vulnerable. She tried to tell herself it was because of Kay Kay and his feelings of sympathy toward her, that it was because they were working so closely together on a dangerous project, that Jane wasn't here and he felt lonely. But her gut instinct told her it was more than that. She was finally admitting to herself that Sprague was attracted to her and that she was attracted to him.

*    *    *

Allison had called this meeting for two reasons. She needed to pull together all the information her staff had been collecting. But she also was using her work as a way to blot out her sorrow. It was the only antidote she had found to the pain.

She had assembled the group in her small dining room on the ground floor of her house, next to the kitchen. That way they could sit around the table, take notes, and eat while they talked. The entrance was on the ground floor so people could come and go depending on how long the meeting lasted. The room had glass French doors that gave out onto her tiny garden, bursting with pink, white, and lavender: dogwoods, cherry blossoms, tulips and wisteria. This was thanks to a gardening service, since she had never held a trowel or gotten dirt in her fingernails. Domesticity was not her strong point.

They had been told to be there between nine and nine-thirty so of course nobody showed up until around nine-thirty. Robin had come early, still smarting over having been given the menial task of getting the food. The rest of them began straggling in after the appointed hour. By ten everyone was there except Sprague. She couldn't hold up the meeting just for him even though she was so anxious that she could barely concentrate. Her dread was that something terrible had happened. Her suspicion was that he hadn't bothered to get there on time.

'Where's Tyson?' asked Walt, sidling up to her so the others wouldn't hear. 'Is everything okay?'

'I told you I talked to him night before last and he said he'd be here at nine-thirty.'

She hadn't meant to sound irritated, it was just that she was so nervous.

'I think we'd better go ahead and start,' she said and turned to the others who were still getting their coffee.

'Okay everyone, we might as well get this thing going. Sprague's the only one not here.'

She sat down at the table and the rest of them joined her.

'I think the purpose of this meeting is to figure

682

out where we are on all this,' she began. 'What we know, what we don't know, share all the information and divide up what's left so we don't have two people working the same angle. I'd like Estrella to give us a briefing for those who are walking in on the second act. By the way, does anyone know where Sprague is?'

She tried to sound casual. She hoped somebody actually did know.

'He said something about an interview with an FBI source,' said Robin. 'He said he'd be here though.'

Once again relief turned to anger.

'Okay. Until he shows up, Estrella, could you fill us in on what you've been doing on your end here in Washington while Sprague has been concentrating on his project?'

'Exactly what is Sprague's project?' asked Rod Taylor. 'He's been straight-arming most of us around the newsroom every time we get near him or any of his sources, but he bigfoots around our agencies and departments as though he owns the story.'

She hadn't expected such overt hostility toward Sprague but it didn't surprise her.

'I'd rather wait until he gets here and let him talk about it,' she said.

'What's the deal with the death threats, the bomb threats, and the bodyguards?' asked Lauren Hope. 'Everyone knows about it but nobody has bothered to tell any of us what's really going on.'

'It's not that complicated,' said Walt. 'Sprague is working on drugs, and threats just go with the territory. Sprague doesn't take it seriously but we do. We've insisted that he send his family away and

683

we're providing the guards. And he's moved to a hotel. The bomb threats at the paper, we believe, are a nuisance threat, but we've reported them and beefed up security. The Miami paper gets them all the time and they've just learned to live with it.'

'Let's get back to Estrella,' said Allison.

'I've been making the usual rounds with the FBI guys,' said Estrella. 'And the DEA, the Bureau of Alcohol, Tobacco and Firearms, the White House, as well as nosing around up on the Hill. Robin's been running names through the research center's data bases of all the big papers, as well as some of the foreign press, trying to put together a chronology for us as well as figure out what's been in the press and what hasn't. Basically we've been focusing on these two guys who met in prison in Connecticut, Juan Bader and Chuck Skinner. We think they're the key to the whole thing, or at least we can use them to illustrate the big picture.'

'Wait,' said Walt. 'I'm confused. Bader and Skinner. Their names don't sound Colombian. And why Connecticut?'

'Bader was born in Colombia,' said Estrella. 'His father's a German engineer, his mother's Colombian. He's a real psycho, hates the United States, calls it an imperialist police state. His two heroes are Che Guevara and Hitler—if that gives you any idea. His favorite magazine is *Soldier of Fortune*. He's power hungry. He'll stop at nothing to get what he wants and he'd steal his mother's purse if he thought there was anything in it he needed.'

'Sounds like Tyson,' said Taylor.

Everyone laughed. Allison felt defensive but she was too pissed at Sprague to say anything.

684

'What about the other guy?' she asked, trying to get away from the subject of Sprague.

'Chuck Skinner? Born and raised in Lincoln, Mass, the classic rebellious rich boy. A hippie in the sixties, a stoner in the seventies, and a dealer in the eighties. He got caught transporting grass from Mexico and California back to East Coast Ivy League schools. His best customers were the fraternities. He's not as scary a character as his buddy Bader, but he's no girl scout. He got busted and sent to Danbury for four years and he drew Bader as his cellmate the first year. Bader got out a year ago and Skinner about six months later. Apparently they set the groundwork for their present operation while they were still in prison. But Sprague can tell you all that. If he ever gets here.'

Allison ignored the dig.

'Have you found anybody official to tell you how and when and if they're going to nail them?' she asked.

The phone rang. Allison answered. It was Warburg for Walt. She passed the phone to him and watched his face closely to see if it was bad news. He hung up and she turned back to Estrella. The doorbell rang. She started to rise but Robin was already headed toward the door. It was a copy aide from the paper with some information they had requested for the meeting. She turned back to Estrella.

'Now where were we? Oh, yeah. Have you found anyone official...?'

'Not yet,' he said. 'I've been doing a dance with the widow of one of the DEA guys who recently got his body parts permanently rearranged,

685

compliments of Bader. I think he was on to them in a major way.'

'Why would she talk?' asked Lauren.

'She's pissed off at the DEA,' said Estrella. 'She thinks they sent her husband into Medellin without adequate protection. He was gunned down during cocktails with an informant at La Margaritas, one of the trafficker's chief watering holes there.'

'Yes, well, even if she'll talk,' said Taylor, 'what makes you think she knows anything?'

'You're obviously not married,' said Allison. 'Ever hear of pillow talk?'

Everyone laughed and she blushed. It was not lost on any of them, her relationship with Des, the fact that they had had problems working for competing news organizations.

'She's hinted around that she's got some internal DEA memos and other documents that her husband brought home,' said Estrella, ignoring the distraction. This was his big moment, with Sprague absent, and he wanted to make the most of it. 'I'm this close to getting her to let me see them.'

'Just don't get too close,' said Allison to more laughter.

'Too close to whom?'

It was Sprague's voice and she practically jumped out of her chair when she heard it.

'Estrella's just giving us a few tips on some in-depth investigative reporting techniques,' said Malkin. Everyone laughed.

Sprague threw his canvas shoulder bag down on the chair reserved for him and went to the buffet for coffee. Robin poured him a cup, suddenly turning flirtatious. Sprague responded in kind. Allison decided to continue as though he weren't there.

686

Neither she nor Sprague had looked at each other.

'Lauren, what about that report the Senate committee on drug trafficking is supposedly working on?'

'I hear rumors that it's three hundred pages,' said Lauren, 'which is beyond the pale even for Washington. Anyway, I've been unable to get an advance copy. It must have some pretty sexy stuff in it because they're practically keeping it locked up in a Brink's truck. It's Senator Gordon's baby. Rod went to Harvard with Gordon's press secretary, Jim Bates, so he's been working on him.'

'Have you been able to empty Bates's pockets?' asked Walt.

'I don't know if I emptied them,' said Taylor, laughing. 'I don't know if anybody's ever emptied them.'

'He has very deep pockets,' said Lauren.

'If you shake the tree hard enough the leaves will fall off,' said Sprague mysteriously. His tone wasn't arrogant but he seemed to bug the rest of them anyhow.

'As an interesting aside,' said Taylor, 'Bates told me that nobody from the New York *World* has shown any interest at all in this story. He said he was at a book party the other night and heard a *World* reporter say, "You know, this Colombian drug story is not intellectually stimulating."'

This was met with hoots.

'Yeah, but it sure makes the juices flow,' said Estrella, grinning.

'Anyway, seriously,' said Taylor, turning to Robin, who was tape-recording the session '—and don't put it on tape—Bates sort of said that one of the sexier parts of the report is they've got an agent . . .'

'They?' asked Allison.

'The CIA,' said Taylor. 'They've got an agent who's of Colombian descent—name, face, the whole thing, but born and raised in the Bronx. Anyway, he's been on the inside for about six months as a bodyguard for Bader. Bader loves him, calls him "mi hermano," which means my brother in Spanish.'

'Jesus. If that isn't a ten on the holy-shit scale I don't know what is,' said Malkin.

'Ten and a half,' said Rod. 'But that's not all. He managed to get wired for a torture session of this DEA agent they kidnapped several months ago.'

'A tape, not a transcript?' asked Walt.

'Right,' said Rod. 'The real thing. Apparently it's pretty gruesome, begging for mercy, screaming.'

'So what's the deal with him now?' asked Estrella, going a little pale around the gills. 'Did he get out?'

Rod shrugged.

'He's dead as a doornail,' said Sprague, speaking for the first time. 'They sent his testicles to his mother. He wasn't married so they sent them to his seventy-eight-year-old mother.'

Taylor first looked stunned, then annoyed that Sprague knew about the DEA captive. It was supposed to be his big scoop.

Allison could see a storm brewing. Sprague was not a team player, but it was her job to be captain of the team even if the quarterback refused to cooperate. This was about as far as she could take the football metaphor.

'So, Sprague,' she said, turning to him for the first time. 'Why don't you tell us how you got that tan?'

She was trying to be nonchalant. She thought he flushed slightly under the tan. He did look especially handsome and he knew it. She just wanted him to know that she knew that he knew.

'Okay. This guy Bader needed a place between Florida and Colombia where his planes could refuel and the drugs could be sorted out and shipped to the States. He found a small island in the Bahamas with an airstrip called Jenkins's Cove, a one-day sail from Nassau. He bought a big compound there and then started intimidating the locals to get them off the island. He finally scared off the owners of the yacht club and some cottages. A few people tried to fight him but he had the local police in his pockets within weeks. Pretty soon the whole island was like a ghost town.'

'What were his scare tactics?' asked Allison. She wasn't sure she wanted to know the answer.

'Huge, mean-looking bodyguards, a squadron of Doberman pinschers, stuff like that. A whole family lost in a suspicious fire on a boat. Then a mysterious drowning of a local retired businessman. After a while, nobody wanted to live there, or even visit.'

'No shit,' said Estrella.

'So what did you do?' asked Lauren.

'I rented a sailboat in Nassau and went over there.'

'By yourself?' asked Lauren.

'I had my trusty bodyguard, Ralph, who unfortunately can't swim. But I had him stay in radio contact with Nassau. Once I got close enough to the island I could see with binoculars these pickup trucks on the shore paralleling my course.

They were watching me through binoculars, too. I jumped overboard and swam to shore. Then I walked up and down the beach, careful to stay on this side of the high-water mark...'

'How do you mean?' asked Lauren. She was the only one who would admit she didn't know, though by now everyone was listening with rapt attention.

'In the Bahamas the sand below the high-water mark is property of the queen and therefore public,' he explained. 'So this big thug appears and says I'm on private property. I tell him the law about the queen's property and I keep walking. Then he comes back with two Germans and one Colombian. They tell me I've got to go. I repeat the thing about the queen's property. Surprisingly they seemed unimpressed, I could see their guns tucked into their pants. They pointed out if I stayed they couldn't guarantee my safety. I was very low key, thanked them, and swam back to the boat.'

'That's a great story, but what did you learn?' asked Rod.

'Well,' said Sprague, unperturbed by Taylor's tone, 'I got to see these two guys and the island firsthand. That beats sitting around the newsroom waiting for the State Department lapdogs to call me back with "no comment."'

A little dig at Taylor.

'I sailed around to the tip and saw the airstrip. The next couple of days I drifted around, keeping a log of the planes flying in and out. I spent the last two days poking around the Bahamian Police Department. I got a couple of leads.'

Allison could see he didn't want to go into that and she wasn't going to push it.

'So where do we go from here?' asked Walt.

'I want to go back,' said Sprague. 'I need to rubberhose some of my leads in the Bahamas.'

'Don't you need an assistant for that?' asked Robin.

Everyone laughed except Allison. Robin was getting too aggressive for her taste. However, she noticed that Sprague didn't seem to mind.

'I don't want anyone going back to the Bahamas, or Colombia for that matter. It's too dangerous.'

'That's ridiculous. We can't limit ourselves like that.'

'Look, Sprague,' she said, her tone was testy, as much from his little flirtation with Robin as from his challenge. 'We've got enough to write the first story and there's plenty to be mined right here in Washington, on the Hill and in the agencies. We don't have any money in the budget for funerals.'

'Well, fine,' he said, picking up her tone, 'but I've got to talk to the CIA station chief in Bogotá. I can't get anybody here to talk to me. I need to track him down. I hear there's been some infighting between DEA and CIA. The DEA apparently doesn't appreciate this CIA guy being on the inside of Bader's operation—DEA suspects that the CIA is hot to start neutralizing Bader's gang one by one and that's not the way the DEA wants to handle it.'

'Neutralize?' asked Robin, looking up from her notetaking.

'That's CIA for assassinate. I have good sources on this; I know this is part of the Hill report that Lauren's trying to get ... there are laws being broken left and right. Whether or not the attorney general or the President's involved is the big question. Whether or not any of it's on paper is obviously crucial to us in being able to prove

691

anything. If either the A.G. or the President knows about it ... there could even be a presidential finding on it. If that's the case then this could be big; bigger than any of us can imagine. We've got to get that report.'

'Lauren's not going to be able to get the Senate report,' piped up Estrella.

'What's that supposed to mean?' She was clearly insulted.

'What I mean is that there is something in that report that the White House has to protect—at all costs. I'm not sure what it is but we've still got our eye on the attorney general—he's connected in some way—we can't figure it out but...'

'Sprague?'

For some reason Allison knew better than to say anything more. She wanted to give him the opportunity to share his theory about Antonia and Foxy and the Foreign Minister with the team. She wasn't at all sure he wanted to or would. She knew it would not be wise to force him.

Everyone looked at him. He shot her a warning look.

'It's too early to say. I have a few leads on that front I'm looking into, nothing solid yet.'

Allison felt the tension mount. They were beginning to realize that Sprague was deeply into the story and had no intention of sharing what he knew.

'Could it possibly have anything to do with the A.G. fucking Antonia Alvarez?' asked Estrella in a hostile tone.

'You're kidding?' said Robin in surprise.

'I'll talk about what I've got when I've got something,' said Sprague. He stood up and reached over for his papers.

'I've got an interview on the Hill,' he said, this time glancing at Allison quickly as he turned to leave. She thought she detected a look of gratitude. She had not blown his story for him. If she had, she knew every reporter on the *Daily* would have been all over it before story conference. Of course, by not doing so she had defeated the purpose of the meeting. Which may not have been the worst tragedy in the world.

'Well, fuck him,' said Rod, after Sprague had left.

'Not a bad idea,' whispered Robin under her breath.

'Let's keep our eyes on the Prize,' said Allison, trying not to show her annoyance at Robin. 'As you may remember, it's been a long time.'

★　　★　　★

She rarely had lunch with Alan Warburg. When she did it was never much fun. Alan was the most sober person she had ever known. He was an intellectual who had little time or interest in small talk or gossip. He had no patience with those he considered intellectually inferior. Which was almost everyone. It always amazed her that he had managed to become editor of the *Daily*, given his lack of touch for 'the people.' Though not particularly well liked, he was highly respected because he was so smart and an undeniably brilliant editor. His saving grace, and what had probably propelled him into his job and kept him there, was that he was a crafty political operator. He was famous for decapitating people and leaving them unaware until they tried to move their heads.

Allison was lucky. Alan Warburg liked her. Which was one of the reasons why he decided to drop off the Pulitzer Prize advisory board and maneuver her election as his replacement. It was already no mean trick to pull that off, but as he had explained to Allison, they needed a woman, and if they didn't get her they'd pick somebody else and then the *Daily* would be without representation on the board. He had only two more years to serve. Members were appointed to three three-year terms so he was willing to step down to assure the *Daily* a position, at least for the next nine years.

Not only that, he had told her, she was good, she was a player, she would understand how the system worked, and that would all be to the *Daily*'s advantage. And they could use an advantage. Several years earlier, while she was still in London, the *Daily* had won a Pulitzer, but less than a year later it was discovered by the *Daily* itself that the reporter had plagiarized the story. They had returned the Pulitzer. Since then, they had not won a single prize. This was one of the reasons Allison had been reluctant to take the position. She was already feeling pressured to redeem the paper. She had never been comfortable with prizes. The awards on the few smaller journalism boards or panels she had been on often ended up seeming so arbitrary. It made her nervous to think that this venerable prize could be manipulated. Alan had said he would take her to lunch before the first board meeting to explain it all.

Today was the day. He was taking her to the Federal City Club. It was one small dreary room in the Sheraton Carlton Hotel that had been roped off

694

for members, most of whom were part of the Washington establishment. Clubs were pretty much out and she didn't believe in them anyway, but she thought it was kind of dumb to belong to a club that had no reason for being in the first place. It wasn't for anything, it wasn't restrictive in any way (which she did not view as a negative, simply a curiosity), and the food wasn't any good. So what was the point? Why not eat in a good restaurant with decent atmosphere.?

They were led to a booth, but Alan asked for a table for two against the wall. The seats in the booths were too far apart, he explained, and they would have to shout to be heard. This way they could have a private conversation.

They both ordered soda water and the filet of sole. There was no small talk.

'So,' he said, furrowing his brow and smoothing the tablecloth with his hands, 'we have two finalists this year: Tyson for investigative and Jeremy Dugan for movie criticism.'

'Well,' said Allison, already irritated by the idea of a potential loss in either case, 'Dugan ought to be a shoo-in. The guy is far and away the best movie critic in the country and he's been passed over three times. And nobody has anything to compare with Sprague's drug stuff...'

Warburg held up both hands to stop her.

'Hold it, hold it, hold it,' he said. 'The first thing you have to learn is that nobody's a shoo-in. Especially in our case. We're being punished for our sins. We've been blanked for three years for that plagiarism case. A lot of talented reporters have suffered because of it. I have a gut feeling that we've served our sentence and they're going to let us out of jail. But if I've done my time and I'm getting out of jail I wouldn't go for two no matter how good they are. I'd take one and run.'

'But Sprague's stories have had a major impact. I've read the other entries. They can't touch what he's done.'

'Allison. Listen to me. Sprague has already won a Pulitzer, so that makes it less likely they'd give him another one anyway. We've got a slim chance of getting one if we're lucky. Sprague is working on a story that is much bigger than what's already happened. If that's true he'll have a better shot next year. One of the most important things to learn is to fight the big fight, to know when to fold 'em. If the movie critic gets it and Sprague doesn't win, then you immediately make sure that the advisory board knows he's working on something that will have a hell of an impact, even more than this.'

'Is that all I can do? Isn't there some way I can help get the message across?'

'We've already sent out reprints of all our best stuff to every newspaper in the country. We can't just send them to the members of the Pulitzer board. That would be too crass. But everybody sends reprints to all the papers now. That's about as blatant as you can get. We have an advantage because we're one of the bigger papers, so more people see what we do and we've got more resources. We'll probably do better now that we've got a professional packaging our prize entry, putting out these brochures. We didn't use to do that but these people like glitz so we've had to spend a lot of time on presentation. As to what you can do. You can go up there and be as charming as you possibly can. But for God's sake don't get caught lobbying because that will work against you. You can't get in the way of an express train. If there's a sentiment developing against your candidate then get out of the way. If you know a reason why somebody else shouldn't get it, then by all means be sure that everybody knows. But you have to have the very lightest touch. If there's a choice between doing nothing and overdoing it, then do nothing.'

'But if you think they're being unfair to one of your candidates what can you do about it?'

'If you can, get someone else to fight your fight. That's all the better.'

'Forgive me for asking, but if you're so good at it, why are you giving me your seat? Why don't you go up and politic yourself?'

Alan sighed and took a sip of his drink.

'Because I'm a lightning rod. I don't think I'm doing the paper any good. And because I'm disgusted with the process. It's so superficial.'

'I don't mean to sound naive, but I still don't see how they can not reward the best people for the best work just because of political reasons alone. This is the Pulitzer Prize, Alan. For Christ's sake!'

'That's the way it's done, my dear. This is not a perfect world. I'm surprised at you. You're supposed to be one of the most cynical reporters in this town. You know how the system works.'

'It isn't fair.'

'Warburg chuckled.

'This whole process isn't fair. It's a game. You just have to know how to play it. Just remember one thing.'

Warburg suddenly had a beatific smile on his face.

697

'What's that, Alan?'

'You're always coming back next year.'

★     ★     ★

Stuart Lanier Davidson IV was an old drinking buddy of Allison's from the campaign days, one of the boys on the bus. They had shared stories and sources, covered for each other on deadline, hung out together, sung hymns together late at night, and been there for each other in bad times.

Once, after a campaign trip years earlier, she had had a group covering the incumbent over for dinner at her house the Saturday night before Easter Sunday. Lanny had gotten completely smashed that night. She didn't hear from him for several days afterward and was beginning to worry when she received a huge bouquet of Easter lilies with a card that said, 'Risen at last.'

Lanny was a Southern good ole boy—or bad boy, depending on how you looked at it. From a prominent Atlanta family, he had gone to the college named after his family and come back to the *Atlanta Herald*, much against his parent's wishes, to start a career in journalism. When he and Allison had known each other he was a political reporter and a controversial columnist. Later, he got on the fast track, and after a series of changes in upper management, ended up, much to the astonishment of his friends and colleagues, as the editor-in-chief of the whole paper. He was also chosen to be on the Pulitzer board and was in his second three-year term. When it was first announced that Allison was going on the board, Lanny had called to congratulate her. He had called again this week to ask her to join him and a few of the other 'bad boys' on the board for dinner the night before the voting.

'You oughtta be there, darlin',' he told her in his Southern drawl. 'That's where all the schmoozin' and the lovin' up goes on.'

Allison laughed in spite of herself.

'So that's how it's done,' she said. 'I must say it can't be a total coincidence that the *Herald* has won so many Pulitzers since you got on the board.'

'Well, I wouldn't want to sound immodest, but those boys just love my Southern ass. And when I start singin' gospels I can just close my eyes and see the Pulitzers rolling in. Sweet Jesus!'

'Oh, c'mon Lanny, seriously.'

'Seriously? Let me give you a few tips. There are three areas of manipulation. The first is in categories. When the juries send up their three choices of finalists, one category may have no strong entry, say foreign, for instance. If another category, like explanatory journalism, has a great series about revolutions, you could get the category changed putting revolution in the foreign category and have a chance to win.

'The second is the permanent secretary of the Pulitzers. He can change entries before the juries even meet. He can accommodate or interfere with the juries' will to change things.

'The third and best chance for manipulation is when there is real dissatisfaction with the jury's selection. If you don't like any of the three finalists the jury sends up, you can go back and say let's see what else there is and overrule the jury by awarding the prize to someone who wasn't in the top three.'

'Yeah, but if you do that kind of thing, won't people know about it?'

'Of course. The place is a fucking sieve. Whatever position you take you have to know it's going to get out.'

'I'm not sure I'm going to be any good at this, Lanny,' said Allison. 'I'm incapable of bargaining for a rug in a Turkish bazaar.'

'Trust me, darlin'. You just bat those baby blue eyes and you'll do just fine.'

*　　　*　　　*

She was nervous as a cat. This was the day of the voting. She had shown up at the Columbia University's Graduate School of Journalism at precisely nine that morning. There were already a few people assembled by the coffee urn outside the World Room. She had seen it the day before when they came in to read the entries. It was very impressive, intimidating really, with huge murals of light and truth painted in blue and gold. It looked like a place a venerable prize like the Pulitzer should be awarded.

She had survived dinner the night before. It had actually been fun. Lanny was full of stories and people couldn't help loosening up around him. Before the night was over everyone was shouting and laughing and having a terrific time. She tried not to appear self-conscious, tried to be adorable without overtly flirting, and managed to restrain herself from ever mentioning the Pulitzer. To her surprise and relief nobody else did either.

When she arrived back at the hotel that night there was a frantic message from the editor of the Living section to call her no matter what time she got in. Allison dialed the number immediately.

700

'Thank God you called, Allison,' she said when she heard Allison's voice. 'Jeremy told me tonight that he hears there's a lot of sympathy building to give the criticism prize to this woman. God I can't even remember her name, a music critic from some small paper in Ohio.'

'Did this just arise out of nowhere?'

'Apparently she would be the first woman music critic to get it and ... are you ready for this? ... she's dying of cancer.'

'Oh God.'

'Exactly.'

'Does she have any credentials?'

'Apparently none. The town doesn't even have a symphony, she's only part time and I hear that she's done p.r. work for the Cincinnati symphony.'

'Okay. I'll try to pass that along to some key people. I don't know what I can really do, though. When criticism comes up for a vote, they send me out of the room.'

'Good luck!'

'Thanks.'

★   ★   ★

Now, this morning, she was faced with how to deal with the problem. She poured herself some tea, looked around at the early arrivals, and decided there was no hope there. Resigned, she wandered over to a small group that was having a solemn discussion about the economy. After several boring minutes she heard what sounded suspiciously like a rebel yell. She turned to see with immense relief that Lanny had appeared, his hair still wet from the shower, looking perfectly groomed if slightly hung over.

She sidled over to the coffee urn while he was pouring himself a cup; making sure she wasn't overheard, she nervously relayed to him what the Living editor had told her the night before.

'You're learning fast,' he said, and she wasn't quite sure whether he was criticizing or praising her.

He casually poured some cream in his coffee, stirred it, and looked her in the eyes.

'I hear ya' was all he said, then he smiled and walked over to another group.

★    ★    ★

Allison was seated at the middle of the oval table. Lanny was on the opposite side of her so that she could see his every expression. It soon became clear that the chairman, the publisher of a small paper in the West, was an ineffectual person who let the meetings drift along without much direction. The leadership gap was filled, as far as she could see, by Lanny, who was a compelling personality, and the charismatic editor of the *Los Angeles Post*, Jordan Sinclair.

The first category on the agenda was public service. The *L.A. Post* was a finalist in three categories but not public service. From Allison's point of view, they should have been, for their exposé and continuing coverage of the Los Angeles Police Department. She had noticed at breakfast that several of the heavy hitters on the board had taken Jordan aside during coffee and had whispered conversations with him. Now one of them spoke up.

'Mr Chairman, I would like to suggest that we take another look at the public service category. We have three finalists here that don't even hold a candle to the *L.A. Post* on the police story. I submit that we rethink this and give the award to Mr Sinclair here for the fine job his paper has done.'

There were several murmurs of approval throughout the room. Allison noticed that Jordan demurred. He had managed to plaster the most incredible humble look on his face she had ever seen. He had obviously done his politicking earlier and well.

'It would seem that this warrants some discussion,' said the chairman. 'Jordan, would you please leave the room?'

After Jordan left it took about three minutes to yank the public service award from the three finalists and give it to the L.A. paper. Jordan came back beaming. And well he should. He had three other finalists in three other categories, all clear winners over their competition. That would mean that the L.A. paper would win four. That had never happened before. She was curious to see how that would fly. Jordan would have to be a master to pull that one off.

The next category was national reporting and again Jordan was sent from the room. There was little discussion on this one as well. She had yet to make a comment. She had decided to lay low. His candidate was the obvious winner. He returned with a shit-eating grin on his face.

Investigative was next. Sprague. Nobody would look her in the eye. She knew he had lost before she even left the room to go sit in the library and wait for the vote. There was no question that the winner wasn't nearly as good, but it was not an embarrassment either. They could get away with it. She wondered whether this meant the *Daily* was still being punished for the plagiarism episode or that it was because Sprague had already won a Pulitzer. She took defeat with grace. She still had another shot. But she did give Lanny a long 'I'm counting on you' look.

Then came Jordan's next candidate, this one for foreign, this one also way ahead of the other two.

'He's already won two,' somebody piped up after he'd left. Everyone else nodded and then began discussing the others. She still hadn't said a word but she was stunned when they voted for one who couldn't compare to the L.A. paper. Jordan was obviously as shocked as she was when he came back into the room.

It happened a second time with his last candidate, only this time nobody had to say it. They just voted for one of the lesser entries, passing over what she considered a brilliant feature series. She was appalled. Several of the members puffed on their pipes or cigarettes, and looked as though nothing unusual had happened.

The next category up was commentary. The *New York World* had by far the weakest of the three. Up until this point they hadn't won a single prize even though they'd had several finalists. This was their last chance. The board was definitely going against them until one of the older and more established members spoke up with alarm.

'But this ... this would mean,' he sputtered, 'that the *New York World* wouldn't get a Pulitzer Prize!'

There was a general rustling of papers and looks

704

of uneasiness as the members looked down at their hands.

Finally someone else said, 'He's right. We can't let that happen.'

And before Allison knew it they had voted the *World* a Pulitzer.

Now it was Allison's turn again. The criticism award was up. She left the room. It was the longest wait she ever had. She pretended to thumb through magazines in the library but she couldn't concentrate on a thing. When the young woman finally came to get her, Allison looked at her as though the doctor had stepped out of the operating room to tell her whether her loved one had lived or died.

'You won,' 'she whispered with excitement, and Allison nearly expired from relief.

Back in the World Room she didn't dare glance at Lanny, who kept clearing his throat to get her attention. She was more interested in the next vote. One of the editors of a small newspaper in the West who was the most disliked person on the board had a woman finalist for sports. His paper hadn't won a Pulitzer for years. Allison knew he had his heart set on it. She also knew that he had been the one who had vociferously advocated punishing the *Daily* for the plagiarism case. The chairman had been soliciting comment throughout the morning but she had yet to speak. This time he said, 'Allison, you've been awfully quiet all morning. What are your thoughts on our choices here?'

She had to weigh her answer carefully. She felt that all three candidates were about equal. She didn't want to screw a deserving journalist out of a prize because her editor was a jerk. On the other hand, given that she wasn't necessarily the best and might only receive the award because she was a woman, she thought she could speak up. She debated whether or not to compliment the woman before she spoke for the other candidates and decided that might be too heavy, too obvious. Instead she spoke only of her choice.

'I think he has a great style and wit,' she said. 'His stuff transcends sports. He makes it magic. It's brilliant reporting and writing. I read him regularly and I never read the sports pages.'

She got general agreement. Her choice won the prize. When the editor of the losing paper came back in Allison couldn't look at him. She couldn't help feeling guilty even though she told herself she would have voted the same way even if he hadn't been responsible for the *Daily*'s jail sentence.

After the journalism awards were over she was able to relax and have a good time. She felt fairly secure in all the categories except for the music one. She was a musical idiot. When the three finalists were presented she hadn't a clue what to do. The member in charge, who fancied himself something of a music connoisseur hummed a few bars of each entry, pronounced all three unworthy and recommended that they not award anyone that year. Since none of the other members had any idea whether or not he was right, they all followed his advice and nobody got the Pulitzer Prize for music.

When the day was over Allison couldn't wait to tell Alan, even though it was supposed to be a secret. She quickly left the room and raced out of the building, bumping into Lanny at the entrance.

'You owe me,' he said and winked.

'Wait till you see Tyson's entry next year!' she

said, laughing.

'You're getting awfully cocky, girl.'

'It's not hard to be cocky when you've just seen the most uplifting example of how true excellence is always rewarded and how those who deserve to win always triumph. You could score that sentiment and win a Pulitzer Prize for music.'

'You're as bad as you always were,' he said, kissing her goodbye. 'Now hurry down to the corner bookstore. There's a phone booth there and you can call Alan Warburg and tell him the good news.'

*     *     *

She and Des had hardly seen each other over the past two months. She had been avoiding him, but even if she had wanted to see him she had been too busy. April and May were unbelievably hectic for her, with the drug story, the Pulitzers, and the campaigns. Not only was she involved with Sprague's project but she was having to oversee all the campaign coverage, and the conventions were coming up in less than two months. She rarely left the office before ten or eleven these days, and she worked every Saturday and part of most Sundays.

Des, who often did the Sunday morning talk show, had been signed on as a regular and was up at dawn on Sundays to go to the studio. His days at the *Weekly* were long towards the end of the week, and lately, because of the campaigns, he'd been staying late on Saturday nights to close the magazine. As if that weren't enough, the 'Good Night' anchor on ABC had a terrible drinking problem that had escalated appreciably in the past few months, so that he was often out 'sick,' a not terribly well-kept secret in Washington. Des had been drafted to fill in for him occasionally and had done so well they were using him most of the time. This meant that he was almost never home, because when he did 'Good Night' he never got home before one-thirty or two in the morning. She had almost forgotten what he looked like. They communicated through notes left on the kitchen counter by the phone. The rare times they did actually meet they were cordial at best.

She was surprised when he called out of the blue the first Monday in June.

'Des? Desmond Shaw? Aren't you the one I used to be married to?'

'Right. Tall, dark, curly hair, chiseled features, crooked smile. You remember me?'

So there was some humor, some life yet in what had begun to look like a marital carcass. Maybe the separation had helped—maybe time.

'What's the occasion?'

'Dinner.'

'Where?'

'Nora's?'

'We always end up at Nora's.'

'Well, where would you like to go?'

'Nora's.'

'See you there at eight.'

\* \* \*

Allison got there first, parked her car illegally in front, and was taken to her favorite round table in the back corner. She ordered a kir, very light, and willed herself to unwind. The atmosphere was

708

conducive to it. Soft lights, pale walls, hanging quilts, candles, tablecloths, plush rugs. She always felt at home at Nora's.

As she was sitting there two television correspondents came in and took a table up front. Seeing her, they got up and came back to say hello. 'Great news about Des!' said one. 'What a coup! He'll be terrific, too. Who would have believed they would be so smart.'

She didn't have a clue. She smiled and nodded. Maybe she'd get an idea if she kept listening. Old journalistic trick.

'The bastard really has nine lives, doesn't he? It's incredible. What's it going to do to his home life?'

'What home life? This is an election year.' She was winging it.

'Good point. Well, tell the ole boy we're proud of him.'

'Tell him yourself, he's right behind you.'

'Hey pal, congratulations,' he said to Des, who had just come in. Des glanced nervously at her, as he was shaking his friend's hand.

After they left he sat down and gave the waitress his order for an Irish whiskey, neat.

'So,' she said, a glacial smile on her face, 'I guess congratulations are in order.'

'Sonny, listen, I—'

'Don't tell me. You've won the lottery and you wanted to surprise me. Well, it worked. I'm surprised.'

'Give me a break, Sonny. It all happened so fast I haven't had time to—'

'I have an idea. Why don't we speak Chinese tonight. Maybe we'll have better luck at communicating with each other.'

'I'm really sorry, I . . .'

'Moo shu pork, egg foo young, kung pau shrimp, hoysin sauce.'

'Very funny.'

'Shanghai, Peking, Hong Kong.'

'I quit my job okay. I quit my fucking job at the *Weekly* and I accepted the job as the anchor of "Good Night".'

'You've got to be kidding!'

She looked at his solemn face.

'You're not kidding.'

'They shit-canned Benton Halloran. The guy was half in the bag every night by the time he got there, and then he'd take little nips when nobody was looking. He's blown it a couple of time on the air, he was so sauced. They finally had no choice. It was hair-raising. They never knew from night to night whether he was going to make it to the office and then whether he was going to make it on the air.'

'Have you told New York?'

'They went crazy. Even though I was sick of the job and I couldn't stand them and they thought I was a pain in the ass, I was still the best damn bureau chief they had ever had and they knew it. They tried to talk me out of it. Even the editor got in the act. "Nobody has your contacts," he said. That's all he thinks about. Contacts. Christ, am I glad to be out of there.'

'I take it you've given this a great deal of thought. You've determined that you can live without writing and reporting and that you can deal with the fact that you don't have much respect for television?'

'Of course.'

The waiter came and they both ordered another

drink, then took long sips in silence.

'Who did you talk it over with?' Her voice was barely audible.

'Jenny and O'Grady.'

'Do you want out of the marriage?'

Her question came as a shock to him and he nearly bolted back in his chair. After he recovered he didn't respond right away.

'What marriage?' he said at last.

'They say that ninety percent of all couples who lose a child eventually break up.'

She felt nothing. No pain, no sadness no relief, nothing. She was totally numb. Even the memory of Kay Kay evoked nothing from her at this moment. Her work and her deliberate estrangement from Des had cauterized her emotions. That was the way she wanted it. That was all she knew she wanted. She wanted not to feel. After that nothing mattered.

'The answer is no. No, I don't want out of the marriage. But I don't want the marriage the way it is either. I'm not getting what I need. And I need more now than I ever have. I'm trying, Sonny. I have tried. I'm doing the best I can. It's obviously not good enough for you. I'm willing to do more or at least to try if you can tell me what you need. But I'm a blind man. I can't see my way to helping you or helping myself alone. I can't clap with one hand and you're not even lifting yours. You ask me the question. Now I'll ask you: Do you want out?'

'Do you want the truth?'

He sighed.

'Do I have a choice?'

'The truth is that I don't know and I don't care. There's nothing left inside me. Intellectually I think

711

we both need each other, that this is a stage of the pain we have to go through, that it will come back. But emotionally it just isn't there. If you said you wanted out right now I would have to say to you, "Fine. Leave." I have no right to ask you to stay. I don't have anything to give you. You have nothing to give me. Maybe it's the best thing. I just don't know, Des. I really don't know.'

The waiter brought them menus. They both declined and ordered a third drink.

'So what are we going to do, Sonny?'

'I don't see that we have to do anything. With my schedule and your new job we'll never see each other anyway. So why bother?'

She suddenly felt exhausted. Almost unable to move. It was all she could do not to slump over the table.

'Des, I'd like to go home now. I need to lie down. I'm so tired.'

She reached for her purse and got out her car keys. She was trying to gather the energy to stand up.

'I love you, Sonny.'

She looked at him, into those deep, dark, needy eyes. The love and pain were practically oozing out of him in equal proportions. If it had been a comic book you could have colored the clouds around him. She wanted to comfort him, to heal the pain, to make the hurt go away. But she couldn't. She just couldn't.

She sighed with every fiber of energy she had, pushed herself up out of her chair. She stood there, looking down at him for a moment before she walked away.

'I know,' she whispered. 'I know you do, Des. I know.'

★    ★    ★

It was eighty-six degrees, not a drop of humidity, not a cloud in the sky. A perfect mid-June day. A perfect day for a picnic.

Allison was feeling cooped up in the office. She had been working so hard she hadn't been outside in weeks. Her skin was beginning to take on a slightly greenish tinge, her eyes were bloodshot and unfocused from staring at the computer screen, and she had a perpetual headache. She also hadn't eaten a decent meal in so long she had forgotten what food tasted like. She was getting ready to go down to the cafeteria for her usual salad and fruit when she saw Sprague heading toward her office.

'We need to talk,' he said, sticking his head in the door.

'Unfortunately it's lunchtime and I'm starving,' she said. 'And since you don't do lunch I'm afraid it will have to wait.'

'Okay. So I'm an asshole. Anything else?'

'Yeah. How about lunch?'

'Great idea.'

'Where had you planned to take me? Jean Pierre? The Jockey Club? The Maison Blanche?'

'Actually I was thinking of Lafayette Park.'

'Brilliant!'

'Are you being sarcastic?'

'On the contrary. It's a gorgeous day. I was just pining to be outdoors when you walked in. Let's get some salads and lemonade from the cafeteria and take them over there.'

'I'll met you at the elevator in five.'

713

* * *

She had forgotten about Ralph. She always forgot
about Ralph. But there he was, joined at the hip
with Sprague.

'What would you do, or rather what would one
do, if one wanted to have an affair and had this
bodyguard tailing you every minute?' she whispered
to Sprague as they walked up 16th Street, past St
John's Church toward the park. She wanted to bite
her tongue the moment it was out of her mouth.

'I'd have an affair,' he said, without hesitation.
He looked at her and caught her eyes before she had
a chance to look away. 'Why?'

'Oh, no reason. I mean, I was just curious how
people...' She was flustered and didn't know
where to look. He wouldn't look away. 'Never
mind. It was a silly question. I was just wondering,
that's all.'

They chose a maple tree to the right of the statue
of General Jackson facing the White House. They
had decided to sit under a tree rather than on a
bench because they could talk more privately.
Ralph took up his post at a bench across from them.
They sat down on the grass and spread out their
food.

They sat there for a while, just taking in the
sights and sounds of summer.

The park looked especially beautiful in June with
its colorful flower beds, velvety green grass, and
large spreading trees. Under the tree next to them
was a group of hippie peace demonstrators with
long beards and braids, leaning on backpacks and
playing the flute and the guitar. The music seemed

714

to drift on the air around them. Bees buzzed around the pollen and the birds flew overhead, in and out of a dark green birdhouse perched high atop one of the trees. Somewhere in the distance the sound of workmen on a construction project hammered almost rhythmically. A group of Japaneses tourists took pictures of each other in front of the White House, and a homeless man slept a drugged sleep on one of the benches near Ralph. To the right of them some old men played chess on the permanent chess tables, a man with a motorized wheelchair sped by, several deaf people were speaking in sign language, and a group of pretty girls strolled by in sundresses, laughing and giggling with each other. Sprague followed them appreciatively with his eyes. A couple holding hands came up to one of the benches along the path to the right of them, sat down, and began to neck rather passionately.

Allison was unexpectedly overcome with lust. Insane, irrational, almost uncontrollable lust. She hadn't felt that way in over a year, since she had gotten pregnant. Certainly not since the baby. It came on her so fast that it made her mouth dry. It was as if she'd suddenly been possessed. It was not undirected. It was lust for Sprague. Lust for that tiny scar over his left eye, the full lower lip, the bedroom eyes and strong, tanned hands; lust for the muscled arms she wanted to be in this very minute. His eyes met hers for an instant and she had no doubt that he knew what she was thinking. She was so horrified that she nearly got up and left.

Sprague cleared his throat and took a sip of his lemonade.

'You may be wondering why I brought you here today,' he started in a husky voice, then blushed.

715

She hadn't seen him blush before. She almost didn't notice it because of his tan but it amused her. He obviously hadn't meant to refer to the necking couple but it came out that way.

'I didn't mean . . .' he said.

She wasn't going to help him out of his misery. Let him suffer, too.

'Anyway, I needed someplace secure where we could talk. I just wanted you to know that I am very very close to nailing Foxy. You know that trip he took down to Colombia last month? Well, it seems that he spent the weekend out at the Foreign Minister's ranch with Antonia. Apparently Antonia got him to do some coke and the Foreign Minister had the whole thing videotaped. Foxy knows about it and they've told him unless he calls the DEA off the Bader-Skinner story they're going to release the tapes.'

'My God. How could he be that stupid?'

'They're all stupid, Ally. You, of all people, should know that by now, after covering Washington for so many years. They're all stupid. Once they get into power they lose sight of reality. They think they own the world and that they're not accountable. It's a disease. A Washington disease. Nobody is immune, there's no vaccine. The only cure is downfall.'

'So how solid do you have it?'

'I may be able to get the tape.'

'What are you going to do with all the money you make on the book and the movie?'

He looked horrified.

'Do you think that's why I'm doing this?'

'Relax. I didn't accuse you of being an ax murderer. I'm just being realistic. I can't help

716

wondering whether you'll stay the same sweet, humble, adorable person you are or whether you'll change, too, the way the very people in power that you're talking about do. Some people just can't handle fame, you know.' She couldn't help smiling at his reaction.

'Will you knock it off?' He wasn't quite sure why he should be teased about this. It was serious.

'Where's your sense of humor today?'

'I have just told you the most incredible piece of news you've ever heard as an editor and you're acting like it's some kind of a joke. What the hell is wrong with you?'

She burst out laughing.

'I'm sorry,' she said. 'I think spring fever. I haven't been out of the office in so long that I'm just overwhelmed with the air and the flowers and...'

They both glanced at the couple near them locked in an embrace.

He looked at her and smiled, then shrugged helplessly.

'I'll try to be serious, Sprague. I promise. It's...'

Suddenly his face changed. His smile disappeared. She had her back to Ralph so she couldn't see what was happening. Sprague pushed her to the ground, leaped up, and starting running toward Ralph. When she turned around she saw Ralph was in some kind of scuffle with two men, both with dark, slicked-back hair, shiny suits, very pale skin, and rosy cheeks. She thought she saw a flash of metal as Sprague reached them, she heard swearing in Spanish, then a crunching noise like somebody had been hit. After that there was a loud crack as if someone had been shot, then a cry of pain. She lay on the ground where Sprague had pushed her in shock. It was all happening so fast.

Several park police spotted them and came running over. The two men took off amid shouts to halt. The police were too late. The men disappeared.

She closed her eyes. She didn't move. She knew what had happened. Sprague had been shot. Sprague was dying. That's what happened. That's what always happened. The people she cared about died. How could she have thought that Sprague would be any different? How could she have been so selfish? How could she not have known? She lay back on the ground, resigned. She tried to stop breathing.

'Ally? Are you all right?'

It was his voice. Was it her imagination? Is that what she wanted to hear or was it really he?

She opened her eyes slowly, afraid of what she would find.

It was Sprague. He was kneeling down by her with a worried look.

She stared at him for a moment, not believing it at first, then, unable to control her emotions, she flung herself into his arms.

'Ally, Ally, it's okay. I'm fine.'

He was stroking her back and holding her tightly. She couldn't stop clinging to him and she couldn't stop crying. She certainly couldn't speak.

'Oh God, it's nothing, Ally. Those two Colombian assholes were so inept they couldn't have hit an elephant with a cannonball. It's okay. I'm fine.'

Finally he let her go and she sat up and leaned against the tree, wiping her eyes with a paper napkin.

'I thought you were dead,' she said in a low voice.

'Why?'

'I heard a shot. It came from where you were standing.'

'I heard it, too, but it wasn't a gun. It was a truck backfiring in front of the White House. Those guys never even got their guns out. Ralph hit one of them in the ribs and the nuts. That was the cry you heard. What a couple of bozos. I don't think they were trying to do anything but scare me.'

'Well they certainly scared me.'

'Oh c'mon. They're harmless.'

'I want you off this story.'

'You sound like Jane.'

'Jane? What did she say?'

'She says she's sick of the fear and the hiding and she wants me off the story. She also says sl  ares Washington. She and Melissa are not comin  ack. She wants me to quit the paper and go home to Savannah.'

'What are you going to do?' She could barely get the words out.

'I'm going to stay here.' He paused. 'I don't want off the story. I don't want out of the paper ... and I don't want to leave you.'

★    ★    ★

For the first time in what seemed like months she and Des were home together at the same time. It was a Sunday evening, July 2, the night before her birthday. She had been working. Des had been out to his cabin in West Virginia. He came back, showered, changed, and joined her on the terrace off the dining room for a drink.

It was a beautiful evening, not at all humid, and the air was redolent of the honeysuckle that climbed along the wooden fence separating her from the neighbors. The fireflies were out in full force and it reminded Allison of her childhood in this house. Sam would punch holes in the top of a jar and she would run around squealing with delight every time she caught one, showing off with pride to her father and Nana.

Kay Kay would be six months old. Old enough to sit up and swat at fireflies. This house should have a child. She should have a child. Des should have one, too. A son maybe. It wasn't too late. She was only in her early forties. She could still get pregnant. She hadn't allowed herself to think that before. She shouldn't now. She didn't trust anything she thought or felt. One minute she thought she was in love with Sprague or deeply attracted to him, the next minute she was thinking about having another baby with Des. What was wrong with her? She didn't know who she was anymore. She was so used to being in control, knowing what she wanted. Now she didn't know anything. Her moods changed by the hour and so quickly that it made her dizzy. She had lost all of her resources. She would just have to accept the fact that she was crazy and would be for a long time.

Still, she was feeling calmer. She and Des were talking about the election and the upcoming conventions. They were going to both of them. They hadn't discussed yet whether they would stay in the same hotel rooms or not. Mainly because they hadn't discussed anything important at all since dinner at Nora's.

She got up to fix herself another drink.

'I've got some fettuccine with fresh tomato sauce and basil in the icebox,' she said. 'Does that interest you?'

'Sounds great.'

Was there hope in the air? The rancor was gone. Her enervating mood swings were gone for the moment. Her surge of sexual energy that day in the park with Sprague had not disappeared. She glanced at Des and remembered how good-looking he was, how sexy and masculine.

She went into the kitchen, got out the pasta and some focaccia, a delicious Italian bread she had bought that day. She brought it out to the terrace, along with some candles, which she placed on the small round table. Des opened a bottle of wine and got the wineglasses.

They sat down, he poured the wine and lifted his glass to her.

'Here's to us, baby.'

He had picked up on the feeling of hope, of renewal in the air.

She didn't demur. She clicked his glass and smiled.

The phone rang.

'Shit,' she said. 'If that's the office . . . I'll get it.'

She reached over to the coffee table, got the cordless phone, and answered it. A young woman, so hysterical that Allison could hardly understand her, asked for Des.

She handed it to him, giving him a quizzical look.

When he answered it a look of horror came over his face.

'Oh, no. Oh, no. Oh my God. Holy Mother.

Where is he? Okay, I'll be right there. Tell her I'll be right there.'

He jumped up from the table, nearly knocking over the chair.

'What is it, Des? What's happened?'

'It's Willie Grey. That was his nanny. He's had an accident, fallen down the stairs, hit his head. He may not live. They're taking him to Georgetown Hospital. Sadie wants me to come. I have to go right away.' He was stumbling over his words, stumbling toward the door, clearly not anxious to answer any questions.

'Willie Grey? But why would Sadie...?'

Des looked at her in such a way that she didn't finish the question.

He came over to her and put his hands on her shoulders.

'Sonny ... Sonny. Oh God, I don't know how to...'

A terrible image was beginning to form in her brain, a slow dawning, a recognition of something that she had never wanted to think about.

'I've wanted to tell you so many times ...' he was saying.

Those pictures in all the magazines and on television, that dark curly hair, those masculine little features, that jaunty strut. They had always reminded her of somebody, but she could never figure out who.

'It's just that I didn't want to hurt you...'

But of course it was because she didn't want to know. It was too awful.

'And we thought, I thought, it was better for Willie's sake if nobody knew...'

She knew. She knew in her gut. She had always

known. Willie was his son.

'Of course,' she said. 'How could I have been so stupid?'

'I'm sorry,' he said. 'I'm really sorry.'

'It's okay,' she said, stricken.

'Try to understand.'

He turned and bolted out the door.

Allison stood there for a long time. Then she went back out on the terrace and sat down on the chaise longue and leaned back. She took a long sip of wine and concentrated on the fireflies. She had just been thinking that Des needed a child. What she hadn't known was that all this time he had one. Now maybe he didn't. Maybe Willie would die, too. She tried to analyze how she felt about this. It hadn't sunk in yet. Did she feel jealous? Angry? Sad? She didn't know. What she did know was that she felt enormous pity for Des. To have a son he couldn't acknowledge must be the worst torture possible for him. To lose a baby daughter, and now, only six months after Kay Kay's death, to face losing that son was unthinkable. And yet if Willie lived, Des would be tied to this woman and this child forever. What she had just learned put a huge distance between them, a distance that might be unbridgeable. She couldn't tell now. It would take time to know. Maybe a very long time.

They announced on the news that night that Willie was in intensive care but stable. Sadie Grey, it said, had been accompanied to Children's Hospital by a family friend. She was glad for Sadie and for Des that Willie would not die. She was not glad about what it meant for her and Des.

★    ★    ★

Des never came home that night. She went to work
the next day. When she came home he was at the
studio. He got home at one-thirty that morning.
She was still awake. He didn't turn on the lights.
He got undressed in the dark and slid into bed.

'How's Willie?'

'He's going to be okay. Thank the good Lord.'

'I'm glad.'

He reached over and took her hand. They were
quiet for a while.

'We're losing each other and it makes me very
sad,' she said.

'I know. I know, Sonny. I know.'

## CHAPTER SEVENTEEN

Her suite at the Ritz Carlton was filled with flowers.
There was a large basket of fruit on the table, a
bottle of champagne in an ice bucket. On the desk
was a folder containing her schedule for that
evening plus messages from Freddy and Blanche.

Nobody knew she was in Atlanta. Her
appearance at the last night of the Democratic
convention was a closely guarded secret. She had
flown in on a private plane in disguise and been
ushered in through the back entrance of the hotel so
as not to be seen. Her suite was on the same floor of
the hotel as the President's, so it was heavily
guarded by Secret Service. There was no chance of
anyone seeing her there.

She had not wanted to come. She had refused at
first. In the end she had succumbed to the pressure

and agreed. Now she was sorry but it was too late to back out.

The plan for her to appear on the platform the last night was the idea of the media types Freddy had surrounded himself with. They were frantic at his slip in the polls. He had gone from an 80 percent approval rating to 26 percent, a free fall of public opinion due, in large part, to Sprague Tyson's stories in the *Daily* linking members of the administration to the drug trade. Since the *Daily* had begun its stories, every other news organization in the country had picked up on them. They were all over Freddy, Foxy, Antonia, Garcia, and the rest of them. Although neither Sprague nor any of the others had nailed anyone yet and the allegations were vague, the perception of corruption and sleaze permeated the administration.

Blanche had done a good job as First Lady. She had overcome her image by reestablishing herself as a country singer and had garnered goodwill for raising funds for AIDS. The problem was that no matter how hard she tried the public didn't really want Freddy back in the White House.

This was all aside from the fact that the President had tested positive for HIV. Of course, nobody knew this except Blanche, Sadie, Michael, and several of his trusted NIH researchers. They all understood that if it were to be made public it would be a disaster. Freddy refused to discuss it, even with Blanche. He was clearly in a state of denial. He never once considered not running, though both Blanche and Sadie felt strongly that he shouldn't.

Sadie didn't think he was worthy of occupying the same office once filled by better men, including her husband. And she couldn't help but think her endorsement was the height of hypocrisy.

Not only that, but she really felt that it was time to get on with it. She was no longer in politics; her life was about other things. She felt as if she were retracing old steps, backtracking. The only thing that had saved her in the last two years was being able to look ahead, to hope. She didn't want to lose that.

She was afraid, too, of sad memories that she had only just begun to bury. The memories were not just of Rosey. They were of Des as well. It had been in Atlanta four years ago, at another convention, that she agonized over whether to leave Rosey. Rosey had told her that if she left him he would give up the presidency. But she was pregnant, possibly, though she wasn't sure then, with Des's child. She loved Rosey. She was in love with Des. Des was demanding an answer from her, not knowing she was pregnant. She had been avoiding him for weeks. In desperation he had had her Secret Service agent deliver a note to her, as she stood on the platform with her husband, accepting the nomination for his first full term. In keeping with their private way of setting up a tryst, it had said, simply, 'Regrets Only.' She had shaken her head, knowing she was giving him up to Allison forever.

These were all perfectly good reasons for her not to appear on the platform that evening. It was Blanche who finally talked her into it. If Freddy was going to run, Blanche wanted him to win.

Blanche had begged her to come on stage with them to present a show of unity in the Democratic party. Sadie knew that she could make a difference. If Freddy lost, the next President would be the

Republican candidate, a right winger, a former evangelist, a bigot. She had finally acquiesced to Blanche's request. Partly because she felt sorry for Blanche. But the most mitigating factor was that Malcolm Sohier was the vice presidential candidate. Freddy would more than likely have to resign and Malcolm would end up being President. If Malcolm hadn't been on the ticket she never would have campaigned for Freddy.

She was to appear at ten o'clock that evening. She would be the last person out on the platform, after the Vice President, a few senators and congressmen, and some Democratic heavies. That gave her time to bathe, rest, and have her hair done by Blanche's hairdresser.

Monica and Willie were in a bedroom off the suite, and Willie had gone down for a nap so he could go to the hall later. She took a long hot bath, trying to steam the tension out of her body. She wrapped herself in the hotel terry-cloth robe that had her name embroidered on it and lay down on the bed. She couldn't sleep so she phoned Outland. Annie Laurie and Outland had their own rooms down the hall. Then she thumbed through a magazine. She was so restless and jittery. Hotel rooms always made her that way. She always felt she should be doing something in them, like making love to someone.

She reached for the folder again to see if she had missed anything on her schedule. That's when she saw the envelope. It was a Ritz Carlton envelope, which was why she hadn't noticed it at first. This time she saw his handwriting. She tore it open almost cutting her finger.

'Sadie,' it said, 'I would like to see you tonight

727

after the convention. Des.'

How did he know she was going to be there?

Jenny. She must have told him. Sadie had made her swear on the Bible that she would tell no one. In a way, she couldn't blame Jenny. Des had given her a job at the *Weekly* as a reporter, his last act before he left to be the anchor of 'Good Night.' Jenny was extremely grateful. She hadn't had any luck finding a job she wanted in journalism after she left the White House. She had been getting a little desperate. Allison, despite the fact that they had renewed their friendship, never offered her a job. Jenny told Sadie everything about Des. She had no reason to think Jenny wouldn't do the same for Des. She was pretty sure that Jenny had no idea when she told Des about Sadie's plans to be at the convention that he would try to see her. Jenny would not betray Allison like that. Especially after what Allison had been through.

She had not seen him in over three weeks, not since Willie's accident. He had not responded to her note. She knew from Jenny that he and Allison were having problems, but Jenny was pretty circumspect about Allison. She also knew from Jenny that Des and Allison were staying in different hotels for the convention. Their hours were so different, according to Jenny, that they had decided it would be more convenient. She couldn't help wondering whether that decision had anything to do with what had happened with Willie. She had no idea what Des had told Allison, but she couldn't imagine that Allison wouldn't have figured out by now, if she hadn't already, that Willie was Des's son.

Rosey, Des, Michael ... visions of all of them

kept swirling around in her mind. Who did she love? Who did she want to see? She had told Michael she couldn't see him again. But that didn't mean she no longer cared about him, didn't think about him, didn't love him.

Willie's accident had shunted Michael off to the side in her thoughts. She was so concerned with Willie and his needs. Willie needed a father. Willie had a father. Des had been wonderful that night in the hospital. She had felt so secure having him there with her. He was the one person in the world who understood how she felt at that moment. No one would ever be able to share that with her. She had told Des in the letter that she needed him. She did. And she loved him. But she wanted Michael.

If she agreed to see Des what would happen? What would they talk about? What would they do? What should she do? What did she want to do?

It was impossible. She couldn't see him. She wouldn't see him. That was final. She had made up her mind. She felt enormously relieved.

*       *       *

The noise was deafening when she walked out onto the platform. The band struck up 'Sweet Georgia Brown' just as it had four years earlier and the crowd went wild. People were jumping up and down, screaming, waving and crying. As the television cameras panned over the packed convention hall there was hardly a face that wasn't glowing, hardly an eye that wasn't wet.

Someone shouted her name and the thousands of delegates in the convention hall picked up on it. An uproarious chant obscured even the music.

'Sa-die, Sa-die, Sa-die,' they yelled.

Balloons were released earlier than planned, confetti thrown, horns blown, flags waved. When the cheers and applause didn't stop, the band began playing 'Georgia on My Mind.' More tears, more shouts, more rebel yells.

She hadn't meant to cry. She had prepared herself not to. She had practiced little exercises, thoughts of things that would make her mad so she wouldn't cry. Nothing worked. When she walked out on the platform and heard that welcome she simply dissolved. It didn't help when Annie Laurie and Outland followed her and embraced her. When Willie came running out a few minutes into the applause and lifted his arms to be picked up, she totally lost it. She picked him up and he wrapped his arms around her neck, his legs around her waist, kissing her cheek to console her. She buried her head in his neck.

Her own emotional reaction to the moment was more than the delegates could bear. People began sobbing in the aisles, holding each other, embracing each other. Some even seemed overcome and collapsed in their chairs, burying their heads in their hands.

At the same time, reporters all over the country, both print and television, told the same story. It was a national catharsis. Nobody had predicted it. Certainly not the image makers who had planned to have her show up the last night as the pièce de résistance of the convention and the campaign. Certainly not Freddy, who had not expected to have the attention taken from him so completely. Certainly not Sadie.

As she began to regain control she lifted up her

head to look around the hall, to try to acknowledge the extraordinary tribute. Her eyes scanned the sea of faces encircling the platform. On either side of it, to her right and to her left, were the press sections where the print journalists had their boxes. One of the most prominent was that of the *Daily*. Standing in the front row, next to the two top editors, was Allison. Next to her was Sprague Tyson. Allison was looking up at the network anchor booth. Sadie's gaze followed hers. The anchormen and commentators had stood up and come to the front of their glass booths to look at the incredible scene below them. Her eyes rested on one of them, standing the closest to the window. He was tall and stocky with black curly hair and a square jaw. Even from a distance, she recognized him immediately. It was Des. From his posture she could tell that he had been wrenched by the spectacle. Instead of standing upright like the rest of the people in the booths, he was leaning forward, both hands pressed against the glass. It was as though he were trying to break through, to get down there to comfort her and Willie. His body was poised in such a way that it seemed he was straining in frustration against this act of fate that had conspired to keep him away from what was rightfully his.

When he saw her looking at him he held her gaze just long enough that he finally balled his hands, which had been spread out on the glass, into fists. For a moment she thought he might actually punch out the window, but then he turned and walked back toward an anchor desk, deliberately trying not to look at her or his son.

Sadie turned toward the other side of the hall. As she did she caught Allison staring at her. For a moment neither of them moved, each compelled by the other, by the irony of the situation. Then just as quickly, they both looked away.

The emotional frenzy lasted for over twenty minutes until everyone was drained. Up on the platform, which was crowded with Democratic superstars, it looked like the end of a group therapy session. There wasn't a woman up there who didn't have mascara running down her cheeks or a man with a red nose. Everyone was begging handkerchiefs from each other to wipe their eyes and aides were scurrying backstage trying to find boxes of tissues to pass around.

Not wanting to miss any opportunity, Freddy had taken Blanche by the hand and dragged her over to where Sadie was standing. He wanted to get in the limelight, have some of her magic rub off on him. She noticed that he didn't touch her but put his arm behind her back to make it look like he had his arm around her. Blanche embraced Sadie with genuine warmth, trying to take her and Willie in with one hug. The three of them, and Willie, stood together, basking in the wave of love and admiration that was pouring out across the hall.

When it was over there was almost a sense of exhilaration, the way there often is after a funeral, when the mourners suddenly realize that they are still alive. After the hall had quieted down there was an eerie stillness for several minutes and then, without warning, another outburst of flag waving, cheering, and song singing, this time a celebration of Rosey and Sadie rather than a dirge.

Freddy had finally gone to the lectern. As she was about to extricate herself from Blanche so that they could listen to the President, her Secret Service agent pressed a note into her hand.

A sense of déjà vu overcame her. At first she didn't dare look down at the note. She willed herself not to look at it. Then curiosity got the best of her. Casually, so no one would notice, she unfolded the note and glanced down. In handwriting that was all too familiar, and in words that even now burned a hole in her brain, the note said, simply, 'Regrets Only.'

Being up on the platform again this day and receiving his query as she had four years ago came as a shock, even though in some ways she had to have been expecting it.

She looked back up at the anchor booth. Des had walked toward the front again, and stood looking down at her, his hands jangling nervously in and out of his pockets.

When he saw her turn toward him he shrugged his shoulders in a questioning gesture.

This time, unlike the last, she smiled and nodded.

The band played 'Happy Days Are Here Again.'

\*　　　\*　　　\*

Freddy was ecstatic, not able to distinguish the adulation for Sadie from the lack of enthusiasm for him. Sadie rode back to the hotel with them in the presidential limousine, with the sirens and motorcycles, passing through crowds of admirers and well-wishers, flashbulbs popping, people screaming and waving. It was very heady stuff. She had a slight twinge of wanting it again for herself. Yet when she had had it, all she wanted was out.

Freddy was on such a high, he wanted a

celebration. Sadie was the reason for his high. How could they celebrate without her? The champagne without the bubbles. She begged off, explaining that she was exhausted. Freddy wouldn't hear of it. She finally had to whisper to Blanche that the evening had been a wrenching experience; she missed Rosey terribly; she needed to be alone with her thoughts and her memories. It wasn't totally a lie.

Yes it was.

She went to her room and waited. How would he contact her? Where would they meet? She examined the damage in the mirror. She looked as if she had just come from a funeral. She freshened her makeup, brushed her teeth, combed her hair, squirted perfume behind her knees. Why was she doing these things? Habit? Anticipation?

The phone rang.

'Will you accept a call from Mr Desmond Shaw?' She would.

'I'm in my limo at the back of the hotel. Can you get your agents to bring you down?'

'I'll be right there.'

She had told Toby she might be going out later. She explained the situation. Both agents could ride in the front of the limo.

She put on her wig, her dark glasses, her scarf. They certainly were getting a lot of wear these days. She smiled to herself. What they didn't know in the women's magazines.

The limo was waiting at the back entrance. She needn't have worried. There was no one around. He opened the door for her from inside and she quickly got in. Her agents got in the front. The window between the front and back seats had been raised so they couldn't be seen or heard.

She took off her disguise and shook her hair out, looked up at him, and smiled.

'My, you've certainly come a long way from a lowly print journalist to a big TV star with a limousine.'

She said this in her most beguiling Southern accent.

'You're so beautiful,' he said.

She sucked in her breath.

They couldn't take their eyes off each other. She was being pulled toward him like a magnet. She had no control.

'We can't,' she whispered as she began moving to him.

He reached out and slid her body across the seat with his arm until she was crushed up against him.

'Not here,' she protested lifting her face to him.

His mouth was on hers, his hands everywhere.

'It's such a cliché,' she said, wrapping her arms around his neck.

He clutched her hair, pulling it back tightly as he laid her down.

'Not with you,' he said. 'Not with you.'

She was overcome. So was he. She had not made love to anyone since Michael. Seven months. Before that almost two years. She suspected Des hadn't either since before the baby.

She didn't know which she missed more—sex or love. Right now it was sex. Pure, down and dirty sex. She'd think about love later.

She helped him take off her jacket and he unzipped the back of her now demolished linen dress. He didn't even bother unhooking her bra. He just pulled it down and took her breast in his mouth.

With the other hand he pulled at her underpants, practically ripping them off.

She managed to get to his zipper and undo it, grabbing him and pulling him out in desperation, as though she would lose him if she didn't get him inside her that minute.

They were both gasping, clawing with need, gnawing and biting each other until their teeth crunched. She wrapped her legs around him. He rammed himself into her as hard as he could. Again. And again. And again.

There was no gentleness, no tenderness, only unfulfilled lust. When it was over they lay together, recovering—their breath, their equilibrium, their senses.

He was the first to move. He released her, pulled himself up, struggled with his pants and leaned heavily against the door. She lay there for a moment, then did the same. They were far apart now, on opposite sides of the car, not touching.

She was the first to speak.

'We seem to be repeating ourselves,' she said.

Their first time had been in a car, in the front seat of his Thunderbird at Great Falls on the way back from lunch.

'Yes.'

There wasn't much else to say.

They rode in silence. She was pleasantly aware of the smooth hum of the limousine, the velvet plush of the seats. She felt spent emotionally and physically. She also felt totally relaxed.

Des turned on the radio and found a soft, smoky ballad. He reached in the cooler and pulled out a bottle of white wine, opened it, and poured two glasses. Their fingers brushed when she took her glass but still they didn't reach for each other.

She leaned back and slowly sipped her wine. She felt utterly content at this moment. She wanted nothing more. She wanted to stay exactly where she was forever.

After a while the limo driver called back on the speaker phone, asking about their plans. Des told him, much to Sadie's disappointment, to head back to the hotel.

As they approached their destination she put on her disguise. The car pulled up to the back entrance. As the agents leaped out of the car and came around to open her door. Des reached over and touched her hand lightly.

'Next time,' he said, as he turned to get out, 'next time, we'll make love.'

*  *  *

They did. Slowly and sadly, wistfully even, they made love. To the sound of the waves lapping the shore they made love in her bedroom in the house in Easthampton, as they had the night they made Willie.

Labor Day weekend, the end of summer. The air was turning cooler in the evening but the sun was still deceptively hot enough to burn. The Republican convention was over. Des had come just for two days.

He had moved out of Allison's house, back to his own house on 21st Street, when he returned from Atlanta. According to Jenny it was mutual. Only after Sadie learned that did she invite him to Easthampton. She never really thought he would

737

say yes.

He spent the first day on the beach with Willie. She didn't go to the beach anymore. Aging and skin cancer had scared her away. They came back at five, tanned and sandy and exuberant. They fell into the pool, laughing and splashing at each other. She joined them, sitting on the edge, dangling her feet while Willie dove off Des's shoulders. He was swimming like a little fish.

'Attaboy, attaboy,' Des kept saying, encouraging Willie to try new things. Des would beam with pride when Willie managed to do something he thought he couldn't. Willie basked in it. She did, too. She felt such love for both of them, and such sorrow, too. Des and Willie together broke her heart. That was all.

They cooked out. Hot dogs and hamburgers and roasted marshmallows. Just a typical American family on Labor Day weekend.

They tucked Willie in together. Des telling him a bedtime story about growing up in Boston. She sat on the edge of the bed and rubbed Willie's head. Willie said his prayers, on his knees. Pressing his palms together he recited, 'Now I lay me down to sleep...' At the end he added 'and God bless Mommy, and Uncle Des, and Monica and...' he listed everyone in his family. Then as an afterthought, 'Please God, let Uncle Des come and live with us and be my daddy.'

Des hugged him so hard she was afraid he would squeeze the life out of him. She had to leave the room.

Later that night they went for a walk on the deserted beach. They held hands as they walked barefoot in their white ducks and T-shirts. The

738

moon was full and Sadie couldn't help studying
Des's features as they walked, listing all his
attributes in her mind. He was so handsome, so
strong and masculine. He was a good person, too,
kind and gentle when he needed to be. He was
smart. He was Willie's father. He loved him very
much. It could be so easy with Des. So perfect.
Why wasn't it? Was there just too much sadness
there for both of them to overcome?

They walked up from Georgica Beach to where
the pond met the ocean, and sat down, protected by
the dunes. She picked a piece of dune grass and
began tickling Des's ear with it.

'What are we going to do, Sadie?' His voice was
solemn.

She sighed. 'I don't know.' She waited. 'What
about Allison?'

'I don't think we can make it. There's too much
pain. She looks at me and sees dead babies.'

'Oh God. Poor Allison . . .' She waited again. He
said nothing.

'Do you still love her?'

She wasn't afraid of the answer as she thought
she would be.

'Of course I still love her. The question is not do
I. The question is can I.'

'How do you mean?'

'How can I love someone who looks at me and
sees what she sees? How can I love someone who
needs to blame me because she's angry at my God
for causing her such suffering? How can I love
someone who's too afraid to love anyone for fear of
losing that person? I just don't think it's possible.'

'Oh Des. It's all so sad, isn't it? What's happened
to us? Is it our ages? Is that what happens to

739

everyone? Is the state of grief just a natural part of life's passage? I don't know anything anymore. I used to think I was a happy person with problems. I generally thought of my friends the same way. There were always a few weirdos in college who were "depressed" in quotes. Somehow I thought then it was an affectation. Now I wonder. I look around me and all I see are people who are hurting, some because of things they have done but mostly because of things that have happened to them. There's nothing that prepares us for this, is there? There ought to be courses at school. Life 101. Pain 304. Grief 65. No one's exempt. Nobody gets off free. I feel as if my whole life is one big exam nightmare; I go to take the test and I haven't been to a class or read an assignment. Somehow, if I've done the work I'd get through it easier. But then I think I have done the work, goddammit. I'm a good person. Why is it so hard for me? Then I look at the starving Africans, the displaced Kurds, the hundreds of thousands who've drowned in Bangladesh and I feel ashamed. How dare I complain? I, who have so much, I who am so privileged. Yes, my husband was assassinated; yes, my child is the child of a man I can never acknowledge; yes, I'm in love with...'

She stopped quickly. He looked at her, not quite understanding.

'I'm in love with that man.'

She wondered if he had caught her dissembling. It wasn't that she didn't love Des. It was just that she had been thinking of Michael. Of how she had failed him, failed to make him accept her love.

Des reached over and put his arm around her and they sat together, looking up at the stars, as though
740

they would find the answers there.

Later, that night, he came to her bed. She had put him in the room next to Willie's for appearances and because she felt awkward about it, him, them.

This time their lovemaking was sweet. They both seemed to be trying not to hurt each other, emotionally or physically. They touched each other's bodies as though they were touching tender wounds, brushing so gently that they could hardly feel fingers pressing on skin.

They lay in the dark afterward listening to the waves and the curtain fluttering in the breeze. On their sides, they faced each other, stretched out naked, a shaft of moonlight falling across them. Softly they traced each other's features with their fingers. Making love made them feel perhaps not fulfilled but not as achingly lonely either.

He kissed her finally, slid out of bed, wrapped a towel around his waist, and disappeared.

Neither one of them had said a word.

The next morning, when she woke, she went to Willie's room. He wasn't there. Monica wasn't up yet so she searched the house. Not being able to find him, she woke Monica. Frantic, she was about to call the police when she decided to check with Des.

Slowly she opened the door to his room. What she saw made her put her hand over her heart, made her eyes blur. Des was lying on his side, curled up, disheveled, and dead to the world. Cupped under his arm, in a little round ball was a miniature, an exact replica, a clone. Sound asleep in his father's embrace was Willie.

★　　　★　　　★

She couldn't believe it was almost the end of October, almost Halloween. Could it have been five months since she had seen Michael or even talked to him?

She had avoided going to any of the AIDS commission meetings when she knew he was going to be there. She had also been trying to avoid Blanche. All Blanche wanted to talk about was Freddy's health. She was understandably obsessed but she kept wanting to get together with Sadie and Michael. She needed the relief of being able to talk about it with someone who knew. Sadie was finding it more and more difficult to dance around that one. She had come up with so many excuses why she couldn't get together with Michael that she had almost run out.

The campaign was going badly. It was not at all sure that Freddy would win, which also had Blanche in a state. To her credit, Blanche was as conflicted about it as Sadie was. Part of her was hoping he would lose. Yet his opponent was totally unacceptable. Sadie had refused to do any campaigning. Happily her convention appearance seemed to have satisfied them. Practically everyone she knew was out on the campaign trail or writing or broadcasting about it. Washington in an election was a ghost town. Nobody was around, nobody saw anybody else. people who were in town didn't like to go out for fear of being seen and considered unimportant.

Des was working extremely hard. Sadie had not considered, when they began seeing each other again, that his hours wouldn't exactly be conducive to a great relationship. He usually went into the office around four in the afternoon and never got home before one-thirty. Though he was not actually living with her, he did spend weekends at her house and tried to see Willie as often as he could. This left Sadie with a lot of time alone.

Des had encouraged her to start writing again, as she had when they first began seeing each other, when Rosey was the Vice President, and he first offered to help her edit a short story. That was how they started. He thought she had talent. She was trying to expand a short story into a novel and was about halfway finished when Rosey was killed. Now Des had talked her into pulling it out of the back drawer and taking another look at it. She was surprised that she still liked it. To her delight, the characters and the story held up. For the past six weeks or so she had holed herself up on the third floor of her house, away from her office downstairs. She tried to write for at least several hours each day. It gave her a sense of accomplishment and distracted her from her many problems. Not the least of which was Des.

What was she going to do about Des? About her and Des? There was no longer any passion there, no excitement even. They were comfortable with each other. Their lovemaking was caring and considerate.

They spent most of their time with Willie on the weekends when Des was not on the air. Des had a cabin in West Virginia, a very rustic cabin. He loved it there and so did Willie. They often took Willie with no nanny, now that he was older. She wasn't really crazy about being there, but she was able to read while Des took Willie out in the woods, so it was pleasant. Pleasant. That was one of the problems. Her time with Des was pleasant.

The other problem was that they were never alone, Allison and Michael were always with them. Uninvited but not unwanted, preoccupying their thoughts, distracting them, challenging their feelings for each other. They never mentioned their phantom visitors. They didn't have to. It was as obvious as if Allison and Michael had driven into the middle of the living room in a bright red Mercedes convertible and parked between them.

'Would you like another glass of wine?' Des would ask.

'No thanks,' Sadie would respond.

'Actually, I'd love it,' Allison would interject.

'Shall I put on some Mozart?' Sadie would ask.

'No thanks,' Des would respond.

'Actually, I'd love it,' Michael would interject.

When it happened they each knew it. One would recognize the distraction in the other's face, as though someone were whispering to them from backstage. Then they would resume the conversation as though nothing had happened. But it was never the same after that. Not for the rest of the evening, anyway.

Des was drinking too much. She only saw him drink on weekends but it worried her. She was afraid he might start up on the job. She didn't know how to broach it to him. She didn't want to put him on the defensive and she understood why he was drinking. The stress of mourning his child, feeling sad about Allison, and his relationship with Willie was enough to make anybody drink. Still, she didn't like it and she could see it was becoming a problem.

The fact was that she wasn't happy. Neither was

744

he. They were taking it day by day but it wasn't wonderful. The main reason, she had to admit, was that she missed Michael. She missed him terribly. She wanted to see him.

*　　*　　*

Sid and Judy were taking Michael to services this morning of Rosh Hashanah, the Day of Remembrance. On Rosh Hashanah one's prayers were supposedly answered. It was obviously a good time to strike.

They would be out by twelve-thirty. Lunchtime. She had a plan.

At twelve-thirty sharp her car pulled up in front of the Washington Hebrew Congregation off Massachusetts Avenue, her two agents in the front, she in the back. Temple was just letting out. She waited until she saw the three of them leave and walk down the street toward the Solokows' car. She had hers follow them until she came up beside Michael. She rolled down the window. He turned to see who it was. She lowered her dark glasses.

'Get in,' she said.

He looked momentarily surprised, then smiled in spite of himself.

'What do you want?' he asked.

'I need to talk to you.'

He didn't move for a moment. He was thinking it over. She opened the door. He got in. They drove in silence. He didn't ask where they were going. The agent headed down Rock Creek Parkway, around the Lincoln Memorial and toward the Jefferson Memorial and the Tidal Basin. They turned off to the side when they got there and parked. She got out of the car and he followed. They started walking toward the monument, around the now leafless cherry trees. He walked beside her. It was hot. Indian summer. He took his jacket off and carried it over his shoulder.

'What do you want to talk to me about?'

His tone was hostile. She could tell he was angry. After all, it was she who had written saying she didn't want to see him again. He would be feeling rejected even though he had actually rejected her.

'Lunch,' she said. 'I'm starving.'

There was a hot-dog vendor in front of them. She walked up to him and asked for a hot dog. He did the same and paid. A dollar each. Two sodas. They took their hot dogs and kept on walking along the water's edge.

'I lied,' she said. 'I don't want to talk to you about lunch.'

She turned to look at him, to force him to look at her.

'I wanted to see you again. Because I love you.'

He looked shaken, disarmed. She didn't take her eyes away from his.

'What is that supposed to mean?' he demanded. 'I don't understand you. I didn't expect to see you again. How the hell am I supposed to deal with that? What do you want from me?'

She didn't answer right away.

'I miss you,' she said finally. 'I just wanted to know how you were. What you're doing.'

'I'm afraid my life is rather boring, compared to yours,' he said. 'I'm just working a lot, trying to spend some time in the lab, going to meetings, giving lectures, writing papers—the same stuff.'

'How are the kids?'

'They're great. Both doing well. One is graduating this year from Harvard, summa. The other wants to be a lawyer. They'll be coming here for Thanksgiving.'

'Do you hear from Giselle?'

Her heart beat faster as she asked the question. She cared more about the answer than she thought she would.

'Not much. We're trying to come to some amicable settlement.'

He was quite terse. He clearly didn't want to talk about it. Did that mean he still loved Giselle?

'How about you? How have you been? How's Willie?'

His curiosity had got the better of him.

'Willie's fine, totally recovered from his accident. But I'm sure you know that. I've been writing again. I've gone back to my novel.'

'What inspired you to do that?'

'Des encouraged me.'

'Des?' he asked a little too quickly.

'Yes, Des. He, uh, he, well, I've been seeing, I mean, he and Allison split up and...'

She was being a little disingenuous. She knew he would go crazy at the idea she was 'seeing' Des again. She did it partly because she wanted to make him jealous. She was aware this game carried big risks. Every other man she had ever been involved with had responded to competition normally. They would fight for what they wanted. She wasn't at all sure about Michael. For him it might well be confirmation of his worst suspicions. She was just another WASP bitch who trifled with men's feelings. She didn't care. She had wanted a rise out of him. She had got it.

'I understand perfectly,' he said.

He was trying to be cool but she could see his face redden. She decided it would be fruitless to pursue the conversation even though he had started. She had made her point.

'What about Freddy, what do you think?' she asked, changing the subject.

'I think he's in danger of getting AIDS, what do you think I think?'

He really was pissed.

'I meant, what do you think he'll do?'

'I'm not exactly his political confidant, but my guess would be he'll resign sometime after the election citing health reasons without being specific. I'm sure you know that's what Blanche wants him to do. He's been sick again. I think he may get sicker a lot faster than we thought.'

'Jesus.'

'My sentiments exactly,' he said.

She started to laugh. At least he had not lost his sense of humor.

They had walked almost around the reflecting pool.

'There's an old Rosh Hashanah tradition,' he said, a little warmer now. He liked making her laugh. It pleased him. 'It's called Tashlich.'

'What's that?'

'You're supposed to cast off your sins, symbolically throw them into a body of water.'

'How do you do that?'

'When we were kids we'd picnic by the lake, then save crumbs from our sandwiches to toss.'

He gave her a corner of his hot-dog bun.

'Tear it up in bits,' he instructed, 'then think of

your sins and throw a piece of bread in the water for each sin you want to cast off.'

'You go first,' she said. 'What are your sins?'

'I only have one.'

'What's that?'

'You.'

With that he picked her up and walked to the edge of the Tidal Basin pretending to heave her into the water.

She shrieked and her two Secret Service agents ran at Michael, practically tackling him to the ground.

'Call off your dogs, lady,' he told her. 'It's only a joke.'

He put her down. She persuaded the agents she was safe and sent them away.

'What now?' he said, after they were alone again.

'What do you want?' She threw it back at him.

He looked at her solemnly.

'I would like to be friends. I want to keep in contact with you. I don't want to be separated, isolated from you the way we have been.'

It was quite an admission from him. Not much. But a start.

'Fine,' she said. 'Then call me.'

She was surprised and a bit suspicious of his response.

'I will,' he said.

So. The Des thing had worked. He was not immune to jealousy or competitiveness. Despite everything he said, the man was not so different after all.

*   *   *

'Sadie?'

'Yes?'

'It's Sprague.'

'Sprague?'

'Yes.'

'How are you?'

'I need to see you.'

'Why?'

'I can't discuss it on the phone.'

'When?'

'How about now?'

'Come, then.'

'I'll be there in half an hour.'

'Goodbye.'

★　　★　　★

Sprague Tyson. The name still gave her chills. She closed her eyes, her hand resting on the receiver. Why did he want to see her again? How had he gotten her private number?

Allison, of course. She would have had Sadie's number from Des. Sadie knew Allison and Sprague worked together, though she and Des had never discussed it. Des refused to talk about her, which upset Sadie. Sprague's name came up a lot because of all the drug stories. Every time it did she saw Des bite his lip, a nervous habit he had when he was agitated.

Could Sprague possibly want to talk to her about Allison? No. That was definitely not his style. What could it be?

She had only seen Sprague once briefly since he'd come to Washington, at that awful dinner at the Colombian embassy. He had been with his wife, Jane, and they hadn't even spoken. Before that it had been almost twenty-five years ago in Savannah.

Sprague had been the mascot of their group growing up, six years younger but old and wise for his age. He admired Sadie's boyfriend Danny O'Neill. Everybody did. Danny. Black hair and blue eyes. Gorgeous and charismatic. Clever and reckless. He thought he was invincible. He wasn't. Sprague was in the car with Danny when Danny was killed in a drag race on Victory Drive one summer.

On the first anniversary of Danny's death Sprague and Sadie went to St. Bonaventure Cemetery to visit his grave under the moss-filled live oaks. They necked and petted heavily and nearly went all the way. Sprague was sixteen. They never saw each other again.

Now he wanted to see her. After all these years. She still felt embarrassed, ashamed, guilty when she thought about it. She always would. But it had been so long ago. She rarely thought about it anymore.

It was close to four-thirty when he arrived. Typical gloomy Thanksgiving weather. She took him into the bright yellow library. Asuncion brought tea and cookies. They sat opposite each other, next to the fire.

She studied him while she poured the tea and offered the cookies.

He had been incredibly handsome as a boy, his childish face just about to carve itself into adult definition. His good looks had been enhanced by his polite, self-contained manner, his stoic countenance. He had had remarkable self-control for someone his age, he was unimpressionable, and he kept his own counsel even then. As much as he had liked Danny, he never did what Danny or the

751

older boys told him to. He would just as soon walk away from them as do something he didn't want to do. She had always been a little in awe of him. That made her uncomfortable, even resentful, especially since he was much younger than she was. That made it all the more shocking to both of them when it happened. They hadn't loved each other, hadn't really liked each other.

Had he told Allison about her? She was certain he hadn't. Allison would never know. Neither would Des. For that she was grateful.

She still found him good-looking, compelling. Yet there was something unreachable and cold about him. Maybe it was the fact that he was a WASP. She had been so brainwashed by Michael that anybody who wasn't Jewish or at least Catholic seemed bloodless to her.

No. There was nothing there. Certainly not for her. And she didn't think for him either. He had another agenda. She couldn't wait to find out what it was.

She offered him another cookie and they chatted about the election.

Yes, it had been close, he allowed, but then it was inevitable that Freddy would win. The other candidate had been too extreme.

Yes, his stories had hurt Freddy, but he hadn't really been able to nail anyone in the administration before the election.

Yes, there was more to come.

Yes, it was dangerous for him, working on the story, and that's why he had sent Jane and Melissa back to Georgia.

His mother was fine. Doing well as could be expected after his father's death.

752

They chatted about her family. Their parents were friends.

Her mother and daddy were fine, too.

Yes, Outland and Annie Laurie had graduated from college. They would both be coming home for Thanksgiving. Outland was working for a producer in Los Angeles making documentaries and Annie Laurie was working at the art museum in Richmond.

Yes, Willie was fine. The accident had turned out to be minor. He was a little hellion.

Did he know about Willie and Des? She studied him carefully. She doubted it. No matter how angry or hurt Allison might be, she didn't believe she would ever betray Des or hurt Willie by telling anyone.

Yes, her work with AIDS had been extremely rewarding and time-consuming. She was very involved, and so was Blanche, and through Blanche, Freddy.

She was giving him a sell job, not suspecting that she was walking right into it.

'Actually,' he said, taking another sip of tea, 'that's why I wanted to see you.'

She felt her stomach drop.

She poured herself another cup, avoiding his eyes.

'I wouldn't have come, but you're the only person we... I could talk to.'

She didn't say anything. Let him do the talking.

'I might as well come right out and ask you. We have information that the President has tested HIV positive.'

'Oh, no!'

He ignored her exclamation.

753

'And if anyone would know, it would be you. You're very close to the First Lady and you work closely with Dr Lanzer.'

Dear God. Could he know about her and Michael, too? You never knew with these damn reporters. Especially an investigative reporter like Sprague. You just suspected that they had a basement full of files, some of it about your private life.

'Sprague,' she said carefully. 'You'll have to ask them.'

She was trying to be too cool.

'I really have nothing to say about this.'

It was getting worse.

'I'd like to talk to Dr Lanzer.'

'He'll never tell you anything. He can't, as a doctor.'

It occurred to her that she could have been more noncommittal if she wanted to. She sensed that Sprague had spotted her unsureness and was coming in for the kill.

'We have been told that you and Blanche Osgood accompanied the President to the NIH for an examination by Dr Lanzer at the National Cancer Institute. It would have been last April, April thirteenth to be exact.'

He really did know. She was so flustered she didn't know what to say. She had never been grilled like this by a reporter, especially a world-class pro like Sprague. He was showing no mercy.

'Actually,' she said, as the blood rushed to her face, 'I wasn't here then, at least I don't think I was. And I believe I was sick, that awful flu was going around.'

'Right,' said Sprague.

754

'It was also my daughter's birthday.'

He didn't say anything.

'So, I don't see how I could possibly have been there.'

She hadn't lied, really, she just equivocated. She didn't say she'd never been there.

'The President has been indisposed several times this fall,' he said.

'So I read.'

'Blanche must be pretty upset.'

She noticed he had gone from 'the First Lady' to 'Blanche Osgood' to 'Blanche'. It was an interesting technique, suggesting mutual intimacy.

They looked at each other.

'He'll have to resign. The question is . . . when?'

'I don't know anything about this. It's ridiculous.'

'Well,' he said, getting up from his seat. 'I won't take up any more of your time.'

He obviously couldn't wait to get back to the office. She understood she had given him enough to call the press secretary, say he had it from two sources and get a denial.

'I'm sorry I wasn't able to be of any more help,' she said as she walked to the door.

'Don't worry,' he said.

What the hell did that mean?

'Give my best to your parents when you talk to them,' he said.

Leave them with a friendly taste in their mouths.

'And to your mother.'

He was gone. She leaned against the door and sighed. He had really done a number on her. She couldn't decide whether to be mad at him or mad at herself.

'Bastard,' she said and banged her fists against the door.

He had used their personal relationship to get to her and then to get her to help him. It was dirty pool.

But then she had betrayed Blanche. She had betrayed her friend and not left a single fingerprint.

'Bitch,' she said to herself, looking in the hall mirror.

She had answered her own question. Both. Sprague and herself. She was mad at both.

Dear Sadie,

I'm sitting here in my San Francisco hotel room looking out the picture window at a blanket of fog. This is appropriate since I feel that my brain is in a similar condition. It is also just fine since it means I can't see all the Santa Claus's reindeer, Christmas trees, and blinking colored lights blanketing this town.

Unfortunately, it makes me think of you, which I have been trying hard with little success, not to do.

I miss you.

It's been six weeks since we met at the Tidal Basin. You may have guessed I was really angry with you that day. The fact that you were 'seeing' Des was a shock. I guess I'm pretty naive, but since you had told me you loved me I never expected you to go to bed with another man. Even if we weren't sleeping with each other. I can see now that this is my problem, not yours, part of my antiquated morality.

I was more than angry. I was hurt. Make that deeply wounded. It's not rational. I have no right to ask you to be faithful to me. I have offered you nothing. I have given you nothing. I have only taken from you. I have taken your friendship and your caring and concern and love, and I have done nothing but turn my back on you. Time and time again. Frankly, I don't understand why you keep coming back for more when all you get is abuse. It baffles me. But then, it's not the only thing about this relationship that baffles me.

I'm used to being in control. I have always been able to control every aspect of my life. Without control I feel helpless and scared. When I met you I lost control. It has been the most exasperating, perplexing, frightening experience I have ever had. I thought I understood about pain but nothing has ever caused me more pain than this. I became obsessed with you. To the point that I have behaved recklessly and thoughtlessly to other people, including Giselle, my children, me, and you. I'm afraid of myself. I'm afraid of you. I'm afraid of it. You are like a tumor in my brain which is getting larger and larger each day. I can't seem to stop it. Pushing you away is radiation but it's not working. The cancer keeps growing. It's always been there, the potential for it. You were the catalyst. I don't know whether it's the same for you or not. Sometimes I suspect it is, which frightens me more.

When I'm not with you I feel lonely and sad. Being with you seems right, makes me feel whole. I shouldn't. It isn't right. I miss talking to you, sharing things with you, laughing with you, making you laugh.

You make me feel clever and sexy and funny.

It's wonderful. But I can't deal with it. I can't deal with you. Why? God I wish I knew. It makes no sense. If you think it baffles you, it baffles me even more. It is not because you're not Jewish. I'm sticking with that as a reason because it's the only one I can think of. But you deserve better. You deserve someone who can love you and be a good husband to you and take care of Willie.

What you don't need is a man who can't even make love to the only woman he has ever really cherished without being sick or drunk.

Forgive me. I love you.
Merry Christmas.
Love, Michael.

Dear Michael,
We seem to be better at communicating on paper than in person.

I don't know where to begin.

There is this thing called erotic obsession. Supposedly it overtakes you, renders you helpless to make any rational judgment. The object of the obsession becomes paramount.

The *Dictionary of Psychology* defines eroticism as 'employed in psychoanalytical literature as a general term for sexual excitement and in psychopathology for an exaggerated display of sexual feelings and responses.'

Obsession is 'a persistent or recurrent idea, usually strongly tinged with emotion, and frequently involving an urge towards some form of action, the whole mental situation being pathological.'

Since it's come up in both definitions, you may

758

be interested to know that pathology is a 'branch of biological or medical science, which concerns itself with abnormal and diseased conditions in organisms.'

Somehow I can't really think of our condition as 'diseased,' can you? I say 'our.' It is the same for me.

The question is, why does it have to be pathology? Why can't it just be love? The answer is because *you won't let it*. And the reason is because *you are an asshole*.

I think I've made my position clear, here. Now let me expound.

The Jewish thing is a crock, I've decided. You're just using that to hide behind. It's convenient and comfortable and requires no effort or self-analysis on your part. You're a lazy coward. As you say yourself, you're scared of you, me, it. And besides, you don't want to do any work. So you throw it off on me. She's not Jewish, she'll never get it. Isn't that clever ... and easy.

Well, sorry, big guy. It won't work. I know you too well now so you can't play your little games with me.

When we first met you were right there for me, right in my face. You came on to me so strongly that it was like an emotional invasive procedure. I remember asking, 'Who are you?' I wondered who this magical person could be who was so completely tuned in to my wavelength. It was as though you were picking up signals from my invisible antenna. I felt we had known each other in another life.

Lately, I've had a different question. 'Where

are you?' Where is the person I fell in love with? It seems that ever since Giselle left you've been hiding from me.

I remember going to open-air shops in the Mediterranean, the ones where all the lovely, tempting wares were displayed right there on the street for you to touch. And how frustrating it was to arrive just at closing time and have the heavy metal doors slam down, locking everything from view. It was the inaccessibility of those treasures that was the ultimate frustration.

You're very clever about it. You know how to distance yourself from me, and I suspect from everyone. You know how to hurt me in a way nobody has ever been able to hurt me before. You ask why I keep coming back for more abuse. The answer is that I know you're not a mean person. I know you love me and it's your way of trying to keep me away so that you won't get hurt. Most of the time I can deal with it. It's only when I'm feeling particularly vulnerable that I can't take it.

I miss you, too.

I haven't really seen you since we made love. Occasionally you've let me have a peek, just a hint, a flash behind those beautiful blues. I know you're in there so you might as well come out with your hands up. Or at least let me in.

We're making headway though. You've learned to reveal yourself when you're sick, drunk, nude, and writing letters. That's progress. Actually I like nude best. I could get raunchy if I don't watch out. Somehow I'm in the mood. Sorry. It's late and I'm tired.

I've been watching Des on 'Good Night.'

760

Speaking of Des. There's a difference between Catholics and Jews, I've discovered. Catholics are motivated by fear. Jews are motivated by guilt. I've decided I like guilt better. Guilt is sexy. Fear is not.

There's another thing. He doesn't love me. I'm not sure he knows it yet. He's trying to because he's lost Allison, and because he cares about me and feels sorry for me and he really does love Willie. But it isn't working. Oh, yes. One more small detail! I don't love him.

Anyway, I'm not dead. I'm very much alive, and I'm not going away and you can't ignore me. You can't sit shiva for me, Lanzer, because I'm a shiksa, remember? And one more thing: I've decided I don't want to 'share the pain.' Pain is boring. So can we please stop this and get on with our lives.

'T.O.T.' pal. In case you don't know, that stands for the Yiddish expression 'tochis afn tish'—It means, loosely translated, 'put up or shut up.'

I love you. You love me. We have a great life together ahead of us. Kineahora.

Love, Sadie.

The network's 'Christmas in Washington' special had always been one of her favorite events of the year. It was a one-hour taped Christmas show held at the beautiful old Pension Building downtown. The building was always decorated with garlands of greenery, ribbons, twinkling lights, and huge Christmas trees. The show itself consisted of a number of well-known performers singing carols as well as a black Baptist choir and the U.S. Naval

761

Academy Glee Club. The President and First Lady always came, and others often included the Vice President, members of the cabinet and Congress, and a lot of heavy-hitting media types. What she loved most about it was that the children were invited. She had brought Willie last year for the first time when he was three, all dressed up in a green velvet suit and white knee socks. It was such fun, dressing him up like that.

This year he wouldn't be wearing any green velvet suit. Not with Des around.

'No son of mine is going to go out looking like a fucking fruitcake' was more or less how he put it.

She refused to have her spirits dampened. She got Willie his first navy blazer, white button-down shirt, striped tie, and gray flannel pants. So he looked like a little English schoolboy instead of a fruitcake.

Blanche hadn't quite known what to do about Des, but she gamely asked them to sit with her. She wasn't alone in her dilemma. Everybody in Washington was somewhat confused by their relationship. They didn't actually live together and they didn't go to parties together but it was clear that they were an item. The whole thing made people quite uncomfortable; the two of them spent most of their time by themselves.

Sadie had trouble persuading Des to sit with them. If Willie hadn't been part of the deal he would probably have said no. It was too public, especially now that he was a big TV star. Also joining them in the front row were the Vice President and his wife, Malcolm and Abigail Sohier, and their three children. Sadie was pleased about that. She adored the Sohiers and Des and

762

Malcolm were old friends from Boston.

Blanche had asked Sadie and Des to come to the back entrance of the Pension Building to meet the cast and the network officials beforehand. It was customary for the President and First Lady to wait there until it was time for the show to begin.

Sadie hadn't realized how nervous she was about appearing for the first time with Des in public. Not to mention with Des and Willie. What if someone noticed how much they looked alike?

As they walked into the large room with the huge Christmas tree and saw the cast lined up to greet them she almost turned and ran out. How could she have been so stupid? What on earth was going through her mind? She had been living such a private life with Des that she had lost touch with reality. She hadn't focused on the kind of commotion their appearance together could cause.

She switched Willie's hand from her right side to her left so that he was no longer between them. If she kept him far enough away from Des maybe people wouldn't put it together. Des noticed. She felt sorry for him. She hadn't wanted to hurt him. He was so proud of Willie that, on some level, he wanted everyone to know that Willie was his son. He also knew it was impossible. He let her pull Willie away from him.

The show's producer introduced them to the cast. Willie put a present under the tree for Children's Hospital. She had told him that that's where he'd been after he'd fallen and hurt his head. Willie's eyes fell on the tables full of candy, cookies, and cakes for the party afterward and she allowed him one chocolate Santa. She was relieved and distracted by his mobility.

Des started up a conversation with one of the stars and she began to relax when she heard a commotion near the door. The President and First Lady had arrived.

To her dismay, walking in with them was Michael.

Blanche had taken to having Michael accompany her on public appearances to reinforce her commitment to her AIDS project. He always went to her country music concerts and occasionally spoke. Tonight his presence was appropriate because there was a country music singer on the program who had performed for Blanche's project, and the show was a benefit for Children's Hospital. Only Sadie knew that Michael was really there for Freddy.

She hadn't seen or spoken to him since their exchange of letters. In fact, she hadn't seen him since September.

She was always shocked when she saw him. It was the oddest sensation, like a light going on in her brain. 'Of course! Why didn't I know that before? Why didn't I see that before?' Why didn't I think of that before? She was an amnesia victim suddenly getting her memory back. Seeing him was like discovering the truth after a long search and realizing that it was the only truth.

Now she had two things to hide. She felt very exposed.

Des knew about Michael, of course. But all he knew was that it hadn't worked out.

Michael knew about both Des and Willie.

She and Michael knew about Freddy.

Things were getting so complicated that she had to concentrate to remember who knew what about

764

whom. Tragedy was in danger of turning into farce.

Blanche came right over to her as if she had found her lost security blanket.

'Oh Sadie,' she whispered. 'Thank God you're here. It's been awful. Freddy is sick. Michael didn't want him to come tonight but he insisted. I made Michael come with us.'

She glanced quickly at the President. Blanche was right. He didn't look great. He had on makeup, so it wasn't too noticeable unless you saw him up close. What was more noticeable was his body language. He held on to Blanche tightly. He refused to look Sadie in the eyes. Grateful, she averted hers as well.

Michael was standing right behind him. She gathered her courage.

'Dr Lanzer,' she said, with a noncommittal smile. 'How nice to see you. It's been months. We seem to keep missing each other ... at these meetings.'

Her heart skipped a tiny beat. He looked at her. She never quite knew how to greet him. She held out her hand. He took it. He wouldn't let her look away.

'You're right,' he said. 'We have been missing each other.'

There was no chance to mention the letter. No chance to mention his. What could they say to each other anyway, with all these people standing around? She searched his face for a reaction. Had he laughed when he got her letter? Did it amuse him? Or was he angry? Did he resent her flippant tone? It could have served to make him more confused, more miserable. She couldn't tell. He wasn't giving anything away.

765

Des walked over.

'Des, you remember Michael Lanzer, don't you? I think you met him at the White House last year.'

Des remembered.

'Doctor,' he said coolly, extending his hand. It amused her. Des really wasn't in love with her. She knew that. Yet when his territory was threatened he reacted.

Michael's response was equally cool. She could see his face shut down, a veil go over the eyes. He was having the same problem.

She expected them to break away from each other immediately, the way she would have. Instead, they struck up a conversation, taking each other's measure, like two dogs sniffing out the competition.

She was about to walk away, when Willie came barreling up to Des with chocolate smeared on his face and held his arms up, begging 'Uncle Des' to pick him up.

She started to lean down and get Willie right away. Before she could, Des had swooped him up into his arms, looking triumphantly at Michael as if to say, 'You see. I'm the father of her child. I have impregnated this woman. I have given her a son. I'm the man here. I'm in charge.' It was so primitive she had to turn away for fear they would see her laughing.

The producer ushered them all into a tiny holding room—Freddy, Blanche, Michael, Sadie, Des, and Willie. Mercifully, he came with them to go over last minute instructions with the President and Blanche about their remarks at the end of the performance.

It was time to go in. Willie was already hyperventilating from candy Des had given him

766

behind her back. Sadie, Des, Willie, and Michael slipped into their seats in the front row. Sadie could hear a low murmur go up when people saw her with Des. Well, the hell with it. They would just have something to talk about for the next few weeks. She had given Washington a little Christmas present. What did she care? It was her life, after all. She could damn well do anything she wanted. That realization calmed her considerably.

The President and First Lady were announced and the crowd stood and applauded.

Sadie was distressed to see that Michael was seated between her and Blanche. Willie was between her and Des. The little gold wooden chairs were so close that one side of her body was pressed against Michael's.

Des took one look at the situation, picked Willie up, sat himself in Willie's seat next to hers and put Willie on his lap.

Your basic nightmare.

As if that wasn't bad enough, Allison and Sprague were sitting three rows behind them.

Allison knew about Willie. Sprague knew about Freddy. Pray God neither of them knew about her and Michael. No matter how sworn to secrecy they were, journalists could not be trusted. She had learned that from Des. 'In the end,' he had told her, 'everything is a story. Nothing is ever off the record. Journalists will always go for a story if it's good enough. Stories are to be told. They can't help it. It's chemical.'

Des and Allison exchanged glances. The pain was evident on both their faces. Though she was still beautiful, Allison seemed terribly pale and gaunt, like some tragic heroine. It had to be difficult for her, seeing Des with Willie for the first time, having lost her own baby exactly a year earlier.

For Des it must have been even harder. He had lost one child and was forbidden to recognize the other. Not only that, seeing Allison with Sprague was obviously killing him. Des's territory was being infringed upon on all sides. She felt bad for him. She put her hand on his arm to reassure him. Michael saw it and tensed. Willie started to whine.

This was too awful. The question was, how were they going to get out of it? She looked around for a distraction. She found it in Foxy and Antonia.

They were sitting in Siberia, off to the left at the very end of the row that faced the side of the stage. Banished.

Sprague had had a huge story in the *Daily* that Sunday morning about Foxy and his links to the drug dealers. It was pretty much the nail in the coffin. There was no question that Foxy would have to resign soon. Up until tonight he and the President had been playing the Washington game, Freddy professing loyalty and Foxy insisting he would stay. The embattled victim. They all thought they could tough it out. The White House never failed to bestow on its occupants a false sense of security, an aggrandized sense of power. Foxy was playing his role as if the script had been written for him. Showing the flag, stiff upper lip. Nobody in his right mind would have shown up in public after a piece like that had run about him. Unless he had White House protection. Yet Foxy's seat assignment had not gone unnoticed. Nobody had even looked at him, much less spoken to him. All those Washington establishment types who had been kissing his ass for the past two years had abandoned him the moment they smelled blood. It was always interesting to watch the stunned sense of betrayal when these people found out that they had no friends, no supporters; that all the power was ephemeral; that nobody really liked them for themselves. Foxy looked like his stay of execution had been revoked.

She jabbed Des in the ribs.

'Look where they are seated,' she whispered.

He looked, smiled, and nodded. He liked the idea that she was whispering to him and not Michael.

'That bastard is history,' he whispered back. 'I never thought I'd see the day when Freddy would abandon him like that. This is what's so great about Washington. The symbolism of power: Where he sits at some little Christmas pageant determines his fate.'

What Des didn't like was that the story was Sprague's triumph. And Allison was Sprague's editor as well as his 'friend.'

The performance opened with a medley of carols beginning with 'Away in a Manger' and 'O Little Town of Bethlehem.'

Every time the name Jesus was sung Michael would jab her in the ribs.

'Makes me feel right at home,' he whispered. 'This certainly is the American way.'

Des put his hand on top of hers.

Next came 'O Holy Night,' sung in a beautiful operatic voice. Sadie had always loved the music to this song but somehow, this evening, all she could concentrate on were the words.

'Long lay the world, in sin and error, pining, till He appeared and the soul felt its worth. A thrill of hope, the weary world rejoices, for yonder breaks a new and glorious morn . . .'

They made her feel tired and sad.

What was to become of them all? How had they managed to screw up their lives so badly, each one of them? Freddy and Blanche, Foxy and Antonia, Des and Michael, Allison and Sprague, and herself. Here they were, listening to songs of birth and hope and joy and every single one of them was suffering. They were all in sin and error, pining. None of their souls felt their worth. For them the world was still weary. There was no hope.

They were all at the pinnacle of power. My God. Look at who they were. She was talking about the President and First Lady, the former First Lady, the attorney general, a legendary Latin female diplomat, a nationally famous television anchor, a Pulitzer Prize-winning reporter, the most powerful woman in journalism, and one of the most distinguished scientists in America.

All this success and power and memory and fame. For what?

The performance was ending with a rousing rendition of 'Here Comes Santa Claus.' The producer was standing at the lectern introducing the President and First Lady. They stood up and walked slowly up the few steps onto the platform. Sadie noticed that Freddy was not steady. Michael was practically on the edge of his chair. Standing in front of the audience, Blanche did not step away from Freddy but stood closely, almost propping him up. He looked straight ahead toward the teleprompter and began to read.

'Good evening, ladies and gentlemen.' His voice was wooden. Blanche had one of those mirthless

'I'm thrilled to be here with my husband' political wife smiles on her face.

Freddy didn't continue.

The audience waited.

Blanche turned her frozen face toward Freddy. The audience began rustling in their seats. Michael was barely touching his seat.

Freddy stared straight ahead. All the color appeared to drain out of his face, leaving it translucent.

'Freddy,' said Blanche.

'Mr President,' said Michael softly, starting to move toward the platform.

He opened his mouth to continue. His lips moved but there was no sound.

'Timmmmmmmmmmbbbbbbber,' said Des under his breath.

Freddy's eyes rolled back in his head and he keeled over, hitting the floor with a terrifying thud.

There was pandemonium.

As everyone was screaming and shouting, Michael calmly ordered the Secret Service to pick him up and get him out to the limousine. It happened so fast that before anyone even realized what was happening Freddy and Blanche and Michael were gone.

She turned to Des. He thrust Willie at her, practically causing her to fall over, and ran in the direction of the telephones. Running in the same direction right behind him were Sprague and Allison.

She stood there alone for a moment, in the midst of the chaos, not quite knowing what to do, where to go.

Willie began to cry, frightened.

'Mommy, Mommy,' he said, tears running down his cheeks. 'What happened?'

She pulled Willie to her and pressed his head on her shoulder.

'I think, my angel,' she said, patting his back to comfort him, 'that our world is falling apart.'

★          ★          ★

Sadie was sitting in bed, a duvet wrapped around her, thumbing a book and waiting for 'Good Night' to start. She tried to watch every night unless she fell asleep, which was not unknown to happen.

She hadn't spoken to Des that day, so she didn't know who was going to be on. She was more than surprised when Des announced that his only guest would be Sprague Tyson and the subject was the attorney general.

It was a few days before the inauguration, on January 20. Sprague had just dropped a bomb. That morning the *Daily* had run a story saying that they were in possession of videotapes of the attorney general snorting cocaine with Antonia Alvarez in Colombia at the private ranch of the Foreign Minister. They had evidence that the attorney general had quashed several DEA investigations of drug dealing between the Colombians and Americans and a special investigation of two drug dealers, Skinner and Bader, whose money was being laundered by the Foreign Minister himself. Antonia and the Foreign Minister had been using the tapes to blackmail Foxy into thwarting the investigations.

The evening news shows had all led with the story, with pictures of Foxy, surrounded by

772

lawyers, dashing from his limousine into the White House to confer with White House lawyers, spin doctors, p.r. people, DEA officials, and Colombian embassy types.

Meanwhile, there were no pictures of Freddy, who, Sadie knew, was getting sicker by the day. The press were having a field day speculating. Delegations of senators and congressmen were making trips to the White House in vain, trying to talk the President into taking some action, making some kind of statement, anything. Freddy was just hiding out. Nobody could get to him except a few close aides and they weren't saying anything. Blanche was on the phone to Sadie several times a day. Freddy was scarcely talking to her anymore. Sadie had spoken to Malcolm and Abigail. They had also heard all the rumors, but Freddy had shut Malcolm out and Sadie couldn't bring herself to tell him the truth. Michael was at the White House every day, more for moral support than anything medical he could do. Even though the HIV story hadn't broken, it was rumored everywhere, and the fact that he had closeted himself only made it worse. Plans were going ahead for all of the inaugural balls and members of the administration were trying to carry on as though everything was normal. The presidency was embattled. The nation was rudderless. There was a funereal pall over the city, over the country, which affected everyone and everything. There was no doubt in her mind that Freddy would have to resign. The only question was when. The world really was falling apart.

The state of the world might have been a metaphor for her own life. The tension between her and Des was mounting rapidly. She used to talk to

773

him three or four times a day on the phone. Now it was once a day at best. Their relationship, which had been warm and protective, was beginning to fray around the edges. Their nerves were shot and they took it out on each other. Des was working at least fourteen hours a day and living at his own house. He had started doing the Sunday show as well, which meant he would have to get up at dawn to go to Mass first. They hardly saw each other.

Des was interviewing Sprague now. Sprague came across as cool, intelligent, and convincing. Des was respectful and challenging. Only she could tell there was an extra edge between the two. She knew Allison would be watching. Did she want Des back? Was she in love with Sprague?

She couldn't watch anymore. It occurred to her that this whole situation was untenable. Somebody had to do something to stop it. If nobody else did then she would have to be the one. She clicked off the TV set and picked up the phone. She got Des's producer on the line and left a message for him to call her when the show was over. He called twenty minutes later.

'Sadie. You called? Did you see the show? How do you think it went?

'I called, I saw the show, it went fine. I need to talk to you right now. Can you come over?'

'Is something wrong with Willie?'

'No. I just think we need to talk.'

'Can it wait until the weekend? I'm really beat.

'No. I'm afraid it can't. I need to talk to you now.' This was the third time she said it. He got the message.

'I guess you need to talk to me. I'll be right over. I hope you've got some Irish.'

774

When he got there she was waiting for him in the library. She had thrown on a pair of sweats, lit a fire, closed the curtains, and fixed herself an Irish whiskey, which she never drank.

It was bone-chilling cold outside. As if everything wasn't bad enough, it was one of the coldest winters on record. Des was red-faced and shivering by the time he got up the stairs and let himself in. She made him a drink and he sat next to the fire. She stood in front of it, warming her hands behind her as she gathered her thoughts.

He took a long swig and rested his head against the back of the sofa. He let out a deep sigh. He was exhausted and clearly apprehensive of any kind of serious talk.

'Jesus H. Christ,' he said. 'The whole fucking country is going to hell in a handbasket.'

'And so are we,' she said.

He didn't respond right away. He sighed again.

'Okay,' he said. 'I'll bite. What do you mean by "we"?'

'You and me.'

'Oh Sadie. Do we have to talk about the relationship tonight. I'm so goddamn tired I can hardly think.'

'We have to. I can't stand it anymore. I can't live this lie another day. Des, don't you feel the same way? I know you do. Why do you want to keep on doing this?'

'Sadie, please, I just can't—'

'Can't what? Des!' She was practically shouting. 'We don't love each other. *We don't love each other.*' She stopped in shock. She hadn't meant to say that. Certainly not like that.

He sat up in his chair as though he'd been

775

electrocuted.

They looked at each other in horror, the dreadful secret finally exposed.

He sat back again, put his hands over his face, rubbed his eyes, and muttered, 'Oh God.'

She knelt in front of him.

'Des, I'm sorry. I didn't mean ... it's just that I had to ... someone had to ... please don't be angry...' She could feel her eyes blur.

He lowered his hands and looked at her.

'We go through the motions, Des. We kiss each other and say "I love you." We act as though we're a married couple. We play parents to Willie. We even used to make love to each other. But it isn't there. It isn't real. It isn't working. We're just acting our roles. Our hearts aren't in it. Our souls aren't either. We're like two dead people.'

She put her head on his knees and held on to him.

'Oh Des. I'm so sorry. I wanted it to work. I know you did, too. For both our sakes. For Willie's too. But it doesn't. I care about you. I always will. But this just hurts too much. I can't do it anymore.'

She was crying softly now.

'How could I be angry with you for having the courage to speak the truth,' he said, his voice cracking.

She lifted her head and looked at him.

'Oh Des,' she said.

He pulled her up onto his lap and she buried her head in his shoulder.

'What are we going to do?' she asked in a whisper.

'I don't know, Sadie, my Sadiebelle. I just don't know. I wish to hell I did.'

'You still love Allison, don't you?'

'Yeah.'

'Does she still love you?'

'I ... can't say. I don't think she knows her own mind. I think she's still grieving. And I think she's been confused by that prick Tyson.'

'Have you seen her?'

He looked taken aback. He hesitated. 'Once,' he said. 'At Thanksgiving.'

'And?'

'Nothing was resolved.'

She got up and walked over to the bar for a tissue. She blew her nose, wiped her eyes, and fixed them both another drink. She handed him his drink, then stood again with her back to the fire. They sipped their drinks quietly, listening to the wind outside and the crackle of the fire. The grandfather clock in the hallway chimed two.

'What about Michael?'

'We've seen each other once, briefly, in September. We've exchanged two letters.'

'And?'

'Nothing. He wrote me. I wrote him back. I haven't heard from him since.'

'Bastard.'

I guess that takes care of him and Sprague,' she said, giggling slightly. Des chuckled, too.

The confessions, the tears, had served to relieve the tension.

Des got up and came to her. He wrapped his arms around her and rocked her back and forth.

'Oh Sadie, Sadie, my beautiful lady. I do love you, you know. It's not right to say I don't love you.'

'I know, Des,' she said, putting her arms around

777

his waist. 'I love you, too. What I meant is that we're just not in love with each other. And we've been killing each other trying to pretend. That's all.'

He kissed her forehead.

'We need each other, Sadie. The whole world is coming apart at the seams. We need each other now.'

'Why can't we be friends, then?'

'We can. But this friend is draggin' ass. So c'mon upstairs, ole buddy, and let's get some shut-eye.'

She pulled away.

'I don't know, Des. Do you think it's a good idea?'

Making love was the last thing she had in mind. She wasn't in the mood and she thought it would be disastrous.

'All I want to do is get in bed with you, put my arms around you, and hold on to you as tightly as I can all night long.'

She smiled and kissed him lightly on the cheek.

'That's the best idea I've heard in a long time.'

## CHAPTER EIGHTEEN

Someone had called it vuja de. Déjà vu all over again.

The Democratic convention. Sadie on the platform, tears in her eyes, waving to an adoring audience. Sadie and Des finding each other, giving each other meaningful looks. Allison in the press section looking on, the pained observer. A few of the names, a few of the details had been changed

778

but the story remained essentially the same, only upgraded from sad to tragic.

This time people were wailing as if they were at a Southern wake. She was trying not to get caught up in it but the scene brought back a lot of painful memories. Memories of Rosey. Memories of her life before Rosey was killed, when Uncle Rog was in the White House. It was a time when she and Des were first in love, before they broke up, before they married, before Kay Kay. A time when she was happy. Or at least as she remembered it now. When you are actually living your life, it always seems so fraught with problems and stress. Yet when you look back on those same events, they are the good ole days. Were those ole days ever really good?

Now Sadie and Des were looking at each other again. She was smiling and nodding.

She looked over at Sprague, standing in the box next to her to see if he had noticed. He hadn't. Nobody had.

Would she care if Des went back to Sadie? She didn't know. She was beyond feeling at this point. Des had moved out. He had gone back to his house on 21st Street. It wasn't such a big deal. He had kept his house. They had both agreed they could use it for guests since her house on Olive Street was so tiny. Somehow, though, it was like avoiding a total commitment. It was like having an escape hatch.

They hadn't told anyone. It wouldn't have made much difference anyway, considering his new television schedule and her long hours. It had been a mutual decision. After Willie's accident it just seemed like the right thing to do. She hadn't asked him about Sadie. She didn't want to know. She had

779

managed to successfully wrap herself in her work cocoon. That was her only reality. Des was in another life.

Rachel had told her that she had no capacity for denial. That may have been true then. Not anymore. She was into total denial now. It was great.

★    ★    ★

The convention was over. President and Mrs Osgood had left with Sadie Grey and the platform cleared out. Within minutes the hall was as dead as it had just been alive.

Allison and the others left the press box and walked out of the hall and across the way to the adjoining building where the news media had their work spaces. Everyone was clearing out. She had a few last minute conversations with the reporters and editors still wrapping up the day's stories. The lead stories would be Malcolm Sohier as the vice presidential candidate and Sadie Grey's reception at the convention hall. It had been a triumphant evening for the Democrats. Walt Fineman and a couple of the other national reporters were headed up to the Ritz Carlton bar where all the celebrity journalists hung out. She agreed to join them. She was much too keyed up to go to bed, especially alone. It had been an emotional evening. As they were heading out of the work space Sprague came toward them. She wanted to ask him to join them but she was afraid to in front of the others. He stood chatting with them for a moment. Finally Walt asked. She noticed Rod Taylor stiffen. Sprague noticed, too. He looked at Taylor, then at her. He nodded his assent to Walt. They finally managed to find cabs. Sprague maneuvered his way into hers.

The same thing happened once they were inside the Ritz bar. The place was packed, not a table to be had. Most of the journalists were standing up and talking, like at a cocktail party. Walt took it upon himself to find a table. They were all starving. She found an empty seat at the bar and ordered a glass of wine. Sprague came up to the bar, leaned over her and ordered a Jack Daniel's on the rocks. When he got his drink, he didn't leave to join the crowd in the middle of the room.

She had decided she would be content to just sit and watch the animals at the watering hole. She was tired and drained and she didn't feel much like talking. He picked up immediately on her mood. He clinked his glass against hers and smiled. Neither of them said a word. They sipped their drinks and stared at the merrymaking. Walt was clearly having no luck getting a table, the noise was beginning to get to her, and she was having second thoughts about wanting to be with people.

'Let's get out of here,' Sprague said.

He was reading her mind.

She looked at him, a bit apprehensive. She didn't want to be seen leaving with him.

'You go first. Go around back to the garage entrance. I'll join you there. I'll slip the guy something and he'll let me get my own car so we won't have to wait until next year to get it.'

Before she could answer he was gone, moving into the crowd as though he had planned to make a night of it. She looked around to make sure that neither Walt nor any of her colleagues were watching, then made a quick exit.

She walked around to the back of the hotel to the entrance of the garage, ducking inside so she wouldn't be seen. A few minutes later Sprague arrived with the keys to his rental car and the two of them made their way down into the garage.

He had shaken Ralph, she was relieved to see. Ralph had been dogging him throughout the convention and Sprague was chafing at the intrusion. He was also taking an enormous amount of razzing from the other reporters and he was not amused. But after the incident in Lafayette Park he was smart enough to realize he couldn't afford to take chances.

It was only as they were halfway down that they spotted the limo pulling up to the elevator entrance right near where they were standing.

Before she knew what was happening Sprague had grabbed her and practically knocked her over as he pulled her to one side and behind a pillar.

She started to protest loudly but he put his hand over her mouth.

'Fuck,' he said under his breath. 'Wouldn't you know. The one time I dump Ralph.'

Of course, she suddenly realized, it was the Colombians. How obvious. They would simply pull up in a limo and grab him and drive away.

She was sure the Colombians hadn't seen them. But they must have been following them to have come down into the garage. Maybe they would think they had both gone into one of the elevators.

They were both standing there, plastered against the pillar, hardly breathing, when the elevator opened and out came a woman in a platinum blond wig and dark glasses, flanked by two beefy guys

782

with earphones.

She looked extremely familiar but Allison couldn't place her at first. As she approached the limo, the back door swung open and a man leaped out to help the woman in, while her two companions climbed into the front seat. For a moment, Allison didn't believe what she saw. Then it all made sense.

The man in the limo was Desmond Shaw. The woman in disguise was Sadie Grey.

★ ★ ★

They drove in silence down the highway.

'Where are we going?' she asked after a while.

'A little place in Smyrna I used to take my dates in the days when I was courting. It's called Aunt Fanny's Cabin. It's out of the way. You're not likely to run into anybody you know. It's a good place to talk.'

They still hadn't said anything. She wasn't at all sure she wanted to talk. She was in a daze. She hadn't quite absorbed what had just happened.

He pulled off the highway onto a small dirt road. At the end of it was a pretty, old, white-columned Southern plantation house in a grove of trees surrounded by meadow. He pulled around to the back of the house into the grove.

It was a perfect summer night, hot but no humidity. There was a slight breeze and the smell of frying chicken wafted through the air. The restaurant was almost empty. There were a few people sitting at the bar and several finishing up their dinner. They chose a table in the room with the bar, a room with old plank floors, a brick fireplace, and red-checkered curtains. The windows were open and the candles on the table flickered in the breeze. They begged the manager to feed them though the kitchen was closed and soon their table was piled with skillet-fried chicken, country ham, okra, Brunswick stew, biscuits, and gravy.

Sprague took off his jacket, rolled up his sleeves, and attacked the food. She took hers off and put a napkin up in front of her short-sleeved silk blouse so she wouldn't get grease on it. Neither of them stopped to remove the chains around their necks with their convention press credentials.

Sprague ordered a bottle of the driest white wine they had for her. He stuck with bourbon. He had the bartender bring him the bottle, which he put on the table next to his elbow.

'I feel as if I'm in a foreign country,' said Allison. 'I don't speak the language or understand the customs or know the food. Or you for that matter. I don't know you. You amaze me. You're like a completely different person here.'

'Take a good look because this is the real me.'

'I think I like the real you better.'

'That's encouraging. I wasn't at all sure you liked the other me.'

'I can't understand what gave you that impression.'

'It must have been a misunderstanding. I could have sworn you once called me a prick under your breath.'

'I say that to all the boys.'

'Spoken like a true Southern belle. I declare, I do believe you have got po-tential, darlin'.'

'To be what?'

'To be a good ole girl.'

'What do you have to do to be a good ole girl?'

'You have to git drunk and git nekkid, that's what.'

She burst out laughing.

'This can't be Sprague Tyson I'm talking to. What happened to the stoic, hard-ass citizen/soldier I used to know and love?'

'We left him back in that ... garage.'

Before the words were out of his mouth he realized he had made a mistake, but it was too late.

Her face went white and she sagged visibly, the air knocked out of her.

'You saw them, didn't you?'

She nodded.

'Well, shit. I'd like to kill that son of a bitch.'

He hit the table with his fist.

'There's no point in being angry with him. I'm just as responsible as he is. We separated three weeks ago, Sprague. We deliberately decided to stay in different hotels. Besides, I'm here with you, aren't I?'

He looked stunned.

'So you are. Though you probably shouldn't be. I shouldn't have brought you here. You don't know what the hell you're doing. You can't Ally. For God's sake, woman, you just lost your baby. What kind of a man am I anyway to take advantage...'

He started to get up from the table.

'Sit down and shut up, Sprague. This is terribly insulting to me, the implication that I don't know exactly what I'm doing. My baby has nothing to do with it.'

Once again she had relied on her old friend anger to save her from an embarrassing emotional scene. Her sorrow had overwhelmed her and she had come

785

very close to losing it there for a moment. This time she had turned the anger away from Des onto Sprague. But it wasn't sticking. It had done an about-face and was coming back to her. Exactly what she had wanted to avoid.

He sat down and looked at her.

'Okay,' he said.

She calmed down slightly.

'Of course I wasn't thrilled to see Des and Sadie together. But I have no right to object. I haven't . . . we haven't been close for a long time.'

Her voice dropped to a near whisper.

'Oh, Ally.' He said it with such sadness. 'What can he expect?'

'He can expect love. Support. Friendship. Understanding. He's gotten none of that from me. I won't even tolerate his religion. He's turned to the Catholic church for solace and I belittle him. I've been terrible. I don't blame him for what he's doing.'

'You're really doing a number on yourself, aren't you, kiddo?'

'I'm facing the truth.'

'There are many truths. You should know that from being a journalist. And I got news for ya. This ain't one of 'em.'

She didn't answer him.

He poured her another glass of wine and poured himself another bourbon.

'I think, Miss Ally,' he said, 'that you and I, we gon' git drunk together and . . .'

She started to gasp in mock horror.

'Tell some stories.'

'You start,' she said.

Maybe it was the wine or the foreign atmosphere.

Maybe it was Sprague, this person she had never met before, this private person whose own defenses were down. Maybe she was having a successful go at denial. She could feel her fears being calmed, her hurt soothed, her sadness subsiding.

'Where do you want me to start?' he asked.

'Tell me why you're so afraid of fear.'

There was a shock of recognition in his eyes.

'Boy, you don't mess around, do you?'

'You're even afraid of discussing it.'

'Very interesting, Miss Ally.'

He tightened his jaw as if he were about to go into mortal combat.

'All right. I'll show you I'm not afraid to talk about it. Fear runs counter to the macho code, the Citadel code. I resent fear in myself. I resent being touched by it. I resent the idea that I could lose my nerve. Fear represents a certain kind of failure. I can't even stand the notion that I would be afraid to fail. I have been brought up and trained to believe that even when it's hard you shoulder through. Anything can be overcome by determination. History is replete with stories of people who wouldn't give up, people who were alone and right against a clamoring mob. Homer's *Odyssey* is about overcoming fear, about a distaste for fear, not giving in to fear.'

'I saw fear on your face when you thought that limo was full of murderous Colombians.'

'When you love people it changes things. I can't be afraid for myself anymore. If they're here, then they are close to my family and that scares me. And I was afraid for you.'

The fact that he alluded to loving her was not lost on her.

787

'And not for yourself?'

'I can't separate that out.'

'Where did you get this aversion to fear?'

'From my daddy, I guess. He was a Citadel man, too, and a World War Two hero. I never saw him afraid. His family owned the Savannah paper. He was publisher. They had a big squabble and my father's side of the family lost. They threw him out. He never showed he was afraid but it killed him. He had a heart attack and died. That's why I quit. After I won the Pulitzer. I wanted to win it and then give them the finger.'

'And you want to win it again in the big time and give them an even bigger finger?'

'Something like that.'

The waiter came over to tell them they were closing the restaurant. Sprague prevailed upon them to let them stay around a little longer. He relented and Sprague poured them both another drink. He had drunk over half a bottle but he still seemed relatively sober. At least to her inebriated eyes.

'What happened with you and Des?'

He was so abrupt it took her by surprise.

'I couldn't let him touch me after Kay Kay. I couldn't stand the idea of getting pregnant, of losing another baby.'

She said it so simply. It was so matter-of-fact, so obvious. She hadn't been able to articulate it until that moment, that moment of drunken clarity.

'Does that go for all men or just Des?'

She hadn't thought about it that way.

'I don't know. No, I do know. It's just Des.'

'There is such a thing as birth control.'

She hadn't thought of that either. She had to

788

come up with another reason. A real reason.

'Sex and grief don't go together,' she said finally. 'Even if I could deal with my own, I can't handle his.'

The bartender came over and gently insisted that they leave. The restaurant had long since been empty.

They walked slowly out to the car together. The bartender was the last to leave. He locked up the restaurant, waved goodnight, and drove off leaving them alone in the grove of trees, in the shadow of the plantation house by the meadow.

The night was completely still except for the crickets chirping in the moonlight.

He opened the car door for her.

'A real Southern gentleman. I can't remember the last time someone opened my door.'

She slid in the passenger's side.

He walked around to the driver's side and got in. He had rented a Cadillac, the kind with one wide front seat instead of two bucket seats.

He didn't put the key in the ignition.

They looked at each other.

'I want to kiss you,' he said.

She hesitated, then leaned over to him, holding up her lips. He brushed them gently with his mouth. She sat back. They looked at each other again.

'I want to kiss you again.'

'What about Jane?'

She hadn't intended to mention her.

'I've never cheated on her.'

There was a silence.

'That's not true,' he said. 'Once. On the road. A bunch of us picked up some girls in a bar. I've regretted it ever since. Jane is a wonderful person. She's tough. She's got grit. She's a dedicated teacher. I admire her a lot.'

'What about Jane?'

She had changed her inflection.

'We seem to have drifted apart.'

They sat looking at each other again.

She leaned toward him. He kissed her again. This time with more fervor.

'Ally. Come here.'

She moved closer to him. He put his arm around her neck and she slid up close to him. He kissed her again, this time with passion.

They necked for a long time, just kissing each other, his hand brushing softly against her breasts over her silk blouse. It seemed to suit them both.

Then simultaneously they both wanted more. He unbuttoned her blouse and undid her bra. He hadn't forgotten how. He was very deft.

She had her hand on his crotch. She unzipped his fly and began to caress him.

He had his hand up her skirt, inside her underpants, softly stroking her.

'Oh God, I can't stand this,' he said finally. He stopped to pull off his trousers.

'I don't know how to ask this,' she whispered, frantic with need. 'I'm embarrassed. I've never asked this question before. Have you got a condom?'

'A condom? I haven't used one of those things for years.'

'Well, we can't . . . I mean, what are we going to do?'

'You've got to be kidding,' he gasped looking down at his priapic state.

'Oh God, I'm sorry, Sprague. But I just can't take the chance.'

'I don't fucking believe this.'

He was panting heavily. He leaned his head back against the seat.

'I think I understand date rape for the first time,' he said, looking at her with a feeble grin.

She was leaning her head back against the seat, too.

'I can't bear it,' she said. 'I just can't bear it.'

He reached over and pulled up her skirt, yanking off her underpants. Then he leaned his head down toward her lap and before she could say anything, he had his mouth on her, his tongue in her.

She was satisfied almost instantly and wordlessly she pushed his head away and bent down to take him in her mouth.

'Oh God,' he said when it was over. 'I don't think I could have survived a bad case of blue balls at my age. And you know the worst thing about this experience?'

'What's that?' she asked. She was nearly asleep in the crook of his arm.

'I've developed a new fear, worse than any of my others.'

'I give up,' she said, too drowsy to play.

'Fear of not having a condom.'

\*      \*      \*

'Hi, Bryan, c'mon in.'

Allison motioned to the young metro reporter who had peered into her office. It was the last week in August, the Republican convention was over with, the campaigns were on hold until after Labor

791

Day, and the office was like a ghost town. She was delighted to have a little diversion.

Bryan came in shyly, then looked over his shoulder.

'Do you mind if I close the door?' he asked.

'No, please.'

She waited until he was seated.

'What's up?'

'May I speak to you confidentially?'

'This sounds promising. Of course.'

The poor guy looked so uncomfortable that Allison wanted to help him out of his misery. He was a thin, frail young man who had a rather gaunt look about him. He had only been with the *Daily* for a few years but had done some perceptive reporting on the homeless, actually living in shelters.

'I haven't told anyone at the paper this but I . . .' His eyes welled up with tears. 'Oh God, this is harder than I thought it might be . . . I have AIDS.'

'Oh, no, Bryan. Oh, I'm so sorry. I had no idea, I . . . are you sure? I mean, have you had several tests? Do you actually have AIDS or do you just test positive for HIV?'

He laughed a rather macabre laugh.

'I wish,' he said. 'No, I'm afraid I have a full-blown case of AIDS. I don't expect to live more than a few years. In fact, I'm in an experimental program at the NIH, at the National Cancer Institute. Dr. Michael Lanzer, the head of the institute, is overseeing my case. I'm being treated with AZT.'

'What can we do for you, Bryan?'

'Nothing. I'll try to work as long as I can. I have no idea how long that will be. I've been doing better

792

on AZT but you never know.'

'Right.'

'That's not why I came to see you. I'm here because I discovered something incredible while I was a patient out there last spring. I was admitted because of a serious bout with pneumonia. I didn't tell anyone here. Anyway, one night I was restless and I just decided to go for a walk. I was going down one of the empty corridors and I saw this man in a wheelchair go into one of the examining rooms with Dr. Lanzer. The man looked familiar but I didn't recognize him right away. It was only afterward that I realized who he was and why he was wearing a disguise. I'm pretty sure it was the President.'

'The President of what?'

'How about the United States of America.'

'That's what I thought you were going to say. You've got to be kidding!'

'I wouldn't be in here if I thought it wasn't true.'

'Why didn't you tell us right away?'

'I don't know. I have AIDS and I know how important it has been to me to keep it confidential and I'm just an anonymous reporter. I could only imagine what it would be like to be the President and have AIDS or have tested positive. I had this notion that I should protect his privacy. I've never agonized over anything as much in my life. But finally, after watching this whole election and the drug stories about Foxy and the people he surrounds himself with, I decided that this concealing his health problems was just another scam and it was irresponsible. I know what I feel like a lot of the time, and I don't think someone should be President if he has AIDS. I think it

793

would be too traumatic for the country. Maybe not now in the early stages, but if he got really sick . . . I mean, who needs it?'

'You don't mind if we go in to see Alan and Walt, do you?'

He sighed. 'I guess not. It had to come out sometime. I just wasn't quite ready to be a pariah.'

'We'll keep it confidential, I promise.'

'Allison. I'm a reporter. Now who's kidding?'

All she could do was shrug. He was right. Once more than one journalist knew something it might as well be on the wire service. Something happened. Information was like yeast. It never just stayed the same. It had to grow. Even though both parties would swear they had never mentioned it to a soul, a secret owned by two journalists was no longer a secret. It was written.

She took Bryan in to see Alan and Walt.

'Holy shit!' they both said.

It was definitely that kind of story.

'Does he have AIDS?' asked Alan.

'All I know is what I told you,' said Bryan. 'The guy was in disguise. But I'm sure it was the President.'

'How sure?'

'Positive.'

Alan looked at Bryan hard, taking in his measure. Then without saying a word, he picked up the phone and dialed a number.

'This is Alan Warburg of the *Daily*,' he said to the person on the other end. 'I'd like to speak to Manolas, please.'

There was a pause.

'Manolas? Warburg. I'm calling to request a meeting with the President on a matter of the

794

highest national security. Today. Just me. Nobody else.'

Walt, Allison, and Bryan exchanged incredulous glances.

'Fine. I would appreciate that very much.'

He hung up the phone and looked at them.

'There's one way to find out. Ask.'

★    ★    ★

It was right before story conference, around six-thirty, when Alan came back from the White House. He called the other three into his office.

'Blanked,' he said. 'The little fucker just stiffed me. I got nothing.'

'Who else was in there with you?' asked Allison.

'Only Manolas. It's my guess he doesn't know anything. He was genuinely outraged.'

'What about the President?'

'My gut feeling? The guy's lying. I think he was there at the NIH and I also think he is not well. He was as nervous as a cat. He was perspiring. He kept jumping up and down making excuses. Too many excuses. He was protesting too much. He was not convincing.'

'So what now?' asked Allison.

'How can we find out more?' asked Walt. 'When are you going back there?' he asked Bryan.

'Next week.'

'Hang around,' said Walt. 'Don't just go in and out. Make friends with the nurses. Find out who the lab technicians are. His chart is obviously in the computer but under an assumed name. See if you can get information on that. Talk to everyone. Go to their houses. Keep going back and back and

795

back. Do a Sprague Tyson on them. Somebody knows something and somebody will talk if you're persistent enough. We've only got two months until the election.'

'I've always thought there was something fishy about Freddy's announcement that his AIDS test was okay,' said Allison. 'It took such a long time and then he made the announcement himself with Blanche standing by him holding hands. It seemed a little like overkill.'

'Jesus, if this is true...' mused Alan. 'This is really something. "President has AIDS." Can you see the headlines? Bryan, do you need anybody else? Can you use some help?'

'I don't think so. I mean, I'd like to keep this thing between us, if that's okay...'

'And we don't want the story to get out in the newsroom. Somebody else might get ahold of it.'

'Don't worry about a thing,' said Alan. 'This will be totally confidential.'

Allison and Bryan looked at each other and smiled.

'Right,' said Allison. 'Totally confidential, Bryan. You can count on it.'

★   ★   ★

The campaign would be heating up for good after Labor Day. Then it would be nonstop until the election in November. She knew she should take a break but she had no place to go. Jenny had a small rented house on the Eastern Shore in St Michaels. She had invited Allison down there but she was having a bunch of single journalists, strays, she called them, and Allison just wasn't in the mood.

Des had written her a note offering her the log cabin in West Virginia, but she was scared to go up there alone and it would be too depressing anyway. She hadn't seen Des since that night at the convention. She had tricked Jenny into telling her that Sadie had invited Des up to Easthampton for the long weekend. She tried to concentrate on how it made her feel but somehow her self-protective mechanism had gone into full gear and she was feeling nothing. Rien. Nada. Zip. It was weird.

She debated volunteering for the duty that weekend but the fact was that she was bone tired. She had been working twelve- to sixteen-hour days and weekends without a break since Kay Kay had died. She had the sense that she would unravel if she didn't at least rest for a few days. Still, she might not have taken a break if Alan and Walt hadn't insisted on it. They claimed they had given instructions to have her thrown out of the building if she tried to come in to work those three days.

She had finally decided to just stay home, sit out on her patio and read mystery novels, take walks around Georgetown, rent movies and go to bed early. Total quiet. No phones. No people.

Part of her was looking forward to it. Part of her was scared to death. On the one hand, she was so tired that she didn't even know how she would make it home that night. On the other, she was absolutely terrified that with nothing to do, nobody to talk to, no distractions, she would do nothing but think about her baby.

Three months ago she would never have attempted this. Now she felt she was ready. Unfortunately, she had no contingency plan. It was sink or swim.

Sprague had been traveling since the Democratic convention. He had left immediately for Florida, New Orleans, and Mexico, then come back while she was at the Republican convention. When she got back from that he had left on vacation to spend time with Jane and Melissa. They had exchanged funny notes but hadn't actually seen each other. He was supposed to be back the day after Labor Day.

She tried to concentrate on how she felt about him and she came up blank. She would only allow herself to feel lust. In the word association game Sprague equaled passion. She spent hours fantasizing about making love to him. It was a great distraction when she had a few minutes to herself. It helped her fall asleep at night without having her mind wander into the dangerous territory occupied by Des and Kay Kay.

The idea of loving him was not in the equation. She didn't want to love anybody. She couldn't. So she focused on his body. Which she had never actually seen entirely since they were both partially clothed during their little episode in the front of his Cadillac. That could keep her occupied for at least the fifteen or twenty minutes it took her to fall asleep. But the Friday night before Labor Day weekend it only took five minutes flat, visions of Sprague Tyson's muscular thighs dancing in her head.

The doorbell woke her up Saturday morning. She thought she was dreaming at first until it became so insistent she opened one eye and peered at the clock. It was after eleven.

When it kept ringing she got up and went to the intercom and called down to see who it was.

798

'It's me,' said the husky voice in a decidedly Southern accent.

Sprague.

'I'll be right down.'

*     *     *

Tippety Wichity was a tiny island, a wooded acre at the head of St Mary's River, a tributary where the mouth of the Potomac gave into the Chesapeake Bay. Behind the island was a small bay into which a creek flowed, the inception of the St Mary's River. The river was so shallow behind the island that one could walk across when the tide was low. Set in the midst of the trees on Tippety Wichity was a one-bedroom pale-green cottage facing south. There was a rickety old pier in front of the house, big enough to accommodate a few small boats.

Sprague kept his motorboat at the pier down the road from the Glen Mary Stables off Route 5. They left the car there and piled the groceries and bags into the small boat for the short ride across the river to the cottage.

It had to be the most beautiful day of the year, eighty degrees, clear blue sky, no humidity, heavenly breeze. It was the kind of day that made you think that life might actually be worth living. It felt good to be outside in the sun, completely away from everything. She couldn't imagine how she could have thought it would be a great idea to stay home by herself for the whole weekend.

They unloaded their boat on the pier next to his twenty-three-foot sailboat, which he called *Bonaventure*, and proceeded up the winding path to the cottage.

There was a large room with a kitchen at one

799

end, a round pine table in the middle, sofas, chairs, and a stone fireplace at the other. Then there was the bedroom and connecting bath. The bedroom had one queen-sized bed, a chair, and a dresser.

She looked around self-consciously, her purse and her overnight bag in hand.

'Just put your stuff anywhere,' said Sprague, as he unpacked the groceries.

She stood there for a moment, then realizing she had no choice, she put her bag on the chair in the bedroom.

'You might as well change into your bathing suit now,' he said, 'so we can swim off the boat. The jellyfish have miraculously disappeared. I don't understand how they know it's Labor Day.'

She went into the bathroom and changed quickly, putting on a pair of white cotton pants and a T-shirt over her bikini. She hadn't been in a bathing suit all summer; in fact, not since she'd had Kay Kay. She was extremely self-conscious about her body. Her stomach had stretch marks and she still hadn't lost all the weight she had gained. Having been so slim all her life it was a shock to see and feel herself one size larger.

He changed after she did, putting a T-shirt over his bathing trunks. They had gotten some sandwiches and salads from the American Café and some soft drinks and they took them down to the sailboat.

Allison had only been sailing a few times in her life and then on large sailboats where there had been several people to crew. She had never jibbed a mast or tacked a sheet or cast a rope or whatever those sailing things were. She enjoyed sitting on a boat and letting the breeze blow her hair, getting a

800

little sun, having a little picnic. Her one concession was getting out of the way when the boom moved back and forth so as not to get hit in the head. It seemed that sailboats required a lot of work and she found that boring. She did not, however, find Sprague boring and she had been amazed to hear herself tell him at her front door that morning that she 'adored sailing.'

They cast off around three with a plan to sail up the middle of the river and around on the Potomac up to Carthagena Creek and the Dennis Point Marina. Sprague had a little nine-horsepower outboard motor on the back of his boat to get started, much to her relief. There was also a small cabin with two bunks. Allison sat in the cockpit as Sprague explained a few things to her about how to sail, most of which escaped her. The sea breeze was southerly and they were heading right into it.

'We'll have to tack all the way to the Potomac,' said Sprague. 'I'll trim the mainsail and steer the boat. You trim the jib sheet.'

'Oh, great,' said Allison.

If he detected a note of caution he ignored it and patiently showed her how to pull in the rope of the small front sail.

They did this for almost an hour and a half as they sailed up the river past the beautiful old campus of St Mary's College, the historic village of St Mary's City, and several historic houses that dotted the banks.

Much to her surprise she was enjoying it. The air was so clear and perfect and the day so spectacular that she felt an exhilarating sense of freedom out on the water like that. Sprague had taken off his shirt and looking at his trim muscular body made her

801

even more exhilarated. Anything felt possible.

They sailed over to the Dennis Point Marina and a bit beyond, up the creek where they anchored in a little cove near a wonderful old farm with a big red barn. She felt a thousand miles away from her life.

They swam and ate their lunch, drank beer and told stories to each other about their childhoods. They were in that heady period at the beginning of a relationship when everything is new and fascinating, the prospect of discovery tantalizing.

Allison talked about spending three years in Japan when her father was a spook, how she spoke Japanese as a child, was taken care of by Japanese nurses, and had always been drawn to the culture of that country ever since.

This information took Sprague completely by surprise.

'I have something interesting to show you when we get back to the cottage,' he said.

'What is it?' His secretiveness made her curious.

'I don't want to spoil it for you,' he said. 'You'll have to wait and see. I've never shown it to anyone before.'

Both of them were totally relaxed, as though they had known each other for a long time. Sprague was not as ebulliently Southern as he had been in Georgia, but he had taken off that protective coloration he wore in the office and he was completely natural with her. He had not seemed to be totally disgusted by her body when she took off her T-shirt and plunged into the water. In fact, she had noticed him admiring her several times when he thought she wasn't looking. The sun and the water and the beer had made her feel looser and freer, so that at the moment she didn't really give a damn what her body looked like. She didn't have to look at it anyway and he didn't seem to mind.

She wondered if he would make any advances toward her, but he never even glanced at the bunk beds. She certainly wasn't about to come on to him either, though he was getting more attractive by the minute. Knowing Sprague, his military background, and his sense of discipline, he was letting the sexual tension build until they got back to the cottage. To the cottage with one bedroom. The cottage with one bed. It was very oriental, actually.

They started back a little after seven. Once they rounded the point and headed back down the St Mary's River, Sprague told her to relax because the wind was behind them and they could just run with it. It was the most beautiful time of the day because the flaming sunset was to the west and it was setting in a clear sky with only a few gathering clouds behind it.

'Looks like it might storm later,' said Sprague. 'We're lucky we're headed back. Sometimes these summer storms come up very quickly in the early evening and they can be fierce.'

'But there're just a few clouds,' she said. 'How can you tell?'

'Just watch,' he told her. She noticed that he looked a little worried and he kept his eye to the west as they headed around the horse-shoe bend at St Mary's College and back to Tippety Wichity.

The wind had come up rather suddenly and had shifted from the south to the west and clouds started moving in.

'We're going to have to beat into the wind,' said Sprague with a certain urgency in his voice as he jumped up to grab a sheet.

They were about fifteen minutes from the island when the sky suddenly turned a reddish brown, and what had only minutes earlier been white wisps became menacing black clouds seemingly hurtling toward them. Rolls of thunder sounded from above and cracks of jagged lightning stretched in front and back of them.

Allison was terrified. She wasn't a great swimmer and she was not particularly comfortable on the water. She was also scared to death of lightning.

She looked at Sprague for reassurance and though he was calm she could see his jaw tighten. He jumped over to the mainsail when the sky changed color and was now trying to force it down.

'You hold the tiller!' he shouted as he released the halyard.

She grabbed the tiller and struggled to keep the boat in the wind.

'Oh shit!' he yelled. 'The fucking halyard is jammed.' He reached in a side compartment of the boat, pulled out a knife and cut the halyard, sending the large mainsail crashing down around them. While she tried desperately to keep the boat under control, he bunched up the sail and stuffed it in the cabin.

By this time the storm was upon them. The thunder was deafening and the lightning seemed to be striking all around them. Sprague had started the motor and he grabbed the tiller to try to steer them toward the pier, which was now in sight.

A huge gust of wind threw a spray of water over the boat, knocking Sprague away from the tiller and practically knocking Allison off the boat. The rain was now driving at them with such force that they

804

could barely see anything in front of them. Allison grabbed Sprague's arm and held on to him as tightly as she could until they felt a bump and realized they had hit the pier. He ran up to the front of the boat to cast a line up on the pier leaving her clinging to the tiller, afraid to let go for fear of being washed overboard.

Sprague came back to get her and pulled her away from the stern, holding her with one arm and the rail of the boat with the other. He jumped up on the docks and pulled her up behind. As he did they heard a loud crack and saw a gigantic white flash as lightning struck one of the trees next to the cottage and split in two, sending shards of wood everywhere.

'Get up to the cottage right now!' he screamed at her and gave her a shove. She hesitated, then decided she was too scared to be brave and she ran up the path to the top of the promontory as fast as she could.

When she got into the house, she turned around and saw Sprague tie another line from the boat to the pier to secure it. Another bolt of lightning struck; this one seemed to be right where he was standing. She cried out his name, her heart practically leaping out of her chest, but he obviously couldn't see her. It was interminable, the rope tying, but finally he had finished and rushed up the path to the cottage.

When he got inside he shut the door and leaned against it panting. She came over to him and put her arms around his bare chest and hugged him, then pulled away. She was half relieved, half angry.

'Oh God, Sprague, I was so worried about you. Why didn't you come in right away? You could have been hit by lightning, you asshole.'

He grinned.

'Danger is exciting. It's kind of sexy, don't you think? This is the other side of fear.'

'Ah,' she said. 'The macho code. Of course. How could I have forgotten?'

They were soaked and shivering. It would still have been dusk were it not for the storm, but now it was pitch-black. They could barely see each other. Sprague went to turn on a lamp but the power was out. He groped around for matches on the table and lit the candles. Then he took them and went around the cottage, lighting all the candles until the whole place had a sort of iridescent glow.

He put on a CD, battery operated—he had thought of everything—a popular sixties singer of romantic songs, and went into the bathroom. He grabbed two towels and gave one to her. She took hers into the bedroom, and took off her wet suit and T-shirt and dried herself off, wrapping the towel around her. She was about to get some dry clothes from her bag when he walked into the bedroom, his towel wrapped around his waist.

'Well,' he said, bowing to her slightly. 'Kon'nichi-wa.'

She smiled, recognizing the Japanese.

'Well, hello yourself,' she said.

★　　★　　★

They lay in each other's arms after they had made love, listening to the rain pelting down on the roof and the thunder and lightning outside.

Allison stretched out her body and raised her arms above her head and let out a contented sigh.

806

She felt completely relaxed and, more importantly, completely sexually satisfied. Sprague was a brilliant lover. She had not been at all sure he would be. She'd had a few unsatisfactory experiences with good ole boys before. They had been the masters of the slam, bam, thank-you-ma'am school of fucking. And it was just that: fucking. Not lovemaking. Sprague understood how to make love. Sprague understood how to please a woman. He was in control and disciplined. It was an interesting combination of a military and oriental approach. He would not allow his own desires to best him. When he finally let go he lost himself completely. He had waited until she was practically begging for him and then when he knew she was ready he let go, which made it all the more sensational for her. It gave her a sense of enormous power at the same time that she was surrendering herself to him. He was also a thoughtful and a gentle lover. He had let her guide him in the most subtle ways without making her show or articulate what pleased her. He had also remembered a condom, which he had discreetly slipped on at the last minute. The boy had taken a magnificent natural talent and fine-tuned it into an extraordinary performance. He was awesome.

'You're very good at this, you know,' she said softly.

'The Twelfth of Never' was playing on the CD.

'There's a whole generation of men who couldn't even get an erection without this music,' said Sprague, smiling down at her.

'He demurs,' she said.

She ran her hands over his arms, his torso, his thighs, taking him in with her eyes.

'How did you get those muscles?'

'Why, Ally. I didn't think you were interested in that sort of thing.'

She moved her hand over and began caressing him until he started to stiffen.

'Speaking of interesting things, is this the surprise you mentioned in the boat, the one you didn't want to spoil for me?'

He burst out laughing.

'Oh, yeah, I forgot. Would you like to see it?'

'If it's anything like this I guess I would. Although I don't see how it could be any better.'

'Girl, you sure do say all the right things.'

'So show me.'

He got up, took her by the hand, and led her into the other room. He unlocked the bottom door of an old pine country cupboard that stood against one wall. Inside were stacks of large picture-type books, scrolls, folders, and prints. He pulled several of them out of the cupboard and carried them over to the sofa, sat down, and motioned for her to join him.

'These are part of my collection of ancient Japanese and other oriental books and art. This is one of my favorites. It's called a bride book. It was given to couples when they got married, supposedly as instruction manuals. But they're so much more than that. They are art and poetry and they depict the joy of lovemaking.'

'I've seen them. Sam collected them when we lived in Japan. He left them to me. It's funny. I've never looked at mine. They're stored in the attic. It always embarrassed me that my father had them. It's hard to think of your parents like that.'

'This is one of my favorite samurai books. I've

808

always been fascinated by the samurai. I love their fierceness, the valiant lone warrior so ready to kill or be killed, and the aesthete contemplating the cherry blossoms, the beauty and the fleetingness of life.'

'Not unlike you.'

'I suppose on some level I have tried to model myself after the ancient samurai. Their philosophy appeals to me. I'm a loner. And I've never figured to live a long life. I think my stint in Vietnam did that for me. It either made you crazy or it made you an existentialist. I'd like to think I'm the latter. But it surely is part of the reason I'm on such a crusade to get these drug dealers. I saw the destruction of souls on drugs in Vietnam. I've seen it covering the cities, the hospitals.'

'Is that why you think it's worth risking your life?'

'Yes. And I'm not afraid of dying . . .' He paused. 'But I wouldn't want to die until I've made love to you at least one more time.'

She looked down at the book she was holding and opened it to a middle page. There was an exquisite woodblock of a Japanese couple making love. They were lying on a tatami mat, completely clothed in heavy kimonos. Only their genitals were exposed and they were extremely large.

'They call this kind of art "Shunga." It means visions of spring.' His voice was husky. They were sitting close together on the sofa, both nude. He made no move to touch her.

'What else have you got here?'

'This is an Indian art book. I've got several of them. Some of them are really beautiful.'

'The lingam and yoni books?' She was teasing

809

him.

'I suppose you could describe them that way.' He was annoyed.

'Oh, look, this one has instructions. But then I suppose you know that?'

She couldn't help herself. She wanted to goad him.

The book was filled with hilarious pictures of people screwing on horseback upside down, on acrobatic poles, sideways, and every imaginable position.

'Let's see,' she said. 'Ah, ha. In this one the man puts ... oh, my God. I don't believe it.' She laughed, incredulous. 'He actually puts a plum into her yoni and then tries to get it out with his tongue.' She stopped and looked up at him, with mock suspicion. 'Have you ever done that?'

'Do you think I'd admit it to you if I had? Not with your irreverent attitude, missy.'

'Let's try it! It'll be a new game. We'll call it Samurai Sucks.' She started to get up from the sofa. 'Oh, dear. We don't have any plums.' She sank back dejectedly. Then her face lit up. 'But we do have grapes! Don't move. I'll be right back.'

She jumped up and ran to the icebox, pulled out a bunch of green grapes and brought them back to the sofa, plucked one, and held it up.

'Will you do the honors, or shall I?' she teased.

'You're making fun of me and my books,' he said. He was only half amused. 'I have a good mind to withhold my favors. And if I weren't so goddamned backed up from no sex I think I would.'

'Well. You're the master of discipline and control. Let's see how well you do at it now.'

She was really taunting him.

She knelt on the sofa in front of him, her body erect.

She took the grape and put it in her mouth, rolling it around on her tongue while she looked down at him. Then she took it out of her mouth and slowly brought it down between her legs and inserted it. She leaned back against the opposite arm of the sofa facing him and crossed her legs.

He sat looking at her defiantly and it occurred to her that he actually might be able to hold out.

The teasing had stopped. Neither one of them was amused anymore. The game had turned serious.

She waited a few more minutes. He didn't budge.

Finally in a low and sultry voice, she challenged him.

'You couldn't get it out,' she said, 'even if you tried.'

★ ★ ★

The next morning was clear and beautiful. They went outside to survey the damage. The tree that had been hit by lightning was split down the middle with a huge brown crater. Branches were lying everywhere. They still had no electricity. Luckily, the stove was gas, so they made coffee and tea and took it down to the pier.

Allison leaned up against a post and basked in the sun with her eyes closed; the water lapped against the pier, and she decided that she felt really happy. She had managed to expunge both her emotional and sexual tension. Aside from everything else, Sprague was a good listener, sympathetic and concerned. She had told him during the night, during bouts of inventive and passionate lovemaking, what had happened between her and Des. She had talked a lot about the religious problem, exploring with him the possibility that she had not been understanding enough. She was in a contemplative mood this morning.

Sprague was sprawled against another post, sipping his coffee quietly.

'I'm thinking about going to church this morning,' he said.

'Oh, no,' said Allison, genuinely alarmed. 'Not another one. I can't stand it.'

'Well, after last night I'm feeling awful guilty. That was pretty heavy stuff for a little Presbyterian boy from Savannah.'

'Say a prayer for me, just in case.'

She had just said that when they both saw a small speedboat coming toward them from downriver. They didn't pay much attention until it got quite close to their pier and they realized that it was actually coming to them, not going around the island.

Sprague sat up and looked closely at the two men driving the boat. They were Colombians.

Allison thought she would faint with fear. This was it. They had no weapons. They were completely alone. There was no phone because the electricity was out. They were dead meat.

The boat pulled up, not to the pier but to the small beach on the right side of the island, a little distance from the pier. They turned off their motor and one of the men got out and waded to shore. Both of them ignored Allison and Sprague. The one on the shore walked up and down the ten feet or so

812

of sand, then turned to Sprague.

'Don't worry, señor,' he said. 'I won't go beyond the high-water mark.'

Sprague didn't move. He sat coiled where he was, ready to spring if he had to.

'If I tell you,' he whispered under his breath. 'I want you to jump in the water and swim to the mainland and get help. I'll keep these two bastards at bay. They don't want you anyway. They want me.'

'I can't do that . . .' she started to say in a louder voice.

'Shut up and do what I say if I tell you,' he whispered back.

'Does your wife know about your lady friend?' asked one of the Colombians.

Sprague didn't answer.

'Maybe your wife will ask you to get off the story,' said the other one.

Sprague still said nothing.

The man on the beach waded back to the boat and got in. The other one started up the motor.

'We won't go past the high-water mark,' said the first one in a menacing voice. 'This time.'

The boat sped away as fast as it had come. The last thing they heard was one of them yelling, 'Adiós, señor; Hasta luego.'

'We're outta here,' said Sprague, leaping up and grabbing her hand.

Allison had managed to calm down, barely, as Sprague led the way up to the cottage.

'Don't forget your Japanese porn. You wouldn't want that stolen,' she said.

'It's not porn, it's art . . .' He turned and saw her grin. 'Oh, go fuck yourself.'

'I'm sure there's an illustration of that, too, in one of those books.'

'Look, Ally,' he said, stopping, and suddenly very serious. 'I'm afraid I'm going to have to stop seeing you.'

'Why?' She could feel her heart drop into her stomach.

'Because it's just too dangerous. Those two bozos could just as easily have killed us as look at us. I can't have that responsibility on my conscience.'

'I thought you said you had no conscience.'

'I said a stiff prick had no conscience. That it had a head of its own. But that was last night. And it was very hard to separate me from it. And stop trying to change the subject. I'm taking you home, right now.'

'But Sprague...'

'No buts, Ally. I'm not going to jeopardize anybody I love.'

Nobody had mentioned the word love the night before. He didn't dare say it to her straight out. He was too much of a gentleman. Gentlemen didn't tell women they loved them unless they had something to offer them. Not only did he not have anything for her, he had broken his code last night. He had fucked the editor and cheated on his wife. This was the closest he could come to apologizing, explaining, confessing. She was relieved. She couldn't cope with emotions at this moment. Love was not part of her vocabulary. She didn't want to learn it. Even with Sprague. For this reason she was willing to abide by his rules.

'Okay,' she said, looking him directly in his eyes. 'You may be right. It might be best if we didn't see each other again.'

814

She had demanded a meeting with Walt, Alan, the boys, and the political reporters to talk over the campaign strategy. It was the first week in October. They had one month to go until the election. She was not happy with the way things were going. No matter how many meetings they'd had, how many times she had objected, they kept going back to their old ways of covering the campaign. It was pack journalism at its worst. These guys had been doing it for so long they had become part of the system, part of the process. They wrote for each other and their buddies, the political in-crowd.

Allison felt that what they wrote meant nothing to the voters and it was why people were turning off to politics. Against her advice, they had covered every primary in every state and nobody gave a shit. As far as she was concerned they were part of the problem. They had set up a schedule a year ago outlining what they would do every week and they had become wedded to it. Consequently, they had had no flexibility. They weren't able to change their coverage if things weren't going the way they had predicted. It was like a train going in one direction that was impossible to turn around. The whole process had a life of its own. She had been in a rough position because she didn't know as much about it as they had. She had been out of the loop, out of the country for three years. Which was why she had been hesitant to force her strategy on them. She also did not want to come up looking stupid if she turned out to be wrong.

These old-time political reporters divided everyone into two groups: insiders and outsiders. If you didn't know who the Republican party chief was in Kansas you weren't worth talking to. Allison thought they felt closer to the people they were covering than to their editors, or at least the editors they felt were outsiders, like herself and Malkin. She did have Walt's support. She wasn't so sure about Alan. She knew that every time anyone had gone in to Walt to complain, he had shut them up by saying, 'Tough shit. I like the way she's doing it.' So far, Walt had managed to keep them at bay. But now it was the rush to the finish line and when the going got tough these guys felt more comfortable doing it their way, not the new way, and especially not her way. With one month to go she thought they needed a little consciousness-raising session. A group encounter.

It was scheduled for Monday morning in place of the national staff meeting. Might as well get right to it.

She was the first into the conference room. She wanted to take a few minutes to collect her thoughts. She had no sooner sat down than Sprague walked in.

He stopped for a moment when he saw her, then came over and sat down beside her.

'Hi,' he said.

'Hi.'

This was the first time they had been alone since Tippety Wichity. They had deliberately avoided each other. He had been traveling a lot and when he was there she had asked Malkin to work with him on the drug staff, claiming she was too busy with the campaign. She had thrown herself once again into her work to avoid dealing with anything in her personal life. She had never been so happy about having so much work to do, so many distractions, as she was now. There simply wasn't any time to think about anything but work. She had put Sprague out of her mind the same way she had put Des and Kay Kay out of her mind. She knew that somewhere down the road she was going to pay a price for it emotionally, but she wasn't ready.

She had not been prepared for Sprague's nearness to agitate her. She didn't welcome it. She felt they had both been thoroughly professional about the whole thing and she didn't want any momentary whim to spoil that. She had to remain detached at all costs.

'So. You're still here, I see. You haven't been mowed down by the crazy Colombians yet.'

'Yeah. Sorry about that.'

He was as nervous as she was. His laugh belied his cool demeanor.

'How's it going? Malkin tells me that you're on to the tapes.'

'Yeah. It's looking good.'

'Great ... that's great.'

'Yeah.'

They had avoided looking directly at each other until now. After a moment or two of silence they dared. It was a mistake.

They spoke in unison.

'Look ... Sorry ... Not going to work ... This is too hard ... We can't ... Maybe if we just ... Unrealistic.'

Laughter.

'Oh Sprague. I don't know what to do. I don't know what I think. I'm trying not to think about it at all. You'll have to decide for both of us.'

'It's too complicated right now, Ally. God knows I want to be with you. I can't get you out of my head. But we've both got too much to deal with.

817

You've got the election coming up. I've got this drug story. I'm not out of danger. I have to go see Melissa whenever I can get any time. We need to get a lot of things in our lives out of the way before we can even talk about anything, before we can see what we have. We're doing the right thing. Professionally and personally.'

'You're right. I know you're right. Only I...'

The door opened and Walt and Alan came in, followed by the rest of the group, about ten in all. They took their places at the table. Alan opened the meeting.

'Welcome to the group encounter, everyone,' he said. 'I suppose you are all aware of some difference of opinion on how the campaign should be covered and how it has been covered up to now. The question before us today is, are we covering it right or are we covering our asses? Is our goal being able to say we had this or that story or is it to make sure that the readers of the Morning Miracle understand what the fuck is going on? Allison, I believe you had something to say on this subject?'

'I'm concerned about our coverage as we head toward the finishing line, particularly of these political consultants,' she said. 'It seems to me that we've been running an awful lot of stuff about the boys in the back room who are making the decisions and creating the images. I don't see what we're doing to help the prospective voter make a choice. I don't think the voter gives a shit about whose idea it was to get the candidate to stand up for the American flag. I think the voters really care about the issues—health care, crime, drugs. The problem with concentrating on the consultants is that we fall into the trap of publicizing them, which creates an

818

issue where there wasn't one. It shows that we know what's happening on the inside and that seems to be all the inside people really care about. The mere fact that we write about it becomes part of the process. So I guess what I'm saying is that we've got exactly one month to go and I would like us to rethink our mandate. Which to me is informing the public in order to help them make an educated decision on the first Tuesday in November.'

She paused and looked around the room. There were several pairs of beady eyes looking daggers at her. Nobody said anything.

'Look. I want you to know that I think you have all worked really hard and done a better job than any other paper in the country. There's no question that ours has been the best coverage and we have the best team. I am also not impugning anybody's motives here. I don't see any malevolence. It's just that everybody talks about how we have the franchise in politics and I'm saying if that's true then we are the ones who can change the way we're doing it. We have the duty to update that franchise. Where is it written that we have to do it the same way over and over again for the next hundred years? I just want, in the next few weeks, for everybody to stop and take a fresh look before they assign a story or write a story. That's all I have to say. Now I'll shut up. Alan.'

'Okay. Let's look at where we are politically. We've got the crap out of the way, we've identified the issues and the key states. We're down to the short strokes. We've got to concentrate now on Texas, California, and Illinois.'

Alan went around the room, soliciting comments

819

from the others. Finally, he turned to Sprague.

'It looks like Freddy Osgood is solid to win. What are the chances of breaking a really big story that could flip it? Sprague?'

'As everyone knows by now,' said Sprague, 'I'm working on getting some tapes that could land the A.G. in jail. The question is when. I'm close but I don't know whether it will come through before the end of October.'

'If you don't have it by the middle of October,' said Walt, 'it won't have the impact that could change the election. We have to be able to plan on that.'

'There you go again. Planning ahead,' teased Allison.

'Give me a break,' said Walt.

By picking up on Walt she had eased the atmosphere. Everyone was tired, stressed, and strung out from having been on the road for nearly a year. They had been sleeping in strange hotels, eating junk food, living without clean laundry, missing their families, working their buns off, and in some cases fucking their brains out. She understood that she had to find a way to show them she appreciated what they had been going through.

'I can't promise anything,' said Sprague. 'I'll get them when I get them. And it may not be until after the election. In any case I don't have any evidence that Osgood's fingerprints are on this one.'

'Okay, everyone,' said Alan, standing up. 'That should do it for this meeting. Any complaints, take them to Allison. And by the way, you're all doing a first-rate job.'

The room cleared out and Allison and Sprague were left standing there together.

'By the way,' she said. 'I've been meaning to ask you. Did you ever know Sadie Grey when you were both living in Savannah?'

She thought he looked a little stricken when she asked the question.

'Yes. Why?'

'We need to talk.'

⋆　　⋆　　⋆

It was the week before Thanksgiving, three weeks after the election. Freddy had won. Despite his sinking polls in the summer, his consultants had finally managed to pull him out of his slide. A series of brilliant TV ads detailing the positions of his religious right opponent and highlighting his running mate, Malcolm Sohier, had done the job. The Republican had been more than the American people could stomach, and Sohier's appeal was more overwhelming. They reluctantly voted Freddy back into office. Sprague had not been able to come up with the tapes of Foxy and Antonia doing dope together in Colombia. Bryan had uncovered nothing at the National Cancer Institute. Freddy had lost weight but otherwise seemed to be in perfectly good health. He had stonewalled Alan Warburg. Allison was frustrated at having both stories that they all believed to be true but unprintable. But she was not ready to give up.

She had an idea. She would send Sprague to talk to Sadie and see if he could get anything out of her. She knew Sadie worked closely with Michael Lanzer and was Blanche's only friend in Washington. If anybody knew anything it would be Sadie. Unfortunately, Allison had only come up

821

with the idea after the election—when she had brought up Sadie's name at the brainstorming meeting it was just out of curiosity. They had never really had a chance to discuss her. Then she found out that Sprague knew Sadie pretty well from Savannah. She had tried to get him to see Sadie about Freddy. For some reason he had resisted at first, saying he needed to concentrate on the Colombian story. It was only after a lot of persuasion that she managed to talk him into going.

Sprague's initial reluctance made her wonder what kind of a relationship he had had with Sadie in Savannah. He was clearly not neutral about her. But Allison decided she didn't want to know. Somehow she knew too much already. She would leave it for now. Maybe later, down the road, if their relationship developed into something, she would ask. But not now.

She herself would go see Michael Lanzer. Though she had seen him on television and seen his picture in the papers, she had only met him once at a White House dinner after Rosey had been killed. She had found him extremely attractive, even more so in person. She had often wondered if he were having a thing with Blanche or Sadie. Both of them spent so much time with him. She would never have dreamed of suspecting a First Lady before, but now, after Sadie and Des, she knew better. She certainly wouldn't have blamed Blanche for having an affair, especially being married to Freddy. Sadie was an even more likely possibility because she was single and Lanzer had apparently split up with his wife. But then Sadie and Des had begun seeing each other again, so that shot down that idea. At any rate, that was all beside the point. She was not going to see him to discuss his sex life. She was going to see him to discuss, well, the President's sex life. Or former sex life.

It was up to her to get something out of Lanzer. Bryan had said Lanzer was adamant about never discussing his patients under any condition. A famous television reporter had called him asking about a famous AIDS patient who was being treated at the National Cancer Institute anonymously. Lanzer had hung up on him. If Allison wanted to talk to Lanzer she better have another reason. She found one.

★     ★     ★

He had agreed to see her the next afternoon at four. She explained to him that they had a potential problem on their hands with AIDS in the newsroom and she would like some advice from him on how to handle it.

His secretary ushered her into the small conference room and offered her a cup of tea. When she was alone she walked over to the picture window overlooking the Bethesda Naval Hospital and the imposing Mormon temple in the background. It was a beautiful view despite the dreary November weather. The clouds were so dark it looked almost like night, and she shivered just looking at the wind blowing the trees. She used to love the fall weather, especially Thanksgiving. Now she dreaded it. It reminded her of death. This time last year she was happier than she had ever been in her life. Christmas was coming, she was a month away from having her baby, and she was madly in love with Des. How things reversed. A year later she was more unhappy than she had ever been. Christmas was coming, the anniversary of her baby's death, and she and Des were not together anymore.

She felt a stab of pain like she hadn't ever remembered and she clutched her stomach reflexively. It lasted only a second. She had trained herself well. She could manage to eradicate the thoughts that had subjected her to that pain almost before they began. It was like some kind of meditation trick. She could just put those thoughts behind her. She did.

She had remembered correctly. He was attractive. He had these eyes that saw through you, and high cheekbones and a sensual mouth. The interesting thing about him was that, unlike most good-looking men, he didn't seem to know it. That was an immensely appealing quality. The white doctor's coat added to his appeal.

It was even more inexplicable, now that she had seen him again, why he and Sadie didn't have something going. It would have been natural since they were both single now and were thrown together so often. There was no point in pondering that. It hadn't happened. She did think, though, that in other circumstances, he would be someone she might be interested in.

He seemed completely oblivious to what she was thinking. He motioned her to a chair and sat down himself.

'What can I do to help you?' he said.

'Actually, we have a reporter on our staff who has AIDS and who is being treated here. His name is Bryan Babbitt. He knows I'm here. I told him I was coming. I don't expect you to acknowledge that he is your patient. However, it will become known soon, since Bryan is developing symptoms and he very much wants to continue working in the newsroom. I've got to know how to handle the fears of other reporters and editors who work with him.'

'AIDS is not contagious that way. There is absolutely no need to discriminate on any level.'

'People are going to ask so I need to get some answers from you. What if someone objects to sharing a phone or a computer terminal with him? What about him using bathrooms and water fountains? What about the cafeteria, the possibility of drinking out of the same glass—these are questions on everyone's mind, even sophisticated journalists. As open-minded as we all are, as we would like to be, I'm afraid everyone is a little apprehensive.'

'There is absolutely no evidence of any possibility of getting AIDS except through sexual intercourse or blood products. All those things you mentioned would be perfectly safe. There is nothing to worry about.'

'Well, you've certainly set my mind at ease on that subject.'

She emphasized the word *that*.

He didn't say anything. She saw that he sensed there was another agenda. She might as well come out with it.

'There's another subject I'd like to discuss with you.'

He kept looking at her with those eyes. He was inscrutable. It was making her nervous and she was a pro at this.

'Bryan tells me that you are treating President Osgood. He saw him in the examining room with you.'

She was going with harder information than she actually had. An old journalistic trick.

'I'm not going to comment about the President or anyone else, so don't even try to ask me questions about him.'

He didn't seem surprised at the question. He didn't gasp in shock. He didn't deny. She would keep going.

'If I had known you were going to ask me this, if I had known this was the real reason you wanted to see me, I would never have agreed to talk to you.'

'Does President Osgood have AIDS or has he tested positive for the HIV?'

'Look, you told me you were coming here for one reason . . .'

'I have my answer.'

'I'm not telling you anything. All I'm telling you is no comment.'

'Dr Lanzer, we are not talking about Joe Ordinary. We are talking about the President of the United States. The state of his health affects all Americans. Are you going to conceal that to the detriment of your country?'

She knew she was going a little too far. She was really playing hard ball here.

'I don't discuss my patients with the press or anyone.'

She raised an eyebrow.

'I don't even say if anyone is a patient or not.'

'Right,' she said.

He realized he had given away more than he had intended. He immediately turned conciliatory.

'I hope we can still have a working relationship . . .'

'Why did it take so long for the President to announce the results of his AIDS test?'

'I'm going to have to go with "no comment" again,' he said. 'I'm sorry.'

He was trying to placate her, but the fact was that his whole no comment, rather than a denial posture, told her everything she needed to know. She didn't have enough to go with a hard story, but she certainly had enough to keep working on. If the President was being treated out here, a good reporter could find it out. It would only be a matter of time.

She stood up. There was no point in pressing him anymore.

'Thank you so much for taking the time to see me, Dr Lanzer,' she said warmly. 'I really appreciate it. And I do understand what a difficult position you are in. I will probably be calling you from time to time. I hope you will speak to me.'

He seemed relieved by her equally conciliatory tone.

'On any subject but who I might or might not be treating ... it would be a pleasure.'

*      *      *

She had no plans for Christmas. She had spent Thanksgiving with Jenny and a group of strays on the Eastern Shore and that had been quite pleasant. Fun actually. She was glad she had done it. Thanksgiving was a relatively neutral holiday with no emotional context for her. Unlike Christmas—Christmas was Sam. Christmas was Kay Kay. She didn't actually know how she was going to make it through this one alive. She wasn't

827

sure even her best defenses would hold up under the strain of this holiday. Jenny was going to be away. She didn't celebrate Christmas anyway. Sprague was going to be in Savannah with Jane and Melissa. Aunt Molly and Uncle Rog had invited her to come out to Colorado to spend it with them, but she didn't think she could hack that either. Aunt Molly was on the sauce most of the time and Uncle Rog had had a series of operations and was so feeble he could barely keep up a conversation. She was afraid that visit might really put her over the edge.

In fact, something terrible was happening to her. Little cracks were beginning to appear in her armor. She was suffering the emotional equivalent of metal fatigue. The campaign was over and there was always what they referred to in the newsroom as the postcoital let-down after a major story. The eighteen-hour days had turned into twelve-hour days, which were not long enough. Nothing much had turned up on the AIDS story. Sprague had gone to see Sadie and had come back with basically the same 'no comment' confirmation that she had gotten from Michael Lanzer. Since then he had been off trying to get the tapes, which meant that he was rarely in the office. They had become friendlier after their initial period of enforced estrangement, but it was not easy. They still made a point of not being alone together. She had asked him to go with her to the NBC Christmas in Washington show at the Pension Building. It was to benefit Children's Hospital and she really wanted to go. She knew Sadie would be there and she didn't want to go alone. When she told Sprague it was for the hospital he accepted immediately. He was very formal and gentlemanly when he picked her up. He seemed to sense this would be a difficult evening for her and he was protective. Neither had any idea how difficult it would be.

She had had no idea that Des would be there with Sadie and Willie. She had gasped when she saw them come in together, and Sprague quickly took her hand and held it through the rest of the show. She could feel herself being sucked down into a spiraling black pit of depression, the same pit she had been in when Kay Kay died, and this time she felt helpless to do anything about it. What saved it for her was the fact that the President passed out on the platform. They had all rushed for the phone, then gone immediately back to the office. The White House claimed Freddy had 'orthostatic hypotension from high blood pressure.' They rushed to get doctors' opinions from all over the country to see if they could connect it to any kind of AIDS symptoms. She had worked half the night and gone to bed exhausted. She would never know what would have happened with Sprague if Freddy hadn't fainted. She suspected they might have started up again. Certainly they would have if she had wanted to. Sprague could not have refused her under the circumstances. It would have been against the 'macho code.' What she didn't know was whether that was what she wanted. The fact was that she did not have any idea at all what she wanted right now. It was the first time in her life she had ever been in that situation and she found it debilitating. The one thing she knew she didn't want was to be alone on Christmas Day, the first anniversary of Kay Kay's death. The problem was that the only person she could possibly spend that day with was Des, and he would be with Sadie and his son, Willie. It was, after all, Willie's birthday as well as Christmas.

She was standing knee-deep in quicksand and she could feel it sucking her down.

*　　*　　*

'Sonny?'

Her heart stopped.

'Hi.'

She could barely get it out.

'Hi.'

Neither of them seemed to know what to say after that.

'Where are you?' she said finally.

'At my house.'

'Oh.'

'It's, uh, it's getting close to uh . . .'

Was he choked up? She couldn't tell. All she knew was that she wanted to cry herself. She could feel the tears coming.

'I know.'

'I don't want to be alone. I mean, I want to be with you.'

'Me, too.'

If she said anything more she would break down.

'May I come over Christmas morning?'

'Yes. Of course.'

If he didn't get off the phone she knew she would lose it completely.

'Good. I'll see you then. Bye.'

He barely got the words out himself.

*　　*　　*

830

It was eight in the morning when he rang the bell on Christmas Day. She crawled out of bed, brushed her teeth, threw on a pair of jeans and a turtleneck, and went down to answer the door.

When she opened it and saw him standing there she threw herself into his arms as though she had been running a marathon and had just crossed the finish line.

He shut the door and put his arms around her and held her and they stood there.

He looked as if he hadn't slept at all. She certainly hadn't.

'Oh Des,' she said. 'I'm so tired. I feel so tired. I feel so sad. I feel so hopeless. I can't do it anymore. I can't hide it and I can't pretend and I can't go on. It isn't worth it. I don't care about anything anymore. I just, I just, I don't know anything anymore. Oh God, it's so hard.'

She broke down, despite herself.

'She would have been so beautiful. She would have been walking now and saying Dada and Mama and we would have been so proud and happy. We would have had a tree and lots of toys and a stocking and maybe her first doll.'

'Don't, Sonny.'

'Des, help me. I can't do this. It hurts too much. Please help me, Des.'

He wrapped his arms around her more tightly and swayed with her back and forth in a rhythmic motion, trying to calm her down, to soothe her, to soothe himself.

'It's okay, Sonny. It's okay. I'm here. It's going to be okay.'

She broke away from him.

'No!' she yelled at him. 'No, it's not okay! Don't

831

you understand? Kay Kay is dead. Our baby is dead. She will never come back again. We will never hold her again. We will never be able to love her again. I will never nurse her again. She will never call me Mama. I am not a mother. I am a woman whose baby has died. That is how I define myself. That is not okay.'

They were standing in the downstairs hallway next to the kitchen. Des leaned against the wall.

'Oh Sonny, I will do anything to make your suffering easier. I want to take on your pain, to wrest it away from you so that you might have some peace. I can carry it because I don't carry it alone. You don't have that. It makes me crazy to think that you've had to deal with this by yourself. I have tried to help you but I don't know how. I can't do more than I know how. All you should know is that I love you and I want to help you any way I can. If you will let me.'

'I'm so sorry, Des,' she said after a while. 'I didn't mean to turn on you. I know I've already done this before. It's just that I haven't known where to direct my anger. It's easy to be mad at you. You're here and you're defenseless. It helps me. Anger has been my religion this past year. The problem is that I'm losing it. It's going away. I can feel it and it's scary. Mainly because I know what will replace it. Sorrow and sadness. I'd rather be angry. The only thing is that I'm having trouble sustaining it. Especially at you. I just realized it when I had that outburst. I didn't have my heart in it. It was sort of a last gasp. The last of my defenses. I'm sorry. I know you're suffering as much as I am. And you have Willie. Your son you cannot claim. I ache for you as much as I do for

832

myself. I despair for you and me. I guess that's what worries me the most. What will make it better, make it easier for either of us? I don't see that it's possible. I see us living in this hell forever, having no control over our pain. I just can't bear it. I don't know what to do.'

He reached out and put his arms around her again and they held on to each other until they were both calm and still.

'I have an idea,' said Des finally. 'If you're looking for something to do?'

'What?' She was dubious.

'You could make me a big breakfast.'

★    ★    ★

Breakfast had given them strength. Literally and psychologically. Des loved huge cholesterol-filled breakfasts and she had bought eggs and bacon and croissants especially for him. She was suddenly starving, though earlier she couldn't have stood the sight of food. Their binge had been cathartic and they were both feeling an enormous release of emotional energy. On some level Allison felt that she had managed to purge her feelings of anger and embrace her feelings of sadness. Now that she faced it, it wasn't nearly as bad as she had thought. In fact, it was easier to be sad about Kay Kay's death than it was to be angry at Des.

They were both wiped out and didn't talk much during breakfast. They ate and read the paper together in the dining room downstairs off the patio. For the first time Allison noticed that it was a gorgeous sunny day, unlike last Christmas when it was so dark and snowy. Maybe it was a good omen.

For the first time she felt a tiny twinge of hope.

After breakfast Des suggested they take a walk. They strolled all around Georgetown, up Wisconsin and over near the university, across to P Street and over by Dumbarton Oaks. It was a lovely walk and she felt invigorated by the time they got back to her house on Olive Street. They kept going, down by the Washington Harbor, where the sun was sparkling on the water, casting brilliant little diamond patterns on the glass of the buildings. It was after 1:00 p.m. so they decided to have Christmas lunch at the Sequoia, a large all-glass restaurant on the second floor of a building with spectacular views of the Potomac River.

They had champagne and turkey and told stories about the campaign and made each other laugh. It was after three when they left and walked arm in arm up to Allison's house.

When they got to the door Des paused. Neither of them wanted the day to be over.

'There's one more thing I'd like to do,' she said.

He waited.

'I'd like to go to Children's Hospital. To the little chapel on the first floor of the atrium. I'd like to go there with you and just think about Kay Kay. Just let her know that we're there and we love her wherever she is.'

Her eyes welled with tears. It was such a relief to be able to do that. And to do it with Des.

They drove to the hospital and parked in the underground garage. They rode up the automatic ramp into the atrium and walked slowly to the tiny chapel at the far end.

They went in hesitantly and sat down in the middle row. Des crossed himself and genuflected.

834

Allison looked at him and reached for his hand. He clasped hers in his and they squeezed very hard. The tears began rolling down her cheeks and she didn't even try to stop them. Des was crying, too.

'Oh Des, I miss her so much,' she whispered. 'I loved her so much. I would have been a good mother. Don't you think, Des?'

'Sonny' was all he could say, and he put his arm around her.

'Do you think she knows we're here? Do you think she knows we love her?'

'I think she does. I believe she does. I know she does,' he said.

'She has to,' she said. 'She has to.'

They sat for a few more minutes. Then they got up to leave.

Allison paused at the door and looked back at the altar.

'Merry Christmas, Kay Kay,' she said. 'Your mommy loves you.'

*    *    *

When Des pulled up in front of the house he hesitated.

'You can just let me off,' she said, putting her hand on the door handle.

He reached over and touched her other hand.

'Where do we go from here, Sonny?'

'I don't know, Des. All I know is that it was impossible before. There was too much anger. Right now, for me, there's still too much pain. Maybe, maybe when the pain changes to hope...'

He leaned toward her and holding her head in one hand, he kissed her softly.

'Just know that I'm here and that I love you,' he said. 'You are not alone.'

'I'm glad,' she said, and smiled at him, then turned and got out of the car.

\* \* \*

Sprague got the tapes. One of his Colombian journalist sources managed to get a copy of them and, unable to use them himself, passed them on to Sprague. The *Daily* stripped the story across the top of the front page. It was late January, several days before the inauguration. The bottom fell out of Washington. It was a great day for journalism. Newspapers, networks, wire services, cable news—all of them were besieging the *Daily* for more information. Sprague was asked on every talk show in America. He chose to go on 'Good Night' with Desmond Shaw.

He came in to tell Allison about it after the evening story conference.

'Maybe we could have a drink afterward,' he suggested. The way he said it made her believe that it was important. She agreed.

Since there was so much happening she decided to stay down at the office and deal with all the reaction, have a quick supper in the cafeteria, and wait until Sprague finished the show. She'd look a mess by then, but she had the feeling that this 'drink' would not turn into romance. Somehow she was relieved.

It was strange seeing Des interview Sprague. She wondered if it was not some sort of conflict of interest, but she couldn't exactly define the conflict. Des had planned the entire show around Sprague and his series of stories on the drug situation in Colombia and the Jenkins's Cove operation in the Bahamas. He introduced Sprague as a Pulitzer Prize winner and a man who would surely win another one for his extraordinary body of work. Des was probably right. After this story there would be no way they could refuse to give the prize to Sprague. At least no honorable way.

Sprague talked about how difficult it had been to work with a bodyguard and the threat against his family. He allowed as how the two guys in the Bahamas had both been arrested. He had told Allison earlier that he felt pretty secure now and that he had let Ralph go. Both Sprague and Des came across looking good, looking intelligent and professional, and looking like hunks. She had to admit she was as amused as anything else.

Sprague called as soon as the show was over to say he would be picking her up shortly. They went to the Ritz Carlton bar, a cozy, low-ceilinged room with love seats and chairs, oriental rugs, and soft lighting. It was the perfect place to sit and talk privately, something they were clearly going to do.

'I want to tell you a little bit about myself,' he said, after they had chosen a selected corner. He had had the waiter put a bottle of bourbon on the coffee table in front of them.

'I've already told you how my daddy got aced out of his job as publisher by the wrong side of the family. But I didn't tell you how it made me feel. I didn't tell you my fantasy. I felt like I wanted to make good, give them the finger, leave the paper, come up North to the big city and make good again in the big time. My fantasy was that after they had fucked up the paper, they would beg me to come down and take it over and I would go back down there and make the bastards eat shit.'

'I guess you forgot to tell me that last part. Sounds like a good plan though.'

He laughed.

'I knew you would approve.'

'The first part works,' he continued. 'I do a series on drugs, I win a Pulitzer, I get offered a job by the *Daily* and quit. I'm lucky. I've got a little family money that makes it possible for me to do things I might not otherwise be able to do. I come to Washington. I bring my wife and child and I think I'm going to break through this cold glass ceiling of a city and make it big. I'm under a lot of internal pressure. The pressure to produce comes not only from my father but from my desire to avenge my father. I have to succeed.'

He took a swig of his bourbon, which he was drinking neat, and turned to look at her.

'And then I met you.'

She took a sip of her kir and said nothing. She didn't know what he was leading up to and it made her feel nervous.

'You, my friend, were not part of the plan.'

She waited.

'You were the Scheherazade of Washington. You told fabulous stories and kept everyone enthralled. You were a brilliant editor. You were a beautiful woman. You were a woman in distress. You were part of the tableau of this city I was trying to beat. I had to stay aloof from you, from the city in order to master it. Once I got too close I was afraid I would fall into the trap, get sucked into the superficial life of this city I was trying to conquer, become a part of it and never manage to do what I set out to do,

838

never make it back to Savannah. That's why I was so hostile at first, that's why I stayed away. I was afraid.'

She raised an eyebrow.

'Yes. I said "afraid." Another of my dreaded fears.'

'I had a very contented if not passionate marriage with Jane. You threw a grenade in the middle of it. Nothing you did on purpose. It was my problem. You were just there.'

'But what—'

'I was glad to send Jane away. I wanted her gone so I could have you. Have you and the story. I got both.'

'Then what—?'

'I'll let you talk in a minute. The problem was that I conquered neither you nor the city. I'll never understand Washington. I'll never like it. I'll never be comfortable here. The drugs story was just that. A drugs story. Foxy was just a dupe. He could have been anywhere. His being attorney general was incidental. The fact is, ma'am, this ain't my town.'

'May I say—'

'Please. One more thing. I never conquered you because you were in love with Des. And I ain't your guy.'

'Oh Sprague, I—'

He held up his hand as he poured another drink.

'All this is a long way to say that I'm leaving the *Daily*, I'm leaving Washington, and I'm leaving you. I'm going back to Savannah to run the paper. The bastards have fucked it up and they're begging me to come back and take over. I'm going back and I'm going to make them eat shit. So the fantasy is fulfilled. And what the hell, Ally. You were never

839

part of my original fantasy in the first place.'

He leaned back against the pillows and smiled at her.

'Okay. You can talk now.'

She couldn't say anything. All she could do was put her arms around his neck and kiss him.

'Oh Sprague,' she said. 'I do love you.'

'That dog won't hunt, lady. Go back to Des. He loves you. He needs you. The two of you belong together.'

'I don't know. I'm not sure it would ever work for us again.'

'I have never seen two people more in love with each other than you two. I know what I'm talking about. You're crazy about that guy, grapes notwithstanding.'

'Plums. It's supposed to be with plums. Next time . . .'

'Next time Des will get the plum.'

## CHAPTER NINETEEN

She had the feeling she was in a dream, completely dissociated from everything. She was floating high above the earth, wafting in and out of the clouds. The sky was painted in vivid pinks and blues. All her troubles had disappeared. She hadn't a care in the world. She was very happy. Very happy.

'May I get you another glass of champagne, Mrs Grey?'

The stewardess was hovering over her, making sure she had everything she needed. She nodded. The stewardess refilled her glass for the third time. Or was it the fourth?

She leaned back in her wide comfortable seat, stretched her feet out in front of her, and took a long sip. Maybe she had died and gone to heaven. This was surely not real life. At least not real life as she had known it lately.

So much had happened in the last four weeks that it seemed like four years.

The President was inaugurated. A week later the President resigned.

All of Washington was in shock. The President cited the drug scandal for his resignation. It would be impossible to carry on the business of governing after having been tainted, however unfairly, by the attorney general's behavior. He had, of course, asked for Foxy's resignation at the same time. There was not a word about AIDS. It had still not surfaced in the press. It had been determined that drugs, theft, murder, corruption, torture, and international humiliation were more acceptable to the American people than AIDS. Sadie despaired over that. It made her realize what a long way they still had to go to educate the people on the subject.

Blanche had been hysterical and had nearly driven Sadie crazy. Once it was over, she had left immediately for Nashville and had been embraced by all her country music buddies. Sadie wasn't worried about her. She would be fine and a lot happier out of the White House and out of Washington.

Freddy was sick. It would get out in a matter of months. By then Malcolm and Abigail Sohier would have a remarkably smooth transition and would have the reins of government firmly in hand.

The Republicans were still screaming and yelling about fraud and how the President had known all along he was going to resign. There was some movement among the far right to demand some sort of reelection, but it wasn't going anywhere. Most of the moderate Republicans were secretly thrilled that Malcolm Sohier was in office rather than their right-wing nut case.

She hadn't seen much of Des. They still talked every day on the phone. They were now best friends. He still came by on Saturdays to see her and play with Willie. Usually they had dinner together. But he had been working so hard, with all the news, that he didn't really have more time than that. It was just as well. After their talk they both realized there wasn't anything left.

She had not seen Michael since the night of the 'Christmas in Washington' show.

The day after the President resigned she had received a short note from him.

Dear Sadie,

I'm sorry I haven't responded before to your very interesting letter, but as you can imagine I have been quite busy. With any luck things should begin to slow down a little now. I'm off next week for an official tour of Eastern European countries. See you in Prague.

Michael

She had had to put her novel writing aside in the last few weeks. There had been a lot of preparation for the AIDS conference in Prague, which was where she was now headed. She had been asked to open the five-day conference. Michael would be there but only for the last two days, arriving in Czechoslovakia in time to make the major

842

presentation at the end of the conference.

Coincidentally, Des would be attending a journalism conference in Prague at the same time. It had been organized to bring together leading American journalists and their Soviet and Eastern European counterparts to exchange ideas. She had also learned from Jenny that Allison was one of those who had been asked to speak at the same conference.

Prague was apparently the hot place these days. Because it was so beautiful, so completely undamaged from the war and undeveloped after the war, it still had the romantic old European atmosphere that so many European cities had lost. Every organization in America was holding its conferences in Prague and it had become a meeting ground for friends from all over the States.

Des and Allison had been obvious choices to be participants, since they were both so well known and so respected. She had been surprised that they both accepted, however, because of the new administration. It was a busy news time. Did they accept because it would be a chance for them to be alone together in a foreign city?

She wanted Des to be happy. She hoped he would end up back with Allison. But she didn't want to lose him when she had no one for herself. It was a selfish attitude but she was lonely and Des filled a need for both her and Willie. He wouldn't be able to do that if he got back together with Allison.

She didn't know what she hoped with Michael. She was going to Prague because she had agreed to do so a year ago. Michael had agreed at the same time. They were speaking to each other then. Were they not speaking to each other now? How would she know? She was so baffled by his response to her letter that she didn't know what to think. How could he possibly write her the kind of letter he wrote to her, get her response, and not respond? It didn't make any sense. He had been busy. He apparently had spent every minute with Freddy toward the end. If Blanche's hunch was right, he was responsible for getting Freddy to resign.

Still, he could have written. He could have had the courtesy to let her know he had received her letter. She was beginning to hate him. He had caused her more pain than any man she had ever known. He had toyed with her mind. He had trifled with her heart. She was sick of his games, sick of him, sick of the whole thing. The awful part was that he still had a hold on her. Every time she thought she was through with him she would see him, talk to him, get a letter from him, and it would stir up all the feelings she thought she had suppressed. The thing to do, obviously, was not to see him again. After this conference she vowed to herself that was exactly what was going to happen. Blanche was gone now, so AIDS would not be the White House project. She would obviously stay involved, but she could be more selective about what she attended. She would make sure that Michael wasn't going to be there. She had her novel to work on. What she really needed was to find another man, to find someone else to fall in love with. Her fear was that until she did she would not be able to get Michael Lanzer out of her life completely.

★      ★      ★

844

Everyone from the AIDS conference was staying at the Intercontinental Hotel in downtown Prague. It was centrally located and within walking distance of all the sights. The participants at the journalism conference were staying at the Praha Hotel out in the suburbs. Des was arriving after she did and was only going to be there for two days. They had discussed the possibility of dinner together if that fit in to their respective schedules. Neither of them seemed terribly enthusiastic about it. In fact, she secretly hoped they couldn't. She really wanted this trip to be an escape. She wanted to forget her life, if only for a few days.

*     *     *

Prague. It was as beautiful as everyone had said it was. She had a suite on the top floor of her hotel overlooking the palace and the old city.

It was the heart of winter and the first afternoon it began to snow. A bus tour of the sights had been arranged in the late afternoon. As they drove around and twilight approached, the white flakes began swirling around, throwing a magical spell over the entire city. For a while Freddy and Blanche and Des and Michael didn't exist. She had an eerie sensation that she was about to embark on a new life, a life that had nothing to do with her old life at all. She was overcome with a sense of excitement and anticipation.

That evening a dinner was planned with all the members of the commission. She had become quite friendly with many of them over the past year and a half. They ate in a wonderful old wood-paneled restaurant with great atmosphere, stained-glass windows, soft candle light, terrific goulash, a violinist playing corny love songs, and lots of wine. It was all so far away from Washington and everything that was familiar, that she was able to relax and enjoy herself in a way that she couldn't remember having done in years.

The next morning she opened the session with a very moving speech she had written herself. She stayed until the end of the day, sitting in on every presentation and discussion. She did the same the following day. By the third day she was tired and wanted a break. Des had called from the Praha to apologize for the fact that he wouldn't be able to see her. They had two full days and working dinners had been planned as well. He hoped she wouldn't be too upset. She let him off the hook. She was in the same boat, too, she explained. It would be impossible for her to get away. She hung up the phone feeling relieved and liberated.

\* \* \*

On the third day after the morning session she arranged for her agents to get a car. She had decided to break away from the conference and do some sightseeing.

It was dark and gray outside. The coal from the stoves had left a thin blanket of soot on the white snow. Everything looked dingy and depressing. She was glad as they got in and out of the car that she had worn high boots, her fur-lined coat, and her fur hat. It was bone-chilling cold, damp, and penetrating. She shivered and pulled her coat closer around her.

It was close to five when they arrived at the old Jewish cemetery. It was getting dark and the snow had begun to fall again, covering the city once more with its magical blanket.

She had read about the cemetery, used from the fifteenth to the eighteenth century, the old-new Gothic synagogue built in the thirteenth century, and the postwar State Jewish museum. She asked the agents to stop and see if it was still open. They pulled up a few minutes before closing and the agents explained who Sadie was. A guide was provided to lead them into the now completely empty cemetery.

She was not prepared for what she would see.

No description could possibly evoke the torrent of emotion she felt when she entered the gate. There were thousands of gravestones, crooked and blackened, crowded into the small courtyard together. They looked as though they were huddled together with their arms wrapped around each other. She had the oddest sensation that they were moving, whispering, moaning in the twilight. But how could they? They were only monuments. They weren't real. Was it her imagination? Or the wind blowing the snow?

She stood gaping.

The guide was silent, accustomed to the first reaction.

After a moment she began to speak slowly and quietly, explaining that there were over ten thousand graves, with over a hundred thousand Jews buried in them, some ten feet deep for lack of space.

At the back of the graveyard, next to a high wall, in a grove of stark trees and branches, was a large tomb. It was covered with stones and candles.

This, explained the guide, was the grave of Rabbi Löw, a very famous rabbi born in 1609. It was the custom to write a wish on a piece of paper and place it on his grave under a stone.

Rabbi Löw! She remembered that night she had made the Sabbath dinner for Michael. He had told her a wonderful story about how his grandfather had wished to be reunited with his grandmother at Rabbi Löw's grave in Prague. They had found each other later in America.

The guide was getting anxious. It was nearly dark and the snow was coming down quite heavily. She glanced at her watch.

Sadie asked for a few minutes by herself and nodded to her agents.

They walked back towards the gate with the guide, leaving Sadie alone at Rabbi Löw's grave.

She fumbled in her purse for a pencil and a notebook. Struggling to see in the twilight, the wet snow sticking to the paper, she wrote her wish.

'Please let Michael believe that I love him.'

She folded up the note and placed it on top of the tomb, weighting it down with a large stone she had found on the path at her feet

She was about to leave when a man's hand reached out from behind her. He picked up the note from under the stone she had just placed there. She almost let out a cry, she was so startled.

As she turned to call her agents she saw his face in the dusk, the snow swirling around his eyes as he tried to read what she had written.

He looked up from the piece of paper and smiled.

'He does.'

This time it was going to be different. This time they were going to make love to each other.

They were back in her hotel suite. He was standing in the middle of the room. She was leaning against the door. He really didn't need to touch her. He was already making love to her with his eyes.

'I'm sober and I'm well,' he said.

'Good,' she said, slowly taking off her coat. 'Because you're going to need your wits about you.'

He took off his coat and threw it on the chair.

She let hers slide to the floor.

He took his tie off. Then his jacket.

She slipped out of her boots, then her pantyhose.

He took off his shoes and socks, then his belt.

She was wearing a long-sleeved cashmere dress that buttoned down the front. She began to unbutton it slowly, one button at a time, the top button first, then the next, then the next.

He stood watching her, never taking his eyes from hers.

She was always amazed at how beautiful he was, when she was not entrapped in his gaze. Those cheekbones and that mouth, which always seemed hungry when he was studying her.

He was unbuttoning his shirt as she undid her dress.

His shirt came off first.

Her fingers were working in slow motion. Finally she parted her dress in the middle revealing her bra, which barely covered her breasts, and the top of her underpants.

She took a deep breath and swallowed.

She let her dress slide to the floor. She couldn't

bear it, she wanted him so much.

He dropped his pants, then his shorts.

She could see he was in the same condition.

Slowly, she slipped off her pants and her bra.

She walked over to him and stood so close that they were almost touching. She held her face up to his, her mouth slightly parted.

He waited.

She put her hand on his chest and pushed him backward to the sofa, then down.

He sat looking up at her, his expression a contrast in amusement, curiosity, and desire.

Before he would ask what she was doing she sat on his lap, straddling him with her legs, wrapping her arms around his neck.

Now it was his mouth held up to hers.

She leaned down and took his lip in her teeth, biting him playfully. She felt his hands grab her waist in back, then slide downward.

She moved her body in toward him as far as she could. He was so hard now that it was impossible to get closer. She lifted herself up slightly and, finding him, she sat on him, thrusting herself to him until he filled her completely.

She bit his lips, tantalizing him, biting, pulling away, biting, pulling away, until he couldn't stand it and grabbed her hair, holding her so he could cover her mouth with his.

They moved together, loving each other, he taking the lead one moment, she the next, breathing in tandem, covered with sweat, devouring each other in the dimly lit room with their eyes, with their mouths, with their bodies.

# CHAPTER TWENTY

There was a balcony off her room at the Hotel Praha, a 1950s hotel in a fashionable suburb of Prague. It overlooked the snow-covered grounds of formerly grand houses and down toward the city, the spires of the palace.

It was midday when she arrived from Washington, having changed planes in Frankfurt. It was a sparkling day and she didn't feel at all jet-lagged. She debated trying to get some sleep now before their cocktail reception with the mayor of Prague later that evening, but she was too excited about being in a new city to rest.

The idea of being away from Washington, from the *Daily*, from the news, from her life, and in a totally foreign place was exhilarating.

She had left Washington and the *Daily* emerging from the turmoil. Freddy had resigned shortly after his inauguration, saying he felt the scandal with Foxy had tainted his administration so badly that he was no longer the person to lead the country. No mention of AIDS. There was no question in her mind that he had tested positive at the very least, and they would still continue to try to get the story. Freddy had had no choice; it was the right thing to do. Malcolm and Abigail Sohier would be wonderful in the White House and already there was a sense of calm and healing after chaos and conspiracy that had been going on this past year.

She had gone back to her eighteen-hour-day schedule when Freddy resigned. By mid-February, with Malcolm and Abigail ensconced, she didn't feel so guilty leaving the office. Besides, she really had to get away. It was a question of survival.

She had been asked to go to this journalism conference sometime last June, before she and Des split up. They had both been asked and both had accepted, welcoming the idea of getting away together somewhere after the campaigns and the inauguration. She had not really focused on it again until January and was about to drop out, just to avoid Des, when Jenny told her that he had decided not to go. She couldn't figure out why, because there was an international AIDS conference being held in Prague at about the same time and Sadie was going to be there. She wasn't going to worry about it though. Her only concern at that point was getting away. Far far away.

She took a shower, washed her hair, put on wool slacks and a heavy sweater, warm boots, and her fur-lined hooded parka, stuffed her guidebooks in her bag and went down to rent a taxi to take her to the central part of Prague.

Her first stop was the castle, the former royal seat of the Hapsburgs. The view from the castle atop one of the highest hills overlooking the river was magnificent. The sun shone on the spires and reflected off the sides of another castle in the distance, the old town, and the Moldau River below.

She took a deep breath and let it out slowly, watching it come in clouds of vapor in the cold winter air. Looking out on this exquisite, romantic city she felt infused with energy, invigorated, exhilarated almost. Why hadn't she done this before? Why hadn't she gone away somewhere, somewhere totally new and different where she could forget everything and start all over? She suddenly had the sense of possibility. Why couldn't she do it now? It wasn't too late. She could ask for another foreign assignment. Maybe Eastern Europe. There was so much excitement and a sense of vitality, of new life and new possibilities. It would suit her mood. Her mood? Was this her new mood? One of hope and possibility? It stunned her to think that. She had been so used to her anger and her pain. It had been hard enough letting go of the anger. Could she do it with the pain, too, so that she could get on with her life? She didn't know. But at this moment, for the first time, she thought it was not completely out of the question.

St Vitus Cathedral was within the castle grounds and she wandered over to have a look inside. It was enormous and impressive, with an extraordinary silver altar, gargoyles at every turn, ancient worn-wood purple-curtained confessionals, and a tiny Wenceslas chapel encrusted with jasper and amethysts.

She marveled at how completely devoid of any sense of spirituality this grand place was, for her especially, compared to Holy Trinity Church in Georgetown, which was so peaceful and meditative. Yet there in the midst of all this grandeur were simple people worshipping.

She thought of Des and his Catholicism and wondered whether they would ever be able to resolve their differences with each other. It baffled her so to know that someone she was close to felt the same way, thought the same way, had so many of the same attitudes but could then believe in something so bizarre. It was not lost on her that she was no longer angry at him for his belief. She just didn't get it. She was, however, beginning to feel something akin to religious tolerance. He had told her Christmas Day that it drove him crazy to think that he had his religion, something to fall back on, to help him through this crisis and she had nothing. She had thought about that a lot. She realized that she was no longer scornful or contemptuous of him. She was envious. What she thought now was that she was glad for him that he had it. Glad for him and sorry for her.

She left the cathedral and wandered slowly down the winding cobblestone path, past the quaint Renaissance buildings, toward the river. There weren't many tourists out in this cold weather, but the ones who were had obviously headed for the Charles Bridge, the main attraction. It was a gorgeous stone arc, which spanned the Moldau River, punctuated with baroque statues. A few artists were out selling etchings of famous local façades, and a pair of musicians played a banjo and sang with a group of students circling around them. There were couples in fur hats strolling across the bridge hand in hand and one pair up against a blackened ancient statue kissing. It was an extremely romantic scene. It made her lonely. Lonely for Des. She was suddenly overwhelmed with a sense of need for him and a realization that she was simply not complete without him.

She shivered. The clouds had covered the sun and it was looking gloomy now. It was about to snow. The temperature had dropped at least ten degrees in the last half hour.

She stopped and leaned over the wall of the bridge looking down. One of her guidebooks had mentioned that there was a gold cross embedded in the top of the waist-high bridge wall somewhere in the middle. If you put your hand on the cross and said a prayer your prayer would be answered. It was hard to find so you had to look closely. It would be on your left side toward the clock tower. She walked slowly along the edge of the wall running her gloved hand along it, looking carefully for the small gold cross. Not that she was religious or anything, but why not say a little prayer? What could it hurt?

As she approached the middle of the bridge she saw a man standing with his back to her next to the wall. He had his hand on the top of it. He was tall and had on a dark coat and a Russian-style fur hat. She would have to go around him. As she got a little closer he turned sideways to face the river, not moving his hand.

It was Des.

He had his hand on top of the gold cross.

She walked up behind him and took the glove off her left hand. She still had on her wedding ring. She had never removed it. They were still married. She leaned over and gently placed her hand on top of his.

He didn't move. He only looked down at her hand. Then softly, without turning to her he spoke, a note of awe in his voice.

'It works,' he said. 'Blessed Mother, it works.'

He wheeled around then and put his arms around her, picking her up and twirling her around.

'Oh God, it works!' he shouted. 'It works! It works! It works!'

She put her arms around his neck to hold on as she was being swung around in a circle and he was laughing and she was laughing and they both had tears in their eyes as they went around and around until they were dizzy with motion and with happiness.

It had begun to snow and the tiny flakes were swirling about their faces as he put her down.

'Sonny, my precious Sonny,' he said, crushing her to him. He held her head in his hands and kissed her face, her eyes, her nose, her lips.

'I've got you now. I'll never let you go. Never.'

She kissed him back playfully on his nose.

'Can we possibly continue this love scene indoors?' she said. 'I'm freezing to death.'

He laughed.

'Isn't it convenient that the Three Ostriches is tucked away right at the foot of this bridge? I was just thinking of stopping in there for a wee taste myself.'

He took her by the arm and led her to a beautiful tiny sixteenth-century building right on the river.

Inside the minuscule fifteen-room hotel was a cozy restaurant overlooking the bridge with soft lamps and candlelight. It was getting dark outside and they slipped into a booth next to the window and ordered hot mulled wine.

Des took her hand from across the table, then got up and came over to her side of the booth.

'I don't want to be separated from you another second,' he said, encircling her with his arm. 'I want to be close to you.'

The waiter brought their drinks and they touched their glasses together.

'To us,' said Des.

Allison grew quiet and Des frowned.

'What is it, Sonny?'

'It's just that I'm afraid for us, Des. I felt so

856

strongly that you were being taken away from me, that I was losing you to some strange cult, that it would always be in the way for us. It's all so strange to me and I felt so shut out by you. So excluded. At the time I needed you most you weren't there for me. You had been body-snatched and had left me all alone. That's mainly why I was so angry at you. And I don't see what's changed that. If it's going to work for us you're going to have to make me understand. And you're going to have to stop pushing me away.'

Des nodded.

'You're looking at a guy who's always judged his whole life on the basis of worldly success,' he said. 'Suddenly he's confronted by the fact that most of the things he cared about are not important. He loses his child and everything else loses its importance to him. Looking for God is looking for understanding. I had to believe that it was providential, that things happen for a reason. I had to find that reason, to understand. Does that make any sense to you?'

'Yes, I think so.'

'My mother lost three children. She had asthma. If all of those children had lived she would probably have died of the strain of having to care for them. God is loving and all powerful. There must be a design. I have to believe that or I couldn't go on.'

'I do understand that part of it, Des. I just don't get the Church part. I don't get that you go to Mass every morning and take communion. I mean, Catholics are supposed to believe that the bread and wine actually turn into the blood and flesh of Christ. Do you believe that?'

She was challenging him again, threatening to

ruin what they had just found. He looked suddenly pained. At first he didn't say anything. Then slowly he reached over and took both her hands in his and held them tightly. He leaned toward her and in a slow, deliberate voice he began speaking to her as though he were talking to a child.

'Sonny. I love you. I will never leave you. Never. And I won't let you use religion to drive us apart again because you are afraid of loving someone, being close to someone. Because you are afraid of being abandoned. Do you understand me?'

She stared at him a long time, as if the message needed time to penetrate her brain, as if she were absorbing the information before she could comprehend it.

Finally, her face softened. Tears came to her eyes. Then she smiled.

'Because if you do believe it,' she said with a mischievous twinkle, 'that would be cannibalism!'

He laughed with relief. She had understood. This was her way of dealing with the message.

'The genius of the Catholic church is that it has a lot of complex arguments to rationalize what people feel,' he said.

'I don't need complex arguments to rationalize what I feel,' she teased.

'And what is you feel, my precious angel.'

'I feel you are an asshole. But you're my asshole.'

'Why, Sonny. That's the most romantic thing I have ever heard you say. When you talk like that I hear violins. I see moonlight and roses.'

'Do you see double beds with fluffy down comforters in adorable little Czech hotels where you have to bribe the concierge to get a room?'

'What makes you ask that?'

'What makes you ask that?'
'I'm suddenly starting to believe in communion.'

## CHAPTER TWENTY-ONE

Michael made a brilliant closing presentation at the
conference and then took off for the rest of his East
European tour. They had not discussed when they
would see each other again. It was up to him now.

She had already made plans to go to La Samanna
when she returned from Prague. She had promised
Willie and she needed the chance to unwind. The
older children were working and wouldn't be
joining them this time.

She couldn't decide whether it was a good idea or
not to go to La Samanna. Would it make Michael
seem closer or farther away?

Willie was old enough to eat in the terrace dining
room so the first night she took him and Monica for
an early dinner, then retired to her room to read.
She had deliberately chosen a juicy novel to distract
her, but every time she picked up the book he was
all she could see, all she could think about.

She decided to take a walk down to the beach. It
was probably a mistake, but she was too restless to
stay in her room. She was adept now at evading her
agents and she slipped out without any trouble.

It was a lovely warm night with hardly a breeze.
The waves were barely lapping at the shore. She
was barefoot and hiked her ankle-length cotton
skirt above her knees so she could walk in the surf.

The walk down to the end of the beach was long
and she was a little nervous. A new moon was
obscured by banks of passing clouds so it was quite

dark. The hotel security people had said there had been several robberies and assaults that winter, and people along the water were buying watchdogs. She put it out of her mind. She needed to get out, to think.

They hadn't talked much that night in Prague. They had already talked too much. They just loved each other.

She hadn't told him how she had felt that afternoon at the cemetery. He didn't seem to need her to. He had sensed it.

As she approached the end of the beach where she always sat to meditate, she noticed a movement from the rocks to her right. The moon was behind a cloud and it was too dark to see who or what it was. She froze.

She looked back toward the hotel. It was nearly a mile and there were no lights anywhere in between. Even if she screamed there was no one to hear. She looked at the water. It was very rocky in front of where she stood and the waves were ferocious. She would have killed herself just trying to get to the water and she wasn't a very good swimmer anyway.

Her heart began to pound. How could she have been so stupid? Here she was with two Secret Service agents to protect her and she had deliberately shaken them just to go for a walk. She thought of Willie and panicked. It was irresponsible of her to take such a risk, with a small child. A child who had already lost his father.

She decided to try to stay calm, casually turn around, and start walking back the other way. If the person attacked her she would try to talk him out of it. She had no money and he would surely recognize her and think better of whatever he had in mind.

As she started to turn, she heard a voice.

'Don't go,' he said.

The cloud over the moon passed on, revealing his face.

It was Michael.

## CHAPTER TWENTY-TWO

'Good Night' was filming the next two weeks of shows in various Eastern European countries and Des had to leave for Hungary the next day after his segment on one of the panels.

She had to stay for her own presentation at the end of the conference, then get back to Washington.

She didn't mind going back now. Sadness had turned to hope. They had not resolved anything. They had only made love to each other all night. It was almost an otherworldly experience, being there in that setting with this man who was her husband, the person she loved most in the world. She almost believed it had not happened. When she tried to re-create it in her mind on the plane going home she couldn't summon up the images.

Des had said he would call her when he got back. Meanwhile she would go about her life trying to act normal until he returned and they could see what they had together.

She sleepwalked through the next two weeks, going to the office, going home, talking to people as though she were actually there instead of miles away.

She thought of nothing but Des. The only problem was she didn't know what to think. What

861

worried her was that even if Des returned and asked her to come back to him, she didn't know what she would say. Somehow she felt she needed a sign that it was right. Standing between them, in their way every waking moment, was Kay Kay. It wasn't that she wanted to eradicate Kay Kay's memory. She would always be there in her heart.

What she needed was something that would take her beyond her beloved daughter so that when she and Des looked at each other they didn't see the specter of their dead child.

*  *  *

Des called her from the airport. It was early evening and he had just come in from London.

Somehow she knew it was he when the phone rang. She had been waiting. She ran to pick it up, then hesitated before she could answer. It rang a few more times.

'Hello,' she said finally.

'Sonny?'

'Des?'

She put her hand over her heart.

'How are you?'

Her mouth went dry. She wasn't sure she could say the words. She hadn't expected to cry, she didn't want to cry, but now the tears were coming. She hesitated again, not wanting to break down on the phone.

'Sonny? Are you there?'

There was a slight panic in his voice.

'Des?'

'Yes?'

'I'm, uh, I... I think I'm pregnant.'

862

# Caring for People God's Way

## Personal and Emotional Issues, Addictions, Grief, and Trauma

■ ■ ■

*Edited by*

TIM CLINTON, ED.D, LPC, LMFT

ARCHIBALD HART, PH.D., FPPR

GEORGE OHLSCHLAGER, J.D., LCSW

*A Joint Publication and Service Ministry of*
*the AACC and Thomas Nelson Publishers*

NELSON REFERENCE & ELECTRONIC
A Division of Thomas Nelson Publishers
*Since 1798*
www.thomasnelson.com

ISBN 1-4185-0894-2

Library of Congress Cataloging-in-Publication Data available upon request

*Printed in the United States of America*

2 3 4 5 6 7 — 10 09 08 07 06

# Contents

## Part 3: Addictions and Impulse Control Problems

## Part 4: Counseling for Grief and Trauma

# Acknowledgments

Those of you who write—and especially those who write books—know that many people are responsible for getting a finished book into the hands of the reading public. This book, in particular, had a very long gestation and, it felt at times, a rather torturous birth. It was begun many years ago as the natural sequel to our work on *Competent Christian Counseling*, and is tied closely to that seminal volume.

Great thanks is given to the many contributors to this volume—your tireless patience and continued encouragement to complete this work have been, in large part, the needed motivation to see this thing through to the end. The richness and higher value of these books are revealed by the expert contributions that so many of you made to this volume, and continue to make to our ever-growing field of Christian counseling. There is no way that we alone could have written a book of this quality—thank you all so much.

Special thanks to you, Arch Hart, for your inspiration and steady goading. And thank you, Greg Janz and Mark Laaser, for coming through at the near-midnight hour with excellent contributions that completed the subjects we needed for this volume.

We wish we had a "suffering servants" award for those of you who still have not seen your contribution in print. We can only ask for continued long-suffering patience with us, as we do have your work planned in future volumes. In fact, a fair share of the very best leaders in our field will have contributed to this series before it is done.

Special thanks and high praise for a job well done to Anthony Centore and Joshua Straub, our resident Ph.D. counseling students who have done a tremendous job at checking and cleaning up our references, building lists, and assisting us in the last-minute completion tasks that can be so overwhelming. Anthony also made written contributions to two chapters in the book, and is on his way to making a significant contribution in our burgeoning field.

One of the reasons this project took so long to fruition was our struggle to find the right publisher for this book and for the series. Thomas Nelson Publishers have come through with everything that we asked, and we are delighted to be back in partnership with the company that did *The Soul Care Bible*, the primary work that we are connecting to the entire series.

Finally, we are delighted to thank and acknowledge our wives and children—surely those who "long-suffered" the most in this project. Bless you, Julie, Megan, and Zachary, and you, Lorraine, Noelle, and her husband Josh Bronz, Justin, and Rea, for all that you mean to us. Thank you, always, for all the love and patience and succor that you pour out to us, even when it is not deserved.

# Editors and Contributors

**Tim Clinton**, Ed.D., LPC, LMFT, is President of the 50,000-member American Association of Christian Counselors (AACC), the largest and most diverse Christian counseling association in the world; and is Publisher of the award-winning *Christian Counseling Today* magazine. He is Professor of Counseling and Pastoral Care, and Executive Director of the Liberty University Center for Counseling and Family Studies; and was recently Distinguished Visiting Professor in the Regent University School of Psychology and Counseling.

Licensed in Virginia as both a Professional Counselor (LPC) and Marriage and Family Therapist (LMFT), Tim is President and maintains a part-time counseling practice with Light Counseling, Inc., in Lynchburg, Virginia. He recently became Chairman of the Covenant Marriage Movement, and is a member of the Arlington Group, a national marriage policy leadership group based in Washington, DC.

Tim is Executive Editor and co-author of *Competent Christian Counseling:*

*Foundations and Practice of Compassionate Soul Care* (WaterBrook, 2002). He is lead author of *Attachments: Unlock the Secret to Loving and Being Loved* (Integrity, 2003). He was Executive Editor and a primary writer for *The Soul Care Bible* (2001), the NKJV Bible project by AACC and Thomas Nelson Publishers.

He has authored over 150 articles, chapters, notes, and columns on Christian counseling and on marriage and family life. He is co-author of *Baby Boomer Blues* in Word's Contemporary Christian Counselor series, and author of *Before a Bad Goodbye: How to Turn Your Marriage Around,* and the newly-released *The Marriage You Always Wanted,* both by Word.

Tim is a Liberty University honors graduate with B.S. and M.A. degrees in pastoral ministries and counseling. He then earned Ed.S. and Ed.D. degrees in counselor education from the College of William and Mary in Virginia.

Tim and his wife Julie have been married for 25 years, have two children—Megan and Zachary—and the family lives in Forest, Virginia.

**Archibald D. Hart,** Ph.D., is Senior Professor of Psychology and Dean Emeritus in the Department of Clinical Psychology at Fuller Theological Seminary in Pasadena, California. He was recently Executive Editor of International Relations for the AACC, and remains on AACC's Executive Board. Dr. Hart is a licensed psychologist, certified biofeedback practitioner, and is a board certified fellow in psychopharmacology. He is an internationally known speaker on Christian counseling and managing the stress of ministry.

Dr. Hart is best known for his research and writing on the hazards of ministry, depression, anxiety, divorce, stress, and sexuality. Among his numerous books are recent publications *Safe Haven Marriage* with daughter Dr. Sharon Hart May, *Unveiling Depression in Women* with daughter Dr. Catherine Hart Weber, *Unmasking Male Depression,* and *The Anxiety Cure.* He is now involved with these two daughters in the Hart Institute, an international caring and consulting ministry for the church. He is president of the International Association of Christian Counselors, a global umbrella group for national Christian counseling organizations.

Dr. Hart is an active member of the Prescribing Psychologists Register. A native South African, he holds the BSc from the University of South Africa, and the M.Sc. and Ph.D. from University of Natal.

He lives in Southern California with his wife Kathleen (they just celebrated 50 years together!), and he is surrounded by the love of his three daughters and nine grandchildren.

**George Ohlschlager**, J.D., LCSW, is Executive Director and Co-Founder of the American Board of Christian Counselors, the national Christian counselor credentialing and program accreditation agency affiliated with the AACC. He is Director of Policy and Professional Affairs for the AACC, and is Senior Editor and Writer of the award-winning *Christian Counseling Today* magazine, and the *Christian Counseling Connection* newsletter.

A Licensed Clinical Social Worker in California, George chairs the AACC Law & Ethics Committee, drafted and revised the *AACC Christian Counseling Code of Ethics*, and maintains a nationwide clinical, ethics, and forensic consulting and training practice. As a member of the Arlington Group, he does policy and political advocacy work in Washington, DC, on marital and family issues—especially to support the passage of a Federal Marriage Amendment to the U.S. Constitution. He teaches in the Ph.D. programs in professional counseling, and in pastoral care and counseling in the Liberty University Center for Counseling and Family Studies, and at St. Petersburg Theological Seminary.

George was honored as Consulting Editor and one of the primary writers of *The Soul Care Bible* (Thomas Nelson, 2001). He is Executive Editor and co-author of *Competent Christian Counseling* (WaterBrook, 2002), and also co-authored *Law for the Christian Counselor* (Word, 1992), and *Sexual Misconduct in Counseling and Ministry* (Word, 1995). He has authored and co-authored over 200 articles, chapters, columns, codes, reviews, memoranda and notes in his many fields of interest.

A B.A. psychology graduate of Humboldt State University in California, George holds an M.A. in counseling psychology and biblical/theological studies from Trinity Evangelical Divinity School (now part of Trinity International University). He then earned M.S.W. and J.D. degrees in a dual-degree, interdisciplinary studies program in social work and law at The University of Iowa.

George lives near Lynchburg, Virginia, with his wife, Lorraine, and they have three adult and teenaged children, Noelle, Justin and Rea—all are attending college.

**Diane M. Langberg**, Ph.D., is a member of the AACC's Executive Board and a Licensed Psychologist with *Diane Langberg, Ph.D. & Associates* in Jenkintown, Pennsylvania. She is also the author of *Counseling Survivors of Sexual Abuse* and *On the Threshold of Hope.*

**Sharon Hart May**, Ph.D., is Director of The Marriage, Family, and Relationship Institute at *La Vie Counseling Center* in Pasadena, California.

**Catherine Hart Weber**, Ph.D., is the co-author of *Secrets of Eve*, which reports on a recent national study of Christian female sexuality, and *Unveiling Depression in Women*. She serves on the International Board at C.A.R.E., a counseling resource for pastors and their families.

**Anthony J. Centore**, M.A., Ph.D. cand., is the Executive Assistant to Dr. Tim Clinton of the AACC, and works for the *Center for Counseling and Family Studies* at *Liberty University*, where he is a Ph.D. candidate in the Professional Counseling program.

**Everett Worthington**, Ph.D., is Professor of Psychology and Director of the Graduate Counseling Psychology Program at *Virginia Commonwealth University*, and he is Executive Director of *A Campaign for Forgiveness Research*.

**Gary Stewart**, D. Min., is a military chaplain trained in communications and crisis intervention. He is co-author of *Suicide: A Christian Response*.

**Michael R. Lyles**, M.D., is an AACC Executive Board Member and has a private psychiatric practice with Lyles & Crawford Clinical Consulting in Roswell, Georgia.

**Mark R. Laaser**, Ph.D., CCSAS, is Executive Director at Faithful and True Ministries in Eden Prairie, Minnesota.

**Mark Crawford**, Ph.D., is a Clinical Psychologist and a partner in Lyles & Crawford Clinical Consulting in Roswell, Georgia.

**Siang-Yang Tan**, Ph.D., is Professor of Psychology at the Graduate School of Psychology at Fuller Theological Seminary, and is also Senior Pastor of *First Evangelical Church* in Glendale, California.

**Gary J. Oliver**, Th.M., Ph.D. is Executive Director of The Center for Relationship Enrichment and Professor of Psychology and Practical Theology at John Brown University in Siloam Springs, Arkansas. He is a popular conference speaker and the author of numerous books including *A Woman's Forbidden Emotion* with H. Norman Wright.

**Carrie Oliver**, M.A., is a graduate of Denver Seminary, director of the University Relationships Initiative at JBU, a counselor specializing in marriage and family and women's issues, a conference speaker and an author. Gary and Carrie are parents of three boys and coauthors of *Raising Sons . . . and Loving It!*

**Ian Jones**, Ph.D., is Professor of Counseling and Director of the Baptist Marriage and Family Counseling Center at Southwestern Baptist Theological Seminary in Fort Worth, Texas.

**Theresa Burke**, Ph.D., LPC, is the Founder of Rachel's Vineyard Ministries and the author of *Forbidden Grief: The Unspoken Pain of Abortion*, as well as the *Rachel's Vineyard Weekend Retreat Manuals*, which serve as the basis for retreats offered in 45 states.

**Greg Jantz**, Ph.D., is a Psychologist, Author, Speaker, and the Founder of *The Center for Counseling & Health Resources,* which to date has helped almost 30,000 people. The Center has five locations in the Seattle, Washington area and an affiliate in Quito, Ecuador.

**Linda Mintle**, Ph.D., is a Virginia-based Therapist, Speaker, and Author of *A Daughter's Journey Home: Finding a Way to Love, Honor and Connect with Your Mother.*

**Henry Virkler**, Ph.D., has been training Christian Counselors at the graduate level for the past 25 years and is currently a Professor of Psychology at Palm Beach Atlantic University.

**Mark Shandoan**, LCSW, A.B.D., is a full-time Clinician at Light Counseling in Lynchburg, Virginia, and is completing his doctorate in Counseling Psychology at Argosy University of Sarasota.

# Preface:

## Introduction to the Book and the Series

On behalf of the American Association of Christian Counselors (AACC), we are delighted to announce our newest book and book series, *Caring for People God's Way*. This new ministry project is a joint publication venture of the AACC and Thomas Nelson Publishers, and follows the name and spirit of AACC's Caring for People God's Way video training series.

This highly usable, practice-oriented book, denoted as Volume 1A, is the bridging volume of our 2002 work on *Competent Christian Counseling* and the three volumes to follow in the format of this book. We intend this to become the Christian Counseling Practice Library for the 21st century, the leading edge of Christ-centered, research-savvy and user-friendly counseling books that takes Christian and pastoral counseling to a new standard of competent and caring delivery in this new millennium.

This entire Library is intended for professional Christian counselors, pastors and pastoral counselors, and anyone doing helping ministry in church-based ministry roles. The professional will appreciate the integration of biblical and psychosocial research material and the comprehensive way that treatment issues are covered, while the church-based helper will respond to the clear language and practical way that complex issues are defined and dealt with.

Each volume will present a discrete and clearly definable area of application—personal and emotional concerns, marriage, sexuality, trauma, addictions, grief, and loss, for example—and will cover the breadth of issues that are most commonly addressed in doing counseling in those arenas. In 20–22 chapters across 400+ pages, each volume is designed to cover material quickly and yet also comprehensively, honoring your busy schedules and need for practical, relevant data to assist you in your ministry or professional practice.

Christian Counseling has become so large and diverse that no one or two persons can write with expertise across the breadth of our burgeoning field. Beyond our own written contributions, we already have chapters for the various volumes written by over 30 of the best practitioner/teacher/writers in Christian counseling. Before this series is completed in 2007, we plan to invite over 60 people to contribute. Including *Competent Christian Counseling* with this series, you will be influenced by nearly 100 of the very best practitioners and leading academics we have in the field today.

Volume 1A, *Caring for People God's Way*, is foundational to the rest of the series. This new book encapsulates and advances the Paracentric counseling model of the earlier work on *Competent Christian Counseling* and presents it in a systematic, step-by-step fashion that outlines the process very practically for the reader. It is then applied to the most common issues faced by Christian counselors: personal and emotional issues, addiction problems, trauma disorders, grief, loss, and suicide.

This model is then superimposed on the counseling issues that are presented in each of the subsequent volumes, outlining the assessment, treatment planning and intervention strategies of the model for that area of application.

Volume 2 will address Christian counseling applied to marriage, divorce, family, and sexual issues, an arena where both the "cultural wars" and values issues in the counseling field are very hot topics right now.

Volume 3 tackles the tougher issues we all face as counselors, including counseling around medical and health care issues, working with more difficult personality disorders, and dealing with controversial treatment issues. Each of these areas is exploding as a major focus of training, research and practice throughout the world.

Finally, Volume 4 presents "The Ethical Helper." This last volume meets a crying need in the church by outlining the ethical, legal, and business issues related to Christian counseling in both professional and church-based settings, as well as delivering a "nuts-and-bolts" outline of counseling practice development in both church and clinic settings.

This library, this *Caring for People God's Way* project, intends to become the "must have" counseling and ministry resource for every professional therapist, pastor, pastoral counselor, and church-based lay helping ministry in the United States and throughout the world. We plan to finish this entire 4-volume series together so that the full project—all 4+1 volumes as a complete set—can be available for the first time by the 2007 AACC "No Greater Love" World Conference in Nashville.

Our hope—our prayer from this day forward—is that God will call you to loving service and anoint you with wisdom and power to lead others into that healing place that only He can transform. May this book and the volumes to come bless you for your work as Christian counselors in these last days.

TIM AND GEORGE
Forest, Virginia
August 2005

ARCH
Arcadia, California
August 2005

Caring for People God's Way

## Part 1

# 21st-Century Christian Counseling

# 1

## Introduction to Christian Counseling:
## The 21st-Century State of the Art

*Tim Clinton and George Ohlschlager*

And we proclaim Him, admonishing every man and teaching every man
with all wisdom, that we may present every man [and woman] complete
in Christ.

COLOSSIANS 2:28

When good King Josiah died around 609 B.C., Israel was prosperous,
strong, and safe in the world. Yet the people of Israel quickly declined both
morally and spiritually, and their leaders grew corrupt. The whole nation
refused to hear the prophets God sent, including Jeremiah, to call them to
repentance and restoration.

Amid the ongoing search for the good life, a great terror was about to
befall them—the complete destruction of Jerusalem and the forced slavery
of the Jews by the Babylonians in 586 B.C.—but they would not turn their
hearts. Jeremiah 6:14 captures the essence of that day, "They have healed
the brokenness of my people superficially, saying, 'Peace, peace,' but there
is no peace" (NASB).

Interestingly, as today's prosperous generations search for purpose,
meaning and value, many are experiencing a pervasive sense of emptiness
and isolation. And why shouldn't they? In a world flooded with distresses
like father absence, abuse, violence, marital discord, and emotional prob-

lems there is a natural epidemic of escapism through consumerism, drugs, alcohol, sex, and suicide. Earnest Becker accents this thought concluding "Modern man is drinking or drugging himself to death . . . or he is shopping which is the same thing."[1]

Living in denial, today's powerful and pampered generations have become "tranquilized by the trivial," though they find neither solace nor healing—crying "'Peace, peace,' but there is no peace." Dallas Willard alludes to this modern journey in his book on spiritual disciplines and concludes, "Obviously, the problem is a spiritual one. And so must be the cure."[2] We agree.

In 1978, Scott Peck opened his near-classic work *The Road Less Traveled* with the profound truth assertion that "Life is difficult." In the quarter century following, everything has changed. Relativism, cynicism, and the deconstruction of traditional morality have run their course leaving a socio-cultural travesty in their wake. Hence, what was accurate and profound then, "Life is difficult," hardly grasps the needs or silent cries of many today; the trauma, loss, the present terror of neglect and abuse that touch the lives of so many.

Our pressing concern at the inception of the 21st century is that *people are hurting*—and searching frantically for hope and new life. If there is ever a time for godly leadership, servanthood and biblical counsel, it is now.

Consider the following facts about our modern world:

*Marital Discord.* Studies show 35% of persons who marry get a divorce, and 18% of those divorced are divorced multiple times. Currently, for African Americans, single-parent households outnumber married-couple families.[3] In addition, almost half (46%) of persons from the Baby Boomer generation have undergone a marital split, and millions more are expected to divorce in the next 10 years.[4]

It should be noticed that the destruction of the American family is troubling kids too. Reportedly, many children 10 to 15 years after the divorce of their parents continue to battle with resulting unhappiness.[5] In addition, younger generations are likely to reach record heights of divorce and it is estimated that somewhere between 40 and 50% of marriages that begin this year will end in divorce.[6]

Christians are far from exempt. According to The Barna Group, although churches try to dissuade congregants, rates of divorce among Christians are about the same as the non-Christian population. Moreover, data shows such divorces occur *after* the married persons have accepted Christ as their Savior. Also, multiple divorces are extraordinarily common among born again Christians, for 23% are divorced two or more times![7]

*Fatherlessness.* Each night, nearly 40% of children fall asleep in homes where their fathers are not present.[8] The deterioration of fatherhood in America—by 72.2% of the U.S. population—is considered by some our most serious social ill. Encumbering the development of youth, fatherlessness promotes mental disorders, crime, suicide, poverty, teenaged pregnancy, drug and alcohol abuse, and incarceration.[9]

A study of nearly 6,000 children found that youth from single-parent homes have more physical and mental health problems than children living with married parents, and another study confirms single-parent children are 2–3 times as likely to develop emotional and behavioral problems. In addition, almost 75% of children living in fatherless homes will experience poverty, and are 10 times as likely—as compared to children living with 2 parents—to experience extreme poverty.[10]

*Sexual Abuse and Assault.* The present evidence of widespread sexual abuse is daunting. By age 18, 1 in 3 girls and 1 in 6 boys will be sexually abused by someone they love or should be able to trust.[11] According to recent surveys, about 1 in 4 women during their college years, and 1 in 33 men, have experienced an attempted (or completed) rape. Moreover, according to a national survey of high school students, approximately 9% reported having been forced to have sexual intercourse against their will.[12]

*Domestic Violence.* Violence at the hand of an intimate partner occurs across all populations, irrespective of economic, religious, social, or cultural affiliation—and accounts for 20% of all nonfatal violent crime against women. The occurrence of nearly 5.3 million acts of domestic violence each year (among women 18 and older) results in almost 2 million injuries and 1,300 deaths. These deaths are not without warning, a staggering 44% of women murdered by their intimate partner enter emergency care within 2 years prior to the homicide, 93% seeking care for an injury.[13]

*Suicide.* A suicide occurs approximately every 20 minutes in the United States.[14] According to a 2004 study, over 30,000 U.S. residents commit suicide each year, and over 130,000 are hospitalized following a suicide attempt. For men, suicide is the eighth leading cause of death. For women (as compared to men), suicide attempts are 3 times as common. Also, suicide is the third leading cause of death for children 10–14, and adolescents 15–24.[15] These high rates of self-destruction are exacerbated by social isolation, being a victim of child abuse, having feelings of hopelessness, or sustained depression. Shawn Shea writes that suicide can be considered as an only option for those feeling deeply alone or ashamed.[16]

*Alcoholism.* In the year 2000 there were approximately 85,000 deaths in the U.S. attributable to either excessive or hazardous drinking—making alcohol the third actual leading cause of death. Recent studies show that approximately 40% of all crimes are committed under the influence of alcohol, 40% of persons convicted of rape or sexual assault state they were drinking at the time of the offense, and 72% of rapes on college campuses occur while victims are intoxicated to the point that they are unable to consent or refuse sex.

In addition, 50% of child abuse and neglect cases are connected with the alcohol or drug use of a guardian, two-thirds of domestic violence victims report the involvement of alcohol, and in 2001 there were 1.4 million arrests for driving under the influence of alcohol or narcotics: that is a rate of 1 out of 137 licensed drivers.[17]

*Substance Abuse.* The results of a 2003 poll show that 8.2% of persons 12 and older have used illicit drugs in the last month.[18] Though it is known that the motivation of substance use is to increase comfort of one's psychological state, less is known about what places one at risk for abuse. Genetics, learning, environment, intrapsychic issues, personal relationships, and early life experiences all seem to have influence, though there is no absolute determinant.[19]

Recently, in investigating these issues, it was found that 56% of substance abusers admitted for treatment met the diagnostic criteria for borderline disorder, a high percentage of abusers display self-damaging impulsive tendencies, and a recent analysis of literature involving the comorbidity of drug abuse and personality disorders shows that 80% of studies find a positive correlation.[20]

There are many abuse recovery treatments, which procure varying rates of success. Review of some programs has found treatment to be ineffective when compared to a control group. One study investigating inpatient care found a relapse of substance abuse in 90% of instances, if psychosocial intervention is not part of treatment.[21]

*Depression.* An estimated 20% of the U.S. population will experience clinical depression at some point in their lifetime.[22] More than just "the blues," clinical depression is distinct in that symptoms are of a severity that disrupt one's daily routine. Often ubiquitous, these symptoms include decreased energy, fluctuating body weight, depleted concentration, irritability, bouts of crying, and thoughts of suicide.

According to recent studies, depression appears to be on the rise—those born after 1950 are 10 times as likely to experience depression as compared to their predecessors. Currently, individuals between ages 25 and 45 occupy the greatest percentage of depression, though adolescent groups possess the fastest rate of depression growth.[23] Causing inestimable pain for both those enduring the disorder and persons closest to the sufferer, depression unnecessarily consumes and profoundly impacts both the life of the victim, and that of his/her family. Unfortunately, most sufferers do not seek treatment or believe their depression to be treatable.[24]

*Anxiety.* Maladaptive anxiety has become a common plague that affects approximately 19 million U.S. adults—or up to 25% of the general population—and is distinct in that it progresses to consume one with overwhelming irrational fear, panic and dread.[25] In many instances, symptoms are intense to the point that they cripple one's personal relationships, career, and quality of life.[26]

Even in its severity, anxiety can go misidentified by a sufferer, becoming deeply routed in one's personality. For example, currently 25% of persons who visit an emergency care unit presenting chest pain are actually suffering from Panic Disorder.[27]

Issues like financial setbacks, workplace demands, loss, unplanned pregnancies, cancer, obesity, and other physical problems and the stresses of our day quickly get overwhelming. Whoever described our times as "The Aspirin Age" didn't miss it by much.

But these problems are only one form of suffering in our groaning world. Demonic oppression is still rampant. Abject poverty and life-threatening disease beset nearly one-third of the world's population. Last year, AIDS became the largest pandemic of death in world history—exceeding the 75 million deaths of the Black Plague. The ongoing horror of terrorism and war has touched every corner of the world. Last but not least, political and religious persecution, torture, and murder affect half a billion people across the earth.

## Global Recognition of Mental Disorders

We are also beginning to know a lot about mental disorders, not only in America, but around the world as well. In 2004, the World Health Organization presented the findings from its global study that analyzed data from 60,463 face-to-face surveys with adults in 14 countries—to estimate the prevalence, severity, and treatment of mental disorders.[28] All surveys used the World Mental Health-Composite International Diagnostic Interview (WMH-CIDI), a structured diagnostic interview to assess disorders and treatment. The surveys were conducted in the Americas (Columbia, Mexico, United States), Europe (Belgium, France, Germany, Italy, Netherlands, Spain, Ukraine), the Middle East and Africa (Lebanon, Nigeria), and Asia (Japan, separate surveys in Beijing and Shanghai in the People's Republic of China).

Mental health issues included anxiety disorders, mood disorders (i.e. depression), disorders with features of impulse control (i.e. the eating disorder bulimia), and substance abuse disorders. Treatment was also studied, and in the United States (US) treatment was found to be more strongly related to the ability to pay and less to the need for care, compared to other countries—many others having universal health insurance.

Despite differences in treatment, researchers found remarkably similar high proportions of mental disorders (17 to 29%, with the rates in the U.S. in the higher ranges at 26.4%), early age of onset (mostly childhood through the early adult years), high rates of chronic mental illness, and high levels of adverse effects on jobs, marriages, and other aspects of life.

*Inadequacy of treatment.* Over the last several decades, research studies have repeatedly proven the efficacy of counseling. Moreover, religious and faith-based psychotherapy have skyrocketed, showing again and again the great value that ensues when "faith meets counseling." What's sad is the gap between persons needing help, and the lack of trained individuals available to provide quality care.

For example, though there is a great client demand for spiritual care, a troublesome incongruity exists between Christian clients and mental health professionals. One survey shows that while 72% of the American population says religious faith is among the most important factors in their lives, only 33% of psychologists state the same.[29] Also, a Gallup poll suggests that above 60% of prospective clients prefer counselors with spiritual values, and 80% want their beliefs brought into the counseling process.[30] With a great many of mental health professionals deficient in an understanding of spiritual importance, the notion of finding suitable Christian counselors for all clients seems problematic, if not daunting.

Dr. Ronald Kessler, professor at Harvard Medical School, writes regarding the lack of counseling treatment in general, "The consistency of these patterns across a wide variety of countries is striking. Issue number one is that we can't wait as long as we do to get young people into treatment. Issue number two is that we have to do a better job of making sure patients are treated with the best available therapies once we manage to get them into treatment."[31]

In all countries, young, poorly educated males with serious mental disorders are the least likely to receive treatment, and it is suggested that school-based interventions in low-income school districts may help reach these young men to prevent progression from mild to more serious disorders. Early intervention is uncommon but important, according to the report, for "people with mild mental disorders, if left untreated, have a significant risk of future serious outcomes, such as attempted suicide, hospitalization, and work disability," the authors write.

Kessler said he and his coauthors were struck by the inadequate treatments in America stating, "This involves both medical care that fails to conform with accepted treatment guidelines, such as a homeopathic dose of a psychopharmacological medication prescribed by a family doctor, or care in some other sector of the treatment system, such as self-help or religious counseling, that has not been shown to be effective in treatment of clinically significant mental disorders."[32] In sum, there is a call for an increase in quality care, the necessity of which is inestimable.

## Problems in the Pew

If the population in our pews is representative of the world around us, 1 in 4 of those pew-sitters in the U.S. wrestles with a diagnosable mental disorder with few receiving any help or direction. Moreover, churches involved in evangelism and outreach may show even higher rates of disorder because if they are succeeding in their job of fulfilling the Great Commission, then many entering these churches could be beset with chaos and trouble like the church has never seen.

*A crisis of leadership.* There is widespread acknowledgment that the American and Western Church is mired in a major leadership crisis. The Catholic Church's sexual abuse crisis, of course, immediately stands out for its severity and pervasiveness. Not only are there thousands of still-suffering victims of hundreds of serial sex-abusing priests, but the cover-up and shuffling of these priests to new parishes to replay their crimes over and over is a scandal that has implicated dozens of bishops and archbishops, and two American cardinals!

Not that the Protestant church has any reason to gloat or be smug about its own status. Nearly 6,000 Southern Baptist pastors leave the ministry prematurely every year. More than 200 pastors are fired every month! Former SBC president Jimmy Draper asserted that a third of the SBC's 62,000 churches have staff suffering from significant stress or emotional problems.[33]

Dr. Freddie Gage, former SBC evangelist and leader, pioneered a ministry to burned-out and abused pastors, called Wounded Heroes. After suffering from major bouts of anxiety and depression in his 40s, and receiving real help via psychiatric treatment, he worked for Rapha for many years as a liaison between that Christian counseling ministry and the SBC: "The majority of Southern Baptist ministers do not offer grace, compassion, and restoration to their fellow ministers. When a pastor stumbles, we purchase him a coffin and bury him," said Gage.[34]

*Shooting our wounded leaders.* The recent scandals of pastoral leadership only confound a wider issue: the abuse of church leaders by the church itself. A friend of ours was recently fired as pastor of his church. It was an unjust act—akin to shooting a bleeding soldier lying prone on the hospital cot rather than tending to his wounds and restoring him to health. Arguably, it was an act of soul-murder, and something that the conservative church does all too often, not just to its hurting people in the pews, but also to its wounded leaders.

This man—an author with a long history of successful pastoral ministry—wasn't caught in adultery, wasn't embezzling church monies, and wasn't engaged in fraud or wrongdoing of any kind. He simply got sick. He was stricken by a depression that adversely affected his ministry, no doubt about it, but in no way was a firing offense. His church should have rallied around, shown him love and mercy, given him a health-restoring sabbatical, and found him the resources to repair his life and return to ministry when able. Instead they wrote him off and kicked him out.

The great blessing for the woman caught in adultery was that she was hauled before Christ as the object lesson of a higher purpose—which was to entrap the Son of God in some violation of the law. For although the Pharisees had only one target audience—callously using this woman as if she didn't count, or even exist—Jesus never discounted her and always kept in view his two audiences, the abused woman and her powerful accusers. And it was surely the love of Jesus that intervened on her behalf, saved her life, and probably saved her soul with his merciful challenge to "go and sin no more."

The scandal of modern-day Pharisees who abuse and mistreat those needing mercy and a "safe-haven" is that these people are never brought before Christ. Instead, the abusers think they have the "mind of Christ" and those who suffer depression and chronic mental disorders—those among the "least of these" that Jesus calls us to special ministerial commitment—are often among the first that many churches scrub from their ranks.

Think about this being normative in the American church. The mentally and emotionally disabled are often too embarrassing and unrepresentative of the bright and shiny Christians the church wants to show off to the world. Stepping down to care for those with ugly dispositions and repulsive traits is exactly opposite to the step up we want to take in a life of ever-growing satisfaction with the abundant life that God promises on the other side.

No wonder Jesus wept. No wonder the scandal of the church shooting its wounded keeps growing. And no wonder there will be many expressions of shock and disbelief on judgment day when many will hear the Lord say, "Depart from me, for I never knew you."

However, it is also true that even some Pharisees and legalists in the modern church can be persuaded to provide care—even if it is condescending care—to the most needy and chronic sufferers. More and more people are understanding that many mental/emotional disorders are serious issues like cancer and diabetes. They understand the influence and mutual reinforcement of mental illness with poverty, illiteracy, family chaos and child abuse, drug abuse, and the like. And some people even understand the cyclical and repetitive nature of depression and various disorders that were once thought to be solely a product of sin or character defect.

But a pastor, a Christian leader, is expected to overcome trouble even if that trouble arrives through no fault of his own. A leader may suffer as any other mere mortal, but fault is attached if he does not overcome it, or carry through it with grace and aplomb.

The sad and harsh truth is that there is no room in Christian leadership for debilitating trouble. Tragically, there is no place to go for most—nowhere but down in flames and shame.

### Living in a Hard-Hearted Age

We cannot escape the truth that we live in a cold and hard-hearted age. Without dedication, spiritual fullness, good health, good training, perseverance, and on occasion, a willingness to suffer with those one serves, helping ministry does not work all that well. Even with these things in place, it does not always work consistently, for there is one thing that must infuse and flow from the servant in order for counseling to be redemptive. That is the caring love of Christ, a love that must transcend the best love we can muster by ourselves.

*Charles Colson and the TV interviewer.* Years ago, in one of his columns for *Christianity Today*, Charles Colson tells the poignant story of an interview on PBS that demonstrates the power of caring, sacrificial love. In pointing out the limits of our best efforts to reform culture through political activism and persuasive argument, Colson asserts that "there is only one way people will genuinely 'hear' the gospel message: by observing how the church itself lives . . . They should see in the Christian community a unifying love that resonates with their own deepest longings—and points to a supernatural source." Then he told this wonderful story:

The interviewer had an aggressive manner and a hard expression under layers of make-up and mascara. "How can you be so sure about your faith," she challenged me. I answered by telling her a story of my time behind bars after Watergate, when several Christian men stunned me with a quality of love I had never known before.

> I'll never forget that day because one of them—Al Quie—called to say, "Chuck, because of your family problems, I'm going to ask the President if you can go home, while I serve the rest of your prison term." I gasped in disbelief. At the time, Al was the sixth-ranking Republican in the House, one of the most respected public figures in Washington. Yet he was willing to jeopardize it all out of love for me. It was a powerful witness that Jesus was real: that a believer would lay down his life for another.

As I retold the story for the cameras, the interviewer broke down and waved her hand, saying, "Stop, stop." Tears mixed with mascara were streaming down her cheeks. She excused herself, repaired her make-up, and—injecting confidence back into her voice—said, "Let's film that sequence once more." But hearing the story again, she could not hold back her tears. Later, she confessed that Al's willingness to sacrifice had touched her deeply, and she vowed to return to the church she had left years earlier.[35]

A Christian community united in love attracts attention in the most jaded culture. Sacrificial and caring love does offer up the best remedy to influence and change the hardest hearts. This is the difference that the love of Christ makes, and it is this kind of love that must make a difference in our service to hurting souls. When the love of Christ is truly shown the Spirit of God infuses it with power that changes lives.

## Searching for God

Though it appears to be the worst of times, something else seems to be happening across America—people are searching for God. According to the work of George Gallup and Timothy Jones, 82% of Americans desire for a more intimate relationship with God: This is up 24% in just a 4 year period! Further, according to the research, in the last 24 hours some 66% had prayed to God seeking not only help but also direction in life. Some 50% had sensed a strong presence of God in their lives and had even gone out of their way to help another person with spiritual or religious issues.[36] A new Gallup book, *The Next American Spirituality*, cites how a spiritual movement in the hearts of Americans is contrasting what has become an overwhelming secular culture.[37]

With this we are reminded of Isaiah 6:8 when God asks, "And whom shall I send, and who will go for me?" We never cease to be amazed that God's desire is to send persons like you and each one of us to carry His message of hope in Christ to a searching and hurting world.

*Preparing pastors, clinicians, paraprofessionals, and lay helpers.* That is why we are so excited about what God is doing in and through the Christian counseling movement today, especially in the American Association of Christian Counselors (AACC), which is so dedicated to the entire community of care and to training and filling the church with lay helpers and caregivers beyond anything that has been done in history. Pastors and professional Christian counselors alone cannot possibly meet the needs that exist in the church and in the world today.

The helping ministry of the church must have *four* strong legs to properly function, to even begin to meet its ministry call in the 21st century world. Unless pastor, professional clinician, paraprofessional, and lay helper all work together—in harmony and with mutual respect and support for the role that each serves—the church will surely be overwhelmed by its sins and mental health troubles.

### The Call to Care

Remember the story of Jesus' call to discipleship of Phillip and Nathanael in John 1? All he had to say to Philip was "Follow Me," and he did. Because of his great skepticism, Jesus did not approach Nathanael directly (he knew that a direct approach might likely yield a rejection of the call). Instead, he sent his friend Philip to persuade him to "come and see" the one that Moses and the prophets wrote about. And when Nathanael came, Jesus revealed to him his best character and self-perceptions, banishing all skepticism and leading him to exclaim, "You are the son of God! You are the King of Israel!" (John 1:43–50).

Are you called to Christian counseling? Are you called by God to lead others into a life-changing encounter with the living God? Just as God calls us and uses us to help others enter into a unique healing encounter with him, Jesus used Philip to draw his skeptical friend into a life-changing encounter with Jesus Himself.

### God Will Make a Way

In a sense much like Paul's words in 1 Corinthians 4:1, "Let a man so consider us, as servants of Christ and stewards of the mysteries of God," we often assert in Christian counseling that "God never wastes a wound." Although he is not the author of evil or sorrow, he is wise to use every kind of wrong suffered and dream dashed to reach out to us to grab hold of his healing hand. He is the "God of all comfort, who comforts us in all our tribulation, that we may be able to comfort those in any trouble, with the comfort with which we are comforted by God" (2 Cor. 1:3b–4).

What a glorious circle of care! God comforts us, enabling us to turn and comfort others with that same care given by God, enabling both to worship God and give to others again. We are his agents, his regents, his care-giving disciples given to a call to "bear one another's burdens, and so fulfill the law of Christ" (Gal. 6:2).

*Healing power in caring relationships.* We believe, then, that Christian counseling and pastoral care is grounded upon the centrality of healing relationships with both vertical and horizontal dimensions. Like all counseling, it is dyadic in its horizontal dimension between at least two persons. As truly Christian counseling, it becomes uniquely triadic due to God's presence in the vertical, supernatural dimension. In Christian counseling, the Holy Spirit is the third person in every counseling situation. Since this vertical dimension is unique to Christian counseling, it is essential that we begin healing pursuits with the relational God—with Father, Son, and Holy Spirit.

Yes, the one God existing in three persons pushes beyond the boundaries of rational thought. God in three persons is the blessed Trinity, the spiritual lifeblood through which flows the meaning of our existence. It is to this triune God that we are called—wooed to participate in an intimate, lifelong relationship—now on this earth, and forever in a heavenly eternity. Come to the Father, Son, and Holy Spirit. When we encounter one, we encounter all three. When we worship one, we worship all.

Why does God exist this way? Why does He reveal himself to humanity in this difficult and complex manner? When it is so hard to understand God even in the best of circumstances, couldn't He have made it easier to know Him? Struggling with these questions, the disciples queried Jesus in John 14:8, "Show us the Father and that will be sufficient for us."

The cynic might say that God does this to confuse and distress us with mysteries we cannot understand, puzzles we cannot unravel. The believer might assert a simpler, more direct reason: *God does this to show us the beauty and value of relationship.*

*Christian counseling reflects the Trinity.* We tell of this important truth about the triune God of the Bible because it is an apt analogy for the development of Christian counseling, and of Christian counselors. Moving from a one or even two-dimensional practice to a triune, or three-dimensional practice means that one is maturing as a clinician in ways that more closely reflect the God who is there.

## Counseling that Is Truly Christian

Christian counseling, then, may be defined as *a triadic healing encounter with the living Christ, facilitated by a helper who assists this redemptive, healing process, helping another get unstuck and moving forward on the path to spiritual maturity and psycho-social-emotional health.*

As with everything else in our triune approach here, this definition has three distinct clauses. To be "on the path to spiritual maturity and psycho-social-emotional health," focusing on the back end first, is to be committed to becoming like Jesus himself. It states the ultimate goal of sanctification, and hints at our ultimate state of glorification. God is at work at every turn in every Christian to make him/her more like Christ. The right metaphor is marriage, not cloning or robotics. Two travel on and become one in spirit and mutual purpose, all the while retaining their distinctive personalities and identities.

Secondly, getting "unstuck and moving forward" states a fundamental reason people come into counseling in the first place. Despite being panned by some recent critics, it is nonetheless true that people seek help and come into therapy on the basis of felt needs that go unresolved by the known efforts of the client.

Finally, the clients engage the counselor to assist them to experience a "healing encounter with the living Christ." Stated another way, the client should interact with and be touched by the Healer, who is Christ. Christ comes alive through the agency of the counselor, and makes himself dependent on the invitation of the people engaged in the process.

Christian counseling facilitates a supernatural encounter between the human spirit and the Holy Spirit wherein Christ is made alive in the life of the person in a fresh and healing way. The Holy Spirit is present to bring conviction and guide us into all truth (John 16:8, 13). And in this life the Holy Spirit comforts us (Acts 9:31), renews us (Titus 3:5), convicts of sin (John 16:8) and searches all things (1 Cor. 2:10). The apostle Paul proclaimed, "Likewise the Spirit helps us in our weakness. For we do not know what to pray for as we ought, but the Spirit himself intercedes for us with groanings too deep for words. And he who searches hearts knows what is the mind of the Spirit because the Spirit intercedes for the saints according to his purpose" (Rom. 8:26–27 ESV).

## Embracing a Wisdom Theology of Caregiving

As we asserted in *Competent Christian Counseling*, every counselor has a theology—and a spirituality, bio-medical theory, and psychosocial theory—that directly influences the counseling process. We believe that Christian counseling is largely deficient in its theological roots and spiritual practices. Lamenting the current state of Christian counseling in this regard, Arch Hart, one of our pioneering leaders and co-author of this book, has challenged us:

> For some time now [speaking in 2001], experts have been telling us that the stock market is due for a major correction. Already we are beginning to see the economy "cool" with stocks jumping around like a cat on a hot tin roof. Well, I have the same fears about where we are headed in some of the things we do as Christian counselors, particularly our uncritical adoption of the secular psychological concepts. We have run ahead of our theological foundations in developing our understanding of a "Christian" approach to counseling—and we are due a major correction here as well![38]

A wisdom theology of caregiving, therefore, is especially commended to counselors, as it incorporates both the creation and redemptive visions of God and is most applicable to problems in daily living (see chapter 3). Consider this value as expressed in The Wisdom of Solomon:

> I called for help, and there came to me a spirit of wisdom. I valued her above sceptre and throne, and reckoned riches as nothing beside her...I loved her more than health or beauty, I preferred her to the light of day ...So all good things together came to me with her, and in her hands was wealth beyond counting, and all was mine to enjoy, for all follows where wisdom leads.[39]

Mark McMinn recently called attention to the importance of theology in counseling when he stated: "Effective Christian counselors also consider theological perspectives at the same time that they engage in the various psychological tasks of counseling. Historical and systematic theology, biblical understanding, and Christian tradition are all valued and considered essential components of counseling."[40] Effective counselors, in McMinn's view, are those given to "multitasking"—the ability to utilize insights and skills gained from the study of theology, psychology and spirituality simultaneously and appropriately for the benefit of the client.

Allen Bergin[41] and Ev Worthington,[42] among others, have clearly shown us that we cannot divorce counseling from its moral, theological and philosophical roots. All counseling and psychotherapy—especially that which denies it—is deeply values-based. This makes it a given that we are all doing theology when we practice counseling. The obvious questions, then, are these: Are we doing theology well? Is the theology we are doing biblical theology or bad theology?

Counselor competence is greatly enhanced when we build from a solid theological foundation, for at theology's core is the study of God Himself. Our hope is that Christian counselors will learn and impart to their clients a *living, caring, and experiential theology*—revealing the truth of His Person and His desire for relationship with us. Answering these questions and reflecting upon the significance of the answers for counseling will provide the structure for the rest of this chapter.[43]

### Caring Enough to Challenge Transforming Change

A very significant area of study and debate in counseling today surrounds the issue of change. Questions abound, like, What is meaningful change? What is the true goal of counseling? Is it self-actualization? Helping people become less dysfunctional? Cultivating more self-awareness? Becoming unstuck? Getting in touch with the inner self? Personal congruence? Enlightenment? If you have studied psychology you could probably easily add to this list.

Most outcome research studies, however, simply hinge on symptom reduction. An example would be; Johnny started out smoking two packs of cigarettes a day and now only smokes one. While noble, change also needs to go deeper and affect key issues of the heart. This is where the importance of redeemed relationships and transforming change, versus change as mere adjustment or "coped-with" relationships, spills over into our understanding of Christian counseling as caring ministry. A major challenge to Christian therapists is the incorporation of a biblical spirituality into counseling—

yielding ourselves and our work to the lordship of Christ in the counseling goal and process.

Yet we would also assert that counseling, by itself, is not enough. To revise, slightly, the language of Carl Rogers, counseling models that do not consciously set Christ at the center may be useful to some degree, but are insufficient models because clinically we have all encountered persons who, after years of work, are still stuck, still oppressed. There are many people who will not be freed without a healing *encounter* with the living God through the Holy Spirit. And most importantly, we assert true freedom only comes through faith in Christ.

Christ-empowered change, which can be understood as the power in counseling and psychotherapy, is transformative. It is not merely the process by which adaptive forces are placed in greater harmony, but the process by which "new life" itself is discovered and applied to one's existence.

Theologically, James Edwards has made a cogent case on the scandal of the Incarnation. Jesus—God come in the flesh—not only scandalizes the world and the acceptance of Christianity among the panoply of comparative religions, it is a scandal in the church itself. He argues that much of the church—in order to make the Christian gospel more palatable to the non-Christian world—shifts to and adopts a creation, rather than a redemptive theology.

A creation theology alone, in its acceptance of the natural order as God's created design, essentially denies sin and the need for a transforming redemption of the human personality. In this subtle sophistry, what is good and therefore must be affirmed and celebrated—redemption from sin and a Christ-transformed life—are not needed, nor are they wanted in a sin-denying/Jesus-rejecting world.

However, when God is truly present in counseling, sin can be redemptively accepted and honestly disclosed—as the Holy Spirit leads us. Wounds and traumas that still bind us—things we thought were resolved or that we simply live in denial about—can be revealed and washed away in supernatural healing. Jesus is magnified and glorified, and is known to us as a fellow sufferer and divine lover. God Himself is transformed in our perceptions of Him, becoming a divine object of attraction, rather than One of fear and avoidance. All things are genuinely possible when God is present in Christian counseling.

## Caring vs. Curing

Systemically, in the same way that medicine is better balancing the demands of acute care and chronic care in the treatment of disease, Christian counseling must learn to do the same with its bio-psycho-social-spiritual interventions. In other words, we must learn to become much more focused on caring than solely on curing in our ministry work.

Of course, this is not a screed against counseling as a curative process. To be sure, many client problems are curable and will never beset that person again. This is especially true—and is far more possible in Christian counseling—because of the miraculous power of Christ. In fact, in this book we explicitly incorporate the necessity for supernatural healing encounters with the Holy Spirit as an essential part of true Christian counseling.

However, some of the issues that clients bring to us—including our dedicated Christian clients—are repetitive and long-term problems that appear over and over again in different contexts and at different times in the life of the client. While this borders on the definition of personality disorders (and personality quirks pushed to extremes by severe stress do exhibit many of these disorders), our point here is to acknowledge the chronic nature of many of the problems that are brought to us in counseling.

Problem chronicity demands a different approach, something other than the curative orientation of acute medicine. It demands a coping and caregiving approach that teaches problem management instead of cure. Theologically, this is about recognizing that we still live in a fallen world, and that sanctification should not be confused with glorification—as it often is in so much Christian advertising and book marketing. It is not the event of being made perfect by a major miraculous encounter with the risen Christ. It is about recognizing the distinction between acute and chronic care—that chronic pain, like the ongoing struggle for sanctification, has a quite different treatment from that applied to acute pain.

For example, most of the cases of depression that you will see will be seen again by you or someone else. For most sufferers, depression is a recurrent, even lifelong problem that erupts time and again at different junctures of living. Same with many anxiety disorders, social phobias, addictions, and anger and impulse control disorders. And, believe it or not, this is true with most of the Christians you will see in counseling, and in the church.

Moreover, our curative theology must change. Many Christians falsely believe that accepting a chronic understanding of a disorder is tantamount to a failed faith—even to a denial of Christ Himself. It is cure or nothing, as any alternative to a curative approach denies the power and desire of Christ to heal—and to heal now. We do not agree that this is a failed faith, but a failed hermeneutic, a distorted understanding of Scripture that is often reinforced by a "Pollyannish" view of God, and a "too magical" expectation about living. We certainly believe in soul healing but we also acknowledge that God sometimes chooses not to heal or that the healing comes in and through the pain.

Sanctification is a lifelong process of being made incrementally more like Christ as we travel the high road of Christian maturation. Or to state it from the negative reality: every one of us has chronic problems—including chronic sin problems—as detailed by Paul in Romans 7, that we will battle with at various stages throughout our lives. Also, the author of Hebrews (12:1) writes that we strive to "throw off everything that hinders and the sin that so easily entangles."

Therefore, much counseling has to do with problem management or reduction. To state this positively, much Christian counseling has to do with learning and applying the principles of kingdom living to the chronically recurring sins, fears, failures, and dark areas of our life.

## The Foundation and Scope of this Book

We establish, once again in this book, the authoritative foundations for competent Christian counseling. For our purposes, in this book and in this library series, this authority is grounded on these four sources:

1. The revelation of God in Christ Jesus. Jesus is our Wonderful Counselor and the model for both therapist and client of that which calls us to maturity and excellence in life and in ministry. He is the Way, the Truth, and the Life, the guide upon whom we ground all our work as Christian counselors.
2. The preeminent role of the Bible (Old and New Testaments) and Scriptural truth as the final authority and primary revealer of Christ, of God's redemptive story on planet Earth, and his purpose for humankind, both individually and corporately.
3. The important, though secondary role of science and logic and also of history in the development of Christian counseling, as in all counseling.

4.  The person of the counselor, including the training, experience, and credentials of the therapist. The helper's character and orientation to counseling, including primary values and ethical commitments, are central determinants in facilitating consistent, constructive, and ethical client change.

Therefore, as we did in *Competent Christian Counseling*, this work also melds together and takes further:

1.  The foundations and teachings of Scripture, salted with the writings of the giants of church history on spiritual formation and pastoral care, with
2.  some of the very latest research, theory, and practice in Christian counseling, in the broader fields of counseling and psychotherapy, and in the bio-psycho-social sciences, to
3.  construct a biblically-based, strength-oriented, Spirit-directed, 21st century meta-model of Christian counseling—a model that is "counselor friendly," is effective in facilitating change, and is geared to help people mature in the ways and wisdom of Jesus Christ.

We also asserted in *The Soul Care Bible* that the church should become—that it is called by God and has the best people to be—a spiritual hospital in the best sense of that term: "The church is critical to the care and solace of those suffering with mental disorders. These people are very often isolated, fearful, confused, and in need of unconditional love of Christians to repair and return to vital living."[44]

This book, then, is not just about caring for people well, but *caring for people God's way*—the way revealed in the person and love of Jesus Christ. It is our hope—our prayer that goes out with this book—that you who are Christian counselors and pastors would renew your commitment to sacrificial love in service to hurting souls. We cannot do it alone, nor merely in the power of our own energies and desires.

By the Holy Spirit and bound together in Christ, however, it can and will be done. Be part of a redemptive revolution in this new millennium. It may not make the work of ministry any easier, but it surely will be a wonderful ride that bears great fruit for the kingdom of Christ.

## Conclusion

Years ago the liberal religious magazine *Christian Century* told two stories of mainline church pastors who were transformed by Christ and became, in their words, "post-liberals." Embedded in both stories was the delightful telling of their conversions to Christ through their work in pastoral care, and the discovery of the wonder and power of the Scriptures. What you find in the stories are conversions to Christ that evince his healing love and wonder-working power.

These pastors became Christians as they witnessed Christ come alive in caring ministry to people who cried out for God's touch. Though we are committed evangelicals we recognize that God is at work mightily in the world far beyond evangelical boundaries. Whether Catholic, Orthodox, or Protestant "post-liberal," the church is being challenged by Christ himself and Christian counseling is called to serve it in all its varieties.

So then, let us renounce any dedications to dead religious formalism or hot new psychological programs and, instead, renew our relationships with the God of power and wonder. Jesus promised us that this kind of love freely given to the most wounded and desperate lives will move a jaded culture that has largely abandoned the Truth.

Christian counseling is wonderful, maddening, joyous work. Those called to walk with and serve the hurting are sometimes overwhelmed, often confused, and occasionally avoidant of walking committedly in this calling. We understand this because we ourselves know this joy and are beset, at times, with these very same struggles.

The wonder of it all is that Jesus sends the Spirit—all the time and in every way—to comfort us and to set us free of ourselves. Truly, our real life—and that of our clients and parishioners—is hidden with Christ in God. If we look for it, He always reveals it. Finding Him in the midst of every counseling situation—meeting Him in the midst of every need—is what this book is about.

## ENDNOTES

1.  Earnest Becker, *The denial of death* (New York: The Free Press, 1973).
2.  Dallas Willard, *The spirit of the disciplines: Understanding how God changes lives* (San Francisco: Harper and Row, 1988), viii.

3.    Population Reference Bureau, 2000 census data—living arrangements profile for United States, *Analysis of Data from the U.S. Census Bureau, for The Annie E. Casey Foundation.*

4.    The Barna Group, Born again Christians just as likely to divorce as non-Christians, *The Barna Update* (8 September 2004) [journal online]; available from <http://www.barna.org.

5.    Judith S. Wallerstein and Sandra Blakeslee, *The good marriage: How & why love lasts* (New York: Houghton Mifflin Company, 1995), 6.

6.    Scott Stanley, Personal communication.

7.    The Barna Group, Born again Christians just as likely to divorce as non-Christians, *The Barna Update,*(8 September 2004).

8.    David Blackenhorn, *Fatherless America: Confronting our most urgent social problem* (New York: BasicBooks, 1995).

9.    Rebecca O'Neill, *Experiments in living: The fatherless family,*<http://www.civitas.org.: The Institute for the Study of Civil Society, September 2002; The National Center for Fathering, *National surveys on fathers and fathering,* http://www.fathers.com/research/.

10.    The National Center for Fathering, *The consequences of fatherlessness,* <http://www.fathers.com/research/consequences.html>.

11.    D. Finkelhor, Hotaling, G., Lewis, I. A., and Smith, C., Sexual abuse in a national survey of adult men and women: Prevalence, characteristics, and risk factors, *Child abuse & neglect 14,* 19–28, (1990); C. Bagley, Development of a measure of unwanted sexual contact in childhood, for use in community mental health surveys," *Psychological Reports, 66,* 401–2 (1990).

12.    National Center for Injury Prevention and Control, *Sexual violence: Fact sheet* (April 2005), <http://www.cdc.gov/ncipc/factsheets/svfacts.htm>.

13.    National Center for Injury Prevention and Control, *Intimate partner violence: fact sheet* (November 2004), <http://www.cdc.gov/ncipc/factsheets/ipvfacts.htm>.

14.    Shawn Christopher Shea, *The practical art of suicide assessment: A guide for mental health professionals and substance abuse counselors* (New York: John Wiley & Sons, Inc, 1999), 6.

15.    National Institute of Mental Health, *In harm's way: Suicide in America* (2003), <http://www.nimh.nih.gov/publicat/harmaway.cfm>.

16.    Shea, *The practical art of suicide assessment,*6.

17.    National Center for Chronic Disease Prevention and Health Promotion, *General alcohol information* (September 2004), <http://www.cdc.gov/alcohol/factsheets/general_information.htm>.

18.    National Center for Health Statistics, Health, United States, 2004: With chartbook on trends in the health of Americans(Hyattsville, Maryland: Author, 2004).

19.    Lynn F. Ranew and D. A. Serritella, *Handbook of differential treatments for addictions* (Allyn and Bacon, 1992), 85.

20.    Ibid.

21.    Ranew and Serritella, *Handbook of differential treatments for addictions,* 33.

22.    Archibald D. Hart and C. H. Weber, *Unveiling depression in women: A practical guide to understanding and overcoming depression* (Grand Rapids, MI: Fleming H. Revell, 2002), 23.

23.    Hart and Weber, *Unveiling depression in women,* 23.

24.    *Margaret Strock, et al., Depression,* National Institute of Health publication No. 00–3561 (2000): (originally published 1994 *as* Plain talk about depression) [journal online]; available from <http://www.nimh.nih.gov/publicat/depression.cfm.

25. National Institute of Mental Health, *Anxiety,* http://www.nimh.nih.gov/publi-cat/anxiety.cfm#anx1: (Author, 2000); Archibald Hart, *The anxiety cure: You can find emotional tranquility and wholeness* (United States: W Publishing Group, 1999); N. Short and N. Kitchner, Panic disorder: Nature assessment and treatment, *Continuing professional development,* Royal College of Nursing 5(7) (April 2002).

26. Carol M. Christensen, *Power over panic: Answers for anxiety* (Colorado Springs: Life Journey, 2003), 17.

27. J. Lee and L. Dade, The buck stops where? What is the role of the emergency physician in managing panic disorder in chest pain patients? *Journal of the Canadian Association of Emergency Physicians,* 5(4), (2003), 237–238; Hart, *The anxiety cure*; Short and Kitchner, Panic disorder: Nature assessment and treatment.

28. R. C. Kessler et al., The epidemiology of major depressive disorder: Results from the national comorbidity survey replication (NCS-R), *JAMA,* 289, (2003), 3095–3105.

29. A. E. Bergin and J. P. Jensen, Religiosity of psychotherapists: A national survey, *Psychotherapy,* 27, (1990), 3–7.

30. E. W. Kelly, *Religion and spirituality in counseling and psychotherapy* (Alexandria, VA: American Counseling Association, 1995).

31. Kessler et al., The epidemiology of major depressive disorder, 3095–3105.

32. Ibid.

33. Jeffrey Weiss, Wounded heroes, *The Dallas News* (7 March, 1998), <http://www.dallasnews.com>.

34. Ibid.

35. Charles Colson, "Wanted: Christians who love, *Christianity Today* (1995, October 2), 112.

36. George Gallup Jr. and T. Jones, *The next American spirituality: Finding God in the twenty-first century* (Colorado Springs, CO: Victor/Cook Communications, 2000).

37. George Gallup Jr., *The next American spirituality: Finding God in the twenty-first century* (USA: Chariot Victor Publishers, 2000).

38. Archibald Hart, Has self-esteem lost its way? *Christian Counseling Today* 9(1) (2001), 8.

39. The Wisdom of Solomon.

40. Mark R. McMinn, *Psychology, theology, and spirituality in Christian counseling* (Tyndale, 1996), 270.

41. A. E. Bergin, Values and religious issues in psychotherapy and mental health, *American Psychologist,* 46, (1991), 394–403.

42. Everett Worthington, Understanding the values of religious clients: A model and its application to counseling, *Journal of Counseling Psychology* 35(2) (1988), 166–174.

43. See R. Hawkins et al., in Timothy Clinton and G. Ohlschlager, *Competent Christian counseling, volume one: Foundations and practice of compassionate soul care* (Colorado Springs: WaterBrook, 2002).

44. Paul Meier, T. Clinton, and G. Ohlschlager, Mental illness: Reducing suffering in the church, *The Soul Care Bible.* (Nashville: Thomas Nelson, 2001), 364–365.

# The Person of the Counselor:
# Growing in Knowledge, Character, and Skill

*Tim Clinton, George Ohlschlager, and Anthony J. Centore*

As counselors, we should convene our sessions deeply aware of how dependent we are on divine wisdom. We all live in a fallen world...

RON HAWKINS, IN *Competent Christian Counseling*[1]

I hadn't seen Eileen for nearly a year, so I was delighted when she called to come back into counseling. Eileen had been a model client. She worked diligently to understand her problem and her situation. She was intent to incorporate and learn from my insights and interpretations, and was always polite and thankful about gains she had made. The problem was that she really didn't get any better.

She had come into counseling complaining of depression, anxiety, and other symptoms that looked like a classic case of SAD—seasonal affective disorder. Since she could trace the onset of tail-spin symptoms from November onward the two previous years, I was convinced the diagnosis was a no-brainer.

As a mild SAD sufferer myself who has struggled with it for numerous winters, I was confident in both my assessment and treatment plan. Eileen purchased a set of UV lights to work under in the evening, simplified and focused her life, worked effectively at scrubbing some toxic "depressogenic" thinking out of her self-talk, and was praying and growing closer to the Lord in all this. She was doing everything right—and, I thought, so was I—but *she wasn't getting well.*

In fact, as the winter wore on, she complained of worsening depression and anxiety. I knew that anxiety was present in most depressive episodes, and, being the resourceful counselor I like to think I am, I thought I was dealing with a treatment-resistant form of depression that underlay the SAD disorder. I did what most good counselors do in this situation—I punted and referred Eileen to a local psychiatrist.

The psychiatrist diagnosed Eileen with a recurrent major depression, and a SAD disorder only secondarily. She prescribed Serzone, a stronger antidepressant that worked both serotonin and dopamine receptors in the brain. Eileen dutifully began the medication, worked through her body's adjustment to it, and showed some improvement in about two weeks. Now we were getting at the core of it—and it looked like a biological disorder at its root!

After a couple more sessions, Eileen's HMO benefits ran out and she decided to end counseling with me. We reviewed her progress—and lack of it—and Eileen was extremely grateful for all the help I had given her. We didn't discuss the nagging question that seemed to be in the back of both of our minds—that we were missing something. I think we still weren't quite sure what was going on—but, hey, we couldn't afford such expensive speculations anyway.

When she came in again, I was amazed how healthy and alive she was. My first thought was so self-inflated—that I really had helped her the year before, and the fruit of that work was shining a healthy glow in her face. She was happy to see me again and thanked me all over for the work that we had done together. I then queried what she had come in for, thinking there were some loose ends or unresolved issues that she was now ready to work on.

No, she replied, she had merely come to tell me what happened that last year—what the problem really was. That summer she had cleaned out an old storage room in her basement and had found stachybotris—black mold—covering most of a wall behind a large storage shelf. During the winter, when she had her house closed up, the heating system provoked mold growth and carried its microscopic spores throughout the house.

Eileen had been sick with black mold poisoning—something that, just like the course of SAD, got progressively worse as winter carried on—and cleared up each spring when she opened up her house. Eileen had the mold removed professionally and repainted her storage room—presto, mold gone and no more trouble.

I was dumbstruck as she told her story. I must have looked quite guilty, because at one point she stopped and said, "George, no, I'm not blaming you! If anyone is at fault it's my doctor and the psychiatrist who are probably most responsible for missing it. But I don't blame anyone here—who knew??!"

Who knew, indeed! This episode taught me that, as a clinician, it's more than what you know and don't know that counts for competence. Sometimes it's what you think you know that, in fact, you really don't.

The pearl-of-conclusive-wisdom to be drawn here is this: stay humble and be tentative about what you think you know in counseling. Just when you start to think you have it all figured out—that you're an expert and ready to start writing books on the subject—*bang*, along comes someone whom God uses to bring you down a few pegs on the humility scale. Life and counseling for that matter, are so complex, so full of mystery that overconfident assurance can be just as wrong, just as toxic for your patients as ignorance and a lack of confidence.

### Becoming a Trustworthy Christian Counselor

As one studies and spends time doing counseling, it doesn't take long to learn that one of the most important ingredients in the counseling relationship is the counselor him- or herself. While empirical data now shows that client variables are most potent in affecting outcome, the counselor and the quality of the counselor-client relationship follows closely.[2] As a counselor, what you believe, how you feel and act, what you do and don't do, matters—a lot. Hence, building an effective caring and counseling ministry starts with you.

The essence of Christian counseling, as are all things Christian, is hidden in the person of Christ (Col. 1:26–27). The challenge of Matthew 22:42 (KJV) must be clearly understood and embraced by those who would call themselves a Christian counselor, "What think ye of Christ? Whose son is he?" It is a wonderful and, at times, elusive knowledge this revelation of Christ Himself, but one that is freely given to us when we seek it earnestly (Matt. 7:7–11). And our greatest calling/responsibility is to take Paul's words to heart as we seek to counsel: "follow my example, as I follow the example of Christ" (1 Cor. 11:1). We labor to outline this essence—the essence of Christ the caregiver—in this chapter, as well as the process by which Christian counseling works *in and through the person of the counselor.*

We do this so that Christian counselors are guided by a "road map" that helps them serve those in need in a way that honors Christ and brings unity to the church. This tall order we see as an important centralizing goal—in no way do we presume to fulfill it with this book or those that follow. We endeavor to be catalysts, acknowledging our small part in a growing field, pointing the way and encouraging action that will bring the ministry-movement to a fuller maturity.

### Developing a Personal Style for Counseling Ministry

Making sense of all the counseling information, theories, and techniques now available; shaping them into a useful treatment approach, and applying it effectively and consistently in the lives of hurting people requires the adoption of a counseling model that is intensely personal at its core. As a counselor, "you can't treat what you don't see" and "you can't see what you don't understand." Therefore, cultivating a meaningful counseling relationship and process that answers core questions like "What works for this client, with this problem, in this situation, at this time in his life with you as the counselor under the direction of the Holy Spirit," is the challenge of your time together.

In fact, in the practice of ministry with people expecting or wanting change, the theoretical must be transformed into the personal. Clients are usually unwilling or are not interested in exploring the nuances and ramifications of some theoretical position that you, as a counselor, have embraced and are high about. Rather, they merely want to know "will this work for me and mine?"

On the other hand, they are almost always interested in you as a counselor—what you do, and say, and believe, which as we stated earlier really does affect counseling outcome. Constructing a personal model or style of intervention is a developmental process that every counselor must engage in to be fruitful in one's work.

## Foundations of Christian Counseling

One cannot delegate responsibility without authority. How does a counselor establish a position of strength and authority in counseling? It all starts with a sure foundation—a foundation built on the Bible and cultivating an eternal perspective.

*Scripture first.* The foundation for Truth is given to us in the Bible—the standard by which everything else is evaluated. Second Timothy 3:16 boldly declares that "all Scripture is given to us by inspiration of the Holy Spirit and is profitable for teaching, for reproof, for correction and for training in righteousness."

Further, 2 Peter 1:3 reminds that "His divine power has granted to us all things that pertain to life and godliness, through the knowledge of him who called us to his own glory and excellence." If we are going to help people break free in this life, we start by knowing that "they are darkened in their understanding and separated from the life of God because of the ignorance that is in them due to the hardening of their hearts" (Eph. 4:18). Hence, new life is tied directly to one's relationship with God in Christ and that "the fear of the Lord is the beginning of wisdom" (Prov. 9:10).

The journey then becomes a life of faith that focuses on the washing and renewing of our minds and "destroying arguments and every lofty opinion raised against the knowledge of God, and to take every thought captive to the obedience of Christ" (2 Cor. 10:5). His way is not ours. Why? Because as Proverbs 16:25 declares, we naturally follow after our own ways and not necessarily God's ways: "There is a way that seemeth right unto a man but the ends thereof are the ways of death."

Hence an effective system for responsible Christian counseling involves the Chalcedonian pattern of logic. This occupies three features:

1.  Two terms are placed in a relationship where they exist unaltered and autonomous.
2.  The terms are related so that they coexist inseparably.
3.  One term is deemed logically prior, given authority over the other.

When two disciplines conflict on some point (such as psychology and theology) the logically prior discipline (theology) prevails. For example, considering the purpose of prayer, in practice secular psychology often overrules theology (wrongly) and prayer is used primarily as a means to request healing.[3]

By using the Chalcedonian model, prayer is brought back to its proper (theological) main purpose—communion with God. One of the great dangers here would involve both disciplines—where truth is tainted by our fallible interpretations and understanding of it. The wise counselor will approach the pursuit of truth with both a spirit of expectation and humility.

*Eternal perspective.* Christians must also approach the counseling relationship with an eternal perspective of life, and of hope in Christ. Psalm 42:5 evinces this point: "Why are you downcast, O my soul? Why so disturbed within me? Put your hope in God, for I will yet praise him, my Savior..."

As Christians we believe that if a person struggles with emotional disorders, that the Lord is "near unto the brokenhearted and saves the crushed in spirit" (Prov. 34:18 ESV) whether in this life or in the one to come. However, if one dies without Christ the consequences are eternally devastating. As Christian workers, we wish to create better people on earth, so that they may serve God more fully. However, we do not wish to promote better-adjusted people at the expense of their salvation, or by denying their need for sanctifying growth.

*A war of the mind and spirit.* Christian counseling, in large part, is a war for the mind. Failure identity and negative thinking lead one with a serious drinking problem to think "I am an alcoholic" versus the truth "I am a child of God who struggles with alcoholism." Of course, we do not mean to minimize that man presents a fallen sin nature. First John 1:8 tells us, "If we say we have no sin we are deceiving ourselves and the truth is not in us."

However, there is a serious difference, as theologians teach, between *having* a sin problem and *being* sin (Col. 2:6–10; Rom. 6:11; Gal. 5:16; Eph. 1:18). This is an important distinction for Christian counselors. If we accept the theology that our clients *are* sin, there is no helping them. However, as we correctly show our clients that they are created in the image and glory of God and that sin is something that mars that image, help becomes a process of aiding a client to repent, accept forgiveness, and mature as a child of God.

## Roles and Characteristics of Effective Counselors

As the counseling movement has matured and expanded, so have counselor roles and responsibilities. The following list is a general overview of the numerous roles in our modern-day profession:

1. Counselor—Although this word can be ambiguous, having multiple meanings (i.e. see wardrobe counseling), counseling generally focuses on helping clients navigate problem issues: relational, behavioral, spiritual, or emotional.

2. Consultant—Often understood as the role of an "expert guide," here a counselor helps the client to troubleshoot a situation or make important life decisions.

3. Teacher—Sometimes known as "psycho-education," teaching is a significant part of the helping process. With teaching, the counselor imparts insight into a client's issues and strategies for coping (i.e. answers to the questions "What is stress?" and "How can I decrease my stress?"). With Christian counseling, teaching also encompasses presenting solid biblical truths.

4. Supervisor—This is a professional-to-professional relationship where counselors participate in "peer-supervision," or it is where an experienced counselor oversees, and is held liable for, the practice and progress of a novice counselor.

5. Researcher—The practice of research is what allows counselors to know whether what they are doing is working, and is an empirical method of discovering the Truth of God. Research is what promotes positive revisions in counseling treatments, to meet changing contemporary needs for care.

## Motivations for Becoming a Counselor

Counseling, as a profession, usually attracts kind and noble persons.[4] Healthy motivators for one pursuing a career in counseling, or a lay counseling ministry, include the desire to help others and a perceived "calling" that is confirmed by a body of Christian believers. However, not everyone in counseling is motivated by such pure desires; even the better counselors usually show a mixture of noble and not-so-noble motivations for their pursuits.

Therefore, before one makes the decision to pursue the practice of counseling, a prospective counselor is wise to complete some self-exploration. If you are considering a counseling ministry, a few of the major introspective questions include:

1.   Do I have any unresolved personal issues I should "work on" before attempting to become a counselor?
2.   Am I spiritually grounded and mature enough to lead others to a place of spiritual maturity?
3.   Am I willing to be open, dependable, compassionate, and generally nonjudgmental—even when clients frustrate me?
4.   Am I willing to repeatedly expose myself to the stress that is intrinsic to the counseling process?
5.   Am I willing to provide care to clients that I do not like, and do I offer Christlike compassion when I struggle with those that I intensely dislike?
6.   Do I understand that not everyone will improve through counseling?
7.   Am I willing to undertake the necessary preparation, training, and supervision?
8.   Am I willing to participate in ongoing continuing education for as long as I practice counseling?

## Personality and Spirit

A Christian counselor's success depends on several distinguishing characteristics including personality, spiritual gifts, professional training, commitment to the gospel, and biblical worldview.

*Personality.* Regarding personal qualities, an effective counselor will often possess:

- a natural interest in and compassion for people[5]
- emotional intelligence and the ability to accurately assess feelings
- the facility to engage a variety of persons in conversation
- a disposition that allows one to listen well

- an understanding and mastery of empathy
- meaningful introspection and self-reflection
- the capacity to suspend one's personal needs to help others
- the ability to tolerate relational intimacy (therapeutic alliance)
- the ability to lessen, not increase, a client's anxiety
- the ability to establish healthy boundaries
- the aptitude to not let counseling relationships adversely affect the counselor's home life
- unwavering ethics and integrity

*Spiritual gifts.* It is true that God has equipped some people with gifts to be counselors (1 Cor. 12:7), and this calling is good motivation to become a counselor. However, as one writer states, "people helping is everybody's business,"[6] each of us has the ability through meaningful, empathic relationships to help someone every day of our lives.

*Professional or other counselor training.* Christian counselors, to truly be equipped, must be knowledgeable about a wide variety of topics and issues. They must be educated toward understanding the many needs and complaints that are prevalent today, as well as their treatment. This means formal education and specialized clinical trainings for anyone desiring to practice as a mental health professional. For the lay helper in church-based ministry, it demands some degree of structured training in basic helping skills and process to properly direct the gift that has already shown forth.

Second, for the helping professional particularly, one's training should involve learning how to see contemporary mental health issues in the light of Christian theology. Third, continuing education is key for a Christian counselor to stay current with his/her counseling approach! It is not only our strong recommendation—it is an important ethical standard.

*Commitment to the gospel.* Remember, the goal of Christian counseling is the restoration of the image of God in man, and maturity in Christ. Unlike secular psychology, the elimination of suffering is not necessarily the end-all of life's objective. Christian counselors must be dedicated not only to helping clients heal their emotional, maladaptive, and social problems, but also to restoring clients' relationship with God.

*Biblical worldview.* This characteristic involves an awareness of life and the world including, especially, the nature of the eternal, spiritual world as presented in Scripture. A discerning counselor accepts the truth about good and evil in the world, is able to clearly discriminate one from the other, engages in genuine warfare with the "enemy," and is willing and prepared to seek the Holy Spirit's guidance in the counseling process. The expert counselor also shows the facility to bring forth good fruit, and the wisdom to know when to convict and admonish, or when to comfort a client.

First Timothy 3:2–4 list qualities of a pastor that would benefit a Christian counselor. The character qualities, social relations, and circumspect behavior of a Christian leader are all noted herein:

> Now the overseer must be above reproach, the husband of but one wife, temperate, self-controlled, respectable, hospitable, able to teach, not given to drunkenness, not violent but gentle, not quarrelsome, not a lover of money. He must manage his own family well and see that his children obey him with proper respect.

A comprehensive biblical worldview also involves a clear and useful understanding of natural revelation—respect and facility with the world of science. This encompasses all useful knowledge of human emotions, thoughts, relationships, and physiology, as presented in clinical research, and is discussed in more depth later.

*Integrating training, experience and character.* This involves the amalgamation of one's scriptural knowledge and clinical education with practice. In metaphor, experience is the bridge between the understanding of art theory and creating great art.

Great art for Christian counselors is using biblically sound, research-based treatments at the right time, in the right way, with the right client. Moreover, it is encouraging the supernatural healing touch of God in counseling—fully expressing both sides of the Parakaleo philosophy, which is the ability to both admonish and give comfort as need requires. Lastly, great art is reinforcing a commitment bond with clients, building and maintaining strong rapport from intake to termination—and beyond.

### The Interpersonal Environment

While there are many counseling approaches, theories, and techniques, and while the way a counselor engages a client will be influenced by situation and presenting needs, there is a series of core conditions for establishing an effective environment that are almost universally seen as important in the counseling relationship.[7]

*Genuineness.* In order to be effective, a counselor must live out the change he/she desires to see in a client. For example, a counselor with anger problems is not in suitable condition to counsel a client to better manage anger. Moreover, a counselor who is not living out his/her faith in Christ is not spiritually prepared to participate in Christian counseling (as a counselor, that is).

*Warmth.* This characteristic is simply necessary to promote a sense of comfort in the client. A counselor who comes off cold or abrasive will be ineffective in establishing relationship or rapport with those seeking help. Without rapport, the core of the counseling alliance is void.

*Positive regard.* Though this differs from the secular concept of "unconditional positive regard" where anything the client believes, desires, or does is acceptable, positive regard should be given universally to the *client as a person* created in the image of God. This is widely known as the principle of hating the sin, loving the sinner. In addition, Christian counselors need to know when to "hold off" on conviction for a time, and simply console and show compassion for a hurting client.

*Support and challenge.* There is an intricate balance of supporting clients through the "tough stuff" they are dealing with, while at the same time challenging their destructive beliefs and sinful choices. Counselors must strive to find a healthy balance in their relationship with clients; one where a client can approach the counselor with confession and feel *supported*, while at the same time be *moved to grow* in a healthy, Christlike direction.

## Core Skills in Counseling Care

In *Competent Christian Counseling* we promoted 1 Thessalonians 5:14–18 as the penultimate biblical statement of Christian counseling:

> And we urge you, brothers, warn those who are idle, encourage the timid, help the weak, be patient with everyone. Make sure that nobody pays back wrong for wrong, but always try to be kind to each other and to everyone else. Be joyful always; pray continually; and give thanks in all circumstances, for this is God's will for you in Christ Jesus.

This extraordinarily powerful mandate should be the motto of every Christian counselor. In fact, when taken back to the full color of the Greek language this passage incorporates every Greek term that denotes the helping endeavor in the Scriptures, and reflects the many dimensions of counseling today:

*Urge (parakaleo)*: Literally meaning to call to one's side, and incorporates a wider range of responsive behaviors in counseling, traveling among and between "comforting," "consoling," "encouraging," and "beseeching" or "admonishing."

*Warn (noutheteo)*: Coming from the root meaning "mind," it is the seat of consciousness that includes "understanding," "feeling," "judging," and "determining." It is characterized by a confrontational style of directive challenge to root out sin and follow the right path.

*Encourage (paramutheomai)*: Means to "comfort," "soothe," "console," or "encourage;" especially in connection with someone experiencing deep grief.

*Help (antechomai)*: Refers to holding up or supporting someone who is weak and in deep need of assistance; to support something very fragile.

*Be patient (makrothumeo)*: Literally meaning "long-tempered," this carries the idea of "forbearing," "suffering," and "enduring." It connotes the idea that we tend to be impatient and expect too much too quickly from those engaged in the change challenge.

Several other "core skills" of Christian counseling that are compatible with the theme of this passage include the following:

*Active listening.* Have you ever shared your heart with someone and it seemed his or her mind was a million miles away from you? In contrast, known also as "effective listening," active listening is a process where the counselor contains his/her biases, inner-conflicts, and disagreements as he or she focuses completely on the client. Active listening involves:

- verbal and nonverbal expressions to encourage the client to tell his/her story
- withholding of judgment (or revulsion) even while the client presents disquieting information
- attending to both what the client is saying and what the client is omitting (the ability to accomplish this will increase with training and experience)

- attending to a client's nonverbal communication and emotional themes
- waiting out moments of silence

*Attending.* This means to provide undivided attention to the counselee. In addition, the counselor attends by maintaining an open posture, eye contact (without staring), forward lean, and courteous gestures that assure the client the counselor is "present" in the counseling session.

*Empathic response.* This is responding to the client's dialogue in a way that reframes what the client has said and that focuses on the emotion being communicated. This assures the client that you are understanding what he/she shares in session, and it also provides the client with the therapeutic opportunity to hear his/her story told from another perspective.

*Probing.* This is the process of asking questions for the purpose of deepening the content of the therapeutic encounter (skills will greatly increase with continuing education and training). Probes often begin with the words *who, what, where, when,* or *how* (though not generally *why*) and should be designed in a way that the counselee can provide extensive feedback from a single query (i.e., When did you first feel depressed?).

*Goal setting.* Deciding the specific objective(s) of the counseling relationship: includes developing a course of action, and using research-supported biblically-based methods to lead the client from his/her current condition to a more functional, healthy, Christ-centered state.

### Pitfalls and Ineffective Care

Robert Kellemen in his recent work *Soul Physicians* provides a vignette called "The Tale of Two Counselors" where two professionals are both ineffective in treatment of a client for different reasons. The first counselor (a pastoral counselor), after a client sobbingly tells him about the sexual abuse he endured at the hand of an uncle, responds with a 30 minute sermon on the client's sinfulness. The second (a professional Christian counselor) was equally ineffective, responding with empathy and compassion, but lacking any skills in helping the client "move forward" or deal pragmatically with his present relationship problems.[8]

Counseling is not simple, and there are many ways a counselor can go wrong in the (what should be) therapeutic process. Some mistakes are rooted in the motivation of the counselor, others in the counselor's approach.

*Poor motivators for prospective counselors.* Individuals become counselors for one of two reasons; either they wish to help others, or they wish to help themselves overcome their own issues. Most often it is a combination of the two. Prospective Christian counselors should examine their motivations for desiring to minister through the practice of counseling.

Simply put, Christian counselors must evince both emotional health and spiritual maturity to be effective. Even with proper education—or a clinical license—not everyone is prepared to serve as a counselor. Following are a few of the common pitfalls, motivators common to persons who decide to practice counseling.

1. *Hunger for Relationships:* Counselors must have their intimacy needs filled adequately if they intend to help clients with their interrelational problems. If a counselor is motivated by a need for intimacy, he/she will be inclined to use relationships with clients to fill emotional emptiness.

2. *Having a Messiah Complex:* Counselors (often novice counselors) believe they can heal everyone. This unfortunately is not the case. As a counselor you may find that some clients may not even like you and do not improve much, or at all. As a counselor, there may be areas that are not strengths for you. Learning to refer to another counselor, or even an inpatient program, then becomes a sign of maturity, not weakness. Hence, counselors need to accept their limits, and at times the limits of the counseling process.

3. *Needing to Have Control or Power:* For one desiring power or control over others, counseling is not the proper profession. Effective counselors operate under the premise that clients have rights and ultimately need to be in control of their own lives. Also, counseling is generally a collaborative process that operates upon a foundation of mutuality and collegiality, one not governed by the counselor as ultimate "authority."

4. *Living Vicariously:* Parents often try to live or relive their lives through their children. Likewise, counselors often try to fulfill their needs through the experiences and lives of clients.

5. *Vicarious Rebellion:* Sometimes counselors with unresolved issues will live out their rebellion through the dysfunction of their clients.

6. *Atonement:* Some may feel motivated to help others as a service of atonement—to compensate for some wrong one has done in his/her past. Counselors should first repent of their sins and fully accept the forgiveness given by God, before counseling.

7. *Self-Significance:* Wishing to make a difference in people's lives is different from desiring to be a counselor in order to be a person who has made a difference, for with the latter the focus is on the counselor, not the client. Counselors should understand their innate significance as children of God and not approach counseling as an avenue to becoming a significant person.

## Mistakes in the Process of Counseling

Here is a list of several common mistakes that can be made in the counseling process:

1. *Rescuing*—Saving a client instead of empowering a client to save him/herself.

2. *Excessive Self-Disclosure and Transparency*—Extreme openness that moves the focus of the counseling session off of the client and onto the counselor.

3. *Assuming the Meaning of the Problem*—Presuming without adequate investigation, testing or data.

4. *Catching the Panic*—Instead of the counselor decreasing a client's anxiety, it is when the client's anxiety disrupts the stability of the counselor. Note: A client's crisis is *not* the counselor's crisis.

5. *Breaking the Silence*—Silence is sometimes more meaningful than words and is necessary for deep introspection. Counselors should not feel the need to fill the void of silence in counseling.

6. *Giving in to Demanding Clients*—Counseling is a mutual, collaborative engagement. Neither the counselor nor the client should have a disposition that is "demanding." Counselors should establish benevolent, though securely established, boundaries to protect themselves from overly demanding clients.

7. *Giving Advice*—Counseling is not advice giving. Instead, it is heavily rooted in empowering clients to advise themselves, to draw out and magnify the 'Truth of Christ' that lives in every believer.

8. *Not Setting Realistic Goals*—Setting grandiose goals will only discourage. Instead, create small objectives and encourage clients as they succeed.

9. *Being Controlled by One's Sexuality*—Healthy sexuality means the counselor deflects sexual advances made by clients.

10. *Lacking Empathy, and at Times Sympathy*—Remember, many people who enter counseling are broken and hurting. A counselor therefore must maintain an attitude of grace and sympathy to promote healing.

11. *Being Overly Emotionally Involved*—It is good to desire the best for your clients, and it is normal to feel upset when clients are hurting, or are not improving. However, counselors must establish emotional boundaries so that they can continue to objectively and effectively help clients.

You may be overwhelmed with all this, thinking to yourself "I am not this perfect!" Indeed, if this is the first time you have been exposed to these issues of motivation and competence and you are *not* beleaguered, reconsidering whether you should continue down the road of counselor training, something is wrong.

Counselors should be responsibly concerned about their competence, ability, stability, spirituality, and more. It is the constant introspection that makes them good counselors; and it is their prolonged growth that makes them great counselors. This is only the launching ground, and the journey is long for the person of the counselor: *for they are to be always growing in knowledge, character, and skill.*

**ENDNOTES**

1. Ron Hawkins, E. Hindson, T. Clinton, Theological roots: Synthesizing and systematizing a biblical theology of helping, in T. Clinton and G. Ohlschlager (eds.), *Competent Christian counseling* (Colorado Springs: WaterBrook, (2002), 101.

2. Timothy Clinton, and G. Ohlschlager, *Competent Christian counseling, volume one: Foundations and practice of compassionate soul care* (Colorado Springs: WaterBrook, 2002), 101.

3. Jay Adams, *Competent to counsel* (United States: Presbyterian and Reformed Publishing Company, 1970).

4. D. Hunsinger, An interdisciplinary map for Christian counselors, in M. McMinn & T. Phillips (eds.), *Care for the soul: Exploring the intersections of psychology and theology* (Downers Grove, Ill.: InterVarsity Press, 2001), 218–240.

5. S. T. Gladding, *Counseling: A comprehensive profession* (4th ed.) (Upper Saddle River, NJ: Prentice-Hall, 2005).

6. Gary R. Collins, *How to be a people helper* (Carol Stream, Ill.: Tyndale,1995).

7. Carl Rogers, *Client centered therapy* (Boston, MA: Houghton Mifflin, 1951); Carl Rogers, The necessary and sufficient conditions of therapeutic personality change, *Journal of Consulting Psychology 21* (1957), 95–103; Carl Rogers, *On becoming a person* (Boston, MA: Houghton Mifflin, 1961); G. Egan, *The skilled helper: A problem-management approach to helping* (6th ed.) (Pacific Grove, CA: Brooks/Cole, 1998); S. Strong, Counseling: An interpersonal influence process, *Journal of Counseling Psychology 15,* (1968):215–224.

8. Robert W. Kellemen, *Soul physicians: A theology of soul care and spiritual direction* (Taneytown, MD: RPM Books, 2005).

# 3

# Christian Counseling
# and Essential Biblical Principles

*Ian Jones, Tim Clinton, and George Ohlschlager*

True Christian counseling is "built upon a biblical understanding of people (Creation), problems (Fall), and solutions (Redemption). It focuses upon the process of sanctification—growing to reflect increasingly the relational, rational, volitional, and emotional image of Christ. Its goal is clear: the inner life of your spiritual friend is to look more and more like the inner life of Christ."

ROBERT KELLEMAN, IN *Spiritual Friends*[1]

In his delightful book, *The Gift of Therapy*,[2] psychiatrist and Stanford professor Irvin Yalom tells the story of two master healers, Joseph and Dion, ancient desert characters from Hermann Hesse's classic novel, *Magister Ludi*. It is a story that, reframed once again by us beyond both Hesse and Yalom, encapsulates our hopes and dreams for the future of Christian counseling.

Joseph was the classic Christian psychologist, integrating the best Christian truth with the data of the psychosocial sciences. He was the empathic master, whose inspired listening and thoughtful responsiveness brought insight and healing to all who came to his tent. As Yalom tells it, "Pilgrims trusted Joseph. Suffering and anxiety [that] entered his ears vanished like water on the desert... and penitents left his presence emptied and calmed."

Dion was just as effective as Joseph in his healing work, but he worked from the directive orientation of the biblical counselor. His healing power was based on his ability to "divine their unconfessed sins" and guide the pathway to righteousness by his "active intervention." Dion treated his "penitents as children, he gave advice, . . . assign[ed] penance, ordered pilgrimages . . . , and compelled enemies to make up."

Though they had never met, Joseph and Dion knew of each other's stellar reputations, and secretly competed with each other for many years. Then came a time when Joseph fell ill in mind and spirit. He became filled with despair and thoughts of suicide that he could not shake. Unable to heal himself, he set out on a journey to find Dion and seek his help. While resting at an oasis, he recounted his search to a fellow traveler, who immediately offered his help to find Dion. After many days of continued journey together, the traveler revealed to Joseph that he was, in fact, Dion.

Joseph went home with Dion and found healing under his tutelage and care. He continued to live in Dion's home for many years, eventually becoming his most trusted and valued healing colleague. For years they worked collaboratively and found great success, far beyond that which either knew on his own.

Then one day Dion fell ill and, bereft of any recovery, called Joseph to his side to make to him a deathbed confession. He told Joseph that he, too, isolated and living alone, had become sick of heart and was on his way to find Joseph when they had met years before. As Joseph's eyes flared in question and surprise, Dion confessed how empty and despairing his life had become and what a miracle it had been to meet Joseph and become partners in the way it had all come about.

Dion told Joseph how he had been healed of his own sickness by his care for Joseph. He admitted how proud he had been—a pride that God had healed by Dion making Joseph his healing colleague. Before he died, he thanked Joseph for his love and friendship, who expressed the same to Dion. At the end, they had become fully honest, fully transparent, fully friends.

*True metaphor?* Are we at an end, and at a new beginning, in Christian counseling? Although tension between the two main rival camps in Christian counseling remains, we are heartened by the way the diverse development of our increasingly complex discipline is already resolving this dispute.[3] It is a dispute being resolved not so much by the assertion of bridge-building models—which we do present in this chapter—but by the goodwill and mutual commitments of bridge-building people. A new generation of leaders is arising on both sides of this increasingly fading divide and is coming together because of our common bond in Christ and mutual recognition that our real war is "out there," and not within the fences of our own camp.

## Necessary but Deficient Roots

Christian counseling has far too long suffered the conflict between biblical counseling and the integrationist movement. And in denying the influence of twelve-step, lay counseling models, and the inner healing and prayer ministries—other prominent lines in our history—this dichotomy was not even an accurate picture of Christian counseling at the height of the debate.

Furthermore, in *Competent Christian Counseling*, we challenged this false dichotomy by indicating at least ten distinctive counseling theories or identities across the nearly 50,000 members of the American Association of Christian Counselors.[4] We now torpedo this false dichotomy one last time in this volume by presenting a theoretical perspective, a unitary model of Christian counseling that we believe both fair-minded biblical counselors and integration therapists can embrace.

*Nouthetic roots and biblical counseling.* Jay Adams brought a biblical revolution to Christian and pastoral counseling in the 1970s, challenging a field that was racing toward rancor, even dissolution by its fascination with all manner of anti-Christian psychobabble.[5] The clarion call to maintain theological orthodoxy, the centrality of Scripture in counseling and pastoral care, and the necessity of holy living by dealing with sin and overcoming evil were its prophetic markers in a larger counseling movement that too easily forgot such truths.

However, its reliance on *noutheteo*—confrontational warning about sin and wrongdoing—as the near-exclusive means to godliness was a fatal flaw that denied it wider acceptance among even evangelical counselors. That and the fact that some of its leaders maintained an adversarial, inflammatory style and ongoing animus toward integration over the years has deeply limited its reach as an intervention model.

We believe that *parakaleo*—coming alongside someone to offer encouragement and succor as well as godly challenge—is a more normative New Testament value, and offers a unique basis for Christian counseling ministry.[6] Parakaleo not only includes the role of admonishment and confrontation about sin that noutheteo exclusively promotes, but also includes the roles of comfort, consolation, and encouragement for the brokenhearted souls in one's care.

A recent article on treating sexual abuse victims reveals the challenge of an exclusive use of a sin-confrontation approach in all of one's caregiving. Many in the biblical counseling field today are moving beyond mere proclamation to living lives of caring demonstration—one that is inherently challenging of the truth—and attractive in the way that love is shown to be true.

> Sarah is five. Her parents drop her off at Sunday school every week. She learned to sing, "Jesus loves me, this I know, for the Bible tells me so," "Little ones to Him belong," and "They are weak but He is strong." Sarah's daddy rapes her several times a week. Sometimes she gets a break because he rapes her sister instead. The song says Jesus loves her. It says He is strong. So Sarah asks Jesus to stop her daddy from hurting her and her sister. Nothing happens. Maybe Jesus is not so strong after all. Or at least, He is not as strong as her daddy. Nothing, not even Jesus, can stop her daddy. The people who wrote the Bible must not have known about her daddy.
>
> ... You do not have to know very much about learning theory to grasp the profound impact of such experiences on a life. The abuse, due to the intensity of the traumatic experience, shapes the control beliefs by which all other information is processed.
>
> What response can a counselor or pastor give that will be powerful enough to overcome such obstacles? If simply speaking or teaching the truth is not sufficient, then what else is required? I believe that those members of the body of Christ who have been called to walk with survivors become the representative of God to them. The reputation of God is at stake in our lives. We are called to live out in the seen, in flesh and blood, what is true about who God is....
>
> In other words, we are to demonstrate in the flesh the character of God over time so that who we are reveals the truth about God to the survivor. This is not in any way to deny or underestimate the power of the Word of God. However, often that Word needs to be fleshed out and not just spoken for us to truly grasp what it means.[7]

*Christian cognitive-behavior therapy.* Much Christian counseling is now done as a variant of cognitive-behavioral therapy. This seems to certainly be the common preference of those who have identified with the integration movement. It is also the most preferred model of practice among members of the American Association of Christian Counselors.[8]

At the core of this practice is the process of assessing, identifying, and renouncing faulty thinking, adopting instead the truths and insights of Scripture and right thinking. Exposing the "lies" clients still live by after regeneration and exchanging them with the truths of Scripture is a central method of numerous models of Christian therapy now being practiced.[9] The best Christian cognitive therapists have incorporated Christ and the centrality of Christian maturity in the counseling goal and process. And whether they recognize it or not, many nouthetic counselors are essentially practicing a form of cognitive-behavior therapy in the name of biblical counseling.

Yet we would also assert that the best cognitive therapies are not enough. In the classic language of Carl Rogers, cognitive-behavioral models are necessary but insufficient for a full Christian counseling. Changed thinking is not enough—a changed heart is also required. In fact, it can be cogently argued that changed thinking flows primarily from a transformed heart in the process of Christian maturity. From a theological perspective, a purely cognitive therapy would be like counseling without the Holy Spirit, or lacking the Spirit's fullness and power. Systemically, however, the order of influence is not as important as recognizing the cyclical, mutually reinforcing influence that both a change of heart and a transformed mind have on each other.

Clinical and pastoral experience, moreover, reveals this insufficiency. For example, most pastors and clinicians have encountered Christians who, after years of Bible study and growth in Truth by the Scriptures, are still stuck, still oppressed. And this has nothing to do with the limits of salvation or the "need for" something more than the Bible—the Scriptures are complete in themselves, revealing all the truth that we need.

*From proposition to encounter.* Transformative change becomes a matter of translating the Truth from a proposition to an encounter—oftentimes a series of life-changing encounters—with the living God. There are many people who will not be freed—including freed enough to grow into maturity—without a supernatural healing encounter with the Holy Spirit. Russ Willingham states this truth well in the context of sexual addiction treatment:

No one is transformed by a purely cognitive approach, even if that approach is biblical. Healing of the self *requires a spiritual-emotional attachment to a nurturing parenting figure* . . . Identity formation . . . comes about as the sexually broken person *learns to attach to Christ subsequent to conversion.*

Contrary to popular evangelical belief, this doesn't happen solely through the accumulation of biblical facts or by religiously following the propositions and instructions of Scripture. This happens by interpersonal interaction with Christ, similar to the interaction between parent and child in a healthy family . . . The processes are identical, yet obviously different, in that Christ will not literally take a person up in his lap and speak audibly into his ears . . . But a *similar work must be accomplished by the indwelling Spirit, which is no less real.*

In addition, since attempts to form a Christian identity are often based on the learning and memorization of biblical truths—largely an impersonal acquisition of facts—this also will not suffice. Please don't misunderstand me here, as I am dedicated to the study and learning of the Bible—God's revelation of Himself to us. *What I am opposed to is the mere learning of facts about God, and substituting that for a relationship, the intimate knowing of God. Far too many Christians, and most addicts, make this basic mistake.*[10] (emphases ours).

So then, do we forsake both biblical counseling and cognitive-behavior therapy and turn wholesale to inner healing strategies, a twelve-step program, or ministry? Not at all. Sole reliance on these interventions (eventually) tends to rigidly program the uncontainable movement of the Holy Spirit, and often fail to attend to the aftercare dimensions of growth and maturity. Whether the fault of the practitioner or recipient, there is often the false expectation that the dramatic healing encounter is all that is needed—that healing and maturing growth are included in the same touch. The hard work of discipleship or the ongoing challenge of spiritual formation and godly maturity revealed in the Bible is too often forsaken by a quick and easy approach that mirrors the "you can have it all and have it now" lie of the culture.

However, we must incorporate inner healing—facilitating true and life-changing encounters with the risen Christ—into our Christian counseling regimen. Such ministry not only is necessary for some who need a profound healing touch, but it is the growing currency for reaching a postmodern generation that is no longer moved by modernist approaches to the Truth—empirical evidence and rational persuasion. Those opposed to this because "an unbelieving generation always seeks a miraculous sign" (Matt. 12:39) end up denying the fact that while Jesus rightly challenged such unbelief, he then went ahead and performed many miracles.

In fact, we now believe that critical aspects of all three approaches are necessary for a complete and comprehensive Christian counseling. In this book *biblical counseling, Christian cognitive-behavioral therapy* approaches, and *inner healing* therapies are all incorporated into the construction of a new-century model for Christian counseling.

## A Comprehensive Orientation

Christian counseling has perpetually searched for a comprehensive theory—a metaperspective that can help integrate biblical wisdom, personality theory, developmental constructs, psychopathology, and spiritual formation. Such a theoretical perspective would help us better understand how people grow, not only emotionally and psychologically, but spiritually. A metaperspective would also offer us more powerful insights into how normal development can go awry, leading to psychopathology and a wide array of spiritual maladies (i.e., psycho-spiritual pathology) such as spiritual apathy, turning-away from God, and chronic doubt.

Most important, this theory would guide counseling practice in a dynamic way, becoming wedded to practice so that each realm helps shape the other as both theory and practice grow to maturity. Christian counseling needs a metaperspective that will help guide our helping efforts, especially as many of us try to sort our way through a myriad of counseling schools, or theoretical perspectives. A biblically sound metaperspective would not necessarily compete with any one theory of counseling so much as it would help us make sense of how each theory can offer unique insights into a particular client's problems.

Finally, a useful metaperspective would be an empirical one—using clinical science to help Christian counselors devise and deliver more effective intervention programs. A Christian perspective on empirically-supported treatments (EST's) could be known as the BEST interventions— biblically-based, empirically-supported treatments. Such a model will never be slavish to empiricism or a naturalistic worldview, but will be open to supernatural intervention, with methodologies constructed to allow for and observe those interventions in practice.

In addition, we hope this metaperspective would encourage churches to focus more attention on prevention and wellness, incorporating the best of the bio-psycho-social sciences and the positive psychology movement. Understanding how to promote healthy relationships and God-honoring psycho-spiritual behavior, and how to prevent the development of unhealthy and potentially detrimental outcomes would seem to us to have a profound future in the Church.

## A Model for Christian Churches

The importance of the church for promoting spiritual and emotional health, and for the development of meaningful counseling that disciples its members can hardly be overstated.[11]

For this endeavor, Larry Crabb has suggested a comprehensive, three-tiered model.[12]

*Encouragement.* Regarding the first tier, encouragement, all church members can and should be involved with providing counseling at this basic level, which will help in subduing problem feelings. Though persons are often hurting, and though Christians share a profound unity in membership with Christ's body, interaction is usually—though friendly—shallow and utterly trivial. Stated, Christians warmly shake hands each Sunday with those who are about to come apart at the seams—people who could be drastically helped by the encouragement of ordinary people who care.[13]

From a clinical perspective, this first tier is an example of the church providing proactive "primary care" to its congregants. In brief, the level one counselor in the church maintains awareness in regards to brothers or sisters, and notices counseling need; uncharacteristic quietness, distant or strained conversation, a gloomy or indefinably different affect. Then the level one counselor engages such a person in meaningful conversation, to help him/her.

*Exhortation.* The second tier, which concerns problem behaviors, implements counseling by exhortation. Candidates for level two counseling include elders, deacons, Sunday school teachers, and pastors. Level two counseling requires knowledge of Scripture, an ability to reflect feelings accurately (empathic response), counseling technique, and (most importantly) a strong interpersonal connection. The approach of the second level counselor will be accepted well by the client if his or her motivation strongly includes wanting to please God.

This second tier aligns well with what is clinically known as "secondary care," the providing of counseling in milieu of a presenting problem.

*Enlightenment.* The third, and highest tier, concerns problem thinking, and counseling is implemented by enlightenment. Accordingly, only a few select persons can be equipped to handle these more drastic, complicated issues, for training should be more extensive: a recommended three hours per week for six months to a year. In level three counseling, to observe a person's erroneous thoughts, one must look under the existing problem behaviors. It is said to change a behavior, first belief must be modified. This includes the understanding of the gospel, which also directly effects one's commitment to Christ.

Categorized clinically, the third tier of help in the church provides a type of "tertiary care," which is counseling amid more serious problems, or a client's personal crisis.

## Biblical Principles in Counseling Theory and Practice

How do you evaluate the biblical authenticity of the variety of counseling theories and practices that lay claim to a biblical or Christian foundation? The field of Christian counseling has come a long way from a time when its theoretical development reflected either secular models baptized in a biblical framework or narrow exegetical models of biblical terms and phrases, lacking rigorous hermeneutical examination or empirical validation. The robust nature of the field has yielded numerous approaches to caregiving, with an assortment of techniques and interventions.

### Scripture as Foundation

As we indicated earlier, 2 Timothy 3:16–17 states, "All Scripture is given by inspiration of God and is useful for teaching, rebuking, correcting and training in righteousness, so that the man of God may be thoroughly equipped for every good work." Hence, the foundation for Truth by which everything else is evaluated is the Bible, and the Scriptures in themselves provide us with a plethora of information in instructing one on how to live a proper life.

For example, a man comes to his pastor with a confession of adultery, and is consumed in guilt and depression over his error. The best and most proper way to help the client in such a case is the traditional biblical design that includes "the classic interventions of compassionate and humble listening; confrontation over sin; consolation, comfort and companionship in despair; receiving of confession, assurance of pardon, and reconstruction of that man's life in accord with proper virtues of self-control, fidelity, respect for life and so forth."[14]

The Bible provides the singular authoritative standard for both generating and evaluating a caregiving ministry. The essential qualities of a complete Christian counseling theory and practice should incorporate our creation in the image of God, the model of Jesus Christ, and the empowerment of the Holy Spirit. The components necessary for an adequate model of personality and counseling include an explanation of (1) our origin, (2) our essential nature or the things that we all share in common, (3) our current condition or a diagnosis of what is basically wrong with mankind, and (4) a prescription for remedying our problems based on an adequate understanding of human motivation, development, and the processes of change.[15]

Christian counselors help people to find their location in relationship to God, self, and others. They accept the authority of Scripture, recognize the uniqueness of human creation in the image of God and the effects of sin, acknowledge the redemptive initiative of God, and help people to find and follow a godly plan for healing. The Greatest Commandment guides them in their communication and service to others, as they seek to discover the provision and goodness of God in every situation. Such counselors try to model the example of Christ, the Messiah and Master Counselor, in wisdom and understanding, planning and power, and the knowledge and fear of the Lord, as they engage in the theory and practice of caregiving.

Christian counselors allow the Holy Spirit to do His work through the ministry of counseling. They nurture the fruit of the Spirit, the gifts of the Spirit, biblical traits, and spiritual disciplines. In the process, they draw others to God and build up the church, the body of Christ.

## Creator and Creation: The Bedrock

There is a temptation to align ourselves with the familiar. Our ethnocentric predisposition draws us toward counseling models that reflect our own needs and interests. Indeed, modern secular counseling theories often mirror the culture, historical context, and biographical character of their creators. Christian approaches to counseling generally mirror preferred theological orientations along with supporting verses from Scripture, usually from the New Testament and, in particular, from the Pauline epistles.[16] The challenge for all Christian counselors who desire to be truly biblical is to develop counseling approaches that embrace foundational principles of caregiving cultivated and mined out in Scripture, from Genesis to Revelation.

## Our Design and Purpose

An understanding of our divine origin is essential to the development of a fully Christian counseling theory and practice. The opening chapters of the book of Genesis reveal that all creation owes its existence to God. Humans are unique among creation in that they bear a special imprint of their Creator. They were originally designed for the purpose of having communion with Him and being caretakers over His world. We bear the image (Hebrew: *tselem*) and likeness (Hebrew: *demuth*) of our Creator (Gen. 1:26–27), but our relationship with God has been broken due to sin.

*Created for relationship.* We are designed by God for fellowship with Him and with other people. The desire for relationship is a basic component of our human nature, and this quality is found in the nature of our triune God.[17] We do not exist as a result of chance or arbitrary genetic mutation. Each person is part of a divine design and plan. Knowing our Creator and having relationship with Him is the primary task of all people, including biblical counselors.

*Our fallen nature.* Adam and Eve's decision to listen to an authority other than God's and reject His will has resulted in a fallen world, filled with deception and disobedience. Our original purpose of relationship with God and with others has been shattered. Sin has led to disobedience to the Word of God, destruction of the unique relationship with our Creator, and to conflict in our relationships with others. Only through the initiative, grace, and power of God will we find the ultimate solution to our dilemma. We are incapable of resolving these problems ourselves.

All secular counseling theories present an incomplete picture of human nature. They are unable to account adequately for both our attraction to the eternal, the spiritual, and the altruistic, and our pull toward the temporal, evil, and the selfish. These theories will emphasize either a basic goodness (e.g., Carl Rogers) or a basic depravity (e.g., Freud) in the soul. These counseling models place the individual self, social forces or biological drives at the center of all change.

Such theories may rest upon a belief in free will or biological or social determinism; cognitive, affective, or behavioral reprogramming; a problem-solving or solution-focused orientation; depth analysis or minimalist intervention. Ultimately, they all seek resolution of human dilemmas in some expression of personal or social power. Mankind is central, while God is relegated to a peripheral function. He is created in the image and for the needs of humanity or He is entirely ignored. The result is a form of idolatry or a cult of self worship.[18] Christian counselors understand that all biblical care giving and assistance falls within the larger plans and purposes of God, and that Christian counseling should begin with God and model His actions.

## The Genesis Model of Intervention

The first question asked by God in human history occurred in the context of a crisis counseling situation. Adam and Eve had listened to a different voice of authority and their disobedience led to a breakdown in fellowship with God, as well as their relationship with each other (Gen. 3:1–19). They were in a state of spiritual and relational crisis, with their very souls at stake. Adam blamed both God and Eve ("The woman whom You gave to me" [Gen. 3:12]), while Eve accused the serpent of causing the problem. The communion between the couple and their Creator was broken and a dissonance had entered the relationship between the man and the woman.

*The initiative of God.* The response of God to the Fall serves as a model for the church and its ministry, particularly in the fields of evangelism, discipleship, service and counseling. God took the initiative in reestablishing contact with Adam and Eve. He is a pursuing God.

"Then the Lord God called to the man, and said to him, 'Where are you?'" (Gen. 3:9 NASB). This passage is one of the most interesting, and perhaps one of the most significant in all of Scripture. Humans had just freely chosen to turn their backs on their Creator and reject His Word and authority. They were in a state of sin. We would expect God to react to their behavior with righteous judgment, condemning them for their sin, demanding repentance, and dictating their punishment. Although the consequences of their sin was revealed, God did not open His conversation with words of condemnation. Instead, we see Him beginning His intervention with a question: "Where are you?" (Gen. 3:9).

*The importance of location.* The question of location is basic to a biblical model of Christian counseling. If you have ever been lost, then you will understand the importance of knowing your location. Your very survival may depend upon such knowledge. There are three things that you need to know to reach safety when you are lost: your current position, the place of safety or your goal, and the path(s) that will lead you safely to your destination. Effective Christian counseling addresses these three areas.

The temptation for Christian counselors is to step into a counseling situation and direct people toward answers based upon a particular theory or selective verses from the Bible without taking the time to get to know the people in need and to allow them to define their situation. Often, we expect people to conform to our interpretation of the problem and to act on our terms. God shows us a different approach. His question gave Adam an opportunity to define his current condition and accept responsibility. Jesus followed this approach on a number of occasions.[19]

*The application of location and relationship in counseling.* Christian counseling seeks to discover a person, family, or group's position in relationship to God, self, and others. Locating clients becomes difficult when they are overwhelmed by their problems, being deceptive or deceived, hiding from or unwilling to accept the truth of their condition, or confused by their situation. Effective counseling focuses on the three dimensions of relationship (God, self, and others) and the client answering the following basic questions concerning location.

### Current Location, Problem Definition

- Where do you say that you are located? What do you believe is the problem?
- Where do others say that you are located? What do they say is your problem?
- Where does God say that you are located? What is the biblical view of your situation?

### Goal, Destination, or Solution

- Where do you believe that you want to be? What is the solution to your problem and what changes do you want? Where do you have control? What changes are you willing and able to make?
- Where does your counselor and others say that you need to be? What do they suggest?

- Where does God say that you need to be? What does Scripture say is the solution to your problem and what changes does God expect?

## Plan for Change

- How do you propose to get to your goal? What resources do you have?
- What suggestions do your counselor and others have for reaching your goal?
- What is God's plan for your life in this situation? What spiritual resources has God provided for you?[20]

In the ideal counseling situation, there is complete agreement between a counselee, the counselor, and the Word of God on the answers to these questions. Of course, not every case works an ideal result.

## The Greatest Commandment: Guiding Principle for Treatment and Healing

Christian counseling follows the biblical model of caregiving by seeking to achieve healing in the relationship with an individual, family, or group and God, the self, or others. The guiding principle that provides the spiritual and ethical standard of practice in this task of healing is the Greatest Commandment. Jesus identified the greatest commandment as *the call upon us to love God with all our hearts, souls, minds, and strength, and to love other people as much as we love ourselves* (Matt. 22:34–40; Mark 12:28–34; Luke 10:25–28). The commandment summarizes the message of the Ten Commandments into two distinct dimensions, our relationship to God and our relationship to others.

## The Three Dimensions of Healing

Jesus proclaimed that the kingdom of heaven was at hand. He revealed the healing and redemptive activity of God in the world and in the process addressed the essential issue of Eden: our location and lostness in relationship to God, to self, and to other people. Biblically-based therapy needs to address a client's current spiritual, cognitive, social, behavioral, and affective condition in relationship to these three dimensions. We find this subject clearly presented in the theme of the Greatest Commandment.

Our priority must be to seek and love God, placing Him first in our lives (Deut. 6:5, 10:12, 30:6). We show our devotion to God by accepting His love for us. The godly love of self is not an egoistic selfishness; rather, it is the recognition of our creation in the image of God. We show a true love of self by seeking the best for ourselves, by answering His call and being obedient to His will. We express our love toward God by joining with Him in loving others (Lev. 19:18; Rom. 13:9; Gal. 5:14; James 2:8).

*Adjusting interventions to individual location and needs.* Jesus gives us an example of finding the location of people in need and adjusting His intervention when, on two occasions, He is asked a question related to the Greatest Commandment. Both the rich young ruler and a scribe or lawyer approached Jesus with the same question, "What must I do to inherit eternal life?" (Luke 18:18–21, 10:25–28), but He gave different responses to each of His inquirers. The two situations provide insight into the biblical counseling principles of location and intervention.

1. *Address the questions raised by the clients and begin with their understanding of the problem.* Jesus responded to the questions raised by the young ruler and the scribe. Since they were interested in a theological issue, Jesus focused on this area. If they had asked a question on some other matter, then we can assume that Jesus would have shifted His response to meet their needs as they defined them.

2. *Look for ways to connect or join with clients.* Jesus responded to the youthful zeal of the young ruler with warmth and affection (Mark 10:21). With the scribe, He deferred to the status of the scholar by asking him to answer the question. When the scribe correctly cited the Greatest Commandment, Jesus affirmed the man's knowledge of the Law.

3. *Do not assume that people who ask the same question have the same problem.* Jesus understood that while these two men were asking the same question, they, nevertheless, were wrestling with different fundamental issues in their relationship with God and with others. We see these issues revealed as Jesus adjusted His intervention according to the theological and spiritual position or location of each of the men.[21]

4.  *Begin interventions, if possible, at the points of agreement.* If our relationship to God is more important than our love of neighbor, then why did Jesus begin His response to the young ruler by referring to the second table of the Ten Commandments? Surely a pious and godly biblical counselor must start every counseling session by focusing on God and insisting that the client start there also! Yet, Jesus did not begin by identifying the first commandments. Instead, He listed commandments that dealt with adultery, murder, stealing, false witness, and honoring parents.

    The young ruler's claim that he had kept all these commandments gives us a clue to the strategy of Christ. He connected with His inquirer by focusing first upon the person's spiritual and relational strengths. Beginning with areas of agreement lessens the likelihood of rancor, defensiveness, and debate. Instead, it increases the chances that a client will be open and receptive to the truth. The young ruler's problem lay elsewhere, with the first commandment and his relationship to God. In contrast, the scribe did not have a problem with the first commandment and the importance of placing God first in his life. Jesus seemed to agree with the scribe on this point, but His response elicited a question from the man that went to the heart of his real problem: "Who is my neighbor?" (Luke 10:29).

5.  *Encourage clients to wrestle with the truth using techniques that illuminate biblical principles as clearly as possible for them.* The young ruler's problem was a common idolatry for many of us today. He was placing his material wealth before God. Jesus used a direct approach to test the man and prove the point. He told him to sell his possessions and give all he had to the poor. In the case of the scribe, Jesus told him the story of the Good Samaritan and concluded with a question (Luke 10:30–36) designed to reveal the scribe's inadequate understanding of the biblical view of neighbor.

6.  *Allow clients to take personal responsibility and apply biblical truths to their lives.* The young ruler was faced with a choice, and he went away sad, because he was very wealthy and he was unwilling to express his total commitment to God (Luke 18:22–24). The scribe revealed his struggle with biblical truth by identifying the true neighbor only as "the one who showed mercy" toward the victim

of the attack (Luke 10:37). He still could not bring himself to say the word "Samaritan." Jesus challenged him to show the same mercy toward all people.

Not all clients will make the right decision, or even arrive at one. Counselors cannot decide or act for their clients, but they look for the most effective means of joining with clients and revealing the paths to truth in ways that make the most sense to them. If a counselor can facilitate a client encounter with God, wrestling with His way, then much is accomplished, and a holy seed has been planted that God will water and nurture.

### The Messianic Example

If Jesus Christ is the perfect and only answer to the problem of sin, then He is also the supreme model for counseling. While it is beneficial to study the examples of caregiving found in the ministry of Jesus, we find the foundation for His ministry in the Old Testament, and, in particular, in the messianic passages. Isaiah 9:6 gives us an overall description of the Messiah:

> For a child will be born to us, a son will be given to us;
> And the government will rest on His shoulders;
> And His name will be called Wonderful Counselor, Mighty God,
> Eternal Father, Prince of Peace (Isa. 9:6, NASB).

### The Authority of Jesus

"I have been given *complete authority in heaven and on earth.* Therefore, go and make disciples of all the nations, baptizing them in the name of the Father and of the Son and of the Holy Spirit. Teach these new disciples to obey all the commands I have given you. And be sure of this: I am with you always, even to the end of the age."

This Great Commission of Christ, His last words recorded in Matthew's Gospel (24:18–20), are much more than a charge to evangelize the world. He reveals that God the Father has given Him all authority over all the powers of heaven and earth. From this power the disciple-making challenge is possible—the very same power to lead the church into maturity in Christ. Christ is the Source of this power, and He promises to be always available to accomplish this task—He is the Source of all authority, and He will never leave us!

The Messiah will come as a gift from God (cf. John 3:16), as a child who will be given all authority in heaven and on earth (Matt. 28:18). We will find His authority and His character revealed in His names.

*Wonderful Counselor.* The Hebrew word for counselor (*yaats*) should not be confused with the formal concept of modern psychotherapy; rather, it conveys the incomprehensible vastness of the wisdom and knowledge of the Messiah. He will be able to discern the truth in all situations and determine the appropriate way to proceed. The term "wonderful" (Heb: *pali*) is a descriptive adjective, and accentuates the supernatural nature of the Messiah, indicating that His counsel will lie beyond our comprehension and ability. It will be so exceptional that human wisdom would appear as foolishness by comparison (1 Cor. 1:25, 3:19).[22]

*Mighty God.* The Messiah will express the creative and miraculous power of God. His authority will extend over heaven and earth, body and spirit, and the temporal and eternal.

*Eternal Father.* The Messiah will express the nature of our heavenly Father, our Creator and Redeemer. He will come as an everlasting presence with whom we may share a personal relationship as adopted children (Rom. 8:15, 23; Gal. 4:5; Eph. 1:5).

*Prince of Peace.* The Messiah will bring eternal peace and salvation (Luke 2:14). He will be the One who brings reconciliation between God and fallen mankind (Eph. 2:14–19). His peace will be beyond any peace that the world can offer. It will be capable of calming all fears and bringing the grace of God and His redeeming presence into all situations (John 14:27).

The Messiah will come as Savior. He will locate us in our sin and provide us with the only path to salvation. In so doing, He will serve as the standard or model for counseling intervention.

## The "Spirit of the Lord" in Christian Counseling

The nature of the Messiah is revealed in the form of three spirits, each spirit having two characteristics.

> Then a shoot will spring from the stem of Jesse,
> And a branch from his roots will bear fruit.
> The Spirit of the Lord will rest on Him,

The spirit of wisdom and understanding,

The spirit of counsel and strength,

> The spirit of knowledge and the fear of the Lord (Isa. 11:1–2 NASB).

The three spirits (wisdom and understanding, counsel and strength, and knowledge and fear of the Lord) are all expressions of the one Spirit of Jehovah. The three groupings and the pairing of characteristics indicate distinct dimensions with overlapping meanings.[23] The six terms give us insight into the personal nature of the Messiah. They provide us with an ideal picture not only of God, but also of the perfect Man, unblemished by sin. The six characteristics are expressed in the life of Christ, and through His example, they provide us with a framework for developing a model of care and counseling.

*Wisdom* (Hebrew: *hokmah*; LXX: *sophias*).[24] The Messiah will not make judgments based on external appearances and circumstances (Isa. 11:3–5). Instead, He will possess a divine awareness of the broader context of a situation as well as supernatural insight into the true nature of a person. Godly wisdom is the ability to see into the heart of a matter, beyond the visible and superficial, and correctly discern the most appropriate response.

In the context of a counseling ministry, this godly wisdom indicates the need for a comprehensive theoretical basis for caregiving that encompasses a full awareness of human nature, including the social, cognitive, behavioral, affective, and spiritual dimensions. Such complete wisdom is not accessible outside of the guidance of God (Job 28:12–28). Proverbs 8:1–36 connects this wisdom to four other expressions in Isaiah 11:2: knowledge (*daath*), sound advice (*etzah*), understanding (*binah*) and strength (*geburah*).

Jesus kept increasing in wisdom (Luke 2:52). His wise counsel is expressed in the Sermon on the Mount (Matt. 5–7) and the many occasions when He looked beyond external appearance and circumstances to see the broader spiritual, social, and psychological factors in a situation.

*Understanding* (Hebrew: *binah*; LXX: *suneseos*). The Messiah will possess a deep and practical understanding of individuals and events. Understanding is the ability to discern and discriminate between the various parts of a situation; to know how the different components relate to one another. In counseling, we need such understanding to look beyond the external and the superficial and to identify the motivations and complex social forces that influence human interaction and individual behavior.

We find an example of such understanding in King Solomon's order to divide a child in two when two mothers both had claimed the same baby (1 Kin. 3:16–28). Solomon knew the true mother would relinquish her claim rather than see her child harmed. He understood the motivating forces and emotions at work in both the biological mother and the false claimant, and he used this knowledge to reveal the truth.

Jesus understood human motivation and what lay in the heart of a person (John 2:25). He used this understanding with His disciples, people in need, and others who opposed Him. In the case of the woman caught in adultery, His awareness of the motives, needs, and attitudes of the Pharisees and the woman enabled Jesus to join relationally with both the accusers and the accused, deescalate a dangerous situation, biblically confront the religious authorities, save a woman from physical harm and minister to her spiritual needs (John 8:3–11).

The brilliance of His counseling intervention was revealed in His ability to address the issues in a way that revealed the therapeutic path for both parties. Both the Pharisees and the woman were confronted with a choice. How they responded was their personal responsibility.

*Counsel or Knowledge* (Hebrew: *etzah*; LXX: *boules*). The Messiah will have a spirit of knowledge that will enable Him to evaluate a situation correctly in order to determine the appropriate response and develop the best plan. The Hebrew word *etzah* conveys the idea of giving counsel or advice based upon wise planning and an accurate assessment of a situation.

Both appropriate and inappropriate counsel is found in the story of Rehoboam, who chose to ignore the recommendation of his older counselors for reform by lightening the burden of the people. Their advice (*etzah*) was based upon their knowledge of the hearts of the people and insight into the political climate. Instead, Rehoboam listened to his young and immature peers who argued for further oppression. Their counsel did not reflect a careful examination of the situation nor wise planning. The king's decision had disastrous consequences (1 Kin. 12:13–14).

Wise Christian counselors gather and examine all the data in a situation. They carefully identify the important information and they assist people in designing a course of action that accounts for the circumstances, possible dangers, and abilities of the person or people in need. Such counsel, however, wisely acknowledges that behind every situation God is still in control. Consequently, it is imperative that a godly path be chosen. "Many plans (plots, thoughts, schemes) are in a man's heart, But the counsel (*etzah*) of the Lord will stand" (Prov. 19:21).

Jesus clearly articulated His mission plan in Luke 4:18 where He quoted from Isaiah 58:6 and Isaiah 11:3–4: "The Spirit of the Lord has come to me because he has chosen me to tell the good news to the poor. The Lord has sent me to announce freedom for prisoners, to give sight to the blind, to free everyone who suffers, and to proclaim that this is the year the Lord has chosen." His Great Commission outlined His plan for all Christians (Matt. 28:18–20).

Christians have the promise of Christ's power, presence, and authority. As we obey Christ's call, the Holy Spirit, our Divine Comforter and Counselor, will guide and help us. An important role of the Holy Spirit is to reveal to us the true nature of things, teaching us, reminding us, and helping us to witness for Christ (John 14:15–17, 26; 15:26–27). All Christian counselors possess at least one of God's many gifts to be used in service to others and for His glory (1 Pet. 4:10–11). In addition, God has given us a Spirit of power and of love and of a sound mind to care for others (2 Tim. 1:7).

Christian counselors assist their fellow believers to grow and mature in Christ and in their relationship with other people. Such counseling also provides Christians with an opportunity to represent Christ in a therapeutic encounter with non-believers. The process of revealing Christ is an essential component of competent Christian counseling; however, it must be done in a way that honors client choice and follows accepted ethical practice.[25]

Christian counselors must seek the Spirit of Knowledge, but wise planning is not enough to ensure that changes will take place in a person's life. There must be a source of power strong enough to execute the plan and produce change.

*Power* (Hebrew: *geburah*; LXX: *ischuos*). Power is the strength or might to produce change; the ability to execute a plan; and the capacity to remain firm and constant in a situation, despite opposition. The Bible calls upon us to recognize and sing praises to the power and strength of God (Ps. 21:13). Job acknowledged his complete dependence upon God, who possessed wisdom (*hokmah*), strength (*geburah*), counsel (*etzah*), and understanding (*binah*) (Job 12:13). God knew human nature. He understood the strengths and limitations of Job and the dilemma that he faced. God's message to Job was that He also had the power to deal with any problem or situation and to determine the future.

This power is found in Christ, who worked in the power of the Holy

Spirit (John 4:14), and who was given all power and authority in heaven and on earth (Matt. 28:18). His power is revealed clearly in John 10:17–18, where He proclaimed that He not only had the power to lay down His life for others, but He also had the power to take it up again. Jesus had power over death. He had the plan for salvation and the power to execute the plan. Christian counselors have access to the supernatural power of Christ, who has the strength to overcome all the forces, authorities, and rulers in the world (Eph. 1:17–23).

Many plans fail because people lack the strength to implement them. Wise counselors consider the skills and abilities of their clients in the process of developing treatment plans. Attempts to impose changes and place unrealistic expectations upon clients can leave people feeling frustrated and overwhelmed. Repeated failures due to poor planning and inadequate power resources can lead people to experience habitual or learned helplessness. They just give up.[26] Consequently, it is essential that each client's location in relationship to God, self, and others is determined and that an assessment is made of the resources available to the one in need.

*The Knowledge of God* (Hebrew: *daath*; LXX: *gnoseos*). The Messiah will possess a perfect understanding of the will of God. The knowledge of God is the ability to see a situation through the eyes of God who is all knowing, and to possess the information necessary to determine God's intention or direction. Proverbs 2 tells us that we will understand the fear (*yir'ath*) of Jehovah and the knowledge (*daath*) of God if we bow our ears to wisdom (*hokmah*), extend our hearts to understanding (*binah*), cry out and seek discernment (*binah*), and lift up our voices for understanding (*binah*).

The Messiah possessed this knowledge of God (cf., Isa. 53:11) and Christ embodied this knowledge as the Way, the Truth, and the Life (John 14:6). Christians have access to the knowledge of God through their relationship to Jesus Christ and the presence of the Holy Spirit in their lives. The Spirit enables Christian counselors to commune with God and access the knowledge of God revealed in Scripture.

*The Fear of God* (Hebrew: *yirath*; LXX: *eusebeias*). The fear of God is a holy reverence of and respect or honor toward God. It is the loyalty and duty that we owe God by placing Him first above everything else. The fear of God in its fullness represents a perfect relationship with the Creator. "The fear (*yirath*) of the Lord is the beginning of knowledge (*daath*); fools despise wisdom (*hokmah*) and instruction" (Prov. 1:7). Wisdom and knowledge begin when God is placed first in our lives and we seek to live our lives in accordance with His will.

Fear of God and obedience to His Word allows us to make sense of this world (Eccl. 12:13–14). True fear is based upon an awareness of who God is and a desire to find Him in every situation in life. The true believer continually seeks the will of God and fears the possibility of ever losing sight of God. False fear is rooted in a doubt of God's existence (Ps. 14:1, 53:1) and the subsequent dread of death and a future judgment. Such people live their lives in rebellion to the will of God. [27]

Godly people express their fear of the Lord by refusing to engage in sinful attitudes and actions. Jesus perfectly manifested the fear of God, as He lived a perfect and sinless life. He was in the Father and the Father was in Him (John 14:10). He was in His very nature God (Phil. 2:6–11). "I and the Father are one," He said (John 10:30). His life exemplified a person who never took His eyes off the Father, one who reflected the absolute holiness of God and the rejection of evil.

> The fear of the Lord is to hate evil;
> Pride and arrogance and the evil way
> And the perverted mouth, I hate.
> Counsel is mine and sound wisdom;
>     I am understanding, power is mine (Prov. 8:13–14 NASB).

Counselors need to help people distinguish between true and godly fear and the false fears that mislead and debilitate. An important role of biblical counselors is to represent Christ and to look for the hand of God working in every counseling situation.

## The Holy Spirit and Spiritual Gifts in Counseling

Jesus said that He would ask the Father to give His followers another Counselor or Helper (Greek: *parakletos*), the Spirit of Truth, to abide with them and teach them (John 14:26). As the Divine Advocate or representative of Christ (John 15:26) in the life of Christian counselors, the Holy Spirit strengthens and directs them. The traits attributed to the Messiah in Isaiah 11:2 (wisdom, understanding, knowledge, power, the knowledge of God, and the fear of God) are now expressed through the Holy Spirit.

Christian counselors are filled with the Spirit (Eph. 5:18), bear the fruit of the Spirit (John 15:16; Gal. 5:22), and receive the gifts of the Spirit. The fruit of the Spirit (love, joy, peace, patience, gentleness, goodness, faithfulness, meekness and self-control) are necessary components of mature Christian counseling (Gal. 5:22–23). They are more accurate measures of our identity in Christ than the possession of gifts, which can be misused.

The spiritual gifts reveal God and the eternal presence of His Spirit, as well as minister to and edify the believer and others. Paul identified nine gifts in 1 Corinthians 12:8–10: the word of wisdom, the word of knowledge, special faith, healing gifts, the working of miracles, prophecy, discernment between spirits, tongues, and the interpretation of tongues. Paul clearly stated that the gifts were not distributed equally and that certain Christians were blessed with particular gifts of the Spirit.

Additional gifts include service to others and helping, teaching, encouragement, giving, leadership, mercy, apostleship, missionary evangelism, and pastoring (Rom. 12:6–8; 1 Cor. 12:28; Eph. 4:11). We are expected to speak the words of God accurately and to work in the power of the Spirit as we minister to others with our gifts (1 Pet. 4:10–11).

### The Spiritual Disciplines in Counseling

Christian counselors need to develop the biblical traits and spiritual disciplines associated with caregiving. One survey identified nearly 50 biblical traits and 20 spiritual disciplines that are related to counseling, including the traits of patience, gentleness, self-control, compassion, truthfulness, approachableness, ability to teach, discernment, empathy, giving comfort and encouragement, confrontation, integrity, thoughts obedient to Christ, hope, ability to relate well to others, a longing for God, and an example to those served. Spiritual disciplines included prayer, service, maintaining purity, compassion, accountability, forgiveness, obedience, confession and repentance, wisdom, agape love, listening and guidance.[28] Such encounters with the living God changes everything for both counselor and client.

## Conclusion

We are honored that our friend and colleague, Professor Ian Jones of Southwestern Baptist Theological Seminary joined us in this chapter and consented to contribute the essence of his soon-to-be-published manuscript as the core content here. His careful exegesis of the "whole counsel of God" on the counseling endeavor has yielded a rich treasure of revelation that will guide our field in our research, practice, and theory-building for the rest of this century.

### ENDNOTES

1. Robert W. Kellemen, *Spiritual friends: A methodology of soul care and spiritual direction*, (Taneytown, MD: RPM Books, 2004), 77.
2. Irvin D. Yalom, *The gift of therapy: An open letter to a new generation of therapists and their patients* (NY: HarperCollins, 2002).
3. Timothy Clinton, and Ohlschlager, G., *Competent Christian counseling, volume one: Foundations and practice of compassionate soul care* (Colorado Springs: WaterBrook, 2002), chapter 3.
4. Timothy Clinton, and Ohlschlager, G., *Competent Christian counseling, Volume One.*
5. Jay Adams, *Competent to counsel* (Presbyterian and Reformed Publishing Company, 1970).
6. Timothy Clinton, and Ohlschlager, G., *Competent Christian counseling, Volume One.*
7. Diane Langberg, *On the threshold of hope: Opening the door to healing for survivors of sexual abuse* (Wheaton, IL: Tyndale, 1999).
8. AACC members survey.
9. W. Backus, *Telling the truth to trouble people: A manual for Christian counselors* (Minneapolis: Bethany House, 1985); W. Backus, *What your counselor never told you: Conquer the power of sin in your life* (Minneapolis, MN: Bethany House, 2000); L. Vernick, *The TRUTH principle: A life changing model for spiritual growth and renewal* (Colorado Springs: WaterBrook Press, 2000); C. Thurman, *The lies we believe* (Nashville: Thomas Nelson, 1989).
10. Russ Willingham, *Breaking free* (Downers Grove, IL: Intervarsity, 1999).
11. Mark McMinn, and A. Dominguez, Psychology collaborating with the church, *Journal of Psychology and Christianity*, 22(4), (2003), 291–294.
12. Larry Crabb, *Effective biblical counseling: A model for helping caring Christians become capable counselors* (Grand Rapids, MI: Zondervan, 1977).
13. Larry Crabb, *Connecting* (Nashville: W Pubishing Group, 1997), 25.
14. This section is a summary of the biblical foundations of counseling addressed in Ian F. Jones, *The counsel of heaven on earth* (Manuscript submitted for publication, 2003).
15. Leslie Stevenson, *Seven theories of human nature*, second edition (New York: Oxford University Press, 1974), 5–7; Mary Stewart Van Leeuwin, *The person in psychology: A contemporary Christian appraisal* (Grand Rapids, MI: Eerdmans, 1985), 46. The four features of a complete theory of human nature are identified by Stevenson and developed by Van Leeuwin within a Christian worldview. They overlook the crucial fifth criterion: a clear articulation of the source of authority for the truth claims.

16.    A challenge for all Christian counselors is to examine their preferred counseling model in light of their personal history, personality, and culture. Failure to do so is likely to result in a theory that inadvertently reflects the needs, character, and experiences of individual theorists, who then assume that their particular approach is universally applicable for all people at all times—a fault found, in particular, among the pioneers in secular psychology and counseling. Subsequently, any other approach encountered by these Christian counselors must be, by their own definition, less than biblical.

17.    Francis Schaeffer argues that the Christian doctrine of the Trinity is essential, in that it reveals that God has no need for relationship outside of Himself. He was not compelled to create us in order to have fellowship, but we are absolutely dependent upon Him for our existence and survival. See Francis A. Schaeffer, *He is there and He is not silent* (Wheaton, IL: Tyndale, 1972), 14–17.

18.    See Paul Vitz, *Psychology as religion: The cult of self worship*, second ed. (Grand Rapids, MI: Eerdmans, 1994).

19.    Variations on the question of location are found in the response of Jesus to people seeking healing and many of the questions He asked and discussions He had with His disciples. Most of His post-resurrection appearances are examples of God locating people in need and directing them toward an understanding of His will and truth.

20.    These questions reflect general areas of inquiry in counseling. They should not be used in a rote manner, without considering the location of the client in terms of language, temperament, concerns, context, and physical, spiritual, social, and emotional condition.

21.    Counselors need to be cautious about automatically responding to an identified problem with a pre-selected technique or verse of Scripture, without investigating a client's location in such areas as context and motives.

22.    If the terms *Wonderful* and *Counselor* are considered to be separate names or titles, as some translations prefer [e.g., King James Version], then "Wonderful" conveys a sense of the incomprehensible and mysterious nature of God.

23.    Isaiah is not describing three or even six different entities in the passage, but a single Spirit manifest in different attributes. While parallelisms involving synonyms that convey identical meaning are used in Hebrew literature, the terms used in this passage appear to have discrete, although overlapping meaning. See, e.g., Joseph Addison Alexander, *The earlier prophecies of Isaiah* (New York: Wiley and Putnam, 1846), 220; and Edward J. Young, *The book of Isaiah: The English text, with introduction, exposition, and notes, New International Commentary on the Old Testament*, ed. by R. K. Harrison (Grand Rapids, MI: Eerdmans, 1965), 380–381.

24.    LXX refers to the Septuagint—a Greek translation of the Old Testament.

25.    George Ohlschlager and Clinton, T., Inside law and ethics: The ethics of evangelism and spiritual formation in professional counseling, *Christian Counseling Connection* (Issue 1, 2000), 6–7.

26.    Martin E. P. Seligman, *Helplessness: On depression, development, and death* (San Francisco: W. H. Freeman and Company, 1975), 21–44.

27.    Blaise Pascal, *Pensèes and the provincial letters* (New York: The Modern Library, 1941), 92, (Pensèe #262).

28.    Kevin Scott Forrester, Determining the Biblical traits and spiritual disciplines Christian counselors employ in practice: A delphi study, PhD diss., Southwestern Baptist Theological Seminary, (2002), 151–157. The biblical traits were love, joy,

peace, patience, kindness, goodness, faithfulness, gentleness, self-control, compassion, living in the Spirit, humility, forgiveness, truthfulness, holding others accountable, approachable, wisdom, self-giving, able to teach, meekness, hunger and thirst for righteousness, merciful, pure in heart, peacemakers, walking with the Lord, prayerful attitude, giving God the glory, discernment, thankfulness, empathy, respect, biblical morality, giving comfort and encouragement, confrontation, integrity, renewed mind, thoughts obedient to Christ, using the armor of God, knowledge of God's Word, endurance, hope, acceptance, ability to relate well to others, a longing for God, knowing self, avoiding quarrels, work toward biblical goals, an example to those served, and not practicing worldliness. The spiritual disciplines were prayer, listening prayer, service, Scripture: counselor proactive, maintaining purity, compassion, praise, being an example, accountability, forgiveness, discernment, obedience, confession/repentance, wisdom, agape love, growth, caring, listening and guidance, thought life, and ministering to all needs.

# 4

# Christian Counseling Process: Goals, Traits, Stages, and Plan

*George Ohlschlager and Tim Clinton*

The path of life runs in and out of darkness, confusion, uncertainty, loss, and heartache—not a path we would choose naturally. It compels us to walk as aliens and strangers through the desert and through the valley of the shadow of death.

DAN ALLENDER, IN *The Healing Path*[1]

This chapter is for the analyst, the rational logician in every reader. It delivers the cognitive road map of competent Christian counseling—a map that will assist you when you get stuck in counseling, and one that you will necessarily teach to many of your clients. This chapter outlines the structural matrix of Christian counseling—a perspectival grasp of the track, traits, goals, and session-by-session plan of counseling—that easily facilitates left-brain understanding and analysis.

Novice helpers will want to study this chapter—all five chapters in this first section—carefully and in depth, working to engrave this matrix into your thinking until it becomes "second nature" to your own analytical process. Experienced helpers will want to return and review these chapters from time to time as a refresher, to remember what should never be forgotten in the counseling endeavor.

Knowing the road map richly and in great detail will always serve your mission as a helper in all kinds of cases, and will mark you as a wise counselor and a confident teacher. This, of course, is true about any life journey, not just counseling. Let's begin with a common dilemma in counseling—misunderstandings between counselor and client.

The client was devastated. We were near the end of our eighth session and I had just raised the question of terminating counseling with her. A divorcee in her mid-thirties with two children she was raising on her own, she had brought a thorny relationship problem with her new fiancé into counseling. She had worked through most of the trouble she originally presented with courage and, it seemed, real success. Termination was a natural and logical step to now consider.

Her reaction surprised me, or I should say that the strength of her reaction was the surprise, as termination issues are often fraught with strong emotions. Though I raised it as a tentative question, as I had long ago learned to do, it was clear she had heard it as a threat, as an inflexible demand to end our relationship as soon as possible. First she was hurt, then she became increasingly angry as she talked about ending counseling (triggering some abandonment questions in my mind that came out later in therapy, as she explored her fear of and resistance to remarriage).

Client:  *I can't believe* you want to terminate me now. I thought we were starting to work together really well.

G.O.:  We are working well together... In fact, it's working so well that you are telling me, in effect, that you've accomplished most of what you wanted when you came in.

Client:  Well if I have given you that impression, I am sorry. There is so much more to do... and then you broadside me with talk of ending counseling.

G.O.:  Termination is a proper subject to consider when you've reached your goals... but if there is something else?... [I left it hanging as a question.]

Client:  Well... there is something... something that I hadn't planned on bringing up in counseling... at least not when I started...

G.O.:  And maybe you're wondering whether you should bring it up now?...

Client:  Yea, I'm afraid that things could spin out-of-control if I do... I mean I KNOW you're a mandatory reporter and all....

G.O.: Oh, and if you tell me about some child abuse situation or something... I'm going to have CPS (child protective services) all over you and your boyfriend.... [Again, I left the question hanging.]

Client: Yea, something like that.... I mean I know I need to talk to someone about this, and I really do trust you to do right by me... but I don't want to lose.... [her voice started to crack and tears welled up.]

G.O.: [I sat back and went as soft and non-threatening as I possibly could.] You know, most clients fear the worst will happen, and it rarely does. I know some people at CPS who are very good at what they do, and are committed to maintaining the integrity of the marriage and family... Compared to carrying this thing any further all by yourself, sometimes the best thing to do is to get it out and let others take on the burden with you...

That was all it took for the story I hadn't yet heard to come pouring out. As it happened, I did have to make a report, but CPS in Northern California is so overwhelmed with truly horrendous cases that they did not get involved in the matter. I ended up continuing to work with this client, her husband-to-be, and their blended family-to-be for another two and a half years, including a year after they were married.

### Getting and Staying Oriented to Your Client's World

Counselors will often find themselves backing off going forward—pausing instead to find common ground with their clients in our increasingly pluralistic world—a world where common understanding of issues and terms is less and less likely as we proceed into the 21st century. Not only is it getting difficult to establish a common cultural understanding in America, but a common Christian culture is harder and harder to agree upon. Helpers will necessarily borrow the language of science to "operationalize" terms— to define common meanings that will resonate in mutually understood language and goals with their clients.

All counselors need to deeply understand their clients—to get oriented to their clients' ways of perceiving and understanding the world—and to reinforce this understanding by adapting to the language that they use. Some have suggested that focusing on how people think, feel, and act is essential for increasing counseling effectiveness.[2] Such a belief led Hutchins and colleagues to espouse a model called the "TFA System."[3] His model is designed as a means for "examining theories, techniques, behavioral problems, and interactional patterns that exist between people."[4]

*Thinking orientation.* Generally, thinking persons are characterized by intellectual, cognitively-oriented behavior. They tend to behave in logical, rational, deliberate, and systematic ways. They are fascinated by the world of concepts, ideas, theories, words, and analytic relationships. The range of behavior in this category runs from minimal thought to considerable depth in quality and quantity of thinking. Organization of thoughts ranges from scattered to highly logical and rational.

Counselors with this orientation tend to focus on what clients think and the consequences. Special attention is paid to what the client says or does not say. Frequently, illogical, irrational thinking is seen as a major cause of client problems. A primary goal of this approach is to change irrational thinking, thus enabling the client to see things more rationally and to resolve problems. Counselors who use this approach are likely to be influenced by the work of Ellis (Rational-emotive therapy), Beck (Cognitive therapy), Maultsby (Rational behavior therapy), and Meichenbaum (Cognitive behavior modification).

*Feeling Orientation.* Feeling persons generally tend to behave in emotionally expressive ways. They are likely to go with their feelings in making decisions: "If it feels good, do it!" The expression and display of emotions, feelings, and affect provide clues to people with a primary feeling orientation. A person's look can range from angry, anxious, bitter, hostile, or depressed to one of elation, joy, or enthusiasm. One's emotional energy level can vary from low to high.

Counselors with this orientation are likely to be regarded as especially caring persons. They tend to focus on the client's feelings, paying special attention to the expression of emotion by how the person talks. Knotted and tangled emotions are seen as a major source of the client's problems. These counselors help the client describe, clarify, and understand mixed up and immobilizing emotions. As emotional distress is straightened out, the client is frequently able to perceive things more clearly (insight). Counselors using this approach are likely to be influenced by the work of Rogers (Non-Directive/Client-Centered/Person-Centered Therapy), Perls (Gestalt Therapy), Maslow, and a host of phenomenological, humanistic, and existential writers.[5]

*Acting Orientation.* Acting persons are generally characterized by their involvement in doing things, and their strong goal orientation. They are frequently involved with others, and tend to plunge into the thick of things. Action types get the job done, one way or another. To them, doing something is better than doing nothing; thus, they are frequently involved in a variety of activities. Their behavior may range from loud, aggressive, and public-oriented, to quiet, subtle, and private.

Counselors with an action orientation tend to see client problems as arising from inappropriate actions or lack of action. These counselors focus particularly on what the client does or does not do, and they tend to encourage clients to begin programs designed to eliminate, modify, or teach new behavior. An action-oriented counselor is likely to be influenced by the work of Bandura (Behavior Modification), Wolpe (Behavior Therapy), Krumboltz and Thoresen (Behavioral Counseling), and others espousing a behavioral approach to change.

A more learned expression of these modes would be in the form: cognition/affect/behavior. A cognitive person is a thinker, a feeling person is very affective, and behavior and action are obviously synonymous terms.

## Proposed Correlates for Christians

We would encourage this next generation of Christian counselors to develop client-centered models of understanding based on the religious and cultural traditions of various Christian populations that we tend to work with most heavily. Two ideas, for example, that may have some merit for future research and theory building are noted below.

*Theology/Spirituality/Religion.* The religious correlates to the thinking/feeling/acting aspects of a psychological orientation are proposed as theology/spirituality/religion. Theology literally means the knowledge of God and correlates to thinking or cognitive modes. Spirituality is more feeling oriented—an affective mode of perceiving and understanding the world. Religion correlates with action—the behavior of belief.

*Head/Heart/Hands.* The body orientation of many clients might express itself by way of head/heart/hands. The head obviously correlates with thinking and theology—with a cognitive orientation. Heart is the grand metaphor for feeling, for affect, and for spiritual life. And hands have to do with action and behavior—they are the prime tools (along with our feet) by which we take action and get things done.

## Motivation from the Client's Perspective

Client motivation is a huge issue in successful counseling. There has been some significant research done on identifying the motivation levels and developmental progression of counseling as experienced by the client.[6] Again, this can vary depending on specific circumstance. However, this general six-stage outline provides a useful introduction to this important work.

*Pre-contemplation.* Though a client can be in counseling and in this stage, the client in pre-contemplation has little desire for change, or does not believe change is necessary. A case example of this is someone mandated by a court of law to participate in counseling, or a husband pressured to see a counselor by his spouse.

*Contemplation.* In this phase a client observes that he/she needs to change, though may not be convinced he/she wishes to exert the effort to do so. In essence the client is weighing the pros and cons of taking steps to change. It is said persons can spend years in this stage, and often counselors mistake a client's "contemplation" for the next phase, "preparation."

*Preparation.* With preparation, clients have made the decision to begin working toward their goals within one month's time. Nothing has technically been "done" in terms of progress, except that the client has agreed to and intends to carry out a plan of action.

*Action.* Here a client actively makes steps to change. Whether it is outward behavior modification (i.e. stop drinking; begin attending Bible study) or inward (i.e. establish a healthy thought life; use positive thinking), the results of this stage are the most obvious—the most observable change takes place.

*Maintenance.* This involves the establishment of a "post-treatment program," which is designed to solidify the positive changes and actions that have taken place in the preceding stage. In essence, the maintenance stage is concerned with preventing relapse.

*Termination.* Termination involves looking back at the journey that was made, and concludes the counseling relationship while at the same time establishing that the counselor is available later, if necessary for the client. Moreover, some counselors schedule a "checkup" appointment about 3 to 6 months after termination to help the client address any related issues that may manifest after the end of therapy. In general however, termination after successful counseling is a time of reflection and celebration of the change, maturity, and healing that have taken place.

## The Goals and Traits of Christian Counseling

### Christian Counseling Goals

Constructive client change—improving how to think, feel, and act in a goal-directed way—is the primary mission of all counseling. Christian counseling would qualify or add to this universal goal statement to assert the importance of improved belief or better faith in Christ—growing up into Christian maturity. The definition of these goals must ultimately be stated and owned by the client, with the counselor's help. Proverbs 27:19 reveals that, "As in water, face reflects face, so the heart of a man reflects a man."

Counseling, it could be argued, is a process of shifting the locus of one's dreams from the present into the future. That is, the counselor helps the client overcome their obsessions with the past and directionless daydreaming and fantasy to honestly locate themselves in the present, while they define an attainable goal they are willing to pursue into the future. Clients must be able to honestly admit their current status—their present location, as we argued in the last chapter—while assessing the resources and barriers to goal attainment.

A client who has come to pursue God's will in their life as the biggest dream they have, as the most important thing in their life, is far down the road of sanctification, of Christian maturity. "The good person out of the good treasure of his heart produces good; and the evil person out of his evil treasure produces evil, for out of the abundance of his heart his mouth speaks." (Luke 6:45)

A key challenge, then, in Christian counseling goal discussion and negotiation is to influence—to artfully argue for and persuade—a client to "turn your eyes upon Jesus," as the famous hymn states. This demands a maturity in the counselor that clearly distinguishes the unethical imposition of values and, at the other extreme, acceding to "anything goes" from the client, from exposition of the goodness of God and the high road of following Christ. Consistently seeing the relationship between the client's immediate interests and goals and the higher goals of Christ takes an experienced wisdom forged over many years of practice.

*Short term and long-term goals.* Distinguishing short and long-term goals is an effective way for counselors to resolve the otherwise incompatible conflicts that arise in defining client goals and God's will in a person's life, between merely coping in this life versus liberating the heart of man. As Proverbs 9:10 states, "The fear of the Lord is the beginning of wisdom." The wise counselor learns to connect client goals in the present with God's long-term design for the sanctified life.

We know biblically that the primary issues in life are related to brokenness in relationship with God and others (insecurity and lack of safety). Attachment wounds affect our core relational beliefs about God, self, others and the world in which we live. If we can understand that our emotional life and hence, our goals in living, are directly tied to our sense of safety and stability in relationships with God and others, it is easier to see how a client's short-term goals are linked to God's design.

Some clients are in open rebellion toward God, and destructive to themselves and others. Ephesians 4:18, "They are darkened in their understanding and separated from the life of God because of the ignorance that is in them due to the hardening of their hearts." Warnings and admonishment are more often the challenge for helpers in such cases. Second Corinthians 10:5 states it best: "We destroy arguments and every lofty opinion raised against the knowledge of God, and take every thought captive to obey Christ. . . . " believing that "I am a child of God, the evil one cannot touch me . . . " (1 John 5:18) for what the heart takes in also tends to become its master . . . "A characteristic of the heart and the center of man is its propensity to give itself to a master and to live toward some desired goal."[7]

### Seven Synthesizing Traits

Competent Christian counseling can also be described by its most salient traits. These seven synthesizing S traits are the features of this counseling model with which every learner should become most familiar.

*Scripturally anchored.* True Christian counseling is as dependent on Scripture as people are on food and water to live. The Scriptures are the food and water of spiritual life, and the resource to be constantly tapped in the practice of helping others grow to Christian maturity. As we cogently argued in the last chapter, reliance on the Bible must be based, not on a few proof texts, but on the entire revelation of God from Genesis to Revelation.

*Spiritual-forming.* As we highlighted in Chapter 2, Christian counseling at some level involves growth toward Christian maturity. Christian counselors are called to help form the Spirit of God into the lives of those who come for help. Whether such a goal is explicit and mutually agreed between counselor and client, or more covert, linked to a long-term strategy and prayer on behalf of the client, spiritual formation and growth in faith is central to this Christian counseling endeavor.

*Short-term (initially).* Modern Christian counseling, like all other counseling, is bending to the realities of the marketplace. It is transforming into a brief counseling modality, one in which the majority of cases are concluded in ten sessions or less. Acknowledging the marketplace is not merely a recognition of the influence of managed care on modern mental health practice. It reflects, primarily, the growing consumer reality that most clients also conclude counseling themselves in less than ten sessions. Most clients today do not want to be in counseling interminably; counseling, like everything else in our frenetic existence, must yield to the demands of busy, modern lives.

Therefore, we restate and emphasize here the two-phased model of counseling we introduced in *Competent Christian Counseling:* Brief therapy is mandatory for every client, with long-term therapy being a discretionary option for those who want and can afford it.[8]

*Solution-focused.* Brief therapy is necessarily focused on finding solutions—solutions that are often based (incorporating the next section) on targeting and building upon selected client strengths. It is not merely that there is not enough time to explore and reduce or scrub away the problems or pathological elements of a person's life. It is a recognition that, often, the most effective way of doing that is to seek strength-based solutions, concentrate on and grow them stronger, and let them constructively compete with and replace the problems that exist.[9]

*Strength-based skills.* Another essential aspect of brief Christian therapy is its strength-based approach to change. In its essence, a strength-based orientation de-focuses problems and pathology in order to highlight, to strengthen the best and most constructive things going on in a person's life.

Pragmatically, this means that much problem solving involves helping others focus on and do more of what they are already doing well and right. Since most Christian counselors practice cognitive-behavioral therapy, there is widespread recognition that change involves an educative/learning process that concentrates the acquisition and mastery of current and new skills.

*Storied narratives.* Years ago, the editors of *Futurist* magazine made the outlandish prediction that "Story-tellers will be the most valued workers of the 21st century." The further we travel into this very young new century, the more we believe this to be true. Narrative, in fact, is the way we live, the way we reveal ourselves and understand the story of our lives. We are story-tellers and story-sharers from the earliest times of our lives right through to the day of our death.

Narrative—and especially relationship narrative—is the way God tells us His story in the Bible. Yes there are wonderful books laid out in the form of precepts and propositions—Scripture covers all the ways that truth can be revealed—but it is primarily a book of stories. God is revealed as the Author and Finisher of our faith, the grand Narrator who is writing our lives into a beautiful story of faith, redemption, hope, and courage.[10]

*Scientific.* All Christian counseling is being called to an empirical accountability. We heartily support this and invite any and all aspects of this model to be applied and tested empirically. We want to encourage the 21st century development of BEST interventions—biblically-based, empirically-supported treatments. Again, we are not slavish to empiricism or a naturalistic worldview, as we actively invite supernatural intervention by God, hoping to observe, record, and then replicate these interventions in practice. But we are committed to empirically test and validate all our models of Christian intervention.

## The Process and Content of Christian Counseling

In our first volume we introduced a brief, solution-focused, two-phased model of eclectic therapy that fits the counseling process to the motivation and needs of the client. This model, in the first and mandatory phase of counseling, ordinarily accomplishes essential counseling goals in five to ten sessions. It is action-oriented, directed toward solutions that enhance spiritual maturity in Christ, and relies heavily on specific, task-related questions to assess client need and direct client behavior (see the last section of this chapter).

At the end of the short-term phase of brief therapy, clients should be able to report positive change in the direction of their goals and accomplishment in their lives, coupled with noticeable problem/symptom reduction.

The second phase of our model is longer-term and discretionary, oriented toward a deeper level of healing and characterological change. This is depth therapy that can run anywhere from ten to fifty or more sessions—running from a few months to a few years to accomplish stated goals. This therapy is discretionary in that both the costs and the time incurred by clients is substantial, and most if not all of these costs are borne by the client alone. Therefore, since managed care and insurance no longer pay for this kind of long-term care, consent to such care is an important discretionary choice by the client. The transition from one to the other comes about in a hundred different ways—even in the revelation of child abuse that will not be revealed until there has been a successful period of counseling on another issue.

## A Seven-step Process

The counseling relationship can take many forms depending on the counseling theory the counselor maintains, the presenting problem(s) of the client, and the unique style of the interpersonal relationship that counselor and client develop. Despite these differences, there is a series of stages in the process of counseling that are generally consistent across the spectrum of differing theories. The process of Christian counseling tracks through these seven interrelated and overlapping steps. Competent helpers should be able to locate themselves and their client at the proper stage along this road map, and to be able to define the necessary work to be done to move the process along to the next stage.

*Intake.* Remember that well-worn adage: "You never get a second chance to make a first impression." Since many people come into counseling with some anxiety and skepticism, first impressions by counselors and their staff are vitally important.

You want to do everything you can to reduce anxiety, inspire hope, and promote confidence in others who may be looking for any excuse to turn and run. It has long been accepted that the rapport between client and counselor is the most important part of the counseling process. Known as the "therapeutic alliance," relationship formation includes a commitment on the part of the client and counselor to participate in therapy, and a mutual perception that both can communicate effectively. These are critical to the construction of a bond of interpersonal trust, and that begins with the first contact.

*Assessment.* Counseling is much like medicine in that it involves an accurate assessment of the patient's problems, goals, and abilities and deficits that will impact the process of goal attainment. There are many different methods for assessment of a client's situation. These range from psychological testing, to neurological CAT-scans that show cross sections of the brain, to an in depth counseling interview. Some of the most basic questions a counselor can ask a client are:

1.   What do you want? What kind of changes are you hoping for?
2.   What are you doing to get what you want?
3.   Is it working? Or what's working and what's not? and
4.   If not, what do you have to think/do/maintain/relate differently to make it work?

*Gaining insight,* or improving support-building, explanation and understanding. Support-building combines both the intangible qualities of relational trust with the practical enrichment of professional and social support that is built around the client during therapy. The supportive aspects of an ever-increasing trust relationship allows the therapist to explain, to challenge, even to goad the client toward a deepening understanding of avoided pain and change-oriented risk-taking.

Though identifying the problem begins early on, understanding develops progressively throughout the counseling process until genuine insight into life—especially God's invisible interior life—is attained. For example, a woman in counseling is diagnosed with depression, and may begin to understand some causes of her depression. However, only after continued counseling does she understand the full root source of the problem. It should be noted—from a pastoral aspect—it is in this part of the counseling relationship that confession and repentance take place.

*Yielding to His healing touch.* Can counseling be truly Christian without an encounter with the living God? We think not. We believe that the essential experience in Christian counseling—and that which produces lasting, even eternal change—is a result of encountering God via the relationship between Christian counselor and client. Christian counselors, when functioning at their highest, are truly the healing regents of the living God, and are engaged in the triadic relationship we defined and described in Chapter 1. The Christian counselor, as an agent of supernatural change, guides the helpee into that otherwise scary zone of meeting and yielding to the Master of all healing. This reminds us of 1 Corinthians 4:1–2 where Paul writes, "So then, men ought to regard us as servants of Christ and as those entrusted with the secret things of God. Now it is required that those who have been given a trust must prove faithful."

*Active change (brief counseling for all).* Interventions that facilitate client change in thinking, decision making, and goal-directed behavior reach their peak during this phase of active change. This mandatory and, for most, only time in counseling requires skillful treatment planning and goal setting. Treatment planning involves pinpointing an end goal—the purpose of the counseling—and then developing a course of action for achieving said goal. A good treatment plan will be research based and present many small objectives on the course to an end goal.

Implementation is the effort to carry out the treatment plan. Here the counselor may assign specific tasks for the completion of small objectives in pursuit of the final treatment goal.

*Transformative change (long-term therapy for some).* The focused time spent in active change (brief therapy) will, for many clients, cascade into a longer period of transformative change. This will come about, essentially, in two ways. Some clients will elect to continue in long-term therapy, with a goal of effecting deep healing and core characterological change. Others will terminate counseling but will seek out a coach or pastor or spiritual guide to engage more fully the journey of spiritual formation and life transformation.

*Counseling as discipleship.* The final step of the model involves the very natural progression of counseling to discipleship. We recognize and strongly support the view of Christian counseling as a necessary and very effective form of intensive discipleship in the overall plan of God to bring the entire church to maturity and service. This is God's universal goal—and His constant work through the Christian counseling endeavor—to help us become more like Christ and to motivate us to give that same gift away to others.

## The Outline of Brief Christian Therapy

Since most clients terminate counseling within 8-to-10 sessions, and since managed care rarely authorizes more, we have developed a 10-session outline of Christian counseling that addresses both content and process issues a counselor will most commonly face. Bathing each session and the client in prayer, we begin with:

### 1. First Contact: First Impressions Always Count

- The first phone call: Take basic information and build rapport.
- Maintain calm in client crisis, while countering skepticism and promoting optimism.
- Convey to clients the likelihood of a successful outcome (to build confidence).
- Is the client presenting a problem I am competent to work with? Do I need to refer now?
- Schedule an appointment and pray to invite God to begin change now.

### FIRST SESSION

### 2. Trust Building and Beginning Assessment

- *Directed facilitation:* Striking the balance between relationship building and intentional interviewing to gain both rapport and necessary information about the client and his/her life.
- *Facilitating client storytelling and collecting client information.* Beginning a mental status exam and collecting data on personal history, family history, medical history (and medications), and psychosocial treatment history.
- *Assessing suicide and dangerousness, and religion and spirituality.*
- Is the client a danger to himself or others? Is the risk severe and immediate?
- Has the client reported the abuse of a child, the elderly, or a handicapped individual?
- Does the client find solace or pain in his/her religious faith?
- Is the client striving toward spiritual obedience and maturity?

- *Informed Consent:* Begin to tell the client about the treatment/ services you provide, and about the rights and limits of confidentiality

### 3. Life-enhancing Goal Setting (LeGS)

- *Understanding ultimate and immediate goals.* What is the Christ-centered end goal, and what are the smaller, client-stated objectives to be obtained along the way?—assess and link the two!
- *Facilitating client goal-setting:* Does the client claim ownership of the treatment goals and have they made a firm resolve to participate in treatment?
- *Using the miracle question:* Ask, "If you woke up tomorrow and everything was perfect, what would it look like?"
- *Fee-setting and service contracting*: Be very specific about your counseling rates, cancellation policy, time of payment due, warranties, and other financial matters.
  ACTION 1: SHOW the client the beginning way out by giving them a Simple Homework task that Overcomes the World—that begins to resolve the problem.

### SECOND SESSION

### 4. Comprehensive & Diagnostic History-taking

Using the BECHRISTLIKE Christ-centered Multimodal Assessment tool

**B**—*Behavior:* Focuses on observable behavior and assesses whether helpful or harmful. Defines key behavior patterns around problem issues. Assesses antecedents and consequences of behavior. Notes behavioral strengths and deficits.

**E**—*Emotions:* Assesses primary emotional disturbance and the emotional patterns. Describes desired feelings. How does client value emotions in relation to beliefs, thoughts, and behavior? How do emotional themes reveal relations with God?

**C**—*Cognition:* Assesses thought content and process. What are the lies and distortions that animate this client? Reasoning ability? Psychotic or delusional symptoms? Self-talk? Is client imagery helpful vs. traumatic? What is imagery content, intensity, and frequency?

**H**—*Health:* What is client's overall health status? Notes medical problems, and whether or not under a physician's care. Notes sensory/somatic complaints and psychosocial interactions, whether for better or for worse. Assesses sleeping, eating, and exercise habits and conditions. Is MD referral called for?

**R**—*Religion:* Where is the client in Christ? Saved or not? Maturing or not? Assesses church life and Christian practices. Conducts a biblical analysis of problem behavior. Assesses receptivity vs. resistance to spiritual interventions.

**I**—*Idols and false beliefs:* What desires and values compete with God, with God's priorities? What values line up biblically and need strengthening? How is problem related to value conflicts and discrepancies, biblically understood?

**S**—*Substances:* Assesses what drugs client is taking, both prescribed and/or illicit. What are drug interactions? Does client need MD referral for psychotropic meds? Does client need a program for detox and substance abuse treatment?

**T**—*Teachability:* Is client motivated or resistant, and is it global or specific, dependent on problem or other variables? Hope vs. hopelessness? Does client trust the counselor? Are there racial, ethnic, or gender differences that need to be bridged?

**L**—*Law/ethics:* Assesses whether client is a danger to self or others. Any current legal trouble? Any other red-flag issues that demand immediate attention? Does client need to be referred to a lawyer?

**I**—*Interpersonal relations:* Describes current issues and history with family and friends—rich web or deficient? Who is best and worst family member? Best and worst friend? Best and worst traits in father and mother? Describe spousal relations, satisfying and dissatisfying. Describe sexual behavior and problems.

**K**—*Knowledge:* Does client have sufficient knowledge/skill to change? Assesses skill strengths and deficits. Notes formal education and what, if anything, client does to improve knowledge. Considers resources for further learning, formal and informal.

**E**—*Environment:* What are the external obstacles and reaction triggers? What are strengths and resources available to client? What is client's locus of control—does s/he perceive they are controlled by events or free to influence them?

See our text on *Competent Christian Counseling,* for a more in depth discussion of this anagrammatic tool. Through interview or testing, obtain a diagnostic analysis of the client.

*Screening for psycho-social problems,* and for addictions and psychosis, and for medical/legal referral. Complete mental status exam with clear indications of any referrals and with a narrowing focus on the treatment goals that you will be working toward with your client.

ACTION 2: Review homework from week one and build on what was done well, or evaluate why nothing was completed and recalibrate homework task.

## THIRD SESSION

*5. Treatment Planning and Ongoing Prayer*

- *Making a DSM diagnosis:* Usually for the process of insurance reimbursement; include axes 1–4 even if *diagnosis is deferred.*
- *Translating goals and data into a plan:* A research-based treatment protocol should be used to treat the presenting problem.
- *Continual prayer for wisdom, discernment, guidance:* Do not overlook the healing touch and spirit of God by taking a fully cognitive approach to therapy.

ACTION 3: Review week two homework and continue to build on what was done well, generalizing this initial success to another, more central issue of concern.

## THIRD/FOURTH SESSION

*6. Working from the Therapeutic Frame*

- *Therapy rules that enhance client safety and motivation:* Instituting structure and boundaries in the counseling process is an important part of treatment.
- *Working toward goals that will likely succeed:* Do not set your clients up for failure by establishing unreasonable or grandiose goals (small steps in the right direction make more sense than big ones in the wrong).

- *Fostering attachment to God in Christ:* The goal of Christian counseling is not symptom relief but reestablishing the image of God in man, and maturity in Christ. Is your treatment promoting this objective?
- *As you think, so shall you act:* From the good treasure stored up in the client's heart—thus says Luke. Clients must experience internal sanctification if they are going to sustain a positive external change.

ACTION 4: Review last session homework, praising and reinforcing any success shown and pointing its effects across the bio-psycho-social-spiritual spectrum of the client's life. Move further in the generalization of successful to other, more difficult problems.

## FIFTH–TENTH SESSIONS

### 7. Working with Client Resistance and Dependency

- *Resistance is normal—use it, don't fight it.* When resistance occurs, use the opportunity to investigate what is keeping the client "stuck."
- *Client phone calls—emergencies or dependencies.* It is not uncommon for clients with attachment issues or borderline tendencies to call counselors under the ruse of a crisis, as a way to attempt to control or sabotage a counseling relationship. Counselors must handle these clients with boundaries, and also with compassion—for their intrusiveness is rooted in need and dependency.
- *Dealing with no-shows and late arrivals.* Payment for missed sessions omitted, counselors should communicate with clients their policy of starting counseling sessions late, and the issue of no-shows. Sometimes missed sessions are an action used by clients to regain control of a dynamic, or to avoid progress of the counseling endeavor.

ACTION 5: Review last session homework, praising and reinforcing any success shown and pointing out and strengthening its effects across the bio-psycho-social-spiritual spectrum of the client's life. Address any issues of entropy or resistance by talking and working through them.

*8. Working through Your Lapses and Frustrations*

- *Boredom and empathic lapses.* A good counselor can set aside his or her needs and be completely present for a client. This includes the counselor's needs for fun and emotional rest. Counseling is a draining process for all parties involved; counselors should prayerfully ask for strength to remain empathetic and involved amid a long day of sessions.

- *Managing frustration with clients.* Clients can frustrate counselors through their lies, deceit, and sin. Others will purposefully attempt to frustrate counselors, for doing so is part of their dysfunction. In addition, counselors are not immune to counter-transference issues, and react to client traits and behavior with annoyance and avoidance or denial.

- *Maintaining constructive work.* The counselor should A) assess if they are able to work with the frustrating type of client (i.e. some counselors will not work with men who abuse) and B) should work diligently to be supportive and therapeutic of frustrating clients they do agree to work with.

- *Using your anger wisely.* Anger is not a sin but a God-given response to a real or perceived injustice or wrong. Used wisely anger is gently assertive, and takes into account the needs of the client. Counselors should understand healthy and constructive expression of anger.

ACTION 6: Review last session homework, praising and reinforcing any success shown and pointing its effects across the bio-psycho-social-spiritual spectrum of the client's life. Address any issues of entropy or resistance by talking and working through them.

*9. Managing Ethical Tasks and Dilemmas*

- *Knowing when consent is withdrawn.* Consent is more than merely a formal legal construct—clients may withdraw it psychologically and show, by resistance maintained or refusing to return to therapy—that they have disengaged altogether.

- *Confidentiality and reporting duties.* Make sure you follow through with these demands in a timely fashion, giving your client notice of intended action.

- *When clients want to see their records.* Give them a summary statement of their records. If they want more, set a date to copy and give clients what they are due.
- *Dealing with sexual feelings in therapy.* Acknowledge them, pray about them, and DON'T ACT THEM OUT WITH YOUR CLIENT. If they persist, go find a trusted colleague of the same sex, and talk them through with honesty and wisdom.

ACTIONS 7/8/9: Review last session homework, same as before, praising and reinforcing any success shown and pointing its effects across the bio-psycho-social-spiritual spectrum of the client's life. Address any issues of entropy or resistance by talking and working through them. Continue to encourage and assist client along to goal acquisition.

LAST SESSION

*10. Terminating Treatment*

- *Don't abandon your clients.* When counselors can no longer provide service, they are ethically obligated to refer clients to another mental health service provider.
- *When the client simply drops out of counseling.* This is not uncommon, and preventing dropout is often outside the power of the counselor. Counselors should discuss a dropout policy with clients during the intake process that answers questions like "Are clients welcome to return if they drop out of counseling?"
- *When ending counseling is raised in-session.* Clients can have apprehension about ending counseling, even when the goals have been achieved. Counselors should reinforce their client's independence while also making themselves available in the instance of client need.
- *Once a client, always so?* Counselors maintain some ethical and legal responsibility long after the counseling relationship ends. For example, if a client commits violence against himself or others after termination, the counselor may be called into question. Also, romantic relationships and other dual roles are typically forbidden with past clients.

ACTION 10: Review the entire course of counseling, discussing what went well and what didn't. Discuss and secure client commitment to continue in working and maintaining change. Terminate with a clear invitation to return in the future if needed.

## Documentation

A final word must be said about note taking and documentation. This is a very important part of the counseling process that should begin with the first contact by a client (or prospective client) and continue until termination. Counselors are ethically responsible to maintain a client record for each person they counsel: including a diagnosis, treatment plan, progress notes, etc. Some counselors will make parts of the file available to clients, while others will provide an interpretation of the record upon a client's request. For pastoral counselors and lay helpers, a full record may not be necessary, though one should check with the practice laws in his/her state of residence.

**ENDNOTES**

1. Dan B. Allender, *The healing path: How the hurts in your past can lead you to a more abundant life* (Colorado Springs: Waterbrook, 1999), 19.

2. G. Corey, *Theory and practice of counseling and psychotherapy 6th.ed* (Pacific Grove, CA: Brooks/Cole, 2000); Albert Ellis, *The Albert Ellis reader: A guide to well-being using rational emotive behavior therapy* (NY: Citadel Press, 1998); L. L'Abate, Classification of counseling and therapy, theorists, method process, and goals: The E-R-A model, *The Personnel and Guidance Journal,* 59 (1981), 263–265.

3. D. Hutchins, and Cole, C., Helping relationships and strategies 2d ed. (Pacific Grove, CA: Brooks/Cole, 1992); D. Hutchins, Improving the counseling relationship, *The Personnel and Guidance Journal,* 62(10), (1984), 572–575.

4. D. Hutchins, Improving the counseling relationship, *The Personnel and Guidance Journal,* 62(10), (1984), 573.

5. Ibid.

6. Timothy Clinton, and Ohlschlager, G., *Competent Christian counseling, volume one: Foundations and practice of compassionate soul care* (Colorado Springs: WaterBrook, 2002), 101; James O. Prochaska, Norcross, J. and DiClemente, C., *Changing for good* (NY: Avon Books, 1994).

7. Neil Anderson, *Discipleship counseling* (Ventura, CA: Regal Books, 2003), quote by Robert Jewett.

8. Timothy Clinton, and Ohlschlager, G., *Competant Christian Counseling, Volume One: Foundations and Practice of Compassionate Soul Care* (Colorado Springs: Waterbrook, 2002).

9. Gary J. Oliver, Hasz, M., and Richburg, M., *Promoting Change Through Brief Therapy in Christian Counseling,* (Wheaton, IL: Tyndale House, 1997).

10. Dan B. Allender, *To be told* (Colorado Springs: WaterBrook Press, 2005).

# Christian Counseling Ethics:
# Honoring a Clear Moral Structure

*George Ohlschlager and Tim Clinton*

Counseling is often a moral, legal and emotional "minefield." Pastors and lay helpers should not attempt long-term, in-depth counseling and psychotherapy unless they are specifically trained to do so. The subtle but powerful moral conflicts and ego dynamics inherent to counseling have trapped many well-meaning pastors and their counselees in moral compromise and spiritual defeat...I recommend that pastors develop and honor a three-part policy of pastoral counseling and referral. (1) Set clear limits to the time, number of sessions, and kinds and depth of problems that you will work with, referring parishioners when these limits are reached...(2) Develop and train lay ministers for both one-to-one help and, especially, small support group ministry that can be a first source of referral...(3) Finally, refer the more difficult and long-term problems to ...professional Christian counselors.

*Pastor Amos Clemmons*[1]

As Christian counseling is drawn into greater intimacy with God and service to the church, not only are professional Christian counselors serving more frequently in church staff and consultative roles, but pastoral counseling and lay helping ministry is mushrooming. This is a wonderful development, and goes far toward fulfilling the promise of Christian counseling in the 21st century.[2]

However, there is increasing concern over the ethical-legal issues of Christian counseling from a number of power centers—the church and the law being the two most obvious. Calls to the AACC for consultation, mediation, and training about the ethical practice of Christian counseling has seen an exponential rise in recent years. We believe that if every pastor honored the framing ethic of pastoral counseling practice stated above by Pastor Clemmons, then the church's entire helping ministry would operate like a well-oiled machine.

Some look at ethical codes, state and nationally legislated counseling laws, and all the "legalese" present for the practice of counseling, and cringe! However, in truth such guidelines are designed just as much for the protection of the *counselor* as they are for the *client*. Anyone looking to function in the role of Christian counselor should be familiar with (at least) the major counseling ethical standards.

Also, ethical decision-making is mired in crisis and confusion in our values-relative and pluralistic world. The moral elasticity of our postmodern, post-Christian culture has even infected the church. Whether it is pulpit exaggeration, printed hyperbole, the abuse of conferred power, sexual misconduct, or other serious forms of client/parishioner exploitation, too many church leaders and counselors today are losing the battle of moral purity and ethical integrity. As a result, Christians are ridiculed, and the cause of Christ suffers.

Although we are witnessing an increasing frequency of lawsuits against counselors and clergy, we believe that the majority of these lawsuits are preventable. We noted in *Law for the Christian Counselor*[3] that most suits were a function of these problems:

1. Sexual involvement with a counselee—still the most frequent source of trouble, by far.
2. Counseling beyond your competence, ability, or training.
3. Advice against medical or psychological treatment, including medications.
4. The administration, interpretation, and scoring of personality and psychological tests.
5. Inadequate records or the improper care of records.
6. Inadequately trained and supervised lay and pastoral counselors.
7. The failure to give credence to violent intentions or statements.
8. Misdiagnosing psychotics (or others) as demon-possessed.
9. Misrepresenting one's title, position, degrees, or abilities.
10. Recommending for or against divorce.
11. Violations of confidentiality (in both clinical and church settings).
12. Denial of the existence or severity of a psychological or psychosomatic disorder.

13. The belief that all problems are spiritual or physical with denial of the psychological dimensions.

14. The belief that pastoral and lay counselors need only biblical training to solve such severe problems as neuroses, psychoses, suicide issues, and the like.

### Getting Oriented to Christian and Counseling Ethics

Webster defines "ethics" as the "study of standards of conduct and moral judgment," and the "system or code of moral conduct of a particular person, religion, group, profession, etc." Corey, Corey, and Callanan further distinguish ethics from values: "Although values and ethics are frequently used interchangeably, the two terms are not identical. Values pertain to beliefs and attitudes that provide direction to everyday living, whereas ethics pertain to the beliefs we hold about what constitutes right conduct. Ethics are moral principles adopted by an individual or group to provide rules for right conduct . . . "[4]

A code of ethics is a systematic statement of ethical standards that represent the moral convictions and guide the practice behavior of a group—in this case, the pastoral and lay counseling ministry of the church. Every one of the primary counseling disciplines—psychiatry, psychology, social work, marriage and family therapy, and professional counseling—has an ethics code. These codes are revised and updated every few years to stay current with emerging issues and to develop a refined sense of ethical clarity and direction. Christian counseling has developed ethical codes, including the *AACC Christian Counseling Code of Ethics* (Code), parts of which are detailed in the remainder of this chapter.[5]

Accountability is central to our consideration of what it means to be an ethical helper. Jesus practiced a divine accountability to His Heavenly Father at every step of His public ministry—and He asserted that, in similar fashion, His disciples were accountable to Him and His Father as well. "All those who love Me will do what I say. My Father will love them, and We will come to them and live with them. And remember, My words are not My own. This message is from the Father who sent Me." (John 14:23–24) The most powerful being in the universe was dedicated, not to His own agenda, but constantly yielded to He who sent Him. Imagine it. We are to do no less.

## Ferment over Ethical Foundations: Three Views

Ethical decision making in the modern world is now influenced by three major orientations:

1. *Divine revelation yielding moral absolutes.* For two millennia of church and Western history, most ethical systems have been rooted in Judeo-Christian values flowing out of God's revelation in the Scriptures. This view asserts that the infinite-personal God of the Bible has revealed the perfect law—a transcendent and universal order of right and wrong—and has given us grace through Jesus Christ to know and attain it.

God's moral absolutes are held to be universal, not culture or time-bound, but applicable across all space and time. With the Law of Moses, the ethics of Jesus Christ—revealed in their highest form in the Sermon on the Mount—are the basis of ethical, legal, political, and economic principles that have shaped the development of Western history and culture. Honoring these ethics promises to bring order, peace, prosperity, and dignity to the people and cultures that do so. Transgressing these ethics results in personal distress, interpersonal conflict, political and cultural decline and, if not halted and godly ethics restored, national anarchy and dissolution.

2. *Radical individualism yielding moral relativism.* The ethical history of the 20th century reveals the incremental and systematic rejection of divine authority and the rise of secular humanism. Individual autonomy is supreme in this worldview and moral relativism—"do your own thing, just don't hurt me doing it"—is the result. The root value of this perspective is that "man is the measure of all things" including his or her own judgment about right and wrong. Also known as subjectivism, or "situational ethics" as an applied practice, this view yields an extreme form of moral relativism—"I will decide for myself what is right and wrong; whatever is right for you may not be so for me."

Proponents of this view consider personal freedom to be the ultimate value and autonomous living the grand pursuit. Hence the value of individualism is radicalized—placed above and over all other values—and any recourse to social convention or moral absolutes is denied. Laws, custom, and social convention is held to be a constraining, even oppressive force that only serves to unjustly inhibit personal freedom.[6] Politically, anarchy is the result of this view when pushed to its systemic conclusion.

3. *Social constructionism yielding moral consensus.* A third model gaining

current force is influenced by family and social systems theory as well as our democratic political tradition. The social constructionist view posits that ethics are forged in the interactive consensus-building process of people and systems in relationship. By negotiation, mediation, and arbitration, derived ethics reflect a group or social consensus whereby the best values as agreed upon by the participants in the process are expressed as ethics and codified into law.

Moral absolutes are not controlling in this approach, but may be reflected in the consensus values and ethics that are reached by majority rule. Biblical values may or may not survive this process of ethical and legal decision-making. The group or the "body politic"—whatever its size and function—is the creator of the moral consensus, and the final arbiter of right and wrong. This view seems to be ascendant among those who recognize the social and political risks of a purely subjective and individualized ethic, but do not want to adhere to the revealed ethics flowing from God's revelation.

## 1. Above All, Do No Harm

The first rule of ethics in any profession—especially the counseling professions—that serves human need is: do no harm. At first blush this may seem absurdly obvious and simple. On reading and reflection the depth and importance of this rule comes to light. Consider both our general statement and one of its applications—euthanasia and assisted suicide:

> 1–100 Christian counselors acknowledge that the first rule of professional-ministerial ethical conduct is: do no harm to those served.
> 1–101 Affirming the God-given Dignity of All Persons
> Affirmatively, Christian counselors recognize and uphold the inherent, God-given dignity of every human person, from the pre-born to those on death's bed. Human beings are God's creation—the crown of His creation—and are therefore due all the rights and respect that this fact of creation entails. Therefore, regardless of how we respond to and challenge harmful attitudes and actions, Christian counselors will express a loving care to any client, service-inquiring person, or anyone encountered in the course of practice or ministry, without regard to race, ethnicity, gender, sexual behavior or orientation, socio-economic status,

education, denomination, belief system, values, or political affiliation. God's love is unconditional and, at this level of concern, so must that of the Christian counselor.

1–120 Refusal to Participate in the Harmful Actions of Clients

Christian counselors refuse to participate in, condone, advocate for, or assist the harmful actions of clients, especially those that imperil human life from conception to death. This includes suicidal, homicidal, or assaultive/abusive harm done to self or others—the protection of human life is always a priority value. We will not abandon clients who do or intend harm, will terminate helping relations only in the most compelling circumstances, and will continue to serve clients in these troubles as far as it is possible.

1–122 Application to Euthanasia and Assisted Suicide

Christian counselors refuse to participate in, condone, advocate for, or assist clients in active forms of euthanasia and assisted suicide. We may agree to and support the wish not to prolong life by artificial means, and will often advocate for hospice care, more effective application of medicine, and other reasonable means to reduce pain and suffering.

Regarding patients or clients who wish to die, we will not deliver, nor advocate for, nor support the use of drugs or devices to be utilized for the purpose of ending a patient's life. We recognize that the death of a patient may occur as the unintended and secondary result of aggressive action to alleviate a terminally ill patient's extreme pain and suffering. So long as there are no other reasonable methods to alleviate such pain and suffering, the Christian counselor is free to support, advocate for, and participate in such aggressive pain management in accordance with sound medical practice, and with the informed consent of the patient or patient's representative.

For physicians the call to "do no harm" may translate into doing nothing medically, or always considering the least intrusive action first. Christian counseling ethics also presumes this all-encompassing first rule: that to help someone, we must first ensure that we do not harm them. This is not as easy or as obvious as it seems. Understanding that harm is possible in any kind of human intervention yields an ethic enlightened and humbled by the fact that even though saved by Christ and sanctified by the Spirit, humans remain susceptible to sin and wrongdoing (and do frequently sin on a regular basis).

Research indicates that negative outcomes affect a stubborn minority of all counseling cases, and hurtful yet unintended consequences are unyielding phenomena of human interaction. We give children the grace to continually say, "But I didn't mean to hurt them." As adults, we are usually allowed only one or two such excuses before we are barred from doing the thing we hope will be helpful, not harmful.

## 2. Supervision and Training in the Church

We state in the preface to this section to Christian counseling leaders that "Some Christian counselors serve in senior professional roles—as administrators, supervisors, teachers, consultants, researchers, and writers. They are recognized for their counseling expertise, their dedication to Christ and the ministry or profession to which they belong, and for their exemplary ethics. These leaders are responsible for the development and maturation of the Christian counseling profession, for serving as active and ethical role models, and for raising up the next generation of Christian counselors and leaders."

We are opposed to all forms of "lone ranger" ministry, and do not advocate for or distribute our lay helper training programs without a commitment to pastoral oversight and supervision in the church. Pastors and counseling professionals in the church should be involved in every step of the selection, training, and supervision of lay helpers and church counseling staff.

2–110 Ethics and Excellence in Supervision and Teaching
Christian counseling supervisors and educators maintain the highest levels of clinical knowledge, professional skill, and ethical excellence in all supervision and teaching. They are knowledgeable about the latest professional and ministerial developments and responsibly transmit this knowledge to students and supervisees.

2–111 Preparation for Teaching and Supervision
Christian counseling supervisors and educators have received adequate training and experience in teaching and supervision methods before they deliver these services. Supervisors and educators are encouraged to maintain and enhance their skills through continued clinical practice, advanced training, and continuing education.

2–120 Supervisors and Educators Do Not Exploit Students and Trainees

Christian counseling supervisors and educators avoid exploitation, appearances of exploitation, and harmful dual relations with students and trainees. Students and trainees are taught by example and by explanation, with the mentor responsible to define and maintain clear, proper, and ethical professional and social boundaries.

## 3. Competent Counseling: Doing Well at Consultation and Referral

Being a competent Christian counselor means that one is highly aware of and honors the limits of his/her counseling knowledge and skill. Lay helpers must embrace this rule with enthusiasm, and most pastors do so out of necessity due to the myriad demands of pastoral life. Here is an excerpt of this ethical rule.

210 Honoring the Call to Competent Christian Counseling

Christian counselors maintain the highest standards of competence with integrity. We know and respect the boundaries of competence in ourselves and others, especially those under our supervision. We make only truthful, realistic statements about our identity, education, experience, credentials, and about counseling goals and process, avoiding exaggerated and sensational claims. We do not offer services or work beyond the limits of our competence and do not aid or abet the work of Christian counseling by untrained, unqualified, or unethical helpers.

1–220 Duties to Consult and/or Refer

Christian counselors consult with and/or refer to more competent colleagues or supervisors when these limits of counseling competence are reached: (1) when facing issues not dealt with before or not experienced in handling, (2) when clients need further help outside the scope of our training and practice, (3) when either counselor or clients are feeling stuck or confused about counseling and neither is clear what to do about it, or (4) when counselees are deteriorating or making no realistic gain over a number of sessions. Christian counselors shall honor the client's goals and confidential privacy interests in all consultations and referrals.

1–221 Consultation Practice

When counseling help is needed, and with client consent, consultation may be attempted first, when in the client's best interest and to improve helper's knowledge and skill where some competence exists. Counselors shall take all reasonable action to apply consultative help to the case in order to gain/maintain ground toward client objectives. The consultant shall maintain a balanced concern for the client discussed and the practice/education needs of the consultee, directing the counselor-consultee to further training or special resources, if needed.

1–222 Referral Practice

Referral shall be made in situations where client need is beyond the counselor's ability or scope of practice or when consultation is inappropriate, unavailable, or unsuccessful. Referrals should be done only after the client is provided with informed choices among referral sources. As much as possible, counselors referred to shall honor prior commitments between client and referring counselor or church.

1–223 Seek Christian Help, If Available

When consulting or referring, Christian counselors seek out the best Christian help at a higher level of knowledge, skill, and expertise. If Christian help is not available, or when professional skill is more important than the professional's beliefs, Christian counselors shall use the entire network of professional services available.

1–224 Avoid Counsel Against Professional Treatment

Christian counselors do not counsel or advise against professional counseling, medical or psychiatric treatment, the use of medications, legal counsel, or other forms of professional service merely because we believe such practice is per se wrong or because the provider may not be a Christian.

Dr. Gary Collins,[7] one of the pioneers of our field who trained and mentored us both, advocates that, "Sometimes we help counselees most by referring them to someone else whose training, expertise and availability can be of special assistance ... referral can reflect the counselor's concern for the counselee, and can show that no one person is skilled enough to counsel everyone."[8] The counselor has the moral, ethical and professional responsibility to admit to herself, and to her client, when the relationship fails, or the client's situation exceeds her ability to help.

It is not always the counselor's lack of expertise that is the determining factor for a referral. Therapeutic relationships can fail when:

1. Counselor and client have incompatible personalities
2. Transference or counter-transference issues occur that cannot be resolved (such as sexual attraction)
3. When there is incongruity between counselor's and client's beliefs or values
4. When the counselor is unable to break through a client's resistance to change
5. Dual roles manifest (such as a client becoming a college student of the counselor)

Lastly, the responsibility to refer implies counselors be familiar with all resources and persons available for referral.

## 4. Informed Consent for Church-based Counseling

The need for informed consent increases as intervention increases or as a specialized kind of counseling method takes place (i.e a brief meeting vs. biofeedback therapy). Pastoral and lay helpers should use a simple one-page agreement that covers some of the issues (in 1–320 below) and indicates that the clients understand they are engaged in pastoral or lay helping, not professional counseling.

1–310 Securing Informed Consent

Christian counselors secure client consent for all counseling and related services. This includes the video/audio-taping of client sessions, the use of supervisory and consultative help, the application of special procedures and evaluations, and the communication of client data with other professionals and institutions.

Christian counselors take care that (1) the client has the capacity to give consent; (2) we have discussed counseling together and the client reasonably understands the nature and process of counseling; the costs, time, and work required; the limits of counseling; and any appropriate alternatives; and (3) the client freely gives consent to counseling, without coercion or undue influence.

1–320 Consent for the Structure and Process of Counseling

Christian counselors respect the need for informed consent regarding the structure and process of counseling. Early in counseling, counselor and client should discuss and agree upon these issues: the nature of and course of therapy; client issues and goals; potential problems and reasonable alternatives to counseling; counselor status and credentials; confidentiality and its limits; fees and financial procedures; limitations about time and access to the counselor, including directions in emergency situations; and procedures for resolution of disputes and misunderstandings. If the counselor is supervised, that fact shall be disclosed and the supervisor's name and role indicated to the client.

1–321 Consent from Parent or Client Representative

Christian counselors obtain consent from parents or the client's legally authorized representative when clients are minors or adults who are legally incapable of giving consent.

1–330 Consent for Biblical-Spiritual Practices in Counseling

Christian counselors do not presume that all clients want or will be receptive to explicit spiritual interventions in counseling. We obtain consent that honors client choice, receptivity to these practices, and the timing and manner in which these things are introduced: prayer for and with clients, Bible reading and reference, spiritual meditation, the use of biblical and religious imagery, assistance with spiritual formation and discipline, and other common spiritual practices.

1–331 Special Consent for More Difficult Interventions

Close or special consent is obtained for more difficult and controversial practices. These include, but are not limited to: deliverance and spiritual warfare activities; cult de-programming work; recovering memories and treatment of past abuse or trauma; use of hypnosis and any kind of induction of altered states; authorizing (by MDs) medications, electroconvulsive therapy, or patient restraints; use of aversive, involuntary, or experimental therapies; engaging in reparative therapy with homosexual persons; and counseling around abortion and end-of-life issues. These interventions require a more detailed discussion with patient-clients or client representatives of the procedures, risks, and treatment alternatives, and we secure detailed written agreement for the procedure.

## 5. Multiple Clients: Working with Groups, Couples, and Families

Most pastors work with couples and families, and church-based counselors lead all kinds of groups—counseling groups, Bible study groups, growth groups, spiritual formation groups, 12-step and recovery groups, supervision groups, and education groups of all sorts. Here are our ethical guidelines for group work.

1–540 Working with Couples, Families, and Groups

Christian counselors often work with multiple persons in session—marriage couples, families or parts of families, and small groups—and should know when these forms of counseling are preferred over or used as an adjunct to individual counseling. In these relationships we will identify a primary client—the group as a unit or the individual members—and will discuss with our client(s) how our differing roles, counseling goals, and confidentiality and consent issues are affected by these dynamics.

1–541 Safety and Integrity in Family and Group Counseling

Christian counselors will maintain their role as fair, unbiased, and effective helpers in all marital, family, and group work. We will remain accessible to all persons, avoiding enmeshed alliances and taking sides unjustly. As group or family counseling leaders, Christian counselors respect the boundary between constructive confrontation and verbal abuse, and will take reasonable precautions to protect client members from any physical, psychological, or verbal abuse from other members of a family or group.

## 6. Confidentiality and Its Exceptions

Since confidentiality reaches the very core of the maintenance of trust in helping relationships, we recommend that pastors and lay helpers take it as seriously as do professional therapists. Here are the primary rules that govern modern-day confidentiality and privilege.

1–410 Maintaining Client Confidentiality

Christian counselors maintain client confidentiality to the fullest extent allowed by law, professional ethics, and church or organizational rules. Confidential client communications include all verbal, written, telephonic, audio or video-taped, or electronic communications arising within the helping relationship. Apart from the exceptions below, Christian counselors shall not disclose confidential client communications without first discussing the intended disclosure and securing written consent from the client or client representative.

1–411 Discussing the Limits of Confidentiality and Privilege

Clients should be informed about both the counselor's commitment to confidentiality and its limits before engaging in counseling. Christian counselors avoid stating or implying that confidentiality is guaranteed or absolute. We will discuss the limits of confidentiality and privacy with clients at the outset of counseling.

1–420 Asserting Confidentiality or Privilege Following Demands for Disclosure

Protecting confidential communications, including the assertion of privilege in the face of legal or court demands, shall be the first response of counselors to demands or requests for client communications and records.

1–421 Disclosure of Confidential Client Communications

Christian counselors disclose only that client information they have written permission from the client to disclose or that which is required by legal or ethical mandates. The counselor shall maintain confidentiality of client information outside the bounds of that narrowly required to fulfill the disclosure and shall limit disclosures only to those people having a direct professional interest in the case. In the face of a subpoena, counselors shall neither deny nor immediately comply with disclosure demands, but will assert privilege in order to give the client time to consult with a lawyer to direct disclosures.

1–430 Protecting Persons from Deadly Harm: The Rule of Mandatory Disclosure

Christian counselors accept the limits of confidentiality when human life is imperiled or abused. We will take appropriate action, including necessary disclosures of confidential information, to protect life in the face of client threats of suicide, homicide, and/or the abuse of children, elders, and dependent persons.

1–431 The Duty to Protect Others

The duty to take protective action is triggered when the counselor (1) has reasonable suspicion, as stated in your state statute, that a minor child (under 18 years), elder person (65 years and older), or dependent adult (regardless of age) has been harmed by the client; or (2) has direct client admissions of serious and imminent suicidal threats; or (3) has direct client admissions of harmful acts or threatened action that is serious, imminent, and attainable against a clearly identified third person or group of persons.

1–432 Guidelines to Ethical Disclosure and Protective Action

Action to protect life, whether your client or a third-person, shall be that which is reasonably necessary to stop or forestall deadly or harmful action in the present situation. This could involve hospitalizing the client, intensifying clinical intervention to the degree necessary to reasonably protect against harmful action, consultation and referral with other professionals, or disclosure of harm or threats to law enforcement, protective services, identifiable third-persons, and/or family members able to help with protective action.

1–433 Special Guidelines When Violence Is Threatened Against Others

Action to protect third-persons from client violence may involve or, in states that have a third-person protection (Tarasoff) duty, require disclosure of imminent harm to the intended victim, to their family or close friends, and to law enforcement. When child abuse or elder abuse or abuse of dependent adults exists, as defined by state law, Christian counselors shall report to child or elder protective services, or to any designated agency established for protective services. We shall also attempt to defuse the situation and/or take preventive action by whatever means are available and appropriate.

When clients threaten serious and imminent homicide or violence against an identifiable third-person, the Christian counselor shall inform appropriate law enforcement, and/or medical-crisis personnel, and the at-risk person or close family member of the threat, except when precluded by compelling circumstances or by state law.

When the client threat is serious but not imminent, the Christian counselor shall take preventive clinical action that seeks to forestall any further escalation of threat toward violent behavior.

1–470 Advocacy for Privacy Rights Against Intrusive Powers

Christian counselors hear the most private and sensitive details of their clients' lives—information that must be zealously guarded from public disclosure. Rapidly expanding and interlocking electronic information networks are increasingly threatening client privacy rights. Though federal and state laws exist to protect client privacy, these laws are weak, are routinely violated at many levels, and the record of privacy right enforcement is dismal. Accordingly, Christian counselors are called to wisely protect and assertively advocate for privacy protection on behalf of our clients against the pervasive intrusion of personal, corporate, governmental, even religious powers.

Clients rightly expect that whatever they reveal to the counselor will be kept confidential. But competent counselors must be aware of limitations, and they have a responsibility to advise clients of these up-front. As you can see, we have incorporated Tarasoff principles into our ethics code—referring to the now-famous California Supreme Court decision establishing the duty to warn others if a client threatens homicide. We did so because the policy behind Tarasoff—that human life is more important than confidentiality—is good biblical ethics and law.

In addition, counselors will need to familiarize themselves with: (1) individual state laws concerning responsibilities related to suicide, child and elder abuse, abuse of the handicapped, and threats of violence; (2) available resources in their areas for emergency action regarding suicidal and homicidal clients; (3) who to contact regarding child and elder abuse reports; and (4) information regarding AIDS reporting and limits, which is increasingly regulated by state statutes that affect all health care professionals.

## 7. Dual and Multiple Relations in Church-based Counseling

No area of ethical development has given us more trouble. Defining the principle and the boundaries of dual relations is highly dependent on the application of the rule—whether in a church or in a professional clinical setting. The ethical guidelines concerning this are as follows.

1–140 Dual and Multiple Relationships
Dual relationships involve the breakdown of proper professional or ministerial boundaries. A dual relationship is where two or more roles are mixed in a manner that can harm the counseling relationship. Examples include counseling plus personal, fraternal, business, financial, or sexual and romantic relations.

Some dual relationships are not unethical—it is client exploitation that is wrong, not the dual relationship itself. Based on an absolute application that harms membership bonds in the body of Christ, we oppose the ethical-legal view that all dual relationships are per se harmful and therefore invalid on their face. Many dual relations are wrong and indefensible, but some dual relationships are worthwhile and defensible (per 1–142 below).

1–141 The Rule of Dual Relationships

While in therapy, or when counseling relations are imminent, or for an appropriate time after termination of counseling, Christian counselors do not engage in dual relations with counselees. Some dual relationships are always avoided—sexual or romantic relations, and counseling close friends, family members, employees, or supervisees. Other dual relationships should be presumed troublesome and avoided wherever possible.

1–142 Proving an Exception to the Rule

The Christian counselor has the burden of proving a justified dual relationship by showing (1) informed consent, including discussion of how the counseling relationship might be harmed as other relations proceed, and (2) lack of harm or exploitation to the client. As a general rule, all close relations are unethical if they become counselor-client or formal lay helping relations. Dual relations may be allowable, requiring justification by the foregoing rule, if the client is an arms-length acquaintance—if the relationship is not a close one. This distinction is crucial in the applications below.

1–143 Counseling with Family, Friends, and Acquaintances

Christian counselors do not provide counseling to close family or friends. We presume that dual relations with other family members, acquaintances, and fraternal, club, association, or group members are potentially troublesome and best avoided, otherwise requiring justification.

1–144 Business and Economic Relations

Christian counselors avoid partnerships, employment relations, and close business associations with clients. Barter relations are normally avoided as potentially troublesome, and require justification; therefore if done, barter is a rare and not a common occurrence. Unless justified by compelling necessity, customer relations with clients are normally avoided.

1–145 Counseling with Fellow Church Members

Christian counselors do not provide counseling to fellow church members with whom they have close personal, business, or shared ministry relations. We presume that dual relations with any other church members who are clients are potentially troublesome and best avoided, otherwise requiring justification. Pastors and church staff helpers will take all reasonable precautions to limit the adverse impact of any dual relationships.

1–146 Termination to Engage in Dual Relations Prohibited

Christian counselors do not terminate counseling to engage in dual relationships of any kind. Some counselors and their former clients will agree that any future counseling will be done by someone else if, after legitimate termination, they decide to pursue another form of relationship.

## 8. Sexual Misconduct: Getting Under Control or Going Underground?

Nothing is more harmful to clients than to be exploited sexually by a therapist that one has hired to help with the most private secrets and sensitive life issues. It is a betrayal like no other in counseling and is being criminalized by a growing number of states as a grave and serious offence.[9]

1–130 Sexual Misconduct Forbidden

All forms of sexual misconduct in pastoral, professional, or lay relationships are unethical. This includes every kind of sexual exploitation, deception, manipulation, abuse, harassment, relations where the sexual involvement is invited, and relations where informed consent presumably exists. Due to the inherent power imbalance of helping relationships and the immoral nature of sexual behavior outside of marriage, such apparent consent is illusory and illegitimate.

Forbidden sexual activities and deceptions include, but are not limited to, direct sexual touch or contact; seductive sexual speech or nonverbal behavior; solicitation of sexual or romantic relations; erotic contact or behavior as a response to the sexual invitation or seductive behavior of clients; unnecessary questioning and/or excessive probing into the client's sexual history and practices; inappropriate counselor disclosures of client attractiveness, sexual opinions, or sexual humor; advocacy of the healing value of counselor-client sexual relations; secretive sexual communications and anonymous virtual interaction via the Internet or other electronic and informational means; sexual harassment by comments, touch, or promises/threats of special action; and sexual misconduct as defined by all applicable laws, ethics, and church, organizational, or practice policies.

1–131 Sexual Relations with Former Clients Forbidden

All sexual relations as defined in 1–130 above with former clients are unethical. Furthermore, we do not terminate and refer clients or parishioners, even at first contact, in order to pursue sexual or romantic relations.

1–132 Counseling with Marital/Sexual Partners

Christian counselors do not counsel, but make appropriate referral, with current or former sexual and/or marital partners.

1–133 Marriage with Former Clients/Patients

Since marriage is honorable before God, the lone exception to this rule is marriage to a former client, so long as (1) counseling relations were properly terminated, and not for the purpose of pursuing marriage or romantic relations, (2) the client is fully informed that any further counseling must be done by another, (3) there is no harm or exploitation of the client or the client's family as a result of different relations with the counselor, and (4) the marriage takes place two years or more after the conclusion of a counseling or helping relationship.

### 9. Ending Counseling: Termination, Abandonment, and Inept Care

Ending counseling is as important as beginning it—doing it well means clients leave with hope and encouragement that they can carry on the change they have experienced. Consequently, poor termination has become a troublesome ethical issue.

1–560 Continuity of Care and Service Interruption

Christian counselors maintain continuity of care for all patients and clients. We avoid interruptions in service to clients that are too lengthy or disruptive. Care is taken to refer clients and network to provide emergency services when faced with counselor vacations, illnesses, job changes, financial hardships, or any other reason services are interrupted or limited.

1–570 Avoiding Abandonment and Improper Counseling Termination

Christian counselors do not abandon clients. To the extent the counselor is able, client services are never abruptly cut-off or ended without giving notice and adequately preparing the client for termination or referral.

1–571 Ethical Termination of Counseling

Discussion and action toward counseling termination and/or referral is indicated when (1) counseling goals have been achieved; (2) when the client no longer wants or does not return to counseling; (3) when the client is no longer benefiting from counseling; or (4) when counseling is harmful to the client. Christian counselors shall discuss termination and/or referral with clients, offer referral if wanted or appropriate, and facilitate termination in the client's best interest. If crisis events alter, even end counseling prematurely the counselor, if it is safe and proper, should follow-through with the client to ensure proper termination and referral.

It is time to consider termination when clients (1) have achieved their therapeutic goals; (2) appear stable emotionally, psychologically and spiritually; (3) maintain behavioral changes or goals for a reasonable amount of time; (4) possess a new perspective of their world as a whole; (5) appear to have taken control of their lives; (6) personal relationships have improved; and (7) tell you they believe it is time to go.

Termination should be a gradual process when possible, and often is not absolutely final. Some clients return off and on for years; some for a periodic "check up." Others soar to new emotional, psychological and spiritual heights and never return. Kottler asserts, "There is nothing like that feeling of elation we sometimes experience when we know beyond a shadow of a doubt that our efforts have helped redeem a human life."[10]

## 10. Values Conflicts with Parishioners and Clients

We show in this book a variety of ways that counseling is a values-laden experience, one that we believe requires that the values of every counselor be made known, if possible, at the start of counseling.

1–550 Working with Persons of Different Faiths, Religions, and Values

Christian counselors do not withhold services to anyone of a different faith, religion, denomination, or value system. We work to understand the client's belief system and always maintain respect for the client. We strive to understand when faith and values issues are important to the client and foster values-informed client decision-making in counseling. We share our own faith only as a function of legitimate self-disclosure and when appropriate to client need, always maintaining a humility that exposes and never imposes the way of Christ.

1–551 Action If Value Differences Interfere with Counseling

Christian counselors work to resolve problems—always in the client's best interest—when differences between counselor and client values become too great, adversely affecting counseling. This may include discussion of the issue as a therapeutic matter, renegotiation of the counseling agreement, consultation with a supervisor or trusted colleague or, as a last resort, referral to another counselor if the differences cannot be reduced or bridged.

We recognize a continuum of Christian counselors who emphasize varying degrees of Christian practices in counseling. At one pole is the helper who plans and practices every session as a discipling experience—praying overtly with clients in every session, referencing Scripture, encouraging yieldedness to Christ, exhorting confession and forgiveness, and reinforcing any movement toward Christian growth.

At the other pole is the helper who, although confessing Christ, believes that inclusion of Christ in therapy is an unjust imposition of religious values, one that violates client self-determination. Although some may engage in Christian practices with Christian clients who ask for it—especially prayer—these brothers and sisters emphasize a psychological practice where evangelism and overt forms of spiritual exhortation and advocacy of Christ are not done.

While our bias is clearly toward Christian counseling that incorporates spiritual disciplines, we take an inclusionary approach and see all believers as welcome within Christian counseling's "big tent." We suggest that excellence and positive outcome is better correlated with an active inclusion of Christ and Christian principles, but one that respects the working environments and the limits, capabilities, learning styles, and the readiness of clients. What good is forcing a message upon deaf ears? Then again, what good is mere psychological adaptation if one adapts better to evil ways? Both polar extremes are too doctrinaire, putting ideology, absolute ethics, and rigid theology above people. Nonetheless, we recognize all practitioners who name the name of Christ as citizens of God's kingdom and want to encourage them as brothers and sisters in the Christian counseling fold.

## Moving from Law to Love: Helping Others Be Like Christ

In their 1998 volume, Corey, Corey, and Callanan discuss two basic kinds of ethics in counseling—what they call principle ethics and virtue ethics. Principle ethics are specific and applied; virtue ethics are global and aspirational. Therefore, a respect for client privacy is a virtue ethic; when and how to responsibly breach confidentiality is a principle ethic. I (George) followed this distinction—one that is rooted first in the Scriptures—in an article that revealed the zone of ethical behavior between conforming ethics and transforming ethics.[11] Essentially, it is a study on the differences and relationship between law and love.

Conforming (or principle) ethics are the baseline standards, the floor below which no one should fall in their practice with others. Transforming ethics are the ethical ideals reflected in the law of love that Christ Himself showed toward us by willingly going to a cross to die on our behalf. These are the perfect virtue ethics toward which all Christian counselors should strive.

Remember that when a counselor is dedicated to fully revealing the love of Christ—against this kind of love there is no law. In this love, there is no harm to another. Because of this love, people's lives are transformed into something beautiful and holy. This is the love of Jesus, and the Holy Spirit just loves to pour it out to those who seek it. The relationship between the two kinds of ethics is suggested in the Christian Counselor's golden rule expressed below.

## The Christian Counselor's Golden Rule

This Christian counselor's application of the Golden Rule is adapted from Romans 13:8–10. It expresses the cardinal values and core rules of Christian counseling ethics.

Christian counselor, hear this:

Do not be indebted to any client or parishioner, except the debt to love them.

For if you love your clients, you honor all your professional and ministerial duties.

You know the rules of counseling and pastoral care:

Do not engage in any form of sexual misconduct with your clients, whether current or past.

Do not, as far as is possible with you, let them kill or harm themselves or anyone else.

Do not steal your clients' money or disregard your time with them.

Do not harm, or envy, or look down on, or manipulate, or fight with, or in any way exploit those Christ has sent to you for help.

In fact, to sum it up and state it conclusively:

Practice the Golden Rule with all wisdom and grace.

Love your clients as yourself.

Don't do anything to your clients or those they love that you wouldn't want done to yourself.

For love does no wrong to any client.

Therefore, to love your clients as Christ loves you is to fulfill all your obligations—all your moral-ethical-legal duties—as a Christian counselor.

## ENDNOTES

1.    Amos Clemmons, The pastor and the institute, *Parakaleo* (Eureka, CA: The Redwood Family Institute, 3, 1991), 1–2.

2.    Tim Clinton and Ohlschlager, G., *Competent Christian counseling: Practicing and pursuing compassionate soul care* (Colorado Springs: WaterBrook Press, 2002).

3.    George Ohlschlager and Mosgofian, P., *Law for the Christian counselor: A guidebook for clinicians and pastors* (Dallas: Word, 1992) and adapted from Thomas Needham, Helping when the risks are great, in *Clergy malpractice*, 89–90.

4.    G. Corey, Corey, M., and Callanan, P., *Issues and ethics in the helping professions* 5th ed. (Pacific Grove, CA: Brooks/Cole, 1998).

5.    American Association of Christian Counselors, *AACC Christian counseling code of ethics* (Forest, VA: AACC, 2001).

6.    See *Lawrence v. Texas*, 2003, on the establishment of the right to homosexual sodomy via the elevation of the Autonomous Self, for an extreme example of this ethic being anchored into American law by the U.S. Supreme Court.

7.    Gary R. Collins is another pioneer who taught and mentored us both.

8.    Gary R. Collins, *Christian counseling: A comprehensive guide*, rev. ed.(Nashville: W Publishing Group, 1988), 54.

9.    Glenn Gabbard, *Sexual exploitation in professional relationships* (Washington: American Psychiatric Association, 1989); George Ohlschlager, and Mosgofian, P., *Law for the Christian counselor*; Kenneth Pope, Sonne, J., and Holroyd, J., *Sexual feelings in psychotherapy* (Washington: American Psychological Association, 1993).

10.    Jeffrey Kottler, *On being a therapist* rev. ed. (San Francisco: Jossey-Bass, 1993), 46.

11.    George Ohlschlager, Avoiding ethical-legal pitfalls: embracing conformative behavior and transformative virtues, *Christian Counseling Today*, 7(3), (1999), 40–43.

Part 2

# Counseling for Personal and Emotional Issues

# 6

# Helping People Forgive:
# Getting to the Heart of the Matter

*Everett L. Worthington Jr.*

Be kind one to another, tender-hearted, forgiving one another, as God in
Christ has forgiven you.

Ephesians 4:32 (ESV)

We can forgive because we have been forgiven.

At age 8, little girls are *not* supposed to be raped or molested by their
fathers. It is one of the most horrific experiences imaginable. We hear an
adult molested as a child affirm, "I can't forgive him!" She clenches her
fists, looks you square in the face, and asserts with certitude, "I *won't* do it."
More often than not, we find ourselves automatically shaking our heads in
agreement. For how can anyone forgive—and then be reconciled—to a sex
offender who was supposed to be the child's primary defender in life? The
thought is reprehensible, beyond the pale. Yet forgiveness is the centerpiece
of Christianity—and of effective Christian counseling.[1]

We are impelled by two motivations to forgive. On one hand, we are
commanded to forgive. Jesus clearly says that if we forgive, we will be forgiven, but if we do not forgive, we will not be forgiven (Matt. 6:12, 14–15;
Luke 6:37–38). The parable of the unforgiving servant encourages us to forgive because God holds us accountable for forgiving (Matt. 18: 23–35). So
duty, responsibility, accountability, desire to please God, and desire to
avoid displeasing God motivate us to forgive.

On the other hand, we are admonished to forgive spontaneously and emotionally as Christ forgave us (Eph. 4:31–32), and as God forgives (Jer. 31:34; Heb. 8:12, 10:17; Ps. 103:12). We see examples in Scripture of forgiveness from the heart—like Jesus on the cross (Luke 23:34) and Stephen facing his executioners (Acts 7:55–56). We see parables of unfathomable grace, like the prodigal son, in which the father's heart of forgiveness is almost incomprehensible (Luke 15:11–32). On that hand, forgiveness is an altruistic gift we freely give to those people who harm us and who do not deserve forgiveness.

With those two motivations to forgive, and the believer's experience of God's mercy and grace in giving Jesus freely to die for us (Rom. 5:1; Col. 2:13–14), Christians should hope that all Christians are ever-merciful—always forgiving. Yet, mostly, we see with great sympathy Peter, plaintively whining to Jesus, "How many times must I forgive one who harms me?" (Matt. 18: 21–22; see also Luke 17:3–4). How many, Lord? We identify with Peter. We almost daily catch ourselves judging others for not forgiving. We feel the deserved shame of knowing how short we fall of forgiving anyone 70 times 7 (Luke 17:5).

As helpers, people come to us and pour out their woes, their unforgiveness, their sorrow at the pain of relationships ruined. They ask us to help them find solace. Yet, their pleas inform us of how far we are from being examples of forgiveness.

I know in my heart how much resentment I harbor, and I know that my heart is deceitful so that I am not aware of much of my own sin (Jer. 17:9–10). My intentions are often good. I want to forgive. Yet I repeatedly fail. How can I help someone forgive?

I can forgive and help others to do so only by the grace and mercy of God. I am an unworthy vessel. I know that what might flow from me is muddy clay-stained water, not pure cleansing water. Yet, somehow a profound mystery exists. I am part of Jesus' church (Eph. 1:22–23), and the mystery is that despite the muddy water flowing from me, people can often be cleaned.

There is no mystery in counseling techniques. Counseling techniques cannot help people forgive any more than a physician can heal a person's body. Counseling techniques, like a physician's tools, are merely structures through which God sometimes sovereignly acts. He acts more often through some structures than through others. He brings more forgiveness about through counseling than through football, for example.

In this chapter, my goal is to provide one structure that I hope will help counselors assist people to forgive after a transgression and to become more forgiving people. To accomplish this, I will combine the Scriptures about forgiveness with the scientific studies done in our lab and elsewhere to provide an understanding of unforgiveness and forgiveness that complements and fleshes out what is said in Scripture. I describe a method of helping people forgive—which I describe first within a psychoeducational group,[2] and second show its use within a counseling session with a couple.[3]

The ideas I will talk about in this chapter are useful at a number of levels. They might help readers to understand forgiveness and to forgive more successfully in their own lives. They might help readers to counsel others in ways that promote forgiveness and reconciliation. These applications might occur in psychoeducational groups. We can teach forgiveness in Bible studies, Sunday school classes, teaching seminars in church or other settings, adjunct groups to psychotherapy, psychoeducational groups aimed at a particular problem like romantic betrayals, forgiving a more general collection of offenses, or abuse, or psychoeducational groups aimed at becoming a more forgiving person.

We can also teach forgiveness in individual, couple, family, or group counseling or therapy. These interventions can be conducted by laypeople, clergy, or professional therapists. Even community interventions such as disseminating the information through sermons or to community organizations could produce change in larger bodies of Christians.

## Understanding Unforgiveness and Forgiveness

When people are wronged or hurt, they experience an "injustice gap"—the difference between the way the person would like a transgression to be resolved (i.e., desired outcome) and the way things are perceived to be currently (i.e., current outcome). They also respond with immediate anger in response to perceived offenses or wrongs, or they respond with anger plus fear in response to perceived hurts.[4] They might inhibit their motivations to act in revenge or avoidance. McCullough, Fincham, and Tsang call that inhibition of expression of negative motivations, "forbearance."[5]

There are two types of forgiveness. First, "decisional forgiveness" can cancel an interpersonal debt caused by a transgression. A person simply decides to forgive. Often this occurs because people feel that it is their duty to forgive, that God holds them accountable for forgiving, that they are responsible for forgiving. Their decision to forgive is a statement of intent not to pursue the natural motivation to seek revenge or avoid the person who harmed one. Once it is made, that decision prescribes some behaviors (like acting as one did prior to the transgression) and proscribes other behaviors (like retaliating). Decisional forgiveness does not deal with the emotions. It reflects a preference for or understanding that duty, accountability, and responsibility—what we call "conscientiousness-based virtues"—are highly valued.[6]

Second, when people are hurt or offended, they respond in immediate anger or fear or a combination. They might ruminate about the event and the consequences to the victim until they develop emotional feelings of "unforgiveness," which is a combination of resentment, bitterness, hostility, hatred, anger, and fear.[7] In tandem, rumination produces motivational desires to act on that unforgiveness (even though they may have struggled to forbear or have foresworn revenge and avoidance in a decisional statement of forgiveness). Those emotional feelings of unforgiveness (and associated negative motivations) will eat at a person who does not reduce those negative emotions in some way.

"Emotional forgiveness" juxtaposes positive emotions toward the offender such as empathy, sympathy, compassion, agape love, or romantic love against the negative unforgiving emotions. Emotional forgiveness is born out of a valuing of the "warmth-based virtues" (such as love, compassion, gratitude, humility, sympathy, and compassion)[8] in contrast to the conscientiousness-based virtues that motivate decisional forgiving. The emotional juxtaposition first neutralizes negative emotions and second builds in positive emotions such as a net positive love, until emotional replacement occurs.

Because emotions and motivations are so closely linked, with emotions stirring up motivations on occasion and changes in motivation changing emotions on other occasions, motivations are inevitably changed as emotional forgiveness occurs. Emotional forgiveness is indeed both a change in emotions and motivations simultaneously. (Parenthetically, there are numerous ways to reduce unforgiveness—such as seeing civil, criminal, or personal justice done, turning the matter over to God, renarrating the event to excuse or justify the transgression, or defending against the threat psychologically).[9]

Decisional forgiveness and emotional forgiveness are related, but they respond to different rules. Different circumstances can promote or inhibit each one separately. Michael McCullough and I have, together and separately, described emotional forgiveness. McCullough has concentrated on the motivational aspects of emotional forgiveness.[10] I have concentrated on the emotional aspects.[11]

Emotional forgiveness changes over time. Emotions may change, and associated motivational desires to avoid or to seek revenge against a person may also decay as time passes. This is especially true if intervening events do not intercede to make things worse. When positive events occur (such as receiving a sincere apology or restitution), those events can help neutralize negative unforgiving emotions, increase positive forgiving emotions, reduce the motivation for avoidance and for revenge, and increase the motivation for conciliation even further.

### Helping People Forgive Using a Psychoeducational Group

Under normal circumstances people forgive in many ways. They might forgive in response to God's prompting, to worship, to reading a book, to their own prayer or meditation, to conversation with a friend, upon the advice of a pastor, or because they were exposed to some intervention. Therefore under normal circumstances, God has an amazing array of avenues by which He can move people from the state of unforgiveness to the state of forgiveness.

These avenues are as numerous as the possible routes one could use in moving from the state of Virginia to the state of California. Helpers take many routes to guide people through a process of forgiving. We have examined the published research on interventions to promote forgiveness.[12] Through that review of the literature, we have discovered that almost every program that helps people forgive, whether it is psychotherapeutic or psychoeducational, leads people through similar events. This is similar to saying that leading people from Virginia to California can be done through many routes; however, these routes pass through the same six or seven cities as a person navigates across the country.

I have been conducting research on how to help people forgive using psychoeducational and therapeutic methods in a variety of formats since the mid-1980s. This has culminated in a method that I call a Pyramid Model to REACH Forgiveness, where REACH is an acrostic in which each letter stands for one of the five major steps. Below, I will describe the steps in helping people reach emotional forgiveness using my Pyramid Model to REACH Forgiveness as a way of structuring the steps.[13] However, I must point out that other people put these elements together in different orders and different ways. So there is a freedom involved in how people organize and present these steps.

The steps to REACH forgiveness can be used in psychoeducational groups and in counseling. First, I will describe one way to conduct a psychoeducational group (based on my book, *Forgiving and Reconciling*, plus additional exercises derived from my experience since I wrote the book). Then, I will illustrate how to use it in couples counseling.

## Who Should Participate in Forgiveness Groups?

People who can benefit from an intervention to help them forgive are those who want to forgive but have not been able to do so. They might have tried repeatedly to forgive or they forgave and back-slid. Sometimes we helpers want to take over one of the roles of the Holy Spirit and convict people that they need to forgive. We quote Scripture and admonish people to be responsive to God's Word. These methods to follow, however, help people experience emotional forgiveness. This group is aimed at 13 one-hour sessions—making up a Sunday school quarter or 13 hourly counseling sessions.

## Agreement on Goals and Definitions

*Goal setting (Hour 1).* Because people understand forgiveness in many ways, and those ways can result in disagreement, begin the group by stating the goal of the group. The goal might be aimed at three levels. At level one, we hope to help people forgive a single past or current transgression. At level two, we hope to help people learn *how to* forgive transgressions. These skills cannot be effectively taught in the abstract. They must be learned by applying them to one event and by being explicit as to how that event is forgiven. At level three, we hope to help people become more forgiving people. Just as skills to forgive a transgression cannot be learned in the abstract, people cannot learn how to become more forgiving people in the abstract. Rather, people must forgive transgression after transgression and person after person.

The leader should solicit from group members their goals. After everyone has shared, the group leader can describe the three levels of forgiveness. The leader either states the advertised purpose of the group, or decides on the goal based on the sharing of the members.

At whatever level of goal is aimed at—forgiving a particular hurt, learning how to forgive better, or becoming a more forgiving person—the person must learn to forgive one transgression. The steps will then be applied more generally and more repeatedly if more levels are addressed. Therefore I will describe carefully how to help people forgive one transgression.

*Definitions of forgiveness (Hour 2).* The leader should circulate a list of definitions of forgiveness. Most are incorrect definitions such as "forgiveness means forgetting," "forgiveness means excusing the person for having done something wrong," or "forgiveness means realizing that the person was justified in transgressing." Two of the definitions within the list might be those that will be used in the group. Decisional forgiveness will be identified with the definition "forgiveness involves declaring that one is not going to seek revenge or avoid the other person but will do his or her best to get along in the future." Emotional forgiveness will be identified with the definition, "forgiveness involves a change of heart in which one replaces negative emotions of resentment, bitterness, hostility, anger, hatred, and fear with more positive emotions toward the person, such as empathy, sympathy, compassion, or love."

Group members discuss in triads which definitions of forgiveness they consider to be correct and incorrect, and why. After three-person discussion, the group reconvenes. Group discussion is held. The group comes to agree on the two definitions as being forgiveness. The leader should differentiate between decisional and emotional forgiveness. The leader suggests that the group will be aimed at forgiving from the heart (i.e., emotional forgiveness)—and depending on the goal, on building skills to forgive or being a more forgiving person.

*Christian views of forgiveness.* Scriptures pertaining to the two types of forgiveness are considered by asking people to contrast the parable of the unforgiving servant (Matt. 18:23–35) with the parable of the prodigal son (Luke 15:11–32). The leader makes it clear that there are two distinct types of forgiving—with decisional forgiveness governed by duty, accountability, and responsibility, and emotional forgiveness governed by love.

*Unforgiveness (Hour 3).* In the group, people describe what it feels like to be unforgiving. The group leader lists emotion-words as members discuss. The leader refers to the definition of emotional forgiveness, which describes the six negative emotions that make up unforgiveness, and then defines unforgiveness. The leader draws a flow path that describes how people develop unforgiveness after a transgression. A transgression leads to a perception of a hurt or offense, which generates an immediate emotion of anger, fear, or their mixture. Rumination—continual replaying of the event—leads to unforgiveness. The group lists physical, mental, and relational effects of unforgiveness. The leader briefly refers to research on the effects of unforgiveness on physical, mental, and relational health.

### R = Recall the Hurt

The leader directs each person to describe (in writing) the event that he or she hopes to forgive. The Transgression-Related Inventory of Motivations (TRIM) scale should be completed, the single-item measure of forgiveness, and the Forgiveness-Perceptions, Emotions, Actions, and Cognition (F-PEAC) should be completed[14] (see Table 1).

People discuss the event in dyads. They are directed to discuss how their unforgiveness developed over time, using stimulus questions about the kind of emotion they felt in the beginning, whether they could turn loose of the event, or how they tried to deal with the event and their feelings? The leader reconvenes the group. Three volunteers share their experiences.

Participants are asked to focus on how they have tried to deal with the event and their emotions. The leader defines the injustice gap as the difference between desired and current outcomes. The group lists ways that people attempt to close the injustice gap and reduce unforgiveness. The list is compared with a table of ways to reduce unforgiveness.[15] Ways that better the current situation include (1) receiving an apology or restitution, (2) understanding the transgressor better, and (3) seeing civil or divine justice enacted. Ways to lessen expectations of desired outcomes include accepting the transgression and moving on with one's life or giving the judgment to God. Group members discuss which methods are biblical (the answer is that all are consistent with Scripture) and whether people who have tried them have found them to work.

The leader tells the group that recalling the hurt is effective, but only if people move past feeling how badly we have been victimized or what a jerk the other person is. Group members must express themselves but then work toward a different understanding of the transgression.

### E = Empathize with the Transgressor (Hours 4 through 7)

To forgive the transgressor, victims must change negative unforgiving emotions to less negative or more positive emotions. Typically, people will not jump from a negative to a positive emotional state, but will reduce negative emotions gradually by neutralizing them as they experience positive emotional states.

*Empathy.* If people who feel unforgiveness can empathize with the transgressor temporarily, then empathy can erode some unforgiveness. If people can sympathize with, feel compassion for, or experience love toward the transgressor, they will reduce their unforgiveness. Finally, they might feel more positive emotions toward the transgressor. Because people forgive as they feel positive emotions while thinking about the transgression, group members must be helped to experience positive emotions toward the transgressor.

We first take people through several methods to help them understand more about what might have been going on in the transgressor's life. Each group member writes some notes about what he or she thought might be going on in the transgressor's life. In dyads, partners share with each other. The facilitator demonstrates the empty-chair technique—moving from chair to chair in a mock conversation between transgressor and victim, which stimulates understanding and empathy. Members of dyads take turns enacting empty-chair dialogues while the dyadic partner observes. After the empty-chair conversations are complete, the group is reconvened and members share reactions.

We assign homework: each group member should write a letter giving an account of the transgression as if he or she were the transgressor. The letter should describe the thoughts, feelings, and motivations of the transgressor, who usually had positive intentions yet offended or hurt the group member because things seemed to just "go wrong." In the following session, people read their letters to a partner. We reconvene the group and ask two or three people to read their letters to the group. We ask how successful group members were in empathizing with the transgressor. At this point, some people raise objections—they could not empathize or empathy had only a small effect. Others were more successful in empathizing.

*Sympathy, compassion, and agape love.* Because several positive emotions can replace unforgiveness, we ask that people sympathize with the transgressor. Empathy is merely feeling what the transgressor felt; sympathy is also feeling sorry for the transgressor. We process the results of the sympathy discussion. We ask people whether they can feel compassion for the other person. Compassion is empathy plus sympathy plus a motivation to do something for the person. Finally, we ask people whether they can experience agape love for the other person. Perhaps the love might be motivated by Christian commands to love one's enemies (Matt. 5:44; Luke 6:27–28) or one's brother (1 John 4:20–21). We discuss what this love would look like and if the person were to love one's enemy, how would each person act?

*Symbolizing positive feelings for the transgressor.* These interventions have been aimed at helping people experience positive emotions that replace unforgiveness. In the group, we ask people to discuss how successful this was. People readily symbolize the extent of emotional replacement for the person who transgressed against them.

In advance, we prepare two dark pieces of construction paper with a piece of golden construction paper inside, and we cut the three pieces of paper, together, into the shape of a heart. They are taped into a three-layered heart. Group members are given one of the hearts. They look at the dark exterior and think about their judgment toward the person who hurt them and the times they had wished that person ill. They are then told that if they have now become more empathic, sympathetic, compassionate, or loving toward the person, their hearts have been lightened. They tear away the dark exterior and reveal the heart of gold (sunshine) within.

### A = Altruistic Gift of Forgiveness (Hour 8)

People forgive best if they are motivated to forgive altruistically—to bless the other person—rather than to get a blessing for themselves (such as better physical or mental health). People recall a time when they transgressed against someone who forgave them. We give people time to reflect on that and to write a description of the event. In dyads, people describe the event. We convene the group and ask two or three people to share with the entire group. People report feeling free and unburdened when they received forgiveness.

We then say, "You have now empathized with (and perhaps sympathized with, felt compassion for, and experienced love for) the person who hurt you. You also now have realized how good you felt when you received forgiveness. Would you like to give that gift to the person who had hurt you so that person could feel forgiven?" Some people forgive totally, but others answer that they are not yet ready to fully forgive. We accept anything as a valid answer and ask each person to quantify how much forgiveness they are willing to grant—10%, 25%, 50%, 75%, or whatever. They answer aloud within the group.

## C = Commit Publicly to the Forgiveness One Experiences (Hour 9)

To assist in maintaining the forgiveness, when almost unavoidable doubts about whether one has completely forgiven occur, we ask people to commit publicly to the forgiveness they have experienced. People write a certificate of forgiveness stating the degree of forgiveness experienced. They share the certificate with others in the group as they talk about the forgiveness that they have experienced. This provides another public commitment that they have forgiven to some degree.

We solicit expression of the roadblocks to complete forgiveness. Group members discuss what it would take to help them forgive. We note that there are many paths to forgiveness. Some say that they would forgive if the other person simply apologized or made restitution. We agree with them. Then we say, "Are you going to allow your transgressor to dictate whether you will experience perhaps years of unforgiveness?" We suggest decisional forgiveness, trusting God to then change the feelings as they act as if they had forgiven the transgressor. We also might recycle through steps E and A, and then again ask people to rate the degree to which they had forgiven.

In a group, some people will have fully forgiven, but others not. We invite the people who have forgiven to take a different transgression by the person or even a different person's transgression while others work further on the initial transgression.

We symbolize the forgiveness people have experienced through a ceremony. We might have each person bring in a rock weighing about two pounds. People hold the rock at arm's length as we discuss the weight of unforgiveness that people have carried. As arms droop, we invite people to symbolize their forgiveness by putting down the rock—laying down the burden of unforgiveness they have carried for so long.

Another way of symbolizing the forgiveness is through writing a brief description of the offense and burning it or pinning it to a cross. Still another way of symbolizing the forgiveness is to write a word describing the offense on the person's hand, then try to wash the hand clean. We note that the ink does not come off easily. It lightens as the soap of forgiveness cleanses the person's feelings, but it will take time before the word is gone.

### H = Hold on to Forgiveness When You Doubt (Hour 10)

Maintenance of gains of forgiveness is always difficult. People who feel that they have fully forgiven an offender can merely see the offender and feel anger and fear stir their hearts. Usually people will then conclude that they have not really forgiven, because *if I had really forgiven*, they think, *I should feel no anger or fear toward the transgressor*. However, this is not a true perception. Anger and fear are their God-given natural bodily mechanisms to protect them from a harmful situation.

We explain an analogy to help people remember and understand this. "Assume that you burn your hand very badly on a stove. After it has healed, your hand passes near a hot eye again. Immediately a fear rushes back into your entire body. It is not that you are unforgiving of the stove eye for "burning" you. Rather, the fear and anger is a natural bodily response to having been injured. This is what happens when a person has been transgressed against and suffered a psychological or physical injury and forgives, and then sees the person and transgressor again.

Unforgiveness might be rekindled if the person ruminates about the event. Rumination is persevering on the negativity and negative consequences of the event. So the person needs to have some mechanisms to get his or her mind off the rumination. Daniel Wegner's white-bear studies illustrate the almost impossibility of stopping intrusive thoughts consciously. In Wegner's studies, people are told *not* to think about white bears. If they fail at the task (and thus think about white bears), they must ring a bell. The command to try to inhibit thoughts increases the thoughts rather than decrease them. Thus, people must not merely seek to stop rumination but think of other things in place of the negative thoughts. For example, they might think positively of the person, or simply distract themselves to think of something else altogether.

## Talking About Transgressions (Hours 11 and 12)

*Content of the teaching.* The way people talk about transgressions can affect forgiving. If people talk destructively about transgressions, unforgiveness multiplies. We teach two skills. One is to make good reproaches. A reproach is a request for an explanation if a person believes that he or she has been transgressed against. A good reproach assumes that the transgressor had positive motives and love for the victim. It does not blame and accuse the transgressor. A good reproach says, "Usually, you are very sensitive. I was puzzled when you [forgot our anniversary]. I didn't understand; that doesn't fit my concept of you. Can you help me understand what was going on with you that caused you to [forget]?"

Once a victim reproaches, the offender tries to make a good account of the behavior. There are four types of accounts. One type is a denial. A denial says, "I did not do what you're accusing me of." A second type of account is a justification, which admits transgressing but claims that the transgression was justified (usually because of what the other person did to provoke the act). Denials and justifications are called aggravating accounts. They make matters worse.

Mitigating accounts make things better. One type of mitigating account is an excuse. An excuse admits to the wrongdoing but tells the pressures and stresses that make the behavior more understandable. Importantly, the timing of the excuse is crucial. Excuses should not be given right away, but instead should be given only after a good confession is made. The person can then say, "Would it help your consideration of forgiving if I described what was happening so that you understand what was going on with me?"

A confession is an admission of wrongdoing without excuse. Again, from my book, *Forgiving and Reconciling*, we use an acrostic to structure the confession.

- C = Confess without excuse
- O = Offer an apology (and it must be believable and sincere)
- N = Note the other person's pain (i.e., communicate your empathy)

- F = Forever value the person (i.e., say that repairing the relationship is more important to you than being "right")
- E = Equalize the situation (i.e., make restitution if appropriate)
- S = Say, "I'll try to never do it again."
- S = Seek forgiveness

*Introduce the topic.* Set up a role-play for people to demonstrate the worst possible communication. Describe the scenario—a forgotten anniversary. Let volunteers act out an example of terrible communication. Have group members describe ways that communication was poor. Describe in general what reproaches and accounts are.

*Teach reproaches.* Solicit ideas about what makes a good reproach. Demonstrate a good reproach. Have dyads practice making a good reproach.

*Teach accounts.* Describe aggravating accounts and refer back to the terrible-communication role-play for examples. Teach about excuses (and their proper timing) and making a good confession. Solicit discussion that identifies elements of a good confession. Summarize by teaching the CONFESS acrostic. Give people a handout summarizing CONFESS. Demonstrate a good confession. Have dyads practice giving a good confession to each other.

*Discussion.* Numerous issues arise as group members discuss how and when to make good reproaches and confessions. These often revolve around the other person not apologizing, not making a good confession, or not seeming sincere or regretful. People complain of the transgressor repeatedly confessing (and seeming to mean well) but continuing to offend. People describe times in which the transgressor intentionally hurts or offends. They talk about how the transgressor may be unwilling to stop the offenses. They describe having forgiven repeatedly, and they ask when it is enough.

Usually, the discussion boils down to a realization that one cannot be responsible for the other person. Rather, a group member is responsible only for his or her own behavior. On the other hand, the necessity of setting limits arises. Forgiving does not mean being a doormat. Nor does it mean putting oneself in harm's way if the transgressor is likely to inflict permanent physical or psychological damage.

Often, there are no good answers to the really difficult issues with which people must deal. The leader of the group must not feel that he or she must satisfactorily answer every question and erase all objections. Some things must simply be matters of conscience between the group member and God.

### Becoming a More Forgiving Person (Hour 13)

Despite the practical objections that surface, most people want to become a more forgiving person. So, in the last session, the leader attempts to leave the person with positive motivation to practice forgiving. Becoming a more forgiving person requires that the person practice forgiving many different transgressions with many different people. However, part of becoming a more forgiving person involves having a motivation, or increasing one's motivation, to be a more forgiving person. This means that people will need to cue themselves to forgive when they become angry. Besides practicing repeatedly, there are several ways that we help people try to become a more forgiving person. One of those is to have them reflect on the Scriptures prayerfully. People can be given a list of Scriptures to meditate on, and can pray through those Scriptures. This can increase the person's desire to be more forgiving.

Another way to become a more forgiving person is to adopt a journal and each day reflect on forgiveness. A third way to become more forgiving is to get a good book on forgiveness and read it for morning or evening devotions. Each of these ways is aimed at getting people to think about forgiveness in more situations in their lives throughout the day, and sustain that interest and attention over time.

### Helping People Forgive Using Couple Therapy

I have described how we conduct the Pyramid Model to REACH Forgiveness using psychoeducational groups. However, it can also be used within counseling, as I show below. The flow is not as linear as in psychoeducation. Counseling simply cannot be controlled as well as a structured group. Also, in counseling, the problems have usually become more chronic and more distressing and might be entangled with other issues. For the transcript below, W = Worthington, R = Ron, and C = Cindy.

*The situation*: A year before counseling began, Ron signed up for a class at a health club. Ron knew that Cindy did not approve. When the health club sent a bill for $1,000, Cindy opened it and hit the roof. After the argument settled down, both partners brought it up periodically. Now, after counseling had worked on their communication and resolution of conflicts within the hope-focused marriage framework,[16] they identified that event as the hurt that generated the most unforgiveness in each.

### Counseling Transcript

W:   Ron, tell me more about this issue. *(Comment: I encourage them to R=Recall the Hurt. I will work with one person at a time.)*

R:   We were back in this time when we were really fighting. I felt I needed to be in a health club, so I felt justified in joining. We were at the point where if Cindy said she thought something— anything—was a bad idea, that meant I would almost certainly do it. I only went to the spa about 3 weeks. I know that decision was a pretty large screw-up. I've admitted that. I've asked for forgiveness. I recognize my fault.

W:   And yet...

C:   And yet, we still had to deal with a $1,000 bill, which meant our vacation plans for that summer were changed. We had to read-just some priorities. I was not happy about that at all.

R:   That's putting it mildly.

W:   I understand that this has not been one-sided. Ron, you felt like once you apologized, said you were sorry, and admitted to mess-ing up, that should end it. But that didn't end it.

R:   Right. I felt like I went as far as I could go. Yet it's still an issue. It's frustrating. I find a lot of anger building up as that issue keeps resurfacing.

W:   So you said last week that you were having trouble forgiving *her* for not forgiving you.

R:   Right. It's a big spiral. I did something wrong. She recognized that and accused me of it. I came around to seeing some of her side of it. But she can't let it go. So now, I don't like her response. I was being humble. I made myself vulnerable. I did what was right. But we still haven't resolved anything.

W:   So both of you feel unforgiving but for different reasons. Today, let's see whether we can make some progress toward a more forgiving spirit for each of you. Ron, I think I'll start with you. Would you pretend for a minute that you are Cindy? *(Comment: In this couple, Cindy seemed a bit more insightful, so I wanted to begin with Ron. I hope to help Ron empathize with Cindy. E=Empathize with the one who hurt you.)* As "Cindy," tell "Ron" there [points to Cindy] what you have felt about all this. What are your feelings about what Ron did?

R: That's hard. I'm an intellectual person. I rationalize and justify. Now you're asking me to put aside my understanding of what's right and be somebody else.

W: I know you can do this.

R: Okay, from me being "Cindy": I saw Ron act irresponsibly. He didn't consider us as a couple. He was financially irresponsible. It just wasn't a very smart choice.

W: And what was your emotional reaction? *(Comment: Because I want to help him eventually replace his negative unforgiving emotions with more positive emotions—like empathy and love—I pay a lot of attention to his emotions.)*

R: That jerk.

W: Anger.

R: Anger at stupidity. Offended. My values weren't considered. What else can I say?

C: *I know.* [Cindy raises her hand.]

W: Wait a minute, let's let "Cindy" here tell us more. "Cindy," did you only feel anger? Nothing else?

R: That's tough. Sure. It wasn't just anger; it was irreverence towards me, "Cindy's" person, disregard or disrespect. I don't know what other words to put on there.

W: It's like a wound that's been dealt to you. *(Comment: Both anger and hurt are mixed. Because Ron is aware of and sees Cindy's anger, I want to call attention to the other side, so that he sees her reaction as "softer" toward him. If he had attended to the hurt, I probably would have mentioned the anger briefly, but I would have gone back and focused on the hurt—the softer emotion. Accurate empathy demands that he see both sides, but the therapeutic use of empathy demands that he focus on the softer emotion if he is to forgive.)*

R: Sure.

W: So what kind of emotion would you think having been *hurt* by this ...

R: I was going to say, "hurt." What kind of emotion? I don't know if this counts as an emotion but a kind of deflated feeling—like "that guy doesn't see the worth in me."

W: So, "Cindy," you feel sadness, depression, lower self-esteem because of this.

R: Right. Yeah, that certainly causes me to evaluate who I am. Am I really insignificant like "Ron" keeps telling me I am.

W: Now, Ron, this has gone on awhile. Why would this go on? What might she be feeling? Or, I should say, what might *you* be feeling "Cindy" that would make this last so long. (Pause) There's anger, there's hurt, depression.

R: It's a big anger and a deep wound. And I'm trying to deal with it using a little Band-Aid.

W: So, "Cindy," you feel helplessness, thinking *What we can do? That apology wasn't enough.*

R: Sure, a big gap, a big divide that never did get bridged.

W: So, "Cindy," if you didn't care about Ron, it seems to me that this wouldn't bother you at all. But somehow it bothers you a lot.

R: Hmm, that's true.

W: So, you must care a lot about him to be so worried, so afraid that this might happen again, and so distraught and distressed. Do you think that might ...?

R: That sounds right. I'm trying to put myself in Cindy's shoes, but you got me thinking.

W: Let me change. You're Ron again here for a minute.

R: I can do *him* better.

W: Would you think a minute about your relationship with Cindy. Can you recall whether you've seen somebody, not you, hurt her. (*Comment: I want him to experience even more empathy for Cindy—and to show her that he can understand her.*)

R: We work at church and she was in charge of the nursery. There was another Mom that lit into her one morning about something. I don't even remember why.

C: About her child.

R: She let everybody know—loudly—that she thought Cindy really screwed something up. It was a very personal and public attack. The issue was insignificant. I don't remember what it was.

W: But it certainly was a *personal and public* attack. And how did that make you feel—as her husband?

R: Oh, wow, a mixture of things. Part of me, the angry male, wanted to go plunk (that woman) on the head and say, "Quit being an idiot!" Part of me wanted to put my arms around Cindy and say. "That wasn't accurate. It didn't treat you fairly, honestly, and correctly." Protect her. *(Comment: He is directly telling her of his love.)*

W: You could sense the way that y'all are tied together as one flesh. That attack on her was...

R: It was on me, too [overlapping].

W: ...was an attack on you.

R: Yeah.

W: *(Comment: Ron seems "softer" toward Cindy after expressing his love for her. I sense that it might be good timing to try to get him to give a good apology.)* You know you've said that you have confessed your part in this betrayal with the health club before. And thinking about what she's gone through, I wonder if you'd be willing to tell her again, in my presence, how you feel about your part in the health-club incident.

R: Part of me feels like she attacked me over it, and so I'm defensive. She might attack again. Also I don't want to admit I've been so wrong. I feel really guilty. But [turns to Cindy], I guess what I really want to try to say is I never meant to do something so personally hurtful to you. It wasn't about *you*. I don't want that to stay between us.

W: So, can you tell her that what you did was wrong?

R: I knew it was wrong when I did it. Even more, over the last year. But today, I realized that this affects you in a very deep and personal way. I know how deeply it hurt you. What I've been writing off as a small incident is really a big and important one to you. *(Comment: He expresses his empathy, but he has trouble using "feeling" words. I encourage him.)*

W: I can hear in your voice real sorrow and regret. Can you express how sorry you are?

R: I can't find the words that could capture it, other than "a lot."

W:   I guess, let me say that eventually if Cindy is going to be able to forgive this, she needs to know what impact it had on you. She needs to believe how sorry you are that this happened.

C:   That would help.

R:   As I sit here right now, I recognize that we aren't talking about $1,000. We aren't talking about it was only a few weeks. We are talking about *I hurt you*. And that's a big difference. You weren't supported.

W:   I think that seemed to me to be a wonderfully sincere expression of your feelings. I don't know whether it felt that way to you, Cindy?

C:   I hear he understood. It feels more now like he understands than he ever did. But he chose to do something without me knowing. And that hurt. *(Comment: Cindy wants reassurance.)*

W:   Ron, I guess if I were Cindy and had worried for a year about this betrayal, I might think, *Oh, my, what if it happened again? That would be horrible if it happened again.* Do you think something like this could happen again?

R:   I know something now that I didn't before. It could never happen *this way* again. But I guess there's a real fear in there too. I could still screw up again and hurt you by accident—not *planning* to hurt you, or not *trying* to hurt you. *(Comment: Ron waffles on giving unconditional reassurance, so I must put as good a spin on it as possible.)*

W:   You're saying you really want to *try* never to do anything like this again. But you also are aware of your own *humanness*, that you might mess up. You know it could happen, but you don't *want* it to happen. *(Comment: I want to positively reframe Cindy's reluctance to turn loose of the incident, in order to bring out their love, which will foster more forgiving.)* Let me shift gears a little. Can you see why Cindy might have continued to bring this up repeatedly?

R:   Sure. I was addressing the superficial issues, not the real deep ones, the ones that really hurt, the ones that affect her personally.

W:   But also she was worried. She loved you. And she didn't want to lose the relationship. She was coming out of a position of love over this.

R:   It was harder to see when I felt I was getting emotionally blasted.

W: That's right, her anger made a lot of noise and fireworks. It was hard to see in the darkness behind those fireworks.

R: Right. *(Comment: Remember, we are working on helping Ron forgive Cindy for bringing this up repeatedly. He has demonstrated some empathy for her, sees his part in provoking her, but he might not be ready to forgive her by giving her an altruistic gift of forgiveness.)*

W: Can I get you to do one other thing for me? I would like for you to think back on your life. Can you recall a time when you might have hurt somebody else—not Cindy—but somebody from your past? Yet they forgave you for it and told you.

R: I can think of a fairly recent one. It was my son. He's 11. He broke a lamp. I let him have it, just verbally. I didn't throw him across the room or anything, but I really tore into him about watching what he was doing, paying attention, quit being irresponsible— the whole spiel. And it was obvious looking at him that I was hurting him. It took me several hours to go back and tell him that I knew I overreacted. I told him that compared to a lamp he was infinitely more important. So I told him I was sorry. He didn't hesitate at all. He just put his arms around me and said, "I forgive you, Daddy." I felt like somebody who was really wrong. Yet when I said I was sorry, he said "That's okay." He forgave me, and we could still love each other.

W: You could really *feel* that forgiveness. When he granted forgiveness and hugged you, you knew it was okay. It was a freedom for you.

R: Oh, absolutely. Yeah, very much.

W: As you've talked through your health-club incident here, you've thought about how Cindy brought this up many times. You see now what was going through her head. You said you were holding some unforgiveness about this.

R: Yes.

W: And you have understood that she was bringing it up because she loves you and was worried about your relationship. Also, you saw that when you received forgiveness from your son how good and free it made you feel. I was just wondering if you'd want to give that gift of the freedom of forgiveness to Cindy—if you really *feel* forgiving, that is. *(Comment: I ask him to give A=Altruistic Gift of Forgiveness.)*

R:    I'd like to do that. [Faces Cindy] I know you love me. I love you very much. I see now that your mentioning my having hurt you often was saying that you care for me, for us. I want you to know that I forgive you for bringing this up. In a way, I'm glad that you did 'cause I didn't honor you when I tried to deceive you. I'm sorry I did that. I'm glad I could say that to you. Anyway, I love you. [They kiss and hug] *(Comment: Ron commits in front of Cindy—and in front of me—to the forgiveness he experienced in his heart. C=Commit publicly to the forgiveness.)*

## Conclusion

Scripture and counseling practice coincide. Some aspects of forgiveness require us to forgive simply because we know it is the right thing for Christians to do. Other aspects of forgiveness require a gradual change in emotions over time. I have provided an understanding of unforgiveness and two types of forgiveness, and have outlined an organized structure that can be used to help people forgive.

I end this chapter the same way I began it. Forgiving others their sins and transgressions is not due to technique. In shaping the graceful steel of a beautiful Christian character, psychoeducational or therapeutic actions by group leaders, teachers, or therapists are merely the hammer and anvil. Life experiences supply the heat that makes us malleable, and God's hands provide the material and use us as tools to shape His church into something beautiful.

### ENDNOTES

1.    Martin E. Marty, The ethos of Christian forgiveness, in E.L. Worthington, Jr. (ed.), *Dimensions of forgiveness: Psychological research and theological perspectives* (Philadelphia: The Templeton Foundation Press, 1998), 9–28.

2.    Michael E. McCullough, and Worthington, E. L., Jr., Promoting forgiveness: A comparison of two psychoeducational group interventions with a waiting-list control, *Counseling and Values, 40,* (1995), 55–68; J.S Ripley, and Worthington, E.L., Jr., Comparison of hope-focused communication and empathy-based forgiveness group interventions to promote marital enrichment, *Journal of Counseling and Development, 80,* (2002), 452–463; E. L. Worthington, Jr., Kurusu, T., McCullough, M.E., and Sandage, S., Empirical research on religion and psychotherapeutic processes and outcomes: A 10-year review and research prospectus, *Psychological Bulletin, 199,* (1996), 448–487; S.J. Sandage, *An ego-humility model of forgiveness: A theory-driven empirical test of group intervention,* PhD diss., Virginia Commonwealth University (1997); for the best summary see E.L. Worthington, Jr., *Forgiv-*

*ing and reconciling: Bridges to wholeness and hope* (Downers Grove, IL: InterVarsity Press, 2003), which summarizes and discusses the full model.

3. Everett L. Worthington, Jr., An empathy-humility-commitment model of forgiveness applied within family dyads, *Journal of Family Therapy, 20,* (1998), 59–76.

4. Everett L. Worthington, Jr., Is there a place for forgiveness in the justice system? *Fordham Urban Law Journal, 27,* (2000a), 1721–1734.

5. Michael E. McCullough, Fincham, F.D. and Tsang, J-A., Forgiveness, forbearance, and time: The temporal unfolding of transgression-related interpersonal motivations, *Journal of Personality and Social Psychology, 84,* (2003), 540–557.

6. Everett L. Worthington, Jr., Berry, J.W., and Parrott, L. III., Unforgiveness, forgiveness, religion, and health, in T. G. Plante and A. Sherman (eds.), *Faith and health: Psychological perspectives* (New York: Guilford Press, 2001), 107–138.

7. Everett L. Worthington, Jr., and Wade, N.G., The social psychology of unforgiveness and forgiveness and implications for clinical practice, *Journal of Social and Clinical Psychology, 18,* (1999),385–418.

8. See Everett L. Worthington, Jr., Berry, J.W., and Parrott, L. III., Unforgiveness, forgiveness, religion, and health. In T. G. Plante and A. Sherman (eds.), *Faith and Health,* 107–138.

9. See Nathaniel G. Wade, and Worthington, E.L., Jr., Overcoming interpersonal offenses: Is forgiveness the only way to deal with unforgiveness? *Journal of Counseling and Development, 81,* (2003a), 343–353; E. L. Worthington, Jr., Unforgiveness, forgiveness, and reconciliation in societies, in Raymond G. Helmick and Rodney L. Petersen (eds.), *Forgiveness and reconciliation: Religion, public policy, and conflict transformation* (Philadelphia: The Templeton Foundation Press, 2001a), 161–182.

10. Michael E. McCullough, Bellah, C. G., Kilpatrick, S. D., and Johnson, J. L., Vengefulness: Relationships with forgiveness, rumination, well-being, and the big five, *Personality and Social Psychology Bulletin, 27,*(2001), 601–610; M. E. McCullough, Fincham, F.D. and Tsang, J-A., Forgiveness, forbearance, and time: The temporal unfolding of transgression-related interpersonal motivations, *Journal of Personality and Social Psychology, 84,* (2003), 540–557; M. E. McCullough, Rachal, K. C., Sandage, S. J., Worthington, E. L. Jr., Brown, S. W., and Hight, T. L., Interpersonal forgiveness in close relationships II: Theoretical elaboration and measurement, *Journal of Personality and Social Psychology, 75,* (1998), 1586–1603; M.E. McCullough, Sandage, S. J., and Worthington, E. L., Jr., *To forgive is human: How to put your past in the past* (Downers Grove, IL: InterVarsity Press, 1997); M. E. McCullough, Worthington, E. L. Jr., and Rachal, K. C., Interpersonal forgiving in close relationships, *Journal of Personality and Social Psychology, 73,*(1997), 321–336.

11. Nathaniel G. Wade, and Worthington, E.L., Jr., Overcoming interpersonal offenses: Is forgiveness the only way to deal with unforgiveness? *Journal of Counseling and Development, 81,* (2003a), 343–535; E. L. Worthington, Jr., On chaos, fractals, and stress: Response to fincham's 'Optimism and the Family,' in J. Gillam (ed.), *The science of optimism and hope* (Philadelphia: The Templeton Foundation Press, 2000b), 313–318; E. L.Worthington, Jr., Unforgiveness, forgiveness, and reconciliation in societies, in Raymond G. Helmick and Rodney L. Petersen (eds.), *Forgiveness and reconciliation: Religion, public policy, and conflict transformation* (Philadelphia: The Templeton Foundation Press, 2001a), 161–182; E. L.Worthington, Jr., *Five steps to forgiveness: The art and science of forgiving* (New York: Crown Publishers, 2001b); E. L. Worthington, Jr., and Scherer, M, Forgiveness is an emotion-focused coping strategy that can reduce health risks and promote health

resilience: Theory, review, and hypotheses, *Psychology and Health, 19*, (2003), 385–405; E. L. Worthington, Jr., and Wade, N.G., The social psychology of unforgiveness and forgiveness and implications for clinical practice, *Journal of Social and Clinical Psychology, 18*, (1999), 385–418.

12.     Nathaniel G. Wade, and Worthington, E.L., Jr., Overcoming interpersonal offenses: Is forgiveness the only way to deal with unforgiveness? *Journal of Counseling and Development, 81*, (2003a), 343–353; Nathaniel G. Wade, and Worthington E.L., Jr., Content and meta-analysis of interventions to promote forgiveness, Manuscript under editorial review, Virginia Commonwealth University (2003b).

13.     Everett L. Worthington, Jr., *Five steps to forgiveness: The art and science of forgiving* (New York: Crown Publishers 2001b); E. L. Worthington, Jr., *Forgiving and reconciling: Bridges to wholeness and love* (Downers Grove, IL: InterVarsity Press, 2003).

14.     Michael E. McCullough, Rachal, K. C., Sandage, S. J., Worthington, E. L. Jr., Brown, S. W., and Hight, T. L., Interpersonal forgiveness in close relationships II: Theoretical elaboration and measurement, *Journal of Personality and Social Psychology, 75*,(1998), 1586–1603; E. L. Worthington, Jr., Sandage, S. J., and Berry, J.W., Group interventions to promote forgiveness: What researchers and clinicians ought to know, in M.E. McCullough, K.I. Pargament, and C.E. Thoresen (eds.), *Forgiveness: Theory, research and practice* (New York: Guilford Press, 2000), 228–253; Nathaniel G. Wade, and Worthington, E.L., Jr., Overcoming interpersonal offenses: Is forgiveness the only way to deal with unforgiveness? *Journal of Counseling and Development, 81*, (2003a), 343–353.

15.     Everett L. Worthington, Jr., Unforgiveness, forgiveness, and reconciliation in societies, in Raymond G. Helmick and Rodney L. Petersen (eds.), *Forgiveness and reconciliation: Religion, public policy, and Conflict Transformation* (Philadelphia: The Templeton Foundation Press, 2001a), 161–182.

16.     Everett L. Worthington, Jr., *Hope-focused marriage counseling* (Downers Grove, IL: InterVarsity Press, 1999).

# 7

# Depression and Bipolar Disorders

*Siang-Yang Tan and Michael Lyles*

Hear my prayer O Lord, and let my cry come to You. Do not hide your
face from me in the day of my trouble...For my days are consumed like
smoke, and my bones are burned like a hearth. My heart is stricken and
withered like grass, so that I forgot to eat my bread...I lie awake...for I
have eaten ashes like bread, and mingled my drink with weeping.

PSALM 102:1–9

Jim awoke with a groan and rolled over and checked his clock on the bed
stand: 1:30 in the afternoon. Not that time or routine meant anything anymore, as he was as likely to be wide awake at 1:30 A.M. as asleep in the middle of the day.

Jim had lost his job at the sawmill three months earlier due to his
chronic depression. His boss could no longer count on him showing up, let
alone accomplishing a solid day's work when he was there. Jim decided to
go into business for himself—he made fine redwood boxes and gifts in his
shop—but his shop was a chaotic mess and his lack of attention to business
detail made it nearly impossible for others to count on timely delivery of
goods.

Thankfully, his wife worked full time or they'd be in serious financial
trouble. However, she was complaining of leaving him due to being overwhelmed with the hopeless job of caring for him and carrying all the family
responsibilities. Jim had felt alienated from her for some time now—in fact,

he noticed that all social relations were a real chore and he was systematically avoiding them, lost increasingly in his own dark thoughts.

When Jim thought about all this, he felt nothing—he was numb. He knew this was odd and a real change from the frustration and anger that he experienced over his conditions in the early months of "the black cloud" (as he had long described it). He noticed, now, that he would just shrug his shoulders, as if he were witnessing his own demise in a dreamlike stupor that he could neither shake himself out of nor did he really care to do so.

Jim also noticed that he was no longer overeating and drinking heavily, which he had done for the first 7 to 8 months of his depression. His appetite for food—in fact, for anything enjoyable—had dried up almost completely. He smiled at the irony of it all. Although he was no longer so angry, even violent at times, he had broken so many good relationships then that he had no one around to enjoy his newly detached self. Sad thing was, he told himself, that he didn't really care—about anything.

Jim had long since overcome his denial of naming his problem correctly. He knew he was depressed and had long accepted the fact that he was in deep suffering. He had visited his pastor, and much prayer had been given on his behalf, but he had refused to see a counselor, believing for a long time that he merely had a case of "the blues" that would eventually pass. He did see a physician, who prescribed Prozac, but Jim quit the drug after a week because he "felt weird" and it wasn't helping him get better (he had shut out his wife's nag that the doctor said it would take 3–4 weeks to work).

Now he was plagued by thoughts of suicide, and wondered whether it would simply be easier to just shoot himself and end this unending misery for himself and his family. Of course, he told no one about this. He didn't want anyone to think he was beginning to "go crazy."

### A Most Prevalent Disorder

Depression is one of the most prevalent and serious mental disorders in the United States. It has been called the common cold of emotional disorders and appears to be on the rise, affecting up to 20% of the population at some time in their lives, with women being twice as likely as men to suffer from major depressive and dysthymic disorders (a milder form of chronic depression), but *not* bipolar disorders.

More specifically, major depressive disorder as one type of clinical depression is the most frequently diagnosed adult psychiatric disorder in the United States, with lifetime prevalence rates of 20 to 25% for women and 9 to 12% for men or point prevalence rates of about 6% for women and 3% for men.[1] In fact, the National Institute of Mental Health (NIMH) has noted that over 19 million adult Americans will experience some form of depression each year, with depression being the leading cause of disability and annual associated costs totaling more than $30 billion! Depression also increases the risk of heart attacks and is a serious and frequent complicating factor in stroke, diabetes, and cancer.[2]

Bipolar disorder (previously called manic-depressive disorder) with extreme mood swings or ups and downs, and a vulnerability to future episodes has also received increasing attention in recent years. It is estimated that about 1.5% of the adult population has classic bipolar disorder, affecting men and women equally, but with the inclusion of subtypes the prevalence can be as high as 5%[3] or even 6.5%![4] Both depression and bipolar disorder are therefore crucial ones to understand in order to be of effective help to the many who suffer from these conditions.

## Diagnosing Depression and Bipolar Disorder

Misdiagnosis of depression is very common at both ends of the spectrum. Not only do a lot of laypeople mislabel a variety of sadness and grief reactions as depression, but many physicians will misdiagnose depression as anxiety (a common affect with many depressions) or other mood disorders. Accurate assessment is the first step to proper treatment.

## (a) Depression

Depression can have a variety of meanings because there are different types of depression. Clinical depression as a disorder is not the same as brief mood fluctuations or the feelings of sadness, disappointment, and frustration that everyone experiences from time to time and that last from minutes to a few days at most. Clinical depression is a more serious condition that lasts weeks to months, and sometimes even years.

The *DSM-IV* (American Psychiatric Association, 1994), or more recently the *DSM-IV-TR* (American Psychiatric Association, 2000), identifies five major categories of mood disorders: depressive disorders, bipolar disorders, mood disorders due to a general medical condition, substance-induced mood disorders, and mood disorders not otherwise specified.[5] This chapter will focus on depressive and bipolar disorders.

In order for *Major Depressive Disorder* to be diagnosed, one or more major depressive episodes must have occurred. This means that the depressed person must have experienced at least two weeks of depressed mood (or irritable mood in children or adolescents) or loss of interest or pleasure in almost all activities, together with a minimum of four other symptoms of depression (only three if both depressed mood and loss of interest or pleasure occur) such as: (1) marked weight loss when not dieting, weight gain, or change in appetite; (2) insomnia or excessive sleep; (3) slowed movements or agitation; (4) decreased energy or fatigue; (5) feelings of worthlessness or inappropriate or excessive guilt; (6) indecisiveness or decreased ability to concentrate; and (7) recurrent thoughts of death or suicide. These symptoms (the second to the sixth) must occur almost every day.

A milder form of a depressive disorder is *dysthymic disorder*. Here the depressive symptoms are not serious enough to meet the criteria for major depressive disorder, but the person has a depressed mood more days than not for a minimum of two years. The other category of depressive disorder is *depressive disorder not otherwise specified*.

### (b) Bipolar Disorder

*DSM-IV* lists 4 major types of bipolar disorder: Bipolar I Disorder, Bipolar II Disorder (Recurrent Major Depressive Episodes with Hypomanic Episodes), Cyclothymic Disorder, and Bipolar Disorder Not Otherwise Specified.

In order for *Bipolar I Disorder* to be diagnosed there must be: (1) one or more *manic episodes* in which the patient feels hyper, extremely "high," wired, or unusually irritable, and gets into trouble, is unable to function at school or work, or ends up being hospitalized; (2) during the *manic episodes,* at least 3 of the following symptoms present: feeling overly self-confident or even grandiose; needing significantly less sleep than usual; being unable to stop talking; having racing thoughts; being easily distracted; being much more active socially or sexually, or being much more productive at work or at school than usual, or feeling agitated much of the time; getting involved in pleasurable activities without thinking of the consequences (e.g., buying things that are not affordable or having unprotected sex with a stranger);

and (3) one or more *depressive episodes* as described earlier for *major depressive disorder*.

In order for *Bipolar II Disorder* to be diagnosed, there must be: (1) one or more *depressive episodes* as described for *Major Depressive Disorder;* and (2) one or more *hypomanic episodes* which are similar to manic episodes but are not as impairing or severe. The hypomanic episodes usually last two to four days, causing Bipolar II patients to have far more depression than hypomania. They are often misdiagnosed with Major Depression but are worsened by antidepressant treatments. The suicide rate for this disorder is slightly higher than the rate for Major Depression.

In order for *Cyclothymic Disorder* to be diagnosed, there must be: (1) mood swings that are unpredictable, with the "ups" less severe than manic episodes and the "downs" less severe than major depressive episodes; (2) reduced productivity and unreliability in the patient due to the unstable mood even though it does not cause significant problems per se.[6]

### What Causes Depression?

There are various possible causes of depression. Different authors emphasize different causes depending on their theoretical viewpoints, but in general the possible causes (which are not mutually exclusive) can be grouped into six categories or factors: biological-genetic, physical, spiritual, personality and psychological, interpersonal, and environmental or societal.[7]

### Biological or Genetic Factors

Biologically oriented counselors and psychiatrists often view severe depression and bipolar disorders as being due to imbalances in brain biochemistry. These may be related to genetic influences and/or constitutional predispositions, as well as to environmental and life stress. More specifically, depression may be due to a deficiency in norepinephrine, dopamine, or serotonin, neurochemicals needed for proper brain functioning. Medical treatments such as antidepressants and/or electroconvulsive shock treatment are often recommended for severe depressive disorders. Antidepressants differ in mechanisms of action and side effect profile, leading patients to respond to some better than others. Mood stabilizers or medications such as lithium, depakote (divalproex), lamictal (lamotrigine), and atypical neuroleptics such as abilify (aripiprazole), geodon (ziprasidone), seroquel (quetiapine), and risperdal (risperidone), are crucial to the treatment of bipolar disorder. An interesting recent development is the use of mega-3 fatty acids (or fish oils) for bipolar disorder.[8] Antidepressants can worsen bipolar disorder and should be used sparingly and with a mood stabilizer.

It takes antidepressants four to six weeks to work. Mood stabilizers and atypical neuroleptics tend to work quicker to stabilize acute symptoms. However, they also can take four to six weeks to begin to maximize the benefit. Neither antidepressants nor mood stabilizers/atypical neuroleptics are addictive. They do, however, need close monitoring to avoid side effects or medical complications.

## Physical Factors

Lack of sleep, lack of regular exercise, poor diet or nutrition, substance abuse (e.g., cocaine, alcohol), overwork or exhaustion, some physical illnesses and conditions (for example, an underactive thyroid, chronic illness, or traumatic injuries), or certain types of medication (e.g., tranquilizers, steroids) can contribute to depression. Postpartum depression is an example of how physical or biological factors can lead to depression. It occurs after childbirth in about 10–15% of all deliveries. Another example concerns sunlight exposure and its effects on our biological systems. Seasonal affective disorder, or SAD, is an acute form of winter depression. It affects about 5–6% of the population, and exposure to sunlight is a natural and effective treatment. Artificial sunlight fixtures that mimic full spectrum bright sunlight are useful for this population.

## Spiritual Factors

*Sin.* Does sin cause depression? There are cases where depression appears to be a consequence of sin in a person's life, although this does not mean that depression is always due to personal sin. Possible sin-related causes of depression include negative attitudes or feelings like bitterness and hatred, guilt and lack of repentance over sinful behavior or attitudes, turning away from God and His Word, fear of the future and lack of trust in God as sufficient Provider, and unbelief in general.

*God-sent trials.* Difficult, painful, stressful times of trial or struggle may lead to periods of depression. Such God-sent trials are meant, however, to prune or purify us, so that we can bear more fruit (John 15:2; 1 Pet. 1:6–7).

*Demonic attacks.* Satan and his demonic forces may attack and oppress people. This in turn may sometimes lead to depression. Inner healing prayer and prayer for deliverance may be helpful.

*Existential vacuum.* At times depression may be due to feelings of meaninglessness and emptiness—an existential vacuum in life. Milder depression, experienced by almost every person at times, may come from the pain of being human in a fallen world.

*"Dark night of the soul."* There are times when depression is associated with spiritual dryness and an experience that St. John of the Cross called "the dark night of the soul" (Isa. 50:10). Richard Foster, in his excellent book, *Celebration of Discipline*, describes it: "The 'dark night'... is not something bad or destructive....The purpose of the darkness is not to punish or afflict us. It is to set us free....

What is involved in entering the dark night of the soul? It may be a sense of dryness, depression, even feeling lost. It strips us of overdependence on the emotional life. The notion, often heard today, that such experiences can be avoided and that we should live in peace, comfort, joy, and celebration only betrays the fact that much contemporary experience is surface slush. The dark night is one of the ways God brings us to a hush, a stillness, so that he can work an inner transformation of the soul....Recognize the dark night for what it is. Be grateful that God is lovingly drawing you away from every distraction so that you can see him."[9]

## Personality and Psychological Factors

*Temperamental vulnerability (Depression-prone personality).* Are some people innately prone to being depressed? Two decades ago, Frederic Flach described the depression-prone person who has a temperamental vulnerability to depression. Such people often have experienced loss early in life, such as the death of a parent. They are conscientious and responsible, with high morals and a tendency to feel guilty even when they have done nothing wrong. When they are not depressed, they may be energetic and competitive. They are introspective but concerned with the feelings of others, often to the point that they try hard to avoid hurting anyone's feelings.

Many are overinvolved in activities and overly dependent on others. They are easily hurt, sensitive to rejection and loss of self-esteem, and have a high need for control. Often they are not aware of the intense anger they feel and have trouble expressing anger appropriately when necessary. [10]

Although this description is somewhat general, it is a helpful reminder that some people are more susceptible than others to depression. These people may need to take special steps to avoid depression-producing situations or relationships.

*Loneliness.* Sometimes loneliness is seen as the consequence of a fear of love or a fear of rejection. This can result in depression if a person withdraws from much needed fellowship and interaction with friends.

*Triggering situations.* A number of situations can trigger depression or depressive reactions. These include insult, rejection, or failure; loss—especially of a loved one or object; life stress and change, especially if it occurs too often or too quickly; lack of positive, reinforcing, or rewarding events (or loss of the power of such events); success (when it is very taxing or stressful, or sometimes just before a success occurs); or learned helplessness, in which a person discovers, as a result of numerous experiences, that he or she can do nothing to change life events.

*Irrational, unbiblical self-talk, or misbeliefs.* Cognitive therapists have emphasized that triggering situations do not cause depression per se. Instead, depression is due to a person's mental attitude or self-talk (reactions, interpretations, expectations, and implicit beliefs) in response to such situations. Perfectionistic and rigid ways of thinking, often with logical errors (for example, blowing things out of proportion, taking things too personally, focusing only on the negative, jumping to conclusions) can distort views of oneself, the world, and the future. Depression follows and is likely to persist unless such distorted thinking is challenged and corrected, sometimes with the help of a counselor.

*Anger turned inward against the self.* Some mental health professionals, especially those with a more psychodynamic (Freudian) perspective, suggest that unresolved anger turned inward against oneself can result in depression. Such anger initially may have been directed toward a loved one or object that has been lost. Hurt may underlie the anger, and eventually this results in depression.

### Interpersonal Factors

Serious interpersonal disturbance or relationship problems also may lead to depression. For example, about 50% of depressed people also experience chronic marital discord. Recent research has shown that marital difficulties and family dysfunction have a significant impact on the course of depression. Relapse following therapy is more common among individuals whose families have high levels of criticism in their communication. Marital counseling can be a crucial approach to helping depressed individuals.

### Environmental or Societal Factors

Larger environmental, societal, and cultural factors like political unrest, economic recession, modernization and industrialization, high divorce rates, and poverty also may contribute to higher rates of depression. In addition, the ways people express their depression in terms of specific symptoms is affected by ethnic and cultural influences. For example, Asians tend to "somaticize" their depressions, showing physical symptoms, including loss of appetite, sleep difficulties, and headaches or other aches or pains.

## What Causes Bipolar Disorder?

Briefly, as Miklowitz has pointed out, genetics, biological vulnerabilities, and, to a lesser extent, stress, may all be possible causes of bipolar disorder. The biological vulnerabilities may include disturbances in the production and chemical breakdown (catabolism) of neurotransmitters such as norepinephrine, dopamine, glutanate, serotonin, and abnormal production of hormones like cortisol when under stress. The tendencies toward these biological vulnerabilities appear to be genetically mediated. While stress does *not* cause bipolar disorder per se without the crucial roles played by genetics and biological vulnerabilities, stress may increase the likelihood of having another episode of mania or depression for someone who already has bipolar disorder. Three kinds of environmental stress may be particularly significant: major life change (positive or negative), sleep-wake cycle disruptions, and conflicts with significant others.[11]

### Psychosocial Treatments for Major Depressive Disorder

Our goal here is to outline a reliable treatment approach to depression that combines biological, psychosocial, and spiritual elements of care. The good news is that depression is very treatable, if it is accurately recognized and rightly approached by caring family, pastors, and professional helpers.

*Behavior therapy*, *cognitive-behavior therapy*, and *interpersonal psychotherapy* have all been found to be effective psychosocial treatments for major depressive disorder. Psychosocial and pharmacological interventions for major depressive episodes appear to be equally effective, with some support found for the superior effectiveness of combined psychosocial and pharmacological treatments, although this is less clear for *severely* depressed patients.[12]

The following are some helpful books that provide clinical guidelines and methods for the psychosocial treatment of depression: Martell, Addis, and Jacobson on *Behavioral Activation, an approach to Behavior Therapy*, and McCullough on *Cognitive Behavioral Analysis System of Psychotherapy*; Beck, Rush, Shaw, and Emery, Klosko and Sanderson, and Persons, Davidson, and Tompkins, on Cognitive Therapy or *Cognitive-Behavior Therapy*; and Klerman, Weissman, Rounsaville, and Chevron, as well as Weissman, Markowitz, and Klerman on *Interpersonal Therapy*.[13]

### A Spiritually Oriented Psychosocial Approach to Treating Depression

In a short-term structured approach to strategic pastoral counseling with depressed parishioners or clients, Tan and Ortberg[14] have integrated some of the main aspects or components of behavior therapy, cognitive-behavior therapy, and interpersonal therapy within a biblical or spiritual perspective as follows:

A. (Affect): *Strategies for Exploring and Dealing with Feelings Associated with Depression*

1.  *Permission-Giving* to clients to talk openly about their struggles with depression
2.  *Attentive Listening*
3.  *Empathic Responding*
4.  *Use of Feeling Words, Imagery, and/or Role-Playing* to help clients better express their feelings
5.  *Appropriate Self-Disclosure*
6.  *Identifying Losses and Working Through the Grieving Process*
7.  *Inner Healing Prayer* for past hurts and painful memories, using a 7-step model developed by Tan: (a) begin with prayer for the Lord's guidance and blessing as well as protection; (b) use a relaxation strategy (e.g., slow, deep breathing, calming self-talk, and pleasant imagery, prayer, and biblical imagery or verses) to help

the client relax deeply; (c) once deeply relaxed, guide the client to go back in imagination to reenact a past event that is particularly painful or hurtful still. Ask the client at appropriate times, "What's happening right now? What are you feeling or experiencing?"; (d) after sufficient time has gone by, pray aloud for the Holy Spirit to come and minister His healing grace to the client in whatever way is needed or appropriate; (e) after some waiting, ask the client again, "What's happening? What are you experiencing or feeling now?"; (f) close with a brief prayer by both the counselor or client if possible; and (g) debrief the inner healing prayer experience with the client, and assign homework inner healing prayer to the client if appropriate.

B. (Behavior): *Behavioral Interventions for Treating Depression*

1. *Self-Monitoring*, using a Weekly Activity Schedule or Log, and rating activities engaged in with a Mastery (sense of achievement) and Pleasure (sense of enjoyment) scale of 0–5, gradually scheduling in more pleasant activities and events over time (Activity Scheduling).
2. *Use of Graded Task Assignment*, breaking down bigger tasks into smaller, more "doable" or manageable units.
3. *Use of a "Behavioral Experiment"* to overcome perfectionism or shame (e.g., by intentionally losing at a board game).
4. *Assertiveness Training*, using role-playing and modeling of appropriate, assertive responses.
5. *Relaxation/Coping Skills Training* to reduce tension and help to control negative thinking and feelings.
6. *Listening to Music and Engaging in Other Pleasant Activities.*
7. *Taking Care of the Body* (e.g., with good nutrition, regular exercise, and adequate sleep of 8 hours a night).
8. *Use of "light boxes" or special light bulbs* if the client is suffering specifically from Seasonal Affective Disorder (SAD).

C. (Cognition): *Helping Depressed People Change Distorted Thinking*

1. *Use of an "ABC" Diary*, with A for Activating Event or Situation, B for Belief or Self-Talk, and C for Consequences (Feelings and Behaviors).

2. *Thought-Stopping* to temporarily stop recurrent negative thinking by shouting "STOP" and eventually saying "STOP" sub-vocally to oneself.

3. *Cognitive Restructuring,* the mainstay of cognitive therapy, to help the client change negative, distorted thinking into more accurate, realistic, biblical thinking, with the following helpful questions:

- On what basis do you say that? Where is the evidence for your belief or conclusion?
- What's another way of looking at the situation? (alternative interpretation)
- Assuming that your conclusion or belief is correct, what then does it mean to you? (the "so what" question)
- What do you think God's view of this might be? What does the Bible have to say?

4. *Prayer with Thanksgiving* (Phil. 4:6–7)
5. *Use of humor*
6. *Bibliotherapy (Homework Reading)*
7. *Use of Contemplative Prayer and Meditation on Scripture and Other Spiritual Disciplines for Learning to Rest in the Lord.*[15]

## Psychosocial Treatments for Bipolar Disorder

Psychosocial treatments for bipolar disorder are *adjunctive* or secondary to the primary treatment involving pharmacological interventions or medications. Psychosocial treatments have the potential to increase medication adherence, improve quality of life, and enhance strategies for coping with stress. Combining pharmacotherapy and psychosocial treatments for bipolar disorder may therefore significantly lower the risk of relapse and rehospitalization, and improve the quality of life for patients.

*Psychoeducation,* involving the provision of information about bipolar disorder and its pharmacological treatment and treatment side effects to patients and their families, has been found to increase medication adherence.

*Cognitive-behavior therapy* as an ancillary or adjunctive treatment is effective in increasing medication adherence, decreasing rehospitalizations, and improving occupational and social functioning. *IPSRT* (a combination of Interpersonal Psychotherapy or IPT and Social Rhythm Therapies or SRT) has demonstrated its greatest impact on symptoms of depression. Consistency of psychosocial treatments over time may also be an important factor in the effective helping of bipolar patients.

Finally, *marital/family therapy* can be successfully combined with pharmacotherapy to decrease recurrences of bipolar disorder and improve occupational and social functioning.[16]

The following are helpful books that contain clinical guidelines and methods for the psychosocial treatment of bipolar disorder: Newman, Leahy, Beck, Reilly-Harrington, and Gyulai, Basco and Rush, and Lam, Jones, Hayward, and Bright on *Cognitive Therapy or Cognitive-Behavior Therapy*; Weissman, Markowitz, and Klerman on *Interpersonal Therapy and Social Rhythm Therapies* or IPSRT; and Miklowitz and Goldstein on a *Family-Focused Treatment Approach*.[17]

## A Spiritually Oriented Psychosocial Approach to Treating Bipolar Disorder

Many of the strategies covered for treating depression also apply to bipolar disorder, especially the "downswings" of the disorder. Miklowitz[18] has provided the following more specific aspects or components of effective psychosocial treatments (i.e., psychoeducation, cognitive-behavior therapy, IPSRT, and a family-focused treatment approach) for bipolar disorder, aimed at reducing risk factors and enhancing protective factors for the client:

A. *Reducing Risk Factors such as:*

1. *Stressful Life Changes*
2. *Alcohol and Drug Abuse* (and Caffeine Use)
3. *Sleep Deprivation* (e.g., jet lagging or changing time zones, staying up all night, sudden changes in sleep-wake cycles)
4. *Family Distress or Other Interpersonal Conflicts* (e.g., high levels of criticism from a spouse or parent, hostile interactions with coworkers or family members)
5. *Inconsistency with medication* (e.g., frequently missing one or more dosages, suddenly stopping taking mood stabilizing medication)

B. *Enhancing Protective Factors such as:*

1. *Observing and self-monitoring of client's mood and triggers for mood swings* (e.g., by keeping a daily mood chart or social rhythm chart)
2. *Maintaining regular daily and nightly routines* (e.g., by having a predictable or stable social schedule and going to bed and waking up around the same time each day)
3. *Relying on family and social supports* (e.g., by clearly communicating with family or relatives and asking for their help in emergencies)
4. *Receiving regular medical and psychosocial treatment* (e.g., by taking medications regularly, attending support groups, and by seeing a psychotherapist or counselor)

Miklowitz also listed the following objectives of psychotherapy for persons with bipolar disorder: to help the client make sense of current or past bipolar episodes; to do long-term planning, given the client's vulnerability to future episodes; to help the client accept and adjust to a long-term medication regimen; to identify and develop strategies for effectively coping with stress; to improve the client's functioning at work or in school; to help the client deal with the stigma of having bipolar disorder; and to improve family or marital/romantic relationships.[19]

### Depression, Bipolar Disorder, and Suicide

It is well known that severe depression and bipolar disorder have a high risk for suicide. Some have described suicide as a current "epidemic," especially among children, prisoners, the elderly, young adults, and particularly teenagers. Risks are highest among men, especially those over 65, people who feel hopelessness, and those who have experienced severe stress. Other factors associated with a high suicide risk include a prior history of suicide attempts, alcoholism, the presence of an organized and detailed plan for killing oneself, the lack of supportive family or friends, rejection by others, and, for many, the presence of a chronic, debilitating illness.

Most counselors are aware that when counseling depressed individuals or those with bipolar disorder who may be at risk for suicide, it is crucial to ask openly whether they have been thinking of taking their lives, and if so, whether they have specific plans. Open discussion, sometimes followed by hospitalization or referral, can reduce the likelihood of suicide.

Within recent years depression has become so common, within the church and without, that many people are aware of its symptoms and potential for impacting lives and families. Bipolar disorder involving extreme mood swings is also beginning to receive more attention. Helping others to understand the basics of depression and bipolar disorder can be a first step toward effective treatment for people suffering from these disorders.

After many years of denial and misunderstanding, Christians are coming to recognize that depression and bipolar disorder are complex conditions. They can be effectively treated, but they are not likely to be dismissed by simplistic explanations or approaches to treatment.

## When God Comes Near

Elijah is a great example of how depression can strike even the boldest and most godly of men. He became so stricken he retreated to a cave and wanted to die (1 Kin. 19:4). Yet God—in contravention of the common belief among depressives that He is angry with or doesn't care about the depressed sufferer—came and ministered to Elijah's every need. God provided him with food, sent angels to minister to his loneliness, and called him a godly rest. Elijah received God's loving care and was eventually restored in strength and purpose. God ministers the very same way today to anyone who suffers in the dark places of depression.

**ENDNOTES**

1.  W. E. Craighead, Hart, A. B., Craighead, L.W., and Ilardi, S.S., Psychosocial treatments for major depressive disorder, in P. E. Nathan and J. M. Gorman (eds.), *A guide to treatments that work*, second edition (New York: Oxford University Press, 2002), 245–261. Also see I. H. Gotlib and C. L. Hammen (eds.), *Handbook of depression* (NY: Guilford, 2002).

2.  National Institute of Mental Health (NIMH), *The numbers count*, NIH Publication No. NIH 99–4584, (1999) [Online]. Available:<http://www.NIMH.NIH.gov/pulicat/members.CFM

3.  M. Maj, Akiskal, H.S., Lopez-Ibor, J.J., and Sartorius, N. (eds.), *Bipolar disorder* (New York: Wiley, 2002).

4.  M. R. Lyles, Will the real mood stabilizer please stand up? *Christian Counseling Today*, 9(3), (2001), 60–61.

5.  American Psychiatric Association, *Diagnostic and statistical manual of mental disorders, fourth edition* (Washington, DC: American Psychiatric Association, 1994), 317–391. Also see American Psychiatric Association, *Diagnostic and statistical manual of mental disorders, fourth edition, text revision* (Washington, DC: American Psychiatric Association, 2000), 345–428.

6.  See A. Frances and M. B. First, *Your mental health: A layman's guide to the Psychiatrist's Bible* (New York: Scribner, 1998), 59–78.

7.  Some of the material in this chapter is based on a more detailed description of depression and strategic pastoral counseling found in S.-Y. Tan and J. Ortberg, Jr., *Understanding depression* and *Coping with depression*, (Grand Rapids, MI: Baker, 1995). From a Christian perspective, also see: A. Hart, *Counseling the depressed* (Waco, TX: Word, 1987); A. Hart, *Unmasking male depression* (Nashville: W Publishing Group, 2001); A. Hart and Weber, C.H., *Unveiling depression in women* (Grand Rapids, MI: Revell, 2002); F. Minirth and Meier, P., *Happiness is a choice*, second edition (Grand Rapids, MI: Baker, 1994); P. Meier, Arterburn, S. and Minirth, F., *Mood swings* (Nashville: Thomas Nelson, 2001).

8.  A. L. Stoll, *The Omega-3 connection* (New York: Simon & Schuster, 2001).

9.  R. Foster, *Celebration of discipline* (San Francisco: Harper & Row, 1978), 89–91.

10. F. F. Flach, *The secret strength of depression* (Philadelphia: Lippincott, 1974), 41–42.

11. D. J. Miklowitz, *The bipolar disorder survival guide* (New York: Guilford Press, 2002), 73–97. Also see E. F. Torrey and Knable, M. B., *Surviving manic depression* (New York: Basic Books, 2002); J. Fawcett, Golden, B., and Rosenfeld, N., *New hope for people with bipolar disorder* (Roseville, CA: Prima Publishing, 2000); F. M. Mondimore, *Bipolar disorder* (Baltimore: Johns Hopkins University Press, 1999); J. Scott, *Overcoming mood swings* (New York: New York University Press, 2001); D. Papolos and Papolos, J., *The bipolar child* (New York: Broadway Books, 1999). For secular self-help books on depression see: D. Burns, *Feeling good* (New York: William Morrow, 1999); D. Greenberger and Padeskey, C.A., *Mind over mood* (New York: Guilford Press, 1995); P. M. Lewinsohn, Munoz, R.F., Youngren, M. A., and Zeiss, A.M., *Control your depression* (New York: Fireside/Simon and Schuster, 1992); D. Papolos and Papolos, J., *Overcoming depression*, third edition (New York: Harper Collins, 1997); M. Broida, *New hope for people with depression* (Roseville, CA: Prima Publishing, 2001); M. E. Copeland, *The depression workbook,* second edition (Oakland, CA: New Harbinger, 2001).

12. Craighead, Hart, Craighead, and Ilardi (see note 1), 245. See also R. J. DeRubeis, S. D. Hollon, J. D. Amsterdam, R. C. Shelton, P. R. Young, R. M. Salomon, et al., Cognitive therapy vs. medications in the treatment of moderate to severe depression, *Archives of General Psychiatry*, 62 (2005): 409–416, and S. D. Hollon, R. J. DeRubeis, R. C. Shelton, J. D. Amsterdam, R. M. Salomon, J. P. O'Reardon, et al., Prevention of relapse following cognitive therapy vs. medications in moderate to severe depression, *Archives of General Psychiatry*, 62 (2005): 417–422.

13. See C. R. Martell, Addis, M.E. and Jacobson, N. S., *Depression in context: Strategies for guided action* (New York: W. W. Norton, 2001); J. P. McCullough, *Treatment of chronic depression: Cognitive behavioral analysis system of psychotherapy* (New York: Guilford Press, 2000); A. T. Beck, Rush, A.J., Shaw, B.F., and Emery G., *Cognitive therapy of depression* (New York: Guilford Press, 1979); J. S. Klosko and Sanderson, W.C., *Cognitive-behavioral treatment of depression* (Northvale, NJ: Jason Aronson, 1999); J. B. Persons, Davidson, J., and Tompkins, M.A., *Essential components of cognitive-behavior therapy for depression* (Washington, DC: American Psychological Association, 2001); G. L. Klerman, Weissman, M. M., Rounsaville, B. J., and Chevron, E.S., *Interpersonal psychotherapy of depression* (New York: Basic Books, 1984); M. M. Weissman, Markowitz, J.C., and Klerman, G. L., *Comprehensive guide to interpersonal psychotherapy* (New York: Basic Books, 2000).

14. S.-Y. Tan and J. Ortberg, *Understanding depression* (see note 7). See also Tan and Ortberg, *Coping with depression*, rev. ed. (Grand Rapids, MI: Baker, 2004).

15. See S.-Y. Tan and Gregg, D.H., *Disciplines of the Holy Spirit*, (Grand Rapids, MI: Zondervan, 1997); and S.-Y. Tan, *Rest: Experiencing God's peace in a restless world* (Ann Arbor, MI: Vine Books, 2000).

16. W. E. Craighead, Miklowitz, D. J., Frank, E., and Vajk, F.C., Psychosocial treatments for bipolar disorder, in P. E. Nathan and J. M. Gorman (eds.), *A guide to treatments that work*, second edition (New York: Oxford University Press, 2002), 263–275.

17. See C. F. Newman, Leahy, R. L., Beck, A.T., Reilly-Harrington, N. A., and Gyulai, L., *Bipolar disorder: A cognitive therapy approach* (Washington, DC: American Psychological Association, 2002); M. Basco, and Rush, A. J., *Cognitive-behavioral therapy for bipolar disorder* (New York: Guilford Press, 1996); D. H. Lam, Jones, S. H., Hayward, P., and Bright, J. A., *Cognitive therapy for bipolar disorder: A therapist's guide to concepts, methods, and practice* (Chichester, UK: Wiley, 1999); Weisman, Markowitz, and Klerman (see note 13); D. J. Miklowitz, and Goldstein, M. J., *Bipolar disorder: A family-focused treatment approach* (New York: Guilford Press, 1997).

18. Miklowitz, *The bipolar disorder survival guide* (see note 11), 153.

19. Ibid., 122.

# 8

## Stress and Anxiety

*Archibald Hart and Catherine Hart Weber*

The only thing we have to fear is fear itself.

Franklin D. Roosevelt

At first John enjoyed the excitement, the exhilaration and rush of the adrenaline surges. He felt a sense of profound urgency that propelled him to long working hours. He missed lunch often and had little time for his declining marriage and activities such as exercise and recreation. He had to focus. There were a lot of changes his business was going through, reorganizing and integrating many new systems.

His symptoms were subtle at first, nothing to be alarmed about, just annoyance. A low-grade sense of discomfort hovered over his life. Physically, he battled frequent colds. He didn't eat well and battled exhaustion. He masked the unresolved grief of several losses in his life. Drinking and other addictions had been temporary solutions to dealing with his pain. And then there was the occasional pounding heart, pains in his chest and muscle tension. Insomnia kept him awake at night, which gave opportunity for his mind to strategize anxiously and worry.

He tried to trust God and let go, but his faith and hope were clouded by a stronger force that had hold of him. He withheld his feelings of being overwhelmed, helpless, frustrated and disconnected, even from his wife.

Then, on a Friday afternoon, out of the blue, while driving home from work, John started having severe pains down his left arm and across his chest. He started to hyperventilate and panic. Tearfully, in desperation he called his wife on the cell phone. "Honey, I'm having a heart attack! I'm going to die!" She calmly instructed him to hang up and call 911. But he decided to drive himself to the nearest emergency room, stumbling in a state of fear and panic declaring he was having a heart attack.

He got immediate response, with extensive testing. No, it was not a heart attack, but a close resemblance: a panic attack (also known as a "stress attack" or "anxiety attack"). That is when he realized he needed to get some help.

### Epidemic Disorders

Behind the emotional pressure, fear, worry, catastrophizing, wandering thoughts and physical discomfort of stress and anxiety that John and millions of others experience was a powerful and intricately designed system created by God and centered in the mind, nervous system, and the brain. While this natural defense mechanism is designed to alert us to danger, keep us growing, vigilant and productive, it can also be pushed too far and become toxic.

When the immediate threat or call for action is long gone, the nervous system can sometimes continue to stay activated, intensifying symptoms resulting in stress or anxiety disorders, depression and many other health problems. Quite simply, our bodies and being aren't physiologically capable of dealing with the prolonged pressures of modern-day living that so many are experiencing.

Stress, anxiety, and related depression are now considered epidemic and the leading mental health disorders in our nation. Christian counselors will increasingly be challenged with connecting this array of overlapping and sometimes confusing symptoms with understanding the underlying causes and providing effective comprehensive treatment that brings complete healing to the whole person, not merely eliminating symptoms.

Christian counseling can provide effective lasting recovery through utilizing a combination of approaches in caring for the whole person. Effective counseling will augment conventional psychotherapy addressing areas of change and growth, cognitive-behavioral and medication treatments along with other complementary approaches.

## Stress

First, let us examine the nature of stress. Hans Selye, Ph.D., the Canadian endocrinologist who first discovered "the stress response" in the mid-1930s, clearly described the physiological changes that occur when a person experiences difficulties or pressures in life. Science has made much progress since then in understanding the stress response and long-term effects. We now know that it is not stress itself that is the problem, but our *responses* to stress, the sense of *helplessness*, the *duration* of the stress, and the *lack of recovery* from the stressors bombarding us which cause damage emotionally and physically.

*Eustress*, or so-called normal healthy stress, is an essential natural part of life enabling us to change, grow, and produce good results in our lives. God uses times of difficulty and adversity to stretch us and develop our character. This mechanism also keeps life exciting, enabling us to be creative and productive. *Acute*, short-lived stress keeps us alert to the protective response, equipping us to deal with challenges, unless they are too traumatizing. However, when any stress is prolonged (good or bad), *chronic*, excessive and intense—when we aren't able to recover, or remove ourselves from it, there is a transition into *distress* (stress disease). This causes adrenaline exhaustion and begins to erode the foundations of mental and physical health. The mind and body are not equipped to handle the process of ongoing chronic stress.

## Causes and Symptoms of Stress

So what is causing this epidemic of stress? The source of stress can come from external or internal factors.

*External Stressors* include adverse physical conditions such as pain, illness, extreme temperatures, noise, foul air, hurried schedule; or stressful psychological environments such as work demands, abusive or conflictual relationships, the environment and unpredictable events.

*Internal Stressors* can also be physical such as infections, inflammation, hormonal imbalances, poor health habits; or psychological such as intense worry about finances, work, family and relationship problems, worrying about a harmful event that may or may not occur, an emptiness, lack of fulfillment, irresponsible behavior, unrealistic expectations, negative attitudes and feelings, personality traits such as perfectionism, trying to do too much, change and loss.

Whether seeking help for primarily psychological or physical ailments, doctors say that their patients complain about stress, anxiety and other related emotional and physical symptoms more than anything else.[1, 2] An estimated 20 million Americans are experiencing nervous tension, sleep disturbances, physical aches and pains and many other symptoms due to these conditions.

In Table 1, we provide a way to differentiate some of the symptoms of stress from anxiety. Table 2 differentiates symptoms of depression from the stress/anxiety complex. Although some of these symptoms also overlap with other physical and psychological conditions, many have been overlooked as evidence of stress, anxiety and depression, resulting in patients being frustrated with undiagnosed conditions and unhappy lives. Others are shocked to realize that the numbness in the limbs or frequent urination are actually the result of stress and anxiety. Encourage clients to not merely focus on symptom relief, but what these symptoms are alerting them to. Once they understand the underlying cause(s), complete, lasting recovery is then possible.

### The Stress Response

To expand your understanding and assist you to effectively counsel those who suffer from excessive stress, here is a brief summary of the stress response. The stress response starts in the brain. When a stressor is detected as a threat, the *amygdala, hypothalamus,* and *pituitary glands* trigger the "flight-or-fight" stress response. The *sympathetic nervous system* activates several different physical responses to mobilize for action. The *adrenal glands* increase the output of *adrenaline* (also called *epinephrine*), *cortisol* and other *glucocorticoids*. These are the stress hormones. In turn, nerve cells release *norepinephrine,* which tightens and contracts the muscles and sharpens the senses to prepare for action.[3]

An outpouring of these stress hormones impacts virtually every system

## TABLE 1:

## DIFFERENTIATING STRESS FROM ANXIETY

### Symptoms of General Stress
### (Consult the DSM-IV for criteria of specific stress disorders)

**Physical Discomforts (which are not due to another illness):**
Muscle and skeletal problems such as tics, headaches, dizziness, aches and pains due to muscle tension, trembling. Gastrointestinal difficulties such as indigestion, nausea, stomach aches, diarrhea. Cardiovascular changes—pounding heart, high blood pressure, fatigue, lack of energy, insomnia, weight gain—especially around the abdomen.

**Behavioral changes:** Withdrawal. Avoidance. Increased alcohol and/or substance use, change in eating habits, appetite and weight. Change in sleeping habits. Sleep disturbances.

**Social, Emotional, Mental uneasiness:** Chronic fatigue, irritability, feeling out of sorts, interpersonal conflict, reduced concentration, lower levels of creativity, negative, pessimistic thinking, depression, an inability to switch off and relax.

### Symptoms of General Anxiety
### (Consult the DSM-IV for criteria of specific anxiety disorders)

**Physical, mental, emotional changes:** Heart palpitations, mitral valve prolapse, sensations of smothering/ choking, stabbing pains, chest pain, headaches, back pain, muscle spasms, sweating (hot or cold), constant need to urinate or defecate, apprehension, nervousness, worry, uncertainty, jitteriness, fear or panic, feeling of doom, dizziness, nausea, diarrhea and stomach problems, depersonalization, paresthesias (arms, legs, mouth), preoccupation with symptoms, irrational fears about: dying, losing control, losing your mind, embarrassing yourself, having a heart attack.

**Behavioral and social changes:** Erratic or consistent impairment in functioning, hostile angry outbursts, verbal and emotional attacks, social withdrawal, dependent clingy behavior, compulsive behaviors, phobic fears, self-destructive irrational behavior.

**Indications for anxiety in children:** Refusing to go to school; overly clinging behavior; frequent stomach aches; headaches and other physical complaints; persistent nightmares; not getting work completed.

**Indications for anxiety in adolescents:** Substance abuse; frequent truancy; risk-taking behavior; "acting out"; decline in academic performance; inability/ fearfulness of engaging in social relationships.

**Symptoms of General Stress and Anxiety**

Fast heart rate, rapid or shallow breathing; increased muscle tension; loss of concentration; diarrhea; substance abuse; avoidance behaviors; sleep disturbances; appetite disturbance; repetitive behaviors; intrusive thoughts; interpersonal conflict; depression.

Also listen for some common complaints such as:

Tension, feeling on edge, up-tight, hassled, nervous, jittery, jumpy, wound up, scared, terrified, insecure, pressured, alarmed, anxious, worried, dreading what might happen, uncertainty, vulnerability, apprehension, edgy, troubled.

of the body. Four main systems respond to stress and can be compromised by prolonged stress: the cardiovascular system, immune system, nervous system, endocrine or glandular system and metabolic response. The heart and pulse rate increase, breathing becomes shallow and rapid, muscles get tense, the digestive system shuts down and the hands and feet become icy cold. Eventually, when the danger or pressure passes, the level of stress hormones drop.

*Negative consequences of chronic stress.* However, chronic low or high levels of stress can keep the *glucocorticoids and catecholamines* (stress hormones) in circulation, causing all systems involved in the stress response to be compromised. Fatigue, exhaustion and illness results when the body doesn't get enough rest, relaxation and recovery time to restore equilibrium. The body also forms free radicals that are associated with degenerative diseases, illness and acceleration of the aging process. Table 3 presents a list of some of the negative consequences of prolonged, chronic stress.

### Diagnostic Criteria for Stress

Most stress related problems would be categorized under the heading of Adjustment Disorders in the DSM-IV. The first criteria states: "The development of emotional or behavioral symptoms in response to an identifiable stressor(s) occurring within 3 months of the onset of the stressor(s)." Here is the range of classifications:

**TABLE 3**

**CONSEQUENCES OF PROLONGED STRESS**

**Negative consequences of prolonged, chronic stress**

Physical and emotional exhaustion, Anxiety, Depression, Heart disease, Stroke, Depletion of calcium from the bones, Immune system vulnerability, Immune disorders, Cancer, Gastrointestinal problems, Eating problems, Weight gain—especially around the abdomen, Diabetes, Pain, Sleep disturbances, Sexual and reproductive dysfunction, Self medication and unhealthy lifestyles, Damage to the brain causing Hippocampal atrophy, killing of brain cells, memory loss and diminished concentration.

*Adjustment Disorders*

| | |
|---|---|
| 309.0 | With Depressed Mood |
| 309.24 | With Anxiety |
| 309.28 | With Mixed Anxiety and Depressed Mood |
| 309.3 | With Disturbance of Conduct |
| 309.4 | With Mixed Disturbance of Emotions and Conduct |
| 309.9 | Unspecified |

The nature of the stressor can be indicated by listing it on Axis IV (e.g., Divorce).

**Categories of Stress**

Serious stress disorders can be divided into two main categories:

*Acute Stress.* This is the reaction to an immediate threat, danger or loss eliciting the fight or flight response. Acute stress meets the diagnostic criteria if it lasts less than 6 months. It is sudden in onset then usually diminishes once the threat is over.

*Chronic Stress.* Constant ongoing stressful situations, even seemingly minor ones, that are not short-lived can cause continual pressure that then become chronic. This is a more serious form of stress disorder, even though it may not seem as intense as acute stress. Ongoing highly pressured work, long-term relationship problems, loneliness, complicated bereavement, persistent financial worries—all could meet the diagnostic criteria if these disturbance lasts for 6 months or more. Eventually this form of stress can weaken the immune system and have many damaging effects to health and well-being.

## Anxiety

Now, let us examine the nature of anxiety. Anxiety results from a combination of chemical reactions in the brain to a stimulus, fearful and worrisome thinking, troubled feelings and an exaggerated and persistent stress response. Anxiety, in effect, can be a stressor OR can be caused by stress. There is a body-mind connection where every change in the mind (anxiety) produces a corresponding change in the body (alarm and stress) and vice versa. This reaction impacts every part of a person's being all at once.[4]

Anxiety, like stress is an inevitable part of life. Symptoms and intensity range from a "mild" response to stressful or challenging situations to "intense" fear and a troublesome disorder, which interferes with daily functioning and a sense of well-being.[5] Some people have a lower threshold for stress and are more susceptible to develop anxiety. For example, in some people, stress hormones remain elevated instead of returning to normal levels. This may occur in highly competitive athletes or people with a history of depression, or early childhood anxiety. Anxiety can result from a number of other factors such as: genetic predisposition, a painful childhood, major stress or trauma, medical illness, alcohol or drug abuse—and can also occur for no obvious or apparent reason.

### The Anatomy of Anxiety

When faced with a stressful, anxious thought, feeling or startling sensory trigger, the emotional and fear center in the brain, the *amygdala* is activated and alerts other parts of the brain for a *fear response*. This powerful mechanism, begins in the brain, and also involves the spinal cord and the peripheral nerves. The *locus ceruleus* receives signals from the amygdala initiating many responses in the body's *sympathetic nervous system*, such as sweaty palms, rapid heartbeat, increased blood pressure and pupil dialation. The *hypothalamus and pituitary gland* signals the adrenal glands to pump out high levels of the stress hormone *cortisol.*

The physiological response to anxiety or stress is the same no matter what the initial stressor is (physical danger or imaginary threat). After the initial fear response, the conscious mind is activated. Some of the sensory information through sight, sound and smell doesn't go directly to the amygdala but takes a route through the *hypothalamus, hippocampus* then the *cortex*, where the threatening or traumatic stimuli it is analyzed. If the decision is yes, then the cortex signals the *amygdala* and the body stays on alert. The *bed nucleus of the stria terminalis* in the brain perpetuates the fear response, causing the symptoms typical of anxiety.[6]

Each anxiety response and disorder has its own distinct features, but they are all bound together by the common theme of excessive, irrational fear and dread. Presented below are the primary types of anxiety disorders and the diagnostic categories, which are outlined in the DSM-IV under *Anxiety Disorders.* Each has distinct criteria, requiring specific treatment.

*Diagnostic Categories for Anxiety*

| | |
|---|---|
| 300.01 | Panic Disorder Without Agoraphobia |
| 300.21 | Panic Disorder With Agoraphobia |
| 300.22 | Agoraphobia Without History of Panic Disorder |
| 300.29 | Specific Phobias |
| 300.23 | Social Phobias (Social Anxiety Disorder) |
| 300.3 | Obsessive-Compulsive Disorder |
| 309.81 | Post Traumatic Stress Disorder |
| 308.3 | Acute Stress Disorder |
| 300.02 | Generalized Anxiety Disorder |
| 293.89 | Anxiety Disorder Due to...(indicate the General Medical Condition) |

Substance-Induced Anxiety Disorder

300.00   Anxiety Disorder Not Otherwise Specified

## Comorbidity Between Stress, Anxiety and Depression

Many who suffer from stress and anxiety slowly become depressed to some degree. Comorbidity between depression and any of the anxiety disorders is well over 50%. This has crucial implications for accurate diagnose and effective treatment for those experiencing both anxiety and depression.[7] According to the National Institute of Mental Health, anxiety disorders can also co-exist with eating disorders, substance abuse, depression, other anxiety disorders and illnesses such as cancer or heart disease. Anxiety disorders can precede the onset of depression or follow it, and successful treatment of an anxiety disorder may delay or minimize the severity of depression.

A combination of determinants work together to predispose someone to stress, anxiety and depression disorders: life events, childhood experience (brain becomes vulnerable to depression), faulty parenting, heredity, individual personality (inhibited, introverted), cumulative chronic stress, lifestyle, interpersonal conflicts, biochemical imbalance in the brain, abnormalities in the emotional processing center of the brain (the amygdala). Other complicating problems can increase symptoms of depression such as hypoglycemia, premenstrual syndrome and alcoholism.[8] These causes and the factors that maintain the disorders are varied and experienced in every level of life.

### Treating Stress and Anxiety: A Comprehensive Approach

For lasting healing in treating stress and anxiety, an integrative combination of approaches in caring for the whole person and the full range of contributing factors has proven to be most effective. The physiological response, cognitive, emotional, relational, behavioral, spiritual and lifestyle factors all interact to trigger and overcome the causes and effects of stress and anxiety. Clinical practice usually utilizes the conventional scientifically proven combination of cognitive-behavioral therapy along with medication, for more moderate to severe anxiety disorders. However, although these treatments are helpful, not everyone is able to achieve complete recovery, or may get better for a while and then relapse, because treatment wasn't sufficient for complete healing.[9]

To ensure lasting recovery, the *whole person* and their *whole life* need to get better. Effective treatment will go beyond learning specific strategies and techniques to reduce symptoms of physiological anxiety, redirecting fear-provoking thoughts and overcoming negative behavior. As an integrative Christian counselor, address other areas of change and growth such as a healthy lifestyle, diet and exercise, overcoming anxiety-prone personality traits, interpersonal conflicts, grieving, spiritual hope, strategies for reducing and managing stress.

## Treatment Summary

Treatment of stress and anxiety problems will require a specific treatment plan for each client depending on their diagnostic features. Utilizing conventional and integrative resources will most-likely span several interventions and disciplines. Here is a summary of primary considerations:

1. *Do a comprehensive diagnostic evaluation.* Review *current problems and concerns,* and their perceptions (such as helplessness and hoplessness). Depending on the presenting issues, use whatever *measures* for determining levels of stress, anxiety and depression you are trained to use. If you are not trained to do assessment, refer to someone who is. Identify typical as well as atypical signs and symptoms and the underlying cause(s). (The client might be more comfortable describing physical symptoms than admitting to emotions associated with depression or anxiety.)

Take a complete *patient history,* as well as family of origin. Assess for *medical conditions, genetic factors, medical history and underlying causes of stress* as well as *negative coping patterns* such as substance abuse, alcoholism, addictions, eating disorders, excessive behavior, anxiety disorder, depression and suicide. Anxiety disorders are not all treated the same and coexisting conditions will determine treatment. Establish the specific problem before continuing treatment. A condition such as alcoholism would need to be treated before or along with anxiety disorder.

2. *Refer client to their primary physician for an updated complete physical.* This should include a blood workup to rule out a physical illness and medications. Get a release to access their past medical and psychiatric history as well.

3. *For severe symptoms of anxiety, refer to a psychiatrist.* Consider further testing and possible prescription medications to be combined along with cognitive-behavioral therapy for the best results. Medication is critical in treating those with severe symptoms of panic attacks, agorophobia, obsessive compulsive disorders or those who do not respond to other treatments. Anxiety is considered "severe" when the client meets one of the following criteria:

- Anxiety is disruptive to their life, prohibiting functioning at work.
- Anxiety interferes with their ability to be in relationship with others.
- Anxiety causes distress at least 50% of the time they're awake.

4. *Develop a comprehensive treatment plan for recovery.* This plan is customized to the specific needs of your client. Work with them to outline changes and strategies for each area of their life, as well as treating any co-existing disorders. Physical—Mental—Emotional—Spiritual—Behavioral—Social. Begin with progressive, practical action strategies that moves them toward overcoming a sense of helplessness, but is not overwhelming. Educate client on the stress response—what is normal, how to discern when it is not. For successful recovery, use practice and repetition to strengthen the longevity of skills and resources gained in therapy.

5. *Consider consultation with a dedicated treatment team.* If the case is complicated indicating comorbidity with other disorders such as substance abuse, and/or physical illness, you will need to work together with a team of health professionals. This might include their primary physician, psychiatrist, specialist, nutritionist, outpatient rehab, pastor or social worker. Get consultation and utilize support networks in order for the client to receive the most comprehensive effective treatment.

6. *Help your client understand the nature of the underlying cause(s) of stress/anxiety.* They might deny that they are even "stressed out". Regard symptoms as a signal with a message, to assist them to understand themselves more and make changes. *What are my body and mind trying to tell me? What is causing me stress? How am I alleviating and recovering from stress? What is behind my developing the anxiety? What led to my developing these symptoms? What changes are necessary in order for me to recover? What can't I change, but learn to live with better? How can I gain a more optimistic sense of control?*

The goal may be to reduce stress, resolve relationship conflict, grieve a loss, change personality patterns, grow in trust and faith spiritually or make healthier lifestyle changes. When they are able to heed the symptom's warning signals and identify and make the necessary underlying changes in all areas of life, not only will the stress, anxiety and depression symptoms improve, but their whole life will get well. Address each coexisting diagnosis separately, treating each progressively along with the overall treatment goals.

7. *Help treat the milder physical symptoms.* Milder physical symptoms of

pain, headaches, stomachaches, tension and insomnia could be managed by over-the-counter medications or calming herbs such as Kava Kava, if their physician permits.[10]

8. *Practice the best Christian cognitive-behavioral therapy you can.* Conventional interventions that have been found effective in treating stress and anxiety are cognitive-behavioral therapy along with medication (for moderate to severe anxiety). If you are not trained in these techniques, seek consultation. (See a brief description following.) In order to get the benefit from cognitive-behavioral therapy, it takes consistent effort and time practicing these basic strategies and techniques. This can be difficult to do, especially after therapy is terminated. To ensure ongoing recovery, you could suggest the use of cassette tapes and occasional sessions with the client after termination, in order to brush up and stay on track with the strategies they learned. Referral to an anxiety support group will also enhance recovery.

9. *Address personality and other issues.* There are often issues that go beyond fears and distorted thinking that contribute to stress and anxiety problems. *Personality traits most associated with stress, anxiety and depression are*: excessive need to please (fear of rejection); anger, hostility; over-control; perfectionism; over-cautiousness (fear of illness, injury or death); fear of confinement; extremely analytical; emotionally sensitive; over reactive; low self-esteem; and being guilt ridden. Equip and empower clients to overcome these challenges with resources such as: assertiveness training, anger management, healthy emotional expression, learning to trust and let go, positive self-talk, dealing with disappointments guilt and worry, overcoming an emotional sense of helplessness and gaining a sense of control.

10. *Encourage optimism and a sense of control.* Acute and chronic stress can have negative effects, but what really determines the toll on health is the extent to which one feels an emotional sense of being *helpless* and *hopeless*. The stressor isn't usually the problem, but the perceived *sense of control*. This helplessness can lead to physical and emotional degeneration including depression. It is essential then, to help clients be optimistic, to do something—anything against the chronic stressor to reduce helplessness and being overwhelmed. If there is some way to contribute to and predict what will happen next, to remain optimistic, there is a higher resistance to hopelessness. Learning a relaxation response, exercising regularly, prayer, meditation on the Word and hope in God—all contribute to gaining a sense of

control over the stressor and damages from chronic exposure of stress-induced chemicals.

11. *Spirituality is important for complete healing.* In addition to counseling and medication, the healing power of relationship with God, the Bible, prayer and connection with others are essential. As a Christian counselor you are uniquely equipped to be sensitive to the client's spiritual experience and issues that could be contributing to the root of anxiety. Do they feel distant from God, empty, lacking meaning, vision, and purpose, confused, fearful, directionless, unloved, not knowing their unique gifts or creativity? Are they experiencing a spiritual battle in their mind? Peace of mind, tranquility, hope, and unconditional love can be viewed as the ultimate remedy for fear, worry, and anxiety. Explore with them ways they can strengthen their relationship with God through spiritual direction resources of reading, applying Scripture to their life, prayer, meditation, and connection with others.

12. *Adopting a healthy lifestyle, with proper self-care should be encouraged.* Even if the client is receiving good care through conventional medication and therapy, full recovery will be limited if they fail to place importance on their peace of mind, practical lifestyle, reducing and managing stress, and staying aware of their vulnerability to external and internal stress that can lead to anxiety and depression. Encourage them to:

    a.    Eat well-balanced, nutritious meals. Eliminate harmful substances.

    b.    Learn mind-body techniques to help relax and reduce stress response.

    c.    Get enough sleep, rest and relaxation.

    d.    Develop a relationship with God. Practice prayer and Christian meditation.

    e.    Exercise regularly. At least 30–45 minutes of exercise a day.

    f.    Counteract negative self-talk and mistaken beliefs with positive reality and God's Word.

12. *Address stress management and anxiety reduction interventions.* Relaxation techniques and stress reducing outlets are absolutely essential to recovery. An essential passive way to counteract the physiological stress response is to elicit a relaxation response. The body can't be relaxed and

tranquil as well as tense and anxious at the same time. An active lifestyle including regular exercise is another effective antidote to recovering from the physiological strain of stress and anxiety. Explore how the client can reduce stressors—what they can change, what they cannot. Infuse a *sense of control* over the stressor and stress response through these following strategies, which counteract helplessness and hopelessness.

Deep breathing exercises:

    a.   Progressive muscle relaxation
    b.   Prayer and Christian meditation
    c.   Mindfulness training
    d.   Biofeedback
    e.   Massage therapy
    f.   Exercise

13. *Strengthen or establish the client's support network.* Meaningful connection with others and safe, trustworthy people can be helpful in difficult times. Discourage isolation, which is a symptom of depression, and only further complicates the healing process. Encourage connections with family, friends, church, community, and support groups.

## Integrative Therapeutic Interventions

In closing this chapter let us review in more detail the primary therapeutic interventions that need to be utilized in treating stress and anxiety problems.

## Cognitive-Behavioral Therapy

Cognitive-behavioral therapy (CBT) is solution focused psychotherapy enabling the client to learn skills that they can continue to utilize and improve the quality of their life. From a Christian perspective, cognitive therapy can be integrated as an effective resource for those seeking answers in their life, and as a means of changing and gaining control over faulty thinking and behaviors. A combination of the following strategies have been proven to be effective therapeutic treatments for stress and anxiety disorders:

- Abdominal breathing training,
- Muscle relaxation training,
- Cognitive restructuring,
- Systematic desensitization, and
- In vivo exposure.

The cognitive therapy process identifies distorted thoughts and perceptions which contribute to the anxiety, and are then challenged and redirected. Here are some of the basic fundamentals:

1.  Help the client identify the sources of stress and anxiety by asking the client to keep a journal of daily events, activities and thoughts, feelings, physical discomfort and the severity. This helps to make connections between negative thoughts, and the resulting emotions and behaviors.

2.  Once a list of automatic distorted thoughts and fears are identified, begin to teach clients to monitor and challenge these with contrary evidence and reality. Using the Word of God is a helpful mainstay for this process.

3.  Teach strategies to dispute the negative irrational thinking, substituting new ways of thinking, believing and responding, and help them deal with reality.

4.  The client then learns how to monitor their negative thinking, ruminating and self-talk by having better control of their thoughts and thus over their lives.

5.  Then they are able to identify, question and change the irrational thinking and replace them with empowering, positive thoughts and beliefs.

### Antidepressants

SSRI's such as Paxil, Zoloft, Buspar or Celexa are often used in the treatment of anxiety. A new group of antidepressants known as serotonin-norepinephrine reuptake inhibitors (SNRI's), are being considered to be even more effective in treating anxiety disorders. These newer antidepressants act on both serotonin and norepinephrine and are preferred medications in the treatment of comorbid anxiety and depression disorders due to their broader spectrum of effect on multiple neurotransmitter systems. The effectiveness is due to being able to target several neurotransmitters, which can stabilize mood as well as the fight-or-flight response. These can be used for long periods of time provided patients have regular liver function tests.

When treating anxiety, in order to avoid relapse, clients will need to take antidepressant medication at least eighteen months or longer. Staying on the medication longer enables the brain to rest, regenerate and recover from the initial trauma of severe anxiety symptoms. Relapse is higher for those who take medication for a shorter period of time, especially without psychotherapeutic resources.

## Tranquilizers

Faster acting relaxants can be used as short-term temporary intervention until the longer-acting medications kick in, but only under very limited and severe circumstances. Benzodiazephines such as Xanax, Ativan or Klonopin must be used for a limited time under strict limit refills because they can be addictive, and can be harmful if not used properly.

### Alternative Therapies

There is increasing interest in exploring alternative approaches either instead of prescription drugs, or along with conventional treatment.[11] Herbs, supplements and deep relaxation approaches have been found to be helpful in treating mild to moderate anxiety and depression and can be used in conjuction with therapy. Natural tranquilizers having a calming effect are Kava, Valerian, and passionflower. For mild depression accompanying anxiety, Sam-e, tryptophan and St. John's Wort can be helpful.[12] Other helpful herbs are Gotu Kola and Ginkgo Biloba. Amino acids used to treat anxiety and mood disorders are Tryptophan, Gamma Amino Butyric Acid, DL-Phynylalanine and Tyrosine. Natural hormones such as melatonin is used to help with sleep and DHEA, which improves mood. Due to the lack of getting adequate nutrients from food, and the wear and tear on the body, stress and anxiety patients need vitamin supplements to replace the deficiencies. The following is recommended: Vitamin B complex, Vitamin C, Calcium and Magnesium, Zinc, Chromium and Iron.

If your clients are exploring these, caution them regarding not self-medicating by taking more than is recommended, taking natural pharmaceuticals along with other medications and the exposure to "new age" practices that often accompany alternative remedies. A helpful resource to guide clients through alternative treatments is the book *Christian Guide to Alternative Medicine.*

## Healthy Lifestyle Changes

*Eat well.* Food does impact mood and is essential for fueling the body, enhancing recovery and reducing symptoms of stress and anxiety. Here are the essential considerations:

1. Eat five to six small, balanced mini-meals throughout the day, to help keep blood sugar stabilized. Don't skip breakfast.
2. Use olive and canola oil, but no hydrogenated oil products.
3. Eat whole, unprocessed foods, organic when possible. Choose brightly colored fruits and vegetables.
4. Eat balanced meals including lean protein and complex carbohydrates at every meal.
5. Take a good quality vitamin and mineral supplement, and adequate amounts of calcium, magnesium, folic acid, selenium and vitamin B complex.
6. Avoid or eliminate substances and stimulants such as caffeine, refined foods, sugar, MSG, saturated animal fats and foods that cause allergies. Check with primary physician regarding any prescription drugs being taken, to see if they could be contributing to symptoms.
7. Drink 8–10 glasses of water a day.

*Exercise.* Regular exercise is a beneficial form of stress, as it is an effective way to train the body to actively withstand and recover from stress.[13] Chemical and hormonal changes released while exercising have a positive impact on emotions. Physical activity also protects against possible health problems associated with stress, anxiety and depression such as obesity, heart disease and cancer. The most effective form of exercise is interval training—when waves of energy expenditure are followed by recovery. Raise and lower the heart rate between 60%–75% of maximum, creating cycles of stress and recovery during the activity. Two 12–20 minute sessions can be done a day, or one 45–60 minute session. As physical endurance improves, so will endurance for dealing with stress.[14]

## Prayer and Biblical Meditation

"Anxiety in the heart of man causes depression, but a good word makes it glad." *Prov. 12:25*

"The Lord God has given Me (Jesus) the tongue of the learned . . . that I should know how to speak a Word in season to him who is weary." *Isa. 50:4*

Scientific research is now validating the power of prayer in healing and recovery. Why worry, when you can pray? Take it to the Lord in prayer. Besides, worry never changes anything, but prayer does. And we have proof. Regular prayer and biblical meditation leads to increased peace and tranquility, a very effective passive approach for reducing worry and generalized anxiety. However, the benefits of the power of prayer and meditation are more profound than the calming effect on our body, mind and emotions. Like the healing infusion of hope and encouragement that builds faith knowing people are praying for us. The ultimate transformation comes as we come into relationship and a complete encounter with the living God, Christ His Son, the Holy Spirit and the changing power of His Word. He sets us free from the wounds and strongholds of the past, bringing reconciliation with Himself, ourselves and others.[15]

The discipline of Christian meditation on Christ and the Word is an important heritage since the first days of the church, but misunderstood and distorted by new age and eastern religions. It is a dynamic way to change the thought life by focusing on God and His Word, and thus changing the rest of life—and can be utilized effectively into cognitive therapy. It instills a sense of control, optimism and hope. Direct your clients to learn more through Christian resources such as the books *Biblical Meditation for Spiritual Breakthrough* by Elmer L. Towns, *Praying God's Word* by Beth Moore, and the Christian relaxation tape available through *The Anxiety Cure* by Dr. Archibald Hart.

**ENDNOTES**

1. Susan M. Lark, *Anxiety and stress* (Berkely, CA: Celestialarts,1996), 10.

2. Richard A. Swensen, *Margin* (Colorado: NavPress, 1995), 20.

3. Michael Lemonick, How stress takes its toll, *Time,* special issue (20 January 2003), 67.

4. Harold H. Bloomfield, *Healing anxiety naturally* (New York: HarperPerennial, 1998.), 31.

5. Archibald D. Hart, *The anxiety cure* (Nashville: Word, 1999), 5.

6. Christine Gorman, The science of anxiety, *Time* (10 June, 2002), 46.

7. Steffany Fredman, and Rosenbaum, G. F., Treatment of anxiety disorders with co-morbid depression, available from <http:// www.medscape.com>.

8. Archibald D. Hart, *The anxiety cure* (Nashville: Word, 1999), 170.

9. Edmund J. Bourne, *Beyond anxiety and phobia* (Oakland: New Harbinger, 2001), 6.

10. N.D. Murray, and Pizzorno, N.D., *Encyclopedia of natural medicine* (Rocklin, CA: Prima Health, 1998).

11. Donal O'Mathuna, and Larimore, W., *Alternative medicine: The Christian handbook* (Grand Rapids, MI: Zondervan, 2001).

12. Archibald D.Hart, and Hart Weber, C., *Unveiling depression in women* (Grand Rapids, MI: Fleming H. Revell, 2002), 165–185.

13. Robert M. Sapolsky, *Why zebras don't get ulcers* (New York: W.H. Freeman and Company, 1998), 321.

14. Nicholas Hall, Stress: A psychoneuroimmunological perspective, available from <www.psychjournal.com/interviews>; Stress and exercise, available from <http://www.saluminternational.com/articleshall.htm>.

15. Archibald D. Hart, *Adrenaline and stress,* (Dallas: Word, 1995), 201.

# Perfectionism and Obsessive-Compulsive Disorders

*Mark E. Crawford*

Few ways of thinking are as harmful as perfectionism. Perfectionists believe that they should never make mistakes and that it is a catastrophe when they do. They tend to become quite upset when people or situations are out of their control and don't go the way they "should." They expect more from themselves and others than is reasonable and often become angry and bitter as a result. Though perfectionism in people is fairly common, it carries a high price tag in terms of causing emotional problems, relationship difficulties, and spiritual burnout.

CHRIS THURMAN[1]

Dr. Molar returned to his office six times that weekend to check whether or not his doors were locked and the security system turned on. The robbery of his thriving dental practice just a few months before was constantly on his mind, distracting his thoughts and disturbing his sleep like nothing ever had before.

His wife was not aware of how many times he had checked that weekend, but this fifth visit (he checked again that evening) did get her notice. He drove all the way across town before church on Sunday morning to check things again, and they ended up being a half-hour late for church. That made her upset, as she did not understand why he couldn't wait until after church to check things out. His reasoning made perfect sense to him, however, "My office manager had been there Saturday night to pull charts for Monday, and may have left things open." He had almost gotten into his car to drive over to check the office at 3 A.M. because he was up pacing and obsessing about it most of the night.

Dr. Molar was a prompt and meticulous professional, who demanded of himself and his staff near perfection in the operations of his dental practice. His staff, more afraid of his wrath for anything done out of order, joked about him being "an obsessive sicko." The past month had been no joke, however, as Dr. Molar so constantly complained and pushed on their behavior that half the staff were on the lookout for a better job.

Molar's wife and family had also lived a miserable month with their insufferable husband and father. Mrs. Molar began to suspect something more, however, that Sunday while the family was out to dinner after church. Her husband had not only left church at the beginning of the sermon to check whether or not the car was locked, he did the same thing in the middle of dinner. She wasn't sure how to broach the subject, for she knew how well defended and hyper-rational her husband was, but she took a deep breath and plunged in anyway, "Honey? . . . ."


## Defining Our Terms

"Perfectionistic," "compulsive," and "obsessive" are all terms that most of us have used to describe our own or others' behavior at one time or another. For example, a person who may be preoccupied about an upcoming project may be described as obsessing about it. I have heard many parents tell me that their child "compulsively" played video games. A person who is very conscientious about his performance at work or a homemaker who is fastidious regarding housework may be described as perfectionistic in these roles. However, much of the time, these behaviors or traits do not represent pathological behavior.

*The functional/dysfunctional continuum.* But like most human traits and behaviors, these aspects of functioning exist on a continuum. When they increase to a level that *begins to interfere with effective daily functioning, then they can be considered pathological.* Obsessive-compulsive disorder (OCD) is the term for a specific clinical disorder that significantly interferes with daily living, and is characterized by two primary symptoms: obsessive thoughts or images and compulsive behaviors. Defining these terms is essential to proper understanding, diagnosis, and treatment of this disorder.

## Obsessions

Obsessions refer to intense thoughts, worries, or images that are experienced as intrusive and unwanted. These obsessions cause great anxiety for an individual. One of the simplest ways to describe an obsession is an unrealistic or over-exaggerated worry or concern about something. The person experiencing an obsessive worry will frequently describe a thought or concern that sounds magnified or "catastrophized" to others. In other words, they will talk about a fear or worry that is far beyond what most people consider "normal."

In fact a person with OCD can sometimes tell you that they realize that their fears or worries are irrational or illogical. However, the anxiety is very real and overpowering. I've talked with many patients who tell me that they know their worries are irrational; however, they can't control the overwhelming fear and anxiety that these obsessive thoughts produce.

In his book, *Secret Thoughts and Tormenting Rituals* by Ian Osborn,[2] Dr. Osborn states that four qualities distinguish obsessive thoughts from everyday preoccupations, temptations, and worries. These four qualities include: 1) the thoughts are *intrusive*; 2) the thoughts are *unwanted* by the individual; 3) the thoughts are *recurrent*; and 4) the thoughts are *inappropriate*. In OCD, obsessions often fall within one of several categories including, but not limited to:

*Contamination obsessions:* worries about being contaminated by germs, toxins, or diseases. These worries frequently involve being contaminated by everyday contact with the outside world (doorknobs, money, handshakes, etc.). The person may also worry excessively about contaminating others.

*The need for symmetry or exactness:* a need for things to be "even" or symmetrical in their environment or on one's body. Examples include needing to have the same number of objects on each side of one's desk; needing to have one's shoes tied to the same tension on each foot; or having to tap or touch the left arm if one accidentally bumps the right one.

*Violent or aggressive obsessions:* these include either being bothered by intense and troubling images of violence or aggression and/or worries or fears that one may suddenly act out violent or aggressive impulses. Examples include sudden thoughts or images of horrible or violent things happening, particularly to a loved one and fears that one may act out in a violent or aggressive manner, such as hurting someone or oneself.

*Sexual obsessions:* these types of obsessions involve experiencing severe anxiety regarding normal sexual thoughts or feelings. These symptoms are particularly common among adolescents who may become very anxious about normal sexual thoughts and feelings.

*Doubting obsessions:* As in Dr. Molar's case, this category involves excessive questioning oneself regarding thoughts or behaviors. For example, a person may question whether they locked the door or turned off the stove.

*"Just so" obsessions:* this includes the need to do something in a particular manner that is known only to the individual. In other words, only they know when they have completed the activity "just right."

*Blasphemous obsessions:* obsessive thoughts and worries about possible blasphemy are common among patients with OCD. These obsessions include worries that one may have committed the unpardonable sin or blasphemed the Holy Spirit.

*Disturbing religious imagery:* many people with OCD report intrusive images that involve spiritual or religious themes, but include inappropriate or blasphemous imagery.

*Obsessing about losing salvation:* many Christians with OCD report being plagued by the fear that they have lost their salvation.

These are just a few examples of the types of obsessions that are common among OCD patients. However, obsessions can take any form and include any type of content. Remember, the definition of an obsession is any thought, worry or image that is experienced as intrusive, unwanted, recurrent, and inappropriate to the person.

## Compulsions

Compulsions are behaviors that are usually done in an attempt to decrease the anxiety caused by obsessive thoughts. These behaviors typically feel like they "must be done." Consequently, the person with OCD feels unable to control them. Usually, compulsions are done to accomplish one of the following:

1.  to prevent something bad from happening
2.  to "undo" the thought or feeling associated with an obsession
3.  to minimize or temporarily eliminate the anxiety caused by an obsessive thought

### ON PERFECTIONISM, BY CHRIS THURMAN[3]

#### What is Perfectionism?

Two perspectives are helpful to consider when defining perfectionism.

Theologically, perfectionism is the destructive belief that people can be equal to God. Specifically, perfectionistic people think they should be all-knowing (omniscient), all-powerful (omnipotent), and everywhere at once (omnipresent). When people think they should know everything, they beat themselves up for mistakes. When they think they should be totally powerful, they become upset when things are out of their control. When they believe that they should accomplish the work of ten people in a given day, they become depressed and discourage over what "little" they did accomplish. While God calls us to be "perfect," it is an ideal that He is asking us to move in the direction of, not something we can literally be. Only God knows it all, controls it all, and fills up the universe with His presence. Finite human beings know very little, can't control others, and can only accomplish the work of one person on a given day. God accepts that about us, and we need to as well.

Psychologically, perfectionism has several facets as well. Perfectionists are idealistic in that they frequently think about how things "should" be, not how they really are. Perfectionists set *impossibly high goals* which lead to discouragement, failure, and ultimately quitting. They are *product-minded,* believing that contentment, happiness, and a sense of accomplishment are not permissible until their current project or activity has been completed. The "process" is overlooked because the end result has not been reached, thus there is no "joy in the journey." Perfectionists often feel that they have to be the best at what they do. To simply do one's best is not good enough. Perfectionists also *equate their worth with their performance*. They only feel worthwhile as people if they perform well. Since day-to-day performance in various areas of life fluctuates, a perfectionist's sense of worth fluctuates as well.

The theological and psychological components of perfectionism destroy any chance at an emotionally and spiritually healthy life. So what can be done to help the perfectionist?

#### How to Defeat Perfectionism

Several steps can be taken to help perfectionists become more realistic in their view of life and personal abilities.

- *Be humble*—Perfectionists must humble themselves before God and repent of being prideful enough to think they can be His equal.
- *Be reality-focused*—Perfectionists need to face life as it really is, not focus on how it "should" be.

- *Set attainable goals*—Perfectionists need to set goals that are small, realistic, and achievable in the here and now. Long-term goals need to be broken into short-term, tangible goals.
- *Set reasonable time limits*—Spending too much time on an activity in order to do it perfectly needs to be replaced with prioritizing activities so that each is given a reasonable amount of time.
- *Accept doing "good enough" on certain tasks*—Given the number of tasks people must complete each day, not every one of those tasks has to be, or can be, done exceptionally well. In areas of less importance, perfectionists need to allow themselves to do "good enough" and move on to the next task.
- *Stop black-white thinking*—Thinking in all-or-nothing terms often makes perfectionists miss the shade of gray in a given situation. By not thinking in extremes, perfectionists can have a more accurate perspective.
- *Learn from mistakes*—Everyone makes mistakes. The key is to learn from the mistakes.
- *Confess sin to others*—Acknowledging imperfections to others (rather than keeping them secret) can help release people from perfectionism. By sharing moral imperfections and personality flaws, perfectionists invite others to see them as they really are. Living a more transparent life builds healthy relationships and is critical for personal growth.
- *Find joy in the journey*—Becoming more like Christ is a process. Each step people take toward being more mature is pleasing to God and is a step further than where they were before. Perfectionists need to take time to stop and enjoy where they are in life.
- *Find worth in God*—Perfectionists need to find their worth not in what they do or how well they do it, but in being God's creation.

Knowing the theological and psychological aspect of perfectionism is only the beginning. Perfectionists must continue to grow in their knowledge of and love for Christ. Perfectionists must remember Paul's words, "Not that I have already attained, or am already perfected; but I press on" (Phil. 3:12). God will bless them as they seek to live for Him every day.

Compulsions often must be done in a certain manner, and at times, must be repeated over and over. They can be behavioral or mental in nature and typically fall under these categories:

*Cleaning/Washing Compulsions:* this involves cleaning or washing excessively in response to the fear of contamination. Common examples include excessive hand washing or compulsively cleaning one's home or environment. In fact, some people wash their hands so frequently, they develop severe skin irritation.

*Checking compulsions:* this includes the need to check and recheck things e.g., making sure appliances have been turned off; doors have been locked; or that something was done (an entry was made in a checkbook) or *not* done (making sure someone was not hurt by an action). Checking once does not bring reassurance; consequently, checking is done repeatedly.

*Repeating compulsions:* repeating compulsions are similar to checking in the repetitive nature of the behavior. However, unlike checking, the compulsion may not be in response to a doubting obsession. Repeating compulsions may appear more random. Examples include rewriting letters or words; retracing steps; or repeating words or phrases.

*Hoarding compulsions:* the hallmark of this type of compulsion is the inability to discard useless or worn out items. Patients with hoarding compulsions become "pack rats," compiling piles of useless "junk."

*Ordering/Arranging Compulsions:* this type of compulsion refers to the need for objects to be placed in a specific manner. Frequently, items are arranged or catalogued alphabetically or chronologically. Inanimate objects may be lined up or spaced perfectly or symmetrically. At times, objects must face a certain direction.

*Rubbing, touching, tapping compulsions:* these types of compulsive behaviors involve touching or tapping objects for no better reason than not doing it causes significant anxiety and distress. Often, there is no obvious or logical reason for touching or tapping the object. However, *not* doing it can cause a nagging or persistent preoccupation that it *should* have been done, and the OCD sufferer fears that if they don't touch, rub, or tap the object, they will never be able to get the thought out of their head.

*Blinking or staring compulsions:* this involves the need to stare at objects for a certain period of time or blink a certain number of times or in a certain pattern.

*Counting compulsions:* this is a common compulsive behavior and includes the need to count things such as the number of stairs climbed; count the number of steps taken; or count the number of mailboxes passed on a car trip.

*Compulsive confessing:* this compulsive behavior involves the need to confess any and all behaviors that the person feels may have been wrong. It differs from normal or healthy disclosure of genuine misbehavior. In compulsive confessing, the person "confesses" normal behavior that is neither wrong nor inappropriate.

*Compulsive prayer:* this differs from the type of genuine prayer that is essential for all Christians. Compulsive prayer is simply a ritualistic type of prayer that the person feels they *must* recite—much like a magic phrase.

Compulsive behaviors are behaviors that are typically done in response to anxiety caused by obsessive thoughts. The person feels unable to resist the urge to perform the compulsive behaviors and experiences severe anxiety if they do not perform the compulsions.

According to the *Diagnostic and Statistical Manual of Mental Disorders— Fourth Edition (DSM-IV)*,[4] in order to receive a diagnosis of OCD, one must have either obsessions, compulsions, or both (as described above). A person must recognize that these symptoms are excessive or unreasonable (except in children), and the symptoms cause significant distress; are time consuming (taking more than one hour per day); and significantly interfere with the person's normal routine. In addition, the symptoms cannot be due to another medical condition or the physiological effects of a substance.

### Prevalence, Course, and Causes

According to research, approximately 1 in 40 adults (2.5% of the general population) suffers from OCD at some point in their lives. This makes OCD one of the most common psychiatric disorders. OCD affects both adults and children. While some individuals report that OCD symptoms first manifested in adulthood, it is common for symptoms to begin in childhood. Some studies indicate the average age of onset of OCD in children to be around 10 years of age. However, many children show symptoms much earlier.

The typical course of OCD is a waxing and waning of symptoms throughout one's lifetime with exacerbation of symptoms when the person is experiencing significant stress. People typically wait several years after experiencing symptoms before seeking help for the disorder. In fact, on average, a person waits 7 years after the emergence of symptoms before seeking help from a professional.

OCD is frequently misunderstood. Many people mistakenly believe that OCD is caused by unconscious and unresolved psychological conflicts. Because the symptoms frequently manifest with religious or spiritual themes, some people erroneously attribute disorder to spiritual determinants such as unconfessed sin and even demonic activity. *It is essential to understand that OCD is now primarily understood and treated as a biological disorder that is the result of abnormal brain activity.*

Genetic studies clearly support the fact that OCD runs in families. In fact, genetic researchers have suggested that OCD is approximately 60% genetically caused. If a person has OCD, the chance of a first degree relative having the disorder is approximately 10–25%. In twin studies, the concordance rate of OCD in identical twins is approximately 67% and in fraternal twins is approximately 47%. Like most disorders with a genetic component, it is believed that OCD is best explained using a diathesis-stress model. In other words, one may inherit a genetic vulnerability or predisposition towards OCD which interacts with other variables (particularly stress) to result in the presence of the disorder.

Brain imaging studies have been helpful in identifying which areas of the brain appear to be implicated in OCD. Both the basal ganglia and orbital frontal regions of the brain appear to be over-stimulated in individuals with OCD. The basal ganglia is an area of the brain involving several structures. These areas work together to control initiation and modulation of movement, and to process and filter information that is fed back to help control behavior and thinking. The primary functions of the orbital frontal region of the brain include filtering, prioritizing, and organizing information received by the brain; inhibiting responses to irrelevant stimuli; engaging in logical and consequence-based decision making; and regulating movements and complex behaviors activated by the basal ganglia.

Finally, the most helpful discovery regarding the causes of OCD has been the understanding of the role of the neurotransmitter serotonin. Neurotransmitters are chemicals in the brain that are essential for communication between the nerve cells of the brain. Patients with OCD have a significant decrease in serotonin activity. Numerous studies indicate that treating OCD with medications that enhance serotonin activity decrease OCD symptoms while giving a patient with OCD a substance that opposes serotonin activity in the brain worsens symptoms.

## Comorbid Disorders

There are a number of other disorders that frequently exist *with* OCD. These are known as comorbid disorders. These include the following:

*Tourette's disorder:* Tourette's disorder is defined as the presence of multiple motor tics and one or more vocal tics which occur many times daily nearly every day for a period of more than a year. A tic is a sudden, rapid, recurrent, stereotyped motor movement or vocalization. Tics are experienced by individuals as irresistible; however, they can be suppressed for some time. Motor tics take many forms: eye blinking; eye rolling/squinting; finger tapping; head jerking/ rolling; nose twitching; eye twitching; facial grimacing; hand clenching/unclenching; jaw/mouth moving; lip licking/smacking; muscle flexing/unflexing; shoulder shrugging/ rolling; teeth clenching/unclenching; and tongue thrusting.

Vocal tics also manifest in myriad ways including: barking; belching; coughing; throat clearing; sniffing; grunting; humming; making animal noises; making "tsk," or "pft" noises; making guttural sounds; screeching; shouting; calling out; snorting; moaning; blowing noises; shrieking; and whistling. Studies show that approximately 1 in 5 of OCD patients also have a diagnosis of Tourette's disorder. This is in contrast to rates of 1 in 100 boys and 1 in 600 girls in the general population.

*Attention-Deficit Hyperactivity Disorder:* ADHD is a neurological disorder that consists of difficulties in the areas of sustained attention and concentration and/or impulse control. ADHD affects approximately 5% of the general population. However, it is a frequent coexisting disorder among OCD patients—15–30% of ADHD patients also have OCD.

*Trichotillomania (TTM):* Trichotillomania is a disorder that involves the recurrent pulling out of one's hair resulting in noticeable hair loss. This typically begins in childhood with onset beginning around age 5–8 years. In some cases, children may show transient periods of hair pulling that stop with no intervention. However, some individuals experience hair pulling into adulthood. For some, hair pulling is continuous while for others, it may be episodic (e.g., symptoms may come and go for weeks, months, or years at a time).

*Body Dysmorphic Disorder (BDD):* BDD is a disorder diagnosed when a person develops a preoccupation with what they believe to be a defect in the way they look. Patients with BDD become focused on a slight or imagined defect in their physical appearance. They may become preoccupied by the belief that an aspect of their body is asymmetrical; that a body part is too large or too small; that a certain aspect of their body is misshapen; etc. There is no specific aspect of appearance on which patients with BDD might focus. In fact, patients with BDD may change the focus of their distress over time.

*Compulsive Skin Picking:* While this is not a disorder listed in the DSM-IV, in his book *Obsessive-Compulsive Disorders: A Complete Guide to Getting Well and Staying Well,*[5] Fred Penzel lists compulsive skin picking as one of the *obsessive-compulsive spectrum disorders* along with BDD, TTM, and Tourette's disorder. Compulsive skin picking is defined as picking to the point of creating open sores and then picking at the scabs that result. It also includes squeezing and digging at pimples and blackheads with fingers or other implements to the point of causing infections and scarring of the tissue. Compulsive nail biting is defined as biting the nails to the point of bleeding and disfigured fingertips. Infections are often the result.

*Depression:* Clinical depression also co-occurs with OCD. Studies have found that approximately 25% of OCD patients meet criteria for a major depressive episode. Left untreated, the symptoms of OCD can lead to the development of clinical depression.

*Substance Abuse:* Some patients with OCD attempt to relieve the anxiety associated with the disorder through alcohol or other illegal or non-prescribed drugs. Marijuana is a drug that is frequently used to "self-medicate" the anxiety associated with OCD. At times, patients develop substance abuse problems due to overuse of these substances.

## Treatment

The good news for patients with OCD is that it is a treatable disorder. In fact, studies show that with appropriate treatment, 80–90% of OCD patients show significant improvement and 75% show long-term improvement in their symptoms. There are two main types of treatment, and combinations of treatment, that have been shown to be effective for the treatment of OCD: cognitive-behavior therapy and medication.

### Cognitive-Behavior Therapy (CBT)

Cognitive-behavior therapy involves several components: education; exposure and response prevention; cognitive restructuring; and the 4 R's.

*Education.* It is imperative to educate patients about OCD. Patients need to understand that OCD is primarily a biological disorder caused by abnormal brain functioning. They need to see their symptoms as *external* to themselves. Treatment goals must be realistically explained and realistic goals must be established. Analogies can be helpful such as explaining obsessive thoughts as similar to junk mail; spam e-mail; or a heckler at a sporting event. This often helps patients to learn to respond differently to their obsessive thoughts.

Education should also discuss outcome, as some patients are resistant to treatment due to their *dichotomous thinking* about the outcome. Dichotomous thinking refers to the tendency to see the world in terms of one extreme or the other. Many individuals see their OCD tendencies as adaptive, describing their punctuality, orderliness, and attention to details as valued functions. They mistakenly see these as part of their disorder and believe that if treatment works, they will move to the opposite end of the continuum of these traits. Instead of being obsessively punctual and perfectionistic, treatment will make them chronically late, hopelessly disorganized, and laissez faire or careless about everything.

It is important to remind these individuals that virtually all characteristics of human functioning exist on a continuum. I often draw a continuum that looks something like this:

I explain that the OCD end is that area that includes all of their OCD symptoms including all of the obsessive thoughts and worries and compulsive behaviors that currently cause them such misery. The anti-OCD end of

the continuum includes the opposite traits—disorganization, carelessness, tardiness, lack of scruples, messiness, etc. The fear for many OCD patients is that if they let go of the OCD end, they will automatically swing to the other end. This, of course, is unacceptable.

I point out that it is perfectly acceptable to live a healthy and happy life closer to the OCD end, as long as they are not on the extreme end. I explain that it is even fine to be closer to the OCD end than to the middle. Many high functioning people show a tendency toward obsessiveness or compulsiveness, but do not suffer from OCD. I call this area "the zone" and indicate that the goal of treatment can be to eliminate or reduce the OCD symptoms without decreasing their effectiveness or productivity. In fact, by eliminating or reducing the OCD symptoms and staying in "the zone," they will actually become *more* effective and productive.

*Exposure and response prevention.* Current research indicates that the most effective form of non-pharmacological treatment for OCD is Exposure and Response Prevention (E/RP). This consists of a therapist and patient cooperating together to gradually expose the patient to anxiety provoking obsessive thoughts while resisting the urge to engage in the compulsive behaviors that serve to decrease the anxiety that follows the obsessive thoughts. When done correctly, this form of treatment is highly effective in reducing obsessive thoughts and compulsive behaviors, and the improvement lasts over time.

The initial phase of this approach requires the patient to "rank" anxiety producing situations (those that elicit obsessive thoughts) from least to most severe. It is usually helpful to ask the patient to assign a number value from 1 to 100 with 1 being a non-anxiety situation and 100 being the worst type of anxiety possible. This is helpful for both the patient and the therapist to communicate with each other about anxiety producing situations.

The technique of E/RP is relatively simple, but wonderfully effective. The patient starts out by resisting the typical compulsive behavior associated with their least anxiety producing situation. I use the diagram below to illustrate how it works:

## Response Prevention

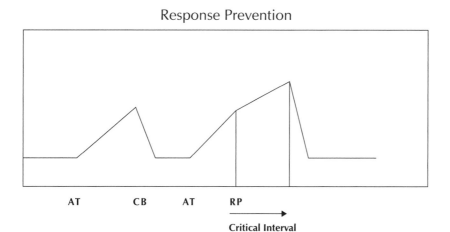

AT    CB    AT    RP

**Critical Interval**

In the diagram, the x-axis represents the passage of time while the y-axis represents anxiety levels from low to high. AT refers to an "anxiety thought." This is any situation that results in the type of obsessive doubt, worry, thought, image, etc. which begins to raise anxiety. CB represents any type of compulsive behavior (e.g., washing, checking, compulsive praying; etc.). As the diagram shows, performing a compulsive behavior immediately results in a reduction of anxiety to same level as before the anxiety thought occurred. Prior to treatment, this pattern would continue ad infinitum. The patient may have different anxiety producing thoughts and perform different compulsive behaviors. However, the pattern would continue in the same predictable way.

On the diagram, the second AT still refers to an anxiety producing thought. However, in this example, at the point the patient would previously perform a compulsive behavior (CB), I ask them to resist the compulsive behavior (Response Prevention or RP). At this point, you see that the anxiety level actually increases beyond the point the patient normally allows anxiety to rise. It is important to predict this rise in anxiety and to explain that this is to be anticipated. The graph also shows that if the patient continues to resist the urge to perform the compulsive behavior, their anxiety level will ultimately decrease spontaneously and will return to the normal level without having to perform a compulsive behavior.

I have labeled the time from the moment the patient resists the compulsion (RP) to the time when the anxiety level falls as the *critical interval.* This is the interval of time that *must be endured* in order to break the pattern of OCD. Without fail, most patients who attempt to do this on their own are unable to endure the critical interval. Many patients erroneously believe that their anxiety may continue to rise to an intolerable level, or that their anxiety will never decrease unless they perform the compulsive behavior. Most patients who successfully endure the critical interval tell me that it normally takes only about 10–20 minutes before their anxiety begins to fall. This may sound like a brief time, but for the patient with OCD, it can seem like an eternity. This is particularly true if the fear is that their anxiety may never stop.

I have found that it is much easier to make it through the critical interval if the patient has something to distract him during this time. I often instruct the patient to have something else that they can get involved in to help them not to sit and dwell on the fact that they are anxious. If a patient can make it through a critical interval without performing a compulsive behavior, it is a great success which should be celebrated. Each time a patient is successful with E/RP, he is in fact weakening the grip of OCD on his life.

*Cognitive restructuring.* Most people with OCD are able to identify thoughts or beliefs that are extreme or slightly distorted. These thoughts and beliefs are referred to as errors in thinking and need to be identified and modified in order to effectively treat OCD. Examples of common cognitive errors include:

1. *Emotional reasoning:* this refers to reaching conclusions based upon feelings rather than facts. For example, a person with OCD shakes hands with a person he just met and *feels* contaminated, therefore he believes that he *is* contaminated.

2. *Catastrophizing:* this refers to imagining the worst case scenario of a situation and reacting to the imagined "catastrophe" rather than the actual situation.

3. *Dichotomous thinking:* this refers to the tendency to think in absolute terms (either-or thinking). This is often the origin of perfectionism. A person may have unrealistic standards for performance. Anything short of perfection is experienced and viewed as a failure.

4. *Selective Attention:* this type of cognitive error refers to the tendency of a person to notice and consider only certain aspects (usually negative) of a situation.

5. *Personalization:* this belief refers to the tendency to make everything that happens somehow related to the person (i.e., "everything's my fault").

These are just a few of the cognitive distortions related to OCD. For a person with OCD, cognitive distortions typically involve such areas as overestimating negative outcome in situations; exaggerations of "normal" concerns about situations; owning too great a share of responsibility for the outcome of situations; and having unrealistic expectations for performance.

## Biblical Thought Modification

Scripture tells us in John 8:31–32, "If you hold to My teaching, you are really My disciples. Then you will know the truth, and the truth will set you free."

Second Corinthians 10:5 tells us, "...we take captive every thought to make it obedient to Christ." I use these Scriptures to help patients understand the importance of cognitive therapy in the treatment of OCD. It is important to recognize the truth of our thinking as opposed to simply accepting our cognitive distortions as fact. Also, we do have the ability to "take our thoughts captive," i.e., we can control what we think if we work at it. For specific cognitive errors, the following modifications may be helpful:

*Emotional Reasoning:* Your feelings are like a faulty navigation system on an airplane. Most pilots know that you can fly an airplane by determining your direction and location from objects on the ground, or by using instrumentation on the control panel. At night, or in inclement weather, you don't have much choice but to rely on instrumentation. I explain that feelings are an unreliable source for drawing conclusions. Recall that in emotional reasoning, a person reaches conclusions based upon how they feel rather than on facts. Therefore, I encourage patients to question their feelings and to make sure that they draw conclusions about situations based on the facts rather than on their emotions which will often lead them astray.

*Catastrophizing:* Recall that this refers to reacting to the imagined worst-case scenario. I encourage my patients to make sure that they are living in the *"what is"* instead of in the *"what if."* Many people with OCD find themselves living in the future rather than in the present. At least 90% of the things people with an anxiety disorder worry *might* happen never do. I think Jesus illustrated this point best when He said, "Therefore do not worry about tomorrow, for tomorrow will worry about itself. Each day has enough trouble of its own." (Matt. 6:34)

Another tool that is useful for people who tend to "catastrophize" is called *probability estimation.* In probability estimation, the person is asked to estimate the likelihood that a particular event will actually occur. Through logically evaluating the probability of something happening, the person often reaches the conclusion that they are worrying about something that has a remote chance of actually happening.

*Dichotomous thinking:* For people who tend to think in only two categories, I try to help them create a "third file" for thinking about things. I explain that it is as if they have just two files—one for one extreme and one for the other extreme. Most things in their lives actually fit best into a third file that is somewhere between the two extremes. One example of this involves performance expectations. As we discussed earlier, OCD patients often have perfectionistic tendencies. They see their performance in a diagram that looks something like this:

| |
|---|
| Perfect |
| Failure |

In the diagram, there are only two categories of performance: perfect and failure. Because perfection is difficult, and sometimes impossible to attain, these individuals usually feel that their performance is a failure. I explain that this model is unrealistic and needs to be modified to create a third category:

| |
|---|
| Perfect |
| Good Enough |
| Failure |

In the revised diagram, a third category called "good enough" has been added to the model. In this model, perfection is still present, as is failure. However, failure is a much smaller category now, and the largest area is "good enough." Most of our performance is, in fact, good enough—not perfect, but certainly acceptable. Creating a third category enables the perfectionist to accept their less than perfect performance without feeling like a failure. For patients with OCD, third categories need to be established in many different areas in order to avoid the dichotomous thinking errors that exacerbate anxiety and obsessiveness.

*Personalization:* For this type of error, I help patients challenge the belief that all things that happen are related to or caused by them. I encourage patients to consider whether there is sufficient evidence to indict them for the crime they feel they committed. I use the example of "putting OCD on trial" instead of them. Most of the time, a person with OCD will feel responsible for something when there is no evidence that they are responsible. They need to reconsider the evidence, to rationally and logically evaluate their conclusion that they are somehow always responsible for the negative outcomes in their lives.

*Selective attention:* For this type of cognitive error, it is important to get and keep a perspective. Recall that in selective attention, the person has a filter that results in ignoring some aspects of a situation and focusing only on the negative aspects of it. I explain that selective attention is like viewing a situation through a camera lens that is focused to only one small aspect of the picture. In this case, the only thing the person is going to see is what the camera lens is focused on. It is important to back up the lens in order to allow the picture to contain all aspects of the scene in order to get an accurate view of the situation.

## The Four R's

Because E/RP and cognitive therapy have been found effective for treatment of OCD, I always use both techniques to treat patients. I have developed a technique known as the Four R's to help patients remember the essential elements of beating OCD.

*Recognize:* This step uses cognitive therapy tools to enable the patient to identify the thinking that is behind the anxiety. In treating OCD, this inevitably results in identifying the obsessive thought, worry, or image and correctly defining it as an irrational obsessive thought.

*Resist:* This step refers to RP in the Response Prevention diagram. In this step, the patient is aware of the urge to perform a compulsive behavior. He has been educated regarding the importance of employing RP as essential in breaking the power of OCD and is prepared to resist the urge to perform the compulsive behavior.

*Replace:* In step 3, the patient begins the process of modifying the obsessive thought or worry with one that is based on truth.

*Redirect:* In the final step, the patient is taught to use the tools mentioned earlier to get through the critical interval of response prevention until the anxiety passes and the pattern of obsessive thoughts followed by compulsive behaviors is weakened.

The Four R's sounds easy, but is actually a simplified model that requires the individual to have a great deal of knowledge about the techniques used to treat OCD, including understanding the principles behind response prevention as well as the theory of cognitive therapy. Once a patient becomes familiar with these concepts, the Four R's is an easy way to remember how to employ these new tools. Learning this method of treatment requires homework assignments, keeping journal entries of thoughts and behavior patterns, and much trial and error. It is a process that takes time, but is ultimately effective in treating OCD.

## Medication

Because of the biological basis of OCD, medications that enhance serotonin activity are essential to treating this disorder effectively. While there are several medications used to treat OCD, the ones most often used include the following: Prozac (fluoxetine); Zoloft (sertraline); Paxil (paroxetine); fluvoxamine; and clomipramine (the latter two are available in generic form only. These medications are typically used in combination with CBT. Treatment using a combination of medication and CBT is highly effective.

Treatment with medication alone is effective in symptom reduction. However, if medication is used without CBT; there is a high likelihood of a return of symptoms after medication is discontinued. Medications used to treat OCD do have some side effects, the most common of which include sexual side effects (decreased libido and responsiveness); weight gain; and fatigue. The decision to use medication is ultimately made by a physician. It is recommended that medication be used (rather than CBT alone) when a person is having difficulty with normal daily activity; when they may not be able to complete CBT without medication; or when comorbid depression is severe. Medications are typically taken from 12–18 months. They usually take 4–6 weeks before results are realized.

### Summary

OCD is a neurological disorder that is the result of abnormal brain functioning. Symptoms can be confusing and debilitating for individuals. Many, but not all people with OCD manifest pockets of perfectionism in their lives as a result of dichotomous thinking. Correctly diagnosing OCD can bring immediate hope for recovery. OCD does respond well to treatment, which is often a combination of cognitive-behavior therapy and medication.

### ENDNOTES

1.  Chris Thurman, Perfectionism, in T. Clinton, Hindson, E. and Ohlschlager G. (eds.), *The soul care Bible* (Nashville: Thomas Nelson, 2001).

2.  Ian Osborne, *Tormenting thoughts and secret rituals: The hidden epidemic of obsessive-compulsive disorder* (New York: Dell, 1998).

3.  Chris Thurman, Perfectionism, in T. Clinton, Hindson, E., & Ohlschlager, G. (eds.), *The soul care Bible* (Nashville: Thomas Nelson, 2001).

4.  American Psychiatric Association, *Diagnostic and statistical manual of mental disorders,* 4th ed. (Washington, DC: Author, 1994).

5.  Fred Penzel, *Obsessive-compulsive disorder: A complete guide to getting well and staying well* (New York: Oxford University Press, 2000).

# 10

## Managing Your Anger

*Gary J. Oliver and Carrie E. Oliver*

Don't sin by letting anger gain control over you. Don't let the sun go down
while you are still angry, for anger gives a mighty foothold to the Devil.

Ephesians 4:26–27 nlt

David Augustus Burke's last words were tainted by vengeance. "Hi, Ray, I
think it's sort of ironical that we end up like this," he scribbled on an air
sickness bag. "I asked for some leniency for my family, remember. Well I
got none and you'll get none."

His last telephone message was tinged with love. "Jackie, this is David.
I'm on my way to San Francisco, Flight 1771. I love you. I really wish I
could say more, but I do love you."

No one knows what Ray Thomson told David Burke when he fired him
November 19 for allegedly pocketing $69 of in-flight cocktail receipts.
Those who knew Thomson described him as quiet but confident, the kind
of guy who didn't take guff. Whatever Thomson said, Burke didn't buy it.
Unemployed, spurned by his girlfriend, he apparently began making quiet
but methodical preparations for a bizarre murder-suicide mission that
would kill a planeload of people.

On Monday all of the rejection, all of the suppressed and hidden anger exploded 22,000 feet over Central California. Shots splintered the calm of a routine commuter flight, and if his calculated death plan of revenge succeeded, at least one shot probably tore into Thomson.

The pilot radioed, "I have an emergency...gunfire." Sounds of a tremendous scuffle would be heard later on a cockpit voice recorder tape. A groan. A gasp. Then PSA Flight 1771 plunged nose-first into a cattle ranch in San Luis Obispo County.

A few days later, David's father, Altamont Burke, tried to make sense of the dichotomy. "My son was a gentle guy, *but don't talk any trash to him,*" he said. Burke, Thomson and 41 other persons died, their bodies ripped apart and flung across acres of green hillside. Lying in the rubble was the .44 caliber magnum that Burke had borrowed from a friend with six cartridges spent.

Also found in the horrid carnage was the air sickness bag that spelled out the apparent motive for mass murder.[1]

From many of the newspaper reports and interviews with family and friends it was clear that David Augustus Burke did not appear to be the "typical" angry person. You might be asking yourself just what do we mean by a "typical angry person"? That's an important question! But let's turn it around. How would YOU describe the "typical" angry person? When you think of anger or angry people what comes into your mind? Who do you think of first? A father or mother, a brother or sister, a husband or wife, a good friend...yourself? What do angry people look like? What do angry people sound like? What does it FEEL like to be around someone who is frequently and visibly angry?

For over twenty years we've had the privilege of helping people understand that being made in the image of God means that we have emotions, and that includes the emotion of anger. In our seminars people ask us: What is the emotion of anger? Why did God create it? How can anything good come from anger? Where does my anger come from? Why is anger such a difficult emotion to deal with? Why are my anger responses so hard to change? How can I make my anger work for me rather than against me?

In this chapter you will find practical answers to each of these questions. The essential starting place is to define this emotion. If we are going to learn how to make anger work for us rather than against us there are a few things we need to understand.

## Anger Is a God-Given Emotion

We were amazed to discover how much the Bible has to say about anger. God clearly acknowledges the significance of this powerful emotion. In fact, the only emotion the Bible mentions more than anger is love. Anger first appears in Genesis 4:5 and the last reference to anger is found in Revelation 19:15. In the Old Testament alone, anger is mentioned 455 times, with 375 of those references dealing with God's anger. [2]

The New Testament uses several Greek words for anger. It is critical to understand the distinction between these words. We have had many people remark that Scripture appears to contradict itself because in one verse we are taught not to be angry and in another we are admonished to "be angry and sin not." Which is the correct interpretation and which should we follow?

The most common New Testament word for anger is *orge*. It is used forty-five times and means a more settled and long-lasting attitude of anger, which is slower in its onset but more enduring. This kind of anger is similar to coals on a barbecue slowly warming up to red and then white hot and holding this temperature until the cooking is done. This kind of long-lasting anger often includes revenge.

There are two exceptions where this word is used and revenge is not included in its meaning. In Ephesians 4:26a we are taught to not "let the sun go down on your anger." Notice that the anger in the first part of this verse (*orge*) is different from the anger in the second half (*parorgismos*) where we are told not to let the sun go down upon this anger. Mark 3:5 records Jesus as having looked upon the Pharisees "with anger." In these two verses the word means an abiding habit of the mind that is aroused under certain conditions against evil and injustice. This is the healthy type of anger that Christians are encouraged to have—the anger at wrongdoing and evil that includes no revenge or rage.

Another frequently used word for anger in the New Testament is *thumas*. It describes anger as a turbulent commotion or a boiling agitation of feelings. This type of anger blazes up into a sudden explosion, whereas in *orge* there is an occasional element of deliberate thought. It is an outburst from inner indignation and is similar to a match that quickly ignites into a blaze but then burns out rapidly. This type of anger is mentioned eighteen times (see for example Ephesians 4:31 and Galatians 5:20) and is the type of anger we are called upon to control.[3]

### Anger as a Secondary Emotion

Most people have no idea that anger is a secondary emotion that is usually experienced in response to a primary emotion such as hurt and fear. Anger can be an almost automatic response to any kind of pain. It is the emotion most of us feel shortly after we have been hurt. When you trip and fall or drop a hammer on your toe, it hurts, and you may experience mild anger. When your son corrects or talks back to you in public, it hurts, and you may respond to him (probably in the car on the way home) in anger.

Anger is usually the first emotion we see. For males it's often the only emotion that they are aware of.[4] However, it is rarely the only one they have experienced. Just below the surface there are almost always other, deeper emotions that need to be identified and acknowledged. Hidden deep underneath that surface anger is the fear, the hurt, the frustration, the disappointment, the vulnerability, and the longing for connection.

At a very early age many people learn that anger can help them divert attention from these more painful emotions. Anger is safer. It provides a sense of protection for the frightened and vulnerable self. Angry people respond verbally or physically to their seeming helplessness. It doesn't take long for some people to learn that it's easier to feel anger than it is to feel pain. Anger provides an increase of energy. It can decrease our sense of vulnerability and thus increase our sense of security. It is often a false security, but it is a kind of security nonetheless.

### Anger Is a Signal

Anger is an emotion that God can use to get our attention and make us more aware of opportunities to learn, to grow, to deepen, to mature, and to make significant changes for the good. Anger, like love, is an emotion that has tremendous potential for both good and evil. That's why it is so important for us to understand it.

In her helpful book *The Dance of Anger* Harriet Lerner notes:

> Anger is a signal and one worth listening to. Our anger may be a message that we are being hurt, that our rights are being violated, that our needs or wants are not being adequately met, or simply that something isn't right. Our anger may tell us that we are not addressing an important emotional issue in our lives, or that too much of our self—our beliefs, values, desires or ambitions—is being compromised in a relationship. Our anger may be a signal that we are doing more and giving

more than we can comfortably do or give. Or our anger may warn us that others are doing too much for us, at the expense of our own competence and growth. Just as physical pain tells us to take our hand off the hot stove, the pain of our anger preserves the very integrity of our self. Our anger can motivate us to say no to the ways in which we are defined by others and "yes" to the dictates of our inner self.[5]

Anger is to our lives like a smoke detector is to a house, like a dash warning light is to a car, and like a flashing yellow light is to a driver. Each of those serve as a kind of warning or alarm to stop, look, and listen. They say, "Take caution, something might be wrong."

## Anger Is a Powerful Emotion

Anger involves power. When you are angry you feel "charged up" and ready for action. Physiologically anger triggers an outpouring of adrenalin and other stress hormones to our central and peripheral nervous systems with noticeable physical consequences. Your voice changes to a higher pitch. The rate and depth of your breathing increases. Your perspiration increases. Your heart beats faster and harder. The muscles of your arms and legs may tighten up. The digestive process is slowed down. Many feel as if a war is being waged in their head and stomach.

In our experience when most people think about anger they associate it with the most painful and violent expression of anger they have seen or heard. Anger is often associated with (and confused with) hostility, rage, aggression, violence and destruction. And it's true that when anger gets out of control it can be expressed in horrible ways. But the problem isn't the anger. The problem is that people haven't learned how to understand and value their anger, how to listen to their anger, how to hear the warnings their anger provides them.

## Anger Is the "Most Likely To Be Mislabeled" Emotion

In our counseling practice we've spent many hours with people who are confused, frustrated and stuck in their efforts to grow and live effectively. Much of this is due to their failure or inability to acknowledge, understand and constructively deal with anger. With the taboos on anger in many evangelical circles Christians can be particularly blind to the value of this powerful emotion. Instead of identifying the emotion and facing it squarely as a fact of life, they either try to shut out and silence their anger or they allow it to dominate and control their lives.

Anger can come packaged in many different shapes and sizes. It hides behind many different masks. Over our lifetime each one of us has developed our own unique style of dealing with anger.

> Of all the emotions anger is the one most likely to be labeled as something else. Of all the emotions anger is the one most likely to be identified as dangerous. What are some of the most common disguises anger can take? When we begrudge, scorn, insult, and disdain others or when we are annoyed, offended, bitter, fed up, repulsed, irritated, infuriated, incensed, mad, sarcastic, up tight, cross or when we experience frustration, indignation, exasperation, fury, wrath or rage, we are probably experiencing some form of anger. Anger can also manifest itself as criticism, silence, intimidation, hypochondria, numerous petty complaints, depression, gossip, sarcasm, blame, passive-aggressive behaviors such as stubbornness, half-hearted efforts, forgetfulness, and laziness. [6]

A person who is worried usually looks and acts worried. A person who is depressed usually looks and acts depressed. A person who is overcome by fear usually looks and acts afraid. But a person who is angry may or may not look and act angry. They may appear to be worried, depressed, afraid or there may not be any external indication of their anger.

### Healthy Anger Has Tremendous Potential for Good

Anger is energy and we can choose whether we are going to spend it or invest it. While we may have minimal control over when we experience anger, we have almost total control over how we choose to express that anger. When we choose to harness and direct that energy in healthy, positive and constructive way and communicate it in biblically-consistent ways, we are able to solve problems and increase our trust and actually deepen our intimacy.

God has given us that choice. We can allow our anger to control us, or we can, with God's help, pursue "healthy" anger. Healthy anger involves open, honest and direct communication. It involves speaking the truth in love. It involves investing the energy God has given us to declare truth, to right wrongs, and to help ourselves and others "become conformed to the image of His Son" (Romans 8:29).

As we move on to the next section remember that anger is not necessarily or wholly negative. Anger involves physiological arousal, a state of readiness. When we are angry our body has increased energy that can be directed in whatever way choose. Anger is a natural and normal response to a variety of life's situations and stresses. Anger is a God-given emotion intended to protect and provide energy for developing solutions to life's inevitable problems. Anger, the ability to understand it and appropriately express it, is a sign of emotional and spiritual maturity.

### What's Your Anger Style?

The first and easiest step in the change process is to identify your characteristic style of experiencing and expressing anger. When it comes to dealing with anger most people tend to fall into one of three reactive styles. What do we mean by reactive? A person who is reactive has an automatic and seemingly unconscious response to a situation. They may not always react in the exact same way but the majority of their responses fall into similar styles.

It's easy for people who don't identify and work on their anger style to get in an emotional rut and once there they are likely to stay there. They are vulnerable to becoming puppets of their past and slaves to their circumstances. While everyone is unique most people tend to fall into one of three characteristic styles of reacting to anger. As you read through them, think of which one might best describe your usual way of reacting. How do you see yourself? How do others see you? Where did you learn this style?

### Cream-Puffs: Repressed

The main characteristic of the Cream-Puff is passivity. Cream-Puffs avoid making clear statements about what they think and feel, especially when their opinion might make someone else uncomfortable. Their energy is focused on protecting themselves or others, and maintaining harmonious relationships. Cream-Puffs avoid conflict like the plague.

Cream-Puffs often fail to share their own legitimate needs and concerns and thus those around them are unaware of their pain. Over time they become less and less aware of their own feelings, thoughts and needs. They can become so focused on hearing what everyone else has to say that they fail to hear what the Lord has to say. God's truths become real to everyone else but them.

Cream-Puffs characteristically avoid any direct experience or expression of anger. In situations that in healthy people would evoke appropriate expressions of anger and protest they are likely to remain silent. They are more likely to say "I'm sorry" rather than "I'm hurt," "I'm afraid," "I'm frustrated," or "I'm angry."

Do Cream-Puffs ever experience anger? Of course they do! However, when provoked they will usually say nothing. Most people think of anger as something hot such as in seething rage or an erupting volcano. But the Cream-Puff's anger is usually more subtle and cold. He or she is someone whose immediate and automatic response to even the slightest hint of anger is to suppress it.

*What does it mean to suppress anger?* Suppress means to hold in, to put down by force, to prevent the natural or normal expression, activity or development of an emotion. When I suppress my anger I'm aware of it but through a lot of practice I'm able to keep it down. Few people are even aware that I'm angry.

If over a period of time I continue to suppress my *anger it is likely that my anger will become repressed.* Repressed anger is kept from consciousness and I'm no longer even aware of it. People who have anger they're not aware of often express it in ways that are destructive to themselves and others. They are almost powerless to deal with it because they aren't really aware of it.

"The Cream-Puff is like a boat drifting aimlessly on the ocean with no motor, oars or sails. They are forced to go wherever the winds of circumstances blow them. The God-given emotion of anger can be a source of propulsion to move them out of their doldrums and help them move in healthy and constructive directions."[7]

Cream-Puff

| | | | |
|---|---|---|---|
| ▪ anger | ▪ suppressed anger turned inward | ▪ apathetic | ▪ toxic shame |
| ▪ overcontrolled | ▪ passive reactor | ▪ guilt-prone | ▪ avoids problems |
| ▪ self-condemnation | ▪ denial | ▪ responsible for others | ▪ self-pity |
| ▪ conflict avoider | ▪ dependent | | |

## Locomotives: Explosive

The exact opposite of the Cream-Puff is the Locomotive. In fact one of the fears that keeps many Cream-Puffs locked in their prison of passivity is the fear that if they ever let themselves get in touch with their anger, they will become like the Locomotive.

What is a locomotive? He doesn't have much time for the feelings or opinions of others. He has a sharp tongue and can be quick to criticize, put-down and humiliate others. On the outside he appears confident but inside he is riddled with fears and insecurities. Because he needs so much accept-ance it is difficult for him to compliment others. It gives them the attention that he believes he deserves and needs for himself. He needs to be right all of the time and when he errs it will be on the side of being tough and not tender.

While the Cream-Puff is a passive reactor the Locomotive is an aggressive reactor. While the passive reactor doesn't give adequate attention to legiti-mate personal needs, the aggressive reactor doesn't give adequate attention to the needs and rights of others. They are often so preoccupied with them-selves that they become insensitive to and unaware of the needs of others.

Whereas the anger of the Cream-Puff (passive reactor) is usually implo-sive the anger of the Locomotive (aggressive reactor) is most often explo-sive. When provoked the Locomotive, who already has a full head of steam, is likely to attack, label, put down, and humiliate others. They often communicate in ways that violate the dignity and rights of other people.

In Philippians 2:3 we are exhorted to regard one another as more important than ourselves. In I Peter 4:15 we read that "If you suffer, it must not be for murder, theft or sorcery, nor for infringing on the rights of oth-ers." The locomotive consistently ignores these biblical principles or twists them as a basis for blaming others for not esteeming them (the Locomotive) as most important.

What are some characteristics of the Locomotive?

When it comes to identifying their unhealthy anger style the majority of

## Locomotive

| | | | |
|---|---|---|---|
| hostile | rage –cruel teasing | blatant sarcasm | |
| anger against others | over-concern for self | loud –obnoxious | |
| quick to blame | critical | underresponsible | has all the answers |
| shallow | few intimate friends | prone to violence | suspicious |
| punitive | combative | overcompetitive | driven –power hungry |

people would put themselves in the Cream-Puff or Locomotive category. However there is a third anger style that in some ways is more subtle and complicated than the first two but just as unhealthy.

## Steel Magnolias: Passive Aggressive

The term passive aggressive was first coined during World War II to describe the behaviors of certain soldiers. We've already talked about this in chapter one but it is such a common response it deserves more attention. The military is highly structured for uniformity and compliance and individuality is not encouraged. Some soldiers thrived under this kind of environment. Others dealt with this enforced change by resisting, ignoring orders, withdrawing, or simply wanting out.

On the outside the Steel Magnolia appears very soft and tender. At times you will see the lovely and sweet-smelling magnolia blossom. But more than just a casual encounter will reveal hardened steel. She is a contradiction to herself and to others. She is the master of the "end-run." A part of you wants to trust her but the other part of you says that she can't be trusted.

You can trust the Cream-Puff to yield to the desires and expectations of others in order to gain approval. You can trust the Locomotive to ignore other peoples' desires and expectations. They are both fairly consistent. But you don't dare trust the Steel Magnolia. She can appear to be sensitive to the desires and expectations of others, but will often go ahead and do whatever she wants. She may appear to be passive but is actually quite aggressive.

On one hand she appears very soft and tender but more than just a casual encounter will reveal hardened steel. She may appear calm on the outside but there is a cauldron of bitterness and resentment boiling on the inside. The reality is that anger is frequently at the core of passive aggression, even when it is denied, suppressed, repressed or called something else. But however much she may try to disguise it, her anger will never be entirely hidden.

The Steel Magnolia is a contradiction to herself and to others. She looks like a cream-puff—she doesn't state her needs, she is indirect. Yet if you cross her or get in her way you are in serious trouble. On the outside she appears to be sensitive and tender but don't get too comfortable because the tough side is sneaking up behind you.

One of the most effective tools of the Steel Magnolia is sarcasm. Sarcasm is one way to express your anger while playing it safe. By pretending to be funny the anger is disguised and retaliation is discouraged. If you respond to the sarcasm you may be accused of being negative, assuming the worst, or of not having a sense of humor. "What's the matter—can't you take a joke?" may be the immediate response.

Sarcasm involves assault by misdirection, disguise, and sarcasm. It is a way of attacking while avoiding a clearly hostile intent. Over time they may even convince themselves that they don't have any aggressive feelings. They may come across as being shocked that anyone could misunderstand their pure motives and sincere intentions.

What are some characteristics of the Steel Magnolias?

### Steel Magnolias

| | | | |
|---|---|---|---|
| ■ procrastination | ■ subtle sarcasm | ■ forgetfulness | ■ stubbornness |
| ■ fosters confusion | ■ obstructionism | ■ fear of intimacy | ■ makes excuses |
| ■ misunderstanding | ■ silent treatment | ■ sulking –lies | ■ mixed messages |
| ■ chronic lateness | ■ inconsistency | ■ ambiguity | |
| ■ carelessness | ■ resentful | | |

### Are There Any Healthy Options?

One of the main reasons why the Cream-Puff, Locomotive and Steel Magnolias represent unhealthy anger styles is that they involve a denial of our real self. When we stuff, repress, suppress, deny, ignore or hurl our anger we are ignoring anger's potentially important message. We have lost touch with the primary emotion that triggered our anger.

All three of the anger styles we have discussed thus far involve unhealthy reactions. They are usually an automatic and unconscious reaction to some real or perceived threat to our sense of significance, safety or security. Each style is dysfunctional. Each one falls short of God's plan and purpose in giving us the gift of anger.

Reactors deny their real grief and pain. Resentment and rage keep them from dealing with legitimate fears and hurts and limit God's ability to bring recovery and restoration. If we refuse to allow God to help us face the real issues of our lives, how can we understand, how can we forgive ourselves, how can we forgive others, how can we grow?

### The Mature and Assertive Responder

Fortunately God has given us a healthy option. God can help people trade in their unhealthy reactive style for a mature, healthy and biblically sound way of understanding and expressing their anger. There is a way of responding that allows us to "be angry and sin not." It is the assertive response.

The mature responder has a clear sense of who they are in Christ. Their emotions, mind and will work together and function in a balanced way. They can express their opinions but don't need to put others down. They delight in serving but aren't servile. They can be tough and tender. They aren't reactive, they are proactive. They have taken the time to look at, understand, and develop a healthy plan for dealing with their God-given emotion of anger.[8]

The mature response is a style of responding to anger without which this world of ours would be a much poorer place. What are some characteristics of a mature responder?

### Mature Responder

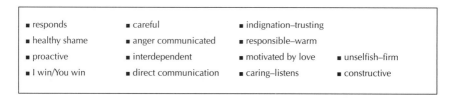

| | | | |
|---|---|---|---|
| ▪ responds | ▪ careful | ▪ indignation–trusting | |
| ▪ healthy shame | ▪ anger communicated | ▪ responsible–warm | |
| ▪ proactive | ▪ interdependent | ▪ motivated by love | ▪ unselfish–firm |
| ▪ I win/You win | ▪ direct communication | ▪ caring–listens | ▪ constructive |

The mature responder is free to "speak the truth in love." When provoked the mature responder is less likely to immediately react without thinking but rather responds in a way that reflects some discipline and thought. She has learned the value of anger. She has learned to be aware of and choose her expressions of anger. She is more likely to have trained herself to think, act and feel more constructively. She expresses her thoughts, preferences and emotions directly to the other person in healthy ways that communicate a respect for the dignity and the rights of both herself and others. Her response is more likely to move her towards achieving both her personal goals and her relational goals.

Anger can be an invaluable tool in the hands of a responsible person. It is a force capable of being directed and used constructively. Aristotle acknowledged these positive aspects of anger when he said, "Those who do not show anger at things that ought to arouse anger are regarded as fools; so too if they do not show anger in the right way, at the right time or at the right person."

## When Is the Best Time to Deal With Anger?

The best time to deal with anger is before one gets angry. That's right, *before* the anger. Why? Because one needs to learn how to seize opportunities to deal with discouraging, frustrating and painful situations *before* one reaches the boiling point. It is easier to be clear and objective when one plans ahead. Hence, with planning your client's perspective is less likely to be clouded by the intensity of his/her anger.

You might want to start counseling by asking, "Is your anger a problem for you or for others?" Just because one becomes angry once in awhile doesn't mean that one has an anger problem. Anger is a God-given emotion that is a normal part of everyday life. Healthy anger has tremendous potential for good. Anger only becomes a problem when we deny, suppress, repress, stuff and ignore it or when we don't listen to it understand it and allow it to serve its God-intended function.

Anger can become a problem when a client lets it get out of control and move into more destructive emotions such as hostility, rage and aggression. It becomes a problem when clients continue to allow themselves to be puppets of past patterns rather than using the resources that God has given to redirect the energy of this powerful emotion. It's a problem when clients haven't disciplined themselves to express it in healthy and constructive kinds of ways.

## What Are the Benefits of Dealing With Anger?

Upon educating clients about their anger, some may be tempted to ask, "Working on this anger stuff is a lot more work than I had anticipated. Is it really worth it?" This is a query only the client can answer. Many people have found that one of the most helpful ways to answer that question is to remind themselves of the benefits of understanding and learning how to appropriately express their anger.

Over the years we've asked clients, "What have you found are the benefits of dealing with your anger?" Here are some of their answers:

- Understanding and dealing with my anger has improved my overall physical, emotional, mental and spiritual health.
- It gives me an increased source of energy to make the hard choices.

- It has improved the quality of my marriage.
- It has strengthened my relationships with the kids.
- It has alleviated my fear of someone else's anger.
- Now my children have a healthy model for this God-given emotion.
- It helps me keep things in perspective.
- The appropriate expression of my anger has helped others better understand me and what is important to me.
- It helps me clarify and protect personal boundaries.
- It helps me to protect myself physically and emotionally.
- It's given me the power and courage to remove myself from the victim role.

If one's desire is to become the person God wants him/her to be, one will make the time to learn how to make their anger work for them. Hebrews 12:15 says, "See to it that no one misses the grace of God and that no bitter root grows up to cause trouble and defile many." It is easy for a bitter root to grow up in the lives of clients. Some may think they are doing the right thing by not dealing with or dwelling on the past. There is a big difference between not dealing with the past and not dwelling on it!

### What Are Some Constructive Steps for Dealing with Anger?

The first step in making a client's anger work for, rather than against, the client is to have the client decide in advance to invest his/her anger-energy and express it in a healthy way. This early decision is important because when anger is in control it can block one's ability to think clearly. Think back to the last time you, the counselor, experienced strong anger. How objective were you? How clearly were you thinking? It is important to develop a plan for dealing with anger before one becomes angry. Here are some simple steps to help clients make their anger work for them.

### Step 1: Be Aware of It

One of the many myths regarding anger is that if a person doesn't look or appear on the outside to be angry, then they don't have a problem with anger, and they are clearly not an angry person. Someone may not appear to be an angry person on the outside but can be like a battlefield on the inside.

Therefore, do not assume, but ask clients: How often are you aware of being angry? What situations do you encounter that might make you more vulnerable to anger? How does your body respond to anger? What are your physical manifestations of anger?

## Step 2: Put First Things First

As soon as one becomes aware of it, before doing anything else, one should ask oneself: What is meant by putting first things first? Take it to the Lord in prayer. In 2 Corinthians 10:5 Paul exhorts us to take every thought captive to the obedience of Christ. I don't think it does any injustice to the intent of that passage to suggest that we also need to get into the habit of taking every emotion to the obedience of Christ. This is especially true of the emotion of anger.

Before deciding what we are going to do, we need to set aside focused time to take all of our concerns, including our struggles with our emotions, to the Lord in prayer. In Psalm 42:4 David talks about pouring out his soul and in Psalm 68:8 David wrote, "Trust in Him at all times, O people; Pour out your heart before Him; God is a refuge for us." (NASB)

If a client is frustrated, hurt, discouraged and experiencing anger with someone, have the client talk to the Lord about it; first in silent prayer and then perhaps even out loud. Instruct the client to ask God for His help and His guidance. Have clients take advantage of the power of the Holy Spirit. In James 1:5 we are told that if we lack wisdom we only need to ask for it. In 1 Peter 5:7 we are told to cast all of our concerns on Him "because He cares for you." (NASB)

Many people have found the following simple prayer to be of help.

Dear Lord, Thank You for creating me in Your image with the ability to experience and express the emotion of anger. While sin has damaged and distorted anger in my life, I thank You that You have promised to be at work within me both to will and to work for Your good pleasure. I thank You that You can cause all things to work together for good and that I can do all things through You who strengthens me. I ask You to help me to change my anger patterns. Help me to experience and express this emotion in ways that are good and that bring honor and glory to You. Amen

### Step 3: Accept Responsibility for Anger

One of the major effects of original sin is seen in our tendency to blame someone else for our problems. When God confronted Eve in the garden and asked her what happened she blamed the serpent. When God confronted Adam he first blamed Eve and then he blamed God. When clients are angry it is easy for them to say, "It's your fault, you made me angry." However, clients should be educated that they are responsible for how they choose to respond to their anger.

### Step 4: Decide Who or What Is Going to Have Control

This is a critical step. When one experiences anger one is faced with a choice. One can either allow the anger to dominate and control, or with the help of the Holy Spirit one can choose to control the anger and invest the anger-energy in a healthy way. While a client can't always control when he/she will experience anger, with God's help one can choose how it is expressed. As your clients take their anger to God in prayer He will help them find creative and constructive ways to deal with it.

### Step 5: Define It! Identify the Source and Cause of It

Anger is a secondary emotion that is experienced in response to a primary emotion such us hurt, frustration or fear.

*Hurt* is usually caused by something that has already happened . . . something in the past. When we are hurt we feel vulnerable and open to more hurt. This is especially true of people who are very sensitive. For many people anger is an automatic defense mechanism to protect against hurt.

*Frustration* takes place in the present. We can become frustrated by blocked goals or desires or by unmet expectations. Frequently the things that lead to the greatest frustrations have one main characteristic . . . they really aren't that important.

What kinds of situations cause your clients to become frustrated? Are there any specific individuals they find more frustrating than others? What situations frustrate your clients?

*Fear* is an emotion that tends to focus on things in the future. Many people associate fear with vulnerability and weakness. Some people, especially men, find it more comfortable to express anger than fear and so may respond to situations in which they are anxious or afraid by getting angry. If you suspect this, consider asking an angry client, "Is there something that you are afraid of that could be triggering your anger?"

### Step 6: Choose Your Response: Spending and Investing Anger-Energy

When one becomes angry the first step is to identify the primary emotion. Then ask, "Is this really that important?" If it isn't, simply let it pass. If it is important then have the client ask him/herself, "How can I express my anger in a way that is biblically consistent and that will enhance the probability of resolution?"

Instruct your client to look at some of the key passages that deal with anger: Proverbs 15:18, 16:32, 29:11; Mark 3:5; Ephesians 4:26, 31; Colossians 3:8, 21. Have the client ask God to help; "speak the truth in love." Have the client take time to acknowledge the other persons' feelings, and remain open to an apology or an explanation. Facilitate a client to make the primary goal understanding, and then work toward a resolution.

### Step 7: Evaluate It

Perhaps your client successfully navigates that emotional rapid. Or perhaps he/she was more successful than in the past but still needs to work on it. Whatever the result of the six steps was, the client is not quite finished yet. The last step in dealing with anger is to discover all one can from the experience. What went well? What was different than usual? Were there any positive surprises? What could one have done differently?

In order to complete the learning process it is important for the client to reflect on the question: "What have I learned from this experience?" One of the most encouraging aspects of being a Christian is that, whatever the experience, good or bad, with God's help we can learn from it. If you've been a Christian very long you have learned that Romans 8:28 is true. God carefully recorded the experiences of many men and women in the Bible. For over two thousand years God protected the record of those experiences. Why? So that we could learn from them.

## Some Final Observations

For many Christians both the experience and expression of anger have become a habit. Habits can take some time to change. The good news is that with God's help we can change, we can grow, we can be more than conquerors. As we allow the Holy Spirit to fill us and apply promises in God's Word we can take the old unhealthy ways of responding and develop new, healthy and biblically consistent emotional responses.

In Daniel 1:8 we are told that Daniel "purposed in his heart" not to defile himself with the kings meat. And he didn't. We can purpose in our hearts not to allow our anger to control us but rather to put our anger as well as our other emotions under God's control. While we can't always control when or why we will experience anger we can with God's help control how we express that anger.

God has given us that choice. We can allow ourselves to be controlled by our anger or we can pursue "quality anger." Quality anger involves open, honest and direct communication. It involves speaking the truth in love. It involves investing the energy God has given us to declare truth, to right wrongs, and to help ourselves and others "become conformed to the image of His Son." (Romans 8:29)

As you help others develop creative ways to invest the God-given anger-energy, as you help them develop more effective anger management skills, as you learn how to approach anger from a biblical perspective, you will find one of the most powerful sources of motivation available to mankind. Martin Luther said, "When I am angry I can write, pray and preach well, for then my whole temperament is quickened, my understanding sharpened, and all mundane vexations and temptations are gone."

If you or your clients have struggled with unhealthy anger, we want to encourage and support you in your struggle. In our work with a wide range of people—university students here at John Brown University, couples in our marriage enrichment seminars across the country, corporate leaders—we have seen time and again that God can and will transform long-term unhealthy anger patterns into a healthy and constructive anger that strengthens individuals, marriages, families and work-teams.

## ENDNOTES

1. S. Peck, Mission of madness, *Long Beach Telegram*, (18 December, 1997), A1, A6–7.
2. Gary R. Oliver and Oliver, Carrie, *Raising Sons and Loving It!* (Grand Rapids: Zondervan, 2004), 135.
3. Oliver and Oliver, *Raising Sons and Loving It!*, 134–136.
4. Gary R. Oliver, *Real men have feelings too* (Chicago: Moody Press, 1993).
5. Harriet Lerner, *The dance of anger* (New York: Harper & Row, 1985).
6. Gary R. Oliver, and Wright H. N., *A Woman's Forbidden Emotion* (Ventura, CA: Regal, 2005), 39–40.
7. Oliver and Wright, *A Woman's Forbidden Emotion*, 78.
8. R. Walters, *Anger: Yours & mine & what to do about it* (Grand Rapids, MI: Zondervan, 1981).

# 11

# Personality Disorders

*Henry A. Virkler*

A personality disorder is more a [dysfunctional] way of life than an illness.

JAMES MORRISON

John was late for staff case consultation due to a crisis he had to intervene in, and came in to hear Jerry exclaim in exasperation and anger, "...she not only has her whole family 'walking on egg-shells,' she now has me on egg-shells as well!"

John knew exactly who Jerry was talking about with other clinical staff, and wondered whether he should have assigned her to a more experienced staff member. "What is Stella up to now?" he queried as he settled into supervisory role as Clinical Director of the Outpatient Mental Health Unit.

"She's threatening to kill herself again if I don't spend time with her on the phone over every alleged emergency!" Jerry was gesturing strongly and his anger was evident.

"Alleged emergencies....?" John let the question trail off, putting the issue squarely back in Jerry's lap.

"Yes, of course," Jerry asserted, "You know she is just trying to manipulate me...to control me in order to quell her raging fear that I'll abandon her . . . isn't that what all borderlines do?" Jerry shot back, more defiant than questioning.

"But what if she cuts herself again?" John queried, as he had seen Stella on the Unit three times over the past seven years, "or worse, finally kills herself in a drunken stupor . . . she has been hitting the bottle more seriously lately, hasn't she?"

"Yes she has . . . " Jerry sat back in resignation, "and I have to admit . . . (he paused and looked around at the staff as if to anticipate a shocked response) that at times I wish she would just go ahead and get it done!" His anger was rising again as he realized how seriously his statement reflected a lack of caring and positive emotional connection to his patient.

John knew that Jerry was a committed though still somewhat inexperienced clinician who was speaking more out of his anger and frustration, something he wanted his staff to be able to do without fearing retribution. He said to him, "Jerry we've all worked with borderline patients that, at times, we felt like strangling more than helping, and I know from experience that Stella will drive you right up the wall with her anger, threats, and demands. But it is important to maintain your boundaries, and follow through with a clear professional intervention here. It's likely that she will stabilize if you continue to work with her, but she must know that you still care and haven't given up on her. Can you do that, or should we consider transferring her case to some other staff?"

Jerry heard both the support and the challenge by John, and he resolved his moral and clinical dilemma the only way he knew how to grow further as a resilient clinician. He recommitted himself to stay with and reconnect with Stella, realizing all too well why borderline personality disorders were among the toughest kinds of cases to work with as a counselor.

### An Entrenched, Long-term Pattern Disorder

A personality disorder is a long-term pattern of thinking, feeling, and behavior that differs significantly from the expected norms for one's culture. When a person has a personality disorder, he or she typically responds in the same way across a variety of interpersonal situations—the behavior is entrenched and repetitive, and is not simply a response to a particular person or situation. People with personality disorders tend to respond in similar ways to every situation, even when different responses would be more appropriate. Personality disorders usually appear in adolescence or early adulthood and tend to change little over time. They cause either stress or impairment in social, occupational or other areas of functioning.[1]

## The Twelve Disorders of Personality

There are ten specific personality disorders identified in the main text of the DSM-IV—the psychiatric diagnostic system used by nearly all mental health professionals—and there are at least two experimental personality disorders that are likely to appear with some frequency in the counseling office. Brief descriptions of each of those twelve appear below.

Persons with *Dependent Personality Disorder* are typically overly submissive and have great fear of making decisions or being independent. They look for others who will lead and make decisions for them. People with Dependent Personality Disorder don't disagree with others for fear they will reject them, and seek an excessive amount of reassurance and advice from others. These people fit many of the characteristics of the literature on codependency, although some clinicians view codependency as a specific way of attempting to control others, whereas this concept is not included in the DSM-IV definition of Dependent Personality Disorder.

Persons with *Avoidant Personality Disorder* have the capacity and desire for intimacy, but are very shy and insecure, and are unwilling to reach out to people unless guaranteed acceptance. They typically feel socially inadequate and are overly sensitive to any signs of criticism or rejection. As a result, they are usually reluctant to take the risks necessary to develop new relationships, even though they sincerely would like to have them.

Persons with *Obsessive-Compulsive Personality Disorder* are overly concerned with doing things perfectly, and with ensuring that anything done by other people that reflects on them also be done perfectly. As a result they often manifest perfectionism that interferes with completion of their own tasks, and are over-controlling in their relationships to family members or work subordinates. Their concern with orderliness and perfectionism also affects them in the realm of morality and ethics, where they tend to be overly conscientious and inflexible.

Persons with *Histrionic Personality Disorder* tend to be lively and overly dramatic. They feel frustrated if they are not the center of attention. They frequently over-emphasize physical appearance and often engage in sexually provocative or seductive behavior. They tend to have a long history of brief romantic relationships that end as quickly as they start.

Persons with *Narcissistic Personality Disorder* have an exaggerated sense of self-importance. They expect to be recognized as superior without earning such recognition. They typically expect excessive admiration and believe they are entitled to favorable treatment and automatic compliance with their expectations. They tend to be exploitive and lack empathy and true concern for others. Other people often view them as arrogant and haughty.

Persons with *Antisocial Personality Disorder* have a pervasive pattern of disregard for and violation of the rights of others. They are typically impulsive, deceitful, and seem to lack remorse for the harm their behavior often causes. They enjoy the challenge of successfully "conning" other people. Some have good interpersonal skills and elicit trust (at least temporarily). From a Christian perspective, these would be people who grew up without a properly developed conscience code.

People with *Borderline Personality Disorder* have a very unstable sense of identity, and frequently feel empty inside. As a result they are constantly looking for someone stable with whom to form a relationship. When they find such a person they frequently become very demanding and jealous of any attention this person pays to anyone else. They constantly worry about being abandoned, and will engage in frantic efforts—including suicidal attempts or gestures—to avoid abandonment.

People with Borderline Personality Disorder are often impulsive in ways that are self-damaging, engaging in activities such as impulsive spending, promiscuous sex, substance abuse or reckless driving. They often express either adoration (when people are giving them the attention they want) or inappropriate, intense anger (when they believe they are being abandoned). They sometimes have episodes that look like mini-psychoses, especially when they feel lonely or afraid.

People with *Paranoid Personality Disorder* have a pervasive pattern of distrust and suspiciousness. They often believe others' motives are malevolent without any substantial reason for such a belief, and frequently read demeaning meanings into benign remarks or behavior. They typically bear grudges and are quick to react angrily.

People with *Schizoid Personality Disorder* are emotionally detached from those around them, but unlike the person with Avoidant Personality Disorder, they have no desire to develop close relationships. They usually have flattened affect. They rarely come to therapy because they are usually satisfied with their solitary existence, but sometimes come because family members (e.g., parents) want them to change, and those family members urge them to see a counselor.

Persons with *Schizotypal Personality Disorder* are also uncomfortable in close relationships, but in addition to their discomfort with intimacy, often have eccentric thinking and behavior. They often appear stiff in social settings, and their clothing is sometimes unkempt. They frequently have paranoid ideation. There is some evidence suggesting a relationship between Schizotypal Personality Disorder and the schizophrenias.

*Passive-Aggressive Personality Disorder* and *Depressive Personality Disorder* are two experimental personality disorders that may appear with some frequency in Christian counseling offices. Persons with Passive-Aggressive Personality Disorder may not indicate disagreement initially when asked to do something, but often resent demands or requests, and express these feelings indirectly by passively resisting social or occupational tasks. They are typically sullen, argumentative, envious and resentful of others. Some persons with this personality style will alternate between hostile defiance and contrition.[2]

Depressive Personality Disorder is different from Dysthymic Disorder, which is a chronic (at least two years) mild to moderate depression that seems to have significant somatic symptoms related to biological depression.[3] In contrast, Depressive Personality Disorder is a chronic lifestyle dominated by feelings of inadequacy and criticalness about self, pessimism about the world and the future, and negativism and criticalness toward others.[4] Thus it seems to be more likely to have a psychological etiology (a cognitive habit of always seeing the world from a dark, negative perspective) than a biological etiology (as Dysthymic Disorder seems to have).

It is estimated that 10 to 13% of the population—over 30 million people in the United States—have personality disorders.[5] Because of the distress or impairment personality disorders cause in relationships and in life functioning, they are likely to appear in counseling offices in higher percentages than they appear in the general population. Thus every counselor in general practice is likely to be faced with the prospect of treating people with personality disorders on a regular basis.

Up to the present time the general consensus has been that the prognosis for successful treatment of people with personality disorders was low, especially within the severe time constraints imposed by managed care. What this chapter will attempt to do is discuss a Christian cognitive-behavioral model for conceptualizing how the personality disorders develop, and how to treat personality disorders within a relatively short time frame (12 to 18 sessions). I will also suggest some ways to begin treatment, or to treat portions of a personality disorder if managed care or other financial considerations do not allow even that amount of counseling time.

### How Personality Disorders Develop

This outline follows a cognitive-behavioral approach to personality development and builds on the work of Adler[6] and Young.[7] Alfred Adler believed that young children attempt to find ways to achieve significance and identity in their world. Assessing their own abilities, courage and confidence, they choose either to develop their identity through socially useful, constructive behavior, or they become discouraged at being able to achieve a unique identity in positive ways, and find their identity instead through unhealthy behavior.

The result of this choice is what Adler referred to as a "style of living" or a "life-style." In contemporary terminology we might say that all people have a personality style. We have no specific names for the healthy personalities of those who choose constructive life-styles—although the trend toward positive psychology and our dedication to redemptive living should challenge Christian counselors to construct such a taxonomy. Various kinds of Personality Disorders are the names we give to those who choose or live out unhealthy life-styles.

Each personality disorder can be identified with one or more of what Adler would call "mistaken beliefs." Psychologist-pastor Bill Backus calls these misbeliefs,[8] and Christian psychologist Chris Thurman[9] describes them as "the lies we believe." Adler believed that we often adopt beliefs about what is true, and then we act "as if" those things were true, whether or not they are.

For example, the mistaken belief that underlies Dependent Personality Disorder might go something like this: "I am not capable of making decisions or taking care of myself, and must find someone strong and wise who can do these things for me." The belief that underlies Avoidant Personality Disorder might be: "People would probably reject me if they truly knew me, so I must be careful what I allow them to see." A person with Obsessive-Compulsive Personality Disorder might be operating on the assumption that "I am only okay if I do things perfectly. If I let myself (or others whose behavior reflects on me) be satisfied with less than excellence, I will soon be overwhelmed with mediocrity and no one will respect me." The person with Histrionic Personality Disorder may be operating on the mistaken belief that "I am only okay if people are paying attention to me." The same kind of analysis could be done for each of the personality disorders.

Young[10] has extended this analysis further in his work with schemas (or core beliefs). He believes that, based on our early life experience, we all develop a set of core beliefs, or schemas, that encompass our view (1) of ourselves, (2) of the world (other people), and (3) of our relationship to the world. These core beliefs may be either healthy ones (adaptive schema), or unhealthy ones (maladaptive schema). Unhealthy core beliefs can result from trauma that occur anytime during the lifespan, but they most commonly develop during childhood. Young has identified 18 different *early maladaptive schema* (i.e., those that develop during the first five years of life). These early maladaptive schema lay the groundwork, without some sort of beneficent intervention, for various personality disorders.

### Proposal for a Christian Taxonomy of Schema Development

From a Christian perspective, one could argue that core beliefs (the early, often unarticulated beliefs children develop based on their early experience in the world) should be expanded from these basic three *to at least eight categories*. These beliefs (either correct or mistaken), form the basis for our early views of ourselves, and determine whether we develop a socially-contributing lifestyle or an unhealthy one (a personality disorder). The eight types of core beliefs I would like to propose include the following:

1. *Beliefs about self* (e.g., Am I loveable or unlovable, worthwhile or not worthwhile?)
2. *Beliefs about others* (e.g., Are people trustworthy, untrustworthy, predictable or unpredictable?)
3. *Beliefs about the relationship between self and others* (e.g., Am I

optimistic that most of my needs will be met through my relationships with others, or am I pessimistic about this happening? Do I
believe I have the power to exert a reasonable amount of influence
on the world around me [self-efficacy], or do I see myself as relatively powerless in influencing what happens?). [Each of the following five kinds of core beliefs are not frequently mentioned by
secular theorists.]

4. *Beliefs about God* (e.g., Does He exist? What is His nature? How much
   control does He have over what happens in the universe? Does He
   have a personal interest in human beings? Does God care?)

5. *Beliefs about God's feelings towards oneself* (Does God like me, dislike
   me, or is He indifferent to my existence? Do His feelings about me
   change when I make errors? When I sin? Does He reject me or
   punish me when I do wrong?).

6. *Beliefs about what one should and should not do* (Wolterstorff has
   called these "control beliefs").[11] This concept of moral direction
   has been typically avoided or pathologized in secular theorizing,
   yet it is evident that some sort of moral control beliefs are necessary, and failure to impart them to children has significant negative consequences.

7. *Beliefs about one's purpose in life* (What is the purpose in living? Is
   my most important purpose in life to minimize pain and maximize
   pleasure? Is it to achieve status, attention, wealth, or security? Is it
   to make a difference in the world by giving of myself to others?)

8. *Beliefs about expression of affection and sexuality* (e.g., What are
   appropriate ways of expressing love and affection? What are
   appropriate ways of expressing and receiving sexual love?)

## Conceptualizing Human Personality Style

Knowledge about personality development is useful for understanding
how personality disorders arise. A healthy personality style (and the dysfunctional personality disorders) can be conceptualized in terms of four
activities:

- cognitive beliefs,
- cognitive processes,

- feelings, and
- resultant overt behavior.

In healthy people there is likely to be relative health in each of these four processes. In people with personality disorders there are likely to be a dysfunctioning mode of activity in one or more of these processes.

## Cognitive Beliefs

Cognitive beliefs refer to *the content of what we believe.* Cognitive beliefs occur at three discernible levels—core beliefs, intermediate beliefs, and automatic thoughts.[12] Core beliefs are often formed by children based on their early observations about the way the world works. We usually are not aware of the fact that these core beliefs are assumptions or hypotheses about reality: unless someone draws our attention to this fact, we typically act "as if" they were true and base our responses to the world on these assumptions. As mentioned above, children and adolescents develop core beliefs in at least eight areas.

Intermediate beliefs are those rules, assumptions and expectations that people develop from their core beliefs. They also include expectancies (e.g., optimism or pessimism about how life in general and situations in particular are likely to turn out). They also include assumptions are how people are and rules about how people ought to behave.[13] Intermediate beliefs serve as the connection between core beliefs and automatic thoughts. For example, if a person developed the core belief in childhood, based on interactions with his family, that "I am inadequate," he might develop the intermediate beliefs (in this case a rule and an expectancy for himself that) "If I work very hard, I may be able to succeed, although there is a good likelihood that I won't." When faced with a problem in his daily life, the core belief and intermediate beliefs are likely to produce automatic thoughts such as "I'm probably going to mess up, and that will be terrible."

Automatic thoughts include the self-talk that people constantly give themselves. People with healthy personality styles tend to be more likely to give themselves healthy self-talk, whereas people with personality disorders are more likely to engage in *disabling* self-talk (e.g., Dependent Personality Disorder, Avoidant Personality Disorder, Depressive Personality Disorder, Obsessive-Compulsive Personality Disorder), *overly self-centered* self-talk (e.g., Histrionic Personality Disorder, Narcissistic Personality Disorder, Antisocial Personality Disorder), or *overly suspicious* self-talk (e.g., Paranoid Personality Disorder, Schizoid Personality Disorder, Schizotypal Personality Disorder).

Adler suggested that the word "unconscious" be used as an adjective rather than a noun—that these cognitions (core beliefs, intermediate beliefs, and automatic thoughts) sometimes affect us without us being fully consciously aware of their presence (they are to some extent operating outside of our conscious awareness). He broke with Freud, however, in terms of believing that there is an unconscious mind where these core beliefs reside which is ordinarily inaccessible to conscious thinking.

## Cognitive Processes

Interacting with the cognitive beliefs that we hold are certain cognitive processes that keep data in or out of our awareness, and also determine the meaning we make of the data available to us. The three most important cognitive processes are selective attention, attributions, and cognitive avoidance processes.

*Selective attention:* According to Tor Norretrander,[14] a leading science writer in Denmark, conscious experience represents a miniscule portion of the stimuli we process. Norretrander asserts that our brains process approximately 11 million bits of information per second, but our consciousness processes only about 16 bits in that same time period. While some might argue with the exact figures Norretrander gives, even if he is off by several fold it is clear that our conscious mind cannot attend to all the internal and external data available to it. We have learned a variety of ways to selectively attend to the data that is most important to our survival, and find some way of not attending to that data that is less important or unimportant.

People with healthy personality styles tend to have cognitive selective attention processes that help them attain a relatively representative sample of the available data. They receive accurate data about the situations where they are doing well, and also receive accurate data about situations where they are doing less well and need to change. In contrast, people with personality disorders are likely to selectively attend to data in such a way that they receive a distorted view of reality and their performance.

People with certain of the personality disorders appear to have developed the cognitive habit of selectively attending to negative data about themselves and their performance (e.g., the Depressive, Dependent, Avoidant and Obsessive-Compulsive Personality Disorders). People with other personality disorders appear to have developed the cognitive habit of selectively attending to only the data that highlights their positives (e.g., Histrionic, Narcissistic, and Antisocial Personality Disorder). People with a third type of personality disorder appear to selectively focus on the data suggesting that others are not trustworthy and that one must always be on guard (e.g., the Paranoid, Schizoid and Schizotypal Personality Disorders).

*Attributions:* Attributions refer to the interpretations people make of their behavior and the behavior of others. People with normal personality styles tend to make relatively objective interpretations of events. People with personality disorders tend to make interpretations that are consistent with the core beliefs they hold. For example, if a person with Dependent Personality Disorder happens to make an independent decision that turns out well, they are likely to attribute this to "luck" rather than interpret it to mean that they can occasionally make good decisions on their own.

Similarly, if someone does something nice to someone who has Paranoid Personality Disorder, that person is likely to look for some "hidden agenda" rather than accept it as a genuinely caring behavior with no strings attached. Thus all people (those with and without personality disorders) tend to make interpretations that are consistent with the core beliefs they already hold and that allow them to keep their core beliefs intact.

*Cognitive avoidance processes:* One of the aspects of Freud's theory that most therapists have accepted as having some validity, whether or not they accept the validity of the rest of his constructs, is his theory of ego defense mechanisms. Ego defense mechanisms are mental processes that serve to keep overwhelming or anxiety-producing data out of conscious awareness, either temporarily, or if the data would be extremely overwhelming, out of conscious awareness for long periods of time. The DSM-IV has a very thorough and interesting description of the ego defenses, and organizes them from the more healthy to the less healthy.[15] Cognitive behavior therapists have recognized the value of having a way to incorporate these concepts into their theorizing, and have termed them "cognitive avoidance processes."

These four concepts—cognitive beliefs, selective attention, attributions, and cognitive avoidance processes—seem to exist in dynamic equilibrium. That is, once people have accepted a certain set of cognitive beliefs as true, they tend to selectively attend to data that confirms those beliefs, make consistent attributions about that data, and engage in cognitive avoidance processes that serve to reinforce those cognitive beliefs.

Normally it is only through some sort of significant event or intervention—a major life crisis, or conversion, or a significant breakthrough with God as a Christian, or therapy—that peoples' cognitive beliefs and cognitive processing style change significantly.

### Emotions and Behavior

In a cognitive-behavioral model, emotions are considered to primarily be the result of the cognitions a person holds and the cognitive processes they engage in. Emotions are important for a number of reasons—they are an integral part of the total human experience, and it is important that a therapist recognize and respect them in order for a client to feel understood. From a therapeutic standpoint, they are a valuable entry point into understanding the cognitive content and cognitive processes that are producing them.

Whether or not thoughts and emotions are expressed in *overt behavior* depends on a number of things—how intense the emotions are, the client's appraisal of the benefits or risks of expressing those feelings in behavior, and the behavioral repertoire they possess. The combination of one's cognitive beliefs, cognitive processes, emotions, and behaviors produce their personality style, or in the case of unhealthy processes, their personality disorder.

### Getting Oriented and Treating Personality Disorders

If the cognitive-behavioral model of understanding the personality disorders described above is valid, then it is possible to approach treatment of personality disorders by asking the following questions:

1.  Is this person's difficulty caused by mistaken cognitive beliefs? If so, what are they?
2.  Is this person's difficulty caused by faulty cognitive processes which they are using to assimilate the internal and external data

available to them? If so, how can they be helped to develop a more balanced awareness of those data?

3. Is this person's difficulty caused because they have either (a) learned unhealthy behavioral responses or (b) failed to learn the behavioral skills they need in order to be successful? Or

4. Is this person's difficulty caused by problems in one or more of these areas?

Since emotions are considered, in a cognitive-behavioral model, to be secondary to the cognitive content and processes people experience, painful emotions are not treated directly. It is assumed that helping people change their beliefs, their faulty cognitive processes, and their dysfunctional behavior will be the best way to help them change their maladaptive emotions.

## Identifying Mistaken Beliefs or Unhealthy Cognitions

Mistaken cognitive beliefs may be either mistaken core beliefs, intermediate beliefs, or automatic thoughts (i.e., self-talk). Therefore the therapist may ask himself or herself the following questions (these questions do not have to be asked to the client, but serve as a template as the counselor listens to the client). Is this client hampered by mistaken beliefs about:

1. Themselves and their own lovability or worthwhileness
2. The nature of other human beings
3. Their relationship to others
4. Their beliefs about God
5. Their moral standards (e.g., too strict, non-existent, inconsistent, etc.), and the value they place on living within their moral values
6. Their beliefs about God's feelings toward them
7. Their beliefs about how they will find purpose and meaning for their life, or
8. Their beliefs about how one should express affection and sexuality.

Since intermediate beliefs and automatic thoughts are related to (and generally outgrowths of one's core beliefs), the therapist can also be listening for the intermediate beliefs and automatic thoughts that have developed from those core beliefs.

## Identifying Cognitive Processes that Interfere with Healthy Living

Using the above model, one can also be listening for the presence of cognitive processes that contribute to the personality disorder by distorting the internal and external data the client is receiving. Three processes to listen for specifically include

1.  Selective attention to internal or external data that reinforces the unhealthy personality style.
2.  Misattributions (misinterpretations of that data), or
3.  Unhealthy overuse of cognitive avoidance mechanisms (ego defenses).

## Identifying Behaviors and Skill Deficits that Interfere with Healthy Living

The unhealthy behavioral responses in which clients with personality disorders engage may be a result of at least two very different sources. First, clients may have learned unhealthy behavioral responses through modeling unhealthy behavioral responses that need to be replaced with healthier ones. Secondly, they may fail to respond appropriately because they have never had an opportunity to learn the appropriate skill. Some of the skills that clients with personality disorders sometimes lack include:

1.  Conversational skills
2.  Knowledge of how to deepen friendships
3.  Communication skills
4.  Conflict-resolution skills
5.  Assertiveness and anger management skills
6.  Relaxation skills
7.  Study skills
8.  Decision-making skills
9.  Knowledge of how to solve complex problems
10. Time-management skills
11. Money-management skills

12.  Knowledge of how to move to a new developmental stage
13.  Parenting skills for children without disabilities (normal parenting skills)
14.  Parenting skills for children with specific disabilities (e.g., how to parent children with ADHD, developmental disabilities, chronic health problems, etc.)
15.  Thus therapy in this area may include unlearning unhealthy responses, learning adaptive responses, or both.

## Integration of the Above Three Areas

Since people are integrated functioning personalities, those who have a personality disorder may have things that could be changed in all three areas, i.e., in their cognitive content, in their cognitive processing, and in their behavioral responses. For example, with persons with Dependent Personality Disorder it may be helpful to help them (1) learn to change their core beliefs about their own abilities and identify and replace their disabling self-talk (cognitive content), (2) help them become aware of how they are selectively attending only to data that supports their feelings of inadequacy and ignoring data that shows they have strengths (cognitive processing), and (3) help them learn decision-making skills (a cognitive-behavioral skill).

Since people differ with regard to their openness to these various means of entry, therapists have the opportunity to choose the avenue that they believe a specific client will be most open to at a given point in time, whether it be looking a the historical roots from which they developed a certain core belief, learning to identify and dispute with the disabling self-talk in which they are presently engaging, or practicing and learning a new skill.

The fact that people are integrated bio-psycho-social-spiritual units also means that it may not be necessary to address every component of the personality disorder. For example, as clients learn to dispute their disabling automatic thoughts and learn new skills, the changes that happen as a result in their personal relationships may cause their intermediate thoughts and core beliefs (or their tendencies to selectively attend or misinterpret data) to change in healthy directions.

Thus by choosing (1) the part of the personality disorder that the person is most willing to change and (2) the part which, if changed, would produce the most overall benefit, the therapist may be able to initiate a process of change that can continue even after therapy is over. This is particularly the case when the therapist *uses methods that teach clients cognitive and behavioral skills that they can use to continue to move toward healthiness without the presence of the therapist.* When working under severe time constraints, as is necessary in some managed care situations, the therapist may need to ask which *single* change would produce the most benefit for the client, and simply focus on that.

The process may be likened to lumberjacks called to break up a logjam on a crowded river. By careful assessment of which key "logs" are most critical in preventing movement and focusing on them, a process of movement toward health may be started in which it is not necessary to personally attend to every log. A clear understanding of how cognitive beliefs, cognitive processes, emotions and behavior are interconnected and which ones are most critical in causing the present impasse can help therapists determine where best to focus their attention.

### Practical Aspects to Treating Clients with Personality Disorders

### Ways of Changing Cognitive Content

This section (of the following three sections) is the one where Christian therapy can differ most from secular therapy. One of the differences is that Christian therapy recognizes the importance of core beliefs in the last five areas mentioned above (beliefs about God, about moral control beliefs, about God's feelings toward the person, about finding a meaningful purpose for one's life, and about the appropriate expression of affection and sexuality). Since 81% of clients say that they would like their religious values integrated into counseling,[16] it seems that most clients realize that such integration will in some way help them with the difficulties they are facing, and hope that their counselors will help them do so.

Secular cognitive behavior therapy usually begins by helping a client become aware of how their cognitive self-talk affects their emotions and behavior, and then teaches them, via Socratic questioning and behavioral experiments, to develop data by which to dispute and eventually replace the disabling self-talk in which they have been engaging. As clients become adept at changing their automatic thoughts, emphasis gradually moves to doing a similar process with intermediate and core beliefs.[17]

Christian therapists can, and often do use this same process with Christian clients. But most Christian therapists can probably also attest to the fact that God is not limited to always working "from the top down." Through the process of conversion, personal devotions, Bible studies, worship, fellowship with other Christians, inner healing experiences, Christian journaling, etc., God sometimes changes intermediate and core beliefs much more rapidly than one would expect simply using the secular cognitive-behavioral methods.

As we help clients appropriate the promises found in God's Word, these promises can provide an antidote for much of the disabling self-talk with which clients often struggle. The following list (adapted from an unknown source) gives examples:

| CLIENT SELF-TALK | GOD'S PROMISE |
| --- | --- |
| It's impossible. | With My help, all things are possible. |
| I'm exhausted. I can't go on. | I will strengthen you and will uphold you. |
| Nobody really loves me. | I love you, and nothing can ever separate you from My love. |
| I can't do it. | You can do all things with My strength. |
| I'm not able. | But I (God) am able. |
| It's not worth it. | It will be worth it. |
| I can't forgive myself. | I forgive you. |
| I can't manage. | I will supply all your needs. |
| I'm afraid. | Cast all your anxieties on Me, and I will give you My peace. |
| I'm not smart enough. | I will give you wisdom. |
| I feel all alone. | I will never leave you or forsake you. |

## Ways of Changing Cognitive Processes

The ways that Christian therapists can help clients change the dysfunctional processes that underlie personality disorders are similar to how secular therapists would work. Therapists can, through gentle, supportive questioning, help clients attend to a more balanced sample of the data available to them, and help them gradually assimilate that more accurate picture of themselves and the world into their core beliefs. They can also teach clients how to "check out" the interpretations they are making, and see whether there are other possible interpretations than the ones they are making. They can also support them as they examine data that they had previously been avoiding through use of their ego defense mechanisms.

But Christian therapists may also experience some advantages in the above process. Usually clients selectively attend, make misattributions, and overuse cognitive avoidance mechanisms out of fear of something. As counselors help clients know that, with God's help and support, they don't have to fear, these unhealthy cognitive processes can sometimes relax at a pace one would not expect if clients believe they are all alone in this battle with their fears.

## Ways of Changing Behavioral Deficits

Some clients need to unlearn old behavioral habits before learning new ones. For others, it is simply a matter of learning cognitive or behavioral skills they never learned as they were growing up.

Not all clients need skills training. For some, they may have observed healthy role models and know how to do certain things, but have never done them because disabling self-talk held them back. For this group, simply teaching them how to dispute with their disabling self-talk and then encouraging them to apply what they already know in a gradual hierarchy of real-life situations may be all that is needed.

Even with clients who do not believe they know how to do a certain skill, it may not be necessary to go through explicit skills training. They can be assigned to think about how to do a certain thing, and/or to carefully observe how someone they respect does it, discuss a plan for trying out the new skill with their therapist, then go out and work their plan.

For those skills that are more complex there is value in each counselor knowing how to teach each of the 14 sets of skills listed in the previous section, or in having pamphlets, books, cassettes, or videos that can introduce the client to the needed skills. It may be helpful to roleplay the skills in a counseling session, giving clients feedback as they try them, and also identifying any self-talk that would interfere with using the skills in real life situations outside the counseling session.

### Documenting Therapy for Clients with Personality Disorders

At least two forces point to the importance of ever-increasing specificity in treatment planning, not only for treatment of personality disorders, but for all therapy. One factor is the research indicating that, as therapists become more specific about identifying the treatment goals, identified problems, and treatment objectives, the efficiency of their interventions increases. To simply list "depression" or "anxiety" as an identified problem gives us little understanding of the causes of that specific client's depression or anxiety, nor does it lead to a meaningful or efficient treatment plan.

The second factor is that managed care providers and government agencies are demanding treatment plans that include identification of specific presenting problems and of interventions that follow logically from those problems.

The following is a suggested approach to writing more specific treatment plans. It involves identifying—for each problem the client is experiencing—treatment objectives, treatment plans (or interventions), and a way to measure whether each objective has been achieved. This model conforms to trends for treatment planning that are increasingly being required by the Joint Commission on Accreditation of Healthcare Organizations (JCAHO) and managed care systems. Some of the following points are from an article entitled "Basic Rules of Writing Treatment Goals and Objectives" found in *Practical Communications: Accreditation and Certification*, Vol. IV, No. 3, pp. 2–9.

### Treatment Goals

Treatment goals are *general* statements that specify the results you hope to accomplish through therapy. They are general, abstract statements that will eventually be transformed into treatment *objectives*, which are observable and measurable.

Whenever possible, treatment goals should be stated positively (something the client accomplishes), rather than negatively (something the client eliminates or reduces). Examples of treatment goals might be "Client will be comfortable initiating and maintaining a variety of close friendships and work relationships as desired" (Avoidant Personality Disorder) or "Increase client's comfort in making decisions, initiating projects, assuming responsibility for personal life, and disagreeing with others when appropriate" (Dependent Personality Disorder).

### The Identified Problem(s)

This step involves breaking the client's dysfunctionality down into component parts. For example, with each DSM-IV personality disorder, select those descriptors from the symptom list that are true for that specific client and are severe enough to be clinically significant in the person's life. (See examples in the tables that follow. The tables include illustrations using all the symptoms in the DSM-IV(TR). In real life situations choose only those symptoms that are important enough to be the focus of clinical attention, and that can realistically be addressed in the time insurance, or the client's financial resources, allow for treatment).

If the client is in a hospital setting for crisis stabilization, it may still be valuable to list all important problem areas, whether or not they will be dealt with during the hospital stay. Those identified problems not dealt with during the hospital stay will help give the outpatient therapist (or partial hospitalization program) direction for follow-up therapy.

Listing all important problems that are evident during the time of crisis is important for a second reason: After a crisis is partially stabilized and clients are discharged, they may sometimes be less willing to admit problems that need to be addressed in therapy. By having the problems already listed as part of the post-discharge treatment plan increases the likelihood that they will be addressed in follow-up therapy. A crucial ingredient in this step is to define the problems in ways that can be changed, either through therapy, medication, education, or some environmental intervention over which the client has some influence.

Sometimes the DSM-IV symptom lists contain criteria that are redundant from a treatment perspective. For example on the treatment planning sheet for Depressive Personality Disorder which follows, Symptoms 2, 3 and 6 are combined because they can all be treated using the same approach (review now).

## Treatment Objectives

Each treatment objective should follow from the respective identified problem. Each treatment objective should be a specific, measurable behavior or cognitive goal. Objectives will usually be the "flip-side" of the identified problem. For example, if the identified problem (IP) is the absence of some necessary skill, the objective will be to learn that skill. If the IP is the presence of some dysfunctional behavior, the objective will be to decrease or eliminate the occurrence of that behavior and replace it with a more functional one. It may be helpful to identify Pre-discharge Treatment Objectives and objectives that, if the outpatient therapist is in agreement, would become Post-Discharge Treatment Objectives.

## Treatment Plans (or Interventions)

This involves a succinct identification of the method you plan to use to accomplish the treatment objectives. The treatment plan chosen will vary depending on the theoretical orientation of the therapist, anticipated openness of the client to a specific approach, agency expectations and policies, insurance restrictions (some insurance companies restrict the types of interventions for which they will pay), and time available. In a time of managed care, the therapist should normally choose methods that have proven effectiveness in treating each specific identified problem, and will do so most efficiently.

## Measure of Achievement and Target Date

This column lists the way you will measure whether or not you have achieved each objective and when. See following examples.

On the closing pages of this chapter are examples of treatment plans for two personality disorders—Avoidant Personality Disorder and Depressive Personality Disorder. The interventions are illustrative only, and not intended to be prescriptive—they represent *one possible way* a therapist could choose to treat each issue, and not the only way. It is hoped that they will spur further thinking and discussion about the treatment of persons with personality disorders.

**Example of Treatment Planning Sheet: Avoidant Personality Disorder**

*Overall Goal: The client will be comfortable initiating and maintaining a variety of close friendships and work relationships as desired.*

| # | Identified Problem | Goal or Objective | Treatment Plan | Measure of Achievement and Target Date | Achieved Yes/No/ Provider/ Client Date |
|---|---|---|---|---|---|
| 1 | Views self as socially inept, personally unappealing, and inferior to others | Increase view of self as socially skillful, appealing, and equal to others in worth and lovability | Teach social skills. Teach how to dispute negative self-talk and how to engage in more positive self-talk about one's social acceptability | 1. Teach social skills by [date]. 2. Use social skills twice per day by [date]. 3. Teach how to recognize negative self-talk and replace it with positive self-talk when it occurs by [date]. | |
| 2 | Is mentally preoccupied with being criticized and rejected | Decrease cognitive preoccupation with being criticized and rejected by changing cognitive focus | Help client recognize how his preoccupation harms him and how to shift his focus from an emphasis on being criticized and rejected to an emphasis on accepting and caring for others | 1. Help client recognize how his preoccupation harms him by [date]. 2. Teach client to recognize when focusing on being criticized or rejected, and how to shift focus to caring for others by [date] | |
| 3+4 | Client is unwilling to be involved with others unless certain of being liked. | Help client become willing to take social risks, even if acceptance by others is not guaranteed | Teach client to dispute with his catastrophizing self-talk, and shift his focus to those who respond positively to his initiatives | Client risk taking social initiatives twice per day and keep record of results starting on [date]. | |
| 5 | Avoids vocational activities that involve significant interpersonal contact, thus hampering his career advancement | Help client overcome his vocational avoidance behavior | Assign small increases in vocational social interaction. Have client evaluate whether his negative expectations prove valid | Attempt at least one vocational social interaction per day by [date]. Evaluate results and use self-evaluation to improve next attempt. | |
| 6 | Client remembers a socially traumatic event, and expects future events will turn out similarly (not from DSM-IV symptom list). | Reduce impact of past trauma on present and future behavior | Help client recognize his overgeneralization and use memory of positive events to combat that tendency. | Identify overgeneralizations by [date]. Develop ability to dispute with them using memories of positive events by [date]. | |

**Example of Treatment Planning Sheet: Depressive Personality Disorder**

*Overall Goal(s): Help client develop a more balanced and positive set of attitudes toward self, others and the future (or the world)*

| # | Identified Problem | Goal or Objective | Treatment Plan | Measure of Achievement and Target Date | Achieved Yes/No Provider/ Client Date |
|---|---|---|---|---|---|
| 1 | IP₁ Usual mood is dominated by dejection, gloominess, cheerlessness, joylessness, unhappiness | TO₁ Increase correlation between mood and a realistic appraisal of the present | TP₁ (1) Help client recognize the relationship between cognitions and mood. (2) Help client learn to dispute with dysphoria-producing cognitions and replace with more realistic ones. | 1. Have client track relationship between cognitions and mood for 1 week starting [date]. 2. Have client start replacing negative cognitions with positive ones starting [date], and evaluate the results. 3. Have client become aware of cognitive processes (e.g., constant repetition of negatives) which produces brooding and reduce frequency by _ by [date] | |
| 4 | IP₄ Is brooding and given to worry | TO₄ Help client replace habitually negative cognitions with habitually positive ones. | TP₄ Help client become aware of the cognitions and cognitive processes that lead to brooding and worry, and replace them with more hope-inspiring ones. | | |
| 2 | IP₂ Self-concept centers around beliefs of inadequacy, worthlessness, and low self-esteem | TO₂ and TO₃ Increase realistic view of one's strengths, ability to make contributions, and a realistic view of self. | TP₂ and TP₃ (1) Help client learn to affirm own strengths and realistically accept that everyone has growth areas. (2) Help client identify contributions he or she can make. (3) Develop healthy self-talk about one's self and contributions (or potential contributions) | Accomplish item 1 by [date] Accomplish item 2 by [date] Accomplish item 3 by [date] | |
| 3 | IP₃ Is critical, blaming, and derogatory toward self | | | Accomplish item 1 by [date] | |
| 6 | IP₆ Is prone to feeling guilty or remorseful | TO₆ Reduce unnecessary and inappropriate guilt feelings | TP₆ (1) Teach client to distinguish between true guilt and unnecessary guilt. (2) Teach client to distinguish between healthy guilt responses and unhealthy ones. | Accomplish item 1 by [date] Accomplish item 2 by [date] | |
| 5 | Is negativistic, critical, and judgmental toward others | Increase acceptance of others, despite their imperfections | (1) Help client become aware of the unhealthiness of the cognitions and cognitive processes that produce judgmentalism and negativism. (2) Help client change those cognitions and cognitive processes. | Accomplish item 1 by [date] Accomplish item 2 by [date] | |

**ENDNOTES**

1.  American Psychiatric Association, *Diagnostic and statistical manual of mental disorders*, fourth edition, text revision, (Washington, D.C.: American Psychiatric Association, 2000), 685–686.

2.  American Psychiatric Association, 791.

3.  American Psychiatric Association, 380.

4.  American Psychiatric Association, 789.

5.  American Psychiatric Association, *Diagnostic and statistical manual of mental disorders*, third edition (Washington, D.C.: American Psychiatric Association, 1980); American Psychiatric Association, *Diagnostic and statistical manual of mental disorders*, third edition, rev. (Washington, D.C.: American Psychiatric Association, 1987). American Psychiatric Association, *Diagnostic and statistical manual of mental disorders*, fourth edition, text revision (Washington, D.C.: American Psychiatric Association, 2000). M.M. Weissman, The epidemiology of personality disorders: A 1990 update, *Journal of Personality Disorders, Supplement, Spring*, (1993), 44–62.

6.  Alfred Adler, *Understanding human nature* (New York: Premier Books, 1959); Alfred Adler, *The Practice and theory of individual psychology* (Patterson, NJ: Littlefield, 1963).

7.  Jeffrey Young, *Cognitive therapy for personality disorders: A schema-focused approach*, 3rd ed. (Sarasota, FL: Professional Resource Press, 1999).

8.  William Backus, *Telling each other the truth* (Minneapolis, MN: Bethany House, 1985).

9.  Chris Thurman, *The lies we believe* (Nashville: Thomas Nelson, 1991).

10. Young, 1999.

11. Nicholas Wolterstorff, *Reason within the bounds of religion*, 2nd ed. (Grand Rapids, MI: Eerdmans, 1984).

12. Judith Beck, *Cognitive therapy: Basics and beyond* (New York: Guilford, 1995), 140.

13. D. H. Baucom, Epstein, N., Sayers, S., and Sher, T.G., The role of cognitions in marital relationships: Definitional, methodological, and conceptual issues, *Journal of Consulting and Clinical Psychology, 57*, (1989), 31–38.

14. Torr Norretrander, *The user illusion* (New York: Viking, 1998).

15. American Psychiatric Association, *Diagnostic and statistical manual of mental disorders*, fourth ed. (Washington, D.C.: American Psychiatric Association, 1994), 751–757. American Psychiatric Association, *Diagnostic and statistical manual of mental disorders*, fourth ed., text revision (Washington, D.C.: American Psychiatric Association, 2000), 807–813.

16. M. Bart, Spirituality in counseling finding believers, *Counseling Today* (Alexandria, VA: American Counseling Association, December 1998), 1, 6.

17. Judith Beck, *Cognitive therapy: Basics and beyond* (New York: Guilford, 1995).

# Part 3

# Addictions and Impulse Control Problems

# 12

# Addictions

*Mark R. Laaser, George Ohlschlager, and Tim Clinton*

> ...addicts can't change their behaviors without help from God and wise
> counsel. None of us can find sufficient relief from pain without help. To
> expect something different from the...addict is to heap more shame on
> [him] and encourage Christians to respond to tough issues with simplistic
> solutions...We learn that we can make it if we just try harder and believe
> that those who haven't made it didn't try hard enough. But believing in
> ourselves and the fruit of our efforts works against the fact that we are
> sinful and can escape sinful behaviors only with God's help.
>
> HARRY SCHAUMBURG

Howard Hillman was an executive consultant living with his second wife
and her children in a tiny suburb on the north Chicago shore. He was also
an alcoholic who lived in denial of it due to his fairly competent functioning (which he grossly exaggerated).

His wholesome and successful veneer started to crack, however, after his
second DUI in which he lost his license and had to hire his stepson to chauf-
feur him around. He also had to engage in counseling in order to clear his
record and get his license back, and was required to take a routine medical
drug screen following his counseling intake. It was then that Howard's secret
addiction to OxyContin[(r)] was discovered, which he had taken two years previously due to a severe back sprain. During his group confrontation about
this, he also admitted his addiction to internet sexual pornography.

Now it all made sense to his wife. Howard had been cutting back on his
drinking—she knew that as they had been fighting about it—but she didn't
understand why he slept in a stuporous state so much, had so many

"minor" accidents around the house, and no longer seemed to be interested in having sex with her. He was mixing alcohol with narcotics and internet pornography.

Worst of all, Howard had become a very accomplished liar. He was lying to cover his lies and now it had all started to breakdown. He had been in a drunken car accident six months earlier, and had just paid cash to "persuade" the other party to get their car fixed and keep quiet. His finances weren't in good shape though, as he was buying his OxyContin[r] on the black market, paying huge credit card bills for internet sex, and his consulting business was starting to slip.

For weeks Howard vascillated between anger at being found out, fear of losing his marriage, and depression at facing reality. He was shedding both real and crocodile tears as he promised over and over to "get sober" and turn his life around. The addictions group he was part of would hear none of it, as they confronted his lies, denial, and avoidance of the truth for weeks.

His counselor knew he was finally ready to get serious about change when he came to group one night and admitted to everyone there that he couldn't change, that he really didn't want to, but that he knew he had to if he was going to live. After this session, things started turning for the better.

Addictions are a very common scourge, the desperate expression of life in a sin-sick world. When addictions are piled on top of one another, or are mixed with mental illness, the suffering is multiplied and the cure is complex, difficult to accurately assess and easily achieve. Medicating the pain and symptoms of psychopathology—whether done under a doctor's treatment or illicitly—is a primary pathway to addiction for many dual-disordered patients.

Dual disorders refer to someone who suffers both an addiction and a mental/emotional disorder of some kind. The prototypical sufferer is someone with depression or an anxiety disorder—some kind of felt dysphoria—who is also addicted to alcohol or other drugs that are usually used to medicate the pain of that dysphoric unpleasantness. And it is not unusual to encounter persons who live the process in reverse, as addictions will induce mental and physical suffering of various kinds, if carried on long and deep enough. Whether working with persons with an addiction, multiple addictions, or dual disorders, it is usually necessary to address the primary addiction first, and that is the focus of this chapter.

The following national data is from the 2003 National Survey on Drug Use and Health,[1] a project of the Substance Abuse and Mental Health Services Administration (SAMHSA) that interviews approximately 67,500 persons each year. It is the primary source of information on the use and abuse of alcohol and illicit drugs by people in the United States, aged 12 years and older.

## Alcohol Use

An estimated 119 million Americans aged 12 or older were current drinkers of alcohol in 2003 (50.1%). About 54 million (22.6%) participated in binge drinking at least once in the 30 days prior to the survey, and 16.1 million (6.8%) were heavy drinkers. The highest prevalence of binge and heavy drinking was for young adults aged 18 to 25. The rate of binge drinking was 41.6% for this group and was highest (47.8%) at age 21. Heavy alcohol use was reported by 15.1% of this group, and by 18.7% of persons aged 21 (also highest). An estimated 13.6% of persons aged 12 or older (32.3 million) drove under the influence of alcohol at least once in the 12 months prior to the interview in 2003 (a decrease from 14.2% in 2002).

## Illicit Drug Use

In 2003, an estimated 19.5 million Americans, (8.2%) were current illicit drug users, the same overall rate as in 2002. The rate of current illicit drug use among youths aged 12 to 17 dropped slightly between 2002 (11.6%) and 2003 (11.2%). Current marijuana use among youths was 8.2% in 2002 and 7.9% in 2003. There was a decline in lifetime marijuana use among youths, from 20.6% in 2002 to 19.6% in 2003. There were also decreases in rates of past year use of LSD (1.3 to 0.6%), Ecstasy (2.2 to 1.3%), and methamphetamine (0.9 to 0.7%).

Marijuana is the most commonly used illicit drug, with a rate of 6.2% (14.6 million) in 2003. 2.3 million persons (1.0%) were current cocaine users, 604,000 of whom used crack. Hallucinogens were used by 1.0 million persons, and there were 119,000 current heroin users. These 2003 figures are similar to the estimates for 2002. Ecstasy (MDMA) users decreased between 2002 and 2003, from 676,000 (0.3%) to 470,000 (0.2%). Although there were no significant changes in the past year use of other hallucinogens, there were significant declines in past year use of LSD (from 1 million to 558,000) and in past year overall hallucinogen use (from 4.7 million to 3.9 million), as well as in past year use of Ecstasy (from 3.2 million to 2.1 million).

6.3 million persons were current users of psychotherapeutic drugs taken nonmedically (2.7%). 4.7 million used pain relievers, 1.8 million used tranquilizers, 1.2 million used stimulants, and 0.3 million used sedatives. The 2003 estimates are all similar to 2002. A significant increase in lifetime nonmedical use of pain relievers between 2002 and 2003 was shown, from 29.6 million to 31.2 million. Specific pain relievers with statistically significant increases in lifetime use were Vicodin[r], Lortab[r], or Lorcet[r] (from 13.1 million to 15.7 million); Percocet[r], Percodan[r], or Tylox[r] (from 9.7 million to 10.8 million); Hydrocodone (from 4.5 million to 5.7 million); OxyContin[r] (from 1.9 million to 2.8 million); methadone (from 0.9 million to 1.2 million); and Tramadol (from 52,000 to 186,000).

There were 2.6 million new marijuana users in 2003, or an average of 7,000 new users each day. 69% of these new marijuana users were under age 18, and 53% were female. Decreases in initiation of both LSD (from 631,000 to 272,000) and Ecstasy (from 1.8 million to 1.1 million) were evident, and hallucinogen initiation dropped from 1.6 million to 1.1 million. However, in the past decade, pain reliever use increased from 573,000 initiates) to 2.5 million initiates annually.

Rates of current illicit drug use varied significantly among the major racial/ethnic groups in 2003. Rates were highest among American Indians or Alaska Natives (12.1%), persons reporting two or more races (12.0%), and Native Hawaiians or Other Pacific Islanders (11.1%). Rates were 8.7% for blacks, 8.3% for whites, and 8.0% for Hispanics. Asians had the lowest rate at 3.8%. An estimated 18.2% of unemployed adults were current illicit drug users, compared with 7.9% employed full time and 10.7% employed part time. However, of the 16.7 million illicit drug users in 2003, 12.4 million (74.3%) were employed either full or part time.

## Substance Dependence or Abuse

Americans numbering 21.6 million in 2003 were substance dependent or abusers (9.1% of the population). Of these, 3.1 million were dependent on or abused both alcohol and illicit drugs, 3.8 million were dependent on or abused illicit drugs but not alcohol, and 14.8 million were dependent on or abused alcohol but not illicit drugs. Between 2002 and 2003, a slight drop was noted in the number of persons with substance dependence or abuse (22.0 million in 2002 and 21.6 million in 2003).

In 2003, 17.0% of unemployed adults were dependent or abusers, while 10.2% of full-time employed adults and 10.3% of part-time employed adults were classified as such. However, most adults with substance dependence or abuse were employed either full or part time. Of the 19.4 million adults with dependence or abuse, 14.9 million (76.8%) were employed.

## Substance Abuse Treatment

3.3 million people aged 12 or older (1.4% of the population) received treatment related to the use of alcohol or illicit drugs in 2003. Of these, 1.2 million received treatment at a rehabilitation facility as an outpatient, 752,000 at a rehabilitation facility as an inpatient, 729,000 at a mental health center as an outpatient, 587,000 at a hospital as an inpatient, 377,000 at a private doctor's office, 251,000 at an emergency room, and 206,000 at a prison or jail. Between 2002 and 2003, there were decreases in the number of persons treated for a substance use problem at a hospital as an inpatient, at a rehabilitation facility as an inpatient, at a mental health center as an outpatient, and at an emergency room.

In 2003, 22.2 million people (9.3%) needed treatment for an alcohol or illicit drug problem, about the same as in 2002 (22.8 million). The number needing but not receiving treatment also did not change between 2002 (20.5 million) and 2003 (20.3 million). Of the 20.3 million people who needed but did not receive treatment, an estimated 1.0 million (5.1%) reported that they felt they needed treatment for their alcohol or drug problem. Of the 1.0 million persons who felt they needed treatment, 273,000 (26.3%) reported that they made an effort but were unable to get treatment and 764,000 (73.7%) reported making no effort to get treatment.

Among the 1.0 million people who needed but did not receive treatment and felt they needed treatment, the most often reported reasons for not receiving treatment were (1) they were not ready to stop using (41.2%), (2) cost or insurance barriers (33.2%), (3) reasons related to stigma (19.6%), and

(4) they did not feel the need for treatment (at the time), or they could handle the problem without treatment (17.2%).

## Symptoms and Etiology of the Addict

The following list is, in our opinion, a good set of common symptomatic behaviors and characteristics—a universal diagnostic set—that could be generalized to all substance or behavioral addictions and compulsions.

1. A pattern of out-of-control substance usage or behavior for a year or more
2. Mood swings associated with usage or behavior
3. An increasing pattern of usage or behavior over time, this increase may be a constant elevation or marked by periods of abstinence alternating with elevation
4. The presence of major or milder forms of depression
5. The feeling of shame or self-worthlessness
6. The consistent need to be liked and find approval from others
7. Impulse control problems, especially with food, sex, drugs, or money/spending/gambling
8. Use of the substance or behavior to reward oneself or to reduce anxiety
9. Obsessing about the substance or behavior, and spending great amounts of time around it
10. Obtaining or doing the behavior becomes the central organizing principle of life
11. Failed efforts to control the addiction
12. Negative consequences due to the substance or behavior
13. Alternating pattern of out-of-control behavior with over-controlling behavior
14. A history of emotional, physical, sexual, or spiritual abuse
15. A family history of addiction, rigidity, divorce, or disengagement
16. Marked feelings of loneliness or abandonment
17. Arrested developmental issues

The addict represents someone who has become trapped in a web of deceit and dark forces too powerful to overcome without significant help from God and others. The Scriptures reveal the truth about it:

So I find this law at work: When I want to do good, evil is right there with me. For in my inner being I delight in God's law; but I see another law at work in the members of my body, waging war against the law of my mind and making me a prisoner of the law of sin at work within my members. What a wretched man I am! Who will rescue me from this body of death? Thanks be to God—through Jesus Christ our Lord! (Romans 7:21–25, NIV)

These words of the apostle Paul embody the spiritual journey of those struggling with addiction. The mind of an addict knows that he or she needs to stop using certain substances or doing certain behaviors, but seemingly can't. The addict knows that he or she must start doing positive behaviors, but will not. It is the great conflict that Bill Wilson, the co-founder of Alcoholics Anonymous, captured in step one: *"I admitted that I was powerless over alcohol and that my life had become unmanageable."*

Paul's self description also reflects the shameful nature an addict's self-perception when he says, "What a wretched man I am!" The feeling of being a bad and worthless person is common to all addicts. It is not only that addictive behavior produces shame; shame is a basic feeling that addicts have felt most of their lives. It is that addictive behavior perpetuates and inflames shame.

Addictive behaviors are problems per se, and they are also symptoms of deeper physical, emotional, and spiritual issues. Maintaining this dual awareness—as well as tolerating and appreciating the inherent tensions between these sometimes competing ideas—is important when working with addicts. Depending on the issues of therapeutic focus, the course of treatment, and the progress (or lack thereof) toward goal attainment, the addiction is best viewed as either symptomatic of the underlying mental disorder or as the primary problem itself.

Addicts by their very nature feel helpless and unworthy. They are desperately asking as Paul did, "Who will rescue me?" Addicts cycle through feelings of the high of addiction and the despair of worthlessness. They may be stubbornly resisting giving up the high because they feel it is the only solution to the despair.

Counseling addicts is often frustrating as they frequently sabotage the most basic answers, and tear down the most fragile progress. Competent Christian counseling must point them to the only lasting answer, a relationship with Jesus Christ. Treating persons with addiction and dual disorders assumes that competent Christian counselors will assess and understand the nature of what they are actually dealing with. The following are the classic factors that define addiction.

## Mood Alteration

Understanding addiction must begin with what scientists are only beginning to understand about the human brain. Brain chemistry is at the heart of what creates and sustains addiction.[2] Addicts seek to either raise or lower their mood using complex (and sometimes criminal) rituals of self-medicating behavior. If they are depressed, sad, or lonely they seek to raise their mood. If they are anxious, frightened, or stressed they seek to lower their mood. In doing so, addicts will eventually train their brains to neurochemically "depend" on the substance or behavior.

We have long accepted that alcohol affects the chemistry of the brain. We can easily understand that other drugs such as marijuana, heroin, and cocaine (to name a few) change brain chemistry. Some scientists believe that nicotine might be the most addictive of all substances. Even caffeine can be considered as an addictive substance in its ability to raise mood as a facilitator or certain powerful brain chemicals, most notably dopamine, that elevate mood.

*Addictive behavior and the brain.* What has long been debated is whether or not certain behaviors can affect the chemistry of the brain. As scientists have increased their ability to scan and produce images of the brain (through MRI and PET studies, for example), research projects have begun to demonstrate that behaviors alone, without the use of substances, can also do this.

When a person looks at another person who he or she loves or has feelings of sexual attraction for, certain opiates (catecholamines) are produced more rapidly in the brain. These neurochemicals have a heroin-like quality in the pleasure centers of the brain. That is why some have suggested that we can become *Addicted to Love*.[3] At Vanderbilt University, researchers are showing the dramatic effects on the brain of looking at pornography.[4] Little doubt remains that all sexual thought and activity produce these same neurochemical effects.

Any behavior that causes a sense of fear or excitement can raise levels of norepinephrine, more commonly referred to as adrenalin, in the brain. Norepinephrine can elevate levels of dopamine and serotonin and, as such, has a mood elevating quality. Gambling, working hard to meet deadlines, shopping, sports, even mountain climbing can become addictive for some.

The need for constant stimulation that some addicts experience means that their brains need "rapid firing" to function properly. These persons are easily bored and distracted. They have problems thinking into the future and planning. As such, they may seem at times to be lazy or lacking discipline. In their academic careers they may have been labeled underachievers. Some addicts, then, may have neurological symptoms that reflect a level of attention deficit or hyperactivity disorder. Christian counselors will be careful to refer addicts for competent psychiatric and neuropsychological evaluation to evaluate these symptoms. Medications may be needed to balance an addict's brain, at least for a time.

*Multiple addictions.* As our case example noted, many addicts suffer from more than one addiction. It is not uncommon for them to use a variety of substances and behaviors to alter their mood. Carnes found, in a research project on addiction,[5] that half of all sex addicts suffer from chemical dependency. He also found that the more serious the wounds of childhood, the more likely there would be multiple addictions.

This dynamic has led to many speculating about "cross addictions," or the "comorbidity" of addictions. Carnes is currently proposing a new and broader diagnosis, "Multiple Addiction Disorder" (MAD—an appropriate acronym). Christian counselors need to evaluate a broad pattern of addiction and triage which of the addictions is the most immediately destructive.

### The Tolerance Effect

God has made us "fearfully and wonderfully" (Ps. 139:14). One of the amazing qualities of the body is its ability to adapt. Whatever happens to the body, it will always seek to return to a normal state. Scientists and systems therapists call this homeostasis. A virus enters our body and the body works itself into a fever to expel it. If a person gets frightened, his heart and respiration rate increases to prepare the body to fight or flee. When the threat is gone, the body works to return it to the normal rate. What the body interprets as normal, however, can change if there is repeated challenge to the normal state of affairs. This is a powerful ability that God has created in all people, the power to adapt.

The first time an alcoholic drinks a beer, for example, he or she experiences the effects of that in the brain. Brain chemistry changes and feelings of intoxication begin. Eventually, the brain returns to normal and the person "sobers up." If the pattern is repeated over and over again, however, the state of what normal is will change. More and more alcohol will be needed to have the same effect. This is what scientists refer to as "tolerance."

The "tolerance effect" can be experienced with any neurochemical change. Whether it is a substance that is ingested or a behavior that produces the change, the brain and body will eventually adapt. More and more of the substance or of the behavior will be needed. Over time a pattern develops and the activity increases. Addiction specialists usually describe this as "escalation" or as "deterioration" because the pattern gets worse.

Counselors must evaluate this pattern over time. Some addicts can quit the substance for a time but will eventually come back to it, alternating between periods of usage and abstinence. Some alcoholics, for example, don't drink during the week, but binge on the weekend. They may convince themselves that they have control because they can occasionally or regularly stop.

An 86-year-old minister's wife presented with chemical dependency. She was addicted to alcohol and to prescription anxiety medicine. In her 20s she started having a glass of wine every few months. In her denomination, this was a major problem, so she kept doing it in secret. Over the next 60 years her pattern increased. She drank once a month, then once a week, then once a day. When I met her she was consuming a bottle of alcohol a day. Her drinking pattern was causing substance-induced anxiety and her doctor was medicating that. The pattern became a vicious cycle.

### Unmanageability

Neurochemical tolerance is the reason addicts crave a substance or some repetitive behavior. These cravings are what can seem to the addict to be out-of-control. They intend to stop but find themselves "drawn" back in. Smokers quit smoking many times but feel the urge to start again, and dieters start their dieting over many times, for example. Cycles like these fuel the feelings of being out-of-control.

Addicts often believe that sobriety is merely an act of the will, and therefore often come to feel they have no willpower. As Christians, they assume that they should be able to stay "sober" without much effort, or if they were just a little bit stronger spiritually they could stick with a decision to quit. Sometimes these attempts at self-control are extreme. In my (Mark) first book about sexual addiction I described a case in which a man plucked out both of his eyes because Jesus said that "If your eye offends you, pluck it out," and he was addicted to pornography.[6]

Addicts pray fervently for help, even "deliverance" from their problems. They may try a variety of spiritual disciplines to stop. They pray, memorize Scripture, meditate, join new churches, and attend Christian 12-step groups galore. Eventually they become discouraged. They have a critical choice to make. Either there is something wrong with them or with God. Anger at self produces shame. Anger at God produces periods of despair and spiritual alienation. It is a terrible dilemma but it can also become the beginning of wisdom, *for self-effort in all its myriad disguises must die.*

Pride, fear, the need to be in control, and the unwillingness to completely surrender to God are also features of addiction and easily become inflamed at this stage.[7] Some addicts are afraid of giving something up that they think has been helping them cope with life for years. Some believe that they can quit when they really want to. Others are afraid that if they confess their problems they will be judged and condemned. Fear of their feelings and fear of rejection lead addicts to deny their problem and hold on to them. In the midst of this chaos, some just give up trying. It is important for Christian counselors to assess for the willingness to get well.

### Need for Nurture

Many addicts feel lonely and abandoned. They long for love, affirmation, nurture, and touch. In many cases the substance or behavior is a substitute for true love and fellowship. This may take many forms. Alcoholics may find a friend in the bottle or in the community of other drinkers. Alcohol allows many to be less inhibited; while intoxicated, they may be friendlier and more outgoing. Food addicts may have certain comfort foods that they binge on. They remember that the act of eating may have been the only time they were being held as infants or gathered as a family. Sex addicts equate sex with love and assume that those who would be willing

to be sexual with them, even prostitutes, offer them the only love, attention, and touch that they receive. Some sex addicts may even be more in
need of the romance and love experienced in their fantasies or in their
affairs.[8]

Feelings of loneliness and abandonment lead to feelings of anger and
resentment. Addicts wonder why their needs haven't or aren't being met.
These feelings may be very old going back into childhood. They can be mad
at their spouses or others for not meeting their needs. The sense of anger
produces a sense of entitlement, not unlike an angry child. Addicts think
that they deserve to get their needs met and they deserve a reward. Loneliness drives anger and anger drives addicts past their own discipline and
morals.

### Assessment and Diagnosis

Most chemical addictions including alcoholism are defined by standard
diagnostic codes (DSM-IV) as being Addiction or a lesser form of addiction,
such as Substance Abuse. Behavioral addictions such as a gambling addiction, and sex addiction are being debated in the medical and psychological
communities on how to accurately define and include these disorders in
the diagnostic system.

The ICD model—the International Classification of Diseases—defines
six clear criteria for diagnosing a Substance Abuse disorder, whereby three
or more of the following must have been experienced or exhibited at some
time during the previous year:

1. *Control problems:* Difficulties in controlling substance-taking
   behavior in terms of its onset, termination, or levels of use
2. *Compulsive use:* A strong desire or sense of compulsion—of being
   driven—to take the substance
3. *Increasing/exclusive focus:* Progressive neglect of alternative pleas-
   ures or interests plus the increased amount of time necessary to
   obtain or take the substance or to recover from its effects
4. *Continuing harm of denial:* Persisting with substance use despite
   clear evidence of overtly harmful consequences, depressive mood
   states consequent to heavy use, or drug related impairment of reasoning, judgment, and cognitive functionin

5. *Tolerance effect:* Evidence of tolerance—increased doses of the psychoactive substance or mixing in new drugs are required in order to achieve effects originally produced by lower doses

6. *Withdrawal symptoms:* A physiological withdrawal state when substance use has ceased or been reduced, as evidence by: the characteristic withdrawal syndrome for the substance; or use of the same (or a closely related) substance with the intention of relieving or avoiding withdrawal symptoms

Most addiction diagnostic codes provide similar lists and suggest that addiction is present if a constellation of similar and interrelated symptom indicators is present. The competent Christian counselor will always remember that he or she is looking for a pattern of behaviors and vulnerabilities. Each field of addiction has developed checklists, true and false tests, and other diagnostic guides to assist in the assessment of addiction.

*Intuition and discernment.* The spiritual discernment and experiential intuition of the counselor is also important in diagnosis, as the self-perception of the addict are often inaccurate. Addicts who have come to a point of helplessness and perceived unmanageability are on the verge of owning their addiction, yet may also fight and deny that reality. The competent Christian counselor will be able to discern this struggle and will also know when the addicted person has not come to this point, even when they claim they have. Some addicts will still be in some state of denial and delusion about their problems, and will often lie about their readiness for change.

Accurate self-reporting may not be possible. The report of others, such as the spouse or other family members will be important. An interesting form of assessment is to ask a potential addict how he or she theologically justifies acting out behavior. For example, how does an alcohol drinker justify drunken behavior, or how does a food addict justify the poor stewardship of being overweight, or how does a sex addict justify adultery, or how does a gambler justify chronic debt?

## Multifaceted Addiction Treatment

The reasons for addiction are multi-faceted. The treatment of addiction, therefore, will also require a variety of approaches. Treatment must maintain a careful balance between confronting the addict's denial and minimization and supporting them when they do the painful and difficult work of honest disclosure and directed change. At times, direct and intense confrontation is necessary because of the tendency for denial and minimization, but also remember that it is quite a threatening and shame-filled experience for a person to openly discuss the secrets and sins and despairs of their addictions. Following are the five classic areas that must be addressed:

## Physical Stabilization and Self-care

Addicts may have caused physical damage to their bodies. Alcoholics will have possible neurological, gastrointestinal, or liver complications. Food addicts may starve themselves to death or suffer the effects of chronic obesity. Sex addicts run the risk of sexually transmitted diseases or a variety of sexual dysfunctions. Any addict also runs the risk of stress resulting from chronic fear and anxiety, often due to the consequences of the addiction.

It is always wise for addicts to undergo a complete medical evaluation. Alcoholics and some drug addicts may need to be hospitalized in order to stabilize the detoxification effect of stopping use. Anorexics may also need to be stabilized in the hospital to prevent the effects of chronic malnutrition.

When stabilization has been achieved, it is also wise for an addict to undergo a thorough neuropsychiatric evaluation. Levels of depression must be determined. Assessment for the presence of a variety of forms of attention deficit disorder is also important. Some addicts will need pharmacological help for depression. Others will need different drugs that help manage the brains needs for constant stimulation. It is always wise to develop a relationship with a competent psychiatrist who can perform these kinds of evaluations and services.

Abstinence from the drug of choice will, over time, change the level of neurochemical tolerance the addict has developed over the years. With help and sure accountability, alcoholics and drug users are able to achieve total abstinence from a substance. Food addicts may be able to abstain from certain kinds of food.

Behavior addicts often have a harder time at abstaining, as secrecy is easier to maintain and accountability is so much more difficult. Some, like gamblers, can stop certain behaviors altogether. Sex addicts, however, can arouse themselves by fantasizing about sexual behavior. The protocol with sex addicts is to have them abstain from all forms of sexual activity for a period of time, even if married, in order to achieve a detoxification effect from sinful sexual activity.

Finally, addicts will need to learn adequate self-care. As opposed to Paul's teaching, they have been treating their body more like the city dump than the temple. Being tired or physically depleted makes any addict more vulnerable to acting out behavior.

## Behavioral Change

Addicts have developed strong, highly programmed, even automatic behavior patterns in order to maintain their addiction. They will go to extraordinary lengths to deny, minimize, or rationalize this addictive behavior.

*Focus honesty and behavior change.* Therapist must maintain a strong initial focus on honesty and behavior change. When the addict seeks to divert discussion to family, emotional, or relationship concerns prematurely, the therapist must redirect attention to behavior. While effective treatment may eventually address these issues, the clinician must help the addict stop using them to escape dealing with his or her addictive behavior.

One way of doing this is to link the tangential topics the client raises with the central issue of their addiction. For example, a counselor might refocus a client's response toward the behavior in this way: "So how is the way you approach your anger toward your wife similar to the way you acted out your anger in your sex addiction?" "How is your tendency to denigrate yourself reflected in your addiction ritual?" The assumption here is that addiction has a life of its own and operates apart from other concerns. Unlike many other clinical issues, addiction is both symptom and disease.

*Changing ritual behavior patterns.* All addicts will need to change certain behavior patterns that lead them into their use. These behaviors are referred to in the addiction community as "rituals." The competent Christian counselor will help an addict assess the cycle of ritual behavior and how he or she acts out. Taking detailed histories of usage and behavioral patterns is essential. When this information has been sorted out, addicts must establish boundaries against those behaviors. Alcoholics will need to avoid certain friends, areas of towns, or stressful situations that lead them to drink. Food addicts may need to avoid going to the grocery store in the early days of recovery, or they may need to schedule meals at regular times and find help to eat at those times religiously. Sex addicts will need to avoid people and places that trigger them into their fantasies or "connecting" rituals. For example, those sex addicts who use the computer to connect will need to become accountable for every minute of access to it.

*Can't do it alone.* No addict can recover by him or herself. Yet, most feel that he or she should be strong enough to overcome this alone. Shame increases as the number of attempts to do so increases. The Bible teaches that we should never undertake a long journey or complicated project alone. In Nehemiah 2, for example, the king allows Nehemiah to go home to rebuild the wall of the city of Jerusalem, but he also sends the army officers and cavalry. Later in chapter 4 of Nehemiah, the strategy is that half the men build and half the men stand guard.

*Accountability in recovery.* The key to overcoming any addiction is accountability. All addicts need a number of people around them who help monitor and maintain behavior. These people will also provide support, encouragement, and affirmation. In the 12-step tradition of Alcoholics Anonymous, this is the power of the meeting and the people in it. Alcoholics have also learned they need a sponsor to help guide the process of accountability.

Addicts should not think that only one person can hold them accountable. They begin recovery believing that they are alone and abandoned. If they only have one person for accountability, they may fall into their abandonment routine if that one person is not available. Addicts will need an accountability group, at least four or five people who really know them and whom they can call any time, day or night. Remembering that loneliness is a major factor in addiction, finding the fellowship of a group will be extremely important.[9]

There are innumerable 12-step groups today for many different addictions. These phone numbers can usually be found in the local yellow pages. More and more, Christians are trying to set up Christ-centered support groups in local churches. In the field of sexual addiction, for example, several ministries are creating materials for such groups. Consult Web sites like *www.faithfulandtrueministries.com* for useful information. One Christian group, *Overcomers Outreach* (1994), has tried to create Christian materials for general addiction support groups.

*The Nehemiah principle.* Nehemiah, again in chapter 4, knew that the attack of the enemy could come at any time, and at the weakest place. He prepared for this. Addicts will need to prepare in their times of strength and resolve to change their thinking and behavior in times of weakness and attack. It is not enough to wait until the attack comes. Automatic and daily preparations should happen. For example, any addict should have daily phone calls from the accountability group and regular attendance at support groups even on those days when they don't feel like they need to. Following is a short list of accountability principles that should be followed by all addicts.

1. Never try to recover alone.
2. Fellowship is equal to freedom from addiction.
3. Prepare in times of strength and resolve for times of attack and weakness.
4. Be in intimate accountability with at least four people.

## Emotional and Cognitive Restructuring

Addicts tend to come from families that have wounded them emotionally, physically, sexually, and/or spiritually.[10] They have deep sadness, feelings of shame, and loneliness.

*Protect against emotional triggers.* It is vitally important for these family and emotional issues to be addressed, once the behavior of addiction changes. Remember that *unhealed wounds raise painful feelings that often result in relapse.* Any stimulus that potentially triggers an addict into old, painful feelings can provoke the old answers and addictive activities that were used to medicate and change those feelings. These rationalizations and lies are referred to as *"stinkin' thinkin'"* in the AA vernacular. Cognitive restructuring involves identification, confrontation, and correction of this erroneous thinking and this requires a psychoeducational approach that should not be avoided. It is irresponsible to suggest that a person should just "forgive and forget." It is also irresponsible to suggest that a person who never let go of their anger so as not to get hurt again. Healing of life's hurt can be a lifetime journey but there are ways to get stuck in sadness and anger.

The competent Christian counselor will either be skilled in this kind of work or will know good cognitive therapists for referral. The process of healing requires several factors:

1.  Understanding the nature of the harm that caused the woundedness
2.  Providing support for the importance of dealing with it
3.  Addressing any anger or bitterness that was part of the experience
4.  Allowing the person to grieve the losses associated with the woundedness
5.  Helping the person find meaning in the suffering of the experience
6.  Guiding the person in the process of forgiveness of those who caused the harm
7.  Adopting healthy new biblical thinking and self-talk

*Thought-stopping interventions.* Every addict starts his or her acting out behavior by obsessing or fantasizing about the substance or behavior. This very thought life is an attempt to alter mood, to relieve pain. Christian counselors will hear the fantasies of addicts and know that they are windows into the mind and heart of the addicted person. Substances and behaviors are often ways that addicts seek to heal wounds from the past. It is mostly useless to tell an addict to stop thinking about a substance or behavior. Seek understanding for what the thought life, the fantasies, mean. If healing can be achieved for the wound that the fantasy seeks to correct, the fantasy will eventually disappear.

*Covert sensitization.* Another approach is to directly intervene in an addict's fantasies. These fantasies are self-reinforcing because they are typically followed, in the case of a sex addict for example, by sexual arousal. In covert sensitization, the addict is instructed to articulate his or her preferred fantasy, and then to add to that fantasy an imagined aversive scene (such as the embarrassment of being caught and punished). Both exposing the secret fantasy and associating an aversive outcome reduces its attracting power. The goal is to reduce the reinforcement value of the fantasy by pairing it with an aversive consequence. Finally, the offender also adds a reward scene to the failed fantasy, emphasizing a positive outcome associated with successful control.

## Relationship Repair

People who live with addicts know how painfully difficult it can be. Some-times the spouses of addicts are referred to as "co-addicts" or "co-depend-ents."[11] The assumption of terms like these is that they somehow ignore, tolerate and even enable addiction. Competent counseling will need to assess the emotional and spiritual health of people living with addicts. It is safe to continue to live with them if they don't get help? Do co-addicts also suffer from their own wounds or addictions? It would not be uncommon for a spouse who lives with an alcoholic to also have drinking problems. My (Mark) research has shown that about one third of spouses who live with sex addicts are also sex addicts.[12]

Counselors should assess factors that brought spouses together. New theories are being developed which suggest that people find each other and seek to play out patterns of family of origin trauma with each other. Sex abuse survivors may, even unconsciously, find another sex abuse survivor to be in relationship. The theory is that addicts may be trying to replay old patterns, in order to find a different result. A corollary of this is that addicts will replay old family patterns, trying to be the one who controls the situa-tion rather than the one who is victimized. The attempt to find healing from a relationship to a spouse for early life wounds is generally referred to as "trauma bonding."[13]

Counselors who deal with addicts and their spouses know that some-times even the slightest of triggers can provoke rage, anxiety, or sadness. Deep healing work with both addict and spouse, together or individually, is vital to the restoration of marriage. Simple communication strategies or intimacy building exercises will not work in these situations. Work on the deep wounds with both partners is essential to helping these partners relate on the most basic of levels.

*Suffer the little children.* The children of addicts will be wounded by addic-tion. Counselors will do well if they are able to address these issues and be of support for the entire family. It is not easy to engage family members, even spouses, if there is the addict to blame for all problems. Gentle forms of education and support can be helpful. Helping family members to be in support groups for others with similar problems can help them see their own responsibilities for the dysfunctions of entire family systems. Support groups of many kinds exist for those who live in relationship with addicts.

The healing of relationships is an essential part of treatment for addicts. Couples counseling and family counseling are important. Addicts and those around them should be encouraged to be in networks of support. One of the best antidotes for addiction and co-addiction is fellowship with other growing Christians. Addicts have a profound longing for nurture. Christian counselors must be able to help them find it in true and lasting relationships.[14]

The potential for developing intimacy and self-honesty is crucial to addiction recovery. Addicts, in their shame, may feel that no one loves them and that if they talk about their most intimate feelings or reveal their worst acting out experiences, others will run from them. They will need to "practice" telling the truth to counselors and those in a support group, who are less emotionally threatening than lifetime loved ones (e.g. spouses). They will then be able to take greater risks by being honest with loved ones.

*Victim empathy.* Multifaceted addiction treatment encourages addicts to develop empathy for loved ones hurt by their addiction. The addict is taught to understand, and even experience the pain they cause their victims. By maximizing empathy for others, it becomes more likely that the addict will treat others as persons, rather than as objects to be used for their own gratification. As addicts develop victim empathy and consider the consequences of their actions, they may present with suicidal ideation, shame, and guilt. Jesus incarnated victim empathy, and a counselor's Christian background can aid in connecting the incongruence between client behavior and their spiritual worldviews.

The road to recovery in relationship is long and labor intensive, but the possibility of profound intimacy with others is well worth the task.

### Spiritual Renewal

Addicts are spiritually immature by nature. They often search for child-like, black-and-white answers to their problems. If addicts have developmental issues it is easy to see that they will also have childish and adolescent beliefs about God.[15] They may have become angry with God for not "delivering" them of their cravings, longings, and lust. There are several spiritual challenges for addicts when working with Christian counselors, pastors, and lay helpers:

*Addicts must address their own need to control.* Many of them may have committed to Christ intellectually but not emotionally. They may be angry with God for not healing or delivering them. They have a hard time letting go of the high and the mood alteration of their addictive activities. Addicts have become accustomed to their ways. Being enslaved to addiction is what they know.

In the 13th and 14th chapters of Numbers, God is trying to prepare the people of Israel to go to the Promised Land. God has already done a mighty work in delivering them out of the land of Egypt. They are being led by one of the greatest religious leaders of all time, Moses. Spies who have been sent to survey the new land give a negative report of how difficult it will be to go there because of "giants" in the land. In the opening of the 14th chapter, the people cry out for a new leader and declare that it would be better to go back to Egypt and die as slaves than to go to a place they don't know.

This is how addicts often react. They don't know a new place or a better way. They will want to hang on to the familiar. They are unable to trust God to see them through unknown and frightening future events. It is an issue of trust and total surrender. They will need to be guided to totally turn their lives over to God and face their own fears and need to control. In John 5, Jesus (our master psychologist) asks the paralyzed man at the pool of Bethesda, "Do you want to get well?" It seems like a silly question for a man who has been lying by this healing water for 38 years. The man, however, doesn't answer affirmatively but instead gives excuses for why he hasn't been able to get into the pool.

Christian counselors will also have to ask this hard question, "Do you want to get well and are you willing to take the risks, make the surrender, and do the hard work that will be necessary?" In Numbers 14, it is Joshua who says to the stubborn people, "We can do this with God's help."

*Much of what has motivated addicts historically is fear and anxiety.* They have sought to avoid consequences and trouble. They have been selfish in their pursuits. In recovery they will need to learn to be motivated for others. In Nehemiah 4, Nehemiah offers a great battle cry to the people. He tells them to fight for the brothers, sons and daughters, wives, and their homes. This is better motivation for addicts. I have never known an addict who has recovered and found sobriety just for him or herself. The 12th step of Alcoholics Anonymous says that having had a spiritual awakening; addicts should carry the message to others. Service to others is an important part of maturing spiritually, and is vital to getting well.

In Ephesians 5:1–3, Paul tells us that we should be "imitators of God, just as dearly loved children," and that we should "lead a life of sacrifice, just as Christ loved the church." Addicts must learn to lead a life of sacrifice, giving over their lusts and cravings. Addiction is selfish; recovery is selfless.

*Addicts don't know a better life.* In most cases addicts don't know true love and intimacy—they don't know a true relationship with God. Addictions are embraced as the perverse substitutes—false love and false intimacy.[16] Christian counselors must be able to model to them what these things are like. An addict needs a true spiritual vision. One of the great challenges in working with addicts is in helping them exchange the short-term highs for long-term truth. Intimacy with God and others is so much more satisfying than the high of any addiction.

When the Jewish people wanted to return to Egypt and live as slaves rather than go to the Promised Land, it was Joshua who reminded them to depend on God. Christian counselors will need to be like Joshua. Leaders like Joshua can also be found in those recovering people who have achieved a number of years of sobriety. These recovering people have assembled a more serene life and testimony of God's ongoing work in their lives. Networking newly assessed and willing to recover addicts with these "old timers" is often one of the joys of Christian counseling.

Christian counselors are able to place more emphasis on spirituality in an appropriate clinical manner as the cornerstone of treatment. It is likely that addicts seeking Christian counselors have done so on purpose, and this can be a powerful beginning to recovery, as well as prognosis for continued alliance, rapport, and investment in treatment. Attitudes toward religion can also provide diagnostic clues. "By examining the patient's religious views in the context of his or her personality dysfunctions, the clinician can differentiate between valid expression of spirituality and defensive religiosity."[17]

## Putting It All Together

Nearly three decades of scientific research have yielded 13 fundamental principles that characterize effective drug abuse treatment. These principles are detailed in *NIDA's Principles of Drug Addiction Treatment: A Research-Based Guide*,[18] from the National Institute of Drug Abuse.

1. No single treatment is appropriate for all individuals. Matching treatment settings, interventions, and services to each patient's problems and needs is critical.

2. Treatment needs to be readily available. Treatment applicants can be lost if treatment is not immediately available or readily accessible.

3. Effective treatment attends to multiple needs of the individual, not just his or her drug use. Treatment must address the individual's drug use and associated medical, psychological, social, vocational, and legal problems.

4. At different times during treatment, a patient may develop a need for medical services, family therapy, vocational rehabilitation, and social and legal services.

5. Remaining in treatment for an adequate period of time is critical for treatment effectiveness. The time depends on an individual's needs. For most patients, the threshold of significant improvement is reached at about 3 months in treatment. Additional treatment can produce further progress. Programs should include strategies to prevent patients from leaving treatment prematurely.

6. Individual and/or group counseling and other behavioral therapies are critical components of effective treatment for addiction. In therapy, patients address motivation, build skills to resist drug use, replace drug-using activities with constructive and rewarding non-drug-using activities, and improve problem-solving abilities. Behavioral therapy also facilitates interpersonal relationships.

7. Medications are an important element of treatment for many patients, especially when combined with counseling and other behavioral therapies. Methadone and levo-alpha-acetylmethodol (LAAM) help persons addicted to opiates stabilize their lives and reduce their drug use. Naltrexone is effective for some opiate addicts and some patients with co-occurring alcohol dependence. Nicotine patches or gum, or an oral medication, such as buproprion, can help persons addicted to nicotine.

8. Addicted or drug-abusing individuals with coexisting mental disorders should have both disorders treated in an integrated way.

9. Medical detoxification is only the first stage of addiction treatment and by itself does little to change long-term drug use. Medical

detoxification manages the acute physical symptoms of with-drawal. For some individuals it is a precursor to effective drug addiction treatment.

10. Treatment does not need to be voluntary to be effective. Sanctions or enticements in the family, employment setting, or criminal jus-tice system can significantly increase treatment entry, retention, and success.

11. Possible drug use during treatment must be monitored continu-ously. Monitoring a patient's drug and alcohol use during treat-ment, such as through urinalysis, can help the patient withstand urges to use drugs. Such monitoring also can provide early evi-dence of drug use so that treatment can be adjusted.

12. Treatment programs should provide assessment for HIV/AIDS, hepatitis B and C, tuberculosis and other infectious diseases, and counseling to help patients modify or change behaviors that place them or others at risk of infection. Counseling can help patients avoid high-risk behavior and help people who are already infected manage their illness.

13. Recovery from drug addiction can be a long-term process and fre-quently requires multiple episodes of treatment. As with other chronic illnesses, relapses to drug use can occur during or after successful treatment episodes. Participation in self-help support programs during and following treatment often helps maintain abstinence.

### Restoration and Relapse

In aftercare treatment planning, one must include a clear plan of restora-tion. This plan must include a great deal of accountability and ongoing oversight. Relapse and recidivism rates for addicts still remain relatively high after completion of treatment. One must be on guard to discern the role of spiritual transformation in the life of the addict. Addicts will say—and genuinely believe, along with many others supporting the addict—that they have committed or recommitted their lives to Christ, that God has for-given their sin, and they have been healed from their addictive desires.

The implication here involves an odd paradox—that if the therapist con-tinues to insist on strong accountability or a need for continued treatment, they are doubting the power of God to change lives. This is a very difficult bind for Christian counselors. On one hand we must seriously believe in the power of God to heal and change lives, while also being aware that healing is almost always a gradual process. Furthermore, the Christian counselor knows as well as anyone the subtle power of sin and the ways of the world to tempt the addict to use again. Even in the midst of the healing process, offenders can and do experience relapse—some relapse numerous times—before eventually getting control over the problem.

We must balance the need to affirm healing in the offender with appropriate concern for the reality of relapse and renewed addiction. The church, as a community of grace and healing, looks to the hope of the gospel for the power to change the behavior of addicted persons, to heal the wounds of their victims, and to provide reconciliation with the body of Christ.

## Conclusion

Working with addicts is usually both challenging and frustrating. A competent Christian counselor will often direct and guide an addict through a variety of resources and network of people. Sometimes the counselor will be like a team leader, shepherding counselors and others who are working with the addict, his or her spouse and children, and addressing other aspects of the problem.

Beware of those who don't have willingness. One sign of an addict willing to recover is a felt sense of brokenness and humility. If you continue to encounter denial, selfishness, or stubbornness, don't think that you have to be the one to make the final breakthrough. Establish your own boundaries of whom you are willing to work with. Even Jesus let some walk away. I often wonder how successful He must have felt as He hung on the cross and looked at the lack of faith in those around Him.

When you are thanked by those who have been broken, felt powerless, and who are working hard, you will see a growing life of peace and serenity, major life changes, and restored relationships. The personal, familial, and intergenerational cycle of addiction can be broken. This is what makes what we do so worthwhile.

## ENDNOTES

1.    2003 National survey on drug use and health, available from, <http://oas.samhsa.gov/nhsda.htm>.

2. See Daniel Amen, *Change your brain change your life* (New York: Random House, 1998); and H. Milkman, and Sunderwirth, S., *Craving for ecstasy: The consciousness and chemistry of escape* (Lexington, MA: Lexington Books, 1987).

3. Steven Arterburn, *Addicted to love* (United Kingdom: Vine Books, 2003).

4. Patrick Carnes, *Don't call it love* (New York: Bantam Books, 1991).

5. Ibid.

6. Mark Laaser, *Faithful and true,* (Grand Rapids, MI: Zondervan, 1996).

7. E. Kurtz, *Not God: A history of alcoholics anonymous* (Center City, MN: Hazelden, 1979).

8. B. Schaeffer, *Is it love or is it addiction* (Center City, MN: Hazelden, 2000).

9. *The twelve steps: A spiritual journey* (San Diego: Recovery Publications, 1988).

10. Patrick Carnes, *The betrayal bond* (Deerfield Beach, FL: Health Communications, Inc., 1997).

11. Melody Beattie, *Codependent no more* (New York: Harper/Hazelden, 1987).

12. These results are as yet unpublished but were discussed at the First Annual Vanderbilt Symposium On Sexual Addiction/Compulsivity in March, 2001.

13. Patrick Carnes, *The betrayal bond* (Deerfield Beach, FL: Health Communications, Inc., 1997).

14. Patrick Carnes, Laaser, D., and Laaser, M., *Open hearts* (Wickensburg, AZ: Gentle Path Press, 2000).

15. Gerald May, *Addiction and grace* (San Francisco: Harper and Row, 1988); and J. Miller, *Sin: Overcoming the ultimate deadly addiction* (San Francisco: Harper and Row, 1987).

16. Harry Schaumburg, *False intimacy: Understanding the struggle of sexual addiction* (Colorado Springs: NavPress, 1992).

17. R. H. Earle, Earle, M. R., and Osborn, K., *Sex addiction: Case studies and management* (New York: Brunner/Mazel, Inc., 1995).

18. NIDA's Principles of Drug Addiction Treatment: A Research-Based Guide, available at<http://www.nida.nih.gov/PODAT/PODATIndex.html>.

# 13

## Sexual Addiction

*Mark R. Laaser*

In our current sexually absorbed culture, working with sex addicts is a growth industry.

<small>RECENT STATEMENT OF A COLLEAGUE OF MINE.</small>

"Warren" was a pillar of his church. He was always seen as a great family man. He attended church all the time and often taught Bible classes. His wife and family seemed happy and content. As a Christian counselor at this church, you were surprised when he came in one day because he had been fired from his job for looking at internet pornography.

In the late 1970s, in three separate parts of the country, groups of men started gathering to use the 12 steps of Alcoholics Anonymous to try to get free of their sexual sins.[1] Many of them were recovering alcoholics at first and knew that these principles had helped them get sober. It was the first time that the word addiction came to be applied to sex and the term sex addiction was born.

In 1981, Dr. Patrick Carnes, a clinical psychologist, wrote the first book on the subject, *Out of the Shadows*.[2] Today there is still a clinical debate in the medical and psychological communities as to whether or not sex can truly be addictive. Thousands of recovering sex addicts would attest that using this diagnosis is helpful in knowing how to find freedom.

I write myself from the perspective of being a recovering sex addict. I began looking at pornography at age 11 and progressed into daily acts of masturbation. I started to visit massage parlors while in graduate school. In my early professional life I began having sexual encounters with a variety of women even to the point of being sexual with some women I counseled.

In 1987 I was intervened on and fired from every job I was doing. Fortunately a recovering alcoholic was a part of that intervention and knew that there was a treatment center directed by Dr. Carnes in Minneapolis where I went for in-patient treatment. I have been sober since that time and God has been gracious to me (Phil. 1:6) and allowed me to have a worldwide ministry trying to bring hope to others that they can be free.

My wife, Deb, stayed with me and has been a faithful companion in the journey of healing. From 1988 through 1992 I trained and worked with Dr. Carnes at the same hospital where I was treated. In 1992, I published the first book in the Christian community to address sexual addiction. This book has recently been revised.[3]

There have been other wise counselors who have written helpful books in this field: Harry Schaumberg[4], Ralph Earle[5], Pat Means[6], Russ Willingham[7], Earl Wilson,[8] and Steve Arterburn and Fred Stoeker.[9] We now know much more about how to identify sexual addiction and how to treat it. This is of paramount importance in our current culture. Cases like Warren's are becoming more and more common.

To realize how sexually saturated our culture is, simply remember what the availability of pornography was in the 1950s when Hugh Hefner published the first issue of *Playboy* and what it is today given the availability of it on the Internet. Now take note of every sexual stimulus that hits you on a daily basis as you watch TV, read a magazine, listen to the radio, go to a movie, or visit a shopping mall. You might even think about it when you go to church and notice what even the girls in the youth groups are wearing.

At a recent conference of the Coalition of Christian Colleges, one president told me that in one recent study 50% of his students lost their virginity while at school. Even in an attempt to stay "virgins" our youth are turning to all kinds of practices short of intercourse, most notably oral sex. Kids today are "hooking up" and having "friends with benefits." Sex has become part of even casual friendships.

*Christianity Today* magazine through its *Leadership Journal* discovered in a survey of pastors that 40% of evangelical pastors admitted to looking at

Internet pornography.[10] One third of those said they had looked at it in the last year. There is a moral crisis in Christian leadership and rarely a day goes by when we don't hear of some pastor or leader who has fallen. Satan has been attacking great church leaders since the beginning of time. Think of Samson who visited a prostitute in Gaza and had perhaps a love addiction with Delilah. Then there was King David who had an affair with Bathsheba and committed murder to cover it up. What of Solomon whose 700 wives and 300 hundred concubines turned him away from the true worship of God.

While there has not been pure empirical research on the prevalence of sexual addiction in the general population, conservative estimates in the field would place it as around 10%. Some also speculate that the incidence amongst Christians might be higher. In informal and unpublished research it has been found that the use of in-room pornography increases at hotels hosting Christian conferences. The Leadership study cited above would also cause us to wonder. Promise Keepers did a study several years ago and found that as many as 60% of the attendees at its conferences said they struggled with pornography.

If ever there was time to understand how sexual sin can become addictive, it is now. Paul's time was not much different when he said in Romans 12:2, "Don't be conformed to the ways of the world." Roman culture was also saturated with sex. What is even more frightening today is how available sex is electronically on the Internet. Pornography is the number one selling product on the Internet. People who might have been otherwise inhibited are using the relative privacy of the Internet to see levels of pornography that used to be available only in the darkest of places. Prostitutes now have their own web sites. Matching services can find you a sexual partner, willing to do all manner of sexual practices, in less than 24 hours.

What we are seeing is a dramatic rise in the number of cases of sexual addiction. Our churches are being attacked by the moral failure of the members and leaders. It is time for Christian counselors to get the knowledge they need to be able to identify and treat this terrible disease.

### Definition of Sexual Addiction

There are five classic criteria that define sexual addiction:

*Unmanageability.* A sex addict believes that his problems with sex are out of control and that he or she is powerless. They have tried to stop and can't. They have prayed and beseeched God to remove their lust. Many have sought salvation in different churches and denominations. What is really true is that sex addicts hang on to wanting to control their own lives. They are participants in original sin, the inability to trust God. Sex addicts are "double-minded" (James 1:8). A part of them wants to get well and a part of them doesn't. Sex has been the way they seek love and nurture most of their lives. They may be Christians, but they want God to magically cure them without them doing any work. What is unmanageable is that they haven't totally surrendered to God.

Carnes was the first to describe that unmanageability leads to a cycle of addiction.[11] It starts with fantasy or preoccupation with sexual thoughts at the top of the cycle. It then progresses to rituals, which lead to acting out at the bottom of the cycle. Acting out brings despair. Most sex addicts experience depression at some level and many have even thought of suicide. Despair is a feeling that sex addicts cope with by turning back to fantasies and the whole cycle repeats endlessly.

*Neurochemical Tolerance.* For anything to be addictive, according to modern psychiatry, it must produce a chemical tolerance in the brain. This means that the brain will literally crave more and more of the same substance or activity to achieve the same effect. This is because receptor sites on nerve endings become desensitized to the chemicals that the addiction creates in the brain.

For an activity like sex to create this chemical tolerance it must be capable of producing powerful neurochemicals. Such effects have been well discussed by researchers like Milkman and Sunderwirth among others.[12] Depending on what kind of sex, love, or romance a person is thinking about or doing, he or she can elevate adrenaline, serotonin, dopamine, and the powerful heroin-like catecholamines.

*Progression.* Because of the tolerance effect sex addiction will progress over time. It will get worse. This does not mean necessarily that an addict will progress from basic sexual activities like pornography or masturbation, but it always will mean that more and more activity will be needed. Over the life of an addict there will be a steady progression. This may take weeks, especially with Internet types of addiction, or years to develop. An addict may go through periods of time when he or she controls the addiction, sometimes referred to as "white knuckling." Eventually, the addiction will progress. In taking a sexual history of an addict a counselor will see how the level of sexual activity has increased over time.

*Feeling Avoidance.* Addicts are lonely, angry, and anxious. They need to deal with these "negative" feelings by ignoring them or by changing them. The neurochemistry of sex addiction can either elevate their mood (through adrenaline, serotonin, or dopamine) or if they are stressed it can moderate their mood (through the catecholamines). Sex addicts are literally "pharmacologists of their own brains." It is really true to say that they are drug addicts.

*Consequences.* Immoral sexual activity will always lead to negative consequences. These can be spiritual as in estrangement from God, emotional as in greater loneliness and stress, financial, legal, physical, vocational, and social. Addicts can be arrested, lose their jobs, spends hundreds of thousands of dollars, get AIDS or STDs, or wind up divorced. Part of the unmanageability is that the fear of consequences is not enough to stop them from their sexual sins.

Sex addiction can be expressed in any sexual behavior. At one end of the spectrum are those who simply fantasize and masturbate. On the other end are those who commit sexual crimes. Even marital sexuality can be addictive if an addict is engaging in it simply for the purposes of avoiding, and not expressing, intimacy. Do not equate sexual sin with sexual addiction. There are many who sexually sin but who do not become involved in repetitive, progressive, and unmanageable behaviors. To have an affair, look at pornography, or even commit a sexual crime is not automatically addictive. Applying the criteria is always the answer.

There are no diagnostic codes for sexual addiction in the Diagnostic and Statistical Manual (DSM) of the American Psychiatric Association. We hope that one day this will change. In the meantime, we often use comorbid mental health diagnoses such as Depression, Anxiety, Post-Traumatic Stress Disorder, and Adjustment Disorder. Some forms of sexual acting out fit into existing categories such as the paraphilias, voyeurism, or exhibitionism.

More and more we believe that women suffer from sexual addiction just as frequently as men do. With women, sex addiction is more often experienced with romance or love addiction. Young women, however, are being trained through culture to be more visually stimulated by pornography and to be more sexually aggressive than originally thought. According to one pioneer in the field, Marnie Ferree, women also experience a harder time asking for help and submitting to treatment as the stigma for women is often greater.[13] While a man may be seen as a "stud," a woman may be seen as a "slut" or "whore."

## Etiology

Causative factors can be understood in five categories:

*Emotional.* Sex addicts are emotionally wounded. In a classic study Carnes found that 81% of them were sexually abused; 74% were physically abused; and 97% were emotionally abused.[14] More study is needed to see if the same kind of abuse statistics apply to the legions of men and women who are getting addicted to the Internet. My own experience would suggest that they are lower and that it is more the factor of cultural enticement that seduces the average Internet addict. Abuse can take two forms: invasive types (such as being sexually molested, physically hit, or emotionally yelled at) and abandonment types (sometimes called neglect). I, personally, have never known a sex addict that was not abandoned in some way. These two types of abuse leave an addict starving for love and nurture but not feeling that he or she deserves it.

Abuse leaves addicts lonely, angry, frightened, and confused. They develop core beliefs: I am a bad and worthless person. No one will love me as I am. No one will take care of me but me. Sex is my most important need. At some time in the life of an addict sex becomes a solution to the feelings. When it does it gets "cemented" in the brain as the way out or escape from the feelings. This is referred to in our field as the "arousal template." It could happen at any time in the life cycle. Whatever age the addict is, he or she will get developmentally arrested, or stuck, at that age. This leaves most at very immature levels.

The arousal template may also determine what kinds of sex a person will get addicted to later on. For example, his mother profoundly emotionally abused Larry when he was a boy. He thought she hated him. There was a family down the street that had four girls in it that were roughly his age. This was in the 1950s. They would play together. The girls would always be dressed in dresses with frilly white socks and patent leather shoes. Play would sometimes involve the old "I'll show you mine, if you show me yours" games. When he was married, Larry longed for his wife to dress up in fancy dresses with white frilly socks and patent leather shoes. He said that he couldn't get aroused if she didn't do this.

For some addicts it may simply be that looking at pornography or masturbating brought the pleasurable feelings that were a way out of the lonely and negative ones. Later in life, when they find themselves compulsively looking at the Internet, it is really one of the oldest solutions they know to deal with their feelings.

*Relational.* Abuse can lead to relationship and intimacy difficulties. If a child does not learn healthy connections, how will he or she know about them as adults? Lately, attachment theory has begun to explain how devastating this can be.[15] Addicts suffer from intimacy disorder. They feel that if they were really known, people would hate them and leave them. This predisposes them to lying and avoiding the truth. They long for approval and usually develop approval disorders which many have called "co-dependency." This is at a deep level of their soul.

Addicts hope that their relationships, especially their marriages will solve all these attachment and intimacy issues. When they don't seem to, at least in the magical way addicts would like, they get angry with themselves and others. They may think that they have found the wrong spouses or friends. As they take this feeling further, it may lead them to think that they need, and even deserve, to find better relationships. This can obviously lead to affairs and other unhealthy relationships. Their co-dependency can keep them locked into these relationship and they wind up feeling trapped.

The bottom line etiologically is that sex addicts may feel that the only way they get their needs for love and nurture met is through sex and/or infatuated romance.

*Physical.* I have already described that one of the main features of addiction is that addicts become neurochemically tolerant to the chemicals that sex, love, and romance produce. They are literally physically dependent. When sex is combined with excitement and danger, adrenaline can be dependently involved. It is very common for sex addicts to be addicted to other substances or activities that produce these same chemicals. Addicts can be addicted to one or the other and, sometimes, trade them off against each other. This is referred to as "Addiction Interaction Disorder." For example, Carnes found that roughly 50% of all sex addicts are also alcoholics.[16] In the same study Carnes also found that the more severe the abuse was to the addict as a child, the more likely he/she will have multiple addictions.

Mike realized that he was an alcoholic in his early 20s. It took him several years to finally go to AA, but eventually he achieved sobriety. Over the next years he discovered that smoking, eating, and his sexual activity (mainly pornography and masturbation) gradually increased. He was bewildered by the ongoing difficulties he had. Finally, someone introduced him to a program for sex addiction and he found recovery in this area of his life too. Today he knows that recovering from sex addiction was even harder than his alcohol recovery because he didn't need to go to a bar, just his head, to get his supply.

Addicts like Mike realize that recovering from food or sex is more difficult than recovering from a substance because with food and sex they can't totally stop. These are normal, natural, and necessary desires of the body.

Many researchers now believe that there is a correlation between Attention Deficit Disorder (ADD or ADHD) and addiction. One belief is that untreated ADD will "metastasize" to addiction. Suffering from ADD can mean that a person is bored and craves stimulation in whatever way they can get it. He or she may also be distracted more easily by the stimuli of sex so prevalent in the world.

In one study, conducted by me and my colleague Richard Blankenship, we found that in a population of positively diagnosed sex addicts, roughly 70% tested as possibly having ADD and roughly 50% tested as highly probable for ADD. I have become very impressed with the work of Dr. Daniel Amen who does SPEC brain scans.[17] He is doing pioneering work in distinguishing types of ADD. We are working together to research what correlations there are between these types and sex addiction.

*Cognitive and Behavioral.* Sex addicts, like alcoholics and other addicts, suffer from "stinking thinking." We might call this "distorted cognitive beliefs." They have lost touch with who they really are in Christ and believe themselves to be worthless. They suffer from the core beliefs listed above. They have unrealistic expectations of themselves and others. This kind of thinking can lead them to totally irrational justifications for why it is OK for them to sexually sin.

Gary didn't think much of himself. He had prayed for God to help him but had come to the conclusion that God either didn't really care about his sexual sin or that God didn't really care for him. "Why not go for it," he would say as he deluded himself into thinking that he wouldn't suffer any consequences of his acting out.

Because of their beliefs and relational issues, sex addicts don't connect with others. It is hard for them to participate in community. They become or remain isolated or alone. No one knows the truth about them and they lead a "double life." Since no one really knows them they are accountable to no one. They may think they have accountability partners, but if one of them would ask if they were OK, they would always reply, "Sure, I'm fine." They wouldn't want their accountability partners to really know them for fear that they would be judged and left alone.

*Spiritual.* Sexual addiction is, at its deepest core, a spiritual act of rebellion against God. Sex becomes the false idol. Sex addicts are spiritually immature and often into black and white thinking. They may be angry at God for not giving them the magic answer. They have not truly surrendered to God and continue to be self-centered and selfish, which in its more profound form is narcissism. Sex addicts have fantasies of an imagined answer that they think will solve all their problems. They don't have a vision of God's true calling in their lives.

## Assessment

A diagnosis of sex addiction can be made mainly and most reliably through a psychosocial interview. The entire life of the person must be understood including a very rigorous sexual history. Develop your skills at asking probing questions and help the addict feel safe to answer them. You can do this by being non-judgmental of them as people. Never ask for graphic specifics. That can get verbally exhibitionistic or voyeuristic.

Nevertheless, be direct. For example, you might not want to ask, "Were you ever sexually abused?" Rather, ask, "When was your first sexual experience?" An addict might not interpret early sexual activity as abusive. You need to know the history and development of sexual activity. When you believe that the five criteria listed above are met, you are dealing with a sex addict.

There is also a very commonly used test that is available without copyright infringement. It is called the Sexual Addiction Screening Test (SAST) and consists of 25 true and false questions. It first appeared in Carnes' book, *Contrary to Love.*[18] Answering 13 or more "yes" connotes a diagnosis of sex addiction. This test has been modified for female sex addicts by some authorities in the field of female sex addiction, such as Marnie Ferree.[19]

**Treatment**

Treatment for sex addiction, whether in a counseling office or treatment center can be understood in the same five categories described in the section on etiology:

*Emotional.* Since sex addicts are so profoundly abused, treating trauma wounds will be one major goal of treatment. The treatment of trauma usually consists of using various counseling methods to identify the history of trauma and allowing the person to express and understand feelings about this history. Next, learning how people have coped with trauma is vital. Carnes, for example, has identified 8 ways that people cope.[20] Using sex as a coping strategy is one of the ways, according to him, that we "numb" trauma. Sex may also be a way we repeat the trauma hoping for a different result (the old definition of insanity).

Shame is the by-product of trauma and spiritual truth is an essential part of the treatment of trauma. Reminding addicts that they are "fearfully and wonderfully made" (Psalm 139) and that Christ died for them is vital. Grieving the loss of so much love and nurture is often a part of the process of healing from trauma.

I have found that the only way to truly heal trauma is to help addicts find meaning in it. Addicts can spend lots of time being victims and feeling sorry for themselves; or they can ask, "What meaning can I make of this?" It is true that God can "work for good" in any situation (Rom. 8:28). God can use our experience of trauma to make us stronger and more sensitive to others. It can also be true that when we experience the pain of our trauma, we are experiencing the pain of all humanity.

Addicts can learn that they grow together in community when they share their pain with others who also have pain. I believe that is what Jesus asks us to do when He says in Matthew 11:28–30 that we can find comfort in our weariness when we take upon ourselves His yoke. When we know that Jesus shares our pain through the cross and that He thereby takes it upon Himself, it becomes a whole lot lighter and easier burden to bear.

Ultimately, the final act of healing from trauma is to forgive those who "persecuted us." That is clearly our spiritual calling. Addicts know that when they carry the burden of anger and resentment, it leads to despair. When they decide to forgive they will start acting like they do and will feel like it later.

Finally, most treatment for addiction would seek to help addicts stop fantasizing about sex. Some would have them "take every thought captive" by just avoiding the thoughts or by guarding the mind against them. Some would say that we have 3 seconds to stop thinking about the fantasy. Finally, some very popular but misguided therapy would have addicts do painful things to themselves when they fantasize, such as using rubber bands about the wrist and popping them when they think sexual thoughts. These strategies may work for a time during the early days of treatment but, ultimately they serve to recreate the trauma that the addicts experienced in the first place and thereby re-injure the brain.

I have found that it is better to ask what the fantasies are trying to teach us about pain. I believe that every fantasy is an attempt to heal a wound from the past. In the fantasy a person will create ways to stop the memory of harm or ways to get the love and nurture that was missed. To turn off a fantasy will miss the message in it. If addicts will ask themselves what the fantasy means about their past, and if they will seek healing from the wounds it seeks to deal with, the fantasy will go away. The addict doesn't need it anymore to bring the message.[21] Ralph Earle and I describe how therapists can help addicts interpret their fantasies in our book *The Pornography Trap*.

*Relational.* Sex addicts will need to learn how to connect intimately. That is why the honesty of support groups can be a vital part of treatment. Just as others may not trust addicts, addicts don't trust that they can be honest with others. They will need to learn in a healthy and safe community that there are trustworthy people. I have never known a sex addict who has recovered alone.

In order to build trust, addicts will need to be completely sober and to become completely honest about their thoughts and behaviors. That is why I believe it is vital for an addict to disclose his or her story to spouses, children, and close friends and family. This can be daunting. The actual specifics of the story are not as important as the exact nature of the activity. It is morally imperative to do so particularly if the addict has put others in physical danger (such as exposure to disease). Others, like spouses, will need to know why they want to know specifics of acting out behaviors. Do they want to connect intimately or do they want to punish or become better private eyes?

My wife, Debbie, and I believe that there are three acts of surrender for couples to recover from sexual addiction. First, each spouse must be surrendered to Christ. Second, each spouse must surrender each other to Christ knowing that they can't control each other. Third, the couple must surrender their marriage to Christ. Only in this act of "one flesh union" can couples build a better relationship.

Carnes found that the spouses of addicts are equally wounded in their childhoods.[22] This means that they will need to honestly heal from their trauma and not blame the addict for all of their pain. Couples who are equally wounded might be what Carnes called "trauma bonded." They have found each other in the pain. This can seem like all the wrong reasons for being married. We have found, however, that this can be part of God's design. We are called together and may well trigger each other into the deepest places of pain, but this is God's way of helping us grow and be each other's healer. When we know this, we can become companions and soul mates in the journey of growth.

Couples therapy for sex addiction will involve three equal pieces of work: the addict, the spouse, and the couple. Couples' counseling, from day one, is vital in facilitating growth. Today, there are workbooks to help couples on the journey.[23]

*Physical.* Because sex addicts have become neurochemically tolerant to sex, they will need to go through a period of total abstinence from sexual expression in any form. They should sign a contract not to be "sexual with themselves or others." This would include spouses. It is important to help spouses understand the need for this and to agree with it. Paul said in 1 Corinthians 7 that couples "should not deprive each other except by mutual consent and for a time so that they may devote themselves to prayer." (v. 5) When addicts do this, they will detoxify their brains and may go to similar, albeit less severe, symptoms as an alcoholic would. It is important during this time to find them support.

After about 7–14 days of abstinence, addicts will notice that it becomes easier to stay free of sexual acting out. My experience would suggest that it is easier to be completely abstinent than to be regularly sexual with a spouse. This is a neurochemical phenomenon. Single people, therefore, may have an easier time being sober than married people. For an addict, at least, there is no amount of sex that is ever enough to satisfy biological desire. They will always want more. I have found that the only way to satisfy sexual desire ultimately is in the spiritual intimacy of marriage.

Addicts may need to have physical evaluation of the possibility of any STDs. They may also need help with any sexual dysfunctions that have developed. Getting competent Christian sex therapy could be important. Physical self-care is also vital. Lack of exercise, proper nutrition, and rest could make addicts more vulnerable to temptation.

Finally, psychiatric treatment for any imbalances of neurochemistry is incredibly important. Since ADD/HD may be a comorbid condition, treatment for it could often be the missing link in staying sober. In my personal experience, brain scan imaging (such as Daniel Amen's work) can be indicated especially in those cases where traditional psychiatry does not seem to be able to adequately diagnose the problem.

*Cognitive/Behavioral.* Talk therapy and spiritual direction will be essential parts of a treatment plan. Helping addicts understand their own wounded core beliefs and the truth of the gospel will be a life journey of healing.

Helping addicts find and maintain accountability is a critical part of treatment, especially in the early months. I have found that the book of Nehemiah is a virtual blueprint of how to do this. In two separate books I have completely outlined an 18-principle approach to accountability based on this book.[24] To highlight several of these principles:

- Accountability begins with willingness and with brokenness.
- Accountability begins with confession and a spirit of repentance. (Neh. 1)
- Accountability is maintained in groups of men or of women dedicated to sexual purity. These are the "warriors" of an addict's life. (Neh. 2:9)
- Addicts must get rid of all "dung" in their lives (Neh. 3:14). Pornography, affairs, secret phone numbers, and irrational thinking are examples of this.
- Addicts must identify the enemy. This is to discover how they become vulnerable in their rituals.
- Addicts must prepare when they are strong for the temptations that will come. They must not wait until it happens for that is part of the temptation.
- Addicts must be accountable to do positive actions and defend against negative ones.

- Addicts must find a higher calling and purpose for which to recover, like fighting for their families and their homes. (Neh. 4:14)

Addicts will learn how to define their sobriety and the rituals that lead them into this acting out. For most Christian addicts sobriety will mean no acting out with self (masturbation) and others outside of marriage. Masturbation has sometimes been controversial in the Christian community especially with singles. My experience is that masturbation is never possible in that it conditions a person emotionally and physically to be dissatisfied with marital and genital intercourse.

Finding sobriety from sex addiction is in some ways more like an eating disorder than it is like alcoholism. Both sex and eating are natural desires of the body. Just as eating can't be totally abstained from, so sex (for those married) can't be given up either. Learning how to be sexual or to eat for the healthy purposes of it is vital to the journey of accountability.

*Spiritual.* Sex addicts will need to answer three spiritual questions in order to begin the journey of healing. First, "Do you want to get well?" This is the question that Jesus asks the paralyzed man in John 5:6. Had this man adopted the attitude of being paralyzed? Addicts do. They must be willing to change and give up their own control and give it to God.

Second, "What are you thirsty for?" In the story of the Samaritan woman in John 4, Jesus tells her that earthly water does not satisfy thirst and that only "living water" does. Recovering sex addicts know that they have been thirsty for sexual solutions and that now they must be thirsty for Christ.

Third, "Are you willing to die to yourself?" In John 11 when Jesus heals Lazarus, He is demonstrating that He will let someone die in order for them to experience the resurrecting power of a relationship with Him. Addicts are often like Lazarus's two sisters, Mary and Martha, and think that if Jesus would only have come, they wouldn't have died. Only addicts who stop looking for the magic answer and who are willing to die to their own control and power, will find true healing.

Ultimately, addicts must have a vision of God's calling in their lives. They have created fantasies of their solutions and must now find God's. Addicts without a vision will perish. A vision is the motivation to follow God and not the self. Fantasy is a magic answer; vision is God's. Vision directs all we do and gives us an appetite and thirst for "things above" and not "things below." When addicts start a cycle of vision it will lead to healthy discipline, healthy behavior, and joy. This is opposed to the addict's historical cycle of fantasy, ritual, acting out, and despair.

## Conclusion

As one of my colleagues recently put it, a statement I penned for the epigraph of this chapter, "In our current sexually absorbed culture, working with sex addicts is a growth industry." There is no shortage of work to go around. I encourage you to be involved if you feel capable. There are plenty of ways to acquire further training and to even get certification. AACC conferences and video series are great sources.

There is one last word of caution. Working with sex addicts will challenge a counselor's own sexuality. Listening to the stories can be troubling at some times and sexually provocative at others. If a counselor's own sexual health is not in good order, working with addicts can be dangerous. When in doubt, refer to a competent therapist in your area.

When successful work with sex addicts and their spouses is accomplished, however, transformation of lives and marriages is a very fulfilling result.

## ENDNOTES

1.  These groups are: Sex Addicts Anonymous, Sexaholics Anonymous, and Sex and Love Addicts Anonymous. Phone numbers and contact information are listed in the resource section.
2.  Patrick Carnes, *Out of the shadows* (Center City, MN: Hazelden Books, 1984).
3.  Mark R. Laaser, *Healing the wounds of sexual addiction* (Grand Rapids, MI: Zondervan, 2004).
4.  Harry Schaumberg, *False intimacy* (Downers Grove, IL: InterVarsity, 1992).
5.  Ralph Earle, Earle M., and Osborn, K., *Sex addiction: Case studies and management* (New York: Brunner/Mazel, 1995). and Ralph Earle and Crow, G., *Lonely all the time* (New York: Pocket, 1989).
6.  Pat Means, *Men's secret wars* (Grand Rapids, MI: Revell, 1996).
7.  Russ Willingham, *Breaking free* (Downers Grove, IL: InterVarsity, 1999).
8.  Earl Wilson, *Steering clear* (Downers Grove, IL: InterVarsity, 2002).
9.  Steve Arteburn and Stoeker, F., *Every man's battle* (Colorado Springs, CO.: WaterBrook Press, 2000).
10. The Leadership survey on pastors and internet pornography, *Leadership Journal* 2001:001
11. Carnes, 1984.

12. Harvey Milkman, and Sunderwirth, S., *Craving for ecstasy: The consciousness and chemistry of escape* (Lexington, MA: Lexington Books, 1987).

13. Marnie Ferree, *No stones: Women redeemed from sexual shame* (Fairfax, VA: Xulon, 2002).

14. Pat Carnes, *Don't call it love* (New York: Bantam Books, 1991).

15. Tim Clinton and Sibcy, G., *Attachments,* (Brentwood, TN: Integrity, 2002).

16. Carnes, 1991.

17. Daniel Amen, *Change your brain change your life* (New York: Random House, 1998).

18. Pat Carnes, *Contrary to love* (Minneapolis: CompCare 1989).

19. Marnie Ferree, 2002.

20. Pat Carnes, *The betrayal bond* (Deerfield Beach, FL: Health Communications, Inc., 1997).

21. Mark Laaser and Earle, R., *The pornography trap* (Kansas City, KS: Beacon Hill Press, 2002).

22. Carnes, 1997.

23. Patrick Carnes, Laaser, D., and Laaser, M., *Open hearts* (Wickensburg, AZ: Gentle Path Press, 2000).

24. Laaser and Earle, 2002. and Mark Laaser, *A L.I.F.E. guide: Men living in freedom everyday* (Fairfax, VA.: Xulon, 2002).

# 14

# Gambling, Spending, and Credit Abuse

*Gregory L. Jantz*

Many individuals with Pathological Gambling believe that money is both
the cause of and the solution to all their problems.

DSM-IV[1]

For the love of money is a root of all kinds of evil.

1 Timothy 6:10a

Jerry and Susan came in for counseling. Married eleven years, with two
boys, they found themselves growing apart. Jerry described sexual difficulties. Susan complained of financial struggles and a general feeling of
estrangement. Both were cautiously willing to enter into therapy, each convinced the other was mostly at fault.

Deep down, Susan expressed a fear that Jerry was having an affair. He
came home later and later from work. Money was missing from the checking account and Jerry became angry when she asked about it. One time, she
said, she'd called him at work, a rare occurrence, only to find he'd "gone
home sick." When she'd driven home to check on him during her lunch
break, he wasn't there. His explanation of where he'd actually gone just
didn't sound plausible. It seemed to Susan that Jerry was becoming more
irritable with her and the boys, as if he resented them. His beer on the
weekends was turning into a nightly routine. Susan felt afraid and angry.

Jerry was frustrated in his marriage. He said Susan didn't respond sexually the way he wanted and that she put more time into the boys than him. The stress of providing for a family, especially in a tight job market, was taking its toll and Jerry didn't like having to answer to Susan every time he was late getting home. He felt he had to schedule his entire day in order to get everything done. All the things he did to help handle the stress seemed to cause strife and irritation in Susan. Jerry felt confined and stressed.

Susan came into counseling expecting to be told that Jerry was in love with another woman. Jerry came into counseling expecting Susan to be told to be a more understanding wife. The key to resolving their difficulties lay in a completely different direction, one that did not surface immediately. Pressed by the demands of family responsibilities, Jerry had indeed sought out an alternative relationship, one that was exciting, energizing. Not with another woman, as Susan feared, but with an activity. Jerry had fallen in love with the thrill and promise of gambling.

Dinner with a friend at a local restaurant and casino, while Susan and the kids were out of town, led to a night of slots and blackjack. More than a year later, Jerry still continued to gamble. Even when confronted with the negative consequences, he tried to downplay them and insisted there was nothing wrong with his newfound recreation.

What started out as marital difficulties to Susan and a necessary outlet for Jerry was fast approaching a DSM-IV classification of 312.31.

### Pathological Gambling

Pathological gambling, in the DSM-IV, 4th Edition, "is characterized by recurrent and persistent maladaptive gambling behavior that disrupts personal, family, or vocational pursuits." What it meant in Jerry and Susan's life was financial stress, deterioration of personal credit, loss of affection and heightened anxiety. The following is taken from the DSM-IV Diagnostic Criteria for 312.31 Pathological Gambling:

A. Persistent and recurrent maladaptive gambling behavior is indicated by five (or more) of the following criteria:

    1.    is preoccupied with gambling (e.g., preoccupied with reliving past gambling experiences, handicapping or planning the next venture, or thinking of ways to get money with which to gamble)

2.  needs to gamble with increasing amounts of money in order to achieve the desired excitement

3.  has repeated unsuccessful efforts to control, cut back, or stop gambling

4.  is restless or irritable when attempting to cut down or stop gambling

5.  gambles as a way of escaping from problems or of relieving a dysphoric mood (e.g., feelings of helplessness, guilt, anxiety, depression)

6.  after losing money gambling, often returns another day to get even ("chasing" one's losses)

7.  lies to family members, therapist, or others to conceal the extent of involvement with gambling

8.  has committed illegal acts such as forgery, fraud, theft, or embezzlement to finance gambling

9.  has jeopardized or lost a significant relationship, job, or educational or career opportunity because of gambling

10. relies on others to provide money to relieve a desperate financial situation caused by gambling

B. A diagnosis is not made if the gambling behavior can be associated with a Manic Episode.

### New Twist to an Ancient Malady

Prior to 1980, there wasn't even a diagnostic code for pathological gambling. Since that time, gambling has moved in and made itself accessible. It used to be if you wanted to gamble, you had to go to Las Vegas or Atlantic City. Now, you need go no further than the blackjack room down the block or the tribal casino out on the interstate. With the rise of internet gambling, you need go no further than your den or bedroom.

Accessibility can prove problematic to those with an impulse-control disorder, such as pathological gambling. The more communities welcome gambling, the higher the likelihood you will see gambling-related issues coming in the front door of your counseling practice or ministry. The greater the types of gambling allowed, the higher the lifetime rates of pathological and problem gamblers (Volberg, 1994).

It has generally been my experience that gambling does not surface immediately as a primary reason for a person or a family to seek counseling. More often, I've seen the Jerry-Susan scenario, with gambling interwoven around other issues. One of the most common companions to pathological gambling is alcohol abuse and a current study suggests that those with problematic gambling behaviors should undergo a chemical dependency screening.[2]

### Gambling Gaining Ground

Most Americans gamble. A study for Arizona's state-run lottery reported that "the majority of adults in the United States have gambled at some time in their lives. Nationally, the proportion of the population that has ever gambled ranges from 81% in the Southern states to 89% in the Northeast."[3] In Arizona, 7 in 10 adults gambled within the past year and 23% gambled within the past month. Ten percent gambled within the past week, with the majority of gambling occurring through visiting a casino or playing the lottery.

According to information put out by the National Council on Problem Gambling, an average of 3 million adults meet the criteria for pathological gambling each year. They are more likely to have problems with alcohol, drugs, smoking, and depression. Serious gambling problems can lead to suicide. While the poor appear to be an at-risk population for pathological gambling (Ladd, Petry, 2002), in the Arizona study, 60% of those identified as problem gamblers worked full-time, with only 10% disabled or unemployed, a rate half of that of non-problem gamblers (20%).

Gamblers now come in both genders, across age groups and in all colors. Three million of our fellow Americans. At-risk populations appear to be the elderly, the young, minorities and the poor. Because of this, "the National Council on Problem Gambling has advocated a public health perspective, pointing out that pathological gambling is more prevalent where gambling is more available, and advocating a national gambling policy to restrict the availability of gambling (National Council on Problem Gambling, 1993)."[4]

Thirty years ago, this issue wasn't even on the horizon. "Since the mid-1970s, America has evolved from a country in which gambling was a relatively rare activity—casinos operating only in the distant Nevada desert, a few states operating lotteries, and pari-mutuel gambling relatively small scale and sedate—into a nation in which legalized gambling, in one form or another, is permitted in 47 states and the District of Columbia."[5] Over time, and with the continued increase in gambling, attitudes have incrementally changed. According to research by the Barna Group, "Of the ten moral behaviors evaluated, a majority of Americans believed that each of three activities were "morally acceptable." Those included gambling (61%), cohabitation (60%), and sexual fantasies (59%)."[6] Moral acceptability of gambling is currently directly related to age, according to Barna. For the oldest Americans, half find gambling acceptable, while the number jumps to 3 in 4 for those just graduating from high school. This culture increasingly finds gambling an acceptable behavior. The more who engage in it, the more who will become trapped.

## The Downward Spiral

Looking back over the past five years, I realized I lost a good portion of my life. I remember the pain and the continuous deception as I awoke each and every morning. I lied to my wife and I lied to my friends. I cannot believe how my personality changed as I became more and more manipulative over time. I knew I had a problem. I did not know how to face it when I lost all of my money, maxed out my credit cards and kept this secret from my wife and kids. I was a good husband and I was a good person but life all changed as I became more and more involved with gambling. My wife found out since bills were mounting. I sat down and told her what I had done. She was in shock and disbelief. She told me either to get help or get out.[7]

Even with other issues present, it is imperative that gambling be addressed, because of the destructive and progressive nature of the disorder. What starts as a preoccupation with thinking about gambling can lead to criminal activity to obtain funds to gamble, the loss of family relationships, financial resources, and employment. Simply stated, pathological gambling wrecks lives and ruins families.

There are three distinct phases in the progression leading to pathological gambling. Counseling may be sought during any of these phases, although the financial, personal, and peer pressure to confront gambling consequences may increase in the later stages and motivate a person to seek help.

The initial phase is known as the *winning phase*. It is during this phase that the gambler does not perceive any negative consequences to the gambling behavior. On the contrary, this phase is characterized by a sense of excitement and even euphoria. (For this reason, a manic episode involving excessive gambling and loss of judgment can sometimes appear to be pathological gambling. It is important to differentiate whether or not the manic characteristics are sustained outside of the gambling behavior, hence item B in the DSM-IV criteria.) About half those identified as compulsive gamblers begin with a big win early on. This early win is identified as pleasurable by the gambler, who then seeks to replicate the feeling. Even if there is not an initial win, the sheer excitement of the act of gambling is interpreted as pleasurable, enticing the person to continue the behavior.

The more the person gambles to replicate the pleasure, the higher the odds s/he will lose. In the *losing phase*, the person starts to increase the amount of gambling in order to recoup losses (known as "chasing" losses) to recapture that initial feeling of excitement. The magnitude of the bets and/or the frequency of the activity increases to produce the same level of thrill or financial windfall. It is at this stage that the gambler will begin to alienate family and friends, jeopardize employment, and borrow money. Sometimes, the gambler will experience a win during this phase or be enabled by family and friends to continue. These events merely forestall the inevitable. The heavier reliance on gambling, however, does not produce the desired results long-term and the gambler sinks into the final phase.

As the person continues to gamble, s/he enters the *desperation phase*. Gambling has now taken precedence over other, important considerations such as family, friends, work, finances. In a desperate attempt to gain funds to maintain or even increase the amount of gambling, the person may resort to unethical or criminal behavior. Family members or friends may be lied to about the true reason for needing money. The person may cheat or steal from employers. Gamblers have been known to embezzle funds entrusted to them. (One sad example in my home state of Washington involved a high-school band director who gambled away $4,000 raised by students and parents through a bake sale, car washes, and other fundraising events for a trip.) It is during the desperation phase that pathological gamblers will have increased incidences of suicidal ideation as a way out of their difficulties brought by gambling.

## At War, At-Risk

Those who provide gaming resources, services and equipment are adept at developing gambling venues that are most effective. Internet gambling combines immediacy, convenience and anonymity. This potent combination can prove overpowering to someone on the edge of pathological gambling behaviors.

In addition, there is another form of gambling that is proving to be highly addictive—machine gambling, including slots and video poker. Called the "crack cocaine" of gambling, this "analogy implies that machines are more addictive than other, more "traditional" forms of gambling, such as horse-racing and card games."[8]

It is in the financial interest of gaming business, even state governments that rely on gambling revenues, to become even "better" marketers of gambling venues and products. Their efficiency, however, easily translates into higher rates of pathological gambling. Gambling has become another skirmish in the ongoing culture war, with pathological gamblers and their families caught in the crosshairs.

## Warning Signs

In some instances, a pathological gambler, realizing the devastation his or her compulsion is causing, will come in for counseling specifically on this issue. However, pathological gamblers are not always forthcoming about their gambling behaviors, so there are specific signs to watch for during counseling on other issues that may point to the existence of a gambling addiction:

- Unexplained withdrawal of personal or family funds
- Unexplained time away from school, work, or home
- Heightened irritability and hostility over financial matters
- Increased signs of depression and/or anxiety
- Increased isolation from family members
- Withdrawal from previously enjoyed social activities
- Unexplained mood swings
- Selling personal possessions
- Unexplained gifts or excessive generosity

- Borrowing from family and friends
- Unexplained indebtedness to credit cards
- Associated disorders

There are a variety of diagnostic tools available to help assess the presence of pathological gambling. The least "clinical" in my view can be obtained through the National Council on Problem Gambling (www.ncpgambling.org), which presents the person with ten statements about his or her gambling behavior. They are:

1. You have often gambled longer than you had planned.
2. You have often gambled until your last dollar was gone.
3. Thoughts of gambling have caused you to lose sleep.
4. You have used your income or savings to gamble while letting bills go unpaid.
5. You have made repeated, unsuccessful attempts to stop gambling.
6. You have broken the law or considered breaking the law to finance your gambling.
7. You have borrowed money to finance your gambling.
8. You have felt depressed or suicidal because of your gambling losses.
9. You have been remorseful after gambling.
10. You have gambled to get money to meet your financial obligations.
11. According to the "Problem Gambling Resource & Fact Sheet" put out by the NCPG, if the person answers "yes" to any of these, he or she should consider help from a professional.

*Twenty Questions.* Gamblers Anonymous was started by two compulsive gamblers in 1957 in Los Angeles, California. It was decidedly ahead of its time, and has a checklist of twenty questions that are still valuable diagnostic tools:

1. Did you ever lose time from work or school due to gambling?
2. Has gambling ever made your home life unhappy?
3. Did gambling affect your reputation?
4. Have you ever felt remorse after gambling?

5.  Did you ever gamble to get money with which to pay debts or otherwise solve financial difficulties?

6.  Did gambling cause a decrease in your ambition or efficiency?

7.  After losing did you feel you must return as soon as possible and win back your losses?

8.  After a win did you have a strong urge to return and win more?

9.  Did you often gamble until your last dollar was gone?

10.  Did you ever borrow to finance your gambling?

11.  Have you ever sold anything to finance gambling?

12.  Were you reluctant to use "gambling money" for normal expenditures?

13.  Did gambling make you careless of the welfare of yourself or your family?

14.  Did you ever gamble longer than you had planned?

15.  Have you ever gambled to escape worry or trouble?

16.  Have you ever committed, or considered committing, an illegal act to finance gambling?

17.  Did gambling cause you to have difficulty in sleeping?

18.  Do arguments, disappointments or frustrations create within you an urge to gamble?

19.  Did you ever have an urge to celebrate any good fortune by a few hours of gambling?

20.  Have you ever considered self-destruction or suicide as a result of your gambling?

According to Gamblers Anonymous, most compulsive gamblers will answer yes to at least seven of those questions.[9]

The National Council on Problem Gambling has a "Problem Gambling Self Test" on-line that can be found at http://www.ncpgambling.org/about_problem/about_problem_test.asp.

There are other diagnostic screening tools that can be utilized. Two are the South Oaks Gambling Screen (SOGS)[10] and the NORC (National Opinion Research Center) DSM-IV Screen for Gambling Problems[11], both of which were used in the Arizona study. The SOGS was used in the 1999 report to the Washington State Lottery on my state's gambling and problem gambling behaviors.

## Associated Disorders

In my research, I believe that people become trapped in gambling behaviors for the same reasons that any addict uses whatever their "drug of choice" may be: out of a desire to obtain a euphoric thrill, to gain control over their lives through money, or to provide an escape from uncomfortable feelings and/or situations. Where one disorder takes hold, another can follow.

A link appears to exist between gambling behaviors and substance abuse through alcohol or drugs. These are not the only companions to gambling. The DSM-IV identifies "Mood Disorders, Attention-Deficit/Hyperactivity Disorder, Substance Abuse or Dependence, other Impulse-Control Disorders, and Antisocial, Narcissistic, and Borderline Personality Disorders"[12] as being linked to Pathological Gambling. In some cases, these associated disorders precede and intensify the gambling behaviors, making it difficult to identify which came first. At some point, the only effective treatment is to recognize all of the associated disorders and factor them into a comprehensive treatment plan. In the case of Substance Abuse or Dependence, this would require treating the person under a dual diagnosis of mental health and chemical dependency.

## Treating the Whole Person

It is my belief that recovery from pathological gambling is possible and best achieved through a whole-person treatment model. By whole-person, I mean addressing the emotional, relational, physical, and spiritual components contributing to the person's compulsion to gamble. The Jerry-Susan scenario provides an example of how the whole-person treatment model functions.

Jerry's sense of dissatisfaction with his life and marriage preceded his gambling experience. Emotionally, Jerry felt anxious and overwhelmed by the pressures of providing for his family financially. He also resented the increasing amounts of time necessary to fulfill his family and employment responsibilities. He felt squeezed out and marginalized by his family. Jerry was able to articulate how he felt but it took longer to identify why he felt that way and where the thoughts supporting those feelings originated.

When Jerry was growing up, his father was the sole support for the family. As such, he was exempted from household chores, which were accomplished by Jerry's mother, Jerry and siblings. Jerry perceived that if you worked and brought income into the home, this activity exempted you from the mundane tasks of the family. It also seemed to Jerry that he and his younger sister were burdened with the worse jobs around the house and yard, while his older brother was increasingly excused from chores. Jerry grew up feeling deep resentment over this family inequity. He determined that being an adult and bread-winner, he would be relieved of these types of responsibilities. Adulthood, to Jerry, meant getting to do more of what you wanted to, of having more control of your life.

At a time when Jerry was experiencing increased stress in his work and family, the gambling opportunity arose. It was exciting, self-focused, more of what he always thought being an adult should bring. It was, after all, his money and his time and he should have the freedom to spend it on whatever he wanted, not have to explain every penny to Susan. He was tired of handing over each paycheck and finding out how little was left at the end of each month, after everyone else's items were paid for. Jerry began to fantasize on how much better his life would be if he could just win some extra money so the pressure would be off. He thought if he could just bring home enough money, his life would be eased and he'd be able to gain more control over his time.

As Jerry sought to incorporate his hidden gambling into an already busy schedule, however, his stress increased. He began to lose sleep. His consumption of alcohol, caffeine, and tobacco increased. His eating habits deteriorated and he developed headaches, which made him even more irritable around his family and coworkers. Productivity at work fell, causing additional stress about the permanency of his position. The less sure his job became, the greater the desire to hedge his bets through anticipated winnings.

The more Jerry turned to gambling and alcohol to numb his problems, the less he became available to Susan and his children. As his isolation increased, Jerry began to lose touch with his identity as a husband and father, substituting his identity as gambler. This precipitated a spiritual crisis: Jerry began to question his purpose in life.

Created as complex beings of mind, body, and spirit, recovery and wholeness are best achieved when these factors are integrated into treatment. Through therapy Jerry examined the source of his feelings of discontent and learned skills to help make intentional choices to redirect his negative thoughts. He identified unrecognized family-of-origin patterns affecting his current family relationships. Working with a medical professional, Jerry cut down on his consumption of alcohol, caffeine, and tobacco. He also began a regular exercise routine in order to provide physical release for feelings of restlessness or anxiety. His church was able to provide Jerry with pastoral counseling regarding his faith questions and Jerry and Susan began work with a financial planner to reconstruct their finances.

Susan, working with her own therapist, examined how her relationship with Jerry was altered by the birth of their sons, especially her sexual response to Jerry. They worked as a couple on relationship issues. Jerry and Susan learned how to manage conflicts and effectively communicate needs. They spent time together alone and placed renewed emphasis on their own identity as a couple.

Jerry, of course, had to stop gambling. He began attending a local Gamblers Anonymous meeting to provide support for his gambling abstinence. Approaching every person whom he owed money, both family members and friends, he explained his gambling addiction and obtained a promise from them that they would not loan him any more money, no matter the reason. He also made arrangements to pay each of them back the money he'd borrowed for his gambling. At his church, Jerry was open about his need for prayer and support in his desire to stop gambling. Several men in the congregation pledged to form an accountability group with Jerry and meet on a regular basis with him.

### Community Resources

Recovery from pathological gambling requires a concerted effort not only by the individual but also by the community surrounding that individual. As a counselor, you can provide an important piece of understanding and clarity of the true nature of the disorder. You can assist the person to make positive behavioral changes. You can provide motivation for the person to assemble outside resources from family, friends, support groups, financial counseling, and churches.

As the course of recovery progresses, the more additional resources the person has, the greater the success in overcoming an inevitable relapse. As a counselor, you will not be available to this person 24 hours a day and a relapse could occur during non-business hours. The more community support available to the individual, the better.

As a counselor, you recognize the need to be creative and flexible when dealing with individual situations of gambling. The following is presented as examples for potential auxiliary recommendations:

- If the person lives near a gambling establishment, map out a route to work or home that avoids the area.

- Have a family member or friend go with the recovering gambler to every gambling establishment that will allow him or her to "self-exclude" from that business. (Self-exclusion has been an option for Washington state gamblers since 1999. Under a self-banning agreement, a gambling establishment has the authority to call the police and charge the person with criminal trespass. However, some local police departments have refused to become involved and make an arrest.)

- Have the person cut up all credit cards and deal only from a cash or check basis.

- Determine if there was a specific day/time element to the gambling behavior (for example, Friday nights after work) and assist the person to substitute an appropriate activity into that time slot.

- If the person is going to be apart from his or her support structure, such as on a business trip out of town, have them arrange to check in with and be accountable to others during their time away.

- Go on-line and locate a Gamblers Anonymous support group, if possible, in the destination city.

- If they have participated in gambling activities with any family members or friends, have them contact that person and explain that they will not be able to continue gambling together and suggest they find alternate ways to maintain the relationship. If any of them refuses to respect the person's desire not to continue to gamble, assist the person in finding a way to terminate the relationship until that changes.

- If the person engages in Internet gambling, engage a protection program to restrict access to the Internet during vulnerable hours.

**Family Support**

It is an unhappy reality that some pathological gamblers will choose not to stop. Even when presented with the truth of the damage they are causing to themselves and others, the lure of the disorder will exert too strong a pull. As a counselor, you may be left with the task of working to shore up a family torn apart by the person's behavior. In some situations, the person left in your office will not be the gambler, but the spouse, the parent, or the child. Again, your assistance in identifying, creating, and maintaining a community support structure will be crucial. That left-behind person or family will benefit from the resources of the community—the love of extended family and friends, financial council, legal options, and support from their family of faith. If the person cannot be redeemed from gambling, the family still can.

Unfortunately, resources on the issue of pathological and problem gambling are slim. Gamblers Anonymous (www.gamblersanonymous.org) and the National Council on Problem Gambling (www.ncpgambling.org) have a national reach. From the National Council on Problem Gambling website, you can find state affiliates (www.ncpgambling.org/state_affiliates/), however only about half the states have this resource available. One of the greatest sources of biblically based information is Focus on the Family (www.family.org). Just type in "Gambling" in the Search field on their homepage. This organization has a research document on problem and pathological gambling by Ronald A. Reno, as well as a policy statement by Dr. James Dobson, an informational video, and information on gambling activities by state.

For a more clinical approach, Nancy M. Petry, Ph.D., cited under References, has a book available entitled, *Pathological Gambling: Etiology, Comorbidity, and Treatment* (2004, APA Books). Petry takes a three-pronged approach in this book, going over the most common treatment modalities in use for pathological gambling, non-professional intervention and self-help through groups such as Gamblers Anonymous and a cognitive-behavioral approach she uses. This book is written for an audience of mostly researchers and clinicians.

Especially for pastors or church or ministry leaders I recommend my book, *Turning the Tables on Gambling* (Waterbrook Press, 2001), available through my website at www.aplaceofhope.com. Written from a whole-person approach, it provides information and insight from a biblical perspective. Its commonsense presentation makes it accessible to the lay counselor or ministry leader, as well as valuable for the professional.

## Spending and Credit Abuse

*The rich rule over the poor, and the borrower is servant to the lender.*
Proverbs 22:7

There are no diagnostic criteria for spending too much or ringing up high credit card balances while binge shopping. If there were, many of us would probably fall into that category. While an official "disorder" has not been named, some are already calling this "compulsive shopping disorder" or "shopaholism" and it has attracted the eye of big business.

Pharmaceutical companies have taken note and are interested in providing relief to problem shoppers in a pill. According to a May 23, 2000, article in *Mother Jones* by Chris Berdik entitled, "Selling the Cure for Shopaholism," Stanford University researchers are looking into a pharmaceutical answer for overspending.[13] Relief, however, is unlikely to arrive in a small brown bottle.

No matter how you characterize it, as a society we are overburdened with debt. While you may not experience this on a personal level, my guess is you've seen it first-hand in your counseling practice. I'd also venture to guess that several people, who should have continued working with you on other issues, found they were unable to continue counseling due to their high debt load and payments. They needed to see you because of their spending, but couldn't afford to because of their debt.

The burden of debt creates an atmosphere of oppression and hopelessness. As such, debt becomes a breeding ground for depression, anxiety, marital stress, and avoidance behaviors such as substance abuse. Debt can be caused by a variety of factors. In my practice, I have seen spending and credit abuse due to ignorance, lack of impulse control, and tied to obsessive-compulsive behaviors.

Sometimes, young adults will come in to work on relationship issues and one partner will express distress over the spending and charging habits of the other. In this case, often resolution can be achieved through an understanding of family-of-origin issues concerning the handling of money, as well as a recommendation to seek a financial counselor to establish goals and a budget. Ideally, the whole concept of family budgeting and fiscal responsibility should be addressed within the umbrella of premarital counseling. Disagreements over financial matters consistently rank high on marital stressor lists.

Lack of impulse control can also lie at the root of a problem with spending and credit abuse. This is exacerbated by the sheer volume of credit card invitations the average person receives in the mail each week. The first one might be resisted, while the tenth accepted. Even without a specific diagnosis code, there is still a great deal of help counselors can provide to those challenged by an overwhelming desire to spend beyond their means. By utilizing a whole-person approach, the origins of the desire to spend can be identified and addressed.

Many times, spending contains a highly emotional component. I have had people sit in my office and explain how buying even unneeded items made them feel better. If they felt upset or sad, spending was their chosen method of providing comfort. Buying something enabled them to feel empowered and special. The greater the worth of the item bought, the higher their feelings of personal value. Some have explained that they viewed spending as a reward and whenever they felt unappreciated or undervalued by others, they would counter those feelings by rewarding themselves through shopping.

Almost universally, spending and credit abuse behavior can be linked to family-of-origin issues. The family is the first schoolhouse for how and why to spend money and children are quite perceptive to links made between personal worth and monetary value. Often, I've found the reason given for extravagant spending is to make up for a perceived lack of care by parents growing up. Adults attempt to compensate for a sense of depravation as a child by spending to fill the void as an adult.

Purchasing an item, whether with cash, check, or credit, can be an emotional action with a physical component. Feelings of sadness and depression can be given as a reason for spending money on an unneeded or extravagant item. In some ways, finding just the right item to purchase can be similar to the type of physical response produced by gambling behavior, triggering activity in the pleasure-center of the brain. When people tell me it feels good to shop and spend, this isn't just hyperbole—it actually does produce a physical pleasure response. As such, people can become dependent upon this physical response and seek to replicate it through spending or shopping, regardless of the financial cost.

Often, an important component of a desire to spend is a spiritual one. A person has prayed for something. God has answered "no" or "not now." The person then decides to take it upon him or herself to go ahead and obtain the item or a substitute anyway. The tension of not having creates an impetus, not for more prayer, but for gratification.

Often, God delays the presentation of something we want in order to teach us patience. Patience is never gained instantly. Rather, patience is perfected only through the passage of time and the sure knowledge that God will provide what we need.

The difference between needs and wants can also be a spiritual issue. Jesus expressed this concept so eloquently during the Sermon on the Mount when He said, "So do not worry, saying 'What shall we eat?' or 'What shall we drink?' or 'What shall we wear?' For the pagans run after all these things, and your heavenly Father knows that you need them. But seek first His kingdom and His righteousness, and all these things will be given to you as well." (Matt. 6:31–33) As a counselor, you can assist people in determining whether psychological factors have obscured their ability to accurately distinguish between a need and a want, and how to regain emotional equilibrium.

God has made it clear in Scripture of the value of delayed gratification. Society says now, today. God explains that a day could be a thousand years. That's not necessarily a lesson we want to learn. And the only delay a credit card company considers gratifying is a delay in you actually paying off your principle so they can continue to charge you interest, on the interest.

I believe it is possible to work with people to help develop and strengthen their internal controls over spending. At some point, it might be helpful for the person to work with you on the reasons why they spend and work with a financial counselor to determine how and when they will spend. Your primary role is to assist them in understanding what needs they are attempting to fill through their spending and credit abuse, and to develop the ability to be objective about whether their desires are needs or wants. Again, creative suggestions to individual situations can provide real-life answers to those seeking help:

- For those struggling with spending and, specifically, credit abuse, the number one suggestion from financial counselors is to cut up all credit cards. Learning to live on available resources is vital.

- Some people have found value in working with a financial consultant to whom they give over control of their finances, to increase accountability and provide an established system for accomplishing larger purchases beyond life's necessities. The process often can provide the brakes needed to slow down an impulsive drive to spend.

- Because the impulse to shop can really be a cry for pleasure, or relief from sadness or boredom, the person can be assisted in determining other activities that can be replaced and still achieve the desired effect. If a person finds they shop to relieve boredom and they have a great deal of free time on their hands, they could, for example, be motivated to identify a local volunteer opportunity that would provide contact with other people, connection to a worthwhile goal or purpose, and be mentally engaging.

- As in the case of someone whose finances are devastated by a gambling addiction, out-of-control spending and credit abuse can also destroy personal finances. In this case, the person would most probably benefit from financial counseling. In most major cities, there are consumer credit counseling bureaus that work with individuals and families to create repayment plans with creditors and reestablish a healthy income-debt ratio. Of course, after a person comes to understand the reason for their debt, they still are in debt. And while they seek to not incur more debt, they may need real help in working their way out of debt. Just knowing there is a plan in place can help give people hope as they make the sacrifices necessary to reduce or eliminate their debt.

Sometimes, when working with an individual on spending or credit abuse issues, it can take persistence and patience to uncover the root of the behavior. Just as eating disorders often mask histories of abuse and neglect, these spending behaviors may have been developed by the person to compensate for deep-seated psychological trauma. As such, no amount of financial counseling or creative action steps will significantly alter the behavior in the long-term.

A successful outcome can only be gained by detaching the behavior from the causal event or situation, sometimes a process requiring great patience and perseverance. A person may start out masking their pain through one compulsive behavior and transfer it on to another and then another. This is similar to people giving up smoking only to find they've begun to compulsively overeat. This shell game does little to truly alleviate the root cause. However, by continuing to work through each behavior, it is possible to peel back the layers and uncover the heart of the behavior.

## The True Value of Money

For good or ill, money means power and control in our society. As such, how and why we use it will continue to be an issue for people. Some of those people will wind up in our offices and homes, seeking help. From a psychological standpoint, we have ways to assess whether a disorder exists and ways to treat it. From a spiritual standpoint, we have a wealth of scriptural teaching on money, value, and worth.

Therapeutically, each individual will need a slightly different mix of psychological intervention, common sense, and spiritual help. As Christian counselors and ministers, we are blessed to have all of those palettes in our paint box, unlike purely secular counselors who reject the efficacy, or even existence, of the power of the Spirit of God.

Jesus notes also in the Sermon on the Mount, "no one can serve two masters. Either he will hate the one and love the other, or he will be devoted to the one and despise the other. You cannot serve both God and Money." (Matt. 6:24) It is significant to note that the lure of money is powerful enough to replace God as master in our lives. It was true 2,000 years ago and it's still true today. Our ultimate goal as Christian counselors is to help those suffering from whatever compulsion—gambling, spending, or credit abuse—to return God to His rightful place. As we labor in this task, with those entrusted to us, it is comforting to realize we are not alone. We are in complete agreement with the will of God in the lives of those we seek to help.

## ENDNOTES

1.  American Psychiatric Association, *Diagnostic and statistical manual of mental disorders* 4th ed. (Washington, DC: APA, 1994), 672.
2.  J. E. Grant, Kushner, M.G., and Kim, S.W., Pathological gambling and alcohol use disorder, *Alcohol Research & Health*, 26, (2002),143–150.
3.  R. A.Volberg, *Gambling and problem gambling in Arizona: Report to the Arizona*

*lottery,* (2003), available from <http://www.problemgambling.az.gov/prevalencestudy.pdf.

4.   J. W. Welte, Wieczorek, W. F., Barnes, G. M, Tidwell, M. C., and Hoffman, J. H., *The relationship of ecological and geographic factors to gambling behavior and pathology,* (2003), 4.

5.   National Gambling Impact Commission, *National Gambling Impact Study Commission final report* (Washington, DC, 1999), 1.

6.   Barna Group, Morality continues to decay, *The Barna Update* (3 November, 2003), available from <http://www.barna.org/FlexPage.aspx?Page=BarnaUpdate&BarnaUpdateID=152>.

7.   <http://www.istoppedgambling.com/view1gambler.htm>.

8.   R.B. Breen, and Zimmerman, M., Rapid onset of pathological gambling in machine gamblers, *Department of Psychiatry and Human Behavior, Brown University School of Medicine,* (2000), 1.

9.   <http://www.gamblersanonymous.org/20questions.html>.

10.  <http://www.gamblinghelper.com/staticpages/index.php?page=south-oaks

11.  <http://www.npgaw.org/pdfs/PDF4.pdf>.

12.  American Psychiatric Association, *Diagnostic and statistical manual of mental disorders* 4th ed. (Washington, DC: APA, 1994), 672.

13.  <http://www.motherjones.com/news/feature/2000/05/shopaholic.html>.

# 15

# Eating Disorders

*Linda S. Mintle*

Whatever you eat or drink, or whatever you do, do it all to the glory of God.

1 CORINTHIANS 10:31

One of the guiding lights of modern life is that "you can't be too thin or too rich." Whether or not you agree with the cultural values expressed in this phrase, it is undeniable that a vulnerable sub-population of America lives literally by these words. We pass on the greedy and money-obsessed herein to concentrate on the other group of focus: those whose lives are controlled by how and what and when and why they eat.

Millions of Americans live on a permanent cycle of dieting—now a multibillion dollar industry.[1] America is increasingly obsessed with physical culture, with looking good, good health, being thin, being fit, being and functioning at all times at peak levels. This growing obsessiveness drives millions to shape their daily lives around time-consuming regimens of dieting, exercise, muscle toning, cosmetics, plastic surgery, sports competition, and sweat-producing activity of every kind imaginable.

At the same time, tens of millions of Americans are so fat that obesity has recently been tagged a national health problem, affecting one-third of the children, youth, adults, and elderly of the nation—nearly 100 million people![2] We are a nation that has embraced self-indulgence over self-discipline, and now eat for taste and pleasure rather than for sustenance and health. A multibillion dollar culture of fast food, fried food, and junk food has created millions of "couch potatoes" who neither exercise nor control their eating habits in any meaningful way.

While a case may be made that these many millions are beset with eating disorders of myriad types and styles, embedded within this large mass of humanity is our target group of concern—those with truly life-threatening eating disorders. The anorexic, the bulimic, and the severely obese persons suffer uniquely, with psychological, spiritual, familial, and medical problems all converging in a potentially deadly mix of issues that requires a concerted wisdom to help untangle and resolve.

### Identifying the Eating Disorders

The psychiatric eating disorders are considered a major public health problem and have the highest morbidity and mortality rates among the psychiatric disorders. Contrary to popular opinion, eating disorder clients are not helped by messages to "just eat" or "get control." Their disorders are serious, even life-threatening, but they are treatable and require careful intervention.

The three types of classified eating disorders from the DSM-IV include anorexia nervosa, bulimia nervosa, and eating disorders not otherwise specified (ED-NOS).[3] The DSM-IV criteria for diagnosing each disorder are indicated in tables 15.1 and 15.2.

Clients diagnosed with anorexia self-starve and may reduce their weight through purging. Purging by vomiting, excessively exercising, using laxatives, diuretics, enemas, or other weight control methods creates more physical damage to the emaciated body than food restricting alone.

An anorexic client may wear baggy clothes to cover her body form. Food may be cut up and moved around the plate to give an illusion of eating. Eating in front of others is often avoided. Food choices are limited, with food categorized as "good" or "bad." Repeated daily weigh-ins are common. The fear of weight gain is beyond reasonable and motivates one to dangerously low weights.

Medical complications often include but are not limited to primary or

**TABLE 15.1:**

**ANOREXIA NERVOSA (307.1)**

A. Refusal to maintain body weight at or above a minimally normal weight for age and height (e.g., weight loss leading to maintenance of body weight less than 85% of that expected; or failure to make expected weight gain during period of growth, leading to body weight less than 85% of that expected.
B. Intense fear of gaining weight or becoming fat, even though underweight.
C. Disturbance in the way in which one's body weight or shape is experienced, undue influence of body weight or shape on self-evaluation, or denial of the seriousness of the current low body weight.
D. In postmenarcheal females, amenorrhea, or the absence of at least three consecutive menstrual cycles. (A woman is considered to have amenorrhea if her periods occur only following hormone, e.g., estrogen administration.)

*Specify* subtype:

**Restrictive Type:** during the current episode of Anorexia Nervosa, the person has not regularly engaged in binge-eating or purging behavior (i.e., self-induced vomiting or the misuse of laxatives, diuretics, or enemas).

**Binge-Eating /Purging Type:** during the current episode of Anorexia Nervosa, the person has regularly engaged in binge-eating or purging behavior (i.e., self-induced vomiting or the misuse of laxatives, diuretics, or enemas).

secondary amenorrhea, sexual disinterest or dysfunction, failure of normal breast development in prepubertal females, fetal risk for lower birth rate with active anorexia in pregnancy, dehydration, possible fertility problems even after weight is restored, osteoporosis, GI complications, constipation, abdominal pain, EEG abnormalities, sinus bradycardia, electrolyte disturbances, decrease in muscle mass, MVP, congestive heart failure in aggressive refeeding, cardiac causes of sudden death, anemia, leukopenia and thrombocytopenia, lanugo, and hand calluses from vomiting.

Bulimia usually begins in adolescence and is related to intense feelings of being out of control. While food is the substance used to numb out emotional pain and difficulty, underlying issues must be faced. Food is often

**TABLE 15.2**

**BULIMIA NERVOSA (307.51)**

A. Recurrent episodes of binge eating. An episode of binge eating is characterized by both of the following:

    (1) eating, in a discrete period of time (e.g., within any 2-hour period), an amount of food that is definitely larger than most people would eat during a similar period of time and under similar circumstances

    (2) a sense of lack of control over eating during the episode (e.g., a feeling that one cannot stop eating or control what or how much one is eating)

B. Recurrent inappropriate compensatory behavior in order to prevent weight gain, such as self-induced vomiting; misuse of laxatives, diuretics, enemas, or other medications; fasting; or excessive exercise

C. The binge eating and inappropriate compensatory behaviors both occur, on average, at least twice a week for 3 months

D. Self-evaluation is unduly influenced by body shape and weight.

E. The disturbance does not occur exclusively during episodes of Anorexia Nervosa.

#### *Specify* type:

**Purging type:** during the current episode of Bulimia Nervosa, the person has regularly engaged in self-induced vomiting or the misuse of laxatives, diuretics, or enemas.

**Nonpurging type:** during the current episode of Bulimia Nervosa, the person has used other inappropriate compensatory behaviors, such as fasting or excessive exercise, but has not regularly engaged in self-induced vomiting or the misuse of laxatives, diuretics, or enemas.

used as the coping mechanism for anger, anxiety, depression, and stress related to many areas of life. The shame and guilt that accompanies bingeing is relieved through the act of purging. This cycle of shame then relief lends itself to secrecy. It is not uncommon for family members or spouses to be unaware that the client is engaging in bulimic behavior.

Bulimia is not always observable. Weight can be normal because of the compensatory mechanism of purging that stabilizes possible weight gain from bingeing. Weight gain is feared and body dissatisfaction is high.

Medical complications can include but are not limited to: dehydration, hypochloremia, hyperkalemia, pulmonary symptoms associated with vomiting, erosion of dental enamel, salivary gland hypotrophy, pancreatitus, esophagitis and perforation, gastric dilatation, reflex constipation, idiopathic edema, EKG abnormalities, MVP, dry skin, finger and hand abrasions, abnormal EEG, endocrine and metabolic abnormalities.

### Eating Disorder Not Otherwise Specified (307.50)

According to the DSM-IV, this category is reserved for "disorders of eating that do not meet the criteria for any specific Eating Disorder."[4] Six examples are given and include clients who

1. have anorexic symptoms but are menstruating,
2. self-starvers with a weight loss less than 15% of ideal body weight,
3. binge eaters who binge less often than the determined criteria,
4. those who purge after eating small amounts of food,
5. not swallowing but chewing and spitting out food, and
6. those who binge eat but do not purge.

*Binge eating disorder.* It is this last subclinical category—binge eating disorder—that accounts for a large proportion of clients who enter treatment. Research criteria for this disorder are found on p. 731 of the DSM-IV.

The major difference with bulimia nervosa is that these clients do not purge their bodies of excess calories by vomiting, laxative abuse, diuretics, etc. They gain weight and basically engage in a form of compulsive eating.

Binge eaters present with more depression, anxiety and other psychological disturbances when compared to people with similar weight problems. It is estimated that 30% of people who participate in hospital-based weight programs; 10–15% of participants in nonmedical diet programs; 4% of college students; and 2% of people in the general population may be defined as binge eaters.[5]

Binge eating has serious emotional and physical side effects. The constant battle with feeling out-of-control often leads to feelings of self-disgust, low self-worth and self-esteem. Overweight or obesity can bring social bias, discrimination and prejudice, as well as body image problems. Dieting leads to a yo-yo cycle of weight loss and gain that takes a physical toll on the body.

Binge eaters may suffer medical risk similar to obesity—diabetes (Type II, or adult onset), hypertension, stroke, dyslipidemia, cardiovascular disease, gallbladder disease, respiratory disease, cancer, arthritis and gout.

## Etiology of Eating Disorders

Eating is a behavior of complex influence. Researchers continue to study why some people move from occasional struggles with food and weight to preoccupation and obsession. What causes a 16-year-old to jeopardize her health by repeated laxative abuse? What makes an honor student starve herself to the point of serious metabolic imbalance? What motivates a young adult to think only of her next binge?

Eating disorders are primarily of psychological and spiritual origin even though they have physical complications and may be influenced by genetic/biological factors. There is no one single cause but rather a host of variables that may contribute to onset. The combination of multiple influences and vulnerability to those influences over time, can lead to development of a disorder.

Clinical presentation involves abnormal eating patterns that include self-starvation, compulsive eating, or compulsive eating and self-induced purging. While dieting and weight focus may be an obvious entrée to an eating disorder, there is more to consider. All three patterns share in common certain symptoms: intense fear of gaining weight, excessive preoccupation with food and eating, chronic dieting, poor body image, depression and the need for approval by others.

## Age, Gender, Race and Ethnicity

Development of eating disorders favors females more so than males. The ratio for anorexia and bulimia is approximately one male to ten females in community based epidemiology studies. This ratio also holds true in larger clinical-based studies. Binge eating disorder claims a higher percentage (35%) of males, with the overall rate of eating disorders increasing in males.[6]

Males who develop eating disorders are influenced by a culture that promotes a fit and buffed body as a sign of masculinity and success. Body shape versus weight is more the concern of men. Exercise, as opposed to dieting, is often the entrée into symptom development. Dieting plays a role related to playing sports, past obesity, gender identity conflicts, and avoidance of feared medical illness.

Anorexia is estimated to affect 0.5% to 3.7% of females in their lifetime; bulimia will affect 1.1% to 4.2% of females;[7] and binge eating in a six-month period will be experienced by 2–5% of both genders.[8] Approximately half of all Americans are overweight, with one-third falling into the category of obese (usually measured by at least 20% over ideal body weight).[9]

In the past, eating disorders were most prevalent among higher socioeconomic Caucasian groups. Now they cut across all classes, races and ethnicities. No longer relegated to the Western world, eating disorders have appeared in remote places like the Fiji Islands. What was once only a concern of the Western world has taken on global significance.

No other psychiatric disorder has higher morbidity or mortality rates. The mortality rate for people with anorexia is 0.56% per year. This rate is 12 times higher than the annual death rate due to all causes of death among females ages 15–24 in the general population.[10] Generally, about one-third of eating disorders fully recover; one third recovers with periodic problems; and one-third remains chronically ill.[11]

## Family and Life Cycle Development

The clinician should identify the client's life and family developmental stage. Typically, these disorders emerge at transition to puberty and launching from the family home. Adolescence is also a developmental hot bed for onset because it is a time of identity formation and definition. Anorexia not only keeps a client childlike in physical appearance but also retards the normal development of separation and individuation.[12]

Dating, sexuality, gender identity and assertion of the forming self are put on hold for pursuit of a false identity that becomes enslaving, but protective. Progressive growth toward independence is expected but frightening given the challenges faced by the culture, family, interpersonal relationships and self-expectations. Anorexic symptoms may represent a failed attempt to separate and individuate.

Bulimia usually develops later in adolescence and young adulthood related to similar developmental transitions. A crisis time for many is the launching phase from family to independent functioning outside the family system. Bulimia can signify difficulty making this transition. Bulimics tend to approach life from an all or nothing mind set, thus mimicking the binge-purge cycle of their symptoms.

It should be noted that failure to discover a spiritual identity in Christ is also lacking with these clients. Often they have distorted views of God the Father and are unaware of accurate biblical descriptions of who they are in relationship to God and others.

## Cultural Influences

Cultural influences, particularly attitudes about weight and the feminine ideal, play a role in the development of eating disorders. Women are expected to be thin and attractive, men to be buffed and in shape. Media vilify overweight people and convince girls early on that they need to be thin to be successful or accepted.

Other cultural influencers include the food, diet, fashion, beauty and health industries. All dangle the "thin" carrot promising a life of happiness and love through attainment of the perfect body. This message stands in stark contrast to the words of Jesus. He looks on the heart, prioritizing the building of inner character conformed to His image. To be like Him is often counter to the message promulgated by our culture.

## Personality Factors

Those who develop eating disorders often have difficulty coping with stress. Other problem areas include dealing with conflict, appropriately asserting the self, negative thinking and holding unrealistic expectations.

Studies link avoidant personalities with anorexia, citing the tendency towards perfectionism and emotional and sexual inhibition as characteristic. Other studies on bulimia have found connections between borderline and narcissistic personalities, hallmarked by impulsivity, unstable mood, thoughts, behavior and self-image. Chaos is a chronic state. Hypersensitivity to criticism along with an inability to sooth the self or empathize with others describes many bulimics.[13]

## Comorbid Disorders

In many cases, eating disorders coexist with other psychiatric disorders. Most frequently noted are depression, anxiety, obsessive-compulsive disorder, post-traumatic stress disorder, personality disorders (as noted above) and occasionally psychotic disorders. Eating disorders also correlate highly with sexual abuse and bulimics have high rates of substance abuse.[14]

Mood, thinking, concentration and behavior are all affected by starvation and should be assessed as they relate to the eating disorder. The same is true for other medical conditions that may mimic eating disorder symptoms.

## Assessment of Eating Disorders

Assessment—which is, in fact, the beginning of intervention—includes a structured interview with the client and the family; a complete physical to rule out medical causes and assess the client's physiological state related to the disorder; and nutritional work-up to determine eating habits, calorie intake, refeeding strategy and food choices. In addition, self-report measures may be used to help assess severity of the disorder and treatment progress. Commonly used surveys are the EAT,[15] the EDI—2[16], and the BULIT—R,[17] a reliable measure of the severity of bulimia nervosa.

The eating disorder evaluation should cover presenting problem, history of presenting problem, height, weight, dieting efforts, weight history, frequency and type of binges and purges, substance abuse or use, exercise behavior, weight phobia, past psychiatric history, mental status, medical complaints and history (including amenhorrea), and family history of functioning and psychiatric disorders, losses, changes, and stressors. During evaluation, particular attention should be paid to the psychosocial barriers to treatment, with reducing them an implicit goal even at this stage. Diagnosis of co-morbid conditions also should be made at this time.

### Assess Family and Interpersonal Influences

Negative family patterns influence the development and/or maintenance of eating symptoms. Parental and sibling behavior and attitudes towards dieting and appearance are frequently mentioned as negative. The level of enmeshment or detachment among family members plays a role and should be evaluated. Marital distress, substance abuse and sexual abuse should be areas of investigation.

Anorexic families tend to be more rigid and have less clear interpersonal boundaries. Disagreement between members rarely surfaces because of the premium placed on family consensus. In an attempt to appear adequate and respectable, families often hide their indirect communication, chronic unhappiness, fear of their daughters' emerging sexuality, and preoccupation with their own looks and dieting. The family typically tries to please the therapist and appear socially desirable. An ideal view of family life is often purported. Under the surface may lurk parental conflict, need, anger and stress.

Bulimic families tend to be more unstable in their organization. It often appears that parents are somewhat neglectful or hostile in parenting, with the bulimic daughter angrily submitting to their authority. Mothers of bulimic daughters are commonly described as "neglectful" and fathers as "affectionless." Criticism toward the child is higher than in anorexic families.[18]

In both family systems, joint parental authority is questionable. Parents often struggle with giving their child age-appropriate autonomy or reasonable control. Child-rearing differences may be a function of lack of agreement or distress in the marital subsystem.

### Do Genetics and Biology Play a Role?

At present, researchers are investigating the role genetics and biology play in the transmission of eating disorders. Eating disorders run in families with anorexics having an eight times higher chance of developing the disorder if a relative has it.[19]

### Peg a Target Weight

Important to the initial evaluation is establishing an ideal and target weight to be used throughout treatment. *Ideal weight* is usually determined by locating numbers on the most recent insurance charts that provide weight ranges by height and body frame. Body mass index (BMI) is a more accurate measure of body fatness but few clinicians can work easily with this index.

A *target weight* (the lowest safe weight acceptable for treatment) is calculated by taking 90% of the midpoint of the ideal range. It is best to have agreement on the target weight with the physician and dietitian because clients regularly try to negotiate this number. Calculate the target weight, talk to the client and team and make the number nonnegotiable.

To estimate the client's percentage of weight below ideal, divide the client's current weight by the ideal midpoint (It helps to have a doctor's scale or access to one in order to weigh the client.). For example, a client is 5'6" tall, weighs 110 pounds. According to the insurance table, her ideal range is 128–143. The midpoint of that number is 135.5.

Divide her current weight (110) by the midpoint (135) to obtain a percentage of her weight against her ideal. In this example, the percentage is 81. Then subtract that percentage from 100 and you have the percent below ideal weight to use for diagnosis (DSM-IV criteria for anorexia is 15% or more below expected body weight). This client is 19% below ideal and meets clinical criteria.

### Define the Level of Care

Two important questions should be asked prior to determining level of care:

1. How chronic are the symptoms? Generally, the longer an eating disorder is untreated, the more difficult it is to remit.
2. How severe are the symptoms? Hospitalization or residential services should be seriously considered when clients are suicidal or psychotic, have very low weight, refeeding must be supervised, purging is excessive, there is repeated outpatient failure and/or immediate medical danger (e.g., severe electrolyte imbalance).

### Reduce Barriers to Treatment

This population is especially difficult to treat because of numerous psychological and physical barriers. Barriers to successful treatment that should be assessed include:

1. Labeling these disorders as acts of will and self-control. Clients and family members often believe they should be able to *will* themselves out of these disorders and take control. Usually there is little to no understanding of the emotional, spiritual and interpersonal complexities involved in healing.
2. Denial. Clients usually have distorted body images. They often deny the level of self-harm they inflict. A low weight anorexic

truly sees herself as fat no matter what people say to her. This deception allows her to continue self-harm. Spiritually, denial and deception are married in an unholy union that leaves the client paralyzed to move out of this bondage. Past hurts and woundings are gateways for deceptive thinking to enter the mind. Denial serves a secondary gain function to push away painful feelings and experiences. Pain is redirected to the body through false control of food.

3. Idols in the form of food and restraint. Food is less about sustenance and more about preoccupation and obsession. When a client loses weight, she is often complimented. After significant weight loss, worry replaces compliments. The client begins to idolize the pursuit of thinness. Food restriction feels self-righteous and is often described as a desired "high." Food claims the client's loyalty. What began as a method of control, ends as idol worship. "The thinner I am, the better I am. Denial of the self brings suffering that elevates me above others."

4. Minimizing the problem. Many clients delay treatment because they hope the eating disorder will resolve itself with time. The eating disorder may be reframed as "a phase," "a fad" or "experimentation."

5. Shame and guilt. It is very unpleasant to admit to bingeing and then vomiting. Secrecy and shame surround these disorders and often block cries for help.

6. Pride. It is difficult to admit to a therapist and to God that you are out-of-control and need outside help. Pride prevents clients from laying down the self-sufficiency gauntlet and depending on God.

7. Lack of faith. To trust someone to help you requires an act of faith. When a client is bound by an eating disorder there is no evidence of eating returning to normal. Preoccupation and obsession take hold. Freedom is unseen but hoped for. Faith requires a client to say, "I see no way out of my bondage, but I will trust the therapist, and more importantly God, to help me be free."

8. Fear of treatment. Freedom means giving up a false identity and doing the hard work to create whom you were intended to be. It means facing pain, emptiness and hurt. It means discomfort, struggle and reorganization.

9. Financial barriers. Unfortunately, eating disorders treatment can be expensive. Lack of health insurance coverage, high hospital and program costs prevent many from accessing or continuing care.

10. Access: Available programs and specialty therapists. There may be few to no eating disorder programs or therapists available in a community. Shorter hospital stays, combined with rigid admission criteria, may prevent many from getting needed services. In addition, managed care policies limit visits, services, and choice of providers. Treatment options may be limited to availability of affordable services.

## Treatment: A Multidisciplinary and Multifaceted Approach

The therapist assesses a client's clinical picture and knows when to act. Care giving for this population requires participation with a multidisciplinary team of professionals, all playing an important role in the transformation and healing of the client.

## Assembling the Multidisciplinary Team

The multidisciplinary team should include the following:

1. A psychiatrist (MD). A complete physical is highly recommended for all clients entering treatment and becomes part of the three-pronged assessment process (see Assessment). The use of medication is a treatment decision made collaboratively by the therapist, the psychiatrist and the client. Not all eating disorder clients need medication. And in many cases, medications may be counter indicated. However, when appropriate, particularly when comorbid conditions exist, a psychiatrist or knowledgeable physician prescribes these medications as therapy adjuncts.

2. Other medical doctors (MD). A working relationship with an internist, endocrinologist, family practitioner, or in the case of younger children, a pediatrician is essential. The MD follows the client's physical condition and offers baseline and ongoing monitoring of physical status (e.g., electrolyte imbalance, weight gain, gastric distress, amenhorrea, etc.). It is important to find a

physician who is empathetic to eating disorder clients and
understands his/her role on the team.

3.  An individual therapist. This person should be trained in the specialty practice of eating disorders so that cognitive and behavioral
connections with eating and weight issues can be directly linked
to underlying problems. The individual therapist works with the
client to address those personal issues leading to symptomatic eating behavior and monitors progress towards healing.

4.  A family therapist. The family therapist works with the individual
in the context of his/her intimate relationships and family. Families influence the development and maintenance of eating disorders and are an integral part of treatment. Generally, the younger
the client, the more essential it is to have the family directly participate in treatment.

5.  A group therapist. Eating disorder clients can benefit from group
work whether it is supportive, psychoeducational or interperson-
ally focused. Group needs to be a safe place to share struggles
with fellow sojourners. It can be an adjunct to therapy or a hot bed
for dealing with dynamics in interpersonal functioning. Group
work is particularly meaningful for college students and young
adults living away from their families because it provides a therapeutic arena for interpersonal work.

6.  A registered dietitian (RD). The RD completes an evaluation of
eating habits, food choices and caloric intake. He/she then works
with the client to develop healthy eating patterns and food
choices. Often this requires the client to keep a food journal. If
weight gain is needed, the RD, along with the physician, directs
that path. If weight loss is an appropriate goal, the RD sets a sensi-
ble course based on healthy eating. The client's frequency of RD
visits depends on treatment goals, weight and/or the client's need
for on-going food supervision and accountability.

7.  An exercise physiologist. This person provides input regarding exercise. Very low weight patients may need to stop exercise and temporarily be placed on bed rest during refeeding. An exercise
physiologist can instruct the client how to safely add exercise into a
daily living plan. Since exercise is often an area of obsession and
excess, regulating the amount and intensity may be a treatment goal.

8. Supervision and peer consultation. The seriousness of symptoms, the power of denial and resistance, a therapist's own biases and tendency to be inducted into the family system are all reasons to have access to supervision and peer consultation.

## Treatment Planning

Post evaluation, you should develop a working plan with the client and establish a workable treatment plan. The plan should include recommendations for intervention from the physician and dietitian, input from the exercise physiologist, psychiatric follow up for medication if needed, a target and ideal weight goal, level of care (inpatient, outpatient, day treatment, etc.), modalities of treatment (individual, family and/or group therapy, adjunctive therapies and supports), collaborative goals, and estimated length and frequency of treatment.

## Treatment Goals

Treatment goals would include but should not be limited to:

1. attaining and maintaining a healthy weight
2. restoration/establishment of healthy eating habits
3. treatment and stabilization of comorbid conditions
4. behavioral and cognitive changes regarding eating, food and weight
5. affect regulation—maintaining a stable mood and learning how to regulate mood without resort to destructive behaviors
6. increased acceptance of self and body
7. reducing drives toward perfectionism, control, and distorted (fat) perceptions of self and body
8. clearer sense of identity—especially attaining a new and deeper sense of one's identity in Christ
9. family changes that support separation-individuation, launching and independent functioning
10. relapse prevention (and what to do if one relapses)
11. reintegration into family, school, and peer groups

## The Role of Individual Therapy

The individual therapist is usually the point of contact for the client. The individual therapist manages the patient's care like a quarterback leads the team. It is important for him/her to understand the life-threatening nature of these disorders. Treatment is usually intense and prolonged. The therapist must be able to manage his/her countertransference and be genuinely caring and empathetic.

The therapist should be knowledgeable concerning the connection of eating with psychological issues, be truthful about treatment plans and tolerate hopelessness from the client. An ability to be firm, yet loving, consistent and challenging, and have a sense of humor helps. The work is often slow but rewarding.

It is helpful for the therapist to be at a healthy weight and have resolved any issues concerning his/her weight and body image. A vibrant Christian life and spiritual passion fuels the work as well. Emotional, spiritual and interpersonal issues are played out through the arena of food and weight preoccupation. The most effective models of individual therapy use a cognitive-behavioral or interpersonal therapy approach.[20]

*Challenges to identity, denial, and faith.* Individual therapy challenges the client to relinquish the false identity of the eating disorder. Preoccupation and obsession with food and weight distracts from individual development. Letting go of symptoms may be desired, but frightening. The client must face what feels like an overwhelming world without her false sense of security. This is why change is so powerfully resisted.

Individual therapy must also address eating symptoms, i.e., decreasing the binge/purge cycle and food restriction. Denial of the severity and power of symptoms creates resistance. Surrender requires an act of faith. The client must choose to uncover underlying symptoms and have the courage to make change. Trust in the therapist is needed. Since other people are perceived as a mistrustful, trust is not quickly established. It is an act of faith to relinquish control and trust.

Repentance is also required in that the client, through spiritual pride, has concluded, "I must handle life on my own. I cannot trust God nor will I be dependent on Him. I must take control." This position, born out of pain, confronts the reality that control is elusive. A cycle ensues—pain and failure followed by attempts to seize control (through the food), followed by loss of control that leads to pain and failure.

The client must understand that to be whole and function with a sound mind is not accomplished by perfection or success, but by allowing God to work through her for His glory. He will direct her path if she is willing to be led. He unconditionally accepts her. Walking down this unseen and unfamiliar path requires faith.

The eating disordered person lives by some powerful lies about God and self. These must be exposed and the truth learned and recited and practiced on a daily, even hourly basis. Dependence on God is not weakness. God, unlike people, does not disappoint. Belief in self-sufficiency ends in continual striving. Anorexia is a misguided attempt to be self-sufficient; bulimia utilizes self-striving in an effort to gain control.

## Symptom Tracking

The therapist helps the client connect eating symptoms with underlying psychological issues and directs her towards health. Underlying issues have to do with separation/individuation from family of origin, facing developmental tasks such as dating, budding sexuality, and launching from the home, finding identity through Christ, correcting distorted views of self, identifying and appropriately expressing emotion, working though personal experiences such as sexual abuse, substance abuse or other losses and trauma, tackling perfectionism and dichotomous thinking, learning to be less hypersensitive to criticism, identifying fears of intimacy and closeness, confronting conflict, learning to problem-solve and becoming appropriately assertive. Overall, the therapist helps empower the client to discover and be her authentic self.

A simple tracking chart can be used to help clients connect symptoms to situations, emotions and thoughts. Consider using the Dysfunctional Thought Record (DTR) to track key behavior, emotions, and thinking.[21]

Once the client begins tracking her eating behavior, she can identify patterns with situations, emotions or thoughts that trigger symptomatic behavior. Intervention can focus on changing the situation (antecedent or consequence), working through the emotion and developing better coping skills. The DTR is useful not only for correcting dysfunctional thoughts in the process of renewing the mind, but for finding positive thoughts and situations that can be reinforced and encouraged (such as the last interaction noted above).

## DYSFUNCTIONAL THOUGHT RECORD

Basically, the client keeps a record under three columns—Situation (a brief description of what was happening when the eating behavior occurred), Emotion(s) (What did the client feel? On a scale from 0–100, how strong was the feeling?), Automatic Thought(s) (What was the thought that ran through the client's head? On a scale from 0–100, how strongly did the client believe the thought?). Adding a fourth column entitled "Behavior" is used to record a binge, purge or food restriction. The client lists the eating behavior under the first column "Behavior", then the "Situation" under which it occurred, next the felt "Emotion" and it's intensity, and finally the "Automatic Thought" that ran through his/her mind, rating how strongly he/she believed it. For example:

| Behavior | Situation | Emotion | Automatic Thought |
|----------|-----------|---------|-------------------|
| Binged/purged | Break up with boyfriend | Hurt 90% | I am unlovable (80%) |
| Food restricted | Mom telling me to eat | Angry (40%) | I am not a child (90%) |
| Looking at self in mirror | Morning habit | Discouraged (70%) | Still too fat (90%) |
| Flirting w/ boyfriend | After school | Pleased/confused | He's wrong—I can't look that good (70%) |

## Identity in Christ

Central to the work of healing is developing a strong identity based in Christ. While family, peers and culture influence who we become, it is through an understanding and experience of the one true Christ that a client is empowered to be who God intended him/her to be.

A Christ-based identity is not easily shaken and is a point of reference when facing turmoil from the stresses of life. The client must understand that God cares more about his/her character and conformity to Him than his/her outward appearance and accomplishments. Perfection is unachievable and works do not warrant God's grace.

As respected apologist Os Guinness notes, "A life lived listening to the decisive call of God is a life lived before one audience that trumps all others—the Audience of One." Twenty Scripture references such as Ephesians 1:4, Psalm 139:2 & 14, Hebrews 13:5 lay the foundation for discovery of true identity and pleasing only the "Audience of One."[22]

Thinking is often distorted leading to a negative view of the self and others. A renewing of the mind is also essential to healing. Distorted thoughts should be challenged in therapy and the client asked to generate more rational thoughts based on biblical knowledge and an enlightened view of self.

For example, the thought, "I am no good because I am not thin enough" can be challenged by asking the client to defend that position biblically and uncover fears of inadequacy. "Thin enough" is an attempt to achieve "goodness." It is a failed solution. We can never be "good enough" for God's grace. His Holy Spirit can help us accept our "good enough" status as God's creation and beloved.

## Family Therapy

Family therapy is especially needed when working with younger clients. However, it is highly recommended for treatment of all eating disorders. Typically the eating disorder client has been the caretaker of others in the family. This role preempts focus on critical self needs and development.

In general, fathers tend to be emotionally unavailable and mothers over- or under-involved. Siblings do not form a cohesive subsystem. Communication is often indirect and conflict is poorly managed. Eating and weight issues are symptomatic of these struggles.

Marital tension is usually present but unresolved. The client is often the peacemaker or apex of a marital triangle. One or both parents may confide their unhappiness, burdening the client who has no way to make repair. Client needs are usually sacrificed for family needs.

In the case of anorexic families, emotions are constricted as the family strives to give the impression of happiness and perfection. In bulimic families, problems are more clearly identified but not resolved. The eating disorder is an attempt to bring order to a chaotic system. The "identified patient" requires the family to rally around the problem, thus bringing order and solution to an out-of-order system.

Parenting is often characterized by extremes—either enmeshed and overprotective or under-involved and disconnected. Symptoms serve to help the client separate but still be cared for and nurtured.

The work of the family is to free the eating disorder client from her assumed role of solving family problems or reorganizing relationships through illness. The eating disorder is reframed as a system problem with the client responsible for symptom reduction. Stopping food restriction or bingeing and purging are reframed as responses to interpersonal and intrapersonal pain and emptiness. New responses are possible and more adaptive. The family has the choice to grow and learn new ways of nurturing each other and deal with their pain. This family context must be addressed directly with the family system or indirectly in individual therapy with a systemic therapist.

## Transformation, Not Just Recovery

As noted, about one-third of all clients with eating disorders recover. This statistic is disheartening when you consider two-thirds remain ill or chronically trying to cope. From a faith perspective, healing, through the grace and mercy of our sovereign God, is always possible. Therefore, the Christian seeks more than recovery. The desired outcome is personal transformation through the power of Jesus Christ. Everything old becomes new when surrendered to Christ.

The power of the Holy Spirit can heal and transform in ways unknown to our limited understanding. While we use all the training and knowledge extracted from research and clinical practice, we recognize the supernatural realm as greater than our comprehension. Both therapists and clients should depend on the work of the Holy Spirit to give wisdom and intervene to change lives.

There is hope for even the most desperate case because of Christ. Because of the abiding presence of God, the hope and future promised in Him, promised freedom from bondage and enslavement, and the radical message that, in Christ, past is not prologue to future, we can be transformed and set free.

"Therefore, if anyone is in Christ, he is a new creation; old things have past away; behold all things have become new." (2 Cor. 5:17)

**ENDNOTES**

1. Statistics: *How many people have eating and exercise disorders?* Available from <http://www.anred.com.
2. Statistics,<http://www.anred.com.
3. American Psychiatric Association, *Diagnostic and statistical manual of mental disor-*

*ders*, fourth ed. (Washington, D.C.: American Psychiatric Association, 1994).

4.  American Psychiatric Association, 550.

5.  J. E. Brody, Study defines "Binge Eating Disorder": Report from Dr. Robert L. Spitzer at the Annual Scientific Meeting of the Society of Behavioral Medicine, *New York Times*, (March 27, 1992), A16.

6.  A. Anderson, Eating disorders in males, in K.D. Brownell, and Fairburn, C.G. (eds.), *Eating disorders and obesity: A comprehensive handbook* (New York: The Guilford Press, 1995).

7.  American Psychiatric Association Work Group on Eating Disorders, Practical guidelines for the treatment of patients with eating disorders (rev.), *American Journal of Psychiatry* 157 (1 Suppl), (2000), 1–39.

8.  Robert Spitzer, Yanovski, S., Wadden, T., Wing, R., Marcus, M. D., Stunkard, A., Devlin, M., Mitchell, J., Hasin, D., and Horne, R. L., Binge eating disorder: Its further validation in a multisite study, *International Journal of Eating Disorders* 12, (1992), 137–53.

9.  Statistics,<http://www.anred.com.

10. P. F.Sullivan, Mortality in anorexia nervosa, *American Journal of Psychiatry* 152(7), (1995), 1073–1074.

11. M. Maine, AAMFT clinical update: Eating disorders, *A supplement to the Family Therapy News* 1 (6), (November 1999), 1.

12. W. Vandereycken, The families of patients with an eating disorder, in K.D. Brownell, and Fairburn, C.G. (eds.), *Eating disorders and obesity: A comprehensive handbook* (New York: The Guilford Press, 1995).

13. WebMD Health On-line, what are eating disorders?, Available from <http://www.webmd.com.

14. Maine, 1999

15. D. M. Garner, Garfinkle, P.E., Olmstead, M.P., and Bohr, Y., The eating attitudes test: Psychometric features and clinical correlations, *Psychological Medicine* 12, (1982), 871–878.

16. D. M. Garner, *Eating disorders inventory—2* (Odessa, FL: Psychological Assessment Resources, 1991).

17. M. H. Thelen, Farmer, J., Wonderlich, S., and Smith, M., A revision of the bulimic test: The BULIT-R. psychological assessment, *Journal of Consulting and Clinical Psychology*, 3, (1991), 119–124.

18. Vandereycken, 1995.

19. WebMD Health Online.

20. National Institute of Mental Health, *NIMH eating disorders: Facts about eating disorders and the search for solutions* (NIH Publication No. 01–4901, 2001).

21. A. T. Beck, Rush, A.J., Shaw, B.F., & Emery, G., *Cognitive therapy of depression* (New York: Guilford Press, 1979).

22. Os Guinness, *The call* (Nashville: Word, 1998).

# 16

## Suicide Intervention

*George Ohlschlager, Mark Shadoan, and Gary Stewart*[*]

> Suicide is not abominable because God prohibits it; God prohibits it because it is abominable.
>
> IMMANUEL KANT

The room was packed. It was full of experienced helpers—really, of shell-shocked and tough-minded New York counselors, pastors, and emergency workers who had been living with 9–11 and its aftermath for over a month. In 40 days they had seen, smelled, tasted, and soaked in more death than most of us will in a 40-year career. We at AACC had collected some of our best therapists and academics, grief workers, crisis interventionists, and pastors from all over the country to join us in New York City in late October 2001 and intensively train nearly 1,500 Christian leaders who were helping people deal with the death and trauma.

As I surveyed the audience I could already see the exhaustion, the beginnings of a long-term vicarious trauma in too many faces—the impact

---

[*] This chapter adapts and updates the first author's chapter on suicide from his coauthored book on *Law for the Christian Counselor* (Word Books, 1992). Additional material, on treatment process and on the attributes and orientation to God of the suicidal person, was graciously contributed by the 2nd and 3rd authors.

of 9–11 was thick and heavy among the group. Yet, at the historic Calvary Baptist Church in mid-town Manhattan, they were ready to hear me speak about "Suicidal Distress." I was going to pile death to come upon the mass death that already existed. I prayed silently for divine guidance, took a deep breath, and dove right in:

*Increased suicide and suicidal thinking is one perverse outcome—one that is fairly predictable—of the terrorist trauma of September 11 and the crisis of post-traumatic stress that is growing in New York City. This great city will likely experience a level of suicidal distress—which will include many suicidal attempts and far too many successful attempts—over the next few years unlike anything previous in its spiritual and mental health history. We can expect a rise of suicidal distress—and should target our precious intervention resource—among three groups:*

- *those directly affected—people injured and families who have lost loved ones,*
- *the heroes of 9–11—police, firemen, rescue workers, and other emergency personnel, and*
- *those vicariously affected by the September 11 terror strike who already live on a fragile edge.*

*That's the bad news. And the worst of this bad news is that the pool of at-risk people likely numbers in the tens of thousands, maybe over a hundred thousand people. The possibility of overwhelming the care and response systems of this city is significant.*

*The good news is that you—the Christian counselor armed with this foreknowledge—can be available to help pre-empt and cut-off some (and we mean just some) of this horrible and further death before it strikes those survivors who will lose hope of living. And among those who succeed in the terrible tragedy of self-murder, you will be prepared to give succor and solace to the grieving ones who loved the suicide victim.*

*The seeds of lost hope are contained in many of the stories now being told by the families who lost a loved one on that black day in New York. At the funeral of her 45 year-old son, one widowed woman carried on with her friend about how her son's coffin contained just a picture and a rock-n-roll CD he particularly enjoyed. At the end of the service, she cried and exclaimed to whoever would listen, "This can't be for my son . . . I don't even have a body! This isn't a death. It's a disintegration, an abolishment."[1]*

*Powerful words that are now spoken in shock and anger, in a state of surreal confusion. In the months and years to come, however, these same words may just as easily be spoken in despair and hopelessness, by an old woman now alone in the world and longing for death in a brutal and horrible world. This first winter after the terror there will be hundreds of fragile victims who, overcome by the evil of this mass murder, the craziness of it, the horror of it, will look upon death—will embrace a hoped-for painless suicide—as sweet release from a life that has turned ugly, painful, bitter, and meaningless. When all the help and hoopla are gone, things may even be worse.*

*If this sounds bad, it is because it is bad. There are literally tens of thousands of traumatized, struggling people who have suffered through the hardest winters of their lives over the last few years. All the more reason to pray for and call down a spiritual revival of enormous proportions. God alone can transform the evil, can make straight the crooked way, can bring life out of death and ashes and despair.*

## The Data and Dynamics of Suicide

Facing a suicidal client or parishioner is one of the most stressful—and most fearful—times in the life of a counselor or pastor. Suicide is surely one of counseling's most difficult "occupational hazards." A client or parishioner who kills themselves not only devastates family and friends, but also adversely impacts the counselor long after the event.[2] We explore this tragedy and the moral, clinical and pastoral aspects of suicide assessment and intervention in this chapter.

Friedrich Nietzsche, the famous 19th-century German philosopher, asserted in *Beyond Good and Evil* that "The thought of suicide is a great consolation; with the help of it one gets successfully through many a bad night." This statement reveals a number of reasons why suicide is such a paradox; why it has a complex and controversial history in America and Western culture. Suicidal thinking in time of crisis is fairly common, even attractive to the desperate, yet there exists great fear and a seemingly cultural taboo that bars open acknowledgment of its attraction and familiarity.

This strange attraction, the tragic choice of death over life, is what so greatly confounds us and strikes us with fear. It makes no sense to the well-living how suicide could be such "great consolation." To the person who has lost all hope of relieving intense and unending pain, whether physical or psychological, suicide can easily become an obsessive consolation, a final solution when nothing else beckons.

In the distorted and pain-dominated judgment of the sufferer, suicide may be the most logical and effective choice to resolve what is perceived as an impossible problem. And for family and friends left behind, it is a shocking trauma that leaves scars that can take a lifetime to heal. The gripping story of her son's suicide by Corrine Chilstrom, a pastoral consultant in the Evangelical Lutheran Church of America, reveals the unique tragedy of suicide.

As a pastor and mother, I have witnessed the tragic death of my youngest son by suicide...Eighteen, a freshman in college, [Andrew] was home for the weekend when he died of a self-inflicted wound to his head...It happened about 3 A.M...Sleeping in our bedroom, buffered from the sound...we slept through the shot which would forever change our lives.

It was our Sunday off. We had planned a leisurely breakfast, worship with Andrew, brunch at a restaurant...Those well-made plans suddenly turned into chaos, finding his room empty, lights and TV on, and his note by the phone...his words grabbed us with panic. We rushed to the basement...

Herb was first to the landing. As if he had been grabbed, he stopped short, gasping, "Oh, my God!" White as a sheet, he held me back, saying, "Don't look." All I saw was Andrew's legs. Favorite old khaki pants and black high top canvas shoes.

There are no words to describe the fright of finding him. Or the stumbling up the stairs. Or the frenzy to make those first calls for help. Or what followed. Police. Coroner. Sisters and friends coming on the run. Getting our children home. Crying with his friends. Choosing a casket. Facing the fact of family suicide. Missing him. Wanting him. Becoming suicide survivors.[3]

We must pull back, however, and not let an empathy that helps us understand the suicidal mind push us to accept suicide as a right to be exercised by all those wishing it. Ideas have consequences; good ones have good consequences and bad ones have bad consequences. One bad idea, increasingly prevalent in our day, is that suicide is acceptable in all its forms (self-murder, euthanasia, physician-assisted). The euthanasia movement that asserts a "right to die" and to assist those wanting to die is a growing and powerful assault against our moral and legal prohibition that forbids suicide assistance.

Suicide has pushed its way into the eighth leading cause of death in the United States—tragically, it is the third leading cause of death among teenagers. Approximately 3/4 million suicide attempts take place in America every year—over 2,000 people attempt to kill themselves every day, and 85 of these succeed; 31,000 die every year, or about 4% of those who make attempts.[4] Roughly 40% of these deaths are by persons over 65 years of age, most suffering in pain from terminal and debilitating disease. A quarter of all suicides are by young people between the age of 15 and 24, a three-fold increase in the rate of suicide within this age group in a quarter-century.

The dynamics of suicide are highly complex; simplistic reasons to explain it and easy solutions to prevent it are nonexistent. It is not just a matter of acute and severe depression, although the National Institute of Mental Health considers depression the leading cause. It requires more than restraining or avoiding lethal behavior, although individuals must act aggressively to kill themselves. Though options always exist, the suicidal person is overcome by constricting choices, sabotaged by a perverse tunnel-vision that survivors often express as, "It became *the only thing left* to do."

Finally, it is not just a problem of meaningless and existential despair, although Aaron Beck and his colleagues[5] have shown that hopelessness is even more influential than depression in completed suicides. A pastor and Christian psychologist cogently argue that "suicide is primarily, although not entirely, a spiritual problem. Persons who are suicidal are asking, either explicitly or implicitly, such critical existential questions as: Does my life have meaning or purpose? Do I have any worth? Is forgiveness possible? Is there any hope for a new life beyond this current mess?"[6]

## We Are All Vulnerable

Under certain circumstances, most of us can be tempted to opt for "deadly peace" at the expense of life itself. Whether we are speaking of self-execution in our formidable years or assisted suicide because of the ravages of disease at the end of our life, it is essential that each of us realize our own vulnerability to suicide when the pressures of persistent physical, intellectual, emotional and, yes, even spiritual weakness mount and threaten us.

We would do well to heed the warning of the apostle Peter, "Be of sober spirit, be on the alert. Your adversary, the devil, prowls about like a roaring lion, seeking someone to devour. But resist him, firm in your faith, . . ." (1 Pet. 5:8–9a). However we struggle with the adversary's destructive efforts against us, or our family, our church and community, each of us must keep vigil over our lives to ensure that the normal chaos and assaults we all face are consistently and regularly resolved. Normal pressures that go unresolved gradually mount, one upon the other, eventually threatening potentially lethal responses.

Sometimes difficulties come so rapidly or require such long-term attention, that immediate or timely resolve is impossible. In these circumstances, we can become so mentally and emotionally burdened that our vulnerability to self-diminishing and destructive thoughts is considerably heightened. We can entertain risks that under normal circumstances would never cross our minds. In a sense, we are exactly where our adversary wants us—where our sinful disposition must not remain. So the struggle against suicide in our society must begin with the safeguarding of our own soul.

### Embracing a Biblical Worldview: The Culture of Life

Everyone has a worldview—Christian and non-Christian alike. Christianity proclaims the certainty of truth, the sufficiency of Scripture, and the sacredness of life. The Christian worldview applies just as much to our emotional trials in life as to our intellectual ones, asserts the truth in the public sphere as well as sacredness in our private lives. It touches every area of life. In *The Universe Next Door*, James Sire reminds us that our theistic Christian worldview encompasses much more than intellectual assent.

To accept Christian theism only as an intellectual construct is not to accept it fully. There is a deeply personal dimension involved with grasping and living within this worldview, for it involves acknowledging our own individual dependence on God as His creatures, our own individual rebellion against God and our own individual reliance on God for restoration to fellowship with Him. And it means accepting Christ as both our Liberator from bondage and Lord of our future. To be a Christian theist is not just to have an intellectual worldview; it is to be personally committed to the infinite-personal Lord of the Universe. And it leads to an examined life that is well worth living.[7]

For the Christian it is not enough, in this encroaching 21st-century culture of death, to rest upon the security of a Christian worldview. The Christian must also apply one's worldview and cling to it during the crises of life. Through God's grace, the application of Scripture, and fervent prayer, the worldview of the Christian gives indispensable direction and protects individuals from deadly, detrimental and debilitating thoughts and emotions.

It is a constant challenge to maintain a biblical worldview in a contemporary society slipping from the moorings of truth and the God of the Bible, adrift in an ocean of God-rejecting relativism and self-indulgence. In the free-fall of chaotic emotions that push suicidal ideation, one's worldview is a critical safety net. Our belief system provides not only theological and philosophical security, but psychological safety as well. Our worldview affects how we think about life and death, and what we do about it. A Christian worldview, biblically grounded and consistently applied, will generate valid theological conclusions and assist personal resolution to these issues.

The relevance of Christianity to every area of life cannot be discarded. When faith and religious principles are abandoned, we should not be surprised that Dr. Jack Kevorkian advocates the goodness of "planned death."[8] He understands that in order for this to be accepted in "our modern world, medicine and religion should be completely divorced from one another."[9] Our present culture is coming to a radically different view of humanity. Having jettisoned God, the biblical perspective of humanity as created and sacred is now also being cast away. As Robert Bork ominously noted, "Convenience is becoming the theme of our culture. Humans tend to be inconvenient at both ends of their lives."[10]

## Suicide and a Biblical Worldview

A consistent biblical worldview is relevant to every aspect of suicide in our present culture. Only when we fully embrace the biblical worldview, with all of its ramifications, will we be able to adequately respond to the personal, social, and cultural crises of our time. Even for those who are old and dying, for the infirm, or those who feel worthless and helpless, there must still be the conviction of human dignity. Every living person is significant and worthwhile, even if all circumstances suggest the opposite.

Ultimately only a biblical perspective can accomplish and sustain this truth with any certainty or permanence. Writing of his experiences at Auschwitz, Dachau, and other Nazi death camps, physician Viktor Frankl commented frequently on suicide and its rejection even in the midst of unspeakable personal horror. He tells of talking to fellow prisoners on one occasion after food had been taken away from them.[11]

> Then I spoke of the many opportunities of giving life a meaning. I told my comrades (who lay motionless, although occasionally a sigh could be heard) that human life, under any circumstances, never ceases to have a meaning, and that this infinite meaning of life includes suffering and dying, privation and death. I asked the poor creatures who listened to me attentively in the darkness of the hut to face up to the seriousness of our situation. They must not lose hope but keep their courage in the certainty that the hopelessness of our struggle did not detract from its dignity and its meaning.

For the Christian, then, the creation of humanity in the image of God has far-reaching personal, theological, and cultural ramifications that must be considered; among them, the rejection of suicide in all of its manifestations. As we daily face the issues of suicide in our personal, professional and public lives, we must move beyond the rhetoric, slogans, and euphemisms. In a culture of convenience and bumper-sticker ethics, we must adhere to sound doctrine and biblical perspectives.

A nominal Christian worldview—one that gives only casual attention to God and to the knowledge of "the Holy"—is weak and inconsistent. Therefore, it may not forestall a personal or cultural slide into the acceptance of suicide, and of physician-assisted suicide.

Christians must hold firmly to God and apply central doctrines to their faith. In part, it is through a love and understanding of God the Father, acceptance and devotion to the person and work of God the Son, and application and appreciation of the life of God the Holy Spirit that the option of suicide is diminished and discarded. Knowing who it is that brings us out of the depths of despair can instill immeasurable comfort and consolation when those depths drown us.

## The Immanent/Transcendent God

David Wells believes that modern evangelicalism has lost sight of God's transcendent nature in favor of his immanent qualities.[12] He observed that when a society overemphasizes transcendence, there emerges

> ...a deism with a remote God, cool rationalism, and complete loss of Christological interest. On the other side [a focus on immanence], there emerged modern evangelicalism, which looked to a God "invested with all the gospel's transformative passion" but with a greatly diminished aura of transcendence—the God "below," warmer, closer, more engaging, and more susceptible to be translated into a purely private deity. In other words, evangelicals tended to dispense with God's otherness in the interests of promoting his relatedness through Christ and gospel faith.[13]

To live the Christian life effectively—including the suicide-inducing struggle with pain and suffering—we must strike a balance between the God who loves us and the God who will forever be outside our complete understanding, to whom we are ever subject. To miss or ignore this balance is to impinge upon life an unstable pride in one's spirituality or, to the other extreme, in one's humility. An overemphasis of immanence means that God is too much "for us" (we become too self-centered and, therefore, overconfident in our willingness to speak for God or discouraged when it appears that God is not "meeting our needs" the way we think He should). An overemphasis of transcendence means that God is too much "from us" (we become legalists or skeptics, doubting that a holy and incomprehensible God would be involved in our personal problems, and thinking that God is undaunted by human tragedy).

Erroneous thoughts and decisions rooted in these unbalanced misbeliefs about God in the area of suicide and physician-assisted suicide include:

- "I'll be better off with the Lord."
- "God wouldn't want me to go through this kind of suffering."

- "He'll understand our decision—God is so much more compassionate than we are."
- "The Lord wouldn't want anyone to sacrifice financial security to
  prolong a life unnecessarily."
- "If God was so concerned about my life, He would not cause me
  so much difficulty."
- "I'll never be what God wants me to be; life's just too hard for
  some of us."
- "God doesn't have time for a mess-up like me."

Because God is immanent, He is keenly interested in the way we live
our lives and the way we care for the lives of others. Because He is transcendent, His greatness, power, knowledge, compassion, goodness and
purity establish a standard that is above and not subject to human experience. He is who He is and *not* what we make or want Him to be (Isa.
55:8–9). Consequently, human value is divinely established and, therefore,
not subject to the elastic judgments of human wisdom.

There is something that gives value to man from above. The value of
man is not that he is the highest of the evolutionary process thus far, but
that the Supreme Eternal Being made man in His own image. It is not
man's estimation of himself, but the judgment of the holy God that gives
man value.[14]

Human life cannot be qualified by degree of function (healthiness vs.
disability), age, race, net worth, or any of the many ways the world judges
human worth. Life, in and of itself, is valuable because it comes from
God—to live is to be valued. And since both the suffering and the dying
have life, their value is equal to anyone else's. All decisions that involve the
termination of life must be made in the context of God's view of life. As
long as an individual has life, there remains purpose to that life.

Even the life and death decisions regarding a non-cognitive terminally
ill patient are filled with theological implications for those who must
decide when to acquiesce to the disease.[15] The decision to kill oneself or to
allow oneself to be killed *circumvents the divine purpose of one's life*, which is
an open book, with a finite understanding of one's present experience,
which is but one of many chapters. We must always remember that our
story is comprised of more than one character, and therefore, the purpose
of our life intertwines with that of others (cf. Phil. 2:3–4).

## The Incarnate God

The most visible expression of God's immanence and transcendence is seen in the Incarnation of God's Son, the Lord Jesus Christ. He who was "equal with God" became one of us, even "to the point of death." How does the truth of the Incarnation impact the way we view suffering and the way we die? From the heavens God entered His creation as a human being, as the perfect image of God, not to help us escape physical death, but to give us abundant and eternal life before and after death.

Without the earthly existence of the God-Man, we would not have a perfect reflection of the image of God or a living example of God's commitment to the redemption of humanity. We would be subjects of a King who would seem distant or uninvolved (transcendent) and whose understanding of our human weakness would, therefore, be suspect. We would have no sacrifice for our sin which would leave us without hope, victims of our incessant guilt or our seared and unfeeling consciences. Without the Incarnation, suffering would be meaningless and death would be a welcome relief.

How we live and die is inextricably linked to our understanding and commitment to the incarnate God. Our joys and our sufferings have purpose, just as our Savior's did. The work that Jesus loved was devoted to providing insight, through instruction and personal example, into the value of living life in communion with God and others. However, even the unrelenting accusations of an ungrateful and blind hierarchy and the incomparable agony in the Garden of Gethsemane delineate purpose and direction to the difficulties that confronted our Savior (cf. Heb. 12:3–4).

The incarnate God impacts every aspect of our lives. Jesus Christ teaches us about the will and character of God. He provides a path to fellowship with God, and instructs us in our dealings with the world. He encourages us to struggle through the trials that threaten to undo us, and guarantees purpose of effort and an eventual end to all manner of suffering. He grounds our hope beyond our present experience. The incarnation is truly the central fact around which all human history revolves.

To align oneself with the Incarnate God is to become a prophet in favor of healing, not a proponent or actor of premature death. It is to be an advocate for sure intervention and palliative care, not an adversary of suffering. It is to be an acquirer of solutions, not an acquiescer to the final solution.

The fruits of the Spirit of God that describe the life of the Incarnate Christ are incompatible with the depressive and hopeless characteristics of a person considering self-termination. They are also uncharacteristic of a human being who looks at suffering terminal patients as individuals who have lost their value as human beings simply because their quality of life does not meet a subjective societal standard.

Suffering is a difficult experience to endure, but we must not be too quick to eliminate it, for even the Lord "who for the joy that was set before him endured the cross, despising the shame, . . . " (Heb. 12:2). It was an act of obedience that provided hope to the entire human race. Suffering is the product of physical, intellectual, or spiritual conflict. It is neither moral nor immoral, and it is not something to be stoically endured for the sake of character or higher purpose.

Suffering is an experience that demands serious attention, and demands serious treatment when it becomes chronic and severe. It is surely an event that changes the lives of those who pass through it. Its greatest purpose is to bring us face to face with our finite humanity so that we might more clearly see the face of the divine (1 Pet. 1:6–12). Like the suffering of the blind man, our suffering can become a testimony to the glory of God (John 9:1–5). And like the suffering of the Incarnate God, our suffering can reflect His effect on our lives and possibly lead some, who are ignorant of His grace, into the presence of the Father.

### The Resurrected God

The solution to the complexities of the world is the simplicity of the gospel and its attending consequences. The simplicity of the gospel rests on the message of the resurrection of the Son of God. Paul's words in 1 Corinthians 15 emphasize the importance of the resurrection for the Christian faith: "And if Christ has not been raised, your faith is worthless; you are still in your sins" (15:17). With Christ there is hope, without Christ there is no hope.

*Helpless, hopeless,* and *worthless* are three words frequently used to describe the feelings of those who are suicidal. Such feelings are not restricted solely to non-Christians—suicide claims believers as well. Yet, an understanding of, appreciation of, and daily application of the reality of the resurrection of Jesus Christ provides daily hope for the believer that reaches into the depths of the human heart.

The resurrection of Christ offers not only hope for the next life: it offers hope in this life. Pain, fear, frustration, uncertainty, loneliness, discouragement are all real and debilitating physical and emotional experiences. The reality of the resurrection of Jesus Christ, through which we have present and eternal hope, is equally real but in no way debilitating. Because of the resurrection we are not *helpless*, for we have a risen Priest; we are not *hopeless* for we hear the risen Prophet; and we are not *worthless*, for we serve the risen King. Because Jesus rose from the dead, the Christian has "a living hope" (cf. Titus 2:13). The Resurrected God offers to all who respond a hope for living—a hope beyond suffering, pain, and despair.

## The Loving God

"We have come to know and have believed the love which God has for us. God is love, and the one who abides in love abides in God, and God abides in him" (1 John 4:26). The apostle John's words proclaim that relying on the love of God is an integral part of the Christian life. Knowing and understanding God's love for humanity, and for us as individuals, has enormous consequence. *The human need for acceptance is finally and fully realized in the character of God when there is a proper relationship with Him.*

Describing God's attribute of love, J. I. Packer writes, "God's love is an exercise of his goodness toward individual sinners whereby, having identified himself with their welfare, he has given his Son to be their Savior, and now brings them to know and enjoy him in a covenant relation."[16] God's love toward humanity is observed in four dimensions: benevolence, grace, mercy, and persistence.[17] God's benevolence is expressed through the attention He pays to those He loves. It is His unselfish interest in each of us for our own sake. Intrinsic to His love is a concern for every aspect of our life which is expressed indirectly (Matt. 5:45; Acts 14:17) and directly, the most obvious expression evidenced by the sending of His Son to redeem those who would believe (Rom. 5:6–10; 1 John 4:10).

It is through God's grace that He deals with us, not on the basis of our merit but according to our need, requiring nothing from us in return (Eph. 1:5–8; 2:8–9). To speak of God's mercy is to address the tenderhearted compassion He has for His people. Erickson notes, "It is his tenderness of heart toward the needy. If grace contemplates man as sinful, guilty, and condemned, mercy sees him as miserable and needy." (1983, p. 295) It is in this dimension of God's love that he responds to our spiritual and physical infirmities, frailties, and fears (cf. Exod. 3:7; Matt. 34:14; Mark 1:41). The persistence of God reveals His love in that He is patient in withholding judgement (2 Pet. 3:9).

Each of these dimensions touches on suicide and the suicidal person in that they help us to see the *depth* of God's care and concern for us. The intense introspection of the suicidal individual and the anthropocentric focus of those who would assist in suicide ignore the active love and concern of God. The difficulties we face in life are very real, but so also is the loving God to whom we can take them. An inadequate view of God will always lead to an inadequate view of humanity. When the former is diminished the latter is exalted with the inevitable result, not of "Thy will be done," but, "my will be done." Such an end leads to suicidal thoughts and other related inhumane acts in individuals and cultures that abandon the infinite and selfless love of God for finite and self-serving human reason.

## Suicide Assessment and Intervention

Guidelines for assessment and intervention with the suicidal person are made with both the counseling professional and pastor in mind. It is assumed that pastors and churches will adapt policies from these recommendations that incorporate some, if not all the suggestions offered. This analysis further assumes the historic duty of the care-giver to intervene for the purpose of saving and prolonging life.

### 1. General Policy Guidelines

A. *Work from a written policy.* Develop and follow clear step-by-step procedures for yourself and your staff that will guide decision-making throughout a suicidal crisis. Clearly written policies help guide you through moral and ethical dilemmas and provide a reference or "common language" for consultation and referral. A well-written policy also communicates favorably to courts and lawyers that you are a thoughtful and serious professional, not one prone to negligence, foolishness or exaggeration in your decision-making about people in your care. This evidence will carry great weight in the event you are sued or have to defend yourself in any forum.

B. *Set clear limits on yourself, then consult and refer*. Every clinician and pastor must be able to define clear limits of competence and the level of intervention beyond which you will not work. *Working within your competence is the first line of malpractice defense, a "safety zone" within which the court will not intrude to find you liable if you stay inside its shelter*. When events push beyond the limits of your competence, then consult and refer. Sullender and Malony strongly challenge clergy—a challenge appropriate to all Christian counselors—to "not work in isolation."[18] There will be trouble for those who don't respect this key requirement of risk-avoidant ministry.

The clergyperson's own needs and self-deceptions are common barriers to effective referrals. Clergy must be mature enough and professional enough to know their limits when it comes to counseling troubled persons. These limits may involve training, available time, conflict of interest, or just available energy. They must not feel obligated to "save" everyone who enters the door seeking help. Unfortunately, not all clergypersons are that mature or that professional. Some have messiah complexes that get in the way of effectively using referrals.[19]

C. *Consult first, then refer*. The clinical professional and committed pastoral counselor should first consult with a respected and knowledgeable colleague when dealing with suicidal crises. Referral may not be necessary with close consultation to confirm and add to clinical decision-making on behalf of the person in crisis. This not only improves and advances the professional's clinical skills, it also serves the client who may be confused and mistrusting by having to face referral to a probable stranger. If referral is indicated, however, by all means do it. It is far better to refer to an expert stranger than to carry on a case that may lead to suicide.

D. *Work with your own "flock."* We agree with Sullender and Malony that pastors and churches should not counsel with those outside their own "flock." The inherent moral and legal protection of the clergy-congregant relationship is lost to a pastor counseling someone outside his church. Other than in short-term crisis situations that would lead to early referral, pastors should limit their counseling help to their own parishioners. Beyond the time and energy that such work demands in lieu of service to one's own church, there are simply too many legal, ethical and moral risks to the counseling pastor in working with persons outside the local church or parish.

## 2. Suicide Assessment

Assessment of suicidal risk involves gathering information from multiple sources across a number of key variables. The essential two-part question of suicide assessment is:

- Is this person at risk for committing suicide, and
- If so, how serious is the risk?

The competent counselor will assess this risk according to history, trait, mood, personality, and situational factors.

E. *Begin counseling with assessment of suicide risk.* The easiest way to get information about suicide risk is to ask questions at the beginning of counseling. We incorporate questions about suicide (and homicidal and assaultive behavior) in our clinical intake forms. This gives us direct access to these issues at the start of professional relations and allows us to intervene early in cases where these issues are pressing. Structuring assessment this way and addressing these questions on initial interview puts clients more at ease as they see it as part of the routine we follow with all new clients. Evaluate suicide risk across the seven key variables that follow. Risk for suicide increases according to:

1. *Past suicide attempts and their seriousness.* Clinically and empirically, past behavior is the best predictor of future behavior. Careful assessment of both the incidence and seriousness of past suicide attempts is a significant factor in assessing current risk. Also, assessment of the seriousness—the degree of lethality of past attempts—can give important clues distinguishing whether one has an intent to die or whether one is using suicide to manipulate others. Superficial wrist slashing or "overdosing" on aspirin may yield a different hypothesis about client intent compared to the person hospitalized in intensive care following a failed gunshot wound or massive overdose on sleeping or pain medications. Suicide is also a higher risk for those who have a family history of suicide, especially suicide by the same-sex parent.

2. *Communication of intent / denial of intent.* A second factor, estimated in 75–80% of all suicides (Maris, 1992), is a client who communicates or gives other clues to suicidal intent or, following a serious attempt, denies any intent to further harm themself. This information is rarely offered by the person at risk. You must ask directly and matter-of-factly about suicidal

thoughts and intent. Incorporating these questions into your intake will serve this interest well.

3. *Assessing the violent-angry-impulsive person.* Clinical researchers have identified two major constellations of behavior and mood that correlate strongly with suicide risk.[20] One is the impulsive person revealing a history of violence and unmanaged anger, which empowers suicidal and, sometimes, murderous action as well. Suicide by this kind of person has, in fact, been deemed to be "murder in the 180th degree".[21] The second type (below) shows a history of depression and hopelessness without violence. The violent-angry-impulsive person will:

a.  show a history of violent and assaultive behavior—assault, hitting and injuring others, destroying or damaging property, and injury to self for such action;

b.  reveal impulsive anger or rage that is explosively triggered by various people or events—the person quickly gets out-of-control and becomes destructive to things or people and relationships;

c.  show a tendency to hurt others and vengefully react when angry—using cutting, harmful words or hiding or destroying things special to the person who is the focus of one's anger;

d.  project blame onto others—is critical and condemning of others while being unable to receive and react against any criticism from others;

e.  justify anger and harmful expression, unable to forgive, tending to hold grudges and resentments over a long period of time;

f.  suppress anger—deny anger in the face of obvious evidence— flushed face, clenched teeth and muscles, harsh and loud tone of voice, threatening posture;

g.  repress anger—deny anger problems (contrary to history) without obvious anger signals—passive-aggressive, aloof, sarcasm-cynicism, conflict-avoidant;

h.  show associated physical complaints and symptoms—gastric-intestinal distress, ulcers, spastic colon, headache, hypertension, and cardiac irregularities.

4. *Assessing the nonviolent-depressed-hopeless person.* The other key pattern in assessment of suicide risk is the person showing depression with little or

no history of violence, but who exhibits much hopelessness and a very pessimistic cognitive style.[22] Clinical depression with a strong streak of hopelessness is implicated in over 75% of all suicides.[23] Of critical concern with
the depressed person is the "rebound suicide" where the person is empowered to act destructively as the depression lifts. Depression of this nature is
much more than a bad case of "the blues;" a variety of clinical and medical
indicators exist for suicide risk, including:

    a.   recurrent, hard-to-control, sometimes obsessive thoughts of
worthlessness, hopelessness, helplessness, death or suicide;

    b.   problems in mental function: inability to concentrate, short-term
memory lapses, and difficulty with reasoning, decision-making
and problem-solving abilities;

    c.   mood disorders: sad, flat, "numb" feelings, or strong anxiety, agi-
tation or quick-tempered irritability, or swings between these
moods;

    d.   crying easily and frequently or an inability to cry at all;

    e.   sleep disturbance: sleeping too much but not feeling rested, or not
getting enough sleep, awakening often in the night and sleeping
fitfully;

    f.   appetite disturbance: overeating and weight gain or undereating
with resultant weight loss;

    g.   disinterest in people and self: increased social withdrawal and iso-
lation, poor diet, and/or increased neglect of personal appearance
and hygiene;

    h.   loss of interest in sex, hobbies and things that have been pleasurable;

    i.   various physical complaints: chronically fatigued and tired,
headaches, floating aches and pains, gastric distress, constipation,
fast heartbeat in some.

    5. *Other marked changes in personality and behavior.* Other cumulative or
sudden changes in personality and behavior changes that correlate with
suicidal risk include:

    a.   increased alcohol and drug abuse: combining drugs with depres-
sion and suicidal threats is serious as the last internal barriers to
suicidal action may be relaxed by the drug;

b. recently filling out a new will or purchasing life insurance;

c. a recent injury or illness or loss of ability that leaves the individual with a handicapping condition or in significant or chronic pain;

d. quitting work or leaving school for no good or apparent reason;

e. giving away favorite or treasured possessions and "putting one's affairs in order" may precede deadly action that has been secretly decided upon by the person;

f. failed or declining performance: school grades plunge or work performance falters and high level of absenteeism may precede an attempt;

g. trivial things become important and important things are trivialized.

6. *Environmental stressors.* A key correlate with suicide is the sudden, massive experience of recent loss. The tragic death of a spouse, child or best friend may precipitate suicidal crisis, especially if one is left living alone after such death. A conflictual divorce, coupled with loss of child custody is all too common these days in headlines about murder-suicides. Loss of physical or mental ability following an accident or medical crisis is a risk, especially if one is left with chronic, intractable pain. Major financial or job loss can also be critical, especially if criminal behavior is involved. Acute suicide risk begins to decline, however, after two or three months following such loss.

7. *Demographic factors.* Seventy percent of all suicides are white males (which also reflects the no-turning-back lethality of shooting oneself in the head). Of the remaining 30% of all suicides, 22% are white females (although women attempt suicide at over twice the male rate), and just 8% are people of color of either gender.[24] Increased risk of suicide is also indicated for:

- non-believers over religious believers,
- Protestants over Catholics and Jews,
- higher incomes over lower incomes,
- homosexuals over heterosexuals,
- men between the ages of fifteen to thirty-five, and
- women between the ages of twenty-five to seventy-five,
- singles, who commit suicide at twice the rate of married persons, and

- divorced and widowed persons, who commit suicide at a rate four to five times that of the married.

### 3. Suicide Intervention

F. *Discuss suicide openly and matter-of-factly.* Contrary to seemingly popular opinion, talking about suicide doesn't make it happen. Keeping it secret and not hearing the cry for help are far more likely to facilitate a tragic death. Getting the issue out in the open robs it of some of its mystique and power, including Satan's power to tempt the at-risk person with deadly thoughts. Questioning about suicide openly and discussing it in a matter-of-fact tone helps the one in crisis see it more normally and easily. Communicating that suicidal thinking and feelings are common in crisis also helps people evaluate themselves more soberly and realistically. They are much more able to conclude they aren't "going crazy" even though they're struggling with or attracted to suicidal ideas.

G. *Expand alternate thinking and options to suicide.* The suicidal person's thinking often "tunnels" and fixates on suicide to the exclusion of alternate ways to deal with the crisis. Explore, reinforce, and gain client commitment to alternate courses of action. Often, they will protest that they've tried your suggestions or are convinced that nothing will work. Help the client focus the least offensive option or refocus something they've tried in the past that was partially successful. Assist the client to develop and work simple behavior plans, reporting frequently to you about progress and revision of the plan.

This part of suicidal intervention is crucial to your ongoing assessment of continued risk. A client who will explore and work options to suicide is resolving his or her suicidal crisis. The client who does not engage this part of your intervention—or who engages you without any real motivation or seriousness—is displaying continued risk and may need further or more comprehensive intervention to live.

H. *Respect and use the fears that block suicide.* Discuss and constructively use the things that block the person from further suicidal thinking or action. Many things stop people from suicide: fear of death and going to hell (believing there is no chance to repent), failing to die and being left an invalid, the pain of dying, being found by spouse or family, leaving children to be raised by spouse or parents, or leaving children a suicidal legacy. These things are important internal boundaries that are better nurtured than challenged when suicide is at issue.

I. *Increase clinical or counseling intervention.* Keys to increase and intensify the level of intervention to increase protection against suicidal risk include:

1.  *Increase frequency of sessions.* Meeting more frequently should always be considered in suicidal crisis, with daily contact justifiable in high risk cases. Setting limits here and respecting referral needs is critical, especially if the person is manipulative or overly dependent.

2.  *Use the telephone wisely.* Meeting more frequently without major schedule disruptions or excessive use of time can be facilitated by brief telephone contacts. Daily five-to-ten minute calls may be far more helpful and protective than the weekly one-hour session. Again, some can abuse the phone and clear limits need to be set here as well.

3.  *Get friends and family involved.* With consent from your client or congregant, disclose the risk to family or friends who can make a commitment to assist the person through the crisis. Surrounding the suicidal person with caring, praying, supportive, non-judgmental and available people can greatly reduce the risk of isolated, deadly action. Temporary helping networks can be powerful channels through which God's power can flow mightily to the needy person. We frequently rely on this means of suicide intervention because it is so effective.

J. *Act assertively to protect in crisis situations.* In a serious suicidal crisis, referral should be made to a hospital emergency center, acute psychiatric care facility, suicide prevention center or even the police. Connect the person in crisis with resources able to handle emergencies and act quickly to intervene to protect life. Less serious or acute crises widen the range of potential referral sources. Sending the suicidal parishioner to a trusted Christian mental health professional is a valuable resource for the busy pastor. If none exist, make referral to an honorable professional who respects and will not denigrate Christian values. Also important is referral to a psychiatrist or competent family physician who can evaluate depression and respond medically, either to facilitate hospitalization or to prescribe antidepressant medications.

K. *Make good referrals to people you know and trust.* Know and trust the person to whom you refer—your client will want to know these things and will carry your trust to another person when they are in crisis. If you are new in an area, ask your colleagues to list their referral sources and develop a list of trusted people as one of your first professional tasks. Make an effort to meet and discuss referral situations with community professionals if you do not have a good referral network. Maintain contact with these referral sources during the crisis and afterwards for a time until the client or parishioner is resettled into a normal life routine.

L. *Remove access to lethal weapons and means of death.* Having the client or family remove or reduce easy access to the means of death can be critical to suicide prevention. Help the client agree to give up or lock away guns or ammunition, allowing a third-party to control access to guns and lethal instruments. This can also be necessary for drugs, prescription medications, and car keys as well. Increasing the difficulty of killing oneself can be a crucial factor at the height of a crisis when, if easy means were available, tragedy might well occur.

M. *Contract for "no suicide" and community care.* When non-acute risk exists, negotiate and contract with your client or congregant against suicide. Help them agree with you not to take suicidal action for a time-limited period that is as long as possible—months preferably, session to session at the very least. Let them know you realize they can kill themselves if they choose, but that if they contract with you they will be counted on to maintain their agreement with integrity. If possible, get them to agree to call you or someone else before they take deadly action. Formalize the agreement and reinforce its power by putting it in writing and having both of you sign and date it.

Recent research has called into question the reliability of no-suicide contracts—showing that 41% of psychiatrists who used them had patients go on to kill themselves or make a serious attempt.[25] We have found that the most useful contracts are those that incorporate and gain commitment from many people to work in the prevention circle (as in I.3. above).

When a group of caring people covenant to stay close to, pray for, call on and visit an at-risk person, that kind of community support is a major aid to prevention. Contracting against suicide in this manner is an effective and flexible procedure that increases protection and aids the clinical process through the crisis period. This helps clients realize they have caring people surrounding them, and more control than they often perceive they have when in crisis. It can also serve to distract the one whose obsession with suicide is so isolated, creating a clearer mental picture of how suicide would take place.

## 4. Case Management

N. *Help hospitalize the suicidal person.* Again, hospitalizing a suicidal person may be necessary to save his or her life. Seek agreement to admit themselves to a hospital voluntarily and refer them, even take them to the nearest Christian or other inpatient facility. If they will not agree to admit voluntarily, seek involuntary admission for crisis assessment and intervention. If admission criteria is met—serious mental illness and danger to self—most states allow a person to be held for 48 to 72 hours initially. If the risk is serious and protracted, a hearing will be held to prove the need for longer detention, which may last for a number of weeks. This often is all that is necessary to help a person get beyond the acute and deadly phase of a suicidal crisis.

O. *Monitor your client closely.* Staying with your client or congregant is essential through a suicidal crisis. Even if you refer, they will likely return to you, so your legal duty does not end with referral. It is usually necessary to walk a "second mile" with them, sacrificing some time and energy to insure their safe passage through "the valley of the shadow of death." Since suicidal risk is transient and the great majority of people live through the crisis, you will gain significant influence in their lives if you have walked with them. Your ability to assist them to grow in Christ and to maturity may be keyed to your crisis commitment to the person.

## 5. When Suicide Intervention Fails

The suicide of a 12-year-old male client nearly drove me (George) out of counseling months after beginning my full-time clinical career in community mental health practice. Living with his grandmother and rebounding from the deep anger and depression of his father's drug overdose death and mother's subsequent suicide, I was convinced we were past the worst of his own suicidal threats. The lifting of his depression merely empowered him to fulfill his threat as his grandmother came home one day and found him hanging by his belt in his bedroom closet.

P. *Take time off and get counseling yourself.* Client suicide touches all kinds of emotions and triggers all kinds of thoughts in a counselor—many of them that are not good. Time off or reduced time in your clinical practice to debrief, reflect, and renew-review your basic values and commitments is a wise policy. Talk through your own issues and questions with a trusted colleague or counselor with some real experience with the tragedy of life. Above all, don't deny the impact of client suicide and try to go it alone.

Q. *Help the victim's family get counseling or debriefing.* The family of the suicide victim is going through its own turmoil and trauma, multiplied by the family interactional patterns. If possible, assist them to find a resource for counseling and debriefing. If you have worked with them, you might be the best resources for this, but if there is tension, or mistrust, or rumors of lawsuit, refer them to someone else.

## A Note on Legal Liability in Suicide Intervention

The Christian counselor owes a broad duty to intervene in the life of the suicidal person to give that person a fair chance to live. Professional clinicians are increasingly at legal risk for the suicide of their clients and patients. Indeed, the clinician working in an inpatient or restrictive treatment setting has a strong duty to intervene in the life of someone judged to be a substantial risk for suicide. In contrast, a pastor in a church setting may be ethically and morally, but not legally bound to a duty of suicide intervention.

There is no pure legal duty to prevent suicide—the duty is to intervene appropriately—the law recognizes limits in the ability to stop a determined person from killing himself. The duty to intervene is judged according to the degree of suicidal risk exhibited by a client and the counselor's ability to accurately assess and control that risk. The counselor's liability increases as the risk of suicide increases and the counselor is able to foresee and control the client's actions. Since the clinician in an inpatient facility can control the patient's behavior far more than in an outpatient setting, liability is greater when suicide occurs in a hospital, day treatment, or residential care facility.

Lawsuits following suicide have risen dramatically over the past quarter-century. Among the litigation fears of psychiatrists, Messinger and Taubnoted suicide risk at the top of their list of clinical problems of concern.[26] In the first comprehensive APA Insurance Trust study, client death, predominantly from suicide, made up 10% of the cases against psychologists.[27] Lawsuits have increased here not so much because the law itself is changing—but because of the seriousness of the harm—the unexpected death of a client that shocks the family—that is driving suit in this field. One commentator revealed this connection between emotions and lawsuit very well:

> Wrongful death (to compensate survivors for monetary loss) and malpractice suits for the suicide of a patient are more frequent than other causes of death for two reasons that are peculiar to suicide. Unlike other types of serious illness, there is usually no expectation that mental illness will be terminal. It is assumed that given proper medical care the patient will survive. Premature death, the likely outcome of some maladies, is felt to be preventable for the depressed patient. Hence, the outcome of suicide is per se unreasonable, bizarre, unexpected, and often irrational.

Prior to the suicide, the relationships between the deceased and close family members are bound to be emotionally charged and at the same time ambivalent. Typically, relatives who love him and have his best interests at heart become angered and frustrated by his helpless and despondent behavior. His suicide may be perceived as a personal attack, for it "represents the ultimate in undiluted hostility." Family members are plunged into a morass of contradictory feelings: sadness, shame, guilt, shock, bewilderment, and hostility toward the deceased. They alternately blame themselves and the deceased. To resolve this apparent contradiction, the bereaved may displace their hostility on to the treating psychiatrist or psychologist. The resulting malpractice suit absolves the family of both guilt and helplessness and gives them a reasonable outlet for their anger by blaming the psychotherapist for the suicide.[28]

## The Legal Dilemma for the Church

There is no legal duty for pastors, churches, or counselors working under church supervision to assess and intervene effectively to prevent suicide. The famous California case of *Nally v. Grace Community Church* (1988) reaffirmed historic common law protection of clergy against liability for parishioner suicide. But in practice, churches should disregard this apparent protection and act as if liability does exist, because they may be sued anyway. The church, then, must intervene effectively with the suicidal person, not so much because of legal duty, but rather to fulfill the call of love and to avoid the massive costs of legal defense.

*Should clergy counsel the suicidal?* Following the *Nally* case, there has been increasing debate as to whether clergy should even counsel suicidal persons.[29] The arguments against such clergy counseling assert growing legal liability, the lack of effective training, the demands of a suicidal crisis, the lack of time and energy to address it, and the failure of many pastoral counselors to recognize and respect these limitations. Those making these arguments assert that clergy not engage in this counseling, but instead refer the suicidal person on to psychiatrists or other professional helpers.

On the other side of this argument is the thoughtful analysis of Sullender and Malony, who support the role of the clergy counselor in work with suicidal persons.[30]

To treat suicide or suicidal depression as just a psychiatric problem—a problem to be treated primarily through medication or hospitalization—is to miss the complexity of the dynamics and do sufferers a disservice. And to argue from the false premise that pastors should never work with suicidal persons and always refer them elsewhere for "real" professional help is to belittle the expertise of clergy and the contribution that the religious community can make to the healing of persons. There are clear religious and spiritual dimensions to most if not all suicidal dynamics, and therefore religious professionals have a definite and significant contribution to make in the overall treatment of depressed and suicidal persons.[31]

These writers, while cautioning against attempts to "save" everyone who comes in crisis, assert that "suicidal persons really need to hear and experience anew . . . the 'good news' of God's forgiveness and new life."[32] To experience this life afresh requires pastoral intervention for many. "Often, the average parishioner perceives a pastor to be more available and more trustworthy than most mental health professionals. Furthermore, many people see their problems primarily as spiritual and moral in nature and specifically want the counsel of their pastor regarding their troubling situation."[33] The question, then, needs to be reframed—not should clergy counsel the suicidal, but how best to do it, a question we have sought to answer in this chapter.

## Conclusion

My conclusion in *Law for the Christian Counselor* still holds true today: If Nietzsche is right and suicide is "great consolation," it could only be so to a very pained and desperate few. For most, especially for those who loved the deceased, it is much more a tragedy and painful heartache carried throughout life. Even though never fully washed away, the grief of suicide can be redeemed by the Crucified and Risen Savior, the "man of sorrows" who was and is "well acquainted with grief." Counselors who lose a client or congregant to suicide are sometimes devastated, but must still go on in the work of ministry. To go on without great sorrow, or fear that it will happen again, or without anger and repressed hostility toward the deceased requires great faith in response to unyielding grace from God.

**ENDNOTES**

1. In order to protect the privacy of individual identities, this story is a compilation of reports from recent newspapers and personal stories told to the first author during the AACC Trauma Response and Intervention Project in New York City, October 23–24, 2001.

2. C. Chemtob, Bauer, G., Hamada, R., S. Pelowski, S., and Muraoka, M., Patient suicide: Occupational hazard for psychologists and psychiatrists, *Professional Psychology:Research and Practice*, 20 (5), (1989), 294–300.

3. C. Chilstrom, Suicide and pastoral care, *The Journal of Pastoral Care*, 43(3), (1989), 199–208.

4. Centers for Disease Control and Prevention, *Suicide injury fact book*, <http://www.cdc.gov/ncipc/fact_book/26_Suicide.htm>: Author.

5. Aaron Beck, Brown, G., Berchick, R., Stewart, B., and Steer, R., Relationship between hopelessness and ultimate suicide: A replication with psychiatric outpatients, *American Journal of Psychiatry*, 147(2), (1990), 190–195.; Aaron Beck, Resnik, H., and Lettieri, D. (eds.), *The prediction of suicide* (Bowie, MD: Charles Press, 1974); M. Weishaar, and Beck, A., Clinical and cognitive predictors of suicide, in R. Maris, Berman A., Maltsberger, J. and Yufit R. (eds), *Assessment and prediction of suicide* (New York: Guilford Press, 1992).

6. R. S. Sullender, and Malony, H.N., Should clergy counsel suicidal persons? *The Journal of Pastoral Care*, 44 (3), 203–211, (1990), 204.

7. J. Sire, *The universe next door: A basic worldview catalog*, 3rd ed. (Downers Grove, IL: InterVarsity Press, 1997).

8. We recognize that the boundary between life and death, between passive and active forms of euthanasia can be very narrow, and will address "end-of-life" issues and ethics more fully in volume 3 of this series.

9. J. Kevorkian, *Prescription—medicine:The goodness of planned death* (Buffalo: Prometheus Books, 1991).

10. Robert Bork, Inconvenient lives, *First Things* 68, (1996), 13.

11.   Victor Frankl, *Man's search for meaning*, rev. ed. (New York: Pocket Books, 1984).

12.   David Wells, *God in the wasteland: The reality of truth in a world of fading dreams* (Grand Rapids, MI: Eerdmans, 1994).

13.   David Wells, *God in the Wasteland*, 129.

14.   Millard Erickson, *Christian theology* (Grand Rapids, MI: Baker, 1983).

15.   J. E. Tada, Decision-making and dad, in G. Stewart and Demy T. (eds.), *Suicide: A Christian response, crucial considerations for choosing life* (Grand Rapids, MI: Kregel, 1997), 471–475; T. Oden, *Should treatment be terminated?* (New York: Harper and Row, 1976).

16.   J. I. Packer, *Knowing God*, rev. ed. (Downers Grove, IL: InterVarsity Press, 1993), 116–117.

17.   Erickson, *Christian theology*, 292.

18.   Sullender and Malony (1990), 206.

19.   Sullender and Malony (1990), 206.

20.   A. Apter, Kotler, M., Levy, S., Plutchik, R., Brown, S., Foster, H., Hillbrand, M., Korn, M., and van Praag, H., Correlates of risk of suicide in violent and nonviolent psychiatric patients, *American Journal of Psychiatry, 148* (7), (1991), 883–887; M. Weishaar, and A. Beck, 1992; J. Motto, An integrated approach to estimating suicide risk, in R. Maris, Berman, A., Maltsberger, J., and Yufit, R. (eds). *Assessment and prediction of suicide* (New York: Guilford Press, 1992).

21.   K. Menninger, *Man against himself* (New York: Harcourt, Brace, and World, 1938).

22.   Beck, et al, (1990), 190–195; Beck, et al, (1974).

23.   D. Black, and Winokur, G., Prospective studies of suicide and mortality in psychiatric patients, *Annals of the New York Academy of Sciences, 487,* (1986), 106–113.

24.   R. Maris, Overview of the study of suicide assessment and prediction, in R. Maris, Berman, A., Maltsberger, J. and Yufit, R. (eds), *Assessment and prediction of suicide* (New York: Guilford, 1992).

25.   J. Kroll, No-suicide contracts, *American Journal of Psychiatry*, (2000).

26.   Messinger, Malpractice suits—the psychiatrist's turn, *Journal of Legal Medicine* 3, (1975), 21; Taub, Psychiatric malpractice in the 1980's: A look at some areas of concern, *Law, Medicine and Health Care* (1983), 97.

27.   S. Fulero, Insurance trust releases malpractice statistics, *State Psychological Association Affairs 19*(1), (1987), 4–5.

28.   Swenson, *Margin: Restoring emotional, physical, financial, and time reserves to overloaded lives* (Colorado Springs, CO: NavPress, 1992), 411–412.

29.   Sullender and Malony (1990).

30.   Ibid.

31.   Sullender and Malony (1990), 205.

32.   Sullender and Malony (1990).

33.   Sullender and Malony (1990), 204.

**Part 4**

# Counseling for Grief and Trauma

# 17

# Loss and Grief Work

*Sharon Hart May*

Death is about life, as birth is.

The death of a family member or close friend *is a grievous event*—one of the most difficult of all challenges confronting individuals and families.[1] Expert researcher John Bowlby states clearly, "Family doctors, priests, and perceptive laymen have long been aware that there are few blows to the human spirit so great as the loss of someone near and dear."[2]

The death of a loved one deeply impacts the souls of individuals bereaved, and can shake the foundation of one's family system. Counselors seeking to help sufferers of such loss should understand the current theories of bereavement that focus on the *individual's* intrapsychic (within/personal) experience and the *family system's* interpsychic (between/relational) impact from loss.[3]

## A More Comprehensive Model

This chapter challenges the Christian counselor to broaden their understanding of bereavement counseling by placing the bereaved in a holistic context that emphasizes *the systemic nature of attachment.*

Although the death of a loved one impacts the attachment bond between the living and the deceased, the effect of death is not confined to that dyadic relationship. Furthermore, according to systems theory, even with death the relationship is not "removed from the system in which it is embedded—most particularly the family system."[4]

Usually presented alone, attachment theory and systems theory need not be exclusive and together provide a comprehensive model of bereavement, one that broadly informs the Christian counseling treatment plan when working with grieving individuals and families.

### An Attachment Perspective on Loss

Bereavement is different from the other necessary losses we experience in our lives, such as leaving home, changing jobs, aging, and living an imperfect life. With most, the connection we have with others is deeper and more profound than the ties we have with our possessions, purses, or positions. Bowlby described relationships between two people (such as between child and parent, husband and wife, or siblings) as close emotional attachments or bonds.

In the shelter of these close relationships, we develop as infants, grow as children, and continue to flourish as adults. We turn to these relationships for comfort and support and from these relationships we venture out into life. When children, or adults, perceive their loved one to be available, accessible and responsive, they experience a felt security. When these close bonds are threatened, or if the attachment figure is inaccessible or unresponsive, then an innate set of behaviors (attachment system) are triggered, designed to maintain proximity and restore the disrupted bond.

According to attachment theory, when a loved one dies, the attachment system is triggered. The response is similar to the response children exhibit when they experience their mother to not be there for them. The distressed child, or the bereaved, attempts to restore the bond by first protesting, then clinging, then becoming angry. If the bond is not restored, the anger gives way to sadness and despair, and finally to resignation and defensive detachment.

Freud originally believed that a person mourning the loss of their loved one eventually "detaches" or "decathects" him or herself from the loved one.[5] Freud suggested that "mourning has a quite precise psychical task to perform: its function is to detach the survivor's memories and hopes from the dead."[6] Based on this, psychoanalytic clinicians aimed at moving a person through a process of "detaching." The mourning reactions were seen as immature and pathological, and clinicians tended to hurry the grieving process, in an attempt to get the griever to "let go" and "get on with life."

Bowlby reacted to the orthodox psychoanalytic thinking and viewed the mourning reactions of grievers as natural components of the attachment system. Rather than viewing the grieving process as detachment or the severing of the emotional bond, Bowbly viewed grief as the process of readjusting the attachment bond and reorganizing life in light of the loss. Continuing a bond with the deceased loved one is "a natural result of the dynamics of the attachment system designed to ensure proximity" with the loved one whether or not the loved one is available.[7] In a nutshell, attachment theory, as opposed to psychoanalytic thought, views loss and its resultant grief not as something primarily to "get over" but as a natural part of life that requires adjustment to a new reality.

Fraley and Shaver outline the importance for the bereaved to find a way "to maintain a secure bond with the attachment figure while simultaneously acknowledging that the person is not physically available to provide comfort and care."[8] This "comfort and care" is then derived from personal faith, prayer, and a sense that the loved one is still there. Studies show that the ability for children and adults to alter and then continue their relationship with their deceased loved one was both comforting and productive. The assurance of the continued bond allowed the bereaved to cope with the loss and make necessary changes in light of it.[9]

## A Systems Perspective on Loss

A social system is a bounded set of people, such as a family or a neighborhood, and "the relationships between them, and the relationships between the attributes or characteristics of the elements."[10] Systems theory aims at understanding the relationships within a family and the interactional patterns between the members. As with attachment theory, it does not view causality as linear but rather as a more circular, repetitive, and shared experience between members of the system. In the context of a relationship, each person influences the other and "both are equally cause and effect of each other's behavior."[11] The grieving process of the bereaved takes place not in isolation, but within the greater context of family relationships. The emotions experienced by the bereaved during grief include the grief over the lost loved one, as well as the emotional responses to the family system's reactions.[12]

The family life cycle model of McGoldrick and her colleagues offers a systemic framework for understanding the "reciprocal influences of several generations as they move forward over time and as they approach and respond to loss."[13] Walsh & McGoldrick identify two major family tasks that need to be continually addressed for the long-term well-being of the family. First, the family needs to share in acknowledging the reality of the death and share the experience of the loss. The family comes to accept the reality of the death and the subsequent impact on the family unit. Rituals such as visiting the grave help families share the experience of the loss.

Second, the family system needs to reorganize and reinvest in other relationships and life pursuits. The task of the family is to redefine their identity and purpose as well as reorganize themselves around the loss. This will need to occur over the life cycle of the family and across the developmental stages of each individual family member. The research and clinical experience of Carter and McGoldrick concludes that if the family is not able to adapt to the changes, then the risk of family difficulties and dissolution greatly increases.

### The Main Task of Grief

The main task of grief, according to a systemic approach of attachment theory, then, is to help the bereaved reorganize their inner and outer worlds in accordance with the loss, while negotiating the impact of the family system upon their bereavement, and in turn, their bereavement upon the family. The grieving process is a natural, innate, God-given means for humans to accept, adjust to, and live on in light of the death of loved ones. This means that both the (a) family as a unit, as well as (b) each member of the family needs to:

1. mourn the loss of the bond in its previous form (not physically here anymore)
2. readjust, thus allowing a more appropriate continuing bond with the lost loved one

3. reorganize themselves, their relationships, and their life pursuits in light of the loss.

In light of the close, emotional bonds and reciprocal connections between family members, what does the grieving process look like for the individual and the family? What factors foster the natural grieving process? And how can the counselor be part of their healing process?

It is important to view the grieving process as a natural and productive process of restructuring a bond and a new life in light of the death of a loved one. Therefore, understanding the different facets of mourning will guide you (the counselor) through the bereaved person's grief experience. It will alert you to when the grieving process is stuck or compounded, and it will direct you to the possible needs of your client. Use these analytical tools as guidelines, but don't hold fast and firm to them (or any set of stages) as no person or family will follow them neatly.

## The Five Stages of Grief Process

The classic process outline of grief was conceptualized by physician Elizabeth Kubler-Ross, in her now-famous work *On Death and Dying*.[14] She defines five stages through which the grieving live and resolve their loss, including:

1. *Denial:* a dazed numbness that is much like the shock reaction of physical trauma; a refusal to accept the loss. In this stage, most people try to return to normal routine and intellectualize loss.

2. *Anger:* normal and unavoidable reality sets in that often creates much somatic distress. Too many people internalize anger and block the grief process, ending up with guilt, depression, and long-term physical problems. Many people will exhibit avoidance and blame others for the loss, in this stage.

3. *Bargaining:* people try to recover the lost person by bargaining with God. In addition, the grieved is often obsessed with meta-questions such as "Why?" "How could You let this happen, God?!" and "Why me?" Sufferers may also get trapped in "If only . . ." thinking: "*If only* they had done this that day . . . *If only* I had said [something different]."

4.  *Depression*: depression is often mixed with guilt, and sometimes anger, during this stage for the bereaved will blame themselves for not doing what they "should have done." Give permission for one to feel the pain of the loss and allow them to grieve. It is important for the church family to allow people the "luxury" of being depressed as they face the loss of a unique person or opportunity.

5.  *Acceptance:* resolving the loss by accepting the hurt and the memories; moving on with a focus for what is yet to come.

The process of grief is just that—a process. Visualize the grieving process, not as linear stages to grow through, but rather as layers of an onion unfolding, or as a spiral, or roller-coaster. Few experience the process in the linear way presented here. Many will report living one or more stages at the same time, or rolling through parts of the process again and again.

Allow the bereaved to inform you of where they are and what they need. Although grief is universally similar, it is also very personal. It is continually impacted by individual as well as systemic dynamics. The entire grief process normally takes from 1 to 3 years to resolve, and must be respected as part of living.

### How Grief Is Experienced by the Individual

*When grief is like shock and numbness.* Each of us who have lost a loved one can recall the sharp words confirming the finality of death. The initial reaction is one of shock, numbness, and disbelief which usually lasts a few hours or even a few weeks. It is interjected with intense sadness or anger, and even laughter and acting like nothing has happened.

> Mr. Wolterstorff, Eric is dead. For three seconds I felt the peace of resignation: arms extended, limp son in hand, peacefully offering him to someone—Someone. Then the pain—cold burning pain. [15]

For some the news of death ends a long period of illness. Therefore, initial emotions may include relief, followed by guilt, anger and sadness. For others the news comes out of the blue, shocking and numbing and disorienting. At first, the news and reality of the death just does not seem real. The mind, emotion, and soul pause to register the reality of loss. It is similar to a car having to come to a full stop before being able to be put into another gear. It is in the moment of pause that the gears are shifted, heading the car in a new direction.

It is important for the family to share in this experience together, openly and honestly. Children should not be isolated from the news, and they should also be included in the rituals that confirm the reality of the death. Since each family is tending to their own shock, it would be important for extended family and friends to be there, providing a sense of stability and continuity to such necessities as meals, care of children and house.

Glen Davidson followed 1,200 adult mourners for 2 years after the death of their loved ones.[16] From their experiences, he found that the phase of shock and numbness peaks during the first two weeks after the death of a loved one. Mourners also reported experiencing a sense of disbelief again after one year. At this time the bereaved reviews from whence they have come and says "oh my goodness, has this really happened? It is hard to believe it!"

*When grief is like yearning, searching, and anger.* As the reality of the death begins to register, pangs of intense pain, sadness, restlessness, anger, guilt, and deep sorrow are felt.

> For that grief, what consolation can there be other than having him (his deceased son) back. [17]

There is also great restlessness, sleep and eating difficulties. Mourners express an inability to relax, and often are unable to concentrate or keep a flow of thought. Sometimes mourners fear they will go crazy, and hold in emotions lest they become out of control. Also, they may worry their intense emotions will burden family and friends, furthering the urge to suppress their grief while in the company of others. Often if the bereaved does not feel they can suitably hide their brokenness, they will isolate themselves from social contact.

Anger arises that is often directed toward the deceased, the comforters, and those who may be remotely responsible for the death of the loved one. When this anger is turned inward the bereaved experiences a sense of guilt, blaming him or herself for not having done more, having done the wrong thing, or having done too little. Many, especially children, fear that their indifference, angry feelings, or wishful prayers played a part in the death. It is important for the family system to allow the expression and experience of grief by each family member. Mourners need to express their guilt in a safe and supportive environment to sort out what they realistically are, and are not, responsible for.

During the first year after a death, there is a preoccupation with thoughts of the loved one that includes attempts to find pieces of the loved one in everyday activity. The longitudinal research of Balk suggests that rather than letting go, the bereaved "seemed to be continuing the relationship" with the deceased. Balk found that the bereaved, in the process of healing, were "altering and then continuing their relationship to the lost or dead person."[18] It was found progress toward recovery is enhanced by one's continued sense of attachment with their lost loved one. Stated, the "abiding sense of the lost person's continuing and benevolent presence" helps a person heal, and "reorganize their lives along lines they find meaningful."[19]

*When grief looks like disorganization and despair.* Between the 5th and 9th month after the death of a loved one, the bereaved may find oneself disorientated, though it is still not until one year that the pain of grief tends to peak.

> Loss can also be transformative if we set a new course for our lives. (Our) loneliness and isolation force (us) to see life from another point of view.[20]

This season is also marked by depression, guilt, fluctuation of weight, and an awareness of the reality of the death. There is a loss of joy and meaning in life, and getting through the day requires much effort. Common experiences of confusion, loss of memory, and impairment of fine motor skills can leave the bereaved feeling concerned that they are "losing it." Often, physical complaints and ailments arise, and the bereaved find themselves worried that they may have some serious illness.

This season, if used productively, becomes a season of reexamining personal values and philosophies of life. In this time the bereaved can come to gradually accepting the loss and realize life must be "shaped anew." Life is reassessed and new priorities emerge.[21]

Although life will never be the same, mourners adapt to the changes forced on them by the loss. This becomes a season of "relearning the world." It involves "finding our bearings in the world and give direction to, and seek a sense of purpose in, our ongoing living."[22] The task of the bereaved, and the family, is to find their way by learning how to be and act in the world differently. Habits, motivations, and behaviors are impacted, as well as the connections and interactions with others. The world is relearned, and this way life becomes anew.

*When grief looks like reorganization.* This phase is marked by a sense of release and it is experienced around one to two years after the death, depending on the nature of the loss. Some widows and widowers, report this phase only after 3 years.

> Eventually I had to decide, however, to become a contributing member of the community once again, not only willing to receive but also to give love.[23]

During this time, the bereaved begins to give more focus to the challenges and opportunities for living. New rituals begin to form, bringing meaning and renewed enthusiasm and interest for life. The bereaved begins to reinvest emotional energy into life, in light of their loss.

The bereaved will need to learn new skills and take on added responsibilities and what will impact the reorganization phase is the bereaved's ability to successfully master and adapt to these new roles. This is impacted by the response of the bereaved's community to their reorganization of life. The bereaved's community system will need to be flexible and accepting to allow the bereaved to master the new roles, foster new relationships, establish new rituals, and seek lifestyle changes.

It is at this phase that the bereaved, and family, can visualize themselves living beyond the pain and making a life for themselves. As they look into the future, they can see life blossoming up around them. And they want to be part of it.

## How Grief Is Experienced by the Family

The impact and meaning of the death on the family unit should be carefully considered, even if you only see one member of the family. As previously shown, the bereavement process is not experienced alone, but rather in the context of the individual's family system. Since the counselor will effectively have only one or two hours with the client a week, it will be important to focus on integrating the client back into their family system for emotional and social support during the grieving process. Therefore, the greater context of the individual should be assessed and taken into consideration when outlining therapeutic interventions. This context should also include the wider cultural and ethnic influences upon the family's beliefs. According to Walsh & McGoldrick, coming to terms with the loss and adjusting to its implications is a task revisited throughout the life cycle.

*The timing and type of loss.* The timing of the death has an impact on the family. Sudden deaths impact families differently than long-term illnesses. The unexpected deaths don't allow for good-byes or preparation for the loss. Many family members are left with regrets, guilt and unfinished business. In contrast, prolonged illnesses have the potential to place strain on the family system as well as on the finances, time, energy, and emotional availability of family members.

The farther along in the natural life cycle the death occurs, the less distress on the family. Death of an elderly grandparent is viewed as much more natural than the death of a thirty-six year old husband or, especially, a young child.

The death of a child is likely the most tragic of griefs as it appears so unnatural to the life cycle. The impact of a child's long-term illness and death has profound impact on the marital relationship. Studies found that in cases where the children were hospitalized, 70 to 90% of those marriages resulted in separation or divorce.[24] Hospice studies found that families who were able to care for their dying children at home, had fewer marital problems and a greater sense of power and control. Unusual circumstances surrounding the loss, such as traumatic accidents, violence, suicide, abortion, or other complications increase the family distress and compound the grieving process.

*Nature of the relationship.* If there are unsettled feelings toward the deceased or if the relationship was cut-off, the grieving process will be complicated. Also, if the bereaved's sense of well-being is significantly tied to the deceased, the grieving process will be prolonged and complicated.

Death does not change the nature of the relationship. One's mother, whether dead or alive, will always be one's mother. Whenever a deceased loved one is remembered, the memories can trigger emotions causing the bereaved to sigh, yearn, or even have a good cry.

*Family structure.* The more securely attached (rather than clingy or disengaged) a family is the more able they are to adapt to the loss. Flexible, rather than chaotic or rigid boundaries enable a family to accept the changes ahead. A family needs to be a haven of safety where each individual's process of mourning is supported. It is important for the family to openly talk about the pain of the loss as well as the restructuring of the family.

A family came into my counseling room where the mother had lost both her parents tragically just several months earlier. The family was rigid and did not allow one another to cry, mourn, or talk openly about the grandparents' death. Consequently, the mother longed to express her sadness, but could only find rage. With counseling, rather than attempting to keep things the way they were, the family learned to mourn together and reorganize themselves around the loss.

*Family connections to social networks.* The experience of loss is buffered by the family's ability to draw upon emotional and practical resources from extended family, friends, and other communities such as the church. The lack of connection to these communities leaves the family without a sense of support and structure. It would be of great benefit for you, the counselor, to encourage the bereaved's reaching out and participation in a greater community. For example, after the tragic death of his 36-year old son, a father reconciled with his 85-year old mother after years of hurt and disconnection. This provided added support and family cohesion.

*Concurrent losses or life cycle changes.* Often the death of a loved one is compounded by concurrent loss or life cycle changes. When one loss is stacked upon another, the original loss is compounded. Each loss needs to be separated and mourned appropriately.

Developmental markers such as graduations and weddings add to the distress of grief. Even though they should be times of great joy and celebration, they become reminders of the absence of the loved one. Each life event without the loved one will need to be both mourned and celebrated.

## Counseling the Bereaved

The mourning process lasts longer than most expect. Bowlby emphasized that many clinicians sometimes have "unrealistic expectations of the speed and completeness with which someone is expected to get over a major bereavement"[25] Healing and reorganizing one's life without the physical presence of the lost loved one takes time, approximately 1 to 3 years, or longer. For some, the mourning process is delayed, or it gets stuck, so the process is revisited numerous times over many years.

Furthermore, just having time pass does not necessarily heal the soul. It is what a person chooses to do during their healing time that determines the new meaning life takes on. Remember, each family member will have their own timeline of mourning. It is possible that when one member is at one phase, the other members are at other phases.

## Children and Grief

As you are working with bereaved children, the emotions of grief don't seem all consuming for children as they are for adults. However, children still experience the same range of emotions as adults.[26] Features of child bereavement are diverse, ranging from regression, fear of separation, clinginess, aggressive behavior and discipline problems. Children need time and a haven of safety to reorganize their inner and outer worlds in light of the loss.

The adolescent years are already filled with turmoil as teenagers face new tasks and responsibilities of growing up. Similar to adults, a teenager's response to the death of a loved one will often include anger, guilt, sadness, confusion, depression as well as physical symptoms such as aches, pains, eating and sleep disturbances. Unique to adolescents is that they commonly try to control their emotions, but also act out, in an attempt to make sense of the loss. This usually places added distress onto the family and complicates the adolescent's developmental task.

## Physical Well-being and Medication

It is of great importance to consider the medical and physical well-being of the bereaved, for there is a high correlation between physical ailments or illness, and the loss of a loved one. Mourning is as much a physical process as it is an emotional one; it can be physically draining, is linked to a weaker immune system, and brings with it medical conditions of many sorts. Adequate exercise, enough sleep, small frequent meals, and keeping hydrated will help fortify one's grieving body.

During the months and years of mourning, the bereaved can become physically and emotionally exhausted and anxious. Reaching for sleeping pills, alcohol, antidepressants, antianxiety medications, or other substances should be done with wisdom and caution. A study found that 87% of physicians in Illinois "assumed a standard care that called for prescribing either a barbiturate or tranquilizer for mourners at the time of the loss."[27]

There are times that medications are necessary to assist in a good night's sleep, or enable the bereaved to function in everyday living. Yet, there are other times when the numbing of the grief experience can complicate the healing process. As you are working with the bereaved, help them explore more natural and holistic methods to aid in stress reduction and sleep disturbances such as relaxation techniques and soothing rituals before bedtime, like taking a bath or listening to music.

## Expression of Emotions

It is of value to help family members express their emotions in a manner that is consistent with who they are. Some mourners view expression of emotions as humiliating, or even as inviting criticism and contempt. Sometimes the unspoken messages from family members and friends include "get on with your life," "snap out of it," or "pull yourself together"—which further increases the need to work through emotions in the counseling session.

Stifling emotions does not help the mourning process. Yet, not everyone will express emotions the same way. Respect the quiet, gentle grievers. It is more so those who long to give their grief a bolder voice—but for some reason can't—who potentially complicate their mourning process.[28]

## Real Loss and Imagined Loss

Concrete losses are tangible losses, such as the actual person who has died, loss of marital status, loss of income. Abstract or intangible losses are those such as loss of hope in the future, or loss of ambition. Imagined losses are not based in actual reality, yet are powerful influences on the grieving process. These losses are only in our minds and emotions, and their meanings need to be understood and put into perspective.

There are also losses I call "feared" or anticipated losses, such as the fear of never loving again, or never having a happy life. Threatened losses are those lurking in the wings, threatening to become real. These include the possible loss of income resulting in the possible loss of the family house.

Whether the loss is real, imagined, feared, or anticipated, each loss triggers a deep emotional response. It is important to help the bereaved separate out actual losses from the imagined or feared losses, while avoiding being dismissive or underplaying the importance of the feared/imagined losses.

## Making Sense of God

It will be important to allow the bereaved to make sense of why God allowed the death, and why He did not intervene. We think that we are protected from the deeper hurts of living because we are Christians. But all human beings have been given only a finite number of years to live here on earth. And that reality is sometimes too hard to understand or too difficult to trust God for the outcome.

At one stage or another, all who have lost loved ones wrestle with God. Sittser describes how "We move toward God, then away from Him. We wrestle in our souls to believe. Finally we choose God...we decide to be in relationship with Him"[29] As counselors, we should allow our clients to actively wrestle with God, and in doing so move them toward understanding and walking close with Him.

## Developing the Treatment Plan

A good treatment plan is helpful for the counselor as it outlines what will be done during the counseling sessions. The theoretical framework outlined in this chapter serves as a foundation on which the counselor can build a treatment plan. An effective treatment plan will include therapeutic parameters, assessment, diagnosis, and interventions.

### A. Therapeutic Parameters

1.   Who will be the client? The individual, couple, or family?
2.   Would they benefit from other therapies such as a grief group,

family or individual therapy? Do they need to be referred to a medical doctor as well?

3.  How many sessions will you see them? Adjust your interventions to fit your time frame.

4.  Will the counseling be supportive counseling (walking the bereaved through the grief process) or more in-depth grief counseling (complicated or compounded grief)?

## B. Assessment and Diagnostic Considerations

1.  Gather the story around the death including: who died, how, where, and when?

2.  How would the relationship between the client, the family, and the deceased be described?

3.  What role did the deceased play in the life of the bereaved and greater family context? What roles or responsibilities will the client need to learn and take over in light of the loss?

4.  Consider the developmental stage of the client and each family member. Also assess the family life cycle stage. In light of this, keep in mind what tasks and adjustments the bereaved and the family will be facing. Be aware of coming life markers—births, graduations, and weddings.

5.  Consider cultural, ethnic, gender, and economic factors that may impact the bereaved and family.

6.  What previous loss has the client and family faced, and how was it dealt with?

7.  How do the client and family express emotional pain?

8.  What cultural, gender, ethnic, and spiritual beliefs need to be considered?

9.  Assess for suicidal thoughts, and a sense of hopelessness, or worthlessness.

10. What support system is the client and family a part of? Are they able to ask for needs to be met and utilize the support?

11. Refer back to the previously listed concerns and phases of mourning and ask questions that will give you a broader picture of the client, their experience, and the system in which they live.

## C. Treatment Strategies

1.  If the grieving event is anticipated, such as with a terminal illness, talk openly about it with the dying and their family members. Make sure that preparations for the death are in order.

2.  Give accurate information about the grieving process, especially the possible range and intensity of emotions, and time it will take to heal, so that any false expectations or beliefs may be discussed and corrected.

3.  Encourage decision-making and follow through on the little things that keep day-to-day life functioning in at least a minimally healthy way. Help out and make sure the grieving person is eating properly, maintaining personal hygiene, keeping bills paid, and basic appointments kept. Discourage major decisions and action on big changes until the crisis event has subsided and some time for perspective is gained.

4.  Challenge any hostile, irrational, or slanderous judgments, and reframe any inaccurate expressions about the one lost, communicating your commitment to honesty and truth and how important that is to the healing process.

5.  Encourage discussions about and assist planning regarding the future, including how to go about finishing any "unfinished" business that may be expressed.

## Assessment and Diagnosis

To develop well-informed interventions, it would be in the client's best interest to understand whether your client is going through the normal bereavement process, or if there are other compounding factors that need to be addressed. Diagnosis is valuable for helping you rule out more serious conditions. It would be of value to read the DSM-IV diagnosis of conditions similar to bereavement. It is important to note that the three main symptoms distinguishing bereavement from major depression is suicidation, hopelessness, and unworthiness continuing for more than 2 weeks. If trauma surrounds the death, such as violence, murder, a car accident, a child's discovery of the deceased, then it is important to rule out post traumatic stress disorder (PTSD). If you discover that your client is going through more than just the normal bereavement process, it would be wise to get supervision, further training, or refer your client to a trained professional.

| | | |
|---|---|---|
| Axis I: | 296.2x | Major Depressive Disorder, Single Episode |
| | 296.3x | Major Depressive Disorder, Recurrent |
| | V62.82 | Bereavement |
| | 309.0 | Adjustment Disorder with Depressed Mood |
| | 309.3 | Adjustment Disorder with Disturbance of Conduct |
| | 309.04 | Dysthymic Disorder |

## Interventions

Be there and listen. Most people come to counseling to make sense of the intense and confusing emotions they experience. Research and experience has found that most people are able to adapt to their loss. Key to their healing is an adequate and stable support system. Your ability to listen and enabling them to give their grief a voice will be very healing.

*Listen actively and respond reflectively.* During the crisis, grieving persons are not so desirous (or ready) to hear complex answers to the questions about tragedy and suffering, even though these things come up from time to time. Allowing them the opportunity to talk out their concerns, confusions, and affirmations is important. Listening and reflecting back their communications is often more helpful than engaging in long treatises about God's purposes in these things.

*Normalize their experience.* The emotional experience of bereavement is very painful and often disturbing to the bereaved if they have never experienced it before. It would be good to begin by normalizing the experience, and helping the client understand the experience of bereavement and what to expect. Give permission to talk about the lost person or object, to express fears and emotions, but don't push it. Don't be surprised if strong feelings and displays go on. If you are able, cry when others cry, and laugh when they laugh.

*Encourage and participate in grieving rituals.* Funerals, wakes, family gatherings, memorials, sorting through photos, and watching videos are usually healthy and necessary events that both recall the best times and assist in mourning the loss. The rituals around the death repeatedly confirm that the loved one is not returning. The funeral, memorial service, and visiting the grave-site are rituals that your client and their family can do together. They are healthy aspects of mourning, and it is important to participate in these events.

Explore and expand the dynamics of the family system. A broader picture of the client's family system can be drawn through a genogram, as well as a time line of family life events. Allow the client to tell the history of the family through stories, pictures and memorabilia.

Rituals for staying connected as a family are important. Explore with your client other rituals of remembrance they can do to help them stay connected to their loved one. A 10 year old boy asked me whether or not he should continue to keep his deceased father in his prayers. Together we came up with a prayer that thanked God for allowing him to have his father, even though it was only for 10 years. Still being able to pray for his dad kept him in a continued bond with his father. One woman placed a single flower in a vase on her mantel every Friday in honor of her deceased mother. It was one way she continued to feel the beauty of her mother's countenance.

*Explore and expand the life story of the lost loved one.* Old documents, scrap books, high school yearbooks, newspaper articles, pieces of clothing and hobby tools can be gathered to help tell the story of the loved one.

*Exploring and expanding the feelings and experiences of the client.* As clinicians, it is easy to get caught up in the content, or story of the client and be fogged in regarding the process. To help expand the feelings and experience of the client consider the following:

1.  Allow the expression of emotions, remembering to help and encourage the client to identify and label the feelings.
2.  Help the client understand the link between their behavior and their emotions. This enables them to realize that there is more going on than just what is on the surface. For example, you might say, "When you feel sad you are unable to share your sadness with your family. So, instead you get angry and yell because being mad is more acceptable than being sad. Being sad is more painful than being mad."
3.  Provide corrective emotional experiences. That is when you

respond with understanding and acceptance of emotions and behavior that your client anticipates rejection and criticism. A corrective emotional experience is when your client expresses a negative emotion and receives understanding and acceptance rather than the anticipated punishment or rejection.

4. Help the client lean on God. The Bible is a treasure-store of comfort and consolation in the face of grief. The grieving experience is a time to know the grieving heart and tender heart of God in a way that no other experience allows.

Isaiah 53 presents one of the most powerful pictures of Christ in the Scriptures—a picture of the "man of sorrows," well "acquainted with bitterest grief." (v. 3). Wounded and abused for our sins, "He was beaten that we might have peace. He was whipped, and we are healed." (v. 5). Those who allow the Suffering Servant, Jesus Christ, to minister to them in their sorrow come to know a beautiful Savior, a Wonderful Counselor to whom their devotion can soar.

Psalm 23 has been a favorite verse to grieving hearts throughout history, for it invites God to come alongside and walk with us "through the dark valley of death." (v. 4) God never abandons us. He never fails us, even in the worst hours.

No one is able to carry the wounds of loss alone without eventually being overcome. By letting God, and God's people help us, we are able to bear our slow healing wounds of grief.

## Other Considerations

There is more to therapy than one-on-one dialogue. Techniques such as sand tray, play therapy, art therapy, journaling, telling stories, creating a memory book, and letter writing are other ways that allow the client to make sense of their feelings and experience. Often more emotions and behaviors come out in these modes of therapy than in just plain talking. Again, allow your client to lead you in what best fits for them.

*Counseling with children.* Cook and Dworkin identified six common topics that can be discussed and explored. It will be necessary to adjust the discussion according to the age of each child.[30]

## FROM SUFFERING TO SURRENDER,
## BY TIM CLINTON AND GEORGE OHLSCHLAGER

When we suffer [in our grief], it is not uncommon to believe that God has forsaken us and broken our trust in Him. When others tell us to 'trust in God' during this time, the words suddenly make no sense. They sometimes sound absurd, like a huge cosmic joke.

How can we trust God when our hopes and dreams with our loved one have been unexpectedly shattered? How can we trust the One who took our loved one away? How do we trust Someone with the very power of life and death in their hands? These are common questions—questions we must take to God and wait for Him to answer. At some point we will realize that God wants us to trust Him even when we don't understand why. Since God is the only One who can fix the problem, He often becomes the focus of our anger. The more intimate our relationship with God, the more betrayed we feel by the One who was supposed to intervene in our hour of need.

Lazarus' sister Mary is an excellent example. She was angry at Jesus when He failed to prevent her brother's death. "If You had been here," she admonished Him, "my brother would not have died!" We assume that Mary's trust in Jesus had definitely diminished.

Trust is one of two aspects of faith. Faith is comprised of trusting God and believing what He has said. With this in mind, we need to remind ourselves that our understanding is limited to an earthly perspective. Death makes us feel small, vulnerable, insecure—we come face-to-face with the fact of our own mortality—that death may just as easily (and soon) take us as well.

Grieving the death of a loved one challenges us—to our very core—to believe and trust that God's eternal perspective is better, even far superior to our own. We wrestle with the holes in our knowledge of the future—will God take care of me, will I eventually be privy to His plan? We wrestle with faith in God's goodness—uncomfortable in the awareness that our faith is so weak in the face of such tragedy. Psalm 130:5 tells us; "I wait for the Lord, my soul waits, and in His Word I put my hope."

As the intensity of our emotions levels out and we begin to live with the reality of this death, it is not uncommon for family and friends to suggest disposing of personal items in order to "get over" the loss. While they may have your best interest in mind, do not get rid of anything until you are ready to. (When you do discard some things, it can be difficult to decide which ones to throw away and which ones to keep. Separate those that hold significant meaning and those that don't. For example, disposable items may include deodorant, toothbrushes, razors, etc. More personal items may include family pictures, heirlooms, and other items that hold memories for family and friends.)

It is hard to trust and believe in God, to take His Word as His sure promise. Trying to will ourselves to believe doesn't work—we see it for the weak, self-centered, will-powered sham that it is. We recognize the absurdity of our dilemma—I must go to the One I don't trust to find the trust to trust in Him once again. Sometimes if we don't laugh at the situation, we will do nothing else but cry and lament.

One of Shakespeare's famous characters, Macbeth, said, "Give sorrow words; the grief that does not speak knits up the o'er wrought heart and bids it break."

Grief forces us to face this grand paradox—I am going to get better or become bitter. Too many get embittered. A long-term study indicated that the death rate of widows and widowers is from two to seventeen times higher during the first year following the death of a spouse. Dr. Glen Davidson has discovered that about 25% of those who mourn experience a dramatic decrease in the body's immune system six to nine months after their loss. This is one of the reasons why grieving people are more susceptible to illness.

However if the grieving process is handled in a healthy manner—if the bereaved one pursues God's design to get better—this immune deficiency is avoidable. And in order to believe Him, to put our faith in His Word, we are driven to search Him out in prayer, in the Bible, in the hands and faces of others—compelled to seek Him in order that He may reveal Himself even more—more than ever before.

While you may be ready to accept that God is not your enemy because of your loved one's death, you still may not understand why He chose to take them. As mentioned earlier, our questions may not find full answers while we are here on earth. But we have chosen to walk by faith, believing that God was, is, and will be with us on earth and in heaven. And though grief is an inescapable part of the human condition, He demonstrates His love for us through His loving compassion (Lamentations, ch. 3).

At some point we will arrive at a partial understanding of this process called grief: to grapple with overwhelming loss and eventually adapt to it. During this time, necessary changes must be made so that we can live with our loss in a healthy way. This occurs when our questions change from, "Why did this happen to me?" to "What can I learn from this and how can I best proceed with my life?"

Even as we move—as we begin to grow—through the grieving process we will experience days that are more difficult than others. Tears, fears, anger and confusion are still ahead, but God gives them to us to help release our feelings. We slowly begin to understand, to accept this death.

We also realize that grieving is a two-part process: the loss of a loved one, and the recovery of our spirit. It is natural to want to return to the life we knew before this traumatic event occurred, but it's imperative we create a new "game plan." We do this by refusing to be locked away in a tomb of agony for the remainder of our lives, and instead, come to a place of surrender.

God promises to deliver those who seek Him. Surrender comes when we finally accept that we could not have changed the events that led up to our loved one's death. We accept that we are unable to turn back the hands of time—we cannot bring them back, nor are they coming back. No matter how much we would like to, we cannot change the circumstances.

But we have a choice, and this choice is critical to our healing, to getting better or becoming bitter. We can remain angry at God, blaming Him for everything. Tragically, far too many people get stuck in exactly that. I'm sure you know some, still angry over events that transpired decades ago! On the other hand, we can surrender to God and seek His comfort, healing, and direction. In the midst of grief's pain neither choice seems attractive or acceptable. However, it is inevitable that we choose one or the other.

Most believers, at some point, surrender their grieving to the Lord. In so doing, He comes to our side and answers our cries. God comes to our rescue. Surrender occurs when the bereaved acknowledges the loss of their loved one, readjusts their bond with this person on a more spiritual level, and eventually reorganizes their life following this loss. Death is a life-changing event—one that alters our nature, our view of life, our priorities, our spiritual perception of God and His goodness, and every other aspect of our life. It is inevitable that change will affect every area of our life because loss is not singular.

Resolving our loss and surrendering it occurs when we accept the hurt and the memories but we can move on with a focus when we accept God's promise:

"I tell you the truth, you will weep and mourn while the world rejoices. You will grieve, but your grief will turn to joy." —John 16:20

1. Have the child describe the loved one who died, how they died and how they heard about the death. This can be done verbally, through art, writing of a play, or putting together a scrapbook.
2. Examine thoughts and feelings about the funeral and other rituals that the family shared to confirm the death of the loved one.
3. Discuss changes that have occurred in the family since the death, and how the changes feel. As you listen to the child, assess for coping strategies, family support of their experience, and how the child is making sense of life without the loved one.
4. Discuss the future and what it will look like without the loved one.
5. Find ways that the child can still feel connected with the loved one. Through the enjoyment of memories and the review of hopes the loved one had for them, the child can sense the loved one's continued security and comfort. This can be done through the writing of notes, putting together a scrapbook, or recalling how the loved one valued them and hoped they would do well in life.

6. Again, be creative and allow the child to lead you. Begin each session with play therapy, art work, story writing, or some form of activity that allows the child to express himself creatively.

### Counselor Self-care

Like vicarious or secondary trauma, counselors working with the bereaved are susceptible to carrying too much of their client's grief within themselves. It is important to be able to distinguish between empathic grieving—burden-bearing within proper and manageable limits—and being overladen with sorrow. Unfortunately, this boundary is rarely clear, so counselors need to engage in ongoing self-assessment of the impact of grief work. So then:

1. Do your own grief work. What losses have you faced, or are you facing?
2. Be aware of your limitations. Be aware when the story of your client is affecting you and you can't seem to leave it behind at the office. Also, be honest when you need further training or need to refer your client to someone with more experience. Growing your skills as a counselor will make you more effective.
3. Find your own support system where you can share your concerns, emotions and experiences.
4. Always check your stance in the room. Don't be condescending. Your client is the expert of their own experience; respect that. No matter how many degrees you do or don't have, remember that it is the Holy Spirit at work in your client, not you. You are about the work of the Lord, so allow God to use your expertise to do His work. Bless you. Sitting with the pain of the bereaved is not always easy.

### Conclusion

The death of a loved one is painful and difficult for both individuals and the families in which they live. Gerald Sittser, after an accident that took the lives of his wife, mother and one of his daughters wrote, "I believe that "recovery" from such loss is an unrealistic and even harmful expectation, if by recovery we mean resuming the way we lived and felt prior to the loss."[31]

Life does not get back to normal, life is reorganized and a new "normal" must be created. Our clients are not the same after a loss, nor do they return back to how things were. They are changed, and a new routine, a new normal becomes familiar. Kate Convissor, with five children and five years after the death of her husband explained it this way, "Still the effect of Richard's death lingers. Whatever effort I expend, "normal" will never be as I remember it. To continue living I must accept, adapt, and create something new."[32]

As counselors, our task is to come alongside the bereaved and create a safe place where they can accept, adapt, and reorganize life in light of their loss. As outlined in this chapter, attachment and systems theory together adequately expand the understanding of bereavement by appropriately placing the bereaved within their natural context of the family. Bereavement, then, is seen as a natural healing process that is reciprocally influenced by the bereaved and their family.

Even though the family of the bereaved may never enter your counseling room, when the bereaved leaves your office after one hour, he or she will return back into their family system. Therefore, it would benefit both the bereaved and the family for the counselor to consider both intrapsychic and interpsychic levels of the grieving process. In this way, the Christian counselor is better equipped to formulate a holistic and effective treatment plan fostering healing and wholeness within the souls of those who lost a loved one.

**ENDNOTES**

1.  F. Walsh, and McGoldrick, M., A family systems perspective on loss, recovery and resilience, in P. Sutcliffe, Tufnell, G. and Cornish, U., *Working with the dying and bereaved* (New York: Routledge, 1998); John Bowlby, *The Making and breaking of affectional bond* (New York: Routledge, 1979); R. C. Fraley, and Shaver, P. R., Loss and bereavement: Attachment theory and recent controversies concerning "grief work" and the nature of detachment, in J. Cassidy and Shaver P.R.(eds.), *Handbook of attachment: Theory, research, and clinical applications* (New York: Guilford, 1999).
2.  John Bowlby (1979), 67.
3.  John Bowlby, *Attachment and loss: Vol. 3. Loss: Sadness and depression* (New York: Basic Books, 1980); F. Walsh, and McGoldrick, M., A family systems perspective on loss, recovery and resilience, in P. Sutcliffe, Tufnell, G. and Cornish, U., *Working with the dying and bereaved* (New York: Routledge, 1998).
4.  P. Sutcliffe, Tufnell, G., and Cornish, U. (eds.), *Working with the dying and bereaved* (New York: Routledge, 1998), X.
5.  Sigmund Freud, *Mourning and melancholia*, SE, 14, (1917), 243–58; Fraley & Shaver (1999).
6.  John Bowlby (1980), 100.
7.  John Bowlby (1980), 19–21, 93–100.

8.    Fraley and Shaver (1999), 754.
9.    D. Klass, Silverman, P.R., and Nickman, S. L. (eds.), *Continuing bonds: New under-standings of grief* (Washington, DC: Taylor and Francis, 1996); N. Hogan, and DeSantis, L., Adolescent sibling bereavement: An ongoing attachment, *Qualitative Health Research, 2,* (1992), 159–177; P. R. Silverman, Nickman, S., and Worden, J. W., Detachment revisited: The child's reconstruction of a dead parent, *American Journal of Orthopsychiatry, 62,* (1992), 494–503; K. Tyson-Rawson, Relationship and heritage: Manifestations of ongoing attachment following father death, in D. Klass, Silverman, P.R. and Nickman S. L. (eds.), *Continuing bonds: New under-standings of grief* (Washington DC: Taylor and Francis, 1996), 125–145.
10.   N. Frude, *Understanding family problems,* (Chichester: J. Wiley and Sons, 1990), chapter 10.
11.   D. Becvar, and Becvar, R., *Family therapy: A systemic integration* (Boston: Allyn and Bacon, 1993), 9.
12.   Walsh and McGoldrick (1998).
13.   Walsh and McGoldrick (1998), 6; B. Carter, and McGoldrick, M., *The changing fam-ily life cycle* (Boston: Allyn and Bacon, 1989).
14.   Elizabeth Kubler-Ross, *On death and dying* (New York: MacMillan, 1969).
15.   N. Wolterstorff (1987). *Lament for a son* (Grand Rapids, MI: Eerdmans, 1987), 9.
16.   Glen Davidson, *Understanding mourning: A guide for those who grieve* (Minneapolis: Augsburg, 1984).
17.   Wolterstorff (1987), 31.
18.   D. E. Balk, Attachment and the reactions of bereaved college students: A longitu-dinal study, in D. Klass, Silverman, P. R., and Nickman, S. L. (eds.), *Continuing bonds: New understandings of grief* (Washington, DC: Taylor and Francis, 1996), xvii, 311–328.
19.   John Bowlby (1980), 243, 98.
20.   Gerald L. Sittser, *A grace disguised* (Grand Rapids, MI: Zondervan, 1996), 91.
21.   John Bowlby (1980), 94.
22.   T. Attig, *How we grieve: Relearning the world* (New York: Oxford University Press, 1996), 107.
23.   Gerald. L. Sittser (1996), 164.
24.   Carter and McGoldrick (1989).
25.   Bowlby (1980), 101.
26.   S. A. Cook, and Dworkin, D. S., *Helping the bereaved* (New York: Basic Books, 1992).
27.   G. W. Davidson, *Understanding mourning: A guide for those who grieve* (Minneapo-lis: Augsburg, 1984), 22.
28.   John Bowlby (1980); R.C. Fraley, and Shaver, P. R., Loss and bereavement: Attach-ment theory and recent controversies concerning "grief work" and the nature of detachment, in J. Cassidy and Shaver, P.R. (eds.), *Handbook of attachment: Theory, research, and clinical applications* (New York: Guilford, 1999).
29.   Gerald L. Sittser (1996), 144.
30.   Cook and Dworkin (1992).
31.   Gerald L. Sittser (1996), 9–10.
32.   Kate Convissor, *Young widow: Learning to live again* (Grand Rapids, MI: Zonder-van, 1992), 161.

# 18

# Trauma and PTSD: A Clinical Overview

*Michael Lyles, Tim Clinton, and Anthony J. Centore*

The increasing stress of living in the 21st century, on both a global and personal level, has been sufficient to considerably elevate the numbers of people who suffer from PTSD.

FROM HEALTHYPLACE.COM

The headline said it all: "Low-flying Plane Spooks New Yorkers."

A 777 airliner bringing troops back from Iraq was given permission by the FAA to fly low near the Statue of Liberty and over Manhattan as a special welcome-home gift. The sight of the low flying jet triggered hundreds of calls by frightened New Yorkers, presumably post-traumatic stress sufferers reliving the trauma of 9–11.

Whether one is directly involved or a witness, situations concerning the threat of serious injury, or death, in which one feels intense fear or helplessness, is experiential trauma and places one at risk of Post-Traumatic Stress Disorder (PTSD). During the terrorist attacks of 9–11 thousands of Americans felt the threat of harm, and a PTSD epidemic began.[1]

### A Common Disorder

PTSD is extremely common—the 5th most prevalent psychiatric illness behind anxiety, depression, phobias, and substance abuse. Currently, 5.2

million Americans ages 18–54 are diagnosed with PTSD and statistics show that in any one year 5.6% of the U.S. population will suffer from PTSD, with females at about twice the rate of males.[2]

In addition, some studies suggest rates of PTSD to be even higher. A general population sample of 1007 Detroit residents ages 21–30 presented a 9% occurrence of persons who met the DSM-IV criteria for PTSD. In another study, researchers randomly selected 4,008 females and found life-time prevalence of PTSD to be 12.3%. According to the American Psychiatric Association, 10% of the U.S. population at some point presents clinically diagnosable PTSD, and higher numbers show symptoms of the disorder.[3]

## Risk Factors

It is said over 75% of people will experience some type of severe trauma in their lifetime, and 20% of those will develop PTSD. In review of this discrepancy, much research has taken place to investigate the question of why some people experience PTSD in response to trauma, while others do not. Results suggest several major risk factors.

*Trauma type.* The probability of one developing PTSD varies strongly depending on the type of traumatic event experienced. For example, traumas that are not of human design including natural disasters (e.g. a hurricane, earthquake), technological disasters (e.g. a train wreck, nuclear power-plant meltdown), or human mistakes (e.g. motor vehicle accidents, pilot error) tend to be less often catalysts for PTSD. On the other hand, trauma of human design is much more powerful in promoting PTSD as a result.[4]

In specific to trauma of human design, though statistics vary, soldiers held captive or tortured have the highest incidence for male PTSD, one study showing World War II prisoners experiencing PTSD in 50% of cases.[5] For women, rape (or sexual molestation) is the number one cause, at 49%.[6] Crime victims in general have a PTSD prevalence of 25.8%, while research shows 38.5% of females exposed to a physical assault will develop PTSD.[7]

*Duration and severity.* Apart from trauma *type*, increased duration and severity of trauma are positively correlated with PTSD onset. One's resiliency is depleted with repeated stressors, and it is said trauma and PTSD have a dose-response relationship—the more trauma one endures the more post-traumatic stress one experiences.[8] In confirmation of this, a study investigating posttraumatic stress in *twin* Vietnam Veterans shows decisively that increased trauma exposure leads to increased PTSD symptoms.[9]

Reviewing the 9–11 attack, the actual event was relatively short. However, graphic video footage that aired for several weeks promoted a continuous traumatic experience that may have increased the psychological damage to the nationwide witnesses of the event.[10] Of course, local New York residents experienced the most sustained trauma, having repercussions long after the attack (and long after media focused on newer headlines). This may explain that though the trauma of 9–11 was felt nationwide, 8% of Manhattan residents living below 110th street (approximately 67,000 people) have PTSD related to 9–11, as compared to 2–4% of the coast-to-coast population.

*Early childhood experiences.* Often described as "family history," early childhood experiences can be either a defense against, or risk factor for, developing both PTSD and Complex PTSD (CP, discussed later). Expert John Briere, addressing risk factors, categorizes child trauma as either abuse by omission or commission.[11]

*Omission.* According to Briere, omission involves the neglect of a child through parent unresponsiveness, and psychological or physical unavailability. Described as "the great unrecognized trauma," with omission a child does not receive normal social stimulation, soothing, or support from a parent—and lacks the opportunity to learn how to regulate emotions (decreasing the child's ability to cope with stressors).[12] Also with omission, there are no parent-child interactions that promote self-awareness, security, and positive views of others. Lastly, research by attachment expert John Bowlby shows that neglect is a severe traumatic experience, depriving a child of its innate needs for nurturance and love.[13]

The essence of attachment is displayed when children remain in close proximity to their parents. This is a God-given safeguard, since they are dependant on their guardians for survival and protection. Hence, when physically separated from parents, children may experience severe trauma.[14] The following vignette shows an adaptive response to temporary omission.

A little girl skips down the isle of a department store. She feels safe, knowing her mother is following right behind. Things are going just fine for the young girl until she looks back and notices that her mother is gone! At that moment the little girl's knees buckle. She crumbles to the floor, letting out at the same time an ear piercing scream. People from every direction come to her aid and her mother one aisle over, runs back to her immediately.

In this vignette, the child experiences trauma for a brief moment. However, her God-given survival mechanisms (being unable to stand, screaming) worked to quickly reunite her with her mother, and assuage her stress. With the abuse of omission, children remain in a persistent state of neglect, and experience similar trauma constantly.

*Commission.* The sibling of abuse by omission, act of commission, is abusive behavior—psychological, physical, or sexual—directed toward the child. Such abuse is the single most powerful risk factor for developing a mental disorder of any kind for it creates longstanding attachment issues that distort one's core perceptions of self, others, and the world.[15]

*Brain Development.* Whether it is commission or omission, early childhood trauma is many times more powerful than that experienced as an adult for it not only generates extreme stress, it disrupts one's development of mental and emotional abilities to cope with interpersonal challenges.[16] In place of healthy regulation, sufferers of early trauma develop maladaptive conditioned emotional responses (CERs) to interpersonal and external stimuli.

As the brain develops, it does so from the bottom up—beginning with the limbic system, a non-verbal section of the brain that controls the formation of one's memories and emotions. For a child who has experienced abuse, negative schemas are rooted in this part of the mind. For example, a child abused by his/her caregivers may infer that he/she is unacceptable, bad, worthy of punishment, and that he/she is weak, inadequate, not deserving of love, and helpless. At the same time the world becomes to that child dangerous, rejecting, and uncaring.

Later, a neocortex develops above the limbic part of the brain, providing a person with verbal, rational, higher level thought processes. With normal development, one can regulate his/her emotions by rationally considering the safety of his/her present environment. However, for those with negative perceptions deeply rooted in the (non-verbal) limbic system, rational thought is not sufficient for affect regulation, and one may constantly experience stress due to negative CERs. Consider the following vignette:

Growing up, Ryan's parents were rarely ever home. When they were, they would tell Ryan, "I wish you were never born," or "You were an accident!" Now, at 26, Ryan lives alone and experiences extreme stress anytime he receives the slightest social rejection. For example, today one of Ryan's friends "took a rain check" for dinner because she had to work. Though Ryan rationally tells himself that his friend cares about him, and is not rejecting him, he feels extreme rejection. Memories of Ryan's childhood flash in his mind, and he quickly pushes them away.

Ryan's schema is such that he believes he is unacceptable, and that people do not want to be with him. Therefore, his CER is a pervasive feeling of rejection, even when he knows rationally that he has not been rejected. Though discussed later, it should be mentioned that since the limbic brain can be both incongruent and autonomous from one's rational thought, treatment must involve in large part experiential learning.

Here is a quick summary of symptoms that may become present in direct relation to early childhood trauma.

- Preverbal negative beliefs about one's self
- Preverbal negative beliefs about the world and others
- Negative conditioned emotional responses (CERs)
- Poor emotion/affect regulation
- Inadequate ability to gain or accept social support

*Genetics.* When assessing whether one is genetically disposed to PTSD, a practitioner should remember that genes are not closed symptoms. Hence, genetics will never exclusively determine whether one will develop PTSD—one must encounter trauma.

However, some persons are genetically "wired" in ways that make them more attuned to stress. Recalling principles of survival, our God-given reactions to stress are extremely powerful, and in the wild, one's stress response provides a quick reflex to run from or fight predators. When humans transitioned from the wilderness to modern society, our biological systems did not adapt perfectly, and some of us present similar responses to more benign stresses—memories of trauma, for instance.

Medication may be a wise choice to assist the biological regulation of such trauma survivors (described further below).

*Personality.* Though PTSD is not evidence of personal weakness, individual personality uniqueness plays a role in susceptibility. Reportedly, someone who has a tendency toward fear, worry or anxiety is more at risk than his or her less anxious counterparts. This is because trauma is in fact a subjective experience of objective events, and what is traumatic for one may not be traumatic for another.

Trauma expert Jon Allen tells of a drug dealer placed into a trauma support group because he had witnessed multiple homicides. However, the drug dealer, having an anti-social bent, was not traumatized and instead felt invulnerable and excited by the events.[17] Also showing the subjectivity of trauma, one study found that the post-traumatic stress of burn patients was often not due to the severity of burns, but instead to individual subjective experiences.[18]

Due to their personal vulnerabilities, some clients may feel inferior because they are unable to fully cope with their traumatic experience, while others seem to have experienced similar trauma unscathed. A counselor should always reiterate to clients, they are trauma *survivors*, as opposed to victims of PTSD.

*Comorbidity.* Comorbid psychiatric disorders may exacerbate the symptoms of PTSD,[19] or make one more prone to developing PTSD after a trauma. Counselors be aware that preexisting disorders may make PTSD difficult to identify, for past sufferers of depression or panic disorder often confuse PTSD with a relapse. A client may ask, "Is my depression returning?" when PTSD is the root cause of discomfort.

## Onset

Though many persons immediately following a trauma endure a reaction that meets the criteria for Acute Stress Disorder, symptoms of PTSD usually surface within the first three months after a trauma. The following vignette elaborates:

> Ronald, a family man, while driving is sideswiped by a pickup truck running a stop sign. In the wreckage, his wife dies while he is severely injured. Ron is hospitalized for a time, then immediately returns to work so to financially support his children. After several months, when things "settle down" he begins reexperiencing the trauma of his wife's death, along with sleeplessness, social withdrawal, and other post-traumatic symptoms.

In contrast, onset may be delayed for decades.[20] For example:

> Susan experienced neglect and physical abuse at the hand of her parents. She left home at 17 and never looked back. While attending college she managed to build healthy relationships, despite her past trauma, and she moved on with her life to get married, raise children, and sustain a career. At 45 years old, minor stressors begin to pile up: marital conflict, financial problems, a friend's death, and in her state of heightened stress she begins to reexperience—and avoid—painful childhood memories.

## Symptoms and Patterns

The modern understanding of PTSD has a long history with combat-related trauma. After World War I, "shell shock," was the designated title for supposed brain damage related to soldiers' exposure to explosions. During World War II, the term "combat fatigue syndrome" was popularized. It was not until 1980 that the diagnostic term PTSD was adopted after extensive research and treatment of Vietnam veterans.[21] Whatever the term, it is said persons with PTSD are nearly "walking around in a constant state of shock."

### Reexperiencing the Trauma

With PTSD, a traumatic event is persistently reexperienced by the sufferer in three possible ways—memory, dreams, and flashbacks.[22] In powerful form memories are distressing and intrusive, dreams become night terrors, and flashbacks are vivid hallucinations specific to the trauma. In extreme cases—most common with sexual abuse—persons with PTSD experience dissociation and numbing during the recall of traumatic memories.

When reexperiencing trauma, perceptual and emotional reverberations cause intense psychological or physiological distress, sometimes in response to a triggering cue and at other times with no identifiable catalyst. Cues (when identified) may be related to the trauma: in the instance of someone reexperiencing the 9–11 attack in response to seeing a low flying plane. Cues can be unrelated as well. For example, a woman out of breath from exercising recalls being smothered by a perpetrator.

### Pervasive Avoidance

Recalling trauma, though uncomfortable, is a therapeutic opportunity for the mind to process an upsetting past; and reexperiencing alone is not sufficient for a PTSD diagnosis. However, diagnosis is justified when the intensity of memories is severe to a degree that sufferers avoid thoughts, feelings, people, places, situations, or conversations connected to the trauma. Those with PTSD often forget or repress significant aspects of stressful events. They lose interest in previously enjoyable activities, and they detach from others—often becoming isolated and emotionally restricted.[23] In addition, such persons often avoid counseling because it involves recalling and discussing stressful memories.

### Hyperarousal

PTSD sufferers are very nervous with no present cause, for post-traumatic stress makes an event from the past seem evasively present in one's day-to-day functioning. The stress of this evasive presence produces symptoms of constant arousal—one cannot sleep, presents anger and irritable affect, has difficulty concentrating, hypervigilance, and may become very short with spouse and children.[24] One in a state of hyperarousal is said to be "on pins and needles," suffers from exaggerated anxiety, and physiologically has increased adrenaline and sympathetic nervous system activity.

### Somatic Symptoms

It is now accepted that psychological trauma effects biological homeostasis and can cause both short- and long-term disruptions in organs and systems of the body. Persons with PTSD are frequently ill with psychosomatic symptoms that may appear to be exclusively biological. Common physical complaints include stomach pain, chest discomfort, irregular heart rhythms/palpitations, shortness of breath, back and joint pain, and headaches. Moreover, the inability of a physician to identify a biological cause of these problems can further increase frustration and anxiety in a PTSD sufferer.

The physical symptoms of PTSD are not anecdotal. In fact, people with PTSD present many health problems and utilize more health services than sufferers of any other psychiatric disorder. In addition, sufferers frequently become functionally impaired, they are often unable to fill the role of spouse or parent, and suffer in vocational performance.[25]

## Spiritual Issues

Research shows that persons with PTSD often develop spiritual problems. Avoidance of church, prayer and Christian fellowship are common, as are pervasive doubt and crises of faith. Sufferers display strong anger toward God, and suffer the same detachment from God that they do from other social interactions.

However, very recent studies find that traumatic experiences can lead to a deepening of religiousness and spirituality, and that religion and spirituality are usually beneficial in the recovery of those dealing with trauma's aftermath. One study shows that when writing about their traumatic experiences, 80% of participants wrote narratives with religious themes, with some participants detailing their use of specific religious behaviors, such as prayer.[26]

## Traumatic Guilt

Guilt and shame are common for PTSD sufferers. Sometimes justified, one study shows guilt among reckless drivers with PTSD and another among a group of Veterans with PTSD who committed atrocities at war.[27]

However, often guilt is not justified. For example, some have shame over their perceived undeserved fortune to survive a traumatic event.[28] Others display backwards thinking, a type of traumatic guilt where the client thinks "I should have been able to stop this!" This magical thought provides a sense that one can control the world; they just weren't ready at the time of the trauma.

A counselor's role when presented traumatic guilt is to reiterate the truth that the earth is a fallen place, where at times bad things happen that are outside the client's control. For those with justified guilt, clients— through confession—can begin the journey toward repentance and healing.

## Suicidal Thinking

Approximately 20% of people with PTSD attempt suicide, compared to only 15% of people with untreated clinical depression. Hence, the suicide rate in people with PTSD (without intervention) is nothing less than tragic.[29]

Suicide is a crucial topic when addressing the church, for many Christians with suicidal thoughts will not seek help due to shame, assumptions that they will be blamed, or even considered sinful for struggling with suicide. This dynamic must be reformed if the church wishes to minister to its suffering congregants. Thankfully, when one forfeits the secrecy of suicide, it loses much of its power and the probability of a completed suicide decreases.

## Comorbidity

PTSD often brings on other problems. It increases the risk of developing depression, alcohol or drug abuse (self-medicating), social phobias, and other anxiety disorders. Roughly 79% of women and 88% of men will develop at least one more psychiatric problem besides PTSD, and 40% of women and 59% of men will develop at least three other psychiatric problems.

Though some researchers are dogmatic that technically for two disorders to be truly comorbid they must be independent of one another, not overlapping in symptomatology or increasing the risk of having the other,[30] the following disorders have been traditionally considered often comorbid with PTSD.

*Depression.* Depression affects 20% of the U.S. population at any time, and women twice as much as men. While alone depression can be incapacitating, when occurring with PTSD it is significantly worse.[31]

*Panic Anxiety.* In the DSM-IV, PTSD is categorized as an anxiety disorder. Hence, it presents an increased risk of developing symptoms from other anxiety diseases. In reverse, a past history of anxiety disorders also increases one's susceptibility to PTSD.

A panic attack is not an uncommon occurrence for those with PTSD. Described as 3–30 minutes of extreme emotional and physical stress, one may experience increased heart rate, sweating, shortness of breath, nausea, dizziness, asphyxiation, and chest pains (to name a few). Panic anxiety severely exacerbates PTSD because trauma survivors will have increased avoidance to stress provoking thoughts and situations.

*Obsessive-compulsive disorder (OCD).* OCD is very similar to PTSD in that those with OCD are remarkably afraid of their thoughts, and have difficulty distinguishing their thoughts from the present environment. One may exhibit obsessive-compulsive behavior as a way to manage the painful symptoms of PTSD; participating in compulsive rituals (washing hands, checking locks, meticulously folding clothes, counting) to assuage obsessive thoughts.

*Sleep disorders.* One of the major problems for PTSD sufferers is decreased sleep.[32] Having immediate consequences, one becomes fatigued, sore, irritable, lacks concentration, creativity, and work performance. In addition, insomnia increases the risk of one developing PTSD. During sleep, brain activity decreases while neurotransmitters are replenished. Necessary for normal brain functioning, sufficient sleep increases one's resilience to stressors, including those that facilitate PTSD.

## Complex PTSD

Previously known as complicated PTSD, the first requirement for the diagnosis of complex PTSD (CP) is that an individual has experienced a prolonged period—months to years—of total control by a perpetrator, or perpetrators.[33] Victims of CP are generally held in a state of captivity such as with a POW or concentration camp, sex-trafficking ring, incest victimization, or long-term domestic violence situations,[34] and are exposed to extreme personal stress.

The result of such victimization is the destruction of one's psychological integrity, or "mental death." In detail, it is the loss of a victim's pre-trauma identity, and incorporates a sense of being permanently damaged.[35] Those suffering from CP present a combination of the following symptoms:

1.  *Diminished Regulation of Affect*
    The inability to control emotions or CERs; may include emotional outbursts, suicidal thoughts, catatonic states, and risk taking behaviors.
2.  *Distorted Attention or Consciousness*
    This may involve amnesia, repression or suppression of traumatic events, as well as numbing or dissociation.
3.  *Distorted Self-Perception*
    Includes shame, guilt, perceived helplessness or weakness, or a sense of being permanently damaged.

4.  *Distorted Perception of the Perpetrator*
    Victims may attribute god-like power to, or idealize, the victim-
    izer. Victims may also evince a preoccupation with revenge.

5.  *Damaged Relationships with Others*
    A diminished ability to trust, social isolation, victimizing others,
    feelings of interpersonal rejection, and the repeated search for a
    rescuer are common.

6.  *Somatic Symptoms*
    Physical manifestations of CP include digestive problems, chronic
    pain, cardiopulmonary symptoms, and sexual dysfunction.

7.  *Loss of Value or Belief Systems*
    Hopelessness, despair, spiritual crisis, and a loss of religious faith
    are common occurences.

The assemblage of possible symptoms under the CP nomenclature is consistent with developmental models regarding the long-term impact of victimization. For example, health problems without known etiology, dissociation,
self destructive behavior, and maladaptive affective and cognitive construc-
tions of one's self, world, or others have been noted among incest survivors.
In addition, developmental research reveals that many brain chemical and
hormonal changes may occur as a result of early prolonged trauma, and these
changes contribute to difficulties with memory and learning.[36]

As adults, victims of CP are often diagnosed with depressive disorders,
personality disorders, or dissociative disorders. Treatment often takes
much longer than with regular PTSD—progressing at a much slower rate—
and requires a sensitive and structured treatment program delivered by a
trauma specialist.

## PTSD Treatment

At the core of PTSD is the issue of affect deregulation and at the root of
treatment is the development of emotional regulation skills. Very basically,
since one who possesses PTSD is impaired in his/her ability to cope with
traumatic memories, treatment must involve equipping a client such that
he/she no longer relies on avoidant strategies (i.e. dissociation, numbing,
self-medication, or tension reducing behaviors (TRBs) such as cutting, sexual acting out, etc.).

Coping involves both mentally and viscerally dividing the past from the present and gaining control over both painful memories and emotions, and the avoidant defenses erected against them. Moreover, a therapist must attempt to instill in a client new relational and behavioral schemas that will lead to more benign and adaptive CERs.

## Education and Orientation

A good PTSD treatment plan covers medical, psychosocial, spiritual, familial, and even vocational factors. PTSD-specific treatment is begun only after the survivor has been safely removed from a crisis situation.[37] If a survivor is still being exposed to trauma (such as ongoing domestic violence, abuse, or homelessness), is severely depressed or suicidal, is experiencing panic or disorganized thinking, or is in need of drug or alcohol detoxification, it is important to address these crisis problems as part of the first phase of treatment.

It is important that the first phase of treatment includes educating trauma survivors and their families about how persons develop PTSD, how PTSD affects survivors and their loved ones, and other problems that commonly accompany PTSD symptoms.[38] The client's understanding that PTSD is a medically recognized disorder that occurs in normal individuals under extremely stressful conditions is essential for effective treatment.

One aspect of the first treatment phase is to have the client examine and resolve strong feelings such as anger, shame or guilt, which are common among survivors of trauma.

Another step is to teach the client strategies to cope with post-traumatic memories, reminders, reactions and feelings without becoming overwhelmed or emotionally numb. Trauma memories usually do not go away entirely as a result of therapy; instead they become manageable with the mastery of new coping skills.

## Pace of Therapy

Due to shame or guilt that is often co-present, there can be reluctance on behalf of the client to disclose meaningfully. In addition, since avoidant behaviors are seen as necessary to survival, overzealous attempts by a counselor to remove either denial or dissociative symptoms can overwhelm a client and facilitate use of such defenses in therapy.

A counselor may need to wait for a client to take the initiative to disclose, and will need to operate within what is called the "therapeutic window." Interventions operating within the therapeutic window challenge, but do not overwhelm the emotional or cognitive processes of a client.[39] A counselor must have his/her finger on the pulse of the counseling relationship at all times, for disclosure will be tightly correlated to a client's level of trust, and perception of safety in the counseling environment.

### Relationships as the Antidote for PTSD

*Affect Regulation.* Mentioned earlier, those who suffer early childhood trauma are deprived of growth-promoting opportunities, and instead develop destructive schemas. This can be thought of as a developmental retardation, one which—over time—can be reversed with the integration of healthy relationships. One author states about persons traumatized:

> But sooner or later, many persons *are* able to leave traumatic environments. They *can* find environments conducive to putting their development back on course. Even if you have undergone prolonged trauma, you can potentially choose and construct a healthier environment for yourself. The new environment will foster new learning: The world is dangerous; people are dangerous, but not *that* dangerous. The world can be relatively safe, and many people can be trusted.[40]

It is said that learning to trust one person enables one to trust others, and as persons consistently prove themselves trustworthy, one's capacity to trust society in general will increase (and when the world is perceived as safe, PTSD has much less of a stronghold).

*Social Support.* In addition, social support helps with the coping of new traumas. Take for example the following vignette of two women who experienced the same traumatic situation:

> Two separate woman, each alone, are nearly attacked in a parking garage but escape without physical harm. One woman arrives home upset and is immediately encountered by her husband who is emotion-

ally supportive, reassuring, calls local authorities, and who asks her to talk about the experience. After several minutes the woman calms and begins to feel relief from the stress. A few minutes later her children arrive home from school smiling and calling "Mommy, Mommy!" further confirming that the world is generally safe and good.

In contrast, the second woman arrives home to an empty apartment—she does not talk about the encounter, and instead rethinks the event many times without resolve before she begins to try and distract herself from the memory. She feels nervous, on edge, and she double checks the locks on her doors before retreating to her bedroom for the first of many sleepless nights.

Because relationships are healing, empowering one to establish secure attachment is a cornerstone of PTSD treatment.[41]

## Group Therapy

Group treatment is often an ideal therapeutic setting because trauma survivors are able to share experiences within the safety, cohesion, and empathy of other survivors. As group members achieve greater understanding of their trauma, they often feel more confident in the integrity of themselves and others. As they share trauma-related shame, guilt, rage, fear, doubt, and self-condemnation, they focus themselves on the present rather than the past.[42] Telling one's story—known as the "trauma narrative"—and directly facing the grief and anxiety related to trauma, enables many survivors to cope with their symptoms, memories, and other aspects of their lives.

## Therapeutic Relationship

Also utilizing the power of relationship, brief psychodynamic psychotherapy focuses on the emotional conflicts caused by the traumatic event, particularly as it relates to early life experiences. Client centered therapies promote the retelling of the traumatic event to a calm, empathic, compassionate, and nonjudgmental therapist. With either relationship, the trauma survivor achieves a greater sense of self-esteem, develops effective ways of thinking and coping, and learns to deal more successfully with intense emotions.

## Medication

Due to the stress and anxiety involved with severe PTSD, chemical imbalances (serotonin disturbances for example) are not uncommon. Therefore, for some there is a need of medication as a means of chemical regulation—to correct serious neurological problems facilitated by the trauma.

Medication can reduce the anxiety, depression, and insomnia often experienced with PTSD; and in some cases it may help relieve the distress and emotional numbness caused by trauma memories.[43] Several kinds of antidepressant drugs have contributed to patient improvement in clinical trials, and some other classes of drugs have also shown promise. At this time, no particular drug has emerged as a definitive treatment for PTSD, but serotonin enhancing antidepressants appear to hold the most promise. However, medication is clearly useful for symptom relief, which makes it possible for survivors to participate in psychotherapy.

Christian counselors should have a working relationship with physicians—general practitioners and psychiatrists—in their local community. Antidepressants used to treat PTSD are not addictive, and they do not produce a "high." On the contrary, they require 2 to 3 weeks (and sometimes as long as six weeks) to deliver therapeutic effects. On average, clients will need to take medicine for about 6 to 12 months before experiencing the most therapeutic effects.

## Cognitive Behavioral Approaches

Cognitive-behavioral therapy (CBT) involves addressing disruptive cognitions as a means to change one's emotions and behaviors. Cognitive-behavioral techniques are important in PTSD treatment because they help to challenge the distorted thoughts and exaggerated fears present with the disorder. However, due to CERs based in the non-verbal brain, a practitioner will find PTSD treatment similar to phobia treatment, in that rationalization does not produce a cure.

*Exposure therapy.* Exposure therapy is one form of CBT unique to trauma treatment. It uses careful, repeated, detailed exposure of the trauma in a safe, controlled context to help the survivor face and gain control of overwhelming fear and distress.[44] Though in some cases trauma memories can be confronted all at once with "flooding,"[45] with PTSD it is preferable to use "systematic desensitization" and increase exposure anxiety gradually by using relaxation techniques, and by exploring traumatic memories "one piece at a time."

*EMDR.* Eye Movement Desensitization and Reprocessing (EMDR) is a treatment that attempts to move memories from the limbic brain to the cerebral cortex with therapy that includes top-down (cognitive) and bottom-up (affect/body) processing. In brief, a client is asked to recall traumatic memories while grounded in the present by incorporating eye movements, hand taps, or sounds. While research is still evolving, a recent study investigating EMDR efficacy in treating PTSD found it to be helpful but less effective than systematic desensitization. The most therapeutic aspect of EMDR seems to be the telling of the narrative, with the grounding aspects often seen as more ancillary.[46]

### How Long Does PTSD Treatment Take?

Treatment outcome and duration will depend on several factors, including the length of time between the PTSD symptom onset and the start of treatment. Someone who solicits help very soon after developing symptoms might experience relief in a matter of weeks, or a few months. However, 50% of those with PTSD develop chronic problems and do not seek treatment for months or years after experiencing the disorder. Unfortunately, the longer one has existed without care, the longer treatment will take. It cannot be overstated that, with any instance of PTSD, early intervention is extremely important.

Lastly, issues of disorder severity, CP, and comorbidity will influence the length of PTSD treatment.

### Conclusion

Trauma and PTSD are becoming an all too common experience in modern life—one that will be exaggerated and exploited by a culture bent on victimhood and dependency, but one that should never be minimized in those suffering its ill effects. Christian counselors are poised to become compassionate advocates and effective interveners for trauma sufferers and should do everything possible to prepare—from the first of graduate courses to continuing education—to be the best helpers possible.

The apostle Paul's life was replete with trauma: "...five times I received forty stripes minus one. Three times I was beaten with rods; once I was stoned; three times I was shipwrecked...in perils...in perils...in perils..." (2 Cor. 11:24–27). Furthermore, he was given "a thorn in the flesh" which caused him to plead with God over and over again that it be removed from his life. But these troubles were not removed (2 Cor. 12:7–8). Instead, God told Paul that "My grace is sufficient for you, for My strength is made perfect in your weakness" (2 Cor. 12:9a) and in response Paul learned the deep mystery of power and perseverance in the face of trauma, "...I will rather boast in infirmities, that the power of Christ may rest on me. Therefore I take pleasure in infirmities, in reproaches, in needs, in persecutions, in distresses, for Christ's sake. For when I am weak, then I am strong" (2 Cor. 12:9b–10).

Paul beat the onset of PTSD by embracing trauma that could not be avoided, by seeing God's hand at work in the further training of His disciple, for the glory of God and the building up of the new church in a hostile world; "I will very gladly spend and be spent for your souls..." he told the young Corinthian church (2 Cor. 12:15). So then, let us not look for and revel in trauma—we are not called to be foolish masochists. But when trauma comes unavoidably, let's embrace it and ask God to work His will in and through it for His glory and our growth. Then let it be gone!

## ENDNOTES

1.  Nikki N. Jordan, Hoge, C. W., Tobler, S. K., Wells, J., Dydek, G. J., and Egerton, W. E., Mental health impact of 9/11 Pentagon attack: Validation of a rapid assessment tool, *American Journal of Preventive Medicine*, 26(4) (April 2004), 284–294.

2.  National Institute of Mental Health, *Reliving trauma: Post-traumatic stress disorder: A brief overview of the symptoms, treatments, and research findings* (2001); O Frans, Rimmö, P.A., Åberg, L., and Fredrikson, M., Trauma exposure and post-traumatic stress disorder in the general population, *Acta Psychiatrica Scandinavica*, 111(4) (April 2005), 291–293.

3.  N. Breslau, and Davis, G.C., Post-traumatic stress disorder in an urban population of young adults: Risk factors for chronicity, *American Journal of Psychiatry*, 149 (1992), 671–675; Heidi S Resnick, Kilpatrick, D.G., Dansky, B.S., Saunders, B.E. et al, Prevalence of civilian trauma and post-traumatic stress disorder in a representative national sample of women, *Journal of Consulting & Clinical Psychology*, 61(6) (December 1993), 984–991; American Psychiatric Association, *Let's talk facts about post-traumatic stress disorder* (Accessed June 20, 2005 from <http://www.psych.org/public_info/ptsd.cfm: Author, 1999).

4.  Jon G. Allen, *Coping with trauma: A guide to self-understanding* (American Psychiatric Press Inc, 1999); D.J. Gelinas, Relational patterns in incestuous families, malevolent variations, and specific interventions with the adult survivor, in P.L.

Paddison (ed.), *Treatment of adult survivors of incest* (Washington, D.C., American Psychiatric Press, 1993), 1–34.

5.  Kathleen McCullough-Zander, and Larson, S., The fear is still in me: Caring for survivors of torture, *American Journal of Nursing, 104*(10), (October 2004), 54–65; Allen S. Keller, Rosenfeld, B., Trinh-Shevrin, C., Meserve, C., Sachs, E., Leviss, J. A., Singer, E., Smith, H., Wilkinson, J., Kim, G., Allden, K., and Ford, D., Mental health of detained asylum seekers, *Lancet, 362*(9397), (November 2003), 1721–1724; A.S. Blank Jr., The longitudinal course of post-traumatic stress disorder, in *Post-traumatic stress disorder: DSM IV and beyond* (Washington DC: American Psychiatric Press, 1993).

6.  Steven Cufee, Addy, C., Garrison, C., Waller, J., Jackson, K., Mckeown, R., and Chilappagari, S., Prevalence of PTSD in a community sample of older adolescents, *Journal of the American Academy of Child & Adolescent Psychiatry, 37*(2), (February 1998), 147–154.; R.C. Kessler, Sonnega, A., Bromet, E., Hughes, M., and Nelson, C.B., Post-traumatic stress disorder in the national comorbidity survey, *Archives of General Psychiatry, 52*(12) (December 1995), 1048–1060.

7.  Heidi S Resnick, Kilpatrick, D.G., Dansky, B.S., Saunders, B.E. et al, Prevalence of civilian trauma and post-traumatic stress disorder in a representative national sample of women, *Journal of Consulting & Clinical Psychology, 61*(6) (December 1993), 984–991.

8.  Catlina M. Arata, Sexual revictimization and PTSD: An exploratory study, *Journal of Child Sexual Abuse, 8*(1), (1999), 49–66; O Frans, Rimmö, P.A., Åberg, L., and Fredrikson, M., Trauma exposure and post-traumatic stress disorder in the general population," *Acta Psychiatrica Scandinavica, 111*(4) (April 2005), 291–293.

9.  W. R. True, Rice, J., Eisen, S. A., Heath, A. C., Goldberg, J., Lyons M. J., and Nowak, J., A twin study of genetic and environmental contributions to liability for post-traumatic stress symptoms, *JAMA & Archives, Archives of General Psychiatry*, accessed June 20, 2005 from http://archpsyc.amaassn.org/cgi/content/abstract/50/4/257.

10. Jennifer Ahern, Galea, S., Resnick, H., Kilpatrick, D., Bucuvalas, M., Gold, J., and Vlahov, D., Television images and psychological symptoms after the September 11 terrorist attacks, *Psychiatry:Interpersonal & Biological Processes, 65*(4), (Winter 2002), 289–301; O Frans, Rimmö, P.A., Åberg, L., and Fredrikson, M., Trauma exposure and post-traumatic stress disorder in the general population, *Acta Psychiatrica Scandinavica, 111*(4) (April 2005), 291–293.

11. Atia Daud, Skoglund, E., and Rydelius, P., Children in families of torture victims: Transgenerational transmission of parents' traumatic experiences to their children, *International Journal of Social Welfare, 14*(1), (January 2005), 23–33; John Briere, Treating adult survivors of severe childhood abuse and neglect: Further development of an integrative model, in *The APSAC handbook on child maltreatment, 2nd Edition* (Newbury Park, CA: Sage Publications, 1996).

12. Gary Sibcy, Lecture: Advanced psychopathology, *Liberty University,* (June 2005); John Briere, Treating adult survivors of severe childhood abuse and neglect: Further development of an integrative model, in *The APSAC handbook on child maltreatment, 2nd Edition* (Newbury Park, CA: Sage Publications, 1996).

13. John Bowlby, *A secure base: Parent-child attachment and healthy human development* (New York: Basic Books, 1988).

14. C. Dissanayake, and Crossley, S. A., Proximity and sociable behaviours in autism: Evidence for attachment, *Journal of Child Psychol Psychiatry. 37*(2), (February 1996), 149–156; Mary Ainsworth, Blehar, M. C., Waters, E., Wall, S., *Patterns of attachment: A psychological study of the strange situation* (Hillsdale, NJ: Erlbaum, 1978).

15. John Briere, Treating adult survivors of severe childhood abuse and neglect: Further development of an integrative model, in *The APSAC handbook on child maltreatment, 2nd Edition* (Newbury Park, CA: Sage Publications, 1996); John Bowlby, *A secure base.*

16. P. Fonagy, *Pathological attachments and therapeutic action* (Paper Presented at the Annual Meeting of the California Branch of the American Academy of Child and Adolescent Psychiatry, Yosemite Valley, CA., 1999).

17. Jon G. Allen, *Coping with trauma: A guide to self-understanding* (American Psychiatric Press Inc., 1999), 6.

18. Michael G. Madianos, Papaghelis, M., Ioannovich, J., Dafni, R., Psychiatric disorders in burn patients: A follow-up study, *Psychotherapy and Psychosomatics, 70,* (2001), 30–37.

19. Maria Oquendo, Brent, D. A., Birmaher, B., Greenhill, L, Kolko, D., Stanley, B., Zelazny, J., Burke, A. K., Firinciogullari, S., Ellis, S. P., and Mann, J. J., Post-traumatic stress disorder comorbid with major depression: Factors mediating the association with suicidal behavior, *American Journal of Psychiatry, 162*(3), (March 2005), 560–567; Ill Holtzheimer, Russo, P. E., Zatzick, J., Bundy, D., Roy-Byrne, C., and Peter P., The impact of comorbid post-traumatic stress disorder on short-term clinical outcome in hospitalized patients with depression, *American Journal of Psychiatry, 162*(5), (May 2005), 970–977; Sandra Anton, and Mrdenovi_, S., Working ability of patients with post-traumatic stress disorder (demographic and social features): Comparative study, *Journal of Loss & Trauma, 10*(2), (March/April 2005), 155–162.

20. Cynthia Lindman Port, Engdahl, B., and Frazier, P., A longitudinal and retrospective study of PTSD among older prisoners of war, *American Journal of Psychiatry, 158*(9), (September 2001), 1474–1480.

21. American Psychiatric Association, *Let's talk facts about post-traumatic stress disorder* (accessed June 20, 2005 from <http://www.psych.org/public_info/ptsd.cfm: Author, 1999); Jon G. Allen, *Coping with trauma: A guide to self-understanding* (American Psychiatric Press Inc., 1999).

22. Nancy Fagan, and Freme, K., Confronting post-traumatic stress disorder, *Nursing, 34*(2), (February 2004), 52–54; National Institute of Mental Health, *Reliving trauma: Post-traumatic stress disorder: A brief overview of the symptoms, treatments, and research findings* (2001).

23. Hans Peter Söndergaard, Ekblad, S., and Theorell, T., Screening for post-traumatic stress disorder among refugees in Stockholm, *Nordic Journal of Psychiatry, 57*(3), (May 2003), 185–190.

24. Eldra P. Solomon, and Heide, K. M., The biology of trauma, *Journal of Interpersonal Violence, 20*(1), (January 2005), 51–61; Thomas A. Mellman, and David, D., Sleep disturbance and its relationship to psychiatric morbidity after Hurricane Andrew, *American Journal of Psychiatry, 152*(11), (November 1995), 1659–1664; Jean M. Thomas, Traumatic stress disorder presents as hyperactivity and disruptive behavior: Case presentation, diagnoses, and treatment, *Infant Mental Health Journal, 16*(4), (Winter 1995), 306–318; Kathy A. Pearce, Schauer, A. H., Garfield, N. J., Ohlde, C. O., and Patterson, T.W., A study of post-traumatic stress disorder in Vietnam veterans, *Journal of Clinical Psychology, 41*(1), (January 1985), 9–15.

25. Dorcas Dobie, Kivlahan, D. R., Maynard, C., Bush, K. R., Davis, T.M., and Bradley, K.A., Post-traumatic stress disorder in female veterans: Association with self-reported health problems and functional impairment" *Archives of Internal*

*Medicine*, 164(4), (February 2004), 394–401; P. Niels Christensen, Cohan, S. L., and Stein, M. B., The relationship between interpersonal perception and post-traumatic stress disorder-related functional impairment: A social relations model analysis, *Cognitive Behaviour Therapy*, 33(3), (2004), 151–161.

26.  Annick Shaw, Joseph, S., and Linley, A. P., Religion, spirituality, and post-traumatic growth: A systematic review, *Mental Health, Religion & Culture*, 8(1), (March 2005), 1–11; Julie J. Exline, Smyth, J.M., Gregory, J., Hockemeyer, J., and Tulloch, H., Religious framing by individuals with PTSD when writing about traumatic experiences, *International Journal for the Psychology of Religion*, 15(1), (2005), 17–34.

27.  Tamar Lowinger, and Solomon, T. Z., PTSD, guilt, and shame among reckless drivers," *Journal of Loss & Trauma*, 9(4), (October-December 2004), 327–345; Mel Singer, Shame, guilt, self-hatred and remorse in the psychotherapy of Vietnam combat veterans who committed atrocities, *American Journal of Psychotherapy*, 58(4), (2004), 377–386.

28.  Jennie Leskela, Dieperink, M., Thuras, P., Shame and post-traumatic stress disorder, *Journal of Traumatic Stress*, 15(3), (June 2002), 223–227.

29.  Marcelle Ferrada-Noli, Asberg, M., Ormstad, K., Lundin, T., and Sundbom, E., Suicidal behavior after severe trauma. Part 1: PTSD diagnoses, psychiatric co-morbidity, and assessments of suicidal behavior, *Journal of Traumatic Stress*, 11(1), (January 1998), 103–113; Rani A Desai, Dausey, D. J., and Rosenheck, R., Mental health service delivery and suicide risk: The role of individual patient and facility factors, *American Journal of Psychiatry*, 162(2) (February 2005), 311–319.

30.  R. D. Alacorn, Glover, S.G., and Deering, C.G., The cascade model: An alternative to comorbidity in the pathogenesis of post-traumatic stress disorder, *Psychiatry*, 62 (1999), 114–124.

31.  Archibald Hart, and Weber, C.H., *Unveiling depression in women: A practical guide to understanding and overcoming depression* (Grand Rapids, MI: Fleming H. Revell, 2002), 20; Reginald D.V. Nixon, Resick, P. A., and Nishith, P., An exploration of co-morbid depression among female victims of intimate partner violence with post-traumatic stress disorder, *Journal of Affective Disorders*, 82(2), (October 2004), 315–321.

32.  Johnathan D. Huppert, Moser, J. S., Gershuny, B. S., Riggs, D. S., Spokas, M., Filip, J., Hajcak, G., Parker, H. A., Baer, L., and Foa, E. B., The relationship between obsessive-compulsive and post-traumatic stress symptoms in clinical and non-clinical samples, *Journal of Anxiety Disorders*, 19(1), (January 2005), 127–137; Anne Germain, Hall, M., Krakow, B., Shear, M. K., and Buysse, D. J., A brief sleep scale for post-traumatic stress disorder: Pittsburgh Sleep Quality Index addendum for PTSD, *Journal of Anxiety Disorders*, 19(2), (March 2005), 233–245.; Pallavi Nishith, Resick, P. A., and Mueser, K. T., Sleep difficulties and alcohol use motives in female rape victims with post-traumatic stress disorder, *Journal of Traumatic Stress*, 14(3), (July 2001), 469–480.; Javaid I. Sheikh, Woodward, S. H., and Leskin, G. A., Sleep in post-traumatic stress disorder and panic: Convergence and divergence, *Depression & Anxiety*, 18(4), (2003), 187–198.

33.  S. Roth, Newman, E., Pelcovitz, D., Van der Kolk, B., and Mandel, F. S., Complex PTSD in victims exposed to sexual and physical abuse: Results from the DSM-IV field trial for post-traumatic stress disorder, *Journal of Traumatic Stress*, 10, (1997), 539–555.

34.  Julia M. Whealin, *Complex PTSD a national center for PTSD fact sheet* (accessed on June 20, 2005 from <http://www.ncptsd.va.gov/facts/specific/

fs_complex_ptsd.html>: Department of Veterans Affairs).

35.   Angela Ebert, and Dyck, M. J., The experience of mental death: The core feature of complex post-traumatic stress disorder, *Clinical Psychology Review*, *24*(6), (October 2004), 617–36.

36.   Martin H. Teicher, Andersen, S. L., Polcari, A., Anderson, C. M., Navalta, C. P., and Kim, D. M., The neurobiological consequences of early stress and childhood maltreatment, *Neuroscience & Biobehavioral Reviews*, *27*(1/2), (January 2003), 33–45.; Michael D. De Bellis, Keshavan, M.S., Shifflett, H., Iyengar, S., Beers, S.R., Hall, J., and Moritz, G., Brain structures in pediatric maltreatment-related post-traumatic stress disorder: A sociodemographically matched study, *Biological Psychiatry*, *52*(11), (December 2002), 1066–1079.

37.   Jonathan I. Bisson, McFarlane, A. C., and Rose, S., *Psychological debriefing, effective treatments for PTSD* (New York: Guilford Press, 2000), 41.

38.   Matt J. Gray, Elhai, J. D., and Frueh, C. B., Enhancing patient satisfaction and increasing treatment compliance: Patient education as a fundamental component of PTSD treatment, *Psychiatric Quarterly*, *75*(4) (December 2004), 321–333.

39.   John Briere, Treating adult survivors of severe childhood abuse and neglect: Further development of an integrative model, in *The APSAC handbook on child maltreatment, 2nd Edition*, (Newbury Park, CA: Sage Publications, 1996).

40.   Jon G. Allen, *Coping with trauma: A guide to self-understanding* (American Psychiatric Press Inc., 1999).

41.   Tim Clinton, and Sibcy, G., *Attachments: Why you love, feel and act the way you do* (Brentwood, TN: Integrity, 2002).

42.   American Psychiatric Association, *Let's talk facts about post-traumatic stress disorder* (accessed June 20, 2005 from <http://www.psych.org/public_info/ptsd.cfm>: Author, 1999); Irvin D. Yalom, *The theory and practice of group psychotherapy* (New York: Basic Books, 1995).

43.   Ulrich Frommberger, Stieglitz, R., Nyberg, E., Richter, H., Novelli-Fischer, U., Angenendt, J., Zaninelli, R., and Berger, M., Comparison between paroxetine and behaviour therapy in patients with post-traumatic stress disorder (PTSD): A pilot study, *International Journal of Psychiatry in Clinical Practice*, *8*(1), (March 2004), 19–24.

44.   Jaye Wald, and Taylor, S., Interoceptive exposure therapy combined with trauma-related exposure therapy for post-traumatic stress disorder: A case report, *Cognitive Behaviour Therapy*, *34*(1), (2005), 34–41.

45.   Philip A. Saigh, In vitro flooding of an adolescent's post-traumatic stress disorder, *Journal of Clinical Child Psychology*, *16*(2), (June 1987), 147–151.

46.   Eldra P. Solomon, and Heide, K. M. The biology of trauma, *Journal of Interpersonal Violence*, *20*(1), (January 2005), 51–61; Steven Taylor, Thordarson, D. S., Fedoroff, I.C., Maxfield, L., and Ogrodniczuk, J., Comparative efficacy, speed, and adverse effects of three PTSD treatments: exposure therapy, EMDR, and relaxation training, *Journal of Consulting & Clinical Psychology*, *71*(2), (April 2003), 330–339; Gary Sibcy, Lecture: Advanced Psychopathology, *Liberty University* (June 2005).

# 19

# Adult Survivors of Sexual Abuse:
# Trauma, Treatment, and Living in the Truth

*Diane Langberg*

Rarely in human history...has there been this degree of wanton...violence [done against] helpless victims, ranging from child abuse to state-sanctioned torture. Although a historical perspective will not directly help the victims of child sexual and physical abuse...it undergirds the observation that the trauma done to humans by other humans is considerably more damaging and enduring in its...effects than trauma done by floods, earthquakes [and other natural disasters]. It is not that natural traumas are trivial, but rather that there is something about being hurt intentionally and gratuitously by other human beings...that is particularly gripping in its destructiveness and demoralization.

JEROME KROLL[1]

"My father raped me."

It has been thirty years since I first heard the words. I had just finished a Master's degree in psychology and was entering a doctoral program. Nothing in my personal life or in my training to that point had prepared me for such a statement. But I did what all good students do when they hit a wall—I went to talk to my supervisor. The response I got was that women sometimes tell these hysterical stories and your job is to not get hooked by them. They are essentially looking for attention and if you give it to them you will contribute to their pathology.

As time passed I began to hear more stories of sexual abuse from other women. I decided to listen. I basically told my clients that I knew nothing about such things, nor did I know anyone to ask. I wanted to help and was willing to learn if they would teach me what they knew while I struggled to find what would be helpful for them. They, probably out of desperation, agreed and thus began an aspect of my professional life that has changed me irrevocably, challenged me constantly, and continues to teach me to this day.

To give you a full presentation on the treatment of sexual abuse in one chapter is, of course, impossible. My fuller thinking about treatment is in a book entitled *Counseling Survivors of Sexual Abuse.*[2] So rather than simply give you what you can go read I have chosen to present an overview of treatment as a backdrop for specific consideration of the spiritual impact on the survivor and the resultant struggles you will face as a counselor.

Human beings, as you know, commit atrocious acts against other human beings. One of the most horrible of these is the sexual abuse of a child. Most of the men and women I have worked with are survivors of chronic and often violent sexual abuse. I acknowledge without question that all sexual abuse is not traumatic. However, for most victims it is traumatic beyond words and because of my experience, and for the purpose of this chapter, I will treat abuse as trauma.

A child is by definition developing or in process. The sexual abuse of a child shatters and violates every aspect of their being—their world, their self, their faith and their future. Such violation forces the child to adapt in ways that are often maladaptive in the larger world. Such violation causes the child to develop a view of himself and his world that is based on repeated and destructive lies. Obviously an understanding of this must inform treatment or we will be ineffective.

These are the stories I listen to in my practice. When I first began to hear them, there were no books on the subject, no articles, no TV shows, no workshops. I learned from my clients. Those women taught me what it felt like to be molested as children, what it felt like to be adults with such memories, and what they needed to start on the road to healing. I made many mistakes. I missed a lot of clues. I'm sure they suffered needlessly as a result. But they grew, and I grew with them. I owe them, as do my later clients, a great debt. Now I hope to pass on to you some of what I have learned.

### Prevalence: Prying Open a Secret World

A therapist tells the story that during an initial therapy session with a senior citizen, she asked a routine interview question: "Have you ever been sexually abused?" The older woman paused, then nodded slowly. Although she had been in therapy most of her adult life, there was no

## A CASE-BASED VIEW OF CHILD SEXUAL ABUSE

I would like to define sexual abuse for you—not a technical one (we will do that next) but a graphic one—seeing abuse through the eyes of the victim. Think about a little girl, around 6 years old, who is ready for bed. What images come to mind? Clean, safe, protected, stories, trust, closeness. I am sure many of you reading this have lived this image out with your own daughters and know there is something very special and tender about tucking your child in bed at night.

The reality of sexual abuse shatters that image. The little girl lies in bed in paralyzing fear. She is listening for footsteps, for the sound of her door opening. She wraps her covers around her in a mummy-like fashion—a desperate attempt to provide safety for herself. But she is little and he is big, and she has no place to go. He confuses and frightens her. He touches and hurts her and tells her it's their secret. She's not to tell anyone, or she will lose her daddy forever—and it will be her fault.

His fondling intensifies and he starts doing other things, things she doesn't understand. It hurts so badly and she wants it to stop. She tells him, but he says this is what father's do for their daughters and it's for her good. He also says it's her fault for leading him on. What does that mean? All she did was get in bed to go to sleep.

It's especially confusing because in the morning everything goes back to normal. He greets her at breakfast like nothing happened and she goes off to school. Then he begins doing some of the same things in the daytime if they are alone. She dreads the times when her mother leaves the house. She tries to go to her friend's house after school as much as possible. One night she tried sleeping in her closet—but he always finds her. Nothing works.

She thinks about telling her Mom, but is afraid. Mom encourages her to be with Dad. Maybe she knows and thinks it's okay. Maybe she would be angry and say it was all her fault. She is very confused about all this. One time Mom caught Dad in her room, but he said she'd had a bad dream and he was calming her down. Mom believed him.

Sometimes when it's happening she pretends she's real little and can hide under the flowers in her wallpaper. It's funny, because she feels like she's watching herself from faraway. She digs her fingernails into her palms and sometimes pulls on her hair so hard it comes out. The pain from those things distracts her. She thinks often about running away. Just wait till she's older.

In the meantime, his pursuit is relentless, and his anger toward her increases. He calls her terrible names and tells her how bad she is for making him do this. Doesn't he understand that she doesn't want to do this? What could she possibly be doing to make him do these things? Then, after she does just what he wants so he won't get mad, he gets mad anyway. It just doesn't make any sense. *Nothing she can think of is successful in stopping it*... Maybe it would stop if she were dead...

record of sexual victimization in her overflowing patient file. Her stark response, "No one ever asked."[3]

Too often, we do not ask. We survey clients on alcohol use, drug use, suicidality, depression, physical abuse, and sometimes consensual sexual contact. But we fail to ask about sexual victimization. The nature of the crime constituting child sexual abuse is enmeshed in victim secrecy. Research began exposing sexual abuse as a problem of sizable proportions in the late 1960s and early 1970s. One theme remains consistent: sexual abuse is extensively undisclosed and underreported.[4]

There are many factors relating to the dynamics of the insufferable crime that may impact victim failure to disclose. Abuse victims frequently experience feelings of shame, guilt, isolation, powerlessness, embarrassment, and inadequacy. They may even accept responsibility for the abuse by blaming themselves. Victims often feel that "something is wrong with me," or that the abuse is their fault.[5]

### Research on Victims

David Finkelhor and his colleagues [6] conducted the first national telephone survey of men and women victims of abuse. Of the 2,626 Americans questioned regarding prior sexual abuse, victimization was reported by 27% of the women and 16% of the men. One of the major findings was that many victims never disclosed the experiences to anyone. Of those participants who confirmed sexual abuse, 42% of the women and 33% of the men acknowledged never having disclosed.

Based on his extensive research on sexual abuse, Bagley affirmed that child sexual abuse is much more frequent than previously assumed. He reported 32% of the sampled adult females in his community study responded they experienced child sexual abuse, with sexual abuse greater for women born after 1960 than before.[7] These figures coincide with best estimates that range from 1 in 4 to 40% of the female population as having had an experience of sexual abuse at sometime in their childhood. Estimates for males usually are around 1 in 6.

Most child sexual abuse is perpetrated either by a family member or someone known to the child. The majority of abusers of both male and female victims are male, however, some unknown percentage of abusers are female. The ultimate irony is that abuse may be the biggest cause and effect of abuse...among abusing parents 30 to 60% say that they were abused as children.[8]

Child sexual abuse usually begins between ages 6 and 12, but for many children it begins at a much younger age. Abuse that occurs at a very young age and is forceful and repeated is most likely to be forgotten or repressed by the child. This is because children do not have sophisticated defense mechanisms in their repertoire, so they are limited to dealing with trauma in relatively primitive ways.

Most sexual abuse does not involve force, but rather involves some sort of manipulation and misrepresentation to the child. However, it is important to note that even when abuse in non-forceful, it is violative, and therefore is a form of violence. In other cases, physical force, violence, threats and coercion are used. Children may be frightened into participation by an abuser who threatens harm, abandonment and rejection.

## Definitions of Abuse

Let's move on to a technical definition for sexual abuse and then describe its effects. Then we will consider the treatment process, with an emphasis on what therapy needs to include. Later, we will discuss the dangers inherent for the therapist in doing this kind of work, as well as some of the lessons I have learned that have not only been helpful, but necessary, in maintaining my sanity, my compassion, and my endurance.

I am going to focus on adult female survivors because I do not work with children—my expertise is with adults and, for the most part, victims tend to be female and perpetrators male.[9] Most of the work and research that has been done concerns this particular dyad. However, I would like to add that in recent years I find myself seeing more and more men who have been sexually abused and who have entered therapy for the express purpose of dealing with it.

Sexual abuse is defined in *Renewal: Hope for Victims of Sexual Abuse* as "any sexual activity, verbal, visual or physical, engaged in without consent, which may be emotionally or physically harmful and which exploits a person in order to meet another person's sexual or emotional needs. The person does not consent if he or she cannot reasonably choose to consent or refuse because of age, circumstances, level of understanding and dependency or relationship to the offender."[10]

*Verbal sexual abuse* includes things like sexual threats, innuendoes, comments about a person's body, harassment, sexual and pornographic jokes, coarse jesting, etc.

*Visual sexual abuse* includes voyeurism, exhibitionism, viewing of pornographic material, genitals, or of any sexual activity, and displaying pornography in public or the workplace.

*Physical sexual abuse* can range from intercourse with seeming "consent," to intercourse by force, and attempted intercourse, primarily fondling of breasts and genitals.

As can be seen from the above, sexual abuse involves a wide range of behaviors, alone or in combination with other behaviors.

### The Effects of Sexual Abuse

First and foremost, we must keep in mind that sexual abuse is traumatic. Trauma involves "intense fear, helplessness, loss of control, and threat of annihilation."[11] *These are natural emotions and behaviors in response to catastrophe*, its immediate aftermath, and the memories of it. Judith Herman, in her book *Trauma and Recovery* says, "Traumatic events are extraordinary, not because they occur rarely, but rather because they overwhelm the ordinary human adaptations to life."[12]

We know from experience and from the literature that trauma results in silence, isolation, and helplessness.[13] Silence because words are inadequate for communicating the unspeakable. Isolation because no one knows, no one comes to help, no one enters in. Helplessness because every attempt to stop the abuse is ineffective, and indeed often exacerbates the abuse.

Finkelhor and Browne acknowledged that the effects of childhood molestation may be delayed into adulthood. Long-term effects that are frequently reported and associated with sexual abuse include depression, self-destructive behavior, anxiety, feelings of isolation and stigma, poor self-esteem, difficulty in trusting others, tendency toward revictimization, substance abuse, and sexual maladjustment.[14]

*Arrested development.* There are three other things to keep in mind about sexual abuse trauma—three effects of the arrested development of abuse. The first is that much of a survivor's thinking is "frozen" in time. A woman who was chronically abused by her father for fifteen years, thinks about her self, her life and her relationships through the grid of the abuse. She may have encountered situations where people proved trustworthy, but she does not trust. She may have heard thousands of words about how God loves her, but she believes she is trash, an exception to the rule. Trauma stops growth because it shuts everything down. Abuse trauma brings death. The input from many other experiences, relationally and spiritually, does not usually impact the thinking that originated within the context of the abuse.

Second, the abuse occurred to a child, not an adult. Children think concretely, not abstractly. Children learn about abstract concepts like trust, truth, and love from the concrete experiences they have with significant others in their lives. They learn what love is by how mommy and daddy treat them. They learn about trust by the trustworthiness (or lack of trust) of mommy and daddy. In essence, they learn about intangible things, ideas, values, through the tangible. If those who teach them are repeatedly untrustworthy, cruel, hurtful, and lying, then to grasp and live out concepts like trustworthy, safe, loving and truthful seems like an exercise in the ridiculous.

Third, not only do children think concretely, and learn about the abstract by way of the concrete, I believe that as adults, we continue to be taught about the unseen through the seen. We are of the earth, earthy. God teaches us eternal truths through things in the natural world. We grasp a bit of eternity by looking at the sea. We get a glimmer of infinity by staring into space. We learn about the shortness of time by the quick disappearance of a vapor.

Jesus taught us eternal truths the same way. He said He was the Bread, the Light, the Living Water, the Vine. We look at the seen and learn about the unseen. Consider the sacraments—water, bread, and wine. We are taught about the holiest of all things through the diet of a peasant. This method is used all the way through understanding the character of God Himself. God in the flesh, God with skin on. God explains Himself to us through the natural and the temporal.

If we consider the combined impact of these factors, we see that many survivors exhibit this quality of thinking, frozen in time, in that they learned repeatedly through the concrete how to think about the abstract, and they learned repeatedly through the seen what to believe about the unseen.

These reactions can occur anytime after the trauma, even decades later. The reactions can be acute, which is the immediate response to the stressor;

chronic effects that persist over time; or delayed, obviously symptoms which develop later. Some women react in all three ways. Post-traumatic stress reactions include three major sets of symptoms.

1.  Numbing of emotional responsiveness.
2.  Increased arousal and vigilant reactiveness to anything reminiscent of the event—often referred to as the "fight-or-flight" syndrome.
3.  Avoidance, even the running away from of anything that reminds one of the event—the "flight" side of the syndrome.

Some of the common characteristics in women experiencing post-traumatic stress are:

-  sleep and dream disturbances,
-  irritability and an increased startle response,
-  explosive anger (toward self or others),
-  reduced ability to function,
-  prone to drug, alcohol, gambling, shopping, sexual, and food/diet addictions,
-  increased fantasy, helplessness, and inability to differentiate between emotions,
-  trouble forming attachments and being satisfied in relationships,
-  repeating traumatic relationships, including poor marital and sexual relations,
-  self-blame and self-hatred.[15]

*Severity of effects.* The severity of an individual woman's reaction to sexual abuse depends on many factors. Abuse that occurs more frequently and is of longer duration is potentially more harmful. Sexual abuse involving penetration of any sort is typically more harmful. The more closely related the victim and the perpetrator and the wider the age difference, the greater the damage. Women who responded to the abuse passively or willingly, tend to engage in more self-blame. Disclosed abuse that receives no help has more potential for damage, as does either negative parental reactions or ineffective or stigmatizing institutional responses (the death of hope).

*Duration of effects.* Long-term effects of child sexual abuse can be quite extensive. It is important to recognize that the following list consists of indicators, they are not proof that sexual abuse has occurred. Adult survivors often have very distorted images of self, are unable to trust others, need to be in control to feel safe, and deny feelings and needs or do not even recognize them. Because they were betrayed and used by people who should have protected them, they end up fearing and mistrusting others.

*Psycho-sexual effects.* Abuse victims often feel vulnerable and fear danger, rather than feeling comfortable when they get too close to others. Relationships may be fraught with difficulty, and intimacy and parenting may be especially threatening. Survivors commonly feel isolated, and different from others, and may attempt to gain approval by either taking care of others or by being excessively dependent or some combination of these. Some try to cope with their fears by being controlling or extremely rigid.

Child sexual abuse often results in psychological problems including chronic depression, phobias, shame, physical problems, emotional numbness, dissociation, eating disorders, self-mutilation and suicide attempts. Victim relations and revictimizations such as battering relationships are far too common, as are addictions and compulsions.

Sexual dysfunctions can sometimes be traced to child sexual abuse, such as: sexual aversion, pain, desire disorder, arousal problems and orgasmic difficulties. Survivors may be confused about their sexual orientation. It is not uncommon, when the perpetrator was male, to be so fearful of or "turned off" by men that a woman feels unsure of her sexual identity. Sexual abuse and homosexual behavior have some strong correlations.[16]

*Effects on father-image and self-image.* In the movie *"Forrest Gump,"* Jenny kneels down in a cornfield, asking God to please make her a bird so she can fly away. While she is praying her drunken, sexually abusive father comes in pursuit. God does not make her into a bird and she is left to her father. A child is told to get down on her knees nightly by her bed and pray with her father. As he tucks her in, he molests her, saying, "Why are you such a whore that you make me do this after we have prayed?"

What does incest teach about fathers? That they are untrustworthy. They have a great deal of power. They are unpredictable. They inflict pain on those they are supposed to care for. They betray, they abandon, deceive, use, and rip apart. They speak love and reassuring words and then suddenly abuse. Rest and peace is out of the question.

What does abuse teach the survivor about herself? That she is unworthy, trash. She is not loved and probably never will be. That her prayers are useless.

That she brings evil to people or makes them do evil things. That no effort on her part brings change or relief.

What does the survivor learn about things like trust, faith? Those are things you never do unless you are an idiot. Love? Love is a word you use when you want to make someone do something they do not want to do. Hope? Hope is a set-up. Nothing ever changes anyway.

It is important to remember, however, that abuse does not automatically cause sexual dysfunction, nor does a dysfunction in this area automatically prove the existence of sexual abuse.


## Spiritual Impact of Trauma

Finally, abuse profoundly impacts the spiritual realm. What does it teach about God? That He is cruel, impotent or uncaring. He does not hear or if He hears, He does not answer. He thinks children are expendable. He does not keep His word. He is not who He says He is. Who God is and what He thinks about the survivor, is understood based on who daddy was, or grandfather, or youth pastor or whoever. They have learned about love, trust, hope, faith, through the experience of sexual abuse.

They have also learned about the unseen through the seen. The ins and outs of ordinary life have taught them many lessons about who God is. The sexual violation of a child can have many spiritual effects—a distorted image of God, coupled with a distorted image of self, creates multiple barriers to experiencing God's love and grace. God is often seen as punitive, an impossible taskmaster, capricious or dead, nonexistent. Sometimes children are even abused in God's name, being told it is God's will for them to submit to the abuse in order to "obey their parents." (Example: abuse followed by bedtime prayers.)

That is why a therapist or pastor may have the experience of speaking the truths of Scripture to a survivor, truths desperately needed, and yet finding that they seem to have no impact. *They don't go in*. Many times I find that survivors can speak eloquently to me of the truths of Scripture, but on an experiential level their lives are lived out in the context of what the abuse taught them, rather than the truths of the Word of God. Intellectually, truth is rooted in the Word of God. Experientially, or personally applied, the truth is rooted in the lessons of abuse.

Sometimes, of course, we find an exception to that. God is certainly still capable of the miraculous. They are few and far between however. There are also those who seem to experientially know the truths of Scripture and apply them to themselves, but on closer look are found able to do so because they have yet to face the truth of the abuse they endured.

*Self-deceit to believe in God.* Oftentimes I find that survivors can hold on to their belief in God because they are living in self-deceit. "It was not really abuse." "It wasn't that bad." "He didn't mean it." In other words, "I can believe God is really alive, or truly loves me, because I have in essence 'gone to a nearby room' away from the abuse, so I can think God is still alive."

Elie Wiesel, one of the foremost writers of the Holocaust, states the problem eloquently. Throughout his books he tells the reader not to assume the consolation of believing that God is alive. Rather than being the solution, saying "God is alive" simply reinforces the problem. He struggles again and again with two irreconcilable realities—the reality of God and the reality of Auschwitz. Each seems to cancel out the other, yet neither will disappear. Either alone could be managed—Auschwitz and no God, or God and no Auschwitz. But together? Auschwitz *and* God? How is that possible?[17]

For many survivors of sexual abuse, the same two irreconcilable realities exist: the reality of a God who says He is loving and a refuge for the weak, and the reality of the ongoing sexual violation of a child. Each seems to cancel out the other, yet both exist. Again, the human mind can manage either alternative—the sexual abuse of a child and no God, or God and protection from sexual abuse.

What is one to do with the rape of a child *and* the reality of God? Most survivors will come down on one side or the other. They have faced the rape and God is not to be trusted. Or they hang on tightly to God and the rape is a blur, a fantasy, a blip on the screen. Believe me, the dilemma is not easily resolved. For some, in fact, it is never resolved.

Many survivors do not struggle with these issues so articulately. I use them because they clearly demonstrate the grappling that goes on and carefully delineate between the lies and the truth (a process that is often very muddy for survivors). This woman has allowed me to not only show these today, but has also given me permission to use them with other survivors. I have found them extremely helpful with adults for two reasons. One, they respond to their thinking. Their questions and thinking are

## SEXUAL ABUSE AND THE
## TWISTED KNOWLEDGE OF GOD

Before we go on I want to make sure that we grasp the profound impact of ongoing abuse to a child's understanding of God. Let us consider some specific examples.

Sarah is five. Her parents drop her off at Sunday school every week. She has learned to sing "Jesus loves me, this I know, for the Bible tells me so. Little ones to Him belong. They are weak, but He is strong." Sarah's daddy rapes her several times a week. Sometimes she gets a break because he rapes her eight-year-old sister instead. The song says that Jesus loves her. It says that He is strong. So she asks Jesus to stop her daddy from hurting her and her sister. Nothing happens. Maybe Jesus isn't so strong after all. Or at least not as strong as daddy. Nothing, not even Jesus, can stop daddy. The people who wrote the Bible must not have known about her daddy.

Mary is seven. She lives in a house where she is taught about God. God seems to have a lot of rules. God says children have to do whatever their parents tell them to do. Mary tries very hard to do what her mommy and daddy say. When she doesn't obey then daddy hurts her and says this is how God told daddies to teach their little girls. Mommy sends her to daddy when she is angry with Mary and daddy hurts her then too. She guesses that if you don't do what God says then He will hurt you too. She will try very hard to be good.

Stan is a young boy whose father abandoned them. Many nights his mother requires him to get in bed with her. She tells him that God gave him to her to take care of her since his dad left. She says God knew she couldn't live without him. Stan feels angry with God and wonders why He demands such confusing and repulsive behavior. He is full of shame because he also finds pleasure in it. God seems an enigma, at best, or at worst, cruel.

A young woman in her twenties was sexually abused by her father and others for all of her childhood. She wrote about what it means to be raped by the man you call daddy. She has struggled long and hard, and continues to do so, with why God did not stop it. What was God thinking and feeling while my daddy raped me? She wrestles with both the lies she learned from her father and the truths of the Word of God. She has written four exceptional little books on the struggle to apply the truth of the Word of God to herself and the lies she learned as a result of the abuse.

1. Mister Jesus Cried
2. Mister Jesus Knows All About That
3. Mister Jesus Knows That It's Not Your Fault
4. Mister Jesus Wants You

frozen in these areas. These adults still talk and think and reason like a child about God. Also, these books keep the work of Christ on the cross central. That truth, and that alone, is the sufficient answer to the thinking, questions, and struggles that the abuse causes. We will focus on that now in treatment considerations.

## Treatment and Healing

You have an appointment with a woman in her 30s who complains of depression. In some fashion—perhaps with shame and a quiet voice and dropped head, perhaps glibly and with the wave of a hand on the first visit, maybe six months later after weeks of you both feeling stuck—she tells you: "My father used to do weird things to me," or "My father would touch me."

"Ah-ah!" you think, "no wonder we're stuck. But now what?"

Stay focused. Keep in mind that the motivation for entering therapy is related to presenting symptoms, not the sexual abuse. Often a crisis has developed due to delayed after-effects of the original trauma, a re-experiencing of the trauma in some form or exposure to events that trigger symptoms. Please note that all of these meet DSM-IV diagnostic criteria for Post-Traumatic Stress Disorder (PTSD). Anyone who is going to work with abuse survivors needs a good understanding of this diagnosis. If/when these symptoms are stabilized, you then have the opportunity to focus on abuse treatment.

The model that I use for treating survivors of sexual abuse has three phases. The initial phase of treatment involves: safety, symptom relief, and memory work. Safety is an unknown to those who have been chronically abused. Many patients respond to the question, "Couldn't you get to a safe place?" with incredulity. Often they tried to create one only to have it discovered and then destroyed. Others had safe places that were not physical in nature, but rather a place they created within their own minds. Safety then, is often defined as the absence of people.

Any of you who have worked with survivors of chronic abuse know the intense need for safety and the ongoing disbelief that it is real. Survivors always want to know where the door is. They want an explanation for every sound. Your movements are watched and anything sudden or not explained results in fear and defensiveness. Most prefer to follow me down the hall to my office rather than have me behind them. Many stand for their sessions in close proximity to the door. It is crucial that I do not sit between them and the exit.

## Intake and Assessment

Whatever the mode of presentation, a therapist should ask about childhood sexual experience with adults as part of routine intake procedures. The best approach is a straightforward one, such as: "Did you have any sexual experiences with adults in childhood or adolescence? Words like incest, sexual abuse, or victim are so loaded today, that I would suggest not introducing them initially unless the client herself does.

A disclosure of incest is not always uncomfortable for the client, and a therapist should not assume that it is. You should proceed with caution and sensitivity, demonstrating approachability, understanding and responsiveness. You will assist your client in making fuller disclosures by avoiding such responses as rage toward the perpetrator, minimizing the abuse or its effects, showing excessive interest in sexual details, ignoring the disclosure or pushing the client to say more.

Many clients hold certain beliefs about what will happen if they tell. It is important for you to learn what disclosure means to your client. Respond with belief, a confirmation of her safety with you, and let her know that you will not rush her nor try to force her to deal with more than she is able or chooses. Make it clear to her, however, that disclosure does not equal resolution.

Many women often feel such relief at telling that they eagerly assume they are now "all better." It is important that you communicate that disclosure is the first step in the working-through process. Reassure the client of your willingness and commitment to see her through that process, being careful not to coerce nor frighten her into continuing. Choice-making in therapy is crucial with incest survivors because one of the key components of sexual abuse is the inability to refuse. It is vital that dynamic not be reenacted in therapy.

*Adults coping as children.* Not only the inability to refuse, but most coping that the adult attempts shadows the ways (and failures) of coping learned during the abuse. Each child who undergoes sexual abuse develops certain coping strategies in order to survive the trauma and its concomitant feelings. When out of the context of abuse, coping strategies sometimes seem strange.

This was made very clear to me many years ago when I was visiting in the home of a holocaust survivor. Every time a police or ambulance siren sounded this woman became terrified and ran and hid in a closet, under a bed, any place she could find. To put yourself in a closet at the sound of a far off siren is strange behavior indeed—out of the context of the specter of being sent to a death camp. Within that context it made perfect sense.

Coping strategies are numerous and diverse. Some are highly individualized. Others are more universal. Let's consider a few:

1.  *Denial and distortion of self.* Many children deny what is happening to them, as well as deny the feelings they have about it. They hide who they really are (a child who is being neglected and abused) to maintain approval within the family. As reality is denied and distorted, the true self is denied. A "false self" develops that is dependent on others for self esteem. The "true self" is hidden and seen as not trustworthy for it threatens her ability to cope. As time goes by this affects her ability to delineate the true from the false.

2.  *Dissociation and splitting.* This occurs when the survivor alters her identity, consciousness and memory. She copes by splitting off conflicting aspects of consciousness, memory and identity. One way to do this is via amnesia or blocking out memory. Another way is to psychologically separate from the abuse. Survivors talk about spacing out, leaving the body, or making themselves disappear into the wallpaper. It is a way of removing the "me."
    We have all had the experience of something that feels so bad we find ourselves thinking, "This can't be happening to me." This can become so automatic that it is done in response to any stressor in the survivor's life, not just sexual abuse. The most extreme from of dissociation is, of course, Dissociative Identity Disorder (DID, or more commonly known as multiple personality disorder), where the split truly becomes other than "me" and entirely distinct personalities come into play (see chapter 20).

3.  *Rationalizing and minimizing.* Many victims engage in this to cope: "He was lonely, drunk, etc." or "It wasn't so bad. At least he didn't..."

4.  *Addictions and other physical mechanisms.* Self-mutilation, suicide attempts, compulsive behaviors and addictions, such as: drugs, alcohol, spending, sex, food, chaos, danger and crises.

5. *Deviant behaviors.* Some live out the "bad-girl" persona that the perpetrator foisted on them: lying, manipulation, violence, prostitution.

6. *Relational coping mechanisms.* Over involvement and codependent attachments, withdrawal, repeating the abuse, abusing others, being abandoned, abandoning others.

7. *Magical spirituality.* Commenting on the movie *"Forest Gump"* again, there is that one small but incredible scene of what effect abuse can have spiritually. When Jenny is running from her drunken father and hides in the cornfield, getting down on her knees and asking God to turn her into a bird so she can fly away—this is an excellent example of the magical spirituality that is carried into adulthood.

It is crucial in working with a survivor of any trauma to keep in mind that these coping mechanisms make sense or are reasonable in the context of the trauma. Another illustration is from a Holocaust survivor—standing on an airfield on a brilliant summer day watching a fun-filled, daredevil air show. This woman standing next to a friend screams, clutches her friend's arm, and buries her face in her shoulder. Reasonable in the present context? No—but when she was young, growing up in Europe, the sound of airplanes close by meant chaos and death.

## Beginning Treatment: Safety and Symptom Relief

Most clients come initially in need of symptom relief. The beginning phase of therapy involves both the building of a trust relationship with the therapist and the facilitation of symptom relief. The symptoms are often debilitating and they generally are what brought the client into therapy.

I find it very helpful to begin by normalizing my clients' symptoms. They are usually terrified that they are "losing it," "going crazy," are "weird," etc. As I educate them regarding how their symptoms are reactions to severe trauma it enables them to relax somewhat, thus providing some immediate relief. Just as a holocaust survivor's response to sirens was normal in World War II, so the incest survivor's reactions are normal in the context of sexual abuse.

It is important to do this even with the more severe symptoms, such as self-mutilation. You can normalize without condoning by showing how such a reaction makes sense in context, yet saying that the point of working together is to find healthy ways of expressing feelings and needs. You will find frequent repetition necessary in this area. Ongoing reassurance that your client is not crazy and that her symptoms are normal within the context of abuse is vital.

Presenting symptoms need not only to be normalized, but new ways of coping need to be found. This stage usually involves work with anxieties, phobias, depression and addictive behaviors. Often a medical examination is warranted (e.g. in the case of ongoing headaches or intestinal problems). Stabilizing the client and making certain she is safe is crucial before proceeding with any memory work. If, for example, your client is an alcoholic, it is necessary to get her into treatment for that before considering the trauma. If you do not, looking at the trauma will simply increase her drinking.

It is also important to find out about suicidal ideation or any other destructive or life-threatening behaviors. To proceed to consider the history of a survivor with the tremendous emotional upheaval that usually produces without first helping a client learn some ways to feel safe, find some measure of safety with you as the therapist and learn how to monitor self-destructive behaviors so her life is not at risk, is irresponsible therapy indeed.

This phase of therapy involves trust-building, safety education, symptom relief, and giving comfort. Normalizing your client's reactions to the sexual abuse is part of the educational process. Comforting her, reassuring her, affirming her courage in surviving and now in dealing with the trauma will all enable her to squarely face the truth about her life and form a strong alliance with you. Establishing safety lays the foundation for trust to develop and is also how you prevent the therapeutic process from re-traumatizing your client. It also prepares you both for the plunge into memory work.

*Healing of memories.* Memory work, the third component of phase one must be done with great care. It is essentially a search for truth. The memory of something does not guarantee its truth. But it is also true that the fact that a memory was "lost" for years and later recovered does not mean it is untrue. When something terrible happens to us we often do not want to remember because of the pain involved in that memory.

At the same time, we do not want to forget because of the significance of the memory. It is a place of great ambivalence and fear. A client recently said to me that she desperately wanted her memories to be false. She did not want such things to be true about her life. After a brief moment of silence she realized with horror that it would be equally terrifying to learn that the things her mind was throwing at her were false. There was no good answer.

The purpose of memory work is not simply to retrieve memories. The act of remembering something is not, in and of itself, healing. God has called us to truth. He is truth. He reveals truth. Two very important things begin to occur during the process of memory work. One is that the survivor is afforded a safe relationship where she can give voice to the truth of her life and her response to it. As she does this, healing begins to occur to her damaged person. She is heard. She is cared for. She matters.

Second, as the events of abuse are exposed so are their accompanying lies. There are lies told by the actions of abuse. There are lies told by the abuser. There are lies the survivor told herself. As that which was carried out in darkness is exposed, the lies too are revealed for what they are. This becomes very important when we begin to look at the spiritual issues with which the survivor grapples.

*Memories and emotions.* As memories surface they produce powerful emotional reactions. Your response is critical, because it is what will, in large measure, determine the trust relationship that develops. These memories afford you the opportunity to respond differently from those people who surrounded your client when the abuse was actually occurring.

This memory retrieval is necessary. What was hidden needs to be exposed, what has been in the dark needs to be brought to the light. One of the reasons for this is that memories are stored with their concomitant distortions, lies, accompanying emotions and interpretations. As they come to the light, your job will be to help your client to separate the truth from the lies.

This process can be quite difficult, for both client and therapist. For the client two things can happen. First, her own reactions to the events that occurred are stirred up as she recalls them. She will feel rage, hate, terror, loss of control. Sometimes she will feel in her body the pain she felt when the abuse was actually occurring. These are all feelings that she has worked hard not to experience. You will find her resistant to them again.

Second, for some the horrors remembered become a new traumatizing event. The thought of the upcoming therapy hour can produce fear and flight reactions. The client may respond by becoming severely depressed, or acting out in some way, such as self-mutilation or suicidal gestures. Therapy must proceed at a pace that the client can tolerate. You will have to be vigilant, and if things get too intense or your client is too self-destructive, then the memory work needs to be temporarily shelved. As her trust in you and attachment to you grows, she will be able to pursue it again. Often extra contact via phone, or emergency sessions are necessary during this time.

This is a critical time, for your own reactions to her traumatic memories and your need to distance from them, could easily cause you to emotionally remove yourself in some way. However slight, this distancing will be traumatic for your client. An awareness of your own responses, your ability to cope and what you are communicating to your client are essential.

*The goal of memory work.* As her therapist, where do you want to help her move on to? Once she has recognized what was done to her by the perpetrator as well as by the non-protecting family members and her presenting symptoms have begun to abate, the focus shifts to helping her see herself, not as traumatized child-victim, but as responsible adult.

I find that many therapists do not understand this shift, nor do they know how to help their clients make it. Many clients, and their therapists with them, end up stuck in the victim stage. More writing is being done about what is often referred to as a "victim mentality," which many rightly see as being far too prevalent in our society. One only has to look at the ridiculous litigation today to see this.

However, those who are troubled by this mentality are frequently in danger of forgetting that there are true victims. Scripture not only makes it clear that humans put other humans in the position of being victimized or oppressed, but that those of us who know Christ are to tenderly reach out and assist such people. Any man or woman who has been sexually abused or raped is a victim.

At the same time, part of our assistance to those who are indeed victims is to appropriately, and in a timely fashion, help them grow beyond that place. That is not to say that the issues of sexual abuse will cease to exist or be a struggle for them. The grave sins of others against us often reverberate through our lives for years and we do not want to be naive about this. But neither do we want to fail to empower people to grow beyond the evil that has been done to them.

## The Middle Phase of Treatment

The middle phase of treatment is a turning point. Up to this point the therapist has assumed the role of educator, comforter, listener. These roles are not abandoned by any means; however, as we move into the middle phase more active and directive responses are called for. The more a survivor deals with her history and the lies embedded there, the more she will find she has choice. She has learned to speak. How will she use her voice? She has learned something about relationship. How will she use her ability to relate? She has learned that she has impact. How will she use her power to affect others?

It is during this middle phase that the lies are articulated more fully, that they are renounced, and the work is done to put truth in their place. Many lies will be found to be deeply embedded in the survivor's mind and heart: "Abuse occurred because I was bad." "I was not worth protecting." "It is always bad to be weak." "No one is trustworthy." "Safety only comes in isolation." "I am unforgivable." It is not hard to see how misconceptions about God and how He thinks about us are very closely intertwined with such lies.

Client empowerment to overcome these lies is what the middle phase of therapy is all about. It will prove to be a crisis and a turning point for both the therapist and survivor. I believe the challenge of turning as a therapist is a key reason it does not occur. It requires the therapist to assume a more directive and active stance toward a person whom they are comfortable nurturing and comforting. These behaviors should not cease, but if they continue without more directive approaches being added, the client will stalemate. However much courage is required to face the terror of incest and its aftereffects, this is not a sufficient condition for change. The therapist now needs to carefully begin to treat the survivor like an adult who has power and can make choices, characteristics which the abuse crushed.

One of the reasons treatment can get stuck here is that the survivor will usually put up a good deal of resistance. The major fear in her life, up to this time, has been facing the incest. She has done that and lived to tell the tale, and wants to settle in to enjoy that fact. It is a far more comfortable place than she has experienced previously, and it looks like a good place to live. The therapist can help her verbalize this, and show understanding for those feelings, but must also gently nudge her along.

Part of that is to help the client see that to stay in such a place is to basically stay crippled—and in some sense her abuser will have won. Part of God's work in our life is to bring us into truth. One of the pieces of that is facing the truth of the past. However, it doesn't stop there. Not only is another piece of truth that your client is now an adult, but also the fact that a second aspect of God's work in our lives is growth. God does not produce "stuckness" in our lives, but change—a constant growing up into Him.

Difficult work also surrounds the issues of grief, confrontation and forgiveness. To face abuse means to confront loss. She never got to be a child. She never really had a daddy. She never had a sense of moral integrity. She may have lost children. Such grieving is a dark and painful process. God is seen as impotent, absent or cruel. Those whose faith remained strong during memory work are often rocked hard during this time.

**The End Phase**

The final phase of treatment is in many ways a time of joy and hope. Therapist and client have formed a strong alliance. The client has faced memories and feelings she thought would destroy her. She has exchanged many destructive coping skills for healthy ones. She has established relationships outside the therapy room that are supportive and safe. She has grieved (though of course such grief is never done). She has dealt with her family and her abuser in ways she decided were both safe and wise. What remains is far more present and future oriented.

What happens in the final phase of therapy? Once the family of origin issues have been handled and relational skills built up, the client feels stronger and individuated. It is this that sets the stage for separation from the therapist. This stage continues to include marriage counseling if the survivor is in a marriage. Most of the work that is done is in the present tense. The survivor feels much less encumbered by her past and more capable of handling issues that exist in her marriage. As that relationship (or in the case of a single woman, a network of relationships) becomes more solidified and healthy, the thought that perhaps the therapist is not so necessary anymore begins to surface.

It is initially a frightening thought and requires a response of reassurance, as well as a statement that indicates that termination is the client's choice, not something that will be forced by the therapist. I usually proceed at a careful rate of digression, reducing sessions to every two weeks, then once a month, every other month, in three months, in six months, and finally a year later. Each step is held until the client signals readiness to move on. Some will want to proceed too quickly due to fears of saying good-bye. I suggest being firm in suggesting a more cautious approach and explaining why. Some will get stuck at a particular point and fear moving on. In that case, you need to back up and deal with the underlying anxieties.

This phase will include more extensive work in the area of relationships. I work hard with my clients to help and encourage them to develop a strong and healthy support network. The friendships they have, the churches they attend, all will be the places they will continue to grow in long after they have left me behind. This phase usually includes marriage counseling. Working with the marriage of the survivor is inevitable, in part because the person who started in treatment with you is not the one who ends—spouses tend to not know what to do with the changes. In fact, they don't always like all the changes! This phase also involves increased focus and strengthening of the survivor's relationship with God.

Another area that gets attention during this phase is the body. Learning how to live on friendly terms with a body that has been viewed as the enemy for all of one's life is no small task. How to care for a body rather than ignore or destroy it requires hard work and much repetition. Learning to be connected rather than dissociated is frightening. The possibility of some level of control over one's feelings and one's physical body is an astounding discovery.

The final pieces of the last phase involve the desire of the survivor to give to others in some fashion what has been given to her. Anyone who has experienced some measure of redemption in their own life knows that an eagerness to give naturally flows out of that. There is great joy in seeing someone who came to you simply trying to survive, now leave with a desire and readiness to serve others. I would just like to make a few comments about confronting the perpetrator and family-of-origin issues (since it is currently such a hot topic).

This work will bump hard into many spiritual issues if your client is a Christian. One of the main issues will be that of forgiveness. Again I think we tend to fall off on one of two sides of the horse. One side is that of cheap and hasty forgiveness. The two words, "I'm sorry," immediately are to eradicate years of suffering, lying and abuse. Repentance is verbal, certainly, but it is far more than verbal—it is transformation from the inside out, demonstrated over time.

Many Christians also abuse Paul's words regarding forgetting what is behind, superficially stating "Just put it behind you. Forgive and forget. Forgive and move on." Such an approach is ludicrous. We know from research that the mind doesn't forget anything, it is recall that is the problem. To tell a holocaust survivor to forget is nonsensical. It is equally ridiculous to tell that to an incest survivor, as well as a complete misreading of the New Testament text.

Scripture takes sin seriously, not lightly. Repentance from sin is seen as change in words yes, but also in attitude and behavior, indeed in the whole person. For us to do less is to cheapen what God has named radically expensive. If the perpetrator or silent parent says, "I'm sorry," a response might be, "I am so glad to hear you say that to your daughter. Now let's talk about how you would like to demonstrate it to her."

On the other hand, much of the secular literature states that forgiveness is not a necessary part of healing for the survivor. I disagree. As a believer, that would mean asserting the antithesis to Jesus' words. God says it is not okay to remain bitter and unforgiving. He makes no exceptions for certain sins. Scripture gives a radical picture of forgiveness. It is costly, sacrificial and repetitive. Repentance is significant and sustained change—it unfolds and is evident over time.

God's children are called to forgive. Both repentance and forgiveness are the work of the Spirit of God, not man, and yet they require tremendous, ongoing work on our part. We are to hold our clients (and ourselves) to the highest before God, yet acknowledge that it is God who brings about such mysterious and awesome changes in the human heart.

Again, obviously much more could be said about these issues and this phase of therapy. The topic warrants extensive handling and I am keenly aware that I am referring to serious subject matter. I am hoping that you

## CONFRONTING THE PERPETRATOR

I have found with many of my clients that there often arises a need/desire to confront their family of origin. It is also strongly resisted and feared. It is important to note that I have said that the need/desire arises from the client, NOT the therapist! Example: A counselor who is working with a survivor is insisting that she confront her mother and her grandmother regarding the sexual abuse she experienced from her grandfather. Now she may indeed need to do so at some point. But he is insisting, telling her nothing more can be done unless she does what he tells her, etc.

My question is, Who is it here who has unresolved family issues? Such a confrontation is not to be based on my need nor do I insist that it happens. I do not make a rule that all survivors have to do this. I think for some it is a necessary and helpful part of growth. To maintain silence continues the feeling that the incest is somehow unreal or "made up." It is to actively support a lie, to pretend as if something horrific is not there. I discuss all of this with my client, the topic almost always being initiated by her.

If this confrontation is to take place, much work must be done. It should never be handled quickly or superficially. The client's choices should be respected at all points. If at some point she chooses to back down, honor that choice. A good many of the false memory accusations seem to have risen out of hasty and even coerced confrontations, with the therapist often being the one who insists it had to occur.

You must also keep in mind that a confrontation involves two sides and your goal here is not to destroy a family or verbally beat up on a perpetrator. You need to be keenly aware of your own reactions and motives throughout. You are there for your client. She is your primary focus. But you are also responsible for how you treat the family. God's standard for all communications is that we speak the truth in love and this kind of confrontation is no exception to that.

It is extremely difficult to speak the truth of incest. No one wants to hear it, least of all the family in which it occurred. To name it is to crash through an almost impenetrable barrier that family members have colluded to erect. However, to confront evil and abuse in a manner that reflects the love of God in Christ is no less difficult. The inner work you will need to do as a therapist is no less massive than that of your client.

Preparing your client for this very difficult part of her therapy requires several things: establishing realistic goals, confronting her fairy-tale endings and expectations, deciding how to contact the family and how to conduct the sessions. Role-playing is often a very helpful tool at this juncture. Part of the therapist's responsibility is to assess the level of danger or acting out with respect to family members. Ongoing substance abuse, a history of violence or a history of suicidal or homicidal threats are all serious contraindications to a family confrontation.

Especially when violence is a threat, the usual outcome is to break off contact with the family due to the level of danger.

The goals of such a meeting include disclosure, or a speaking of the truth. That usually involves not simply a telling about the incest, but includes education as to its after-effects, an acknowledgement of guilt with a true apology, the beginning of a reconciliation process defined, and goals carefully set out for the family to assist them in accomplishing this. These are high goals, and again the therapist must work carefully with her client to ensure that she stay realistic in applying them to her particular family. It is difficult to find a balance between expecting far too much on the one hand, and settling for a superficial apology that the client is too quick to name repentance. Caution is needed on both sides.

The therapist's role throughout is to actively support the client, model for both the client and family how to confront and interact, as well as direct the meeting. Sessions such as these require confidence and assertiveness. They usually require saying things like, "Stop negating your daughter like that," "You need to listen to what your daughter is saying rather than simply focusing on your own feelings," "I will not allow you to demean your daughter that way as long as you are in my office." Responses such as these greatly assist the client in her own growth toward being able to assert herself with family members, without curling up, slinking away, or belittling in return.

Such sessions need to include drawing up a definite plan so that all family members have a clear idea about how the relationship is to proceed and what behaviors are appropriate. Reparative work needs to follow an apology. This can be introduced by asking your client what the family needs to do to demonstrate the professed apology.

will use these things to motivate you to pursue the subject through reading and perhaps some workshops.

## The Role and Approach of the Counselor

What is the role of the therapist in this area? From my perspective, this is a huge question, one that I take very seriously. Let us remind ourselves of what we have in front of us. First of all, we have a human being who does not understand safety, love, trust, hope, truth and many other concepts. Second, we have someone who was still undeveloped in every way (physically, cognitively, emotionally, spiritually, etc.) and was taught lies repetitively during times of intense emotion with reinforcing behavior.

You do not have to be very sophisticated about the learning process to comprehend how embedded those lies are. The mind and body of a six-year-old is being repeatedly raped by an adult male who is telling her such things as: "God told me to do this," "God has daddies teach their little girls this way," "If you weren't such a whore I wouldn't have to do this," "You are nothing but trash."

Now how many times do you suppose that has to happen for that little girl to be sure those things are true? The abuse becomes the overriding experience, the abuse provides her control beliefs. God may be strong but daddy is stronger. Jesus loves little children, but not me. Those control beliefs become the basis by which all other information is processed. Again, that is why speaking the truth to a survivor, as crucial as that is, is not sufficient.

So we come again to our question, What is the role of the therapist? What response does a therapist need to give? The survivor is struggling with the most basic questions about God: Who is God? What does He think? What does He think about me? What was He thinking while daddy was raping me? Am I forgivable? Does His patience run out? Why should I have hope? Why should I believe in Him?

## Be Like Christ

The therapist becomes the representative of this God to the survivor. The work of the therapist is to teach in the seen, that which is true in the unseen. The therapist's words, tone of voice, actions, body movements, responses to rage, fear, and failure all become ways that the survivor learns about God. I believe that the reputation of God Himself is at stake in the life of the therapist. We are called first and foremost, to represent Him well.

Words are how we do therapy. They are the "stuff" of the trade. Words, however, in this case are initially meaningless. What are words when you grew up hearing, "Daddy loves you," and then daddy raped you. Or when grandfather called you over to sit on his lap, and when you were afraid he said not to worry because this time it would be okay, but it never was. So the therapist says, "This is a safe place." The survivor's response? "Right." "Oh, sure." Or perhaps, she has become so desperate, words are believed no matter what actions might suggest.

And so our task becomes that of living out before them the character of God Himself. I first began to understand this early on in my work with survivors. I was working with a woman who had been chronically abused and longed for her to truly know the love of God. I tried telling her about it but realized at some point that she was politely tolerating what I was saying, but it was not going in. I clearly remember getting down on my knees before begging Him to help her see what she so desperately needed to see—that He loved her.

What I heard back from God was, "You want to know how much I love her? Then you go love her in a way that demonstrates that. You want her to know that I am trustworthy and safe? Then you go be trustworthy and safe." Demonstrate in the flesh the character of God over time so that who you are reveals God to the survivor.

That is the incarnation, isn't it? Jesus, in the flesh, explaining God to us. Jesus, bringing the unseen down into flesh and blood realities. *The survivor needs us to incarnate God* for two reasons. One, we all need that. That is why Jesus came in the flesh. He came to explain God to us. We have already spoken about the fact that human beings learn about the unseen from the seen. Jesus knew that and used countless examples in the seen to teach His disciples about the unseen.

Secondly, this need is intensified for the survivor because what has been repeatedly taught to a child in the seen is the antithesis of the truth of God. She has learned about fathers, trust, love, and refuge from one who emulated the father of lies. The unseen has been lived out before her and she has learned her lessons well.

If you want the survivor to understand that God is a refuge, then be one for her. If you want her to grasp the faithfulness of God, then be faithful to her. If you want her to understand the truthfulness of God, then never lie to her. If you want her to understand the infinite patience of God, then be patient with her. And where you are not a refuge, or are tired of being faithful, or are fudging in your answers or growing impatient with the necessary repetition, then get down on your knees and ask God to give you more of Himself so that you might represent Him well.

The second aspect of the response of the therapist is to speak truth. We have talked about the deeply embedded lies that the survivor carries within her. Such lies need to be exposed, gently and slowly, so the light of the truth of God can begin to take their place. I find it very important to learn, not just what the lies are, but also what memories taught that lie. There are usually particular aspects of certain memories that burned those lies into the brain and help keep it there.

For example, a woman who was sadistically abused told the story of being forced to kill a loved pet with her own hands or risk further pain. She was told repeatedly during childhood that she was evil and that was why no one would ever love her. Her vivid memory of killing her pet and the blood on her hands provided tangible proof of her evil and burned that lie into her brain in profound ways. It took a long, long time of carefully picking our way through that memory and all its pieces for her to even begin to grasp the subtlety and hideousness of the lies it had taught her.

Working through memories and the lies they hold is arduous and slow. It requires tremendous patience. The rewards are wonderful for you begin to see light dawn in a darkened and confused mind. It is quite different however, from simply telling someone God loves them and having them believe it. Speak it; live it; be it; repeat again.


## Reflect the Man of Sorrows

The third part of the therapist's response is contained in the little book *Mister Jesus Knows All About That*. In that book the woman who wrote it is beginning to grasp that this Mister Jesus is the Man of Sorrows and acquainted with grief—*with her grief*. Mister Jesus says, "I was hurt too. The bad men took my clothes just like your daddy took yours." There is tremendous healing for survivors as they begin to study and truly grasp the suffering and death of Jesus.

*He knows*—that is a phenomenal revelation. I recently had a woman come in to a session who is working through some of the Scripture on the Crucifixion. She had barely sat down on the couch when she said, "They took His clothes. I never saw it before. They took His clothes." This is a woman who had many perpetrators and has countless memories of standing naked as an adolescent in a group of men. Something way down deep gets touched when such things are seen and understood.

The cross of Christ demonstrates the extent of the evil. The cross of Christ demonstrates the infinite love of God. The cross of Christ covers any evil done by the survivor herself. Any inadequacy in the cross of Christ means that none of us is safe. The cross of Christ is God with us—in our sin, our suffering, our grief, our sorrows. In order to redeem He became like us.

*Self-directed client work.* I do not do this work for my clients. I send them to do it. I often direct them to a particular passage or raise a specific question but I do not simply teach them about the Crucifixion. I send them to learn and study as I teach. The work has far more power when they wrestle with it themselves. This is not something I do early on in therapy. It falls more toward the end of the second phase and into the third.

One of the major reasons for this is that I find they will grasp the profound truths of the cross far more readily and deeply if they have seen some representation of those truths in their relationship with me. They have been able to speak the unspeakable. They are known. They are loved. No matter what they tell, they remain safe. I can forgive. I have hope for them. They have found in their relationship with me an aroma of the person of Christ. Out of that experience in the seen, in flesh and blood, they can then turn to the person and work of Christ and His identification with them. I have without exception found it a powerful way of teaching truth and of bringing healing.

## Manage Vicarious Trauma

Any of you who have done this work or have listened carefully today have some grasp of the potential impact on the person of the therapist. We are more and more in the literature about vicarious trauma and secondary traumatic stress disorder. Those of you who heard my presentation on personhood remember that I spoke about all of us being image bearers. It is the nature of human beings that they are impacted by what they sit with. If I habitually reflect trauma or sit with trauma, I will bear the image of trauma in my person. We see this even in the person of Jesus, who though He was perfect bears in His person the image of our sin and suffering. If it was true of Him how much more so for us who are sinners ourselves!

I want to close by giving you three elements which are necessary if we are to do this work and do it well. First, know about people. Know about trauma. Understand what trauma does to human beings. And yet, in knowing, never assume you know. No matter how many survivors you see, each is unique. If we do not understand such things we will make wrong judgments. We will prematurely expect change. We will give wrong answers. We will fail to hear because we think we already know. Listen acutely. Study avidly. Live among the facts.

Second, know God. Know His Word. Be an avid student of that Word. If we are going to serve as His representative to others we need to know Him well. We are often so presumptuous and we speak for Him where we do not really know Him. We need to be so permeated by His Word that we learn to think His thoughts. May we never forget that to know His Word, according to Him, means we have woven it into our lives and live obedient to it. Where we do not live according to His Word, we do not know God.

Finally, do not do this work (or any other for that matter) without utter dependence on the Spirit of God. Where else will you find wisdom? How will you know when to speak and when to be silent? How will you discern the lies from the truth? How else will you love when you are tired or be patient when you are weary? How can you know the mind of God apart from the Spirit of God? How can you possibly expect to live as a person who demonstrates the character of God apart from the Spirit of God? How do we think that the life-giving power to the work of Christ crucified will be released into other lives unless we have allowed that cross to do its work in our own lives?

To work with sexual abuse is to work with lies, darkness, and evil. It is hell brought up from below to the earth's surface. You cannot fight the fetid litter of hell in someone's life unless you walk dependent on the Spirit of God. You cannot bring life to the place of death unless you walk dependent on the Spirit of God.

This work—in spite of its foul nature at times—is a privilege to do. It is a work that is difficult to do. The task of serving as a representative of God in the seen so that the unseen can be grasped, understood and believed in some measure, is far beyond any capability of yours or of mine. It is a work however, that if you let it, will take you to your knees with a heart hungry for more of God that you might in turn bring His presence in very concrete ways into places and lives where He has not yet been known.

## Conclusion

What I have given you is a brief overview of therapy with an incest survivor. Though it is brief, you need to also see it as comprehensive in the sense that I have given you a general cognitive map or outline for how to proceed. Obviously, not all clients will proceed through all of these phases. Some will choose not to confront their family of origin, some will stay bitter, others will divorce their spouses, or terminate therapy prematurely. I have given you these stages so you can have some kind of structure in mind, some picture of what it would look like optimally. I also think this helps us not to sell our clients short. Therapists often fail to encourage further growth because they have no idea what it would look like.

Therapy with survivors is long and hard. It is inexpressibly rewarding. It is the joy of seeing someone stand up straight or find her voice for the first time in her life. It is the marvel of watching a crushed and broken human being, who has faced evil and darkness while yet a child, seek after truth and light. It is the gift of saying good-bye to someone who came to you stuck in a destructive past, and is leaving as someone who is growing and changing, with hope for a future.

It is a work that will demand much of you. However, I want to say here that anyone who attempts this without careful training and supervision is unwise, and runs a great risk of being hurtful to an already injured person. Continuing education and ongoing supervision have often not been stressed in the Christian community. I feel these tasks cannot be emphasized enough.

Therapy is an isolated experience in many ways. You sit in an office with people, one after another, day after day. You can go on and on for years with no input to challenge or stretch you. Couple that with high-stress therapy such as work with survivors and the possibility of mistakes and staleness escalate proportionately. Good therapy requires a good understanding of yourself and a growing understanding of the problems you are confronting. Humility is a key component in both.

Sexual abuse recovery is often long and difficult, but it is not impossible. It will require courage and stamina from your client and from you as well. You and your client need to remember that not only are your efforts helping her, but also the generations that will come after her. I often tell my clients that they are the "pivotal generation," for their family has faced one

## SUGGESTIONS OF ABUSE
## AND FALSE MEMORY SYNDROME

I would like to insert something here about the current psychotherapeutic rage: false memory syndrome. First of all, though I am saddened to say so—even reluctant—there are more than enough ineffective, unethical, and unwise therapists who work with survivors though they have no specific training in this area. Even a Ph.D. in clinical or counseling psychology does not necessarily equip one to work with sexual abuse survivors. I have no question but that some have led dependent, suggestible clients down the sexual abuse road without clinical justification.

Second, as in any area of therapy, and most certainly in this one, it is not helpful—and may even be harmful for some—to ask blatant leading questions. I have read the transcripts of some sessions and they are appalling. Did he do such and such? Even when the answer is no, or 'I don't know,' the therapist goes on to push with an implicit certainty. It is obvious that the interview is being guided by a therapist who presumptuously assumes they "know" something the client does not—that sexual abuse HAS occurred. This is arrogance, not competent therapy.

I don't care how long you have done therapy or how much you think you know, *you cannot read another person's mind, nor can you tell them what is in there.* As a matter of fact, I think the more experience we have the more aware we are of the complexity of another's mind and our inability to not only not know theirs, but our own as well. A healthy dose of humility is in order when tromping around in other people's heads.

Third, any scholar or student worth their salt knows the difference between correlation and cause and effect. It is lousy reasoning to say "if these symptoms are present, therefore *this has to be* the cause." Any time you interview a client the mindset needs to be, "It looks like this could have happened, but I need to rule out a and b first."

Good clinical reasoning engages in differential diagnosis—it is rooted in ruling out competing diagnoses and theories of causation. There must be an investigative, and even tentative quality to our approach. You can have someone with many similar symptoms to someone who has been sexually abused (distorted image of self, emotional numbing, an eating disorder, sees God as punitive) who has never been sexually abused.

Obviously asking the question, 'Have you ever been sexually abused?' is necessary. Then we must respect the answer. If it is no, and later it continues to nag at you, bring it up in a different context. Some clients may wait months to tell you, because they absolutely must believe they can trust you first.

*Never tell a client "You have been sexually abused."* Even with someone who *is* a survivor, to insist that there was abuse *and it must be dealt with,* when she has slipped back into denial and is not ready to proceed, is destructive and grossly unethical. It reinforces rather than heals the original trauma as it is a re-enactment of two of the major factors of abuse:

(1) coercion, and
(2) a denial of where they are.

Fourth, a good understanding of the human mind includes a keen awareness that there are some very dependent people out there who are capable of suggestibility and grave distortions. As a therapist, you are in a position of power. You have been given authority and your words will have tremendous impact. Choose them wisely and carefully.

Fifth, research has shown that memory is not usually photographic (with exceptions) and is stored concomitant with the perceiver's interpretations of that memory. Anyone who has returned to a childhood home as an adult knows this—it is amazing how small things have gotten in twenty years' time!

Sixth, a good understanding of the human heart, which Scripture clearly gives us, tells us that every heart, no matter how nice or wounded a person it dwells in, is capable of deceit, hate, and slander.

All of this is not said so you will not believe those who come to you. I always begin by accepting what they say is true. If a client says she has been abused, I believe her. If she says she has not, I do not force the issue. In over 20 years and hundreds of cases, I have encountered only two situations (to my knowledge, of course) which involved false accusations. It is my suspicion that a small proportion of those aligned with the false memory association have indeed been unjustly accused. If the human heart is capable of coming up with sexual abuse, it is certainly capable of lying about it as well.

A larger proportion of those making accusations against their parents have probably been led to do so through unwise or unethical therapy. Even if the accusations are true, I am aware of many situations where the therapist has insisted on a family confrontation when the client either did not want it or was not prepared for it. Such an encounter is inevitably a disaster.

However, since the key characteristic of a perpetrator is denial, I suspect a significant proportion of those screaming false, have been rightly accused. Some good and helpful writing has come out of the FMSF, but it is important to note that you sign up by simply saying you have been falsely accused. Membership is in no way proof of innocence.

In saying all of this I do not want to induce paranoia in the challenge of working in this difficult arena. I simply want to underscore some basic precepts of the therapeutic endeavor: your position of power, your finiteness, and the deceitfulness of the human heart. The result should be humility, wisdom and an ever-growing dependence on the Holy Spirit as you work with your clients.

way, perpetuating abuse for generations, and they are now turning in a radically different direction.

What a beautiful unfolding of God's promise that, "He who has begun a good work in you will continue to perform it..." What a marvelous privilege it is as a therapist to be a vehicle for the redemptive work of God in another's life. Because of the redemptive work of Christ, you and I have a solid basis for giving a survivor the gift of hope.

## ENDNOTES

1. Jerome Kroll, *PTSD/borderlines in therapy: finding the balance* (New York: W.W. Norton & Co., 1993).

2. Diane Langberg, *Counseling survivors of sexual abuse* (Fairfax, VA: Xulon, 2003).

3. Nancy Faulkner, *Sexual abuse recognition and non-disclosure inventory of young adolescents* (Ann Arbor, MI: UMI, 1996).

4. Bagley, C., The prevalence and mental health sequelae of child sexual abuse in a community sample of women aged 18 to 27, *Canadian Journal of Community Mental Health, 10*, (1991), 103–116; D. Finkelhor, and Browne, A., Impact of child sexual abuse: A review of the research, *Psychological Bulletin, 99*,(1986), 66–77; L. Swanson, and Biaggio, M. K., Therapeutic perspectives on father-daughter incest, *American Journal of Psychiatry, 142*(6), (1985), 667–674; M. Tsai, and Wagner, N. N., Therapy groups for women sexually molested as children, *Archives of Sexual Behavior, 7* (1978), 417–427.

5. C. A. Courtois, and Watts, D. L., Counseling adult women who experienced incest in childhood or adolescence, *The Personnel and Guidance Journal* (January 1982), 275–279; B. B. Johnson, Sexual abuse prevention: A rural interdisciplinary effort, *Child Welfare, 66* (1987),165–73.

6. D. Finkelhor, Hotaling, G., Lewis, I. A., and Smith, C., Sexual abuse in a national survey of adult men and women: Prevalence, characteristics, and risk factors, *Child Abuse & Neglect, 14* (1990), 19–28.

7. C. Bagley, Development of a measure of unwanted sexual contact in childhood, for use in community mental health surveys, *Psychological Reports, 66* (1990), 401–2.

8. D. Graybill, Aggression in college students who were abused as children, *Journal of College Student Personnel 26* (1985).

9. P. Mosgofian, and Ohlschlager, G., *Sexual misconduct in counseling and ministry* (Dallas: Word, 1995).

10. R. McGee, and Schaumberg., H., *Renew: Hope for victims of sexual abuse* (Houston: Rapha, 1990).

11. N. C. Andreasen, Post-traumatic stress disorder, in H.I. Kaplan and Sadock B.J. (eds.), *Comprehensive textbook of psychiatry* 4th ed. (Baltimore: Williams and Wilkins, 1985), 38.

12. J. L. Herman, *Trauma and recovery* (New York: Basic Books, 1992), 38.

13. R. Janof-Bulman, *Shattered assumptions: Toward a new psychology of trauma* (New York: The Free Press, 1992); B. van der Kolk, McFarlane, A., and Weisaeth, L., (eds.), *Traumatic stress: The effects of overwhelming experience on mind, body, and society* (New York: The Guildford Press, 1996).

14. C. A. Courtois, and Watts, D. L., Counseling adult women who experienced incest in childhood or adolescence, *The Personnel and Guidance Journal,* (January, 1982), 275–279; D. Finkelhor, and Browne, A., Impact of child sexual abuse: A review of the research, *Psychological Bulletin, 99* (1986), 66–77.

15. American Psychiatric Association, *Diagnostic and statistical manual of mental disorders* 4th ed. (Washington, DC: 1994), 424–425.

16. S. Jones, and Yarhouse, M., *Homosexuality: The use of scientific research in the church's moral debate* (Downer's Grove, IL: InterVarsity Press, 2000).

17. See R. M. Brown, *Elie Wiesel: Messenger to all humanity* (South Bend, IN: Notre Dame University Press, 1983).

# 20

# Abortion:

## Crisis Decision and Post-Abortion Syndrome

*Theresa Burke, Tim Clinton, and George Ohlschlager*

Think about this for a moment. How many women do you know who have earned a college degree? Let's make it harder: how many women do you know who have been divorced? Some names come to mind, right? Now, how many women do you know who have had an abortion?

Amazingly, according to the prestigious Alan Guttmacher Institute, up to 43% of all women in America have had an abortion—as many women as are divorced, and twice as many as have earned a college degree.[1] The great disconnect on abortion is that while many talk about it as an issue, hardly anyone talks about their own abortion. Why? There are many reasons of course; the fear of judgment, stigma, and for some the shame and hurt that is inherent to post-abortion syndrome (PAS). As clinicians who have worked with women who have had abortions, we believe the problem is not just about the terminated child. We believe the problem also has to do with the pervasive suffering attached to PAS, experienced by so many women.

For more than 25 years, Judith lived with a secret. A secret she hid from everyone, including her husband: *I spent so many years with this gnawing pain buried deep within my heart. Buried so deep, I was not even aware of what caused it. I suffered from depression, bulimia, and some serious marital problems. I felt distant from God and hated whenever the subject of abortion came up!"*

There are many women like Judith who exist in a private world of grief shrouded with loss and despair. The secret of abortion is locked tightly in the deep recess of the heart, admitted to no one. Like the leper who cringes from the sunlight, a wounded heart seeks solace in the dark. Most women simply try to forget about their abortion experience and move on with their lives. This stuffing away of secret memory strikes at the heart of one's spiritual life causing feelings of guilt, shame, self-loathing and alienation from God. Many are afraid to deal with this deep pain because they fear opening up an injury of the soul that may never stop bleeding.

Perhaps no other issue in our culture elicits the same passion and divisiveness as abortion. Friends and family are alienated, churches and communities are divided, and people everywhere are charged up on both sides of the debate. Why? Because millions of lives are affected, and millions of lives are at stake. Since the (in)famous Supreme Court decision in *Roe v. Wade* in 1973, abortion has been legal in all 50 states, and nearly 1.5 million abortions are performed in America every year.

Abortion is a medical procedure that terminates the life of an unborn child and extracts it from the mother's womb in order to end the pregnancy. These induced or "therapeutic" abortions are ostensibly performed to

- preserve the life of the mother,
- end a pregnancy that resulted from rape or incest, or to,
- prevent the birth of a deformed or genetically abnormal child.

No matter the questionable morality of "therapeutic" abortion, the cold hard fact is that only 2% of abortions meet one or more of these criteria. Fully 98% of all abortions in the United States are done essentially as an act of birth control—because having a child is "inconvenient" to the parents. Forty percent of abortions—600,000 fetuses, or 50,000 unborn lives every month—are performed on repeat patients.[2]

*Violating the sanctity of life.* Abortion is wrong because it is the unjust taking of human life—the deliberate death of an unborn human being. Abortion proponents deny this truth—they firmly reject God's divine act of creating human life at the moment of conception: "For you formed my inward parts; you covered me in my mother's womb. I will praise you, for I am fearfully and wonderfully made; marvelous are your works, and that my soul knows very well" (Ps. 139:13–14).

There is no excuse, for all people know very well that life is not a "biological accident"; we know deep inside that the developing fetus is more than an "unviable tissue mass." No clinical terms can dehumanize what God has created and we will neither—as individuals, nor as a nation—escape the truth that abortion is a corrupt business that "devises evil by law" in order "to condemn innocent blood" (Ps. 94: 20, 21).

*The merciful reach of God.* Yet our God is also a God of great and tender mercy, a God of patience and long-suffering. He has heard the cries of the innocent slaughter that piles higher year after year, and only He can bear this grief, only He can carry this great sorrow. One of the more incredible facts about our current national crisis is how so many people trapped in the deadly lie of abortion have come to know Christ, have come to be champions of life. The kingdom is filling up with former abortionists, clinic owners, abortion advocates, and abortion victims in every corner of the land.

Even in the midst of mass death, the life of Jesus shines forth. Even as the thief comes to kill, steal, and destroy, Jesus comes to give life, and give it abundantly (John 10:10). There is absolutely no doubt that God will have the last word in the abortion wars, and that Word will bring forth life, sweet life, precious life. No issue is out of His ultimate control. No person is beyond His blessed reach.

### The Abortion Decision

Let's turn our attention to how the abortion decision and the abortion itself complicates and confounds the tasks of what is a natural developmental process. The decision to have an abortion depends on many factors: maturity, childhood wounds, personal and religious ethics, a law that permits and encourages the destruction of the baby in the womb, or the common pressure women feel from those who actively encourage abortion as a reasonable, responsible, and even loving thing to do.

Once a pregnancy is confirmed, the mother longs for approval, nurture and support. She is afraid of being judged or rejected for what her body has done. A younger mother will realize that she cannot raise a child on her own. She begins to imagine how her boyfriend, parents and friends will react. The real or imagined responses very much dictate the choice to keep the baby or seek an abortion.

Another significant motivation is the desire to conceal sexual activity. The abortion industry itself seeks to maintain a woman's secret autonomy by encouraging her "privacy." In turn, the end result is that women do not learn to ask for the support they need, but instead "take care of the problem" by themselves.

Many people mistakenly assume that no woman has an abortion if she does not want one. In fact, while many women believe they *need* an abortion, very few, if any, *want* an abortion. This reality is described in a rather famous line by Frederica Mathewes-Green, who wrote: "No woman wants an abortion as she wants an ice cream cone or a Porsche. She wants an abortion as an animal caught in a trap wants to gnaw off its own leg."[3] This quote was widely circulated by Planned Parenthood and other advocates of abortion,[4] but the next two sentences from Mathewes-Green's insightful commentary are not included: "Abortion is a tragic attempt to escape a desperate situation by an act of violence and self-loss. Abortion is not a sign that women are free, but a sign that they are desperate."

Many of the problems that follow abortion are not due solely to the traumatic effects of the surgery itself. Often, the problems that follow abortion are simply a magnification of problems that existed beforehand. In other cases, the problems stem back to the flawed, misinformed, compromising, self-defeating, or simply short-sighted *decision* to have an abortion. For many women, the decision to abort is itself sufficient to provoke feelings of depression, guilt, shame, and more.


### Decision Making

The notion that women should be "free to choose" abortion without question or hindrance is extremely irresponsible. It is based on an ideal divorced from reality; that of a fully informed, emancipated, emotionally stable woman. In contrast, most women are not well informed about the dangers abortion poses to both their psychological and physical health, and most women are not truly "emancipated." Instead, many are emotionally dependant on or easily influenced by parents, boyfriends, husbands, counselors, employers, or others who may want them to choose abortion far more than they want to choose it for themselves. Finally, many women considering abortion are simply not emotionally stable, and this lack of stability makes them more prone to hasty, ill-considered, or self-destructive decisions.

Even if one does not have a prior psychological illness or trauma to deal with, any woman confronted with an unintended pregnancy will face feelings of shock and fear about how the birth of a child will change her life. The destabilizing effects of a surprise pregnancy are further aggravated by the great hormonal shifts that occur during early pregnancy. These chemical changes in a woman's body may make her feel more emotional, dependant, exhausted, and physically ill and weak. Any and all of these factors can degrade her ability to make an informed and well-considered decision about abortion.

For most women, abortion is an ambivalent and irresolute choice. Consider the following findings from a survey of 252 women who joined a post-abortion support group:

- Approximately 70% had a prior negative moral view of abortion and chose it in violation of their consciences;
- Between 30 and 60% had a positive desire to carry the pregnancy to term and keep their babies; Over 80% said they would have carried to term under better circumstances or with the support of loved ones;
- Fifty-three percent felt "forced" to have the abortion by other people in their lives; Sixty-four percent felt "forced by outside circumstances" to have the abortion;
- Approximately 40% were still hoping to discover some alternative to abortion when they sat down for counseling at the abortion clinic.[5]

For most women, abortion is more likely to be perceived as an "evil necessity" than a great civil right. Indeed, a major *Los Angeles Times* poll found that 74% of women who admitted having had an abortion stated that they believe abortion is morally wrong.[6]

The fact that most women having abortions see it as posing a moral dilemma is itself problematic. Moral dilemmas, by their very nature, involve emotional and intellectual conflict about the options from which one must choose. These conflicts produce tension and, for many, a powerful sense of crisis. Many women feel completely overwhelmed by their situation[7] and under such pressures many will rush into an abortion without ever examining the full range of their beliefs, needs, and feelings.

Crisis counseling experts have found that those in a state of crisis are more vulnerable to outside influences than they would otherwise be in a non-crisis situation. The state of crisis, especially when it involves moral dilemmas, causes people to have less trust in their own opinions and abilities to make the right decision. This leads them into a state of "heightened psychological accessibility" in which they become reliant on the opinions of others, especially authority figures. When faced with such a crisis situation, "a relatively minor force, acting for a relatively short time, can switch the whole balance from one side or to the other—to the side of mental health or to the side of ill health."[8]

In the case of a woman named Joanna, the abortion clinic counselor's suggestion that she needed to "decide quickly" created emotional pressure that led her to choose abortion immediately, before the opportunity to escape her crisis situation was gone. It is not a coincidence that this same tension-provoking, "choose now" approach is regularly used in marketing programs where consumers are told to "buy now" before a sale price is gone forever.

Persons in crisis "are often less in touch with reality and more vulnerable to change than [when] they are in non-crisis situations."[9] They often experience feelings of tiredness, lethargy, hopelessness, inadequacy, confusion, anxiety and disorganization. Also, a person upset and "trapped" in a crisis, like Joanna, wants to reestablish stability.[10] Thus, one is more likely to stand back and let other people (i.e. a mental health professional, family member, minister, or male partner) make their decisions for them, instead of protecting themselves from decisions that may not be in their best interests.

Uta Landy, an abortion counselor and former executive director of the National Abortion Federation, an association for abortion providers, has admitted that the decision-making processes of women seeking abortion can be temporarily impaired by feelings of crisis related to their pregnancy. Landy defines four types of defective decision-making styles which she has observed in abortion clinics:[11]

The first defective process is the "spontaneous approach," wherein the decision is made too quickly, without taking sufficient time to resolve internal conflicts or explore options.

The second defective decision-making process is the "rational-analytical approach," which focuses on the practical reasons to terminate the pregnancy (financial problems, single parenthood, etc.) without consideration of emotional needs (attachment to the pregnancy, maternal desires, etc.).

The third defective process is the "denying-procrastinating" approach which is typical of women who have delayed making a decision precisely because they have a conflicting desire to keep their babies. When such a "denying-procrastinator" finally agrees to an abortion, it is likely that she has still not resolved her internal conflicts, but is submitting to the abortion only because she has "run out of time."

Fourth, there is the "no-decision making approach," wherein a woman refuses to make her own decision but allows others, such as her male partner, parents, counselors, or physician, to make the decision for her.

Landy encourages counselors to be aware of the fact that some women's feelings about their pregnancy are not simply ambivalent but deeply confused. This confusion is not necessarily expressed in a straightforward manner, but can hide behind such outward behavior as:

1. being uncommunicative,
2. being extremely self assured,
3. being impatient (how long is this going to take, I have other important things to do),
4. being hostile (this is an awful place; you are an awful doctor, counselor, nurse; I hate being here).[12]

Despite her recognition of the fact that many women are making ill-considered decisions, Landy does not recognize any obligation on abortion providers to refuse to perform an abortion on such women, who are at higher risk of severe emotional problems later.

To escape the trap of a crisis pregnancy, women who abort must sacrifice some part of themselves. The experience of abortion is an experience of violence. The decision to expose oneself to abortion often entails a betrayal of one's own moral values or maternal instincts, and thereby a loss of some part of one's self. As the psychiatrist and abortionist Dr. Fogel observed:

"This is a part of her own life. When she destroys a pregnancy, she is destroying herself...I know that as a psychiatrist."[13]

Any number of factors can drive women to this act of desperation:

- Rejection of the pregnancy by partner or family,
- Self-doubt: perceived inability to care for a child,
- The advice or pressure of other people,
- Being driven to choose abortion by psychological compulsions, such as sexual abuse or prior abortions, which incline them to reenact previous losses through abortion.

### Abortion Decision as a Symptom

With some exceptions, many crisis pregnancies are not a complete accident (unplanned or unwanted). Our propensity to permit or create crisis frequently stems from unresolved conflicts. This is why there is a need for intervention and exploration into family history and patterns. Once a woman is aware of the psychological underpinnings which provide motivation for her behaviors, only then can she redirect her life in a way that identifies life goals and a plan to reach them which is not self-destructive. Perhaps more important, is the fact that when a woman sees her abortion decision in the context of her entire life, she is often more tolerant, forgiving, and accepting of herself. This is an extremely essential ingredient to permitting God's love and grace to enter her life.

In working with women who have crisis pregnancies, an insightful therapist may also discover some very clear metaphors. Sometimes a woman is trying to resolve a past conflict or loss. Yet often, her attempts to resolve life's losses through recreating or reenacting the conflict does not succeed in changing the patterns, but rather aggravates and reinforces them. Abortion, in particular validates an already inadequate and fragile self image with the unspoken message that she is incapable and inept—that it is better to destroy the developing child than to be mothered by a woman who is not ready or can't give her child the perfect life. The nurturing, accepting and receptive qualities unique to feminine personhood have been violated.

Human beings are architects of their own misfortune, though, with the help and grace of God, can become ministers of their own healing. It is in removing our defenses, and discovering our brokenness and mistakes, that guides us toward the path of healing and redemption. Healing is not found by hiding from the truth, but by facing it with an honest courage and a humble spirit. This includes taking a look at the personal and situational factors which made one vulnerable to choose abortion in the first place.

Here are a few common examples of how crisis pregnancy and abortion can be a symptom of other conflicts:

*Testing the relationship's commitment.* There are women who become pregnant to test the commitment of a love relationship. When the fruit of their love is not met with wonder and excitement, the woman may turn the blame and rejection inward—and out of powerlessness she may scapegoat her developing child—to maintain peace in the relationship, or avoid embarrassment. It is not uncommon for relationships to end after abortion, and for some it gives the final excuse to be assertive once they realize there is no commitment.

*Anger and control.* Abortion can be a way to express anger, and it may be an attempt to punish another, or regain control. A woman may try to prove her independence and deny her need for others who have let her down. Women in this situation often disavow their need for significant others—because others in their past have disappointed or emotionally abandoned them. Their attempts to compensate for this loss are seen by outward displays of independence, abortion being one of them, though inwardly they may experience themselves as fearful, rejected children.

*Absent fathers.* Statistics reveal that a woman who comes from a family where her father is physically absent or emotionally distant is more likely to become pregnant as a teenager. Such women seek the affirmation and acceptance of a male or father image, but unfortunately this need for love and validation is frequently sexualized. Some women with absent fathers choose abortion because they do not want their child growing up in a home without a father. Again, the theme of choices made is an attempt to resolve a previous loss.

For the woman who invites uncaring and uncommitted men to get them pregnant, usually a fear of abandonment and a history of not having been loved can be identified. Their low self-esteem is validated through a relationship that recreates their sense of rejection. Sparing an "unwanted" child this grief by denying him life, is another painful attempt to take control of unwanted feelings of rejection.

*Maternal identity.* It is not uncommon for abortion to represent a rejection of mother and motherhood itself. When a woman has had a tumultuous relationship with her mother, she is often unwilling to take on that identity herself. Abortion becomes a way to redeem her from ever becoming like her mother. The relationship which craves redemption is the broken connection between mother and child—painfully recreated through abortion.

Sometimes the identity crisis is complicated by present personal problems of the mother. Our mental picture of "mother" is determined first by our own mothers. When a woman's childhood experience was one of poor or absent mothering, accepting the cloak of mother identity can be difficult.

For such a woman, becoming a mother constitutes a threat to the self. Motherhood demands that she is required now to be the caregiver, to be responsible for nurturing, supporting and loving a baby. To her picture of herself as an abandoned or abused child needing nurture, such looms like an overwhelming and impossible demand; "I didn't get enough love myself! I still want to be taken care of! How can I possibly give love and care to a baby?"

*Developmental arrest.* Pregnancy is an important phase in a young woman's unending task of separation and individuation from her own mother. Some women may view the pregnancy as a way to test their sexual identity and capacity to procreate. When abortion enters the picture, the next stages in the developmental process are thwarted because internal parent objects will not give permission for the woman/child to become a mother herself. The developmental phase is arrested and two critical aspects of emotional identification in pregnancy become unsalvagable: identification with her own mother and identification with the child as an acceptable part of herself.

*Histories of sexual abuse.* There is a remarkable clinical finding which suggests a high proportion of women have histories of molestation, sexual abuse, or incest. In such cases, an abortion is a clear metaphor of a recreation of conflict for an internalized and damaged sense of self and sexuality, induced through sexual abuse of some kind.

In an abortion, the abortionist's hand or instrument forces her to undergo a penetrating violation deep into the protective and sacred part of her womb. Life is ended through this intrusion, similar to the death and destruction of her sense of self which commonly results from sexual abuse. In this sense, abortion can be seen as a symbolic suicide, a reenactment of this conflict acting out the rejection of the wounded inner child.

Even the grief of abortion, like the grief of sexual abuse, is held in unspoken cries of secrecy. It is a literal re-creation of the intrusion forced upon her during sexual abuse as she remains helpless and powerless consenting to the invasion while overwrought with unspoken shame and guilt, despair and grief.

*Atonement baby and repeat abortions.* It is not uncommon for a woman to have an atonement baby after a previous abortion. The desire to replace what was lost or make up for the lost pregnancy with another reflects the natural instinct to procreate. However, this desire is often overridden by the concept that we should all be responsible and ready for parenthood. Many times a woman will re-create the crisis of an unplanned pregnancy as an attempt to carry it out this time by getting it right, or as a symptom of psychic trauma and reenactment. Often, the woman's circumstances are still the same and she has another abortion. Repeat abortions can become a ritualized outlet for continued grief and loss. Repeat abortions are a symptom of deep psychic trauma—as repetition is one of the greatest indicators we have to demonstrate trauma. Note that 46% of all abortions are repeat abortions.

It is not uncommon to see women having 4, 5 or 6 abortions. The psychological motivation is to gain mastery over the trauma, and therefore many women become stuck in such a very self-destructive pattern. With each abortion, a woman may become more anesthetized until the process is just a routine event. In other cases, the reenactment can be a ritualized means through which a woman will intensely grieve and mourn.

*Alcoholic families.* The woman who chooses an abusive or alcoholic partner statistically comes from a familial history of abusive or alcoholic parents. A reenactment of conflict will include the intense desire to change him, make things better, or to continue in the familiar lifestyle of denigration and instability. When the woman becomes pregnant, abortion is a way to save the child from experiencing the pain she knew as a child. It can also be a signal to grieve her wounded and rejected "inner child" and express feelings of despair and powerlessness.

*Pressure by others.* It is not uncommon for women who did not want to have abortions, to experience coercion and have no voice to stop the process once it is suggested. This sense of powerlessness is frequently experienced as a type of paralysis on the abortion table—an inability to stop the procedure from happening. This indicates a lack of assertiveness, and the pain of that diminished sense of self, along with the lost child, is what is grieved after an abortion: "Why did I let them do this to my baby? How could I have gone through with this?" the woman will ask herself. The abortion is not an empowering experience, but one of complete and utter devastation upon the realization that someone talked her into violating a basic female instinct to nurture and protect her offspring. In post abortion healing, this lost sense of self must be reclaimed.

### Post-Abortion Syndrome and the Conspiracy of Silence

PAS is defined as the inability to

- adequately process the painful emotions attached to abortion—especially guilt, anger, and grief;
- properly identify and grieve the loss experienced; or to
- come to peace with God, and within oneself, about the abortion.[14]

*Etiology.* Much controversy exists about how many women experience PAS, and to what degree. It is clear that some women who have abortions do not struggle with PAS, and that many do. The secrecy around personal disclosure and controversies associated with abortion has made gathering accurate data a difficult task. We do know that women who struggle with PAS have tended to have[15]

1. been coerced, to some degree by family or father, into having an abortion,
2. been young and immature, most between the ages of 14 and 24,
3. had a stormy relationship with little to no support from sex partner,
4. expressed psychological and moral ambivalence about it,
5. had a religious upbringing and expressed some spiritual convictions,
6. had more than one abortion,
7. had a late term abortion, in the second or third trimester,
8. had a pregnancy due to rape or incest,
9. had an abortion due to fetal or other abnormality,

10. had been awake during the abortion procedure,

11. been unable to conceive after the abortion,

12. had a recent pregnancy with a "wanted" child.

A common pattern of events that influences PAS has long been recognized by doctors and counselors working with post-abortion women: The pregnancy was a crisis event, unexpected and a source of surprise and shame for the pregnant girl and her family. The crisis precipitates a moral dilemma as abortion is considered as one way to "solve" the crisis. An abortion is performed as the expedient, though ambivalent solution, and brings a period of transient relief. The moral dilemma resurfaces, as the question is asked, "Did we do the right thing?" The pain of the act and the ensuing dilemma are dealt with poorly—by denial, suppression of feelings, and avoidance. Efforts of denial and the avoidance of pain go on for years, but erupt again to disrupt life after some event that triggers a traumatic recall of the abortion event, often a later pregnancy.[16]

*Assessment and treatment.* The symptomatology of PAS is remarkable for its similarity to post-traumatic stress disorder (PTSD). In fact, PAS is appropriately characterized by some as a unique form of PTSD, and we believe it is accurate to conceptualize and treat it as a trauma-based disorder. The usual pattern of symptoms include:

- *anxiety:* increased anxiety and guilt are the two "felt" emotions that dominate the feeling world of the PAS sufferer.
- *guilt:* often exacerbated and expressed as a three-strike proposition—(1) "I murdered an innocent" who was also (2) "my child," and (3) "I survived" though I did not deserve to.
- *depression:* often with all the classic symptoms—sleep disturbance, social withdrawal, helpless/hopeless syndrome, crying episodes, reduced sex and pleasure drives, amotivation, and struggles with suicide,
- *lost faith and spiritual deadness:* believing that God is enraged, or uncaring, or that one is unforgivable. Many women lose their faith and dry up spiritually following an abortion.
- *self-abuse and self-hatred:* some women become self-abusive and self-punishing, with suicidal ideation mixing together in a sometimes deadly combination.

- *flashbacks and intrusive memories:* very much like PTSD episodes where vivid dreams, memories, flashbacks, and recalls are experienced as if the event is being re-lived.

- *debilitating avoidance:* anxiety provoked behavior where people and situations with the slightest risk of eliciting a recall of the abortion are systematically avoided.

- *numbing:* when all else fails—when avoidance, self-abuse, or suicide attempts do not stop the pain—the PAS sufferer will learn to "numb out" or "flat-line" their emotional and relational lives.

- *bonding problems, including child abuse and neglect:* PAS struggles can interfere with the normal bonding process with other children—in the worst cases, child abuse and neglect is the result.

- *substance abuse:* many women abuse alcohol and drugs—including prescription medications—and quickly learn to "self-medicate" as a way to numb the pain and guilt of abortion.

- *eating disorders:* a few women, either in lieu of or in combination with drugs or other addictive agents, will develop an eating disorder of some kind.

- *barrenness and pregnancy problems:* some women transfer their psycho-spiritual distress physically, experiencing ongoing difficulty with pregnancy and fertility subsequent to an abortion.

- *anniversary reactions:* as with grief recovery, anniversaries of the abortion and related events increase emotional turmoil and distress.

Treatment planning and intervention with PAS clients concentrates on five goals:

1. *Facing the truth and accepting the loss.* The counselor must give the client permission—encourage and challenge her—to yield to what she has been fighting for months or years. She must honestly face the fact that she underwent an abortion and her child is gone. This will usually release a torrent of emotions and memories and the counselor must be able to assist the client to identify and handle each one. Telling the truth about what happened and discovering that it will not kill or crush her is a huge first step in the healing process.

2. *Deal with the guilt and renew relations with God.* No sin exists that God cannot and does not want to forgive, and to experience anew God's forgiveness and love is a wonderful renewal of spiritual and emotional life. The process of repentance and reconciliation with God is also frightening, and fraught with much unbelief and resistance, so counselors must be patient and gentle to stay with a client, not allowing her to lose focus, but acknowledging and reinforcing the evidence of God's continual entreaty to take His hand and walk together again.

3. *Address the abortion decision and deal with the anger.* Abortion represents a failure of nerve, the expedient submission to the seductive lie by the client and so many other people. The client will be angry with herself, with her sex partner, often with her parents, with the abortion doctors, counselors, clinic, and with the whole abortion system. She may want to exact vengeance or become a crusader for the right to life. Help by acknowledging her anger, working through it, checking the vengeful impulses, and affirming intent toward right action. Give her active things to do to vent the anger and reengage with the world around once again.

4. *Grieve the loss.* A child is dead. Now the client is becoming free enough to mourn the enormity of this awful truth, and to rejoice in the heavenly home of that absent child. Often the client allows herself to do what she has refused to this point—to fantasize about the child's age-appropriate behavior and interactions as if the child were still alive. It is alright to allow and facilitate this now, and to record the crying, laughter, sorrow and pain that will be elicited as the client remembers her lost child. Prepare the client to expect to experience a wide range of now "unfreezing" emotions that, at times, will surprise, even disturb the client at their appearance. All of this is normal to the grieving process and it will take much time to work through.

5. *Reconstruct a new future.* The last phase of the healing process is coming to a place of renewed commitment to living, a refreshment and release of new desires for life. Forgiveness does not mean forgetting, but the memories of the child and its absence no longer debilitate, or create despair. God is able to build palaces out of ashes. Even the pain of abortion must yield to His miraculous

restorative power—the same power that brought Jesus back to life from the grave.[17]

## Further Study of Outreach and Treatment

Developing an effective and meaningful outreach to those wounded by abortion requires education of the manifestations of trauma and in the techniques grief work that have proven to be effective with this population. Reportedly, the often self-destructive behaviors after an abortion are an attempt to work through unresolved psychological conflicts and can be acted out through eating disorders, multiple abortions, obsessive compulsive rituals, anxiety over fertility, stress over maternal and sexual identity, and other physical or behavioral disturbances.

Insights into traumatic reenactments will help the counselor assist clients in interpreting their symptoms so that they can confront the trauma rooted beneath their behaviors. An illuminating work on this subject helpful to counselors and pastoral ministers is *Forbidden Grief—The Unspoken Pain of Abortion.*[18]

### ENDNOTES

1. Alan Guttmacher Institute, *Facts in brief: induced abortion* (Washington, D.C., January 1997).
2. Frank Minirth, Meier, P., and Arterburn, S., Abortion, in *The complete life encyclopedia* (Nashville: Thomas Nelson, 1995).
3. Frederica Mathewes-Green, Unplanned Parenthood, *Policy Review*, (Summer 1991).
4. This quote was reprinted as "Quote of the Week" in the *Planned Parenthood Federation of America Public Affairs Action Letter*, (September 25, 1992) and as "Quote of the Month" in *The Pro-Choice Network Newsletter*, (May 1993), and reprinted in a commentary column by Ellen Goodman, "Not 'Choice,' but 'Better Choices,'" *The Baltimore Sun* (September 18, 1992).
5. David C. Reardon, *Aborted women: silent no more* (Chicago: Loyola University Press, 1987), 11–21; See also, Mary K. Zimmerman, *Passage through abortion* (New York: Praeger Publishers, 1977), 62–70; and Miller, W. B., An empirical study of the psychological antecedents and consequences of induced abortion, *J Social Issues, 48*(3), (1992), 67–93.
6. *Los Angeles Times* Poll, (March 19, 1989), question 76.
7. Vincent M. Rue and Speckhard, A. C., Informed consent and abortion: Issues in medicine and counseling, *Med. & Mind, 6*(1), (1992), 75–94.
8. Gerald Caplan, *Principals of preventive psychiatry* (New York: Basic Books, 1964).
9. Howard W. Stone, *Crisis counseling* (Fortress Press, 1976).

10. Wilbur E. Morely, Theory of crisis intervention, *Pastoral Psychology*, 21(203), (April 1970), 16.

11. Uta Landy, Abortion counseling—a new component of medical care, *Clinics in Obs/Gyn*, 13(1), (1986), 33–41.

12. Ibid.

13. Colman McCarthy, A psychological view of abortion, St. Paul Sunday Pioneer Press, *Washington Post* (March 7, 1971). Dr. Fogel, who did 20,000 abortions over the subsequent decades, reiterated the same view in a second interview with McCarthy in 1989. The real anguish of abortions, *The Washington Post* (Feb. 5, 1989).

14. T. Reisser, and Reisser, P., *A solitary sorrow: Finding healing and wholeness after abortion* (Wheaton, IL: Harold Shaw, 1999).

15. Ibid.; R. Payne, Kravitz, A., Notman, M., and Anderson, J., Outcomes following therapeutic abortion, *Archives of General Psychiatry 33*, (1976), 725; D. Reardon, *Aborted women: silent no more* (Westchester, IL: Crossway, 1987); N. Adler, Emotional responses of women following therapeutic abortion, *American Journal of Orthopsychiatry 45*, (1975), 446–454.

16. T. Reisser, and Reisser, P., *A solitary sorrow: Finding healing and wholeness after abortion* (Wheaton, IL: Harold Shaw, 1999).

17. Ibid.; T. Reisser, and Coe, J., Post-abortion counseling, in D. Benner and P. Hill, (eds.), *Baker encyclopedia of psychology and counseling*, 2nd ed. (Grand Rapids, MI: Baker, 1999).

18. Theresa Burke, with David C. Reardon, *Forbidden grief: The unspoken pain of abortion*, (Acorn Books, 2002).

# Appendices

# Forms and Templates for Christian Counseling

## Appendix A: Professional Services Agreement

This agreement for _____services
between (your practice's name) and
client(s)_____shall govern all professional relations between the parties.

### A. THE STAFF THERAPIST is

_____.

He or she is a professional therapist, qualified and trained as an

- ❏ LMFT, LPC, LMHC, LCPC, LCSW, LISW, licensed psychologist
  or psychiatrist; or
- ❏ pre-licensed intern, trainee, associate, or psychological assistant
  working under supervision of a licensed therapist who will
  know something about your case.

### B. FEES AND INSURANCE POLICY.

Client fees are to be determined at the first session. Full or partial payment shall be made by the client at the end of each session. Clients agree to pay part of their fee out-of-pocket even if covered by insurance. *As a courtesy to you* we can bill insurance and other vendors on a monthly basis. We will not extend credit or schedule appointments beyond three unpaid sessions until payment is made. Clients understand that a therapist with pre-license status (as checked above) may or may not be able to receive insurance reimbursement. *Clients understand they are fully responsible for all fees if insurance or other vendor does not pay.*

## C. CANCELLATION POLICY.

We agree to and ask that clients maintain responsible relations regarding appointment times. Any appointment *cancelled after 6 P.M. the day before the appointment or that the client does not show will be charged to the client at (1) half the fee rate for the first incident and (2) the full fee rate for any incidents thereafter.* Most insurances will not reimburse for this charge, *so clients understand they are responsible to pay for missed sessions per this policy.*

## D. CONFIDENTIALITY POLICY.

All therapeutic communications, records, and contacts with professional and support staff will be held in strict confidence. Information may be released, in accordance with state law, only when (1) the client signs a written release of information indicating informed consent to such release; (2) the client expresses serious intent to harm himself/herself or someone else, clearly identified; (3) there is evidence or reasonable suspicion of abuse against a minor child, elder person (sixty-five years or older), or dependent adult; or (4) a subpoena or other court order is received directing the disclosure of information.

It is our policy to assert either (a) privileged communication in the event of #4 or (b) the right to consult with clients, if at all possible barring an emergency, before mandated disclosure in the event of #2 or #3. Although we cannot guarantee it, we will endeavor to apprise the client of all mandated disclosure.

Clients with any concerns or questions about this policy agree to raise them with their counselor at the earliest possible time to resolve them in the client's best interest.

## E. WORK AGREEMENT.

It is agreed that the client shall make a good-faith effort at personal growth and engage in the counseling process as an important priority at this time in his or her life. Client gain is most important in professional counseling. Suspension, termination, or referral shall be discussed between counselor and client for a pattern of behavior showing disinterest or lack of commitment, or for any unresolved conflict or impasse between counselor and client.

(You or your practice's name) and client further agree that the following needs or problem issues will be addressed in both counseling sessions and in client homework, with future revisions possible as need arises:

_____

_____

_____

_____

_____

### F. FEE AGREEMENT.

The agreed *fee for each intake interview session is* _____ ; and
*per 50 minute session*, the fee is _____ ; and
*per 25 minute session*, the fee is _____ ; and
*for each group session*, the fee is _____ ; and
for any special or emergency session, the fee is _____ .

If a sliding fee scale is elected, fill in the first two categories below:
monthly family gross income_____
number of persons in family _____
sliding fee scale is _____ per session.

### G. MODIFICATION & CONFLICT RESOLUTION.

It is agreed that any disputes or modifications of agreement shall be negotiated directly between the parties. If these negotiations are not satisfactory, then the parties *agree to mediate any differences with a mutual acceptable third-party mediator, considering first either the Executive Director or Associate*

*Director of the practice.* If these are unsatisfactory, then the parties shall move to arbitration, and then binding arbitration, choosing an arbitrator mutually agreeable to both. Litigation shall be considered only if and after all of these methods of resolution are given a good faith effort and are unsatisfactory.

## Service Agreement

We, the undersigned therapist and client, have read, discussed together, and fully understand this agreement and the stated policies. We agree to honor these policies, including the commitment to negotiate and mediate as stated above, and will respect one another's views and differences in their outworking. We have also agreed to an initial definition of professional work and to the fee to be paid by the client.

Client signature_____Date_____

Therapist signature_____Date_____

# Appendix B: Pastoral Counseling Services Agreement

This agreement for _____services between (your church or practice's name) and client(s)_____shall govern all counseling relations between the parties.

A. **THE PASTORAL COUNSELOR is**
_____. He or she is an Ordained Minister and/or Pastoral Counselor, NOT a licensed therapist, and does not provide professional counseling or psychotherapy, but only time-limited pastoral counseling interventions.

B. **PASTORAL COUNSELING AT (YOUR CHURCH OR PRACTICE'S NAME)** is confidential, Bible-based counseling by one trained and experienced in both pastoral and counseling ministry. Pastoral counseling will be limited to ____ sessions overall with an evaluation at the end of this program of counseling. Counseling shall then be terminated, or referral for further treatment may be made at this time, whichever is in the client's best interest.

## C. FEES AND INSURANCE POLICY.

Client fees are to be determined at the first session. Full or partial payment shall be made at the end of each session by the client. Clients understand that a Pastoral Counselor will not be able to receive insurance reimbursement under most policies—clients are responsible to bill their own insurance if they believe a Pastoral Counselor is covered. We will not extend credit or schedule appointments beyond three unpaid sessions until payment is made. *Clients are fully responsible for the payment of all fees.*

## D. CANCELLATION POLICY.

We agree to and ask that clients maintain responsible relations regarding appointment times. Any appointment *cancelled after 6 P.M. the day before the appointment or that the client does not show will be charged to the client at (1) half the fee rate for the first incident and (2) the full fee rate for any incidents thereafter.* Most insurance companies will not reimburse *you for this charge.*

## E. CONFIDENTIALITY POLICY.

All therapeutic communications, records, and contact with professional and support staff will be held in strict confidence. Information may be released, in accordance with state law, only when (1) the client signs a written release of information indicating informed consent to such release; (2) the client expresses serious intent to harm himself/herself or someone else; (3) there is evidence or reasonable suspicion of abuse against a minor child, elder person (sixty- years or older), or dependent adult; or (4) a subpoena or other court order is received directing the disclosure of information. It is our policy to assert either (a) privileged communication in the event of #4 or (b) the right to consult with clients, if at all possible baring an emergency, before mandated disclosure in the event of #2 or #3. Although we cannot guarantee it, we will endeavor to apprise clients of all mandated disclosures.

Clients with any concerns or questions about this policy agree to raise them with their counselor at the earliest possible time to resolve them in the client's best interest.

## F. WORK AGREEMENT.

It is agreed that the parishioner-client shall make a good-faith effort at change and personal growth, and engage in the counseling process as an important priority at this time in his or her life. Client gain is most important in pastoral counseling. Suspension, termination, or referral shall be discussed between counselor and client for a pattern of behavior that reveals disinterest or lack of commitment to counseling or for any unresolved conflict or impasse between counselor and client.

(Your practice's name) and client further agree that the following needs or problem issues will be addressed in both counseling sessions and in client homework, with future revisions possible as need arises:

_____

_____

_____

_____

_____

## G. FEE AGREEMENT.

The agreed *fee per 50 minute session* is _____for the base rate. If the fee scale is elected, fill in the first two categories below:

    monthly family gross income_____

    number in family_____

    fee scale_____per session.

## H. MODIFICATION & CONFLICT RESOLUTION.

It is agreed that any disputes or modifications of agreement shall be negoti-ated directly between the parties. If these negotiations are not satisfactory, then the parties *agree to mediate any differences with a mutual acceptable third-party mediator.* If these are unsatisfactory, then the parties shall move to arbitration, and then binding arbitration, choosing an arbitrator mutually agreeable to both. Litigation is not acceptable between Christians, and will only be considered if these methods of dispute resolution are given a good faith effort and are found unsatisfactory.

### Service Agreement

We, the undersigned pastoral counselor and client, have read, discussed together and fully understand this agreement and the stated policies. We agree to honor these policies, including the commitment to negotiate and mediate as stated above, and will respect one another's views and differ-ences in their outworking. We have also agreed to an initial definition of counseling work and to the fee to be paid by the client.

Client signature_____Date_____

Counselor signature_____ Date_____

# Appendix C: Lay Helping Services Agreement

This agreement for lay helping services between (your church or practice's name) and parishioner(s)_____shall govern all helping ministry relations between the parties.

A. **THE LAY HELPER is**
_____. He or she is NOT an Ordained Minister and/or Pastoral Counselor, is NOT a licensed therapist, and does NOT provide professional counseling or psychotherapy, but only time-limited lay helping ministry.

B. **LAY HELPING AT (YOUR CHURCH OR PRACTICE'S NAME)** is confidential, Bible-based ministry by one trained and supervised by _____. Lay helping will be limited to ____ sessions overall with an evaluation at the end of this program of ministry. Lay helping shall then be terminated, or referral for further pastoral care or professional counseling treatment may be made at this time, whichever is in the parishioner's best interest.

## C. FEES AND INSURANCE POLICY.

Lay helping is a servant's service of this church and no client fees or anything of monetary value shall be charged or given for this ministry.

## D. CANCELLATION POLICY.

We agree to and ask that clients maintain responsible relations regarding appointment times.

## E. CONFIDENTIALITY POLICY.

All ministry communications, records, and contact with church and support staff will be held in strict confidence. Information may be released, in accordance with church policy, only when (1) the parishioner signs a written release of information indicating informed consent to such release; (2) the parishioner expresses serious intent to harm himself/herself or someone else; (3) there is evidence or reasonable suspicion of abuse against a minor child, elder person (sixty- years or older), or dependent adult; or (4) a subpoena or other court order is received directing the disclosure of information. It is our church policy to assert either (a) privileged communication in the event of #4 or (b) the right to consult with clients, if at all possible baring an emergency, before any disclosure is made in the event of #2 or #3. Parishioners with any concerns or questions about this policy agree to raise them at the earliest possible time to resolve them in the parishioner's best interest.

### F. WORK AGREEMENT.

It is agreed that the parishioner-client shall make a good-faith effort at change and personal growth, and engage in the helping process as an important priority at this time in his or her life. Parishioner growth and spiritual maturity is most important in this care-giving ministry. Suspension, termination, or referral shall be discussed between helper and parishioner for a pattern of behavior that reveals disinterest or lack of commitment, or for any unresolved conflict or impasse between helper and parishioner.

(Your church's name) and _____ further agree that the following needs or problem issues will be addressed in sessions and in any homework, with future revisions possible as need arises:

_____

_____

_____

_____

_____

### G. MODIFICATION & CONFLICT RESOLUTION.

It is agreed that any disputes or modifications of agreement shall be negotiated directly between the parties. If these negotiations are not satisfactory, then the parties agree to mediate any differences with the helper's supervisor, or any other mutually acceptable third-party mediator who is a member of this church. If these are unsatisfactory, then the parties shall move to arbitration, and then binding arbitration, choosing an arbitrator mutually agreeable to both. Litigation is not acceptable between Christians, and will only be considered if these methods of dispute resolution are given a good faith effort and are found unsatisfactory.

## Service Agreement

We, the undersigned lay helper and parishioner, have read, discussed together and fully understand this agreement and the stated policies. We agree to honor these policies, including the commitment to negotiate and mediate as stated above, and will respect one another's views and differences in their outworking. We have also agreed to an initial definition of counseling work.

Parishioner signature_____ Date_____

Lay Helper signature_____ Date_____

# Appendix D: Client Insurance Information/Consent

**A.** Client's Name _____ Age _____ Birthdate_____
Address_____
        street                    city       state       zip
Phone (home) _____ (work) _____
best time to call _____
If Client a Minor, Parent /Guardian name(s)

_____

Client Education _____ SSN _____ Occupation

_____

Employer Name and Address

_____

Marital Status(circle):  sing  wid  eng  mar  sep  div  liv-tog

_____

Spouse's Name _____ Age _____
Birthdate _____

**B.** Family Status: List name, birthdate, sex, relationship of all children, and whether they live at home with you.

      Name                      Birthdate  Sex   Relationship at Home?

_____

_____

_____

_____

_____

**C.** Home church(if any)_____
    Pastor _____

**D.** Person to call in emergency (name, phone(s), relationship)

_____

**E.** Referring physician name & address

_____

**F.** Insurance Information and Release. As a courtesy to you, we will bill your primary insurance. You are responsible for getting a physician's referral for insurance payment and are responsible for your entire bill if insurance does not pay.

   At your request, we will provide you with an itemized statement so you can bill your secondary insurance.

Insured's Name_____ SSN _____
Relationship to you_____
Insured's Employer (name and address)

_____

Name of insurance_____ Policy#_____
Group# _____
Secondary insurance? _____ Policy# _____
Group# _____
2nd Insured's name _____
Birthdate _____ SSN _____
If any other person or agency will be covering the cost of counseling, give their name and address:

_____

_____

I HEREBY AUTHORIZE RELEASE OF INFORMATION NECESSARY TO FILE A CLAIM WITH MY INSURANCE COMPANY AND ASSIGN ALL MY BENEFITS TO THIS COUNSELOR.

Signature _____ Date _____

# Appendix E: Client Intake Form

Today's Date_____

**A.** Client's Name _____
Age _____ Birthdate_____
Parent /Guardian name(s) _____
Age(s) _____
Address _____
Phone (home) _____ (work) _____ best time to call ____
Marital Status: single ____ engaged ____ married ____ (how long _____)
times married _____ separated _____ (how long _____)
divorced ____ (how long_____)
Education _____ Occupation _____ SSN _____
Spouse's Name _____ Age _____Birthdate _____
Spouse's Education_____
Spouse's Occupation _____

**B.** List name, birthdate, sex, relationship of all children, and whether they live at home with you.

| Name | Birthdate | Sex | Relationship at Home? |
|------|-----------|-----|------------------------|
| | | | |
| | | | |
| | | | |
| | | | |

**C.** Who is coming for counseling? _____
Any prior counseling? Y___N___
If yes, when? _____Where? _____
With whom? _____
Why? _____

Are you or another family member currently seeing a psychiatrist or another counselor? Y\_\_\_\_ N\_\_\_\_

If so, what family member?_____

Name of helper _____

For what purpose?_____

Person to contact in emergency (name, relationship, address, phone).

_____

_____

PLEASE FILL OUT THE FOLLOWING INFORMATION AS IT APPLIES TO THE CLIENT

**D.** State the nature of the problem in your own words.

What is your most difficult relationship right now?

What is your most difficult emotion right now?

**E.** CRISIS INFORMATION: Any current suicidal thoughts, feelings or actions? Y\_\_\_\_\_ N_____ If yes, explain

Any current homicidal or assaultive thoughts or feelings, or anger-control problems? Y\_\_\_\_\_ N\_\_\_\_\_ If yes, explain

Any past problems, hospitalizations, or jailings for suicidal or assaultive behavior? Y_____ N\_\_\_\_\_ If yes, describe

Any current threats of significant loss or harm (illness, divorce, custody, job loss, etc.)? Y____ N____ If yes, describe

_____

**F.** MEDICAL INFORMATION: Doctor's name, address and phone

_____

_____

Are you presently taking any medication? Y__N___ If so, what?_____

For what purpose?

_____

Any problems with eating_____ sleeping _____ chronic pain _____ recent weight changes _____ Describe any answers checked above_____

Any other medical problems?

_____

Have you or a family member ever been hospitalized for mental or emotional illness? Y_____ N_____
If yes, please explain—dates, where, reason:

_____

_____

**G.** Common problem/symptom checklist. Fill in: 0 – none, 1 – mild, 2 – moderate, 3 – severe.

| | | |
|---|---|---|
| ___marriage | ___divorce/separation | ___alcohol/drugs |
| ___God/faith | ___pre-marital | ___child custody |
| ___other addictions | ___church/ministry | ___being single |
| ___disabled | ___grief/loss | ___past hurts |
| ___sexual issues | ___work/career | ___depression |
| ___codependency | ___family | ___school/learning |

___fear/anxiety        ___intimacy            ___children

___money/budgeting     ___anger control       ___communication

___parents             ___aging/dependency    ___loneliness

___self-esteem         ___in-laws             ___weight control

___mood swings         ___stress control

Other
(specify)_____


**H.** Who referred you to us? (name, relationship and phone number)

_____

_____


THANK YOU for taking the time to fill out this information sheet. Your counselor will review this with you in the first session and use it to best assist you in your counseling work. We will maintain your strict confidence regarding this information, subject to the exceptions noted in your service contract. Be sure you review and sign the elements of agreement detailed in your service contract.

## Appendix F:

## Helping Dangerous Clients: Clinical Care and Ethical/Legal

## Management of Suicide and Homicide Risk

### I. Client Information

**1.** Onset of suicidal ideation_____
__Recent or __Acute
__Ongoing or __Chronic

**2.** Lethality:
  Previous attempts
  __Yes: Details: How many? How did it fail? Date(s)
  __No

_____

_____

_____

_____

History of family suicide completion __Yes __No
Abuse alcohol or drugs __Yes: __alcohol ___drugs __No
___in recovery: how long_____
__AA or NA : __Yes __ No  Sponsored?  __ Yes __No

**A.** __Presence of activating event that elicits
Intensity of Suicidal ideation:
__Low/somewhat troubled __Moderately troubled __Highly troubled
Frequency of ideation:
__Occasional: How often_____
__Intermittent: How often:

_____

__Daily: How long:

_____

__Feelings of sudden shame or beliefs that one is letting down the family

Intensity: __Low/ Somewhat troubled__Moderately troubled
___Highly troubled
Frequency of feelings/beliefs:
__Occasional: How often_____
__Intermittent: How often: _____
__Daily: How long: _____
__Access to lethal means (guns, medications, alcohol)
  List:

_____

Plan to deal with access_____
When_____

**B.** Plan __Specific __Vague __Immediate __Open ended

**C.** Activating Event involves: ___Personal loss (es) __Death of friend or
family member
__Financial __Home __Independent living __Employment
__Interpersonal loss/ relationship, separation /divorce, empty nest
__ Dx of terminal or chronic illness __Chronic pain

**3.** DSM Symptoms/Dx, check all that apply
__Major affective disorder: depression ___and/or mania__ bipolar__
__With psychosis ___with command hallucinations to harm self or others
__Severe hopelessness __Severe helplessness
__Severe loss of interest in pleasurable or highly interesting activities
__Constricted problem solving ability __ Poor coping history __Yes __No
Successful coping history __Yes __No
Rigidity __Yes __No

## II. Checklist for Assessing Suicide Risk and Protective Factors

### A. RISK FACTORS

*Mental Health/Medical History*
1 ___Mental disorder associated with suicidal behavior (angry-impulsive,
    depression, schizophrenia, alcohol dependence, substance abuse, and
    combination of mental disorders)
2 ___Communication/denial of intent
3 ___Prior suicidal behavior (e.g., suicide threats, suicide attempts)

4 ___Family history of suicidal behavior
5 ___Suicidal behavior within the past 3 months
6 ___Major medical problems, particularly chronic, incurable, or painful
    conditions (AIDS, brain disease, renal failure, cancer, and Hunting-
    ton's disease)
7 ___Major medical problem, with prognosis/expectation of death

*Psychosocial History*
8 ___Unattached (never married, separated, divorced, or lack of significant
    relationships)
9 ___Spotty work history ___ Chronic unemployment
10 ___Childhood abuse
11 ___History of violent behavior

*Psychosocial/Environmental Risk Factors*
12 ___Major life stressors (e.g., physical or sexual assault, threats against
    life, diagnosis of serious medical problem, dissolution of significant
    relationship, sexual identity issues)
13 ___Any significant loss
14 ___Breakdown of support systems
15 ___Social isolation

*Personal Risk Factors*
16 ___Emotional instability (chronic) ___Poor problem solving
    ___Low stress tolerance
17 ___Impulsivity or aggression (chronic) ___Poor coping skills
    ___Poor judgment
18 ___Personality Disorder associated with suicide (borderline, antisocial)
19 ___ Problem thinking ___Rigid thinking ___Distorted thinking
    ___Irrational beliefs

*Clinical Risk Factors*
20 ___Specific behaviors suggestive of suicide planning (giving away possessions; writing or saying good-bye to friends/family; thinking about suicide; talking about death, suicide, or both; verbalizing specific plans to
commit suicide; rehearsing suicidal act; asking about ways to die; accumu-
lating medications; and threatening suicide)
21 ___Changes in mental status (acute deterioration in mental functioning;
    onset of major mental illness, particularly early phase of schizophrenia

or depression; psychosis with agitation, command hallucinations, or both; extreme anxiety, paranoia, or both; and severe depression)

22 ___Changes in behavior (social withdrawal, agitation, provocativeness, increased or decreased appetite, disturbed sleep, impulsivity, and aggressive behavior)

23 ___Changes in mood (depression, fearfulness, unfounded happiness, anger, anxiety, lability)

24 ___ Strong expression of hopelessness and/or helplessness

25 ___Changes in attitude (unrealistic, apathy, overly optimistic, overly pessimistic)

26 ___Lack of compliance with treatment

## B. PROTECTIVE FACTORS

a ___Married (or committed to significant relationship)

b ___Having children who are under the age of 18 years

c ___Employed or involved in an educational or vocational training program

d ___Support system (e.g., family, friends, church, social clubs)

e ___Religious faith that is active and internalized

f ___Constructive use of leisure time (enjoyable activities)

g ___General purpose for living

h ___Overall good health/lack of chronic disorders

i ___Involved in mental health treatment

j ___Effective coping and problem-solving skills

## C. RISK ASSESSMENT

Add up check-offs in section A, "Risk Factors," then subtract checks from section B, 'Protective Factors," to get risk score. Evaluate risk score against risk assessment grid below and decide on appropriate protective action, taking all client and systemic information into account.

| Scores: | 25 to 34 | VERY HIGH RISK |
|---|---|---|
| | 17 to 24 | HIGH RISK |
| | 9 to 16 | MODERATE RISK |
| | 8 or less | LOW RISK |

## D. RISK-BASED INTERVENTION

**RI-1**: Hospitalize or closely monitor your very high risk client.

**RI-2**: Closely monitor and intensify outpatient contact with your high risk client.

**RI-3**: Monitor and increase outpatient contact with your moderate risk client.

**RI-4**: Monitor your low risk client.

## II: Threat/Response Matrix for Homicidal and Assaultive Clients

*The Five-step Progression*

1.  One Principle Above All: LIFE trumps all other values—here: your commitment to confidentiality—when these important values clash. When confused, remember this first.
2.  Two Key Communications to deliver at the start of all clinical and professional relations.
    a. Your unswerving commitment to honor confidentiality as far as it is allowed
    b. The limits of the rule—excepted for abuse, suicide, and homicide threats
3.  Three (3x3) Conditions that trigger your duty to protect others from client harm.
    a. Direct client statements of intent to kill to seriously harm,
    b. a clearly identifiable 3rd person or group of persons,
    c. and that threatened harm is
    (1) serious, (2) imminent, and (3) doable.
4.  Four Targets of Disclosure of your client's threats if duty to protect is triggered.
    a. The intended victim or group,
    b. Family or close friend of the victim if unable to contact victim
    c. Law enforcement with jurisdiction,
    d. Psychiatric/emergency response personnel.
5.  Five Clinical Response Principles/Interventions with your dangerous/threatening client.
    a. Adopt a crisis mode of planning and intervention with your client (very short-term, quick-response, highly directive).
    b. Honor your legal-ethical duty to the least restrictive intervention,

but don't be slavish to it (take whatever protective action necessary to save lives).

c. Increase the frequency and intensity of your interventions in order to reduce/defuse the risk of violence.

d. Wrap 3rd party warnings into your client's therapy—use as both a "reality check" to your client about the seriousness and consequences of threats, and as a call to safety that triggers a broad range of threat-reducing actions rather than those that are threat increasing.

e. Facilitate and assist the hospitalization or law enforcement action toward your client to show that you are continuing to maintain your clinical commitment to them.

Determination of Appropriateness of outpatient or inpatient care:

_____

_____

Inpatient referral: __ Yes __No

_____

_____

Reason for decision:

_____

_____

_____

Outpatient services: __ Yes __No

Reason for decision. Note any precautions and what steps will be taken:

_____

_____

_____

# Appendix G: Consent For Release Of Information

I, _____, do consent and authorize
this counselor _____ to:
(check off and fill in the blanks)

(A) release all records _____ of my (or my dependent's) counseling or
other work done by the Institute to the following person or organization

_____

(except for the record of_____).

(B) obtain all records _____of my (or my dependent's) counseling or
other work done by this person or organization

_____

(except for the records of _____)

and send to _____.

(C) exchange all records _____
(except for the records of _____)

 as may be necessary between

_____

and this person or organization_____
for the best interests of my (or my dependent's) goals in counseling or
other work.

*****************************************************************************

This consent is valid and is to be acted on upon receipt of this form regarding the records of this client or patient:_____.

This consent will terminate without express written revocation by the client named herein on or when_____.

Client/Guardian Signature _____ Date ____

Client Address _____

Client Birthdate _____ Client Social Security Number _____

Signature of Institute Staff _____ Date _____

NOTE: *Federal regulations require ALL blanks to be filled in, including date, event, or condition that terminates consent for release of confidential client information.*

## Appendix H: Authorization To Treat Minor Children

I, _____ give my permission to
       (name of parent or guardian)

_____ to see my son/daughter,
       (staff counselor)

_____ for treatment or counseling,
       (name of minor child)

with and/or without me being present in the same session. I/WE understand that we are the holder of confidential privilege—the right to withhold
disclosure of private counseling information about my/our child(ren).
However, in the interest of developing a trust relationship between the
counselor and my/our child(ren), I/WE give the counselor permission to
reveal or withhold information that in her/his clinical judgment is necessary to best help and protect my/our child(ren).

The only exception to this discretion would be in the case of :

_____

_____

_____


Parent/Guardian/Authorized Signature

_____

Date _____

Therapist/Witness _____ Date _____

## Appendix I: Consent For Treatment Governed
## By An HMO Or Managed Care

Third party payment for this treatment of _____
is provided by _____ ,
a managed care company. Requirements of that payor include:

1. A release of information/waiver of confidentiality must be signed by the payor. In order to certify treatment, the managed care company will require the therapist to provide considerable personal information, including, but not limited to, current life situations, current and past functioning, personal and family history, past and present alcohol/drug use, previous treatment and diagnosis of mental disorder.

2. All treatment must be pre-certified. If treatment continues beyond the initial certification period, the therapist will make all reasonable efforts to arrange for continuing care without interruption. This may not always be possible. If a lapse in certification occurs, treatment may be temporarily discontinued. Alternately, the consumer may pay for sessions that are provided between or after certifications (if allowed by the managed care company involved.)

3. Any sessions that are missed without notification to this office at least 24 hours before the appointment will be the financial responsibility of the consumer.

I understand and agree to the above terms of this Consent.

_____     _____

Signature                                                                    Date

Name (printed)

_____

# Appendix J: Christian Counseling Treatment Plan

Patient Name
_____

Date of
Intake_____

Referral
Source_____

Reason for
Referral_____

Medications _____
_____
_____

Physicians: _____
_____
_____

Collaborative Contacts:
_____
_____

Release of Information discussed and signed. __Yes __ No __Refused

Reason for refusal_____

Client Assessments None -Low-Average-High

Level of motivation:          0 1 2 3 4 5 6 7 8 9 10
Level of cooperation:         0 1 2 3 4 5 6 7 8 9 10

Insight into problem:         0 1 2 3 4 5 6 7 8 9 10
Level of distress:            0 1 2 3 4 5 6 7 8 9 10

Level of hopefulness:                          0 1 2 3 4 5 6 7 8 9 10
Level of belief:                               0 1 2 3 4 5 6 7 8 9 10
Self described closeness to God:               0 1 2 3 4 5 6 7 8 9 10
Level of obedience to biblical directives:     0 1 2 3 4 5 6 7 8 9 10
Level of spiritual temptation:                 0 1 2 3 4 5 6 7 8 9 10


Level of Spiritual Disciplines

Prayer __active __fair __poor ___none
Worship __active __fair __poor ___none

Fellowship __active __fair __poor ___none
Quiet time __active __fair __poor ___none

Bible Study __active __fair __poor ___none
Service __active __fair __poor ___none

Accountability __active __fair __poor ___none
Self control __active __fair __poor ___none

Presenting Problem(s) in Clients Own Words

_____

_____

_____

_____

Onset

_____

_____

Duration

_____

_____

Previous therapy No__ Yes___
Problem focus_____

Therapist name_____

Date of service_____

Release of Information __Yes __No __Declined
Reason for refusal_____

Axis I symptom:

Cognitive:

Emotional:

Social:

Behavioral:

Physical/Medical:

Spiritual:

*Axis I Primary*
DX_____
Dual_____
Secondary Dx_____Comorbidity_____
Other, including V. codes that may be of clinical concern or attention.

_____

_____

*Axis II*
__Personality Disorder_____
__Mental Retardation_____
__No diagnosis, V.71.09

*Axis III General Medical Conditions:* None ____

_____

_____

*Axis IV Psychosocial and/or Environmental Stressors*

Stressor Chronic/Acute Mild Moderate Severe
__ with primary support group
(divorce, separation, death, illness, conflict, birth of child, discord with
family member, abuse, neglect, family member abuse of substances, child
discipline, removal from home, caring for ill or aged family member,
remarriage, estrangement, over-controlling behaviors, health or disability
problems)

__related to social environment
(a long distance move, retirement, loss of social support, death of friend,
discrimination, single parent, living alone, limited transportation, crime,
limited access to resources)

__with educational problems
(discord with teachers, academic noncompliance, bullying, and problems
with classmates, truancy, adjustment to academic disability, illiteracy, limited or restricted use of educational resources)

__with occupation
(loss of job, new job, threat of job loss, boss or coworker discord, stressful
work donations, overwork schedule, job dissatisfaction, discrimination,
demotion)

__with housing
( recent move, homelessness, overcrowding, waiting to get a home, unsafe
neighborhood, discord with neighbors, landlord, poor housing conditions,
displaced due to fire or natural disasters)

__with financiers
(poverty, loss of income, bankruptcy, inadequate finances, high credit debt,
loss of credit, creditor conflicts, loss of income due to health problems,
inadequate child or welfare support, audit, loss of business)

__health care availability
(inadequate or loss of insurance, inadequate health care services or
transportation to such, services unavailable, change in health lifestyle)

__related to legal system
(arrest, court appearance, investigation, litigation, crime victim, incarceration or incarceration of loved one, probation/parole, suspended license)

__related to medical condition
(chronic illness or disability, family member who is seriously sick, caring for ill loved one, recent physical accident, recent diagnosis of a life changing disorder, loss of appendage, physical disfigurement, or organ, miscarriage)

__ traumatic exposure
(witness to crime or accident, violent crime victim, secondary trauma, natural disaster, war, riot, severe disaster like a fire, animal attack, abortion)

*Axis V. Global Assessment of Functioning Scale (GAF)*

__0–10 Persistent severity of danger TO SELF OR OTHERS or inability to maintain personal hygiene.
__11–20 Some danger to self or others, occasionally fails to maintain hygiene, incoherent.
__21–30 Psychotic influence on behavior, seriously impaired judgment or communication, incapacitated in all areas of functioning.
__31–40 Minimal impairment to reality testing and communication, or major impairment in several areas of social functioning, judgment, thinking or mood.
__41–50 Serious symptoms of suicidal ideation, obsession, impulse controls, or in any serious impairment in social, occupational or school functioning.
__51–60 Moderate psychological symptoms or moderate impairment in social, occupational or school functioning.
__61–70 Mild psychological symptoms or impairment in social, occupational or school functioning. Overall functioning is adequate.
__71–80 Transient, expected symptoms to psychosocial stressors. Slight impairment in social, occupational or school functioning.
__81–90 Absent or minimal symptoms, generally satisfied with life, effective personal and social functioning.
__91–100 Superior functioning in a wide range of activities. No symptoms.

Treatment Modality: __Cognitive Behavioral Therapy
__Cognitive-Behavioral Conjoint Therapy
__Cognitive-Behavioral Family Therapy
__Cognitive-Behavioral Marital Therapy

__individual __conjoint __family __marital __group

Treatment Plan
1. Problem Focus

_____

_____

Likert Scale of severity 0 1 2 3 4 5 6 7 8 9 10
Mild——————————-severe
Goal_____

Planned Interventions

_____

_____

2. Problem Focus

_____

_____

Likert Scale of severity 0 1 2 3 4 5 6 7 8 9 10

Goal_____

_____

_____

Planned Interventions

_____

_____

3. Problem Focus

_____

_____

Likert Scale of severity 1 2 3 4 5 6 7 8 9 10

Goal_____

_____

_____

Planned Interventions

_____

_____

4. Problem Focus

_____

_____

Likert Scale of severity 01 2 3 4 6 7 8 9 10

Goal_____

_____

_____

Planned Interventions

_____

_____

Estimated number of session_____ Estimated date of termination_____

Signature of therapist_____Date_____

## Appendix K: Case Record Form

Client's Name_____Date_____
___Dx._____Code_____

Others present_____

Modality: Cogntive-Behavioral

Therapy/other_____

| Progress/Goal # | __Progress/Goal# | __Progress/Goal # |
|---|---|---|
| __Completed | __Completed | __Completed |
| __Excellent | __Excellent | __Excellent |
| __Adequate | __Adequate | __Adequate |
| __Poor | __Poor | __ Poor |
| __None | __None | __ None |

GAF___

Notes_____
_____

Outcome of Session_____

Plan/Homework_____

Change of Goals _____

Additional Notes _____

_____
Signature of Therapist                              Date

# Appendix L: Treatment Summary Form

Client's Name _____

Initial Session _____Last Session_____

Total Sessions to date_____ Missed Sessions_____

Anticipated number of sessions to complete treatment_____

Referral Source_____

Medications_____

Reasons for counseling _____
_____

Final DX
Axis I _____

Axis II _____

Axis III_____

Axis IV _____

Axis V current_____at intake_____highest past year_____

Goal(s) Status
Goal 1 _____ Goal 2_____

Completed ___                    Completed___
Noncompliance__                  Noncompliance___

Partial completion__                    Partial completion___
Relapse prevention/booster__            Relapse prevention/booster____


Goal 3_____           Goal 4_____


Completed__                             Completed___
Noncompliance__                         Noncompliance___
Partial completion__                    Partial completion___
Relapse prevention/booster__            Relapse prevention/booster__
Relapse__                               Relapse__

Intervention_____

modality __ individual __ conjoint __ family __ group___ marital___

Reasons for termination_____

_____

Referral to other therapist_____

Signature_____Date_____

# Appendix M: Counseling Exit Assessment Form

Please take a few minutes to fill out this exit form. This will help us know how helpful (or not) we were to you and how to improve our services in the future. Please leave this form at the front desk or send it to

_____.

We will maintain your strict confidence about this form. Thank you.

1. Your name_____

2. Today's date_____

3. Address_____

4. Phone_____

5. Therapist(s) name_____

6. Type of service rendered:
___individual counseling/child
___family counseling
___psychosocial/custody evaluation
___pre-marital
___education/training
___other (describe)_____

___individual counseling/adult
___marital counseling
___group counseling/education
___separation/divorce mediation
___consultation

7. Approx. dates of services (mo/yr to mo/yr) _____

8. Overall, were you satisfied with the help you received from counseling or other services?
___highly satisfied
___mixed feelings
___somewhat dissatisfied

___somewhat satisfied

___highly dissatisfied

9. Compared to the start of counseling, how would you now rate your improvement in counseling?

___worse than before              ___about the same

___slightly improved              ___much improved

___greatly improved

10. If satisfied, what did you like most (one or two things)?

_____

_____

11. If dissatisfied, what is your complaint?

_____

_____

12. Did your counselor understand your problem and needs?

___yes, great understanding        ___yes, mostly understood

___no, didn't understand           ___not sure

13. Did your counselor respect your views and values?

___yes, greatly respected          ___yes, mostly respected

___no, didn't respect              ___not sure

14. Did your counselor rely on Christian resources—prayer, use of the Bible, respect for God and Christ—in helpful ways?

___yes, very helpful               ___yes, somewhat helpful

___no, not helpful                 ___no, not wanted or appropriate

___not sure

15. Were there any problems during counseling with any of the following issues?

___fee disputes/problems           ___confidentiality

___sexual actions or communications

___too passive/not enough advice

___too controlling/not enough listening and support

___lack of/inaccurate knowledge

___timely and adequate phone response

___ competent response to emergencies

____friendliness/helpfulness of office staff

____improper/incompetent treatment

____late/poor preparation for sessions

____inadequate/poor referral or consultation with other helping professionals

16. Explain any issues checked above or not listed_____

_____

_____

# Appendix N: Subpoena Response Letter

## George Ohlschlager, j.d., lcsw
### counseling & psychotherapy · mediation & peacemaking
### consulting & speaking

Date

Address

Dear Lawyer Such-and-so:

I have received your subpoena dated _____. As you are probably aware, at this stage I am duty-bound as a licensed mental health professional to assert privilege—to zealously protect the confidences of my client—about the records you demand under *Section 1010 of the California Evidence Code.* I am also instructed to assert privilege as the first step in response to legal or court demands according to sections 1–420 and 1–421 of the *AACC Christian Counseling Code of Ethics,* to which I also adhere.

Of course my assertion of privilege in no way means that I am resisting compliance with this subpoena. I am merely fulfilling the intent of any privilege statute—protecting my client's confidence and giving them the needed time he/she deserves in order to consult with a lawyer about this action. All relevant clinical records will be turned over to my client's attorney. I trust that after appropriate legal consultation, my client and his/her lawyer will respond to this subpoena as required by law.

Any further correspondence on this matter should take place directly with my client's attorney. Thank you.

Sincerely,



George Ohlschlager, JD, LCSW



Office: 3015 F Street, Eureka, CA 95501 · Mail: PO Box 6638, Eureka, CA 95502

# Appendix O: Professional Christian Counseling

**Definition of an Emerging Profession-Specialty**

**A Proposal for Credentialing and Public Communication
to be advocated by the American Association of Christian Counselors
and the American Board of Christian Counselors**

August 2005

*Base Definition*

Professional Christian counseling integrates Christian spiritual formation with the best of modern mental health practice for client and community betterment. Christian counseling is holistic in that it is oriented toward a bio-psycho-social-*spiritual* assessment and intervention. Furthermore, the treatment and prevention of mental/emotional/character disorders is joined with the goal of growing up into Christian maturity. Christian counselors combine, in complementary fashion, the very best of Christian ministry and clinical mental health knowledge with dedicated, caring service to individuals, marriages, families, churches, organizations, and communities. At its best, professional Christian counseling integrates the best theory and proven methods of the mental health professions with biblical truths and spiritual practices to produce "Christ-like" character, behavior, and contentment in the lives of the people and systems served.

Professional Christian counseling, then, is Christ-centered soul-care, melding modern clinical science with ancient biblical truths to the honor of God and the wellness-maturity of clients and client systems.

*Christian Counselors*

Professional Christian counselors are both confessing Christians and licensed/certified/registered mental health professionals dedicated to serve others in the integrative manner described above. Whenever appropriate, these professionals bring the life of Jesus Christ into the work of counseling, psychotherapy, medical and psychiatric treatment, testing and evaluation, mediation and arbitration, counselor supervision, teaching and research, administration, consultation, speaking, and church, courtroom, and legislative testimony.

Christian counselors also—when in the client's interest, with their consent, and when appropriate in therapy—pray for and with clients, read the Bible and make reference to Scripture, encourage the confession of sin, the practice of forgiveness, the making of amends, support the practice of spiritual disciplines, and give assistance or make referral for spiritual warfare and other specialized practices. When consent does not exist, Christian counselors may be engaged in these activities silently and implicitly, always functioning in the best interests of their clients.

These spiritual practices are not illegal, unethical, or illegitimate, nor are they antagonistic to the forementioned clinical purposes and practices. Christian counseling is not dichotomized into sacred and secular compartments but, from the perspective of the mental health professions, is rightly seen as holistic, adjunctive and integrative.

This integrative work is a central aspect of the Christian counselor's lifelong challenge to become a helper of excellence and ethical integrity. Christian counseling integration is not excessively complex nor is it simplistic and reductionistic. Christian counselors understand and revere the spiritual dimension of human nature and change—best known through encountering Christ and growing in a life of faith in Him. They also diligently search for and apply the best data and practices of the behavioral and social sciences.

Tying these various threads together in clinical practice, Christian counselors understand and respect the role of cognitive, behavioral, moral, emotional, relational, and environmental forces in human and social change. They also invite God's power to transform and sanctify this change, properly using God's Word and the ministry of His church.


*Common Values, Practices, and Ethics*

Christian counselors accord the highest respect to the triune God revealed in the Holy Scriptures, our foundation of faith and ethical conduct. They are also dedicated to the best interests of their patients and clients, to the law and the ethical standards of their respective clinical professions, to their contractual obligations in the workplace, and to select and proven data from the bio-psycho-social sciences.

However, regardless of religious creed or preferred clinical theory, Christian counselors are bound together by these common goals:

- knowing and loving God;
- loving and serving others;
- avoiding all harm toward clients and others;
- bringing truth, healing, and agreed change into people's lives;
- helping set people free from sin, bondage, mental disorder, and emotional distress;
- making peace and doing justice; and assisting the church, community, and profession to grow to its full maturity.

Christian counselors strive to come alongside those seeking help, listen with the heart, and speak the truth-in-love. They are dedicated to listen carefully to clients, to respect them, to understand their hurts, sins, and fears, and to encourage faith, hope, and love. Christian counselors humbly challenge client distortions and wrongdoing and, by mutual agreement, help clients renounce the ways of sin and change in the direction of growth and maturity in Christ. They offer the empathic heart of understanding, the consoling voice of comfort, the guiding hope of godly reason, and the assertive challenge to change, whichever is needed at the proper time in therapy.

Christian counselors are committed to disciplined learning and faithful growth in counseling knowledge, gifts, and skills. When appropriate, Christian counselors testify to the saving grace and sanctifying power of Jesus Christ. They avoid imposing their values and beliefs on clients and, at the other extreme, they are not silent about God's love and grace. Christian counselors strive to maintain their integrity to Christ and His revelation in Scripture, while also contributing to the growth of psychosocial knowledge and clinical skill that is inherent to all professional practice and development. They are dedicated to a continual evaluation and improvement of their practices in order to fulfill the call to excellence as mental health practitioners and as Christian counselors.

Christian counselors serve clients with excellence and ethical integrity—practicing with the utmost respect, sensitivity, honesty, energy, and capability. They do not use clients for their own personal gain and strictly avoid all client harm and exploitation. They avoid activities that violate or diminish the civil and legal rights of clients and client systems. They do not discriminate in the provision of client services on the basis of gender, race, ethnicity, disability, religious creed, denomination, socio-economic status, national origin, or sexual orientation.

Aspiring to honor Christ in all things, Christian counselors are committed to moral purity and honesty, committed to maintain personal, professional, and organizational integrity. Aspiring for excellence in service, they know and respect the limits of their competence, do consult, refer, and network with other service providers, and continually study to improve their excellence in service to Christ and to others. Christian counselors maintain professional integrity in relations with the state, with state licensure boards, with the church, with professional associations, and with employers and colleagues. They understand both their duties to the state and other organizations and the limits of the authoritative powers these state and private institutions hold.

Christian counselors have the right—a right grounded in the Scriptures and protected by the religion and free speech clauses of the First Amendment and the Fourteenth Amendment to the United States Constitution—to identify publicly as Christian counselors and to always maintain this integrated clinical-spiritual practice regardless of professional association or licensure status. This right cannot be abrogated or substantially diminished by any court, state legislature, licensure board, or any professional association.

### The Christian Counseling Profession

Christian counseling is a dynamic, expanding, and multidisciplinary field of practice. Over a half-century of development and growth has witnessed a complex professional-ministerial-social organism come to fruition. There are numerous Christian counseling professional associations that are national in scope at the inception of the 21st century, including the largest group, the 50,000 member *American Association of Christian Counselors* (AACC). Dozens of graduate training programs exist in all parts of the country, integrated with programs in psychology, social work, marriage and family therapy, and professional counselor training. There are at least 25,000 mental health professionals across the 50 states who also identify in some manner as Christian counselors.

More specifically, the AACC has published a *Christian Counseling Code of Ethics* and, with the *American Board of Christian Counselors,* is moving toward delivery of national practice standards and credentials in Christian counseling. Many national, refereed journals on Christian counseling now exist, over one hundred books are published annually, and training, seminar, and conference resources are mushrooming at many levels. Numerous managed care groups across America have recognized and refer specifically to Christian counselors as more and more subscribers demand this service. Finally, dubious though it may be as a mark of professional maturity, liability insurance can now be purchased for Christian counseling practice.

Christ is the bridge by which Christian counseling integrates both spiritual ministry and professional mental health practice. Since all truth is from God, Christian counseling facilitates understanding and integration between the empirical truths of general revelation and the truth of God's special revelation in Christ. Christian counseling is an emerging profession that is distinctive in its ministry to Christendom and society-at-large. Moreover, in relationship to the mental health professions it is also adjunctive and integrative, a specialty form of traditional mental health practice in every discipline—psychology, psychiatry, social work, marriage and family therapy, professional counseling, and nursing.

Christian counseling is an emerging profession wherein people are able to identify as Christian counselors and grow in their personal and professional lives. It is also an interdisciplinary organism by which professional unity is genuinely achievable in Christ. Because of Christ, the Christian counseling profession holds out the promise of overshadowing the turf-protecting enmity and professional prejudice that can otherwise infect relations between the people and disciplines of the mental health enterprise. In Christ, helpers from all recognized groups are challenged to stand together, in mutual and humble service, proclaiming both their professional distinctives and their common Christian mission.

# References

Adams, J. (1970). *Competent to counsel*. United States: Presbyterian and Reformed Publishing Company.

Adler, A. (1959). *Understanding human nature*. New York: Premier Books.

Adler, A. (1963). *The practice and theory of individual psychology*. Patterson, NJ: Littlefield.

Adler, N. (1975). Emotional responses of women following therapeutic abortion. *American Journal of Orthopsychiatry, 45*, 446–454.

Ahern, J., Galea, S., Resnick, H., Kilpatrick, D., Bucuvalas, M., Gold, J., & Vlahov, D. (2002). Television images and psychological symptoms after the September 11 terrorist attacks. *Psychiatry: Interpersonal & Biological Processes, 65*(4), 289–301.

Ainsworth, M., Blehar, M. C., Waters, E., & Wall, S. (1978). *Patterns of attachment: A psychological study of the strange situation*. Hillsdale, NJ: Erlbaum.

Alacorn, R. D., Glover, S. G., & Deering, C. G. (1999). The cascade model: An alternative to comorbidity in the pathogenesis of post-traumatic stress disorder. *Psychiatry, 62*, 114–124.

Alan Guttmacher Institute. (1997, January). *Facts in brief: Induced abortion*, Washington, DC.

Alexander, J. A. (1846). *The Earlier Prophecies of Isaiah*. New York: Wiley and Putnam.

Allen, J. G. (1999). *Coping with trauma: A guide to self-understanding*. American Psychiatric Press Inc.

Allender, D. B. (1999). *The healing path: How the hurts in your past can lead you to a more abundant life*. Colorado Springs: WaterBrook.

Allender, D. B. (2005). *To be told*. Colorado Springs: WaterBrook Press.

Amen, D. (1998). *Change your brain change your life*. New York: Random House.

American Association of Christian Counselors. (2001). *AACC Christian counseling code of ethics*. Forest, VA: AACC.

American Psychiatric Association Work Group on Eating Disorders. (2000). Practical guidelines for the treatment of patients with eating disorders (revision). *American Journal of Psychiatry, 157*, (1 Suppl): 1–39.

American Psychiatric Association. (1980). *Diagnostic and statistical manual of mental disorders* (3rd ed.). Washington, DC: APA.

American Psychiatric Association. (1987). *Diagnostic and statistical manual of mental disorders* (3rd ed. revised). Washington, DC: APA.

American Psychiatric Association. (1994). *Diagnostic and statistical manual of mental disorders* (4th ed.). Washington, DC: APA.

American Psychiatric Association. (1999). *Let's talk facts about post-traumatic stress disorder.* Retrieved on June 20, 2005 from http://www.psych.org/public_info/ptsd.cfm.

American Psychiatric Association. (2000). *Diagnostic and statistical manual of mental disorders* (4th ed., text rev.). Washington, DC: APA.

Anderson, A. (1995). Eating disorders in males. In K.D. Brownell, & C G. Fairburn, (Eds.), *Eating disorders and obesity: A comprehensive handbook.* New York: The Guilford Press.

Anderson, N. T. (2003). *Discipleship counseling.* Ventura, CA: Regal Books.

Andreasen, N.C. (1985). Post-traumatic stress disorder. In H.I. Kaplan and B.J. Sadock (Eds.). *Comprehensive textbook of psychiatry* (4th ed.). Baltimore: Williams and Wilkins.

Anton, S., & Mrdenovi, S. (2005). Working ability of patients with post-traumatic stress disorder (demographic and social features): Comparative study. *Journal of Loss & Trauma. 10*(2), 155–162.

Apter, A., Kotler, M., Levy, S., Plutchik, R., Brown, S., Foster, H., Hillbrand, M., Korn, M., & van Praag, H. (1991). Correlates of risk of suicide in violent and nonviolent psychiatric patients. *American Journal of Psychiatry, 148* (7), 883–887.

Arata, C. M. (1999). Sexual revictimization and PTSD: An exploratory study. *Journal of Child Sexual Abuse. 8(1),* 49–66.

Arteburn, S. & Stoeker, F. (2000). *Every Man's Battle.* Colorado Springs, CO.: WaterBrook Press.

Arterburn, S. (2003). *Addicted to love.* United Kingdom: Vine Books.

Attig, T. (1996). *How we grieve: Relearning the world.* New York: Oxford University Press.

Backus, W. (1985). *Telling each other the truth.* Minneapolis, MN: Bethany House.

Backus, W. (1985). *Telling the truth to troubled people: A manual for Christian counselors.* Minneapolis, MN: Bethany House.

Backus, W. (2000). *What your counselor never told you: Conquer the power of sin in your life.* Minneapolis, MN: Bethany House.

Bagley, C. (1990). Development of a measure of unwanted sexual contact in childhood for use in community mental health surveys. *Psychological Reports, 66,* 401–2.

Bagley, C. (1991). The prevalence and mental health sequelae of child sexual abuse in a community sample of women aged 18 to 27. *Canadian Journal of Community Mental Health, 10,* 103–116.

Balk, D. E. (1996). Attachment and the reactions of bereaved college students: A longitudinal study. In D. Klass, P. R. Silverman, & S. L. Nickman (Eds.). *Continuing bonds: New understandings of grief* (pp. 311–328). Washington, DC: Taylor & Francis.

Barna Group. (2003, November 3). Morality continues to decay. *The Barna Update.* Retrieved from http://www.barna.org.

Bart, M. (1998, December). Spirituality in counseling finding believers. *Counseling Today.* Alexandria, VA: American Counseling Association.

Basco, M., & Rush, A. J. (1996). *Cognitive-behavioral therapy for bipolar disorder.* New York: Guilford Press.

Baucom, D.H., Epstein, N., Sayers, S., & Sher, T.G. (1989). The role of cognitions in marital relationships: Definitional, methodological, and conceptual issues. *Journal of Consulting and Clinical Psychology, 57,* 31–38.

Beattie, M. (1987). *Codependent no more.* New York: Harper/Hazelden.

Beck, A. T., Rush, A. J., Shaw, B. F., & Emery, G. (1979). *Cognitive therapy of depression.* New York: Guilford Press.

Beck, A., Brown, G., Berchick, R., Stewart, B., & Steer, R. (1990). Relationship between hopelessness and ultimate suicide: A replication with psychiatric outpatients. *American Journal of Psychiatry, 147*(2), 190–195.

Beck, A., Resnik, H., & Lettieri, D. (Eds.). (1974). *The prediction of suicide.* Bowie, Maryland: Charles Press.

Beck, A.T., Rush, A.J., Shaw, B.F., & Emery, G. (1979). *Cognitive therapy of depression.* New York: Guilford Press.

Beck, J. (1995). *Cognitive therapy: Basics and beyond.* New York: Guilford.

Becker, E. (1973). *The denial of death.* New York: The Free Press.

Becvar, D. S., and Becvar, R. J. (1993). *Family therapy: A systemic integration.* Boston: Allyn and Bacon.

Bergin, A. E. (1991). Values and religious issues in psychotherapy and mental health. *American Psychologist, 46,* 394–403.

Bergin, A. E., & Jensen, J. P. (1990). Religiosity of psychotherapists: A national survey. *Psychotherapy, 27,* 3–7.

Bisson, J. I., McFarlane, A. C., & Rose, S. (2000). Psychological debriefing. In E. B. Foa (Ed.), *Effective treatments for PTSD,* (pp. 39–59). New York: Guilford Press.

Black, D. & Winokur, G. (1986). Prospective studies of suicide and mortality in psychiatric patients. *Annals of the New York Academy of Sciences, 487,* 106–113.

Blackenhorn, D. (1995). *Fatherless America: Confronting our most urgent social problem.* New York: Basic Books.

Blank, A. S. (1993). The longitudinal course of posttraumatic stress disorder, *In Post-traumatic stress disorder: DSM IV and beyond.* Washington DC: American Psychiatric Press.

Bloomfield, H. (1998). *Healing anxiety naturally.* New York: HarperPerennial.

Bork, R. (1996). Inconvenient lives. *First Things, 68,* 13.

Bourne, E. J. (2001). *Beyond anxiety and phobia.* Oakland: New Harbinger.

Bowlby, J. (1979). *The making and breaking of affectional bonds.* New York: Routledge.

Bowlby, J. (1980). *Attachment and loss (Vol. 3). Loss: sadness and depression.* New York: Basic Books.

Bowlby, J. (1988). *A secure base: Parent-child attachment and healthy human development.* New York: Basic Books.

Brammer, L., Abrego, P., & Shostrom, E. (1998). *Therapeutic counseling and psychotherapy* (7th ed.). Englewood Cliffs, NJ: Prentice-Hall.

Breen, R.B. & Zimmerman, M. (2000). Rapid onset of pathological gambling in machine gamblers. *Department of Psychiatry and Human Behavior, Brown University School of Medicine.*

Breslau, N., & Davis, G. C. (1992). Posttraumatic stress disorder in an urban population of young adults: Risk factors for chronicity. *American Journal of Psychiatry, 149,* 671–675.

Briere, J. (1996). Treating adult survivors of severe childhood abuse and neglect: Further development of an integrative model. In *The APSAC handbook on child maltreatment, (2nd Ed.).* Newbury Park, CA: Sage Publications.

Brody, J. E. (1992, March 27). Study defines 'binge eating disorder': Report from Dr. Robert L. Spitzer at the Annual Scientific Meeting of the Society of Behavioral Medicine. *New York Times,* A16.

Broida, M. (2001). *New hope for people with depression.* Roseville, CA: Prima Publishing.

Brown, R. (1983). *Elie Wiesel: Messenger to all humanity.* South Bend, IN: Notre Dame Univ. Press.

Burke, T., & Reardon, D. C. (2002). *Forbidden grief: The unspoken pain of abortion.* USA: Acorn Books.

Burns, D. (1999). *Feeling good.* New York: William Morrow.

Caplan, G. (1964). *Principals of preventive psychiatry.* New York: Basic Books.

Carnes, P. (1984). *Out of the shadows.* Minneapolis: Comp Care.

Carnes, P. (1989). *Contrary to love.* Minneapolis: CompCare.

Carnes, P. (1991). *Don't call it love.* New York: Bantam Books.

Carnes, P. (1997). *The betrayal bond.* Deerfield Beach, FL: Health Communications, Inc.

Carnes, P., Laaser, D., & Laaser, M. (2000). *Open hearts.* Wickensburg, AZ: Gentle Path Press.

Carter, B., and McGoldrick, M. (1989). *The changing family life cycle.* Boston: Allyn and Bacon.

Centers for Disease Control and Prevention (2002). *Suicide injury fact book.* Retrieved August, 2005 from http://www.cdc.gov/ncipc/fact_book/26_Suicide.htm.

Chemtob, C., Bauer, G., Hamada, R., Pelowski, S., & Muraoka, M. (1989). Patient suicide: Occupational hazard for psychologists and psychiatrists. *Professional Psychology: Research and Practice, 20* (5), 294–300.

Chilstrom, C. (1989). Suicide and pastoral care. *The Journal of Pastoral Care, 43*(3), 199–208.

Christensen, C. M. (2003). *Power over panic: Answers for anxiety.* Colorado Springs: Life Journey.

Christensen, P. N., Cohan, S. L., & Stein, M. B. (2004). The relationship between interpersonal perception and post-traumatic stress disorder-related functional impairment: A social relations model analysis. *Cognitive Behaviour Therapy, 33*(3), 151–161.

Clemmons, A. (1991). The pastor and the institute. *Parakaleo,* 3, 1–2. Eureka, CA: The Redwood Family Institute.

Clinton, T, & Ohlschlager, G. (2002). *Competent Christian counseling, volume one: Foundations and practice of compassionate soul care.* Colorado Springs: WaterBrook Press.

Clinton, T., & Sibcy, G. (2002). *Attachments: Why you love, feel and act the way you do.* Brentwood, TN: Integrity.

Collins, G. (1995). *How to be a people helper.* USA: Tyndale.

Collins, G. R. (1988). *Christian counseling: A comprehensive guide,* rev. ed. Nashville: W Publishing Group.

Colson, C. (1995, October 2). Wanted: Christians who love. *Christianity Today,* 112.

Convissor, K. (1992). *Young widow: Learning to live again.* Grand Rapids, MI: Zondervan.

Cook, S. A. and Dworkin, D. S. (1992). *Helping the bereaved.* New York: Basic Books.

Copeland, M. E. (2001). *The depression workbook* (2nd ed.). Oakland, CA: New Harbinger.

Corey, G. (2000). *Theory and practice of counseling and psychotherapy* (6th ed.). Pacific Grove, CA: Brooks/Cole.

Corey, G., Corey, M., & Callanan, P. (1998). *Issues and ethics in the helping professions* (5th ed.). Pacific Grove, CA: Brooks/Cole.

Courtois, C. A. & Watts, D. L. (1982, January). Counseling adult women who experienced incest in childhood or adolescence. *The Personnel and Guidance Journal,* 275–279.

Crabb, L (1977). *Effective biblical counseling: A model for helping caring Christians become capable counselors.* Grand Rapids, MI: Zondervan.

Crabb, L. (1997). *Connecting.* Nashville: W Publishing Group.

Craighead, W. E., Hart, A. B., Craighead, L. W., & Ilardi, S. S. (2002). Psychosocial treatments for major depressive disorder. In P. E. Nathan & J. M. Gorman (Eds.), *A guide to treatments that work* (2nd ed., pp. 245–261). New York: Oxford University Press.

Craighead, W. E., Miklowitz, D. J., Frank, E., & Vajk, F. C. (2002). Psychosocial treatments for bipolar disorder. In P. E. Nathan & J. M. Gorman (Eds.), *A guide to treatments that work* (2nd ed., pp. 263–275). New York: Oxford University Press.

Cufee, S., Addy, C., Garrison, C., Waller, J., Jackson, K., Mckeown, R., & Chilappagari, S. (1998, February). Prevalence of PTSD in a community sample of older adolescents. *Journal of the American Academy of Child & Adolescent Psychiatry,* 37(2), 147–154.

Daud, A., Skoglund, E., Rydelius, P. (2005). Children in families of torture victims: Transgenerational transmission of parents' traumatic experiences to their children. *International Journal of Social Welfare,* 14(1), 23–33.

Davidson, G. W. (1984). *Understanding mourning: A guide for those who grieve.* Minneapolis: Augsburg.

De Bellis, M. D., Keshavan, M. S., Shifflett, H., Iyengar, S., Beers, S. R., Hall, J., & Moritz, G. (2002, December). Brain structures in pediatric maltreatment-related posttraumatic stress disorder: A sociodemographically matched study. *Biological Psychiatry,* 52(11), 1066–1079.

Desai, R. A., Dausey, D. J., Rosenheck, R. A. (2005, February). Mental health service delivery and suicide risk: The role of individual patient and facility factors. *American Journal of Psychiatry,* 162(2), 311–319.

Dissanayake, C., & Crossley, S. A. (1996, February). Proximity and sociable behaviours in autism: Evidence for attachment. *Journal of Child Psychol Psychiatry, 37*(2), 149–156.

Dobie, D. J., Kivlahan, D. R., Maynard, C., Bush, K. R., Davis, T. M., & Bradley, K. A. (2004, February). Post-traumatic stress disorder in female veterans: Association with self-reported health problems and functional impairment. *Archives of Internal Medicine, 164*(4), 394–401.

Egan, G. (1998). *The skilled helper: A problem-management approach to helping* (6th ed.). Pacific Grove, CA: Brooks/Cole.

Earle, R. & Crow, G. (1989). *Lonely all the time.* New York: Pocket.

Earle, R. H., Earle, M. R., & Osborn, K. (1995). *Sex addiction: Case studies and management.* New York, NY: Brunner/Mazel, Inc.

Ebert, A., & Dyck, M. J. (2004, October). The experience of mental death: The core feature of complex post-traumatic stress disorder. *Clinical Psychology Review, 24*(6), 617–36.

Ehrenreich, B. (1992, January). Cauldron of anger. *Life, 15,* 62–68.

Ellis, A. (1998). *The Albert Ellis reader: A guide to well-being using rational emotive behavior therapy.* NY: Citadel Press.

Engelhardt, H. T. (2000). *The foundations of Christian bioethics.* Exton, PA: Swets and Zeitlinger.

Erickson, M. (1983). *Christian theology,* Grand Rapids, MI: Baker.

Exline, J. J., Smyth, J. M., Gregory, J., Hockemeyer, J., & Tulloch, H. (2005). Religious framing by individuals with PTSD when writing about traumatic experiences. *International Journal for the Psychology of Religion, 15*(1), 17–34.

Fagan, N., & Freme, K. (2004, February). Confronting posttraumatic stress disorder. *Nursing, 34*(2), 52–54.

Faulkner, N. (1996). *Sexual abuse recognition and non-disclosure inventory of young adolescents.* Ann Arbor, MI: UMI.

Fawcett, J., Golden, B., & Rosenfeld, N. (2000). *New hope for people with bipolar disorder.* Roseville, CA: Prima Publishing.

Ferrada-Noli, M., Asberg, M., Ormstad, K., Lundin, T., & Sundbom, E. (1998, January).

Ferree, M. (2002). *No stones: Women redeemed from sexual shame.* Fairfax, VA: Xulon.

Finkelhor, D. & Browne, A. (1986). Impact of child sexual abuse: a review of the research. *Psychological Bulletin, 99,* 66–77.

Finkelhor, D., Hotaling, G., Lewis, I. A., & Smith, C. (1990). Sexual abuse in a national survey of adult men and women: Prevalence, characteristics, and risk factors. *Child Abuse & Neglect, 14,* 19–28.

Flach, F. F. (1974). *The secret strength of depression.* Philadelphia: Lippincott.

Fonagy, P. (1999). *Pathological attachments and therapeutic action.* Paper presented at the annual meeting of the California Branch of the American Academy of Child and Adolescent Psychiatry, Yosemite Valley, CA.

Forrester, K. S. (2002). *Determining the Biblical traits and spiritual disciplines Christian counselors employ in practice: A delphi study.* PhD dissertation, Southwestern Baptist Theological Seminary. Fort Worth, TX.

Foster, R. (1978). *Celebration of discipline.* San Francisco: Harper & Row.

Fraley, R. C. and Shaver, P. R. (1999). Loss and bereavement: Attachment theory and recent controversies concerning "grief work" and the nature of detachment. In J. Cassidy & P.R. Shaver (Eds.). *Handbook of attachment: Theory, research, and clinical applications.* New York: Guilford.

Frances, A., & First, A. B. (1998). *Your mental health: A layman's guide to the psychiatrist's bible.* New York: Scribner.

Frankl, V. (1984). *Man's search for meaning* (rev. ed). New York: Pocket Books.

Frans, Ö., Rimmö, P. A., Åberg, L., Fredrikson, M. (2005, April). Trauma exposure and *post-traumatic stress disorder* in the general population. *Acta Psychiatrica Scandinavica,* 111(4), 291–293.

Fredman, S., and Rosenbaum G. F. (n.d.). *Treatment of anxiety disorders with comorbid depression.* Retrieved from <http:// www.medscape.com>

Freud, S. (1917). *Mourning and melancholia. SE,* 14:243–58.

Frommberger, U., Stieglitz, R., Nyberg, E., Richter, H., Novelli-Fischer, U., Angenendt, J., Zaninelli, R., & Berger, M. (2004, March). Comparison between paroxetine and behaviour therapy in patients with post-traumatic *stress disorder* (PTSD): A pilot study. *International Journal of Psychiatry in Clinical Practice,* 8(1), 19–24.

Frude, N. (1990). *Understanding family problems.* Chichester: J. Wiley & Sons.

Fulero, S. (1987). Insurance trust releases malpractice statistics. *State Psychological Association Affairs* 19(1), 4–5.

Gabbard, G. (1989). *Sexual exploitation in professional relationships.* Washington, DC: American Psychiatric Association.

Gallup, G., & Jones, T. (2000). *The next American spirituality: Finding God in the twenty-first century.* Colorado Springs: Victor/Cook Communications.

Garner, D.M. (1991). *Eating disorders inventory—2.* Odessa, FL: Psychological Assessment Resources.

Garner, D.M., Garfinkle, P.E., Olmstead, M.P., & Bohr, Y. (1982). The eating attitudes test: Psychometric features and clinical correlations. *Psychological Medicine,* 12, 871–878.

Gelinas, D. J. (1993). Relational patterns in incestuous families, malevolent variations, and specific interventions with the adult survivor. Pages 1–34 in P.L. Paddison (Ed.). *Treatment of adult survivors of incest,* (pp.). Washington, D.C.: American Psychiatric Press.

Germain, A., Hall, M., Krakow, B., Shear, M., & Buysse, D. J. (2005, March). A brief sleep scale for post-traumatic stress disorder: Pittsburgh Sleep Quality Index addendum for PTSD. *Journal of Anxiety Disorders,* 19(2), 233–245.

Gladding, S. T. (2005). *Counseling: A comprehensive profession* (4th ed.). Upper Saddle River, NJ: Prentice-Hall.

Gorman, C. (10 June, 2002). The science of anxiety. *Time,* 46.

Grant, J. E., Kushner, M.G., & Kim, S.W. (2002). Pathological gambling and alcohol use disorder. *Alcohol Research & Health,* 26, 143–150.

Gray, M. J., Elhai, J. D., & Frueh, B. C. (2004, December). Enhancing patient satisfaction and increasing treatment compliance: Patient education as a fundamental component of PTSD treatment. *Psychiatric Quarterly,* 75(4), 321–333.

Graybill, D. (1985). Aggression in college students who were abused as children. *Journal of College Student Personnel, 26.*

Greenberger, D., & Padeskey, C. A. (1995). *Mind over mood.* New York: Guilford Press.

Guinness, O. (1998). *The call.* Nashville: Word.

Hall, N. (n.d.). *Stress: A psychoneuroimmunological perspective.* Retrieved from www.psychjournal.com/interviews. *Stress and Exercise* <http://www.saluminternational.com/articleshall.htm>

Hart, A. D. (1987). *Counseling the depressed.* Waco, TX: Word.

Hart, A. D. (1995). *Adrenaline and stress.* Dallas: Word.

Hart, A. D. (1999). *The anxiety cure: You can find emotional tranquility and wholeness.* Nashville: W Publishing Group.

Hart, A. D. (2001). Has self-esteem lost its way? *Christian Counseling Today, 9*(1), 8.

Hart, A. D. (2001). *Unmasking male depression.* Nashville: W Publishing Group.

Hart, A. D., & Weber, C. H. (2002). *Unveiling depression in women: A practical guide to understanding and overcoming depression.* Grand Rapids, MI: Fleming H. Revell.

Hawkins, R., Hindson, E., & Clinton, T. (2002). Theological roots: Synthesizing and systematizing a Biblical theology of helping. In T. Clinton & G. Ohlschlager (Eds.), *Competent Christian Counseling.* Colorado Springs: WaterBrook Press.

Herman, J.L. (1992). *Trauma and recovery.* New York: Basic Books.

Hogan, N., & DeSantis, L. (1992). Adolescent sibling bereavement: An ongoing attachment. *Qualitative Health Research, 2,* 159–177.

Holtzheimer, I., Russo, P. E., Zatzick, J., Bundy, D., Roy-Byrne, C., & Peter, P. (2005, May). The impact of comorbid post-traumatic stress disorder on short-term clinical outcome
in hospitalized patients with depression. *American Journal of Psychiatry, 165*(5), 970–977.

Hunsinger, D. (2001). An interdisciplinary map for Christian counselors. In M. McMinn, & T. Phillips (Eds.), *Care for the soul: Exploring the intersection of psychology & theology* (pp. 218–240). Downers Grove, IL: InterVarsity Press.

Huppert, J. D., Moser, J. S., Gershuny, B. S., Riggs, D. S., Spokas, M., Filip, J., Hajcak, G., Parker, H. A., Baer, L., & Foa, E. B. (2005, January). The relationship between obsessive-compulsive and post-traumatic *stress* symptoms in clinical and non-clinical samples. *Journal of Anxiety Disorders, 19*(1), 127–137.

Hutchins, D. (1984). Improving the counseling relationship. *The Personnel and Guidance Journal, 62*(10), (1984), 572–575.

Hutchins, D., & Cole, C. (1992). *Helping relationships and strategies* (2nd ed.). Pacific Grove, CA: Brooks/Cole.

Janof-Bulman, R. (1992). *Shattered assumptions: Toward a new psychology of trauma.* New York: The Free Press.

Johnson, B. (1987). Sexual abuse prevention: A rural interdisciplinary effort. *Child Welfare, 66,* 165–73.

Jones, I. F. (2003). *The counsel of heaven on earth*. Manuscript submitted for publication.

Jones, S., & Yarhouse, M. (2000). *Homosexuality: The use of scientific research in the church's moral debate*. Downer's Grove, IL: InterVarsity Press.

Jordan, N. N., Hoge, C. W., Tobler, S. K., Wells, J., Dydek, G. J. Egerton, & Walter E. (2004, April). Mental health impact of 9/11 Pentagon attack: Validation of a rapid assessment tool. *American Journal of Preventive Medicine, 26(4)*, 284–294.

Kellemen R. W. (2005). *Soul physicians: A theology of soul care and spiritual direction.* Taneytown, MD: RPM Books.

Kellemen, R.W. (2004). *Spiritual friends: A methodology of soul care and spiritual direction.* Taneytown MD: RPM Books.

Keller, A. S., Rosenfeld, B., Trinh-Shevrin, C., Meserve, C., Sachs, E., Leviss, J. A., Singer, M. (2004). Shame, guilt, self-hatred and remorse in the psychotherapy of Vietnam combat veterans who committed atrocities. *American Journal of Psychotherapy, 58(4)*, 377–386.

Kelly, E. W. (1995). *Religion and spirituality in counseling and psychotherapy*. Alexandria, VA: American Counseling Association.

Kessler, R. C., Berglund, P., Demler, O., Jin, R., Koretz, D., Merikangas, K.R., Rush, A.J., Walters, E.E., & Wang, P.S. (2003). The epidemiology of major depressive disorder: Results from the National Comorbidity Survey Replication (NCS-R). *JAMA, 289*, 3095–3105.

Kessler, R. C., Sonnega, A., Bromet, E., Hughes, M., & Nelson, C. B. (1995, December). Post-traumatic stress disorder in the national comorbidity survey. *Archives of General Psychiatry, 52(12)*, 1048–1060.

Kevorkian, J. (1996). *Prescription—medicine: The goodness of planned death*. Buffalo: Prometheus Books.

Klass, D., Silverman, P. R., & Nickman, S. L. (Eds.). (1996). *Continuing bonds: New understandings of grief*. Washington, DC: Taylor & Francis.

Klerman, G. L., Weissman, M. M., Rounsaville, B. J., & Chevron, E. S. (1984). *Interpersonal psychotherapy of depression*. New York: Basic Books.

Klosko, J. S., & Sanderson, W. C. (1999). *Cognitive-behavioral treatment of depression*. Northvale, NJ: Jason Aronson.

Kottler, J. (1993). *On being a therapist* (Rev. ed.). San Francisco: Jossey-Bass.

Kroll J. (2000). No-suicide contracts. *American Journal of Psychiatry.*

Kroll, J., (1993). *PTSD/Borderlines in therapy: Finding the balance*. New York: W.W. Norton & Co.

Kubler-Ross, E. (1969). *On death and dying*. New York: MacMillan.

Kurtz, E. (1979). *Not God: A history of Alcoholics Anonymous*. Center City, MN: Hazelden.

Laaser, M. (1996). *Faithful and true*. Grand Rapids, MI: Zondervan.

Laaser, M. (2002). *A L.I.F.E. guide: Men living in freedom everyday*. Fairfax, VA.: Xulon.

Laaser, M. (2004). *Healing the wound of sexual addiction*. Grand Rapids, MI: Zondervan.

Laaser, M. and Earle, R. (2002). *The pornography trap*. Kansas City: Beacon Hill.

L'Abate, L. (1981). Classification of counseling and therapy, theorists, method process, and goals: The E-R-A model. *The Personnel and Guidance Journal, 59,* 263–265.

Lam, D. H., Jones, S. H., Hayward, P., & Bright, J. A. (1999). *Cognitive therapy for bipolar disorder: A therapist's guide to concepts, methods, and practice.* Chichester, UK: Wiley.

Landy, U. (1986). Abortion counseling: A new component of medical care. *Clinics in Obs/Gyn,* 13(1):33–41.

Langberg, D. M. (1997). *Counseling survivors of sexual abuse.* Wheaton, IL.: Tyndale.

Langberg, D. M. (1999). *On the threshold of hope: Opening the door to healing for survivors of sexual abuse.* Wheaton, IL: Tyndale.

Lark, S. M. (1996). *Anxiety and stress.* Berkeley, CA: Celestialarts.

Lee. J., & Dade, L. (2003). The buck stops where? What is the role of the emergency physician in managing panic disorder in chest pain patients? *Journal of the Canadian Association of Emergency Physicians,* 5(4), 237–238.

Lemonick, M. (2003, January 20). How stress takes its toll. *Time.* (Special Issue).

Lerner, H. (1985). *The dance of anger.* New York: Harper & Row.

Leskela, J., Dieperink, M., & Thuras, P. (2002, June). Shame and posttraumatic stress disorder. *Journal of Traumatic Stress,* 15(3), 223–227.

Lewinsohn, P. M., Munoz, R. F., Youngren, M. A., & Zeiss, A. M. (1992). *Control your depression.* New York: Fireside/Simon and Schuster.

Lindman Port, C. Engdahl, B., & Frazier, P. (2001, September). A longitudinal and retrospective study of PTSD among older prisoners of war. *American Journal of Psychiatry,* 158(9), 1474–1480.

Los Angeles Times Poll. (1989 March 19). *Los Angeles Times,* question 76.

Lowinger, T., & Solomon, T. Z. (2004, October-December). PTSD, guilt, and shame among reckless drivers. *Journal of Loss & Trauma,* 9(4), 327–345.

Lyles, M. R. (2001). Will the real mood stabilizer please stand up? *Christian Counseling Today,* 9(3), 60–61.

Madianos, M. G., Papaghelis, M., Ioannovich, J. & Dafni, R. (2001). Psychiatric disorders in burn patients: A follow-up study. *Psychotherapy and Psychosomatics, 70,* 30–37.

Maine, M. (1999). AAMFT clinical update: Eating disorders. *A Supplement to the Family Therapy News,* 1(6), 1.

Maj, M., Akiskal, H. S., Lopez-Ibor, J. J., & Sartorius, N. (Eds.). (2002). *Bipolar disorder.* New York: Wiley.

Maris, R. (1992). Overview of the study of suicide assessment and prediction. In R. Maris, A. Berman, J. Maltsberger, and R. Yufit, (Eds.). *Assessment and prediction of suicide.* New York: Guilford.

Martell, C. R., Addis, M. E., & Jacobson, N. S. (2001). *Depression in context: Strategies for guided action.* New York: W. W. Norton.

Marty, M.E. (1998). The ethos of Christian forgiveness. In E.L. Worthington, Jr. (Ed.), *Dimensions of forgiveness: Psychological research and theological perspectives.* Philadelphia: The Templeton Foundation Press.

Mathewes-Green, F. (1991, Summer). Unplanned parenthood. *Policy Review*.

May, G. (1988). *Addiction and grace*. San Francisco: Harper and Row.

McCarthy, C. (1971, March 7). A psychological view of abortion. *Washington Post*.

McCullough, J. P. (2000). *Treatment of chronic depression: Cognitive behavioral analysis system of psychotherapy*. New York: Guilford Press.

McCullough, M. E., & Worthington, E. L., Jr. (1995). Promoting forgiveness: A comparison of two psychoeducational group interventions with a waiting-list control. *Counseling and Values, 40*, 55–68.

McCullough, M. E., Bellah, C. G., Kilpatrick, S. D., & Johnson, J. L. (2001). Vengefulness: Relationships with forgiveness, rumination, well-being, and the big five. *Personality and Social Psychology Bulletin, 27*, 601–610.

McCullough, M. E., Rachal, K. C., Sandage, S. J., Worthington, E. L. Jr., Brown, S. W., & Hight, T. L. (1998). Interpersonal forgiveness in close relationships II: Theoretical elaboration and measurement. *Journal of Personality and Social Psychology, 75*, 1586–1603.

McCullough, M. E., Sandage, S. J., & Worthington, E. L., Jr. (1997). *To forgive is human: How to put your past in the past*. Downers Grove, IL: InterVarsity Press.

McCullough, M. E., Worthington, E. L. Jr., & Rachal, K. C. (1997). Interpersonal forgiving in close relationships. *Journal of Personality and Social Psychology, 73*, 321–336.

McCullough, M.E., Fincham, F.D. & Tsang, J-A. (2003). Forgiveness, forbearance, and time: The temporal unfolding of transgression-related interpersonal motivations. *Journal of Personality and Social Psychology 84*, 540–557.

McCullough-Zander, K., & Larson, S. (2004, October). 'The fear is still in me': Caring for survivors of torture. *American Journal of Nursing, 104* (10), 54–65.

McGee, R., & Schaumberg., H. (1990). *Renew: Hope for victims of sexual abuse*. Houston: Rapha.

McMinn, M. R. (1996). *Psychology, theology, and spirituality in Christian counseling*. USA: Tyndale.

McMinn, M., & Dominguez, A. (2003). Psychology collaborating with the church. *Journal of Psychology and Christianity, 22*(4), 291–294.

Means, P. (1996). *Men's secret wars*. Grand Rapids, MI: Revell.

Meier, P., Arterburn, S., & Minirth, F. (2001). *Mood swings*. Nashville: Thomas Nelson.

Meier, P., Clinton, T., & Ohlschlager, G. (2001). Mental illness: Reducing suffering in the church.Pages 364–365. *The soul care Bible*. Nashville: Thomas Nelson,.

Mellman, T. A., & David, D. (1995, November). Sleep disturbance and its relationship to psychiatric morbidity after Hurricane Andrew. *American Journal of Psychiatry, 152*(11), 1659–1664.

Menninger, K. (1938). *Man against himself*. New York: Harcourt, Brace, & World.

Messinger. (1975). Malpractice suits—The psychiatrist's turn. *Journal of Legal Medicine, 3*, 21.

Miklowitz, . J. (2002). *The bipolar disorder survival guide*. New York: Guilford Press.

Miklowitz, D. J. & Goldstein, M. J. (1997). *Bipolar disorder: A family-focused treatment approach.* New York: Guilford Press.

Milkman H., & Sunderwirth, S. (1987). *Craving for ecstasy: The consciousness and chemistry of escape.* Lexington, MA: Lexington Books.

Milkman H., & Sunderwirth, S. (1987). *Craving for ecstasy: The consciousness and chemistry of escape.* Lexington, MA: Lexington Books.

Miller, J. (1987). *Sin: Overcoming the ultimate deadly addiction.* San Francisco: Harper and Row.

Miller, W. B. (1992). An empirical study of the psychological antecedents and consequences of induced abortion. *J Social Issues, 48*(3), 67–93.

Minirth, F., & Meier, P. (1994). *Happiness is a choice* (2nd ed.). Grand Rapids, MI: Baker.

Minirth, F., Meier, P., & Arterburn, S. (1995). Abortion. In *The complete life encyclopedia.* Nashville: Thomas Nelson.

Minuchin, S. (1974). *Families and family therapy.* London: Tavistock.

Mondimore, F. M. (1999). *Bipolar Disorder.* Baltimore: Johns Hopkins University Press.

Morely, W. E. (1970, April). Theory of crisis intervention. *Pastoral Psychology, 21*(203), 16.

Mosgofian, P., & Ohlschlager, G. (1995). *Sexual misconduct in counseling and ministry.* Dallas: Word.

Motto, J. (1992). An integrated approach to estimating suicide risk. In R. Maris, A. Berman, J. Maltsberger, and R. Yufit, (Eds.). *Assessment and Prediction of Suicide.* New York: Guilford Press.

Murray, N.D. and Pizzorno, N.D. (1998). *Encyclopedia of natural medicine.* Rocklin, California: Prima Health.

National Center for Chronic Disease Prevention and Health Promotion. (2004, September). *General alcohol information.* Retrieved May 19, 2005, from http://www.cdc.gov/alcohol/factsheets/general_information.htm.

National Center for Health Statistics. (2004). *Health, United States, 2004: With chartbook on trends in the health of Americans.* Hyattsville, Maryland: Author.

National Center for Injury Prevention and Control. (2004, November). *Intimate partner violence: Fact sheet.* Retrieved May 19, 2005, from http://www.cdc.gov/ncipc/factsheets/ipvfacts.htm.

National Center for Injury Prevention and Control. (2004, November). *Suicide: Fact sheet.* Retrieved May 2005, from www.cdc.gov/ncipc/factsheets/suifacts.htm.

National Center for Injury Prevention and Control. (2005, April). *Sexual violence: Fact sheet.* Retrieved May 19, 2005, from http://www.cdc.gov/ncipc/factsheets/svfacts.htm.

National Impact Gambling Impact Commission. (1999). *National gambling impact study commission final report.* Washington, DC.

National Institute of Mental Health (NIMH). (1999). *The numbers count.* (NIH Publication No. NIH 99–4584) [Online]. Available: http://www.NIMH.NIH.gov/pulicat/members.CFM.

National Institute of Mental Health. (2000). *Anxiety.* Retrieved May 2005, from http://www.nimh.nih.gov/publicat/anxiety.cfm#anx1.

National Institute of Mental Health. (2001). *NIMH Eating Disorders: Facts about eating disorders and the search for solutions.* NIH Publication No. 01–4901. Retrieved from http://www.nimh.nih.gov/publicat/eatingdisorder.cfm

National Institute of Mental Health. (2001). *Reliving trauma: Post-traumatic stress disorder: A brief overview of the symptoms, treatments, and research findings.*

National Institute of Mental Health. (2003). *In Harm's Way: Suicide in America.* Retrieved May 19, 2005, from http://www.nimh.nih.gov/publicat/harmaway.cfm.

National Institute on Drug Abuse. (n.d.). *NIDA's Principles of Drug Addiction Treatment: A Research-Based Guide.* Available from, http://www.nida.nih.gov/PODAT/PODATIndex.html.

*National Survey on Drug Use and Health.* (2003). Available from, http://oas.samhsa.gov/nhsda.htm.

Newman, C. F., Leahy, R. L., Beck, A. T., Reilly-Harrington, N. A., & Gyulai, L. (2002). *Bipolar disorder: A cognitive therapy approach.* Washington, DC: American Psychological Association.

Nishith, P., Resick, P. A., & Mueser, K. T. (2001, July). Sleep difficulties and alcohol use motives in female rape victims with post-traumatic stress disorder. *Journal of Traumatic Stress, 14*(3), 469–480.

Nixon, R., Resick, P. A., & Nishith, P. (2004, October). An exploration of comorbid depression among female victims of intimate partner violence with post-traumatic stress disorder. *Journal of Affective Disorders. 82*(2), 315–321.

Norretrander, T. (1998). *The user illusion.* New York: Viking.

O'Mathuna, D. and Larimore, W. (2001). *Alternative medicine: The Christian handbook.* Grand Rapids, MI: Zondervan.

O'Neill, R. (2002, September). *Experiments in living: The fatherless family.* Retrieved June 2005, from http://www.civitas.org.uk.

Oden, T. (1976). *Should treatment be terminated?* New York: Harper and Row.

Ohlschlager, G. & Clinton, T. (2000). Inside law and ethics: The ethics of evangelism and spiritual formation in professional counseling. *Christian Counseling Connection.* Issue 1, 6–7.

Ohlschlager, G. (1999). Avoiding ethical-legal pitfalls: Embracing conformative behavior and transformative virtues. *Christian Counseling Today, 7*(3), 40–43.

Ohlschlager, G., & Mosgofian, P. (1992). *Law for the Christian counselor: A guidebook for clinicians and pastors.* Dallas: Word.

Oliver, G. J. (1993). *Real men have feelings too.* Chicago: Moody Press.

Oliver, G. J., Hasz, M., & Richburg, M. (1997). *Promoting Change Through Brief Therapy in Christian Counseling.* Wheaton, IL: Tyndale House.

Oliver, G. J., & Wright, H. N. (1992). *When anger hits home.* Chicago: Moody Press.

Oliver, G. J., & Wright, H. N. (1996). *Good women get angry.* Ann Arbor, MI: Servant Publications.

Oquendo, M., Brent, D. A., Birmaher, B., Greenhill, L., Kolko, D., Stanley, B., Zelazny, J., Burke, A. K., Firinciogullari, S., Ellis, S. P., & Mann, J. J. (2005, March). Post-traumatic stress disorder comorbid with major depression: Factors mediating the association with suicidal behavior. *American Journal of Psychiatry, 162*(3), 560–567.

Osborne, I. (1998). *Tormenting thoughts and secret rituals: The hidden epidemic of obsessive-compulsive disorder.* New York: Dell.

Packer, J. I. (1993). *Knowing God* (rev. ed.). Downers Grove, IL: InterVarsity Press.

Papolos, D., & Papolos, J. (1997). *Overcoming depression* (3rd ed.). New York: Harper Collins.

Papolos, D., & Papolos, J. (1999). *The bipolar child.* New York: Broadway Books.

Pascal, B. (1941). *Pensèes and the provincial letters.* New York: The Modern Library.

Payne, R., Kravitz, A., Notman, M., & Anderson, J. (1976). Outcomes following therapeutic abortion. *Archives of General Psychiatry, 33,* 725.

Pearce, K. A., Schauer, A. H., Garfield, N. J., Ohlde, C. O., & Patterson, T. W. (1985). A study of post-traumatic stress disorder in Vietnam Veterans. *Journal of Clinical Psychology, 41*(1), 9–15.

Peck, S. (1997, December 18). Mission of madness. *Long Beach Telegram,* A1, A6–7.

Penzel, F. (2000). *Obsessive-compulsive disorder: A complete guide to getting well and staying well.* Oxford: New York.

Persons, J. B., Davidson, J., & Tompkins, M. A. (2001). *Essential components of cognitive-behavior therapy for depression.* Washington, DC: American Psychological Association.

Planned Parenthood Federation of America Public Affairs Action Letter. (1992 September 25). *Quote of the week.*

Pope, K., Sonne, J., & Holroyd, J. (1993). *Sexual feelings in psychotherapy: Explorations for therapists and therapists-in-training.* Washington, DC: American Psychological Association.

Population Reference Bureau. (n.d.). 2000 census data: Living arrangements profile for United States. *Analysis of Data from the U.S. Census Bureau, for The Annie E. Casey Foundation,* Retrieved May 2005, from www.aecf.org

Prochaska J. O., Norcross, J., & DiClemente C. (1994). *Changing for good.* NY: Avon Books.

Ranew, L. F., & Serritella, D. A. (1992). *Handbook of differential treatments for addictions.* Boston: Allyn and Bacon.

Reardon, D. (1987). *Aborted women: Silent no more.* Westchester, IL: Crossway.

Reisser, T., & Coe, J. (1999). Post-abortion counseling. In D. Benner & P. Hill, (Eds.). *Baker Encyclopedia of Psychology and Counseling,* 2nd ed. Grand Rapids, MI: Baker.

Reisser, T., & Reisser, P. (1999). *A solitary sorrow: Finding healing and wholeness after abortion.* Wheaton, IL: Harold Shaw.

Resnick, H. S., Kilpatrick, D. G., Dansky, B. S. Saunders, B. E., et al. (1993, December). Prevalence of civilian trauma and post-traumatic stress disorder in a representative national sample of women. *Journal of Consulting & Clinical Psychology, 61*(6), 984–991.

Richards, P.S., & Bergin, A.E. (1997). *A spiritual strategy for counseling and psychotherapy.* Washington, DC: American Psychological Association.

Ripley, J.S., & Worthington, E.L., Jr. (2002). Comparison of hope-focused communication and empathy-based forgiveness group interventions to promote marital enrichment. *Journal of Counseling and Development, 80,* 452–463.

Rogers, C. (1951). *Client centered therapy.* Boston: Houghton Mifflin.

Rogers, C. (1957). The necessary and sufficient conditions of therapeutic personality change. *Journal of Consulting Psychology, 21,* 95–103.

Rogers, C. (1961). *On becoming a person.* Boston: Houghton Mifflin.

Roth, S., Newman, E., Pelcovitz, D., Van der Kolk, B., & Mandel, F. S. (1997). Complex PTSD in victims exposed to sexual and physical abuse: Results from the DSM-IV field trial for post-traumatic stress disorder. *Journal of Traumatic Stress, 10,* 539–555.

Rue, V. M., & Speckhard, A. C. (1992). Informed consent and abortion: Issues in medicine and counseling. *Med. & Mind, 6*(1), 75–94.

Saigh, P. A. (1987, June). In vitro flooding of an adolescent's post-traumatic stress disorder. *Journal of Clinical Child Psychology, 16*(2), 147–151.

Sandage, S.J. (1997). *An ego-humility model of forgiveness: A theory-driven empirical test of group interventions.* PhD dissertation, Virginia Commonwealth University, Richmond, VA.

Sapolsky, R. M. (1998). *Why zebras don't get ulcers.* New York: W.H. Freeman and Company.

Schaeffer, B. (2000). *Is it love or is it addiction.* Center City, MN: Hazelden.

Schaeffer, F. A. (1972). *He is there and He is not silent.* Wheaton, IL: Tyndale.

Schaumburg, H. (1992). *False intimacy: Understanding the struggle of sexual addiction.* Colorado Springs: NavPress.

Scott, J. (2001). *Overcoming mood swings.* New York: New York University Press.

Seligman, M. E. P. (1975). *Helplessness: On depression, development, and death.* San Francisco: W. H. Freeman and Company.

Shaw, A., Joseph, S., & Linley, A. P. (2005, March). Religion, spirituality, and post-traumatic growth: A systematic review. *Mental Health, Religion & Culture, 8*(1), 1–11.

Shea, S. C. (1999). *The practical art of suicide assessment: A guide for mental health professionals and substance abuse counselors.* New York: John Wiley & Sons, Inc.

Sheikh, J. I., Woodward, S. H., & Leskin, G. A. (2003). Sleep in post-traumatic stress disorder and panic: Convergence and divergence. *Depression & Anxiety, 18*(4), 187–198.

Short, N., & Kitchner, N. (2002, April). Panic disorder: Nature assessment and treatment. *Continuing Professional Development.* Royal College of Nursing, *5*(7).

Sibcy, G. (2005, June). Lecture: Advanced psychopathology. Liberty University.

Silverman, P. R., Nickman, S., & Worden, J. W. (1992). Detachment revisited: The child's reconstruction of a dead parent. *American Journal of Orthopsychiatry, 62,* 494–503.

Singer, E., Smith, H., Wilkinson, J., Kim, G., Allden, K., & Ford, D. (2003, November). Mental health of detained asylum seekers. *Lancet, 362*(9397), 1721–1724.

Sire, J. (1997). *The universe next door: A basic worldview catalog* (3rd ed.). Downers Grove, IL: InterVarsity Press.

Sittser, G. L. (1996). *A grace disguised.* Grand Rapids, MI: Zondervan.

Solomon, E. P., & Heide, K. M. (2005). The biology of trauma. *Journal of Interpersonal Violence, 20*(1), 51–61.

Söndergaard, H. P., Ekblad, S., & Theorell, T. (2003, May). Screening for post-traumatic stress disorder among refugees in Stockholm. *Nordic Journal of Psychiatry, 57*(3), 185–190.

Spitzer, R.L., Yanovski, S., Wadden, T., Wing, R., Marcus, MD., Stunkard, A., Devlin, M.,

Mitchell, J., Hasin, D., & Horne, RL., (1992). Binge eating disorder: Its further validation in a multisite study. *International Journal of Eating Disorders, 12*: 137–53.

Statistics. (n.d.). *How many people have eating and exercise disorders?* Retrieved from
http://www.anred.com.

Stevenson, L. (1974). *Seven theories of human nature* (2nd ed.). New York: Oxford University Press.

Stoll, A. L. (2001). *The omega-3 connection.* New York: Simon & Schuster.

Stone, H. W. (1976). *Crisis counseling.* Fortress Press.

Strock, M., et al. (2000). Depression. *National Institute of Health Publication* No. 00–3561.
Retrieved February 25, 2005, from http://www.nimh.nih.gov/publicat/depression.cfm

Strong, S. (1968). Counseling: An interpersonal influence process. *Journal of Counseling
Psychology, 15,* 215–224.

Suicidal behavior after severe trauma. Part 1: PTSD diagnoses, psychiatric comorbidity,
and assessments of suicidal behavior. *Journal of Traumatic Stress, 11*(1), 103–113.

Sullender, R. S., & Malony, H. N. (1990). Should clergy counsel suicidal persons? *The
Journal of Pastoral Care, 44* (3), 203–211, 204–206.

Sullivan, P.F. (1995). Mortality in anorexia nervosa. *American Journal of Psychiatry* 152(7):
1073–1074.

Sutcliffe, P., Tufnell, G., & Cornish, U. (Eds.). (1998). *Working with the dying and bereaved.*
New York: Routledge.

Swanson, L., & Biaggio, M. K. (1985). Therapeutic perspectives on father-daughter
incest. *American Journal of Psychiatry, 142,* (6), 667–674.

Swenson R. A. (1995). *Margin.* Colorado Springs, CO: NavPress.

Swenson, R.A. (1992). *Margin: Restoring emotional, physical, financial, and time reserves to
overloaded lives.* Colorado Springs, CO: NavPress.

Tada, J. E. (1997). Decision-making and dad. Pages 471–475 in G. Stewart & T. Demy
(Eds.). *Suicide: A Christian response, crucial considerations for choosing life.* Grand
Rapids, MI: Kregel.

Tan, S.-Y. (2000). *Rest: Experiencing God's peace in a restless world.* Ann Arbor, MI: Vine
Books.

Tan, S.-Y., & Gregg, D. H. (1997). *Disciplines of the Holy Spirit.* Grand Rapids, MI:
Zondervan.

Tan, S.-Y., & Ortberg, J., Jr. (1995a). *Coping with depression.* Grand Rapids, MI: Baker.

Tan, S.-Y., & Ortberg, J., Jr. (1995b). *Understanding depression.* Grand Rapids, MI: Baker.

Taub. (1983). Psychiatric malpractice in the 1980's: A look at some areas of concern. *Law,
Medicine and Health Care,* 97.

Taylor, S., Thordarson, D. S., Fedoroff, I. C., Maxfield, L., & Ogrodniczuk, J. (2003, April).
Comparative efficacy, speed, and adverse effects of three PTSD treatments: Exposure
therapy, EMDR, and relaxation training. *Journal of Consulting & Clinical Psychology,
71*(2), 330–339.

Teicher, M. H., Andersen, S. L., Polcari, A., Anderson, C. M., Navalta, C. P., & Kim, D. M. (2003). The neurobiological consequences of early stress and childhood maltreatment. *Neuroscience & Biobehavioral Reviews, 27*(1/2), 33–45.

The Barna Group. (2004, September). Born again Christians just as likely to divorce as non-Christians. The Barna Update. Retrieved May 2005, from http://www.barna.org.

The leadership survey on pastors and internet pornography. (2001). *Leadership Journal,* 001.

The National Center for Fathering. (n.d.). *National surveys on fathers and fathering.* Retrieved June 2005, from http://www.fathers.com/research.

The National Center for Fathering. (n.d.). *The consequences of fatherlessness.* Retrieved June 2005, from http://www.fathers.com/research/consequences.html.

*The twelve steps: A spiritual journey.* (1988). San Diego: Recovery Publications.

Thelen, M.H. Farmer, J., Wonderlich, S., & Smith, M. (1991). A revision of the bulimic test: The BULIT-R. *Psychological Assessment: A Journal of Consulting and Clinical Psychology, 3,* 119–124.

Thomas, J. M. (1995). Traumatic stress disorder presents as hyperactivity and disruptive behavior: Case presentation, diagnoses, and treatment. *Infant Mental Health Journal, 16*(4), 306–318.

Thurman, C. (1991). *The lies we believe.* Nashville: Thomas Nelson.

Thurman, C. (1995). *The lies we believe workbook.* Nashville: Thomas Nelson.

Thurman, C. (2001). Perfectionism. In T. Clinton, E. Hindson, & G. Ohlschlager (Eds.), *The soul care Bible.* Nashville: Thomas Nelson.

Torrey, E. F., & Knable, M. B. (2002). *Surviving manic depression.* New York: Basic Books.

True, W. R., Rice, J., Eisen, S. A., Heath, A. C., Goldberg, J., Lyons, M. J., & Nowak J. (n.d.). A twin study of genetic and environmental contributions to liability for post-traumatic stress symptoms. *JAMA & Archives, Archives of General Psychiatry, accessed June 20, 2005 from* http://archpsyc.ama-assn.org/cgi/content/abstract/50/4/257

Tsai, M., & Wagner, N. N. (1978). Therapy groups for women sexually molested as children. *Archives of Sexual Behavior, 7,* 417–427.

Tyson-Rawson, K. (1996). Relationship and heritage: Manifestations of ongoing attachment following father death. Pages 125–145 in D. Klass, P.R. Silverman, & S. L. Nickman (Eds.). *Continuing bonds: New understandings of grief.* Washington DC: Taylor & Francis.

van der Kolk, B., McFarlane, A., & Weisaeth, L. (Eds.). (1996). *Traumatic stress: The effects of overwhelming experience on mind, body, and society.* New York: The Guildford Press.

Van Leeuwin, M.S. (1985). *The Person in psychology: A contemporary Christian appraisal.* Grand Rapids, MI: Eerdmans.

Vandereycken, W. (1995). The families of patients with an eating disorder, in K.D. Brownell, & C.G. Fairburn (Eds.), *Eating disorders and obesity: A comprehensive handbook.* New York: The Guilford Press.

Vernick, L. (2000). *The TRUTH principle: A life changing model for spiritual growth and renewal.* Colorado Springs, CO: WaterBrook Press.

Vitz, P. (1994). *Psychology as religion: The cult of self worship* (2nd ed.). Grand Rapids, MI: Eerdmans.

Volberg, R.A. (2003). *Gambling and problem gambling in Arizona: Report to the Arizona lottery.* Retrieved from http://www.problemgambling.az.gov/prevalencestudy.pdf.

Wade, N.G., & Worthington, E.L., Jr. (2003a). Overcoming interpersonal offenses: Is forgiveness the only way to deal with unforgiveness? *Journal of Counseling and Development, 81,* 343–353.

Wade, N.G., & Worthington, E.L., Jr. (2003b). *Content and meta-analysis of interventions to promote forgiveness.* Manuscript under editorial review, Virginia Commonwealth University, Richmond.

Wald, J., Taylor, S. (2005). Interoceptive exposure therapy combined with trauma-related exposure therapy for post-traumatic stress disorder: A case report. *Cognitive Behaviour Therapy, 34*(1), 34–41.

Wallerstein, J. S., & Blakeslee, S. (1995). *The good marriage: How & why love lasts.* New York: Houghton Mifflin Company.

Walsh, F., and McGoldrick, M. (1998). A family systems perspective on loss, recovery and resilience. In P. Sutcliffe, G. Tufnell, & U. Cornish. *Working with the dying and bereaved.* New York: Routledge.

Walters, R. (1981*). Anger: Yours & mine & what to do about it.* Grand Rapids, MI: Zondervan.

WebMD Health On-line. (n.d.). What are eating disorders? Retrieved from http://www.webmd.com.

Weishaar, M. & Beck, A. (1992). Clinical and cognitive predictors of suicide. In R. Maris, A. Berman, J. Maltsberger, & R. Yufit (Eds.). *Assessment and prediction of suicide.* New York: Guilford Press.

Weiss, J. (1998, March 7). Wounded Heroes. *The Dallas News.* Retrieved May, 2005, from http://www.dallasnews.com.

Weissman, M. M., Markowitz, J. C., & Klerman G. L. (2000). *Comprehensive guide to interpersonal psychotherapy.* New York: Basic Books.

Weissman, M.M. (1993). The epidemiology of personality disorders: A 1990 update. *Journal of Personality Disorders, Supplement, Spring,* 44–62.

Wells, D. (1994). *God in the wasteland: The reality of truth in a world of fading dreams.* Grand Rapids, MI: Eerdmans.

Welte, J.W., Wieczorek, W.F., Barnes, G.M, Tidwell, M.C., & Hoffman, J.H. (2003). The relationship of ecological and geographic factors to gambling behavior and pathology. (Accepted for publication by the *Journal of Gambling Studies).*

Whealin, J. M. (n.d.). *Complex PTSD a national center for PTSD fact sheet.* Retrieved on June 20, 2005 from http://www.ncptsd.va.gov/facts/specific/fs_complex_ptsd.html.

Willard, D. (1988). *The spirit of the disciplines: Understanding how God changes lives.* San Francisco, CA: Harper and Row.

Willingham, R. (1999). *Breaking free.* Downers Grove, IL: InterVarsity.

Wilson, E. (2002). *Steering clear*. Downers Grove, IL: InterVarsity.

Wolterstorff, N. (1984). *Reason within the bounds of religion: 2nd edition*. Grand Rapids, MI: Eerdmans.

Wolterstorff, N. (1987). *Lament for a son*. Grand Rapids, MI: Eerdmans.

Worthington, E. (1988). Understanding the values of religious clients: A model and its application to counseling. *Journal of Counseling Psychology, 35*(2), 166–174.

Worthington, E. L., Jr. (1998). An empathy-humility-commitment model of forgiveness applied within family dyads. *Journal of Family Therapy, 20,* 59–76.

Worthington, E. L., Jr. (2000b). On chaos, fractals, and stress: Response to Fincham's "Optimism and the Family." In J. Gillam (Ed.), *The science of optimism and hope*. Philadelphia: The Templeton Foundation Press.

Worthington, E.L., Jr. (1999). *Hope-focused marriage counseling*. Downers Grove, IL: Inter-Varsity Press.

Worthington, E.L., Jr. (2000a). Is there a place for forgiveness in the justice system? *Fordham Urban Law Journal, 27,* 1721–1734.

Worthington, E.L., Jr. (2001a). Unforgiveness, forgiveness, and reconciliation in societies. In Raymond G. Helmick & Rodney L. Petersen (Eds.), *Forgiveness and reconciliation: Religion, public policy, and conflict transformation*. Philadelphia: The Templeton Foundation Press.

Worthington, E.L., Jr. (2001b). *Five steps to forgiveness: The art and science of forgiving*. New York: Crown Publishers.

Worthington, E.L., Jr. (2003). *Forgiving and reconciling: Bridges to wholeness and hope*. Downers Rove, IL: InterVarsity Press

Worthington, E.L., Jr., & Scherer, M. (2003). Forgiveness is an emotion-focused coping strategy that can reduce health risks and promote health resilience: Theory, review, and hypotheses. *Psychology and Health, 19,* 385–405.

Worthington, E.L., Jr., & Wade, N.G. (1999). The social psychology of unforgiveness and forgiveness and implications for clinical practice. *Journal of Social and Clinical Psychology, 18,* 385–418.

Worthington, E.L., Jr., Berry, J.W., & Parrott, L. III. (2001). Unforgiveness, forgiveness, religion, and health. In T. G. Plante & A. Sherman (Eds.), *Faith and health: Psychological perspectives*. New York: Guilford Press.

Worthington, E.L., Jr., Kurusu, T., McCullough, M.E., & Sandage, S. (1996). Empirical research on religion and psychotherapeutic processes and outcomes: A 10-year review and research prospectus. *Psychological Bulletin, 199,* 448–487.

Worthington, E.L., Jr., Sandage, S. J., & Berry, J.W. (2000). Group interventions to promote forgiveness: What researchers and clinicians ought to know. In M.E. McCullough, K.I. Pargament, & C.E. Thoresen (Eds.), *Forgiveness: Theory, research and practice*. New York: Guilford Press.

Yalom, I. D. (1995). *The theory and practice of group psychotherapy*, New York: Basic Books.

Yalom, I. D. (2002). *The gift of therapy: An open letter to a new generation of therapists and their patients*. NY: HarperCollins.

Young, E. J. (1965). *The book of Isaiah: The English text, with introduction, exposition, and notes*. In R. K. Harrison (Ed.), *New International Commentary on the Old Testament*. Grand Rapids, MI: Eerdmans.

Young, J. (1999). *Cognitive therapy for personality disorders: A schema-focused approach: 3rd Ed*. Sarasota, FL: Professional Resource Press.

Zimmerman, M. K. (1977). *Passage through abortion*. New York: Praeger Publishers.

# Index